The Adventures of Mr Marigold

a novel by

Michael Charles Tobias

paperback and ebook editions
published by

Zorba Press
Ithaca, New York, USA
www.ZorbaPress.com

Copyright

Acknowledgements

I wish first and foremost to acknowledge the generous collaboration and kinship of Craig Potton whose artistic soul, photography, and stunning commitment to the global environment, I have long admired; and to Robbie Burton, ever enthusiastic and informed Managing Director of Craig Potton Publishing. To Tina Delceg, who has labored so long and intensively on the production design and management of this little novel, as well as Sarah Maxey for critical production aesthetic issues, and to Jane Parkin, the finest literary editor I have ever had the good fortune to work with.

I want especially to thank my Father, William Tobias, for his cover photograph on the boxed deluxe edition, and his other images scattered like jewels throughout the book, which mirror his own yearnings and wisdom. And deeply and enduringly, my Mother, Betty May Weber Tobias, my fiercest critic, and advocate, and the one person to whom I owe nearly everything, and much more. She alone understands how this odd colossus came about. A profound debt to Jean, whose own marvelous passions, ensconced in Santa Fe, have been passed down to me by way of one miracle after another. As well as our dear friend, the painter/philosopher Alvaro, a blithe spirit. And my comrade-in-arms, Roberto, who has joined me on so many expeditions. Finally, my Brother, Marc, the world's most brilliant and memorable eccentric, whose crazy élan I share.

Disclaimer

Dedication

This novel is a love letter, and a tribute to a remarkable woman whose personal history helped inspire the work. Her endless compassion and companionship have been my salvation. My muse, my conscience, my joy. The love of my life, my wife, Jane Gray Morrison. With eternal gratitude.

CONTENTS

Part One

The Hermit of Tesuque

CHAPTER 1
A Boy Blowing Bubbles in the Presidential Palace

HE WAS A BRIGHTLY tarrying lad, five feet four inches of gumption, lean as the gopher snake, privileged truancy obliging over centuries, gamboling and shaggy, ringlets red, irises gray, but 115 months out of the womb, give or take, this most recent of Marigolds, the family Junior —Murillo.

At that time, his widower father, Pecos Marigold, was invited to Ecuador by the highest-ranking transportation official in the beleaguered government of Jose Velasco Ibarra (the man whose voice carried his country with the protest "Just give me your balcony and I shall be your President!") for the purpose of building a national highway that would unify a nation. The road was conceived so as to pass directly before the great glacial volcano Chimborazo. It could be said that Ibarra had it in for the Eiffel Tower and Empire State Building. El Presidente was convinced that Ecuador should stand without rival, touting a grandiose symbol of the country's sovereignty that was bold and handcrafted—a lapidary coup with the fanfare of the Champs-Élysées that could be celebrated by all peasants and party hacks alike. Without so much as a bullet fired, this highway should establish political and economic pre-eminence, affording an international Silk Route to show off the magnetic zenith, a mountain 7,000 feet higher than Everest, as measured from the center of the planet. Oddly, Chimborazo was not the highest peak in Ecuador. That favor was reserved for Frederick Church's great fumarole-ridden Cotopaxi. Nor was it by any stretch the world's highest as taken from its base—an attribution endowed singly upon Hawaii's Mauna Kea, at 32,000 feet. Yet, Chimborazo was indeed the highest point on earth, a peculiar riddle of obscure inferences and extrapolations that would, in the case of the Marigold family, pit heartbreaking hindsight against blinding destiny.

The special-delivery package with its maps, blueprints and detailed instructions arrived at the semi-retired surveyor's door as a complete surprise, though the postage stamps were not altogether unfamiliar to him, stirring memories of family heirlooms that were gathering dust in the attic. Those stamps with their exotic imagery, sun-burnished iguanas, steaming calderas and native dress, exerted an uncanny effect on Pecos' son as well. He examined them with a magnifying glass and the attention normally paid to baseball cards or purloined girly magazines.

The cognominal, Marigold, with its family history of surveyors, renowned in some parts of South America, made receipt of the letter not entirely surprising. What clinched the solicitation was the fact Ecuador had lost nearly half its territory to Peru in a war in 1941 and the road was deemed a security buffer, to overlay the earlier royal passage of the Incas known as the Avenue of the Volcanoes. That was dirt. Ibarra wanted smooth black pavement, two lanes, tunnels carved deep in the cavernous bedrock, mountain passes with clean white guardrails, a veritable freeway with all the modernizations: pit stops, gas pumps, pay telephones. A road that could withstand the abrasive loads of armored tanks with (in army parlance) full-track driving trains traveling between Quito and Guayaquil.

In those years the people of New Mexico and Ecuador were similar in some respects: strange melanges of Europeans whose blood was mixed to various degrees with Indians'. In the case of Ecuador, the locals were mostly Quichua speaking, but there were also several thousand others—moribund, fading, sorrowful Shuar and Achuar, and the nearly extinct Cofán descended from the little-known Valdivians. Once tens of thousands of these tribals had flourished around Ecuador's ancient capital of Real Alto. Now, their descendants, marginalized to its far fringes, struggled to make sense of the modern world.

Pecos and his son arrived in Quito during the week of Corpus Christi. The country was gripped by ceremonies and rituals that, to the young Murillo, were nothing short of astonishing. Young women jumped over fires, flipping their skirts up in the belief that this display to the rearing flames would ensure swift pregnancies. By starlight, Murillo had his first glimpse of a vagina. Dozens of them. He passed out, quite unexpectedly. The canny historian might adduce the boy's later history of untreatable reveries as dating from that stubbornly delicious fainting spell.

Aboard every street in Quito gangs roamed amidst musicians, gypsies and gauchos. Thespians relived the Nativity; ghosts and goblins dressed in white plaster masks, adorned in tropical head feathers, sang, marched, got drunk, fought, laughed, loitered, toiled beneath dark oak crosses, and generally caroused with abandon. The celebrants fanned out to the showy percussion of fire rockets, while the church's great carillons rang forth. Along every streetside were flamenco dancers, players of the 20-horned bocinas made of bull bones, Andean harps, mandolins and zompoña panpipes, and singers belting out their plaintive ballads.

The two Marigolds wandered through this euphoric maze before returning to their hotel room. At 2 a.m. they looked out from the verandah at the continuing roman candles, and by bright moonlight could decipher the white thrones of Illiniza and Rucu Pichincha, two of the many ice-caked summits nearby.

In the days that followed, young Marigold—who preferred the animated market places whose profusion of caged birds he first conspired to set free—was instead dragged along by his father to half a dozen meeting rooms overlooking the Avenida 6 de Diciembre. Murillo played with his yo-yo and struck several officials in the side, and one, Romero, Deputy Vice Counsel to the Transport Minister, in the jowls. The requisite papers were signed at the Palacio Presidencial, commissioning Pecos to spend the next twelve months connecting the north with the south. The yo-yo was written into the contract, a piece of marginalia denominated with a humorous eye as both "a deterrent and formidable negotiating strategy" that has perplexed seven successive government archivists in downtown Quito. Whatever it meant, one thing was sure: the President of Ecuador liked this wayward boy and thought he boded well for the endeavor.

While Pecos was lending his ink on the dotted lines, his son blew doting bubbles with the aid of a little hollowed-out wooden spoon and an ink bottle filled with liquid soapsuds. He watched the largest of these float across the room and hang undecided. A breathless pause, epiphany becoming international incident: it landed squarely, ever so delicately upon El Presidente's sinus-enflamed nose, where it sat perfectly still, mockingly, for a solid 40 seconds. Those across the room were death still. Ibarra had ruined men's careers or imprisoned them for far less, but presently gave no clear indication which way his temper might stride.

"Ahh...to be young again," he mused aloud.

"Yes, indeed," Pecos avowed nervously.

As for the boy, Murillo gazed intently, hushed by the reverence for chance which dictated that if it burst, bad luck, they go home; if not, they stay on.

"Do I dare touch it?" El Presidente asked the boy.

"Let me," volunteered Marigold, Jr, who took possession of the bubble like the munitions expert disarming a terrorist's bomb—with a sureness and probity that much impressed Ecuador's leader.

Everyone in the room stared into that fair weather of childhood where the fate of the world, and all its deeper physics, hung in the balance of a blue soap bubble.

Now the transparent globule of foam remained atop the boy's spellbound index finger. No one breathed, not even El Presidente, who was no less credulous than the entire labor class, all those peasants and half-bloods, Spaniards and mestizo from whose ranks he had by means less delicate risen to stardom. Marigold held his raised finger into the light pouring in. There, in that filament of a crystal ball, he saw everything worth seeing in this world, prisms yielding a clear enough picture of the next half-century. He stood surrounded by adults, beside the collection of appointed gold artifacts, bronze statuary, enormous chandeliers of French paste, a portrait of a lion by Delacroix ...

"Open the window, please," said he, nodding toward the south, then he blew upon the bubble and sent it drifting out in the direction of the Andes. The boy went with it, migrating dreams. For those brief seconds, young Marigold thought about the weight on his shoulders, and it was lighter than air.

"A sign, unquestionably," declared El Presidente, the tension in his face visibly easing. He extended his hand, patted the boy on the back and congratulated him on his terrific aim. Relief flooded through the onlookers; minor good cheer resulted.

A moment out of time. A day signified by some footnote in a dusty annal as the day of "the boy who blew bubbles in the Presidential Palace". To the chronicler willing to scour the hacking coughs or detail the dimples of great personages, this interregnum might merit scant notice. Yet, to the boy himself whose tale turns upon the moment, and others like it, there was no more singular event. Not one lyric of equal suspension or augury. In the wild lunatic visages of those tired politicians, the boy sensed the life he must reject, not knowing—at that fateful juncture—that his father was signing more than he had bargained for: that this afternoon's pen-wielding particulars—telling folly, resulting expedition—should affect every subsequent day in his life, and would challenge the nature of religion, of truth, of those things worth living and dying for, without exception.

The road transcended its engineering, was indeed more than the sum of its perilous parts. The myth of the road signaled geopolitical sovereignty, expanded borders, security for an entire people. Its powerful mid-point, and the highest part of the endeavor, was Chimborazo, forever remembered as a promontory, the point at which the north and south of Ecuador were united by tarmac. There was a hut, with an outhouse, already established at the mountain, for it had first been tackled 71 years before by the rambunctious Matterhorner, Edward Whymper. Alexander von Humboldt had tried, and—testily—failed. But since those times thousands of climbers had made the endless slog (18 hours as a rule), waist-deep in snow, between the mountain's two deceptively distant summits. The climbers all arrived at the entrance to the route via the eastern side, marching up the dirt path which soon would be expanded to allow for truck transport.

Ecuador's network of roads was entirely of dirt when Pecos and his son arrived. What was to become the Ecuadorian portion of the Pan American highway, or Pána, was nothing more than a plague of excruciating switchbacks between connecting nudos, or transversal escarpments. From the Oriente—the country's eastern Amazon, once rumored to contain the elusive capital of gold, El Dorado—to the high Sierra, and on to the oceanic Costa, travel was slow going. An acclimated Indian might walk from Quito to Guayaquil in a week. Militia, using horses, could do it in three days, stopping along the Avenue of the Volcanoes at towns like Valle de los Chillos and Latacunga, passing the ruins of Pachuzala, then on to Ambato or Baños to take advantage of the local beers and hot springs.

In those days, campesinos and serranos were agitating for land reform which meant, simply, more free pasture, and the country was trying to get beyond the numbing inequities of the Spanish yoke after a century of political divisiveness. Dozens of presidents had come and gone. Between 1901 and 1948 the nation had endured the carryings-on of precisely 39 governments, and the writing of four separate constitutions. Amid such chaos, Ibarra would be stubbornly elected five times, giving him the confidence, and control of the treasury, to embark upon his lasting achievement: the road that would dwarf even the legacy left by Flemish missionary Fray Jodoco Ricke, Quito's Church at Plaza San Francisco. Built of 104 Doric columns in 1534 on the site of the former Inca Palace, it was the oldest church in South America, and the highest. Ibarra's road would usurp it in both height and significance. The boy with his bubbles convinced him that it could be done, and Pecos was swept forward by this atmosphere of high hopes.

The officials had heard about Pecos because his father had master-minded the road from Lake Titicaca to Macchu Picchu in neighboring Peru. That had taken a decade out of the Marigold family's life, and involved the most treacherous engineering pyrotechnics in South American history. Mules, horses, children, women and men all died in the service of that unlikely vision of a highway, which engendered no happy precedent for future such endeavors. Of course, surveyors-general were rightly immune to blame when tragic mishaps, both during construction and later on, frequently occurred. One night eight European residents of Lima, car buffs inching their Bugattis along some chasm ridge, were swept into geological anonymity by an avalanche. Local Indians recovered few remains from the Vilcabamaba gorge. Family records in Brugge are left with only a sorry inventory of remaining axles, burnt leather seats, a steering column and ruptured engine parts, an emerald ring, a blue beret, a silk ascot, and one corpse, mangled and unrecognizable.

Such disasters happen, of course, and human history is littered with the senseless swathes of fickle Mother Nature. Father Nature no less so, which members of the expedition to Taita Chimborazo, as local indígenas called it, would soon discover for themselves. If there were any lesson to be gleaned, it might be that all the great divides in one's life are strewn with unforeseen turmoils. The road to paradise is paved with corpses; and, as an eloquent samurai once casually managed, we all walk on the roof of hell, gazing at the flowers.

Leave cautions and prefatory bromides to the wind. Suffice to say that father and son arrived in Quito, full of anticipation. Pecos' anxieties were the result of his having nearly retired his former skills upon which the authorities now counted. True, he'd marked the occasional perimeter in Santa Fe County by foot. But this was merely an excuse to get his heart pounding again. The invitation had spurred an old flame, and unaware of the scope of his responsibilities he had ventured forward in the hopes of gifting his son a memorable connection to a family tradition whose strengths had long before blanched. Expertise befallen, memories dissimulated. A most comfortable if ramshackle heritability held sway over the remaining life of the Marigold dynasty—all two surviving members—and there was no need for other glories or truths amid a perfectly respectable desuetude: a life, in other words, whose energies, peripheries and aspirations had, for several decades, been reined in by the coziest of homesteads in a village named Tesuque.

However removed from past generations, one's forebears *do* exert gravity, and dispatch decrees of frightening persuasion. So that when Pecos received the inquiry as to his availability, a vague clamor of fond South American recollections surfaced in the New Mexican's veins. The aura was there of some nearly forgotten crescent, a royal imprimatur of namesakes and family pride. In the strange existential bubble floating across the imperial seat, a microcosm of evolution from nose to finger to window, he too foresaw destiny—a splendid evanescence one does not usually question.

CHAPTER 2
The Outhouse at Chimborazo

PECOS HAD BUT one son, and this highway skirting the clouds would be his final passing of the torch, the family album woven of altitude. Pecos' own father had stubbornly clung to the side of a road and the edge of a materialist ideal, leaving a beacon winding its way for hundreds of miles through the Andean wilds for future generations to follow. Now Pecos might at least honor that legacy with a final testament of two lanes.

There existed at that time in the world but one other equally flamboyant motorable road: to a gumpa (a Buddhist shrine) at 18,500 feet in the interior of Himalayan Ladakh. But the oblate spheroid of the planet, as it is lugubriously described, and the unique hump which is geophysically insinuated by Ecuador's distinctive setting, much like a tired shrimp on her side, meant that the country's—and hence the intended road's—height would reign supreme at the very apex of nation states. Nearly twice as high, in effect, as the one in Ladakh.

Still mourning the recent loss of his wife, raising his one son with the aid of a housekeeper (Alma), and calmly given over to a sedentary middle age, Pecos registered little commentary on the eventualities to come, or none that Marigold, Jr would ever recall. He was little buttressed by heavy-handed cogitations, attuned to a carefree attendance where a more attentive father might have suffered pause before such an exploit with so young and innocent a boy in tow. Stiff penalties accrue on childhood sleepwalking in foreign lands, or at least disaster is possible. To roam somnambulantly the confines of an historic setting, familiar and called home, is one thing. To purvey beyond geopolitical pales, outside known bedrooms and hallways, and into the hamadryad's hegemony, where passenger pigeons often fail to catch a current and newcomers are subject to periodic cholera, is simply asking for misadventure.

But these pitfalls had no purchase over either Marigold. What, after all, could go so wrong, with the Government of Ecuador sparing no expenditure to see the project quickly and efficiently executed? The road-building involved thousands of licorice-breathed laborers, mostly mitmakuna, those squat tribals—able to bench-press 200 pounds of granite per man, nearly the same for women—descended from similar peoples of Incan times. These extended families dwelt in tar-paper tents as the building proceeded from north to south. Murillo learned Spanish, and smatterings of Indian palaver. Both he and his father protected their hearing from all the dynamite blasts by stuffing bubble gum in their ears. Hundreds of sticks of the Bazooka were passed around—Murillo had been the one to rifle through the storehouse, upon learning of the dynamiting back in New Mexico—though many of the laborers got them inextricably lodged for weeks at a time, which caused endless confusion. One woman absorbed the gum into her brain. A father of twelve was blown up after failing to hear the evacuation instructions which preceded each explosion. Pecos saw to it that compensation for the dead father's survivors would exceed by an enormous margin any paid out by a government or corporation to date: one million dollars. Murillo took note. The precedent was historic, increasing the legal and economic value attached to a human being.

At night, from their various hotels near the construction sites, father and son dined at all those haciendas which since have become tourist hotels. Splendid dinners. Every variety of potato, and particularly the local llapingachos (a kind of pancake fried in cheese and onions) was consumed, along with salads of yucca, passionfruit and avocado. Soups known as locro and chupe were prepared with fried maize and quinua, and served up by bulky farting men and women on plates weighted down by shanks of chicken and beef. Typically, one washed the three-pound dinner away with buckets of cold agua aromatica.

Pecos' son never touched flesh, however. Murillo had embraced the diet proffered by his own late mother, a disciple of Leonardo da Vinci, whose words ...*future generations shall scarce believe that we could have been so cruel to animals*, or some to that effect, had greatly affected her. Pecos, too, though on occasion he faltered. The son never had. Understanding a child's dietary choices has never absorbed too much speculation, neither in Locke nor in Mills, where it should have been described, if it were going to be. In Murillo's case, his mother's example, a life of non-violence, was amplified by other life-altering experiences: a viewing of *Bambi* and *Black Beauty*, even Pecos' 1668 edition of *Aesop's Fables*, illustrated by W. Hollars, who had learned to re-gouge and chaff his copper plates over and over again, deepening the engraver's commentary on the rift between the Creation and human behavior, particularly the hunting boasts. Such a large volume within easy reach could easily have transformed any young sensibility.

After dinner, both Marigolds would sample a variety of cerveza beers, while musicians and dancers entertained them, and local officials and swindlers hovered round seeking special workmen compensations for any number of alleged excesses. This one, a father of seven, severed his tongue on a shovel; another crushed his testicles and was demanding appropriate compensation for six future generations that would never exist. The million-dollar payout came back to haunt the generous surveyor who was made to atone for all the oversights and labor-deficient policies of the country. This road, he would proclaim, shall transform the status of all you underdogs in Ecuador. He vocalized a scheme whereby the workers would each own a fraction of the road, a touch of tarmac, a nuance of every railing, and tariffs from tourism would accrue to their accounts. The highest road, the highest levels of worker benefits.

Throughout these celestial-high forays Murillo caught rare glimmers of a would-be revolutionary in his father. Ordinarily given to a decorum of self-rule and silence, to an acceptance of absolute obscurity in the rugged heart of America, this Andean idyll was the elder socialist's final hurrah, as it turned out, making up for half a lifetime of lost causes and suppressed sympathies. Pecos had always been a cultural outcast, unimpressed by social standing, which he had in spades. His age ensured immunity to both of the great wars. While others had endured a Depression, he and his lovely young bride were secured by a small fortune left from previous eons. They had a garden to attend, travels throughout the southwest for diversion. Pecos had all the 4-by-5 photographic equipment and prime lenses of his immediate ancestors—the Zeiss sonar, Bertele's triplet, Cooke's distortionless telephoto—and used them to document his love affair with his bride. Images from half a dozen pueblos—her haloed beauty framed in platinum overexposure, a perpetual Jean Harlow blur, amid Indian friends seen as if for the last time in their relic artillery shells, layers of limned silver and turquoise, and feathered riding boots—were scattered throughout the hacienda, along with the countless antiques, books, paintings, scrolls, assorted handicrafts and broken hardwares which populated the Marigold household, crowding out contemporary America.

The boy remembered his mother in this way, passing her days rambling with no concerns for money, with a freedom to be idle or rumbustious; to drive into town for nothing more than a brandy with lady friends at the La Fonda, to gaze with critical aptitude at the latest exhibit of Steiglitz, or go riding. She was a regular at the town library, donating her scandalous first editions of Joyce and Henry Miller, as well as the complete works of Marx and Engels. She became something of a regular at the town bulletin boards, a clearing house for homeless dogs and cats, or goats and rabbits, parakeets and injured owls, always returning to the hacienda with some new life form. Somehow she managed to accumulate a dozen Italian greyhounds, none standing more than a foot tall, and a zebra which quite exceeded their collective size. She would turn over the "winged victims of this cruel world" with great ceremony to a profusion of traditional nesting boxes she herself constructed throughout the surrounding woods of quickthorn, pedunculate oak and hazel: boxes with tiny holes for the blue tits, open-fronted ones for tree sparrows, narrow slots for the brown bats. Canadian jays, tree creepers and a gymnastic trio of endemic magpies that lived for many years in the family pergola.

A señorita flew across the dance floor of a brightly lit tavern. She stopped abruptly before the reminiscing boy at his rigid-backed dinner place, an alluring feminine body in tightly fitting cotton skirt, 100 burning candles revealing all her curves, points and cups, her dyed shiny hair with its beaded hourglass receiving tangled tresses on her deliciously exposed shoulders, recalling for him in so many bestowed nuances his mother.

Murillo, now accustomed to drinking beer, would often drink too much, as would his father, who took much to heart some New Mexico version of Falstaff's "If I had a thousand sons, the first human principle I would teach them should be—to forbear thin potations, and addict themselves to sack." But unlike Pecos, who was drinking to forget the death of a beautiful young wife, his son was drinking to remember. They would afterwards stagger back to the hotel room, prey to other importunes along the way. Pecos aspired to his bed, that it should be kept warm by one of the many lovely ladies who reached out to his zipper. But he never came closer than a kiss or occasional feel on account of his conflicted son. Murillo was paradoxically twisted, craving a real nudie but utterly incapable of bearing up to the one moment of truth, the whore's shocking finger soliciting her own inside moistures, then shoving herself animal-like up on to the benumbed and defenseless Pecos, who sprawled in alcoholic stupefaction atop his bed.

In the event, the boy's practiced custom was to shoo the woman off with a meager tip, remove his father's leg boots, fix his quilted pillows, and cover him with an alpaca blanket.

During the construction of the road, many children were born on its fringes, in earshot of discs and dozers, the grinding of concrete cutters, the droning of boiling tar barrels, the myriad high-decibel sledgehammers and rock hammers. When the final spur of road was completed, there was a celebration in Riobamba's main plaza. Traditional healers were on hand, the yachaj mamas and taitas, as well as countless artesaniás plying their ornate wares—including baskets woven of a rush that purifies donkey urine, not that anyone knew why.

The spur departed the main highway, four miles of impressively blasted road surface hewn through hard-packed desert all the way to the lower Refugio at Chimborazo. At sunset, from Parque 21 de Abril, in Riobamba, the father and son admired the view over the glacial giant, with its lower astral twin, Ventimilla, and neighboring peaks that soared to 20,570 feet. Glaciers sprawled chaotically in the skies over the patchwork of emerald and turquoise fields cultivated aboard the sheer sides of dusty mountains.

"We'll be going home in a few days," Pecos informed his son, patting him affectionately, taming a wild part where the boy's shoulder-length mane had bunched up. "A year's been quite sufficient to get acclimated, don't you agree?"

It was a tired statement of fact, quite underplaying the truth of an engineering behemoth: machinations completed on time and under budget. One death, despite more than 30,000 dynamite blasts. Seven Indians had lost their hearing, but this was as much a consequence of all that bubble gum getting lost in the vicinity of the inner ear. (The gum had an added effect on Murillo, who'd thrown his jaw out by it. Thereafter the bones of his gustatory apparatus would not permit him the pleasure of eating large tomatoes, and for years to come even inhibited his ability to yawn unfettered, condemning him to perpetual facial exasperations.)

The next morning, a procession of shamans was going to consecrate the road by trekking up to the glaciers at the base of Chimborazo and drinking from the falls. It would be an arduous ascent.

The local Mayor smashed a fine French champagne amid the boulder field, then all proceeded to the first refuge, a substantial two-story outlier of local stone and hybrid concrete. From there a trail led to the Whymper Refugio, visible high on a ridge 500 feet above them, at an altitude of nearly 17,000 feet: a 40-foot high hut amassed of heavy rock, a wellhewn frame of timbers, solid bolts and screws, glass windows with indoor oak shutters, and golden banners sputtering in the wind. The air was bittersweet. It stung the lungs if one advanced too many steps without halting to take in a dozen deep gulps of the meager oxygen.

It was 8:30: cobalt mist, scudding morn. The Indians continued up a long corpus of talus toward the base of the icefall. Here the slope, tortured by ages of successive cataclysms, had been reduced to a fine pedigree of petit debris, detritus forming the characteristically lunar-like surface. Murillo, who had the sniffles and first true hangover of his life, opted to stay at the hut and play with two foxes who were scrounging for scraps, intrigued by the odor of Murillo's extended hand. Andean condors cruised overhead. From time to time the lad fixed his gaze through the binoculars, marveling at the fantastical glacial wall with its maze of hanging seracs and gaping crevasses disappearing into the fast-moving clouds. Huge walls of red rock jutted out in the middle portions of the glacier, bulging with unsteadiness.

Before long the 100-strong Indian procession, with Pecos somewhere in the rear, was no more than a string of little wobbly beads, minute pointilla—Seurat's treatment, or Descartes' theorems pertaining to the impact of light on the imagination, which he located in the eye— distinguishable from the rocky slope only by their slow plodding momentum.

It was sometime in the early afternoon. Murillo had slept for a few hours on one of the upstairs wooden bunk beds where climbers usually threw down their sleeping bags before setting off in the middle of the night to attempt an ascent of the mountain. It was a room redolent with flatus, strewn with broken boot-strings, a dulled wrench for tightening crampons, spare lanterns, lead batteries, wooden pickaxes. A wool mitten left from an ill-fated German expedition years before. On the wall, a cracked photo of the first woman to climb the mountain, in skirts. Scurrying mice whose genes had drifted, then shifted, a new species inhabiting the beds. Even the fleas populating the dark crannies were of a new kind, yet to find their Alfred Wallace.

He remembered scrounging throughout the kitchen of the refuge, consuming a peanut butter and jelly sandwich, some potato chips and a rather considerable quantity of foul-tasting water from a plastic jug. He was parched. At this altitude, the climate was a double dose of desert. He studied the walls above, catching sight of the procession. All were up against the cliffs. The Indians were roaming the lower peripheries of the ice, drinking with their mouths directly off the glacier. In a large semi-circle men and women held hands, sang, moved rhythmically. Murillo searched for his father but would never pick him out from the crowd at such distance.

He put down his binoculars and trudged out to the outhouse in front of the hut. It was a large concrete structure, walls three feet thick. Inside the outer rampart was a small betoiletted chamber whose equally dense walls offered additional seclusion from the outer structure, where the two foxes reclined quietly, awaiting the profferings—mince, bacon, perhaps?—of this generous boy whom they could hear tinkling.

Now all three were distracted by an ominous rumble. Did Ecuador have an airforce? A fierce wind, amplified by thunder, closing in too fast.

He remembered his freezing in fear, not knowing what was best. Just time enough to zip up his woolen trousers. The explosion that wracked the thin air after that was no dynamite—was nothing Murillo had heard before. He threw his face out of the toilet room, peered round the outer barrier of the outhouse, and saw what was happening: the two foxes turning, their hair now electrically on end, a wall as high as the mountain rushing down. Murillo threw himself back into the toilet room, lunging to his hands and knees in the corner. Just as the entire world went dark. The foxes cowered flat out to their bellies, hissing mouths agape, absolutely still. Holding fast was the best move they ever made.

He remembered the sound of the toilet seat hitting his head with a clang. Whereupon a rather peaceful, analgesic spate of black night descended. He was a toilet dreaming he was a fox imagining a childhood. In some order thereof.

He was not in terrible pain, or cold. The peanut butter sandwich went a long way. His thirst was resolved by the dripping water from above which percolated down along dozens of newly fissured hairline cracks in the caved-in cement. The entire bulwark had collapsed, though miraculously lodged ten inches behind where Murillo lay on his side and elbow: enough room, barely, to articulate appendages, keep the blood flowing, but completely sealed in. Anne Frank of the mountains. His greatest solace was the sound of the foxes, two feet away, separated by a wall but clearly alive, by their many hours of crying.

He had no idea what time it was, or even how many days he was confined thus. Oxygen was getting in from somewhere, but in the darkness he was unable to determine anything more. He waited, engaging in sustained milksop and consolation, he and the foxes commiserating— gruffing scrunches, howls, gnawing and biting, growling and consoling. Murillo had not been raised in an atmosphere of prayer, but pray he did. For his father, for the foxes, and for all the others up that mountain. Common sense allowed for a fairly clear idea of what had happened. But more interestingly, his mother's angel air surrounded him. He saw her there, surprisingly close, appareled in gossamer clouds, her smile radiant and gathering. He had grown up in a tradition of calm resignation, as if in the lap of a Rafael. Nothing about this sudden situation so very frightened him. He accepted his fate, and that of his father, though the wellbeing of the foxes was of paramount concern; and he knew that whatever happened could not detract him from some greater purpose. He thought about it for long hours, amazed by his own tranquillity in the face of death, grateful to his parents and all of his ancestors, to Tesuque itself, for having passed down this penchant, some generous gene, for philosophy in the midst of the world's turmoil.

The first squeak of light announced itself many hours before his actual removal, along with the ever so faint sound of pickaxes and hollerings from above. Now Murillo was all screams and cries for help. He could not tell if they heard him, and he howled until his throat was raw and he could speak no more. The foxes grew silent, terrified by what was happening.

Finally, the full candescent force of light broke through, and with it a team of first-time rescuers. Murillo and the foxes had been in the outhouse for five and a half days. Everyone who'd gone up the mountain was gone. Most bodies were not recoverable. Pecos and 100 others had been obliterated by the worst avalanche in Chimborazo's history.

The foxes had survived without injury, though were not a little incommoded by their mountain, which would be set aright in time. Murillo ensured that bowls of milk, and hot biscuits and dozens of cans of pork, sausage rolls and sloppy joes be left out for them in their private stash—as well as any remaining stores that otherwise would have gone to survivors.

Murillo was doted over with national fixation in Ambato. Each nurse, he noted, was more bountifully bosomed than the last—these disasters brought out the best in girls—then he was removed to Quito where El Presidente draped the Legion of Such and Such round his aching neck—(whiplash for years to come): gold chains, tin medallions, one for the boy, and one for his father.

"For you, lad, the bubble will never burst," whispered El Presidente in Murillo's ear. But there was a caveat, characteristically presidential: "Young man, from now on you wear the pants, you understand?"

Murillo did not, exactly.

"What I'm saying is, though nobody can replace a father, you are now forever the Mister of your family. Keep your wits about you. And just between us, that open road you and your father built—" He paused and Mister Marigold wondered what the pregnant moment could possibly amount to. "It's yours. Any time you need a road. All yours."

There was an applause, radio and newspaper reporters got their story, and the nine-year-old was driven in a shining silver Studebaker right on to the airport runway's red carpet. A Pan Am stewardess—(smaller boobs)—looked after him all the way to Miami. From there, another airport official saw that he was properly delivered to Albuquerque.

It was mid morning when Murillo arrived in New Mexico. The ringing of thunder blurred by high altitude, a low annoying hum, had only just died down in his ears. (A piece of bubble gum remained.) Francis Hidalgo, Pecos' lawyer, a young man just out of law school, was there to meet him.

"I'm so sorry, Son," Hidalgo proffered.

Murillo had still not shown any signs of trauma. He was too excited to be home, too curious about his situation, to regard the tragedy as anything more than a remarkable occurrence. A moment's harsh magic in the stream of unpredictable existence. And it was that. It was the concrete, the desert ice of Ecuador (a more friable species, admitting to hidden oxygenation) and the thickness of the toilet bowl that had saved his life, of course. That and his impeccable timing. Had he not eaten those potato chips and peanut butter, and subsequently gulped down all that water in the kitchen, he would not have needed to pee. What spared the foxes was a similar configuration of cement. The outhouse itself, enshrouded in Armageddon, must remain one of the great imponderables—an icon as sure as a woman's heart or the language of foxes.

From that day on, Mr Marigold drank considerable quantities of liquid. And beheld potato chips and peanut butter sandwiches with all due reverence.

Hidalgo made small talk.

As they approached Santa Fe, just turning the hill by Turquoise Mountain, there was yet another distant rumble.

Murillo, or the Commander, as his late father had frequently addressed him (absolutely no reason for him to have done so, except as loving confirmation of the boy's power and dignity; or was there some distant relative, himself an admiral, a colonel, a commander? Unknown. Between Mister and Commander, however, the lad now had his painful ineffable marching orders), stared out, expectantly. Hidalgo plowed to a scraping halt on the side of the badly pockmarked two-lane highway.

Both listened, ears piqued. The thunder reverberated. Murillo frantically wrestled the door handle, lunged from the passenger seat and ran out into the semi-arid plains, conditioned now to avalanches all around. Hidalgo also evacuated the vehicle, unsure what to make of the strange hullabaloo—an earthquake?

Suddenly, both caught the edge of an enormous wave of pineapple light fanning out like a séance of sulfur over the pinions and lemon peaks of southern New Mexico. Galactic shenanigans.

A thousand feet away, crumpled down and breached amid the juniper and cactus, the boy waited stoically.

By the time Hidalgo reached him, the great expanse of burning light had dissipated, the rumbles ceased.

They returned guardedly to the vehicle. Other cars had swerved to a standstill. The highway was littered with bystanders discussing the event.

For the rest of the drive home, Murillo was silent, an aching contemplation enshrined in innocence. The shock had only then entered his deep self, passing beyond the easy acceptance, the traumatic fact of his newly certified orphanhood—an accumulation of effects marked by the strange occurrence of that November 2nd, about which, for many years to come, the military would only volunteer a name, "Mike", and its author, Edward Teller.

Those back in Santa Fe and Tesuque had some inkling of what it meant, of course. There was no concealing the strange relevancy of the first thermonuclear blast, when it lit up one's own backyard. Hiroshima and Nagasaki were not that far removed.

The introspective, docile nine-year-old who'd gone off to Ecuador had come back a man, wounded, weary of life already. Terrified, as beasts which come into contact with human culture invariably are, he took shelter in the guise of a hermit, to become not quite but nearly a total stranger in America. Freed, sadly, from parental demands, he lived outside all normal parameters or social rules, scarcely speaking and seldom befriended (though he remained an assured source of hand-outs to those who ventured near—red foxes mice squirrels owls...) Some mornings the scene resembled that famed animal cornucopia of Albert Cuyp, "Orpheus met dieren in een landschap" rendered in 1640, or the other, even more patinaed one by some anonymous seventeenth-century disciple, or precursor of Jan Brueghel, *After the Fall*, framed on a wall adjacent to Murillo's ratty silk-ensconced and cantilevered bivouac. He was, in short, a boy who did almost nothing but read and study and proverbially ponder, in the worldly, obsolete sense of it, not failing, on occasion, to venture out, enlisting a solitary shamble. For near on 40-odd years.

CHAPTER 3
The Chicken That Fell Down the Well

MOVE NOW FROM the imaginary Benelux of 1640, its cheetahs and Styx macaw beside the musing minstrel; from the 1950s of a South American avalanche and US-Soviet Cold War, to this day in particular, the year of Our Lord nineteen hundred and ninety-eight, as Mr Marigold is awakened by a mighty commotion emanating (it was suggested to his dulled half-sleep) from every quarter of his neighbor's estate, with its sprawling semi-arid gardens, a certified retreat for spiritualists of international pretension.

Marigold squinted after his timepiece to discover the ungodly hour for such screeches. Though he had heard similar death knells in the past, these were certainly of a fiercer and more bloodcurdling effect than usual:

"Amigo! Come back, Amigo!"

The Commander, a wraith in tattered skivvies, wasted no time in investigating the matter, stepping out the side door and exclaiming, "Dear neighbor, fear not, whatever the wrathful demon who elicits such anguish. Trust in God, or, if God will not suffice, your own heart, which— though we have not frankly spoken in years—is surely of strong and resilient mettle..." and so on. For despite his erratic history of euphoric melancholia—a condition that will, in time, become more clear—he had never quite broken with his fellow humans, was always waiting for the tap at his door, wasting no opportunity for chivalry, seeing in every ballabosta and bulldog caparisoned maidens and sloping almond eyes. He uttered such nonsense without intention or deliberate inflation, thanks to uninterrupted book learning from sources that pre-dated his current century.

"Come quickly, Señor!" issued the continuing cry.

Why the woman Raquel should have bothered the Commander also begs some consideration. In fact it was Rodriguez, her rooster (and long-time companion of the chicken), presently crowing beside the others, very Gijsbert Gillisz d'Hondecoeter-like (speckled strutter, proud parent, defiant derrière, tall purpose, prone to highly imaginative trysts and nervous bouts, its rooster enunciations no less recondite than our Dutch comparison) who most assuredly had reckoned upon the helping hand of Marigold. And how would a rooster have known? Because Marigold, that most peculiar neighbor, so obscure a figure as to have eluded local gossip (for there was nothing to be said of nothing) was, alone among humans, the one who thought to scatter sacks of home-baked banana granola at strategic entrepots used by roosters. No other human put such effort into the avian calculus of preferred diet. Not even Raquel, fine as she was, no doubt a bird herself in an earlier life, had stopped long enough to recognize the enormously refined tastebuds of her feathered compadres.

Mr Marigold pried open the iron gate and hastened up the dirt footpath towards that ongoing nexus of unruly plaints, right to the footstep of his neighbor's housekeeper. That was Raquel, 19-year-old chambermaid employed by Ginevra de Martin (her long lampblack hair tied clumsily, tears draining her olive radiance, the more marked at first light, barefooted, clad with little left to be revealed by her negligee), leaning dangerously over the well in the courtyard, gesticulating with a shovel to no useful endpoint. Beside her was Ginevra's closest friend and permanent boarder, the suavest of all evangelists, Father Alvaro, along with two other resident clergymen who busied themselves with portentous incantations, and all with a zeal that seemed, by Mr Marigold's quick accounting, to gather force as an inverse function of their inertia.

"Amigo has fallen into the well!" Raquel bellowed. "Please! Can you do something?"

Rodriguez heatedly seconded that appeal. It was clear that the parsons were particularly disinterested this time of morning, or perhaps preferred the taste, to the liberation of chickens. That left only himself to blame for any preventable calamity, inasmuch as Rodriguez, mere rooster, had already proved his colors but could not be expected to do much more.

Upon closer scrutiny, Mr Marigold could just make out the terrified bird flopping in the deep dark 20-foot hole below. There was enough water, evidently, to have saved him from a hard knock and shattered pecker, though the water supply was dangerously diminished on account of the persistent drought across New Mexico, the shrinking aquifer and a host of other too complicated causes—cattleranching, global warming, alfalfa growers, and golf courses. Mr Marigold was going on 50 years and by all appearances a study in frailty. His six-foot-two-inch frame, attenuated legs, pale white ankles and wildly gesticulating arms with their pronounced crazy bones should have given him little reason for hope in stemming the cylindrical shaft like a veritable chimney sweep and making his way down into the hellish, hornet-ridden abyss where the chicken's fate was more likely measured in seconds than minutes.

Now the locums tenens, one a deputy rector from Albuquerque, the other a nondescript preacher on sabbatical from Gouda, were crossing themselves on two accounts: Mr Marigold who had by now disappeared below, and the chicken he intended to rescue. Father Alvaro was less engaged in the theological consequences of these goings-on, and watched with some bemusement. He had never been one to turn down a chicken sandwich with mayonnaise.

"Blessed Father, save my one and only, and in so doing, coincidentally, shed some protective shield upon our fearless neighbor as well," cried Raquel.

"Come, chicken," Mr Marigold urged in the near darkness.

He had descended the vertical tunnel which by his thinking must be hundreds of yards deep, and so cavernous as to yield a temperature change. For as is well known, the deeper one journeys towards the earth's molten center, the warmer things become. Mr Marigold was feverish, perhaps on account of the flu bug which had kept him in bed for a week, but there was no denying the present heat that engulfed the scummy lowest surface of the pit. The water was rank, dark and forbidding. The bird, a plump White Wyandotte pullet, his rose comb and yellow skin tainted with watery slime and ruffled by his rapid descent, screeched in a tone as strident and wracked as that of Raquel, above. The two had lived together for more than a year and it was thus no coincidence that they sounded like brother and sister.

"There, now," Mr Marigold coddled, assuaging the chicken which clung to his arms and naked chest with penetrating talons as its good Samaritan prepared to shimmy back up the well, his behind pressed firmly on one side of the dark excavation, his legs pushing against the other, so that he seemed quite comfortably spelunkered and in control like a Reinhold Messner, the world's foremost 8,000 meterer.

"Señor Marigold, are you there!" came screams from above.

"Yes, all is well down here!" Mr Marigold shouted back. "The bird has been spared any further indignity."

"Now that is a strange reply," muttered Father Alvaro, who knew almost nothing of Marigold but had very occasionally encountered him whilst snow shoveling, par exemple, or spray-painting over the perpetual graffiti that found its way on to all the adobe walls in the area.

There were cheers and Hail Mary's from the earth's surface but at that moment the chicken, in understandable panic, fluttered wildly, causing both bird and man to fall back into the rancid pit.

"What was that?" the rector asked the parson.

Both men looked at Raquel, and Raquel, still gripping her shovel, peered into the hole. "Señor?"

Mr Marigold was flopping under water now, turned upside down, blurred bubbles and eutrophic duckweed obscuring his illuminous line up to the surface. Instead, he pondered past civilizations, reading the mind of the ages, unable to gain purchase with his legs which struggled aimlessly in the murky depths, while the chicken hurled itself to and fro, circling around the masthead of the submerged man. Although no one could actually divine this remarkable sight from above, on account of the darkness, it must have looked ridiculous, for it is rare in these times to see a waterlogged chicken circumambulating a sunken hermit.

But, in truth, those moments were in later days to seem to Mr Marigold a rare deliverance. In that watery desolation, dense with visions and the universal altercation of flesh and destiny, he saw the world as he had never quite seen it before—through the eyes of a chicken, luminous mist at roseate dawn. He felt only good will, a warm, fuzzy release from his body of manly obsessions. No longer was he bothered by the cries and benedictions from above, where several other residents of Father Alvaro's retreat had gathered beside the well to inquire of the chicken and the man bent upon rescuing him.

"Moments ago he grabbed hold of the chicken," Raquel informed everyone, her words and cheeks flushed and rapid.

"How wonderful," came the refrain.

"A passing note in the history of the world," said another.

"That calls for a chicken stew most excellent and fair," hailed Alvaro with a naughty smirk.

"Not on your life, bastard!" Raquel ignited.

Still subaqueous, with precious few seconds left of this life, Mr Marigold should have been flailing but was, instead, gliding innocently towards the surface, neither dead nor alive, neither breathing nor notbreathing, but transfigured by a curiosity of passions as strangely feathered as any in the history of water-well incidents.

Wild ducks, quixotic quails, ponderous partridges and loquacious grouse, phlegmatic pheasants and raucous roosters populated his mind; a whole hierarchy of heavenly creatures roamed the vast interior of thought that belonged to him. White ear lobes commingled with feathered shanks, tails black, bodies chestnut-red; Leghorns, Cornish cockerels, Light Brahman hens, Minorca pullets, silver-gray Dorkings, and a speckled Sussex cock all wandered the back roads of his precious dreamtime. From Rhode Island and New Hampshire to England, France and Sri Lanka they strode, pecking at the molecules, freed and inimitable, their loveliness a verity so refreshing, logical and bright as to give loft to an otherwise soaked and sappy gentleman.

With these worldly chicken mentations he broke through the surface, managed to seize upon a steel stanchion protruding from the bedrock in which the well had been blasted out a century or more before, at the time of some great historic land grab, railroad crossing, gold rush, trading adventure and subdivision, raise himself from the noxious depths, gasp for air, and—in one heroic leap of the imagination—grasp the nearly lifeless avian and resurrect his position in the chasm.

To riotous cheers up above. Never had Tesuque so rallied to a rescue.

Now, without to-do, he rocked back and forth, pushing and umphing, humping and cruising, ridiculous bare feet gaining inch by inch of purchase up the slimy walls of his dungeon, a toe-hold here, a cranny in which to lodge a finger there. Until his mountain-climbing epic was completed at the earthly rim of scattered light, multiple laying on of hands and salutations to greet him. Meanwhile, the bird flopped clear of the well wall and on to the dirt, where it rushed off to be with Rodriguez and others of its kind, a confederacy of gravel- and feed-grubbers who agitated in clucking congeries near to their coops.

Raquel did not waste time thanking the Señor but threw herself at her precious chicken, which sought only repeated fawning of its sodden wings and pulsating chest, to douse its eyes in love and gratefulness.

"Oh my little chicken..." her sobs rang out.

Yes, of course all this might seem silly to those unmoved by the plight of a mere chicken. Even Mr Marigold demonstrated other preoccupations at this time, as it would appear he had somehow lost his briefs in the well. No amount of erudition or heroism could neutralize his uniquely ridiculous-looking nakedness.

Father Alvaro, the least roused by these events, congratulated him on a most distinctive show of valor.

"Way to go, Monsieur," he said heartily, alcoholic fumes still rising from his night before.

It might have ended there, had not the Commander happened to catch sight of two mating monarch butterflies in no less peril than the previous chicken. Their wings, catching the light for just an instant, were held captive on the well's surface of fatal scum. Lucky for them—a witness!

"What are you doing?" asked the crowd.

Marigold had once again lowered himself into the dire and dank, drawing later comparison with one Eduard Dekker (Multatuli), author of the celebrated *Max Havelaar,* who twice threw himself into the sea whilst travelling from Holland to Indonesia, despite warnings of great whites. "What, my neighbor's gone mad?" Father Alvaro inferred. "Or is he, perhaps, Dante's chief disciple?"

All gathered around. Mr Marigold carefully maneuvered himself into the position that would allow him to rescue the ever-so-delicate creatures—which he did, jettisoning them upwards into the shaft that gave them vent, incentive and loft. Off they fluttered, emitting just the hintiest of nuance, some sonic gratitude, he perceived, remaining dazzled by all these extraterritorial communiqués, basking in the psychic realms of scuzz. That warm loam of a conceptual bosom, underpinnings of the shady grove, a pastoral ideal that commended all forms of justice in the natural world and in which our Commander had always been steeped. Even the unrelenting horseflies seemed to him, in his present state, little messengers of that figment of the imagination known to some as God.

It was an ideal, of course, for as Father Alvaro commented, one could devote an entire life to a single well. Imagine that within seconds of marooned butterflies, along comes a feckless globe-trotting wasp, shipwrecked on the very same island of mold, then the damselfly, followed by the midge, and that's scarcely accounting for the hundreds of mosquitoes that must see the torchlight in their eyes go out on a daily basis in that sinkhole. Should a man spend his life rescuing each and every one of them? Would God look more favorably upon such efforts, than, say, the work of a missionary among pagans in Brazil? (A subject very close to Alvaro's heart, as shall later be elaborated upon.)

These were not solvable subjects at the time, nor could the very strange occurrences of that morning strike the religious Fathers as anything other than anomalies, the workings of a thoroughly upright eccentric who might well be the sole inhabitant of his very own sanitarium, no address, no diagnosis.

Rising transfigured to the surface, the Savior of the Well, or Knight of the Woeful Chicken as he would later prefer, clambered more deftly than before back up the slimy stonework, his underwear dangling from between his front teeth. Reaching the lip of the cistern, he was no less astonished than the others upon glimpsing the strangest of all presentiments—more surprising, even, than the chicken visions and butterfly whispers that had occluded his vision down below: a personage whose own evident eccentricity put those of Marigold to rest. The oddest of all delight-makers was approaching from 1,000 paces down the road, appearing from out of nowhere, bearing all the blind corners and prehistoric enigmas of New Mexico in his gait.

Let it be known and appreciated that the Commander was not infrequently torn between such blind corners, blurred edges and lost anecdotes, coordinates that translated into despondency or bliss. His illuminations were frequently blinded by their very light, his great urgencies and aspirations no more than pillow stuffing. Whereas, at rare moments, he laid claim to a truth as permanent as a ball bearing, during which a single blink of the eye would certainly miss a revolution or two.

All these commotions in a single morning. To better grasp their meaning, one might do well to step back, if slightly, gain a vantage on the chicken and the man who saved him. Fortunately, there is time enough to utter a few words about that.

CHAPTER 4
A Peach Tree That Gave Birth to the Clown

FIRST, A SPARK was ignited, mineral crystals in what is today the Karakoram—vertiginous spirals of granitic mud playing host to the earliest alpine DNA four billion years ago, long before the first fledgling prokaryotes of Shark's Bay. Eventually there was an egg, then the chicken and, 100 million years later, a man. That is the complete, unabridged history of life on earth. The rest is all an afterthought, or academic exercise. For example, it is well known in the scientific literature, that chickens (*Gallus gallus*) and persons of high standing possess the same number of neurons. According to the newly received wisdom of our gentleman, Mr Marigold, chickens, hens and roosters count among their numerous achievements the abacus, cuneiform, feather beds, alarm clocks and yoga. Of course, they also excel at all the more mundane equivalents: an economic system (without any taxes), an inordinate liking of pineapples and cinnabar, a propensity for dreamtime, the passion of love-making, the duties attendant upon ancestor worship, and a general aptitude for family values hewn of vertical aspiring. While they live on the horizontal plain, they never lose sight for a moment of their Mount Everest. And to that end, they naturally harbor the same hopes as the rest of us—namely, a good life for themselves and their offspring. Like most other sensate organisms, they are prone to great flights of fancy, fits of inspiration, days of despair, months of madness, whole seasons of sadness and apprehension, or, conversely, never-before-described nights of merriment. No doubt the days of despair outnumber those of joviality, except, perhaps, among those few remaining wild ones in Southeast Asia—where, 11,000 years ago, most were first coaxed into bamboo cages—that continue to elude capture.

On account of their widespread domestication, chickens (along with *Rattus rattus)* have lived in immediate proximity to humans throughout all those millennia. The affiliation has not been entirely friendly. Just one company in Arkansas, for example, takes great pride in slaughtering something like three billion chickens each year under conditions that would bring Stalin to blush and Hitler to full bloom. This much was known to Mr Marigold, from his wide reading of the subject during his brief interregnum in the fuzzy waters of the stinkwell; nor was Raquel at all surprised to hear of these learned matters from the Commander following Amigo's salvation. She was herself prepared for every extreme unction and, conversely, disquisition; was ready to face whatever divine powers ordained the life or death of her beloved Amigo.

Now, one might ask, what sort of person could read a chicken so thoroughly? A boy who by presidential decree owned the Avenue of the Volcanoes, had subsequently disappeared by most worldly accounts, had devoted 40-odd years to book learning? What was this monster of loneliness, prone to sudden upstarts and turnabouts? Had he gotten restless? Had the source loomed in his lair? Ideology become stale?

Mr Marigold slept acrest, betwixt, above and below a reef of teeming books, all shades of dust, nuances of molded bindings befitting the pallor of the ages. *Gil Blas*, its spines worm-infested. *Anatomy of Melancholy*, long-boring beetled. Files too numerous for fathoming; papers plastered like a heavy snowfall; diaries in numbers debilitating, stacked high and far, suggesting an intellect that had evidently pondered every last precarious notion, staked out a perch overlooking quotidian affairs of this world like an eagle—dispassionate, removed, but acutely searching. His unread letters to nobody in particular overflowed with commentary; his marginalia cascaded down the sides of clippings from 100 magazines and newspapers. Tomes teetered like some impossible modern sculpture, or were cached in the manner of emergency supplies beneath pillows; opuscules were arrayed like so many blotters beside the beleaguered bed, looseleafs piled perilously against the adobe abutments of his bursting backroom. In every depression of these dense domains, Mr Marigold's arcane addiction could be easily read in so many scratch pads and ledgers. The abstract and theoretical, the lettered and highbrowed were platitudinously propped up in volume after magnificent volume, an erect edifice—call it a utopian tower with its own drawbridge wherein the bibliophage, inspector, registrar and recorder of ideas and civilizations, species and precious matters, dwelt silently and alone in one man.

The man and the house were also one. Understand the hacienda's history, and you know its inhabitant. There was a room for everything, on account of both the architectural influences of the ages that had permeated Santa Fe society and previous Marigold monies lavished on untold imports. Hence, a drawing room with pediments and pilasters; badly painted Hepplewhite oval-back side chairs in the dining room; a pretentious Grand Salon fireplace with its Kurdistan runner rugs atop broken Moravian tiles and not-quite-matching stenciled couches; putti, plateresque, mullioned and eyebrow windowlets, intrados and bargeboards throughout the house. Nearby, the Venetian Room sported garden facades. Such pretensions were the talk of American high society in their day, but had softened, with time, into the oblique and dusty Pleistocene of Tesuque. French and Italianate fantasies, coffered ceilings and Louis XV paneling, murals after Boucher—all had devolved into simple bultos of Our Lady of Guadalupe or Saint Raymond, petite vitrines stuffed with tired Wedgwood, cracked Tucker china, filthy silvered-glass goblets and overlaid urns scattered beside a festive contagion of santos and retablos.

Two worlds mingled at the hacienda, but in the end had taken on the ragged edges of the Commander himself, who was as disinterested and self-effacing an inhabitant as any estate ever witnessed. Much of the porcelain was coming unglued, was shattered, decayed and discarded. Paintings lay ruined in garage heaps; antique habiliments of every style and design were obscured by grime and cobwebs.

In its tenebrous boudoirs and divining chambers were all the voluminous thoughts of their architect, whose lineage had left this rundown, loose-fitting latitude of kunstkamers to the present owner. Their largeness was his saving grace; or, more precisely, his books and paraphernalia, which took up every cubic inch of space, defied the chance visitor to swing a cat or take up quarters. Elbow room was understandably at a premium, what with thousands (possibly tens of thousands) of hardcover, paperback and unbound manuscripts, not to mention all the other furnishings dating to ancestors of obscure taste. Mavens of furniture would know the industrial and aesthetic nomenclature for these myriad riggings, like so much tackle and bric-a-brac, the gouged-out desk counters laden in the oils and resins of centuries, French and Spanish chairs upholstered in Flemish fabrics, heavy Viennese chests, their drawers permanently stuck, and now stuffed with papers like an ill-fated bird at Thanksgiving. Sikale, as they say in Somali.

In this 400-year-old castle, Mr Marigold had entertained his phantasmagorical self for nearly—how many years?—without too much want of satisfaction or obvious storm. His errancy was allowable, given the meager staples needed by him and the fact of an annuity paid out quarterly by his father's executor, Francis Hidalgo the Third. Hidalgo, now in his late sixties, had lived in Santa Fe his whole life. He had watched the boy take to books like a Chiapas horned guan to its preening, and both he and Mr Marigold, Sr had predicted no less an outcome than that the child —motherless from nearly the beginning and mentally excitable by most accounts—should be given every advantage, but none forced upon him, lest he react badly.

He should be, first and foremost, left to his own devices. Such an education was modeled on the equations for happiness of Bertrand Russell, whose mathematics Marigold's grandfather greatly appreciated (along with the Zen logisticos of Ludwig Wittgenstein). He should also be equipped to ride a horse, discharge a firearm, treat dangers and pleasantries with equal disinterest, forsake all elixirs, run barefoot like the Indians of the region (though they did so less and less these days), and write with the same dexterity (and quill) as the great-grandfather, a surveyor in these parts when New Mexico was still a union territory, a profession passed along in the Marigold family from father to son, dating all the way back, it was surmised, to the time of Willebrord Snell, that distinguished Dutch mathematician who had, for what it's worth, succeeded in calculating a single arc of meridian.

The tradition of geodetic big-scale earth-related computations, planetary monitoring, cadastral inspection of local property rights, hydrographic riverine studies and basic topographical survey all figured in the honorable Marigold family tree. Invar wires (of the pure 36% nickel kind), micrometer theodolites, talk of triangulation with its language of steel tape, pickets driven deep, pole holes and base terminals, referring objects, face rights and face lefts, collimation and resection, tachymetry and Beaman arcs, heliozincographics, contouring and deviations had absorbed the Marigold clan for a long time—until, that is, it came time for Murillo to take up the family trade. Alas, he could neither draw, nor see straight, nor think rationally, which automatically precluded his figuring out the most recent 12-volt 60-kilogram telerometers or Japanese Total System Lasers. He was clumsiest the further away he was from his library, and tripped over the slightest irregularity in the earth's surface—stock and trade of the surveying business, but a menace to himself. Lacking perspective, or even the most rudimentary ability to distinguish a detail from a horizon, a particular from the whole shape, a herd of distant buffalo from the idea of ants, his mind permanently in an exalted absentia, Marigold was—by family standards—a cripple.

In recognition of his catastrophic incapacities, but upholding other qualities that deserved every encouragement, his education was tempered by the one ingredient that above all else was consistent with the honor of the Marigold record: that he be instructed in the ways of virtue and steadfastness, so as to remain calm and confident before Mother Nature who so perpetually dashed all hopes of fairness. By this predilection he should be unmoved by the rigors and tumultuous seas of what are normally called "current affairs", let no changing perimeters affect his demeanor, and take no insult or injury personally. As it turned out, Mr Marigold (few would ever resort to his actual first name of Murillo, on account of his father's habit of calling his son, respectfully, Commander, Chef d'atelier, Commandant or Commodore, depending on the season, the mood, the weather, or for no reason at all—and these honorifics were amplified by the boy's own self-description following his claim to "Mister" upon that fateful sanction by El Presidente) was a dreadful learner, distinctly incapable of separating himself from the assaults on the world. Indeed, the more turmoil, the more he seemed counter-intuitively to throw himself into the fray. It was all—America's nuclear arsenal, photochemical oxidants, an earthquake in China, the killing of a wolf in northern New Mexico by bounty hunters—entirely personal to him.

Pecos Marigold was a Western Free Melungin who spoke Volapuk in addition to English, French, Dine (Navajo) and Spanish. Benighted by frequent bouts of depression, unable to accomplish meaningful goals, as he envisioned them, and probably more sensitive to the condition of the world than should be recommended for anyone, his hazy background of mixed blood, he always thought, dictated the terms of his loneliness in later years, though it certainly needn't have been that way. All of the racial slurs haunted him, the heavy burden of bias that resided in the Indian and Hispanic worlds, where they mixed with awkward parlance and distinct class, or *casta* privileges, or lack thereof. In the 18th century such offspring were sometimes labeled as half-burned Mestizas, wolf-like Castizas, mid-air and knock-kneed Mulattas, coyote-born and upside-down Genizaras or spotted white Moriscos and Cambujos. He never remarried, thinking that to do so would be to perpetuate the racism in his own family, albeit by no fault of his own. But he felt shadowed by history, nonetheless. His one hope was that his only son should succeed at some profession. His wife, Madeline, had been all of 21, frail and Bremen blue, an anxious heaving chest, hair freshly colored of corn, succulent curves and lanky unabashed Rachmaninov nature belying a petite, all-vulnerable body, the sweat of her ague accumulating on that forehead he had kissed so often those last days, watching behind the doctor as she perished during her one childbirth: there was nothing to be done.

Pecos was ill-prepared to raise young Marigold, and largely gave over the task to a raw-hide woman of Asian extraction, Alma Khan. This caustic overseer of Murillo's chaste upbringing was herself the descendant of yak herders in the Gobi whose vanished father had been tied somehow to the CIA, airlifts, military camps in South Korea, all in a secret attempt to help the Mongolian people throw off the yoke of Communism, which they did, though long after Alma had emigrated.

Alma had tended to the boy as an employment. Whatever feelings she might have evolved were well concealed within her hard rind; she was a wary woman of calculating extremes who now adjuvated the uncomplex workings of his estate with an arrogant self-importance. After Pecos was killed, and Marigold, Jr arrived back home from Ecuador in a pitiful state, he grew distant from other children, forsaking their games and social hierarchies for a lonely, intellectual existence. Alma and Hidalgo were the extent of his connection not merely to adults but to people in general. Both proved erratic. Hidalgo dropped by only occasionally. Alma ironed, cleaned, prepared meals and did all those things the young man should require, always trusting to the prepared moment she might come into a contractual bonus of substantial sums and flee her servitude. No love lost. Adios Tesuque. Goodbye to mold-rots, trails of snailsilver upon the kitchen floor, methane water, and the call of the presumptuous chicken. It meant no more to her than it had to Father Alvaro. Both of them would have preferred Amigo covered in mayonnaise, between two slabs of Russian rye bread.

On that day of the chicken's terrible adventure and ultimate deliverance, when Ginevra's compound was struck by a second disturbance as unexpected as the first—for who expects a chicken to throw itself down a well on any given morning?—the man-like being who appeared from off the roadside and approached the courtyard stood beside the coyote-tree fence, waiting to be officially recognized. His appearance was marked by a great clucking of bantams in the coop (our Chicken of Mr Marigold was the first to raise the clamor), for he might just have been a ferret.

The terrifying intruder stood motionless, looking round, peculiar in every respect. His nearly naked body was painted in stripes of soot, his ears done up with corn-husk earrings. His eyes were plastered, as in a burlesque show, with exaggerated circles which merged into dominant black lines across his cheeks to his ears. On his right shoulder he wore a kind of rucksack, and from it hung a bizarre part of an animal's hoof. Terrible. Defiant. The product of untold carnage. He carried a rattle, and around his neck dangled a pouch the size of a goiter, its contents unknown. Two horns protruded from his head, in the manner of those scurrilous Renaissance depictions of Moses. On his feet were worn-out sneakers.

All this Raquel particularly observed.

His belly was distended, his bejowled face marked him as a man of late middle age. With a freakish grin he winked at Raquel, admitting one other detail to her list of observances: not one tooth buffered the sensation of mirth monopolized by naked gums.

Raquel knew that he was a clown of some sort, like the famed Hopi Paiyakyamus, a shaman accustomed to bringing delight on special occasions, but normally in plazas at the pueblos, like those painted by the famed George Bellows and Robert Henri, the closest of which— Tesuque—was eight miles away. But there were no Indians here, only dejected Fathers who knew nothing of laughter and forgetting.

She raised a question mark, though the movement was tempered by the softness of Raquel's inner nature, which knew no trace of haughtiness. After all, her own beginnings had been as humble as humility permits. She had grown up in a covered wagon with three fathers, all claiming her, all with the most wildly abandoned lives: a cowboy from northeastern Wyoming, a Peruvian herbalist faker and a circus hand from Guadalajara who'd immigrated to New Mexico in past years. The one woman all had loved—a Guatemalan—had disappeared the night each was granted ten minutes alone with her, at a brothel named appropriately after the saint who had three balls, each weighing the amount of the other two, a whorehouse once located near the village of Nambé, though no more. Raquel was the outcome of that half hour. How she managed to find her three fathers and coax them into raising her in a covered wagon requires more time than our clown, standing impatiently at the gate, would allow. For he had now produced from his bandoleer a little firework, of sorts, or projectile, and seemed intent on relaying a good fortune or another to the inhabitants of this estate.

"Where's the magic chicken?" the Hopi asked, as Raquel stepped up to the fence and peered over the wooden gate at the stranger.

"Why you want that chicken?" declared Raquel, now rightly suspicious. She knew Señor Chicken was back with the dozen or so others in the shed. Keep in mind that Raquel had hand-raised the little birds, all of them, and maintained a constant vigil over the skies for the hawks that patrolled there. This was a wild land, and she knew chickens were ill prepared to defend their bastions against so much hostility from all directions. Evolution had not bothered to shield them from predators. With her broom and apron skirt she made a fitting image of the Protectress, constantly on guard, alert to the slightest decibel at all hours, even during private moments. Consider, before returning to our waiting clown, how at the instant of her most zealous submission to the male member—in this case, Fernando's; he worked at a gas station on the reservation and frequented the bed of Ms Raquel—she'd heard the uncharacteristic clucking refrains emanating after midnight from the coop. Who else could have picked up on so faint an agitation? With all 200 pounds and 212 muscles of Fernando fairly in motion, working towards his heaven, in tow with a fanfare of strident bedsprings the 25-year-old ruffian was thrown from his pleasure like a matchstick. Raquel, who never slept without a negligée, raced into the hallway, passing at least two insomniac priests along the way, and sped out the kitchen door, frantic to undo the locks, so as to check up on her little darlings. That night, it was only a rat or two feeding on the leftovers, but it does prove a point: her loyalty to *Gallus gallus* must never be doubted.

So it should not prejudice the reader one iota that she was less than amicable towards the stranger inquiring after her birds. He had clear motives, though she could not tell you what they were, especially upon examining at close range the strange device the Paiyakyamus, as anthropologists also thought of such wandering priests, had withdrawn from his corduroy haversack.

"What is that gadget?" she began.

"A Space Shuttle," he replied.

"Eh?"

"Muuyaw. Pam tsiro put ev puuyawnuma," said he, knowing she'd not understand, but referring to the moon and a bird flying around inside it, or nearby. A kind of vision quest which he had earlier that day commenced, the way Paiyakyamus are supposed to.

"Eh?" she said again, openly perplexed.

At that moment Father Alvaro, in company with Brother Bernardo, the chocolate-monk (as he was known) from somewhere in the wilderness of Bill Williams in western Arizona (his monastery manufactured organic brownies to maintain its lifestyle) and saffron-robed Ken Isaacs, a novitiate from a community in Urbana, Illinois, that followed the rites laid down over 400 years before by Roberto DeNobili (the famed Italian Jesuit who migrated to southern India) arrived at Raquel's side, as inquisitorial as they were genuinely concerned.

"Is there some problem?" said Father Alvaro in a kindly tone. What a busy day this was shaping up to be.

But before an answer was forthcoming, Mr Marigold also appeared at the gate, having gone home, dried off, then come back to check on the psychological well-being of his new friend, Amigo. He was carrying a thermos and some contraption combining mercury and peanut butter. "Good day, Gentlemen," he exclaimed. "Herewith, warm soup for the chicken. Made with the finest mineral water. A broth confined to lentils and carrots. It should stave off the ill effects of that infernal damp hole."

As he handed Raquel the thermos, still warm from Alma's stove, he could not help but wonder who this curious-looking man might be. But, too polite to appear over-anxious, he merely commented on the ear husks.

"Nice earrings, good sir." Then he noticed the rocket ship in the Hopi's hands. "Ahh, a space enthusiast?"

"Owi," replied the clown, or shaman, or whatever he was (for Mr Marigold was not certain that this man was no enchanter, there being ample evidence of such). Whereupon he produced from the frayed alforja which hung by colored yarns around his shoulder a printout describing the latest news from NASA of a newly ejected probe to the planets.

The Fathers, Brothers and Mr Marigold in particular gathered around the computer printout. There, in so many words and graphs, was evidence of a "Holy Grail of Cosmology", "Great Walls of Galaxies", "six million trillion miles" of space with 119 clustered nebulai all moving in a uniform direction at the speed of 425 miles per second toward the constellation Virgo, revised data from the Cosmic Background Explorer spacecraft, launched in 1989, and pertaining to those peculiar ripples of matter scattered across the very edge of the Birth of Creation, and so forth.

These matters were of great interest to all, save for Raquel who had never ceased focusing on the question at hand: the clown's purpose in asking about her chicken.

"He came to steal my little Amigo," she said, after scrutinizing the typically unkempt thaumaturgist. "Or to hex the whole lot of us."

"Your good name, sir?" Father Alvaro interceded.

"Thomas," came the Hopi's reply. "Thomas Sipaltsoki. Not the Polish pronunciation, by the way. Means Thomas Under the Peach Tree on account of my parents having made me in the fine shadows of such a tree, when the moon was blue, the wind so many knots, the wolf wailing steadily, the crickets in tow, a pure brook gurgling nearby, a cow lowing in the barn, two horses shaking out the day's heat, a cat in high temperature calling to the nearby hills for a good lay, the leaves jostling in the wine-dark night air, and so on and so on. It's become a sort of song in my family, though they're all dead now, and my English scarcely does justice to the original Hopilavayi."

"But why a poet partly attired as a priest, absorbed by details of the cosmos, and all superseded by some interest in a woman's chicken—a woman, I gather, you have never met before this day?" asked Marigold.

"Never met, never would meet, and hope never to meet again, God grant me this one wish," Raquel aired, spitting into the dust, there being much of it on account of the 100-year drought historians will doubtless concern themselves with in future days, as the insects start to arrive early, or not at all.

CHAPTER 5
Amigo Heads Towards the Stars

THE STORY PASSED quickly from village to village, as words have a way of doing," Thomas began. "We used to climb over rooftops, sling wolf shit at newlyweds. They paid us well to do so."

"Why would they do that?" asked the Commander. Where, he wondered, would one even *find* wolf feces in this day and age?

"You see," mumbled Thomas. "Nobody remembers that stuff. Clowns are outta work, or mopping up donut shops. Only a few stubborn fools remaining now. Me and Sammy Hak, old Jerry Pituq'o up along Zuni River, and Yohozro Wuhti who's living with his nephew in Middle Río Grande country. Sells comic books most days. The young ones don't know the old traditions. And the older ones, they think we haven't kept pace. We're just a freak show, veterans of a war that never happened, with trumpets and flags that carry no meaning. Still, sometimes, in the traditional places, the mesas in Arizona, some of the pueblos— San Ildefonso, or herein Tesuque—we are asked to moderate like politicians at town meetings. Toss the odd pile of manure when things get heated— dumping uranium tailings for profit, messing with water rights. Never too late for a little smirk, piss 'em off with a good fistful of belly-laughs. Normally, we shake a rattle, wave an eagle feather or two, threaten with a bear claw (though Fish and Game inspectors have come down hard on us), pee on their floor, just to screw with people's heads and the existing order. Make dungheaps of the sociology. Blur boundaries, upset the parameters, force new avowals and resolutions. That every day should be New Year's. If we're lucky, cower them into a renaissance, jettison the familiar world through concentration."

"But concentrating on what?" asked Alvaro.

Thomas looked off in the direction of a strange world.

"Sometimes, when the brain's all bent and fried, a clown tosses a pinch of good medicine into their skillet and that person can find new balance. At a wedding, or a funeral. At the inauguration of a new casino its owners want blessed. I don't care what the occasion. They give me 30 bucks, a blanket, some whiskey. Doesn't matter. I'm doing it for the Great Spirit, traveling his road. It's all I know."

Mr Marigold watched this sprouting Thomas with keen interest, because during this entire exposition he was doing something with his metallic rocket ship, fitting the fuse, twisting the wax tail, smoothing the eagle feathers that were attached to the backside. It was an odd contraption, and the Indian clearly had intentions for its use.

"But go on, good man. The purpose of your visit? To what do we owe this special encounter?"

"Well, you see, we're not just politicians, not just clowns or acrobats of deep things. I got an idea that that chicken has a special purpose. We know. We've known about them since the first days of the coyote, the quail, the jaguar and the parrot."

"What? Pray tell. Don't dishevel us with such suspense."

"You see that way?" And the Indian pointed towards the high snowy mountains, beyond the Las Truchas peaks and the ski area, behind the towns and four-lane highways, cloistered condo developments, truck stops, bingo parlors, gas stations and Mabel's 24-hour restaurant. Past the satellite dishes and ashen-white details of human colonization—the opera, the big estates, electric fences, private roads, the No Trespassing signs and country stores.

Everyone nodded—except, that is, for Raquel who would not let go of her distrust and apprehension, and remained quite stiff and uneasy about everything.

"Well, to the rear of those mountains, good friends, lies the future. It's always beyond, you see, never right in front of you—that is, unless you link the two. And Señor Chicken is that link on this day of the year, this year of the century. You're very lucky, Señor—" and he nodded at Father Alvaro, who wore the partial mantle of his creed, such that one professional could easily detect it in another.

"You can't trust the government," Thomas continued. "Big things are overhead—galaxies and answers to questions the Elders have been asking since the first days of the—"

"Coyote, the quail, the jaguar and the parrot?" everyone, except Raquel, stated in unison.

"Precisely, by golly," said he, slapping his painted thigh with his one free hand.

Suddenly, Amigo came ambling from behind the house.

"Amigo, what is it!" Raquel inquired, frozen by the illogic of her bird striding soberly and straight in a beeline towards the Indian. "Amigo?" she again cried, intent upon arresting its seemingly decisive intentions. "You see, he already knows," Thomas said.

"Indeed," Mr Marigold threw in, quite intrigued by the course of events.

The chicken came right up to the clown, exercised its wings, then settled down and waited with the most knowing demeanor imaginable in a chicken.

"The rocket ship will carry the chicken to the stars and back. It is a very fast rocket, on account of the fuel which derives from hydrogen—the stuff of the universe, and non-polluting," said Thomas.

Such details engrossed our Mr Marigold, for it was one thing, he believed, to amass the soundbites of forefathers and tricks of tradition, and quite another to admix learned ritual with contemporary trivia.

"A flint stone," said the Indian, withdrawing it from his pouch. Then he stooped to place the rocket—two feet by three feet by three feet, or thereabouts, in dimension—on the ground. Its cockpit, modeled after those of the Mercury missions, was wide open to receive Amigo, who stepped inside without the slightest trepidation.

"No! You can't!" pleaded Raquel, now coming to her senses, for up until this moment, who would have believed that her prize Amigo would of its own accord step into a rocket ship?

"But this is all too preposterous!" protested Ken Isaacs, who had remained utterly quiet and observant until now. He had had his own experiences of saddhus and other holy men in the Far East and so was not entirely unaccustomed to bizarre mornings and magnetic personalities. But this, this voluntarism on the part of the chicken, this plan to probe the galaxies, exerted something unknown over him. A fantastic puzzle as tantalizing as it was absurd.

Thomas recognized the scepticism all around, so rightly figured he had little time to schedule and execute a launch pattern.

"Why don't you come inside for some home-grown fruit punch and we can discuss the matter," Father Alvaro suggested, witnessing the sullen flare rising in the female company, and knowing enough about Raquel's history to predict a serious collision course. Raquel was as dangerous as a chola cactus if she needed to be.

But the Indian had already closed up the rocket, lit the fuse, oriented the launch and prepared his incantation.

"Gentlemen and gentlelady, fear not. Your chicken will make its tour of the universe, absorbing psychic nuances which I will interpret, and he will return within 15 minutes, or days—I never know which. This is my job. I guarantee my work or your money back!"

He chuckled—and kbooommmm!

"Adios, Amigo!"

"You sonofabitch!" screamed Raquel, tossing her full body at the Indian but missing him as he, like everyone else, lunged for cover whilst the mighty blast—an entirely unexpected convulsion of thunder and conflagration from so diminutive a contraption—shook the neighborhood. She spat, threw dirt and rocks, kicked and cursed as the missile left the surface of earth and headed into unknown dimensions.

Into the lambent air sailed *Gallus gallus* on a maiden voyage to discover the hidden background radiation, or black hole, or undetected edge of the Big Bang, or whatever it was Thomas had in mind.

"A whiskey, anyone?" the Indian intoned, inviting himself indoors now, feeling very good about the lift-off. Mission Control had carefully delineated the rocket's coordinates, the fuel was holding steady, the second- and third-stage boosters had all performed according to plan, and the rocket, at last glimpse before disappearing over the ski area, seemed to be headed in a perfect shot at the moon, or Jupiter, or the Crab Nebula. Of course, it being bright daylight, nothing was visible but blue sky and the odd cluster of blanched cumulus, wherein Amigo was last seen speeding upwards at unknown velocities.

"Exquisite!" cried Mr Marigold, dusting off his breeches.

"Monster!" Raquel shouted, tears whisking over her so lovely cheeks.

"I'm stunned," Father Alvaro stated. "Two great unexpected occurrences in one morning. Imagine that!"

"Well I'm calling Leopold," Raquel enflamed, and she headed inside. Leopold was their local cop, whom they all knew well enough.

The others, more generally humored, followed her indoors to indulge in some hard spirits while awaiting transmissions from the stars and Amigo's return.

CHAPTER 6
The Camp of the Spirits

THE ROAD THAT LED to the Camp of the Spirits curved past giant oak, stemming aspen creeks, drawing up along Lombardy poplars and boulder-burgeoning river. A narrow bridge froze over in winter, when hairpin turns were treacherous, the romance of a single lane turned lethal. Along this medieval route, later known as Bishop's Lodge Road, could be discerned the whole history of colonization and economic disparity: peoples who had settled for a century, then moved on, or indigenous poor mestizos; and others, eighth-generation Anglos of mixed blood in hidden trailer courts that once would have been sold off for 4,000 dollars, now commanding a million or more; and the huge estates owned by California movie stars or British regals. A flood of high-cost second homes that ignored the fact Tesuque was in a desert, and the water disappearing.

There was, in addition, another stratum of culture, dating to the 1920s—to those artists who had sought out this western enclave since the days of Victor Higgins and the Taos group. Higgins, went the legend, had not proposed marriage solely to his girlfriend but to all of New Mexico. His prolific canvasses took the spalding skies, Lucretian hills, fetished fields and mixed Indians, and granted them a colorful apotheosis which sought to override the forces of acculturation. On the purely artistic plane, his enthusiasms remained contagious if sometimes fashioned of air and the past tense. While many (Willard Nash et al.) tried to paint like him, few came close; his only real peer was Andrew Dasburg, a man who set his own brilliant precedents. Adobe flats, complexes of rectilinear dab-thick horizons, fecund fields, trees saturated with alpen glow or advancing storm light, clouds peppered with the pall of mountain weather, lavender, pellucid, penultimate hues pinioned by gravity, liberated by unseen forces, sixteenth-notes of energy, and a stark windy wild pervaded his oils and watercolors. All this had become common parlance among that latter-day Santa Fe school, but none got it quite like Higgins, who died in the late 1940s, leaving a beautiful home in Taos, 50 miles north of Santa Fe, adjoining the famed Mabel Dodge estate, where pigeons still roosted in dozens of boxes hanging over the entranceway.

Higgins' nuances could be read at the entrance to the Camp of the Spirits, where visitors were welcomed with a ramshackle post on which were written the following words: "I Fear Nothing, I Hope For Nothing, I am Free—E me lefteros", borrowed from the epitaph of Nikos Kazantzakis. Father Alvaro had visited the great Greek's windy tomb above the city of Heraklion on the island of Crete many years before, and this saying had always stuck with him. That, and the vision of Higgins, both of which Ginevra adopted as her own.

Mr Marigold had seldom been to the main sitting room of the Camp of the Spirits. He was the quintessential loner, not unfriendly but certainly not neighborly, unless, of course, chickens were in peril. Presently he took in the modernized estate, so different from his own. It was old enough to have escaped the fanfare of the "Santa Fe style" for an earthier ensemble of nuances characteristic of the earlier inhabitants, archeologically deeper than the nineteenth, or even eighteenth century, but eccentrically fitted with contemporary touches that lent to the home a luxury.

Mr Marigold could size up quickly that all that industry of repairs and redesign which made the house so habitable was not the work of Father Alvaro. It was not his house, though it had become his base of operations for many years. He was a man of few possessions, and his cares not easily ascertained. Who could have espied that beneath the simple veneer he was burning up inside with love—not of God, as is the general adage, but of a person lost to him years before.

"What can I get you?" Father Alvaro asked the clown, who had led the others inside. "I think we have some cold beer, and there's always a shot of sherry or sangaree to be indulged. Whatever you'd like."

Not the least annoyed by the drunken Indian stereotype, Thomas asked for Pelegrino with lime.

Followed by three hard shots of whiskey.

Drink orders were taken all around: Monsieur Marigold was abstaining, Brother Bernardo, Isaacs—scotch, and then Raquel—"Blood!" she flared, dangerously vinegar. She was beside herself.

The good Father, always wry and several inches past sarcastic, asked her if she'd like that with ice, then raised his portly self, brushed back his dyed mane, got up with a slight groan and shuffled through the dining room into the kitchen, muttering en route, "Amigo will be back, dear.

Why trouble yourself so?" He was wearing sandals and a cassock, and effected the self-confident attitude of the confessor.

It was a communal kitchen, part priory, adobe and parterre, where visitors wolfed down generous portions in generic silence—or that was the unstated rule, though it was applied only during times of international calamity, like the Swedish victory over Brazil's star soccer team in '95, or was it '96? Meals were forever punctuated by the benignly rowdy quips, anecdotes, nightly jive and rampant speculation of any working retreat. Monks commingled with cowhands, pokes and the odd tourist out for a weekend of spiritual uplift. All got deep, philosophical, wound up and rubbery. Conversations were of the salon type, famed for long, heavy-drinking profundities.

The table—a sixteenth-century Peruvian look-alike, with leather-bolted chairs—sat twelve. At the moment there were half a dozen guests at the Camp, in addition to the full-time occupants: Father Alvaro himself; Raquel, who, dangerously stewing, had removed to her bedroom; an old gardener, Sannazaro, about whom Mr Marigold knew little, other than his supposedly miraculous manner with flowers; Christina, a graduate student from a wealthy family in Bergen, who had come to study North American Indian petroglyphs for her dissertation, had passed through Tesuque, seen the sign "Camp of the Spirits" one larkish afternoon, and had had little difficulty carving out a niche for herself for much longer than the intended part of a summer. She still nursed two-year-old Matthew, whom she'd had by some drifter in town. Lastly, there was Barringer, a Persian Gulf war veteran: hair *en flagrante*, unshaved whiskery face, bouldery body altogether lacking fat of any kind, nearly freakish protruding jawbone, a purple velvet patch over one eye. He'd lost that eye to petroleum poisoning in the war, he boasted. Barringer lived behind the garage in a little stone cottage of infinitely Wordsworthian proportions, covered in ivy, distinctly antiquarian. He could do everything, from routing a rattler to fixing a pump. He boasted of taming the bears that were coming down in search of food and water on account of the terrible drought; he always left them a large pot of cold water and something to eat on the far perimeter of the five-acre property. "Fig newtons is their favorite," he'd tell folks. It appeared he was beginning to win Christina's heart. But this was merely his fantasy.

And, of course, there was Ginevra de Martin herself, a Hollywood-style beauty from Corsica, whose family had bred across most of Europe. At least one originated in Hell, a small town in Norway. (Postcards read "Wish you were here.") Others from her past had originated on the Isle of Wight where, according to her, they lived angrily in stone shacks, climbed cliffs in search of puffin egg yolks, wouldn't say much to one another for 500 years, and died out, more or less, on account of ill winds, pneumonia, bad tempers and deliberate genetic miscommunications. But at least one forerunner harkened from royal blood in the Faroes, a gorgeous icon of a queen, or princess, a glacial legend of the Mother, and her long blonde hair, perfect, statuesque beauty and superb manners came singularly across time, transported by the very best working order, indelibly surreal, with just the right touch of impromptu in the ageless pulchritude of Ginevra.

She managed the affairs of the retreat, when it suited her. It was her love of the Great Ideas, and her long friendship with the Father that made the strange configuration of souls possible in the first place. There were, too, palpable benefits of male companionship: a certain security against burglars; someone to walk the dogs, remove the occasional wasp; light conversation laced with French politics—always refreshing; and a helping hand with groceries or shoveling snow, at least when Alvaro wasn't complaining of a hernia. At this juncture in her life, such details counted for something at the end of the day. Her ex-husband lived abroad, and never called. Her one son had died years before.

Soon Father Alvaro returned with a few drinks. "Where's Raquel?"

"She was mad. She left," said Ken Isaacs.

"Ahh, well. She'll be fine when her Amigo returns. Which should be, how long did you say, Thomas?

Fifteen minutes?"

"Should be about that time," the Indian replied. "But then, never know for sure."

Father Alvaro leaned forward and whispered to the Indian, "You don't really think that chicken's coming back, do you? Or that it's possibly alive? But don't worry. There are others down the road that look just like him. She'll never know the difference."

But the Indian was confident. "Of course it's alive. Naturally he'll return. In its own time." He sat back, poured his drink in a glass filled with ice and stared contemplatively at the others.

"But the trajectory—why, it must have been 300 feet, 400, 500 feet in the air," Alvaro went on. "I'm no judge of these things, but I know, as a horse knows its oats, that that chicken must surely have fallen hard on some rock or other by now, and nothing is going to save it."

"Really, Monsignor, why be a doubting Thomas—" Mr Marigold suggested, with the hint of a humor no one connected.

"I'm afraid I too find it hard to accept," Ken Isaacs joined in.

"Now, gentlemen, for Raquel's sake—" Mr Marigold labored. "We all witnessed a very professional launch, the rocket sailing over the mountain until it disappeared. Truly there was enchantment about so terrific a blast-off in these otherwise uneventful wilds. Why not suppose that, like a boomerang or homing pigeon, the rocket will return. Is it not true that all things come around in this world?"

"It is true, friends." Thomas sighed in a Hopi fashion, finished his beverage with a healthy burp, and got up to leave.

"Where are you going?" Father Alvaro inquired.

"I, too, am like a boomerang," Thomas opined, "and have other great unanswerables to attend to up the road."

"But the rocket ... What, are we just to sit and wait?" Brother Bernardo broke in, annoyed now for Raquel's sake. She had, he thought, guessed it correctly: the clown was nothing more than a dubious showman, dangerous at that. A con artist singularly focused on free drinks.

"Wait if you like. Your waiting cannot affect the outcome."

"But what have you accomplished by coming here, other than to tear out the heart of a fair maiden?" Alvaro asked. "What insolence, what crime against animal nature, a chicken only recently saved from that horrible well who'd committed no wrong. Why did you do such a thing? I am, I must confess, utterly befuddled. For a few moments I felt the elation, the mystery, the purpose. I was conspiratorial, I admit it. The heat of the moment, the sense of a presence, a purpose, a mission. Now I feel only regret, helplessness and anger. You, sir, have disappointed me!"

The Indian looked at him, standing now, and tossed out the oddest assortment of words, everyone thought. "Monsieur Cardaillac, forget about the chicken. He has begun his fine little journey, starting with some chicken scratch, where it all began. You must begin your own. Go to your father. I believe he needs you."

With that cryptic message the clown bid his adieu, out the door lickety-split.

"What was that all about?" Ken Isaacs mused, not entirely surprised, having encountered his share of ethnic guilt, of koans, conundrums and holy pranksters throughout Asia.

Brother Bernardo was far more addled. The chocolate monk was not accustomed to these cosmic perturbations, being far more susceptible to tangible proofs of God (i.e. brownies) and a minimum of hocus-pocus.

"My God," the good Father Alvaro said, wincing. "We have been bedeviled—or, worse—hexed, like Raquel figured. I'm shocked."

There was something he was not saying.

"I sense more to this than meets the momentary mind," Mr Marigold foretold, and all were silent for a few seconds, considering the strange occurrence that had transpired before them. It was like a ghost had passed their way, a certain meteorological anomaly forever unexplained, like those rare Blocking Omega Highs one hears about, ball lightning, or the Brocken clouds discerned by tramps abroad summits like Aconcagua's.

"Let us give him that. Quite the thing to do, quite right, quite." Father Alvaro sank back in thought, his fingers now nervously clasping a San Miguel beer.

The shaman, in the briefest of retrospects, had penetrated Alvaro's most inner being, though he was unprepared to grapple with it, or utter another word. How on earth had he come up with "Cardaillac", and towards what end?

CHAPTER 7
Father Alvaro's Secret

GINEVRA HAD OVERHEARD this last exchange from where she was resting beneath the old rusticated Raffles fan. It was late spring, and the temperature had soared that morning. She had snoozed right through the double commotion of the well and rocket ship. Ginevra had no problem sleeping free and clear of revolutions, as she was a barn owl of post-meridians. Information could not daunt her. She would always pass out before the television around two in the morning, hours after everyone else in the household. Prayer transformed their metabolisms into those of children, she often held.

"Don't fret over Raquel. She has, as we all know, a tendency to dramatize the mundane. Anyway, her chicken needed a break from the routine," she said.

"Hello, my fair Lady de Martin," Mr Marigold proclaimed, having leapt from the couch and taken her left hand, kneeling chivalrously to kiss the delicate fingers not once, not twice, but thrice, in a manner becoming the universe in which he dwelt, further from the neighborhood than mere measures of distance could ever reflect. Delicate? Those unmanicured, coffee-stained fingers, working fingers, beauteous but blunt, sinuous yet squarely of this earth? A worker's unpretentious fingers. Hold the rake, lift the shovel, scoop the dog shit, scrub the oven fingers. "Ahh, my lady, to see you is to see the moon rising like a blue swan over the lost continent of Atlantis! To touch those fingers is to feel the heartbeat of puppy love!" Mr Marigold continued. "Hi, Marigold, you foolish old goat."

Despite being neighbors for nearly two decades, she knew next to nothing about Mr Marigold. She never returned his praise, or even called him Mister, and while delighting in his eccentricities, even, in desperate moments, vaguely pulled to him, she'd take her wine, debate at high volumes, but always kept her feet firmly planted. Whereas Mr Marigold, as everyone who knew him realized, was a habitual throw-back. It was easy to label him that dreamer among dreamers, helium balloon of consciousness, succulent grape in the mouth of a blind man, a charlock among domestics, that passing cumulonimbus in frayed knickers.

Now Raquel re-emerged from her lair. "I'm leaving," she declared. "What?" A general, resounding disquiet erupted.

She carried a frayed leather traveling case, and continued holding on to it for dear life.

"Put your bag down, dear child," Father Alvaro pleaded. "I am so sorry if you've been offended. But surely, dear, you must know that Amigo will be fine? And that what occurred between us—"

"I'm not your child," she pouted. "And it's more than that. I don't want to talk about it."

She put her suitcase on the pashmini carpet with its 100 knots per square inch forming an iambic pentameter of lapis blues, trimmed with mauve, articulated in 100 verts, tied in filigrees of stealth on the far-flung shores of Nagin Lake near the beginning of this century. (Such carpets, including Kirmans and heavy ten-by-fourteens from Tabriz, lay all across the floors of the Camp of the Spirits.) Her suitcase, planted there with all the headstrong assurance of a major paradigm shift, bespoke her nomadic itinerary, as it had been and would evidently continue to be.

"Raquel, you do whatever you have to do," Ginevra said soberly. "Always trust that we adore you. We need you. We appreciate you. Your service here is not service but the articulations of family; your help to Father Alvaro has made all the difference. I doubt—speaking for the good Father—that there is anyone who could hope to replace you. And I know, for myself, that you have become more of a daughter and a friend than an assistant. That much is clear, and doesn't even need to be said. I thought, I had hoped, I would like to believe, that it was a mutual affection."

"It is, Ginevra." Raquel fell into her, a near tearful embrace.

"Oh dear dear dear, what is it that eats at you? Excuse us, everyone. And Ginevra took Raquel into her bedroom and shut the door.

"Well," Mr Marigold said with a sigh, "the dramas of every day."

"Indeed," Father Alvaro seconded. "I really don't know what I would do without her."

All people must have their story, though few must tell it. One cannot barge in on personalities who will, in their own time, do something, be it nonsensical or felicitous. Some will become giant rifts of ore, or feckless snots; some taciturn tremblers; others nincompoops of inordinate babble, personages alive with paradox and poignancy and the power of accumulated experience; yet others, just plain catatonic. Men and women, young and old, will inevitably fill every drawer with their memories, or populate a room with their itineraries. It is all about becoming a local person. To inhabit the familiar. To choose a final resting place, mark time measure by measure according to the number of friendships, trusts, love affairs and deeds accomplished. Some are given to handprints, others to footprints. The distinction is minimal, from above.

But down on the ground, every detail, fine point and nuance matters. Such particulars are enshrined and apotheosized in that which is local. To be local, said Bernard Einstein, a Santa Fe dressmaker and self-proclaimed cousin of the other Einstein, was, in the end, the answer. The sublime.

The secret truth of our existence. Everything of worth happened in local terms. Consider: that romantic summer night's tryst in moonlit meadows. Tragedy. Comedy. Senseless stuff. It was all local, as well. Along such avenues of warm reflection, Marigold himself had noticed how the most commonplace snapshots of yesteryear, now faded and anonymous, tended to burgeon with the world's lost horizons of sentiment. Those times—the picnickers, that day blossoming in absolute perfect obscurity beside a river bank, the deep tawny and roseate grass *Melicytus fluxuosis*, the bonnets, the long dresses, those tin-type expressions so delicately etched and preserved in the sepia of exhausted and impressionistic lives. All of it—the world's finest hours, deepest nostalgias, most enduring myths and nagging desires—could be said to be local. Not to belabor it: we want to be protected and vouchsafed in such locales, untouchable before all of the horrible vagaries and oscillations of history, which always happen out there, in the real world. Not at home, or in the neighborhood. To be secured like a dangling modifier over our pleasure on some sunny afternoon in Brigadoon. That was precisely why the hermit remained in Tesuque. There could be no safer burrow. Ferrotypes, gold letters, wild ivy atop gravestones.

Father Alvaro also thought about such photographs at that moment, images which graced his mind throughout a half century of loneliness and comfort: of unfulfilled duty to higher powers, and the longing to be reunited with lost loves; of simple day-in-day-out purpose that would not be stymied by too much introspection; and of just the opposite, whatever it might be. Amusement parks. Subdued backgrounds.

Meanwhile, in the master bedroom, Ginevra held the girl and did her best to convince her to stay. But Raquel was famed for being headstrong, and had been harboring this melancholy long before this day. It was a sadness born of her spectacular, unresolved upbringing which now, at the moment of Amigo's strange disappearance, bore down on her with a colossal and unavoidable injunction. She had to go; she had to find her family, her true family. "You must try to walk sedately," Robert Louis Stevenson had written.

"You know how much I have appreciated all of you," she cried. "But I have to do this. When I find what I'm looking for, perhaps then I'll be ready to come back."

"Then here. I can't stop you, but at least take this." Ginevra took 2,000 dollars in cash from a safe in one of her enormous walk-in closets, and handed it to Raquel. "Hundred-dollar bills. You'll need them. If you run out, I want you to call me collect, dear heart, don't hesitate to. I know you won't abuse my affection for you."

"Oh Ginevra," Raquel wept, clinging to her like a true daughter. They stepped back out into the living room.

"Good-bye, Father," Raquel said to the stunned Alvaro. She kissed him politely on his hand. "I hope I didn't hurt you. I will never forget you." The Father reflected on those words, but then replied, "When Amigo returns, he'll be well cared for. No more rocket ships."

"Good-bye, Mr Marigold, and thank you," she continued, about to hug him, but she was stopped short by the Commander's emphatic obeisance, his own 300-year-old Japanese servant girl's demur.

A unison of voices blocked her path. "Where will you go?"

"Wyoming, to start," she said. "Back to the place where I was born. That shit hole behind Laramie." She laughed maturely. "Fortunately, I must have been numb at the time. All I remember is the good stuff." Christina, baby Matthew and Barringer saw her off to the front gate. Barringer was most affected, as he had nurtured a flame, as he had for most young girls, and it appeared it was about to be snuffed before it had had its moment of incandescence.

"Hey, I won't forget you," he said.

But it was Father Alvaro whom Raquel actually looked at.

"At least let me drive you to the bus station," Barringer protested. Alvaro knew it was hopeless and turned away.

She headed up towards the Tesuque village along Bishop's Lodge Road.

Father Alvaro raced from the living room to the downstairs, and to his locked private chamber that nobody else ever entered. He frantically got the stubborn bolt to open, lunged for a rear wall, sorted through large canvases that had been covered in rugs, and found what he was searching for: a magnificent painting of Raquel, completely nude apart from head feathers and amulets, her nipples and thighs as supple and invigorating as a spring shower in a time of drought. He covered the painting with the blanket, and raced out through the garage onto the gravel driveway and towards the gate, shouting her name.

Out of breath there on the highway, he saw her stepping into a pickup truck.

"Raquel?"

But it was too late. The vehicle sped away.

Father Alvaro stood transfixed by his own flood of emotions. When the other occupants of the house, on seeing this wreck of a man out near the gate, converged, or most of them did—not Ginevra, who had suspected all along, and instead returned indoors—they beheld in his arms a most compelling portrait of an idealized Raquel.

At that moment the clouds through which Amigo had heroically traveled, and which had all morning been moving steadily over the Las Truces mountains towards Tesuque, gathered in a thundering of purple purpose over the Camp of the Spirits, and with a single bolt of lightning let pummel a fury of hailstone-sized rain that forced everyone indoors. They went through the downstairs. Seeing the open doors to Alvaro's private chamber, and noting the Father's uncharacteristically docile, unprotective manner, Ginevra, who had met the party at the door with towels, could not help but state her curiosity, on behalf of everyone present, regarding that long-pent-up chamber. For years—for so long, in fact, that the clandestine bombshell imagined to reside inside was no longer relevant—it had been allowed, ignored, tolerated. It was a cubicle not merely off limits but off everyone's mind. A question mark nobody cared about any longer. Never once dusted or vacuumed. A compartment that had become invisible, attired in cigar smoke.

But now, imagine, its doors had been left wide open. Its sole occupant utterly deflated and uncaring. The invitation was blatant.

"Go ahead, I'm nothing now," Father Alvaro uttered, paralyzed with an austerity of means before the pew of his own confessional.

Everyone drew close, peering into the darkness. What did they expect to find there? Sacred books? A diary? A phonograph machine? Or weird cult things, pornographic literature, pinups on the walls, a bomb factory?

But as they entered, Ginevra, Mr Marigold, Brother Bernardo, Ken Isaacs, Christina and baby Matthew, and Barringer could smell the truth.

"Turpentine? Oil paints," Ginevra stated.

"It's an artist's studio," another voice declared quietly.

"*You* painted her?" all persons present avowed.

"Brilliant!" Mr Marigold shouted. "May I?" And with the Father's unmoved assent, Mr Marigold began to pull out canvas after covered canvas.

"But why keep such talent a secret, dear man?" Ginevra said. "And all these years? How did you manage?" Her voice choked up, for she could not—nor could anyone—quite believe the power and magnificence of the portrait of Raquel.

But it was a mere prelude, for in painting after painting a gallery of divine nudes emerged: dozens of young girls, and older ones, too, who blessed the untreated canvases, or blocks of bare pine, with their provocative imperfections, ambiguous gazes into every known dialectic, each maddening ellipsis of life.

Ginevra was there, and she, of course, had never posed, or not knowingly. Christina, too. None was deliberately erotic, which is what made the primitive female sexuality so unsettling, so perfect and pure and terrifying. The male had reached his highest wildness in these paintings, touching the unspeakable in hints that knew no bounds, dashed all restrictions and taboos, gave himself away to every desire, each latent conjuration. The bodies were connected to the faces, of course, but in a manner that was new—new in the sense that faces and bodies are normally as separate as the DMZs of every war. But Father Alvaro had painted facial outgrowths of the body: faces whose beauty and expressions could be said to be at one with their full length of figure, flanks and musculature, vaginas and pubic hair, breasts of all attitude, derrières divine. So much in the creases and texture, the wrinkles and warmth, the lewd and the liquid, contiguous with faces of Renaissance depth.

"My dear man, you are a double entendre of brilliant proportions," Mr Marigold extolled. "A tour de force of feeling. You should be in galleries, museums..."

"You needn't have hidden them. How silly," another rang out.

"It is contrary to Catholicism," the Father mumbled.

"Nonsense," Marigold scolded. "The Church is nothing but for its paintings, sculpture and music and the sentiments they evoke."

"But wait," Ginevra said, studying the absolutely ravishing portrait done of the maidservant, and noting an obscure signature in a corner.

"This says Cardaillac? Who is Cardaillac?"

"I am Cardaillac," Father Alvaro stated. "And now I have no doubt as to Amigo's safety."

Ginevra pondered all this, then stated, "You loved her, didn't you?", referring to the portrait of Raquel that faced everyone at the front of the pack of 100 other canvases.

"Yes."

"You've loved them all," Mr Marigold said, unconsciously, admiringly, conveying a truth that had been made obvious, the word turned to flesh then to cinder, and finally back to its unearthly ideal. "Yes."

With that single admission, Mr Marigold knelt down as he had done so often, and proceeded to take Father Alvaro's hand with the clear intention of kissing it. He would have succeeded had Father Alvaro not come to his senses and quickly withdrawn. This brought much laughter to all, except to Mr Marigold, who felt rather foolish on his knees, and not without an ache as well. For he was approaching 50 years, and had neglected his body during all his decades of book reading in a room not so very unlike the studio where our occupants presently stood for well over an hour, gazing with the greatest thrall, the most unabashed delight, at the handiwork which constituted Father Alvaro's terrible secret, and wondrous unburdening.

CHAPTER 8
The Spilling of the Beans

SOON THE STORM PASSED ON, as New Mexico tempests always do, and the sun reanimated the Camp of the Spirits.

After the commotions of the morning, concluding with the constellation of naked women arrayed in the late afternoon light like so many precious enticements in Father Alvaro's well-kept secret studio, Mr Marigold and the other present residents of the Camp of the Spirits sat around on barstools in the open French country-style kitchen, beneath the grid of hanging pewter implements, German cutlery, and the finest ceramic cooking pots from Provence and Japan, contemplating one of the great truisms of life, often repeated by Ginevra de Martin: Life is mad, so grow your vegetables, seize your little moments of pleasure, laugh without limit, regret nothing, leave something behind, and don't look back.

"Tell us, then, Monsignor, how so marvelous a talent felt compelled to remain hidden from a world eager to celebrate and adore such passion?" implored Mr Marigold, who'd now stood back up.

Fully purged by his exposure, and the obvious pleasure his long-time friends seemed to take in his artwork, Father Alvaro, alias "Cardaillac", for reasons soon to be revealed, commenced telling his harrowing history, leaving out those details not crucial to the dramatic backbone of his account, or which, he felt, would surely bore his listeners.

"I was born in Paris. My father was a pentecostal priest; my mother, his servant. I grew up on the rue des Martyrs, a few doors away from where the great composer Maurice Ravel lived as a child. That's certainly one of the lasting charms of Paris—everybody lives near somebody. I was baptized in the church on the Isle St Louis where Mozart performed in later years; had coffee next door to a flat in which Joyce once resided; used to lift weights in the back room of a bar adjoining Napoleon's favorite fish vender, and so on.

"I remember how my father's arms flailed, the sweat poured off his temples during his sermons. He was most persuasive when drowning in his own convictions. When I was eight, Father was transferred to a remote jungle in Venezuela where miners had converged and the love of God had been usurped by the glow of gold. We later learned that it was his honest weakness for the opposite sex that necessitated his removal from France. Nonetheless, he was a missionary at heart, and was sent by the Church to convert not local Indians, but the invading industrialists and migrant laborers, to vanquish those monetary aspirations destroying the Amazon.

To the Church's credit, and this must be a first in the history of South American religious matters, greed was deemed the heathen.

"Soon after our arrival in the Serranía de Mata it began to rain. I believe that rain did not cease for the eight years of our time beneath those impenetrable canopies. It was not a hard rain, but a perpetual dripping because of the partial shelter afforded by the ceiling of fronds. But we paid a second price for that covering—chronic ailments of the lungs and the skin, and a continual flood of insects, many poisonous, that turned paradise into an obstacle course.

"My father had something—a will to survive, with which he infected all who came near him. It was that beaming optimism which, over time, won the whole mining establishment to his side. I did not miss a beat, as there was absolutely nothing else for me to do but observe the transformation of men who were animals into animals that were men. They built for my father a modest church of red sandstone, which at night served as a sort of saloon, and was the place where local Indians came for spirits, and to trade. Often, they traded women for short periods of time. My mother suffered, but she persevered. However, one night she found my father administering Catholicism to two young Indian girls in a back room. I had, as chance would permit, been hiding under that bed, and had felt every tantalizing creak of the springs, which churned and bridled inches from my eyes. Those groans were my only aspiration from that night on. The soggy mattress pressed repeatedly down on my side. I thought I would be crushed by the lust of my father and the bouncing beauties he was riding. At one point I choked, but nobody seemed to hear except me. I thought to flee, to save myself, but the prospect of being caught was too horrible.

"My mother said nothing. She dizzied near the door, then stepped back out and staggered off into the night. My father, in the event, tried ineffectually to make altered sense of what Mother had witnessed. He was a tonguesmith, but nothing was going to change the fact of his having been caught in the act of impregnating two teenage Indian girls.

To my father's credit, they were beautiful girls. No man could have resisted them.

"As for myself, I was now altogether desperate to have what my father had.

"My mother slipped out of her ashen skirt and mottled blouse, and leapt into the Chuchivero where she was devoured by piranhas. There was nothing of her to recover.

"Her picture, which Father kept on his reading table, framed in a lovely bamboo carving, tormented us. We, of course, elevated her in our minds to a saint, for having behaved so, so ..." And Father Alvaro grew silent at that moment, unable to find the right words. His listeners averted their downcast eyes, aware of the discomfiture such recollections must have caused him.

After a few minutes, with a vigor of re-affirmation, noting the sun pouring in the french windows, he resumed his story.

"But when my father's two teenage wives each had their babies, a boy and a girl, I was suddenly older brother to two infants, and life became meaningful again. I never used Father's guilt against him. Instead, I started drawing, first on sheets of paper whose infernal dampness caused each mark of my pen to spread slightly, creating nearly Oriental effects—diffused calligraphy, as one might describe it. The inclination took hold in an utterly frenzied way. I could not stop. Women fueled my brush. Initially, pen and ink, later oils.

"I concentrated on women, painting the Indians not as I saw them but as I wanted them. I will not describe the details, but they were innocent, straight out of Eden, unblemished, unafraid, focused on what intimated the greatest pleasures. My father recognized my intense fascination—it was already an addiction—and made no move to alter its course. You see, all the girls were mostly naked in that jungle. Their bodies were a natural fact to me. I had no other reality with which to compare. And one afternoon, I was probably 14, I found myself naked with his two wives (I never thought of them as my mothers, nor did they consider me anything other than fresh game) while Father was away touring a mining pit with a visiting Church functionary from France who came to learn how one missionary had begun a network of mining unions across the Northern Amazon. Throughout the afternoon those two girls gobbled me up. I exploded in and out of every orifice, and felt like a meteor shower. So this was God, I reckoned. And oh how seriously those two girls took their orgasms."

Mr Marigold couldn't help but notice the total fear or paralysis that had come over both Brother Bernardo and Ken Isaacs. Neither could move; neither could blink, or even shut their mouths, which hung open in hypnotic trance. ("It's all right," the Commander assured them. "You'll survive.")

"From that moment on," Alvaro continued, "I obeyed only two taskmasters in life: my lust for women, and my painting. Fortunately, both were exquisitely linked.

"I'll never know whether the two more babies that arrived were because of my sperm or my father's. By then there were nine of us, and two more hardly mattered. Attributions, consanguinity and such were of little consequence in the jungle."

Father Alvaro's listeners sat in silence, stunned as much by his utterly calm oration—as if he were reading from his Bible, which he did each morning—as by the very substance of the spilling of beans.

"A drink, Alvaro?" Ginevra asked, her voice trembling, and stymied by the sheer aura of liberated desire that permeated the room.

"Please, dear," he said. "A San Miguel, with ice."

Brother Bernardo was closest to the refrigerator and brought the Father his beverage. Everyone took a moment's pause to air out and avoid the detonating stares which Father Alvaro would pass from one listener to the next: some kind of terrible irresistible truth that no one dare acknowledge, but which all were on the edge of their seats anticipating.

Then the narration resumed.

"My paintings improved, though were of a subject that my father insisted be kept from public view. He was concerned that there could be an uprising if the local Indians saw their women in such unblushing guises. To be honest with you, I was very naughty. You see, I had no inhibitions. None. The female anatomy drove me wild. I lived for it. From those beginnings in the Amazon, I was caught in a field of forces, taboos and psychological dilemmas. Eventually, I got out, leaving my father behind to fend for himself. By then, he was in his late fifties and had no desire to leave his harem, which had increased in number. Moreover, he was greatly loved and, I suspect, needed by the miners, who—in fairness to the sex fiend—actually took his sermons to heart.

"I eventually found my way back to France, and was ordained as a priest after several years in seminary attempting futilely to work out my sexual dilemmas and the origin of those imbroglios—the delicious guilt, the crucible of known and unknown family, and the memory of my poor, wretched mother. I had done my tutelage at the Sacré-Coeur, where Saint Denis was martyred. I had learned all of the *Martyrium Polycarpi* by heart; had waded through Irenaeus, Donatism and Arianism, Clement and Ignatius, and wrestled with all of the Apostles on the role of men and women in this world. Contemplating St Augustine's inglorious designation of woman as a "sewer" giving birth to children as if defecating, I knew my remaining days with the Church were few.

"But throughout my myriad travails, my devotion to God lay finally in my paintings, which were, in turn, utterly beholden to the female. I lived two lives. Neither was a lie. Both were necessary for my survival. I haunted Paris like a salivating specter, its dick lashed to a cross. Horrible. I was a wastrel, seething inside with these oppressive, carnal cravings. It was inevitable that I should eventually be caught in my duality—and it happened, as such things do, in the most unexpected and therapeutic of ways.

"I had been browsing on the Left Bank one Saturday afternoon, purchasing bread, fruit, the odd chocolate, and gazing in the window of a picture gallery. I'll never forget the particulars—who can forget

Paris in the spring when love bites? She was standing with a liveried chauffeur who held her acquisitions in his arms. Her blue Bentley was parked on the curb adjoining the gallery. I was in my habit, and she must have found it altogether curious that a priest on Saturday would be touring an exhibition that was devoted to the female form, so to speak. I had been so absorbed with the paintings in the window as to forget myself, and the fact there I was, standing in full habiliment gazing at—at you can imagine. *Vive la France*, after all!

"She grinned, I grinned, and within an hour or two of our forgettable small talk I found myself having lunch with her at her apartment near the Luxembourg Gardens. Her home was a masterpiece, hand-me-downs from the last three Kings of France. I studied everything. She was the Marquise de Cardaillac. Her late husband had financed the restoration of the Jardin du Tracadero.

"Our friendship turned to love. Though she was 25 years older than myself, I found in her a lover and surrogate mother, both. She appreciated my artwork, which I was quick to show her. As I had never signed any of my paintings, which by that time had quite proliferated, she suggested a favorable plan. Her husband had attempted painting, but had absolutely no talent for it. It would be a fitting tribute to his memory, which she cherished, if I would agree to sign all of my works with his (and hence, her) name.

"It was of little consequence to me. If anything, I feared posterity for the revelations it might convey about a past which, to my mind, was awash in sin. Far more important was the unstinting, unquestioning love she showered upon me. It was the Marquise who persuaded me to still the priesthood in myself and concentrate on that passion for which I was born.

"We spent every day together for two years. Her largesse was never proffered as a debt or received as a burden. It sprang from the sheer generosity of her heart, which overflowed like the many gardens in Paris she and her husband had underwritten. But, eventually, I grew restless. When it came time for me to leave Paris, she understood. I moved first to New York, then to Boston where, in a gallery on Newbury Street, I first glimpsed the work of the New Mexico masters. I had never tried landscape, though there was ample material in my mind with which to do so. But I did try Taos, then Santa Fe. And I've never left, as Ginevra knows probably too well."

"But what happened to the Marquise?" Mr Marigold ardently inquired, rather breathless about the matter.

"Many years after my leaving France, I received a letter from the servant I had first seen attending to my Lady, in the gallery. I'll never forget his words: 'Dear Father Alvaro' (for that's what the Marquise called me), 'she is ill, and asks for you. Can you come immediately?'

"I went back to France, and was shown to her remarkable, burnished gold bed, the work of Thomas Chippendale, with famed yellow *passementerie* and silk damask. The night was late, and I could scarcely make her out by candlelight. She lay beneath several gauzy layers of rose swags and tassels. Nonetheless, nothing could prevent that glow of suffered youth residing in antiquity from being reflected in those eyes. Though her body was weak and ready to expire, she shone with all the brightness of a young girl on her first date.

"I kissed her hand, we spoke for half the night. Towards morning she went to sleep, comforted, tranquility in her lips and around her eyes. Of course she was never to awaken. It had been a rare form of leukemia and it caused her little pain, I'm grateful to add."

Mr Marigold, greatly moved, as was everyone gathered, was also perplexed. He leaned forward, cleared his throat, then posed the following riddle, which he was not alone in considering: "Dear troubled Monsignor, how then—for some of us heard it with our own ears, saw it with our own eyes—did that Indian shaman, that clown, that master of rocket ships, heavens and earths, who has now vanished to places untraceable, how could he have known the name of Cardaillac?"

For long minutes Father Alvaro pondered the query, and those nearby all contemplated beside him.

Then, "Ah-ha!" the good Father bellowed. "I'd written my father. Years ago. A single letter. I mentioned the Marquise, and must have referred to the signature on the canvases. That's it!"

But then he had doubts. Why would Thomas have gone to such trouble to track him down, and for what purpose?

At length, Father Alvaro grew certain, holding up his suspicions in the light of some great revelation. He'd racked his memory, craned his neck in the direction of every conceivable detail—the manner of the Indian's body movement, the laughter, the breath and pauses and hesitations, the knowing glances, the eyes darting, steadying, alighting, the bone structure, the intonations, any trace of jungle dialect, the slightest sign of a connection in flesh, and all his paraphernalia. It all made sense, now.

Satisfied that he had seen the truth, he got up from his barstool, finished his beer in one impatient swig, and said in the most astonished tone, "I now understand. Thomas is my brother, or my son, or stepson, or cousin, or nephew, or uncle, for there is no way to delineate with any correctness amid such large clans as exist down there. He was, no question about it, sent by my father—who must be dying, or something very grave. I shall go to him. Visa. Passport. Oh, Lord, so much to do. The car keys? The future? Ginevra, will you forgive me? All of you, thanks, really, thank you so very much, a time of tumult, a coming out—I am thrilled—you really like my paintings? Take them, take all of them. If you'd excuse me? When Raquel comes back—she must, you know—tell her I will return for her. You won't forget? I love her, you see."

"Certainly ... certainly ... dear man ..." echoed the present company, all of whom felt as if they'd been touched by the very core of human evolution: the fall from grace, the plunging out of eternity, the rapture of myriad sin, followed by the re-ignition of original innocence, a paradise regained, and so on and so forth: the veritable ascent of one man, right there, in the living room of the Camp of the Spirits.

They watched in awed silence as he stood up, a certain frenzy, or miasma, about the rejuvenation. He had much to do, by his own body language: a gymnastic, more exactly, that should take him out into the wilds, a golden twilight of his family's prehistory. There was admiration and no small measure of joy in the room, for all present were not a little excited by the good Father's sudden crisis of opportunities and expectations. Alvaro repaired hastily to his quarters, where he proceeded to pack his bare essentials for a long journey.

CHAPTER 9
The Dispersal of Spirits

OF COURSE, PEACH TREES in the Venezuelan outback, even a distant relative coming forward with an ominous warning, did not explain Amigo's blast-off, let alone that bird's current whereabouts. Many other peculiarities were left unexamined—a penumbra of the born and unborn, fertile misgivings, missteps, clairvoyant indications and/or omissions that lingered over the Camp of the Spirits, inducing in the coming days a rash of impulses, blind exoduses and sudden sentimentality. In one corner an unrequited love affair. In another, horse hairs and needling doubts: I told you so. Never say never. If only I had done that, gone there, acquired such and such, had the courage of my convictions. A volley of regrets and questions marks crammed the once tranquil abode set amid its 10 acres of parkland. One detected a splash of hope illumined in the arid plateau of a mammoth despondency that was the near-end of the millennium. Or shared in the sexual pangs, of loins crying out in that wilderness of an oppressive frock. No matter what one wondered, there was no way to ascertain ill- or fair-bodings. Opinions kept counsel with meager comfort. Where one might bask in mysterious relief, another just as simply lost faith, despaired of the birth canal, or fancied him or herself a newly established monarch.

But the overwhelming sensation around Ginevra's home was that something had happened that would change all of their lives, perhaps forever. A rift had opened.

And there was no greater emergent chasm than that within Father Alvaro himself. Raquel, with whom he was madly in love, had stepped out on him. His secret double life had been exposed, and the priesthood, to his way of thinking, would no longer suit him. Most importantly, Thomas had signaled a provocative omen he could not ignore. He had to return to the harsh jungles of his upbringing.

The house disassembled. Mr Marigold himself was stupefied by these rapid turns of destiny, noting in that all-observant skull of his how effortlessly lives could be upended and transformed, character, world view, even profession radically altered, and with hardly any manure of resistance.

The spate of disassociations began within minutes of Father Alvaro's hastily organized departure for the shuttle bus in Santa Fe at the La Fonda Hotel which would take him to the Albuquerque airport and onward flight to Caracas. From there, he'd know what to do, what bus to take, what jeep to hire, which mule train to join and specific Indians to follow. He would read smoke signals, catch the never-forgotten scents of acai, tucuma and orange caja, every subspecies of granadilla, and zapote, sifting homeward in the tracks of white-lipped peccaries, kinkajous, sloths and anteaters along the seeping forest floor. Harpy eagles, flocks of garrulous ruby-cheeked conures and guacharos gliding through the Palo de Vaca and Guilielma. Giant river otters frolicking in the mud beside the tall-standing ibises. Fearsome anacondas slight aboard the dripping hours of original creation among the inga and hevea trees.

It all comes back to the boy in the man, fish darting luminescent, the sun's noonday motes and striations penetrating the fan palms and canopy occlusion, barefooted among the floral gardens, swimming in those eddies at specific times of day when piranhas never came. Hours spent among the old women hunched in their long houses chewing various maniocs with their big molars, spitting out the juice in bowls where it would ferment. His memories of his pet mabyas, and of first tasting moriche, whose edible fruit could be squeezed into a beer, its pith pounded into white bread. And the girls, the endless stream of succulent sentience consolidated by his memory into so many sweet lips and gleaming bottoms. All these hopes surrounding the vision of his father and his beautiful young Indian girls.

Of course, ben trovato ... When he actually got near, there were no mule trains, no Indians in loin cloths or untroubled native beauties in body paint, their unrippled bellies and dark nipples punctuating the mottled Italianate sunsets. Rather, a wide open dusty road, the forests having been felled to either side for miles. There were new facts of life in the jungle, great changes in three decades of need and greed: the kaolinite mine had greatly expanded. Now paper-pulp manufacture was the rage: dioxins fanned out across the newly irrigated rice paddies, beneath the pall of smoke and stench of bauxite, and choruses of heavy aluminum traces in the soil, mercury poisoning down every creek. There were filthy rich bankers and their brattish scions from Jakarta, Auckland, Kuala Lumpur, Sydney, Taipei, Tokyo and Seoul; Christian fundamentalists chanting Utopia; refined Dutch chemical experts; German money manipulators; and, of course, American bourgeois, all masked in expensive, UV-protective shades and casual Egyptian cottons, armed with World Monetary Organization documents stamped GATT or NAFTA (which was enough), Mont Blanc pens in their pressed Giorgio Armani shirt pockets, all filing claims in the new berserk boom towns, marking out vast tracts of unthinkable desert where once were deep tropics and, escorted by paramilitary heavies, directing the bulldozer traffic with loud whistles around their burly necks. New deposits of petroleum, asphalt, sulfur, coal, iron, gold and copper stirred the souls of these emissaries from Caracas, Maracaibo and Barquisimeto who were doing everything in their power to sell off the country.

Father Alvaro would spend weeks searching for his tribe, months tracking down leads deeper and deeper into central Venezuela. After a while, the reality began to set in: the tribe he'd grown up with had been a small cluster of vanishing breaths, a phyle distinct in breeding, utterance, heart and soul; their vision of the stars, their treatment of spiders, unique, untroubled, the purest zenith of a humanity at peace in a rain forest—and now, extinct.

"Señor, so many of the tribes have vanished. There is nothing that can be done. Their time was up. Civilization cannot be stopped."

He could not, would not accept this version, as it was relayed by a government tribes official in the town of Las Lajitas. His last letter would reach Ginevra in September of that year, from a camp somewhere in the Sierra de Guampi, along the Paruchito River. The letter, for now, remains unopened, as Ginevra had closed down the Camp of the Spirits, left it to the safe keeping of Señor Sannazaro, botanical extremist, latent eye of the Renaissance, conscience among blossoms. She had retired to the remains of her family's Mansart, a Napoleon III *manoir*, in Corsica, with its original eighteenth-century fireplaces, grand vitraux, eleven belles chambres, batiments d'exploitation, maison de gardien, salle de bain balneo en marbre (or balneotherapy bath, as they say), half-timbered rotting beams of oak, parquet Versailles and peeling plasters. *Beaucoup de charme avec vaste dépendance.*

Before Ginevra's departure, Ken Isaacs had gone out to the wild Andaman Sea. Equally caught up by the events of the day, Brother Bernardo had also abandoned his New Mexico idyll. Though not particularly intimate with Father Alvaro, he was close enough to theological ambivalence to grasp after such liberation, standing most monks of the world on notice.

"Mr Marigold, it was a pleasure meeting you," Isaacs had exclaimed, extending a hearty handshake. "And again, splendid job down there in the well! You put us wishful thinkers to shame. I admire you for that, even if the day's events did turn out rather unfavorably for that hapless chicken."

"Oh, we mustn't leap to conclusions," Mr Marigold admonished. "Hope and pessimism are not among the great incommensurables."

With that, and other salutations, Isaacs took his shoulder bag (the full extent of the ascetic's possessions), and bummed a ride with a neighbor into town, from whence he'd likely catch a bus to Albuquerque. Heading in the direction of Bishop's Lodge, he glanced at the Camp in the rearview mirror and could see others leaving in his wake—Christina, whose erogenous fingers Mr Marigold was stooping to embrace; even the seemingly well-settled Barringer was busy packing the roof of his Explorer jeep and preparing to take leave of the cottage and his duties.

The spirit of evacuation had set in almost instantaneously, the way an earthquake causes people to sit up, swivel on their barstools or race out onto the street naked. Father Alvaro had spawned a great nomadic migration to all corners of the world. The 47-year-old Isaacs had left Mr Marigold his address at a commune in the wildest of Andamans, and invited him to come there to explore the last of a certain genre of missionary work, as if it were a rare form of orchid, or cuisine. He was, in fact, referring to a tribe that had thus far resisted all contact with outsiders, having killed not a few, but he said no more on that score. Perhaps it was Alvaro's vision of the tribal women that had got him to thinking.

As for Christina, she and Matthew were Norway bound. She had filled the drawers of her belfry with shards of Mimbres pottery, and file cards commending Chumash cave paintings and Grand Canyon mortuary data (dozens of eighteenth-century corpses planted on an open plateau, their palms all extended towards the heavens in a clear gesture of welcome.) Suddenly she was anxious to compare these luscious details with her earlier work accomplished in Nord-Trondelag—specifically her important discovery of a slab of rock depicting a 9,000-year-old reindeer drinking from a waterfall.

"And where will you go?" Marigold asked Brother Bernardo, whose whole person also palpably seethed.

"My weaknesses are no secret," he declared.

"You may speak freely, friend. My ears are large and sympathetic."

Bernardo embraced this cue, feeling an enormous urge to unburden his soul. He began, "Sometimes the world just rings you up and you're summoned away. A mission in the middle of the night, a downed aircraft. A rescue operation. I may seem to you the unobtrusive mendicant, but in fact I believe I was born a freedom fighter, a mercenary for hire. Now I feel the urgings to bring down a corporation, or topple a dictator. A good civil war now and then keeps a man vital. Ho Chi Minh uttered those words over dinner in Peking."

"I believe there are 70 such wars at the moment," Marigold ventured. "That is a statement of fact. The numbers would suggest a degree of futility. For myself, I see no reason to leave Tesuque."

"I know," the Brother sighed. "Still, I have an urging to kick ass."

The Commander was unsettled by this air of so much exodus all at once; these were people he did not claim to know, but with whom he felt a neighborly bond. He was not accustomed to intrusions, excitements, invigorations, jolts, rallies, flutters and frissons. *Kick ass* was not in his vocabulary. Mr Marigold never rushed, wound up, inflamed or foamed. He knew no rages, fumes or animation. He was suspicious of pique, careful of chafe, slow to wake up, quick to sleep. He neither encouraged nor discouraged, would rarely prod, never goaded, and had not been truly aroused in many, many years.

These times were surely different. Amidst the cries of Raquel, the look of praise emanating from Ginevra, and the warm thanks passing from a chicken, Mr Marigold had felt his blood rise: piquant hands, elongated fingers, softly painted fingernails, heaving bosoms and several sets of brightly gazing eyes which he imagined had said everything. Add to all that the vision of resolving civil wars, of sun and rain, pulsing ideas, dust in the road, lightning in the sky, purple clouds and far-off passions taking hold, one confession after another, the vast topography of the planet shrinking down to encompass him in his meager self.

They all stood out near the gate; darkness was settling in, and with it, another approaching storm. The thunder could be heard rumbling up near Los Alamos and Bandelier. Soon, a dry wind, a pelting rain and a cavalcade of lightning would be upon them. Such was the routine this time of year.

The Camp of the Spirits was emptied, a quiet dream cinching to an undetectable close. No time frame, no logical sequence of events. Marionettes manipulated by some higher power. Marigold started back across the lawn towards his hacienda. Suddenly, a vehicle drove up, breaking the silence of descending, cicada-laden twilight with the familiar sound of tires upon gravel. It was the gardener, Señor Sannazaro, returning after a few days away on a seed-buying spree among the organic farms in southern Colorado.

Marigold met him at his car, and offered to help carry the sacks of seed into the garage. The two men had scarcely formed an acquaintance, so similar were they in their hermetic styles and anti-social bearing. At times they had chatted whilst digging a ditch, repairing a roof, clipping a hedge or pruning a tree on either side the failing coyote fence that separated the two properties. But neither had invited the other one over even for a drink. Why had Tolstoy and Dostoevsky never met? Pride? Fear? Complacency? Bad timing? There was Marigold, peeling potatoes at 11 Vladimirsky Prospekt, and there Sannazaro, cooking okra on Kazanskaya Ulitsa. Or the Commander, patching a fence at Sennaya Ploshchad, and his neighbor buying fresh vegetables on Malaya Meshchanskaya. It went like that. Asymptotes of the literary imagination.

Ginevra, alone in her emptied house, enthralled by the rapid-fire show of human emotions but also saddened at the sudden silence around her, heartily welcomed the returning gardener and filled him in on all the dramatic events of the day.

"With all that abandonment, I pray you will not join in the evacuation?" she declared, her voice weak with practical concern.

"Where else would I go?" replied he, with a twinge of sadness. "And who would feed Toto, Heidi, Heyboy, the bear, the squirrels, the birds, the grass, the flowers, the trees, the wasps and bats?"

"Precisely," said she.

Mr Marigold was still there, standing with a sack in his arms. "Those old mutts whose groans I've taken to," he applied. He was referring particularly to the Jack Russell, Toto, whose fits of waltzing, bona fide laughter and frenzied leaps over the gate were the life of the neighborhood. Sometimes he'd run circles around Mr Marigold's estate for no apparent purpose, carrying a Siamese cat, Dandelion, in his jaws. The cat would dangle, utterly amused by the ride, and secure in the knowledge that he would be put down one of these days, his mane a little wetter for the adventure but otherwise no harm done. Toto had even been seen chasing dragonflies and floating on his back down the acequia at high water levels.

It started to pour.

"Come in, you two," Ginevra demanded.

Once inside, Mr Marigold was struck by the uncomfortable realization that all these years had gone by with so little social contact of any significance. Had he been so self-absorbed, a curmudgeon? Was he at fault? She was, after all, a beautiful woman, not much older than himself.

And the little Italian a sterling character, as could be gleaned. Now, with no second guessing or forewarning, he felt a need to know them. This was unusual for him. He never gave vent to such desiderata, sought no purchase in the realm of contours, externality or interconnectedness. He was, truly, the world's last great observer, though without a burning motivation to put the details to any use or in any meaningful order. This latter quirk elevated him to a zone all by himself: of unemployed perspicuity and passionless passion, like an iceberg of perfect dimensions drifting in the open seas. No recompense, favor, or notice.

"Say, Señor Sannazaro, I've been meaning to ask you for over 20 years: what brought you to New Mexico?"

The inquiry sprang from the total blueness of blue, whiteness of white. In truth, Sannazaro sported the body of a nicely configured middle-aged man, standing in modest height, with not an excess ounce to trundle, his hair still black and largely in place, a mustache set gently on the beach of his upper lip, where words quietly gathered to watch a sunset, all in the perfect balance of a composed, long-feeling man of the soil. These were the obvious details. But Mr Marigold knew next to nothing of the inobvious: the Gulf of Salerno, Amalfi, the fecund seahills listing south of Mount Vesuvius, that general region from whence, according to Ginevra, the man had once hailed. In fact, he now felt embarrassed, even apologetic that he had never taken an interest, sat back with a bottle of wine for the afternoon and hashed out the various essences that were so silently co-existing. Why, for example, had Sannazaro arrived with no possessions? From whom did he receive, twice a year, a mysterious letter postmarked Positano? Two had mistakenly been left in the Commander's post office box. Were there children, grandchildren, a wife, an estate?

"Ahhh, the ease of questions. That answers were as free."

"I'm sorry," Mr Marigold demurred in hasty retreat.

"No, no, it's quite all right. You see, it is only here, in the New World, that true anonymity can be had by the likes of me," Sannazaro confessed with a whispering circumlocution, implying a heavy truth concealed beneath the veneer of a well-suited satisfaction. He looked to Ginevra for added strength.

"I am confused, dear sir," Mr Marigold said. "What could possibly trouble one whose hands have tasted perpetual youth? Whose life must surely embody the bountiful innocence of earth the addulcent? Lustrous chestnut, lime, green sward, Annibale Carraci's scintillating streams. You are a gardener, after all."

"Never a truth better finessed. This requires a long-overdue drink," Sannazaro hastened, exhaling with pent-up regard. He elected for a fine port from the cellar, and poured three rounds.

"And a fire," added Ginevra, who placed several logs in the adobe pit, then proceeded to fry up some polenta with mushrooms, gorgonzola and scallions for the gentlemen and the patiently waiting canines.

Over the meal, beside the crackling fire, Sannazaro proceeded to unload his heart. It had been a fine day, a remarkable week, a season of disclosures, mused Marigold. A long-overdue punctuation mark in the evolution of the species, when friendships are forged, rivers crossed, the solar system traversed by a chicken: Venus passed before the Sun, and that which heretofore had seemed without cause, company or merit suddenly took on a new life teeming with necessities, opinions and collaborations beneath the canopy of shared New Mexicana.

"I was the last of Arcadia," Sannazaro began. "Shipwrecked, eclipsed, whittled down into the ghost of an anachronism. Worst of all, uninsured against obsolescence."

"Ahh, you were an historian!" Mr Marigold at once divined.

"My family was history," declared Sannazaro. "It was my naiveté to imagine that the future would have any more need of that past than in the margins of a footnote. Fortunately, I managed to salvage a life, and a few rare seeds. Now, Arcadia is being restored here, in Tesuque. Thanks to her." He lifted his glass in genuflection before their hostess. "It does not happen overnight."

CHAPTER 10
The Gardener's Tale

SANNAZARO TOSSED SOME cedar shavings on the fire, poured another glass of aromatic port for each of them, took the drink up to his nostrils with an exaggerated whiff of relief, and continued with his story.

"I am a direct descendent of the great epic poet, Messer Iacobo Sannazaro, Gentilhuomo na Politano."

"I have heard the name, of course," Marigold demurred. He was not overly steeped in Renaissance literature. "And bow to your ancestry. It is nothing short of remarkable to meet one who is part of that litany.

The flame obviously glows still; the spirit abides; your heart must sing each morning like the meadow lark just to know that you carry in your veins some semblance of the gene, passed down, for verse. Still, it must come as a shock to see a cactus, or a shopping mall, for this country is not given to the lyricism or elegant antiquity from which you hail."

"All truly put," Sannazaro said, before underscoring the shock. "In fact, until coming to this country, I still lived in the family home beside a cliff overlooking the Gulf of Salerno. That resplendent abode— the Casa Arcadia—had stood there since the late fifteenth century, upon dozens of acres of garden, complete with a water mill. It was this very vegetable patch, the grandest on the entire Amalfi Coast, whose composition had been borrowed by the creators of the Great Garden of Whitehall, the first English garden to be precisely painted, in 1545, with Henry VIII and his family standing before the archways. And who should be standing quietly behind the royals, off to one side, shadowed beneath the boscage—my beloved ancestor. An unambiguous tribute to our family's botanical lineage. There he is, gazing restlessly across the rough seas of the Mediterranean one winter. Before him, a mixed groundcover of cotton lavender, Welsh and oriental poppies, bearded irises, dappled hellebore. And slightly yonder, profusions of honeysuckle and herbs nestling in crannies among stones hand-picked from the 40 million-year-old shoulders of Vesuvius. The consummation of the garden was the clematis and pansy-profuse pergola, towards which all chaos and order were alternately oriented. Hanging loftily overhead, a rich riot of tree peonies, *Geranium endressii*, fuchsias and North African palms."

"And the artist?"

"None other than the incomparable Tiziano. You call him Titian. Can you envision it?"

"Not in the least," said Mr Marigold, his eyes closed and straining.

"Keep trying, man," the gardener insisted. "How about now? See the blue gums?"

"Nothing."

"But dear fellow, have you never seen the spring come to fruition? Why, between the very girders and cross-rafters of your own hacienda hang a third of such flowers, or at least their relatives. And in the field—for I have traversed that property of yours a thousand times in the course of my watering—I can tell you that you sit upon a wild varicolored symphony of such perennials."

"I do?" Mr Marigold opened his eyes and peered through the third downpour of the day towards his house, out beyond Ginevra's parterre driveway of gravel and grass, and across the creek, which was rising.

"Tomorrow I shall scrutinize the earth around me, if it will please you."

"Fine. Now, eyes open, listen to the sorrows and final triumph of a dreamer, and beware his sad tale, for it is the same wherever grace and beauty have trod, or carved their initials. The world eschews finesse, harmony, the simple stanzas of sweet bygones. I know, I tried to hold on to that tradition."

With those words Sannazaro grew quiet and introspective.

"Here," Mr Marigold said, presenting to his companion a bowl of highly seasoned guacamole, chile and lime chips.

Sannazaro fed most of his to the dogs which looked up mournfully and clamored around his feet, still ravenous despite their ample dinner of mushroom polenta, and dietary fibres.

"So go on, then," Mr Marigold encouraged the gardener. "I'm eager to learn more of your calamity, for, as my people say, painful memories are acquitted among good listeners."

The elegant reveler began. "For all of these centuries my ancestors were devoted to perpetuating the philosophy of Arcadia. My great namesake, Iacobo, had written a masterpiece during the 1490s. It made its first splash in Venice in 1504. Great literary figures like Pietro Bembo, Battista Guarini and Torquato Tasso all vied with one another to invent ever more lyrical canzonette. Petrarch, of course, had first dedicated the tradition. The Sannazaros built the original family home, a bulwark of elegant simplicity against the agonizing wars of futility that raged across southern Italy, then. The idea was to provide and cultivate a garden far from the deadly sins, altogether removed from city states and politics, the infernal, unwinnable contest between religions, ideologies and ethical positions; to rebuke the sinister extremes of sociology—overpopulation, war, disease, hunger, and all of the other ills and mediocrities brought about by man in his quest for utter ephemeral stature, the flip-side of ruin. And to do so as a family, uncluttered, uninvolved, like primitives had done for tens of thousands of years—hands in the soil, eyes among the stars and, in between, every possible rainbow. To re-invent human life, in other words, according to the Golden Age, as described by Herodotus and other ancients, and exemplified by Christ and Buddha and our very own Saint Francis."

"But this is precisely the vision, is it not?" exclaimed Mr Marigold. "Have I myself not silently, in pure uninvolvement, aspired to remain in, been forcibly swayed by, the mad delicious eternal urgings of just such passive exultation? I have read, though claim little fluency with, Bembo and Herodotus; my nose is not particularly acute in the presence of daffodils or thyme. But the scents of nature are my legislature (though, admittedly, in pollen season I'm a wreck). Perhaps I know too few Latin names, nor how to prune the pear tree properly, but I assure you, day by day, year by year, has grown an orientation that I live by— would name—your very same, Arcadia."

Both nodded agreeably to be in such sterling company

"To think that you and I share so much?" the gardener said. "Like faithful shepherds sitting on their hillocks beneath the noble olive tree, immune to the horrors of every age, committed to nonviolence and love, to art and humanity, to the rights of every blossom, every bee, each silent mouse and foraging deer, pining away for loved ones."

"Precisely! But what a fool I've been to have waited this long to make your precious acquaintance."

"Indeed. Two fools in a pod."

"Now please, go on with your narrative."

Sannazaro continued. "Iacobo's and my other ancestors' attempt at paradise made its mark on our great poets and painters and gardeners of later centuries—on Zappi and Frugoni, Rolli, Crescimbeni and Gravina."

"Oh how I wish I could share in the fluency of your rapture, dear friend. I promise, following this little party of ours, to repair to my library and butter my bread with these esteemed names you have so generously conveyed. You kindle my ABCs right from their cradle. Your every utterance I shall embrace both for its instruction and the rhythms of its ether."

"Good," replied the gardener, "for you will then be better equipped to measure the full pageantry, the hidden cornerstones, of which I speak, the very idea of such villas as Capponi at Arcetri and Gamberaia at Settignano which provided ample evidence of the mysterious, overgrown wilderness of secret gardens like those of my family's estate. Think back to Studley Royal or the finest overviews at Stourhead. Of Hebe and Jupiter rising on a cloud; of Robert Adams' imaginary castles; of Friesian heifers mooing aboard dales, statues peeing a kind of lemonade, the infant Cupid drinking sweet white Sauternes (one of Bordeaux's finest) from a nipple, cascades and herbs overwhelming every available niche, adding immeasurable color to the moss-splattered moon-pool edges, hydrology mounts and ancient follies, stairways of granite leading to nowhere. Where bards dreamt atop silken clearings dancing with blue butterflies, strolled through shaded boschi, and there was no better sanctuary on earth in which to first taste a lover's lips, or gaze into those eyes and recite the immortal lines of my distinguished ancestor: 'Oh Summer, Oh Spring, Oh Fall, Oh Winter, Oh rustling winds and feverish sky; Oh Love, My Love, Let me feel your pulsating parts in my hands—'"

Mr Marigold moved away from the stricken gardener to the far end of the couch. Rapture had captured the moment, but the normal perimeters of neighborly affection were too rapidly closing in.

"You are a learned man, Sannazaro," he said. "And a great gardener, for I have often detected your workmanship there across Ginevra's acreage."

"Thank you, thank you, Señor."

"Who would not be moved by such lilies of the field? Lilacs, I presume, and silver lace and trumpet flower, are they not?"

"Excellent. You see, already the botanical will is weaving its mark."

"And, lo, have I not espied the haggard blue wisteria amid those terracotta statues and coyote fences? And the greenest green cineraria presiding over nothing less than your sure artistry beside the adobe walls?"

"Oh, dear friend, to think that this moment of intimacy has been forestalled 20 years—insanity!"

"But necessary, knowing, as we both surely recognize, that all things come about in their own time."

"Quite true."

And then, "Or is it true?"

"Actually, I have avoided that subject. To lend too much gravity to the timing of anything taunts our free will with superstition, inflicts omens where none are necessary, upstages calm, precipitates skin rashes—in short, provides a bridge off which one is likely to leap, and all unnecessarily. I say, avoid too much contemplation. Deny bridges. If we are lucky, no bridge need ever enter into the equation of our lives."

"Would that it were so."

"I detect troubles, friend. What are you alluding to? Thus far, your exposé has been awash in rhapsody."

"Yes, yes, I'm coming to that, having firmly assembled the points, established the fact that such gardens and woods gave birth to all of us. I grew up there, I and my friends, brothers and sisters. Ahh, Mr Marigold, I made love there, under the Italian stars, in earshot of the crashing sea. I echoed the lullabies from Tosca, which could have been written there: 'Bai boschi, dai roveti, dall'arse erbe, dall'imo dei franti seplocreti, odorosi di timo, la notte escon bisbigli ...' It means 'From all the woods and copses, from parching meadows, from towers, from tombs of vanished glory all scented with flowers, the whispers of the night ...' I entered the canvases of Claude Lorrain and Nicolas Poussin. I sat with the anchorites and their lions; embarked in those wilds with St Ursula and Jerome; found Moses; strolled, amid one pastoral landscape after another, beneath the Arch of Titus, beside Hercules and Cacus; watched Bacchus being born; spied two nymphs of enduring appeal; sojourned with Apollo and Daphne, St Ignatius in ecstasy, Christ in the Garden of Olives; and studied every botanical point of fact in *Orpheus and Eurydice, Pyramus and Thisbe* and the great *Et in Arcadia ego*. I, too, in other words, have lived in Arcadia; I, too, was one of the *Les bergers d'Arcadie*.

"In short, dear friend, I was in paradise. Alas, and all the more sadly, that was not the end of it, as presently you will learn."

CHAPTER 11
The Sorrows of Sannazaro

SANNAZARO LETTHE dogs run in their enclosed wilderness on all sides of the house, then continued pouring out his heart, inspired by the sudden breath of this momentous occasion: his neighbor arriving on a morning of such turbulence, almost as if to verify the chasm that had opened up in a single household. It was an undeniable omen that the Hermit of Tesuque, as neighbors often called him, should have chosen this day to emerge from his ancient lair. This same day that Sannazaro turned 70—older than Ginevra imagined, or anyone could believe, to look at him. Resignation knew no greater portent than this fact which presaged a new sky, new convictions, and an absolute turn-about in the face of disintegration. Ginevra, who sat with both gentlemen, had never known the gardener to be so free with his details.

Sannazaro continued with his story. "As pretty a picture as I have just drawn—the palace of flowers, a life laid bare atop the hallowed pillow surface of reveries assured—there was a disastrous end. For it is one thing to comment upon a glorious apparition of woolgathering beneath five centuries of rose petals and quite another to make manifest its modern realization overlooking the most polluted bay in all of Europe, hounded on all sides by the emergent freeway style of big-city Neapolitan life, just to the north of where we lived.

"You enjoyed a large family?"

"I did. Three brothers, two sisters. Two wonderful parents. My father, Alberto, was a landscape architect. My mother, Manuela, was his on-again off-again partner. My siblings all went on to become drones. This was after the war—after the Germans had occupied so many of the great villas in Italy, like Aldobrandini, which became headquarters to the German high command, and Falconieri. Fortunately, our home was small by comparison with those enormous estates. We were not discovered. The Allied bombings which utterly laid waste such great gardens as those of the Villa Torlonia missed us completely. But there were other problems, Señor. Terrible, terrible mishaps. Arcadia had not stopped fascism from overtaking the country. While a few poets and painters and gardeners like myself continued to cling to the ideals of the Renaissance—for that is what Arcadia commends—the country which had allowed itself to be won over by the bureaucrats, the communists, the capitalists, was not about to be reminded of its pastoral origins. There was too much money at stake. And so, in a very short time, Italy became the fifth wealthiest country in the world. Or maybe it's the sixth, after California, as it were—I don't know. I can only confirm that the land taxes, the soil and water pollution, the pressure of so many people added up. In the end, it was too much. I watched a family fight and lose its roots.

"My parents were killed in an airline crash. They were going to Athens for vacation and this happened before they resolved their will or individual trusts. I still cannot speak of it. Only to forewarn you, dear friend: get your house in order. Appoint your executor, carefully bequeath your heritable assets, taking into consideration every detail of any spiritual or aesthetic importance. Build a fortress to fend off probate. My parents, by a matter of a week or two, failed to accomplish this crucial compact with destiny. I use the word advisedly. You see, one's home is, or should be, one's destiny. I believe that. But such convictions were not shared by my brothers and sisters who had all married and moved to other less favored regions in the country, and abroad. They had sired innumerable brats. I cannot count the times that I am an uncle without portfolio.

"In short, there was fiscal chaos, without any cohesive force to fight the tax system. Rather than be mired, they feigned no more interest in Arcadia. They had gone from being golden-minded adolescents who had been raised unabashedly, bound to, born of that paradise and all that it suggested and ethically required, to spineless middle-class bores, mediocre minds, paltry pedants. An accountant for a manufacturer of women's—how do you call it?" He looked to Ginevra for assistance.

"Not tampons—"

"Absorbent pads."

"That's it. Dreadful business. A maker of cheap tiles in Roma. A comptroller for an actuary. An ambulance-chasing lawyer in Milano. Children with braces—screamers, nags, spoiled monsters. All their friends more so. I was isolated, a freak of nature, alone in my pitiful passion. Tied to a past that had no companionship. The courts divided the trust equally between all of us, the grandchildren included. There was, as a result, no money left to pay the taxes or fight off the local real-estate whores. And I, who had spent my life crawling on all fours around that beloved property, I was patronized by the new owners with an olive branch, a job as caretaker—can you imagine?—to supervise the re-engineering of the gardens. 'Re-engineering', Señor. Do you know what they did?"

Mr Marigold shook his head forlornly.

"They built a hotel, stripped all the gardens, sold the Tiziano at auction, as well as the library, and 'restored'—that was the buzzword—'restored' the pergola, with its 400-year-old hand-painted ceilings, to a bright, shiny original, as they imagined it should be. Atrocious morons. What they did was strip the paint and hire some local buffoon to repaint it with a cartoon—after Michelangelo. That's right. I tried in desperation to get the various government authorities to protect Arcadia under national historic treasures legislation. But I did not have the knowledge, or the legal fund to fill out and properly submit the appropriate paperwork. Unlike the English, the Italians and French are little exercised over interiors. Historical grades and listings mean little. Linoleum, plastic, formica are not eschewed where once Breton granite had been laid. Everything in Italy, except revolutions, takes many years. My brother, a lawyer himself as I mentioned, knew only drunk-driving cases. This was beyond him. Moreover, they basically stole our Titian."

"You poor man."

"Too poor, certainly, to vacation at my ancestral home, which now costs, I was last informed, about 500 dollars a night. For that one can reside at the Vesuvius View Chateau, or whatever they call it. My share of the family sale and the inheritance enabled me to gather my things and flee the country. But where could I go? What could I do? Then the idea struck me: to move out into the furthest back reaches of the Amalfi Coast; to go to the islands, perhaps Sardinia, and find the wildest acre in all of Europe. There, slowly, day by day, I might resurrect faith in my traditions, or die out in dignity."

"Go on?"

"That was when I met an intoxicating runaway. A truant of a new order, Señor. Her name was Allegra."

"Allegra?"

"Allegra ... Allegra ... How I took to that infuriating tart. Her very name reeks, slithers, takes its place in the pantheon of calamities."

Marigold looked anxiously at Ginevra. A school of silence.

The Italian groaned. "A tomboy, atheist, revolutionary. Banished from a devoutly Catholic household, thrown out of college. Her firm curves, loose-fitting garments, the twitch between her legs killed me. No man could have resisted such a blatant cry in the wilderness, that damsel-in-distress scenario, nor ignored the temptation to rescue her from the alleged abuse of her parents. Preternatural bonds, the many madnesses of desire. Puppy love magnified by the terror of my growing old. I mooned beside her racing asteroid, whose scars and rampant danger exceeded anything I might have foretold."

He visibly drew the full significance unto himself, as he had no doubt done many times before. With a melancholy grin he tried to explain his lechery by references to "higher definitions", "Platonic arousal", "Socratic séances". The poor defeated gardener insisted that his sheer admiration of her physical beauty transcended the sum of its parts and, in any case, was not germane to the "summital calling" whose essence was tutorial—the schooling of the next generation in that which he had all but lost. Lacking children, siblings or parents, Arcadia having eluded him, he wanted somehow to pass along the rich memory.

"The outcome of all this noble zeal?" Mr Marigold pressed anxiously.

"What happened is that Allegra was a cunning and spectacular manipulator, a young woman of steel and calculation. Her 20-odd years had already left her immune to the slightest compunctions. Hers was a manufactured grace, an affected generosity. I was weak, pushing 50, and she the most beautiful female I had ever laid eyes upon. Mind you, I had had plenty of attractive women. Divinities one and all." (Marigold was no fool: the boast was plain, concealing a desert.) "But I had never married, both out of the habit of imagined freedom, and for reasons that combined the practical morbidity of my denuded financial situation with a resulting poverty of self-esteem. A morose syndrome. Like some fifteenth-century Norman manor of dark trunk set unto itself in the perpetual rain. I detested the notion of suckling alternative hopes. I was living in a mental quagmire, a stalemate of loneliness, of meaningless café lattes, needing urgently to gift my disappearing life—art, landscape, the whole ideal of a splendid and historical seclusion—which was fading for want of either successor or companion. Allegra was my last exit."

"You were naïve."

"I was desperate. Inventing this happy scenario: her dark eyes, oiled skin, impressive lips. She seemed to understand my crisis. I imagined that she adored me and so surprised her with a wild few hectares in Sardinia. I wrote her a lengthy declaration of my love, only to be extorted. My monumental stupidity. My nadir. Naturally, she figured out there must be more where that acreage came from. I depleted a sizeable portion of my remaining funds on a wretched tangle of land, exhuming misshapen stones, evening the slope, exhausting my last stores on the construction of a weeping cottage which served only to incite her vicious machinations. There was an acidic spring. Little potential for plantings. I should have known. I spent an entire summer up there with some local workers, a stonemason, a seriously soft-in-the-head carpenter they called Idesso. She tormented all of them. Shaving her legs before the workmen. A classic *femme fatale*. But so young and pernicious. Who would have guessed the extent of her manipulations?

"I built something wonderful, given the limitations up on that mountain. There was no road. So we took ponies up to the place—poor benighted animals unfit for such heat and heavy loads. After three days she began to complain. We fought. I placated. She insisted on leaving. I was desperate. 'Where will you go?' I implored her. 'America,' she hastened. Each hour my pathetic situation worsened. I had no pride. I thought I would die without my Allegra. She stole my checkbook, purchased first-class air tickets for New York. I joined her, forgiving, senseless, smitten, willing to go anywhere to keep her. I was not content to hide. I had no possibility of a job. No training. No patience. No humility. Only anger—to be young again. How does a man in lonely middle age, bereft of an income, without a single friend, start over? There are abundant widows, to be sure. But they are looking for security, not a sorrowful Sannazaro with only his background to speak of.

"So, that's how I arrived on these shores. With 900 dollars left. We stayed at an upscale hotel on Central Park. Allegra made sure of that. Her bar tab alone would have ruined me within a very few days, so I should have been grateful when one night she slipped out while I was showering, and never returned. I knew she was screwing anyone whose pockets bulged.

Women also bought her favors. Her clothes gave off wrenching signs of her promiscuity, and there were marks on her arms—heroin. The first dark circles under her eyes. What a fool I'd been. One had to feel sorry for her. Not a pretty childhood, obviously. But what to do?"

"I'm terribly sorry, dear man. Of course, feeble-mindedness is less easily detected in the moment. A moron stands out later on."

"I cannot disagree. It was a stupid, witless conclusion to a pathetic impulse. But my troubles were far from over. I went looking for her."

"Idiot!"

"I was addicted. My disease bade me haunt all the likely pick-up joints in New York—a most unsettling odyssey. One night there appeared a knife at my throat, a maniac intent upon my body. I can't even think about it. Moreover, Allegra had vanished with the one treasure I'd managed to hold on to: the first, priceless 1504 edition of the *Arcadia* by my namesake. By that dastardly theft I was the one who got philosophized.

"I drank myself into a fever, I wept shamelessly, and then got dizzy and collapsed. I remember brute faces black leather metal belts and a rapidly spinning mirror at the bar, and the frenzy of screaming jazz or big band, unshaved cheeks ugly eyes mean female mouths hateful swarthy hotheads sarcastic farting musclemen an indifferent bartender swimming all around me 360 degrees or more.

"I awoke in a city hospital, a crammed open sewer of gunblast wounds, motorcycle injuries, hallucinating vets, homeless addicts, the penniless bottom-of-the-barrel New York, many headed for Potter's Field. And there I was sprawled in anonymous fevers.

"My speaking of English was very marginal at that time. I had suffered several mini-strokes. My wallet was gone. I didn't have a lire to my name. The event severely dented my memory. The doctor prescribed some pills and rest. But there was no real tranquillity to be had in a dormitory room of the dying and deranged. A river of death, with all the odors and groans of a conduit into hell. After three days I checked myself out. But I couldn't remember the names—"

Mr Marigold came closer to him now, even held him, for Sannazaro's swollen eyes vented tears. Ginevra produced a handkerchief.

"—the very names of my own brothers and sisters. I was unable to recall any of their whereabouts—the towns, regions, even the name of Italy herself. My few possessions were lodged in a hotel room somewhere in the city, a hotel whose name I could not recall. And I had not a single acquaintance in all of New York. Even the doctor who had treated me was unavailable, somebody insisted."

"My God, man," said Mr Marigold. "What did you do? At least in the hospital you had a place to sleep. The parks of New York City are not known for their hospitality."

"I can attest to that. But—may the Lord hear me—a true miracle occurred. I met a guardian angel, the kindest-hearted woman in the world, who repealed all the woes that her gender (in the instance of this saga, which beggars no conclusion other than my own stupidity) had inflicted. Ginevra de Martin."

CHAPTER 12
The Metamorphosis of Sannazaro

MR MARIGOLD WAS deeply moved by Sannazaro's emotional recounting of his story, the sad plunge of which invoked so much of his own moribund mental abode, with its impenetrable twists and fever blister turns and general despair at the human condition. But that is not to say that Mr Marigold was of a dark temperament.

Much like his new-found Sannazaro, this Tesuque anchorite fronted a rarified form of wits and wisdom that could withstand most devastation bearing a blithe demeanor. Yet for all that, his optimism was not infrequently tainted by the peppered shriek of fatalistic ages. How did such nihilism function in a person? Split personality? In fact, the Tesuque hermit harbored marvelous phantasms, aided and instructed by picture books from Oz to Ozymandia, whose effect could be said to turn the tide on most days, giving him to believe in a permanency of haloed harborage beyond all ruination. Here was a man who had until then spent the whole of his life comfortably bedecked as a sort of prince without portfolio, ramshackled and literary, lost in the upper stratosphere of reflection. Not merely of ancient history, or the Renaissance, but of a considerable malaise of wire services, PhD abstracts, the latest findings from 500 journals and wwws. Data in reams. Until poor Mr Marigold was spinning like a directionless top, quite the opposite of, say, a well-tuned manta ray whose flotation, fixity, and evolution were primed to be secure, balanced and defended.

Perhaps he simply had too much free time for inner cogitation, time translated into apprehension— what to do about all those hungry children whilst sheep were fed to sheep, or the torture of women in Pakistan— with no clear friendship, or spark of amour, or a coffee indulged among others at the café corner; no prepossessing purpose (though some unusual companions from the wild) to lend even a rudimentary outline to a life that most people would call basic. Would a job carried out between nine and five amid 100 square meters of well-defined and properly lit interior have resolved this melancholy? Brought resolution to a wastrel whacked out by too many luxurious dichotomies?

Martyred by his own aimlessness, he never posed to himself the possibility of an alternative lifestyle. By implication—and he well knew it—his crazy keel was the world's own drift of woes. To know too much is neither sin nor salve, but terribly complicated. Indeed, mental obesity affected him badly. No Tylenol could neutralize the fact he had absorbed too much: read too many tales of wonder and valor; fixated on charts, scales, numeric coefficients, percentages, timeframes, the Holocene and earlier Antediluvian, the sheer illimitability of human numbers and their fallout. A car wash or two across his skull would have been no better administered, or boot camp. Better still, Handel's *Giulio Cesare*.

His pedigree had neither shirked duty nor squandered fortunes. His was not a clear-cut case of sleeping through half a lifetime. He showed no disinclination to effect real change, and was not one of those philosophers content to study rather than change the world. Indeed, he was plagued by the opposite of sloth. But the Byronic pilgrimage in his blood was hampered by an astounding lack of any special talent—muscle tone, eagle eyes, even the basic schoolboy's coordination—that might aid him in his ardor.

Add to it a fear of excess, a lack of strong organizational skills, and an absolute horror of group activities, consensus-building, voting, speaking out or acting up, and the combination could only have resulted in his strange inertia, accounting for his peculiar diffidence and isolation despite his great longing to make a difference.

Still, nihilism is a harsh word. There was no shred of explicitly anti-social, neuralgic or ungrateful predilection, simply his defiance of lowly ideals. Mr Marigold thought in urns, vases and Gothic cathedrals, not cups or teaspoons; in the manner of Toynbee, or Peter the Hermit. He followed the thinking of Roman engineer Marcus Vitruvius Pollio, traced the footsteps on his map of Admiral Byrd, memorized the poetry of Auden, knew every line and dash of Duchamps, the moves of Karpov. Yet, his inspired battalions of injunctions were star-tossed between the home-runs of a Babe Ruth and the paradox of Zeno—the arrow that will never reach its mark. In short, his penchant for paradox was wholly self-destructive. He knew he could never accomplish those great deeds he had scoured in his library, even though the contemporary setting had more than once set his blood to boiling. There was too much about the modern world that left him dazed, unspeaking, trapped. A pervasive blight. No matter the punctuations of quiet pleasure. Alone in a house. The ticking of a clock. Cold floors on his warm feet. Communion with the wind. Nothing to do, day after day. Ode to no pressure. Fearless before the aging process. Still, these were not the fuel of previous charms, sagas he visualized from ages past, cave paintings plastered over his nostalgia—a yearning for bold walkabouts and conquest of lore. In fact, the dreamer longed to move out, hurl stones, erect a tower, signal a new wave, fend for himself, rally the good-doers, propagate a Kingdom of Chimpanzees, relinquish all ties to the presumption of human superiority, install the ghosts and remains of Francabigio at the helm of his new sobriety. Make his mark. Establish a new order of his private Ecuador: a one-man existentialism that should remake the very air he breathed, stay out of the newspapers, print it with no more bravado than a tattoo—a small and dignified tattoo.

For the Commander it was nothing less than an unchecked zest for life, a vastly internalized élan, which made for the absolute in impatience. To be around him might be taxing, the danger of a frenzied concision. He rummaged with gigantic appetite across the whole length of literature, art, philosophy, science, religion—whatever it took to penetrate something.

Untried roads. He had led the perfect life of confinement, absorbed by all these adventure stories, equations, architectural renderings (Ruskin's three-volume *Stones of Venice*, for example), wayward etceteras, palaces of Aachen, and the obscure, theoretical reconnoiters for 1,001 expeditions. Unsavory exploits mired in mischance, in absence of garrison, nothing that might shake him off or undermine the tenacity for far-off things. All was honor, such labors. Harp players, luck—a permanently affected shadow play of hazards that he craved. Schooners, northeasterlies, and four-footed beasts. His seraglio of a mind drifting into jungle and misstep. Wendeth danger. Furies intent; places holy, narrative without judgment, enterprises bold and extreme. By every example of the historical antecedents, precedents, frightful adverbials, look-outs, hithers, fracturations, assemblages. No danger frightened this gamester. No shore was unknown, or attack bothersome. Sea voyages, soldiers, private squadrons and gigantesque idealisms.

That was this flower of West Indies and Japanism. All in one. And one for all.

Pipe dreams. Too much work.

So he had settled for a refectory of calm weathers and gentlemanly tidings, sampled or endured conversation over dinner with Alma, who stood waiting on him, more or less—(a handbell assured Mr Marigold of the requisites, though he never abused it) and took the odd telephone call inviting him to purchase life insurance or answer questions for an important-sounding national survey. His finances were limited to a few thousand dollars each month, timed to stay more or less on top of inflation. Hidalgo had seen to that. More significantly, though, he was very well off in terms of land and the house, both inherited from centuries before, and strewn with treasures and books which, if ever consigned to an auctioneer such as Christie's, would certainly have yielded a moderate fortune, particularly in this age of aesthetic patter.

Towing the mundane, a tinkerer of meaningless chores, he hunkered down amid 7,500 square feet of hacienda, half of which held no interest, was just there, extra space for breathing on lonely nights. Standing nearly naked in the dark. Spreading his arms. And in the morning, amid normal quotidian distractions, Mr Marigold hammered the odd nail to move the wherabouts of a painting, but mostly rummaged through his fairy woods and jammieland, inventorying his decaying estate and adding to his little notebook all the fixes that needed to be attended to, before repairing to his study.

His work habits were those of the slow-nosed echidna. There was always tomorrow. When it came to mundane restorations, he was the world's foremost procrastinator. As for great endeavors, he had them in profuse communities but sensed too well that any attempt at true afflatus would surely backfire; that all inspiration and vision was a mere test-case in the proving grounds of self-defeat. Why bother?, thought he. This is a crucial corollary to understanding his secular stasis, abetted by principles which were their own strengths. Were he less cognizant of the logjams and stalemates, willing to ignore mediocrity, refuse tragedy, he might have dismissed the odds, granted wide ruffles and furbelow to human nature, and gotten away from his intransigence. Alas, this break with tradition required a chicken.

As for visits outside of the neighborhood, they were infrequent: browses to no appreciable degree in Santa Fe, or periodic walks among the high pine forests on the mountain above. He occasionally visited Randall Davey's studio, and sometimes built a snowman.

So that, having never had the pleasure of a visit to New York, he was most certainly gripped by each blow-by-blow description of the dregs, shadows, garbage, hunger and humiliation that attended those oppressive days and nights of Sannazaro's sorrow.

"An abyss had opened up before me," the gardener said, gesticulating with garlic flourishes and treacly drama (he was not Italian for nothing), "and I was quite prepared to leap into it. New York offers such despondency ample elbow-room for killing oneself—the Chrysler Building, subways, bad neighborhoods, two rivers. All are suitable for the mentally high-wrought, those who are idyllically doomed."

"But you lived."

"Yes. After two nights in the park, I had the presence of mind, despite my hideous predicament, to visit the Italian Consulate and there explain my situation to the cultural attachée. She was a genuine human being and could not have been kinder. Though my own name was as yet a mystery to me, I was able to convey most of my desolate circumstances. Luckily, I had not forgotten the name of Arcadia, nor of Tiziano, oddly enough. Though I struck a most bedraggled, uninviting demeanor, there was certainly, in her mind, the ring of credibility. My Italian had not left me, nor the melodious meditation by which I conveyed my gushing odyssey."

"So what happened, and may the gods be attentive?" Mr Marigold pressed, anxious to comprehend the transmigration of this towering soul to the wilds of New Mexico, and to discover his connection with Ginevra.

"Her name was Emiliana Edifice, and she took me home with her. The noblest of intentions. A New Yorker of many years, an Italian of several decades, she had no qualms or misgivings. Her apartment overlooked the Hudson, off Riverside Drive, and was a bastion of good taste and superlative comforts, beginning with a hot shower and a home-cooked meal. She was in her early thirties, and had a charcoal purity, thick darkling masses of hair under her arms, on her belly, between her thighs; the upper lip was spared. I read Picasso in those eyes of hers—as did her husband, an art restorer at the Metropolitan Museum of Art. Together, they certainly restored one pitiful emigré. My memory, my whereabouts. The hotel. My passport and other meager possessions. Then, in quick succession, the names of Positano, and my brothers and sisters—Alberto, Jr, Palma and Taddeo, Isabella and Costanza. Nothing else impeded my return to my native land. Nothing accept Ginevra, whom I met at the makeup counter of Bloomingdale's whilst shopping with Emiliana. Imagine, in her bag was a pet gibbon whom she called Cuckoo. She took that creature everywhere. But it was Ginevra, not so much the ape, who dazzled my fragile condition."

"You don't need to flatter me," she said. "It was a mutual regard, you know that."

"But I want to know. How did you come to this place?" Mr Marigold agitated, eager to conquer the ending. He had worked out the hiking trails and plumbing throughout all 600,000 square feet of the Louvre and—like any true poet—was capable of giving birth to himself on a daily basis. But for all that, he had scarcely done anything. Hence, the seismic restlessness that now emerged in the presence of other human beings with their own real-life sagas to relate.

It was Sannazaro who invited consideration of these fine points, inasmuch as the escape from New York involved a journey, logically, out West, in the company of his new-found benefactress.

Ginevra excused herself. She was craving a bath. Sannazaro continued, free to speak even more of his mind.

"In those days, every man who looked at her probably fell away from the encounter enchanted, frustrated, desperate. Ginevra embodied the extremes of a Vargas Girl and Audrey Hepburn that simply penetrated to the male core. She was the nexus of salivations, a carbonated soul without peer, her ebullience sufficient to raise the *Titanic* in ruined beings."

"You fell in love."

"I plunged into the sonnet of pure love. There was my liberation from the odious Allegra; and here—unassailable joys, a coordinated splash of *je ne sais quoi*, her floating anatomy of ultimate promise ..." And he went on prodigiously, capturing the exquisite moment of their first encounter and all that it forebode, so that Mr Marigold himself was suddenly re-orienting the Ginevra he had occasionally known as a neighbor over the years to this new white marble bust of nonpareils.

"It is, then, a wonder that you two were never married?" he asked.

"No regrets, Señor. She was as true a friend as may the very concept of fellowship ever comport. But she did not gaze upon me. Not in the way you mean. All right. I can accept that. The subsequent journey is there before you, proof of my contentment. I did not require the stars when as many blades of grass welcomed me. All these years at the helm of the *hortus conclusus*, where raccoons can wander up the fruit tunnel, and honey bees nibble at their golden hops and hyssop. A dozen rose types grace the potager—'Prospero', 'Wise Portia', 'Fair Bianca' and 'Pretty Jessica'; quart pots, lotus-infested, beneath the dripping yew *Taxus cuspidata*, and stocked with sweet william, Iceland poppy and delphinium." He loved the very sound of all these plants, the musical nuances of English, and it was a love the gardener and the Commander would share forevermore.

And continuing: "Ginevra, who has paid for my health insurance and my food, bought me barbells, a subscription to *Chateaux* and the English *Country Life*, and ... she quite literally saved me from myself. For in recklessly attempting to fill the open wound left by that no-good Allegra, I would surely have perished in some form or other. But I am also proud to point out that I, Señor Sannazaro, saved Ginevra's garden. She turned the desolate hillsides over to me, and said, 'Experiment!' I pondered on the riot of cactus, the pathetic attempt at a poinsettia bush, the apple tree, the lemon vines that bore no fruit, the gravel slowly eroding down a mountain of pines and accumulating in an ugly morass beneath her very bedroom window. The lonely odd flower haphazardly scattered, the attempt at a vegetable garden with no passion or patience behind it. So, with her blessings, I began a five-year plan. It was the garden, but it was myself. A few acres in which I poured my soul, knowing that the very metamorphosis of Sannazaro, the whole philosophy of Arcadia, hinged on the outcome of my daily toil.

"I gave free reign to Appalachia, Himalaya, Japan and Italy. You see—" and he pointed out a window towards a distinguished glen of *Ilex glabra*, known as inkberry crenata, and a thriving race of cedar of Lebanon, winter lilacs and *Senecio veitchianus*. Then he described at maximal length the Camp's well-rotted manures, rootstocks and dressings.

"A piece of Petrograd here and Peking there, of the Inland Sea and the Southwest," he continued. "Father Alvaro, bless his heart, was most attentive to my botanical ventures. He knew how to smell the flowers. Barringer was most helpful when it came to hauling 100-pound bags of soil amendment, or digging out a stump. But I do not mean to bore you with details of the garden. As they say, a gardener's life never ends. He's always planting. Even his remains end up in the garden for his successor to work into the scheme of things."

"Very true," Mr Marigold said, commending him on his Buddhistic approach to his profession.

There was some raucous foreplay at the front door, and Alma's voice calling out, "Captain!", for that is how she often addressed Mr Marigold. "Francis Hidalgo is on the telephone!" And she continued her frantic goings-on as if announcing the winning numbers of a lottery, or a visitor from outer space. Spittle evacuated her mouth as she hollered. She stamped her foot, slapped her hands and hoarsely advised him that the phone was hot, alive, awaiting his attention. That is how rarely anyone called upon the hermit, and how large an impression a bona fide caller was bound to make on a Mongolian housekeeper whose ankles were huge. In any event, she knew that Señor Hidalgo could mean trouble. He never called, except to announce a reduction in the monthly income on account of some hidden expense for which that confounded trust was liable. And, though not understanding one whit of these higgledy-piggledy money matters, she sensed that there were high levels of graft, corruption, pilfering and outright theft occurring behind the innocent Captain's back, probably originating with the bank, and the lawyers, and probably with Señor Hidalgo himself.

Then again, maybe it was something *she* did? Her mind raced to all her misdeeds during the past month, and pieced together the miscreant trails she might have left.

"She's such a work of art, dear Alma, would you not agree, Señor Sannazaro?"

As her shouting and stomping and excitement continued (her descendants had surely ridden with Genghis Khan, burning villages for thousands of miles, impaling the enemy in 100-head heaps, knowing they would impress future historians), Sannazaro concurred: "Delicacy such as hers would terrorize a stone, deplete all future standards of decorum to the realm of a red ant pile, torture the eardrum, convert soft to hard, smooth to rough, refinement to the last ever crudity. In that one woman are all the boulder fields, tumors, coarse grains and unsheathed husks of human history. In fact, in her, womanhood is vanquished forever. You have harbored a new freak of evolution."

Both men's eyes shared a bright bounce which fell several inches to either side of comprehensibility.

CHAPTER 13
News of Mongolia from Larry

MR MARIGOLD FIRMLY grasped Sannazaro's old hands. Considering all the roads open to them, it was remarkable the two men had taken the same one. Never mind the fact they lived next door to one another. They had discovered friendship in a cynical world, and could not be more delighted.

"Dinner tomorrow?" Sannazaro suggested. "Let me fix you the finest Neapolitan pasta in the world."

"I'll come early, bearing every nectar and liqueur."

"No, never!" Sannazaro insisted. "I have the appropriate wine."

"Fine. It's agreed, then."

Mr Marigold started down the white adobe enameled staircase, done in boat paint, skipping his long fingers over the ornate newels and cavetti, spiraling towards the eighteenth-century sacerdotal door panels that Alvaro had acquired from a Nestorian church in Nambé.

There Alma Khan was waiting, clutching her knuckles, impatient to find out the latest news of their insolvency.

"I heard you," Mr Marigold said quietly. "Do all Mongolians fret so over unknowns?"

Scattered lights of neighboring villas shone dim against a moonless firmament. Down the road, a windmill turned with rhythmic creaks. Golden frogs added to the quiet overture, crickets and ant lions, leisure lacewings and crazy-making katydids gave texture and periodicity to the rapturous chorus. A creek was murmuring beneath the bridge, a breeze descending from the heather. In the distant cry of a coyote pack could be read every misery, mob relentlessness or sexual heat; other irregular canines, cavorting along the road, inciting Ginevra's howler mutts, lent additional music to the Tesuque spheres. There were also three fighting cats, two cooing doves and, somewhere, an actual drumbeat bearing down into the marmoreal still of dark New Mexico highlands. Passing cars, the odd one, swooshed tires.

And Alma, of course, of the barking voice. She spoke with a sonority as subtle and soothing as a flood—whole uprooted trees, bridges crashing, bodies cascading. "Hurry, Captain! You know I don't trust that man. Lawyers! Psssh! I don't care if he was your father's best friend!" She spat onto the floor to prove her point.

Mr Marigold strolled unhurriedly into the double reception room of his house with its eclectic appointments—Cumbria, Burgundy, St Petersburg, Acoma—sat down, and took the phone which Alma thrust into his cheek.

"Yes?" he said, with an air of magnificent disinterest.

"Murillo," Francis Hidalgo the Third began, for he, unlike Mr Marigold's late father, had never been so upright and proper in his address. In fact, Francis had good reason to perceive Murillo as the splendid, eternal, unfrowned-upon, untampered-with youth that he was: a perpetual font of favorable weathers, watering holes of fantasy inch-upon-inch, despite nearly five decades having loosened a bit of his wits, colored silver the odd tassel of desiccated red lock, tightened the auric, slightly Eurasian skin, fashioned a double chin and turkey's beard beneath that prominent point of a jaw and faint lines on his radiant, attenuated forehead. All in all, he struck the appearance of an angel riding upon frayed wings, a waterlogged butterfly, a naked looby of a monk stumbling down the back alleys beside a church in Spain, where once, long ago, two of his ancestors were probably married.

"Murillo," Hidalgo continued. "I have a serious matter to discuss with you."

"I'm ruined?" Mr Marigold brightly inquired.

"Hardly that. But I really must see you. Say tomorrow, 9 a.m. Will that suit you?"

"Splendidly, but wait—Alma, dear, check the social calendar for tomorrow—nine did you say?—for 9 a.m. Am I free of state duties?"

"What are you talking about?" she gestured, cockeyed, never one to fathom his pedestrian wit, despite however many years of the same routine.

"Yes, my secretary informs me that 9 a.m. is possible. I shall leave word with the sentries."

"And Murillo," the lawyer warned, "you will have to make a decision that is bigger than all of us."

"Ahoy, and you're not going to tell me? You'd let me sleep on nails? Monster!"

A fearsome torrent of contradictory instincts must have poured through Francis's mind. He had known about the astounding news for some time, but, lacking the full knowledge of such arcane, possibly unprecedented legal matters, had systematically endeavored to make sense of its basics before laying it out. Here was an enormously taxing crisis of opportunity, a very mortality in the analysis, and it was his legal duty to inform the trust's sole beneficiary, Murillo. But a choice confronted the lad, and Francis stood poised and eager to realize the windfall of windfalls, ether of paradises, cash of the ages, power of all times. But only if his "nephew" were to act expeditiously according to a well-crafted greed in the guise of philanthropy.

"Right, good, then. See you tomorrow, Murillo."

"Fine, Francis, fine. We shall all be ready to greet destiny, no questions asked."

"What? Well? Are you going to tell me?" Alma agitated over him like the whole of the Gobi, brawny and menacing.

"Nothing, absolutely nothing to tell. Not before tomorrow, my dear. Now let sweet nocturnes calm those thickening storm clouds. Your face shows off a cyclone, though I've seen and much prefer the Botticelli in your smile. Some tea's in order, no?"

"Yes, Master," she fell in, giving him a good one-two across the hunching shoulder, all in the fun of two cohabitants long, long past the first roseate blush of their living arrangement.

Hidalgo paid Alma well for her services: room, board and 2,000 dollars a month. After all, she was Mr Marigold's only real family, to speak of. She was not without additional comforts, either. Hidalgo knew she'd had more than one man during her 40 years in service to the Marigold estate. Even, in bygone times, a marriage to a rogue, and no charming rogue, who stole her Mongolian heirlooms, though not her virginity—she'd given that up on the great legendary steppes, in a 90-mile gale, on the very site of the discovery of the skeleton of Baluchitherium, a colossal hornless rhinoceros, the largest land mammal in biological history, to hear her rhapsodize the moment. It was also rumored she'd actually killed a man, once, near the Colorado border in a near beer dispute, however queer-sounding. Self-defense.

Subsequently, she diddled with a fiberglass king, who drove the rounds, five states, with ill-fitting sheets jutting dangerously from his land cruiser. This guy was a fast-talking sales whore, who wooed her into the back of Ace Bottoms Bingo Palace on a Saturday night. He was but the first of many other neighborhood slobs, drifters, bartenders, cattle rustlers, poetasters—until, finally, Larry.

She returned now with caffeine-rich Macedonia Mango tea, spiked with arkhi and brewed with local honey. The bees responsible had, in the words of a local Tibetan, propagated Buddhism throughout New Mexico, and had done so for 13,000 years, since Clovis Man. Mr Marigold now took this lesson to heart, propped up against four satin pillows on his abbatial chaise longue.

"I got a letter from Larry," she declared ominously.

"That's nice."

"I'm very upset. He says that Washington is planning an attack on my homeland, and this time it's for real."

"Why would anybody attack Mongolia, least of all the US?"

Mr Marigold sipped his tea with imperturbable ease. He knew that Larry only wrote about peat in disguise, for some important-sounding journal. Actually, he was a spy, according to Alma, a very important one, whose affiliation with all things Mongolian worked in his favor—at least when it came to stupping Alma, which he had been doing on again, off again, for many years.

"Larry got a report from the Buriats of Transbaikalia. It was in cipher, of course. Nuclear espionage at Los Alamos."

"Ahh, that explains it."

Then she launched for the hundredth time into serious points of fact regarding the descendants of the blue wolf, the Dune people, and how the Monroe Doctrine, the Louisiana Purchase, the Cuban Missile Crisis, the Panama Canal, the first flight by the Wright Brothers, the Kennedy assassination, and the current effort on the part of the White House to increase its wiretapping authority were all about Mongolia.

"Something big is going on," she said. "I just know it. Maybe it's time for me to get out, while I still have time."

"But you are out. If my memory serves me, you left Mongolia many decades ago."

"I'm worried about reprisals on the domestic front."

"There are other things to worry about. The house is becoming a sieve. The termites are everywhere."

"I may need to flee the country. Remember what happened to the Japs and Krauts."

"You'll do no such thing," Mr Marigold said, trying to squash her fears. "I personally know the President," he began, referring obliquely to the President of the Santa Fe Chapter of Great Books. He had gone only rarely, some say to meet his imagined goddess. "And let me assure you, he can't even spell Mongolia. He doesn't know 'Inner' from 'Outer', where it is, what it's worth, or whether one can play golf there."

This was just like Alma. When she indulged her little stash of marijuana, which she grew out back, she got all homesick and sentimental. Her grandfather had been present when the Chinese delegates at Ulan Bator (then known as Urga) were banished from the country by the Mongol princes who declared their independence. Her ancestors had lived on the far reaches of the Gobi Desert, among the Kalmuch tribes, dinosaur eggs, vampires and pyramids of yak dung. They were known as Arat, free nomads, and they lived in the wind and were famed for their horsemanship and their defiance of K'ang-hsi, the Chinese warlord. Of course, the great Kublai was her cousin. She, and a few hundred thousand other cousins, had controlled a million and a half square miles of plateau lands—her civilization—and was able to pack up in 20 minutes. The yurts were mobile, the Golden Horde adrift in bricks of silver, ingots of gold, the finest Russian embroideries, and flocks of mutton to every horizon. She could recite the lustrous tales of the House of Jagati, of the spicy national epic poem, Jangar, and—to Mr Marigold's amazement—seemed adept at pronouncing the impossible finals and medians of the Mongolian alphabet, which had to be the most difficult and discombobulating of tongues.

Alma was wild, crazy, convinced that the Western military-industrial establishment was out to get Mongolia; and Larry, her lover, played on her fears to maintain his control over her. She fervently believed that he was her link to the secret government and their ongoing preparations for screwing with Mongolians. One day he whispered in her ear, "You are aware, are you not, that the Republicans in Congress have passed new anti-terrorist legislation authorizing the rounding up and hanging of all relatives of Genghis Khan in the United States?" At first she thought it an amusement, but Larry's deadpan demeanor was unflinching. It was a cruel thing.

One night it dawned upon Mr Marigold that Alma appeared to have barricaded herself in her room, and that her recent request for a raise had been prompted by her having exhausted a considerable sum from her savings on the purchase of ammunition. What an astonishing thing to do, he thought. And it truly frightened him.

Alma's strange paranoia actually indicted the Marigold household as much as it did Larry. This poor superstitious woman was buffeted by isolationism and the curse of capacious hips. And though she was harassed by demons from her past, she should also have had every reason to be grateful. There are people in this world with virtually no requirements or compulsions: no need of company, accoutrements, accolades or commendations. People for whom good health, a steaming blueberry scone and musical air suffice to save the world and make the day right. And in whose fellowship there will issue only the melodies of praise, gratefulness, curiosity and humble origins. These listeners with no special requests, no armaments, no attitude, are a species unto themselves. All is reasonable, courteous, convivial. Their orientation to their allotted life span seeks no alternative, voices no regrets, wants only the sun to shine, the moon to lullaby, a breeze across a wild waterway for contemplation.

But Marigold was not entirely that simple, for he was steeped in anger: anger about nearly everything that was wrong with the twentieth century, anger born of too much reading and too few interactions with real people.

A proportion that left him livid with the rancor of an idealist who had none of the anthropological grounding to temper his complaints. But for all that, his voracious inquiries on the written page, his knowledge of most classics and general lifestyle approached a condition of extreme asceticism that, on most days, could be described as pleasing to the ears and faintly relaxed; a quiet immersion in Ariosto.

His frenzies were internal. He was a magnet of solipsisms. No companion was possible under such circumstances, and Alma's destiny was to clean up the floors, cabinets and table tops. The Commander—whose largesse had made her limited freedom possible—she now held responsible for what she perceived to be the lost years, a life with nothing to show for it. There was no open exchange to indicate ill will. She still served him with a certain attachment, rather as if he were an extended family member. But there was ire lacing the lather, moistening the dust of her daily toil. The routines had gotten terribly old, suffocating any true hope. Marigold's lack of outside female connections, other than the most superficial, compounded his unreality, and hers. He was the definitive case study in asexuality, a fact made strange by his adoration of the ideal female.

Yet, for all this abnormality, this odd couple appeared genuine in their fundamental feelings for one another. Mr Marigold would never let anything untoward happen to Alma, and vice versa. This much was a certainty. An atomic fact, substantiated by all the familiar objects and verbs of their community of two.

Before going to bed, shuffling along in his velvet slippers, heading for late-night munchies from the refrigerator, Mr Marigold happened to pass by Alma's room, where he thought he heard sobbing.

"Alma?" He opened her door. "Are you decent?"

She did not speak, and Mr Marigold saw a sorry sight of a woman: late middle-aged, as dumpy and dreary as she had ever appeared. "What's wrong, dear?"

With great effort she rallied beyond pathos to state, "He left me."

"Who?"

"Larry."

"But when? I thought—"

"That was yesterday. I just got off the phone with—"

"With whom?"

"His wife. One of three!"

"Oh dear, I'm very sorry," Mr Marigold said, applying himself to comforting her. "Maybe it's temporary. Maybe he's just on a secret spy mission."

"And he's not a spy," she said bitterly.

"But I thought—"

"No. He's an undertaker in St George, Utah. He also has a wife in Florida. He's a big phony. He was no spy. And he was no writer. He was a con artist."

Mr Marigold was quiet as he reflected on another loss for this woman more sinned against than sinning.

"An undertaker. So he digs? He does know something about peat, then?" He was trying to exhume anything positive about the scoundrel.

"But I don't mean to say I told you so."

"I'll survive," she whimpered.

He hugged her, which he rarely did. In fact, aside from obsessively kissing the hands of any female who moved before him, Mr Marigold was distinctly unphysical. Had he even lost his virginity? Honor does not recommend exposition. But something altogether unexpected was about to happen to the Commander, and the advice and confessional of Father Alvaro, the world's premier bon vivant, might have been useful, if only he could be located.

By the way, how is the good Father doing?, Mr Marigold mused later that night, as he prayed before an icon over his bed, and drifted off into the strangest dream he'd had in years.

CHAPTER 14
How Francis Hidalgo Raised the Ghost of Alonzo Marigold

PUNCTUALLY, AT 9 a.m., Francis Hidalgo banged on Mr Marigold's gate, which was the old-style *la puerta del zaguan*, wide enough to admit a single-oxen-yoked truckle. The day began bright and bothered. Dust clouds were brewing, hawks carousing overhead.

"Hello, Alma. God is good, God is great, no?"

"Liar," she replied, slapping her dust rag against her apron and looking up at the sultry, uneven sky.

The portly Hidalgo, hoisting a personal history of considerable fillets, labored with his heavy briefcase, breathing hard as he accompanied Alma up the path. He had evidently stuffed too many files into the case; various paper edges, bent and manhandled, stuck out the sides. In his somber, darkening suit, with his free fingers twitching at his black mustache, and one eye squinting on account of the dust, he struck a nervous countenance that forebode, in Alma's mind, some kind of financial fiasco. She was like a Philippine monkey-eating eagle: very attuned to economics. Then again, he had fronted a positive frame of mind when he walked in, so who could tell?

"Hello, Murillo." Business-like, concealing a monument.

"Good morning, Francis. Alma, take Francis's order. Do explain to him that we have no water, power or food, but that he's free to nibble on the plants. Or, as they say, let no one despair as long as he breathes." It was an exaggeration: water and power had been out for four hours in the night, as was common after storms in the area, but had come back in time for this important tryst.

Mr Marigold led his visitor out to the solarium, where they took respective seats on adjoining frayed aubusson couches of russet and mauve, tawdry varieties commonly obtained every weekend at the Marchés des Puces—the flea markets—on the north end of Paris. Alma served them biscuits heated in the microwave, slices of cold Danish sweet butter, and steaming orange spice tea, on a superlative tray of pewter from Antwerp of Rubens' time. Such was Marigold's confluence of discordant amenities and objets d'art.

They sipped in relative silence, enjoying the company of sparrows (the same sparrows, more than 60 percent of whose population was said to have vanished from the British Isles, and perhaps 90 percent from China) and titmice, some of which managed to fly through the rambling sun-rooms before finding their way back out under the cobwebbed eaves. The house, northern Spanish in its details, presented to the south a 60-foot verandah, azotea roofing supported by a dozen old majestic beams, Norman in their thickness, fitted into the adobe and brightly painted, that had been lumbered off the mountains to the northeast three centuries before by men, and a few women possibly, who had perfectly vanished from the record of activity on earth.

Despairing of courtesies, Hidalgo set forth to explain the reason for his sudden visit. He placed a file on the old knotted Japanese cherry table with its brass rims and glass-nugget insets.

"This is an important document, a crucial moment that bears careful consideration," he began.

Alma feared the sobriety.

"I can see it is a document. But what is it?" queried Mr Marigold. "Perhaps the better question would be, what isn't it?" Hidalgo's face blanched; a contagion of monies buzzing on the near horizon in his skull. He heard the multitudinous doubloons just as clearly as if they were bees, nectar dreams consolidated in a feeding frenzy.

Mr Marigold did not exactly follow the best-kept secrets gesticulating in the facial muscles of his guest, though he rightly reckoned there was single-mindedness in the air. "I'm at a loss," he said.

"Let me just lay it out for you, Murillo. Your grandfather's grandfather"—and Hidalgo visibly counted the receding generations with the fingers of his left hand to be certain of his arithmetic—"was an explorer, did you know that?"

"A surveyor."

"No. An explorer. The surveying came later. Thomas Jefferson had just acquired Louisiana from the French."

"1803."

"I believe you are right. It's when my own ancestors, the Spanish, were entrenched right here, in Santa Fe, along with a bunch of poor Indian folk. The whole Southwest was unknown to Americans. Those in the East were not wrong in seizing the opportunities of New Mexico. Your family story."

"I am not unfamiliar with those times. But what of it, Francis?"

"It appears that your great-great-grandfather—that is five removed—"

"I am no mathematician."

"Anyway, around 1804, nearly 200 years after the Spanish settled here, and at the same time such traders as Saunders and Pursley were making the initial contacts with the locals, a merchant of fortune whose name was lost until last month followed Captain Zebulon Pike and 23 of his men—soldiers, buffalo hunters, adventurers—into the furthest reaches of Colorado. They were the first Americans to see the snow-capped Rockies. They got over the Royal Gorge—don't ask me how—and then headed south into New Mexico, passing the first clusters of our unburned-brick houses, where they were met by crowds. Four clamorous shots were fired over their heads to celebrate the auspicious moment. Imagine them riding through our plaza, to cheers of *Los Americanos!*, and finally seated at a large European-style table. The documentation is all there. Even down to the meal that was served. A fine dinner of partridge and muskrat, sautéed beans and crispy potatoes, corn gruel roasted in honey, curdle cheese, and ample spirits, all of which they consumed in the fine company of the local Governor Don Nemesio, as well as the Juez de Hacienda, or Judge of the Customs, whose name is unknown. After the officials collected their various *derechos de arancel*, or tariff imposts, the visitors were warmly seen to a hotel and arrested."

"But where did a lawyer come by so vivid and sanguine a story-telling imagination?"

"Historians abound, Murillo. Every cranny belies an expert, each church its maven; not one rare bookstore lacks for a resident guru, and the city's archives teem with professors of the palimpsest—learned men whose only hope is the past. In this case, the precise details cascaded and, lucky for you, the record is fairly complete."

"Francis, you must recall that I am a history buff, but what suspense is all this leading to?"

Hidalgo paused with a great, disarming grin. "Would you believe me if I told you that, upon their arrival, the man who did the translating for them was a local ranchero and surveyor named Chihuahua Marigold, father of Alonzo, your great-great-grandfather?"

"Why shouldn't I believe you?"

"And that Alonzo Marigold would one day become one of the largest landholders in the territory because of a card game in his favor?"

"That figures." Mr Marigold was not entirely impressed by the news. "But now, *now* we have learned—"

"Francis, who is this imperial 'We'?"

"We, me, myself, and a law student, excellent researcher, whom I have retained for the case—all on your behalf, my dear Murillo—"

"What case? And don't try to charm me—I've never taken to that."

"You're too much like your father. Just listen to me. Details have emerged from your ancestor's diary, recently discovered and purchased at a garage sale right here in Santa Fe. That's right. The original diary, can you imagine! There are countless annotations, whose dates have been confirmed by the greatest experts at the historical society in Albuquerque, confirmations repeated in any number of official books, one of which was authorized by the first Governor of New Mexico. Eyewitness accounts rendered by none other than Pike himself."

"Of what, blast it! Where are you headed with this gibberish?"

"Murillo, look at me."

"I'm looking. Am I not looking? Do you not see both of my eyes—this one on the left, the other to the right, both fairly evenhanded to either side of my nose? Can you not distinguish the perfect symmetry—much like a trapezoid and remarked upon by none other than Leonardo—that conspires between those same eyes and the looming nostrils underneath?

And are they peering forwards or backwards?"

"Enough. This is no joke. Peer forwards henceforth. Much depends on it ..."

And he began to fill in the amazing blanks.

CHAPTER 15
The Provocative Sensation of Dollar Signs

ALMA BUSIED HERSELF in the room, removing each book for dusting—Volney's *Ruins*, Wills' *Wanderings Among the High Alps*— emphatically interested in the conveyances of Hidalgo, whose own excitement was reaching a fever pitch.

"Murillo, Alonzo's giant gains were as easily lost, through sheer apathy. He was cheated by a combination of his genes—given to disinterest in such matters. Just look at your own life, with its academic predilections, massive inertia—"

"I beg your pardon?"

"By destiny. It is proven by the various accounts."

"Cheated!" Alma burst out.

"Just wait—" Hidalgo carried on, tiring of the fools around him. "Cheated? Nonsense. Who? By what means? What are you talking about?" Mr Marigold reddened in the concavity of his cheeks, so that an impatience the color of anger lidded the bone structure and burst like some poisoned sunset upon the sandstone arch of his brow.

"Your great-great—"

"Yes, yes, five removed—or is it four?"

"We can win it back," Hidalgo declared.

"Win it back?" Alma's eyes grew circumpolar.

"Win *what* back!?" Mr Marigold half-exploded.

"Murillo, try to fix this image in your head: thousands of silver ingots, or *barras* as they were called, and a fortune in stamped gold bullion. Add to that exactly 1.2 million acres. It's all yours."

Alma cried out in a joy sounding more like grief. "I'm totally confused."

The Commander, whom Alma often called Don Magnífico, sighed.

"Murillo, you've read 10,000 books. But they were the wrong books. Now listen to me."

And Francis went on to describe the value of such coinage, acreage and thousands of cows, horses and sheep today, as well as the mineral rights—gold, silver, oil ...

"... He owned most of Santa Fe," he concluded. "Who? How? What are you talking about, damn you?"

Another joyous outburst issued from Alma Khan's breast. She got up, strode forward, knelt down and kissed the lawyer's hand, a gesture she had learned from her Commander, who agitated, "Alma, please, show some dignity."

"You may kiss my hand, Alma," the lawyer said. "And you, Murillo, you can kiss my butt for what I'm about to tell you."

"Kiss your butt, will I?—I have a mind to toss you out that gate."

"Shut up!" Alma exploded. "Hear what your father's executor, his closest, most trusted friend, the only salvation left this infernal rut of an existence, has to tell you, or I shall—"

"Oh piss off! I will listen, and then I shall throw you *both* out!" Hidalgo separated certain files, papers, titles, claims, deeds, notes, marginalia, xeroxes of xeroxes, court numbers, dockets, file cards, books and book markers, official copies of articles of incorporation, land grants, transcripts, letters, the original diary, and certain previously sealed court proceedings, until the table, and portions of the floor, were lost beneath a sea of ridiculous legalese. Now it was perfectly clear why his briefcase had been so heavily weighed down.

"All right, so?" Mr Marigold commanded, all fluster.

"Look at this description." Hidalgo delineated with his finger the blow-by-blow obfuscations of which history is made, each second lending more and more credibility to the reversal of fortunes that had stripped bare one of the largest estates in the history of the territory; that had financially raped a modest surveyor before an assemblage of his jealous peers, officials for the state of New Mexico, all of whom, one by one, decade after decade, substantiated the lie by allowing for its escheatment.

He spilled out the guts of the claim, referring to the late nineteenth-century Marigold, grandson of

Alonzo, the Commander's great-grandfather Burrito.

"As of course you know, he sired some children, to be sure, but died in very modest circumstances, owning this property and its contents, but owing even more. If not for the sweat, blood and tears of your own father, Pecos, you'd have lost everything. Burrito had your same lackadaisical charms," Hidalgo admitted. "He never deigned to manage his assets."

"A Wild West Buddhist." Marigold took comfort in the notion.

"A stubborn, foolish man who ignored the protection of his family and, in essence, repudiated his rights. Alonzo's legacy was staked out by his rivals, who did so with the connivance of people in high places during the turbulent transition years following the annexation of New Mexico by the United States. Alonzo lived to see all his properties vanish into the mire of government deceptions and systematic corruption. The treaty of Guadalupe Hidalgo—no relation," Francis said matter-of-factly, "was not sufficient to protect the Spanish and Mexican land grants secured earlier under the Treaty of Cordoba, when New Mexico was transferred from Spain to the Mexican Republic. Subsequent possession was further complicated by local Indian claims. All these conflicting cultural layers were treacherous for the long-lived. Your ancestor, more poet than proprietor, got totally chewed up in the political and ethnic shuffles. He was dealt complexities far beyond his ken."

"So what is the point of all this, I reiterate? What has the card game to do with it, and why, for crying out loud, did you need to come over here at 9 a.m. this particular day to depress me with news of my dis- possessed ancestors a century and a half ago?"

"The point," rallied Hidalgo, "is that your ancestor did not die a poor man. He passed away a victim of deliberate theft, and I am now coming to the conclusion that this can be proven beyond a shadow of a doubt. It can be resolved outside the judicial system, because that is the last thing the state wants. If we are lucky, the judge's hammer will only be heard privately, within his own chambers."

"As in some kind of formal apology?" Mr Marigold's headlands were reeling, a travelogue of hijinks in the Holocene—unclear, desperate not to be dragged into tasks, detail work, anything other than what he was comfortable with: namely, his books, the mottled half-light of his familiar space, the utter lack of responsibility.

"Hardly. I am referring to restitution. Murillo, here's the map of Santa Fe, circa 1860, when your fifth- removed was laid to rest. At that time, the territory surrounding the capital extended from the one hundred third meridian of longitude along the eastern border all the way to California. See that? And that? And that? From here to here to here—"

And he drew the alleged perimeters with a blue magic marker. "There are approximately 75 million acres in New Mexico today. Your ancestor owned 1.2 million of those, give or take (for he was never certain, nor even interested), and they happen to be amongst the finest acreage in the state."

"He's dead, Hidalgo. Surely ownership is a moot point by now."

"No, it belongs to you. There are ample legal precedents for retroactive land cases. The state, as I said, does not want a long and expensive battle. It will settle. I've already made some preliminary checks with the DA's office."

"They've said they will settle?"

"Not exactly. In truth, they think I'm crazy."

Marigold caught the glimmer of far-reaching humor in Hidalgo's eyes, and it struck in him an intriguing chord.

"But they also know I mean business. In fact—and I've got this on tape—Gerald Hemmings, the city district attorney, rather quickly blurted out that you might owe the city and state back-taxes—150 years' worth on a hell of a lot of land."

"That's terrific. Good job. We are surely bankrupt 150 times over."

"Actually, it is terrific. It's an admission, you numbskull. They also—"

"Who's they?" Mr Marigold's dizziness was escalating by the minute. "Lawyers for the state of New Mexico. Certain preliminary issues have already been broached with them. They have acknowledged the diffuse status of the land, the non-contiguous parcels and many of the contingent problems—federal land issues, Native American concerns, and the fact that an estimated 80,000 people and several Indian tribes are currently living on the property in question, believing it to be their own. This poses a dilemma for the state."

"Eighty thousand people, on my land?"

"I fairly believe it's provable, yes. So, what I've been thinking—to avoid impossible tangles, as you can begin to appreciate—is some kind of preemptive suit, a buy-out, a compromise or an unpublicized swap. In exchange for our dissolving any and all claims to the city of Santa Fe, the state should agree to deed over to the Marigold Trust 10,000 acres of forest lands north of Santa Fe, on the condition that you keep it preserved.

And a considerable chunk of cash. I'm still toying with figures—scores of real-estate precedents, the actual seals and documentation of the card game, the players at the table, the later surveyors-general, legal arguments and all the possible rebuttals Hemmings' office might make. I'm trying to anticipate everything. This is complicated stuff. But it's clear that you will be in a position to build on a few pieces, subdivide 5,000 of the acres in large 500-acre sections, if you so desire, to generate income for maintenance and the like, and I would cut a deal so that they pay you for at least some portion of the dollar value of the rest of the 1.2 million acres—say a few billion. That's the chunk I was referring to."

"*Dollars?*"

"Of course."

Alma collapsed, sprawled as if dead, across the rug.

Mr Marigold gazed upon her unmoving body with morbid interest, then smiled imperceptibly at the lawyer. "At the very least, you've done me a colossal favor."

"What is that?"

"Her silence."

CHAPTER 16
Mr Marigold Prepares to Preside Over the Course of Empire

HIDALGO ACKNOWLEDGED the Mongolian slab on the floor. "She'll be well compensated," he said. "You must allow that you are probably not the easiest eccentric to look after."

"What could be easier? Such momentous brooders as myself require nothing at all, neither staunch comrade nor engine room. The specters that loom above my reef are of my own choosing."

"Just listen carefully. Try to understand what I'm telling you. A nature conservancy has expressed keen interest in working with you in a scientific advisory role. They tell me there are badgers up there, rare mushrooms, orchids, cougars and wolverines. That sort of thing."

"Who else knows about this?" Marigold puzzled, deeply stilled, like some frozen fish in a crystallized lake, a mineral salt washed up on the shore of an unexplored ocean, a Potton-like "Improbable Eden."

"Just me, the researcher, a trusted broker, those in the DA's office. It's a tight-lipped conspiracy. Has to be. I want to get as much ammunition as possible before we go to court."

"So, what else? What happens?"

"Among other things, I'd condition the settlement on your retaining most of the Plaza."

"*Which* plaza?"

"*The* Plaza. Well, at least the park, not necessarily the buildings around it."

"What are we going to do with the park?"

"Nothing. Mind you, none of this has actually been discussed yet."

"I surely would have heard."

"That is correct. But my hunch is that we can ask the city to lease it back from us at the rate of 25,000 dollars a month for the rest of your life. That would be a bargain from their point of view. That, in addition to the value of the 10,000 acres, average price of 40,000 an acre, and you are now worth, on paper, 400 million dollars, less the normal commission to the trust of three percent, or 7.5 million. Add to that the big chunk of cash—say, a minimum of two billion dollars. That will make you the wealthiest man in New Mexico."

"I don't like it one bit," Mr Marigold protested.

"What do you mean?"

"I absolutely loathe having to contemplate matters pertaining to money before noon. You've essentially ruined my day. What's more, the money you are referring to was ill gained. Really, Hidalgo, a card game? That I should expect anything from a card game!"

"I've ruined his day!" Hidalgo repeated, as Alma was his witness. She'd now risen from the dead, her eyes ember glowing, new-found rubies in the court of highest hopes.

"Murillo, time is of the essence. No fooling around. As for the card game, it was monte. An innocent wager that appears to have taken advantage of the fact that the Mexican Governor had just lost his job, courtesies of General Kearney, and in his shame he bet more and more of his considerable fortune. He could not bear to lose twice in the same day. Hand upon hand the stakes escalated, whiskey flowed, tempers flared, but Alonzo Marigold kept winning, and La Tules—she was the dealer—kept dealing. Alonzo's luck was uncanny, according to eyewitness accounts gathered in the documents."

"But how did he then lose everything?"

"He had no motivation to maximize his gains. Most of what he won was land. He surveyed it, and had it formally sanctioned by the Acting Secretary of the Interior. That sanction required a Congressional hearing in Washington. They approved the legality of the card game and the debt. We need to find that particular document. I believe it must be in your attic somewhere."

"There are dozens of boxes and crates up there. The spider webs are impenetrable."

"You need to look for it. That document would be incontestable. You see, Alonzo Marigold essentially did nothing. It's as if he was hardly touched by his windfall. Oh, he grazed some cattle, but being a vegetarian—probably one of the first in the whole Territory—did not make him inclined to pursue cattle ranching."

"He loved the cows."

"No doubt. But without a strong utilization of the properties on which they grazed, they were subject to homesteading by others, and piracy. As I mentioned before, he appears to have been uninclined to protect what he had. Which is understandable. He would have needed his own military force to patrol such a vast empire. Other ranchers were keen to pick off his parcels. Prior to his death, Alonzo had become the butt of humor by those with great ambition. They were turbulent times."

"And Burrito?"

"Your great-grandfather did nothing, either," continued Francis. "Moreover, there were those eager to insist that Alonzo had cheated, that the whole thing was a scam masterminded by the gambling hall, for a stake in the winnings. You can't imagine how much history has been rewritten. With the advent of a new flag, new laws, new partitions, your ancestors' bland petitions fell upon deaf ears. The system of government had totally closed out Santa Marigold, as the estate was called. There was no recourse, none. Not then. But there is now."

"So, let me be clear. A diary turns up and you say it was Alonzo Marigold's?"

"Correct."

"And there are additional statements of some form? What, letters, other diaries?"

"An obituary, published in the daily record when Chihuahua died in 1853, and written by his granddaughter, your grandmother four times removed, who was holding up in a small adobe south of Santa Fe. She was an unhappy woman, by all accounts. I think I know why."

"You've actually investigated my great-great-grandmother's happiness?"

"Not in those terms. I'm saying, as part of the documentation of the scam, she described it, corroborated it, even referred to many of the individuals evidently present in the casino when the biggest fortune in New Mexican history changed hands. The letter provides a crucial trail from one document to another, like a bridge paving the way to the night in question. Keep in mind, the whole Santa Fe Trail economy was worth, at best, a million dollars a year. So Alonzo would have been like, I suppose, a Rockefeller or Rothschild. With one major difference: he didn't care for the money, despite the keener interest showed by his parents."

"A true Marigold."

"Well, Santa Fe was marching to a different drum: trade, progress, slicker and slicker consumer goods, and social aspirations. Anyway, the diary is for real, and like I said we've sampled the official response. They'll discuss the matter. They're already doing their own homework. You need to search the attic. Your father entrusted such decisions to me, on your behalf. Naturally I would never do anything unless you approved."

"You just contradicted yourself."

"Murillo, please. Your Trust was set up as an independent mechanism to protect you and to invest assets as is deemed will make the best business sense."

"And if I refuse the settlement, but insist on recovering all 1.2 million acres?"

"That's not an option," Hidalgo replied.

"Why is that?"

"As I stated earlier, you've 80,000 people living on the various properties to contend with."

"I do have the right to kick them off, if I so desire, correct?"

"I doubt that is a desirable course, and I would never recommend such warfare. For that's what it would be—you against the world. A lonely place to be. And what for? Do I detect greed, nephew?"

"Merely an old utopian, at heart. A Gene Kelly to the core. I don't care if Jonathan Swift demolished the genre, made us all out to be nostalgic fools. As you were speaking, relaying these matters of pure historical interest, I began to feel a connection with Chihuahua and Alonzo, with Victor and Burrito, each of whom was evidently overtaken by the speed of the modern world, such as it was back then. Whose inclination, I am sure, was towards the peace and tranquillity of a Luddite's private life."

"He may have been a shepherd musing under a tree, but there was another side to Alonzo. According to known sources, he was as compulsive as the next man. You don't accrue 1.2 million acres in a gambling victory unless you're pretty damned aggressive about it. Granted, I have much more research to do in coming weeks, but I have a fairly good sense of what happened."

"Perhaps, perhaps not. In any event, I am myself, am I not? I have my rights, do I not? You were kind enough, diligent enough and I'm sure self-serving enough to bring this miraculous legal case to my attention, and for that I am in your debt, make no mistake. But from this juncture, I must proceed alone. Oh, do not fear for your commission, inflated though it be. I will not attempt to alter the binding bylaws of my father's will. You have always looked after me and I am forever grateful, as they say. But as to the resolution of this outstanding debt, I shall not fear the fray, mismanage the profound opportunity, flee the fanfare nor shy away from the dream of Arcadia."

"Dream of Arcadia?" Hidalgo looked to Alma who looked up at the ceiling. "And what is that?"

"That, my legal marrow, is the only desirable, durable end on earth: the realization of a human community whose solitaires cannot be faulted for intrusiveness, mean-spiritedness or exploitation of the life force all around them. Montano lends an egg to Amarillis. Mirtillo pursues Corisca, the wanton nymph. Ergasto, friend to Mirtillo, helps Lupino, the goat-herd and servant to Dorinda, fix a barn roof. And so forth." Marigold could not help but marvel at the swirl of coincidences unleashed by that tale told by his very neighbor, Sannazaro.

"If I detect your ecological bent, then we are on the same wavelength. As I mentioned, the Nature Society wants to consult. You have spectacular taxwrite-offs staring up your nose! You'll be celebrated for your generosity! Your wisdom!"

"You are a man of countless exclamation points, Hidalgo."

"Thank you."

"But I must defer to yet higher callings. Mikhail Gorbachev liberated hundreds of millions of people, knowing the price would be the mantle of their opprobrium."

"I don't understand."

"I have grown up obscure and have only my 1.2 million acres—if all that you have said is true—with which to accomplish the liberation of the Southwest, to set the one example worthy of remembrance in a century and a half. I am not the point. The acreage is the point, as Napoleon himself was the Revolution."

"What's he saying?" Alma implored. "What's this about Gorbachev, Napoleon?"

"I'm not sure," Hidalgo conceded. "Murillo, what's that ill-boding meteor flash across your temples?"

"Just that this is bigger than all of us combined, even including your prodigious belly, fine Hidalgo. So rouse the judge, send for the defense team, alert the highest prosecutors, jazz the jury, rattle the sabers, arrest speculation, heighten their uncertainty. Prepare to be brave, friends."

Alma, recognizing the routine signs, soaked a white Egyptian cotton wash rag in mineral water and made to rub her master's forehead and cheeks. Mr Marigold was perspiring slightly, from the ague of the moment.

"He'll be all right, just give him some space," she said, as anxious as Hidalgo to set him straight so that they could all retire.

"I'll call a news conference," Marigold began.

"You'll do no such thing."

"And all the media will be given to understand that Santa Fe, henceforth, shall become the City on the Hill."

"But the town rests upon an arid plain beneath a mountain."

"All right, then: let it be hailed the City Beneath the Hill."

"You don't own the whole city."

"What's left out?"

"The airport, a cemetery, the outlying reaches of St Francis Boulevard, and about half the municipality."

"But the main part, downtown, the old parts—"

"Definitely. Let it be known that those lands belonged to your esteemed ancestors."

"Splendid! Tomorrow morning we begin the process of re-appropriating them."

Hidalgo had spent countless hours on the situation already; had worked out the whole strategy. He dreaded divulging the case to his client for precisely these reasons. He knew Murillo would never understand it, and gobble down the highlights like a compulsive guppy in a fishbowl, risking defeat through over-enthusiasm, unthought-out bravuras. Not that he didn't believe the Commander's intellect to be of the highest caliber. It was just that he still thought of him as a bursting adolescent of terrible extremes, an overgrown zealot lost between a hangnail, a tonsure, shoulder-length hair and stooped shoulders. And with no motivation, ever, to be responsible in this world. A classic dreamer.

"That's not the best approach, Murillo," the lawyer said respectfully, hoping to diffuse any further escalations and arrest all hyperactivity. "The state will never cede that much land. We need to force a swift settlement, which I have been researching and am prepared to argue with a judge and the District Attorney behind closed doors. No fanfare. Otherwise, we might be forced into an unwelcome battle—no compromise, no dialogue—to sue the state, in other words. Which would mean taking our chances in a courtroom. We could lose. I can't afford it. You certainly can't."

"We won't lose."

Mr Marigold's thoughts were flaring like the arc of a ponderosa fire into dizzying heights. A Zone VI 4 x 5 camera and 600mm lens capturing on film inch-wide lightning bolts—the shutter of his thoughts wide open for long minutes—striking the twilight-rich perpetuum that was Marigold's brain-case. Sometimes a silhouette illuminated like tidal sands, or the vertical sacatón grasses of the Animas Valley frenzied in the wind. At other times, a pioneering plant surpassing all expectations, a tenacious lichen, the pounding surf, a hyperthermophile, as witnessed at a thousandth of a second on saturated Velvia film under a Wratten G-orange filter. All in all, his confidence bypassed any conventions and treaties, all constraints or conceits. There occurred an elemental shift in the atomic chart of his computational facility.

"What could you possibly do with a million acres? As it is you have spent 40 years cooped up in a few rooms of adobe, and if I am not mistaken—Alma, tell me if I'm wrong here—have you not been the happiest of men?"

"He has, oh yes," Alma confirmed. "Never a fret, never an unkindness, and never the slightest desire to catch a bus, occupy the berth in a train or chance a 747. The rest of the world has had no bearing on his thoughts. Though my many suitors have come from far and wide, never an inquiry out of his mouth or noodle factory of a helm. One might conclude he was short upstairs, but it's not that: here sits a satisfied man. The horse and buggy can offer him no greater solace than what he has already. And while a fine automobile sits in the garage, his total mileage last year was under 29 miles. Even his bicycle remains unutilized."

"Happiness, true, I have tasted it," Mr Marigold explained. "But what I'm suggesting is the same for the commonweal."

"What's commonweal?" Alma asked.

"The general welfare, dear girl," Mr Marigold went on. "I have been fortunate, sitting all day long since childhood immersed in my books, in every imaginable tale of heroism, pettiness, adventure, lust, weird science, geopolitics, nihilism and passion. The world of ideas has been my pillow. And so all-encompassing that only this week have I really sat down and had a conversation with my neighbors. And, lo! What I have missed out on! Great souls surround me, people of dignity, of promise, and I have no doubt such neighbors populate the whole of Santa Fe, all of New Mexico—indeed, the planet entire. I merely aim to institute a system, a master plan, the blueprint for preserving that neighborhood in all its glory."

"I think," said Hidalgo, "you better talk to a few more people whose good word for the day may well differ from the one you're preparing. Santa Fe is no panacea, as much as I love this town."

Mr Marigold smiled, revealing the Appalachians of his front teeth, an old and worn-down range, slightly yellowed from all the ginseng tea. Across the grin of his aging gaze, Monument Valley at sunrise. "I am no preacher, fear not. You correctly know me to be fearful of the public eye. I shall not bring undue scrutiny down upon the Marigolds, for it would serve no end."

"What do you want to do, Murillo?"

"What do you suggest, Francis?" he replied, in a moment of sober conciliation.

"Precisely what I've recommended. Let me finish the research. Then I will initiate a formal proceeding with a judge. You'll need to be there. I'll brief you to the extent necessary. You're going to be a rich man. But don't talk about a million acres. That's unrealistic and could sabotage the whole deal. Think in terms of money."

Mr Marigold already had his own secret agenda simmering. "Fine. Do it," he said.

He ushered both Francis and Alma away from the table and into his library, pointing to whole sections of dusty volumes on a first-name basis.

"For 40 years I have been building this museum of ideas," he said. "It is more than a collection falling through the floorboards."

Hidalgo, bending down to examine the region where termites had done the most damage to the floor, then poking a finger through the masticated hardwood, replied, "I know someone who can come out and give you an estimate. You're going to have to tent the hacienda."

"You're not listening, Francis. Forget the termites. I'll get to that, for there is a fitting metaphor beneath our feet. My point—what was my point?"

"More than a collection—" Alma reminded him astutely.

"Good. You see that, Francis? A woman, when it comes to money, pays attention. Where was I?"

"More than a collection," Alma repeated.

"Right. As I was saying, I have largely memorized the books, for I was blessed with that capacity, having no other need of it than for what it could glean from the written page. Now, as you can see, there are several thousand volumes here, and together they combine the wisdom of the ages without exaggeration. If a man of better than average intelligence, sitting—for so many years—memorizing such books, could not reinvent the future, then what? What hope for humankind, eh? My point, exactly. I have fathomed the rudiments of Utopia, yes, it's true, but only today do I see that there is reason to speak of this matter; only now have I the incipient confidence to translate this gobbledygook of lore and untried possibility into a local experiment. And only as I am speaking, and seeing the innocent surprise on your two faces, am I emboldened to part the waters of Santa Fe, to stay the relentless onrush of civilization that threatens to homogenize and overturn the pulse of ancestral days; to ensure that no animal is ever threatened, no woman or child abused, no homeless person refused, no old man ignored, and not a single tree cut down. Country life—suffused with the sweetness of horehound—for the urban wreck! The Carob tribals of the Dominican will be reborn as parrots. That will become a relevant fact. As will those law schools all across our conflicted nation awaking to the refinement of animal emotions and their day in court. First sunrise over the Oregon Islands National Wildlife Refuge, or the one and only bloom in its entire lifespan of an Hawaiian silversword, an *Argyroxiphium sandwicense*—unpronounceable, better that way. In Scotland, a hunter will be treated as a poacher. Let all the world become a Scotland; let every idea blossom like the silversword."

He waxed uncommonly, embracing political metaphors right off Wizard Island, mathematical certainties such as are expressed from time to time at the Bald Cypress estuaries in Reelfoot, Kentucky, or the quiet effects of a certain poetry discernible amongst the Brazos Mountains in his own state. No more shying away from the bold declarative; he embraced fully the little voice in whose incomparable freedom he would rejoice—no more saddle breeding; an end to horse carriages, Conestoga wagons, ox carts; the last of that damnable Royal Windsor Horse Show, and so forth—and opened his arms to every fox, badger, mouse and grouse, to the very termites.

"Money can do all that," Hidalgo finally remarked, amused. "If that's what you want."

As Hidalgo and the Commander stepped out into the courtyard for some needed air, Hidalgo felt confident about the weeks ahead. He would come to quiet closure with the state, and secure in writing a lifelong guarantee of Mr Marigold's monthly income and much—*much*—more. Meanwhile, he and Shirley, his wife, would enjoy the percentage owed him as executor, a significant sum, depending on the extent of his success with a judge. It was all in the research, and in the level of intimidation.

The split nerves, blinding details, stultifying knots between the words; the annoyances and ulcers, hurdles and long hours; a relentless, untiring bureaucracy of nullifying dimwits lining up for the explicit purpose of persecution and prosecutorial abuse. Golf with the judges. Church with their wives. Hidalgo needed a new prescription for his reading lenses.

The money would make it all worth while.

"I appreciate your efforts, Francis. I really do," Marigold reassured him.

"I am a new man as of this moment. Ignore my earlier remarks. I would never go this alone. Leave here at once and begin preparations. Let us rally forth with all the particulars when the time is right."

"Now you're talking, kiddo," Hidalgo replied. And he turned to Alma. "It will be fine, dear," he said. He didn't feel it was fair to leave her hanging.

She had a raise, and quite a generous bonus, coming.

Mr Marigold saw Hidalgo to his car, which was a black Cadillac, and stood at the gate watching as it pushed off up the Bishop's Lodge Road toward Santa Fe. A cloud of dark smoke belched from its rear end.

CHAPTER 17
The Commander's First Utopia

SENSING A MIGHTY duty to contribute significantly to the state of cosmic underpinnings here on Earth, fearing no censure, brooking no impediment or damper, mocking all impossibility, dismissing any likely tars, feathers or ridicule, Mr Marigold set about constructing his ideal community. He used his favorite quill and azure bottle of India ink, which he kept beside the old Parisian metronome on the table beneath the south-facing window of Delftian leaded glass. Adjoining it was his Siamese teakwood double-king-sized canopy bed with its 1,000 tassels and bells, circa 1885, painted in gold Buddhas and once exhibited at the World's Fair, that sat comically atop a tattered 12-by-18-foot Zuni rug of impressive antiquity. The headboard was from a tenth-century Viking vessel recovered by archeologists from a fjord. Pecos had acquired it from a dealer in Copenhagen.

The clock was ticking. Hidalgo had made it clear in a follow-up phone conversation with Mr Marigold that the attorneys for the state had given them one week to get back with an answer, or forfeit the deal altogether—in which case, all claims would be remanded to the endless judicial system where costs, vicissitudes and delays (known as continuations) would ensure that Alonzo's fortune languished unclaimed for another 150 years, in Hidalgo's studied opinion. Time was the critical factor now. They had a brief window of maneuverability.

Marigold knew that when he had completed his visionary edifice, he could consult with his new friend Sannazaro for any final touches whilst supping a good dry bottle of the softest amontillado. As they say, *In vino veritas!* And, as they also say, *Alter ego est amicus.* They say many things.

With these inner assurances at the far side of the dark tunnel, he swam through his library in search of memories, clues, links, trade-offs, arguments, contexts, references, primary sources, theories, practices, unambiguities and hallowed reason—in short, the appropriate building blocks for his City Beneath the Hill, as he formally designated it.

Now, consider that this man was no scholar, in the conventional sense. He had been to school, it is true, as a youngster. But by the age of 15, with a monthly provision and no obvious inclination on his part (or that of his executor on his behalf) to pursue or push for a high school diploma, let alone a career out of college, Mr Marigold abandoned all future classrooms without resistance from others and instead embarked on his own regime of learning. A guild of privacy with its handy stipend. It was a different species of grasping the picture, true enough, and not one easily debated by those inside the comfortable precincts and inner sancta of aptitude tests, school boards, regents and governors. Nevertheless, for every book read in the normal American high school, Mr Marigold probably read 1,000 other books, for he could read quite fast, it is said by those who, on rare occasions, glimpsed him at work.

Of course, it is true that he did not necessarily read with any kind of slavish discipline. For he easily tired of books, and would not hesitate to push to the end before the beginning. The speed of his literary consumption might be attributable to the fact that one of his eyeballs exceeded the other in size; one retina saw things differently from the other. There might be two colors instead of one, three mountains instead of two. Four breasts instead of the normal number. The combination made for unexpected conclusions, and might prompt truly unseasonable analysis. Alma had seen her share of visually anomalous manifestations. He had tried, on occasion, to take his soup with a fork, and frequently buttered his toast with a spoon. He had peed in a sink and slept in the tub, and had frequently collided with objects—and not just new objects, but familiar furnishings from childhood, like the floor-to-ceiling mirror. He got into his underwear the wrong way, tried on occasion to stick his legs through shirt sleeves, had driven into more than one tree, and off more than the occasional bridge, and had a problem with his legs, which might have been too long for the chest. His comportment seemed slightly ridiculous, as if he were clad in armor and his joints refused to move easily. But when he looked at you, it was a piercing glance. He almost defied you to look back.

These points aside, Mr Marigold's body and mind contained a certain indefinable grace, or fluency. He kept to few conversations, was a light eater and immune to virtually all normal distractions. Few items of the news day could pull him from the steadfastly centered calm of his benedictory lifestyle. At least until that of his ancestral windfall.

Now those very same inner resources converged, in massive relocation, in the service of a vision—and there is nothing more perilous, less understood or surer to invite lasting melodramas and imbroglios than a vision.

Even a vision has its day, of course, giving weight to smoke and, out of the smoke, into the flame its passing fancy builds before vanishing. But a utopia does not so easily fly away. At the very least, it barges on the world scene with a certain set of hopeless, some would say silly demands, invariably raising echoes of some *ancien régime*, imposing beliefs on those of others (never very practical), and supposing that the human imagination and society's ethical threads, however diverse, can amount to the same quilt. A grandiloquent hope, lost on man, as far as can be discerned.

These countless Zions, Elysia, Blessed Isles and Erewhons of the past, however, make for pleasant enough reading and had certainly—to look at him—cast a spellbinding radiance over Mr Marigold.

Without wasting a minute he moved the stepladder about, gathered his essential texts together and then called upon the live-in vixen for necessary supplements and those trifles that must never be ignored.

"Oh sprite, loveliness borne upon the world, transported hither aboard legs of supple breeze or Bernini bronze, whose fetching eyes have caught all of heaven's light in a girlish glance, be so good as to get me a large glass of lemonade, would you, dearest?"

In the enthusiasm of the hour, he took her furthest-most finger for the purposes of a cavalier kiss whose sincerity was beyond rational discussion, a nurseried Essene bethinking himself a Romeo.

"A charming fool," replied she, with a sheepish enough grin. There was a definite *joie de vivre* to her crudeness. "But a fool nonetheless."

Throughout the coming days he pursued this ultimate puzzle, moving presidentially through the current thinking. He had before him a task as truly monumental as getting blood from a turnip, or learning from an enemy: the construction of a Tower of Babel. What he hoped to spell out, having already envisioned it in one sweeping gesture, his five fingers meditating against his eyes, his head stooped forward in an ecstatic introversion, the sort seen widely at the Café Flora in Paris, so that his body total was more ridiculous in appearance than usual, was a new kind of town, an audacious community, a biology of a higher, kinder order, one in which people were not people but saints, whose unselfconscious good works were necessarily tied to a natural theology. It all ran together, in other words: interconnectedness and incomprehensibility.

He harbored all the great illusions, contradicting those fatalistic schools that had preached a scenario whereby our ancient cousins squatted in caves gnawing on each other's bones, bored silly and bespattered in blood. Rather, argued he, our nature is malleable, if given half a chance.

We are born to be larkish, free of sin and peace-loving, with a genetic determination that will not be stayed for very long. It is a particular sort of society that breeds monsters, perverting the noble savage, undermining the wild child, notwithstanding that the majority of archeological sites suggest only unflattering behavior on the part of our forebears. Nonetheless, he said, these were inconclusive sketches of prehistory. If the same archeologists examined today's funerary evidence, they would note a vast medical field that had exerted countless surgeries and other attempts to heal and prolong human life; they would also necessarily omit for lack of documentation the millions of gestures of sincerity and loveliness that pass unnoticed every day in every community. He was determined to resurrect all those kindnesses and make them adhere as a general principle that one could count on.

Marigold was shrewd enough to place his primitive ideals in specific, limited locations, far removed from the possibility of being thwarted by those scattered cliques of ruffians and brutes, for there was far too much data revealing the fundamentally assholish nature of most aggregates. Could society be rehabilitated? A sisterhood rendered in place of chaos? Fraternities of quietude replacing that age-old party of fiends? All flaws finessed? And by what non-violent means? Mr Marigold was prepared to split as many hairs as necessary to realize his thesis. He believed that there were anthropological benchmarks, selective beacons here and there, a string of nacreous nuggets in the night, both in the past and probably the present, which taken together might provide the basis for extrapolating a workable kingdom.

He began by reviewing the parameters. All of Santa Fe, owned by one man. A great plan. But the 80,000 people could not be owned, only swayed. And what better way to persuade and encourage behavior than by the holding out the promise of rewards, money.

He tried an experiment. "Alma, come here, dearest."

She stood over him where he sat at his writing desk with his fresh lemonade. (After all these years of service, in her heart she held out a mother's compassion for him, despite her ceaseless harangues and clever spurns, her open frustrations and bouts of disapproval; and its greatest expression might be summarized by the fact she never once spat secretly in his lemonade.)

"What is it, master?"

"Suppose I were to pay you to become a vegetarian and stop with all that pork and fatty acid. No more sloppy joes, rib roasts, braised briskets. An end to salmon scales in your belly and cow tongues festering in your intestines. No more fish heads and bull gristle. How much would it cost me?"

She pondered the offer, then: "One hundred dollars. Per day."

"Pork means that much to you?"

"Freedom means that much to me."

"Aren't we philosophical tonight."

"One hundred fifty."

"Thank you, Alma. I'll get back to you on that."

He continued rippling his formulations, sinking down into the grocer paper, tapping his pencil, spinning his magnum opus.

Coercion, he reckoned, was feasible but expensive. It might be more sensible to lever his power by exerting a perpetual menace. To allow the force of a threat to haunt his tenants, much like the Spanish Duke of Alva's reign of terror over Flanders and Brabant in the 1560s. No List of Forbidden Books. No sawing of people in half, of course, or other executions. But fear of exile. That was suasion enough: fear of losing their homes, jobs; the prospect of migration to another part of the state; hunger, at its worst.

On the other hand ... However the gathering clouds might brew, whatever the alarms, Mr Marigold rightly saw the folly in intimidation, for he wished only to ingratiate himself with his subjects, such as they were. To instill a love that would carry over to the flora and fauna. No crucifixions, martyrdoms or terrorizing, after all. That was his first conclusion. Let the eighteenth-century French example stand. Or the Treaty of Versailles worked out by Woodrow Wilson: let them keep their homes but challenge them to behave.

Behavior. This would require massive social re-engineering. The behavior was foul, and he could list the ways. Even in idyllic settings like Santa Fe and Tesuque, he had, out of the book-lined corners of his myopia, ascertained disturbing trends over the years which beggared revolution. No expert, he, but canny enough to have followed the general decay as it was reported upon every day of the year. Everyone spoke of an ecological revolution. Well, maybe not exactly in the service of that particular phrase, but that's what underlay local discontent, no doubt about it.

Which translated into politics. And that meant economics. Jobs, in other words. The Commander was already out on a ledge. The very idea of a job—sitting in a chair, legs under a desk, taking requests (never mind orders), sharpening pencils on demand, the slightest repetition of tasks or focus upon errands—made him quite queasy. The local politics were silly enough—quagmires surrounding barbwire fences enclosing pompous puff-pieces and paid-for advertising: entitlements secured by the few, contested between classical ideologies like Socialism and Capitalism. The jobs, the power, the money, came down to property. But he was no Max Weber, Herbert Spencer, Paul Hawkin, Henry Kissinger or George Kennan to assess the qualitative distinctions. There had to be a system that worked for everyone; a way to juggle the opposing theories that miraculously smoothed over all wrinkles, like the finest French face cream, gave everybody their portion, anesthetized differences of opinion, so that the beast of economics would spark to life, well greased, without the slightest misstep.

He also knew instinctively, as John Dewey had made clear, friction was necessary for any smooth-running machine. How much friction? Enough to spawn a revolution, Marigold assumed.

Where did that leave him, this overnight potentate of manipulations and sociological tyrannies? Do not imagine that Mr Marigold did not wrestle with countless demons, night after night, straining at the limits of his considerable reserves to fathom a New Order. A Benevolent Patriarchy that Worshipped Women. A Benevolent Matriarchy that Guardedly Included Men. A Thorough Dictatorship which Gave a Refreshingly Peaceful Course to the Ship, the Commander at the Helm, of course.

A Kingdom Modeled After the Temper and Ease of Reconciliations Displayed by Butterflies.

To accomplish these High-minded Hat Tricks, Mr Marigold felt compelled to throw out all existing paradigms and begin anew. His prefrontal lobes were now awash with a schemer's heaven: a schooner, more aptly described, plying new waters. He raced to the notion, first instanced by the Nature Conservancy, of trading debt for wilderness, and cottoned early to pollution bubbles, cap and trade methods for limiting what ugly big industries have been getting away with for generations. He embraced every good idea that floated by: carbon sequestration techniques, biodiversity assets and natural capitalism. The value, for example, to future generations of all that forest surrounding the north of Santa Fe, and the various irreplaceable ecosystem services it provided. That should be worth something in real dollars. And he envisioned an exuberantly profligate concordium like that established after the works of Silvio Gessell prior to World War II. The Argentine/German economist had convinced the desperate mayor of a depressed Austrian town, Wörgl, to print its own money, a script to be used exclusively by residents of that town, and which accrued only negative interest, so that the longer one held on to the money, the more one would be punished by exorbitant fees. The idea was to encourage denizens to spend—spend frantically in order to boost the economy: on public works, on gifts, on anything that might engineer a productive facelift for the whole town. The result, claimed a visiting Prime Minister from France, was miraculous. A happy people. A thriving community. Everyone was busy building annexes, planting gardens, purchasing chocolates and books, and commissioning fine art. Other towns throughout Austria aspired to the same model of village utopia, until the country's national bank exerted its muscle and caused the grassroots economic revolution to go underground. Gessell himself was tried for treasonable activity just before he died. But Marigold was not worried about that. These were different times, he reckoned, and the banks could stand some competition.

It is true that the Soviet Union had owned all real estate within its borders, as well, and that such ownership was not, in itself, sufficient to induce a popular naturalism. The Marigold Estate would be different. Compliance might be the operational term. It certainly underscored the approach of all environmental protection agencies worldwide in dealing with the primary culprits.

With this basic approach, he divided up Santa Fe society into The Good Souls and The Nincompoops.

And each with several sub-classes: Contrites, Connivers, Those-With-No-Taste, Assholes, Secondary Assholes, Tertiary Assholes, Offspring-of-Assholes Who Should Have Learned From Their Parents' Sins, Nurturers, Altruists, The Wounded, Those-Who-Smelled-the-Flowers, Cultivators-of-Gardens, Lawyers, Fast Talkers, Those-Who-Paid-Mere-Lip-Service, Volunteers, Good-For-Nothings, Fly-By-Nights, Migrants, People-Content-To-Do-Menial-Tasks, Hypochondriacs, Con Artists, Deviants, Addicts, Poets, Opera Singers, Violin Players, Students, Idealists, Paragons-of-Virtue, Old People, Babies, Animal Lovers, Tree Huggers, and so forth. Until he discovered that there were approximately 100 types of residents in any statistical metropolitan region. Forcing them all into a smooth-flowing stream of city life would, admittedly, constitute a contrivance and contractual arrangement of insurmountable proportions, especially against the wider context of six billion people. But he was convinced it was possible.

These mathematical conundrums were mounting in Mr Marigold's head with a vigor, a terminological staying power and a willfulness that could, if one were to question Alma about it, be described as pivotal in his life. No man was ever so excited about the prospect of an additional million acres added to his household and the geopolitics this boon implied. He had good reason for giddiness. He believed that he was about to change history.

Politics required a legal framework, of which Mr Marigold was not entirely ignorant. He'd studied the old Latin principles—*erga omnes, actio popularis*—referring to international suits and the community of nations as tools for filing motions. In other words, if he could accomplish something grand in old Santa Fe, it might be presented as a model, an ethical and legal standard for other communities. He had a list of every federal code and legal mechanism for pursuing environmental offenders. But none of that was necessary. It was the private ownership issue upon which he had the most confidence to launch his plan. After all, he owned the city now, or most of it. Wasn't it up to him to decide its fate? If he wished to become labeled a greenhouse imperialist, more interested in the fate of methane and nitrogen than the lives of used car salesmen and their families, so be it. He need not worry that his envisioned kingdom might be branded right wing, in the same way as such European political parties as the Swiss Demagogues, the Victuals Block in Belgium, and Northwestern Bowlers in Italy. Even the Essential Trench Party of France.

All suffered for their radical backlashes which ambiguously endorsed certain ecological themes (pollution, miscarriages, uniform genes) while dismissing others, the sum total of their links, assertions and separations spelling doom for the even-minded.

But Marigold's politics should suffer from no ambivalence or untoward economic fallout. For example, his allegiance to taxonomic categories (read: furry critters) and their protection, if properly conducted, might actually abet the more equitable distribution of goods and value according to the so-called "Ben & Jerry's improvement" equation of economists, where at least one person, randomly, equitably emergent, wins (i.e. gets an ice-cream cone) and no one loses—a principle whereby opponents and competitors will always work towards the most efficient reconciliation. That might mean kicking somebody out of town, but at least he'd deserve it and everybody else would be in agreement. And if those kicked out should amass their own army at the gates (an old story)? He was not sure of the details, but they were surely looming large in his meddling upper story.

Simplify the statistics, abridge the arcane, pare down the parameters, spoon-feed the locals. Thus he resolved to propagate a manifesto, one he could read aloud to the judge, or before any municipal forum. He chose to engender a list of 1,000 salubrious maxims, penetrating tenets, happy sayings and one-liners that would form the legal, political, spiritual and economic basis for his Utopia. For example:

1) All children shall be loved, and given every advantage. Notwithstanding, spoiled brats shall be ceremoniously shipped out to boarding school in Iraq.

2) Four hours of every day shall be deemed work-free holidays, and named after particular species or individuals or geographical regions most deserving of our pledges, such special designations to be selected by various committees and clubs, and published weekly, in advance. For example, Tuesday, 8 a.m., in honor of Thoreau's Mother; 9 a.m., to commemorate the South Face of Pumori; 10 a.m., in Remembrance of All Worms, or the Greek Islands; 11 a.m., in grateful thanks to White Caps, Sea Shells and the Equator.

3) Money shall no longer be the primary medium for the exchange of goods and labor, but be replaced by Great Books, seedlings, love poems and any gesture of kindness, all valued according to the scope of their earnestness.

4) All students shall be supported until the age of 80 or more.

5) Each animal, tree, shrub and flower shall have equal representation with humans in any instance where a decision, financial stake, development scheme, financial endeavor, investment, point of access or protocol, vote, investiture, right, interest or election is likely to affect them, directly or indirectly. Insects, bacteria and individual blades of grass shall be assured of their collective rights, as biologically indicated by the presence and voting power of their larger host species.

6) Food vouchers and obsessive attention shall be paid to all endangered parrots, and primates, including in this latter category, but surely not limited to: the West African drill, several tonkins and langurs of Vietnam, the gorillas of East and West Africa, the silky sifakas of Madagascar, and lemurs, tamarins, red colobus, orangutans, mangabeys, capuchins, gibbons and muriquis.

And so on. It seemed to him a good plan. A fine beginning. A resolute conviction of convictions. He was ready to tackle the mob, to vanquish any and all clamjamfreys. Or so he thought.

CHAPTER 18
The Splendid Particulars of the City Beneath the Hill

HE WAS CERTAIN TO THE point of joviality that this document, writ in the blush of optimism, would change the future. Knowing that one mop can clean all tiles, that no truth is too large for a simple mind, that life consists of a wink, a grimace, and then another wink, that knowledge speeds faster than light, and hope more speedily than gloom, he was determined to put this plan into effect, and told Alma so.

"You see, dear—" he always addressed her thus, when on the verge of a great miracle—"it cannot fail to arouse first the curiosity, the mass *déjà vu*, and then the sound confirmation of the many. It is a fantastic plan, combining the best of Pluralism, Preservation and Pantheism, true to all the chivalrous arts, as once played out by my revered predecessors, the various Dons, in accord with the greatest statesmen of lore, and mightily conforming to all those passions that would, at their peril, uphold the livelihood of plants and the intelligence of rocks, and dispense with all misologists. This is no mere frog aspiring to be an oxen, or elephant worshipping the moon."

"I don't want to hear about nothing," she braved, chastising her companion for focusing on anything other than the quick consolidation of his new windfall. "Gather your boons to your bosom and cut out all this philosophy hokum," she decried.

But he was beyond the obvious. Mr Marigold had plunged four-square into that ethereal realm where greatness, so called, collides with stubbornness; where high-flying and flamboyant swans manage to outsmart the hunter; and ideals shall no longer be dragged down by comfortable habit, on the one hand, or menacing mouthfuls on the other.

He repaired to his dusty den and quietly began laying out his architecture, needing no food, no word from the outside, nothing but his own huffing and puffing powers of concentration.

Heroically, he jumbled a concatenation of the obvious and less than obvious grievances sweeping the surface of Santa Fe, and the few precious ideologies, self-reliant communities, projects, ideals, technologies, solutions and personalities that could be mobilized to combat them. His choices were not merely local ones, but ranged across countless extra-territories, riveted by the current debates between digital blob and transmeditational space, between the goals of village Rajasthan and the Getty Museum, the grim conurbations of Jakarta and the Turin-to-Trieste megacity, as well as the nostalgic utopias of history. He threw in whatever had a ring of truth, knowing that he would sort through the ages, narrow the chimes of recognition, translate quintessences, amalgamate opportunistic pragmatisms, and arrive at a manifesto of breathtaking proportions. A veritable pavilion of Biennale Bravura. Let the few cracks and blemishes in the plan remain to remind man of his humility. But no warthogs rummaging in the pantry or lice in the hairdo should lessen the spell or dispel the lesson: Nature must be ushered in, in all her homecoming.

He took as a premier example a most misunderstood, if treasured legacy—namely, the Netherlands Fallacy, as his starting point. Noting that the Dutch were dependent upon their exports and imports, he calculated that 19.4 million flibbertigibbets occupied 41,526 square kilometers of damp, making for a watered-down density of serious proportions, and a virtual absence of natural resources or recipes.

Almost their entire complement of needs came from outside their boundaries, making theirs perhaps the least sustainable nation in the world. The Commander had heard that Holland would soon need 700,000 new homes, each bearing two toilets, two people, but where to place them, with rising sea levels and increasingly denuded, congested surroundings? In short, a thirteenth province was required, and half a million acres or more that simply didn't exist. Perhaps some unknown marine wastes of the North Sea could be dredged, or land reclaimed at the port of Maasvlakte. Meanwhile, millions of farm animals were psychologically readied for re-allocation to skyscrapers, whilst architects in towns like Ijburg were grappling with ways to convert mundane apartments into habitats of the urban wild. Old factories revitalized into penthouses, windmills converted to studios, condominiums rendered portable, like yurts, outmoded sewage lines expanded into underground caverns. Anything to alter the prejudice of space constraints and the stultifying limitations of the "beauty commission". In short, the Dutch were seeking ways to cope with excess regulation and deep-rooted claustrophobia—universal syndromes that resulted, by some accords, in a splendid, tolerant, artistic, happy society.

With these and other analogies to misconstrue, Mr Marigold began his great conjuration, employing all those dazzling intellectual triggers to spawn his enumeration, not the least of which was the famed Illinois biologist Stephen Forbes, and his early use of the word "microcosm" (from his "The Lake as a Microcosm" address given to the Historical Society of Illinois in Peoria in 1887). Tesuque and Santa Fe entire would become his privatized microcosm, a little Holland in the Southwest. A balancing act of compassion-in-action, whereby every coordinate and nuance of the present civilization would be accounted for: animal and plant suffering, cubic meters of wood, hectares of cropland and liters of drinking water consumed, emissions of noxious gases and distribution of toxic substances per person per day. This business-as-usual scenario he now resolved to topple and transform. Naturally, he was fully up to speed on the various psychological, aesthetic and neurological studies pertaining to blood pressure, disease recovery, and the importance of shade trees, humming birds and the pastoralist tradition.

He spent days ciphering the numbers and ponderously scrutinizing between and betwixt every conceivable end-use schema: the philosophy of go-carts as public transportation; orchid cultivation under glass; nutrient diffusion coefficients and the potential for enforcing diets of blue-green algae; energy-intensive materials; the data on ecotourism; unnatural work; the metaphysics of veganism; policy instruments for ethical compliance as indicated among ancient Toltec, Aztec, Greek, Assyrian and Mayan cultures, none all that pretty (note the practice of defiling virgins and tearing out hearts of living sacrifices among some of the above); various ramifications of ecotax reform; environmental liability issues (when is clean clean?); the possibilities for post-materialism among shopping-mall-addicted teens; the cost of cool, new action plans for every sector; the debt problem; novel distributions of environmental space according to natural resource depletion rates; decentralized photovoltaics; the irony of carbon chains; chemical intermediaries like fig newtons; Superfund half-lives; end-product substitutions for Tupperware, zippers, fly paper, spray cans, four-color ink, fungicides and tobacco; raw material conversions; mineral re-use potentials, whether clay or loam or masonry sand; all the ins-and-outs of sustainable land use, export markets, pauperization principles, barter economies; disease infestations; climate changes; leisure-time consumption patterns; food intake in cafeterias versus home-baked meals; tradable pollution rights and bubbles; endangered species mitigation; rectification banks; eco-amortizations; and the polls pertaining to so-called "consciousness raising", that common clucking sound which constitutes a social fabric amongst chickens.

With all that lofty psychobabble spinning his topmost foam upside-down, mushing his neurons, plastering each and every synapse with an unintelligible fog, he was prepared confidently to finger hamburger stands which were the summation of a syndrome of torture of so many bovines, and human flatulence which trapped heat in the troposphere and led to the Greenhouse Effect. He was in a position to indict every major industry, short- and long-range weapons, as well as barbwire fences; he could claim expertise on the subject of impervious surfaces with little or no natural possibility of evapotranspiration, like motorways, and had fully gauged the three most dangerous man-made substances on earth, which everyone knows to be CFCs, chlorine and petroleum. He attacked all sources of noise over 80 decibels, despaired of overpopulation, and waxed rhapsodic on ways to restore habitat and non-human populations to their primeval numbers—a revelation of numeric profundity he prepared to unleash last upon the legal council for the state, or the town hall, whichever loomed with greater immanence. Mr Marigold was in his prime. How rare for a man of his letters and learning, so accustomed to bedside manners and armchair adventures, to transmute his indisputable talent for sideways scanning into something practical, and oriented to this time, this world and this humanity. The effort was almost embarrassingly relevant.

For example, in meditating, trancing and snoozing over alternatives to the existing "civilized" way, he alighted on some of the following: the custom (as opposed to the "tragedy") of the Commons, as practiced in the Massachusetts Bay Colony; the Olmsted/Vaux "Greensward Plan" for New York's Central Park; the Neighborhoods and Greenstreets programs of Chicago; the dragonfly pond refreshment program of the Honmoku Citizens Public Park in Yokohama; the recommendations of the Arizona Corporation Commission for reducing the effects of urban heat islands through energy-efficient landscaping; the introduction of *Gavia immer* (common loons), *Branta canadensis* (Canadian geese) and *Ardea herodias* (great blue herons) to the riparian portions of the county, and the *Euarctos americanus* (black bear), *Cervus canadensis* (elk) and *Canis latrans* (coyote) to the higher quadrants; the widespread introduction of Dutch windmills, hydrogen/fuel cell city buses, a new harmonization scheme involving clean drinking water, the recovery of waste steam, the reforming of the city's grids according to the fuel cell/solar-produced hydrogen plan, and the recycling of all English whisky bottles, condoms and buildings; the creation of a Wildflower Meadow Task Force for the purposes of transforming the downtown into Siberian-style taiga; a complete redesign of all local bingo parlors along the lines of the sherry bars in Madrid; a concerted return to the Baffin Island igloo economy using indigenous adobe; advanced, high energy-efficiency standards for toys; the offer of political asylum to all idealists worldwide who would like to come live out their tormented days in Santa Fe; the use of the *Salix* plant for heat boilers and lucerne for fertilizer, biogas body-cups for ungulates and a collection task force organized among unemployed nurses; a ban on slash-ploughing, inorganic fertilizers and the cutting down of any tree; a universal search for round (rather than square) sand for horses to roll around in; a system of needs-oriented child support; a sleeping-in-hammocks-half-the-day tax incentive; a General Agreement on the Abolition of GATT, NAFTA and the WTO; the rejection of all other acronyms; a comprehensive network of cruelty-free zones; the initiation of a Santa Fe World Monetary System, a substratum of the *arbeitsgemein schafumweltfreundlicher* (a working, ecologically friendly community), with tax advantages for those who can say it; a "Save the Alps" committee for good measure; a fast-growing eucalyptus farm to supply all wood needs; an end to the debate between native and introduced species, such rancor to be replaced by a new index that prizes cool, sweet-smelling shade above all else (he obviously had geriatric burros in mind); no more wood-burning; a restoration of all wetlands, recognizing that New Mexico had lost a third of such ecologically sensitive zones since the late eighteenth century; a draft amendment to outlaw respiratory disorders and their causes as a way of surely reducing medical premiums; a trend towards pedestrianization; tax breaks for the purchase of blue overalls; the restriction of any odds; free services for the chronically ill, the depressed or despised; a procouncil for promoting the phrase "anders gaan leven" (just live differently); a Use The Bathroom Less (Just Hold It) club with distinct tax incentives as part of the overall waste policy for Santa Fe; ecological guilds providing the know-how and labor skills for various conservation corps around town; a security guarantee for Mars, and methane capture plan for cows.

Finally, and most importantly, a legal sanction granting everyone the right to stop everything. Only one man would have final say on any changes or altered interpretations to the above—namely, and as required, the owner of the city, Mr Marigold.

These were but a few of the inspired pieces of the evolving puzzle that now furiously preoccupied the Commander's mind. Between bouts of medieval archeological research into the origins and evolution of the village, in such old relic commons as one still found in the Aisne Valley or Umbria, he was comparing building materials from Scandinavian churches, Anatolian cagoulards, *Homo erectus* cave sites, and medieval stabbau, lost in the jargon of interrupted sill beams, tongue-and-grooved planks and palisade walls. Dry stone, turf block, sunken huts and upright posts drove him mad, while green globalism, the "crisis of labor", the zero hour of scarcity, and John Locke's solution, posed in his *Second Treatise*, of flight into emptiness, gave him hope.

Hope is what drove Marigold to familiarize himself with dozens of previous blueprints for the paradise factor. He dreamt of the great foggy estate at Point Carradale in Argyle, hemmed in by Himalayan rhododendrons planted by Hooker, and the finest grasses in all of Scotland. This was where the prolific author Naomi Mitchison had envisioned her dreamy fictions, cozily ensconced overlooking the Isle of Arran, hosting (with her husband, a Member of Parliament) scientists and artists for much of the twentieth century. Had she found the answer there, amid the lowing of bovines and warmed westerlies?

Or elsewhere in remotest Scotland, in the Outer Hebrides at St Kilda, where during the nineteenth century a tribe lived in perfect harmony, according to anthropologists. Or did they? Cut off from the rest of the world for most of each year, with its storm-tossed beetling cliffs rising just short of 1400 feet, the island saw its last 36 indomitable denizens evacuated to the mainland in 1930—probably a good thing for the two rare endemic species of mice, Soay sheep, and the largest gannetry in the world.

Scotland seemed to germinate this longing for perfection, wherein the history, religion, work ethic and landscape conspired to re-fashion the way people should live, and no more so than at the village of New Lanark, where famed political economist Robert Owen engendered a legendary experiment and Sir Richard Arkwright invented the spinning frame. It was there that David Dale had acquired much land and a complex of factories, later to be sold to Owen, a man devoted to ending poverty in Scotland. It was a noble thought, one supported even by the Duke of Kent, father to Queen Victoria. But when Owen made known his antipathy to all received forms of religion, his support among the wealthy set withered. He went out to the common man, who flocked to him.

New Lanark, with its insistence on commutarian ethics and economics, made a huge splash in the first half of the nineteenth century. It was the right idea for the time, thought Marigold. Later, the sage of Scottish socialism turned his vision to America, where within a decade no fewer than 17 communities inspired by his example sprang up. Over the coming century, another 115 known farming utopias, from the 300 Hutterite Brethren farmers who moved to South Dakota to those at the New Llano settlement of Louisiana, joined the fray, many following the Frenchman, Charles Fourier. There were Mennonites in Manitoba and Mazahua Indians of Mexico, the Separatists of Zohar in Ohio, William Keil Mystics at Bethel, Missouri, and the Ephrata Community of German Seventh Day Baptists in Pennsylvania. Most famed of all were the Harmonists, Harmonites and Rappites who inhabited 39,000 acres in common along the Wabash River in Indiana, and were skilled at weaving and leatherworking. Their founder, George Rapp, would sell out to Robert Owen and resettle at the town of Economy, in Beaver, Pennsylvania.

Owen came out to Indiana, and a number of scientists and artists joined in, but the majority of utopians were impractical dreamers who could not handle a hoe—a fact Marigold was quick to ascertain. Dissent managed to tangle their purpose. A proliferation of Constitutions evolved, and countless inner secessions—10 by 1828, when New Harmony, as it was called, collapsed. All that remained was a Workingmen's Institute and Public Library with its collection of étatist manuscripts.

Marigold took note of these liabilities, secure in the knowledge that there would be no committees to answer to, ultimately, in his City Beneath the Hill. Just one man sitting atop the pyramid of decisive choices. His belief in this autocracy was further solidified upon scrutinizing that too familiar fate which overtook Brook Farm, near Boston, no matter how closely it seemed to invoke Plato's *Republic* and *Timaeus*. There, a grand attempt at ideal education and absolute individualism had played out its finest aspirations, inviting the cream of Boston's intelligentsia to come roll up their sleeves and work with children in the gardens and the library, to wash clothes and memorize Ovid. To air their noblest devices in free concerts of exchange, without forgetting how to gently skin potatoes. The year was 1844. Professors and interns were enjoying a barn dance when Brook Farm's largest structure, known as the Phalanstery, burned down. An arsonist fed up with perfection? In the aftermath, lacking sufficient funds to keep a different flame burning, Brook Farm, like so many other failed experiments, vanished in history, one more lyric in a long and monotonous story of fabulist professions.

In hopes of fully fathoming the germ that compelled great thinkers to take flight, the Commander had schooled himself in that genre which included James Harrington's *The Commonwealth of Oceana*, Bernard de Mandeville's *The Fable of the Bees*, Mersier's *L'an 2440* and James Burgh's *Account of the Cessares*. From Say's *Olbie* and Cabet's *Voyage en Icarie* to Lytton's *Coming Race*, the political theories of Theodor Hertzka, and the Utopian trilogy by H.G. Wells (*Anticipations*, *A Modern Utopia* and *New Worlds for Old*). These treatises and adventure stories had each combined an obsession with establishing, in one form or other, a Kingdom of God on earth— which presupposed there was not one already—or, if not a Kingdom of God, at least free love, equitable labor exchange and enlightened kindergartens. The salubrious metaphysics at Islandia, Middle Earth and Nowhere. The inspired vision of paradise by one Mr Peck, vice-president, of two noisy department stores in Lewiston, Maine and Joliet, Illinois. All the world, if only it were different, might yet salvage a time and a place equivalent to the perfectly organized, utilitarian department store, he seemed to be arguing. Would Neiman's or Bergdorf Goodman or Harrod's have brought him to his cloud? A gallery of delights: 20 shelves devoted to the maintenance of women's nails?

Others before him had seen slightly different versions of what it would take to make its colonists jump up and rejoice. De Foigny and Tyssot de Patot had gazed towards the South Pacific, precursors in their imaginary voyages of Gauguin's and Thor Heyerdahl's respective jaunts in the Marquesas. Edward Bellamy looked in all directions as long as they were backward. Francis Bacon romanced the perfect society of science and philosophy, mounted atop some hidden Mediterranean bulwark, but failed to specify the laws governing such commonwealth, settling ultimately for St Albans, outside London. Whereas Jean-Jacques Rousseau ascribed confidently to the law of the jungle, *jangala*, the mysteries that made life interesting. Others took suggestive variants and spelled out any number of political, economic and fantastical configurations thereof—in the name of C. W. Wooldrige (fiscal paradise in Cleveland?), Lady Mary Fox (somewhere in the heart of New Holland, or Australia), and Gilbert Stevenson (in Santa Monica).

But in tracking these spouts of philosophy and wilderness ethos, peopled phalanxes and grandiose hardware stores, Marigold got all the principles of equality upside down. Unsettled Bawlfredonian fragments admixed in the same bouillabaisse with Mr Oseba's "last discovery". He was not entirely sure which communities were real, which fictional, so that an entire archipelago of ideal islands—even one called Lunarchia, which should have been a give-away—emerged to taunt him with documentation that he had no way of checking. From electric-hosiery communes in Babylon to a Kibbutz along the Puget Sound to a cotton-mill collective at Orbiston outside Glasgow, Marigold so trifled and tumultuated over the "correctness" of the data that, in the end, he needed something far more soothing than Utopia to stay his pathetic nervous condition. He wanted to believe, to go out on every limb, yet what he really required was absolute immobility, a couch, a huge bag of potato chips and cable television, along with several beers and Valiums. These might have settled him, had any existed in his hacienda.

There were ideological difficulties, as well. In truth, Mr Marigold was incapable of integrating all that he had read—or not in a manner of any use to fellow human beings. He inhabited a permanent condition of the paradox of enforced leisure, agitating against effluents and cow pies whilst satisfying himself on the finest chocolates from the Benelux. "Stone age economics", as anthropologist Marshall Sahlins termed it in his seminal work of that name in 1972, held special appeal for Mr Marigold, though he had grossly misinterpreted every word of it. Indeed, by his own taste for poetic licenses, he was led down a series of missteps, from impression to concept, from concept to application, which suggested to his mind that Alma, for example, or Hidalgo for that matter, should have no theoretical difficulty shifting gears and donning the loincloth and lifestyle, say, of the Nyae Nyae Kung. How would Hidalgo get about town? On the back of a giraffe? Where would Alma acquire her salutiferous wines for her various lovers? From the fields? No tampons in the desert, either—though she could use cigars, as the pilgrim women did. But other habits and cravings were not so easily satisfied in his Utopia. The odd tomato and goat cheese sandwich at midnight, chocolate chip cookies, Bach, dental floss, refrigeration, beer from Barcelona—all were points of profound difficulty. And what of Frisbees for the children? Plastic! Hula-hoops! Plastic! Medical emergencies—metallic, plastic, high-tech apparatuses, helicopters, ambulances, buildings, money, insurance, lawyers, an avalanche of issues? Or interstate trade, or the manufacture of photovoltaic arrays, chemical solutions, refining silicon, gallium arsenide conductors, computer chips, light bulbs? And books, the manufacture of books! And what about the fact that animal fats are used in the fabrication of bicycles, bricks, musical instruments, plaster and videotape? Every high hope and ingeniousness conspired against Mr Marigold's new-found ecological altruism, so that in no time he was utterly discombobulated. Partial measures, slow steps, gradients, compromises had none of the dramatic punch and promise he was after. A manifesto needed courage, vision, horizons, absolutes, conclusions, not piecemeal prefatory remarks.

He felt the want of solid experience, the hot sting of so little human interaction. His faculties suffered from this dearth of worldliness. And yet, this very absence of contact gave him a clean room of objectivity. Because he had read everything, his thinking had evolved in a pure space, like a crystal formation outside of gravity. A thorough virgin.

He regrouped and analyzed the nature of work in society. Who were the food producers and were they, short of exports, afflicted by a law of diminishing returns? How could food best be distributed? There were 100 mathematical formulas to characterize the dilemma, like Metcalf's Law, which he failed to grasp entirely, although he sensed its insufficiency to account for famine. He examined news reports from the Calcutta riots of years before, and the UN methods in Somalia—most efficient manners of dispersal, it seemed, though not without incident. Noting that more than 50 percent of the world was urban, and little inclined towards tribal prehistory in its food-gathering methods, Mr Marigold's foremost task was the working out of a plan that could uphold an apparent truism among people: they must eat—not cake or dumplings, but solid, consistently vitamin-rich vittles of a sufficiently diverse and tasty variety, beyond the vagaries of social taboo, stigma, wealth and poverty. Carob powder, gluten flour, the wealth of legumes, prairies full of bulghur and couscous, brown rice and pearled wheat, a bounty of vegetables, fantastic fruits and gentle herbs. The earth dripping in vitamins, a dozen humble micrograms per week of B12, dollops of nutritional yeast, a thermos of soy milk now and then, the sugary excess of a date or unbleached cane, garlic granules, silken tofu, and mashed tempeh amid a discreet concordance of beans. *Et voilà*!

How could Santa Fe pave the way for a methodology of sufficiency— an agrarian renaissance that avoided slavishness, that transcended ennui, ensured freedom and harmed no living being beyond, he imagined, those creatures with the least malice towards their offenders: that magnanimous class of pine cones, broccoli, hibiscus flowers, radishes, potatoes and asparagus most forgiving of the transgressions of herbivores?

This theory of forgiveness—the best form of revenge, according to Rossini's *La Cenerentola*—emerged towards Mr Marigold's left ear one middle of the night during that paroxysmal week, logically adding to the labyrinth of prefigurements. The great Metterlink and the refined Okakura had documented the evolution of intelligence in plants with the gusto of first-hand acquaintance. Clearly, thought Mr Marigold, they had spoken with the pumpkins, gone native among fungi, clambered into evergreens, made peace with lilacs, and intoned all manner of benediction prior to their salads.

All other sentient personages, according to this master plan, were off-limits to human breakfast, lunch, dinner or between-meal snacking, on account of their more sensitive natures or neurotic genotypes. Hence, all animals, even some highly evolved fruits where numerous seeds were involved, were inviolate. The pomegranate, kiwifruit, papaya, fig, watermelon and cantaloupe were the most obvious examples. Chilled and seedless watermelons and honeydew were to be granted most consumable status, sad to think of it, but certainly something to relish on hot summer nights, though their declassification, admittedly, was senseless, much like banishing infertile couples or testing radioactive isotopes on unsuspecting fetuses. The details would have to be worked out later. Mr Marigold had little time. Alma reminded him almost hourly of the deadline, which Hidalgo had been entirely firm about.

But if his theory of forgiveness was laid on shaky ground (did the lordly leech pay discernible heed, a cuttlefish give communion, the spider take an insult to its web, mammals turn the other cheek?), how much more so his plan for "wild stuff "—which, as detailed by E. W. Gifford in his 1926 essay on "Clear Lake Pomo Society", should be sacrosanct, if translated to any urban setting, necessarily transforming every process, ethic and exchange into an impossibility.

Still, through high water and muck, Mr Marigold saw it all. The morally gifted economy; a high degree of genetic reciprocity—that is to say, the apotheosis of generosity. Social status would be achieved on the basis of largesse, not accumulation. Because private ownership would no longer have meaning in the conventional sphere of profit, inasmuch as nothing could be bought or sold, and nothing could be owned—since Mr Marigold already (however paradoxically) owned the land upon which the city had been built, and presently intended to turn it over to the future plant and animal heirs—those who believed themselves landholders would be acquitted of their consumerist fevers. Thus unburdened of the possessive case, such previous owners could focus on what truly mattered during any given day. Marigold intended to compensate those who lost their land with medals (barring civil war).

Nevertheless, amid so much fine wine of passion, even Mr Marigold was vaguely sceptical. The gray areas of reality gnawed at his insides, moment to moment. The kilowatt hours of the prosaic, mundane gallons of water used each day, fancy-wrapped goods one took for granted at the backbone of leisure—all these specific possessions, processes and uses formed one massive contradiction that rather defied his sort of analysis.

It was theory that went nowhere. Idle philosophy. Vitality *in absentia*. He could hear Hidalgo's naysaying amid the nosegays. And though long separated by the mysterious forces of transmigration contained in each of us, the Commander even detected his dearly beloved father's voice cautioning him against over-expectation and excitement. Like a haunting that came to him in the right ear and scribbled caveats, poked fun, breathed chortles and made mockery down his flimsy ribcage, the voice echoed: Come down off your bunk-bed, Son.

Everywhere, he imagined, the unbelievers conspired. Certainly Alma would hear nothing of such highfalutin delicacy. With most of the Camp of the Spirits dismembered, that left only Sannazaro. But what better compatriot with whom to co-fathom destiny?

Mr Marigold caused his live-in gossip to quit the telephone, dialed the necessary numbers, and after some time heard the quiet, reticent voice at the other end, some several hundred yards across the way.

"Señor Sannazaro, it is I, your neighbor, in dire need of your wisdom, good cheer and your wine."

"Ahh! My dear Marigold!" The voice, like a clarion in the morning, a masterstroke of mirth, though it was verging on the witching hour, welcomed his "old" friend at once. "Come quickly, before the red wine stiffens and the white turns warm and poky."

"Alma, fetch me my breeches," Mr Marigold declared, for he was clad only in his long yellow nightgown with its headcover woven in the fashion of a monk's cowl or dunce cap.

She brought him his freshly patched corduroy pantaloons that crunched up just beneath the knees, Kurdistan-style. She also provided him a walking stick, which he rejected—"I'm turning a new page, no more effects!"—and an azure-colored lambswool sweater patterned after an early Mondrian.

"You look dashing, Master," the good woman admitted. "Say, what's the occasion?"

But Mr Marigold was already out the door. Seconds later, he re-entered the hacienda: "My notes." He marched abruptly into his inner sanctum and returned with a pile of rolled papers, tied with a silken magenta scarf, under his arm. He closed the front door in haste.

Something's wrong, contemplated Alma, who proceeded secretly to follow behind, moving with adroit bare feet from tree trunk to bush-camouflage, and leaving the front door inadvertently ajar.

Sannazaro was by the gate to meet his new intimate. With him was a tail-scything, irrepressible cacophony of several dogs. Their welcome was measured by their myriad decibels. Howls, night groans, bright eyes.

"Buena sera."

"Greetings, comrade-in-arms. Hail to the New World!"

With that, and arms flung around one another's waists, the two rapidly concretizing chums, followed by the bounding canines, prepared to alter the magnetic poles, or continental drift, and all headed indoors.

Once upstairs, Sannazaro did the honors, pouring drinks in the kitchen. Mr Marigold was seated near the perdurable fire which sparked redolent and lavender bright from all the fresh cedar shavings. Behind the house was a ready cord of wood from which the gardener daily chopped the necessary faggots.

"So, what news, what great unfoldings?" asked Sannazaro. "How have you gotten along? It's been days since we conversed. Has the rain ceased? Is summer nearly forgotten? Can you quite imagine how many frogs there must be to keep me up each night? Worse, the 17-year locusts. Why, not a limb that isn't home to an army."

"A great experiment, Señor, fallen into my lap by a destiny our ancestors, one and all, have conferred on the living."

"Go on," said Sannazaro, taking a sprawled position on the L-shaped couch beside a low mahogany table with a dozen gardening magazines on top.

"I shan't bore you with excessive minutiae. Only to say that I have nearly taken possession of an entire village beneath a hill, with radical intentions novel and pure, recipes for human reformation both precious and fine, and a whole new vision of the human community that is lovely and good, three crows of the rooster, and Hail Mary!"

And the Commander proceeded fitfully to explain that which offered no clear explanation to either the happy Italian, nor to his own addled and medieval brain, for that matter.

CHAPTER 19
A Pitter Patter, a Truffle and a Lark

BUT BEFORE MR MARIGOLD could expound too far, the dogs went racing through the downstairs portion of the house and scratched convulsively at the door, howling after some thief.

"Silenzio!" Sannazaro railed, but to no avail. "One moment, dear friend—" and he ambled downstairs to let them out.

The dogs charged past the open screen, and Sannazaro scarcely had time to call them off. The hapless Alma was caught out in the dark, screaming with no less a horror. As it was, the dogs were not attack dogs per se, but muscle and brio, lunging speed and hair-raising teeth all put to nothing more than effect—for they were, in truth, a comedy team. When they bared their fangs, they knew how best to elicit terror, and that to them was great fun. They were laughing dogs, with their own stand-up routines and droll mannerisms. They no more knew how to inflict a wound than to cut their meat with knife and fork. They had trained, comedically speaking, on the UPS and FED Ex people, who by now knew the deal.

But none of these embarrassing truths was of much comfort to Alma, who hung with deserting strength from the nearest mulberry branch while the mutts gamboled and frenzied beneath her, before tiring of their prey. They knew Alma, and she them, but in the dark such confrontations can take on wholly unexpected dimensions.

Sannazaro removed a flashlight from the wall and shone it on the intruder whose situation was the size of a gorilla's nest.

"Oh—" And calling up to Mr Marigold: "I believe it is your housekeeper. Stuck in a bush."

"Leave her, then," Mr Marigold advised. "She's just hiding out from the round-up of Mongolians."

Señor Sannazaro called in the dogs, who by that time were more taken with Mr Marigold's Gucci slippers which they proceeded to savage. "To move along, then. Let's see. Did I not hear you mention the possession of some city? Was I incorrect?"

"Not any city, but Sante Fe. I own it."

Now Sannazaro was not one to quibble churlishly with standards set by society for determining a state of mind or degree of mental abnormality. He certainly did not know his neighbor well enough to infer anything about his hygiene or capacity. So he changed the topic by concentrating on his drink.

"You see," Mr Marigold continued, undiluted, and he filled in the essential pieces of information with a verbal facility that inspired Sannazaro's confidence in the veracity of so many odd historical references. By the time he had quite concluded, there could be little doubt.

Sannazaro was plunged deep in thought, for no one could be entirely immune to such news. Moreover, the implications more than likely affected the Camp of the Spirits. Ginevra would have to be consulted. Everyone would.

"Fear not," Mr Marigold rallied, seeing how suddenly tempered, even distant, was his host. "What I mean to do is create your very Garden, city-wide, if that is conceivable."

"But is it possible—you, neighbor, the new and rightful *owner* of Santa Fe? Do I kneel down, polish your suedes, solicit an autograph?"

"Don't be silly. Think of me as a poultice for the collective, a bandage of souls awarded this sober task by all the fates gathering across time. What I have done these last several days and nights is fashion a design for disposition of properties, a strategy for de-constructivism of the so-called civilized world, an ecological shape that will benignly settle in men's hearts, a scale they can live by, a chart that will aid the weary worker, and a prospect that should make it all worthwhile. I have devised a syllabus of action, a procedure for each household, a layout in terms of their new livelihood, a psalm by which to remember the new renaissance of edicts I am contemplating, and a vast series of interdependent arrangements in lieu of the existing structure. I have limned the future, outlined the solutions, drafted a legal position and fashioned my very own manifesto—" a word he flung upwards like a conductor his baton—"by which Santa Feans will henceforth live and dream. What I'm saying, dear friend, is that I now have it in my power to transform this, this—" but he was at a loss for words—"this potpourri of rich and poor into that very

Arcadia of which you have spoken. What do you think about that?"

Sannazaro did not reply all at once, for the news was not inconsiderable. Finally, he asked for a sense of the thing. "But how will you go about it? Your zeal is one thing. The actual facts and complications quite another."

So Mr Marigold took the opportunity to spin his tale of de-, re- and post-constructivism; of flexible specializations, pooling, public trust, *jus publicum*, Vorsorgeprinzip (otherwise known as the "precautionary principle" for anticipating, and protecting against, environmental abuse), household yeomen, and cooperative labor schemes akin to those of Guipúzcoa in the Basque country. Unfortunately, the words tended to befuddle his concepts: his notes shrank in meaning, the thread wound into knots, the coherence pixilated into 1,000 dulled fragments, his vowels broke down, nouns favored adjectives and adjectives adverbs, until Sannazaro was convinced that Mr Marigold's master plan must be so important, dense and indescribable that it would have to work, because nobody could ever argue against such cuneiform.

"Your opacity is stunning," said he. "Nobody will know what in hell you're talking about, and—if history be your guide—you will achieve easily the results you're after, whether it be the transformation of everybody else into serfs or lords. It won't matter. They'll be so confused, so impressed, so insecure, it will take no effort to have your way with them."

But Mr Marigold had not finished. He meant to have a witness to his breakthrough, and in his canny thinking sought to prepare his testimony. He was already anticipating that nerve-wracked moment before some commission or council or angry mob: a vision of the cadres of the French Revolution queuing up with bloodlust, of Shays' Massachusetts rebels of 1782 agitating throughout the East Coast in defense of farmers' rights, or Shelley calling for Irish independence from a bridge on the River Liffey. He wasn't exactly sure what was meant by these intrusive side-glances in his head, shimmering recollections of great change. But he was ready to cross the fork, forge the spoon, blaze the trail, alleviate affluence, canonize poverty, hallow the pub, make massive material substitutions (i.e. "candle-makers to regain jobs"), take the plug out of computations, the rattle out of sabers, the chip out of slide rules and the disproportion out of—he couldn't remember what. But he was tired of "immense challenges", bourgeois ideas, garbage-removal trucks, apocalyptic predictions, the fatalistic scenarios that all argued for the death of god and the collapse of everything else. As if Plato, whilst formulating his Republic, had consulted Proust.

His Utopia was, admittedly, an isolated system. Lodged precariously, like Mr Marigold himself, over the abyss of the most damnable unknown of all: human nature. For it is one thing to recite the old Latin dictum, *Homo sum: humani nil a me alienum puto* (I am a human being, so nothing human is strange to me) and quite another actually to anticipate the vast sprawl of individuals with their too myriad of drools, depravities, goulash and idiosyncrasies.

Reading his friend's exalted, precarious mind, Señor Sannazaro posed the germinal conjecture: "I wonder whether the people will cotton to it? Maybe it won't be so easy."

He knew from experience that not all members of the human race were equally trustworthy. Mr Marigold could not know, given the scarcity of his appearances. He knew not the street or madding mobs of late twentieth-century life. To say he had been sheltered was to miss a more anomalous message of his 49-odd years: the man was a freak, even by the stiffest standards of reclusion—a solitary moose lost in the lower-48, or a butterfly at peace among converging ravens. Who could not fail to notice his trembling fingers, brow given to sweat, a twitch here, a nervous cackle there? Backing off sounds, and, to mask his ill-ease, his one arthritic knee going down, a stoop tantalizingly off the pages of knight errantry, in hopes (as they say) no man could resist an idea whose time had come. Sannazaro worried about the permeability of his friend's cellular organization, or, to put it more clearly, doubted whether he possessed thick skin or even the vaguest idea of rejection, conflict, man to man. Remember to distrust!, said a certain Greek, and Sannazaro re-intoned the point. Perhaps it was his greater affinity to Platonic friendships that egressed at that moment, or simply the universal sensibility of which he possessed a great store, but he suddenly felt terribly protective of the mumbling innocent who had spread his notepapers across the living-room floor, only to watch the comedian canines race over them, stamping and exploding the vulnerable compositions. That, and a pissing match from all the excitement—which may have dampened his piece-of-historical work but not the Commander's enthusiasm. An irony never more true.

"I'm still drawing sides," Mr Marigold replied to the human nature query. "Forming two columns in my mind, one outlining all of the misadventures, pledges gone awry, hideous devices, odious instructions, manhandlings and self-destruct mechanisms by which people have lived and died. But, alas, we mustn't underestimate, nor overlook that second column, the one psychiatrists after World War II discovered: that rich vein of good deeds and restraint that characterized the vast majority of our kind. Men who were more fearful of killing than of being killed. Who had rejected the muscle-man mentality in favor of joy and decency".

He included in this shorthand schematic of human evolution all those telling increments of emotional progress made by our forbears which he induced from a 4.4-million-year-old *Ardipithecus ramidus* sweet tooth and the jaw of *Australopithecus anamensis*. Marigold had grown up reading about the Leakey Dynasty. Names such as Lake Turkana, in Kenya, were second nature to him even in childhood. But what expressly excited him was the evidence for vegetarianism among those who lived so long ago. Anatomical data from brain-cases and small teeth that differed over time, from *A. afarensis* to *H. neanderthalensis*—a dozen examples, explained Marigold, and each a contradiction. Experiments in survival, some doomed to failure, butchery, warfare, depression; others given to quiet miracles, triumphs of restraint, that must yield clues to the human potential.

"You are a dreamer," Sannazaro bubbled, fixated on his wine glass, which he held like some crystal ball from paintings by Robert Wright of Derby or Georges de la Tour. "My kind of man."

Then, of a sudden, with a swashbuckling flurry, Mr Marigold got an idea.

"My God," he exclaimed.

Sannazaro drummed his fingers, silently awaiting the word. Then, impatiently, inquired, "What?"

CHAPTER 20
A Republic of Honey-loving Bears

"I'LL CREATE A whole new country! A member-state. Imagine—we can do it, Señor! Just think how the maps of Africa, the former Soviet Union and southeastern Europe have changed of late! This is no different!"

"I am feeling awash in your stammers and enunciation points," Sannazaro replied. "But oughtn't you first to secede from the United States government?"

"We, Señor, the two of us. You are now a central pillar of my master plan—the most critical zone, I might add. For you bring the gardener's touch, the lexicon of Voltaire, of all those pragmatic peoples throughout time who also kept a hand in the upper ether."

Sannazaro smiled. "I appreciate your confidence, dear friend," he said. "But now I must address the overall scheme. In short, why bother?"

"What do you mean?" Was Marigold to feel wounded, or further amphetamized?

Sannazaro opined the death blow: "What's wrong with the way things are, actually and all things considered? Taking into account the ups and downs, disasters and charities, good thinking, bad thinking; the chocolate-chip cookies and Saddam Husseins; the by and the large, the narrow and small of history—frankly, I would sooner live in these times than Hieronymus Bosch's. Be an American than Hittite, have a police force than none, be a fool than a beggar, read of massacres in the morning paper, if I must, than be caught up in one myself."

Even as he spoke Sannazaro was thinking how mad and Machiavellian the conversation was. But he was also aware of the special situation: mad, maybe. But the man now owned, if his word was to be trusted, the whole damned city! That was peculiar indeed, for it promised of actual mayhem.

There was no telling what this neighbor might try.

Mr Marigold was presently on a cloud of speculation. "It just popped right in there," he repeated, referring to his revelation. "A new country."

"But I repeat. Why bother? You risk making things even worse."

Mr Marigold did not take the provocation lightly. Naturally, he had thought of nothing else for well over 100 hours. In fact, despite his being removed from most exchange and intercourse among fellow humans, much of his life had been absorbed by an effort to understand its "silly face". He was not about to let such personal good fortune be wasted.

"I believe in a moral hierarchy," he began.

"No no no ... *never* use the word moral."

"But why not? Just as you have outlined your aesthetic predilections with respect to the placement of plants in the service of an ideal, I have often wondered about the placement of people in such service. But what is that ideal garden of people? Democracy? Utilitarianism? A common parlance of pleasure? Who am I to remark upon another man's happiness, or the status of his hunger, or the ins and outs of his imagination? I wouldn't dare. I am not so bold or foolish as to desire that kind of omnipotence. In fact, I prefer absolute anonymity. You see how I live, how I have preferred to remain—alone, virtually, at peace with my surroundings. But I have not been blind. I recognize the dissipation of the natural order of which both you and I are a part. Why not seize the day, fix the wagon, so to speak, and get on it?"

"What is broken? How do you fix it? You're speaking about 80,000 human beings and a million more tourists. What if they don't like your ideas? What if—?"

"What if, what if, *what if*, blast it!"

"Well, you can't ignore what-ifs. Who was it that said—Prime Minister Nehru, I think—that India did not have a population problem, but several hundred million population problems?"

"I don't disagree. But fortunately, I am soon to command unique leverage in providing what Adam Smith termed, did he not, 'a visible hand'," adding legs, elbows and eyelashes for effect.

"Which is what? I confess I have not read him."

"A mechanism, organized by the state, to persuade the populace."

"Now you are a state? You would enlarge the size of government?"

"A state of being, of amelioration, a state of—"

"Force. Tyranny. Stupidity! Pardon my French, but these dreams are poppycock fermented in rubbish. Look, Commander, if you truly wish to rule with a benevolent thumb, and happily a green one, you'd better sample public opinion."

"Public opinion?"

"That's right. Between the dust and the shadow lurks a strong-willed right to exist. Or, as we say in Italian, *soto la bianca cenere, sta la brace ardente.* Under the white ash, the glowing embers lie."

Suddenly there was another commotion—the dogs roughhousing atop Mr Marigold's ledgers, demolishing his written ruminations with their stampede, paws shredding precious fabrics of thought, careening down the stairs and bolting for the adobe and enamel door.

"'S'cuse," Sannazaro said, and he once again fetched the flashlight and went downstairs to meet the fray.

There was an audible ruckus issuing from somewhere in the neighborhood. Upon closer scrutiny, it could be detected next door, at Mr Marigold's hacienda. Then the phone rang. Sannazaro picked up.

"Si?"

"Señor, help me, mother of God!" Alma whispered, between major clankings and grunts and wheezes and other assorted high and low pitches too distressing to relate. The sound of one mighty crash after another blazed from the interior, and Alma's faint voice was submerged in that unknowable hell, like the last remnant of an iceberg before total dissolution.

"A bear has gotten in!" she pleaded, still whispering.

By the time Mr Marigold and Señor Sannazaro arrived, with the canine comedians—all four of them—struggling against their leashes, Alma had evacuated the premises and stood, paralyzed with incredulity, at the open gate.

The bear was visible, propped up on Mr Marigold's famous bed, steadfastly comfortable. The Commander assumed it to be a "she", given the daintiness by which she modeled herself after the pashas of the late Ottoman Empire, whose positions in their beds, on their myriad divans and sofas, thrones and satin pillows, as captured by the incomparable Ingres, were oriented for eternity. Seated panda-like on her enormous butt, she was licking her fingers that had found their way into the gallon jug of honey Marigold, in his haste to visit with Sannazaro, had left open beside his bed. A long procession of ants also partook, and not surprisingly. After all, Marigold's tea-honey was the finest in all of northern New Mexico, and scooping it out with his own fingers was an occasional late-night ritual that the Commander had indulged since childhood.

"That is precisely the sort of black bear I mean to introduce in greater number into my new country," he declared. "Any bear that loves honey can only exert a positive influence on the young children of the Republic."

"All bears love honey," Sannazaro pointed out. "And where will the rest of us sleep, when our beds are so occupied?"

"What are we going to do, dear Lord?" Alma managed. "It rampaged through the kitchen. Nearly killed me, I might add, no special thanks to eitherof you, or your idiot dogs. Call 911! Send out the National Guard! Hasten the police, summon fire officials, I don't care, just get rid of it!"

"Alma, shhhhh! You'll scare the poor thing," Mr Marigold said, already in tune with his future tone of voice that would swell to nature, rectify past misdeeds and wrongful intentions, and—like St Francis— embrace all creatures, with no thought of tomorrow. "I intend to populate my new city-state with such noble beasts. We will make special allotments of honey to keep them happy, and distribute barrels of the stuff the way salt licks are evidently laid down every mile throughout parts of Africa."

"Fine, you sleep in your own bed if you're dumb enough to. I'm checking in to Bishop's Lodge. Good night, gentlemen!"

And Alma walked off up the road, clutching her handbag. She then turned around and walked back to the gate.

"Señor, on second thought, I'd prefer to stay at your house, if you don't mind. It's less expensive."

Señor Sannazaro escorted her back into the house. The four comedians who, earlier, had entertained themselves at Alma's expense, were unfazed. They were desperately focused on the real event, clearly able to see the big black ursus feasting on the bed, occasionally peering out the window in some direction that addicts know—a heaven of oblivious ingestion which can conceive, in the moment, of no other transport than the sweet tooth and her blind arrows.

Mr Marigold was tempted to walk into his house and greet the bear, but decided in favor of abandoning the hacienda entirely, at least for this night, and come what may. He, too, headed back inside Señor Sannazaro's domicile, or rather, the now emptied Camp of the Spirits.

Alma repaired to a hot shower downstairs, while Sannazaro and Mr Marigold gazed at the hacienda from upstairs with a pair of binoculars. In some awe they observed as the bear answered the call of nature on the Commander's Russian goosedown pillows. And as, later, the animal stretched out an arm that inadvertently toppled a bookcase right into the steaming pile of fresh bear feces.

"My God, Hakluyt's *Travels* and the complete works of Rousseau— that was a first edition."

"It is still a first edition," Sannazaro said, managing a twinkle.

Some time in the wee hours, and after several disastrous tries, the bear found her way out of the house, having consumed the full jug of honey, and much more. Marigold returned to his rightful bed.

By morning, he could hardly be roused, though both Francis and Sannazaro shook him robustly, standing beside the deflated canopy, amid the ruins of the 500-pound visitor.

Finally, from who can say what terrible grip on his unconscious mind, Mr Marigold lunged upwards with a single, groping "*Huh*?"—the aftershocks of an Aesopean dream.

Hidalgo withdrew a letter from the vest pocket of his three-piece suit and summarized the contents of their appointment with Judge James Bradford in his chambers in two days. He further elaborated on the delicate nature of their presentation.

"I shall be ready," Marigold muttered.

"I'll collect you the day after tomorrow, 9 a.m. sharp. I want us to be clear about our demands. I'm doing this for you. You surely understand that."

"Good bye, Hidalgo," Mr Marigold rejoined, annoyed but ever in a good humor.

Alma presently entered the room, sniffing the putrid air with pronounced disgust, to serve her master's disgraced tea, which he took on a bed tray, sitting up on a new set of pillows. (The ones from the night had been sent to the best dry cleaner in New Mexico, minus their novel addition, for resurrection.) The Commander freshened up, changed his raiment, gathered his notes, some of his papers and a tape recorder with a supply of batteries, and stashed them in his haversack. Then Mr Marigold and Señor Sannazaro headed out the front door, behind Hidalgo, and gathered up two bicycles for their expedition. Hidalgo shook Murillo's hand, bade farewell to the Señor, and drove away.

"I should be back for dinner," Mr Marigold decreed.

Alma watched, her broom in hand, as the two men rode off in wobbly zigzags up the road.

"But why not take the car?" she yelled after them.

"Out of gas for years," Mr Marigold shouted back triumphantly, whether or not it was exactly true.

CHAPTER 21
Mr Marigold and Señor Sannazaro Sample Public Opinion

BOTH BIKES WERE fitted with umbrellas to keep out the intense morning heat. As such, a wind might have given them untoward loft.

As Marigold pedaled strenuously, he recalled such utopian captains as the American geographer Carl Sauer, and the great turn-of-the-century Austrian ecological economist Josef Popper-Lynkeus. It was Sauer who, in a 1956 essay, had clarified the irrational distinctions (normally confused) between production and extraction, the stealing from Peter to pay Paul syndrome. This pattern of fuzzy logic stood at the very crossroads of the ecological money thesis, but had, somehow, been missed by most social thinkers until well into the twentieth century. Deforest Haiti for lumber: it is good, since time is not a factor. That was the old thinking. Rape the Javanese highlands, ruin the soil. Value-added chips today will always count for more than future forests. And when flash floods displace a million Javanese, there will be jobs aplenty in clothing and housing the environmental refugees. Profits can be made on their ruin. Or when all the seas are overfished, a dinner of fresh salmon might cost 1,000 dollars. The market for fish, like oil or platinum (for those investors canny enough to foresee the inflation), will prosper, eventually raising everyone's standard of living (everyone except the fish). That was the conventional wisdom. Marx struggled to rise above such mercenary economics when he tied the prosperity of the laborer to the fruits of the soil—a previously ignored interdependency.

As for Popper-Lynkeus, Mr Marigold had read the scintillating analysis of his work by the influential Spanish economist Juan Martinez-Alier. Popper-Lynkeus had envisioned an egalitarian, sustainable, energy-efficient community that converted at least some of its potatoes to alcohol, for use as a non-polluting alternative to coal. He posited the utilization of vegetable oils for burning in diesel engines, and extrapolated human carrying-capacity (the number of people who could inhabit the earth while maintaining all the vital ecosystems) according to the amount of food that might be produced under greenhouse farming conditions.

Popper railed against fascism, eugenics, social Darwinism and of course anti-Semitism. He himself was Jewish and could read the graffiti on the narrowing walls of German history as the population tripled and the dissonance of unemployment swelled. A group of loyal disciples had formed a society around his works, but few, relatively speaking, were interested. As Martinez-Alier pointed out in chapter 13 of his extraordinary book, *Ecological Economics—Energy, Environment and Society* (published by Blackwell in the UK and the United States, and which Mr Marigold kept close at hand), if only those followers of Popper had managed somehow to implement their teacher's system of reforms, the social turmoil which fueled later Nazism would have been nipped in the bud. If a few vocal advocates of birth control, women's rights, ecological equity, social grace and—above all else—love and courtesy had rallied with sufficient strength around Popper-Lynkeus back in 1912, when he published his seminal work, they might have built a constituency, put different leaders in power, harmonized labor conditions, developed safe sleeping zones for the homeless, improved the employment rate (as was done in Spain by the Mondragon cooperatives), and thus prevented some of the worst atrocities in human memory.

Had Popper's influence been established in the early 1900s, sustainable energy consumption would have set a corrective pattern to 200 years of post-industrial abuse across Europe, prior to the disastrous reliance upon fossil fuels. A hundred other changes would have been triggered as well. Organic beets instead of blast furnaces. Putting greens and Montecito gardens rather than pewter factories and parking lots. Forest idylls, whimsical days, lean black acacias in the place of skyscrapers; nymphs and satyrs substituted for comptrollers and board directors. One man's thinking, lost to most posterity! Even in the early 1970s, only three countries in the world contained any organic farming enterprises. While unabashed racism and more terrorist weapons had swept across most of western Europe by the late 1990s.

What prevented that coterie attached to Popper, chiefly concerned with a form of "conscription for food production" (*allgemeine Nahrpflicht*) from carrying out his plans? Was it their guru's unwillingness to be so easily tagged as a Socialist, or Communist, or Capitalist? Was it the very foresight of his environmentalism—the concern about coal consumption, nitrogen fertilizer use, overpopulation, solar energy? Instruction was not a possibility. The existing paradigm of abuse was not ready to be altered.

As he rode towards town, trying very hard to keep his bike on the straight and narrow—never a small effort for one with knees that rarely collaborated with the feet, and arms that could not always be trusted to act in accordance with the hands—Mr Marigold informed Sannazaro about his visions of the Eritrean National Environmental Policy; of Yasnaya Polyana, Tolstoy's farm devoted to the principles of Christ and Love Thy Neighbor; and of the Swiss utopian community of Monte Verita in the region of Ascona at the turn of the century. In that latter ideological entrepot was gathered a covey of vegetarian literati that included Herman Hesse and Carl Jung, and that later New Mexican prophet of plumed serpents and the sun, D.H. Lawrence, all living in simple rustic huts on the mountain and communing with the elements.

High upon the Alps an all-star cast of well-meaning exemplars got together to stage a unique experiment. Among them, the Austrian psychoanalyst Otto Gross, now considered to be the first hippy *extraordinaire*. Gross died in the winter of 1920 whilst roaming the streets of Berlin. One observer described him during those last days as "starving and ragged". The communing intellects and artists strove to understand the muddles and contradictions that plagued the European imagination in its quest to rediscover Eden and rescue it from the rising tide of Fascism. For months, day and night, they sat like a great photovoltaic array, ready to be converted into current. And now, 80 years later, their impact glittered in the mind of the pedaling Mr Marigold, who related these various tales and tribulations to the vastly perplexed gardener riding at his side. But unlike those early utopic communalists, Sannazaro had made peace with his past and no longer strove to conquer the mountain fastness of Sardinia, had ceased sentimentalizing the gazebos of his childhood in order to better embrace the present and whatever years of good health, god willing, were left to him.

"Where to?" Sannazaro asked, bringing Mr Marigold's head down out of his academic storm cloud.

"We need to locate the most typical modern person," Mr Marigold replied. "Neither too rich nor too poor. Someone, preferably a woman, who has dispensed with the nonsense as well as the pretense; who cares for humanity but is unwilling to sacrifice her dignity in the service of a false conviviality. We need to find a neighborhood where, by necessity, the densification of life requires a certain degree of cooperation. But let it be mutualism, symbiosis, commensuralism."

"What is that?" Sannazaro broke in, for he was no scientist.

Neither was Mr Marigold, who answered him: "A theory of social behavior equivalent to the Dutch national motto: Don't screw with me, I won't screw with you."

On the down slope, the two men passed the enormous pink Church of Freemasonry, and continued into the Plaza area of town, filled with post-Indian Market week tourists, leisurely couples, musicians, low-riders and skateboarders. Native Americans clustered beneath awnings in their colorful leather trousers and full-length cotton skirts, selling off the remainder of their myriad turquoise jewelry, and 300 galleries spewed forth endlessly similar Santa Fe portraits and landscapes at end-of-summer fire sale prices. Crowded chaos prevailed. The sleepy Santa Fe was nowhere to be found. Traffic was thick, parking at a premium, development everywhere in the air.

From Mr Marigold's point of view, the prospect of taking over the helm was disorienting, to say the least.

"We must find our first sample," he said as they steamed downhill towards a residential area near St Francis Boulevard and the big mall.

They turned onto a nebulous-looking street.

"What about that house?" Sannazaro suggested. "It looks absolutely typical of the region."

The house—utterly forgettable, the worst in democratic, do-nothing, cheap, easy, ugly architecture—was, like most homes in the Southwest, made of wood and latter-day adobe, and had a small, unkempt garden to one side, a driveway to the other, and a nondescript pitch black land cruiser—sign of the times—

on enormous wheels parked nearby. The fence was locked. Hoops of barbwire and broken glass had been strewn across the top of the high wall.

"You see! A man's home is his rightful fortress," Mr Marigold observed.

"I have a bad feeling about this one," Sannazaro confided.

There was no bell. All the blinds were closed, so that there was no possibility of peeking inside the house. But the vehicle was there and presumably someone was home.

They stepped up to the gate, where a large sign read: "Keep Out! Rattlesnake Farm!"

"What do we say?" Sannazaro asked. He was a trifle nervous. "Leave all that to me," Mr Marigold replied pluckily.

He had noticed another sign on a wall near the garage: "Liver Flukes, Ticks, Wasps, Mites, Tarantulas, Emperor Scorpions, Termites, Crabs and Driver Ants For Sale!" And, to one side of the driveway, a poster, painted in what looked like blood: "Stay Away! Rabid Dogs, Hanta-Virus, Rats!"

"Jesus, what is this, a zoo?" Sannazaro started back from the gate.

But Mr Marigold had already rattled the fence. He was determined to be impartial in his survey and had read a recent national poll indicating that most people felt closer to their pets than to other humans. Over 60 percent of all men sampled were convinced that dogs and cats—and who knows, maybe rattlesnakes and liver flukes, too—understood them better than their wives or children.

An overhead video surveillance camera tilted down at the two visitors. Eventually, a husky voice issued from the contraption. "What the hell do you want?"

"Good morning, neighbor," said Mr Marigold. "We have come on an official visit of vital importance. We have been authorized to conduct a public survey of opinions pertaining to the coming political upheaval in Santa Fe."

"What upheaval, and what official sent you? Didn't you read the sign?"

Sannazaro backed away, and tried with all his knowledge of human nature to persuade his friend to leave this one household. Of all the homes to have picked, this sickening habitat was definitely the most inopportune. But Mr Marigold was not about to back away from a challenge.

"If there be a black widow spider under one rock, there will be countless such hazards under many other rocks, dear Sannazaro. Better to welcome contest at the beginning, see it through, test the limits, know one's possibilities, than be falsely encouraged by bland and meaningless concord. Every knight worth his elbow grease knew as much."

"That sounds fine, but did you not pick up a distinctive hostility in that man's voice?"

"I did, but he is obviously a person close to nature. And that can't be all bad."

"You didn't answer me and I'm getting tired of seeing your ugly faces in front of my gate!" the occupant shouted.

"Of course we noticed your signs, good sir. I take it you are of a zoological disposition?"

"A what?"

"Entomologist, virologist, snake worshipper—in short, a nature enthusiast, and man of my own leanings. Pray, let us in and I shall explain everything. I sense great communion between us."

"I gotta gun, just so you know," the voice continued, meaning to menace. "And countless metal-shattering bullets."

"You wanted a woman," Sannazaro reminded Mr Marigold in a whisper.

"That is a woman," Mr Marigold presently declared.

"What? That is a man if ever I heard one—a big bully of a voice, a cowman instinct with malevolence. Psychosis haunts these premises. I tell you, there is a horrible feeling in my gut, a yawning pit, a distress call. We should flee this awful place while we are still on the safe side of the gate."

Sannazaro could see another neighbor peering from behind the mostly closed drapes across the way. There seemed to be no small stigma infecting this particular neighborhood.

"A voice cries out for friendship," Mr Marigold insisted instinctively. "I say we exercise all due compassion and frown not upon the possibilities for human redemption. This is Lucretia B. Public speaking. This is the voice of the Projects. Of post-modernist liberation theology. Understand this person who is hidden behind force, trapped by her gender, frightened to go out, necessarily pretending to be the stronger of the sexes for her own preservation. If we can but grasp the shape of trauma obviously inflicted here, resolve the ancient wounds that fester in the shadows, then we will have gathered all the data necessary to shape the program."

"I am no psychoanalyst. I don't care about the said program. I just think it would be better to sample opinions at the city art museum, a local college, even a laundromat among Tide bleach and Downy softeners—in public, anywhere but here."

"Touch the core of a soul in pain, feel the vibrations of the common virulence, taste that vexation which our unholy century has visited upon the innocent, and we will surely have surveyed the typical reaction to the master plan. I am certain of it, Señor."

"Is the survey really that important?"

"Dear man, you yourself suggested it."

"I miscalculated."

"No, you did not. We are at a fateful crossroads. The entire history of the Southwest, of the G-7, hinges on my decision."

"The G-who?"

"Does an architect ignore his rotted two-by-fours, a bird the mites gnawing at its flight feathers? We have no less an obligation than this stocktaking and connoitering."

"I suppose that's two ways of looking at it," Sannazaro conceded. "But have you even figured out what you intend to ask? Surely you are not going to divulge actual details?"

"All in due course. I do not intend to hammer science on its head, or nail down toes with factoids. This is a sensitive area we're treading, half way between a folly and a monument: past future."

The loudspeaker beneath the video camera had evidently picked up most of the present conversation. Whoever was listening had obviously found such talk ludicrous in the extreme, possibly amusing and worth exploring, for at that moment the gate swung open. The two men ventured forward, and there was a loud and vicious barking from inside, clearly the sign of mad dogs straining at their tethers. As they drew closer to the house, heading up to the porch, they found themselves staring up at a gun barrel aimed quite unmistakably on target. But when they reached the screen door, several locks having been opened, Sannazaro was amazed to see a short, rather pretty little woman in a white tennis outfit, a miniskirt, holding a big gun in one hand and a miniature apricot poodle in the other. Her scrawny, almost sexy legs were quite tan, the product of an appetite for outdoors. Marigold had guessed it right.

"So what do you want, Jehovahs? Hare Krishnas? Tupperware? Greenpeace? What is it?"

"Good day, Madam." Mr Marigold bowed, stooping down on one knee, ready to kiss a hand if one were extended, which it was not.

"Cut out the flattery," muttered the woman, lessening the grip on her gun, "'cause I ain't impressed."

Gazing in, Sannazaro noticed a sign in the woman's living room which read, "Extermineighbors Anonymous."

"A great experiment is about to take place, ma'am, right here in Santa Fe," Mr Marigold persisted. "There will be a change of hands. Your property, the whole neighborhood, is going to be converted into a National Park."

"Is that so. And where am I supposed to go?"

"Under modified circumstances, a new Immigration Act and Extirpation Bonds will be applied, enabling those who are discomfited by the radical transition to relocate."

"Say what?"

"Employers will be given tax advantages for helping those in distress. Same-sex couples who recycle will have priority standing in the new tent city to be erected somewhere in the forest. Family planners, farmers, pianists and philosophers, poets, feminists and top-ranking chess players will also enjoy special benefits."

"What about people in sports?"

"Ummm." Mr Marigold rubbed his goatee between his left thumb and index fingers. "Such as?"

"Tennis," she said.

"A great game. Particularly lawn tennis," Mr Marigold replied, having had the good sense to recognize the woman's attire. "Arthur Ashe was the Wright Brother of his day."

"Hell, you can come in then!" The woman's tone had softened almost completely. She put the gun down by her side.

"Perhaps you have some tea?" Sannazaro inquired.

"Don't drink tea."

"Coffee, then."

"Out of it."

"Water?"

"Got water. But my filter's broke. I wouldn't touch the local variety 'cause a' the giardia and all that radiation from the labs."

"Never mind spirits. Let's cut right to the questionnaire. You see, it's an official survey."

"You with the municipality?"

"We will be," Mr Marigold stated.

"I suppose it's all right, then. I've got nothing against you, on account of I don't know you. It's the neighbors I'm gunnin' for. I can't be too careful these days."

She led them in to the living room and turned off the switch of the vicious-dog tape which had been interrupting their little conversation until that time.

Once comfortably seated, Sannazaro glanced about the room. It could only be described as a church devoted to middle-American décor—the velvet artwork, chintzy plastic scrimshaw, fake alabaster statues, frowzy smoke mirrors, blinding overheads, a male pin-up calendar, a tatty red couch (also velvet), a carpet that had seen years of nervous canine leaks, a library of worn paperbacks starring Barbara Cartland, Sidney Sheldon, Judith Krantz and Edgar Wallace, and three simulated pinewood walls plastered in trophies and ribbons from the woman's tennis game. She turned off the television, with its 40-dollar diamonds for sale, and got all calm and pleasant. She felt at ease with her two mysterious visitors.

"Come to think of it, you two aren't from around here, I bet."

"Tesuque, ma'am," Mr Marigold explained.

"Oh, pretty up there. Call me Elizabeth. Elizabeth Herbert Buzzard-Breath. Funny name. Maiden name. I'm not married anymore. Threw that sonofabitch, Barlow Tweed, out the window—" She pointed to the fourth wall where stood the remains of a plate-glass door partly boarded up. "He was screwin' my ten-year-old niece."

"There's still glass on the floor. This must have happened quite recently," Sannazaro noted. "I'm sorry."

"Two years ago. I keep the mess just to remind me that I can do it. I'm empowered. I guess it's a woman's thing."

"Good thinking." Mr Marigold nodded, wanting her to feel excellent and fine about herself. That was an essential ingredient of political and spiritual transformation, that much he knew. "I hope your niece is okay?"

"She's not. Now what's this about a new National Park? Will it have tennis courts?"

"Yes, naturally. But do you mind if I record our conversation? It's important as part of our survey, since I can't write as fast as you can probably talk, okay?"

"I suppose. But you're not gonna publish it in the newspaper are you?"

"Oh no, this is strictly confidential research. City of Santa Fe archives."

"I see. Well, sure, it's all right, then. You do what you have to. I don't want no trouble. Say, you're not with the police or anything?"

"Heavens no," Sannazaro assured her.

"'Cause we've had our share of problems around here. Still fighting several battles in court. Wife beatings, the poisoning of the elm trees, the torture and shooting of pregnant cats, boys exposing themselves, the killings at the high school, suicides, and worst of all, the neighbors."

"The neighbors?"

"Thought you'd ask." And as if already prepared, she launched into a disquieting confession of hardship and hatred; of neighbors left and right—and their 140-decibel dogs—all of whom she would surely havesilenced in the night if the law didn't forbid her from doing so. Extermineighbors Anonymous, a local support group, was her last hope, she explained.

So that before Mr Marigold could even get out a word of explanation about the National Park, and the City Beneath the Hill, which Sannazaro himself was eager to learn more of, Elizabeth had described her life behind the shopping mall, and it was Santa Fe so little like the one Mr Marigold imagined that it was all he and the Señor could do to politely extricate themselves from the social morass and quit, they hoped, the 'burbs for ever.

Indeed, if one were to extrapolate the future from that gal's position on internal community relationships, then Love Thy Neighbor, social cohesion, non-violent conflict resolution, basic courtesy and all virtue would definitely be struck from the annals of human behavior—and all of Marigold's elaborate schemes doomed.

CHAPTER 22
The Remarkable Professor Madame Vignette

"TERRIBLE STORY," Mr Marigold said, deeply moved by the plight of this poor woman.

Sannazaro, on the other hand, was itching all over. Hives had been his reaction to the locale, the woman, the red couch, the shotgun, the whining dog, the very concept of such people and events and personalities. But Mr Marigold had ignored him, utterly wrapped up in the Peyton

Place of neighborhood combat and disgruntlement. If this was the great Western United States, the same Santa Fe in which he had spent the last five decades—indeed, if this little woman represented the majority of locals—then he knew he had his work cut out for him. Elizabeth had been instructive to the point of ground zero. It got no worse than that. But had any Utopia ever been advanced with sufficient elixirs to cope with such distortion of humanity? Such limited spheres and dire obsessions?

Here was a victim, disguised behind the silent veneer of a congenial-looking block—any block in America. Here was charm school charred and ransacked by so much surrounding wickedness; even the lavender lipstick had weathered. Tear stains shone upon the simple register of pale skin and tired eyes. She had been cute in younger years. Her simplicity could not be faulted. But to be so schooled in the avenues and armor of rage, frazzled by demons all around her, did not presage a happy outcome for the Commander's Great Deliverance. She held a job, stood up for her ecological rights: peace and quiet is what she'd said. Was that so difficult to achieve in a town like Santa Fe? And if so, among these unprepossessing relative calms, then where? By what possible means?

All these deep and burning cogitations wound their seedy tentacles around Mr Marigold's mazard as he and Sannazaro sat down for lunch at the Sena Café, their bicycles parked inside the courtyard beside the wild rose beds.

"She was no lunatic," Marigold said, reflecting on her studious mention of certain philosophers of war, like Clausewitz and the Dutch jurist Hugo Grotius. "No mere child, or magic spell." She had boned up, Christianized self-defense; had learned the Congressional definition of a state of war, defined in 1897 as a condition that equally permitted combatants to contend by armed force.

"You are greatly exaggerating her verbal skills," Sannazaro objected.

"I am merely giving her the proper benefit of doubt, based upon her skilled way with skirmishes. She has obviously been well tutored in the art of war. And in those customs of international law which, she argued, were not inappropriate for judging one's behavior towards inclement neighbors, if you recall."

"I remember only a hag in a tennis skirt," the gardener carped.

"My dear man, surely you are not unaware of the fact that since the time of the middle ages, just prior to when you were born, sovereigns were always sanctioned by the Church if a war were waged on account of state security."

"I never followed too closely matters of state security."

"But you were raised in proximity to some church, and must remember from childhood that the great saints all condoned just war."

"If that is so, nobody bothered to inform me of it."

"I'm informing you now. St Paul spoke of helmets and breastplates of faith, and it is clearly written somewhere that the very best Christians stood ready to become armed soldiers of Jesus Christ."

"What does any of that nonsense have to do with Buzzard-Breath?"

"Did you not wonder at the extent of her knowledge? The fact she had become familiar with guns, paraffin-sawdust incendiaries, fire fudge igniters and gelatin-capsule delays?"

"To question such expertise was not called for. I sensed harm to my physical person in her putrid presence—and now that you mention it, I think there is probably no more humiliating way to die than by gelatin capsule or fire fudge."

"I'm merely pointing out by way of sociological example that this woman knew how to build bombs for purposes of eliminating her neighbors. All it required, she alleged, was basic knowledge of the effects of granulated sugar, potassium chlorate, oil of vitriol and battery acid in combination. You heard what I heard."

"I do not pretend to understand the American middle class, its ire, bad taste, oil of vitriol or mediocre aspirations."

"You are more of an elitist than I realized."

"All gardeners are elitist. On the one hand we prefer deer, gophers and rabbits to stay away, and will go to every degree to wall in our creations, but on the other hand I am not immune to the charm of bright flowers and populist plants. Your name itself might terrorize certain refined practitioners of their craft, but not me: I have been known to plant occasional marigolds. But none of this pertains to the gruesome particulars of that woman and her neighborhood and, by implication, the bulk of Santa Fe. Actually, the part I vividly recall, following her tirade, was her mention of the fact Americans produced 12,000 pounds of excrement every second. I wasn't sure where she intended to go with that."

"Another form of weapon, I suspect. Remarkable."

Mr Marigold was deeply disturbed by the woman's outpouring of sad venom. She was, as Sannazaro rightly intuited, the last person on earth the Commander would want inhabiting his Utopia. Everything about her, which he at first tried to excuse and empathize with, grew more and more wearisome, until he had little patience left for her cant and racial slurs. If this was the general public, the caliber of social grace, that element in human nature to be recommended above all others, then he was ruined, his plans undermined from the start. Who would inhabit the paradise he was planning? If not these locals, which ones? Where would all 80,000 people go? Let alone six billion?

"Not in my bed," Sannazaro reiterated.

When, after lunch, the waiter brought them their check, Mr Marigold took the opportunity to question the helpful lad, who was naturally beholden to the waiters' ancient oath of good cheer and accommodation. It was just what these two exhausted and depressed sociologists needed at this moment.

"Say, young fellow, how would you view the transformation of Santa Fe into a National Park?" Mr Marigold asked.

Pausing to collect the impact of so broad and waif-like a speculation, the young man hazarded, "What about me? All my friends—relics? Ousted? Jobless?" His voice crescendoed from neutrality to suspicion in an arc second. "How would you apply park principles to all the thousands of houses and buildings? What about the ethnics? Gangs? Car salesmen? Cars? The economy? I'll be back with your change."

With a reserved smile he took the money away to the cashier.

"He does have a certain point," Sannazaro added. "Bright boy. Who would have predicted?"

"An attitude problem," Mr Marigold reckoned, though he had not entirely ignored the difficulties raised by the smart-ass. Forced to focus upon them, the Commander presently had no other choice than the consideration of the masses—a subject which invited little fondness. Would one leave the buildings alone? Were not people also animals with equal rights to housing? As the beaver to its dam, the rabbit to its warren? He knew, or could well surmise, that beneath the inorganic acreage of stonemasonry and concrete, steel and brick, thrived a whole substratum of earthworms and bacteria and countless subterranean creatures unaffected by the human presence. But that was little consolation to the wilderness aesthete in him. As for roadways: no way.

"Electric cars?" Sannazaro posed.

"Well, maybe during the Great Transition."

"You can't expect to move mountains," Sannazaro said. "And is it a National Park you're really thinking about? I assumed you were going to socialize, or communalize, the city? It did not work in Sweden or England. Actually, I don't really understand what you have in mind, exactly."

"In ecological terms, dear friend, there is what's known as a slippery slope of degradation. Things are getting worse all the time and the goal of minds like mine, for whatever scant imaginings they're worth, is to invent ways to halt the downswing, to maintain a steady state, to stave off further deterioration. If it is not practical to remove the city (which it is probably not), then at least one must invent ways to beautify it, and to curb any further growth. Hence, I envision a massive tree-planting party, a year of voluntarism, the abolition of money—"

"Other than your own, of course?"

"Of course, fair is fair, but I would vouchsafe the adoption of a tribal barter system. Oh, I have scores of innovations—a committee to ensure that legal standing be accorded every living being. Just imagine how the world would change by that one simple edict."

"Simple?"

"Well yes. There are ways to understand it. An emphasis on open space; the adoption of Taoism. I would steer the entire town towards the construction of a mighty hypercomplex, like that underway in Arizona by that great visionary, Paolo what's his name, in order to consolidate the populace in small compounds, and thus liberate surrounding green belts.

This series of interconnected causeways and hyperbuildings combines the best of a tea house and a space station. Think of it like the medieval shopping mall."

"Were there any?"

"Well, I have read of the village of Ez, just off the Middle Corniche, abutting Monte Carlo, where Nietzsche consigned his Zarathustra. The whole community has been likened to a closed ecological life-support system. It produces nothing that cannot be recycled again and again; it involves no profit, only pleasure, and the gratification in knowing that there stands a city devoted to maintaining the biological bounty surrounding it. The reutilization of manure, wood chips, even urine."

Sannazaro rolled his eyes. "I've had lunch and dinner, both, in Ez. And it is no Oz."

"You've been to Ez?"

"Every tourist to Europe has been to Ez, I would imagine. It is expensive, chic and built of stone. Trees are in short supply. There is a little sign, I recall, that says something about Nietzsche. That is all."

The Commander was momentarily distracted, but not stumped. "All right, forget about Ez. Just think of my new Santa Fe as a single cause: the amalgamation of 80,000 conservationists whose sole crusade is the preservation of the natural splendor—with its bears and eagles and tadpoles and forests. Earthworms and bats. Creeks and hillsides. Even the people themselves, indigenous Santa Feans, constitute a cultural treasure that is unequaled and must be preserved."

"What about all the tourists, the curio shops and fast-food chains, the worst parts of St Francis Boulevard, and Elizabeth Herbert Buzzard-Breath? What about her?"

"Nothing with St Francis' name attached to it deserves such scorn, dear Sannazaro. As for those other shadows across the land, we will see."

Sensing irresolution in his friend, and noticing a peculiar-looking old woman, dignified and bespectacled, very European, walking briskly towards some destination that had taken her on a shortcut through the Sena Café outdoor courtyard, Sannazaro suggested, "Why not get another opinion—hers?"

Pausing to consider the approaching woman, who moved gracefully in the luminous day; reflecting on her delicacy, a venerable comportment akin to the insect world; and taking in the spectacle of Woman with the savoring eye, the counter-reflex and inhibitory refinement that certainly marks the more evolved chevaliers of the Empire, Mr Marigold stood up from their table, nodded gently downwards and calmly solicited the Madame.

"My profound pardons, dear Beauteous Dawn. You are a being of pure light, good of heart, gracious of demeanor, whose pulchritudinous passage through the day inspires one and all who are blessed with even a passing reflection of your sumptuous form. Might my friend and I be so bold, brave the framework, presume upon Destiny and the Cosmos, both, to have even a meager word with you?"

Sannazaro was tickled by the show, for in truth Mr Marigold had not yet managed to glimpse even the face of the Empress of his supplications who, by the highlights, might have been from the ranks of Big Time Wrestling.

The woman, turning around, addressed Mr Marigold. "Who is it that is asking for Professor Vignette?"

She peered towards the voices, but did not see them. Mr Marigold and Sannazaro realized at once that she was quite blind. Yet she seemed to have no difficulty pacing herself methodically along a path. She must have taken the same route every day, for she knew it as well or better than a person with normal sight.

"The name is Mr Marigold, and my friend is Señor Iacobo Sannazaro."

Mr Marigold got up to help the Professor to their table. The woman removed her hat, leaned her cane against the fourth, empty chair, and seemed to disport herself with total ease and equanimity so that there was really nothing for Mr Marigold to do but wonder at the efficiency and grace with which she got about.

"You are blind," Mr Marigold said anxiously.

"Yes! Which calls for drinks all around!" rejoiced the Professor, and she slapped Mr Marigold on what she evidently took to be his shoulder, but missed, clobbering him across the face.

This threw the Commander quite off his chair, and he sprawled thunderstruck onto the cobblestone. Sannazaro cracked up.

The Professor did not miss a beat, her own raw laughter continuing as a means of disguising her apparent distress and embarrassment. "I'm so sorry," she appealed. "That happens all the time. Are you all right?"

"Quite, Madame," Marigold replied, retaking his seat, but this time with a healthier regard for their new companion's aim, or lack of one. Sannazaro got the waiter's attention, and drinks and food were ordered. A rum, a brandy, a sherry, a mineral water, some hot buttered scones, some green olives and pieces of bittersweet chocolate. The clouds were gathering, their movement heralded by the cool expanse of shadows and the effect of a garden sprinkler in the courtyard, rousing the afternoon banter of several dozen wrens, song thrushes and uncommon sparrows that had congregated in the lilac bushes and magnolia trees all about. A child sat holding an orange balloon and tossing scraps of onion pizza at the birds, which pecked nonchalantly. A man sketched the woodwork and vega pillars of the old adobe ramparts in which the restaurant was nestled. (He favored a No. 9 pen.) People strolled by, arm in arm; a cool wind had caught an entire tangle of oak seeds, layering the air with velveteen. A woman pushed a pram, her stride the proud mark of womanhood venturing into ether, so happy was her moment. Another woman held a parasol. Two young boys in breeches played jumping jacks. A family of ill-dressed tourists staggered by, beset by evident quarrels of no importance. A man whistled at a woman in harmonic thirds, the product of a cleft lip, or cracked tooth. Foreign languages mingled as mouths, disembodied, seemed to float through the linguistic quadrants of an historical moment, such was the blur of possibilities that circled Mr Marigold's softening brainstem.

Purring cats, belonging to the restaurant, foraged under the tables. Somewhere off in the urban rustic yonder a gypsy violinist could be heard. Two lovers, absorbed in one another's blandishments, fondled on a gilded-iron bench beside a bed of blooming blue and yellow iris.

Aromas of jasmine and cotton candy wafted through the lower galleries of air. The once empty horizon had become a filled-in habitable dream of comforts and city life. Was it so bad? Was ecology necessary, in that moment? In that place?

"So tell me, what's on your mind," Professor Vignette inquired, drinking to the health of whoever was nearby.

"And to you, Madame." Sannazaro lifted his glass, suddenly struck by the universality of the Professor's evident insouciance, and swigging down his portion in one.

"You look to be a penetrating mind, seeing with no eyes what others have been blinded to their whole lives," Mr Marigold incited.

"Well put, and true to the core," said the Professor. "Legally blind, I still confess to deciphering the odd shadow and nuance, outline and relief, however retarded, deformed, distorted and unreal the performance of light on my retina. My rods and cones simply refuse to cooperate with the normal register, I'm proud to announce, battling for custody over even the memory of a glimpse. I cannot see your faces, fair fellows, but I am able to sense the presence of two manly brutes, bodies and all. What more is required?"

She laughed boisterously, a gagging, rakish laugh issuing from a robust chest. She was like a St Bernard (and yes, a big woman), quite content to stop at any table and celebrate, at any time in the day, and sniff the snuff boxes, genitals and molecules of newfound friends, in one manner or another. Such creatures flit, proverbially, for organic reasons, existentialism melting into rhyme, angst expelled and given up to the wind. Like butterflies, which produce the most penetrating pheromones as measured in parts per billion and exhibit the largest sex organs, relative to size, of any creatures in the natural world. To meet a person of such abandon was rare in these times. Mr Marigold at once felt companionship, a nullification of the earlier miasma sensed in the perverse little character of that Buzzard-Breath, whose feeble universe of neighborhood hatreds and obsolete squalls, of exterminating protocols and petty paranoias, had reduced the whole of human nature, in his mind, to one dung heap of putrefaction, the whole of Santa Fe peppered with inward disgrace. Here, in the blind magnificence of the Professor, was ultimate vindication.

With no other introduction she began to speak with Mr Marigold and Sannazaro, conducting a most irregular review of their respective journeys through life.

CHAPTER 23
An Expedition by Hurricane Lantern

YOU SEE, I HAVE nowhere in particular to go, no one to visit, no appointments to keep. Whether I rush or amble, no difference. Where tos, what fors, how comes, why nots, indeeds, whatevers, by joves are all the same to me, at the end of the day. Which is not to say that I have become reclusive or withdrawn. Quite the opposite: a full embrace, Gentlemen, without inhibition or gall, false hopes or dulled expectations; balance at the edge of all zeal; love beyond simple murmurings; no worries; my ballast the geological ages, my only hope that I should know the moment I separate into stardust."

Marigold prized the remarkable encounter, pressing, "May I ask what happened? How you were taken blind?"

Without pausing she replied, "Silly, really—it's quite impossible to say with any precision. In fact, I can't be certain I'm even blind, in as much as I see so many things now. Figments and ideas by the mind's own lantern light I would never have dreamt of deciphering in the old days. Think of me as a mariner of some *belle époque* of darkness, with its own zeitgeist and frivolities, dropping off the last trough of a tidal wave, disappearing into that alluring, ambiguous, god-groveling Unknown to which all adventurers have been oriented since the first tall tales around a campfire, and before."

The Commander knew at once that he was in close company: a woman of fabulist pedigrees and perfectly preposterous peerage, whose every known inkling, animated aura, mercurial manner of elocution was dear to his own. That she lived in Santa Fe and he had never met her was not surprising—it had become a minor metropolis of surpassing congestion. But that two similar souls should reside in such untapped proximity stunned him just then. He wondered how she'd gotten along, what she did, who she was, then pursued these many Champs-Élysées of inquiry.

She discoursed with a free verve born of the Café at the Heart: "We are each entrapped by a colossal and clambering conformity, ensnared by what we wear, the habits of mind, the things we want and believe we can accomplish with effort. Hope harasses. Dreams dement. Aspirations abrade. But we have no short supply of grace, faith, prayer—all those egotistical pontifications which we as a species have always addressed to ourselves with the strictest confidence. There are never any outcomes, but in the meantime we talk on and on and see the world not as it is but as we should like it to be. Running headlong into every substratum, where truth collides with fancy, our bruises are the record of our presence here on earth, out of which our heroes are molded, encyclopedias construed, great monuments erected, history conjured from blistering smoke. In the end, we are doomed to the beginning."

The Commander nodded his assent gracefully. "You will find no contrary quarter at this table."

"Then you will also subscribe to the curious algebra of X," she said. "X?"

"X?" reiterated Sannazaro.

"X is always missing," she went on. "That which is perpetually sought after. X, and X squared even more so, underscores, or nags at, every despair and each consolation. If sight were so simple, wouldn't you suppose that we'd all see the same thing? That X and X squared would be there before us, on every breakfast table and in each closet? In fact, it is not. Each of us sees a poodle or a rose differently. Your X, and mine, might be miles apart."

The Commander fumbled. "But isn't X a mere substitute for whatever we want it to be? I am no mathematician but—"

Unguarded: "Mathematics is not the point. After all, were there mathematics in the first love affair 10,000 eons ago? Or numbers complicating the original day at the beach, the original whiff of fresh air in the pores of an angiosperm, or the sight of a double rainbow after a heavy rain 100 million years ago when a hummingbird hovered mid-air to marvel at it? No, X is something else."

"Well, what is it, Madame? My impatience is no fine art."

She came to the point. "By the time I had somehow slid into the blind of inward seeing, X, and X to any number of powers of ten, was within my grasp. I knew instinctively that by the very condition of an inwardly viewed universe, X and all that it suggests yielded up an unambivalent slate: a picture as pure, reliable and perfect as any oracle could convey."

"But how is that?" Marigold wrestled, ready to be convinced but addled by the sheer volume of her philosophy.

"I still don't know what X is!" Sannazaro remonstrated.

"X, young man, should be everyone's priority. The end of all surmise.

But, lo, it is not, and that is why we fight wars, build jails, put down dogs, ignore the homeless and persecute women. That is why Charles Dickens and Upton Sinclair postulated theories of inhumanity and desperation; why Mark Twain resorted to wit in order to throw some luminance on a rotten beast. But with my sightless situation, oddly enough, I was finally able to focus with a clarity light-years beyond the blurred focal lengths of my previous life. The dust of numbers, the expanse of the sky. All the stars at once. I was suddenly in a position to see past the frosted glass plate with enhanced emulsion speeds; to grasp everything from the vantage, ironically, of one who never grows old."

She smiled, and recited the immortal verse of Victor Hugo which concluded with "... Les étoiles et les fleurs!" She translated, "For six thousand years war has been the pleasure for all quarreling powers. And God, it would seem, wastes his time making for man the stars and the flowers. The stars and the flowers," she repeated. "That's X squared."

"But you are blind. How could you see the stars and flowers?" Sannazaro plowed forward dumbly amidst so much eccentricity. In short, he had no idea what the woman was talking about.

Finally, Marigold himself tried to restore some cogency to the table talk. "Madame, you speak eloquently, there is no doubt. Emulsion speeds and Monsieur Hugo. But surely, beyond all the vagaries of war and the stars, your incapacity has its origins?"

"I would be hard pressed to confirm or deny."

"No accident?"

"Only the accident of luck. I am an archeologist."

"An archeologist! I thought a mathematician?"

"Heavens no." And with a disarming smile: "Do you have a few minutes?"

Thus she proceeded to explain. "For years I had haunted the Valley of Tehuacán in the high semi-desert basin between the Sierra de Zapotitlan and Zonzolica, 1,400 square miles of lush prehistory between Oaxaca and Puebla. I was searching for Godot, as they say; disgusted with a world where one crazed Communist-hating General could push a button and destroy everything. Where—as we now know—you can go to jail and pay 25,000 dollars should you dare to sing "Happy Birthday", or "God Bless America". Where one can be sued for publicly speaking out against meat, or milk, or rallying to the defense of turnips. Who has not rankled at the thought of the five-year-old expelled from school for kissing his girl friend on the cheek? Or endured on behalf of every ethnic minority their absolute humiliation and oppression. That is our Age and I was sick of it. I often thought how much better to be permanently *in absentia*, a blind hermit—blinded, in other words, to the horror of two billion people utterly bereft from the moment they are born. The poorest of the poor, in places like Mozambique or the worst sections of Gary, Indiana. Saner to be insulated from all the man-made mayhem, with a hefty flagon of wine in hand, scratching the subsoils of our ancestors, than to be part of the current madness. By the simple action of disinheriting myself from my era I obtained that rare freedom which the Buddhists dream about. A woman's heart realizes hope at the moment she has a child. My child was this freedom. I was its offspring, a liberty without hesitation, a kiss upon the lips of life."

She helped herself to a cup of tea, then continued: "I threw myself into the past, convinced that there existed once, maybe even twice, a Golden Age. Imagine, if you will, a young woman of great beauty—you cannot see it now—"

"Not true, Madame," the Commander decreed magnanimously. "Every ounce of that former pulchritude exudes its blush and staying power."

"You must be as blind as I am! I was speaking of beauty—but it is the beauty within, the beauty that is joy before gratification, pleasure in the sheer complicity of every sunbeam, breath of air, chill of night, that tragic miracle which is a woman's consciousness. So there I was, on one of these grateful, tragic, blissful treks, robustly straying up a Mexican trail, as truant as a leap year—I remember the brilliant illuminati of quaking aspen leaves. I was giddy with the expedition, like an entomologist at the end of a rope, observing mosquito larvae in the iron rifts of a Saharan caldera; as removed from the normal cares of the world as a marathon monk on Mount Hiei."

Marigold shrugged. "Madame, your itinerary excites the imagination but gives little solidity. Are there longitudes involved?"

She sought to clarify: "There are ways to describe isolation, to embellish the anticipations of a young philosopher which may, or may not, have the slightest impact on one who has never experienced the sensation."

"Oh I know all about isolation," the Commander alleged. "Though in a different blind from yours, of course."

"It's true. He does, he is," reiterated Sannazaro, who was trying, over his hot pumpkin soup, to catch up with the woman's exasperating way of speaking. Was such confusion the way of blindness? He could not say. He noticed that as she spoke her fingers wobbled, entwining invisible webs amongst their tips, toying with ideas, silent collaborators in the fluent mayhem of her memories.

"Well then, you should have little difficulty appreciating my life in those days." She stared backwards, like a fawn examining itself in a mirror. "That trail had led me far away from everyone, other than those in my immediate company: other members of the expedition. I was no more involved in the affairs, duties or distractions of this country than a passing cloud, enamored, rather, of all those ceaseless possibilities for solitude. More than any other buffer or distraction it was the history of these peoples, the traces they had left, the many riddles and spiritual haloes of tribal memories surrounding their entire life span, that truly saved me."

She was referring to those friezes, cradles, stick figures, colorful petroglyphs and bundles of humanity contained in so many artifacts and bare bones along the valley bottoms of that Mexican plateau where she had first immersed herself in the cares of her profession, beginning in 1961, a year after the famed Professor MacNeish had begun his monumental search for the origins of corn.

"After investigating 38 caves," she continued, "he finally discovered a small rock shelter of the pre-ceramic stratum, caked in goat dung. There, to much exaltation from his peers, he uncovered a one-inch-long corn cob that would be tested and shown to have been cooked 6,000 years before. Fifty-odd specialists, myself included, joined the good professor in that green chasm, working in the company of bats, rabbits, peccaries and gophers. We pored ardently over 237 fossilized turds and more than 12,000 bone fragments. A botanist found two of the oldest cotton balls ever recovered.

"In the end, we brought up something like 750,000 pieces of human existence dating back 10,000 years. From what I could divine, no community had ever fostered such unadulterated cohesion."

And she proffered enough examples to convince any dullard of her correctness on the matter, referring to trading partners in the Southwest, including such representatives as the San Nicolinos, Laguna Girl and LA Man; peoples whose radiocarbon testing placed them back thousands of years and suggested societies that had discovered their own paradises. At the very least, they had great corn bread.

This had become her mission: to uncover all those social remnants of lasting harmony, gossamer comportance, and make it work in her own lonely life.

The Commander looked at her and tried to imagine what strange incentives had goaded her. Was it a ruined love affair? Some other unspeakable disappointment or shattered dream? Or, conversely, a spiritual epiphany? Events in life of great significance tend to be short of fuses, long in aftermaths. Something had happened to her; something strange and forbidding.

"That wending cactus-strewn track in Mexico jettisoned me along other pathway in later years, and eventually to a place populated by its own ghosts, called Bandelier. I'm sure you are familiar with it, just over that way."

"The name is certainly familiar, though I have never been," the Commander admitted. As for Sannazaro, he'd heard of it as well.

"A series of cliffs. In those days I had the fortitude and skill to descend without hesitation. With each ten feet down that rope, I was actually traveling back a century in time. Rappelling down dusted walls into absolute oblivion, the picture that emerged of all those mysterious former inhabitants of the yawning chasm seemed to impart a near perfect compact with destiny: the end of my search; the real reason I had pursued such studies in the first place. Destiny that was the better part of valor, and that commended this particular past in so many more ways than the present. *Allez en avant et la foi vous viendra*, said Jean d'Alembert. Go there, act diligently, and faith will follow. It did."

"You refer to the Pueblo peoples, I presume?" asked Mr Marigold.

"Yes," she said. "I had landed with both my feet quite in their realm. I erected my little encampment, with its tent and sleeping bag and various provisions. Each waking morning I put myself there, grappling with the basic sentiments and needs, the urgent survival stratagems of those early inhabitants. If all that was meaningful then, how much more so now?"

The conjecture lingered long in her febrile poet's mouth, for that's where the response seemed fixed and ruminating, like a good thick lump of sugar slowly eroding in thought, falling swoon to the elixir, reformed by sundry. Finally, her blank stare floating, she uttered a disappointed assessment of all those hopes that history had thrust upon the late twentieth century.

"I can say confidently that they were lucky to have disappeared untainted or changed. They lived and died pure. It is a concept that cannot possibly be recorded in any subsequent Western society. John Steinbeck came close to the sentiment in his and E.F. Ricketts' *Log From the Sea of Cortez* when they wrote something to the effect that—wouldn't it be wonderful to live perpetually in that state of fond farewells, that halfway world of taking leave but not quite having departed, so that bystanders kept waving, loved ones weeping, hugging, arousing all the best outpourings between people. An impromptu purgatory of emotive sayonaras, remaining transfixed and sustained by all those heartfelt floods of going away, just prior to actually setting off, as from the human pageantry of a misty wharf before the infinite sea."

She sat back, tantalized by her own recounting.

In Madame Vignette, Mr Marigold had found absolutely the right mentor on the eve of his visit to the Santa Fe courthouse. It was, as Sannazaro later described it, after Puccini, "the force of destiny" that brought them together.

She then leaned forward and launched into modern comparisons with her beloved past: an inventory so dismal and familiar as to uphold the darkest night and condemn the entire so-called civilized world. Her parents, said she, had wished for her a husband, a nice house, children who might receive an inheritance. They skimped and saved for this dream, imagined no other scenario than that their one daughter should have neighbors, join women's clubs, be part of the community and get guidance throughout her adult life from one man. So many ruined hopes, collapsed preconceptions! To have instead produced a hermit of uncompromising obsession and with no sibling was, in their mind, a family tragedy. To become old with no grandchildren. To have accumulated their own lifetime of habits, expectations and possessions with no offspring to whom might be conveyed these bare rubrics of an unexamined life was a Siberia of final exiles. They had grown old quickly. The life of two generations was tangible, could be etched into almost any latter-day conversation. What did it amount to?

"By the time she was in her seventies, my mother continually and openly lamented her disappointment in me. 'There could be no greater heartbreak than this,' she used to cry. 'That you should be such a freak. A loner. A spinster.'"

Eventually, there were deaths in the family, dissolution, as if the Vignettes had never lived.

But there was no other way, not for the Madame, who harbored her own personal silence, its wayward roots illuminated, without remorse, in a quiet, credible tirade that carried its outrage in pellucid prose and courageous calculations. She did not falter in her sweeping appraisals of all the terror, decay and disillusionment. No modern-day utopian master plan or set of coordinates was ever likely to suffice.

It was one thing to draw the cynical connection, to bolster a theory with a megaphone at an outdoor café. And quite another to suggest an expedition back into time. But that is exactly what she presently recommended.

"We can go by hurricane lantern," she suddenly told her listeners, waking to the idea.

Sannazaro could not help but notice her vacant eyes, the upwards-tilting circumspection, so luminous, like a meadow splayed in sunlight, an insomnia of eager embrace, punctuated by the release of intermediary blinks, between whose steadfast darknesses the whole visible world was revealed in spouts of color as vivid as Matisse, but all within her mind.

After more moments of confession—disorders, latitudes and platitudes that coursed through all disciplines, circumambulating X and X squared—the three purveyors routed further discussion by resolving at once to embark on the journey Professor Madame Vignette had suggested.

"This is perfect," she concluded. She had decided upon a course of action that stirred momentous feelings in her warm bosom, the revealing of a secret to her two new intimates.

Both men recognized in her the energy of a circus, though she wore it softly attuned, a heavenly face as polished as sand with no more need to see exactly, having grasped the absurd entirety of life, this archeologist whose knees had become palimpsests of the Southwest.

"But what about your meeting with Hidalgo and the judge?" Sannazaro reminded his compatriot.

"Nothing could be more relevant to my City Beneath the Hill than this expedition," Mr Marigold replied. "And anyway, Bandelier is but an hour from here. There's heaps of time."

Professor Vignette had in mind the stealth of centuries, her own past locked away in a cavernous hold of the last undiscovered piece of a twisting ridge enveloped by a mini-cordillera, absolved from any description by a little-known valley of spurs, arêtes, knots of cliff, shadowed incline too steep for all those successive waves of posterity to have attempted: land that legislated the rare coincidence of inaccessibility, a geological guarantee, the sinecure of the blind. This topography was safe haven to a people whose survival, in their day, was the direct consequence of hundreds of similarly played-out generations of aboriginal conscience.

The Madame, while still employed by the Laboratory of Anthropology in Santa Fe, and still capable of crawling over rocks on her hands and knees and sliding down ravines on her bottom, had espied the one point of entry along a series of sheer granite escarpments. She had retraced the romantic footsteps of Swiss anthropologist Adolph Bandelier who, along with Cochiti Indian guides, had first looked down at the mesmerizing ruins named after him one October in 1880. She had immersed herself in the annals and mysteries of the Eastern Anasazi, a people that thrived between 1160 and 1290. Her passions percolated up across the Paleo-Indian, Archaic, Basketmaker and Pueblo periods, like some blooming purpose, the unquenchable curiosity of youth that is immortal and insists on its mirror image in the remains of others.

Where other students of the past picked up lance heads of Pedernal chert, the Madame discovered poetry to rival Homer's tears. And what to some might simply be of a category, such as the Archaic acorn-gatherers at Jemez, who ground the acorns into a nutritious meal on one-handed manos, or grinding stones, were to Madame a veritable theology of human preoccupations, the metrical passions of *chapalote*, small-cobbed popping corn, the earliest variety, that shaped the human spirit, the deities and wind, the taste of the earth in the early morning and late autumn, the soft suffusion of moonglow on a field cloven between canyon walls, and the scent at twilight of roasted corn in a fire around which a gathering of children dreamed their dreams, knowing only the tourmaline light on their cheeks, and the beauteous virgins, male and female, awaiting one another under the sanction of cliff dwellings, against eternity.

A larger corn arrived in New Mexico, *maiz de ocho*, with eight rows of kernels. It was ground up in metates, cooked in ollas, and served in white ceramic bowls painted with black, red and green designs. For the Madame, this little-mentioned event in the history of passing centuries was marked by more than mere academic surmise. This addition to the Renaissance diet of canyon lands in the Southwest was occasioned by Coronado's expedition dating to 1540—the melancholic finale of the Madame's own formal investigations. She had already seen the writing on the wall, understood the horrors of conquest, fusion, chaos and disappearance. Corn soufflé: that's what remained of paradise. She had touched the dust of scattered souls among the Frijoles, Alamo and Capulín canyons of Bandelier, observed in her mind's eye, on her benumbed hands and knees, the raiding Apaches, the displacement of one tribe by another, century after century, until there was no more the community of origins, no more the poetry. Only the dried-out corn cobs.

But by then she had happed upon the most spectacular of all finds, and would tell no one about it. Never would she provide an opportunity for historians to gain access, to trespass and tamper, disport on behalf of the government, build fences, park stations, remove corpses, invite tourists upon highways in their recreational vehicles. Rather, her secrecy was hallowed in this blindness, which—though she herself could not precisely remember it—had overtaken her some time after a year by herself amid the scintillating ruins of her hidden quadrant. Was it life in the cave, where her eyes, no longer needed, went the way of those dolphins, bats and frogs which—living in certain dark depths of the subterranean, or deep in rivers—also lost the necessity of an iris, an eyeball, a visual reference? She simply could not remember how, why, or even where. For the ease with which her blindness at the age of 30 or 35 had overtaken her had no professional record. She entered seeing; she crawled out, improbable though it seems, utterly blind.

"In that cave I discovered the great secret of time," said she. "The only wall between us and the dark, as Mark Van Doren put it."

"Which was?" asked the Commander.

"We are going," she replied. "You will see for yourself."

Forsaking a fine bottle of Toscana, only partly nursed between dunked scraps of week-old biscotti, Mr Marigold and Sannazaro escorted the Professor to her Upper Canyon adobe where her cheerfully sleeping nephew, Retard (as she called him), kept a spanking-rouge, seldom-used 1957 Studebaker in a tilting, mouse-infested garage.

"Who can drive it?" the Professor inquired.

"No problem," replied Mr Marigold.

"I will drive," Sannazaro promptly decided. "No offense, Commander, but I've seen you on a bicycle and it wasn't pretty."

"He jests."

"Gentlemen, help me gather some necessary provisions," the Madame hastened, greatly enflamed by the madness of a volition she had not entertained in 30, perhaps 40 years. In truth, it was a fantastic plan: a blind woman returning to the cliff, to the secret chambers and cylindrical bastions of the Keresan-speaking Pueblo who populated the Pajarito highlands and mesas, skinny-dipped in creeks shadowed by the cottonwood and willow. Quail darted through the Spanish bayonet; bighorn (*Ovis montana*) nobly preyed upon the wild flowers.

Those people had gathered *shkoa*, an ancient spinach, and their fire shamans, the Hakanyi Chayani, derived countless medicines from the plant known as *apotz*. They would scatter sacred meal into the four winds, the Madame explained, to the *yaya*, the mothers, to the moon, to the earth, into the fire embers, and all in the presence of the household gods.

"Heiti-na!" they cried out, upon prefiguring a cure.

"I'm going to introduce you to several hundred ghosts, Commander Marigold," she said. (She was already distinctly inclined in her address.) "You and Señor are in for a very great surprise."

"For that we thank you, Madame," Mr Marigold replied. "I will not yet weigh the relative advantage of communion with so many spirits, but shall hold off judgment, sensing the strength of your convictions. In any event, one ghost is as remarkable as a pod of them. But if, as you have uttered, we are to be surprised, let it come unstintingly. Bring on as radical a revelation as you can see fit to conjure. We are ready. A chocolate is never as good as three of them, and this principle harbors exponential qualities best tested on the young at heart, whose appetite knows no bounds and who would rather suffer the aftermath of a good bellyache than stymie the impulse to embrace life in the here and now."

They proceeded to gather lanterns and old nylon 11-millimeter diameter climbing ropes; pitons, slings, a hammer and rucksacks; two bottles of pisco Suspiro de Santa Fe (the "sigh of the locals"); two variegated take-out cartons containing lightweight foodstuffs and *papas huancaina,* lest hunger overtake them; three walking sticks; a magnifying glass; an ear horn and tuning fork; an oil torch and matches; silver pendants of squash blossom; red bandanas; a five-gallon *tinaja* for carrying water; hachamoni prayer sticks swathed in green plumes of the mallard duck; a vial of tansy-mustard drink, which the Professor called *asa*; a tobacco pipe of shaped clay from local sources (she knew the very cliff); abalone shell which she kept in a top drawer, along with rattles containing agave seeds; the rather disgusting dried scrotum of an elk; creamy down feathers of a roadrunner, a magpie, an eagle and a turkey; and a coral necklace which Mr

Marigold placed around her neck.

Each put on an armband and red and white moccasins of buckskin (the deer having died of natural causes) and a cotton kilt. For good measure they carried a rattling gourd and a flute fashioned of extinct bone. Thus armed, the Madame informed them they were all ready, albeit weighed down.

She whispered, "Nekamu—let us go."

They drove for three hours into heavy indigenous darkness, bumping along an interstate, then out on to a county road, drawing at length upon a dirt narrows, and finally, rather incredulously, swinging into a thicket in pursuit of an improbable off-road swathe through forest. They continued over flat granite steppes, an impossible knoll of up-country bedrock, then switched to a more improbable ridge, and down a dale, all according to the Madame's unerring memory. Wild cows stood their ground, voiced their resentment, then moved off into the black night.

Professor Vignette periodically sniffed the air. Then, suddenly, with no forewarning, she cried out: "Stop the car!"

Señor Sannazaro—newly deputized sociologist of Santa Fe—snapped back with a fearful reflex, and lurched to a halt.

"I think we must be close," she demurred, less certain of precise coordinates but confident enough. "We'd best go by foot from here."

"But that's extraordinary," Mr Marigold remarked. "How can you know these things, in your state?"

"I just do."

So with some confusion, dread and heavy laboring, they threw on two rucksacks, lit the lanterns and started towards what the Madame believed to be the East Rim of the hidden canyon she now named for the first time: "Hakukue".

CHAPTER 24
The Lost Valley

"HAKUKUE? WHAT IS IT?" both men blurted, in virtual unison.

"It is an old word that refers to drinkers of the dew. That's how I think of them, the delicate civilization that once thrived down there. Now watch your step, I can smell the drop-off," she advised.

They skirted cloud-touching monticules, hugging templed alp. Ponderosa pine of everthickening circumference shrouded their inexpert scrambles.

Hotfooted and premonitory was she, who announced meteorically, "There!" and pointed down slope.

Puffing, battling, bruised and belaboring, all three felt the wind, heard the echoes, and knew—as only drop-offs of such magnitude can make one know—the gut-aching vulnerability of a great and fabulous cliff that plunged but a foot away from them: an entire rim, perhaps half a mile wide, that gave vent to nothing less than a hidden valley, though in darkness such superlatives were still unseen and thus were doubly amplified in imagination.

"Uncoil the ropes, we're going down," the Madame incited.

"In the dark? Heaven help us," Señor Sannazaro exclaimed. "The night is no time for harebrain shenanigans. In any case, I am strictly allergic to ropes. Cliffs and heights, distances, the unknown and, in this instance, even the dark only hasten the unhealthy reaction. In fact, as of this moment, I am allergic to both of you for coercing me along. Shame on you. And twice shame on me for so unprecedented a gullibility."

"Nonsense. I spent years hanging on ropes," the Madame rallied.

"If you please, your Ladyship," Sannazaro politely interjected, "was that before or after your loss of sight?"

"It's of no consequence to you, Señor. The fact remains, I am ready now, this minute, to step over backwards down that cliff, which is the proper Dulfersitz technique. You walk facing in, being sure to clasp tightly that rope between your legs, avoiding any sensitive parts, then lashing it across your chest and down the backside. Hold it against the base of your buttocks, and be certain neither to slip nor allow your legs to step up the face of the cliff at an angle any higher than your waist. Here, I'll show you—"

But Mr Marigold stepped in to prevent any catastrophes. "Madame, surely you can appreciate the trepidation of one so uninitiated. As for myself, fine. I have braved all manner of Karakoram, leaped off unimaginable Chimborazos, even burrowed myself deep in a well. Nothing frightens me. No technique is too taxing. But Señor Sannazaro, he is an older person, more accustomed to the horizontal peace and tranquillity of a garden."

"Ahh, Arcades ambo!" she cried. "He and I. But he should not fear, for as it is frequently said, the thorn arms the roses. I shall see that he is not splattered at the base of the wall."

"A most comforting reassurance, Madame," the good Señor avowed. "Why don't we spend the night here, where it is safe and flat and we can fashion a cozy campfire with make-believe marshmallows, and discuss this insanity solidly fitted on our rear-ends, with no pressure of vertigo to spill out our guts or derange our thinking? By morning, I am certain we will all be of clear head and rational demeanor. I will make you scrambled eggs and we can toast to our salvations, separately or in the fashion of a Greek chorus, if you prefer."

"Well spoken, friend," the Commander declared. "I, too, Madame, would vote for a moment's reflection, a good night's sleep and a reappraisal in the morning of our precarious position."

"In that case, bring out our stores," the Professor decreed. "Let me call the ghosts up the cliff, if you are both unwilling to join them in the night, down below."

They made camp along the unseen rim, beside the Studebaker, whose headlamps provided light for all those practical maneuvers that mark the commencement of any such camping endeavor. All around them hovered 100-foot trees filled with the sound of voices. The Tesuque-bred members of the expedition clustered courageously around a sputtering fire, covered in wool blankets. But there, coursing the darkness, said the Madame, was a cornucopia of spirits, creatures that partook of nearly every avenue of thought, communed in dream time with the indigenes down below, and helped foster the same centered vegetable patch of life that had grown up and prospered (by her reckoning) for nearly 100,000 years. All were vegetarian: the bears and antelopes, American elks, Rocky Mountain sheep. Even the would-be carnivores had converted, strange as it may seem, out of homage to the *salvajes*, or *naturales de pueblos*, as the Madame thought of them. The mountain lions, bobcats, badgers, black-footed ferrets, bats, snakes, lizards, bull frogs, horned toads, turtles, gray timber wolves, coyotes, prairie dogs, red foxes and raccoons had all gone over to vegetative matter, along with the proverbial herbivores, the beavers, skunks, porcupines, jack rabbits, muskrat, mice and wood rats, kaibab and flying squirrels, antelope chipmunks, pocket gophers, and a million and one others—birds, spiders, annelids, insects and so forth.

"One night was an entire season. One season a whole life. That is the fifth season," the Professor explained.

They sat silently for some time. Then, she continued, "You asked about sustainable community, models, beacons, paradigms, tested hypotheses, practical immortality, ways in which a community might live as if every day were enshrined in the concept, the living reality, of a national park. Well, you sit atop that testimony, and if you are really searching for answers, you need search no further."

Mr Marigold roused himself, reacting like a jolt, wrapped in a shock-wave. "If it is true, then surely, my dearest Professor Madame Vignette, I am in your debt, for I have my entire life searched, though not in geographical terms, but across 10,000 fickle, life-affirming, life-renouncing tomes, for the answer to human existence."

"But have you asked the right questions?" she asked.

"Leave it to a woman," Señor Sannazaro rightly inferred out loud, "to recognize the ripe avocado. That's what I love about the sensitive gender."

"No surprise. As Confucius himself stated, happiness is the same height as woman," declared the Commander. "And all questions come home to roost in her bosom."

Sannazaro tossed a bundle of kindling onto the fire, and settled down to a bottle of Tequila and nibbles. For, as old Russians sometimes say, *Solovnya basnyamee ne kormyat*, or, Actions speak louder than words, or, literally, Let's stop talking and get something to eat. Carrots, celery with salt, a jar of extra-crunchy peanut butter, fig wafers and other delights were passed around.

Their own speaking softened, grew faint, and finally died out altogether. A hoot owl swept by, along with uncountable other airborne, grass-tethered, tree-cloying, earth-faring beings. Mr Marigold was accustomed to the wild life, for Tesuque could still claim relative impunity to all things urban. But

Señor Sannazaro was less comfortable with big sounds. Having cultivated roses and lilies, he was better acquainted with the mating behavior of ladybugs and elephant slugs than wolverines and pronghorn antelope. Eventually, however, quiet gathered round them. Sleep took out the Señor, and conspired like a musk over the Commander's heavy eyelids.

All of a sudden, all three felt a terrifying lurch beneath them. "Earthquake!" the Señor bellowed, jostling up out of blankets to stand quivering in his jimmies by a cloud-laced moonlight, clutching to an ant-infested tree.

"Calma calma!" the Madame urged.

Mr Marigold had sat up, long-tempered, unafraid, but now showed some sign of panic as his friend began thrusting about with agonized war-cries. Sannazaro's frantic yelps were punctuated by a rapid-fire of swats and lunges as his hands pounded his thighs and neck, forehead and groin, ankles and arms, for the ants had run riot over him in the dark.

Soon, poor Sannazaro quietened down, the army ants having been annihilated or sufficiently discouraged. But there was more to come.

"That was no earthquake," the Madame clairvoyantly reckoned. "We all felt the earth move, Professor," said the Commander. "Shhh!" The Madame held her finger to her lips.

"What is it?" Sannazaro whispered loudly, still smarting from his thousand ant wounds.

"Footsteps."

"Oh my god!" the Señor cried. "I beg you, one and all. For the sake of the camp, my pillowed sleep, and the very notion of a tomorrow—to arms and bullets and not a moment to spare!"

"Fearless into the wilderness, into battle, even into a woman's arms," Mr Marigold recited in a high-headed manner that conveyed not the slightest jot of security for any of them.

"They're coming," the Madame declared.

"Who? What for?" Sannazaro was not feeling entirely rational.

"I told you. The ancestors."

"What is she talking about? Commander, pray tell?"

"Dear woman," Mr Marigold ventured, "of whom are you speaking?

And what might be the probable cause of this unorthodox invasion by night, when all universal codes of chivalry acclaim the right of the weary to rest?"

But before she could even begin to answer, the spirits were upon them, not in any visible manner, but as some weirdly primeval nervous breeze in which all manner of thought, impulse, disregard of hour or safety inspired them.

"What time is it?" the Madame asked.

"Three thirty-two," Sannazaro replied.

"Go back to sleep," the Commander suggested.

"Impossible, not with monsters about."

"Then we might as well rekindle the lanterns, affix the ropes and begin our journey," the Madame submitted. "And do watch out for mountain lions. They hunt nocturnally in packs here, which is most unusual."

"Packs?" the Señor hastened, grappling to stay between his companions. "I thought you said they were vegetarian?"

"As a last resort, of course."

Within half an hour the three stood on the actual edge. The cliff was real. No veto, no Zeno-like paradox could obfuscate the harrowing death-plunge that lay beneath, though dawn's early light had not yet raised by even a degree the cold blackness in which the well-concealed walls were encinctured. A comfort, in some sense.

"Help me with this," the Madame asked, wrapping the rope around herself in a manner she had learned as a youth. "Now find a solid enough trunk, affix the rope, tighten it." And she proceeded calmly to explain the same techniques that saw Herzog atop Annapurna and Mummery on every Caucasus, the tossing of the double rope over the Ruwenzori edge, and so forth.

"But what if the cliff is higher than the length of our ropes?" Sannazaro deftly inquired. "A whole Kilimanjaro beneath us!"

"That is what the pitons and hammer are for. Halfway down, search for a ledge, as was amply demonstrated by Slingsby, Collie and Brodie on the great Grepon."

She intimated other techniques, as well, with reference to all manner of strange names and places—the Couvercle, that resplendent valley of Ingur whose fame lingers 1,000 inaccessible miles behind it, and a secret hotpool the color of scarlet near the summit of Rakaposhi, where it is said giant Asian butterflies convene every so often.

The Señor signed several Hail Marys, and fondled his own testicles. The Commander trembled, but remained unshaken. Above all else, he was deeply concerned about the blind woman's safety.

"How will you manage, Madame?"

"I shall go in the middle. I'm used to this."

"You go first," the Señor pleaded with the Commander. "I am ready," his friend declared.

His chivalry grew, however, with the same momentum as his agility fled the scene entire, leaving him twisted, tangled and weather-beaten within seconds as he tested the rope, leaned out over the abyss, closed down his eyes and mumbled hysterically to the elements. Now he froze in place, his legs unwilling to take the first horrible step off that odious edge. The cliff dropped sheer and demonic.

"I seem to be ... I am stuck."

"Nonsense," said the Madame. "You're just being careful, which is wise. I can imagine your dilemma. Sit back against the rope—further, further—until you are a 45-degree chair. The tree will hold your weight, no fear in that. The rope is strong. Fifty years old but undying in its affection for the sport. Now, are you in position?"

He was. "I am."

"Good. Then just proceed to walk down the cliff, slowly, gracefully, with no to-do about it."

"I am walking, I am walking, no to-do about it ... walking ... walking ... I am walking and no to-doing ..." And uttering these mantras the Commander began his perilous descent. A hurricane lantern was lassoed over his neck, a stranglehold of mechanical obstruction. "I cannot breathe, though all is illuminated," he cried back up to his companions. "That must be the normal situation."

Sannazaro, terrified to his very appendix, liver and spleen, every neuron having taken total leave of its senses, looked down upon the single dwarfed point of a man ever-descending, diminishing, depleting, evaporating, now engulfed by the greater extremities of a wall that seemed to swell for miles in every direction, until Mr Marigold was only a speculum of light bellowing from a wash-rag-sized ledge 150 feet below.

"I have found a spot," Marigold shouted up the wall. "Not much of a spot—it's the size of a teenage girl's brassiere, but a place nonetheless to take pause."

"Is there a crack?" the Madame hollered back.

"Yes," came the harried reply.

"Hammer two pitons to stay on the safe side. Snap in the carabiners, tie off the two ends of the rope, then tie yourself in, just like I showed you."

Five minutes later, Mr Marigold shouted back up. "I believe it is all accomplished. Madame, I await your eminence."

Sannazaro was astonished to see the blind woman fearlessly step off the wall after a cursory test of the tree. She moved down into the darkness like Edmund Hillary himself. Off to the far east the first rays of sunrise were upon the world. Within ten minutes, it was the Señor's turn.

He had seen twice the technique and so threw caution to the fleas and headed off into a direction from which, he imagined, few ever returned.

"Here I come!" he brayed.

In this methodical manner, as the first glint of light struck the top of the wall and began inching its way down towards the miraculous valley, the three alpinists descended, one by one and from one ledge to another, until they finally reached the ground.

"How do we get back up?" the Señor inquired.

"With these," the Madame stated, pulling out the chrome-molybdenum ascenders, known as jumars, from her rucksack.

It was 5.20, and the river was flowing. The inner New Mexico was waking, as the threesome traveled along the banks, beneath the solid sandstone cliffs, towards a spot the Madame had indicated.

"I find it amazing that no one else has found this miraculous valley," Mr Marigold observed.

"The spirits control all access," the Madame murmured, with no further explanation.

None was needed, the point taken. "But where are we headed?" the Señor fretted, out of breath and slightly dizzy. "I think it's all going to my head. That cliff."

"Let it," advised the Madame. "Mental aberrations are good omens; lunacy the only true precursor for where we're headed. Shipapu."

"What is that?" Mr Marigold asked.

"Paradise," she replied matter-of-factly. "Their Paradise."

CHAPTER 25
The Codex From the Beginning of Time

THEY WERE TREKKING along the creek bed when suddenly the Madame whispered, "Stop!"

They'd come upon another drop-off. Dark memory, detailed in the light of perfect and complete introversion, had come forth upon the lithesome lips of the aged Madame. There, 200 feet below, was a valley within the valley.

"Is there a large oak, with an eagle's nest?"

"There is indeed," the Commander said, gazing directly at it. "A mistletoe compounded by a kind of sea-raft."

"With two spotted gray squirrels lying on their plump bellies, relishing the dawn?"

"My goodness, there are. How did you know that?"

"Cooing doves and a little brackish pond nearby with hundreds of mosquitoes just waking up? Two fawns browsing near its sleepy edge?"

"But that's uncanny."

"Some things never change, never get better, were perfect in the beginning and, with Irish luck, should remain so for all time." Marigold slowly passed his hand before the woman's vacant gaze, just to make sure there wasn't some chicanery as yet unexplained. But she did not react to the passing shadow. Rather, she proceeded to describe from memory all those events of the hour. Hundreds of little bugs exercising their wings in a meadow of petite dew drops, crickets just now heading for bed, a badger digging at a mouse tunnel, a certain flowering plant, a crook in a trunk that resembled a goblin filled with golden mayflies. "Okay, gentlemen. This is it. Let us to the plunge."

They descended the sheer sandstone of the enclosing canyon, at times spinning out into the vertiginous blank of air. No detectable hairs stood up during their group moments on the precarious cliff. Rather, an elegant calm had settled there—perhaps in Señor Sannazaro's case because he held his eyes entirely closed.

"Don't look down," the Madame cautioned her allies aboard the rampart.

"Hail, mighty heart. It be a solid enough tether threads this wall. Fear not!" the Commander spouted in wobbly voice, between anxious mumbles and knuckle-bleeding scrapes. He was showing off, it seemed, with cavalier abandon. The Señor took his cue and, emboldened by a false machismo, made a sport of endangering himself.

At length the threesome topped off, dragging the ropes down from the tree around which the last of them had been fixed.

It was now fine morning. The sun mellowed upon their cheeks like melted salt-free Danish. They sat in the shade of a natural arbor. Exhausted, sweet grass between his teeth, Marigold bade the Madame recite all she could recall of her vanished people. She did, elaborating, highlighting, sifting and sieving that narrative which she had unearthed one fateful day several decades before. Sannazaro covered his eyes with his hat, buttressed his position with pine needles aboard a rock which served as his pillow, and lay down as if forever.

She began: "I had dug through the deep holds and keeps of the language from chalky calcolithic substrata, analyzing pictographs and hieroglyphs, meditating on the vast array of entablatures and fickle faces, animal portraitures and talismans that lay sprinkled throughout the remote canyon. I had scoured the floor of Bandelier on my hands and knees with a voracious appetite for knowledge.

"Until now it had been my wildest vow to withhold the sacred information from a world gone mad. You may ask, 'How had Madame Vignette kept so glorious a secret?' To be precise, my blindness worked in its favor, distracting my colleagues at the Institute and enabling me to maintain only the loosest of affiliations so as to protect the valley from any and all inquiries or intrusions. Anyway, who would have believed a blind archeologist?

"The paper I had been long working on for the Smithsonian Institution, 'The Semiotics of the Eastern Anasazi', was derailed. My many academic colleagues respectfully disappeared as I prepared to take permanent leave of the twentieth century. With a single switch I one day turned off the limelight and the pressure forever. Henceforth, I was utterly at liberty to pursue the phantoms of the canyon without the slightest requirement.

"It was then that—having returned to Bandelier—I made the discovery that would catapult my life into a direction even I, with such built-up hopes, could never have anticipated. I believe—no, I know that it was after that discovery that I lost my outer sight completely."

"But what discovery, Madame?" the Commander asked.

"Patience," she scolded. "Fortunately, I had been living in the canyon long enough to have worked out a survival regime of astonishing precision, even ease. It was the outgrowth of my ability to smell and sense at great distance, and to differentiate one scent or shadow or hard surface from among many: edible plants, specific meadows, caves, stream banks. I culled paths for myself out of the darkness, and though I lost weight initially, my metabolism seemed to stabilize quickly. There have been monks who went for a year without food and had only minimal weight loss.

"But what truly ensured my salvation was the staggering biological equipoise I discovered by not distinguishing between my memory of the exterior and my inward vision. My daily toil became an absolute joy. Metaphysics taking on the power of practical survival. My long persistent night was a starry one; moon glow became grafted onto my dulled lens. The rings of Saturn, the reddish aura of Mars, the green storms of Venus, and the bright plump points of Jupiter and Mercury, betwixt 1,000 constellations, somehow acquired additional luminance in my blindness and showed me the way. I was navigating by a new kind of astronomical and biological Braille. I could touch with barest fingers the warm rock, cuddle 'gainst sylvan sequesters recalled from before the final onset of blindness. I took refuge during winter in mossy caves and slept out naked during summer, oblivious to ants and spiders that might equally take refuge under my arms or in the warm lining of my crotch. We were all one family.

"I grew by mellow hours and submissive tranquilities into the splendid savagery of my situation. I had learned how to live—truly, how to live— after my encounter with the Codex."

"What is that?" Marigold intervened.

"I shall describe it," she said. "But understand, and visualize my life at that time. My foraging betrayed no sign of the scavenger, cannibal or desperado. Mine was the final union off the hidden map, quadrants somewhere between the heart, the stomach and the imagination. Those are precisely the coordinates that history always misses in its details of lost peoples, races and civilizations. Yet, that is precisely where, through my own labors, I learned that the tribes of Bandelier—and by inference, most other human predecessors—had lived for 100,000 years before the perverted change in *Homo sapiens*. I will show you!"

She continued speaking as they made their way along the river. "Can you imagine that these yeomen were a tribe as singular and unsullied as any of the Stone Age, pre-Stone Age or Upper Paleolithic peoples of Europe, right here, in our back yard? They fashioned dwellings in the cliff that bespoke of humility and revealed nature's perpetual experiment, architecturally anticipating every subsequent innovation, from Chartres to Frank Lloyd Wright. But the tutelage was far more impressive than mere roofs over their heads. And, incidentally, unlike that house in Pennsylvania that Wright constructed over falling water, these dwellings never cracked, their beams held fast. I was medicinally washed in the aboriginal virescence. I poured their inspiration over my skin, rinsed myself in their reinvigoration, renewed my bloodstream, apotheosized my hormones, lavished rainwater, sunlight, dirt, air and star-nights in my lymph. My cellular Self re-asserted origins long subsumed in the contemporary. It is the ultimate back-to-nature verbiage I'm speaking of, but I cannot begin to tell you how real, thrilling, viable it was. I had become a time traveler. Not an archeologist imagining the past, sifting through the rubble, but I had actually gone there, lived there, as they lived. Entered a romantic landscape and made it my true home. It was like that day after night after day, month by uncountable month. And as I vanished into this condition of Being which, as I indicated, transcends the imperfect detective work of history, like a tadpole bobbing upstream in warm mottled light, dead eyes awake, listless but full of joy, as in a crevasse, I disappeared, was reborn, was no longer Madame Vignette, no more the archeologist from the Sorbonne. But by the grace of some power, some unknown, I was living proof that the Codex was realizable, even in this crazy world of the twentieth century.

"Nobody knew where I was. My parents eventually notified the police. A search of no consequence was conducted, but since I had no known last whereabouts, it was largely a matter of filing some hypotheses in some cabinet. I was presumed to have flown a coop, however a blind person does that. My picture appeared in post offices. It was assumed I'd been kidnapped, or killed, or who knows what. A few colleagues figured I was onto something and would someday turn up in Arizona or Ethiopia.

"Meanwhile, I had become the tatterdemalion, unfettered Self. And I don't mean to be precious about it: I simply want to emphasize that a woman indeed lived for many years on wild seed, wild fruit, on dust and cold, heat and tears, and became by and by fearless. I knew by the end of the first savagely difficult month or so (for I had no way of keeping track of the passing days and nights) that I could and I would survive. Just as the parrot and the dragonfly, the frog and the chicken, the bat and the lynx—all portrayed in the Codex—survived. I knew that I had somehow become the messenger to further the mission of those ancestors. They had not tilled the soil, or stripped bare the wild vines, or hunted a single creature. I know this because I didn't either. Their gentleness, you might say, is their mystery. Gentleness beyond cognition. How did they survive? The way I survived."

For two hours they continued, skirting deep marsh along a river with no name, no source, no outflow. Visible from many prospects were the distant, high mountains beyond Los Alamos, behind Bandelier, before the plains of Albuquerque, not too far from Tesuque, but far enough from all of these human hotspots to ensure the cirque of inaccessibility that somehow uncannily masked the one last sliver of timelessness in New Mexico, and possibly the whole United States.

"There are nearly 70,000 known ruins in New Mexico," the Professor said, "including the famed Pindi Pueblo, settled by lowlanders around Santa Fe. For hundreds of years they favored small-scale irrigation farming because it provided more security than the high-mesa dry farming employed in the mountainous areas like those around Bandelier. Here, they scarcely farmed at all."

"But you said they were vegetarian," Mr Marigold reminded her.

"My research suggested that they were."

"So no hunting, no farming? How did they eat? What did they eat?"

"They did minimal farming—what some would call today one-straw planting. They'd throw corn seeds around, rarely deigning to till the ground. They'd pluck fruit from the trees, pull up tubers and roots, and consume wild harvestable produce, but never in excess. They had dried chilies and hemps, a whole bakery of breads. See, they used a number of flours, like *mashaish*, white corn meal; *shekaiuoisa hati*, a meal of sweet corn, roasted in the earth; *hati*, which was soaked corn ground up into sweet yellow flour; and a bread meal made of delicious prickly pear. Sometimes they'd prepare their bread paper-thin, from blue corn, baked on smooth stone. That they called *guayave*, and would serve it doused in honey. All these things even a child could manage. The valley was their home for thousands of years. They coexisted perfectly."

The three searchers followed a toe-and-finger trail at the base of the northern cliff, where it narrowed down towards the river. The water was full.

"See that grove?" And indeed, there was a grove of cedars. "That is where I spent several years!"

The Professor Madame kneeled, dipping her open, hollow eyes into the water, reciting a prayer. Then she got up, made her way to a rocky alcove, and removed a metal box, refulgent in the moonlight.

"I left this here in 1953. I knew one day I'd be back."

She opened the box, exposing a number of articles.

"These are all sacred," she said, and she began to mutter some words which were eaten up by her quiet breath. Neither Sannazaro nor Mr Marigold could make them out. Then she explained: "The words I use come from much later Pueblo speakers. I cannot utter the words of these more ancient people. Soon you will understand why that is. For now, just know that *ettow-iyatik* means that one does not disturb the fetish. The language. The hopes and dreams that survived here for so long. *Ettow-iyatik*. Hold it gently, respectful of the spirits that still inhabit it. Here—" and her fingers fondled an object before her—"a pot. Hello old friend ... old friend," she whispered. "I recall it vividly, but, alas, I cannot tell you its color."

"A beautiful red," Mr Marigold informed her.

"Ahh, they got that with crushed red scoria, a volcanic derivative. Notice the hair-lines at the lip."

Both men felt the pot carefully.

"You see how it is open. The Zuni scholar, Frank Cushing, who wrote about fetishes in the early 1880s, called this the 'exit trail of life and being'. For thousands of years it was believed the pottery—fired with dry grease-wood, sagebrush and piñon—had its own personality; spirits were said to dwell within, and they made noise when disturbed. Break the jar and you could almost hear them screaming."

She took the pot and set it down. "And here, *heishi*, from the Spondylus shell, harvested in the Sea of Cortez. Turquoise. Clay-fired pendants of coral, shell and pipestone. And see! A pair of sandals, woven of yucca, 9,000 years old. And a blanket of turkey feather. A lightning stick of spruce, which gives the holder the voice of the oracle." She looked up.

"See, it must be over there ..." She pointed to a magnificent fresco, totally exposed on the rock face. A small sacellum of naked sprites. "Go ahead, rub your chest against it, put your cheek to it. Lick it. That is how you soak up their power temporarily, and imbibe their visions."

"I'll pass. I'm too nervous," Sannazaro said.

"I'll do it," the Commander braved, disrobing. And he proceeded gingerly to apply his spindly body to that of the warming rock.

"Now that is a queer sight," Sannazaro laughed. Two distinct body types, ancient and modern, cavorted momentarily along the cliff.

"I must say, Commander, you are game. I like that about you."

"Is he, now?" inquired the Professor Madame. "We'll see. Come, Gentlemen—" and she hurried off up a sort of trail towards a complicated array of dwellings hewn from the rock and twisting deep into the cliff, and upwards, like Dante's spiral. There must have been 200 dwellings, and it was as if they were still being lived in, protected from the weather by the enormous overhangs of fashioned tuff and mortar.

"Animals everywhere," Mr Marigold observed. "Serpents, lions, masks, men, women bejeweled in turquoise, and robust children. And look at this." He knelt down and stroked the face of a creature that was part human, part animal, part—"Aliens?"

"No," said the Professor. They are simply the imaginings of harmony— harmony between the clans and their namesakes. They envisioned all the snakes of the world, road-runners conversing with ants, cocks discussing matters of great urgency with lizards and turkeys, parrots walking hand in hand with antelopes, and buffalo with grasshoppers. I could go on forever."

"Please do," the Commander beseeched.

"Murillo, the time," Sannazaro reminded him.

"Forget time," he jousted.

"That's the spirit," said the Madame, continuing: "It was the great anthropologist Mrs William Sedgwick who worked out the pantheistic details in the early 1900s. But here, among the Hakukue, that harmony was more than merely imagined. The creatures all understood one another. The dreadful Tower of Babel had not yet sundered human beings from each other and from all other species. They spoke routinely, as we are speaking."

"About?"

"Everything under the sun and the moon. Everything in the wind and the fire. About Love and Death and Sharing and Happiness. Everything Aristotle and Shakespeare, Marcus Aurelius and Han Shan ever dreamt. This was the Kachina to end all Kachinas. The Shipapu at the beginning of all Shipapus."

"But ... how did you come to know about this?" asked the Commander.

"How does one acquire the capability? For I would give anything in the world to be able to speak the language of seagulls. It would change everything!"

"I found the Rosetta Stone of these people," the Madame replied with some finality. "Their Ho-aanite, or oracle. It is written. Up there, in that cave—you can just make out the lip. That recess contains an ancient precursor of what later became known as the kiva. In that shelter rests a large flat slab of marble and onyx, crystal and purple gold, six feet by four feet approximately. On that stone is exquisitely carved a tale that says damn near everything we will ever need to know as a species. Its discovery marked the turning point in my life. I became blind some time shortly after reading it. I feel comfortable telling you what it says, because I don't relish the notion of dying with the knowledge all pent up inside. I have no children. And my nephew, Retard—well, he's only interested in paper bags."

Both men cast her a questioning glance.

"Yes. He is an expert on sacks of all kinds, but holds a patent on extra-strength paper bags. In other words, he is a disaster. Oh, he has his moments, I suppose. He shops for me. That's how he puts his limited genius to use."

"You could have published," the Commander pointed out.

"Never. How quickly you forget—*Ettow-iyatik*! The oracle is sacred. I cannot write of it. Perhaps I should not speak of it, though I am old and willing to take that chance. But I suggest, if you want to keep your eyesight, you not read it yourselves. Illumination exacts a price. As you can well guess, I have never been sorry. But blindness is not a consequence I'd wish for you. So come. Help me along here. The path is obscure. I want you to see the perfect architecture, the Sistine Chapel of Mother Nature, where the forces of all time have come together. The spot where all the animals slept and dreamt the same dream. Someone had the good sense to record it. I will show you. But be careful. Glance, but do not read; intuit, but avert your eyes; divine, but do not dwell on the words. Grasp, but let it go afterwards. He who clings to messages and meanings goes blind. Let reason be your prayer, passion your voice. Do you understand?" She repeated her caveat: "Are you listening to me?"

Both men nodded. "Of course," Marigold replied.

They were impressed by the virago before them, this feminine champion of metaphysical spooks and heavenly rejoinders. Yet, the undulating underworlds of her circumference were also strangely comforting. In her presence, even the downsloping cliff gave reason to be confident.

"What next?" Sannazaro said, his throat dry, his heart pounding.

CHAPTER 26
The Song of the Dragonfly

THE MADAME POUSSINED in the shade of the outer entrance to the cave while the Commander and his Squire groped in the dark of the recess, fetching after the slab.

"The light is just sufficient. I see it," Mr Marigold exclaimed, grasping after handholds in the dark.

"Pray, do not examine it," Sannazaro warned, "or we shall constitute the blind leading the blind. We still have to get out of here."

The Commander gently stroked the surface of the oracle, feeling each minutely carved figure. Around him, poised in the eternal dark, were arrays of twilled weave, plaited wicker, two-rod-and-bundle coiled baskets. It was a living museum atop cool and uncompacted dirt, a choreography arranged by time for visitors long ago. In its private thrall, no hand ever conspired to alter its primordial truth.

Yucca ring and root, bear grass and moss, unborn seeds and pebbles of geological unrest: each laid truant claim to the sediments. All of the origins and subsequent generations of life had put down their mark: *Purpura* snails, peanut worms, keyhole limpets, holothurians, poisonous urchins, gorgonians, tunicates and trilobites from the ancient seas—these were the scattered effects and condiments of a biological web of helium hopes and sunken sighs. The Indians who built their own lives atop the many-storied canopy of antediluvian precursors had manifested a mysterious continuity through the practice of art and sacrament. The result was a proliferation of jewelry, the myriad effigies all constituting some mythological dragonfly. What did it mean? Why these silver-laden insects?

Scattered across the pottery-ensharded floor was this purposeful multiplicity, impervious to rain or thunder, cushioned by marmoreal silence. Inhabitants had come, come to pray—it was clearly so, for these little zinc and leaden crosses, like crucifixes, were of sky-born skill and impressive artistry that made eternal sense in the dark, though none the Commander could as yet understand as he reconnoitered the museum floor. Here, in the precise shape of dragonflies, were shell pendants, hammered ingot silver, cone-shaped finials, double bars, petals and quadruple crescents, beaded and single-stranded lightning.

"The dragonfly is a miraculous beast," the Madame stated. "Its own Ode to Joy."

Crushed abalone lay like sea sand, woven of guano, tiny fired mirrored surfaces and fossilized turds of fox or squirrel or jaguar, all making for a solemnity of calm substance that attached to fingertips willing to trace the outlines of a psalm in the myriad apexes of the little winged flyers. Divine aeronautics. The dragonfly, with its perfect masteries lending it an aerial perspective over the planet, sensory scans far more precise than could be gleaned from any satellite, as it zipped with mathematical precision over every swamp; circumnavigating each of the world's estuaries at stop-and-start speeds, mangrove Mach 7's, past Monet's lily ponds. But no scientific nomenclature could quite capture what the Indian knew about the little miracle that was the flying insect.

The mirrors that Versailled the cave bottoms were smoky gray, carbon-catapulted knots of beadwork framed in square minuscules that served to couple the charges of any incoming light from the entrance, so that—despite the faint interior of the cave—all was bright, once the eyes attuned.

"It is beautiful," Mr Marigold cried. "The graces have sworn every affinity. The soothsayers their communion. Each trust its devotion, all truisms their song."

"You're catching it quickly," the Professor replied, not ten paces to the fore.

"Don't encourage him!" chided Sannazaro, restless and fixated upon the ruination which would surely befall them if they did not soon make exodus from present quarters for the rim—a trip that had penetrated his marrow with every anticipatory anxiety known to canyon dwellers.

"Go on," the Madame urged. "Speak what enters your heart." Ignoring Sannazaro, Mr Marigold kept both palms flattened on the oracle stone and skimmed the surface of his surroundings with a blurred aspect of vision that was all vulnerable and willing. He got down on his wizened belly and carefully placed his high ancestral cheekbones to the dole, buttering his Spaniard's Modigliani face with beginnings and ends. Speech came infallibly, oracular murmurs tied to the earth's own nervous system. He might have been commending a temple to Venus Stratonicis, or Apollo, Sion's Hill and Siloa's Brook; chanting with the fervor of a priest, fluttering wings and voices strange, a medicine world and messenger lips, on the very authority of Oedipus, bells unseen, mystic bills, and witches' brews, omens and holies. For Marigold, fluent senseless ecstasy and, to his mind, a poetry.

"I see the layers of ash, fireclouds and atmospheres. A loud grey pitcher defines the world; a silver squash blossom and a maiden shawl are my last orientations before setting sail herein, though it is a rag-whipped slip of a sail that falls through my fingers like sand. I see a child. An archipelago. A storm. A mighty storm."

"He's becoming more mad than before," Sannazaro declared. "I urge an end to this folly!"

But the onset of trance clung to Marigold like an orphaned orang and he held forth with no recourse to caution. All was palavering dribble. "Go on," the Professor hailed. "Let me hear words not heard in decades."

She leaned back against the cottonwood and smiled as only a blind woman can smile, love lodged in her long-agos.

In a quavering voice the Commander, falling unconscious entirely, laid claim to vocal apostrophes and prepositions, to dative transports and all things desembalaje, as his ancestors might have characterized such rueful ecstasies: not merely to unpack his soul, but desembaldosar, desembanastar—parvar ... buchar (said of birds when they feed their young); desembravecimiento (to reclaim from the wilderness); bozar (to uncover a face, a beauty who has been concealed her entire youth and then, as a dragonfly first takes to the air, to remove her veil and be shattered by desire) ... "Desem desem," he howled. To gather the fresh corn and unbend the bow; to remove everything, become sober, refloat a stranded ship, or clear a thing of mud; to take it full-bodied, like the Hispanic woman of his Tome dreams, in the arms, by the waist, eye-to-eye, lips-to-lips, under the stars, forever and ever; to extricate, relinquish and engage, all in one leap of faith; to wash down with a double shot of Jim Beam, recover an appetite, fall back from amazement and ultimately—desempanar—to polish a looking-glass, and look through it with the eyes of every child.

Like that, Marigold fell in with the spirits—whose embodiment as quicksilvered dragonflies had emerged across 1,000 miles and 10,000 years of romance—of a small boy and his older sister, both orphaned by the winds and left to browse with the deer in winter.

"In his despair the lad brought his older sister toys," Marigold recited. "With switchgrass he embroidered a crochet work, a basket, of indigo blue, spindled with the tail feathers of a flicker and a quail, to delight her ere she starved, and he also. For it was an exceptionally severe winter; there was no food left in the woods and many were falling to their knees. The boy, in giving these, said, 'Here, Sister mine, that you should not suffer.'

"Together, sister and brother sat waiting for the end.

"Then, one bright morning, spring in the air, the siblings all ribcage and yellow skin, cold pinions flowered, and the horizons were whitened with the arrival of sandhill cranes and fluttering song. Pepper fields sprang forth to feed the birds; clouds dissolved in warming moods and gave vent to heat. Within an hour, a holy transformation. Ice rivers cracked, and all was revived.

"The children ate, a resurgence of corn and grasses velvety, accompanied by the rooting of toads and tadpoles.

"For multitudes of centuries, the tribe, all of the tribes, were made strong with the presence of corn maidens, corn stalks, yellow, blue, red and white corn, corn puddings, stews of stuffings, and breads of every sustenance. The corn was the salvation. Later, melons, beans and squash. For generation after generation."

"What is he *talking* about!" Sannazaro despaired.

"Shhh!" the Madame intoned.

"Years went by, weavers, basketmakers, spinners, herders, hammersmiths and gardeners, spirits and kachinas all partaking of the feast the dragonfly lords had prepared. The brother and sister, the elk and wolves, the hares and lions, the ravens and the rest of them lived to be very, very old; lived together in that word—"

"What word?" Sannazaro pleaded. "And Lord forgive him. For he knows not what he's saying."

"The only word," the Madame said. "A word," the Commander revisited, "of all possible intrusions and extrusions—the light in women's eyes, that which will endure forever, minglings and meldings, paragons and paradigms, laughters, lovings, tidings and innocences. Of communities in true harmony. Harmony. Harmony."

"Harmony," the cave buzzed.

The shadow of a magnificent Queen Dragonfly moved across the cave floor. Invisible. From the musical vibrations of her 1,000-knot wings issued a rhapsody that penetrated to the core of the Commander, whose own incipient wings began stirring in a skinny chest that previously had known only human compromise, cave-ins, meaningless breath.

"Harmony..." sang the hallowed late-afternoon breeze, gathering its rosebuds, bewitched in that moment.

"Harmony schmarmony. If we don't get the hell out of here we're going to invite our own disaster. Don't you feel the winter cold fast creeping up your bones?" Sannazaro protested.

His two companions remained oblivious.

"We have at best two hours of sunlight. Keep your harmony. Give me a warm bed and a bowl of minestrone. Pronto! Or, as the great bard, wit in hand, once waxed, 'I would give all my fame for a pot of ale.'"

"Better come down, my suffuse Marigold. He's probably right," the Professor exhaled. "I can tell you, the nights this time of year are frigid, and none of us is acclimated. Words of God, of stone and light may, yes, be lovely. But death by cold is not, is ugly. And I will be going up that canyon wall sluggishly. We must hurry."

Mr Marigold slowly, reluctantly, devolved from his dizzy state. "Hast thou a charm to stay the morning star?" he murmured, quoting his Coleridge.

"No more of that!" his now panicking other enflamed.

"I feel resplendent, completed. You were right. It is everything. Such silence of the spheres, all-knowing."

"You were a demon of purple preposterous discharge, of verbiage meaningless and doggerel fiendish, and you don't even realize it!" Sannazaro upbraided the zealot.

"You, ungrateful heathen, would disgrace my hundreds of days in a quiet sanctuary, adding odium to peasantry—" In a flash, the Commander went for his sword, or sidearm ... even a fist would do.

"I warned you, Madame. He gets crazy."

But Mr Marigold had already put down his imagined sword—nothing more than limp willow branch—and fallen back towards the charm of his perplexity, chiming aloud at his great odyssey. For he had, by his quick calculations, disappeared for at least a year in that cave. "Four seasons with a people whose names are now familiar to me, all bedecked in the loveliest halos man or woman ever wore."

"That cave is truly wicked," Sannazaro said, spitting twice to renounce its memory from his head. "You were in there less than ten minutes. Do not be misled otherwise."

Marigold would hear no such defiance and continued to remark upon each aspect of his year with the Indians, wrapped for warmth in a turkey feather blanket, until it was impossible to believe otherwise. His mumblings were populated by such a throng of plausible individuals— among them strong-shouldered Pinzesbah, Dennehiaji of the furtive waist, Yeibichai, dressed like a wild rooster, Unshagi the mystery-maker, and Mescalero whose ferocity concealed a shy adolescent who preferred to spend his days lounging with the lizards and dreaming of his bride—it seemed impossible for him simply to have made up his story on the spot. Sannazaro did not believe his boss had such capacities or was so clever by nature. Which left only one explanation: the cave was indeed haunted, and spent its time demonizing hapless wanderers.

As the trio departed, fumbling up toward the dreaded place of fixed ropes, the Commander continued recounting every astonishing detail he could of his time travels. Of how he had run with the wild turkeys, witnessed the great drought and, worst of all, seen the arrival of strangers, his own ignorant ancestors.

"Mark that most hateful of days, February 23, 1540, when a man by the name of Francisco Vasquez de Coronado, along with 300 cronies and six friars, left Compestola, Mexico, on thrice as many burdened mules, with no knowledge whatsoever of the song of the dragonfly.

"Once they had subdued my people—"

"*His* people! Do you hear that," Sannazaro bleated, tripping over himself, grabbing after every hold in the tiring light, certain he would at any moment plunge to his final judgment.

"Yes, that's what happens," the blind yet easy-moving Professor replied.

"We transformed ourselves into mystics, ensuring our survival by metallurgical stealth. The dragonfly became the crucifix. The Spaniards, who by this time had perverted our corn into tortillas and 100 other nixtamals, masas, tacos and tamales, had no clue what we were doing. Because in the damnable eyes of the governors and religious brotherhood, we had been successfully converted. Every Indian wore the same necklace of silver and turquoise, which the Christians assumed was a cross. It was not.

"We were patted on the head, as proof the missionaries were doing the bidding of God, as bland assurance we were not animals, as evidence that someday even the Pope himself might bestow upon us the rights of human beings.

"Oh, Madame! I have seen the tragedy. And bore witness to the passing of the Spanish, as well. For there is joy, in the end. Just as there is a dragonfly hovering—right there ... You see it?"

"I hear two," she said.

Sure enough, two dragonflies were mating on the rock face as the threesome managed the last treacherous 80 yards of two-inch crack and irregular face. A gutsy pendulum off the enlarged roots of a silver spruce, a frantic shimmy, a few hauls, and they were back safely in their vehicle on the forested rim.

The forest was weak, sallow, for there had been fires across much of the Los Alamos Laboratory regions in previous years, and it was rumored by reliable investigators that radiation had been unleashed in the flames, aerosolized, and had killed tens of thousands of the trees.

"Thank you, gentlemen," Madame Vignette cried aloud, her tears salty with memory.

It was some time after dusk, a nightfall accented by mobs of stormy cloud. Sannazaro made the sign of the dragonfly as the Studebaker lurched with a grievous clank and took a solid hammering on a rock pit on the forest floor. Within minutes, a flat tire slowed them to a halt. Since neither male had the slightest mechanical penchant, it would take them all night to figure out how to replace it.

CHAPTER 27
The Ashes of Madeline

MADAME VIGNETTE was returned to her home, which offered a prospect of extraordinary botanical collusion: a bathing pool thick in lotus, surrounded by bronze statuary, a few lazy Adirondack chairs, a riot of *Mandevilla splendens*, century-old lanterns, sand-floored cactus and succulents. She had a gardener, she said, but invited Sannazaro—who openly admired her bright poinsettias and obvious Italian passions—to come over any time he liked and hybridize, or fiddle, or simply sleep in a chair by the pond. He thanked her for that, then all bid farewell.

By the time the Commander arrived at his hacienda, he was in a state of profound separation from all mundane matters: deeply moved and carefully disturbed, as in a trance. A picture of enlightenment tempered by the coming-down process—which could not have been more accelerated, thanks to the presence of Hidalgo who was churning in the profuse company of Alma, who had herself been agitating with no less severity over the sudden and uncharacteristic absence and evident absent-mindedness of the Commander.

"I don't know what prevails in me that, after all these thankless years, I should stay on in his berserk company," she cudgeled self-appraisingly before Hidalgo, whose belly full of 1,000 chickens, pork chops and pepper steaks pressed the three-piece Brioni suit out into the furthest reaches of imperial hauteur.

He was sympathetic, and joined Alma in railing and bemoaning the jeopardy into which they mutually believed their dreamt-of fortunes to have been plunged.

Now, with the weary-eyed arrival of the wayfarer, who looked as if he'd been stampeded by mules, the world was set aright.

"Behold, his highness. Where on earth have you been? We were worried you'd forgotten," Hidalgo aired.

But before the Commander could reply, Alma was shoveling him into his changing parlor.

"Hurry up, then," she addled him.

"Out, woman!" he yelled. "I am quite capable of changing my own pants, thank you."

"Freshly pressed, your majesty," she growled back, tossing slacks, argyle socks and Calvin Klein undies onto the pier table of mahogany veneer after the style of Meeks and Hall that abutted the wall. They weren't the trousers Marigold had in mind. He chose, instead, leggings from the Punjab.

Alma had polished his Gucci shoes, fitted him with fine haberdasheries so as to make him presentable before the Emperor, King, Governor, the People, or whoever else might come to hear out and negotiate a truce regarding the New State of Santa Fe and the world's financial markets. For such was the height of monumentality she had divined in Hidalgo's spare remarks regarding the coming contestation. Whole planets were weighed in her heavy ruminations; jeopardies affecting outcomes; truces, war cries, battle axes, Wall Street, the State Department, the masses. All mingled with expectation and dread in her febrile bowsprit.

"Brush that hair back! What, no shave? I'll take a razor to your throat if you don't obey. Best behavior, good as gold, get it arranged. Master, a big day, and these are horse flies you'll be contending with."

In such nagging manner, she drove him out of the house.

As they embarked in Hidalgo's majestic Cadillac with boisterous white leather interior, the lawyer announced, "We've got to formulate our absolute synchronicity on this matter, you understand? I've worked out the essentials of the exchange, the long-term dollar worth, modern portfolio theory, depreciation factors, accounting for public use, the maximal retainable value under fair consideration easement guidelines." Marigold, head fussy with fandangles from the other world, shielded his ears from the assault. "Please. Harass not my contemplativity."

"Murillo, come off your headstool, leave go your angels, just for a few days. We have leverage—incredible historic documents—but you mustn't confuse them by saying a bloody word. I don't mean to be insulting about it, but I know what I'm doing. So what say you?"

"You underestimate me."

"No I don't. Face it, Murillo; this is not your area of expertise. Is that fair?"

Marigold was stern-browed and silent, dark circles ever broadening beneath his eyes.

"All I'm saying is we need to be strong in the predictable face of hostility. I know how to fight, and I'm fighting for you. I've been over this dozens of times. Independent appraisals and opinions. What I have in mind is not entirely unprecedented, but the dollar sums are. Your ancestors, and your father particularly, would be proud."

Such curious assertions evoked complicated feelings in Mr Marigold. To calm himself, he stared into the distance from the top of Bishop's Lodge Road out towards the blurry blue crest above Albuquerque, and reflected upon the strange imbroglios of the previous days. For one so unaccustomed to dealing with people, community and the vague clamors of the current world, such immersion in what the ancient Greeks called praxis constituted an awesome, if vexatious, task. Medieval Arab traders likened such hurdles to the gnat becoming a camel, and showered about such expressions as Hak, Hu, Allah Akbar, Wallah, billah!, or Damagh-i-shuma khushk shuda-ast ("Your brain has dried up", as detailed in *The Adventures of Hajji Baba of Ispahan*). Of equal peril, who in the Mister's situation would not recall those fateful words of Niccolo Machiavelli: "If he whom you join prevails, you are at his mercy"? Mr Marigold had been consumed for so long by daydreams (*the shout of joy*, in Old German) that the prospect of practical design, realization, empowerment, proportion, ratio, persuasion, was suddenly unthinkable, at least after his encounter with the Dragonfly Lord. He'd had no powers-that-be, no conflict, in his life. No historical battlefields, sleepless nights, tyrants, genetic compulsions or translocations (like the Holstein's protein on the 16th gene, turned around in the swirl of machinations, so that it can't remember which way to go for a drink of water). The moment you stake your life or happiness or dreams on anything beyond yourself, Marigold always thought, you're washed up. Or so said his array of antediluvian pundits.

Some people gawked at the Creation for answers, others at a Creator. Some believed in violence as a necessary cleansing mechanism, a spur to evolution, the way astronomers relish the far-away existence of Black Holes, which suck up the old and spit out the new galaxies. Some are pursued by destiny. Others pursued it. Conundrums manifested in too many guises to make any sense of heaven. Murillo's ancestors—Roman Catholics turned heathen—had rejected every basic, but one: the Infallibility of the Falling Apple, which was tantamount to confirming free will—our only hope of redemption, if not in this, then in the next life.

What of the infant, born without limbs or a palpitating heart?, Murillo had asked his father long ago. Or six million innocent Jews slaughtered by the Nazis? Where was the redemption in that? Who was to blame? Why was the exercise of free will limited only to those with power to be cruel?

But it was the demise of Pecos' young bride, Murillo's mother, that had truly clinched his father's departure from the fold. He could no longer believe in a God that allowed for innocents to be short-changed. That was when he ceased visiting the Marigold strip of plots in the venerable cemetery outside the San Estevan del Rey Mission Church at Acoma. For centuries his family had supported this particular relic, built under the controversial guidance of Fray Juan Ramirez between 1629 and 1642. It was the oldest and best preserved church in the southwest, and sacred to the locals. With its 35-foot-high double towers, or torreons, and 6,000 cubic feet of stellar interior, this numeric calculus, known as the pueblo in the sky, sat atop 500-foot cliffs. At least eleven Marigolds were buried there. Pecos, and Murillo himself, vowed they would not be.

To accent his renunciation of the Church, Pecos had Madeline cremated, her ashes scented with her favorite perfumes and scattered across all the furniture of the hacienda, ground into the carpets, sprinkled in the library, the food pantry, under the bed, in the coverlets, clothes and crannies. Other ashes were directed outside, in the garden, across slopes of stunted juniper—wherever Pecos, his son or any additional offspring were likely to circulate in their remaining years.

All these thoughts passed through Murillo's mind as they raced towards town, ten minutes up, then down, the road. For so many years his solipsisms had lounged in his graying matter like a stubborn lozenge. Now, drained of insularity, propelled into a fray of thrilling if queasy possibilities, he likened himself to an astronaut on a mission in a new era, an extra-vehicular foray out of the armchair into the whirlpool. A dragonfly jettisoned into the twenty-first century.

Portly Hidalgo gabbed on in legalese, asserting his hot implacables, the rules of the judicial in-camera process before them. In his head he was closing in on a paradise of percentages, the land of milk and money. But he also knew they would be treading on legal *terra incognita*, so his hands were not without their blend of sweat; his speech tremulous beneath the bluster.

Hidalgo was a lawyer of unscrupulous stature, known for his charms, heavy drinking, ruthless tactics, long business lunches, and young paralegals of the kinder gender whom he was constantly *grooming*. One of them, Anita Sanchez, had recently undergone an abortion. Hidalgo, who had noticeably cheered up in the aftermath, was certainly well versed in the history of legal rights for fetuses, beginning with the case of Mrs Dietrich in 1883, the Annie Walker case in Ireland a few years later, and the Mrs Laveille suit in Canada. But when it was convenient—and Anita's wasn't the first time—he rallied for *Roe v. Wade*. Silence was critical. Action must be swift. The more delicate the situation, the greater the justification for an expedient was his *modus operandi*. Hidalgo was a Democrat because, said he, Republicans attracted fewer cute girls.

Yet, for all his inconsistencies and perditions of character, he could be positively instrumental in other ways, which proved that where there was even a small toehold amid blank walls, humanity was possible. In all, Hidalgo was more grace and sterling than mixed baggage. Pecos had come to trust him with the Marigold estate because he knew him to be a solid friend of the family, and had noted his extremely fatherly affections for the Commander through thickness, darkness and light. The two of them maintained a kidding relationship. It was hard not to smile in company with the Commander, especially whenever he opened his mouth to speak. Did Marigold ever catch a glint of his own silliness? Probably not. But Hidalgo understood, and rather relished the temperament.

As they entered Santa Fe, Mr Marigold examined the proliferation of chaos all around him. With one more generation, a single city of Elizabeth Herbert Buzzard-Breaths would spread from Los Alamos to Albuquerque—just as Boulder became part of Denver to the north. Marigold's sequestered private drive—a microcosm of the world as it once was, wild and free and equitable—was up for grabs. What suit of armor, he wondered, had any chance against the many onslaughts of this strange outer universe, with unnatural boundaries precluding the wandering of baby geese, or shepherds with their flocks? No place for a Theocritus to recite his epistles beneath an Acropolis, or the Renaissance-type Honthorsts and Huets to paint their wild perfect scenes—not with a population explosion happening all around the world. As repressive and grim as it appeared, however, this Marigold had a plan. He would make his romance work for the modern age.

"Murillo," Hidalgo started with some trepidation, "you're going to have to consider an heir, once this is all finished. You can't leave such assets to chance."

"What I do with my money—all respects, Francis—is not for you to trouble yourself over."

"Your father would have wanted—"

"My father wanted only for my happiness."

"Never a truth more rightly propagated."

"To sire offspring for the purposes of preserving capital is preposterous, like climbing a tree to be closer to the clouds. When I am done with my dinner I shall get up from the table, bid adieu to my few loyal friends, walk out the door, and give no thought to tomorrow. Thank you very much."

"I have no problem with that. You just haven't met the right woman. In fact, you haven't met any woman."

"That's not so. I just spent the most remarkable time with a woman, Madame Vignette, a blind archeologist, decades older than myself, but possessed of the spirit and agility of a mountain goat."

"That's not the sort of woman I was referring to. But listen, Son, I ask only one thing of you. And by the way—" he was admiring the Commander's rare suit of clothes, and especially the tie from a museum of modern art, with stencilled Mondrian ferns—"you look great."

"Thank you." Alma had evacuated the Commander from his shredded dungarees and reappointed him in a relatively wrinkle-free pair of respectable jodhpurs for the occasion.

"Now, not to sound condescending towards you, but just let me do the talking once we're inside the courthouse. I think I've got this under some control, and we don't want to give them any ammunition for a delay or a doubt."

"I concur," Marigold replied, far more taken by his previous day's dizzying séance in the chasm of communions than by this upcoming round of legal protocols.

In any case, he harbored his own agenda. Corpuscles blind, blisters bedazzled, rashes raking in the profit of untold perplexities: his was without doubt the most ambitious fever in all of human foolishness. His capital outlays exceeded his wildest modesty, his monkhood ravished by the turn of events: 80,000 people and 2,500 government agencies in Santa Fe to overturn. He worked over his fantasy to patent in mind the one thing worth living for, as he saw it: an impromptu, radical paradise parading the delicate dragonfly teleology beyond all meat- and cheese-eating, unruly masses and the mayhem of *Homo sapiens*. Mr Marigold had become, in other words, his own man.

CHAPTER 28
The Case of *Marigold v. New Mexico*

THE NEW MEXICO Supreme Court overlooks the attenuated remnants of the Santa Fe River. An unprepossessing sign, the only one, graces the Appeals side of the building—"No Skateboarding".

"Still something of a Mecca for the kids," one of two guards at the front entrance commented when Hidalgo made mention of it. But the lawyer had moved on, and he and Marigold strode briskly towards the judge's chambers at 9.15 sharp.

The judge, 53-year-old James Bradford, sat easily in his dark pine-regaled quarters. He wore no robe, but a colorful sweater, and fiddled with a Mont Blanc pen. He had before him documents bearing the stamp of the state of New Mexico and the seal of various testimonies and procedural witnesses. Two other men, the city attorney and his deputy, both known to Hidalgo, and an officious stenographer, were also present. All three had their laptop computers (two PCs, one Mac) open and purring. The judge feigned disinterest, though was vaguely alert to a radio down the hall that carried the latest scores of the Broncos, but the attorneys seemed anxious, observed Mr Marigold, who took this all in with the appropriate spirit of Christmas, multiplied by a thirst, embroidered with something approaching vengeance—financial vengeance oriented to recompensating the world. He must have given off a glow. Though it could easily have been perceived by the judge as sheer annoyance. Each member of the table had a different weight hanging over him, or her, but Marigold alone had the true scent of liberation—potent fumes of global justice—goading him on.

"Have a seat, gentlemen," Bradford offered. "You know Gerald Hemmings, our DA, and his deputy John Michaels. And that's Lisa Ringling, no relation to the circus, who'll be taking notes, strictly off the record."

Hidalgo had already endured weeks of strained communications with the district attorney, a 46-year-old Republican of ranching stock, top of his class at the University of Albuquerque Law School. He knew the DA's reputation, and had heard the brunt of his riot act: the case was frivolous and a waste of taxpayers' money. It could go nowhere. It defied reason. It was groundless. Hidalgo also knew things the DA did not know. Plentiful revelations. But he was saving them. All in due course.

Hemmings wore local designer jeans and a True Grit flannel jacket over a sleek, collarless russet shirt, marked by a polished bolo, an overwrought silver Santa Fe-style belt and expensive Luchese boots. "You must be the troublesome Mr Marigold," he concluded with a calculating grin consistent with his rumored tough-nut-to-crack routine. The Marlboro Man pretending to be from Yale.

"That I am," the Commander said with no other salutation. (He was never one to pause with the scissors before the rose. This was a trait that forever mystified Hidalgo. "Why must you feed so many loaves of bread to the birds?" he would ask. Marigold always had an original reply, garnered from the latest science journals. He might expatiate on tool use ("hooks") among New Caledonian crows. Or some analysis of the Bemba of Zambia, who know no such thing as counting, accumulation, first, middle or last numbers, or money. At other times he waxed on the evolutionary advantages of promiscuity in primates and avians.)

"Some coffee, anyone?" Bradford allowed. Then they got down to business.

"I'm holding your statement of facts as you have declared them," began Bradford, "and I must interject this court's scepticism. I don't know of a similar case that's ever come before this jurisdiction. It begs incredulity, somewhere between a confederacy and absurdity. We will keep an open mind, but you have already gone far to close it down. We've all got copies and I'd like us to read through the pleading together. I'll make my comments as we go."

"Fine," Hidalgo said, fuming.

"Here it is, then." The judge moved forward with his recitation, part redneck, rigged legislature and part Republican selfishness—or these were the airs and sentiments the Commander read into his haughtiness.

"New Mexico versus Murillo Marigold, regarding the alleged Santa Marigold Grant, or debt repayment (such language to be deliberated), submitted to this court January 12th, 1999. The petition alleges the bestowing of a land grant by Governor Manuel Armijo on Christmas Eve 1846 to your ancestor, Alonzo De Resista Marigold—was he from Spain?"

Hidalgo started, only to be interceded by his client, a trend that did not bode well for the comportion of silence he had tried to inculcate in Marigold.

"Spain, via Paris, Russia, Persia and the Far East—" the Commander began. "He was a surveyor and explorer for hire by governments and companies."

"De Resista. Sounds like a Communist. Or guerrilla."

"Possibly."

"A liberal before his time," Hidalgo burrowed in, regaining the high ground. "A man concerned with the poor, with minorities, with civil rights, long before there was a current for such generosity in this or any country."

"Well," the judge went on, "I'm sure he was a colorful fellow. And I gather he was your great-great-great-grandfather—do I have that about right?"

"That is correct," Hidalgo declared, with an accompanying nod of confirmation from the Commander.

"A certain tract of land known as Santa Marigold, said grant being a good and valid one. That the grantee entered upon and took possession of the same, and that he continued to dwell on the estate up to and after the ratification of the *Treaty of December 30, 1853*, between the governments of Mexico and the United States, by the terms of which treaty territory, including the Santa Marigold grant, was transferred to the sovereignty of the United States. Your petition then alleges that in the year 1846, the certificates and deeds of title that had been recorded in Santa Fe were destroyed by the US occupying forces."

Hidalgo intervened at that moment: "We've got some additional records in our possession, your Honor, that will substantiate those lost documents."

"Like what?" DA Hemmings inquired.

"I'd like to get through the pleading, first," Judge Bradford said.

All agreed, although Hidalgo had more to add.

"Also, your Honor, there were numerous heirs who inhabited the estate over successive decades and generations. In 1846 the Marigolds constituted a large family."

"Noted," the judge said. "Now, evidently proceedings had been taken on March 12, 1854, for the purpose of corroborating proof of ownership and clear title on the basis of some judicial re-establishment of boundaries and distinguishing characteristics of the grant. The direct beneficiary was given formal possession of the same by the end of that month, 1854."

"That is correct," Hidalgo confirmed.

"A certified record of these proceedings was alleged to be on file in the office of the US Surveyor General for the Territory of New Mexico, a duplicate copy of the same in the Spanish language. It is further stated that the surveyor held that in the absence of any sufficient attack upon the record or of any evidence on the part of the government to disprove or discredit the statements contained therein, that such forms were sufficient basis for the finding of the court that there was a grant as declared, and that such grant and the record thereof in the archives had been destroyed under the circumstances mentioned. Moreover, you state that in certain previous cases of precedent, including *The United States versus Sutter*, *The United States versus Castro*, and *Peralta versus The United States*, that the courts were of opinion that the evidence of possession was sufficient, in connection with the other evidence referred to, upon which to base a presumption that the petitioners had a title to the land which should be confirmed, within the treaty of 1853 and the provisions of the *Act of 1891*, which established as you know the *Court of Private Land Claims*. The judgment, in your honest and best opinion, should therefore be affirmed. Does that about sum it up?"

"In brief, yes, I believe so, your Honor," Hidalgo replied. "These circumstances were, in essence, a telling precursor—by a century and a half—of the Hegstead."

The Commander, meantime, was falling asleep, bored out of his bunkers and intoning the first telltale snorts. This was no dragonfly prince fanning its melodious wings; no Spenserian sonnet or Ovidian love ode. But ghastly legalese, which exerted an almost instantaneous nervous reaction in him. Hidalgo kicked him under the table, and he awoke with a start.

"Mr Marigold?" The judge had noticed his quizzical expression.

"If you meant to say that my ancestors were given a chunk of land that was rightfully theirs, yes."

"Sir, your own lawyer wrote the brief, not me. I presume you've discussed it with him."

"My client has carefully studied the broad strokes, your Honor. But he is a poet, not a lawyer."

"That's fine."

"Now here's the deal, guys," Gerald Hemmings began. 'We see other retroactive cases in the state all the time. None this large, never this large, except in Alaska, Maine and Canada. But there has never been a successful case brought against the New Mexico State Government that comes anywhere close to this. I'm being frank here. In the old days, adjudication was politically motivated by the government council—they called it the *ayuntamiento*. They doled out grazing rights on stubble according to a commons law that was transparent. Laws were not laws as such, but personal expedients. The governors were wending their way through minefields of competing interests, none of which are legally binding today. Even back then there were community standards that determined the use and ownership of land. You might think you owned it, but there were other interests—Indians, previous Spanish land grants to whole communities, gaps in title claims because of an absence of probate or reliable information pertaining to heirs, water rights that could not be subverted by private ownership. On an acre, no problem. There you can build clear definition. But this—1.2 million acres? Why, you're talking about damn near all of Santa Fe County. Frankly, Jim—" here the DA spoke directly to the judge—"the whole thing is outlandish. I thought so from the beginning, and now that I've had the opportunity to review its particulars, I'm even more convinced today."

But Hidalgo was ready to pounce. "Think again, Gerry!" he said. And he withdrew from his magical briefcase a formidable bundle of documents floating in a sea of heavy oxygen.

Hemmings examined the top papers. Marigold noticed a brimming consternation. "Your Honor, we've never seen these," Hemmings declared, angered. "But I faxed them to your office yesterday. Was your secretary out sick?" Hidalgo lied. He had no intention of allowing an inhospitable disposition time to manufacture a refutation.

He then laid out the series of strange events, all corroborated according to tangible evidence that indicated an exchange of land encompassing hundreds of square miles. The nature of the bequest was complicated because a governor's aide and his confidante—a woman some claimed to be his mistress—were involved, as well as a stranger who had left no trace other than a single night of gambling that was widely attested to.

Mr Marigold had supplied Hidalgo with a crate of letters made fibrous by the activities of several generations of brown recluses in the attic. A real crate, of early nineteenth-century Mexican origins, with rusted latches and colorful roses painted on the cedarwood, more or less unopened. In addition to the formidable slew of evidence already gathered by Hidalgo, it contained a rich medley of data upon which to build the claim of ownership. A tapestry of land grant records, gambling debts and first-hand accounts that, today, would be the equivalent of property abstractions.

Hidalgo had then compared those notes with modern legal texts, filling in the voids. He had conferred with the proceedings before the Court of Private Land Claims by a thorough study of BLM (Bureau of Land Management) documents at the Thomas Benton Catron Collection in the Coronado Room of Zimmerman Library at the University of New Mexico in Albuquerque. That record just happened to contain the papers of the attorney for Marigold's great-great-great-grandfather. The validity of conveyances was checked genealogically. That was the original basis upon which he'd first filed a declaratory action seeking a judgment granting validity to the estate. This, in turn, had triggered a case number in the Santa Fe District Court, and a subsequent preliminary hearing date, of present consequences.

But the pleading being read aloud this day was only the beginning. For Hidalgo was a good lawyer and he intended to win: to win his own glorious future and that of his children and their children—two new luxury vehicles, a second home in Aspen, a lavish apartment in Paris; to secure, by way of his legal fees, a bonus of cash beyond the dreams of his parents and their parents, and a portion of land outside the realm of normal imaginings. It was a case that his old friend, Mr Marigold's father, had often spoken of sadly, like a man in rehab trying against the impossible odds of his own doomed physiology to rebuild his life or find a missing daughter. Such retroactive claims, he had assumed, were simply not possible in this day and age—the idea of a fantastic windfall. Out of kilter with modernity, rueful and winsomely lost because of so much intervening time, Pecos had assumed, and the sheer inertia of excavating the particulars, let alone fighting it in a court of law. Hidalgo, however, had a different take on all this.

Pecos Marigold was smart enough to understand how difficult it would be to prove such a case. He was a surveyor, after all; and he knew that surveyors were never taken on authority, that their numbers were subject to bias and therefore unreliable in any courtroom action. That meant other expert testimony would be required—but from whom? Dead souls? Epitaphs? He'd left it alone. He was comfortable, and his son would not suffer. The rest was a repository of ghosts, better undisturbed in their spider-infested attic.

Had Mr Marigold himself not mentioned the subject years before by way of a poetic *what if?* Hidalgo might never have put two and two together. But, reaching a ripe old age, he had no other obligations, no excitement to look forward to, and this Santa Marigold Grant had come like a rare blow upside: a deliverance in the form of unimaginable wealth. If only he could keep the facts straight and make the case. Moreover, he had what few claims in the history of New Mexico had: a signature by a Governor on one of the letters, the handwriting quite legible and authentic, with a second signature by a witness of eminent standing, and this augmented by the published record of numerous eyewitnesses, as well as the reputable calculations of a Deputy Surveyor General, and a letter from the Secretary of the Interior in Washington.

And so with that seemingly irrefutable weight of leading evidence, he had sought to defy expectations, taking no heed of advice from fellow lawyers who made ribs of his proposition, who viewed him as delusional, his theory preposterous. While they were writing him off, he and a young Spanish-speaking pre-law research assistant at St John's College pored through the extensive archives of New Mexican land rights, whose history had been more fully documented than any in the United States (with the possible exceptions of Boston and Manhattan). This obsession with details was not only the result of that fascination with a past which is, after all, rather briefly laid to rest, but also the product of a considerable bevy of retroactive suits, like those filed by Indian tribes throughout North America—injunctions seeking to retrieve sacred grounds, graveyards and whole territories deeded, then retracted, by the US Government. Most of New Mexico was contested in one way or other. For all its bedrock, the state floated upon cultural differences laced with interruption, conflict, obscurantism—a medley of contested layers that would never cede a way of life or grant real title to ingenues. So that the tenuous peace was only that which had been enforced by larger powers in the rough-riding shape of cavalries and distant Presidents. It was no more solid than the geology of the state—was, in short, a history of upheavals.

And so tenuous, in fact, that one sliver of land—three sections worth—had slipped through the cracks of political history. As late as the mid-1930s, those acres were not part of the United States but of Spain.

Ownership of land, of water, of trees and air was the most difficult of concepts: the pride of the white man, who killed for the glory of possessing so many clods of dirt, whilst previous tenants might well have overlooked any personal attachment for the longer-lasting security of a loosely described spiritual affiliation, today known as tribal trusts. Indians passed down water, agricultural and grazing rights to individual families, but the lands themselves were held in trust by the whole communities.

Indians lived there forever, and they worshipped the dragonfly. Spanish, Mexicans, the Confederacy and then Union Americans had no dragonflies in their vocabularies. The gulf was paramount.

In the thick of these warring discrepancies, there were odd tangential lineages, families and personalities conjuring a way of life that was stamped by all sides, tempered by leniency, favoring victory for one and all, without bias, and the Marigolds were certainly among them. Alonzo probably was a Communist, or commutarian. He gave equal importance to all people and never once thought less of a man because he was red, or black, or white, or some colorful combination thereof.

Abetted by precedent, Hidalgo had reviewed all abstracts, and probed deeply into the Marigolds' neighbors a century before in order to expose any quiet title or unextinguished interests. He had spent months in pursuit, beginning with a detailed analysis of *Private Land Claims in New Mexico*, a four-volume tome issued by the Government Printing Office in Washington DC between 1856 and 1891. And that was merely a prelude to a more finely honed search that began with the first appearance of the Marigold name.

It had emerged, possibly, with the founding of the city itself. The ambiguity was a question of spellings and distant ties—ancestral relations whose true identity could only be faintly fathomed. But now, Hidalgo had gone beyond guesswork, lighting a match to a great experiment of incendiaries.

CHAPTER 29
The Prehistory of a Card Game

THE PHRASE *Mare Goledo* first surfaced on a topographical map describing certain discoveries in the Southwest, particularly a new species of *Zizyphus nymphaea rhamnaceae*, otherwise known as lotos, found floating in diaphanous green colonies across the legendary Silly Sea, an inland body of epieric water once stretching across much of the Great Basin from Molly's Green to Porter's Wood. Spanish explorers in the commission of Don Pámfilo Narvaez set sail (just in time) in 1529 on one such breathing blob, the size of a 50-gun galleon, and remarked upon such passing creatures and look-alike landmarks (the "hypogryphus" and a rare highland manure of no sure origins, the size of a temple edifice) as are no more.

By 1531, the Silly Sea had all but evaporated, leaving vast salt flats populated by a now-extinct silly shrimp that whistled tunes whenever it was breezy and fed upon algae in the sunlight. These shrimp, in turn, were lunch to the last 30 pupfish, whose meat, sadly, proved refreshing to Alvar Nuñez Cabez de Vaca and three other survivors known to history for their agonizing march, naked, across the savage continent.

They reached New Galacia in 1538. But it is also alleged that there was a fourth fellow among them, a stalwart lad who endured the same shipwreck and pan-continental travails, but refused embarkation back to Spain, and in the end remained behind with his various Indian friends. His name—Marigold—as bright as the archives will permit, vanishes, as other early explorers jockey for the same distinction, whatever it is or was: Juan de la Asunción and Marcos de Niza, Francisco Vásquez Coronado, Friar Augustín Ruiz, Castaño de Soa.

Yet, by 1550, when the first temporary camp was established in the area of today's Santa Fe, a proliferation of Marigolds could be deciphered among the marsh reeds and dusty records. Hidalgo had done so. By the time of Juan de Oñate's official christening of the town site in 1608 on the Santa Fe River (after he'd established an earlier capital at San Gabriel near the meeting of the Río Chama and the Río Grande in the county of Río Arriba), there was a small community, and the boy, no longer among the living, had left a son, also a Marigold, who was present in 1610 at the construction of a plaza under the aegis of the first Governor of the Territory, Pedro de Peralta, appointed to the task by the Spanish Viceroy in Mexico. His age or circumstances are unknown, his duties and employers like shades in the remains of an uneventful summer. Though a poem on the eve of obscurity, a Marigold was indeed present—Hidalgo had the evidence. He was there, fixing meridians, establishing boundaries, overseeing mulecarts, crawling around on his hands and knees with a hammer and nails. Letters attested to the fact. Just 45 years after the founding of Saint Augustine, Florida, the first Spanish city in North America, and ten years before pilgrims landed at New England, a Marigold was living in the town of Santa Fe, according to three separate artifacts, handwritten, from the period.

The town itself meant "holy faith", a suitable designation, thought de Peralta, who based it upon the namesake of Santa Fe de Granada, in Spain, which Ferdinand and Isabella had designed like a Roman garrison.

The idea was to fashion an impenetrable fortress of a city, orderly and mathematical, elegant and airy, futuristic and efficient. It worked in Granada; it would work in New Mexico. Human nature is architectural, and northern New Mexico fostered just the sort of crannies in which people were born anew, sojourned in contemplation, struck up a sloe pungent living color amid the inhospitable barrens of the desert high-altitudes. Individuals who would sooner wander down winding alleyways drinking whiskey or inventing rhyme than standing at attention.

The architects tried (successfully) to force a main plaza into a large rectangular space on the north bank of the Santa Fe River. It would be dominated, of course, by a complex known as the Casa Real or Palace of the Governors. To the west was the town hall and jail, with a whipping post. There, too, would grow up many important family residences with their typically Spanish approach to inner courtyards. And for the exclusive use of these wealthy minions, the town's first church, the San Miguel Mission.

The Palace of the Governors was the plenipoteniary center for not just the area of New Mexico but a region extending from the Mississippi River to San Francisco—a hegemony more territorially expansive than most European nation states. Hence, a forerunner of the White House—the Adobe House—where the inner administrative stakes of power, prestige, secrecy, and corruption were lodged, all within the highly fortified complex of offices, secret passageways and residences. In fact, no equivalent structure exerted so much power anywhere in the world, whether Moscow, Peking, Edo, or Paris. Only rural London's Windsor, and the Ducal Palace of early sixteenth-century Venice offer appropriate analogies. Not unlike those corrupting counterparts, during the course of two centuries—from the period of the 1680s to the late nineteenth century—the Palace of the Governors was fraught with untidy truths, constant shifts of treachery and more than a few massacres. Political intrigue pervaded those inner corridors of baked earth. Temptations of one kind or other, and the exigencies of self-preservation, catapulted the times, at the hands of more than 100 successive Governors and Captains-General in charge.

The lures and distractions of power were heralded just adjacent to the Plaza where compulsions were easily fulfilled in the surrounding maze of congested fandangos, brothels, pleasure halls and other notorious hell-raising establishments, particularly the casinos where card games—and the gamestresses who waited in line for the winning sharks—had become the rage of the Southwest.

Travelers had heard of Santa Fe's free women and gambling halls and they would attempt the journey in droves. They arrived from Mexico along the Río Grande. From the east, for most of the nineteenth century, the Santa Fe Trail provided the key link to the rest of North America.

The route came in along what is today Highway 85. When 25-year-old Mary Donoho (the first woman from America) arrived in Santa Fe from Independence in 1833, accompanied by her husband William, a nine-month-old daughter and 150 other Missouri folk, she had journeyed by wagon train, stopping each night at all of the trail's major depots— Diamond Spring, Fort Zarah, Pawnee Rock, Fort Dodge, Cimarron, and so forth. The city extended its welcome to the earliest trappers and explorers by arresting them, briefly. Terms of release were generous ones, contingent upon the size of the traveler's purse.

Land was cheap, but ownership never guaranteed (a point the DA drove home time and again, despite Hidalgo's comprehensive assertions to the contrary). New Mexico under Spanish and Mexican control was divided into sections, Hidalgo argued; they were known as *partidos*, ruled over by prefects. Each *partido* was subdivided into *alcaldías*, administered by the *alcaldía* mayor or *alcaldes* (councils). These procedural definitions adhered until 1852, when New Mexico became a United States territory. But prior to that time, much of Marigold's relevant history had been singled out by conjoining, disparate, unexpected forces and individuals whose measures and choices would shape the present claim.

Hidalgo had scrutinized as many early images as possible in an effort to fix the perimeters of the property in question. The task was simplified on account of the sheer limitations in population density. In 1780, for example, the town's total human count was 2,000. By 1860 it had grown to no more than 4,635—57 percent of Santa Fe County at the time. He had studied Negative #21149 from the Museum of New Mexico, an image of Santa Fe in 1847 in which there were fewer than 60 dwellings, including Fort Marcy on the hill overlooking town. The sum total of four trees, three of them mountain cottonwoods, could be discerned. The number of homes was at odds with the demographics. The discrepancy could not be accounted for by large family sizes alone. Something in the record was ajar. The houses, as cited by contemporary historian Marian Meyer who chronicled some of the earliest observations of Santa Fe, were described as "heaps of unburnt bricks"[1]. Other visitors remarked upon the town's "dazzling whiteness", and the "animals (that) seemed to participate in the humor of their riders". A chaos of goats, pigs, burros and horse-drawn *carretas* crowded the central plaza, upon whose northeast corner the Mexican flag was draped atop a flagstaff. A single cannon of small caliber guarded each entrance, according to Francisco Perea, an emigré from Bernalillo writing in his memoirs of 1837[2] Perea went on to write,

"The square was then a dirty, unsightly place almost to a degree unbelievable ... and the people seemed to be satisfied with these conditions. Opposite the Palace stood the military church, called La Castrense, then the handsomest building of its kind in the capital city ... Don Manuel Chaves, father of Amado Chaves, Esq., built and owned the finest dwelling house in Santa Fe. This structure was built four-square enclosing a court, and was finished with portals all around outside, and also on the insides bordering the court ... There were no gable roofs in the entire capital at that time and the residences were scattered over a large area, with more or less ground enclosed with adobe walls, in which were gardens, orchards, corrals, and stables."[3] Hidalgo explained to Bradford and Hemmings: "I exhibit this lengthy citation, Gentlemen, to remind you of the exactitude of eyewitness accounts from that time. According to Meyer, the town teemed with brick-kilns, cornfields and incessant camp fires. There was little by way of architectural adornment to relieve the monotony of crude adobe. Note this evidence—" which he produced on the table before them—"from the US Signal Corps Collection, part of the Museum of New Mexico, Negative #l 1330, of San Francisco Street, *circa* 1850, looking over the barren row of adobe houses and shops towards the old Parroquia, where the St Francis Cathedral stands today. Or of this 1855 image, Negative #l0685, of the Exchange Hotel, known previously as Fonda, and subsequently the US Hotel, when Kearny came into town in 1846. These glimpses of the past yield a sullen-looking vantage."

It was not all dust and darkness. Hidalgo went on to describe how most of Santa Fe's enthralment figured indoors, or behind streetside escarpments, where each brick or adobe floor was covered in luxuriant fabric, carpets woven thick enough to hold water, just as if they'd been jugs, elegant earthen vessels scattered like Grecian nudes across dirt courtyards that sprang perpetually to life with a multitude of children who were, by one description of a resident woman, marvelous beings, quick, inquisitive and displaying a general politeness that " 'twould put many a mother in the U.S. to the blush".[4]

"The point of this history lesson?" Hemmings asked.

"I am leading, by turns, to a single establishment in Santa Fe at that time: the casino, site of the infamous card game in question. But it is important to establish the basis for land claims in those days, a context that cannot be imagined if one is in any way, shape or form comparing it with the Santa Fe of today, but which, conversely, must argue additionally for a narrow and circumspectual appreciation of the facts."

He went on to elicit other images of the period, in which there was little to distinguish the finest from the most ordinary dwelling (other than those properties owned by Señor Vicar and the Parish Church on the Calle Principal de la Ciudad, site of today's St Francis Cathedral). But what was more clear were the undeveloped surroundings, and these were the very hills and stretches that would become the property of Marigold.

The acquisition occurred at the height of provincial Governor Manuel Armijo's fame, in the middle of his term in 1846. He had been Governor twice before—in 1827 for two years, and again in 1837. Ranked beside his colleagues, such as Melgares, Chavez or Vizcarra, he stood out in Hidalgo's mind as a man who championed consensus-building at a time of revolution and multicultural mayhem. He was generous and fair-minded, and as given to rational governance as he was a good time. Such aspects of his character, Hidalgo believed, would prove crucial to any interpretation of the Governor's losing streak at the monte table, and the fact of his willingness to sign off on his debt.

In this historical vein, one teeming with verifiable details, Hidalgo continued his assault, laying out the particulars, the antecedents, and the between-the-lines. His staff had gone exhaustively through each and every source, he stressed, from Daniel Tyler's authoritative summary of such reference points detailing New Mexican history during the early half of the nineteenth century.[5]

"I hope to convey some appreciation for the depth of research my office has conducted on behalf of the Marigold estate."

"You're not writing a dissertation; or delivering some doctorate oral examine," the judge declared. "Rather an outlandish hold-up."

"I know you think it's frivolous—that was the word you used, Gerry, when I first informed you of our suit. But perhaps you'll begin to think differently after today. Just consider some of the more intriguing corroborations, in one form or other."

"What do you consider corroborative?" Bradford asked.

"Your Honor, by that I mean any document that lends appropriate credence or essential context to the said Santa Marigold Grant. Now this is where I've been—bear with me, because there is not a single citation from the following list that does not in some way shed important light on this case."

He listed the following: Josiah Gregg's two-volume *Commerce of the Prairies*, the full title of which was *The Journal of a Santa Fe Trader, During Eight Expeditions Across the Great Western Prairies, and a Residence of Nearly Nine Years in Northern Mexico*, published in New York in 1844; a study of the land grants and conveyancy files at the New Mexico State Records Center and Archives; all available papers belonging to other historic estates, such as the Archuleta, Bergère, Delgado, Cordova and Borrego-Ortego families; the *hijuelas* (estate inventories) of the Peralta family; and various livestock purchase documents, promissory notes, orders for account audits, and sheep payments.

"Why sheep?" inquired Hemmings, annoyed and intimidated by his opponent's due diligence.

"It will be seen, your Honor, that sheep and other animals—several thousand, in fact—were owned by the Marigolds, and they wandered on some of the property. I've gone so far, you'll be pleased to know, as to have brought in a paleobiologist."

"What the hell for? And what is a paleobiologist, anyway?"

"An expert on fossilized feces of sheep. These people are organic chemists and they do a test and can tell you what animals inhabited a precise region, and in what numbers. Well, we've got several thousand sheep on one part of the property as of 1855."

Hemmings shook his head in wonder. Hidalgo's was, he supposed, a grasping, sick mind.

As for Mr Marigold, he'd had no idea of the extent of Hidalgo's investigations and was duly impressed.

"That's not all," Hidalgo continued, on a rise. "We've examined every record of river and smaller acequia disputes, last wills and testaments, land petitions, registrations, contract awards, assassination reports, divisions of property, and pay and promotion communications from Mexican authorities."

Hidalgo noted that Bradford was both curious and exasperated. He knew how to play the judge, at least to the extent of fixing on his subtle gestures and speaking only when offered a cue. Judges did not like to hear from lawyers, as a rule, which is why "No, your Honor" or "Yes, your Honor" tended to summarize the extent of discussion. But there were moments, rare and unpredictable, when it appeared that the judge had done his homework, or at least appreciated a lawyer who did, which was the present situation.

"Your Honor, we're speaking of a provincial Governor from Mexico, whose lieutenant has screwed up. It looks bad for him. A gambling debt, a mistress and the US cavalry bearing down. The territory is about to be lost, and his ass is personally on the line. What would you do? What would you say? Would you cover it up with a bribe, tell the truth, or simply pay the debt, knowing the US Government would never honor it to begin with? Of course, as we will show, the incoming government *did* honor it."

"There is no proof of such a debt," Hemmings said angrily. "There is, Gerry. In due course."

Hidalgo could see his rival, a bully who had been a high school wrestling champion, beginning to squirm. He knew he'd have to manipulate the melodrama. An enormous amount was at stake. While he had become something of an expert on these matters, he would be the first to admit the state's sovereign power when it came to writing new laws or whimsically repealing old ones. A special legislative session might well be called before this case came to fruition. That assemblage would determine any and all compensation. Gerald Hemmings would be in that State House to sway the legislators. Hidalgo would have only limited time before the congressmen, enough time to speak in broad strokes and indelicate highlights. The amount of land involved was beyond most men's ken; it would strike as greed, or madness, when translated into today's dollars. That was the thorny part of all this: the valuation business. It wasn't as if pregnant women had miscarried, or tobacco smokers perished. But he wasn't there, yet. He was still working out the intimidation phase of his brief.

"We've gone through all public record of permissions from the Superintendent of Indian Affairs, naturalization papers, business correspondence, militia commissions, material pertaining to a smallpox epidemic—Alonzo had a daughter who died of it—and the proceedings of the *ayuntamiento* of Santa Fe over a 50-year period.

"Even the Diligencias Matrimoniales, the prenuptial investigations by the great historian Fray Angelico Chavez, provided valuable insights regarding the appropriate pathways of legal inquiry," Hidalgo plowed on methodically.

He described how he and his "team of researchers" (a slight exaggeration) had culled various land deeds and receipts for funeral expenses, *partido* contracts, an appeal to the Governor pertaining to 59 prisoners condemned to death or awaiting sentence that bore directly on the soundness of mind of the Governor in question and his executable authority, material regarding Indian depredations, recognition of Manuel Alvarez as US Consul, peculiarities of certain land squabbles, citizens' complaints over the changing definitions of community property, and James W. Magoffin's and Secretary of War W.L. Marcy's itemized expenses from the "bloodless conquest" of New Mexico.

He had investigated old notices of extended powers-of-attorney and the expulsion of certain priests, dozens of county registers in which were conveyed most *escritura de venta* (bills of sales), vital statistics, clarifications of boundaries and laws, decrees outlining voting districts, handwritten documents pertaining to expeditions among the Comanches, archives of the Archdiocese of Santa Fe (on 90 reels of film), all the Twitchell Numbers, census records, *Archivo Militar*, the Ritch Collection papers, the Villa de Santa Cruz de la Canada Archives, the Libro de Visita Pastoral of Bishop Zubiria's 1833 visitation to the territory, the remarkable handwritten family records of Mrs Andrea S. Abeyta concerning family lineage and home customs, and the Ruth Garcia, James Josiah Webb, Alvarez-Vigil and *Río Arriba County Deed Book* records. In addition, Hidalgo had personally skimmed through the 240 volumes of the *Historical Records Survey of New Mexico* prepared between 1938 and 1941, various broadsides by such individuals as Donaciano Vigil from January 25th, 1847, countless corporation decrees and *testimonios*, the illuminating William Albert Bork *Muevos Aspectos del Comercio entre Nuevo Mexico y Misuri* from 1822 to 1846, and the 66 reels of Diaz's *Guide to the Microfilm of Papers Relating to New Mexico Land Grants.*

Most of this, said Hidalgo, could be seen in summary form in Malcolm Ebright's *Landgrants & Lawsuits In Northern New Mexico*, published by the University of New Mexico Press in 1994. He brought a copy of the book for the judge, and one for the DA.

He had visited county courthouses to look at the precise deeds, inventories of church properties, baptismal entries, genealogy charts and dispensation notes in order to establish the precise times and arrangements that resulted in the spread of the city of Santa Fe upon Marigold property. This would prove crucial in understanding the dimensions of the case and its significance in the context of recent American legal history. That was the mental framework in which Hidalgo was working: legal history. The Santa Marigold estate now covered and enjoyed most of Santa Fe city proper, and that would cause problems never before encountered in a legal claim for which due compensation would, in turn, take on new levels of reappropriation criteria.

As Hidalgo spoke, the stenographer recorded details, and both lawyers took their own notes. The judge, increasingly hot-headed, just listened. He had pressures hanging over him.

Meanwhile, Mr Marigold mused on the ineluctable advent of Sannazaro's arcadia right there in Santa Fe. As Hidalgo enumerated the daunting array of pieces, the puzzle began to fit together. He'd heard some, not all, of the names and dates; grown up with an inbred acquaintance. But laid out like this, the sum total was frightening. He had not counted on his ancestry being so dense with ties, was not accustomed to this degree of socializing and speechifying, even in theory. Had his family actually lived among such complex entanglements, involving so many people, ties, money? It was wearying just to ponder the fact of such history. To be part of it was downright debilitating.

His mind wandered back to the lost valley, and the people of the dragonfly.

Hidalgo continued: "In 1846 Santa Fe was surrounded by enormous land grants from the Spanish—the Jacona, Ramon Vigil, Las Vegas, Embudo, Cundiyo, the Villa de Santa Cruz, and others. You know them all. Their names are with us still, in every case. We've all grown up with an appreciation for the cultural geography they imply. I intend to prove beyond a shadow of doubt that Santa Marigold ranks supreme among them.

"As for the city itself, history has left a colorful picture, some details of which I have already referred to. But there was nothing more colorful than the mysterious woman from Spain—from the Marigolds' home town in Spain—who landed in New York, made her way to Taos, and then Tome, where she was married. Two years before Alonzo Marigold was to receive the 1.2 million-acre grant, she came to Santa Fe, which was already garrisoned by the US military forces stationed there.

"I have in my possession a handwritten letter of 1846 from the Governor describing the peculiar situation that has brought us all here, and which can be summarized in a word: debt, a certain debt incurred by a first lieutenant at a certain gambling hall in Santa Fe. This is the same document upon which the US Congress later deliberated. A letter which it honored, from a sense of both justice and embarrassment, and in recognition of the powers that had prevailed while New Mexico was still under Mexican rule."

"But who is this mysterious woman? A relative? What is her relationship to the case?" the judge asked.

"Yes, who?" Marigold pressed.

"In due course, a new page in history," Hidalgo replied.

CHAPTER 30
A Beauteous Spanish Gypsy

THEY CALLED HER Señora Dona Maria Gertrudis Barceló," Hidalgo began, "and she hailed from the Malaga coast of Spain, a region I have never visited but one, I'm told, that fosters a blithe disposition, as my client's own people, who similarly emerged from there, adamantly demonstrate. Her lineage could be traced to North Africa, possibly Mauritania, to Saharan tribals who'd spent millennia around campfires under wide, open starry nights. We can only imagine these scenes, and speculate on their importance to the night in question, Christmas Eve, 1846."

So he plowed forward, describing how her ancestors had probably converged into ever-narrowing circles of habitable life, eking out their subsistence in the margins with other nomads of their kind, eventually drifting north towards the sea. How all of this arcana happened to be officially entered into the juridical ears of the Santa Fe courthouse remains a question for debate, but can safely be said to have exasperated its listeners.

"These tribals," Hidalgo continued, "were eventually driven across the Mediterranean, making waves from Algier or Tunisia, to the coast of Spain. Maria's people most likely signed on to Catholicism as an expedient to get through the Inquisition, and re-settled in a lovely palm-laden grove along a beach near modern Marbella, where they were evidently occupied in the trade of making fishing nets. At a young age Maria, the eleventh of 12 offsprings, traveled along the coast to Barcelona with a band of gypsies some time around 1819.

"Of course, it wasn't called Barcelona at that time. The region, Catalonia, was dominated by Mount Tibidabo, the Panades and Valles depressions, the Llobregat and Besos river plains, and the ancient amphitheater of Montjuich, where the Romans were once fortified. Roman tradition also left its flavor in the Barcino on Monte Taber. Today there stands a cathedral and relics to the patron saint Eulalia."

"Francis, none of this bears on why we're all here, and my time—I don't know about yours—is precious," the DA declared.

"It is all material context, your Honor. Señora Dona Maria's background is important to our case. There is not much more known, so if you will permit me."

"Proceed, but please, try to hone in on what is essential," the judge allowed.

Hidalgo went forward: "Here on the one hand, King Ferdinand. On the other, Napoleon, who decides to invade Spain. Revolts ensue. It gets complicated but the resulting fervor succeeds in liberating those Spaniards in America, with the help of President James Monroe. It actually happened on a given day, December 2nd, 1823. She was a teenager when she first set foot in the luxuriant city."

"Which city?" the judge asked.

"Barcelona, your Honor, with its tropical gardens and rocky hills and oceanic vistas. Her language was an odd patchwork of Ossetic, Greek, Persian, Arabic and Spanish. She was a fortune teller by inclination, which separated her out as one of the gypsies. She was this young wild thing in skirts sleeping on a Romany rug in a cave along the city's ramparts with a smattering of others of her kind—musicians, kettlesmiths, jugglers, circus players, tinkers, ferriers, riveters, comb-, spoon- and furniture-makers—and she somehow came unto a pack of cards. She began her profession on that hillside, passing out cards like the dealer she would become, quickly mastering the seasons of the deck, with its mathematical certainties and mystiques."

"Your Honor," Hemmings agitated. "Must we be subjected to these abstruse, and I dare say, irrelevant ramblings?"

The judge cast a stern eye at Hidalgo. "Francis?"

"I'm getting to the essential point, your Honor. Please bear with me."

"But Judge, this is all supposition. There were no witnesses to attest to this narrative. How do we know it is not one colossal fiction?"

"There is sufficient historical evidence to frame these matters and this personage, Mr Hemmings. We know, for example, that the cards were not yet subject to state monopoly, as later they would be in Spain.

Three *pesetas* bought you a pack. In England, where the cost was a farthing and the tax stamp was imprinted on the ace of spades, a tradition of ornate cards had evolved, and this is what attracted our teenager from Marbella. Those beautiful images, descendants of Tarot, which Cardinal Mazarín had utilized to educate his pupil, Louis XIV. This was Maria's education, as well. But her prowess at the gaming aspects was quickly realized, for there is no reason to doubt that she was the one who managed to purchase with her winnings a one-way passage for her and her mother to New York."

Anyone watching would have seen the Commander off in some other land, dreaming of his princess, luminescent with the vision of a woman who would alter his own destiny. But the judge, the DA, the DA's assistant and stenographer were busy enough wondering where on earth this obscure history was leading, and why. They would have done with it. But they knew enough to remain silent by this time; given Hidalgo's reverence for details he had obviously spent a considerable time unearthing. There was a method here, and the judge was as anxious to know its outcome as the others.

"How the young gypsy from Spain arrived in Taos by 1821, and what wonders she encountered in her expedition west, can only be imagined ... the wind through a Kansas wheat field, that first glimpse of the snow-crested Rocky Mountains—were they clouds or mountains? —And the encounters with American Indians, as yet innocent of the carnage soon to overtake them. It is known that young Maria made the journey without her mother, who died of a plague epidemic in New York. A sister shows up later in her life—Maria probably sent for her once her wealth enabled her to do so.

"In Taos, Maria continued fortune telling. But the town was limited, as it remains so today. She had arrived there, as others before her, having come down through those unrelenting icy slopes. Her first winter in Taos was not easy. She was poor, and her beauty got her into difficult situations.

That loveliness would be much commented upon, and here the record becomes quite concrete, for a European gypsy with long red hair and a complexion like dark, seamless cream was no secret for long. Cowboys lost their hearts to her. Puritans at once suspected her, with her loose ways and bawdy talk. She was, as I indicated, and as the history books reveal, a wild child in the body of awesome fertility: deft with her hands, well schooled in throwing a knife, lassoing a mustang or ascertaining the future in a gullible palm, she was also quick-witted and never at a loss for acid, icy or hilarious ripostes. Think of the Marilyn Monroe of *The Misfits*, though far more sultry, exotic, and—if you will permit an old man his preferences—shapely. She loved men, but not inordinately or out of calculation. And she kept her counsel, a trait that would serve her well at the gambling tables. All this we know.

"She would soon hear about a town a few hundred miles out in the desert, warmer than Taos, less dusty and dangerous. She joined a small pack train from Taos, journeyed five days along El Camino Real, the King's Highway, and one evening rode into the intriguing outskirts of the forested Mexican oasis of Nuestra Señora de la Concepcíon de Tome Dominguez—Tome for short. I'm sure you all know it, or have been there. An ancient Indian Pueblo known as Abbey Santo Tomáshad underlaid the village. Father Madariaga, the town's pastor whose chapel in Valencia had been built back in 1750, looked after the more than 2,000 residents. It was a town much larger than Taos. All of New Mexico did not number more than 42,000 then. Albuquerque, long famed by this time for its apricot groves, after which the city was named, numbered a mere 800 souls.

"As Maria entered Tome, she made out a multitude of clambering figures on a large hillock known as El Cerro de Tome. There, to her amazement, she saw fiery crosses being passed along the boulder-strewn mountain, and she learned that a Semana Santa, or passion play, was in progress. The local artisans, *bultos*, had constructed a life-like, bloody and mangled Christ on the cross, and this was being trundled up the cactus-infested slopes. Throughout the day they had sent soldiers into a garden where Christ had been captured; there was Pontius Pilate reigning from a balcony, Veronica wiping the face of Jesus. Now he hung in effigy on the mountain. Fireworks illuminated the scene beneath a sky of encroaching starlight. Priests and shouting children, braying animals and barking dogs, explosives against the last laces of twilight over the western plateau, and the accompanying onset of an abandoning La Cuna and Italiana, the zealous musical steps danced by the locals, together convinced Maria that she had reached a salubrious destination.

"The next morning, the Passion continued with the transport via *las andas* of La Patrona, also life-like, done in wax. Surrounding her portage was a medley of human and animal forms—sumpter horses, howling mules, whirligigish children, hortatorical hogs, frolicsome lambs and a procession of wagons carrying the women who recited prayers in homage to the Virgin. The whole town of Tome had turned out to celebrate the Immaculate Conception.

"But Maria also noticed a considerable share of single girls with their eyes on the men.

"'Pues este es el Mesias que hoy viene a vos, Caminaba la Virgen Nuestra Señora, que gusto! Que alegria, Pues, alma mia,' went the verses.

"This is the Messiah who comes to you today. Our Lady, the Virgin, was traveling along. What pleasure! What joy, my soul!"

"'El amor y los placeres y las pasiones', her heart must have cried out in unison with the rapturous Tomesenos. 'Love and pleasure and passion.'[6]

"These sensations were escalated a few months later, after she had taken up that trade most suited to her gifts—monte, played everywhere in the western territories of North America—for she had cast her own eyes on a certain gentleman who traveled by the name of Manuel Antonio Sisneros and had shown up one evening to play cards. On June 23rd, 1823, the couple, now titled Don and Dona, were married in the Valencia chapel.

"Nobody knows the exact date when Maria and her husband came to Santa Fe, or what her husband did for a living. But at some point Tome must have seemed too small for her. Santa Fe, which numbered nearly 5,000 people, and was the seat of Mexican governance, was ripe for her pickings."

"Where is all this leading us, Francis? The day is going and your time to make a case is limited. Your choice," the impatient judge cried out. "You will see, your Honor, that I am trying to establish the particulars of this woman's credibility, for she is crucial towards a clear understanding of the debt and her resolution of it."

Bradford conceded just a little more time for the exposition. He had his obligations, and a furious District Attorney to contend with. But he could not deny his own fascination with the tale of the beauteous gypsy, nor Hidalgo's manner of telling it.

"Santa Fe in 1827 was probably the hub of women's rights anywhere on earth," began Hidalgo. "The town was famed, or notorious—depending on whether you were inside or outside of the church—for its single women and *scandalous concubinage*, as some looked upon the practice. There were 450 married couples, but 4,185 single persons. Many have cited the exorbitant fees charged by the priests for performing ceremonies. But it was more than that: the culture fostered matriarchal rights. Women were free, legally and sexually. They took as many lovers as they pleased, could sue for divorce, inherit property, work whatever job they wanted.

They had mobility, income and standing. This was all part and parcel of the Spanish psyche, where women do, in fact, reign. A child born out of wedlock was considered normal—indeed, almost obligatory—in Santa Fe. Female chastity was not an issue and illegitimate children were multitudinous. Extended families were defined by an affable chaos of bastards, servants, half-breeds, guests of unknown origins, stepchildren, friends, and orphans from every territory.

"Anglo-Saxon law would try to change all that, ending female independence, prohibiting a woman from signing a contract, even with her husband's consent. A wife, once the US forces came into Santa Fe, had no rights. A woman was to become property. It would be another 80 years, as we all know, before Susan B. Anthony and her colleagues got through to the American public, and to Congress, pressuring an Amendment to the Constitution that granted women certain rights—though even the Constitution, and the much debated Equal Rights Amendment of today, falls short of the spectacular liberties enjoyed by the female sex in early Santa Fe history.

"La Tules, the gambling lady, as Maria would become known, died just one year before the US Government muddied the waters, ending this paradise of female freedoms in the name of American independence. As one who considers himself a true Mejicanos, this legacy of the occupying force is not one I, or any of my fellows, tout with any pride.

"But I'm ahead of myself. Step back to the period between the years 1826 and 1835. That's the period when the cigar-smoking Maria left Tome and appeared well established in Santa Fe, though there is no record of how she achieved her riches so quickly. We can surmise it, however, by the many records of her skill at monte. Monte, meaning a mountain of cards, was a game of pure chance, involving the typical Spanish deck she knew so well from her earliest travails on the slopes of Tibidabo in Barcelona—suits of club, sword, sun and cup, ten cards per suit, ace to seven, no queen but, rather, a horse. Add to that a jack and king, and there you have it. Monte tables were covered in red and green felt, divided into four squares.

Bets were placed on the two cards picked from the bottom and two from the top. No deschapelles coup, only colors. When the deck was turned up, if the suits of the gate matched the two picked cards, it was said to be a layout. If there was no match, the banker won. Maria's calm served as an uncanny disarmament: gaze upon her dealing hands and banking ways—serious, steady, as if working a knitting needle. All who played against her trembled visibly. Drinking whiskey, playing with bags full of gold and Mexican silver dollars, which the croupier swept off the table, she seemed incapable of losing. Surrounded by rough men who carried heavy arsenals of weapons and must have scrutinized her every gesture, cheating was impossible. Some would claim that it was her provocative dress and spectacular cleavage that distracted players at her table, and that might be true. She had forsworn the country dress of other women of the time—loose chemises and short petticoats—and instead adopted the Parisian sex-kitten attire with tight-fitting gowns. They called her the most fashionably dressed woman in town. But cheating was a serious offense, and there were always enough onlookers and exposed rifles to seize upon any prestidigitation. It was simply impossible to switch cards.

"If it ever appeared that she was losing, observers noted her exquisite patience. She might hold out calmly all through the night, never evidencing the slightest discomfiture, receiving the insults of her drunken players as if they were compliments. She was simply imperturbable. Not only was she gorgeous, but she had that innocence, remember, which could undo the most petulant bully. Her skills were much remarked upon. But so was her dignity. Some claimed she must have descended from European royalty, and had married beneath her in order to further flaunt her freedom. Losers at her tables were so charmed by La Tules that they hardly considered the consequences of their bad game. A hayseed might lose his entire year's income from trapping in an hour yet consider himself fortunate to have gazed into her unflinching eyes or caught a telling glimpse of that spectacular bosom. Happy on his flight into poverty."

"You were born in the wrong era," the judge said heartily.

"I've often thought that," replied Hidalgo. "But I would not have had a chance with La Tules. All the men were after her, you can be sure. Her fortunes equaled her fame. She eventually bought and greatly expanded a gambling house, and it was to become the most sought-after den of pleasure in all the Southwest, a place frequented by my client's ancestors, as I shall now endeavor to explain."[7]

"Go on," said the judge, absorbed.

CHAPTER 31
The Night New Mexico Was Saved

BY NOW EVEN a restless DA, the DA's easily perturbable assistant and the overworked stenographer were curious to hear the outcome of this remarkable gypsy lady's story, and her alleged involvement with the Marigolds. The Commander was familiar with some of the tale—after all, he was directly related to the remarkable La Tules—but by now had every expectation that his lawyer would further surprise him.

Hidalgo, relishing the evident impact of his yarn on those in the judge's chambers, continued. "Of course, a swarm of scandals surrounded La Tules. Some claimed she was the mistress of Governor Manuel Armijo.

This is debatable, but she was surely a financial advisor to him, given her wealth, which can be estimated by her last will and testament, and by the sheer size and furnishings of her establishment. In fact, two assassination attempts on the Governor had been planned with a knowledge of his frequent visits to her monte tables.

"La Tules, which was also the name by which she designated her gambling casino, was designed after Versailles, much like the Sports Club in Monte Carlo, a grand haven for all-night merriment amid lavish appointments. Consider the huge crystal chandeliers shipped in from Toledo, the carpets from Provence, the floor-to-ceiling pier glass mirrors from central Belgium, private card rooms set in semi-precious stones mined locally. The main gambling floor was like a gymnasium or disco, with its own formal receiving lines modeled after those of Imperial Russia; walls of amethyst and jade, turquoise and crystal; adobe floors carpeted in thick silken liners from Cyprus; sable cushions for the weary gambler; a bar that served Irish gin, Crimean vodka, and hors d'oeuvres for every demeanor. The whole emporium of pleasure extended an entire city block, the full length of today's San Francisco Street, and taking up part of Burro Avenue. Its complex of rooms, many for purposes other than gambling, butted up against Palace Avenue on the north."

"She lived at the casino?" the DA asked.

"No, her own home was near the marsh, adjacent to the ruins of the old city wall, east of the Governor's Palace. When she'd walk the few blocks to her casino, everyone she passed would greet her. They treated her like a queen, or high priestess. Consider the words of Josiah Gregg, writing in 1844 in his *Commerce of the Prairies*." Hidalgo read from the original source: "'The governor himself and his lady, the grave magistrate, the gay caballero and the titled señora may be seen staking their doubloons upon the turn of a card; while the humbler ranchero, the hired domestic and the ragged pauper all press with equal avidity to test their fortune at the same shrine.'[8]

"It is known that a court decision by the *alcalde*—*La Tules versus Don Santiago Circe*—recognized the legality of debt at the gaming tables involving a claim of 400 pesos. That, gentlemen, was an important benchmark that prefigured the events to come. In 1837, the city was thrown into chaos when there was a rebellion against Governor Albino Perez. The Governor and other officials fled Santa Fe but were captured, and Perez was beheaded on Agua Fría Road on August 8th. The insurgents played a kind of soccer with his head, while Don Santiago Abrevio suffered the evisceration of his tongue. Nasty business in those years. Don Jesus Maria Alarid, the Governor's secretary, was tortured to death. There were, at the time, some 200 foreigners—Americans and a few Europeans—living in the city. Six hundred loaded guns were at the ready, and saddled horses in the courtyards. It was the beginning of the end of Mexico's dominance.

"The following summer, with Manuel Armijo now ruling, La Tules exerted an enormously stabilizing force throughout the community. Why? Because she had a continuous revenue stream. Much like owning an entire shopping mall—Albertsons, McDonald's, the bookstore, Starbucks, the cinemas, everything! She was the Donald Trump of her day. We know that she acquired various pieces of land.

"By this time La Tules' husband has disappeared from the record. Maybe they divorced, or perhaps he moved down to Mexico. We just don't know. There is no indication of a burial in either Santa Fe or Tome."

"And the relationship of La Tules and Alonzo Marigold?" the judge inquired.

"He probably did some or all of her land surveying. One of her great-nieces married one of Alonzo's sons."

"And then?"

Hidalgo, all worked up, had his next installment ready. "James Polk declared war with Mexico on May 13th, 1846. The President's orders to Colonel Stephen Watts Kearny and his steely 1st Dragoons were: subdue all those western territories that had been surveyed by Lieutenant William H. Emory. Kearny's Army of the West left Leavenworth a month later with 1,558 men. The idea was to pick up more volunteers along the way. The problem was, they moved too fast. By the time they entered New Mexico, they were ahead of the cash advances from the War Department. La Tules, at the recommendation of the Governor, came to the rescue. She literally bankrolled the American conquest, which would earn her a place in US history. Had she turned her back on the request, there is no telling what might have ensued: rebellion, mutiny, bloodshed. It's even possible that the US would never have succeeded in acquiring Santa Fe. La Tules had already captured the city's heart. Her allegiance was thus critical to any invading force.

"This is how it probably happened. It was mid-autumn; the Governor's days were numbered. He knew it and had no desire to incur the wrath of the invading army. Kearny was going to officially relieve him of his duties some time soon. It had to be a peaceable transition, given the potential for civil war; and it could happen overnight. Sentiments against the invading forces were high. But La Tules loved the soldiers in their bright uniforms, and especially prized their silver dollars, which they lost promiscuously at her casino.

"The American force, already stationed in Santa Fe unofficially, decided to throw a ball for the Governor and the high echelons of the Mexican Government. It was an effort on Kearny's part—he masterminded the affair—to ease tensions in a social setting. But there was a second purpose, and it was to secure money from the Grand Dame in order to pay the troops. A private earned six dollars a month, which was not much, but more than the expeditionary force could accommodate during those troubled times. Imagine the delicacy of all this: the invading army was there, but they were out of money for salaries or supplies.

Declining morale among his troops had to have been first on Kearny's mind, as well as the need to silence any rumors of a bankrupt army.

"The entrée to La Tules was done through an intermediary, the handsome Lieutenant Colonel Mitchell, who was delegated the task of escorting her to the ball. By the conclusion of the event, she had handed the young lieutenant a considerable sum that he, in turn, would pass along to the Colonel. There was a newspaper in Santa Fe, and a reporter in attendance at the ball tried desperately to get the inside scoop on La Tules and Mitchell. The latter threatened his life if he reported anything.

"We don't know what was said between Mitchell, Kearny and La Tules that evening. They probably slipped away from the dance at some point and convened secretly at Armijo's private quarters of the Palace. We can infer the cementing of a strong allegiance on her part, because a few months later, at the most crucial moment in Santa Fe's history, La Tules conveyed an intelligence report, so called, detailing a Mexican–Indian conspiracy to overtake the American forces.

"Kearny had already taken the Santa Fe Plaza, and all of New Mexico with absolutely no resistance. Convinced of the passivity of the locals, he felt secure in dispatching part of his army towards California and another division, under Colonel Alexander Doniphan, to El Paso. A third unit, commanded by Colonel Sterling Price, stayed at the garrison in Santa Fe. It was this reduced, self-confident force that had inspired two locals, Tomas Ortiz and Diego Archuleta, to secretly spread the word of an uprising that would retake the city by Christmas day. All Americans were to be massacred and the land returned to Mexico. Ortiz would assume the governorship, Archuleta command of the local army. They were both frustrated that Armijo had not done anything to preserve the dignity of Mexico. He seemed, instead, content to gamble all day beside La Tules.

"A servant girl got wind of the goings-on and told our Gypsy Queen. She in turn went straight to Price, as well as to Donaciano Vigil, Kearny's appointee as secretary of the territory, second in command after then Acting Governor Charles Bent.

"That very day, standing in the Plaza, Kearny publicly laid down the new agenda. Armijo was no longer Governor, though he would act in an official capacity during the transition. Charles Bent would replace him formally by year's end, one week from that time. People were to carry on as normal, attend to their jobs, farm their farms, ranch their ranches and trust that the representatives of the US Government would protect them through thick and shine.

"'We are here to respect and protect, regardless of a man's station in life, or his religion,' decreed Kearny. 'But make no mistake—' and these were his words—'those who resist will feel the hangman's noose without reservation. Thank you and God bless you!'

"Now, with word of the insurrection coming directly from La Tules, the Americans acted silently and quickly. That night—Christmas Eve, 1846—saw extraordinary events unfold. Imagine Santa Fe, cowled in a fresh snowfall, the city streets lined with thousands of glowing little luminaria hung in paper baskets from every gaslight and tree, and aboard every coyote fence post, and at each doorstep. But the streets were quiet. A fog pervaded the night. In order to present a picture of supreme confidence, and ignorance of any plot, Kearny placed a few of his top officers at the monte tables of La Tules. Mitchell, Vigil, Price and one Marcus Durango were there, along with Armijo and his deputy. The casino was especially crowded that night. It was the warmest place to be in town. Among the many gaming aspirants was Alonzo Marigold. We know this from the writings of the reporter Chicago Sam, as he was evidently called.

"Marigold found himself on a winning streak. Armijo, who did not bet himself, but rather provided the funds for Durango, was thoroughly sapped of pride, knowing that his days in public service were finished.

Vigil, a no-nonsense conservative, joined in at the game only because Kearny had asked him to be sociable. Vigil was the first to drop out, as the cost of staying in had dramatically increased. We don't know much about Durango except that he was some kind of advisor to the Governor. The stakes were amplified when Mitchell, who'd been drinking heavily, started betting an officer's monthly salary at one go. Then two, then five. He seemed intent on impressing La Tules, which is how it probably always happened. Suddenly, the wagers began groaning under their own weight. Mitchell had already bet, and lost money belonging to the occupying forces, confident the good lady would bail them out. But Durango, or rather his banker, Armijo, took a beating beyond any such debt assistance or forgiveness, and there was nothing anybody could do about it. Durango was quite inebriated, angry and stubborn, and refused to give up. He dug a deeper and deeper hole. He and Mitchell were in neck-deep.

"At one point Armijo, mortified by his mounting debt, requested of La Tules that she and her establishment accept properties which he had accumulated during his long and successful career as a public servant. The three-time Governor was no crook. He was a man of considerable talents and integrity. He had acquired his lands and his outrageous fortune through legitimate means. The history books do not impugn his character or his actions. But this night he lost control of the feckless Durango and, being quite macho and of a sporting nature, did not end the game in time. La Tules was neutral, but gracious, it can be assumed. She dealt the cards throughout the long session. Who knows what looks she cast? Two friends, Alonzo and the Governor, were in a dead heat. By dawn, the Governor's holdings had been whittled away. And who was the happy beneficiary of these gaming piranhas?

"Alonzo Marigold, who walked away with a signed IOU itemizing his new acquisitions: all the lands from Camino De La Canada to San Francisco Street; up Tesuque Road toward Fort Marcy; everything along Camino De Alamo (Agua Fría), including the houses on Cerillos Road, Camino De Galisteo, the Barrio de Analco and Camino De Pecos. A vast territory in the mountains behind town. A tract of land extending from the Tesuque Pueblo to Los Alamos. There were pockets left free of this general swathe: a square mile here, 1,000 hectares there. But his winnings were considerable. We have seen it from the air. A full 1.2 million acres. It is possible that Armijo figured he had nothing to lose because Kearny was planning to appropriate the former Governor's holdings under US law. But that is not true."

"And the insurrection?" Bradford asked.

"It never went down. While this extraordinary card game was going on inside, all of Kearny's Dragoons moved out just after midnight, searching every house for Ortiz and Archuleta. The soldiers confiscated all weapons, and met almost no resistance. The two leaders of the revolt managed, improbably, to escape. Historians now know that they dressed as women, and were to show up in Chihuahua months later, badmouthing the Americans and describing an apocryphal revolution and their own decisive heroism. In fact, Ortiz had hidden atop the church. At the stroke of midnight, he was lowered off the rooftop by a rope, and was met below by an accomplice who carried him on his back. Troops spotted them on what would be Water Street. But they were negligent and failed to check the identity of Ortiz. The man carrying him claimed that 'she' was his daughter, stricken with bubonic plague. The soldiers were keen to stay clear and let the man pass.

"By the following afternoon, Christmas Day, Kearny thanked La Tules for her Christmas gift to American history and named her a national hero. This was before he'd learned of Mitchell's debt. He was not about to plead on behalf of a drunken soldier, but asked for an extension on repayment. To sign such an extension required a signature on the total wager. You see, Mitchell had dropped out just after Vigil. But the wager was written up in a single document, the same one containing the debt of 1.2 million acres."

"I'm confused," said Hemmings.

Hidalgo went on to explain. "You see, by signing off on the Mitchell debt, Kearny officially acknowledged the debt of Durango to my client's ancestor. La Tules kept meticulous records. She was fair, even though it meant a heavy loss for her friend, the former Governor. He could afford it, though. There were other lands in his portfolio, down in Mexico."

The DA scratched his head and eyed Bradford. "Let me get this straight. The Governor, betting through a mysterious associate named Durango, Vigil and Mitchell, a high-ranking officer in Kearny's invading force, and Alonzo Marigold are at the table. Vigil drops out. Marigold takes the pot. Kearny signs off, acknowledging the debt, and so does the Governor."

"That is the story, in highlight. A few months later, a magnificent eighteen-year-old niece of La Tules named Rafaela was seduced by an American whose identity has never been worked out—he could have been a general for all we know. She bore an even more beautiful daughter, Rallitas, whose hair was celebrated in a verse commending 'the color of autumn, her eyes that of a lynx'. The father of this marvelous girl disappeared. When a second suitor for Rafaela climbed, one night, to her bedroom window on the second story overlooking the marsh, La Tules, shotgun in hand, and a priest standing beside her, were waiting in the darkness of the room. The suitor had his way with Rafaela, but La Tules and the priest had their way afterwards. The marriage was prompt, and so were several offspring, all girls.

"We know that La Tules drew up her will four years later. Attending witnesses to its execution, on

October 13th, 1850, included Vigil; Francisco Ortiz y Delgado, Prefect of the jurisdiction; Baca y Ortiz and Juan Estevan Sena, members of the city council; and Samuel Ellison, the official interpreter and translator for the territorial Supreme Court at the time. The document was written out in five succinct paragraphs and duly recorded and executed in the Santa Fe courthouse. Moneys and land were bequeathed to La Tules' sister, Maria de la Luz Barceló, to her niece Rafaela and all her children. She left money—a bag of gold, lost to the records—to her husband, which was kept by the church until such time, if ever, he should return for it. She also conveyed some shekels to a brother named Trinidad, about whom we know nothing.

"La Tules died on January 17th, 1852. Her funeral was grand, costing 1,600 dollars. The first US census of Santa Fe, taken 18 months before, revealed 30 American women living in town at that time. It is clear from the various letters and diaries that they felt no special fondness for La Tules, whom they considered responsible for the corruption of their men. These were women already brainwashed by the American way. They evidently accepted their loss of freedom.

"But the Spanish women and nearly all the men of Santa Fe came out to honor her in lavish style, never mind the fact she had played a pivotal task in what would be described by historians as the final conquest of Spanish holdings in the United States. But to these mavericks of the Wild West, these Old World daredevils, La Tules was a heroine. The American troops fired their rifles 16 times, and her casket lay open for pilgrims to observe for three days and nights. Her casino was taken over by Rafaela, who ran it with less commitment, and in later years it was sold off in pieces, until it disappeared altogether. An enormous painted mural of dancing men turned up in Las Vegas some years back and was eventually auctioned off by an art dealer. It probably originated at the casino.

"And Alonzo's son?" the judge asked. "Why didn't he take up some claim to the 1.2 million acres? What happened?"

The Commander sat up. "That was Victor, my great-great-grandfather, who married Lucinda, one of Rallitas' daughters, and they settled in the family home where I have resided my whole life. He was a simple man, content to graze some sheep, write some poetry and place few demands upon life." He paused, marking his words, then: "When I think of the legendary gambling woman, her gorgeous Rallitas, and her great niece Lucinda, I recall the spirit of the gypsies in southern Spain, my own ancestors, who forever roamed this earth with an abandon. Chivalrous, rambunctious, steeped in the virtues of simplicity and joy. As a child I used to play gin rummy with my father. I was very good, and knew all the tricks. I could pull an ace out of my sleeve, or even three queens from behind his ear. He found such antics quite amusing, but would caution, 'Careful, Murillo. The ghost of La Tules might be watching!' and I hadn't a clue what he meant. In fact, it wasn't until 1992 that I really learned more about her. That's when *Viva Santa Fe!*, a musical depicting part of La Tules' extraordinary life, was invited by the US Commissioner General's Office in Washington to be part of the 1992 World's Fair in Spain. Though I was vague on such details, as my lawyer has now so marvelously conveyed, I knew then that some aspect of myself had come full circle—part African nomad, silly shrimp and gypsy. That's me."

CHAPTER 32
The Surveyor's Tale

GERALD HEMMINGS' office asked for two weeks to absorb Hidalgo's presentation and do some of its own fact checking.

"They know they've got a problem," Hidalgo explained to his client. "Now comes the tough part. They'll screw with us. But don't be alarmed. That's what lawyers do. In this instance, we're talking about a major chunk of the state, and the judge has got to be taking heat from the Governor."

It was true. The Governor was not overjoyed by the prospect of losing Santa Fe. But then, he wasn't exactly worried about it, either.

"Don't go getting over-exercised," he declared into his Nokia cell phone. He was traversing his ranch by Range Rover, looking for any excuse—a dead cow or sheep—to call in the Animal Damage Control people, and speaking to Bradford who was in the kitchen of his Upper Canyon Road home. The judge's daughter, Natalie, was next to him, frying a mushroom and red pepper omelet.

"What's that noise?"

"Natti's frying eggs."

"Now listen, Jim. If necessary, as Governor I'll simply veto this bullshit on grounds of state security."

"They could take it to the Supreme Court. The case has sufficient merits, I believe."

"You're serious?"

"I've done some looking into it."

"And?"

"And nothing. No predictions. But if we lost, it would be dirty."

"Could we lose?"

"If it went to trial? Who knows. These are unknown waters. It would, at the very least, require a community hearing. The community is involved. Hell, the whole state is involved. I'd say if things go badly we might want to consider a quick settlement before they understand the full implications—and leverage—of their position. I'm calling for a short calendar, and a status conference in two weeks."

"Who is this Hidalgo, anyway?"

"He's smart, he's done his homework. He's asked for no continuations."

"You think he's already put his case together?"

"Oh yes. But I truly doubt he's figured the extent of the state's liability in this matter."

"And you have?" the Governor asked, trying to suppress mounting concern.

"I'm not even sure anybody can bring sufficient expertise to the table to figure it out. This is complicated."

"Good," the Governor concluded. "Keep it tied up in the courts for a century. That's the New Mexico style. Say, you know what the state cookie is, Jim?"

"You're breaking up. Did you say state cookie?"

"We've got some cliffs here. Can you hear me? I just found out. It's the bizcochito. What is a bizcochito, and who had the authority to make it the state cookie?"

"Same person who named the roadrunner, the black bear, the yucca cactus and the piñon as emblems of the state. But the cookie I never heard about. I'll look into it, if you like."

When everyone reconvened at Bradford's office, Marigold sensed a change of mood, signaled by Hemmings' attire, a conservative suit. His attitude seemed cool and malevolent. Hidalgo noticed the same thing, although he'd expected it. He was prepared. He'd spent the last two weeks fortifying their position, downloading every relevant case from dozens of sources across the entire spectrum of litigation.

"Good morning," Judge Bradford began. "I hope you've all had some coffee and sleep. This is a mess. I've been studying the decisions of some of the surveyors-general during the period of Alonzo Marigold's life." He read from his notes on a large yellow legal pad. "Men like William Pelham, Alexander Wilbar and particularly James Proudfit. They all seemed to share one thing in common: the community interest, Hispanic custom. The law sided with the public commons. This is where Hispanic and Anglo-Saxon due process meet. These men were in positions to recommend interpretations of physical surveys. They were magnanimous in their determinations, from all that can be gleaned from the record, at least up until the latter part of the century, when the Santa Fe ring came into power."

He was referring to that unscrupulous ensemble of co-conspirators— surveyors-general, crooked politicians and businessmen, judges and lawyers during the mid-1880s—who manipulated the land grants in such a way as to steal tens of millions of acres outright. And by implication, he meant to cast a shadow upon the credibility of Alonzo Marigold aswell. The New Mexico scandals got so bad that President Grover Cleveland himself appointed Surveyor-General George Washington Julianto break the ring and strengthen a whole new Court of Private Land Claims. In the process, Julian also managed to give back to the state several million acres that had been illegally transferred to private hands in preceding years. Bradford was suggesting a precedent that might invalidate the Deputy Governor's debt.

"Julian discovered breaches in community property tradition, and he rectified them. I admire that. Moreover, the law dates to Julian's procedural approach and, I dare say, his ethics."

Hidalgo listened carefully to Bradford's emerging tone, and the suspicions that underpinned it, as well as to the strenuous reaffirmations from Hemmings and Hemmings' assistant, John Michaels. When they had finished, he replied with equal sting, and brought forth from his bundle of files an essential piece of discovery, the Surveyor-General's *Report* from the Spanish Archives of New Mexico, consisting of a letter from the Acting Secretary of the Interior, transmitted in pursuance of laws at that time back to the Surveyor-General. These events occurred some 25 years prior to the arrival in town of Surveyor-General Julian.

He handed prepared copies of the letter to everyone present. All read in silence.

"House Executive Document, dated December 11th, 1855. Sir: Referring to Department letter of July 14th, 1838, I have the honor to transmit herewith, pursuant to the requirement of the eighth section of the act of July 22nd, 1854 (10 Stats., 308), a supplemental report of the Surveyor-General of New Mexico, on the alleged private land claim designated as Santa Margiold, No. 823. H.L. Muldrow, Acting Secretary.

"The President of the Senate Pro Tempore.

"Let it be known that Congress has confirmed and asks that the General Land Office execute a patent for the land to the said owner, and I have therefore required the petition to be so amended as to specify the name of the present claimant, namely, Mr. Alonzo De Resista Marigold, longtime resident of Tesuque, New Mexico.

"The petitioner has claimed a tract of land in Santa Fe County, made pursuant to a debt discharged on December 24th, 1846. There is no controversy as to the genuineness of the document on which this claim is based and the sole question to be considered relates to the boundaries and survey of the grant. The petitioner says: I am the beneficiary of a debt, discharged by signature of the Governor himself, said debt to have accrued as a result of certain excesses at the establishment of La Tules, a night of gambling whose uncanny particulars were witnessed and attested to by presiding officer in charge, Colonel Kearney, by Lieutenant Colonel Mitchell, and by the Governor Manuel Armijo himself. I register the same, and its boundaries are the following: All lands from Camino De La Canada to San Francisco Street; up the entirety of Tesuque Road to the precise base of the Fort Marcy hillside; all acreage along Camino De Alamo excluding the government-owned row houses along the length of Cerillos Road, Camino De Galisteo, the Barrio de Analco, and Camino De Pecos. Allland from the Little Tesuque Canyon extending for 25 miles due north by northeast, with the exception of the Tesuque Pueblo lands, and acknowledging community access to all rivers, acequias and pasture lands. Mineral and lumber rights, and any agricultural yield, however, shall revert to the petitioner as bona fide portions of debt repayment."

There were deep rings under the DA's eyes. The present document, if bona fide, represented a serious blow to his case. Could the letter have been forged? Were there precedents for such conveyances? While 80,000 Santa Feans went about their high desert business, dropped children off at school, served up monotonous salsas to mobs of tourists, unloaded silver trinkets at the Plaza and over-priced works of headier art at 300 galleries, this predator Hidalgo was making ready to drop a bomb on the entire region. And, from the looks of it, had every legal right to do so, Hemmings imagined.

The week before, Hidalgo and Mr Marigold had actually traversed the hundreds of square miles of property, beginning at the northeast corner of the Plaza in downtown Santa Fe. Mr Marigold had retrieved his father's rusted tools of the trade, enabling the two men, after some disagreement, to draw up a transverse Mercator, utilizing the elements of the north and south pole, the earth, a copper cylinder circumscribed by multiple lines (circles, really) of intersection, and a central meridian. They then managed (somehow, incredibly) to translate the drawing onto a plane surface, with its rectangular grid, graticule and equator. The technique had been handed down for generations, and the Commander more or less remembered what to do. Furthermore, he was able to find actual iron pipes sticking out of a rock here, a stone marker there, and these, coming as they did in the middle of nowhere on a mountain, in a forest, at the edge of a meadow, and in the center of the current Governor's own ranch, were spectacular confirmation of the surveyor's work, as described in the Acting Secretary of the Interior's 1855 letter. These relics of the route presaged an outline that was nothing short of destiny to one who observed its signs: trail-heads, patterns and reliefs, stonework, masonry shards, nails, carvings in the canyon wall, holes drilled on exposed slabs. All spoke to their newly enshrined proprietor.

"Do you not realize how peculiar the sensation is?" the Commander pointed out on the second day of their traverse. "I own most of Santa Fe!"

"I couldn't be happier for you, my friend."

They had scrambled over monadnock and downs, driven portions of the circumference and chartered a silent German glider plane for five hours from Santa Fe airport to gain as precise a perspective on the land as possible. The size defied the Commander's contemplative faculties. He was no Leonardo when it came to aerial understandings. Lakes, rivers, a waterfall, snowfields, forests brimming to five horizons, inhabited and uninhabited range land, mesas, ridges, complicated cliffs, much of a National Forest, a State Park, an entire ski area and, to cap if off, a city with its unsuspecting populace. Not the whole city but, by their reckoning, 75 percent of it—a city which in large part had grown up on land undeveloped at the time of the debt discharge. The prospect surrounded Mr Marigold, and left him feeling vulnerable, fearful, disinclined to go through with the suit. He recognized an end to his anonymity and could not fail to sense a coming fanfare that would change his quiet, comfortable life forever. Was this bold scheme worth the personal turmoil that would inevitably avalanche? He could not say. The very thought of going through with it, the open and heated contention, gave him a slack throat. He felt his heart pumping wildly, fearful of all outcomes; he craved his bed, an old book and a nameless status. He sought support upon his shepherd's crook.

Hidalgo, on the other hand, harbored no fiercer boldness than when in plain aerial view of the state now in contest. It shone illimitable beneath the famed New Mexico skies. Geological larks. Labyrinths of desire solidified into land and forest. Sensing the trepidation of his client, he volunteered, "I know this is work. It's big—bigger than the both of us. But it's going to happen and you needn't fear the outcome."

But Mr Marigold was too nervous to hear him above the wind sheer of the sloping aircraft. He reached for the vomit bag, out of tune with the topography closing in all around him. His face blushed like a waterspout, falling swoons and whirling dusts obscuring this line of sight; call it an historical moment that conspired to suffocate the old Marigold and force out the new. Was such rebirth necessary? He wasn't sure, but there was no more stopping their descent into the maelstrom than that a lion should forego his meal, a conductor his baton.

CHAPTER 33
The Metaphysics of Real-estate Law

THE GROUP OF WEARY experts continued their reading of the Acting Secretary's letter, dated December 11th, 1855.

The judge, an unhappy expression outlining an even less readable perturbation from within, presently held forth aloud: "'This office had dispatched a very competent and trustworthy surveyor to familiarize himself with the language of the grant and the evidence in the case, and then, with the assistance of old settlers thoroughly accustomed to the localities around Santa Fe, to examine the ground, and if possible identify the natural objects referred to in said land transfer, given the underlying potential for fraud, inasmuch as Mr Alonzo Marigold, a surveyor by trade, was a self-interested party and had every reason to act in an unscrupulous manner. The petition makes mention of an eastern limit of hills, a western brow of a canada—la ceja de una canada—'" he detailed in chopped Spanish— "'a northern-most road leading to a cerro pelado.'"

"A bald hill, your Honor," Hidalgo thought wise to interpret, pronouncing the Spanish properly.

The judge, annoyed, cleared his throat. "'And on the south, the titled lands of the Church,'" he continued. "In the writ of possession it is stated, 'And I designated to him the boundaries, which are on the east, some black hills on the west, pines, a church, a northern road leading to the base of Fort Marcy. The Surveyor-General has filed a sketch map of some detail representing an area of 1.2 million contiguous acres. Most men in Santa Fe cannot fail to recall such land as previously owned by the Governor's family, and others indebted to that family; that the Governor himself had title to most of the parcels, as did the US military personnel involved in the gambling incident. Inasmuch as no money, only chips, were lost on the monte table, there is no way to understand this debt in dollars, only in the acres that were wagered and lost by the Governor's party. This being the case, as is verified, the public domain is not at issue, as these are definitely private lands. The Surveyor-General did not fail to note the unusualness of said transfer, given the potential for legal morass. But he has acquitted any doubts of the validity of said properties, and the US Congress has resolved to accept his interpretation that the transfer is, under the laws of the United States, the equivalent of a land grant, made legally, and willfully, by properly titled individuals of high standing who have each supplied their signatures as witnesses to the event. Whether the discharge of so huge a debt in such a manner presents an ethical or psychological issue, I will not undertake to decide; but it has about it something of the fascination of a romance and invites the pencil of an artist."'

Hidalgo threw a well-disposed glance at his client. There could be no more positive reading than that, its impact measurably underscoring the judge's serious demeanor.

"'While under the law of Spain in 1742, the mountain and pasture lands in the provinces were common and free to the inhabitants for purposes of establishing their corrals or herdsmen's huts thereon, and to freely enjoy the use thereof, and a penalty of 5,000 ounces of gold to any owner who would infringe the commoner's right, this all began to narrow with the possession by Mexico in 1821 of New Mexico, and such adjustments were again amplified as of 1847.

"'I now come to the evidence,' the Acting Secretary continued." Hidalgo relished the depth of the judge's evident sobriety. The case could not have offered more secure documentation. This was an instance where premonitive instincts were not contrary to superstition. "'Thirteen witnesses were questioned by Surveyor-General Marquez, following his one-month expedition around the perimeters of the property in question. Marquez had carried on cross-examinations of people who were in some knowledgeable position to argue for or against the accuracy of the perimeters, but all testified to the fact of the accumulated debt and the manner of its discharge. Affidavits were properly filled out. Each witness was of lawful age, was duly sworn in, and then answered the following questions: First—State your name, age and place of residence. Second—How do you know the location of this property? Third—Was the Governor, the US Colonel and his Lieutenant Colonel of a right mind by your estimation, the night of the accumulated debt? Fourth— Was there any perceivable or unnatural threat exerted in the recovery of said debt the night of its discharge? Fifth—Have you reason to believe mischief at hand in this exchange, or was it truly won?

"'To every question, and from the myriads attesting, satisfactory answers came forth. We cannot judge the peculiarity of circumstances that would compel a Surveyor-General to administer oaths when the said lands conflict to such an extent with the territorial capital itself. Given the political upheavals of that year, the Congress recognizes extraordinary circumstances for Marquez doing so, and cannot fault either his motives or those of the US military officers involved in this affair.'"

All put down their respective copies. Bradford removed his glasses with one hand and addressed those present. "He's referring of course to the fact that La Tules saved the United States Government's tenuous situation on more than one occasion, and this was one of them. But we will never know, I believe, whether it was extortion, or whether the military officer involved acted illegally. Suppose the Lieutenant Colonel was drunk. Suppose La Tules was the Governor's mistress. Suppose, suppose. This case is full of supposes. Even if they were contemporary supposes, there would be grounds enough for dislodging assumption from fact and tossing the case out. But we are going back a century and a half. There is no case."

Hidalgo bristled. Where confidence had reigned supreme, the first horrifying doubt had now exploded to the surface. But he maintained his decorum. "Your Honor, I must disagree. You have in your hand a letter signed by the Acting Secretary of the Interior authorizing the discharge of a debt involving 120 full sections and the same number of fractional sections that have been surveyed as rightly owned by a small group of men. These very same men have signed over their full property rights to Alonzo Marigold. There is no ambiguity. No hidden titles or highjinks. I have never seen a case more cut and dried."

"Let me ask you a silly question, Hidalgo," Hemmings said. "Why would they do that? Why would they turn over the biggest piece of property in the whole territory to a surveyor?"

"Let me respond with a query of my own, Gerry." He said the name with the kind of sarcasm that lawyers who know they've got the high ground find amusing, and it was not meant to amuse Gerald Hemmings.

"If this whole thing were not what it appears to be, why indeed? The Governor could easily have accused Marigold of cheating, or determined that an appropriate discharge would be, say, a small homestead, enough acreage to grow corn, seedless watermelon—" nobody smiled—"fava beans, and that would have honorably ended it. The reason I believe 1.2 million acres was given over is because the Governor, the Deputy Governor, the Colonel and Lieutenant Colonel, among others of some stature standing beside these goings-on, were all in the public eye at that monte table. Alonzo was the fifth. La Tules was dealing. Du Bain, a croupier both loved and despised, was standing there, and, by all testimony, 75 spectators, 80 percent of whom, based upon the demographics at that time, would have been Mexican. The city was ripe for revolution. Mexicans wanted the Americans out. Alonzo passed as one of them, though he was more recently of Spanish descent. If the debt were not honored, the revolution might well have broken out that night. America would have lost New Mexico, and possibly Arizona and Colorado as well. The Indians would have probably acquired their own nation as part of the shuffle."

There was silence in the room, while everyone digested Hidalgo's reading of that night long ago.

"That, sir, is a ridiculous speculation that adds insult to this proceeding. Fancy compounded by murkiness, complicated by half-truths, multiplied by greed. I do not like it," the judge said.

Hidalgo wasn't sure where he could go, however.

"All due respects, your Honor, but the documentation which you have read is unambiguous. Your negations, conversely, lack any substantiation."

War in the chamber. Trip-line tongues, engine lips, mouths to the motorway where a game of chicken was worth billions of dollars.

"All right, let's suppose you're right," Bradford began testily, throwing out a theory. "That the letter checks out with handwriting, ink, paper and signature analysis."

"It will."

"That still leaves a number of critical issues to address."

"Such as?"

"Clouded title prior to the discharge."

This is where John Michaels, Deputy DA, had found some elbow room for the state.

"Such as the Juan de Gabaldón grant, recommended to Congress for confirmation, the papers showing the grant to have been made in 1752, a total of 11,619 acres. Also, large amounts of the Santiago Ramirez grant—I don't have the precise number of acres with me, but we'll find it—and a small portion of what is called the Talaya grant, recommended to Congress for confirmation, and known as Reported No. 89. The record will show that these lands were illegally confiscated by Mexican forces and became part of the debt discharge."

"Where are these lands?" Mr Marigold asked, speaking up for the first time that morning, casting his weight of support where he could sense it was needed.

Michaels used a pointer on a large map of Santa Fe County that had been placed on an easel in the judge's chambers to pinpoint the three land grants in question. All of them were southwest of Santa Fe, on the far western fringes of what Alonzo Marigold had acquired.

"Fine. Subtract the acreage," the Commander volunteered jauntily.

"Wait a minute," Hidalgo broke in. "What proof do you have of illegal confiscation? By what means are you in any possible position to judge legalities carried out in what was then Spanish territory, by Mexican officials, under laws pertaining to Spain 250 years ago?"

"The same right by which you would vouchsafe a debt under a legal regime of no relevance today," the Deputy DA half vituperated.

But Bradford was shaking his head and interjected, "I don't know, John." He was being politic.

In fact, Michaels was mistaken. Hidalgo knew it. Hemmings knew it. The analogy did not work. By 1855, when the Acting Secretary confirmed Alonzo Marigold as sole property holder of the 1.2 million acres, American law was both consistent with, and justified under terms of, the *Treaty of Ratification of 1853*, which recognized Mexican land grants and accommodated Mexican law as much as possible. This was done out of respect for a sovereign nation, and in the interests of a peaceful transition (always paramount), particularly given the preponderant demographic mix of New Mexico at the time of US annexation—namely, Indians and Mexicans, not Americans.

"US laws and orders had fully encompassed such situations, and that was a fact. Even doubts attributable to fishy surveying had been resolved according to a senior land commissioner's rendering of a decision in the early 1850s," said Hidalgo. He described the views of the Supreme Court at that time regarding Spanish grants, naked claims, irresistible conclusions, bearing upon all matters of physical perimeter. It was a highly technical description, which left those present in a state of utter exhaustion.

Bradford-of-fiddling-pen then took up the fray by citing particulars of the brief history of the *Court of Private Land Claims*, an institution begun in 1891. Three hundred claims had been heard before the turn of the century, covering some 35.5 million acres nationwide, he said. Eighty-two New Mexico grants (about two million acres) were confirmed.

Another 58 were appealed to the US Supreme Court. Petitioners were required to submit to the Court the original grant documents and two copies—not an issue in this case, he acknowledged. But, he said, and this was the clincher, claims were deemed abandoned if not filed within 24 months of the *Act of March 3rd, 1891*. If it appeared that the land had previously been disposed of by the government (lawfully acted upon by Congress), the present claimant was to receive no more indemnity than $1.25 per acre (1890s dollars). Half the cost of a survey had to be paid by the claimant after an affirmative judgment, a lien on the land held until such payment.

Bradford had found this *Act of 1891* in his sleep. It was, like all dreams of deliverance, a measure of his success as a man of the legal system; he had risen spectacularly and now stood poised to become a state Supreme Court Judge. This was a decisive insight, and the Governor could only admire a memory like that, pulling an Act out of a hat, whilst sound asleep. But it was a truism: the Act was as real as any, and it seemed, if there were no other surprises in store, to adhere magnificently in this instance. Of course, he had not gotten entirely up to speed on the value of 1890 dollars, multiplied by 1.2 million acres, but whatever it was, it could not come close to the value at risk otherwise—or so he assumed. Nor had he thought to call the state comptroller's office and request a computer computation of interest during a century and a decade. How bad could it be?

Revving up with an enthusiasm soon to be proved slightly premature, he hailed, "I would say, in stern review of the changing laws, that this is the precise Act for the moment."

Hidalgo felt a dark thud in his chest, parsing the hidden implications and working out a response in the precious seconds left him during Bradford's affront. Of course, he reckoned, there would be the issue of a century and a decade, the accrual of interest, and so forth. A dinner in 1890 was a quarter. A ranch 500 dollars. So the 1.2 million acres had to be worth a sizable fortune. It could be worse. But it could be vastly better.

However, Hidalgo was a man of wherewithal and canny connections. His father had long illustrated the possibilities for turning sudden peril into advantage under fire. Hidalgo had learned well. Now, when the judge thought him least likely to fetch a comeback, Hidalgo surprised them all, like a plumber with his plunger, a market maker, a mint hovering over its coin, seizing upon specifics that appeared likely to crush Bradford and Hemmings.

"It is my understanding that land grants made by special legislative acts—Chaperito, Dona Ana and Nuestra Señora del Rosario San Fernando Y Santiago, for example—are exempt from such time constraints."

"Those grants were of a communal nature. No time frame was involved. They are not relevant," rallied Michaels, although with a lump in his throat: he was not sure about that.

"It is not the timing, but the specialness of the Act that I am thinking about," snapped Hidalgo. "In this case we have a private confirmation, duly given and received without contest. There was no need—certainly none conveyed to Alonzo Marigold—to acquire the property more thoroughly. It was his."

"Look at the other large confirmations that came out of the Private Land Claims Court," said Bradford, heating up at the hint of this threat to his intellectual salvation. "They all hinged upon an active, rather than a passive interest. In the case of Jose Samosa of Socorro county—261,187 acres, all ranched or farmed, or nearly so. The same with Juan Jimmy Bean Hiraldo of Río Arriba county—205,615 acres, the largest watermelon operation in the state." He was running in circles, stabbing at endless permutations.

"Excuse me, your Honor, but I fail to see any connection whatsoever," Hidalgo fired back. "Show me where a man has to farm his land in order to own it. If that were the case, I guess I'd better surrender my own home, because I haven't planted a bean or a watermelon since I was a child. Have you?"

"You don't live on an historic land grant, Francis."

"What is historic today was not so in 1846, your Honor. I fail to see the relevance. The property in question was private land, not communal. Alonzo Marigold was a surveyor who knew well the difference. Incidentally, he was a valid surveyor, used frequently by the Mexican authorities, and he surveyed the lands in question out of a personal interest, as can be surmised. But his documentation met the same standards, tests and specifications as outlined in the Acting Secretary's letter. He did, subsequently, range some cattle and sheep on the land—and their movement can actually be traced by chemical analysis of their petrified dung and turds. As I indicated a few weeks back."

Hidalgo then added a one-two punch to this sudden twist in the game by pointing out that such "quiet title" was always safe (and remained so to this day) from collateral attack. "In fact, that was a freedom of private property enunciated in the US Constitution. And one more thing—"

This was Hidalgo's own surprise bombshell, the one he had discovered in going through the Commander's grandfather's diary—an instance of historical coincidence that could not have garnered more perfect serendipity when called for.

"—The visit of Sir Robert Torrens. Perhaps you've heard of him?"

"Torrens," Hemmings mulled aloud.

"As in the Torrens System?" asked Michaels.

"The very same," Hidalgo said with a smile, noting that neither Bradford nor Hemmings knew what the Torrens System was. Mr Marigold had never heard of it either.

"Let me explain. In truth, there is no single system of records that applies consistently, from state to state, for any given parcel of land in this country. Interests acquired due to a marriage in the family, the execution of a will, estate succession, judicial decree are all in separate files, oddly enough, thus rendering the process of clearing title a gigantic hassle. Such impediments are typically instituted with deliberate craft by those who have something to gain by the imposition of detours and difficulties. There is, however, a system in place to correct this legally suspect obstacle course. That system is known as Torrens, and it was first established in the *1858 Real Property Act of South Australia* by one Sir Robert Torrens. His experiences led him to believe there must be a more streamlined method, a single document that would establish title, eliminating the labyrinth of abstracts and byzantine proceedings such as these. He did this purposefully: to expedite the sales of merchant ships at Port Adelaide. Here's what he came up with, and then I shall tell you why it is relevant to Alonzo Marigold.

"Following the examination of interests by an attorney paid for by the applicant, a report was supplied to the court which rendered not an opinion but a decree that was binding, and this certificate became a title under the Registrar of Titles. In a single stroke it eliminated conflicting titles, occupancies, interests and liens. Now, a little-noted disciple of Torrens, Algernon Quackwick, also of Australian ancestry—"

"All former criminals," Hemmings said. "And with a name like that?"

Hidalgo ignored the remark. "He happened to be in Santa Fe in the year of 1860, during which time a major estate was being contested— that of Captain James Biltmore, a soldier under Kearney who, when his commission ran out, opted to raise a family in Santa Fe. I have something to show you."

The judge glanced upon another of Hidalgo's stacks with foreboding and exasperation. He was suffocating.

Hidalgo continued. "He purchased disputed land, and a big stink was made about it. Quackwick investigated the problem surrounding the Biltmore property and used it as a test case in the United States."

"The US never instituted the Torrens System," Michaels hastened to point out, "let alone, Quackwick!"

"That is true, but other countries have, including New Zealand, Canada, England, even the Philippines. The reason it has failed miserably in the US, particularly in New Mexico is, as I mentioned earlier, because of the existing system that feeds the pockets of combatants and executors, lawyers and title insurance men, abstractors and real-estate whores. Even the distrust of big government, and the resulting unwillingness of landowners to faithfully register their existing possessions (a means for big ranchers to hide acreage from the tax collector), enters into the failure of Torrens in the US. Except for a unique instance in 1860.

"Quackwick showed that a simple metes and bounds description, consistent with the later State Plane Coordinate System, was sufficient to eliminate all obscure title claims to the Biltmore property. And here's the best part. He befriended in the summer of 1860 none other than Alonzo Marigold, who showed him his property—the property in question today. Quackwick noted the particulars, as he was fascinated by the unusual nature of the debt discharge and its implications for the American legal system. He wrote about it in his own diary, in fact, illustrating in a clockwise direction the course and description of the Marigold property lines, beginning at the Plaza, a known monument, of course; and from there he wrote down all bearings and distances, acknowledging actual Land Office brass caps, in the tradition of the US Public Lands Surveys which had, by the way, been initiated by private surveyors under the *Act of May 18th, 1796*. It should come as no surprise that my client's ancestors were among those first private surveyors, and that was the reason Quackwick was keen to meet Marigold in the first place."

"No surprise whatsoever," a humiliated Bradford replied. He was at the base of a burning pyre; all his hopes seemed to be disintegrating at the insistent pile-up of one irrefutable bulwark after another. He had simply underestimated the ferocity of Francis Hidalgo. Perhaps it was because the case had not been taken seriously by the DA; and maybe that was because Hemmings had received so casual a preliminary inquiry from Hidalgo. It was almost a passing observation, lodged more like a theoretical query than a declaration. Of course, that was obviously the strategy at work: understate, then detonate.

Hemmings had not bothered to research the matter for many weeks, and then only to the extent that he delegated a law clerk's time for a few days. The clerk turned up next to nothing and that had suggested to Hemmings that nothing it would be; that Hidalgo was reaching, basing his claim on the gullibility of the District Attorney's office and the blind sense that all claims got settled somehow. Hemmings could not have known that Hidalgo was one of those history junkies who populate western historical libraries.

Now, the judge was rearing beneath the weight of abstruse, nearly metaphysical, evidence: nuances turning to fact; details 150 years old haunting the current administration; the whole edifice of his present balance falling apart.

He mind's eye rested fearfully upon the one emblazoning icon, which spoke to these new legal turnabouts. It was a depressing speech that only serviced to bore cruelly into the judge a singular revelation: New Mexico's state insect was a tarantula wasp, predatory, ever unpredictable and focused on one thing only— its own survival. It spelled the queasy, inevitable demise of his own career. For he had just lost half the state's budget to a madman.

CHAPTER 34
Marigold's Blueprint for the New World

HIDALGO RETURNED with his client after a 20-minute break, during which time they consumed dreadful machine coffee. He'd explained to the Commander how they had made out, in legal terms. Despite a few humps in the road and dark corners, it was looking good, no doubt about it.

"They will counter, and it will be strenuous. But they have no case. You can't invalidate history, not when it comes embroidered in so many pressing details with your living name attached."

"But will they actually give me Santa Fe?" Marigold's eyes tarried in suspended humor, terrified by the potential fanfare yet unable to fully grasp the miracle.

"No. The Governor won't let that happen. On the other hand, the DA's case is such a colossal contretemps they will be forced to settle in your favor. The terms are wide open. Eighty thousand people are not going to be evacuated. But the state will have to pay prettily to maintain the privilege of the city's existence."

"How much?"

"To be determined. Believe me, I've got more ammunition than you can imagine. I've tried to anticipate everything."

And he had, hitting them with Torrens just when Bradford believed Spanish common law would demolish Hidalgo's entire case. With an equanimity learned from his father, he had overturned every possible objection thus far, resurrected in an instant clear title, historic precedent, all the exemptions, signature and congressional affidavit. The judge and DA had very few options left.

Inside Bradford's chamber, the afternoon session resumed. Hidalgo took a solid, measured breath and began.

"Gentlemen, I direct your attention to the *Public Land Survey Act of February 11th, 1805*, which rationalized all of the principles for such surveys, be it the marking of corners, the running of boundary lines, the use of a language of minutes, seconds, quadrants and circles. Nearly every modern concept had been encompassed: geographic centers; township and range lines at six-mile intervals north and south; transverse Mercator projections; elipsoidal adjustments; the diameter of the cylinder; X coordinates in the east-west, Y coordinates north-south, expressed in feet and decimals of a foot. Every tract of land was surveyed within one-half mile of triangulation and traverse stations, all in conformity with the New Mexico Coordinate System. None of this escaped the notice of Quackwick, who urged the Surveyor-General to study the work of Torrens. My point, Gentlemen, is that here we have yet a third confirmation of the survey, of the title, of the precise coordinates, and, as I discovered myself, some of those brass caps are still in place around town."

Bradford seemed confused and conciliatory. "Let's not forget what's at stake here. A lot of money. More than money—a class action suit filed on behalf of the entire city of Santa Fe."

"Do you know that for a fact?" asked Hidalgo.

"No, but I can fairly predict it. That, Francis, would put you and your client in court for a decade or more. I'm guessing. Maybe you'd see nothing in your lifetime. I will tell you, I've already had word from the Governor and the Secretary of State who are ready to throw out the whole deal. I assure you the Supreme Court will be similarly inclined."

"By which legal chutzpah do you dare to make such preemptive assumptions?"

"The *State Security Act*. It works in the same manner, you might say, as the state's right of eminent domain."

Bingo! That was the phrase Hidalgo had been waiting for. Bradford thought he caught a twinkle of suspended animation in the lawyer's eye, the universal lull before a death knell. He knew that would give him something to think about. It was, as far as the judge could see, the only plausible escape from this fantastic quagmire. It could force a quick settlement at terms acceptable to the state, if greatly deflated from the high plateau Hidalgo had probably envisioned. A few hours' delay would no doubt infuse this ambulance-chaser, as the judge thought of Marigold's executor, with profound jitters. He'd succumb to a panic attack. If Bradford could keep up the pressure, maintain his poker face, there would be a settlement, and one acceptable to the Governor and, by implication, the people of New Mexico.

It had to work, thought Bradford. The alternative was catastrophic. Hemmings had spoken with the state comptroller. One hundred and fifty years' accumulated interest was not the pretty sight the judge had imagined. Both he and the Governor would probably be booted out of their respective offices by one mechanism or other. Hundreds of other historical claims would storm the courthouse. The present administration, which won its offices and seats on the basis of the first demonstrated surplus in the state's history, would—overnight—see a whopping deficit.

A freeze on all state employee salaries. The end of any social services. Mental cases turned away. Sex offenders released on their own cognizance. The jails would shut down; pre-schools, state universities, the state franchise board as well. No more money for environmental clean-up; no more salaries for garbage collectors or nurses. No reserves for the homeless, the hungry or for disaster relief. The state—already deemed the poorest in America—would be dependent on its Indian bingo parlors for financing water and power, school lunches, road works.

Bradford took a phone call, listened, then placed the phone back down.

"Something's come up. Meet back here in two hours," he said cryptically.

He knew that eminent domain, by the Governor's personal decree, was the only way to preempt Armageddon in the state of New Mexico. He needed to engineer mitigating circumstances that would necessarily define a finite cap on the value of the debt. The debt itself was real, he now conceded privately to Hemmings and Michaels, before excusing the state's team for lunch. In so doing he sounded an ominous alarm: "This is not over, Gentlemen—" then repaired to his favorite café a block away.

"What did he mean by that?" Marigold asked, somewhat alarmed.

"They're just thinking through strategy—what's left of it," Hidalgo stated confidently. "Don't worry. They're crumbling."

Marigold and Hidalgo went into town. The Commander had seen a rare two-volume biography of Peter Paul Rubens he wanted to purchase. Hidalgo needed lunch.

"Can the Governor do that?" the Commander asked as both he and his lawyer sipped their Margueritas and dipped hot chips in a hotter salsa. "He can try. But don't worry. Eminent domain is always the state's excuse for bullying lawful claims. Bottom line, they'll have to compensate. You may not get anywhere near 1.2 million acres, and certainly no entire city. But you'll get something. We could, of course, take it to trial. But then we'd have to convince 12 citizens."

"Convince them that they should embrace homelessness, you mean?"

"It's your inheritance, Murillo. Just as it was your father's and his father's and so on. If you want to bail out, that's your prerogative. Take the lesser pocket change and run. It would be a considerable sum, and you could avoid any hassles."

"The value? What did he say, a dollar and a quarter per acre, less all kinds of costs?"

"Don't forget appreciation. Today's value is not the value in 1846. You'd be rich, there's no doubt about it. They'll try to whittle away at the value issue, but I've got our counters pretty well nailed." Neither said anything for long minutes as they tucked into their quesadillas, Japanese rice bean soup and sheep cheese salads.

Finally, in a tone of quiet demur, the Commander asked for Hidalgo's advice. These were matters too far removed from his cozy little existence. His head could not deal with the wild scrimmage of points and percentages as thick as chard, legal interpretation without end, and tactics that boded of retribution by strangers.

"What should we do, I mean really?"

"I think you realize that I have only your interests at heart, Murillo."

"You don't need to repeat yourself."

"I know. But at times like these—"

Mr Marigold raised his hand to brush aside all professions of deepest affiliation. Such were understood.

Hidalgo seized his chance. "I would advise the following: We go for the gold and if, at the last moment, it seems that this security business and eminent domain problems become too dangerous, we opt for a quick settlement. By then, the valuation will have skyrocketed because that is their only way to press home the value to the state, the scope of the threat to New Mexico's security. You understand? They are in the perfect double bind. We will allow them to set the cost to the taxpayer of losing Santa Fe. That cost is our price. We will be generous and offer a discount. It's perfect."

"I think I understand. I am to say nothing, as usual."

Hidalgo leaned over and pinched the Commander's cheek. "What a guy you are, eh? My genius."

Back at the judge's chamber, it seemed Hidalgo's strategy could not have been more prescient. This was precisely the tactic initiated by the district attorney. It was obvious that eminent domain had preoccupied the judge and the two lawyers over lunch, for that was their only concern when the proceedings got underway.

"I don't doubt that Alonzo Marigold won 1.2 million acres. You've done an admirable job convincing us of that," said the judge.

"Thank you, your Honor."

"And I'm sure that you, sir—" he was addressing Mr Marigold— "would like nothing more than to take full possession of those 1.2 million acres."

The Commander looked to his lawyer, who gestured that it was fine for him to answer.

"It's all I've got," he said. "I should be pleased to be reunited with my inheritance. Wouldn't you be?"

"Our records show you currently own a large, historic mansion in Tesuque, is that correct?"

"A run-down hacienda would more accurately characterize my home," Marigold conceded.

"And that you have a housekeeper, but no family. I also have a copy of your income tax returns from the last three years. You receive what must be described as an adequate income of 5,000 dollars a month that was entrusted to your lawyer, who serves as the executor of your holdings. In addition, your insurance and real estate taxes, your medical bills and utilities, even the housekeeper, are paid for out of your estate. You don't work. Nothing in this scenario indicates duress or financial need, is that correct?"

"I am not in abject poverty, if that's what you mean."

"Your run-down hacienda, which happens to be listed in the State Historical Society records as the oldest home in Tesuque—"

"Valued at probably over three million dollars, according to the current market," Hemmings added, "— is yours, free and clear. You are a rich man, by any standard."

"What is this all leading to, your Honor?" Hidalgo asked.

"Your client would have a very hard time proving that without his 1.2 million acres he would be dispossessed. In fact, no hardship whatsoever could be linked to the loss of that property, since we are not talking about his hacienda and he has gotten on quite well for his entire life, thus far, in absence of 1.2 million acres."

Hidalgo thought about that for a moment then had to admit, "That is true, but irrelevant."

"The only criterion for making a determination here is the public's welfare. I don't suppose you've considered the impact this land claim, if actually ratified, would have on the people of Santa Fe?" the judge asked.

Hidalgo feigned ignorance, allowing for the conversation to drift directly into his reverse web of detrimental valuations and converse assessments.

"I have, your Honor," the Commander suddenly interjected, dashing Hidalgo's best-laid plans. He had missed the tenor, thought suddenly that Hidalgo may not have fully worked it through, and so hoped to addle and impress the court with his own Blueprint for the New World.

"Tell us, what did you figure out?" Hidalgo kicked Marigold under the table. But it did not have the desired effect.

"I, too, have surveyed the property perimeters and much therein. I own, according to the records, nearly all of Santa Fe, as silly as that sounds."

"Silly, yes. Preposterous, more so. Not gonna happen, best approximation of the truth," the judge declared.

"Understand my point of view, if you dare." The words sent a shiver up Hidalgo's spinal quarters. He knew that Mr Marigold was winding up for one of his big blow-offs.

"Your Honor, my client has his own ideas but this is not the appropriate forum."

"We'd like to hear those ideas, wouldn't we?" He looked at Hemmings, Michaels and the stenographer.

"Very much so," Hemmings reiterated. Hidalgo laid claim to concerned silence.

"I have a vision for this property of mine. Sort of like the City Beneath the Hill, a paradise of urban harmony, in which the wild lands surrounding Santa Fe would be ecologically incorporated, and the entire human settlement gracefully converted into a National Park, one of the first city parks in the world. I've worked it all out. A World Heritage"

"Have you?" Bradford nodded admiringly.

"Nothing would change in a sense, though, in another sense, everything would change. This courthouse, for example. I would turn it into a sanctuary for cats."

Eyes rolled, mouths yawned, chuckles issued.

"You'd have a very difficult time, I'm sure, explaining your vision to all the diverse inhabitants of this city who, for the most part, work for a living. Nine-to-five."

"I have already figured that out."

"They have jobs, sir. They are car mechanics, real-estate brokers, politicians; and they rule, these families with children in school who will drive polluting automobiles when they turn 15, who do drugs and get into trouble, or pregnant and need family planning assistance. There are people out there who consume, and need garbage trucks to haul away their trash. And sanitation services, and water-processing plants, and lawyers likes us who work for a living, too."

Hidalgo was seized by a coughing fit.

"Your Honor, not to be glib, but I know all that. I'm not talking about dispossessing anybody, but cleaning the place up a little bit, and ensuring that none of my undeveloped land is converted to concrete, while spending millions of dollars—whatever's necessary—to plant more trees, preserve more greenbelt, and increase recycling services and alternative energy resources. To outlaw hunting, to enforce a ban on all violence towards other species and, in general, to create something of a Utopia, just as Christ or St Francis or Buddha would have it."

"That all sounds marvelous, but I would caution against too much zeal on your part, Mr Marigold. Don't count your eggs just yet. What you're suggesting would require the complete cooperation of 80,000 people. That, in turn, would necessitate a town forum. A dozen people can't even agree on a single zoning regulation. Don't expect the whole town to agree on your ecotopia. You'll find a few dreamers, like yourself.

And I'm sure our Mayor would be interested to hear what you have to say. But otherwise, you're out to lunch. No, you haven't even gotten close to breakfast. The truth of the matter, and I'll say it now: you're never getting near to those 1.2 million acres. The city has occupied that land. It belongs to the people. Your lawyer will ably prove that it once belonged to your ancestors, but it is now out of your hands, like so many other millions of acres that have passed out of estates by the sheer exigencies of history, and new generations. This isn't to say you aren't entitled to something, and it will be the burden of this court to determine what is fair compensation, but I would caution you against confusing your utopian fantasies with the matter at hand—the true value of 1.2 million acres, under the peculiar circumstances before us."

"What are those circumstances, your Honor?" Hidalgo demanded. "Gerry, you tell him," Bradford pivoted.

"Simply put, the state's right of eminent domain, under which a whole new set of laws and valuations comes into being. I'd be happy to spell them out for you."

Hidalgo's father had taught him never to retreat. Especially when you're winning. Hidalgo was ready for this. They'd taken the bait. But there were no guarantees which way they'd go. Now he had the added problem of his client, who had come unfortunately to life, roused by some undetected tic to speak his mind. If Hidalgo was unable to contain him, that could prove disastrous.

"So spell," Hidalgo said, glaring without a blink at his opponents. Bradford began. "No one in any court of law disputes the fact that the power of eminent domain is a viable mechanism, available to the Fed, and to all state governments, according to the Fifth Amendment and every state constitution across America. Article Two, Part Twenty of the *New Mexico Constitution* describes it as an inherent attribute of sovereignty, under which there are really only two caveats to consider. First, that acquisition must be merited according to what are called 'public use tests'—that is, if some necessary benefit, otherwise denied it, is conferred upon the community, and/or if police security, otherwise deficient, is improved as a result of the acquisition. Second, the previous owner must be compensated, according to criteria that vary on a case-by-case basis."

"Compensation is not entirely discretionary, your Honor," Hidalgo angled. "There have been any number of precedents, as you know, and as Gerry surely knows, that have set stringent requirements for compensation. Sometimes, it is a combination of money and land swaps. Let me draw your attention to the common practice of swapping lands confiscated under government Rico laws with other Resolution Trust Corporation properties. Congress, you may recall, approved a rather enormous land trade in the case of a portion of downtown Phoenix, in order to obtain additional environmentally sensitive lands in the Big Cypress National Preserve in South Florida. I have Xerox copies here of the documentation."[9]

"Mitigation is always a possibility," Bradford said.

"I would also point out that the US Supreme Court has held that aesthetic values can justify a restriction on the use of property, as in the case of Berman versus Parker. My client's own aesthetic standards and values affirm that restriction while re-affirming his own viable claim."[10]

"Aesthetics?" The judge's hostility was marked. "I fail to see a relevant inroad or connection."

"You see, my client is an idealist, as you have just heard." (This was Hidalgo's special talent: the ability to marshal an argument instantly, and integrate it into the overall strategy). "He wants his property back. He's willing to negotiate, but he is anti-development."

"We gathered as much."

"That means that we want his undeveloped land restricted—whether it is ultimately deemed subject to eminent domain, or not."

"You can't have it both ways, Francis."

"In New Jersey, the Green Acres Program—one of the first in the country to rule in favor of open space—provided for the transfer of development rights. California did something similar in its *State Government Code 65560(b)*. My point is, we might consider a smaller sum if the Marigold Estate were left as intact as possible, perhaps converted into a park. I'm speaking of the contiguous portions that have not been urbanized."[11]

"Until we have a map, and surveyor reports, and the input of zoning experts, the situation of water rights, plumbing, traffic patterns, building starts, planned communities and 100 other pieces of information, these are particulars better left to urban administrators. What we have to establish here is the validity and nature of the claim, and the options open to you, your client and the State of New Mexico. As I see it, this boils down to one question: the value of the land and what the state might be willing to settle for. Is that fair?"

Hidalgo thought about that—a pause marked by genuine concern which only he understood as part of his stage presentation—then replied with an air of dignity, "That's fair."

"Good," said the judge. "Let's start with a value of 1.5 million dollars as a total settlement. That would be based upon 1.2 million acres times a dollar and a quarter less surveying fees. What do you think?"

After a careful pause: "Well, let me lend some hard data to the discussion. If I had invested one dollar in 1846, today that dollar would be worth 4,000 dollars. Does that help?"

The judge frowned. Gerald Hemmings closed his eyes.

"Hence," continued Hidalgo, "I estimate a starting price for serious negotiations of eight billion dollars." Hemmings sat back in his chair, eyed intently by his younger colleague.

The judge took a breath, numb, but aware of each painful keystroke of the laptop made by the equally astonished stenographer.

"Keep in mind," Hildalgo continued, "your dollar and a quarter was an arbitrary ruling on another land dispute in 1890. My research shows that acreage in 1846 was more like two dollars an acre, though it varied, obviously. I think eight billion is a very conservative estimate of a fair asking price. It does not begin to account for accumulation of value, which is a whole other issue we'll need to look at. It could top 50 billion, by my estimates."

"You'd like to bankrupt the state, in other words?" Bradford replied with real bemusement. "The whole Southwest, for that matter."

"Of course not, your Honor. I'm simply stating for the record the value of the land in 1846 dollars. In fact, that's only the beginning. The courts have recognized that the true market value of property, as a function of the capitalization of net income loss through a century of contamination, versus the value of uncontaminated land during that same period, acknowledging that the city of Santa Fe constitutes extreme contamination on a private landholder's property—and I can prove that by a simple survey of records from the local EPA—has been determined according to the following mathematical computation: Vu, the value of contaminated property, equals the NOI, the net property income of the property in year T divided by Iu, the market discount for an uncontaminated property, so that the value is the sum of net rents for the life of the property capitalized to the present value."

"I would think I'm speaking for all of us when I admit that you've lost me. What the hell are you trying to do?"

"Judge, I'm merely pointing out a number of issues that would argue for increased value. Alonzo Marigold wins fair and square 1.2 million acres. He doesn't touch the property. He dies. His heirs leave the property unaltered for a century and a half. Now, the present owner argues that his intention is to leave that land in a similarly wild state forever, as is consistent with his belief that wilderness is one of the most important values inherent to American culture and history. However, he discovers, much to his pain and distress, that civilization has overtaken his sweet ecological vision. Now, where once was wilderness, a city stands, teeming with businesses and its share of gross contaminants. His aesthetic belief system has been violated, whittled down, practically speaking. So he concludes that he will compromise: give him fair financial compensation for the land which has been developed—based upon the collective net value of that land to its owners today, a numeric value that would certainly comport with your assertion of value under eminent domain—and let him retain title to those lands that are undeveloped, where no one else is likely to be inconvenienced."

"You're out of your mind. The value of businesses today—why, that's hundreds of billions of dollars, if you wanted really to get in there and compute. That's plain stupid. You can't manipulate the laws that way."

"Your Honor, if you will permit me, it's more than that: it is the aesthetic value of the land that has been compromised. Someone's going to have to pay, and that someone is the State of New Mexico."

"There are absolutely no legal precedents for your assertions," the judge invoked, blind rage barely controlled.

Hemmings removed a handkerchief to wipe a sickly layer of sweat from his brow, and whispered into Michaels' ear, "I'd like to deck this asshole."

"Not so, your Honor. First, consider Justice Brennan's ruling that the government is obliged to repay the owner when and if such regulations destroy the use and enjoyment by the owner or deprive him of all beneficial use of it."

"You're speaking of 'inverse condemnation' proceedings?"

"That's right. They've been upheld throughout the country in case after case—*City of Austin versus Teague 1978, City of Virginia Beach versus Virginia Land Improvement Association 1990, Taub versus City of Deer Park, Texas 1994,* and so forth."

"There are cases to the contrary, Francis."

"Few. And in each instance, the benefit to the public, versus the injury represented by a private loss, was weighed by the courts, particularly if a flood plain were involved, or wetlands, or other ecologically significant values. Such values have factored into decisions including *Agins versus City of Tiburon* in 1980, and the protection of the New Jersey Pinelands region in the 1981 *Wilson versus County of McHenry*. In fact, if you recall the famed Penn Central case of 1978, the court ruled that the New York Landmark Commission was right to reject an application by a company to build a modern office building atop the historic railroad station because that would have affected the integrity of the building.[12] But your Honor, why quibble"—this was, he believed, his knock-out punch—"in New Mexico, the courts have shown that the taking of property for public use without just compensation to the owner is forbidden. I presume you and the Office of the District Attorney know all about that? Or that the taking of property from one individual for the use of other private individuals is prohibited? I am referring to *Threlkeld versus the Third Judicial District Court, 36 N.M.350, 15 P.2d 671 1932."*

James Bradford was tiring of this discussion. He was deeply strung out over its direction and he felt, wherever that might be, he was losing something which the Governor had entrusted to him. The dollar figure had already crossed the threshold of madness; his DA was proving useless; and the laws themselves seemed ill-equipped to deal with this unique situation. Indeed, he was beginning to wonder whether anything like this case had ever arisen, in any city.

Gerald Hemmings was wondering the same thing. He had an eerie foreboding about Mr Marigold, who sat mostly in a state of hibernation, like some cadaver who'd come back to reap weird justice, and about Francis Hidalgo the Third, his lawyer from hell, a man who had done his homework with a greed verging on the insane. Even if the Governor shut the case down, he could not alter the constitutional obligation of the state to compensate fairly the claimant. That would mean bond issues, hikes in state income tax, and probably his own resignation. The Governor would never get re-elected after a tax hike in the highest unemployment state in America. The only solution was to buy Hidalgo. To make him an offer that would appeal to his client's irrational utopianism. But what could that be? This Mr Marigold appeared steadfast, enigmatic and elusive. Was he as greedy and conniving as Hidalgo? Or merely a dreamer, easily swayed by a show of authority?

They adjourned for the evening, the plan being to reassemble the following morning at Bradford's chambers. The judge was feeling ill. His knees trembled. Hemmings tried but could not speak, his words stuttering like those of a diver whose tongue has been refrigerated.

CHAPTER 35
Hidalgo's Final Conquest

THAT NIGHT, the judge, the DA and the Governor convened over rare steaks and baked cheddar potatoes and plenty of San Simeon wine that hung above water. As Bradford laid out the state's dilemma, and their own, the Governor seemed increasingly disinterested, unwilling to face up to the implacable debt emerging before him. Not unlike the Governor 160 years earlier, he would find himself trapped by the echoes and poetry of a grand contradiction, and one the voters would remember for many decades to come.

Bradford explained to the Governor the process of eminent domain, and how it could only work against them, but how they had no other choice but to enforce it. In one case, he said, back in 1981, the *Poletown Neighborhood Council v. the City of Detroit*, the Michigan Supreme Court upheld the City of Detroit's action to acquire by right of eminent domain some 465 acres, home to 3,500 people, and 1,176 buildings—which included 144 businesses, three schools, 16 churches and even a cemetery—at the price of 200 million dollars, in order to give the land to an auto manufacturer, which in turn paid the city eight million.

The reasoning behind this seemingly suicidal swap was that the jobs and eventual accumulating taxes from the auto plant would more than compensate the city.[13]

"So what happened?" the Governor pressed.

"Well, sir, that's what happened," Bradford clarified. "The Supreme Court allowed the displacement.

Hidalgo knows all about such cases.

He's got the law on his side. There are dramatic precedents. He's not going to stop."

"He's one greedy sonofabitch," aired Hemmings, feeling the heat exchange between the judge and Governor.

"How greedy? What will it take to get him off our backs?" the Governor swiped, cutting into a slab of rare beef.

"That's a good question. One we're going to find out tomorrow morning. But I think it's important we make a reasonable offer."

"What's reasonable?"

"I tried 1.5 million. The man laughed."

"One and a half million's a lot of money. What do you mean he laughed?"

Bradford looked at Hemmings.

"You tell him," Bradford said.

"Thanks, Jim. Governor, I think the figure Hidalgo mentioned was eight billion as a starting point."

"Eight billion dollars? Only in America. It's all the goddamned lawyers. I'll re-invoke the *Firing Squad Act*. I'll order a public hanging. Is he Catholic?"

"He is."

"Good. We'll excommunicate."

"I believe that is a tactic reserved for or at the discretion of the Pope."

"He can't do this," the Governor mumbled.

"He can, and it appears—unless we find a way to discredit him—he will."

"I thought I had the right to end this on grounds of security?"

"True. But he has the right to compensation, and any court will agree with him."

"Who decides the value?"

"We spent most of the day looking at that."

"Bottom line."

"The government need not underwrite loss."

"What loss? Whose loss?"

"Hidalgo's client's loss, Governor. Or so he claims. A man who blithely touts principles. An idealist who would like to turn the city of Santa Fe into Utopia."

"Guys, stay on cue. There are standards, criteria. I used to be one of those goddamned lawyers, I haven't forgotten everything."

"You're absolutely right," said Bradford. "The courts may follow their own standards and criteria. But market value is the gold standard and it must always lead to fair compensation."

"You're talking in circles, damn it. What's fair if it's so subjective?"

"It's less subjective than you'd think. The courts recognize what's called present use or highest and best available use as their criteria."

"You're the court. Change the criteria."

"The cost of replacement with a parcel of equal stature is fairly well understood. It can't be manipulated."

"We know that's impossible. There's only one Santa Fe. And it wasn't quite the same city in 1846," the Governor rightly reasoned.

"That's our principal loophole," Bradford said. "Nonetheless, the *Model Eminent Domain Code* is quite clear in its definition of fair market value. What the owner—in this instance Mr Marigold—has lost, not what the condemner—the state of New Mexico—has gained. The full value of the city of Santa Fe to the economy, and to the 80,000 residents, cannot be questioned. But some equation needs to be addressed that provides this Mr Marigold with some equitable portion of his lost income opportunity, based on the economy itself. Now that is a big problem, because it amounts to billions of dollars every year."

"Wait a minute. You just said the value is based on his loss, not the state's gain. If not the gain, then isn't his loss precisely what it was worth at the time of this ridiculous gambling debt, and no more?"

"Yes, and no. Fair compensation requires the accrual of interest, appreciation and the fact the state has, in his eyes, destroyed most of his property in the last century and a half."

"We're being held up by one lunatic. What do we really know about this Marigold?"

"We've done some investigating. He's an ecological communist—that's about as close as we can come to figuring him out. Single, a recluse, no criminal record, no driving tickets, not even a parking ticket. He's never worked a day in his life. Minimal education. Has never distinguished himself in any area. His housekeeper has a Green Card. She's Mongolian."

"Mongolian?"

"She's clean. He pays his taxes, no red herrings. He's also clean. Some say he's crazy, however."

"Criminally insane? Can we file a motion to have him placed in psychiatric stockades?"

"Uh, Governor, he hasn't committed a crime, or hurt anybody, or himself. Or presented the slightest signal that he might be capable of doing so. Hence, there are no reasonable grounds for filing a motion to have him checked out. Nor any living relatives who might be tempted to question his capacity."

"What about insane greed? Isn't that grounds?"

"No, Governor. That's called The American Way."

"What about this lawyer of his? He's obviously a little dirt bag. What's he taking, 50 percent?"

"Actually, he was Mr Marigold's father's closest friend, and executor of the estate. Very smart. You'll recall he was the one who stopped the ski-area expansion on behalf of the local tribes."

"Oh, him. So what do we do?" The Governor was at a loss. Bradford, his hand shaking, tried calmly to top off his wine, then said, "We lay out the state's latitude, blame it on the previous Republican administration, and make him an ultimatum. A fair price, or we're taking it to trial—where he'll lose."

"How do you know he'll lose?"

"Because for him to win means every taxpayer in the state gets socked with the bill, and that includes the jurors. Trust me. Hidalgo is not letting this go to trial. Even before the trial, the law would require town hall meetings. That, too, would prove disastrous for Mr Marigold. They know they've got to keep this whole thing quiet. The only way to do that is to work with the state to peacefully resolve the matter. He mentioned something about preserving some of the land. I see that as a possible face-saving remedy. Much of the acreage is already on National Forest lands. Guarantee no logging or mineral prospecting. That would make him happy. Give him 10,000 acres of his own. And a cash settlement. Probably to be paid off over 30 years like a lottery."

"But how much?"

"A billion dollars."

The Governor was stunned. "That's ridiculous. Let him take it to trial. Like you said, he'll lose. End of story."

"Yes, but then he'll go to the Supreme Court, and he'll win, and he'll sue the state for legal fees and punitive damages which will be augmented by all the bad press he'll be getting from our newspapers. Then we'd have a big problem, because he could easily claim bias and the inability to obtain a fair trial in this state—which is absolutely true. The state is, by definition, an interested party. But in some other state the jurors might not give a damn about New Mexico. Of course, that could take years. And I believe they want to settle quickly. He'll ask for two billion. We give him the 10,000 acres or so, the guaranteed preservation—hell, we could name it the Marigold Wildlife Preserve or whatever—and we settle for the billion dollars. They'll take it."

"He will," Hemmings concurred.

"At a billion, over 30 years," the Governor calculated, "what does it mean to the state's treasury? Let's see, that's 33 million a year, right? We can handle that."

"Plus interest and amortized loss of income."

"How much is that?"

"Another few million annually."

"All right," the Governor reiterated. "But I want to keep this out of the press. They'd surely bastardize the whole pitiful affair." As he spoke, his last piece of steak, covered in sauce, fell on his elegant white Manuel suit. Superstitious, he got up and left the table.

The next day those were precisely the terms laid out for Hidalgo and Mr Marigold.

Hidalgo had come prepared with a dissertation on the dollar value of aesthetics. He'd read the exhortations of Thomas Jefferson who'd written about "Gardening as a Seventh Fine Art", and had studied the records of court skirmishes which have shown increasing resilience on the issue of beauty and the marketplace. In the matter of the *State v. Blair*, a landscape architect's property was taken, including 65 species of plants and shrubs, and 21 varieties of trees. The courts awarded him 7,359 dollars for his troubles. Louisiana courts had been especially noteworthy with respect to their interest in aesthetics. Most homeowner insurance policies allowed for 500 dollars per tree. The Council of Tree and Landscape Appraisers, formed in 1975, had actively promoted the awareness of the value of trees and shrubs and other vegetation, and was supported by hundreds of environmental groups like the American Associations of Nurserymen, Consulting Arborists and Landscape Contractors. Nursery stock, timber and crops all constituted aesthetic value, and Francis Hidalgo was prepared to slap the state of New Mexico with a profound appreciation of vegetative assets.

Moreover, he was poised to position the value of the Commander's estate according to the known existence of mineral deposits—oil, sand, gravel, rotary-drilling clay, manganese, coal, gold and silver, all found in parts of the 1.2 million acres. In 1940, the New Mexico courts ruled that the market value of a mineral deposit had to be compensated for. Hidalgo was certain that Bradford would try to argue that the Marigold family had never shown any interest in mining the land and, therefore, that the value of such mineral deposits was not relevant. But Hidalgo had his own response, and it hinged upon the wording of the *Uniform Eminent Domain Code Rule* for the state which stipulated that a knowing buyer and a knowing seller must come together on a fair disposition of the land, whether or not exploitation of the separate resource was contemplated by either party. The same held true of water and lumber rights.[14]

Bradford hoped to disarm such clever ripostes and sadistic research. Preemptively, he laid it out squarely and firmly.

"Here's what we're prepared to do, and I'm speaking on behalf of the Governor."

Ten thousand acres, a wildlife preserve and a billion dollars: Mr Marigold heard the amazing, numbing, unforgettable words, and he grew vague with the tonality of the incantation, as if it had been uttered down in the Cave of the Dragonfly by past spirits. A sweat lodge of haloed conjurations. As if La Tules herself were there—her burning eyes and ravishing hair, the freckled Spanish pallor that lent to her overall demeanor a pulchritude only for worship, loved from afar, with the discretion of whispers and distant memory—overseeing the rightful execution of this long-standing debt.

He could not imagine a billion dollars. Few people can. But he knew, without the slightest configurations of the mind, that a billion dollars would help the world, could save lives, and he vowed at that supreme junction of miasmas to apply himself to its noble dissemination.

All such lofty ruminations were shattered in an instant as he heard his friend, lawyer and executor decline the offer.

"*What?*" the Commander shouted from the sovereign insulation of his thought.

"Excuse me?" came the faltering reply from the DA.

"Four billion, or we go to trial," Hidalgo repeated. "That's a mere half of what we know to be the truer value."

"You will lose in a trial," Bradford said.

"Probably. But we will win in the Supreme Court, and I have already begun writing the brief. They'll find this very interesting."

The judge and Hemmings had a word with each other.

The Commander had a strong word with his lawyer.

Then, in an exasperated tone, Bradford countered, "There's something we haven't mentioned here, as yet. But since you seem intent upon toying with a state that has been good to your people for centuries, let's get it out."

Hidalgo's hair had risen an inch on the back of his neck but he contained himself. He was used to being rankled.

"Unlike the policy of perpetual sovereign power granted to tribal lands, Hispanic grantees may lose title to their lands through non-use.

Are you aware of that?"

Hidalgo, taking the racial slur in stride, was not. He asked for the citation, and Bradford was quick to give it to him. *Gonzales v. Yturria Land and Livestock Co., 1947.*

"I believe we covered that aspect of the case, Gentlemen. Alonzo Marigold, and his descendants, kept sheep and cattle on the land."

"Maybe so, but they certainly did not open the land to recreational use for wilderness enthusiasts; it was never protected as such, nor exploited for any of its alleged hidden wealth."

Hidalgo was furious. Had they not listened? Understood? Or were they simply denying the evidence out of customary denial, to wear him down, pressure his client, eclipse the underlying merits of the case?

Adding to the hoped-for effect of last-minute intimidation, a desperate Bradford also reminded Hidalgo of *Waterman v. the City of Albuquerque, 1977*, involving a requested zoning change. A Mr Waterman had desired to construct several hundred condominium units. The Supreme Court held that the public be given a timely opportunity to hold a hearing. Which, inevitably, might spell the demise of such projects.

"Any large project in New Mexico requires intense public hearings be held so that all involved may comment," the judge explained. "We send word out for months ahead of time. There will be reporters. Scrutiny. Background checks. In this case, we'd be speaking to 80,000 people and they will be speaking to your client." Bradford directed his glare at Marigold. "Are you ready to lose your privacy for the rest of your life? Can you take the heat? It will be intense."[15]

The judge recognized that Marigold was beginning to sweat and to squirm. He looked to Hemmings, then announced, "Here's our last counter: two billion dollars. Take it or leave it."

There was a pause. The Commander was bursting. Before Hidalgo could speak, he returned the judge's steely gaze.

"We'll take your offer," Hidago understated, "assuming the 10,000 acres are good acres. And the two billion are tax free," he added. "And, in addition, we want the Plaza. Just the parkland. My client owns it. We proved that. We are happy to lease it back to the city. And we want a large selection of other parcels to choose the 10,000 acres from."

Without too much reflection, "The state can manage all that," Bradford replied. "As for the tax ramifications, I wouldn't predict your IRS status. But the state will waive any assessments."

"And one last thing." Hidalgo turned off his computer and handed the judge a confidentiality waiver. "We'd really appreciate an effort to control unwarranted leaks to the press, or anybody else."

Hidalgo shook his client's hand. Then, before everyone adjourned, he handed the judge a copy of his brief containing all the citations he had used to argue his case, and some. "These precedents, and this record, should help you explain what happened here today to any detractors."

"What a thoughtful man, you are."

"Why thank you, your Honor," Hidalgo said.

As the judge was leaving, he turned and fired one last question at Hidalgo. "By the way, how did Armijo ever get 1.2 million acres in the first place? That seems like a stretch, even for a corrupt Governor."

"I believe he, too, won the land at the monte tables, your Honor."

CHAPTER 36
The Marigold Hypothesis

ONCE THE LEGAL PROCEEDING was accomplished, Hidalgo's wife Shirley suggested they take a year's cruise round the world to slowly digest the windfall and contemplate the best way in which to spend all their money. "Spend" was her operative term. Her biggest dilemma was choosing an ocean-going vessel. She wanted state rooms, walk-in closets, a private pool and her own trainer. "Spend until I drop" was her compulsive goal.

The Commander gave 100 million dollars to Hidalgo for his troubles, three million dollars to Alma, and equal portions to Sannazaro, Ginevra, Madame Vignette, the local art museum, and a few other organizations he thought well of. That still left him 1.85 billion dollars, as well as 10,000 acres and the park in the Plaza. Hidalgo had already planned his affront on the IRS, which—he was certain—could claim none of the settlement. There was no income, as such; no capital gain. It was the equivalent of property, possessed in the year 1846.

Hidalgo wanted to stay and help, but not too much, and so the Commander bid farewell and many thanks to his executor and his wife.

"Don't do anything rash," Francis exclaimed to His Holiness at his going-away party. "I know you, and I don't want to read about your ill-conceived exploits whilst sipping Maitais on the *Queen Mab*."

He and Shirley—who had researched the matter thoroughly—had joined several *Queen Mab* journeys into one. Their itinerary would take them to something like 70 countries over the course of 365 days.

After a limousine had picked the couple up and taken them to the Santa Fe airport, the Commander filled Sannazaro in on all the miraculous details of the case. The gardener, who was still aching from his adventures at the Cave of the Dragonfly, could not fail to be impressed.

"You're giving me three million dollars?" he said, utterly astonished.

"That's only so you'll feel free to pay your bills, and not have to fret late at night when you want to run out and buy a Mars bar or plant another bed of roses. The kingdom I promised you is the real incentive here."

"Incentive to do—what?" There was always a catch with Don Magnífico, and Sannazaro knew enough about his strange neighbor to fear for his life at the slightest hint of a sweet-talking Marigold, or his rising enthusiasm.

"Well, a number of things. Firstly, I have 10,000 acres to select somewhere, hopefully, in the vicinity of Santa Fe. I want wild land, and intend to leave it that way, obviously. But I have been thinking. Perhaps it would be worth exploring what biologists refer to as a genetic corridor."

"Which is what?"

"The dream, I believe, of all my ancestors. A theory of biology inherent to finance. A topographical tapestry at the root of all migrations, hybridizations and future offspring. Think of me as a six-year-old. That way, maybe, you'll someday understand me."

"One more time," the befuddled gardener applied.

"You were listening. I'm talking about piecing together acreage so as to provide lifelines for creatures otherwise condemned by sprawling, unchecked development. I have pondered, of late, the so called rarity-weighted richness index."

"What is that?"

"A methodology used to identify biodiversity hotspots."

"What are hotspots?"

"My dear man, there's far more at stake than our puny pleasures. Species are imperiled nationwide. Whether alligator or hummingbird. Creosote bush or prairie grass."

"I have never made the acquaintance of either alligator or creosote. And there would seem to me plenty of prairie to go around."

"A fool's reply. I assure you such grass is in short supply, every alligator crying out for repast. As for the creosote bush, it is older than the bristle cone pine, each living one dating tens of thousands of years into antiquity. Yet our brethren think nothing of dirt-biking over them."

"Well, at least the bush has lived a long and prosperous life. I would happily be struck down by a dirt bike on my 30,000th birthday."

"More than foolish, you add biological insult to ignorance. Let me try to straighten your genius. Imagine, if you dare, if there were a way to infiltrate Santa Fe, or Albuquerque, with 10,000 untouchable acres: a library of trees, causeways untrammeled, a series of creeks enabling fish to spawn within the city proper without fear of either Whirling Disease or Winding Up on a Dinner Plate. One grove of trees leading to another, wending their way in and out of all the parking lots and shopping malls. The soil covered in leaves. Bugs. Every cave teeming with furry mammals. Each garden unencumbered. Do you have any idea how many species inhabit this state? A known 3,266 plants, 762 vertebrates, 147 mammals, 448 birds, 95 reptiles and 25 amphibians. That's fourth in the nation. Think about it."

"I can't think in so many numbers. Tell me about one good meal, or two pearl earrings, and I will drum up some enthusiasm. But not however many thousands of reptiles, did you say? Frankly, I've never cottoned to snakes or lizards."

"You are denser than I imagined. Don't you see, we need an end to the era of pesticides and fungicides."

"In one era, out the other, as Italians say."

"No more lawn-mowing. No males in offices of power. No trading in acreage at three cents a shot, as in Jefferson's day. Let us see the seven-foot tallgrass prairies in their deep dark loam the way Lewis and Clark spied them—to the horizons and forever. An anthem to the manatee. Forbid human entry to Florida's Panhandle. Revere the whitetop pitcher plant, the Torrey pine; rid San Francisco's Delta Estuary of all people; restore the Pleistocene; give back discrete populations to every region. Replace all sovereign political states with ecological nations, beginning with the Republic of Appalachian China, wherein all salamanders, freshwater mussels, fish, crayfish and invertebrates are taught to eschew humankind. Revere endemics; engineer adaptive radiation as it was 17 million years ago, when this was a great country; worship the Oahu tree snail and all his friends; pay proper heed to coastlines; grant riverbanks their loveliness, starting with Alabama's Cahaba—the greatest one in North America—and, though sadly absent, the blue shiner (*Cyprinella caerulea*). To hear once more that little girl's heartbeat—that of the fish, I mean—I should gladly give up my own."

"All this in Santa Fe? The Appalachias? China? But how will you move them? I am utterly confused." The addled (and who wouldn't be?) Squire squirmed.

"And more. I failed to mention my favorite arthropods, pupfish, dune grass, and mixed mesophytic, needleleaf and sclerophyllous forests. I should have added that we in North America are nothing if not for the genius of Cuatro Cienegas, a basin in northeastern Mexico containing more endemics than anywhere else."

"So?"

"So? Ingrate. Where is your thinking cap? Your decency? There is no nation without endemics; no people without prairie; no silence save for the empty spaces. You can have your coffee machine, I am content with oak savanna. Keep your skyscrapers, give me mountain mahogany. If it's a new freezer you require, I shall instead walk across the North Pole. And if the cold gets to you, move to the reaches of cypress, ceinza, fayette and everglade. And right here, downtown, a mesquite bosque. That is my plan."

"That is your plan?"

"You heard me."

"And the people who might be inconvenienced by all these silly-sounding words of yours?"

"I shall move their hearts with a playground."

"A playground?"

"Are you deaf ? A playing field strictly to enable the physically challenged to interact with the non-challenged. A precinct of high grass scattered with fancily clad seesaws and castles, bubbles that are boundless, so that children can remove their wheelchairs, roll in the deep sward and dance free of constraints with others from all neighborhoods. Let the whole city be undermined by play, by tears, by empathy and endemics."

"I am lost, can't see it," Sannazaro confessed. Then, upon second reflection: "Don't we already have playgrounds, baseball fields, tennis courts, wheelchair ramps, flowers in abundance, forests all over downtown?"

"Yes, and no. You are a challenge, Señor. Your headpiece—with its multiplicity of doddypoles, dungcarts and devitrification—I can see is equal to that of every other dunderhead in the world. Make you understand, and all will understand. That is why I admire your company, if for no other reason."

"Thank you."

"You're welcome."

"Convince me, then. Not that your munificence has not already done so, fundamentally, by the gift of three million, for which—grass or no grass—I am forever in your glade."

"Again you're welcome. Now consider the city," began the Commander. "It is unfruitful and haphazard, without concern for the biological needs of the native species, or the inundation of parasites into the rivers..." He found himself speaking with greater clarity and resolve than at any previous time in his existence. A recent fixation with numbers had certainly influenced these ruminations. Always ecologically attuned, now he seemed to blossom with purpose. To rise out of his milk vetch, this master of blasting, a summons in a civil process, his every word a bittersweet celebration of the coming dawn.

"Oh," Sannazaro said dumbly.

The Commander had not yet given up on the idea of converting Santa Fe to a National Park. He'd have to effect the transformation through some kind of buy-out, as coercion was no longer feasible, given Judge Bradford's ruling. He had not garnered anywhere near enough funds to purchase all of the city. Which left him open to turmoil: how to budget his priorities? Green buttons, or red? Roses or violets?

"There's a bigger nut to crack," he explained to the gardener, "and that, of course, is the 1.85 billion. How to spend it in this world, or invest it, in a way that will do the most good. Help the least, remedy the rest. Through Bingo? Churches in South Dakota raise money for non-profits that way. That is not my bailiwick. But I'm not shy about asking. To that end I have called upon a fine woman who lives just up the hill—Catherine Champion, a true source of vital heritage in this town. Do you know her?"

"I don't," the gardener admitted. "How did you meet her?"

"Ginevra made the introduction some time ago. I've invited her for lunch because I believe she is best suited to arrange for a confab of great souls—people whose contributions to this region speak for themselves, who have shown by their example what it means to be a true blue, a contributarian, humanist and ecologist. I want to throw the question of 1.85 billion dollars out into the open. I want suggestions. Naturally, I have one or two ideas of my own."

"Give the man a prize for understatement."

"The point is, I want to hear from people older than myself. Santa Fe abounds with common sense and I'm certain that the ideas that will flow from this think-tank of compassion, as I'm envisioning it, will inspire me in my responsibilities."

"Just as long as you don't invite any tennis players from the suburbs." Catherine Ann Champion, aged 70 going on 20, as they say, arrived at the hacienda in her green hatchback Honda, and carrying a rucksack filled with ideas: notebooks, letters, documents, books which she had written, pieces of calligraphy, marriage certificates, testimonials from those who had been divorced, or had miscarriages, or fallen in love, or died and gone to heaven.

She came inside, threw down her pack, took a look around and declared, "Great house! Who's that?"

She had zeroed in on a photograph of Mr Marigold as a child, seated on an Arabian with his father.

"That's my father, who died in an avalanche when I was a kid."

"How fascinating. And who's that?"

"My mother. I never knew her. She passed away during my childbirth."

"I'm sorry," Catherine said. "She was a beautiful woman."

The Commander stared at the photographs in their bright silver frames and felt a tremor of sadness. His parents would have been proud to learn that Alonzo's wealth had been returned. Pecos would have relished the search for the best 10,000 acres, and the chance to lovingly survey every inch of that land. Now, the Commander was incapable of properly doing so, and would have to hire someone from the state instead.

He thought how his mother would have made good use of nearly two billion dollars. She'd have organized benefits, raised additional moneys, set up all manner of distribution centers for the dispossessed, adopted children, purchased books, rescued animals and abused women, passed out condoms. That was her style, according to Pecos, and it was a persuasive one. Throughout their history Marigolds never cultivated a name; their public presence was a force of self-effacing discretion and beneficence. For his part, the Commander had probably sunk to the lowest ebb of modesty within that family tree by dint of his impractical nature, spindly idealism, disdain for all physical exercise and utter refusal to involve himself in actual issues. His uninvolvement with his fellow humans, however, did not mean that he was not a deeply caring person. He was simply in love with books, whose ease of infection had so manifested great adventures from a single armchair that—quite frankly—there was never a good reason, or even a bad one, for him to get out of bed in the morning. He could feel horrible about starving children on the pages of the *Economist* while drinking his coffee and picking at a blueberry scone. Or imagine fabled kingdoms without the slightest constraint on their architecture or inhabitants.

His role model was Alonzo. From everything Hidalgo had found out, Alonzo De Resista Marigold must have shunned the fame that came with the 1.2 million acres. Indeed, his life played itself out with hardly a notice of the windfall. It changed nothing for him. When he died, in the early 1860s, his children were given the lump sum of land without the slightest modifications, annotations or itemization. There had been no "improvements" because Alonzo knew that none were needed. Wild land was perfect as it was. No planting. No rearranging. No maintenance.

Victor, Chihuahua, Burrito and Pecos Marigold were each equally impelled towards disinterest. We know that they were never caught up in the rage for improvements that came with homesteading Acts and incentives from government, the mad flurry of settlements which the Spanish and the Mexicans and finally the Americans took to be fundamental to community life. Burn, bury and build: that was the motto. Put up barbwire fences, clear forests for pasture, ship the logs, convert them to railroad ties, shoot bison and prairie dogs from passing zephyrs, belch the smoke of iron and steel across the troubled horizon, dam all the rivers and erect squat shelters to imprison citizens who, thinking themselves civilized, soon lost the ability to distinguish between happiness and servitude, liberation and oppression, compassion and cruelty.

But there was a qualitative difference between the Commander and his ancestors. Whereas Murillo had been content to remain more or less self-exiled within the borders of his hacienda, those family members preceding him were bona fide wanderers of intimate renown. Burrito, for example, kept no fixed record, adhered to no routine, and married repeatedly, for short stints. His journeys took him to remote settlements, from Newfoundland (where he practiced meteorology) to Costa Rica (for purposes of finding the world's tastiest banana). But he always returned to the hacienda in Tesuque. He was a lyrical, generous man: poetaster, painter, farmer, gourmet chef and part-time surveyor. In his case, from what could be divined, the earth and heavens were *not* bigger than his philosophy—a capaciousness passed down to Pecos.

None of this heritage was presently lost on Marigold who, following his expedition with Madame Vignette and his courtroom victory, was now ready to turn a new leaf. And by his very first example, it was clear to Sannazaro that the Commander was altogether serious about using his new-found riches to mend the world, however problematic an instinct.

He soon got down to the point with Catherine. There was little time to waste. Hidalgo had suggested, and Mr Marigold had agreed, to invest the 1.85 billion in overnight money markets. The rate would yield him 5.85 percent, and that would simplify matters in the short term, while the Commander figured out what he really wanted to do with all that money. The interest alone would bring him over 50 million dollars a year after taxes. If he needed to borrow against the money, he certainly could. Any bank would be only too happy to extend a billion-dollar line of credit, though Hidalgo didn't advise it. Nor did he favor gambling on margins, going into stock options, buying short or long or inviting penalties. Hidalgo knew that the IRS would be watching him, that audits were guaranteed, and that Mr Marigold was absolutely the worst candidate for dealing with tax people. He had set the Commander up with a great accountant; and a money manager at Merrill Lynch, adept at socially conscious investing, would also watch over the estate. Before boarding his cruise vessel, Hidalgo had negotiated a package fee for the Commander which encompassed all fiduciary responsibilities. Mr Marigold would be in fine hands, no cowboys; his optimization data—the beta, P/E, capitalization and volume quintiles, yield simulations, sigma r squares and tracking errors—importantly sounding and extrapolated. He was protected by an armada of strangely phrased provisions of section 16052 of the *Probate Code* and all those caveats inherent to the *Uniform Prudent Investors Act* that controlled the latitude, scope and discretion of the money manager. Marigold had no clue, as yet, about any of it.

Notwithstanding a total return policy, it was the Commander's money, after all. He might alter the proportion of equities, fixed income and cash; or the maximum average effective maturity of the bonds; or the percentage relation to the so-called Lehman Aggregate Index. He might buy women's bonnets, rather than prune futures; manage cheese-free pizza parlors, if he liked, or purchase part of France. If a set of bonds were called early, he'd have to be the final arbiter and decide the fate of such intermediate-term trends, probability theory and overall investment strategy. Hidalgo would be on his charter, soaking in a hot tub or lawn-bowling above the whitecaps.

On the other hand, waiving better judgement, eschewing all prudent practices, Mr Marigold might choose at any time to take a huge sum of money and put it towards some sudden and unexpected idyll, or lark. A hundred such schemes presently fluttered upwards like spring azures and pearl crescents—from the vast central open area of his headline, blotches and effluvia breaking out and streaming off the impenetrable map of his fixations. He suffered from an eagerness to be parted from his change, to solve all the world's problems as quickly as possible.

"I will not be bullied into patience," he rallied. "No monetary policy for me."

"A dangerous contagion," warned Sannazaro, who dimly perceived trouble, if not outright bodily harm, down the unlit road.

CHAPTER 37
A Parliament of True Blues

LET ME FILL YOU IN on the real me," Catherine began. She had all sorts of wonderful ideas about how 1.85 billion might be spent, but she concurred from the start of their conversation that such money, in truth, was a gigantic responsibility best administered in earshot of good advice from a number of points on the compassion compass. The two seemed absolutely coordinated, even if the Commander's eyes sometimes jerked and spasmed outside the realm of normal understanding. She took this as a sign of eccentricity and high thought. A maverick of fiscal power.

"Some liken me to a miracle worker," she said with a self-mocking grin. "It's other people who are miracle workers, of course. I'm merely a facilitator."

And she went on to explain how she, and several dozen others, belonged to a Tabernacle of the Life Force. As she spoke, she spun a little pendulum which she wore round her neck to get answers: a yes, a no, or a no comment.

"Spin it," she said, "and make a wish."

The Commander did so, and then Sannazaro.

"I won't ask you anything about either wish, but trust that the pendulum is in an agreeable mood this morning." She laughed. "By the way, it never gets any better than this."

"Than what?" Marigold inquired.

"This. This moment. Full of health, sunlight, friendship, discussion. Cold water to drink, food on the table, a hillside behind, and views to take your breath away. No wars or mould underfoot, and only love and smiles and promise emanating from all sides. And look—out the window, a wind blowing apple blossoms hither and yon. No, it doesn't get any better than this."

"You are quite right, Madame. Thank you for that reminder." The woman's comments had sparked in the Commander the realization that all the woes of this age would be eclipsed, so that within a decade, or five, or even one year, today's civil wars and corn blights would be faint memories, infused with a certain romance of history, like so many old sepia tones and tintypes arrayed for purposes of instruction, hieratic snoozes and idle nostalgia. Always important to recall. That this too shall pass.

She showed the two men some of her calligraphy, exquisite work that evidently commended two points of the world book of morals, two laws eternal: forgiveness and paradise. "Paradise is here is here is here," she echoed.

Catherine Champion was raised in Kentucky. She would go on to mother eight children and 32 grandchildren. Voted most important activist in Santa Fe year after year, she had survived a long bout with leukemia without a dent. Dress designer, calligrapher, book binder, basket maker specializing in cross-stitch and paste craft, lobbyist, healer, ordained minister, tree planter, founder of the local theater guild, president of the New Church of Sensitive Beings, recruiter for the Peace Corps, fighter against nuclear proliferation and toxic wastes, a member of the New Mexico Women's Panel on Gender Equity, a high priestess of the Acupuncture Colloquy, head of the local Environmental Task Force on Biophilia, stalwart supporter of the Santa Fe Arts Fund, member of the former Soviet-American Women's Summit, a director of the Global Community for a Better World, a leading delegate of the Green Belt Movement in Africa, director of the World's Woman Congress and the Equity-Through-Unity Program in South Chicago, she was a true blue, as the Commander thought of her. Catherine had chained herself to a fence at Los Alamos, had fasted for 100 days, saved 90 goats from slaughter, and adopted 400 Honduran orphans of a mighty hurricane. She was unstoppable.

"You must be the change you wish to see in the world," she would say. Life for her was "a red-lettuce day".

Through this remarkable profusion of affiliations and commitments, the friends she'd made in Santa Fe, the powerful connections she'd favored or cultivated, all recommended her burning knowledge of how best to delegate, administer, invent, inspire and effect. She was as practical as she was a dreamer, and Sannazaro, for his part, could see a strong affection for this woman in the Commander.

"Who do we invite to our town hall meeting?" Mr Marigold began.

"How long a meeting?" she asked. "I mean, this sort of thing needs planning, time."

"I don't want to spend too much time. I prefer impulse, bursts of the imagination."

"But not impractical."

"We'll see. Remember, 1.85 billion dollars allows for multiple unachievables. It is a big enough sum to relish the theoretical, entertain the crackpot, speculate amongst the starry-eyed, and be diverted by chimeras and potholes. Friction, peripatesis, frisson, silence, even error are each necessary to creation."

"Your decisions, your money. But I do know the people, 100 of them, at the very least. Is that too many?"

"Hmmm," the Commander thought. Then, "Speak up?" He'd noticed Sannazaro's look of concern.

"Too many," the gardener said. "A hundred people cannot agree on a bottle of wine or make for consensus on a cheese dip."

"I don't need consensus on a cheese dip. I simply want to hear good ideas."

"No, he's right," Catherine agreed. "How about 35?"

"A good number, truly," Sannazaro exclaimed. "Done. Get us 35."

Catherine set to work in her ebullient fashion, calling on friends at the Departments of Social Welfare and Public Health, Employment and Rehabilitation. She hand-delivered a rolled invitation, tied with string, at the Temple of Scottish Rites, advising them of a secret meeting that could change the course of destiny. She knew they'd chime to that. She passed along a cryptic directive for the headmaster of the Sacred Hearth in the Sacramento Mountains near Alamogordo where, her hair still in ponytails, she'd gone to boarding school and caused memorable mischief. She faxed contacts at the National Council of Federated Garden Clubs, the head beekeeper at the Santuario de Guadalupe, a zoologist specializing in wood rats at St Catherine's Indian School, a physicist at the New Mexico Solar Energy Group, an archeologist at the Ghost Ranch, an equestrian at the Ranch of the Crows, a writer at the Church of the Eagle, an historian at the Pre-Colonial New Mexico Cultural Trust, the janitor of Manderfield School, and various experts at New Vistas, the Red Cross, the Santa Fe First Presbyterian Church, the American Legion, the Espanola Wildlife Rescue Society, the Chamber of Commerce, Federation of Progressive Women, the Audubon Society atop Upper Canyon Road, the Catholic Maternity Institute, the founder of the Fiesta de Santa Fe, a head honcho at the United Mine Workers Coalition, a midwife at the Bruns Army Hospital who had delivered her first baby when she was eleven, and countless others.

Her many missives and messages induced an avalanche of interest, and within 24 hours the participants had been screened, and the meeting assembled at her solarized abode with its Saltillo-tiled floors, dutch doors, ivy and rose gardens, and a portal looking out over the Sangre de Cristo and Jemez mountains from above Bishop's Lodge Road.

They crammed in like volts or electrons on a live wire, honored to have been invited, and held in some suspense by the actual details of the assembly which had not been explained. All they knew was that the largest bequest in Santa Fe's history was being considered by a local ecologist who had come unto a fortune and who deemed their input of some consequence to the outcome. The gathering buzzed. Many of those present knew each other, of course; were part of Catherine's network of spiritualists: Sally, who performed various women's rituals and earned her living cooking tortillas. The roller-blading Father of the Church of San Lorenzo in the Picuris Pueblo. The biker padre of Kirtland Air Force Base in Albuquerque.

Sannazaro and the Commander watched on, without much mingling. Also at hand was the head chef at the New Mexico School for the Deaf, a former scientist with the National Institutes for Health and a preacher in his own right. This polymath presided over the Ministry of Tea. His name was Lester Okakura, and like any true Cadfael he could correctly identify an epigallocatechin gallate (or EGCG compound) from an antioxidant, a growth inhibitor from a blood glucose level. He knew about ultrasound stimulation and anticoagulants, how to reduce HCA (heterocyclic amine) levels, and the surest method of synthesizing vascular endothelial growth in babies. It all came down to green tea, he explained, parsed out in brick portions, the legacy of Bodhidarma and his own ancestor, Kakuso, a former curator of the Boston Fine Arts Museum. He served tea—powdered green tea from Kyoto—four times a day to the students, preparing it like a conductor, modulating the heat on a half-dozen kettles so that the whistles would blow themselves into a harmonic chorale, which he alleged stabilized the DNA in every living creature. He was an extraordinary nut and his friends swore by his ministrations.

"Folks, folks, attention please. A call to order," Catherine started amid the pell-mell.

Cheerful silence pervaded the open drawing room.

"I'd like to welcome you all this morning. Each of you was selected to join in this summit meeting of the ecological soul, as I'd like to call it, for one reason: you have a lot on the ball. You've been around the briar patch, and you know your turf. Now I can't tell you too much because the donor to this enterprise treasures his anonymity. I can't even tell you if she, or he, is here with us today." (Everybody spied upon his neighbor with most sanguine expectations.) "But what I can tell you is that your ideas, which we hope to elicit during this gathering, will certainly be addressed in the planning of how to spend the money."

"What are the origins of this money?" somebody asked.

"Family inheritance," said Catherine without further explanation. "Now what we're looking for are breakthroughs. We want to know how to transform our little Santa Fe into a Utopia. We all love it here and we want to keep it as perfect as possible. Our benefactor is willing to pay for its preservation. The question is this: what do we preserve, what are the priorities, what's possible, what is our wish list?"

"This is heavy stuff," said Enrique Stefano, once named by the *Detroit Herald* as America's most compelling one-man theater. He'd portrayed Geronimo, the Wright Brothers, Gaudi, Truman and Jean-Paul Sartre, and every year performed as the legendary fire dancer alongside the giant puppet Old Man Gloom, or Zozobra, on the streets of Santa Fe. "The days are short. In my time I've seen the population increase fivefold. Santa Fe will never be a Utopia, if it's the air and water and wildlife you're speaking of. Way too much tarmac, already; too many shopping centers, too many people. I suppose it would benefit from a few more theaters, book stores, comedy clubs and camping sites."

"How much money are we talking about?" asked Bob Jenkins. "As much as it takes," said Catherine.

Jenkins was the State League's Natural Resource Chair, a Harvard graduate who'd moved to New Mexico in the 1930s and was born, many said, to see the passage of the *New Mexico Solid Waste Act of 1990*. He had spearheaded awareness of sludge, going from school to school to sermonize on the dangers of untreated sewage, which once flowed freely down the city's gutters, as in every American city.

"We've got a water problem in Santa Fe. Always have, but it's surely going to get worse with increasing population," he said. "Our waste treatment facilities are underfunded. Waste should be the guiding hand here, the canary in the mineshaft. All other problems and prospects derive from what a city does with its waste. You cannot have Victor Hugo without a good sewage system."

How extraordinary, thought the Commander.

"OK. More money for waste treatment and septic tanks. What else?" asked Catherine, who took diligent notes.

An old fellow raised his hand. "Some of you don't know me. I'm Miguel Maxitodado. I'm the guy who stopped that power line from being laid in the Jemez Mountains. It would'a killed all sorts'a rare medicinal plants my people, the Tewa Indians, have used for centuries. Power lines are bad. Herbal medicine is good. I see that my old friend Lester's here, which is terrific, 'cause he knows. He's been there. And I think I speak for both of us when I say that the sign of a healthy society is the number'a plants in the town, not the number'a power lines. Put 'um underground. Better yet, go solar. It's more trees and flowers we need. Peace be with you all."

"Trees and flowers, fewer power lines. Got it. Thanks, Miguel. You're terrific" Catherine intoned lightly.

The Commander, who languished inconspicuously in a corner like a French semi-colon, not only absorbed the facts of his finding mission but also took special notice of the sheer energy swirling about the room. A barometer would have recorded the ague of every human anxiety.

These assorted visionaries held strong beliefs, such that no opportunity escaped their agitation. They were the fumigators within any democracy, the spoilers amid plenty. They coveted success, counter-amending every process with an annoying, insoluble detail and all those particulars with a multiplication table of complaints that could be counted on to aggravate the least drama, even in absence of the slightest difficulty or opposition. In their hands was vested an interminable dialogue, the contentment of speech without end. A paralysis such that these many hopeless, combative ideologies all rendezvoused towards no outcome. Intellects which would forever remain on the sidelines of the revolution, taking their potions calmly.

"Hi, I'm Lena, and I just want to say I agree with Miguel. After all, St Francis worshipped cedar,

Bonaventura pine, Teresa juniper, Aquinas red oak. God, keep us simple. Keep my family whole. Without trees and flowers, who are we?"

"Hear, hear! Great Spirit, keep the oven warm," said Maria Chaveazio. "And look who's here, speaking of a great spirit!"

The most noble Pima Indian ever to set foot in New Mexico, Tashquent, had just arrived, and sat down on the floor. He'd gotten his PhD from Princeton, in paleobotany, and his cures for all those ills from lightning to whirlwinds, wheat-crop failure to warts were said to be miraculous. He came prepared to list 500 plants that could be saved in the Santa Fe environs and might put the immediate world back in balance. *Euphorbia polycarpa benth*, for example, or rattlesnake weed—Veeipkam in Pima.

"What's that you're chewing?" Catherine asked him.

"Jievut hiawsik," he said. "Makes all the girls love me. Came here to test it out."

"We want to fix Santa Fe," Catherine replied. "Not your love life. Anyway, you already know we all adore you. And if I were just a year or two younger—"

"Catherine, your youth and inspiration shame us all. But not everybody shines quite so refulgently. Since a city is only a reflection of its people, you've got somehow to get it right by everybody."

"There hasn't been a truly unanimous vote since World War II," she replied. "Not in this country, anyway," Tashquent went on to signal the emergence, 2.5 million years ago, of *Homo rudolfensis*, *habilis* and *ergaster*—"the three machos". Ever since then, he said, we've been doing it all wrong. Cutting and chopping and killing. "Time to wake up," his voice rang clear. "The plant kingdom should be our guide. Why, just in America there are nearly 8,000 vegetation tribes, all living in perfect harmony. Their love lives are miraculous, the modesty they espouse, the values they share, the moisture and oxygen they freely give. Even mercy is in plants. The brake fern, poplars, willows and sunflowers, each of which can bio-remediate the soil, neutralize arsenic, detox the rhibosphere, clean up an oil well. There is no greater exemplar than a plant. Let our politics be divided, our leaders fall and cities crumble. Let wilderness retake all that man has aspired to. A jungle of former Cambodian palaces, infiltrated with the bacterial root and poking stem, broken down like so much mulch and humus until only the moss campion and brick-strewn ghosts remain. A nation of vegetables is what we need. I give you that to ponder!"

CHAPTER 38
Goltz the Garbage Collector, and Others of His Kind

STRAIGHT AWAY another man rose heartily to his feet, and stood square like a mean bruiser.

"My name's Sidney Goltz," he said, "and I'm a retired garbage collector from Los Alamos National Laboratory. I'll tell you what: I've seen a few things. It's broken, all right. Somebody was talking about sludge. You think Santa Fe's got a waste problem? Well trust me, folks, you don't know the half of what's in the regional water and air and soil. You want to build Utopia in Santa Fe, first thing you're going to have to do is tear down Los Alamos and replant, just like Tashquent said. Tearing down the legacy of Los Alamos won't be easy.

"He's absolutely right," a woman called Margaret Freemason said. "You all know that I was here in 1902 when 80 acres could be had south of Santa Fe for under 150 dollars, and they'd throw in a gang of Jerseys. There was one automobile in the city. Collars were thick and had to be sent to Albuquerque for laundering. The houses on Agua Fría Street were surrounded by alfalfa fields. The more expensive homes had lumber stamped 'No slave labor used'. I remember when Archbishop Lamy planted Carolina poplars everywhere. I mean thousands of them. The last one was unceremoniously chopped down in 1986. It's presently the site of a laundromat. What more can you say." Everybody nodded.

"It's no secret that Margaret turned 100 this week," someone called out from the crowd. "Some of you were at her party. Biggest hangover in recorded history."

"I'm still working it off," the centenarian who had a paying job at the local hospital cursed fuzzily. A round of applause went up.

"A city that can't even protect its poplars ain't worth shit," said Shoedog Strauss, the famed anti-Nazi cartoonist, speaker of Apache, Hungarian, Czech and broken English. He and his wife Gretel had turned their Espanola photographic studio into a vegetarian cookery, telecommunications center and B&B free to any and all human rights activists. "I motion to replant all the poplars."

"You're all forgetting the health of the people. You can't ask them to replant trees if they're sick, or malnourished, or blind, or undergoing chemo. And we've got all that in spades in Santa Fe County. I'm Cynthia Taylor of the Indian Health Service and I've specialized in such things as vitamin A deficiency for years. You want reforms—reform the health. We need more 24-hour clinics, staff, equipment. And an outreach for nutritional illiteracy. You got this big-time ecologist zillionaire? I ain't impressed because ecology means the ecology of the people. If the people aren't fit, the landscape ain't worth a damn. We had 17,000 murders in this country last year. Add to that more than 100 executions. All the billionaires in the world couldn't stop the killing, even if they wanted to."

"I come at this thing from a different angle," bespoke Barbette Violetta. "You all know how we fought to preserve the city parks. We also struggled with city officials to preserve the baseball team. The health of the children was at stake. But we ran into a real forcefield of conflicts and contradictions. Remember how the city wanted to turn some of the park land over to baseball fields? What were we idealists supposed to do, huh? She was a doozy. Made us re-think. But we figured it out. You can have both with a little planning."

"May I say something?" asked Judge Anselm Tiano, the conscience of Santa Fe. He was famous in town for refusing ever to prosecute; hundreds of traffic tickets crowded his desk, sometimes with checks he refused to cash, money he refused to deposit. A good soul that near everyone loved. City administrators detested him, however. Said he was lazy, spent his days at the Santa Fe Downs watching the horse races. In his fancy cowboy boots and ten-gallon hat, he was known to have more respect for people than for the law.

"I'll tell you how planning works in my office," he said. "All that money I collect from people with parking or traffic tickets—you know where that money goes? Healthcare baskets for the kids on reservations, chocolates and rescued puppies for the elderly at homes, and special meals for prisoners. I've never told anybody this, but it was the good people of Santa Fe whose parking tickets contributed to 5,000 vegetarian meals which the late Linda McCartney sent over as part of her one million vegetarian meals to the refugees of former Yugoslavia. You don't tamper with your ethics, just the money behind the ethics. Catherine, you dodged the bullet when Marvin asked you. So I'll ask it again. How much money we talking about, in rounded figures?"

Catherine glanced towards Marigold, who subtly nodded his assent. "Well over a billion dollars. And it's no TV moghul."

"Holy shit," the judge muttered. "That's a lot of parking tickets. You could damn near buy up the whole town for that amount."

"Well, that's sort of the idea," she said.

"Of course, the people would have to agree. And what, exactly, are we agreeing to?" said Parena Eventide, a famed healer who had managed to blend the techniques of dance choreographer Rudolph Laban with those of the resistance theologian Joseph Pilates. Just to look at her was to be cured of any physical illness. "I've treated sick people, and there is a simple principle behind it: give them the tools to cure themselves. But in the case of the city it's more difficult. Bad wastewater disposal, polluted air, unsightly power lines, the cutting down of trees: these are symptoms of a sickness. What is that sickness? Government intervention? Greed? Ignorance? All of the above? You can't just cure those things with lots of money. There has to be a spiritual healing. My dear friend Tashquent nailed it."

Gloria Angel, the blind drama teacher at the Los Niños Kindergarten, who had literally opened more eyes, stimulated more senses than any teacher west of the Missouri River, nodded her agreement. "We could talk all day about Utopia. But what is Utopia? If you're blind, it's being able to see. If you're in a wheelchair, it's being able to walk. Talk of power lines is pretty academic, as far as I'm concerned. Vitamin A is closer to the truth. More Shakespeare is one answer. Anyway, there is no one answer. Because we don't really know the question."

Joe Barber spoke up. He'd developed the Habitat for Humanity Seminars, focused on hunger, and a ministry for the physically challenged. An indefatigable pioneer of the underdog, his motto was: "A roof over everyone's soul; a cup of hot chocolate for every wayfarer".

"What are we really saying here?" he began. "What does this patron saint expect to accomplish with his billion dollars?"

"I don't even think he knows. That's why we've called on all of you. Only to reaffirm a better quality of life for everyone. And the idea of converting Santa Fe into a National Park."

There was a rumble.

"Now *that's* a notion," cried Maggie Mason, whose discovery of a six-foot phytosaur, the primeval New Mexican alligator, inaugurated her commitment to the paleontological preservation of Santa Fe. Her fingers had stroked twelve million years of wind and sand. To shake her hand was risky business. To look into her eyes, a lawyer once commented, was to confront either the wrath or the love of God, depending on where you stood on the issue of fossils. Presently, she was fixated on the migration patterns of the armadillo, trying to determine whether the shy creatures ever got as far as Colorado. "I'm all for it."

"You would be," said the judge. "And I understand. But what does that mean? How do you turn a city of tens of thousands of people into a city park? I don't quite see it."

"We could still have concerts," said Juanita Molina, the founder of the city's chamber music series, and a staunch defender of myriads of tastes and more funding for music departments in elementary schools. Humming was her answer to everything. Didn't matter what tune, the bright melody, the attitude, the hope inherent was universal, she said.

"I'm all for it too," hailed Boris Henderson, member of the Santa Fe Land Use Advisory Committee, who'd bought space in the local newspaper to publish his essay on The Moral Majority of Plants. "It's a brilliant idea. Imagine: the first National Town. A park, a city, a culture preserved. Why, it's downright inspired!"

Catherine was wise to have invited Henderson. Here was a man who spoke out on all issues, proffered generous particles of faith, semens of soul, conspicules of conscience, stamensworth of plant statutes and roots full of psychological repertoire. A pioneer in red leaf, root rot and dandelion therapy, his roses were famed up and down the state. Senators, auto workers, professors and aeronautic engineers, to name just a few, came to him for private counsel. His wife, Henrietta, was a farmer in her own right, and an esteemed voice in the Santa Fe League of Women Voters. Both could be said to have laid the groundwork for a profusion of flowers in the city, and by this they hoped to be judged in the afterlife.

"I'm sorry. It seems racist to me," said Jose Melrose, the best boxer and wedding singer in Santa Fe (Jose never needed a microphone). When he wasn't punching people out, he did embroidery, sandblasting, brain science, elevator repairs, or metal and tile work. He was massage therapist, Dadaist, bongo drummer, surrealist, concierge at the Holiday Inn, designer of pepper shakers, and mathematician working in the thirteenth dimension.

"The two ideas don't work side by side," he boomed. "Some things in life you accept. It can't all be perfect flower gardens. There's desert, sand dune, parking lot and molten lava. The world's not one thing. This is a city, and a damned good one. It's a people's town. Human beings. Not wolves, or bears, or rattlesnakes. People. Sure, we need our parks. Mental health considerations. But this is where Indians can sell their jewelry, artists their paintings, and where people like me can get an honest wage. All this park talk. Save it for the wilderness. I just don't see where it can possibly lead. We're not going to leave Santa Fe, if that's what this is leading to."

Sannazaro caught his Commander's look of impatience.

"Of course we're not leaving," declared Horatio de Palmieri, once a presidential hopeful. He had founded the Civil Liberties Union in Tesuque, and had cultivated spitting in the dirt and rubbing it out with his left cowboy boot to a fine art. "People first. I built my whole candidacy on that maxim, and I plan to do so again when I run for Governor. Utopia? Bull. We already live in one of the cleanest, most family-oriented towns in America. What arrogance to think that one man—or is it a she?—would dare to try and buy us off."

"Nobody's buying anybody off, or bussing us out!"

"We're not for sale. The land's not for sale. Our freedom's not for sale."

"Have you looked around? Every other house is on the market," said Betsy May Lewis, born on the Pajarito Plateau and fond of a single fact that once, though certainly no longer, dominated American history in her mind: not a single fence for 200 miles. "People are selling out, and it's created this mad dash to cash in without any plan. Have you driven Cerritos Road lately? Seen all the crap to either side? How many more cineplexes, supermarkets, parking lots, condo developments are we going to stand for? I for one would welcome a rich ecological moghul. Let him alienate everybody, kick out the hoi-polloi, stamp out the crude bastards, scrap whatever's ugly, clean up the flotsam, scrape the hovels, take charge and impose some artistic order on what is becoming true capitalistic chaos."

"Bullshit," de Palmieri replied, spitting on Catherine's floor and stomping out the door.

"Oh shut up!" Betsy May looked around the room. "Can you imagine that creep in the Governor's mansion? That's precisely what I mean. We need true leadership, not some fascist two-bit fart telling us what to do. A person with vision who respects all life."

"Not to mention my silk carpet," spouted Catherine, furious.

"I spit on the greedy bastards. May all bad taste rot in hell. May every low-rider be banished, every garage sale burn down, every motorcycle crash and each boom box be trashed. I'm sick and tired of anti-intellectuals, shopping malls, teenagers, four-lane highways, fast-food, mad cow disease, Republicans, advertising, romance novels, bad movies, gas stations, telephone wires, parking meters, country clubs and leaf blowers!"

There was laughter and applause all around, then further discussion, the odd venom competing with a majority grace, anger vented amid respectable congeries. Finally their discombobulated hostess gave the distress sign, broke in, and suggested the meeting adjourn for an hour.

CHAPTER 39
A Symphony of Discords

SAMUEL ("SAM") Turbovsky had suffered damnation in his life prior to his emancipation in New Mexico. A bald and bronzy 220-pound philosopher who wore a chest-tight leather T-shirt, a turquoise earring in his nose and a massive tattoo on both naked forearms, he had arrived in Santa Fe after eleven years' detention in San Quentin for a murder he did not commit. The former professor of economics and anthropology at the University of Chicago had been serving a life sentence for the alleged shooting death of his wife. But when the home in which Ceecee Turbovsky had been killed was put up for sale, the sharp eye of a potential buyer, a doctor, incited new interest in a case long deemed concluded by judges and more than one Governor. It was the heretofore unnoticed droplet of dried blood on a wall, its DNA analysis and a tenacious attorney which finally exonerated Sam, now in his late 60s.

He'd never been to Santa Fe, only dreamt of it, and when he arrived, with a modest settlement provided by his legal vindication, his life was one of humility and gratefulness. Yes, he embodied all the cynicism possible in the span of one life. But he was like a person given his sight back; his sense of smell, of touch, of open space expanded. A living laboratory in biological renascence, Sam Turbovsky knew what was important in life. Having lived in a cell for so many years he came to Catherine's front door with a perspective that those lacking the experience of incarceration would never understand. It greatly affected his thinking with regards to the Commander's own propositions. Sam had had plenty of time to contemplate the human condition, particularly in an overcrowded prison, and his conclusions bore directly upon Mr Marigold's own utopian longings.

Sam stood up to address the group and commenced. "You must try to act without reference to an aggregate larger than 150," he said.

"What does that mean?" said Billy the Kid, Jr, the great-great-grandson of New Mexico's most famous outlaw. Though he owned no weapon, he carried himself with demonstrative air. He worked at Wild Oats grocery.

"It's been amply shown," Sam continued, "that non-human primates never gather in groups larger than 150, with the rare exception of female furrowed blue mandrills. That's how they've managed to maintain such evolutionary equipoise. Brain power is at its most keen in small gatherings, present circumstances exempted." He cited the modest size of Einstein's class at the Zurich Polytechnic, "and, for that matter, the typical number of shoppers at any given moment at Wild Oats, I would imagine", as cases in point, however much a reach.

There was the odd groan.

"Only humans have dissembled the proportions. We need small communities that are integral and sustainable. No more development, no more aid, or trade or global visions. All those lofty ideals of high commerce need to be focused right where you dwell, be it a prison cell or local community. It's too obvious for words. The old neighborhood is where one is able to do the most good. Cause and effect, right where you are. Your food, your clothing, the names of your great-grandparents, and an acquaintance with things that transcend the labels on your trousers. You've got to learn the native names for earthworms and aspen trees, for the birds and the crickets. Such acknowledgements must lead, ultimately, to self-sufficiency in all things which, by most standards of natural capitalism, will reject the public utility and the big automobile.

"This rejection inevitably leads, in my humble opinion, to turning off Mr Multinational," he continued. "I'm saying there's no need for big car plants, computer chips, or any of it. Plant trees, walk, talk to each other, cultivate the arts. Political decentralization. Total authority vested in a household, not a region. You don't need money, either. In times past people used sod, or elephant hair, or tobacco for payment. They used brick tea in Siberia, and wampum or copper in Native North America. A barter system is the key. You spend a decade or more in jail and you start to re-read everything in your life. That and barbells puts a whole new perspective on human economics. A buoyant stock market is meaningless. Quotas, export subsidies, government procurement agendas, wage increases, inflation, percentage points, output, input, capital indexes, total returns—you name it, all arbitrary. Money corrupts. You cannot make it on to the Russell 1000, let alone the S&P 500, without some inclemency."

"How do you get around it?" somebody asked.

"Back to nature," Sam said emotionally.

"We live that way on weekends up in Taos," someone else put forth.

"But I don't see it for all of Santa Fe. It can't work."

"Ahh come on, Sam," railed another detractor, who had heard the same tirade on an earlier occasion at the city high school, where townsfolk had come to discuss ways to defuse crime, violence and drugs in the classroom, out on the streets, in the parking lots of Bingo parlors and casinos, in the very social revolution occurring on the northern outskirts of Santa Fe where rich and poor collided, and Hispanic and Indian sentiments in opposition to the wealthier Anglos was running high. "You're never going to rid America of the dollar or, at the very least, a gold standard."

"You may be correct," Sam countered, "but that doesn't make it right." And he launched into an erudite examination of other tribal cultures whose transition from a state of nature to an assimilated urban ghetto was occurring across the planet that very day, their misery all the result of economic disparities. He referred to some 87 indigenous groups in Brazil who had died out during the last 150 years for reasons strictly pertaining to gold and the acquisition of wealth by the very few. He pointed to the fact that only 5 percent of the world's population was legally protected. The vast majority of indigenous people—the real shepherds of the earth—were without legal or economic recourse whatsoever.

"What does that say to you? You've got to preserve the habitat for all kinds of humanity. Do so, and the tribal wisdom will prevail. With that wisdom, a harmony with nature. As far as I can see, back-to-nature means preservation, and you can do it in the Amazon, or in Santa Fe, but you've got to get started, and a billion dollars—notwithstanding my antipathy toward money—is certainly a plausible shortcut, if carefully expended."

"So what are you suggesting?" Mr Marigold himself asked. "I thought you just said money was the great evil?"

Catherine considered properly introducing him, then thought the better of it. There were enough newcomers from out of town in the group that his presence should not precipitate suspicion or unintended exposure, she figured. Marigold had stressed his anonymity, and it seemed assured among this crowd.

Sam explained, "It's rare in these times that a billionaire isn't swathed in the sins of his ill-begotten wealth. And maybe this local utopian— whoever it is—means to assuage a guilty conscience. How did he inherit his wealth? What did his predecessors do to screw humanity? Does anybody know?"

Catherine herself was suddenly struck by that fact: she didn't have a clue. She hadn't asked.

"Old money," she blurted, seeking a way to change the tenor of the moment. "Centuries old."

"Well," said Sam, "let me put it this way. You've got to be practical. Money is just another tool, if used properly. Assuming the money is clean, and pre-supposing this guy has suddenly got religion, I would encourage him to buy every available lot and convert it to wild park land. Some of that property might be useful for primate enterprise, like growing honey or herbs or making wood chips from downed timber. Or providing healthy distractions for children of all creeds and colors. Feeding stray animals, for example."

Catherine took that as a useful cue, got up and served tea and cookies to her guests.

"Let me open some windows. It's getting awfully warm in here," she volunteered.

Too much intention had been stoked, dreams levitated, hopes stirred. The idea of a local Utopia had triggered a level of fantasy that struck one and all as appealing, though no consensus seemed possible, and that was the most salient impression Marigold could glean. Small groups within the larger collection of disputants harbored their own distinctive techniques for resurrecting paradise on earth. None of the methodologies seemed particularly compatible. Mr Marigold saw through all the many conflicts to the core conclusions, however: amid the many orientations was the one universal impulse to enshrine a sense of place, to restore a lost Eden. One could see it in their faces, divine the glints of yearning, tell-tale wanderlusts that circulated like so many extravagant mists throughout the living room, in glances and figures of speech and nostalgia that were akin to museum sighs. Everyone wanted more than the cards they were dealt. Nobody was satisfied. Big men who put on airs were simply afraid—afraid of change, afraid of women, of losing control. How was that possible? Did no one smell the flowers?

The most troubling aspect of the whole morning, however, was the Commander's realization that 1.85 billion dollars was scarcely meaningful, a sum that would hardly warrant attention in a world that thought nothing of trading trillions of dollars in a week. It would certainly be enough to acquire a truly nice chunk of the planet's real estate, or refurbish thousands of animal shelters or improve the township's sewage lines, but, ultimately, it was a drop in the bucket. It couldn't begin to affect "the three machos" still at large in human culture, the long evolutionary line that had resulted in so much contemporary mayhem, argument and indifference, as well as the occasional Boethius.

The sewage problem was a case in point. In Pojoaque, Santa Clara, San Juan and San Ildefonso, water was showing 400 percent the amount of contamination set by the government as a safe drinking standard. Nitrate levels in the water indicated heavy amounts of human waste, as well as fertilizer runoff. Nitrates—and with them bacteria and other chemicals—dissolved into ground water from the huge number of private septic tanks spread across the region. Private wells then took back up the ground water. To build a regional sewer system would require a considerable sum, and local politicians were fearful of raising taxes to pay for it. People would rather drink dissolved excrement than pay a few extra dollars. That's what it had come down to.

"Let them drink shit," was Sam's motto. He had long reflected on the intransigence of human nature, the fact that he might dream of angels cavorting with humans but humans ultimately must excuse themselves from heavenly concord to eliminate waste. Such a scatological vision of humanity, grotesque and realistic, probably derived from Sam's many years of using uncleaned latrines, of seeing excrement rubbed on walls by way of one protest or other, of dropping off to sleep immersed in the inescapable scent of prison offal and aging urine. Why couldn't we be like kangaroo rats, he often wondered, metabolizing everything? Perfect ecological economists.

"What other creature makes its own water from within?" he said. "The rat can go an entire lifetime without taking from the earth. Not even one drop."

After listening to Sam, the Commander dropped the issue of helping out with the local sewage problem. Alas, it was poetic justice that those responsible for its generation would simply have to deal with it, raising their own 40 million dollars (the estimated cost) to build a system that would pump sewage over the hills between Río Arriba and Santa Fe counties. Mr Marigold was not interested in changing the diapers of his neighbors, or tracking their water-born pathogens.

And this about-face, wherein the public must fear to tread, brought him abruptly to his escalating senses: reason to be cautious, acidic, disheartened. The Commander had divined his own eccentric precepts without a degree of paradox: Paradise would fare better without people, but people there were, and people there would have to be. A globalization of souls that guaranteed a mishmash of ideals and denigrations, exemplary nights and devastating days, in no particular order. For this solitaire of halcyon hours, the present company gave him to understand that human nature, and thus his own human nature, must be willing to contemplate change. But certain questions remained immune to discussion. Sacrosanct, without compromise. Between the malleable fine points of tuning a city, and the indisputable high moral breeding grounds of his own making, he was realizing solid progress, even if his loyal neighbor was utterly amused.

CHAPTER 40
The Arrival of the Experts

AFTER A DAY OF unending sanctimony and expostulations, Marigold was impatient to find some other sweeping mechanism that would short-circuit the endless safety pins, horseshoes, Chlorox bleach, needles and thread, Elmer's glue and blow-dryers of local transformation—bandages, as he viewed them, that could not hope to effect dramatic reconstitution. He was, moreover, convinced that Hidalgo's recommendation to form a Foundation was the most sensible approach to coping with the assured chaos of global injunctions, social reveries and contradictions. High-flying merit swirled around him, a flophouse for stranded causes that paid out the projected 55-odd million dollars in interest each year to Marigold's pet passions but never touched the principal, except in those circumstances demanding fantastic, sudden and eccentric expenditure. That, at least, might enable the Commander to sustain his ongoing learning curve; and if enough young people could be mustered and manhandled with sufficient seriousness, he might realize an army of conscientious souls, thus amplifying the bang for each buck. As a non-profit, of course, he would be in a position to pay no taxes, to trade aggressively in equities and build his portfolio rapidly.

The problem remained. In which directions to kick off the world series, or insinuate a motion, stroke a fancy, incite a novel paradigm, instill a compassion? Sannazaro was right: one person is indecisive; two people together will argue; three will constitute a gang; four start a revolution; five a war. Yet, somehow these same agitators must agree on everything. The dreamer cringed before the rancor and tired rhetoric of the slightest minion. Multiply it by every Times Square and he could not envision anything for humanity, falling speechless and afraid before the disorganization of the human spirit, the space-time warp of wants and irreconcilabilities. He recalled the tragic case of Pulitzer Prize-winning photographer Kevin Carter who, in 1993, took a heartbreaking image of a starving child in Sudan and was subsequently inundated by hate mail. People who themselves had done nothing to end hunger were quick to blame a lone photographer for not saving the child. The social activist in him had expired under the impossible weight of compassion fatigue. The artist killed himself.

Marigold recognized his own signs of burn-out as well, even after just a few days of worrying about problems bigger than he was. The arithmetic, buttressed by insurmountable odds and authentic impasse, did not bode well for his own tenacity, thought Sannazaro.

Barring his own emotional collapse (it was strenuous enough just being in the presence of other human beings), what Marigold had hoped for, in the aftermath of the gatherings, was a higher standard of precision, informed analysis, ecumenical inquiry. A more sober and arresting pathway that was not divided into a bowling alley of discordant personalities, and the divergent flamboyance of every would-be seer and prophet. Not that he was so boring as to ignore the paramount importance of multiple spices. Somewhere in between lay the antidote to a world correction. A philosophical soft landing.

The Commander took his leave, repairing to his quarters of silent solace so that he might reflect upon the confusing fragments of light that had shone sporadically before him that afternoon at Catherine Champion's. In fairness, he thought, there had been voiced some ideas. He had obtained a loud earful of what to do, what not to do: give all his money to beetle preservation, the felling of power lines, abortion clinics, and the fight against Communism. Give his money away on street corners to the homeless. Of course, the laundry list was asphyxiating.

A too-facile glance at a local paper gave some currency to the dilemma. There, arrayed like so many refugees, Appaloosa geldings, tropical fish, blue roan Belgian mares, Chihuahua puppies, Yorkie males, baby parrots, pygmy goats, Texas longhorn females (trophy horns), German shorthair pointer pups, lost Dalmatians, bearded titmice, Gouldins, Peachfronts and cockatiels, Bengal kittens—and on and on— hundreds of animals doomed to misery, in one town, on one day.

Which translated into a concatenation of good ideas, a cursory summary of which made for impossible energy expenditures. One man. Ambitions beyond his wallet size.

Mr Marigold spent the following days tracking down a dazzling group of powerful minds at universities across America in hopes of defining a list of key sectors and experts from throughout the world to help him increase the focus of his considerations. He was, quite simply, dumbfounded by the possibilities, even granting the limited reach of 1.85 billion dollars. Something in him called beyond the confines of Santa Fe.

"Or maybe you've already given up," said Sannazaro. "You just haven't admitted it to yourself."

"What are you saying? Get it out, man."

"It's easier to save a white rhino that's far away and ideological than it is to save all the dogs at the local pound."

"That's nonsense. We will do both, and I have called in experts from throughout the world to help me situate my priorities and face that music which is composed of all the most sobering truths."

Alma, who with the windfall from her employer had rushed out to purchase a new wardrobe and a maroon Rolls Royce, presently remained on at the hacienda, though Marigold would not let her park the new car there. It embarrassed him. Despite such fancy wheels, she had no better place to go—or not yet; and now, with an enormous bank account lodged firmly at Southwestern Federal, felt a surge of hubris that gave her to understand she was on a collegial footing with her former oppressor. Her ill-temper all but melted in this sweet aura of financial breakthroughs.

The Commander wasn't sure what to make of it. As he lay awake one night on a Turkish chaise longue surrounded by one of many tenuously tall-standing piles of obscure masterworks, he reflected on this positive aptitude of fiduciary instruments which Sam and other socialists had so questioned. If warm, artless pieces of eight could soften Alma Khan, anything was possible in these infernal spheres of international mange and global despair.

Sannazaro, meanwhile, resumed his old life next door at the Camp of the Spirits, not about to be shook up, twisted sideways, emboldened or perverted by the onrush of dollar bills. With most of the Camp's inhabitants having flocked to the four winds, he made himself a delicious solitary stew, soft carrots, cauliflowers and braised seitan, got into his overalls, picked up his trusted hand tools, and bent down in the loosening pre-spring soil to greet his crocuses, paper whites, jonquils and hyacinths, Voltaire in exile at the Chateau Cirey on his mind. He was tired of so much calculating in the service of the Commander. He longed for simplicity, and now could well afford it.

It was 1.30 in the afternoon. A knock at the hacienda signaled the arrival of the first of the experts. Mr Marigold had flown two dozen individuals from all over the planet to consult with him. True, there was no grave urgency. His money was growing at the rate of approximately 2.5 million tax-free dollars a week. How many lizards or parakeets or doomed dogs and cats could he buy with 357,000 dollars a day? Where would he put them all? On the 10,000 acres now owed him by the state of New Mexico? That was one way to do it. Once the 10,000 acres got filled up, he'd save his money for a month, and then go buy another 10,000 acres. Surely he could find managers and interns to help organize the purchasing, transport and maintenance of all the critters on their new geography of hope. It seemed slam-dunk, all in one grand vision. Millions, tens of millions of rescued animals, souls, heartbeats. But just when he felt ready to rest easy with the plan, the experts were brought forward into his expansive living room, which Alma had more or less cleaned up for the occasion, and a whole new series of conflicts and confusions was unleashed upon the teetering sinciput that was Marigold's.

The first arrival was a specialist with UNESCO who had drafted the International Union for the Conservation of Nature and Natural Resources Commission document on National Parks and Protected Areas (CNPPA). Shortly after her, three people appeared simultaneously at the imposing worm-wood of a front door: a World Wildlife Fund analyst specializing in ways to preserve endangered habitat by working with local indigenous peoples; an investigator named Sophia from HLAA (Humans that Love All Animals) in Santorini, Greece; and an energy consultant, James, from Montreal, who was helping advise a few power elites that were the undisputed leaders in the fuel cell revolution.

Others arrived throughout the day: a Greenpeace executive director; a senior ecologist with the MacArthur Foundation; the Eritrean Secretary of the Interior; the Danish Minister of Environment; a biologist with the Kenya Wildlife Service responsible for curbing poaching in his country under the famed tutelage of Richard Leakey; a strategic defense expert from the Rand Corporation; a Bhutanese monk,

Wangchuck, famed for his ability to speak with crows; a Stanford University population expert who'd studied with the Ehrlichs; a solar physicist from Princeton University; a parrot authority from Costa Rica; a Dutch jurist based out of The Hague who dealt principally with ecological conflict; a Russian ecosystems researcher from somewhere in Amur tiger country; a tidal wetlands activist from Isahaya, Japan; a Nobel Prize-winning mathematician from Cambridge University; a Yekuana tribal chief from South America; the Lord Mayor of British dependency Tristan da Cunha; a political scientist from Iceland; a rancher-turned-vegetarian with the Argentine Humane Society in Buenos Aires; and an old woman from Algeria who seemed to know everything about social services in poor countries.

All were seated. Marigold eventually quieted the soirée by clanging a teaspoon to his Waterford crystal wine glass. "Thank you all for coming," he began. "I welcome you to my humble hacienda which has been in the family for centuries. Please make yourselves as comfortable as possible after your many long journeys. Collectively, you've just traveled nearly the distance to the moon. There is a bathroom just there, and a shower and towels if anyone wants to freshen up. We Marigolds were surveyors by profession, but I was always more taken with books than measuring rods and compasses. Hence, before you sits a near-sighted enthusiast who can better describe the contents of the Venetian Academia than the surrounding neighborhood. I hope you will excuse my little chaos, with its scorpions and mites. I am a bachelor, and my mind is somewhere between a monastery and a helium balloon. My assistant, Alma, keeps me rooted to the extent possible. Alma, please heat the spanakopitas and bring them in. And take drink orders."

The experts were encouraged to remove their shoes, cuddle up upon throws and pillows, and sample the drinks and antipastos. By five o'clock, all were well settled on French satin cushions or studiously akimbo on the worn kilims in respective corners of the literary salon, keeping watchful eyes for little scorpions. They were not sure if the Commander had been needling them or not. The hacienda shaped the crowd, lowering its tempo, softening a number of harsh edges. The dust had been checked, but not removed, the Commander's "little chaos" pervasive at every seam. One would never decipher too much obvious wealth in this ramshackle cauldron of strange habitation, though to the astute observer a fantastic medley of antiques surfaced at every new glance, whilst cobwebs upon an original Turner must say something about its owner.

The Hermit Freak continued: "Because of an unusual set of benign circumstances I've now acquired nearly two billion dollars—that's cash, ready to spend—and I'm looking for the most virtuous ways to do so. Rescuing orphans in Rio or orchids in Malaysia? Teenagers in Somalia or tigers in Java? DNA research up the street, or new prosthetics for dogs hit by cars? Grants to AIDs or famine victims? Support for girls without birth control pills in Brazil, or boys without condoms in Ethiopia? Bread and butter for hungry New Mexicans, or airlifts of hominy to malnourished Mississippians? To clean up the Delaware River or purify San Francisco's drinking water? And so on and so forth. I've invited all of you here to help me work this through, if it's even possible on such a limited budget."

"That's marvelous," said the Lord Mayor. "But what is your plan?"

"The most good for the largest number of needy—a universal pledge of activism based upon such luminaries in the avant garde of solitude as Jeremy Bentham, John Stuart Mill, Albert Schweitzer, Percy Shelley, Leonardo da Vinci, Nikos Kazantzakis, and the theory of hotspots."

Queer looks emanated from the gathering. These were, by and large, conservative and prudent ambassadors for their specific domains who had not yet gotten the peculiar lunch basket that was the composite Commander. They sat in his home, had been flown first class and underwritten by his largesse, but could not begin to decipher the degree of eccentricity that now assailed them in a silver spoon.

"Needy—? People? Animals? Orchids? Which?" volunteered the World Wildlife Fund representative. "You have to decide," he said gingerly. "Nobody can do it all."

"That is quite true. Initially my concept was to transform Santa Fe into a National Park. The more I've thought about it, though, the more impractical it appears. By all indications, there is in every household a degree of petulance no man could hope to presume upon. I cannot elicit agreement from any two denizens on any one issue. This bodes ill for a national park in these domains. Maybe that is for the best. That is why I've called you all together. Perhaps there are international quagmires and fever blisters in greater need of financial assistance."

"There is no doubting that," rejoined the Kenya Wildlife Service director, Saleho. "This is my first trip to America, but one glance confirms what the rest of the world has always known: it is largely a rich man's playground. Better you should focus your money upon poor countries where every square inch is hemorrhaging." His motion was seconded by nearly everyone present.

"To get back to your idea of a national park," the Eritrean mused. "Always an appealing instinct. But, to cite one example, in my country there is no room for a big park. We do not have the luxurious scope my esteemed colleague from Kenya enjoys. Our President takes home a few hundred dollars a year in salary. However, he was democratically elected. Democracy is our national preserve, with its own endemic species—namely, a constitution and the freedom to vote. But we are poor, with little means of curbing, as yet, a terrible blight of pollution from necessary cottage industries, the systematic fallout from over-fishing, and a debilitating civil war with our foolish neighbor to the south. We need money, pure and simple."

Others chimed in with their own litany of disasters. The Russian ecologist, Vladimir, spoke of their need for hard cash to counter the all-out assault by poachers on tigers and brown bears, as well as sturgeon in the Caspian Sea. Saleho described his anti-poaching aircraft, and the cost of maintaining soldiers in the parks. "We usually shoot first. It sends a message. But there are farmers agitating against elephants; and eco-tourism is out of control. The lions are refusing to mate before camera-clicking crowds. Can you blame them?"

The Dutchman rhymed in with new proposals to grant trees and other non-human life forms legal standing in the World Court. "Holland is an ecological Armageddon," he admitted. "The worms are dying. The trees are limp. We have traded biological rights for the rights of stockholders. We know this. There must be a twenty-first century approach to unraveling priorities—a science, if you will, of figuring out the applicable coefficients and factoring them into a workable scheme."

"There is," started the English mathematician, who launched into an incomprehensible polynomial approach to solving seemingly irreconcilable problems by translating those arenas of contest into eleven ecological and humanitarian dimensions. Marigold detected hints of Madame Vignette's X-squared philosophy.

Picking up from nowhere, the Bhutanese monk described his ten-year meditation on the language of white crows in the region of Lishi, to the extreme north of his country. Which had absolutely nothing to do with the theory of "discriminating priorities" advanced by the social scientist from the Rand Corporation who would have preferred to see Marigold tackle the US immigration issue rather than the plight of dying worms in Holland. Whereas the Princeton physicist tried to impart the fact that ecology and defense were not on equal playing fields. A single war would undermine all the ecological restoration in the world.

"The US Government is spending 95 percent of its energy budget on fossil fuel and nuclear research," he began. "Three hundred billion per year on outright military weapons. We believe that the entire collective of global ecosystems produces something on the order of 33 trillion dollars each year, free of charge to all of us. That is what the earth might be said to be worth on Wall Street. And it is a very conservative figure. If you consider what the value of a life is, and the fact that without those biotic windfalls there would be no life, no dollar-and-cents figure can ever be substituted. Nonetheless, you'd think we'd want to take out a considerable insurance policy on such an asset. Yet, the entire budget worldwide for biodiversity preservation is a paltry five billion, and that is mostly from non-governmental private and corporate foundations. Meanwhile, the US is preparing to construct a 96-billion-dollar space station. We've got our priorities all backwards."

"What would pure wilderness research consist of ?" asked Marigold.

"Dispatch a Brancusi to Borneo, a composer to the North Pole; place James Joyce in a dugout canoe in the Amazon, and send the Pope to Yosemite. Let the spiritual masters retreat to their caves and study their EKGs; provide a year of study in the outbacks of the world to every CEO of the Fortune 500. We need to know what a single flower truly means to the health of the earth; how that connection can be converted to business ethics and economic barometers, extrapolated to policy, legal standing and absolute police protection."

"Yes," said the Canadian fuel cell executive, "but no amount of alternative energy breakthroughs or smelling of flowers will counter the rape of British Columbia, and the burning of Madagascar and the Amazon, or of soft coal in China. We need sustainable technologies, but we also require education, modesty and restraint, as well as firm public consensus."

The Icelandic visitor—a former President—prayed for a generation of silence, and incisively hammered at the ontological crisis of consciousness throughout Scandinavia.

Only two members of the assemblage spoke of true paradise on earth. Easy for them to say. The Lord Mayor of Tristan pointed out that his island—like nearby Nightingale, Gough and Inaccessible, each sequestered in the roaring forties—was lacking in any serious problems.

Tourists almost never came there. The 309 residents could hardly be said to be statistically relevant to the rest of the human world. Yet, as an experiment in cooperative harmony with nature, here was an island society that had maintained itself in strictest isolation and seemed to be thriving. Never a dull moment.

"When the wind merges the sea salt with the sea foam, and the wild south rears its majestic expanse, and the burning late-afternoon sun settles toward the Antarctic, to curl up in a stone cottage on our island, knowing that along with Gough we constitute the most important seabird habitat on earth (northern rockhopper penguins among others), is to be ensured a certain immortality, nestled in mottled shadows of creation. Life could not be more perfect, despite the constant gales and stinging cold. Our heath and grasses are deep, our colorful volcanic cliffs over a mile high.

When the waves lash our beaches—long tortured shorelines scattered with Portuguese and English shipwrecks, the ghosts of explorers and artists—you have never inhaled finer air or tasted purer moisture. Nor is there any shortage of kelp for our salads, ornithocopros for our energy needs, or bird breasts for our steak. Of course, if it's a movie theater you're looking for, a car dealership, ice-cream parlor or disco, you'll have to go several thousand miles to the left or right."

Many of those present were deeply moved. The man was nearly in tears, so homesick was he after only three days away.

"I am a vegetarian," the Bhutanese mystic asserted, "and would not fancy a diet of bird breasts, all respects intended. In one breath you speak with obvious pride of seabird habitat. Then you speak of eating those same birds. That is precisely the crisis of consciousness infecting the human species."

"Different birds," the Lord Mayor assured him. "We are absolutely sensitive to endangered species, and each Tristanite can name the hundreds of plant and animal species and tell you which are threatened or rare, which are not."

Marigold caught the glimmer of revulsion in the Bhutanese emissary's eyes.

"I can assure you," replied the monk, "the bird you pursue with a fork and knife rightly considers himself endangered." But he was polite enough to alter his address and thenceforth spoke at length upon the skewed barometers of wealth, citing the fact that his own country was perceived by those with the IMF and World Bank to be at the bottom of the income ladder when, in fact, it was the richest place on earth with respect to quality of life, as far as his people were concerned.

"No pollution, no stress, no greed, no crime. Our country—the size of your Wisconsin, or Switzerland—is devoted to nonviolence. We have 62 percent of our primary forests intact, and little need of money. Our disability-adjusted life expectancy for babies is quite high—double that of most African nations. My government has rejected nearly all development projects from outside. Our monks love soccer, our King the Lakers. They all wear the traditional bokhus, and there are no drugs. Children look after their parents. Community values are deeply rooted, dating back 1,000 years. Sex invites little controversy. Our children start having premarital relations by the age of 14, a custom that is encouraged by most Bhutanese parents. You want to find out how to create a Paradise on Earth, just visit my country with its snow and clouded leopards and golden langurs. You are welcome any time."

Marigold felt an uneasy chill rippling through the crowd. Two representatives of the most remote Gardens of Eden had come across like picture-postcard hobbyists, country gentlemen who had retired to rose gardening, with no chance of imparting their ethical delineations to the outer world. More problematic still was the fact that even these two diplomats on behalf of paradise differed substantially in their assessment of what constituted harmony.

"Easy for you two," said the MacArthur Foundation advisor, "but how do the rest of us convert Hoboken or Dacca into Bhutan or Tristan? What are the necessary and feasible steps? How does a large nation untangle its millions of competing demands, bureaucratic log-jams, financial constraints? What's perfect is just not possible for six billion people. Of that I am certain. Now, what's acceptable should be possible."

"Who determines standards of acceptability?" Marigold asked. "Based upon what criteria? Some people are more sensitive than others; some eat meat, some do not; others prefer the company of 10,000 pedestrians in Time Square, whereas I suspect the Lord Mayor might find such crowds appalling."

Confessed the Tristanite, "To be honest with you, my travels by bus from the Albuquerque airport was one of the darkest journeys of my life. I wept inside at such ugliness and desecration. Native plants by the millions that had been uprooted to make way for endless building sites.

A six-lane freeway! My God, man, how much tarmac does one town need?"

"I found Albuquerque rather charming," another voice contested. Ruffled feathers, good-humored castigations, swipes and broadsides.

Like a ping-pong table of charged particles going nowhere.

"In fact, if I am not mistaken," said the Rand Corporation representative, "the Bhutanese Government has rejected the bid of Nepalese migrants to her southern borders. Even Bhutan has felt the pangs of an immigration crisis and over-population. As for Tristan, honorable Mayor, I'm sure you will agree that your island is finite. Most of its residents fled to the UK in the sixties, when the island's volcanic underpinnings began to shudder. And what if the tourist trade should suddenly discover you? Where is your infrastructure to receive it, and at what cost? Are your 300 friends up to the debate? Who will sell out, who will not? And in the end, what families will be left that can afford the inevitable escalation of real-estate prices? Even in theory you cannot hide from escalating demographics, or, I'm told, sex scandals."

"They will discover you, and you will have to compromise," said Barbara Quenstrom of the World Wildlife Fund. "Every species—each one of us personally, I might add—is going to face incremental change, most for the worse, some for the better. Our idea at WWF is to try to find ways to keep the slippery slope of degradation from getting any steeper. There are reasons to be hopeful."

So far, these pundits of the global problematique had merely augmented the random effusions of Santa Fe's own subjective citizenry with scarcely a conveyed clue as to how to spend money, or by what rubrics.

Am I feeling the weight of my own stupidity, or is it the inevitable irresolution of being human?, the Commander wondered. Here were all these savants, schooled, mostly, in the real world, with forbidding knowledge bases and vast experience in damage control, exotic customs, anthropological, legal, economic and theoretical sciences, political know-how and managerial prudence. The air of computation was thick, embroidered with every fiendish fact, adjusted argument, fretted brow and squeamish detail. Yet there was not even the making of a single conclusion. Compromise? What did that mean? How to apply its logic, and in which circumstances?

The Commander tried to envision the Lord Mayor and his 300 or so friends, happily marooned on their volcano out in the South Atlantic subantarctic. So too the Bhutanese, who had not yet divulged the secrets of the crow, in his Himalayan bastion.

All of these visitors were somehow hostile, it seemed to the Commander. Angry at his wealth. Probably annoyed by his ignorance. Impatient with his desire to help. What this revealed to him was the extent of their desperation, in one way or other. They all embodied the tense undercurrent of a world in trouble.

Marigold gazed balefully at the assembled visitors. He had his dream, a rambunctious overview. As impractical, inexperienced and unrealistic as he was, there was the undeniable truth of all that money.

"Life is pain," recited the Buddhist. "That is the standard, the only circumstance one must weigh action and intent against. People who have suffered are more apt to understand each other. Happiness does not accomplish similar consensus."

A sobriety severed discussion. Alma prepared dinner. More drinks broke the ice. The Commander (most uncharacteristically) downed several shots of whiskey, and bade his guests to continue.

CHAPTER 41
The Mudskipper's Lament

THE EXPERTS RE-GROUPED, heightening their sociological stakes and ideological demands through a rag-taggle give-and-take exposition. In the middle of it, Sam Turbovksy, the one person from Catherine Champion's gathering whom Marigold had cottoned to (and whom Alma was at once intrigued by), turned up.

"The Lakers game is on!" he announced.

None present shared his enthusiasm or entertained even the slightest curiosity. One did not mention crass, exhausting, purposeless sports in the company of world reformers. Sam let it go, barely amused by the stifling sobriety around him, though glancing every so often at the lost opportunity which was the television.

"Ano..." began the Japanese scientist. He had spent 20 years falling off a slippery slope, immersed in that pain. During that time he'd rallied hard to mobilize public opposition to the largest public works project ever mounted in his country—a disastrous hoax of agricultural reclamation that succeeded only in destroying the most important wetland in Asia, Isahaya Bay on the Ariake Sea.

Hiro spelled out the details: how he and his cohorts had hired PR firms, and attorneys who could fight the government. They had managed to name the endangered mudskipper, a slimy amphibian-like fish that had inhabited the wetlands in question, as the chief plaintiff in a drawn-out lawsuit. But in the end, they didn't have enough money to rouse sufficient public condemnation. On a single day in 1997, 20 miles of steel wall slammed shut, cutting off the ocean's tides in what was described as Japan's very own Watergate scandal. Within weeks, what had been the largest, most productive wetland in Japan had become a parched desert 25 miles across, five miles in length, 90 feet in depth. Millions of animals, many already endangered, were killed. Migratory fowl disappeared. It was an ecological disaster that cost Japanese taxpayers billions of dollars. Yet, no farmers would ever benefit, because the sea wall could not entirely prevent ocean intrusions, particularly during storms, and because pesticides flowed into the dried-out bay from inland rivers that drained farmlands.

This was just one of several tens of thousands of environmental crises occurring simultaneously around the planet. It put the Commander's meager 1.85 billion dollars into some perspective.

"With enough money, we could embarrass the Government," the Japanese activist pointed out. "We could force them to reverse the clock. Already, at least one member of the Diet has come out in support of what we're doing."

"How much money?" the Commander asked.

"I'll have to do a budget. Maybe two million dollars."

"Do your budget. If you need to call your friends in Japan, there's a phone."

"It is true. Money is everything," someone hastened. "The sound of coinage, no more soothing salvo; paper bills and tradable notes that nullify pain and are unto heaven as an oratorio."

"I agree with that," Marigold added. But with my few dollars I can barely scratch the odd surface. I need help. That's why you're all here. Venture philanthropists one and all. Apply the rigors of a business methodology to saving the unseen, the unborn, the unheard."

"I don't know," the Icelandic advocate of silence alleged. "I would have to say, ethics before money. Otherwise, conservationists will start making blue whales, bull elephants and wildebeest earn their daily bread by culling herds and selling off the meat to local markets, as they are doing in South Africa's Kreuger National Park. Once you prescribe money as the answer, any ethical standards are going to crash."

"Fine, fine," someone else's hue and cry rang clear. "Be a poet. Preserve the ethical orientation, long-term values. But if people can't get motivated behind an action, it'll never work. And there is no more guaranteed motivational tool than money."

"Capitalization has certainly been crucial to the private energy field, where the path from investment to perfect planetary solutions has been accomplished," declared the fellow from Montreal. "Hydrogen and fuel cells for every home. This is the ultimate energy source and birth control in one unit: give them electricity and they'll acquire a radio, then a TV, and that's when they'll start watching sitcoms rather than making babies. Moreover, every house will become its own utility, off the grid, providing energy to at least two billion people who are currently too poor to afford what the rest of us have enjoyed for nearly a century. With electricity comes refrigeration, safer drugs and inoculations, ice, medical relief, stored foods, music. The solar/hydrogen fuel cell economy: no pollution, and you can drink the exhaust from an automobile. It's the answer. You combine that with the Bhutanese equation, and Eureka! There's no stopping the human race. I've brought all the schematics if you want to look at them."

The Eritrean was fascinated by the Canadian's ideas. "Our generous host has only so much money. That is the tragic truth. Perhaps others of his ilk would take up the challenge towards matching funds. But if not, the resource will exhaust itself before any of these lovely visions get off the ground. Yes, you could finance a few parks, provide fuel cells for every home in my country. And that would be the end of the rich transferring to the poor. What about my friend here from Kenya who needs more anti-poaching aircraft? Or our Japanese colleague attempting after two decades to persuade one of the wealthiest nations in the world that wetlands are important? Or the good lady from the World Wildlife Fund with her dozens of hotspots around the globe, each crying out for solvency and capital injections? No ... As gratifying as it is to come to Santa Fe and be tantalized by hand-outs, there must be some other way. One man cannot save the rest of us. Take the 20 richest families in the world, whose combined assets probably exceed one trillion, and you are probably in a position to medically, industrially and ecologically stabilize Africa for a decade. But that won't necessarily alter a cultural proclivity in many sub-Saharan countries for forced female circumcision or huge families. You might use that colossal wealth to curb cholera in Chile, hepatitis in Taiwan, slave labor in South Korea and watershed destruction in China for a generation or two. But you won't change the basic pattern of deforestation, water pollution, gender bias in the workplace and racism directed at the non-Han minorities, all of which afflict those four countries respectively. The fact is, there must be some other means of triggering a diffuse altruism. Otherwise, we're just wasting words—and, frankly, I am needed back home."

Someone else summarized. "Adam Smith said it: a visible hand. Let governments intervene to jump-start companies within a free market. What else are they good for?"

"Yes. But what kinds of companies?" said the Icelandic philosopher. "The old regime. The takers, not the givers. We need new governance. That requires a new crop of ethical and practical children who have imagination, and love in their hearts."

The Commander found himself beginning to tire of so many dreamers and antagonists (all sounding too much like himself).

Throughout these illuminating tidbits, Alma stood anxiously in the kitchen putting finishing touches to her masterpiece, which would be served up shortly. But she could not help overhearing the circus and serious fanfare of her new peerage. As she saw it, her windfall from the Commander guaranteed her membership in the club, even if she didn't quite understand the reason for the meeting.

As their conversations continued, it became perfectly clear to the Commander that in spite of the present limitations, there were numerous options open to his preservation ideal. These included the strict reserve concept, which would entail a conservation area that was off limits to all but those with an extreme need-to-know; a natural monument that would lend status to and shape the national perception of individual places; a managed nature reserve—it might be as modest in size as the 300-acre Lew Sarett Nature Center in Benton Township, Michigan; specific protected landscapes which might be limited to no more than an acre (after all, a rare toad inhabited a single pond in Wyoming, and that had triggered a surrounding corridor of buffers contributed free of charge by local ranchers); resource reserves that relied upon the mitigation concept for bartering land swaps—tainted pits and pollution sinks for pure vacuums and bubbles of untarnished acreage (the *Gospel According to St Thomas* of preservation); anthropological reserves, and multiple-use management areas. Marigold was buoyed up atop a pedestal, replete with so many colorful and fabulist options, especially in view of the low cost per acre of wild land in most countries and the possibility of coaxing matching grants from other rich individuals around the world. From people like the former CEO of Esprit who had saved the last great temperate rainforests of Chile, from the Atlantic to the Pacific, and lived there in a little farmhouse as their guardian angel.

Each approach to conservation biology entailed workable compromises and proliferating gradations. But as his invited guests walked him through the labyrinths from their respective home fronts, a Marigold philharmonic emerged in his sunken chest: string sections of confusion, brassy aspiration, woodwindedness and percussive response. In fact, this one hermit gave vent to multiple voices, each sparking into other voices, until he was unto himself a myriad of genders, of child-like wonder and deranged seasons crying out irrationally from his hameau. The Signor was simply overwhelmed by everything and everyone.

Consider the wiry, olive-skinned fisherman whose people, the Imraguen, lived along the Bay of Timiris within the Banc d'Arguin National Park on the Mauritanian coast. In his tall-standing splendor, there could be no better example of indigenous people being employed to save themselves and their surrounding habitat. Yet, to Marigold, the idea of conferring salutations on those who would slaughter the lambs of the sea was a travesty of fascist proportions, and he told the man so.

"A fisherman is a Hitler," he swore up and down. "A fish—no guts, no roe, as those who take the easy line and tackle would tell you, braggadocios at the end of a barb, psychotics toying with their hooks. Rather, each fish I take to be God's most precious manifest in hue and silent cry, the memories of the beginning, the first and last. A fish is not to be fried but venerated, learned from. It wants nothing more than to float free; to it a wave is proof of higher things, a coral reef its home, a group of shimmering truth its true community. Quicksilvered these fleeting gems we denominate by "fish"; veracity in every bubble, complex nerve endings about every underwater glint; a monumental self-consciousness that knows the endlessness of time without so much as saying so. There, mates, the modesty of the ages. Let no man foreswear these precious angels 'neath the tide were made for wonder, not their flesh. Give me that, open your sadly narrow minds, and it will be clear that all the fishermen of the world have erred miserably. And for what? A taste treat, the scent of oil-caked sea, crisp and ruined, flavored in death, twisted in the brine of your own intestines, picked over, shat out, for what? It is sea you crave, then see, you unlettered bully; look squarely into its most innocent of eyes that gaze, asking for nothing, forgiving, like a Christ in the waters, all in their beauteousness; witness in the fish's meanderings the motion of the spheres. Know this, that there was never a greater heart than that which beats beneath these seas, enmeshed in a perfect floater's Paradise." And he fell off, dreamily, tragically, unreachably.

The spell was broken wholly by the Mauritanean's contempt. "'Merde!" he shouted, and he promptly rose from his seat and left the drawing room, still mumbling his four-letter words. Two others went with him, slamming the door behind them.

"You are an idiot. A billionaire who knows nothing!" came the refrain from many of those remaining. "Proving that inheritance confers no brains. A one-way ticket more dangerous than a return. Five dollars more potent than ten. Give a child a quarter, and beware the coming sea of unscrupulousness!" And on and on they chided, unsuited to a radical bent, but sucking up to the truth of a patron nonetheless.

Similar problems arose for the Commander when he assailed a Sherpa whose people had engaged in what is called the *shingi nawas* system of local forest protection in Nepal. Well and good, but for the Sherpas' equally zealous penchant for consuming meat. Among the Kayas in Kenya, or the "Law of the Mother" of the Kogis in the Sierra Nevada of Northern Colombia, Marigold ran into yet other contradictions.

"You cannot buy off human nature," came the addled response. "Either you are serious about change or not. If not, we're wasting our time."

"Of course I'm serious."

"Then put aside your vegetarian ethics. We respect them. But they simply will not fly in the face of bigger problems."

"Bigger problems, is it?" And he growled, spat, stomped and whinnied in ways the eavesdropping Alma—ears flapping—had never witnessed. "Maggot! Murderer! Dunderhead! Have you no shame? To write off the value of life, in whatever form?"

A silence gripped the gathering, a hushed embarrassment that clearly threatened to undermine the entire assembly. In the massive halo of dark lights and chasmed concerns that was at the core of Marigold's lunacy, a dancing fairy surmounted all obstacles, shouting circles around its benefactor.

"No plumbing," Marigold cried. "Not a sewer for 1,000 miles. The lights are out, a cutlass stampedes through the children's choir. A stylish umbrella fashioned in Kyoto conceals the patient. A gaping hole in the heart whilst crowds cheer their heroes forward. A light storm verges on the canyon. One moment there was the innocence of a red fox prancing near the river bank, a scene that had endured for millions of years; and then, not one scratch of warning, the carnage of syphilized nations commanding their hounds into war. Stephen Foster, César Franck, Walter Piston: who listens to them now? Plato, Hsieh Ling-yun, Bernard Shaw— does anybody even remember?"

"Your point, sir?" came the exasperated chorus.

He paused, then responded. But notice how the man had so quickly become the child; the origins of his quixotry, right there, exposed without any other rallying cry than that a stone should be admired, a blade of grass respected. Then he gave way, a calmer voice issuing above the rancor, stabilizing his mast, a gentler Marigold beneath the tempest, full of kindly reason superseding rage.

"Admittedly, there are layers of complexity," he allowed. "If I seemed intolerant a moment ago, understand that I have a serious problem with people and their habits. I want a world free of harm. Pure and simple. I want a world where no injury is tolerated. Is that wrong? I think not. But I will calm down, and grant you the foibles that must make this more interesting, perhaps, than I was willing to concede a moment ago.

Yes. There are strange bipedal carnivores among us. And some can sing in tune, however strange the contradiction. After all, Mozart guzzled oysters, it is well known. Therefore, let us move on. Find a tenable course through all this misery. Come to terms. Equivocate. I shall not impede progress any further. I mean only to speak my soul and hope for what is commonly deemed the best."

Simmering down, conversation resumed: serious questions of ethnographic sovereignty which, thus far, no amount of discussion, or financial offers of aid, had resolved. Only precedent-setting legal statutes could do that. The Dutchman, Henckle, described the Mabo case in the Torres Strait Island which pitted the Meriam people against the High Court of Australia over the question of possession. Who should benefit? The locals, or all Australians?

Even where the legal questions had been settled, there were difficulties with respect to biological management. For example, while Papua New Guineans had seen the Queen Elizabeth II National Park enshrined in 1954, the lands and resident wildlife had been totally devastated since that time, and the park's status all but abandoned by the government through lack of money or responsible stewardship. In some cases parks were mere smoke screens designed by corrupt officials for purposes of concealing outright exploitation—as has been borne out at many tiger reserves in India.

Zimbabwe's Communal Areas Management Plan for Indigenous Resources, CAMPFIRE, started in 1986, had hoped to prevent such corruption by encouraging entrepreneurial indigenous management for preservation and economic benefit, explained Lady Quenstrom of the WWF. Dozens of other efforts could be monitored, from the forests of Zambia to the coastal reserves of Panama and Costa Rica. At the first aboriginally owned national parks in Australia, like Gurig and Nitmiluk. Or at the remote Arfak Mountains Nature Conservation Area in Irian Jaya, managed by the Hatam tribe whose principal occupation was the allegedly sustainable collection of rare butterflies for propagation and sale to buyers in other countries. At the Air-Tenere National Nature Reserve in Niger, where the blue people adopted mud bricks instead of wooden poles for their homes to protect the forest. And among 2.7 million Pwo, Skaw, Thongsu and Kayan Karen of Kanchanaburi and Tak provinces in Thailand and Myanmar, traditional lifestyles had ensured the maintenance of the Huay Kha Khaeng and Thung Yai Naresuan wildlife sanctuaries. The Karen engaged in subsistence rice and vegetable farming, and added to their wealth by collecting forest products. They maintained the soil's fertility by very carefully considering every aspect of their multi-cropping—rice, bananas, potato, sesame and natural fertilizers. Most were vegetarian, as recommended by their Buddhist abbots.

"So it is! Possible?" Marigold waxed aloud, fancying his own scheme to celebrate and engage all of the world's 300 million indigenous peoples, including those of New Mexico, in Earth-saving missions. These were the most crucial endeavors, it was apparent, because these same tribal groups tended to inhabit the most fragile and biologically rich regions of the planet, the very ones destined to be raped by multinationals, or by the expansion of middle-class consumers and their children. It was this meager six percent of the human population that was mostly in tune with the world, lived directly off the provender of the land, knew what to do, how to get there, when to stop. Restraint was their password. Family the catch-all.

"There, you see!" the Commander hailed.

The Greenpeace executive responded. "The tragic irony of the tribes in Thailand, with whom many international NGOs worked to save the forests, is that now some ecologists are calling for their eviction from what was the largest conservation area in Southeast Asia—nearly 2.2 million acres."

"But why?" asked the mathematician, acutely attuned to such illogic.

"Because by some definitions a wilderness should not be inhabited by humans at all. That's the dangerous catch. Humans do chop down trees, kill plants and animals. It's no good, if you're an absolute purist—which, in my opinion, is ridiculous."

All eyes now rested on Venezuela's Yekuana chief, leader of the most sizable confederation of indigenous people still living in their traditional manner anywhere. Collectively, 200 tribes, including their neighbors, the Yanomami, dwelt throughout the Alto Orinoco Biosphere reserve, partly in Venezuela, partly Brazil.

It was the largest rain forest park in existence, and the second largest national park, second only to that of Northeast Greenland.

The chief, wearing faded jeans and a muslin scarf to tie back his long black hair, stood up to address the group. His eyes were bright, his skin glowing. "We now have about 68,000 square miles, inhabited by some 21,000 of my brothers and sisters. My people have lived there for millennia, and for most of that time, all were content."

A young anthropologist translator who had been dwelling with the tribes for some years picked up the story. "The chief say they have maintained perfect relations between all animals. The wasps and honey bees, eagles and macaws, until recently, all very secure, happy. My people, too. But for many years, says the chief, turmoil has been unleashed upon the jungle. First came Christians, then scientists, miners and industrialists. They wanted young girls, gold, oil, wood or animal skins, and the governments of Brazil and Venezuela have only hastened the pace of our suppression. Meanwhile, existing pipelines are leaking. There have been massacres. A great melancholy invades us. More people are going to die. The courts have been bought by the opposition. Yes, we need help. We need honesty."

"You see, Marigold," said Sam, who had been quiet up until this time, all-observant, distilling these many declarations, subsuming and turning over in his mind the rash of polemical pitches and ires, "human nature being what it is. There is no place that will not fall prey to the savage beast in man. Believe me, I got the raw end of it in prison. Santa Fe's no different. Rape clinics, animal shelters that euthanize over 80 percent of their residents, murders... our little paradise here is a mess. You're dreaming if you think it could be any different. Sure, the other day I spoke of what I termed primate enterprise. But even primates kill each other. It's rare, but it happens." And he elaborated with an impressive reference library, culled from behind bars, that fully convinced the Commander of the darkness looming in all hominids, and pushed further back his graspable, peaceable kingdom. A deep and disturbing urge to dominate, not just in people, chimps and savanna baboons, but among paper wasps, sage grouse and red deer, to name but a few.

"So what are you all saying?" asked the Commander, exasperated afresh.

"It won't be easy."

"I don't need to hear that."

"You have to be decisive."

"Give me evidence of a reason to spend money, and I shall do so. Show me there's hope. Otherwise, let's conclude our little tryst, embrace conceptual celibacy and have our dinner. Alma?"

She had been standing guard over her impending fortune, listening in whilst spreading out the various trays and nibbles.

"It's ready, your Highness," she said.

She meant to embarrass him. But the Commander was coming unto his own. He'd never had such a voice, such strength. The very fact that he had opened his hacienda to a convergence of strangers was a sign of punctuated equilibrium—one of those great leaps of evolution which converted one species into another. The hermit into a social gadfly.

Awkward silence met the Commander's ultimatum. Then: "Of course there's hope, or we wouldn't have bothered coming," urged the Danish Minister.

"Or you smelled easy riches, perhaps?" Marigold teased. "A fool whose money might be easily cuckolded."

"I assure you, sir," the Minister declared, "where I come from, in Europe, there are other—I won't say dozens of—billionaires looking for rational ways to be philanthropic."

"And?"

"They have mostly done so for enormous tax write-offs, or for contracts for their subsidiaries, whether their factory retrofitting equipment or some clean-up technology. We have rarely witnessed true altruism. Of course, from time to time, it happens: The Body Shop, STMicroelectronics, a few others. Exquisite companies."

"There, you see?" Marigold exclaimed. "Examples. It is possible. In all its undeniable tenacity, the power of ethics reduces the suasion of other factors. Commence with the passion, poetry, the very salvation which beauty offers the human species, and all other considerations—like my money—must follow dutifully. Well, ladies, and gentlemen, you've come to the right place. I just need to be guided and convinced."

"You said you were looking beyond Santa Fe, to the international arena. Do you want to spread out your money, spend it all at once, focus on a particular country or region? What do your instincts tell you?" asked the representative from the no-slouch MacArthur Foundation.

"In the fullness of blood, dust and tears, I savor an unstinting soft spot for all that I can. I commend wilderness, children, bumblebees; I acknowledge a fondness for bears and 107 acres of *Populus tremuloides* in Utah—47,000 genetically identical aspen trees, the largest super-organism known on Earth; even the cells in the eyeballs of the Namibian chameleon, a real charmer. The fact is, all of Nature's manifest I, too, compulsively enlist; all her puff clouds and fresh icy streams I crave. I require horizons unfettered, lest I lament; human hearts untainted, for a kingdom I should trade. Is that too much to hope for?"

But what Mr Marigold really heard amid the clamor of exotic-sounding place names, Capability Brown-lands, tribes, confusing strategies and experts who had their own pet projects and priorities, was the eerie, complicated plight of the mudskipper, condemned by all the massive forces of a schizophrenic culture: a people who had enshrined, on the one hand, the most beautiful, natural city in the world, Kyoto; and on the other, had wantonly destroyed Isahaya Bay.

It was this that finally saw the Commander kneeling by candlelight at his bedside, saying his prayers on behalf of a fickle human nature:

"Lord, just give me the strength to choose wisely. You are in me, all about me, under every stone, in each piece of wood. I acknowledge."

CHAPTER 42
How Mr Marigold Conspired to Buy the Greek Elections and Topple the Meat Industry Worldwide

TOWARDS TWILIGHT, that stretching hour when the Bandelier escarpment languishes in shadowy slumber and spies move silently across the courtyards at Los Alamos, Alma brought forth tray after tray of assorted dinner nibblings. She was not famed for her preparations, not even within the limited Marigold household, but in this instance she had ordered out for the majority of delicacies from her friend, an assistant chef at Geronimo's, thus wowing her two dozen remaining guests, and inducing a gulp of incredulity from her master, who could not comprehend such a culinary fuss. He had planned on cooking some spinach and mashed yam, served up with microwaved corn, a lentil soup and plenty of fresh-squeezed lemon. Instead, his eyes and those of his guests fastened onto the sautéed and generously garnished *huevos motulenos*, bite-sized corn cakes with dollops of *queso blanco* and sprinkled *calabacitas*; a filo dough smothered in sweet sauce; a large T-bone steak, which all but Marigold and four of the others consumed; polenta with mascarpone and grilled portobellos; and, alternatively for those susceptible to beans, a chilled avocado and green chili soup. She served hearts of romaine with toasted chili pecans and sliced pear beneath a dressing that combined Maytag blue cheese with fire-roasted poblano chilis, and ended the dinner with Mexican hot chocolate and toasted piñon ice cream.

Marigold said nothing about the steak. It was pointless.

By late evening all but three of the guests had departed, though not without substantial donations from the Commander, who acquitted his confusion and sceptical put-ons by simply writing two-million-dollar checks to each of them. This was the price of being a conscientious human being, he was later to tell Alma, who was furious that each of these strangers had received 70 percent of what she had been given—and she had virtually raised him.

"If they each got two million—I don't care how fancy their theories or expert their resumes—would it not have been fairer to give me 10 million?" she whined.

"In time, you weasel," he chided her.

The three guests—the HLAA representative, Sophia; the engineer from Canada, James; and the Bhutanese monk, Wangchuck—remained in the living room of the hacienda. The Commander wanted to pursue with them a few particular initiatives which he'd been struck by during the course of their heated sessions and they seemed most appropriately situated to advise him.

"I'm deeply troubled," the Commander confessed up front. "I hope you can help me."

"Speak up," the venerable Wangchuck replied.

"Look around you. This is where I have spent my youth, and middle years, completely cut off from the world. Even Santa Fe has rarely seen me, and that was only to take in the occasional art exhibit or buy some books. But the truth is, I have been self-absorbed in the life of the mind, happily floating in the clouds of unknowing, carefree and untouched by the Pandemonium of the world, suitably disposed to have no concerns or tribulations. My greatest worry has been the local drought, and the accumulating scum in the well, though I have been fortunate to have enough money to buy bottled water. I have wanted for nothing. Now, upon reflection, I realize that I lack for everything. My heart knows no solace. You saw what happened to me in the presence of a fisherman. Was I wrong? Do I expect too much?"

"You play the fool to hope that Africans will give up fish," applied Sophia. "But what a wonderful ideal."

The monk, declining the drink, offered his appraisal: "Save the animals. They have no voice that speaks for them."

Now Sophia, born of the Cyclades, her genes woven of misty whitecaps, a woman of knowledge and Homeric convictions, wild of eyes, gentle of demeanor, with a flashy black mane of hair, the whitest teeth, lent her own soft appeal, which merely reaffirmed the logic of animal salvation. "I too found it most queer that your guests, all spouting some semblance of ecology, thought nothing of consuming steak, then taking your money. I am impressed that you got over your wrath and helped their causes. I don't know that I could have done that."

"It set my heart back several paces, but I have to learn. I mean to be effective."

"For 15 years we have been struggling to save precious lives in spite of Greece's renunciation of common decency, courtesy, love. Beginning October 15th every year—the day the hotels close their doors and tourists go home—local islanders, some of them, begin poisoning all the dogs for no other reason than hatred. These victims, the wild dogs populating so many of our islands, are the friendliest of all canines. Despite all the years we've been fighting this, trying to educate the Greeks, they refuse to make peace. They are monsters. The only hope is to buy them off.

You want to make a difference in the land that discovered the democratic way, come to my country and make speeches. Acquire a candidate. You can afford it. We have a presidential campaign getting under way just now. With your kind of money, I assure you, you could purchase the election, and it would be the first animal rights presidency in history. The country has a penchant for such things. In 1981, PASOK, the Greek Socialist Party, won on a platform of cleaning up the air. In 1983, we introduced a law mandating the first unleaded gasoline, and monitoring the habits of drivers based upon license plates and certain days of the week. Unfortunately, the wealthier Greeks simply purchased second cars which enabled them to drive at all times, as before."

"There is no Green Party candidate in Greece?"

"Since the death of Petra Kelly in Germany in the early 1990s, there has hardly been a bona fide Green Party candidate anywhere."

"Ralph Nader?"

"No. A superego without decorum or finesse. As a politician we find him, at best, dangerous—he has angry convictions, some of them informed, others less so. We need to pick a winner, one who is pure of heart but understands negotiation, compromise. Make a contribution that is spectacular. That's what it will take."

"What would such a President ordain? And would the people follow, these monsters you speak of ?" asked the Commander.

"You negotiate with an existing liberal. He gets, say, 10 million from you for his campaign—that would be a hell of a lot in Greece. Inundate the media; outlaw all souvlaki, all meat for that matter—the BSE crisis across Europe will work in your favor. Rejuvenate our animal cruelty laws. Assign 1,000 full-time undercover agents throughout the country to curb all violations. Outlaw the biochemical industry in Greece, compel consumers to turn in their furs. Create 10 new national parks and expand existing ones, stepping up regulations that inhibit off-road vehicular traffic. Place a moratorium on any new beachfront development, and—on behalf of those seaside angels of yours—a five- or ten-year moratorium on fishing, as well. Start a new breeding program for the monk seal. Create an anti-dumping patrol as part of the Mediterranean clean-up efforts."

"How would you prevent a fishermen's civil war? You see how hot-headed they can become."

"Pay them compensation. But they don't just get the money. They have to work for it, putting in the same hours they would have killing fish and squid and sponges. Make them clean up the beaches, protect the last nesting sites of our migratory fowl, curb traffic along the tide pools, and work with the Greek Coast Guard to prevent tankers from emptying their bilge tanks filled with used oil. There are so many things they could do. I believe in your country it is called a Conservation Corps of Engineers."

"So I've secretly bought the presidency. Then what?"

"Then think of it: the first vegetarian, cruelty-free nation in the West."

"It should be Greece," Wangchuck added. "Because South Asia, with 98 percent of the population evidently in favor of leather goods, seafood, mutton stew and thermonuclear devices, is certainly not going in that direction."

"I must say, this strikes just right of preposterous," James managed. "I am enthusiastic about revolutions, but there are laws, even in Greece, I'm sure, against such campaign contributions."

Sophia retorted without even blinking. "Fine, add a massive government investment in solar hydrogen fuel cell systems as one of your negotiating points."

"Now it's all coming into focus. Before, my eyes were blurred. Sophia, a toast! You are an inspiration," the Canadian exclaimed.

"If I give you 10 million dollars tonight, how can I be sure you'll spend it in accord with this conversation? You see, my lawyer is off on a cruise somewhere. It's not that I don't have total trust in you."

"I understand. You're saying you'd like to stay out of it."

"I've never been to Greece. I would certainly come for the celebration party. But I want us to win."

"We'll win. And Wangchuck and James will be with me. Gentlemen?"

"Buddhist monks do not as a rule engage in politics. However, there have been some notable exceptions."

"I knew you'd say that," Mr Marigold sighed. And he looked questioningly at James.

"Oh, my company will understand." Everyone smiled.

"I would prefer a budget," said Marigold. "Go back to Athens, discuss it among your closest confidants, figure out the amount that will get the job done. I cannot overstate the importance of our pledge of confidentiality. Agreed?"

Now even the monk indulged in a late-night chinwag. "By the way," Wangchuck added. "Once you've converted the Greeks to animal rights, let's do the rest of Europe. They've already banned leghold traps."

"What about Canada?" said James. "Don't forget it's the largest per capita meat-consuming nation in the world. I didn't start out in life as a vegetarian. But the day I vowed to devote my engineering skills to helping the environment, there was no choice: you cannot be an ecologist if you are not a vegetarian. Ontario, BC, disasters!"

"Actually," the Commander exclaimed, "I've been thinking about a rather global solution to the problem of meat-eating."

"We're all ears."

"It's one of the reasons I asked you to come, Wangchuck. I know it was a particularly long journey for you."

"No, no." He waved his hand apologetically. "Not to worry yourself. You call, I will come. Anywhere, any time."

"You see, I've done some reading on the Bhutanese, and, well, who would not be deeply moved by their example, though I have noticed mention of some meat-eating, have I not?"

"Sadly, not all Buddhists refrain. Their justifications for eating flesh are highly suspect, I must add."

"What are they?" Sophia wondered.

"By consuming an animal some Buddhists believe it will expedite that creature's journey to Nirvana."

"The height of arrogance."

"It is," the monk replied. "Unfortunately, many high lamas have fallen prey to this atrocious propaganda."

Marigold started. "Here is what I've got in mind. Among my various schemes—a quick and easy vegan restaurant to compete with all the fast-food animal hells. I have read in the *Wall Street Journal* that some of the world's most emulated figures relish hamburgers for both lunch and dinner. There is thus much work to be done. I want to open the franchise in every major city from Beijing to Toronto. I need an architect, a food engineer, someone experienced in setting up food chains. I want the meat that goes into burgers to become a thing of the past. As archaic as Nero's savage entertainments in the Colosseum. To save the tens of billions of chickens and cows killed for human consumption every year in the US alone. That, to my way of thinking, is the paramount crisis sweeping the planet. There may be two billion hungry humans, but there are tens of billions of tortured animals, whose nociceptors are capable of feeling far more pain, it may be deduced, than their lesser human cousins. Surpassing acid rain, toxic wastes, nuclear war, our behavior towards chickens and cows—and turkeys and horses and goats and sheep and pigs, of course—must constitute the greatest offence on earth against God's masterplan. No, we are not part of the masterplan. Of that I am quite certain. No God worth his name could have devised the horrors of factory farming. Forced molting. Sow stalls. Battery cages. Debeaking ... Cut off the habit of meat and all the other byproducts, make them illegal, and the animals go free.

"I envisage a vegan restaurant chain as addicting and convenient as the most successful meat-eaters' chains. You all know the ones I mean—I refrain from even uttering their names because they are abominations. Their stockholders are living in denial, like most Germans during World War II. To even refer to such corporations is to bring on the worst karma. What do you think?"

"It can be done. It must be done. Bravo, Mr Marigold! But how will you make it competitive?"

"That is the best part." He mooned on the fly and grubbed on the wing, making everything up as he strode along. "I will not compete. That is an unseemly occupation for a gentleman. Rather, I shall dent world hunger by cornering the global market for soy beans, wheat gluten and gruel of tempe (all unmodified genetically, of course), so that my own factory outlets can cook up 1,000 steams, let loose canola oils for the patties, knead scallions and chipped legumes into the amalgams, formulate a recipe to be admired by one and all, and subsequently distribute several million soyburgers to the poor every day, all for free."

"But how can you possibly afford to pay for the world's hungry? You are not that rich, are you?" asked James. He referred to studies which pegged the cost for long-term amelioration of the world's undernourished and/or chronically malnourished at 600 billion dollars per year. And that did not take into account the existing subsidies of the West by the poorer nations, a flow of dollars from cotton-poor Mali, and other desperate nations that had fallen far behind the twentieth century, victims of farm subsidies, digital divides, and chronic cultural differences which argued against financial gain.

"A man of many questions. Two billion, I am told, are hungry. All right, I admit that I am but a lonely voice, woven of a weak tensile strength, and have limited purchasing power. I cannot overnight erase the plight of two billion. But let us commence with two million. We can easily establish a non-profit corporation devoted to saving some percentage of lives in every precinct. Come close—I whisper now. There will be subtle additives I wish not to broadcast too loudly, metaphysical properties culled from the French countryside—most likely the region of the Vallée de la Blaise in Haute-Marne spanning the Bois de Charmes and Chateau Voltaire: a pinch of chalk water, wild boar's urine that has dried atop truffles, the salt tears of a pike, secretion of wild strawberry, and so forth, all calculated to quite literally addict the human population to vegan food. Imagine those same millions of people obtaining their burgers and bisque of tempe at no cost to themselves. We will design food lines for the twenty-first century, environments like those of the very best health spas at Baden Baden. Dignity. Aroma. Collegial leisure. Do I know what I am speaking of? Not exactly. I have never been to a spa. Not at all. But I can well envision the setting. Lermontov. Lana Turner. Within days the targeted populace will view these free lunches as the ultimate expedient, freeing them from laborious toil. No longer need they work for their sustenance. Liberated thus, they can concentrate on higher thoughts. You can be sure that they, their offspring included, will banish the very memory of meat forever. Then the meatless word shall spread. And behold, a kingdom of grass. I expect that a year will pass and the killing will end. No more exposed ribcages, scurvy, goiters, rickets, and the widespread condition of vitamin B deficiency."

"You paint a romantic picture. But won't the conversion simply substitute one burdensome form of monoculture for another? Vast tracts of land usurped in the rage for a single crop, soy? What of all the other species? What would be the outcome for hundreds of millions of cattle worldwide?"

"Salvation. Beyond that I cannot precisely speculate. Paradise regained."

But the Commander had already seized upon his Vision of Managed Meadows, like some sustainable song cycle from the age of the Duc de Berry: cadres in dozens of countries intensively growing Marigold's crop, whole families employed in the merrymaking, ceremony, ritual gathering, growing, processing and distribution of soyburgers. The New Economy will be galvanized by soyburgers, smothered in the Commander's own brand of sautéed onions, spread with Marigold Mustards, for lunch, dinner and breakfast.

"As for the cows and other creatures, they will live out their lives to old age, assured of a permanent refuge in the thick of our kind's subversive malignancy. Soy will enter their diet as well. While cow birds, starlings, white-throated sparrows and hornets feed on their droppings. This is a win-win, for everybody."

"Nonsense," Alma cried out. "What's wrong with hamburgers, anyway? What's gotten into you people?" And she proceeded into the kitchen to feast on left-over veal chops, which she then paraded throughout the hacienda, insisting in a rare eloquence that meat is what gave mankind its edge over the rest of nature.

"She is from Mongolia," Marigold explained, "where there are few vegetables."

"Then one can hardly blame her," said Wangchuck. "On the other hand..." and the conversation drifted on well into the night.

CHAPTER 43

The Kingdom of Grass

IT HAD BEEN OVER A MONTH since all the momentous events of the grand judicial resolution and the deliberations of the Marigold think-tank. Spring bumblebees and scrub days had come gloriously to Tesuque and environs. The money was in the bank, and Mr Marigold, for all of his continuing anonymity, was now the wealthiest man in New Mexico. In fact, he discovered within weeks that his 1.85 billion dollars was actually worth much more than that, for his broker had proliferated into half-dozen managers whose buys, calls, diversifications, catastrophe and junk bonds, Socrates software-screened ecofunds and other placements had swelled overnight. In one month they had executed 14,000 trades, taking profits on one-, two- and three-dollar upswings, buying short, buying long, investing in tracking stocks and—mostly—getting lucky.

Marigold, who until this moment knew nothing of investments—had made little of money, thought of bullish markets as a disgusting throwback to the worst of human nature, equated personal advantage with the most vicious vice, despised talk of equity and gain, accumulation and profit, saw only disparity and unhappiness—began to come around. He now gained fluency in the language of high-yielding instruments. He changed overnight, in fact, recognizing how he could benefit others with wealth. Henceforth, said he, there would be no stinting, no crimped style, no parsimony. What had been content to remain subject to the fickle modesty of Nature now dressed for warfare in the pursuit of acquisitions and mergers, optimization and performance. He quickly understudied the world of e-commerce, global software, long-distance telecom, future broadband growth, fiber optics, database storage and management, futures, commodities, margins, e-chips, aggressive growth, corporate bonds, debt securitization in Japan, German re-insurance corps, stretches and credit ratings.

What was particularly odd about his investments was their uncanny good fortune. While most ecological stocks and securities were plummeting, those chosen by the Commander utterly and inexplicably soared. They included a well-known firm that had managed to eliminate millions of pounds of CFCs from its operations; an American group that had come up with a user-friendly fuel cell for home use; a waste management fund; a French conglomerate specializing in biodegradable fast-food containers; a Brazilian multinational that had focused much of its workforce on finding ways to recycle lost oil along railroad tracks; a British start-up devoted to protecting snails, leeches, anything that crawled; a mid-European airline whose logo was the rat, and many others, so that in a matter of weeks the Commander had earned another 700 million dollars, 20 million dollars alone on edible diapers.

He was advised to sell, wait out the micro-recession, then re-buy aggressively. Day trading, taking profits, was part of the strategy: buying short, buying long, watching movement from 7.30 a.m. onwards. Which he did, realizing yet another 400 million dollars on bizarre high-tech IPOs.

All of this storm of lucrative activity certainly got his blood running. But his quickly-won laurels were hounded by the scent of scandal and contradiction, echoing the wisdom of Sam Turbovsky. There were no easy marks. No clean profits. That quarter's conference calls by CEOs of the many corporations which interested him provided opportunities to vent his extraordinary confusion and concern. And who wouldn't be massively turned round, he reported, unburdening his doubts by thoroughly assailing the economic cartwheels, accounting fraud, corporate irresponsibility and special interests without end. Here was the celebrated manufacturer of soy bean, a wonderful alternative to animal protein. But then came reports the company was using methyl bromide, an acutely toxic vaporous fumigant, in at least one of its plants. Talks of a dead man, rotting corpse, OSHA violations, nitrogen pollution adding to the Greenhouse Effect. The flipside of every altruism doomed to corporate gigantism. Reduce manure by manufacturing amino acid supplements for animal feed. Excellent. But what about the fate of the animals themselves? Slaughtered. Ferment corn to manufacture ethanol, the cleaner grain alcohol, and thus reduce the use of MTBE, the suspect gasoline additive. Substitute nematodes for chemical insecticides. Terrific. Good things, to be sure. But what about those allegations of noxious waste discharges in South America devastating little boys and girls? Or the secretive genetic engineering of crops? Marigold wanted to invest in natural gas companies but tallied between the half-dozen candidates' potential responsibility at nearly 85 EPA superfund sites. How many dead birds, inundated soils? And all those barbs fired by displaced or poisoned indigenous peoples from India to Bolivia to Texas. Human rights abuses. No women or minorities in senior executive positions, pipelines leaking PCBs, drilling in national wildlife refuges, explosions that killed workers. Even the most squeaky-clean alternative energy component manufacturers had been cited for non-compliance with environmental regulations or violation of water-discharge laws. The same eloquent company that supported environmental classrooms and took on leadership roles in global climate change research had also reaped hundreds of millions in revenues from nuclear weapons-related defense work. All this unsettled the already destabilized mind of the do-gooder.

Were compromises legitimate in the interests of earning money that would, in turn, be donated to good causes?, he asked. Could unstinting largesse ever justify tainted money? If not, who had the right to throw the first stone?

Sin and compromises notwithstanding, there seemed to be no stopping the economic monster; no sign of a bubble or an end to "irrational exuberance". The engine was in place, both in the general marketplace and in the inevitable momentum of Marigold's portfolio. Capacity utilization, unemployment and inflation were low; runaway share and asset prices at an all-time high. Despite rising interest rates, the stock market had continued upwards. But Marigold understood not one principle of economics, and this was probably for the best. A master builder of new excursions and dangerous exploits, his venture capital instincts were primitive, carnivorous and untutored. He was in the jungle of appreciation, refinancing, mortgage packages, in stormy seas of greed. The whole American dream spread its economic legs and he suffered no pause in its swift deflowering.

He knew now what must be done with the profits.

He laid it out with all the instruction his own hacienda had offered to the inquiring mind. "Consider the humble nematode," he began. "Why? What does it mean?" Sannazaro wondered. He had been seated in a corner, quietly nursing a Moose Drool brewed in Missoula, not about to enter the scientific fray where he did not belong.

"I speak of roundworms. The most numerous of all creatures, without whose good graces I assure you your gardens would dry up. The worm is the hallmark of good economic thinking."

"Go on?"

Marigold proceeded to extrapolate 100 principles of trade dividends and monetary policy that were explicitly biological, recognizing a host of kingdoms—Protoctista, Fungi, Plant, Animal—and a dozen other taxonomic groups. These were the basis, he overtured, of absolutely everything worth thinking and caring about. In short, Marigold intended to develop a program for saving amphibians and snails, mammals and skippers, ferns and tiger beetles, along with all the cows and sheep and hungry children.

But he was no simple generalist, making waves for the betterment of all. His specifics entailed an exasperating grasp of the headlines. For example, he reckoned there were some 15,300 native angiosperms, or flowering plants, in the United States, at least 15 to 20 times more worldwide, and they were fast disappearing with little interest shown by humans. Despite an elite effort by a few scientists to crack the genetic code of the *Arabidopsis thaliana*, a seven-inch-high weed in the mustard family that fairly mirrored the 26,500 genes and 121 million units of DNA throughout the plant kingdom, less than one percent of all known plants had ever actually been studied. Read: plucked, sundered, pulverized and dried. A vast manhandling of vascular sentience. Moreover, there could be as many as three million additional plant species as yet undiscovered, unpulverized, according to the Marigold Theory of Ignorance (for every known species, 10 remained to be found). There were clear convergence factors working in opposition to discovery and/or preservation. That vast wave after wave of development projects, be they World Bank and IMF-inspired, or other, had collided with what ecologists referred to as the Net Primary Production Paradox. The stripping of wilderness for farmland, the malling of arable soil for condos. Until a world of ranchettes—too big to mow, too small to farm—had replaced the life of the woods and its natural photosynthesis, with one Los Angeles bearing down on nature every three weeks. Somewhere in the middle was Tesuque, whose one interested inhabitant had made a careful study of the abnegation at large.

In question, to move beyond the plant world, was the preservation of nearly every endangered species in North America. The rare *Aplodontia*, for example, along with their remarkable team-mates, *Hystrichopsylla schefferi*, the world's largest flea, half an inch long, living in the dense hairs of this Pacific Northwest-based mountain beaver. What secrets did they possess? What gossip their nameless ancestors? For a million years they transpired, effected great dreams, silent felicities. Now they were nearly lost, and nobody cared.

Marigold's estate had harbored its own sanctuary for these magnificents. It was an algific slope, like a Paleocene island, with its own relict molluscs doting against moldering walls, a Great Interchange of Splendid and Peculiar Isolations. His ancestors had inadvertently set down roots atop that point of continental separation where fault lines and tectonic plates fractured, took leave, superimposed, collided, or abandoned their primeval positions. The resulting Marigold Line induced something like a latitudinal genetic drift. Even the humble mayfly, winging it throughout the adobe chambers of the hermit's house, showed double, triple the genes of those a few degrees to the south, in the vicinity of Albuquerque. Had the Commander not cared, none of this would have mattered. But presently, in his heightened fiduciary state, he could not help but take note of the microcosm and its ramifications: the two bright yellow Bachman warblers in the greenhouse, seven white wartyback mussels clinging to the inside of the well where he had liberated Amigo, a family of *Cambarus pristinus*—the most imperiled crayfish in America—splashing about in the acequia behind the house. All omens, to be sure. A methodology at his front door. Anybody of common sense would have recognized such particulars, performed a similar deduction, arrived at a pantheism without constraint or compromise.

The Lord Dragonfly was himself part of this mighty string of conceptual pearls, but even more so the mayfly, *Ephemeroptera*, taken to flight as an adult for a mere 24 hours, long enough to mate (but not to take a single mouthful of food), and then to die. The ultimate ecological exemplar. If only humans could learn to live like the mayfly, he reasoned.

As for the 10,000 acres, each and every one had factored exquisitely in the revolution he was prepared to undertake, had been chosen wisely with the help of Sannazaro who could pick soils like a chef of haute cuisine. The Senator (aka Sannazaro) would scrutinize a mere dollop of earth, taste it, smell it and lend his verdict. Hillsides vulnerable to erosion were perfect for his avant-gardening. The two Tesuque geographers, one a Marigold, the other firmly and everlastingly Italian, had mulled over the biological cost/benefits of a single spread versus several, and had come up with a plan of action based upon the works of Victor Higgins and Andrew Dasburg, master painters of New Mexico. Higgins had also been a geographer and his "Little Gems" reflected his roving appetite for pristine views—the Picaris Hills, Santa Clara Canyon, Arroyo Hondo, parcels throughout the Sangre de Cristo Mountains, the Chama Valley, the Río Grande Canyon and a place called "The Valley of Waiting Souls". In Mora, Marigold acquired 800 acres bordering the Pecos Wilderness and Santa Fe National Forest and overlooking the eastern Sangre Range. It was there, amid the large aspen meadows and running brooks, that he established a wild mule and horse sanctuary. Jeanette Mulado, a disciple of the famed Solvang horse whisperer who'd worked out the non-verbal semiotics of *Equus*—down-turned eyes, twisted shoulder, silent glare, pinched mouth, and so forth—moved to the property within weeks, and had already negotiated for the transport of over 100 wild mules rescued from the gunsights of US Fish and Wildlife bounty hunters in the Mohave.

Marigold's overnight contributions—growing by the day—were by no means insignificant. He learned that there were fewer than 1,200 land trusts in all of the United States, protecting four million acres. Most of the trusts were in the East—Massachusetts and New Hampshire particularly. In New Mexico he discovered that fewer than 20,000 acres were protected, 75 percent by the Santa Fe-based Forest Trust. The Commander's patchwork of properties would increase New Mexico's total by 55 percent. The deal with the state provided that his 10,000 acres must be preserved forever. He would pay no taxes as a result.

Most of the Commander's properties were in the ten- to 100-acre size, pieces of a puzzle which was the enigma of his own heart that, as it came of age, seized upon multiple land-lusts, went impulsively into alpine and high-desert cul de sacs, primary forest canopies, rocky canyon lands and riparian labyrinths teeming with eight-inch minnows, scores of darters. He found sylvan glens that were home to western tanagers and Lichtenstein's orioles with their orange bellies and thick beaks. He arrived at the entrance to Apache Canyon and saw within seconds a red-eyed vireo, and two willow flycatchers, and with absolute certainty, without any other criteria, declared, "We'll take this one!" At Pacheco Canyon, north of Tesuque, he watched at sunrise as little hermit hummingbirds and blue buntings sported among flowering cacti. Without further hesitation he acquired the 60 acres. A common potoo, a lesser pauraque, a nocturnal whiskered screech owl, or the sunlight striking a rufous-browed wren were all he needed to be sold on a given piece of turf. His ornithological eye was well advanced, all the more so considering that this expertise came from the picture books he had grown up with. The bleating hawks and the darting quail. Murmuring doves and dive-bombing harriers. The birds, along with the soil, were his most important indications of a desirable habitat. Every added parcel fulfilled another aspect of his newfound gluttony for life, his exploding joy in existence. Truly he had prepared himself to be reborn.

Sannazaro was equally driven by this acquisitive greed for land, because everywhere the soil could take it, he'd come round with bags of grass seed. He had become a firm believer in the wisdom of grass, of worm farming and composting as methods of combating erosion and drought. Indeed, the sun-beaten semi-arid soils of northern New Mexico were similar to those of his native Italy. Once Marigold had acquired the property swap from the State, Sannazaro would drive onto the land in an old red Chevy pickup and simply fling the diverse grass seedlings from large burlap sacks in the manner of the Japanese one-straw revolutionary Masanobu Fukuoka. He was careful to do so on rainy days, just prior to breaking storms.

Sannazaro had acquired large quantities of lyrical-sounding grass: *Pennisetum orientale*, *Stipa pennata*, *Cyperus textili*, nomenclatures that rippled in the wind, off the lips, like velvet; swaying mood shifts, first violins and deep cellos, brass ensembles and metrical follies. *Carex conica* "Snowline", *Miscanthus sinesis* "Cabaret", and Golden Toupee "Glacialis". Names to nestle beside. Precious, life-restoring grass. A kingdom of grasses for which every storm, each burst of wind, gave added delight and possibility. Runnels of rainwater provided sustenance. Snow added minerals. Fire provided the pepper and the salt. The myriad droppings were so much protein. As the grass spread, millions of insects made the land home, and with them all the rodents, reptiles, avians and larger beasts.

In this way, the Italian gardener looked upon the wild hills of New Mexico as his private domain, vast canvases for his colorful palettes of flowers. The Commander himself espied in those same wilds the opportunity to have children—infant birds and crickets and mountain lions and bears. He planned to adopt the entire animal kingdom.

One day both men lay in the high grass of one of their newly acquired properties, staring upwards at the rolling cumuli, daydreaming out loud, bare toes feeling the bite of cold.

"How much money do you think it would take to buy the entire planet, terrestrially speaking?" Marigold conjectured.

"More than you've got, Professor."

"Surely there is a realistic computation not altogether inaccessible?"

"Well, I suppose there would be. Multiplication tables ad nauseam. The number of provinces times the extent of acreage multiplied by the number of countries. Is that right, or shall we gloss over the provinces, sticking to the charts and tables? Accounting for political difficulties, and certain properties explicitly Not For Sale—the White House and Pentagon, for example."

"Everything is for sale," the Commander said sharply. "That's the problem." And he proceeded to figure out a price, based upon some basic arithmetics. "The Earth's land surface comprises 149 million square kilometers. One square kilometer is equivalent to .3861 square miles, which equals roughly 250 acres. Give or take such and such. I am no abacus. But what is that?"

The Commander scratched the equation in the loam under his butt, arriving at a planetary total of 37 billion, 250 million acres.

"Now it would certainly be fair to exclude most deserts and the highest portions of the high mountain ranges, as well as the Arctic regions and Antarctic. I would also subtract from that total those regions currently protected, beginning with Ecuador, Venezuela, Bhutan, Austria and the UK, where between 19 and 38 percent of each country is preserved. That would leave only those biodiverse-rich regions at risk—I am not speaking of the few dozen most critical hotspots, but semi-critical, as well—and I would guess they constitute no more than 10 percent of the total, or, say, 3.7 billion acres. At an average global price of 100 dollars per acre (to be negotiated, of course), I do believe it would be possible to round up enough money to pull off a great coup, engendering a whole kingdom of grass, assuming enough billionaires could be interested in the proposition."

"On the other hand," Sannazaro began, "once you purchased the land, your troubles would only then begin. Have you done a proper budget? Taken note of utilities, insurance, public liability? The ambiguities of No Trespassing signs and representations, hidden potholes in your roads, a teenage dirt-biker topples or sets a fire like the conflagration at Point Reyes, an outbreak of bark beetles, a mudslide. You'll need a bonded guardian—more than one—otherwise who should protect it? And what if lyme disease is tracked to your woods, or an epidemic of malaria when global warming whips every depression into a swamp? With all of your money invested in the land itself, what then? I see the same Santa Fe syndrome: an avalanche of difficulties and dissent. What happens if you can't negotiate at 100 dollars per acre. What if it is 1,000 dollars? How much will the lawyers take? What about revolutions in some of those countries? We'd be out on our noses. Stay clear of Liberia. Iraq. Columbia. You see my point?"

They carried on this way for several hours, going back and forth in their calculations. Finally, the Commander decided it was too much trouble, however inspired his motives, to buy the world, and his gardener friend tended to agree.

CHAPTER 44
A Corsican Tail

ONE AFTERNOON in early summer, Ginevra de Martin returned unannounced to the Camp of the Spirits. She had caught a small article referring to Marigold in a Swiss newspaper.

Sannazaro showed her the envelope he'd left on her vanity table.

"What is it?"

"Open it."

She withdrew the three-million-dollar check made out to her. "I don't understand," she said.

Sannazaro explained as best was humanly possible.

Ginevra immediately called over the Commander, who tried to assuage her shock. "It was the neighborly thing to do," he explained. "I've done the same for Sannazaro."

"Oh, absolutely. Like it's the latest vogue. Murillo, I have my own money. Why would you embarrass me with such generosity?"

"Madame, there is no embarrassment, no encumbrance or indebtedness. Your loveliness offers to the eye a mural of purposeful proportion and stunning symmetry. A tuning fork of ideas, an entire ideology without a shadow. In your gathering of spiritualists and artists, roosters and saints, gardeners and beasts of heaven, you have endowed the neighborhood with a feast for the heart. Who would not be indebted to you?"

She blushed and looked away to Sannazaro for support. "I suppose, now that you're a rich man, you'll no longer be doing my gardening?" she wondered aloud. "I certainly wouldn't blame you."

"Once a gardener, always so," he reassured her. "As for the money, do not fear its corrupt influences, not on me. A dollar does not bloom, nor throw off the scent by which the human psyche alone survives. Man would excise wild weeds and ignore his soul; eschew the buttercup, marvel at the rose, then toss it in the garbage without a thought. He would rout the woods, then have no shade; sever the innocent lily, then die of loneliness; decapitate geraniums, while enshrining his bank account on a palanquin of clouds. If your life depended on it, would you rather have one dollar or one tree peony, a high-yielding money market or magnolia, most Fragrant Lord of the First Spring?"

A whimsical smile. A woman's inward heaven made rare and manifest. Eyes twinkling.

"To commemorate the logic, I shall plant three million peonies around the property to remind you of the good old days, keep your head out of the clouds, out of your checkbook and down to earth. In fact, while you were gone, I endeavored to design for you a New Garden that would be self-sustaining. I've planted a lot of wildflowers and wild grass species.

You'll see the canvas emerging by September, gracing every box elder and silver maple, a pointillism beneath cottonwood and spruce."

Ginevra kissed him on the cheek. Then said to the Commander, "I'm happy for you. What will you do now that you are the richest man in New Mexico?"

"I shall continue to be myself, with any luck," he sighed. "However, there is one new advent I might as well mention, for you are certain to hear word of it. Wherever trouble calls, I feel inclined to dive in, feet first, of course."

"He's decided to save the world," Sannazaro applied instructively, a final tentative brush stroke on the canvas of impossible dreams. "At least some percentage thereof, beginning with Pliocene apes."

"It is a slight exaggeration," Marigold deferred. "But it is fair to add that the countless burdens of biological injustice weigh heavily on my appetite."

"A broad complaint," Ginevra said, frowning. "But I agree with my gardener: money cannot arrest a tidal wave, nor dry a woman's tears."

"Santa Fe is in pain, Ginevra. Cerrillos Road cries out. El Dorado signals the alarm bell. Tesuque teems with doubt. Chimayo and Nambé fall prey to mob rule. Now multiply the regional wrecks by 50 million—" and he prepared to overwhelm her with that contagion of worldwide worries he'd become so deft at reciting. In fact, so persuasive was his discourse of analytical abscesses that it came across as a vivid enthusiasm in the thick of rotted teeth.

In such loquacious presence, most people could not shirk the inherent responsibilities or fascination. But Ginevra was of a different straw, and cut him off before he even reached the adjoining state in his inventory of crises and civil wars.

"Look, I really do find your generosity fantastic, but I am no believer in negative vibrations or self-nullifying information. They tend to replicate. Talk about death, and somebody is bound to die. Refer to tragedy, it will happen. Speak, instead, of hope and happiness, and their possibilities are magnified. That's how I try to live."

"Yes, I agree with the wisdom of positive thinking. But not to the exclusion of reality. It is important to separate, for example, the good Christian from the good scientist."

Sannazaro's eyes widened. Lo, that could not be the entire Commander speaking? Master of surrealities, stretches, leaps and illegible ledgers? Unless responsibility was already growing on him.

Marigold turned down Ginevra's dinner invitation. He had scores of blueprints and mountains of tomes to study. But back at the Camp, Ginevra inquired of Sannazaro about their remarkable neighbor who had only of late shown his apparently true colors.

"Strange," she said, "how we have never really gotten to know this man, after so many years. I am horribly to blame, of course."

As she watered plants and swept up leaves that had blown throughout the house, Sannazaro followed, describing his new friendship with the greatest eccentric of recent centuries: how much the Commander meant to him; the good Madame Vignette and their remarkable adventure; the gathering of diverse personages from around town, and from all over the world. All the incredible particulars of the legal proceeding instituted by Hidalgo—or at least those with which he was familiar.

"Yes, but what about your Commander himself?" she went on, suddenly curious about that which had never entered her mind, but now loomed large for no apparent reason. "Has he no marriage plans?" Sannazaro was humored by the notion, for what could be determined was that the Commander was not of this age, and his fidelities belonged to an ideal, rather than flesh and blood. "He dreams of his princess," he volunteered. "The dying art of chivalry has discovered in the Commander, who is lost in a welter of virtuous ideals and historical antecedents, its truest diplomat."

"A rather strange-looking man, isn't he?"

"There's that universal profile, the pointed Spaniard's chin, the bright temple, the shock of dark ringlets, and his eyes—have you seen his eyes? One aquamarine, the other verging on yellow—a freakish feline thing, undiluted absorption in whatever dream he's dreaming. Never have I witnessed so skinny a branch. The strange thing about it, I have seen him consume a pound of mashed potatoes and three chocolate bars with no apparent ill-effects. He sleeps erratically, and is by most criteria an ascetic, though desserts and café mocha are indeed his principal subject of conversation."

Late that night, Sannazaro persuaded the Commander to drop by for a nightcap, which turned into a most convivial and starlit repast. The conversation veered towards Corsica, for Ginevra had just returned from a two months' stay with a sister who lived outside Bastia. Their mother had died, leaving an estate to be reconciled that included a worthless 2.5 hectares of inaccessible mountain in the center of the island— by an odd coincidence, a patch of squatter's calkstone, infertile slope and fly-infested stagnant brook much along the lines of Sannazaro's own ill-fated idyll on that other nearby Mediterranean isle. Helga, Ginevra's mother, had moved into a condo in town with her dog, Negrescu. The dog was mostly wolf, huge and white, and anyone who came in contact with him was not likely to forget the encounter, for he was, by any scientific yardstick, remarkable.

"Please, tell us," Mr Marigold hastened. For he was a great listener and particularly relished animal tales.

"All right—" and she began. "Before my mother's illness, she and Julia, my sister, managed a trip up the mountain to the property. They had not been in years, and for Negrescu, who was six years old, this was his first time ever out of the city. They drove the 30 windy miles into the mountains, and there a jeep with four-wheel drive took them another three miles up to the 8,000-foot mark. From that point, a shepherd who was grazing his flocks in the area transported them by horseback over the rocky stubble. With his goats, and sheep and odd pig, the fellow produced a smattering of *fromage de brevi* and *jambon de corse*, local products unique to northern Corsica. In the south, in my opinion, the cheese and meats are less tasty. The people are all dour stinkers. They never smile. They worship Napoleon, of course; all the men and boys carry concealed guns; and most of the top policemen and criminals in Paris, Marseilles and Nice come from either Bastia or Ajaccio.

"Anyway, they reached the property which my sister informs me is worth nothing to anybody, save for the shepherd. There was a stone shelter there, but even that had caved in and offered refuge only to the snakes and spiders. Negrescu, who had been named Simon after my father, at least prior to this journey, promptly ran off. The dog had never seen goats, sheep or pigs, all quite able to stand their own ground against a city-slicker. There were red deer up there as well. Now this was a gentle giant of a dog, but it did have that wolf in him. To make a long story shorter, it was impossible to wait for the dog to return, as much as they would have preferred it. There was simply no suitable means by which to survive the night, and so, before darkness endangered them, they were returned to the jeep, and then made their way back to Bastia. Mr Marigold, some more wine?"

"Certainly, Madame. Most kind of you."

Ginevra continued. "My mother was devastated. Understand that following the recent death of my father, that dog had been her life. Not a word from the shepherd for weeks, and then only a call late one afternoon from the village at the foot of the mountain to inform her that the dog had never returned. Then the sciatica set in and there was absolutely nothing for her to do but take painkillers and read. No possibility of her getting back up that mountain. Naturally, she never gave up, for what such adages are worth."

"That's it? What a sad tale."

"No. A month later, that same adage yielded a miracle. My mother received a call from the concierge of the Negrescu Hotel in Nice. He knew my parents, who used to frequent the establishment. Father loved the place. Anyway, the fellow had seen what he described as a white wolf begging for food from tourists in front of the hotel—a sight not witnessed since 1816, when the last French wolf was seen wandering a city street. Evidently, on one of their last trips to Nice before Father died, my parents had mentioned acquiring the dog and the man remembered and assumed it had to be the same one. In her waning emotional state, my mother clung to the coincidence, but in the event the animal disappeared when the concierge tried to coax it."

"It couldn't have been the same? There are plenty of large white dogs loitering about Nice."

"But listen. The story thickens. Two weeks later, the concierge called my mother again. The dog had shown up in the garden. It apparently preferred the leftovers at the Negrescu. However, the concierge was still unable to catch him. He tried everything—fresh broiled shrimp, raw hamburger, ice-cream sundaes. The dog ate everything offered but bared its fangs the moment the concierge made to corner him."

"My kind of dog."

"Presently it seemed a guest at the hotel thought he recognized him. The fellow was the captain of one of two tourist ships that plied the Mediterranean between Nice and the two harbors of Corsica. He was certain the dog was the same one that had been stowing away on board his vessel not once, but three times a week! His crew loved the cunning beast and had adopted him, though nobody had managed to venture very close.

"So can you imagine? Negrescu had found his way off the mountain, all the way to Bastia, had boarded a ship, and was scavenging at the best five-star hotel in Nice—and that's on top of all the goodies he probably copped on board the vessel. But here's the clincher. Mother's condition deteriorated, and somehow Negrescu sensed it."

"But how do you know that?"

"Because a month later the dog showed up at her apartment in the center of Bastia."

"You're kidding."

"They say a wolf has a seventh sense. What I find incredible is the fact that Negrescu knew which steamer to board, for there are boats to Bastia and boats to Ajaccio. And then to find the apartment, in the middle of a city. Anyway, she renamed Simon Negrescu, and the dog's great compassion and companionship kept her alive another year. Of that Julia is certain."

"Where is the dog now?"

"You're about to meet him!"

"What?"

"Yes. My sister lives in the city, which would never do, and the shepherd feared he'd kill his flocks, which is utterly untrue. This dog prefers steak tartare, and dines out most nights each week. Are you ready?"

She opened the door to her bedroom and out poured the creature. One hundred sixty pounds, a wolf by most characterizations, fresh from USDA quarantine, thrilled by all appearances to be in America. It plowed, slobbering, into the Commander with no inhibition or awareness of its colossal size.

Marigold fell off his chair, and the two of them wrestled with astonishing familiarity. The Commander then began working on the dog to convert him to vegetarianism, abetted by a box of chocolate Orioles at hand.

CHAPTER 45
Men Who Love Fliesand the Women Who Adore Them

THE NEXT DAY Ginevra visited Mr Marigold. She couldn't quite fix in her mind the urging. Gratitude, curiosity? Possibly a remote desire. She'd not been with a man for several years, not since her quiet divorce from Jacques.

The Commander had lain on the rug in the living room stroking Negrescu and sharing his cake with the wolf, and Ginevra recognized in this neighbor a strange quirk of a human being to her liking. Sannazaro had at first impressed her in this way, as well. But their familiarity over the years—the decorum of a higher friendship circumscribing their cohabitation—had dampened any sexual ardor, or that's how she explained it to herself. Not so, in the case of Marigold, whose eyes, she imagined, had connected with her own, if the Commander's cockeyed expressions of felicity could be construed as anything other than dementia.

In fact, Marigold had other lofty preoccupations when Ginevra led herself up along the baked-brick pavers, past the dusty blue stucco plaster, beneath the repeating vigas and transom windows, arriving at his doubled-gated zaguán which still bore the historical plaque of the Secretary of Interior's insignia, indicating the antiquity of the estate. It was listed on the National Historic Registry.

She rattled the cow bell at the very moment Alma had admitted to momentous news: she was three months' pregnant by Sam Turbovksy.

"Hello?" Ginevra called out into the sprawling hacienda.

"Alma's pregnant!" issued the frantic electricity from the Commander's own lips, a visceral response of spastic wonderment.

"Why stop there? Alert the whole damned neighborhood, mobilize the national press corps," protested Alma.

But the Commander, rising to the occasion, was inordinately excited.

"You both can stay here, there's plenty of room. You must stay here."

"Very kind of you, Murillo. But, frankly, dear, after all these years, I'm ready for a reprieve. It's time I hired my own maid."

"Surely you don't think I ever thought of you in that way?"

"Of course I do. No need to chip around an old bone."

Alma had met Sam at the bar at La Fonda two days after he'd moved to Santa Fe, his whole being on fire with liberation. The flame burned Alma as well who, needing to weed the low-brow Larry from her mind, drew close to his big smooth hands, his vague evocation of a modern-day Genghis Khan, his beautifully shaped head filled with jail jargon and PhD patter, his muscle-bound throat, the tattoos and motorcycle gang demeanor. It all fitted.

A host of womanly feelings surged unexpectedly in Marigold as he opened the door to find Ginevra in the lambent morning light, mottled and looking like one of Modigliani's women. Perhaps it was the queer excitement spawned in his heart by the living fetus in his midst, the blushing truth of a coming newborn and how he, or she, had evinced such a transformation over the beast of burden that was his maidservant. Now she bore the presence of grace, beginning to show through in bulges and rosy cheeks and other fresh, irrepressible signs of impending motherhood. Enter Ginevra to compound the sensation. His Montparnasse heart skipped several metro stops, his brow flushed. Ginevra was a beautiful woman, and he'd never actually paid attention to her. She was older than himself by some years—he wasn't sure how many—but, after 30, what difference between 50 and 70? Her falling cascade of blonde locks was a lilting breeze along Lake Windermere, her eyes had the same distant passion as her wolf's. These collective features impressed him with a disquiet he recited in a spate of atrociously bad lyrics which did not turn her off so much as enchant.

It took all his steely nerves to restrain himself from grasping her hand.

"I just wanted to say how nice it was to get to know you better, after these many years," she said.

"Good woman, why don't we have tea and toast—we've got some fresh blueberry jam from Zacatecas, and Alma—" He stopped himself, knowing that life would be different from now on. How could he ask a pregnant woman to do anything? To the contrary, he would now serve Alma. But how could he serve Alma—how could he do anything of a time-consuming nature, with so much of the world hanging on his shoulders ... not to mention the brouhaha that had erupted at the Plaza, which he now owned, after he allowed various but selective local groups to use it for their appetizing appeals? Seventh Day Adventists, Predator Friendly Products, Inc., Catherine Ann Champion's Tabernacle of the Life Force, the local Greenpeace chapter, the Espanola Animal Shelter, the Rape Hot Line group, and so on. Nothing could have been more well intentioned.

What caused such consternation was a newspaper article that very morning revealing the identity of the new owner of the Plaza and describing the "10,000 other acres and billions of dollars Mr Murillo Marigold and his lawyer, the notorious Mr Hidalgo the Third, had exacted from the state of New Mexico under circumstances that must appear impromptu and unorthodox. If there are merits to the case, should not the citizenry be informed, given the magnitude of the exchange? If the merits are insufficiently warranted, where is the follow-up investigation?

Why have the lawyer and his wife suddenly disappeared on a cruise ship? Moreover, as details of the case begin to surface, it is also clear that severe stipulations were to have been enforced on the exchange of acreage, but how could the Plaza—the state's most symbolic piece of land—have been turned over to a man of utterly mysterious origins, whose only apparent purpose seems to be to forward his own radical views at the expense of nearly everyone else in the state?"

The article, according to Ginevra, went on to defame the Marigold legacy with a slew of bizarre allegations, fantastic inventions, ridiculous inaccuracies and sinister innuendoes, and to propose a Grand Jury investigation into the possibility, as yet mere supposition, that the judge and DA in the case were somehow on the take.

The reporter had hastily cobbled together interviews with those who claimed to know Marigold—though the very absence of acquaintance with a man whose family history in Santa Fe purported to go back to the late seventeenth century was evidence enough of nefarious goings-on, or so suggested the reporter. He had tried to interview Marigold, but the Commander had obliged no such intrusion.

Ginevra continued. "'His entire purpose seems to be to save flies,' said one anonymous voice from the Santa Fe Institute, unwilling to concede any explanation or official position on the moral rights of flies.'"

"Flies?" wondered Marigold aloud. "Yes, of course I spare flies. But who wouldn't? Have you ever actually examined the anatomy and morphology of *Odonata*?"

Ginevra shook her head. "Fourteen thousand genes. The very same protein-building mechanisms as in humans. Tormented like no other species, for what? For us. We ignore the miracle of flies, whacking them into inertia—a delight that gains atavistically, one imagines, with every pulverization. Yet, show me one that lives unmolested and I shall produce a miracle of sight, of aerial dynamism, and the frenzy to be born and reborn. Let no man forget the fly, whose appetite and cleverness is second only to man's. Was it not Thomas Malthus who asked, What can consume the corpse of a lion with greater dexterity and speed: two flies of the opposite sex, or an entire village of hungry Masai? The question, of course, begs the admiration Malthus shared with all his followers for the logic of exponential growth, and that, dear friend, is inherent to the fly. And consider, if you will, the most tender fly. The one that naively trusts in an arm, or finger, and looks you in the eye, wanders up your forearm, not so much as a hint of fear. Innocence of that kind, framed in so perfect a little body, would otherwise ignite the envy of the rest of us, were we not so consumed by our own self-importance. So much to learn, so little time."

"That may be—a disquieting image, I dare say. But other allegations swoop down upon the moment:

"'He's intent upon forcing an evacuation of the whole city of Santa Fe,' a certain waiter was angrily quoted. 'Like some feudal lord who prefers to turn an historical crossroads into his own private hunting ground, he lusts after stew of wild boar while the rest of us are plunged into unemployment. One can only conclude: a morose fool, a redneck in lambswool, Mussolini posing as John Muir.'"

Ginevra continued on, paraphrasing the article as she went. Some peeping toms described seeing Mr Marigold and a co-conspirator entering the premises of a known Ku Klux Klan organizer months before, a woman repeatedly hauled in to the city jail for unlawful possession of weapons and for harassing her neighbors. Her organization, Extermineighbors Anonymous, had been the subject of an ongoing FBI investigation into suburban terrorism, which now suggested links to Mr Marigold.

A major-domo with the local utilities company even complained about Marigold's water meter, which was notoriously jerry-rigged to the acequia.

Still others, who declined to be named, summarized many of the musings propagated by the more radical sectarians who had attended the gathering at Catherine Ann Champion's house. All these pipe dreams and fascistic interventions were ascribed to Mr Marigold. The reporter, whoever he was, obviously had it in for him. But why?

The answer was clear enough. The same "voice of moderation" that belonged to a new candidate for Mayor, a pro-life, anti-Bingo aspirant, had somehow gotten wind of the Marigold case and decided to use it as her ticket. She was the driving force behind the article.

"This travesty of New Mexican history; this spineless corruption on the part of the Attorney-General's office, and the Governor, is just another symptom of the sickness rotting away any decency in the state capital. These are the same people who stoked the government into a frenzy of greed with a 150 million dollar lottery. They are demons of self-interest masquerading as the people's representatives. They should be prosecuted to the full extent of the law," she declared in her interview.

"I guess you better spend your money quickly," Ginevra suggested. "But that's not what prompted me to drop by." She smiled understandingly, and Marigold served her green tea in the secret garden.

As much as any man, he was quite capable of laughing at himself. He knew well how silly he was: stupidity neutralized by the gift of mirth and the lessons, easily assimilated, of human puniness before the madcap enormity of an unfeeling universe. He had long been attuned to the painter Goya's remark about the monsters of imagination that, when reined in by passion, produced a balance necessary to any temper, curbing the angst of our coming death with the delight of coming day. And thus, without delay, the mood was decorated: crinum and *Rosa* "May Queen" in profusion; the modulations of a vicarage; drifts of stepping stone whose forecourt of quince and asymmetrical three-seasoned charm was amplified by *Geranium* x *magnificum*, pink trumpet, a stone urn awash in *Crambe cordifolia*. All this variegated ivy, *intemporelle exquis*, *emotions d'un monastère*, tranquil and unsuspecting, surrounded their conversation. He stood unbridled and ready to conquer. Softly at ease before this virgin of new proportions that was his neighbor.

"It will all blow over," said the Commander. "I'm not at all fazed by these pedestrian rough edges. You cannot make some people drink clean water. And Hell, in Gustave Doré's palette, was sumptuous"

Though fixed in bourgeois charm, his warmth, Ginevra picked up, was as uncertain as a piece of sixteenth-century porous limestone in Sud Bretagne: subject, in other words, to radical temperature change.

For a brief hour, amid Victorian settees, terracotta figures, sunflowers in bloom, a large Irish bell, bishop's weed and blue Russian sage, the two new friends sat beneath the aspen trees in the al-frescoed pergola of the courtyard. The Commander's head was spinning, his face flushed with the fear of a giant wave washing away his glorious sand castle.

All that romantic neglect which had guaranteed his vintage disinterest, distant dispassion, historic follies—diverted by notoriety. His namesake threatened, the carpet pulled out. And how cruel the timing. Just when his great day, lasting eve, decisive dawn, were working in favor of his abundant largesse and moderating influences. He'd never been in the newspapers before. He felt sick, suddenly at sea. The heat was building. Could his edifice withstand exposure? A newly born heraldic fend off firestorm? Ignore ignominy?

These were turbulent news crowding him beyond experience.

CHAPTER 46
An Inconsolable Macaw of the Upper Amazon

SENSING THE NEED for lighthearted diversion, Ginevra removed a stamped envelope from her bag.

"We received this marvelous letter from Father Alvaro," she began. "You remember him, of course?"

"Certainly. Aka Cardaillac. A fine painter."

"We only discovered his lurid passion recently. You remember—you were there."

"Who could ever forget all those scintillating women locked under bolt and key in his studio."

"That's right. And his unplanned departure for the Amazon following the visitation of that peculiar Indian and a sudden vision of his family in danger."

"What is in the letter? How is he faring?"

"An astonishing report. Shall I read the pertinent parts? I think you'll find this rather poignant."

"Spare no details. Circumambulate, zig-zag, meander, meddle in others' business, cut far away from the chase. Stories of this kind are my protein, tribulations my tofu."

The fine-looking woman before him took his mind off the sharp edge of emotions swirling around the tea table: the FBI, a Grand Jury, reversal of fortune, or worse—his inability to break out from under subterfuge and jealousy in defense of the world. All those elaborate donations, sublime restitutions, animal liberations, misunderstood by the public. He choked in view of the possibility that his life was merely an enormous fiction. An Arcadian backfire. How like this ending century which he despaired of: a mirror of every awry, extinct auk, hooded dodo, shipwreck and defeat. Impotency compounded by the futility of hope. To have come so close to actually accomplishing good, only to see the palace of virtue crumble at the slightest touch of real human nature. Crowds and power caught up in the nervous twitch of self-destruction and those seven deadly sins. How could he ever face himself again? He'd promised the Señor a governorship, at the very least. Instead, a hollow defeat, a swarm of slap-suits, or worse, a jail cell, when, instead, he meant to free every dog and cat from every so-called shelter in America where the vast majority were euthanized.

Humans who solely perpetrated these brazen insanities could not be forcibly sterilized (indeed, the French were moving in the opposite direction, rewarding parents a 10,000-franc prize for every conception, each child then receiving a monthly stipend of 8,000 francs until the age of 18). But the neutering of male animals, the spaying of females, required no permission. He thus imagined an end to the century of pounds, of animal control and abandoned puppies. He dreamt of providing for barefooted vets in their mobile RVs, equipped with acupuncture needles and the necessary sterilization equipment, dispatching them throughout the country, and particularly New Mexico, the state most famed for the sorrowful plight of its domestic animals. He was prepared to fashion 100 square miles of dog and kitty heaven (80,000 acres had gone on sale just southeast of Santa Fe for a mere 75 million dollars); to build tens of thousands of warm huts with dog and cat doors; to hire an enormous army of care-giving families who did nothing but live on the land, ensuring the joy and nutrition of a few dozen of the new denizens. A solution, after a few generations, to the holocausts occurring in every city and town.

In fact, he intended to incorporate his dog and kitty villages; to provide each one with its own Governor and garbage removal service, Internet connects and wool blankets; to endow the children of the care-giving families with the judicial responsibility for all conflict resolution.

To experiment in new modernist forms of tenderness and soul transfers. In time, he hoped to see his villages become a vast metropolitan epicenter of proud dogs and protected cats. And eventually its own state, with its own canine and feline laws, and a carrying capacity of no more than a few million barking residents looked after by a few dedicated human care givers. He could rightly see it, spread out across illimitable canyon lands and high juniper and stunted pine. The true Dog and Cat Town, so generously supplied with delicacies as to void the very need of predator/prey nonsense. A gymnasium to keep the cats in shape. And the outlying 'burbs dedicated to all those fun-loving packs of canines, every hiccup of hybridization, breeds seen nowhere else. Fed only the finest soy tartares. A Customs house for transmigrating tourists, such as curious coyotes or lonely peregrines.

He envisioned similar townships across America for other species, as well, particularly in Hawaii and Alabama, where animals and plants were most at risk. In the case of Alabama the reason for such carnage was twofold: first, the fact the state was spared the Ice Age, meaning an unusually sustained burst of adaptive radiation amongst its endemic biota, and second, the recent human atrocities in the name of poaching, and of damming all the rivers, with the most disastrous consequences for freshwater snails, crayfish, mollusks and countless other riparian-dependent species. Marigold intended to break up the cartel of such dams, liberate the water, restore the ancient eddies and fast currents, and rebuild the sandbars. As for the Hawaiians, he had great plans in store for its 479 species known to be imperiled, which included a concerted effort to hallow the honeysucker, single out the tree snails for state honor, celebrate the hoary bat (the islands' only native mammal), give all of its lobelia a second chance, dignify the more than 1,000 species of native *Drosophila*, and practice hallelujahs to the Haleakala silversword in every school.

Such noble arrangements had been placed in jeopardy as the reckless result of some foul-mouthed reporter for the local newspaper. It was an abominable situation to be in. He held the table to regain his balance. He had to get a telegram through to Hidalgo to warn him, and seek not a little advice.

Now, all these mounting torments were put aside as the lovely Ginevra read from Father Alvaro's dispatch received that very morning:

"A few details of his arrival, etcetera etcetera. And then he begins in earnest. 'By the time I'd reached the final river juncture, I already knew there'd be problems, and the words of that Hopi shaman, the lecherous misdeeds of my alter-ego Cardaillac, my years in Paris, the nude models in Tesuque had come back to haunt me. I have no idea what I'd been thinking. What disguise was this, when my true roots were here, in the jungle? How could I have abandoned my family with such selfish disaffection and callousness? The Indians looked on like doomed mutts. The kaolin mine had covered most of the forest like a cancer. The surrounding region was a disease, populated by yellowing mulattos in their shanty-town back alleyways and lean-tos of corrugated aluminum, TV satellite dishes that had broken down years before, exhausted, sickly prostitutes, and wicked paramilitary goons. The new boom town with its bulldozers and helmeted workers meant the demise of the indigenous Indians. *GATT* and *NAFTA*, silk cravats and Mercedes 450SLs—I have no idea where they came from in such roadless tropics—had conquered this portion of the

Amazon. Fires burned everywhere along the horizons. No expression of pain can quite get at the meaning of such smoke, or of the general agony in its wake. Smoke also inundated the human lungs. Asthmatic responses—angry, wheezing, irritable, disinterested—infected the air between people. Children played checkers and jacks and whistled at the girls who, by the age of 30, looked 60. By then they will have had a dozen abortions. The unwanted fetuses are buried in the jungle, or dumped in the mercury-laden river: the Church forbids abortion, and the country has no population policy. There are no schools for the children. AIDS is rampant. In the distance, you can always hear guns going off. The sound of earth movers continues 24 hours, day and night. When I asked about the tribe in question, nobody knew anything.

"'I did finally get enough information about the missionaries to attempt a journey. I hired two dugout canoes and we ventured up a far tributary of the Río Negre. I suppose we'd been gone more than a week, going ever deeper. At times the river was a mere creek. We saw an anaconda, and slept under two layers of netting at night, or, my Indian guide informed me, we'd have been devoured. He was deadly serious. Three o'clock one morning I awoke—having taken three PM Tylenols and one 5mm tab of Melatonin—to a million stinging insects trying to get inside the netting. They'd eaten through the outer layer. I panicked, and if it had not been for my guide, who had the presence of mind to squirt kerosene all over the both of us, I'm sure we would have become statistics of the grimmest sort.

"'But this was a mere prelude to my coming discovery,' the letter goes on. 'We reached a place I recognized, where I'd grown up as a child. How strange to see the familiar embankment, where we swam naked and played in the water with our bowed arms, and swam through gold dust along the sandy bottoms, always careful to get out of the river before dark, otherwise the piranha babies would get up your dick, our parents told us. How odd to see the site where a church once stood but now was gone, burned down, the ashes overtaken by the jungle. I could still make out the remnants of the landing strip where the occasional plane touched down with supplies.

"'We continued up the river. By this time my Indian boatman was showing signs of wariness. He was out of his territory and I knew that he was going to stop rowing at any moment. But the moment never came—for within a two-day journey of the abandoned settlement we came upon the recent remains of a river encampment. When I kicked up ash in the fire pit, smoke emanated from the still-warm embers. What had happened here? Scarcely any possessions of note. At least a dozen people had spent time at this unlikely entrepôt among the jagged rocks of the river's edge. But there was little else to be gleaned. Then, as we were preparing to put into the river once more, my guide, Jacko, caught the light of the waning sun on something wedged between the boulders and advancing forest. It was the medallion known as the Chevalier of Courage and given by the Prime Minister to outstanding citizens of France. My father had worn it all his life. It was made of platinum.

"'I gazed on balefully. My father would never have allowed himself to be parted from this memento handed down by my grandfather. With this apprehensive perspective, I more fully searched the ruins and detected one clue after another of the last days of a tribe. They had gone extinct, or such was the impression. We spent the night there, and in the morning discovered we had slept among corpses. Heads were missing. Bones as well. The dead had been scavenged, possibly by jaguars, or eaten alive—who knows? Jacko discovered the signs of bloodshed: a curare-tipped arrow lodged in the neck of one of the victims. In the scuffle, the assailant had evidently dropped his blowpipe. The weapon, made from chontawood, with its double hollowed channels, was nine feet long. Jacko informed me that it was precise up to 200 vertical feet. Horizontally, a skilled hunter could take down a sloth or peccary at the distance of a football field. This attack, however, had occurred within speaking proximity of its victims. Also present in the warm ashes was a black-dyed gourd filled with a paste known as kapok. And there were darts as well. My guide sniffed their heads: barbasco, he said. Yet another poison, normally used for killing fish. There had been a terrible battle here.

"'By the middle of the day, when the heat was intolerable, we took cover in the shade. Within minutes I heard a strange voice.

"'I cannot adequately convey the musical sonancy, full cadence or verbal facility that accosted us from the upper canopy of rain forest, but it was a cascade of some tribal language that was entirely alien to me. Jacko, however, could pick up the odd word. The declarative and inquisitive remarks splashed down with increasing desperation. With my binoculars I quickly detected the source of the speaker. It was a bird! A scarlet macaw of magnificent size, plumage and autonomy.

"'Of course, I did not believe it at first. But Jacko was not entirely surprised. I extended a hand, tossed some pieces of huito and achiote fruit from our stores, and the macaw hopped down the 200-foot-high series of branches, one at a time, until he was actually within reach, his powerful beak just inches away from me. He preferred yucca, also known as manioc, Jacko informed me. But we had none.

"'The bird's eyes were as full of wisdom and loss as any I have ever seen in a human. But what shook me to my foundations was his subsequent eloquence, spoken with great feeling. Most of it was incomprehensible. Sentences fired off with a frenzy. The bird craned its head, yearned for something, and it soon became clear that what it missed were its friends, the humans. Another macaw, blue and gold, waited for its mate high above, and was afraid to come down. Both creatures kept thrusting their beaks, taking angry whacks at their talons. Their stomach regions were bereft of feathers and I knew enough to recognize the signs of a terrible frustration and self-infliction. These birds had witnessed horror and the trauma was there, inside them.

"'*You, friends. Where others?* Jacko translated. It was the language of a tribe that existed no more. And these were some of the last words anyone would ever know of them. I suppose a linguist or anthropologist might have reconstructed the whole human society from the adopted speech of that desperate, lonely macaw, which had probably lived in proximity of the tribe for—who knows how many years or generations? Macaws, as I understand it, can live to exceed 100 human years. Perhaps as a child I had even seen that very bird.

"'*Where others?* Again and again. I was utterly devastated. As much on account of the realization that my father and mother were dead as by my inability to determine which corpses belonged to whom. The damage that had been wrought here was so extensive, and the mechanism of decay so accelerated in the Amazon, that the dead were utterly dismembered, burned and rotted beyond any kind of recognition. Lines of biting ants 20 inches across emanated from the entrails. Burial was not even an option. So we left. I safely wrapped the medallion.

"'We continued upriver. I don't know what I expected, and Jacko was certain we would be killed. Maybe I wanted to die. A fitting end to a strange life. Perhaps I gravitated towards the dissolution of the jungle, and the perverse vision of reincarnation among those towering rain forests. There is a poetry in the tropics that cannot be separated from decay and rebirth. I understood why so many Christian missionaries had been attracted to the vast tracts of Amazonia. However inconvenient the stinging insects and snakes, and all the other hazards while one is alive, Lazarus lives in these backwaters; Christ embraces every leaf-cutting ant the same. God's Creation speaks through the miasma as in no other region on Earth of which I am aware. To be enveloped by it all, to have one's very marrow sucked clean, holds an allure that is quite real, and I felt it.

"'But all this contemplation of self-destruction was cut short by a miracle. Just before twilight, rounding a bend in the river, all was revealed. Before us were dozens of tumbledowns and, on a grassy knoll, a church, painted white, with a lovely high steeple. Children would not enter the water, as is customary when visitors arrive, but rather waited on shore. All the villagers—dozens of them—came down to the beach. Among them, to my profound astonishment, was my father.

"'We both wept. He doubly so upon learning of the massacre down-river—the site of carnage to which, I realized in retrospect, the macaws had remained loyal, watching over the spirits of the deceased. My father told me he had given his medallion to a young chief who had not exactly converted, which was never my father's real purpose, but had shown at least an appreciation for the concept of a loving Christ. Amid a chaos of ungainly omens, that was more than enough. It took courage to endorse such a creed, and spread the word, which is what the young man was doing when he and a dozen followers were slaughtered by unknown tribals further back in the jungle. These complex politics were meaningless, of course: grim intrusions into a way of life in the Amazon that, in the end, had no relevancy. None.

"'They were probably one of many tribes that had never been contacted by the outside, my father suggested. As horrifying as the events were, he could not help but feel a certain positive mystery about it all—about the fact that unknown peoples still roamed the shadow world of the Amazon.

That the grip of civilization in these forests was not infallible. As for those two young Indian mistresses that had precipitated my mother's suicide, they had long passed away, suffuse with fevers, dying in their hammocks surrounded by their clan, sipping cool fruit juices, the opiate of spirits, a pantheon of animist saints easing them into the next life. Beneath the ambiguous glare of St Anthony of Padua, St John the Baptist, and my own father, I believe it was cholera that killed them.

"'True to all things French which dwelled in my father (a rogue at heart), he took his fifteenth mistress, a beauty in her twenties whose naked body gleamed like 24-carat gold. But here's the big news, Ginevra. Her sister is equally beautiful. She is the one I have been striving to paint all my life. This is the girl I was searching for in every other woman who disrobed for me. It is true love. I have given up not my faith, but my cassock. She is pregnant. I am very happy. Please keep my paintings safe, but consider them yours. I will always treasure your memory and thank you for the gift you've given me. Hello to everyone. Perhaps someday I shall return to introduce you to my new family. You can write to me c/o ... such and such.' He has provided the details. A river junction. A post office box. And signs off, 'In love and ecstasy, Alvaro.' No more the honorific Father. And that's his letter."

Marigold and Ginevra finished their tea, remarking on the strange and wonderful conclusion to the tale.

"What will you do now?" Ginevra asked.

The Commander, brought back to the reality of the moment, sighed.

"I'm not sure. The last several months have turned me upside down. The written page has been lost in daylight. Books stepping out into glorious crusades, dreams into demonstrations. The surreal has become actual, and actuality a bit of a fog."

"Is it really true you've come into so much money?"

"Oh yes. Amazingly. I would never have thought to pursue history with such a vengeance. But Hidalgo, bless his heart, was more stubbornly convinced by the fairness of it than I. His penchant for unearthing the past was persuasive."

"Sannazaro says he made a cool 100 million dollars in the upshot."

"I would never begrudge him that."

"And you gave all of us three million each. I still can't get over it."

"The price of a good cup of tea with a good friend."

She smiled generously. "I'll lose the best gardener in Santa Fe thanks to you."

"What a funny little man he is," Marigold said. "But he does seem to know his plants."

"Oh yes."

The Commander looked at her quizzically.

"What?" she broached, alarm mingling with self-consciousness.

"What would you do if you were me? You see how I have lived all my life here—a recluse, with hardly a friend, no needs, just my library, my modicum of security, the stable earth underfoot. I call it human scale. But what would you do with two billion dollars? Actually, it may even be closer to three. I've asked dozens of others and gotten all kinds of intriguing answers, some inspired, others less so."

Ginevra hesitated. Then: "You ask me how to live, in other words? The money has little to do with it. I'm not saying two billion isn't a good thing, but certainly not what most people might crack it up to be. More trouble than it's worth, I imagine. As for myself, it's like this. Any time the negative enters a conversation, be it a thought pattern, a suggestion, even a nuance or intimation, we have to immediately reject it. That is the basis of survival. You just watch. The twenty-first century will be about positive thinking, positive approaches, the universal rejection of the negative. It will be the most important revolution in human history. Discount discouraging words. Banish bitterness. Relinquish regrets and recriminations. Move forward. Be hopeful. Have faith. Tie up every loose end. Gratify each heart, hold no grudge, grant amnesty to former foes. There is joy in making amends, and that begins in the heart. Money becomes dust against such eternal bulwarks."

"Words well chosen," said the Commander.

"I believe in the emotional revolution. But I am even more firmly convinced in the wisdom of an action plan," Ginevra continued. "Let activity predominate. An academy of asseveration, a school for pilgrims, every child a candidate. We have the choice. People—oh God, how even to phrase it. Strength is about spreading love and positive thoughts to everyone. I listen to the crickets at night and know that that's exactly what they're doing."

"What an extraordinary notion!"

"And we're not the only species that picks up on it. The year 2000 is going to be incredibly complicated because there is darkness in the world. It's mounting faster and faster and I have no idea how it will all end, but people are going to have to mobilize in support of all that's clear, pellucid and good. The world is full of gravy. Say, the Sikhs are doing a peace walk June 20th through Precious Valley. Why don't you join me and Negrescu?"

"That's weeks away."

"So what?"

"I'm trying to figure it out. So much, so fast."

Ginevra looked away, thinking—distracted, bored, disappointed, full of prophecy, deadlocked with desire? (who could say?)—then returned her gaze to Marigold. "I'm certainly no crusader. I wake up in the morning and I just give thanks to God that I'm alive. Because life is so wonderful. I don't deal with the contradictions of human nature, especially my own, and I never have. I found my home. My spirit soars beneath the Tesuque blue. I feel very, very free. Live and let live. Just go out of your way to recognize the goodness in all people. That helps them. And that helps you. Nothing troubles me more than this vast inertia of despair spreading throughout the world. Each culture seems to capitulate to its chosen mediocrity. These trends are terrible. We need resurrection in the heart, and then a blueprint for action. If that's the goal of all your new-found riches, then consider me your greatest advocate."

Marigold kissed her on the hand, a show of great respect. "I am touched by your kind words."

She brushed off his delicate profusion. "It's the best advice I can give. I don't have any sadness. As I told you—because you asked—my only solution to life's woes is a systematic rejection of all those negatives. A minus times a minus equals a positive. So why should I have any sadness? I only occasionally watch the news or read the newspapers. Why bother? Violence, more violence. You see, this morning was one of those rare occasions, only because Sannazaro brought it to my attention. And what do I get? My beloved neighbor plastered all over the front page. Lies, jealousy, hatred. Best thing you could do, I think, would be to find a few good causes that will increase the chances of happiness in this world for as many people and other creatures as possible, and give all your money over to them. Do it now. Don't over-intellectualize. Don't complain. Just get on with it. Our lives are briefer, even, than we can detect. We build our own pyramids, and climb up them, only to discover they are really tombs. Escape these temptations. Circumvent thralldom. The world happens, with or without you. So be smart, be frank, be unstinting. And forgive an old woman her sermons."

The Commander grinned. "What will you do with the token little gift I gave you?"

"Three million dollars? Token gift? I'll give most of it away! Every time you give, you multiply blessings. Never stint on blessings. Think of it as natural capitalism."

Eventually, they said good-day to one another. With a gracious silence Marigold again took up, and studied, the fine wrinkles in Ginevra's left hand.

"Hmmm," she murmured. "What?"

"Interesting," she said, and walked jauntily back towards the gate where she noticed the behemoth gazing restlessly at her from high above on the forested slope. Enormous eyes, minotaur musculature, fur-lined mystery.

The extended physiognomy of Picasso's bull. Menacing. Magical. Ready to move out.

CHAPTER 47
The Ghosts of Chaco

MARIGOLD, TOO, NEEDED TIME away from the portentous cave-in of familiarities. Tired of complexities, wary of simplicities, meditating on Victor Hugo's power of the idea whose time had come. Sannazaro suggested they head over to the Botanical Garden in Albuquerque to examine their new crop of camellias, freesias, fragrant roses, forget-me-nots and lily-of-the-valley. Or the Japanese baths up on Artist's Road. Ginevra had recommended a dozen other distractions in town as a balm of forgetfulness. She was not yet entirely aware of the extent of Marigold's Scylla and Charybdis, of that frail nature which aspired to correct the imbalances of the modern world beyond the reins of any moribund mortality; but she certainly knew he was not altogether happy with his new-found riches.

"Why not go lose yourself in Handel's *Solomon* at the Sweeney Center— piety, self-sacrifice, the erection of the Great Temple of Jerusalem; or the Madrid annual jazz festival—thousands of people, great sax, clarinet...?"

And she went on with other sundry swing dances, discos, piano and vocal bars, a history lecture, a Hungarian symphony under the stars, classical Latin guitar at a half dozen hotels, a production of *The Ruined Woman's Revenge* at the Engine House of the Old Coal Museum, a National Dance Institute of New Mexico production of *Romeo and Juliet*, a gallery talk on the "Ghost Ranch—Land of Light" taking place at the Museum of Fine Arts, fondue for two somewhere or another, a flea market, an outdoor painters' showing, a Sierra Club hike up the Windsor Trail.

Ginevra could not have known that in his entire life Marigold had never gone for fondue, and only rarely taken in a concert or a film. He did watch classic movies on television, and had an enormous soft-spot for *Brigadoon* (as well as St Hugh's dream, guided by stars, battered heath and weirdly wonderful sisters), *Bringing Up Baby, Love is a Many Splendored Thing*—had always fancied a pilgrimage there to that dreaming hill. But the notion of dancing or going to a piano bar was as alien to Mr Marigold as moving to Rome, New York. As for jazz, he was little amused by it; ballet—enamored of sylphids gliding over light, but couldn't stand sitting in public chairs, hearing coughs or rude ejecta of any kind. All had ruined his one and only *Swan Lake*. Spoiled, priggish, with little sense of his ridiculousness, the Commander was an unlikely candidate for levity or lightening up.

Instead, what gathered force around his little dark ratiocinations were modern throw-backs, his ideas always veering off towards some wild place where history might instruct him on all the foibles to watch for, dialectics and distractions to conquer, hope to fathom, utopias to study and engender.

"Come to thinking of it, we need not sally far. Is not that cypress enough?" Sannazaro suggested. "Just to sit under its kindly shade, face into the foehn, and sort things out?"

But Marigold already had another idea, born of that same tree, that precise mistral, but in the shadows, rather, of ephemeral human investiture. He wanted the connection to all those personal details of a lost era: individuals erased in the sepia storms of temporality, addled adults, nameless children, who had vanished. Who were they? What did they dream at night? Did they live satisfied existences? Wherein, wherefore, wheresoever the streams of prior sentience had accumulated in the guise of real presences, hallowed afterthoughts in the nooks and crannies of bedrock. The Commander cited Rilke in this matter—childhood under every rock, surprises beyond the future; and Wittgenstein, on the nature of poetic incommensurables, the Renaissance Campanella. Rose petals matted between pages of antiquity; Zen koans risen from the complicity of silences; and the quiet particulars of immortality enshrined in all those ruins where human habitation had given birth to the remnants of the everyday in the guise of untouchable, perfect memory.

Ideological doggerel, of little harm to anybody but himself. But he was not alone. Anastasia, that great American bison that for years had inhabited Marigold's back yard, was ready to walk away as well. She always gave her signs—bugle blasts, uprooting bushes, crashing through fences—as a way of telling the Commander in no uncertain terms what was on her mind. In this instance he could read the demolition: she wanted to investigate, inhabit, recreate in her mind's fantastic eye the silent distances and terrible truth of some new place; was itching to go somewhere free of impediments. She was seldom incited beyond the safe and easy confines of the hacienda, inhabiting, ordinarily, the dry uplands of the mountain behind— her gigantic heaven of tongue, lips, nostrils to the grass. But there were times when quite unexpectedly she would rear up in revolutionary volition, drawn to open vistas and every saga of North American prehistory whose snorting immensity reflected the greatness of a landscape—an idea that only bison could quite grasp, but whose momentum was dangerous, in mixed company. She needed free space. It was for animals like Anastasia that Thomas Jefferson acquired the Louisiana Purchase, just after introducing French fries to America.

Dear old Anastasia, age unknown, whom the Commander had named after the singularly exiled Russian princess, had got on famously with certain squirrels back in Tesuque, living more or less simplistically on her small acreage of forest and grass in the rear of the hacienda. She had arrived at Mr Marigold's gate one bitterly cold winter morning, emaciated and near death. Alma fed her a hot scrambled egg with salsa, and onion bagels with cream cheese and chives, which she took to immediately, guzzling, in addition, a jug of hot cider. Once she plumped down, there was no getting her up. She was content to be hand-fed for the remainder of that brutal winter of 1993.

The squirrel closest to her turned out to be a stranger in his own right, a subspecies called Ebert (pronounced Abert), an energetic creature known to live exclusively in the ponderosa forests atop the South Rim of the Grand Canyon many hundreds of miles away. Further illuminating his peculiarly proprietary instincts (and hence compounding the mystery of his arrival in Tesuque), Ebert had a cousin known as Kaibab, a squirrel who lived across the canyon on the North Rim. For 10,000 years these two subspecies—distinguished by their long tasseled ears and white underbellies—had been lost to one another, caught up in the throes of tectonic plates, adaptive radiation, latitudinal genetic distribution and mountain-building; had whispered sweet nothings in blind, groping labors without echo across the uncinchable chasm. Ebert, a true quimichpatlan, consoled himself by living atop Anastasia and constantly chirping in her fantastically huge ears.

Once, a squirrel could range over all of North America without stepping foot on solid ground, so dense was the canopy of forest across the continent. Ebert must have gotten lost, or awakened disoriented from a dream one winter night, and started off—perhaps sleepwalking—in a direction unknown to its species; had pushed the envelope, expanding the frontier, going boldly where no squirrel of its kind had ever gone before: New Mexico. That he should have arrived at Mr Marigold's hacienda, taken warmth atop the lounging bison, and shared in the omelets, bagels, crackers, brownies, granola bars, tofu lasagnes, mixed fruit salads and endless bags of hazelnuts which Alma and the Commander slavishly supplied was all part of the saga that Mr Marigold described to his Squire that day, whilst awaiting the hoped-for return of their bull. Full of sentiment, going on about the white truffles that were Ebert's favorite food type (a fungal growth betwixt the root structures of ponderosa pines that was crucial to the whole ecology of squirreldom, he explained), he went on to describe how the great buffalo was rarely seen without his buddy, who resided flat out atop the bison's broadside, virtually concealed within the heavenly summit of finest fur.

"She's missing Chaco," Marigold reasoned. And so was he. Like Bison, like Marigold.

"Chaco? Where is that?" asked the gardener, presently alerted to the goings-on.

"Several hours away, and then some. A dusty high road, pinions and cloud. Not beyond the possible," said Marigold. He had been there years before, in the company of both the bison and the squirrel, who rode like some Washington crossing his Delaware.

Anastasia needed Chaco, Marigold could tell, with its wide open sunbursts, crumbling edifices, lightness of touch and perfect ancestors. Chaco, with all of its ghosts communing in harmony, might just be the perfect test case for his own Nation of Dogs and Cats, and who knows—of Bison, as well. Wouldn't it be nice, he thought, to get us back to the time when 60 million of them roamed wild?

New Mexico, Route 44, saw Anastasia and Sannazaro next morning accompanying the Commander over the fitted stones before New Alto at Chaco. Getting there had involved an eight-wheeler, and a large sack of oats.

He'd decided on this outing after a sleepless night. Every dollar newly inherited was like a letter from an impoverished lost nephew, a stigmata. He needed to breathe freely, though was grateful for the company of Sannazaro. Besides, handling Anastasia alone would be next to impossible.

A single rub the wrong way could topple a house, trample an entire crop of spring bulghur.

They reached the land of solitary squab and windblown bosque, animal skulls, wild burros, phantoms and sirens. Gnarled debris larded the vision before them: violets, eroding silts, warm shales, morning storms, coral mesas, a glow of light spreading all around the purplish fringe of thunderheads on every horizon, and fast gusts through the stunted shrubbery. No fences.

A dream of that fabulous realm just beyond the horizon: Quivira, as the Spaniards called it. That would be the name of his new Nation.

"*El que quiere celeste que le cueste*," Sannazaro concluded. "He who wants blue sky has to pay for it. And that we have. Both back tires are flat. We're stuck. Not a gas station for 50 miles. I'm craving a root beer float. Are there scorpions? There's dust in my eyes. Aren't you cold? Now what?"

Precisely 1,000 years before, to the day, a ranking philosopher among Chacoan thinkers surveyed the many high-rises of the valley with rare contentment. His eye had swept along the orange outliers of

Chetro Ketl, Pueblo Bonita, Wijiji and Casa Rinconada, all the other great houses, plazas, kivas and stone roadways for walking; and in one happy immeasurable sigh he—more likely she—had reconciled a density of archaic mothers and fathers, daughters and sons, priests, basket makers, mountain climbers, gardeners, sculptors, architects, celestial empiricists, mystics and poets, celebrants of erotica, worshippers of the great dolmen, jewelry designers, minstrels, lazy good-for-nothings, savants like himself (herself?), all diffused across the 25,000 square miles of sandstone expanse and fertile valleys that was their habitat. Like the later C.R. Cockrell, in his book *The Philosopher's Dream*, imagining the great Cheops beside St Paul's Cathedral, adjoining the Tower of Pisa to the Parthenon and the spires of Notre Dame. By reconciliation one refers to a certain calculation of ratios.

Despite Chaco's impressive architectonics, the residing population was petite, even by New World standards of the time. He (she?) could count the women grinding stone in the plaza for an hour, or gathering water for ten minutes, cooking a cornucopia of stews and horsing around. Art was the essence of Chacoan civilization and all else was dictated by it. The business of berries and roots, dry land bean and squash cultivation was actually an art form of culinary precision that could rival any of Santa Fe's late twentieth-century 25-dollar-a-dish delicacy. Even the very best of the Michelin three stars were but muted attempts to revive the once spectacular concoctions rolled into so many doughs, brightened with Tanguey sauces, seasoned with a myriad of desert spices. But the artfulness of the civilization far exceeded the palate.

The entire panoply of inhabitants could be gleaned in a quiet glance, across a vast kingdom of spiritual enclave. As the pre-Socratics would have described this arcadian scene, all was surveyable in a single breath, and hence, sustainable.

No traffic jams in Chaco. And when in August of 1849, Lt James Simpson and his US Army survey team were led by an Indian guide to a horizon overlook, they were overwhelmed by the emergent sense of a transcendental society. Of an entire race of beings who left virtually no skeleton, no trace, of their medieval paradise or subsequent disappearance. Such impressions were fortified 50 years later when the Hyde Expedition uncovered a profusion of inlaid effigies, ceremonial artifacts, mystery objects, the testimonials to an active avaculture that evidently centered around a worship of parrots.

Anastasia, walking freely (her eight-wheeler had been left outside the park boundaries), sniffed the stones, rummaging with a keen olfactory affinity to her ancestral behemoths, leading her two human companions through a maze of mottled walls, towards the divining rod, that central pillar of Chaco's past.

The divining rod was a dolmen, planted in Chaco's only geyser, a favorite of the bison who long supped upon the salt licks along the dried effluvia, travertine pools and efflorescent cauldrons.

They carried an 80-gallon jug of water for the beast. The previous night they had camped outside the park and, lacking a tent, had frozen in their bedrolls. The air was moist and penetrated inside the truck compartment where they were cramped and unable to wrest free of their confinement.

"She is a terrible bother. And keeping her a cruelty. I would leave her here. She'll thank you for it."

"Quiet. She can hear you. What's more, she is my friend, with more grace in a single hoof than you could muster in ten lifetimes."

"Let her carry the water, then."

"You try harnessing her!"

The very exchange alerted the all-knowing Everest of Mutton who reared her 300-pound face with an exquisite grunt and made clear that she did not work for a living.

"Prairie grass its heaven, rain and thunder her only companions, open vistas her eyesight, unfettered meanderings her solace. Tamper not, Señor, with the freedom of the clouds."

With that reverie the Commander aimed his azimuth machine and GPS receiver and took a light reading for purposes of better fixing the precise mark and moment—of what, the Squire had no idea—and sat beside the obscure elongated stone, awaiting the presentiment for which they'd journeyed hundreds of miles in their oblong, 30-year-old borrowed truck, its headlights smashed and rear tail blinkers long gone. Sap had accumulated on the radiator box, the fan belt was worn thin, and the windshield wipers threw up tidbits of dried rubber when engaged. Tires were bare, the gooseneck hitch dangerously close to disconnecting. All told, a perfectly suitable vehicle for the trio.

The whole day they moved hither, yon, to and fro, in search of a specific ruin (though whenever she could, Anastasia would forage on the sweetest short grasses in all the land).

Their movements left everything to three very divergent imaginations, each impenetrable in its own fashion.

By late day, they had moved a few miles out into the hinterlands, where a dirt road circled back upon itself, betwixt rows of cliff, across dried arroyo. It was the exact moment of moments, of orange moonrise and sage-scented Chinook: a vacant wind bellowing acrest the coconino shale and slabs of chinle sandstone.

Sannazaro hunkered down beside the leeward furry mass of the bison. "It'll be dark soon. I am not sure as to the wisdom of repeating another night in this blasted cold, Commander."

"Ahh Señor," the good Mister hailed. "As the ancients so oft declared, Impatience may cover many tracks but seldom in any worthwhile direction."

"There were other ancients, equally eminent, who must have stated, He who lingers, dies. The same ones who initiated the *de lunatico inquirendos*, or writs to inquire of the sanity of another. I believe they have been referring to you ever since."

"Still others," the Commander angrily advised, "whose only valediction was their love of the Madonna, who cried most passionately, '*Io ardentissimamente v'amava!*' You know better than I, this language of the gods. With that indefatigable swoon they forswore all grave discomforts, ruinations and disappointments. Sufficing on broth, doting on virtue, fearing no ensorcelment, outstripping, heathenisms or whippings. Living their lives as knights and messengers of the pure spirit, behooving every hindquarter, each issue of the body, all those companions, Caliphs, ministers, faithful beloveds, chamberlains, daughters and sons, vice-regents and emperors of mercy...? Where was I?"

"Behooving," Sannazaro chimed, exasperated.

"To the Lord!" the Commander rejoined.

"Deliver, grant, spare us. Your nonsense attains new heights. *Ni firmes carta que no leas, ni bebas agua que no veas*," Sannazaro advised. "Never sign a paper you have not read, nor drink water you have not seen."

"I fail your meaning."

"It means gibberish, monsters of claptrap compounded by your normal gargoyles of banter. Your chatters jar—the more zealous, the more unintelligible. I suggest you get a good night's sleep and in the morning we hasten homeward."

Anastasia listened on as late into the night the two friends continued to regale one another in a manner of enchantment, with quotations, pieces of badly digested wisdom and sappy truisms from world literature. Kings, heathens, bazaars thronging with citizens. China, Morocco, magicians and all of the Levant streaming from their archaic liquid lips.

All the while Sannazaro clung to the abundant heat engine that was the buffalo. But this was to no effect when she started emitting elephantine rounds of flatulence which, while warm in and of themselves, would offput an empire; then belched with a mighty lurch to put down an invading army. Sannazaro cupped his nose, and stole to a corner, out of harm's way. Then, with a sudden jolt, in the throes of what might have been a response to an unwelcome show of affection, a freakish ember or a yellow jacket, perhaps even some premonitory memory of long ago, the bison made a complete and flamboyant exit. This was not her first time. The strange enduring beast had a history of such hallucinogenic flights. Racing away, the frightful form narrowly missed stomping the Commander, who had earlier placed his railroad-bag far enough away to avoid the direct swathe of her late-night greenhouse gas emissions.

"Anastasia, what is it! Sannazaro, what now?" Marigold shrieked.

"There is nothing to be done. She'll come back when she smells breakfast," the good Señor concluded wisely, not wishing to expose an inch of flesh from his sleeping bag.

"But what dexterous sorcerers possess this place, to have so agitated our hapless little girl?" the Commander contemplated aloud.

Running off into the endless dark, snorting the freedom of the desert floor, her wonderful bronze eyes picking out stars among the flowering cactus, crazy long-boring beetles and seed-supping kangaroo rats scurrying every which way, the beast stopped eventually at a wend in the wend, where an astonished elderly couple camping in their dismal motor home and least expecting an excited bison—a gopher, perhaps, or raven, but not Anastasia—grabbed for their honeydew melon.

"Go on, Roy, give 'um some!" the woman entreated, filled with the excitement of primitive encounters and massive terror.

Anastasia extended her tongue, then withdrew with her brusquely enveloped prize.

Whatever stinger or specter had inhabited the beast no longer mattered. Her sphincter muscles spasming with relief, she shat a steamy ziggurat beside the trailer, then lingered long, beseeching the couple for more and more melon. None was to be had, but peanut-butter cookies and a freshly microwaved apple pie sufficed.

The beast settled down to her late-night snacks, outfitting her sleeping pattern in such a manner as to slightly upend the small motor home, whose occupants spent a sleepless night sliding to the side.

CHAPTER 48
Anastasia auf Quivira

THAT NIGHT, AFTER scouring the area with forlorn and voluminous appeals, Marigold settled by the crazy historical campfire, listening intently for any semiotic of the returning buffalo. Jacques Lacan. Derrida. The new novel. Saussure. Instead, what greeted his haggard ears were the abundant rhythms of the male members of the family Gryllidae—crickets, ostensibly, *Oecanthus niveus*—with their musical advantage: 150 serrations across minute veins which they were voluminously rubbing 100 times a minute, to produce their legendary love psalms. The Commander noticed two distinct melodies and fathomed that one resulted from members of the orchestra playing the same tune in absence of a conductor, while the second, more feverish performance was the sound emitted by all those mad trysts, one antenna furiously rubbing against another of the opposite sex. There was Georges Balanchine's *Jewellery*, Massenet's *Manon*, Prokofiev's *War and Peace*. To forget oneself in the symphony of crickets was just what he needed. In an earlier age, he might have been a prince retreating for the rest of his days to a monastery; a Garibaldi marching home with a modest sack of dried fish and macaroni after having unified Italy with his band of 1,000. But this night, he prayed only for the return of his truant.

In the dappled dawn, across the burgeoning plains, wafted the scent of blue corn chip and molasses pancakes from an open sizzle. Inspired by this news to her nostrils, Anastasia headed off.

Across those same plains, the Commander was rising to the morn.

"She'll come home eventually," he said. "It might be a legendary case of metempsychosis, transmigration of the soul, or metamorphosis. Who can say?"

But both gentlemen avowed the tacit truth: Anastasia, like so many mutts in Tesuque, loved to pursue foreign objects, such as automobiles, and had given not a few drivers a probable coronary. In northern Thailand tigers were known to go after the spare tires on the rear of jeeps. They loved to shred the rubber. But Anastasia's tastes and impulses were more difficult to decipher. Fruit? Conversation? Brownies? Or the least likely option—to hitch a ride somewhere, to that unknown, never-to-be-gleaned region out of time known as bison paradise?

The Commander thought he had found it out there in the vastness of Chaco itself—the original genetic corridor wherein all bison originated.

Not for any lack of love of Mr Marigold but following her own heart, Anastasia may have sauntered out of the hills from the east into a region totally unaccustomed to the sight of such giants. Perhaps she'd mistaken Montana for New Mexico, where bison commingle inside Yellowstone; or eaten locoweed and gone berserk. Maybe she was lonely, feeling misunderstood, an innocent child in a bull's hide. Perhaps she was a Hindu, enjoying the mammoth proceeds of some unexpected past deed. A voluptuary who suffered bouts of evident malaise. In her slow wanderings, who can say what solitary revelations swarmed in her enormous brain, fueled by loping eyes, colossal nostrils, a cerebellum teeming with sunspots and dandelions and a riot of coyote, prairie dog, goshawk, black-footed ferret and king snake gab.

Still within earshot of his friend, Marigold harnessed his faith to a verbal degree: "Lord, see that she comes back unharmed and humbler for her adventure and I promise to be of good cheer and modest aspiration," he recited, so that his restless Squire might not fear for other ordeals or mysteries, as the Early Church might have thought of them.

But the hours drew long. "What will happen now?" the Commander worried aloud. "This is truly terrible, for both of them. You see, they love each other." He was referring to the squirrel, Ebert.

"Maybe she simply missed her little liquid-eyed companion and took the shortest route back home. That's it: Anastasia will be there when we return," the Squire opined. "On the other hand, do you not think it possible that she pines for a sexual mate of her own size, one who snorts to the same euphorias and conjectures? Whose luscious supine hulk, dark lustrous pools of eyes, monumental face and everlasting grace might strike identical chords in her heart?"

"You speak like an eerie gentleman, Sannazaro. My heart weeps for that very possibility, particularly in consideration of the horrible, horrible past times that have nearly seen the bison go extinct." The Commander recounted for his Squire the long sorrowful saga.

"It is well known that long ago, so many tens of millions of the great gentle giants pranced about North America. Some have argued that as many as 60 million bison roamed the prairies. With such biomass asking for nothing, leisurely strolling across America, it was easy for cowardly demons aboard the first railroads to shoot at them. I tell you, Senator, no more horrible legacy stains this culture: that through the sheer cruelty of sportsmen, the bison's number had been reduced to fewer than 20 individuals which took cover behind the gaseous fumes of Yellowstone one winter in the late 1800s. I ponder this near extinction and my heart is as heavy as a bison. I sink with regret for all her lost genes when I gaze upon the perfect being that is Anastasia. And want to apologize, but know not how."

"But they have come back! I have seen them, multitudes on private ranches," the Señor claimed.

"Not multitudes. Now they number no more than 100,000, a pitifully dwarfed assemblage. Many are still being bred for slaughter by allegedly well-meaning citizens, and ranchers who call themselves environmentalists. Even the park authorities in Yellowstone, wearing the National Park Service badge with its imprinted bison mascot, have vouchsafed the slaughter of bison on untenable grounds that they carry a little bacterium known as bruscella, transmittable to cows—who, in any event, would be slaughtered for their meat. By an *Act of Congress, January 24th, 1923*, the Secretary of the Interior was charged with the right to 'sell or otherwise dispose of the surplus buffalo of the Yellowstone National Park herd'. "By such language, the magnificent bison has been reduced to a commodity, a resource," the Commander continued. "This is the language, and the thinking, that has infected most conservationists in America. The Blackfoot Indians know differently, however. So do those few biologists in touch with their own souls."

And so did Marigold. He had read through the "Environmental Impact Statement For The Interagency Bison Management Plan For The State Of Montana And Yellowstone National Park", a document that infuriated him.

"As bison migrate out of the park and into Montana, they move from one jurisdiction with management objectives to a different jurisdiction with different management objectives," the document read. The goal of the park service was to maintain a herd of between 1,700 and 2,500 animals, vaccinating calves to reduce the alleged seroprevalance of the disease. But the whole program was nothing more than a scientific front to ensure the "economic interest and viability of the livestock industry in the state of Montana". Once the animals crossed over into that state, young punks with rifles were hired to go blow the animals' brains out. Nationally televised footage had shown them doing so—teenagers stepping right up to the placid kings and queens who sat shivering in the deep snowdrifts, placing the rifles to their heads, showing off for their girlfriends, before splattering the snow with blood and guts.

All of these horrors, he believed, Anastasia had heard about through the electromagnetic airwaves. Bison communicated with one another like blue and humpback whales, across all of North America. Their most expressive word, "Gwaaa ..." masked an elaborate vocabulary, evolved emotions, lazy gossip and big brains. Unlike some birds and primates, they never indulged in deception or aggression. Theirs had been an utterly peaceful domain, enshrined in millions of years of honor and nobility.

They emanated sophisticated energy fields, radiant halos, auras thick with information. Their cerebral cortex heaved with mirror neurons granting them advanced cognitive empathy. As with all ruminants, they possessed special cells in their frontal and temporal lobes which made for a remarkable long-term memory. For them, the state of the world was bad, a double-bind, hemorrhaging on both ends. The past was a Holocaust. The future, grim and unexamined.

But the Commander had other plans for Anastasia. She'd return, eventually, moseying along New

Mexico's back roads, copping food scraps from unwary travelers, terrorizing others. She'd find her way because in those nostrils, and in that self-willed full pelt of a hood, brainstem and coiffure in one, were lodged certain homing genes that went back to the very beginnings of mammalian DNA. The Commander believed that. When she did come home, he would take both her and Ebert to one of his newly acquired large properties, and there set them free among 1,000 other bison he would purchase, favor them with a jointly deserved and absolute liberty, a *Magna Carta* for Buffalo and Squirrels. Together they could live out their days in bliss, at home on the range, as some minstrel had once naively intended. Feasting on bagels and cream cheese. Beneath the mistral seasons. Anastasia's very own Quivira. Whatever she wanted, wherever she sauntered. Safely.

For the rest of the day the Commander and Squire moved about with the great bison and her little squirrel constantly in their thoughts, among all those primeval generations of Chacoan Indians. Like the Indians at Bandelier, these, too, had disappeared in what seemed no less a paradise, though one difficult to replicate.

But spirits still roamed the precincts.

CHAPTER 49
The Fainting Couch

THEY HAD COME BACK to the hacienda after endless travails and no success at recovering Anastasia. Melancholy acceptance of whatever fates awaited her. Marigold envisioned that perhaps she had embarked on an odyssey to northern Canada, or down to the Yucatan, with what in mind he could only imagine. He would miss her, though.

It was late in the night when the Commander heard something in the sky and had just enough time to catch a flash of light plummeting to earth. A meteorite, he thought.

All the crickets' rhythmic trills grew silent, replaced by the raucous larynx of Negrescu next door. Along with Toto, Heidi and Heyboy, he had taken to howling at nearly anything at night. Wolves will be wolves, and dogs are quick to join in, but this particular astronomical event induced such an extra-hysterical verbal frenzy among Ginevra's *Canus lupus* that the Commander departed his bed, a nightgown concealing skin and bones, and, candle in hand, went out into a side yard, where a swarm of moths was attracted to the light swirling around him. As he squinted past the glare into the tenebrous beyond there seemed to be a hopping sparkler 30 feet distant. Some weirdly lit canister was moving headless across the lawn, a strange cacophony emanating from within.

When the exhausted clucking reached his ears, the Commander had no doubts. It was the Hopi's rocket ship! He raced up to the contraption but could not touch the metallic lid which was glowing white from the heat of re-entering earth's atmosphere. So he took a hose and doused it off. The steam rose. When the metal was cool enough, the Commander reached in and saw a remarkable sight: a scrunched but nonetheless healthy-looking Amigo, back on Earth after who knows what travails in the cosmos. It groaned pathetically, and the Commander picked him up and hastened back to his bedroom, where he outfitted a blanketed basket and provisioned a bowl of lemon tea and another of seven-grain cereal in soy milk.

How Amigo had found them and crashed down amid such interstellar distances was surely a topic for future discussion. All was enchanted, though the poor bird looked fretted and pinched before its time, feathers frayed for want of the incessant fawning that was Raquel's principal outlet for expressing her abiding desire for a child, or a lover of consequence.

These ever-deferred embraces were now taken up by the Commander, and found uncontested happiness in the chicken.

How many months—in sidereal time, accounting for Einstein's various equations and Eddington's q half-integer—had Amigo been up in space? Had his little bones demineralized? Had he become infertile? What does a chicken feel whilst space-walking? Did he look back at earth and contemplate how small and insignificant are individual chickens, even the whole collective of chickens? Such great inexplicables were now subsumed in the moment, amid a great exodus of giant *Samia cercopia* flying towards the moon.

By morning the human nearest to Marigold, Alma, was in no condition to greet Amigo with anything other than disinterest, for she had fainted on a couch in the living room, overcome by nausea. The Commander was also nearly overcome, for it was one thing to contemplate the ills of the world and quite another to suffer the trials of a pregnant Alma, without cumin in the refrigerator, or any part of Dr Spock's manual at hand. He picked up the phone to call Sam Turbovsky. After all, he was to blame. But she forbade it. Yes, they were having a child and would undoubtedly spend the rest of their blissful lives together. But they were not live-ins, and she did not want to insinuate her petty female grievances into his life, or not yet. It would spoil the romance. The Commander then thought to dial 911 but, tired of so many commotions, put the phone back down and called Ginevra and Sannazaro instead.

The two came right over. Sannazaro assumed the worst: a heart attack from all the drudgery she'd been put through in the service of the Commander, lymphatic TB, a ruptured appendix, elephantiasis, a blood vessel in the meridian. But Ginevra put an end to these flagrant speculations.

"Gentlemen, please. She's pregnant, for God sakes. That's what happens to women. Morning sickness is a universal harbinger of good times," she added. "The continuation of our species."

"Thank you, Madam," Alma murmured.

"Your cheeks are flushed. Have some ice cream. It is, of course, a tried antidote."

Alma did. Half a pound of Vanilla Fudge.

Thereafter, she evidenced complete if temporary recovery. She stood up, and commenced a day of housework with the vengeance of one who was bent on repudiating any and all incapacity. She shook out the drapes, admitting the morning sunlight, and millers fell like lugs and by droves to the floor, still motionless with sleep and the night's chill. She swept them outdoors, then attacked the pavers, cleaning out the occasional brown recluse behind furniture, scrubbing the wash basin, running the dishes (the days of doing it by hand were over), scraping accumulated salts off a shower head, collecting some honey, dusting the scores of library rooms, sweeping out the flies, vacuuming wherever possible—some rooms simply remained off limits to any hygiene. She changed sheets, hung freshly laundered shirts out to dry in the warm sunlight, fixed buttons on the Commander's trousers (he had no zippered pants), filled the bird feeders, tossed walnuts to the greatly agitated Ebert—"Anastasia will come home eventually, little one," she said. She pulled some weeds, planted the odd geranium, watered some new saplings, watched for any emergent hornets' nests, and scrambled an egg for Amigo who wandered about a side yard, patrolling the landscape for annelids whilst keeping a wary eye out for the Siamese, Lavoris, from next door, as well as the latest addition to the Marigold household, a weasel acquired on the desert floors of Chaco.

The bird behaved as if nothing galactic had happened to it.

Alma, in short, was earning her 3 million dollars.

Later, quoting the great and eternal Elizabethan poetess, Jane Gray Morrison, she did her nails, proclaiming, "Beauty is a social responsibility."

Which rather topped off a fine day.

Now Marigold took to the fainting couch, for he was overwhelmed by the agenda before him. A dozen Fed Ex and DHL envelopes had been delivered to his postal box, which stood out beside the long coyote fence on Bishop's Lodge Road, three acres from the entrance to the house. He hesitated to retrieve them, fearful of ... of what he could not say, exactly. But for the first time in his life he truly missed a companion. With no sibling, and no significant other, the Commander was this day staring down the cold calculus of odds that loneliness guaranteed. And adding injury to forlorn, still no bison.

He sat out in the garden and prepared to open his mail. But he did not have the stomach for it, or not yet. So he called the Señor, who was busy with topiary works.

Some time later, fresh from a bath, the now wealthy Squire showed his coifed, prim and proper self at the gate. He was a new man, having shaved, shampooed, doused himself in some tincture of beaver, and donned a fresh pair of white Egyptian cotton trousers and matching bowler hat. He looked ideally suited to a party on the Victorian bowling green. A living, breathing daguerreotype.

"Sit down. We have a decision to make," the Commander began, disarming any complaints by proffering a large cup of hot Mexican chocolate and a blueberry scone, which he knew by now would be irresistible to Sannazaro, and sure to calm his cantankerous nature.

"A lot of mail," Sannazaro noted.

"I'm tempted to burn it."

"What, leave telegrams unopened?"

"Why not, you think it's more money?"

"Or subpoenas, after yesterday's and today's headlines."

"Today's?"

"You don't want to know if you don't know already."

"That bad?"

"Nothing to jump up about. Just more sour grapes. Say, that DHL's from Greece. Didn't you mention—"

Mr Marigold seized the package and ripped it open, reading out loud.

"'Dear Dr Marigold—'"

"Oh, it's Doctor now?"

The letter was from Sophia and it contained a full budget, the name and background on the Greek presidential candidate, as well as countless news articles about her. The estimated cost to assure the election: 22 million dollars. She made it easy by including bank wire, even Swiftcode, information.

Marigold shared the contents of the package with Sannazaro. "Should I do it?" he asked.

"Why not?" the Squire replied.

Other packages contained other budgets—for the elimination of corn blight in the Ukraine, poachers in Paraguay, hunger in the southern Sudan, drought in Somalia, human rights abuses in Yemen, AIDS in Malawi, red mercury in Russia, ICBMs in Sri Lanka, political action committees in Washington, motorized trawlers in Tamil Nadu, gender-selective ultrasound in China, a ghastly hydroelectric project in the Caucasus, a project to mine molybdenum from an ancient indigenous grave site in the Solomon Islands, river blindness in Gabon, DDT in Indonesia, dioxin north of Milan, uranium tailings on an Apache reservation in Arizona, radiation poisoning in Tokyo, and deforestation on Victoria Island in British Columbia. There were countless appeals for money from ambitious film makers and religious revivalists. Projects about gay rhesus monkeys, an epic about the Shakers, a multi-part series on new bacteria of the twenty-first century, something about the last wetland in Los Angeles. Three cable networks wanted to produce biographies about Marigold. A PR person from the United Nations was calling, and the phone was literally ringing nonstop. Fortunately, the Commander had already thought to hire an answering service. He also asked Sannazaro to get him a box up the road at the modern little Tesuque US Post Office and to inform the courier services of the new address. He was desperate for anonymity, as in the old days. A sickening feeling rose in him, which he traced back to the conniving of his lawyer. Why was it necessary to tempt the avalanche? Was that ocean-going cruise so important?

"I feel awful," the Commander moaned. "My head is sweltering." For his part, Sannazaro was ready for anything. He had not slept well, lying awake considering the awesome potential of all the money: riches which were as good as his own, given the nature of his relationship with the Commander, who was, by any estimates, a naif in a big dark forest. The avuncular Sannazaro had seniority in the fat chances, dangerous games and terrifying-brevity part of life. His richer vein of experience assured him of some say in the handling of that hay; his three-and-a-half score conferred privilege and expertise which no sane Commander could fail to appreciate, particularly given the gravity of this *fin de siècle*. Moreover, he'd kept his balance after all this time, even on the tortured end of a rope down the haunted walls at Bandelier.

"None of us can change the tides of the sea," the gardener remarked.

"Meaning?"

"You may think you can. Drink eight large glasses of water a day and pee unceasingly into the waves. Won't do a thing. Even in companionship— the two of us peeing. What are we?—no more than two pees in a pod."

"Say what you mean, blast it!"

"You can't protect every gopher from every hawk. Or substantially lighten the load that it is to be man. Nor would I recommend cutting off one's dick to spite the ocean."

"An ill-suited simile. Truth requires that the mean-spirited can be softened. Of that I am certain."

"Perhaps. But the world is full of starch. Collars get soiled, daffodils weaken and collapse with the first winter snow. We all die alone."

"You didn't sleep well. Care for a prune?"

"No, thank you."

"Some lima beans? They've been cooked in garlic."

Sannazaro shook his head.

"How about a Satsuma plum, cold and ripe?"

"Please, thank you, nothing for me. The hot chocolate is perfect." And then, "You verge on convictions, but I'm leery of such declarations. You start talking about conviction, virtue, trust, altruism, and the next thing your reality becomes a kind of fascism."

"You've lost me," said Marigold, perplexed.

"It's easy to speak about bettering the educational system, or introducing morals into politics. But you could just as easily delude yourself into believing you screwed Marilyn Monroe. One's convictions are better kept to oneself."

"They are worthless, then. A broth without the soup, a soup without a container. I saw you cultivating those empty hills with grass. Was that not conviction?"

"Some people throw a party. I throw grass."

They sat in silence. Then, concealing his tightly wound ball of amazed yarn, Mr Marigold declared, "Come see our visitor from outer space." The two men sat in communion with the chicken, observing its nonchalant earth-pecking behavior. Here was contentment. After a few moments, Amigo ventured over to the Commander's feet and pecked them, too, demanding the equivalent of a toll in the form of some goodie, which Mr Marigold produced from a napkin in his vest pocket: leftovers from breakfast. Down on his chest, eye to eye with Amigo, the Commander felt the stirrings of a tantalizing partiality. Here in the form of Monsieur Chicken were all the attributes of sensate Being, as worldly philosophers had long described it. Its lust for sustenance, the obvious joy it took in plucking after herbs and seeds, dirt and gravel, in moving its toes and craning its neck, in preening its plumage and clearing its throat, in breathing and seeing and knowing and believing: all were the things of man. A wasp hovered annoyingly at its stubble, trying to collect on any available tidbits (though it preferred cat food, none of which was to be had). The wasp and the chicken, unlikely allies this day beneath the fast-gathering storm.

As Mr Marigold contemplated the chicken, and the chicken contemplated Mr Marigold, it came to one or other's attention that the world was forever going to change. It wasn't just the year 2000, on whose cusp every human and each chicken nervously awaited, nor the responsibility of so much money. Because the fortune had come suddenly, the Chevalier de Cash had no attachment to it, no investment or long-standing addiction to the idea of being rich. It had no outstanding lure. In fact, for every righteous scheme and outrageous expedition the money invited, it occasioned double the fears and trepidations. This latest wrinkle of newspaper accusations only heightened the lurking trauma and sinking feeling in his chest. He knew, somehow, that the reality of Tesuque was a marriage that could not last. He would have to re-invent himself elsewhere, become, however inconveniently, a new notch on his evolutionary wheel. Chaco had added to his resolution, though the bison's disappearance gave him terrible pause. He had put in a call to their friend at the local sheriff's office who, in turn, dispatched an all-points watch for Anastasia across a multi-state region. As yet, with no result.

In the meantime, Marigold's personal growth curve had been amphetamized by the prospect of making a difference, changing the world for the better. A vapid expression, Sannazaro sighed, dismissing altruism with a show of comfortable angst, addressing all inclination with the power of retreat, discounting force with the seduction of flight. The Squire's arguments were not easily undermined, for Marigold himself had enough trouble changing his own clothes, let alone re-engineering a failed machinery that was human nature. The thought of becoming a better person entailed work, and he had no fondness for work. He had always recoiled from human relations. And presently, all these spurs to action boded of the horrible unknown, spread out before him in misleading math, entangling emotions. Statistics and grave *sine qua nons* bashing him at every front.

Just some of the particulars which swooshed up and down in his conspiring jungle of a brain ... The million Swiss voting in favor of arming peacekeepers. The threat of another meteor flattening thousands of square miles at random. More than 35 million known fur-bearing animals slaughtered each year, from Kolinsky sable to short-tailed weasel. Lambs sold for a dollar. Profits on pigs a mere penny or two. Even many of the national wildlife refuges open for hunting. No wild animal anywhere safe from humans on the planet. In Indonesia democratic reforms had translated into legalized rape of forests, even in protected areas like Tanjung Putting, with its endangered clouded leopards, proboscis monkeys and sun bears. And when, in rare instances, the cutting of trees was deemed sustainable, market forces often ebbed, leaving, for example, the trade in Borneo camphor, or the rein damar, or rattan, severely compromised. Indigenous peoples were forced to raise cattle, or demolish coral reefs, or encroach excessively on reef fish species. Seventy percent of all Nobel Prizes in medicine and physiology continued to go to those who had killed animals in experiments. "Nuclear warfare next," leaders say (*Sun Herald*). The industry supporting shooting ranges had enjoyed a renaissance of new legalities protecting their right to exist, from Hawaii to Nebraska. In one winter freeze, 250 million monarch butterflies had perished in their oyamel trees at El Rosario near Angangueo, Mexico. Most of the surrounding forests had been logged, making the survivors' plight particularly harrowing. The British Royal Society, the oldest scientific organization in the world, had determined that genetically modified crops were safe. In any case, 75 percent of all US farmlands had been infected. Global warming was threatening the existence of all remaining koalas, as well as the nine-island nation of Tuvalu, with its 10,000 human inhabitants. Worldwide, according to UN estimates, annual remediation costs would start at around 300 billion dollars. Class action suits by NGOs, in the manner of tobacco and Holocaust survivor litigation, were being prepared by lawyers across America. The Reagan-era "gag rule" that forbade foreign NGOs from applying funds to abortion efforts, or even counseling, continued to ensure a catastrophic US bias favoring a population crisis through the world— and so many more consumers of American-made products.

Do I need to deal with all this? Marigold thought to himself. Certainly not, came the response from some distant, unused inner core. What do I do, then? replied his *ba*, as the ancient Egyptian muses referred to the recalcitrant soul.

This melancholy dialogue of unknowing passed for silence throughout the day. And during subsequent days, as well. Amigo would throw in his own caveats: Keep your nose to the ground, clucked he. Focus on edible seeds, and all will be well.

CHAPTER 50
An Imaginary Flag

A HUNDRED OTHER platitudes rushed in to comfort the wearying man. The particulars of those days of mental turmoil provide little record. At some point, perhaps a week later, Sannazaro nodded off to sleep on the russet fiber-covered equipale chair, a glass of agua de jamaica hibiscus juice getting warm on the adjoining mesquite coffee table. A snowfall of bleached button-sized elm seeds fell gently across the painted blue courtyard acrest all of Tesuque, in the summer haze which had blown up from brush fires across northern Mexico. Bumblebees systematically worked the blue columbines, sweet peas, myrtle and lobelia, while three-toed northern woodpeckers scaled the high-standing cottonwood trunks whose bark was testament to all the eons.

The big news, literally, was the return of Anastasia. Her fur was ruffled, her tongue panting. By what adventures she had found her hacienda, only Ebert would ever know. But there she was, relieved to be home, ensconced in the perpetual comforts.

Ebert had cried out upon seeing its mate, leapt onto the bushel-worth of crown, and chattered frantically in what could only be described as a desperate display of the deepest relief. The two cuddled as only a bison and squirrel can. Anastasia rolled over on to her back as Ebert raced down towards her private parts, then—thinking the better of it—headed on to her enormous face where, eyeball to eyeball, they shared a secret slang.

Relieved by this additional omen, as he thought of it, Mr Marigold boarded his bicycle and started off down the Bishop's Lodge Road towards the Shidoni sculpture garden, El Nido and the market. The day had a neutral blessedness about it, and every component impressed itself upon the Commander with a reminiscence rather than a new day. Hills clothed in freshly blooming virescence; butterflies abundant; robin redbreasts, mockingbirds, the brilliant white and black magpies tailing the ravens over the full, rushing river. A narrow winding lane without center divider, Garson's rambling estate and horse pasture, the Tesuque elementary school, Mountain Institute, post office and, further up the road, the Pueblo. Shadows dappled the narrows of luscious pinion and riverine seclusion. The whole effect made for a tranquillity that the odd drunken pickup truck barreling down the road on Friday nights could not expunge.

An intimacy that had protected and mesmerized this sedentary resident for half a century, had formulated his cocoon out of all the best that American history could muster. Family members of exquisite romance and obsolescence; windy nomads who'd thought nothing of themselves. Their sexual energy had been that of the cosmos, not the ego: sex working through them, generation after generation, and vanishing with but one final trace in the name of a simpleton known as Murillo, after the painter, Bartolome Esteban (1617/18–1682) presumably, the fourteenth child, orphaned, who would earn his food by painting at the local fairs. Upon whose tomb are found but two words: *Vive moriturus*—"Live as though about to die". He would sire nine bambini, children in rags. Napoleon's officers stole his paintings, disseminating his fame across Europe. Lovely idealism in an age of crass Christianity and Thirty Years War. Marigold could not be sure which painting, or incident in the painter's life, may have prompted his father, but he thought of it in terms of some splendid gag, based upon a hybridization of *Boys Playing Dice* at the Alta Pinacothek in Munich, the *Immaculate Conception* at the Louvre and *St Francis of Assisi* at the museum in his home town of Seville. Possibly *St Anthony of Padua* in the cathedral there, said to attract pigeons century after century. While Ribera offered a more solid style, and Velasquez greater technical facility, his student—the ranking maven of the so-called Andalusian School—was by far the most sentimental painter in the history of Spain, noted for his sheer love of beauty, grace, charity, chivalry; at one with the soul of the Spanish, the pilgrims and beggars, the lovely virgins and women of the night, flower girls and pauper lads, cool-colored biblical scenes in gray and brown, ashen red and mauve. His scenes were charmed. Christ always a child. His softness bespeaks of the earliest chiaroscuro in Spain and his dark-eyed women are to weep over. All that was the basis upon which the Commander's first name was designed, he rightly assumed.

As for the family heraldic, of course there can be only one universal explanation: Calendula, marigold. *L. calendae*, said to be that first day of any month, the day of interest payments. Marigolds are long-flowering. Even a single flower, sautéed, was proffered by the English to induce a most intoxicating dish, a cure for everything from scurvy to fever. In Amsterdam, there was a marigold soup; in Florence it conferred supernatural vision.

Across Europe, when applied with vinegar, a sure cure for measles.

Not only calendula, but *Tagetes patula et erecta*—the African marigold— and named after an Etruscan deity which, history holds, went leaping out of the fertile earth at the first touch of a plow; and *Mesembryanthemum* marigolds, or figs, one of the more bizarre and unsortable botanical puzzles combining the Greek words for midday and flower—*mesembria*, the flower that had no care in the world, that bloomed morning, noon and night (though the great Linnaeus insisted marigolds closed down by mid-afternoon); also middle fruit, or *mesos embryon*. Not to forget *Caltha*, the marsh marigold, which in Latin takes its most memorable signature, simply, a yellow flower or *fiore d'ogni mese*, but which, in the Americas, became the cowslip, and in England the kingcup, perfect for cheese, or nicely admixed with turpentine, applied like a poultice to the chest, for coronary problems. Finally, the pot marigold, a catch-all of yellow flowers.

Hence, those memorable evocations of a late sixteenth-century herbal: "... It hath pleasant shining yellow flowers which do close at the setting down of the sun and spread and open again with sunrise." Shakespeare himself echoed these sentiments in *A Winter's Tale*. And there was one other insightful detail that should not be overlooked. A certain scholar in eighteenth-century Sweden, M. Haggren, perceived at sunset a most remarkable quality among both *Calendula officinalis* and *Tagetes*, namely, a flashing light emanating from the petals. The light was a brilliant orange, according to Professor Haggren, who conducted a thorough investigation of the phenomenon. At first, he suspected phosphoric worms, but this proved an incorrect supposition. Only after repeated observations did he recognize the source of the strobe—an electrical charge occasioned by the scattering of pollen. The conditions supporting this light show had to be right: July or August, a clear twilight, low humidity. Only two other flowers, to his knowledge, produced this remarkable effect: garden nasturtium (*Tropaeolum majus*) and orange lily (*Lilium bulbiferum*), but none with the strength, durability or sheer wonderment of the marigolds.

So the Marigold dynasty embodied the universal bloom, the color of the sun, electricity, ancient deities, etymological conundrums, kings, marshes, figs, money, Greece, Africa, America, England, the domesticated flower, and the wild, untamable blossom. All characteristics of the place, as well: Tesuque.

There were no covered bridges or honeymoon resorts in Tesuque, but a legacy of artists like the painter, Knee, and the color photographer, Porter, who'd lived and worked there. Saddle makers and on again-off again actors of B-Westerns. There were, as well, lower-income Hispanics whose modest, subdued lives could not be separated from the rugged hills and miraculous valleys and that perennial challenge to coax a tenable wage from the land. Amid a rapid influx of Texans and Californians, Europeans and New Yorkers who boosted real-estate values and, as they did everywhere else that's pretty or has history, tempted the locals to abandon everything, such wages were born of endurance and continuity.

Marigold's Tesuque was rich with all these virtues, pleasing to behold, sensuous in all ways. The ridges teemed with Indian arrow heads and broken shell amulets. Abalone speckles, blue in the thick of the wind-worn dust, seemed to float on the earth, going nowhere, belonging everywhere.

The sacred dance of geometries encircled Tesuque: medieval definitions of God, passing lightning, sudden squalls which posed no dismay, only wonderment to those safely snug within their human borders—adobe, agreed to in hue by the town council (it must be sludge color, they argued), that had been replicated in the image of hillsides and shadowy corners. Adobe garrets, garages, tinkerer sheds. Back fields of clematis, "Albertine". Follies thick in frost-hardy hollyhocks. Mahogany-red triploid trinities. Annuals spread vibrantly abase dark earth-colored stonemasonry that had figured in every human rumination and most procreation for 1,000 years. The occasional teepee stuck up from deep grass and eye-catching low growers; horses wandered amid the copper "Pat Austin" flowers; burros in "Constance Spry"; llamas (descendants of the world's first camel, a New Mexican) grazed on "Prospero" and "Sombreuil". A playwright wrote alone in a barn, smelling the "Frau Dagmar Hastrup" rose, its petals of flesh; a grocer served bags of soy up the road; children slapped down their coinage and demanded the greatest number of candies from the merchant, an innocence rare in these times; some movie star sat in his logged sweat lodge reading a script; and hundredth-generation Indians loaded their trucks with cases of jewelry, bound for the Plaza.

The Commander rode down to the river where a dirt lane descended from the country road and he could be assured of total privacy along the quiet embankment. He sat for 20 minutes, his face a study in near tears. With time, they would turn to salt, and dry on his face, and nobody would know and certainly not care about the grave misgivings and perplexities that had ambushed America's newest billionaire, secretly an innocent in the way of a whole historical avalanche of bodyline bowling. He took off his clothes and stepped gingerly into the waist-deep waters. His ablution brought gusto to contemplative deadlock. In his memory, tricycles, *luminaires* and *lits de bébés*, ebbtide the gurgling flow, an ecology of burial that lives in the present life, where immersion itself is the very religious paradise of closed eyes in the moment of supreme completion.

Eventually he retreated from the rapids, dried himself with his shirt, got dressed and sat a while longer on the thin beach where, as a child, he'd played with Indian friends from the Pueblo nearby. It was up the hillside beyond that he had first seen a bear. And there, on the other mountain top, had made his descent by sled one winter in the early 1950s. The memories came easily, and they were shorn of words or bias. In those sunny times, when his father was still alive, nothing could or ever did interrupt the seamless flow of days and ideas. The library, handed down from the peripatetic cumulations of family eccentrics— Chihuahua, Alonzo, Victor, Burrito and Pecos, and all their wives—boasted of a fabulist iconography: big colorful books replete with bountiful visions, like that endless stream of fantastically illustrated editions of Jules Verne across France, and young Marigold read them all, thirsty for more. Unlike his peers, whoever they were, he did not go on to fancy-sounding schools, or take entrance exams or IQs or SATs. Pecos wanted his son to be schooled in meaningful history; to know the land, as he and his own parents had known it. Without any pressure, Murillo's education came about, with occasional outside local tutors, but the mainstay of his upbringing was the library and the hills all around, with their (then) abundant wildlife.

"Just follow your dreams, Son." How many times Pecos had repeated the adage.

But on this day of raging doubt and wisteria tears, Murillo was grateful for all that legacy; grateful to be alive. A colossal velocity going nowhere threatened to topple his every future, but for the moment, at that

Tesuque River entrepot of childhood and middle-aged memories, he was sacrosanct. Nothing could touch him. Might it remain? Might we ever rest in the nostalgia that is softly snoozing on a park bench for all times? Keep it lodged safely in yourself, was his way of caring for it.

He ventured back home. Pedaling either way was the same, for there were no rude hills to pant the breath or overwork the calves. Just the twining narrow lane acrest shambled rickety fence post, pods of coyote bush, velvet lilac against pink rampart and leaning glen, early to bud for May. High uncut grasses and exotics of golden broom and chokeberry filled in the rest. Shadow play wobbled along overgrown track, quiet lingerings between homesteads. The clucking of a cochi cockerel. Scent of jasmine that physics the cottage, furnishes the pot. Peter Rabbit, Edwardian cabbages, Welsh poppies. A cacophony of leisurely spreads whose nature knew only admixture and casual disregard: lettuces and stepping stones, pelargoniums and love-in-a-mist. The occasional journeyman, UPS truck or wandering soul was no intrusion but a flower compared with the ferocious maw of the rest of America. Here in Tesuque there were no masses of people, throngs of strangers, but individuals of interest.

Sannazaro had just awakened by the time Marigold returned home. Alma was resting. So too Amigo, who sat bunched up in shaded clover, four-leafs all around, dazed and apparently happy.

Across the way, a handyman working by the hour was fixing a gas-pump at Ginevra's. She missed Barringer. The hot winds of early summer always conjured legitimate fears of fire, and with a pump and the acequia running through the property, it would be possible to save several homes.

"Alma said you had a call from your service," Sannazaro advised him.

"Oh?"

He checked in—a new and slightly daunting routine—only to learn there were 117 messages. That, in a few hours, was 117 more than in the previous 15 years. Such a deluge only added panic to Marigold's claustrophobia.

"Well, old man, did you come to any startling conclusions?" Sannazaro inquired.

"Are you up for a ride?"

"On your bicycle? Never."

"Airplane ride."

"Why, what have you decided?"

"I need to get out of here. It's time."

"But where? What? I thought Chaco more than sufficient if exile be your potion."

"Amigo landed last night for a reason," the Commander said with an air of cautious revelation.

"I can tell you what that is," Sannazaro replied. "Somewhere in the vicinity that crazy old Indian is still busy shooting birds, not out of the sky, but into the sky. That's all it means."

Marigold handed him the *Santa Fean*, which featured a description of something horrible happening to Amigo's fellow chickens in Hong Kong.

"Look at this article," he said.

Sannazaro skimmed the news piece, and nodded. "Terrible stuff. But it's far away in Hong Kong, which is now China, which means it's none of our business."

"Nearly three billion dollars makes it our business. Anyway, I skinny-dipped in the river this afternoon."

"Good for you. The water's polluted. So?"

"I think I've made peace with Tesuque or, I should say, with my past. It's a kind of closure. Maybe you can't understand."

"Of course I understand."

"But you're a man of the world. You've been places. I've never been anywhere, except of course Ecuador, long ago. I think I'm ready to begin the next half of my life. And you're invited. In fact, I insist you join me. Think of it as Hadyn's pen for Nelson's sword, and the sword for the pen. An inspired substitution that would have easily swayed Talleyrand or Churchill or Andrew Carnegie."

"Damn it, clear your throat. Which is Hadyn, who is Nelson?"

But the Commander had long ago transcended this too-trying disputant with his lame reservoir of simplicities; had instead gone resolutely indoors to speak with Alma about her future, leaving very specific indications as to the disposition of the hacienda, where he implored her to remain, even after her child was born. "Sam, of course, must come and live with you," he said. "There's plenty of room, and I expect to be gone some time."

Alma was deeply moved by Murillo's generosity but again declared she wanted her own place, and that was that.

"At least wait until I return," he suggested. "Somebody's got to feed all the animals."

Part Two

Fools Abroad

CHAPTER 51
Mr Marigold Tilts at H5N1

PIGS ARE NOTHING. Chickens less than nothing. Cruelty an old cliché. A way of life. No fret. No want. No feel. Food on every table. That is how it goes. Father to son, mother to daughter, since the time of Confucius," grumbled Dr Ling, the famed ornithologist and animal rights activist.

"Surely it can change, even if today proved less than consequential?" declared the agitated inmate beside him, which happened to be the Commander.

Ling calculated the peppered coliseum of odds. Then: "Changing consciousness in China is about as likely as a badger reciting Chaucer, or finding a living moa. In this country, progress moves painstakingly, from funeral to funeral. That is why there is such an unreal emphasis upon reincarnation. Well, that's not good enough. Ultimately, the old guard, the fascist bulwark, the military vice and the culture it has manufactured, will just have to die out. And it will. But in the meantime ... Every day the rape of Nanking. Nagasaki. Minamoto."

The doctor was sharing a dank Hong Kong holding cell with the Commander and Sannazaro, along with several others, pending the process of release on their own recognizance. Basement plaster was peeling; lead paint congealing in the trails of urine on the sunken concrete floor. Steel girders held back light. Flies in larval masses were strewn across the dark drains. Overhead brights never turned off. The Tesuque duo had been away from New Mexico just one week, but to the Italian gourmet the overnight turnaround was galling. He could not wrap his mind around their predicament, nor think what it boded for the future.

The judge, who had sat girded by English and Chinese legal codes, had handed down the order from the Crown Courthouse, an Oriental fortress of procedural pluralities and ambiguities that only added to Sannazaro's despair. Jet-lag, uncertainty, and the realization that this trip to the Far East was colossally stupid, gave him to understand that the warden might well throw away the key. After all, any observer could see that he, Sannazaro, was complicit in attempted murder—certainly that's how it might be interpreted.

Nevertheless, this judge was also wary of global internet fanfare, of the pressure of an increasing animal rights constituency focused upon the irregularities in Hong Kong restaurants (the selling of fresh clouded leopard, for example). He had thus tried, in Robert Kennedy's words, to "bend history" rather than invite any more international scrutinizing. But the Chinese who had for generations persecuted every dissident voice or outbreak, banished every democracy-clinging idealist, tortured Tibetans, induced abortions in their non-Han minorities or killed the infants outright—who had, in short, dispatched brutally with all cant, discord, argument and personality—were unprepared for one as bold, eccentric and unintelligible as Marigold. His motives, methods and madness mired the magistrate in self-doubt; he doubled the difficulties of the case by insinuating a nearly shamanic pall over the proceedings, even cast a spell that would not leave the judge's mind for months to come. In fact, he would be only too eager to see Mr Marigold leave the country.

Dr Ling, Marigold's cellmate, was foremost among those who had taken the chicken's legal rights to heart. He had, in fact, written the definitive *Natural History of Chickens*, published in Mandarin and Dutch, and the Prosecution, on behalf of Hong Kong's medical authorities, had even cited Ling's two-volume work in their allegations against the American. The judge, however, could only fall back on what he believed to be common sense in his attempt to counter the lunacy of the defendant before him.

"We are 1.3 billion people. We very much enjoy the taste of chicken. We can't all be wrong. There you have it," he decreed, summarizing as clearly as possible the reality which Marigold had so blatantly contravened.

Later, Ling lamented the fact. "My people would sooner see 10 million children starve than cross a cricket."

"Surely that is a racist remark," the Commander declared.

"Yes, but it is also the case that where human or animal rights are concerned, the Chinese are among the worst in history. I need not bore you with so many horrible details of my country's conquest of Tibet and massacre of millions of Tibetans. You have, this day, seen that propensity in the slaughter of those innocent birds. I do not hesitate to single out the Chinese, as I am one of them, and I would like to consider myself a citizen of the planet and could as easily cite hundreds of other cultures no less barbaric."

There was no humor in this man. None. Nor one light note in all of the Commander's mindset, which now added military conflict, near death, pandemonium and a jail cell to his rapid onslaught of international experiences.

"A few minutes ago you mentioned a name, moa. What is that?" asked Marigold.

A ray of hue and tone entered the ornithologist's waning eyes, a glint from prehistory that was like some romantically neglected Villa D'Avray, and he described for the Commander what, to his way of thinking, must have been the "gentlest creature ever to walk this world".

"You speak in past tense?"

"Yes. The moa were slaughtered long ago by the early peoples of New Zealand, along with countless other bird species killed by other people throughout the South Pacific. I think of the moa as the poster child for all international wildlife conservation, the reminder of just how deranged, how cruel, human beings tend to be—a fact consolidated in this one gigantic heart of Being, laid waste in ages past, though some have held on to the belief that still a few persist in the most remote of all Australasian gorges. If only that were true."

The scientist pulled himself away from the bars of the jail cell and took a seat in a corner. Twenty other inmates crowded nearby.

"If it could be shown that there were still one moa surviving somewhere in the wild," he concluded, "then I would happily spend the rest of my life in this jail cell."

For Marigold, listening rapt, the moa was only the latest in a cordon of despairs and pathos that had followed horror upon horror in previous days—beginning with the onslaught of truly grotesque events as a result of a perceived outbreak of disease among New Territories chickens.

The day before, he and Sannazaro had strode briskly through Hong Kong Customs, checked into a modest hotel, gone to an antique dealer abase Mount Victoria and acquired two samurai swords, much to the Squire's uneasiness, for Marigold would not divulge too many particulars of his plan, and Sannazaro feared the worst.

The Commander's first encounter with the outside world is going awry, he thought, certain that he was seeing a psychopathology in the making, that near-on 50 years of pent-up madness had found its vent.

That so much talk of saving the world now made him prepared to assault others, even die for the claim. The Commander was out of control, gripped by an ague that offered no obvious remedy. At the very least, he was an embarrassment. Beyond that, real trouble.

Later in the day, Marigold pointed upwards to another mountain and declared their route. Sannazaro was not thrilled with the prospect of a 3,000-foot vertical trudge but conceded the air would do him good after the flight.

They trekked in search of a mystery tree, about which the Commander steadfastly refused any information. Hong Kong from that high elevation is, particularly from the trail around Victoria Peak, a legend quite warranted.

The clue to the right hill—for it is a city of many such apiculi—was an historical British/Chinese hospital with a dome. By late afternoon it appeared they had found it, as well as a path leading above.

There, lonely and choked in grass, was the tree Mr Marigold was seeking. He lay down on his back, swords to either side, face to the early evening moon, and began to hum a doo-dah, his head moving, his toes twitching, his eyes and face visibly betaken.

"What is this chorus that defines for all future ages, the expression 'out of tune'?" Sannazaro bid him.

"Lie down, my inhibited prude," the Commander urged, before proceeding to belt out "Love is a many splendored thing!" with a deep, distinctive *alto vibrato mezzo falsetto*, pinched by a heretofore unknown *contralto coloraturo*—in other words, a wail the likes of which, one implores, will never be heard on earth again.

He did not know other words than those memorable six, so he repeated them with the intermittent doo-dahs half dozen times.

"It was in this very spot, on predecessors of this very grass, beneath this, the most romantic tree in the world, that William Holden's Mark and Jennifer Jones's Han Suyin lay in the grass kissing, spurning both the Chinese Confucianist restrictions and an intolerable spouse who would not give Mark a divorce, rejecting the conventions and gossip of fellow employees at the hospital, and desperately clinging to each other, before Mark went off to report on some senseless war or other, only to be killed—it was here, right here."

Sannazaro, fearing other revelations, placed several more feet between him and the Commander. "But how do you know about that, and why do you care? I thought you were immune to sentiment?"

"How little you or anybody really knows me," Marigold swooned.

"Well, that's entirely your fault, then," Sannazaro rebuffed. He could well see the misanthrope, dense with animal nature, denser still with human mishmash—a love psalm here, a rash of poison oak and polemics there; this "Judith", sweet curls, caviar eyes, liturgical folly, betraying a fallen St John (beheaded); this study in morose bliss heralding a hoax of periodic prosody that was one moment cogent, the next surreal.

"I'm human, I am not," Marigold began. "I was, but will never be so again. How can I be? A clam, a wolverine, a flying chicken, yes. A man, never! Is there hope or is there not? Is my puny life worth even a mortar and pestle? Should I bother fending off dissolution, or embrace the incessant dust of my own chaos? We're all getting old, good man. No other thought but this, this all-embracing nothingness. How sweet a notion, nothingness, as if it were a donnybrook, a slowly-melting chocolate in the shrine which is my mouth. A vast canopy bed intricately Siamesed with silken loft. Twenty Summer Palace pillows, goose of down. Leave me be. Grant me the cool breeze of my distant imaginings. A soft suffusion that shelters the sky where pianissimos rain down upon a valley alit within. Where the lamb like unto a Goltzius sketch communes on sunny burn, a trout frolics a living rainbow. My mind, what fields it would inhabit. A million acres of such beguiling conjurations, dear friend. Can you not see them?"

"The acres or the ideas? Give me half a clue."

"Chickens," he reiterated, convictions stronger by the minute. And on and on he went. During those windswept seconds of portable peace Marigold dreamed of the salvation of all chickens and flew off over Kowloon in a warm, moist cloud with thousands of reclining, talkative birds. His mind had become the Hopi's rocket ship. His heart filled with the American movie classic, schmultz multiplied by memory, magnified by Amigo's ancestral ties to Southeast Asia, where chickens were first discovered, caged and tortured 12,000 years ago.

In this state of musical séance, his mind veered from Mark and Han Suyin to Rimsky-Korsakov's *Snegoo-rochka*, or *Snow Maiden*, and the libretto by Ostrovskovo. He exclaimed, "Hops and lime, poppy and clover, honey that imperceptibly steeps the soul like a snow maiden fine.

This is no vision mere. No, no ... Trust me, Señor, the time is near. My beating heart, great goals lining my nerves, and a day so clear. Hey nanny hey, 100 times beneath pale moon, no chicken shall ever suffer again if I have my say."

Which left the poor Italian tag-along more unhinged and confused than ever before.

The next morning they'd taken a taxi to the Pein Ko Rups poultry market district and plotted their—or, more precisely, his—lost cause.

"I'm telling you, this time you're pushing your luck, such as it distinctly is not," the exhausted subaltern carped. "Two swords stand out. They'll take us for hooligans. Then what? Moreover, I have bruises on my bottom from that long—18 hours—sit-down, not to mention a migraine headache which, in your company, has now become a common enough outbreak. And flea bites from that grassy perch of yours."

"Take your Ibuprofen and pipe down." The Commander lacked all sympathy. "Stealth is all that's required just now."

Mr Marigold paid the taxi driver and the two men tried to merge seamlessly with the hubbub of the market. It was no ordinary day. The Commander had, for a start, shelled out 7,000 dollars on accommodation, weaponry and taxi rides. Even more startlingly, that day four people had died, 15 others been hospitalized, from a new influenza virus known as H5N1 Type A, said to be attributable to chickens. At all the poultry farms throughout the city and New Territories, Agricultural and Fisheries Department henchmen, dressed like warriors from outer space, were poised to begin the slaughter. They carried tanks of carbon dioxide gas, knives, bags, disinfectants, and they planned to asphyxiate as many birds as necessary to rid Hong Kong of any further outbreak. At schools around the city, more than 1,000 workers gathered to slit the throats of yet other chickens.

Mr Marigold was beside himself, but Sannazaro considered the precautions by the authorities altogether justified. His thoughts were with the humans who had died, and those still in anguish, and he found his comrade's agitation misplaced.

"True, it is a sorry day, but would you prefer all the people die, or the chickens?" Sannazaro asked squarely. "In my opinion, the Chinese are doing precisely what we would do, and any other civilized people."

To which Mr Marigold evaded an answer: "Such matters of life and death cannot be so easily reduced to black and white, my young friend."

"I believe I am older in years than yourself."

"Older in accumulated follies, perhaps. Of which this attitude of yours is one. Lest you forget: there is no absolute proof that the chickens are a true threat. I have read the literature quite carefully."

"When did you have time to read the literature?" Sannazaro was astonished by the man's flourish of presumptions, overstatements and underestimates. On the other hand, Marigold did travel with that silly little computer of his, with its extra battery pack, and was rarely not reading something or other.

"I have been in touch with the leading authorities and studied all of their reports. If you were living in the twentieth century, dear friend, you could hardly have escaped some notice of it in every periodical and newspaper on that airplane."

"Blah blah blah," the Italian cried, staying to the corners of the market, where he was least observable.

"And I am convinced that this entire plague, so called, is nothing more than an odious flu which hardly warrants the outright slaughter of millions of precious innocents. It's just like mankind to panic, to vent its wrath. To seek the laziest expedient. The whole biomedical industry, the National Institutes of Health, nearly every university research lab that exploits animals, hangs upon the same easy excuse."

"Which is?"

"Kill the animal, avoid the hard work, refuse the proper questions, perpetuate the madness—*Genesis 1.8, 9.2*—and cash your pay check. It was the founder of the Mayo Clinic, as well as several astute contributors to the *Harvard Medical Journal*, who pointed out that the use of animals in research and in industry has hampered our humanity and set our sciences back countless decades. Inhibiting a cure for cancer, diverting our attention from the true matters at hand, perverting the minds of our children, and lending all the necessary paperwork and credibility to a paradigm of cruelty that has been adopted by one generation of mindless carnivores after another. Never mind that thalidomide proved harmless in animals, or that AIDS might well have entered the human stream from a chimpanzee, via contaminated polio vaccine. That Ronald Reagan insisted man never invented a weapon he didn't ultimately use, or that Henry Spira himself argued that you cannot alter self-interest in humans—a theory I reject. Even the most sympathetic anti-vivisectionists are still walking around in dimwitted circles asking, 'How do you care for another?' In short, my foolish man, this species to which you and I allegedly belong has turned over to all the afflictions of the human heart and spirit a free rein, a dismal license, while fatally dooming tens of millions of precious creatures to unimaginable torment in concrete bunkers. Amid this free-for-all slaughter, all the petite and pretty debutantes, chickens whose hearts are opera-mad, voices symphonic, with more philosophy in one square talon than are to be found in 100 human heavens: rare and precious, sequestered like squashed flies into battery-cages where they spend two years venting calcium, vomiting and suffocating, succumbing to advanced osteoporosis, standing horribly on wire mesh, no room even to spread a wing, their bones broken, feathers plucked, necks slit, blood and guts in their eyes, mouths, noses, infant birds thrown alive into grinding machines. Tens of billions of perfect souls, hopeless, reduced to wax and oil. My dear Sannazaro, have you any idea?"

"It is your grammar waxes, then wanes, victim of a bizarre enthusiasm that seems to want to stamp its place in an imaginary history. The words cannot fail to impress, the after-images pierce. You kill by your sentience, catapult with but a sound. No denying the grim Gogol-like picture of endless despair. No, no denying it. But you seriously think that two swords, which you are surely untrained to wield and which by their looks are as blunt-edged as a telephone book, will reverse a decision which has, no doubt, been taken days, weeks ago in Beijing? So far away? So remote from any legal say-so on anybody's part?"

"Though the Goliaths appeareth invincible, truth will win out in the end."

"And the end is surely near at hand, for I see only hearty collaboration by all those amassing around us, lest you've not been socially observing."

Indeed, where the two loggerheads were presently immersed, swords revealed, the throng had amassed. Thousands of caged chickens lay dumped in the swathe of some unknowable ire, the technicians in their suits and gas masks moving in close. Nervous, innocent sets of chicken eyes gazing wearily upon the flotilla of heinous intentions. Real lives, come down to this moment. Hearts furiously beating. Examine the total picture of chicken physiology, enlarge it, scan the emotions flooding the banks of each delicate synapse, trace back all those individual calamities, coming to know the brief and galling life, without name, that had led from cage to cage, trailed after monstrous agony with more of the same, though multiplied beyond any conceivable compass reading of pain, and only then might the true trenches of conflict, the vastness of precious lives at stake, come into meaningful focus.

Into this maelstrom Mr Marigold had injected himself, one moment a soldier bearing the oriflamme of St Denis at the battle of Agincourt, and the next a banner of the Royal Dragoons.

"Ahoy!" Mr Marigold shrieked, waving both swords every which way, narrowly missing his own head in the upswing, catching a piece of Sannazaro's thigh on the downward thrust.

"My back is giving out, no matter; my arms pressed so, the legs stand firm, all is as prescribed. Kingdoms hinge on my every move. Mother of all Virgins, victory to your sequined abode, where thoughts of all good tidings, deeds of virtue, love and charity abound. But lo! Take flight, ye vermin. My wrath is judge and executioner, those chickens a thorough testimony!"

"Are you nuts?" went the horrific cry, as the Señor, bleeding robustly, toppled to the ground, stupefied and surrounded. But Mr Yellow Flower was oblivious to the damage already wreaked on his erstwhile colleague; he rushed headlong towards the cages, continuing to scream in no less grave a manner than during those heady times of the Austria Netherlands revolt in the Brabant, or the days after the accession of James I when it was the red cross of England that knights and warriors pressed forward into the faces of their enemy.

The Sovereign of the Seas, his terrible face flying at topgallant mast— a fleet, van, rear division and red squadron all in one man—proceeded to disperse the huge mob of technicians and demanded on threat of some terrible beheading or other that the poultry workers release the birds to his care at once.

Of course, his speaking in English had less of an impact than he might have hoped.

A flurry of hostile Cantonese burst upon the air like pepper spray. But by now the Commander had managed to open several of the cages and frighten the birds out into their freedom, and to prevent owners and onlookers alike from seizing the doomed chickens with menacing jabs from either sword.

"Go Amigo, *go!* " he pleaded, addressing by name the First Principal of Chickens. It was thus that Majapahit and the great princes of Siam had gained advantage over all adversaries; that the stalwart disciples of Philip II Augustus of France rode to victory with their pennons of scarlet, banners of gold embroidery emblazoned with white tigers and blue dragons. Fearless. Fully aware that their cause was the right one.

All that said and recollected, it was, thought Sannazaro, a moronic, hopeless gesture. He sat in his blood reflecting on this odd scene, aware full well that a prison, and who knows what else, awaited them. That he had followed a neurotic samurai sworn to the sorties of St George; an errant Robin Hood with no muscles, only gumption. It would be Sannazaro's last cause, of that much he was sure. With his three million dollars, there were any number of options now open to him: two homes, not one. Perhaps he'd even return to Italy and try to resurrect his ancestral legacy above the Amalfi Coast.

While Mr Marigold continued on his reckless liberation tactics, leaping and bounding and screaming with the fierce polish of the Tokugawa era, and a few bewildered chickens managed, for the time, to hide out in remote corridors of the market, the police with shields, sticks, automatic weapons and helmets were arriving by droves and preparing their own counter-offensive.

Prices for domestic chickens were plunging all across mainland China.

The swoop occurred, beginning with a verbal threat delivered by megaphone: "You, there! Lay down your swords and surrender or we will be forced to fire. You have three seconds."

"Give him at least ten seconds!" Sannazaro cried out, knowing that Mr Marigold never did anything in three seconds. "His brain is befuddled and it will take him longer than that to figure out that three seconds actually means three seconds!"

"Ten seconds, then!" the police captain railed.

The crowd which, if one included the birds, must by now have exceeded 10,000, watched, breathless, in anticipation of the terrorist's response.

Sannazaro could see his neighbor's head spinning through the ages, as if cloaked by the dark fancy-infested hood of St Martin, the very same borne by the monks at the abbey of Marmoutier and carried on the battlefields of Clovis and Narbonne by men no less than Charlemagne himself. There was the whole besieged Holy Land of animal rights, the crucifix of virtues, the very germ of a nationality that transcended borders and reached out to all common decency, incarnate in the towering figure of Marigold. He did not shrink one iota before the assembling show of modern-day force.

"I have read all the relevant data!" the Commander shouted at the ninth second. "Is it not true that this slaughter has been ordered merely to quell public fears? A panic that resides entirely in ignorance? Is it not the case—or perhaps you have not been properly informed—that not a single poultry worker has been infected? That there is no explanation for the fact that those who work most intensely on a daily basis with these birds have shown no incidence of harm? Explain that, and then I will put down my swords."

There was mumbling among the policemen, translations and annoyed discussion. This was followed with an ultimatum. "You may or may not be correct, sir. But I must insist, do not sacrifice your life on account of chickens. This is a matter for the authorities, not for you. Please, put down your weapons."

"Do it, you idiot, before you get us both killed!" Sannazaro shrieked, thinking, These are surely the most polite, reasonable and patient police I have ever seen. "Last chance, Captain!" he shouted out to his indefensible neighbor.

At that very instant a freed chicken with the sweetest almond eyes in Hong Kong flew up and took refuge in the Commander's arms. Marigold's only reflex, the one that had evidently guided him his entire life, was to fondle the bird. In so doing he relaxed his grip on both swords.

The second was all that was required for the police to converge upon him, and within minutes both the Tall Standing Chevalier of the Empire and his beleaguered Squire were handcuffed, confined to a police van and driven away, as the cadres of impatient chicken-murderers converged on the hapless lives of all those waiting, wondering birds. Nothing so much as these dashed bird hopes proffered greater sadness, mumbled the subdued madman.

It would be discovered within days of the operation that there had been oversights. Some birds dragged themselves away, still alive. Others escaped outright, while whole urban ranch-loads of the avians were passed over by the authorities. In many cases, when the officials ran out of asphyxiating gas, they did whatever they could to kill the birds, hitting them with any available objects, strangling them or, usually, slitting their throats with sloppy brutality. Pain. Excruciating pain. In some cases, dogs were seen running off with the birds between their teeth. Yet, the Chinese spoke only of their own hardships, speculating on ruined poultry workers who were going bankrupt and might well consider jumping out of windows. Do the world loads of good, remarked Marigold.

Meanwhile, authorities prepared to go after ducks and geese as well, despite there being no true injurious link established between people and these birds. In the town of Jiangcun, just outside Guangzhou, an alleged site of the viral outbreak, farmers contested the data, declaring emphatically that no farmer or chicken had died of unnatural causes in over a century. They cited the strange American as a kind of chicken hero.

Mr Marigold sat in the back of the police van silently contemplating the cruel ways of the world.

"What human being could fail to see the terror in their sweet and hopeful eyes?" he asked. Hundreds of the chickens had been doused in gasoline and set fire to.

"Which eyes, blast it!" replied Sannazaro.

"The chickens', of course."

"I did not. And what is it with you and chickens, anyway? First your descent into the well, and now this. Personally, I love a good teriyaki drumstick every now and then."

"Blasphemy!"

"If it will make you feel any better—though frankly, I am the one with injury here—an *old* chicken's drumstick. One destined for the grave, in any case."

"Smudge monger!"

"Every being has to die sometime."

"Monster!"

"Nor is it at all practical to impose your dietary standards on others."

"Traitor! For your information, I am not concerned with diet. Health. Or my vitality. Not one iota. No, sir. I am focused solely upon the lives of innocent animals. If humans want to eat meat, let them find a way to do so without killing any animals. These bastards turned stone into the Great Wall, divined dim sum in a dollop of mucus, made forbidden forever artful. Well, so too there is meatless meat. Any health-food store the world over and under will show you how."

Sannazaro thought it wise to refocus on the immediate. "Whatever you say, better memorize something fine and polished for the judge, a calligraphy of flattery and stooped brow, humility before trouble, a simpleton's cry. No hortation, or you'll only get us both hung."

Twenty minutes later the police van had stopped and both men were led out and into a room where they were strip-searched. Naked, the margrave Marigold did not flinch, but held up to the barbaric scrutiny with no end to his bravery. He wore, in his mind, the mantle of the Order of the Knights of Alcantara, the Grand Mastership of St James of Compostella. In his courage swirled the nuances of every Templar and the lily-hilted swords of faith that had sustained in rough and thick the penitents of Calatrava.

Sannazaro's thigh wound was entirely superficial, and had not one historical precedent of any value. A small dressing and poultice were sufficient.

The admissions officer made a pronouncement, and with no further ado both men were sentenced to one night in jail and a review of the case the following day.

They found themselves thrown in with a motley assemblage of others—Hong Kong's entire animal rights community, namely 23 persons whose fellow countrymen would not hesitate to hunt down and skewer a clouded leopard or eat out the crown of a writhing monkey.

"You see, I am not the lone madman you'd make me out to be," the Commander told his friend. "There, for example. If I am not mistaken, a military officer of the Order of Merit of St Ferdinand. And look to that corner—a member of the Royal and Illustrious Cavalcade of Charles III."

Mr Marigold then proceeded to introduce himself to the others in his camp, including Dr Ling. Needless to say, they all got along famously.

As they discussed the rudiments of Utopia in China, of Ko Hung's *Pao p'u tzu*, and Kuo Hsi, Sannazaro sulked in a corner.

"This is intolerable," he whined and whittled. "But not surprising." Marigold was having the time of his life. "Tell me more about this moa of yours!" he chimed, on to a new obsession. The first in a lifetime of them. Hence, should anyone inquire, the origins of a disease, the first inkling of a syndrome that had catapulted man beyond his means only to run headlong into himself. The very etymology of hope—and when hope was abandoned, dreams. Even as dreams were dunked and good intentions drowned, a desire, faint and distant, for such and such an outcome. Or by and by a becalmed future. Or now and then a mild mark that advanced a cause, created an impression, made a difference. What some might describe as the soul's true calling. Without heat. Or a laundry anywhere near. Or coffee, running water or floorboards. In short, man born naked, with no clue, or hair to cover himself. No god, either. For what god would tolerate the slaughter of chickens? A refrain constantly on Marigold's mind. The atheism at the beginning of all constructive change.

All this the increasingly dour and desperate Iacobo Sannazaro observed. Never did anthropological remorse yield up so critical a juncture, behooving its believer to abandon all else in favor of going home. Relieved of those adventures that had promised a soft landing, elevated purview, satin pillows, he now simply sought reprieve from barefaced calamity.

The Commander was only just winding up, whereas he was finished. No more promises to keep. Day and night, these two. How he had misread the impetus that now must suffer its own foolishness.

Whilst Marigold filled his ambulance with petrol: "And what about the entrancing terrain you allege they once inhabited?" he inquired.

CHAPTER 52
The Search for Erewhon

COMMANDER MARIGOLD HAD caught the fever of international high-tension wires, ten-million-volt battle cries. He was unto his duplex a nation state of treaty deliberations whose rain gutters were clear, plaster-of-Paris freshly painted. If convictions may be likened to the foundations of a chateau, his orientation was unflinching, an *idée fixe*, remote. Somehow, the fray seemed more urgent and appealing in Hong Kong than in Santa Fe, a paradox of trigger-happy combinations that he was—to Sannazaro's eternal wonderment—ready to embrace full on.

It happened that Dr Ling's tantalizing references to a moa had become wound up in the Commander's thinking processes throughout that fitful night of incarceration. Into its myth he fled to unshackle the asthma of adverse chicken consequences, loosen the choke-hold, wipe away the flood of tears. Ling had prized the legendary bird's cause, given just enough inviting detail to cloud Marigold's uncut diamond of a vortex with all those fantasies to which such cerebral matters are prey: a hodgepodge of righteous aggrandizement, poetic fulfillment, desperate disappearance; crevasses of personal salvation; a complete mind-body separation from the assaults of any normal life. All of prehistory to mesmerize him—and, of course, 80-million-year-old New Zealand herself: secret chasms, heaven-drenched alpines, Cretaceous theropods prancing about fern gullies or skulking along rushing rivers in underground caverns. A painted canvas for dreamers like himself.

Next morning, Marigold and his still furious companion were released from prison and ordered to leave Hong Kong within 12 hours. Sannazaro said nothing during the short taxi ride to the airport.

Marigold finally broke the reign of exile. "Look," he said, "I know you're unhappy with me."

The Italian continued venerably to pout.

"Won't you at least talk about it?"

"What's to discuss?" Sannazaro said.

"I could give you more money if you would come to your senses."

"You don't have enough money in this world to fashion such senses."

"Try me."

"One hundred million dollars."

"Done!" the Commander exclaimed. He would have confirmed all of Indonesia, if need be, to secure the bumbling companionship of the only other male (excepting the world-touring Hidalgo) with whom he might actually engage in intimate conversation, confide desperate thoughts, share forbidden exaltations and pivotal frustrations. Moreover, he liked the Italian enormously.

"You see, that's precisely what I mean."

"What is? Mean what?"

"Your fiscal irresponsibility. A hundred million for the joys of one such as myself?"

"You are no ordinary canker, to coin a concision. Your trifling outbursts and petty complaints are like a salve on a planet without gauze. A cantankerous bloke emblazoned with dimples and love nuts."

"I will take that as a compliment."

"And well you should."

"But the fact remains, you are impulsive as you are impractical. I have noticed over the past few months that your rash of ideas is choking out the saner options. Just as your name implies, at least from the botanist's perspective."

"My name? Marigold?"

"Yes."

"Why, it is a beautiful flower if ever there was one."

"More in keeping with the weed that overgrows its bounds, sprouts at random, imposes its exuberance upon others."

"Only a fool would dictate boundaries of the Creation. Or stipulate how yellow a color yellow should be, or exuberant exuberance."

"You're right. I don't mean to judge or begrudge you," Sannazaro said forgivingly. "But why this frenzied far-away?" He was referring, of course, to New Zealand, where they were, on Marigold's insistence, presently headed. "Nobody goes there; hardly anyone has even heard of New Zealand. It's like New Caledonia. Unless you live there, it really doesn't exist. And with so much to accomplish, in strictest accord with your recently acquired religious principles, back home in Tesuque?"

Marigold knew the Italian was coming around. He had acceded to the terms of debate, and that was everything.

"If," he said, "and I say 'if' with few illusions, only the prayer of a future, a single moa could be discovered to be alive, everything we know and imagine and hope someday to know would be different. Unfurl the flags, ferry the champions to shore, lead the people to priority. A biologist in heaven. To know that that bird, if you will, has returned to the living is to acknowledge a goodness heretofore rescinded; to repeal all of human history. Gladden me to understand this icon of the creation lives in the flesh, and I shall shake loose every oppression, rout fatalism, revivify all those tenuous bonds that could render human existence tolerable."

"Unless my ears betrayed me, Ling's assessment was conclusive. This moa has long been extinct."

"Perhaps, perhaps not."

"But on what grounds could you possibly challenge his authority?"

"Credentials, passion, I grant him all that. But these do not constitute a shred of evidence."

"Why stop with the moa, if that is your driving force. We could as easily mount an expedition to the North Pole in search of Santa Claus."

Even as the words were leaving his lips, Sannazaro regretted having uttered them, for there was no telling what twisted alchemy might be detonated by nuances of Noel. Even now, Marigold's visage seemed to wander off, fixed upon some sentimental journey or Grand Tour across a continent. Vast aerial canvases by John Martin swelled the ranks. Beasts of burden plunged from their alpine crossing. Shadows gathered in the overgrown outback. Years of electrical storm concentrated in a single valley which was his brow. Moments passed, and then—"There was—I swear it—a flash of recognition with universal implications. I was, for an instant, a mirror on the world. A meteorite struck my heart, a third eye winking in the recess." He pointed to the spot.

"That's your receding hairline, boss."

"All is as clear as dawn. The Riddle of Consequences resolved."

"A pence for your pensées."

"What was precipitate is now the unfogged camera eye. I swear to you, hearsay does not certify a verdict. There is more to it. I am new to such hunches, which gives us an advantage. Think of them as the windows in a chalet, or clean rooms enclosing the great question marks. We must go and see for ourselves."

Sannazaro's whole person dangled like that grin which spans the idiot savant. Who could not succumb to the colossal silliness of this billionaire clown? Neither man had ever ventured to New Zealand, that was true. But a flight and two First Class seats were available, and the idea of traipsing about fjords rumored to contain some of the most extraordinary botanical furnishings in the world was not entirely unappealing to an erstwhile gardener.

He conceded one more expedition. "But I warn you, this is the last time."

Two days later they had transferred via drizzling Christchurch to the semi-alpinous plains of Canterbury, outfitted themselves for a foray, and begun their bizarre ascent in the alleged footsteps of Samuel Butler.

"You're certain there is no road that would get us to this lake with greater ease?" pondered the Squire, alarmed, fatigued, poised over a map from the late nineteenth century.

"Absolutely," replied Marigold with every unconvincing assurance. "I am no glutton for punishment."

"But why not examine a modern-day map. What if a new road has been built?"

"Cartography available to Mr Butler is what we require. Any other would miss the mark. Not unlike the misuse of a decanter for gold when it's tailings of silver one is after."

In all this obtuse reconnoitering, outfitting and uncertainty, Sannazaro had much to contemplate. On the one hand, how could he not be extraordinarily indebted to his neighbor for the unexpected gift of 103 million dollars? Yet there were clear signs of dementia in Marigold that could only get worse as his hubris mushroomed, bolstered by the fact his riches seemed to be accumulating at an astronomical rate owing to nothing more precocious than freakish luck in the stock market. He had adopted a policy of triple-plantings, by which he reckoned on three spikes and three troughs per year, like corn or rice. A bullet, a barbell, a barbell a bullet. That was the economic principle he inculcated in one misshapen form or another. Take profits at the spikes the second they exceeded their all-time highs then began to dip, selling short, selling long, and selling short again. Do enough volume to obtain special favors from the largest firms in order to exploit the most promising IPOs; place buy orders alongside the huge pension funds during the trough phases, even if one missed by a few marks...

Sannazaro had no idea what he was talking about. Who would? But he also reckoned his sufferings were worth more than "a mere 103 million", and he told the Commander so: "One million for every 100 feet of elevation gained by sheer donkey force. Are you up to it, old man?"

The Commander assented.

After all, his strategy seemed to be working. And with each added increment of self-confidence, Sannazaro noticed how he made light of increasingly dangerous situations. To follow behind, torture. Still, there was no better comic relief for 10,000 miles than this hermit-turned-philanthropist who had not advanced beyond the Lopa De Vega years of the Spanish court, who espied in a wet bale of hay an Isabella D'Este, or in the severest cactus a lily. Certainly the dangers of his inexperience could prove a liability to anyone who dared come near him. His foolhardy fixations might save the odd chicken, but at the expense of a riot with its share of other casualties. And when he set his sights on such grand expressions as Freedom, Liberation and Virtue, he was bound to upset an entire city, if not the decade. Savor a snack, sever a continent; mince no words, stampede a herd; save the mouse, but lose the bus.

On the other hand, Sannazaro pondered, the Commander could make for an invigorating mistral, as pure as peals of the great bell at Clairvaux or the edifice of Easter; beyond the mealy-mouthed morbidities and mediocrities of his age, an arresting temper that would heed no reason when its eyes were fixed on righting wrong, but a nature as easily prone to the suasion of puppy love. In short, despite his dismissals and redactions, his was a man full of all that contradictory stuff that makes a Titian, or Amos & Andy. Remarkably, these extraordinary distinctions seemed to Sannazaro to be gathering strength the higher they climbed. Altitude was having a dangerous effect upon Marigold, if anything distorting his distortions and exacerbating his modesty. He strode boldly, unflinching, unblushing, without respite or need of breath. And such traits had become more than a nuisance: life and limb were now at risk.

Sannazaro knew he played no supernumerary in this dramaturgy. Was no mere chauffeur. Or dog Friday. But rather, was a full member of the team. Together Gullible's Travels, their alliance was born of an equally vigorous proposition which held that the world, or parts thereof, could be remade, or at least rediscovered. Their principal differences lay in the scope of that ambition. The Commander had broader sights, whereas Iacobo was more than content to see a bed of spring flowers push valiantly through the hard soils of the preceding winter.

"By birth, you were Erewhonian if I am a day," Sannazaro remarked to his Commander, intimidated by the snowy Sinclair Range rising behind the juncture of Forest Creek and the Rangitata, his thinking additionally misted by the tidal surge of the Commander's reverential attention to details that were non-existent: tracks in the snow where there was no snow, flowers, groves of trees, cairns and other markers that simply did not exist, had no contemporary representation. The quantum surreal. "There are no moas here, dear crippled, delusional friend. Or Mr Butler would have surely mentioned them."

"Shhh! Do you hear that?"

"I mean his holiness no shame, but that is the rain."

Mr Marigold poked the small of Sannazaro's back with his alpenstock. "It was the cry of some large monkey, or wolf, or reticulated giraffe in distress."

"No way."

Marigold's face flushed, for he knew when he was right, "Try not the patience of one who alone puts up with such petulance."

"I do not take kindly to your national insults," carped the gardener. "I am no young cauliflower. You promised me a cozy retirement, not a whipping post. True, you've given me a generous handout. Yet, who would not remark upon this irrational wanderlust of yours, in which I seem perpetually marooned? I do not know where it will end, and this leaves me frightened. I must be honest with you. I should never have left the Gardens of Tesuque with my very own Empress Dowager's bathtub. A closet of brandies. No end to supping opportunities. No harsh winds or uncertainties, even. Look at this place! We are lost. The desolation grows with every wearying step. Even the sky seems to shirk our company. Not even Valerie Gergiev could coax such phantoms as surround us now"

"What, you would retreat, give up? Am I a lathered sack of lard to quit after only one hour? Furthermore, think back: the first hour is always the most difficult within any wilderness. Bandelier, if I dare say, went spectacularly well, even if Hong Kong less so."

"Inches away from death in both places!"

"Whiner. You can trust that upon the successful outcome of this adventure, you will be sinecured with full possession of the empire you deserve—the tranquillity, warm hearth, glow of late life a governor of your stature and eminence by every means requires. This much I promise thee."

"I'm not a thee, first of all. And while I can't deny that I, too, share in a roving curiosity that would take all the collective continents for its stomping grounds, I also acknowledge that my back is aching from this march you call a trail. I need codeine. I've got bouts of arthritis, can hear loud murmurs in my heart, and allergies are forcing my uprisen nostrils smack into both burning eyes, puffing the cheeks, creating abscesses in my mouth. They say leprosy is coming back. Ventricular walls collapsing. Gangrene increasingly common. My prostate harasses me; I see piss everywhere that no amount of your millions can conceal. Frankly, I don't cotton to the idea of being so far from a good surgeon. You never know when you'll need one—and you should be thinking along those lines, as well."

In spite of his complaints and a repartee that grew more wearisome by the yard, the two kept on according to a hastily planned itinerary that was not without a certain curiosity factor. The Commander summarized his expeditionary orientation with words glibly hewn from the corpus of H.G. Wells, to the effect: "C'est une erreur de faire les choses trop facilement."

Mr Marigold had made Mesopotamia, New Zealand, a point of pilgrimage on their way to the West Coast. For it was here that English alpinist, painter, photographer, critic, novelist and poet Samuel Butler had, in September 1860, purchased a freehold for purposes of a 42-month lease on the sheep station that would form the basis for his expedition to Utopia, as described in his famed 1872 novel, *Erewhon*. Marigold's appraisal of Zealandish cartography and science in the southern latitudes had persuaded him that Butler was no inventor, however; he insisted that the author had, in fact, been there, committing a loose fiction only by way of strategy.

"Literary interpretation is a dangerous business," he confessed, "when there are cliffs about. All the more reason to stay close."

But the Commander's sixth sense was useless, Sannazaro soon discovered. He had no chance of staying a course; moved neither like a detective nor the mountaineer he fancied himself. While he professed a concern for their reality, it was all a fiction fueling his ardor, and this made for the worst perils. He could not recognize a cul-de-sac; took a corner for a plain, a shadow for a crack. He believed himself endowed with powers of the dragonfly, but where was Madame Vignette to save them now? The Italian thought a blind traverse, carefully articulated, would have been preferable to this rash of unquestioning bushwhack. Marigold saw too much, and it crowded out clear thinking. His love of history furthered their obtuseness, for with every step he poured forth details that had nothing to do with their increasingly precarious situation.

The 24-year-old Butler had finished his painterly studies at Cambridge and chosen to emigrate to the New World, knowing that Merino sheep runs of up to 50,000 acres could be acquired simply on the basis of filling in a form with the Waste Lands Board, and paying a trifling sum of farthings each month. No common agricultural policy to intercede or dissuade his profit motives. Butler parted with but one pound per 1,000 acres for the first two years, halfpenny an acre for the subsequent two. He was one of many transplanted Englishmen to the Canterbury Plains. In his case, following a disagreement with his father, it was either sheep farming in New Zealand, or plantation cotton culling in Liberia. Butler was determined to escape the shroud of patrimony back in England, to be adamantly a Romantic. To do so required surmounting certain legal hurdles. Every runholder, so called, had to stock his land within six months, keeping at least one sheep to every 20 acres; 100 Scottish Highlanders, or Red Angus, a Jersey or Hereford breed perhaps, to every 120 acres. By the time Butler had come to the region, there were over a quarter million sheep on the mountained flatlands of Canterbury and Otago. A good shearer, it was said, could do 350 in a day.

Staring out at Mt Harper and the Ben McLeod Range, Butler had built himself a hut of sod—Marigold knew these details well—and spent the coming years exploring his surroundings of jagged cliff and rugged gorge. He expended his considerable energies up the Hurunui, the Waimakariri, the Rakaia and the Rangitata. Distant glaciers and a miasma of braided riverbeds, collapsing side canyons and mysterious interiors; Mt Alma, Two Thumb Range and the Bush Stream valleys. Above it all, far off toward the West Coast, over horizons of snow, Spaniard spear grass and tussock, the "massy parallelogram" in a "cloudless sky" of Mt Cook itself. Here was the embodiment of Ruskin's *Seven Lamps of Architecture*, which Butler had devoured back in England whilst chewing spears of well-cooked white asparagus in season.

It was this far-off West which most incited him, and would continue to do so back in Europe, where he made an odd prose translation of the *Odyssey*, rediscovered the Northern Italian Gaudenzio Ferrari's remarkable *Madonna of the Orange Tree* at S Cristoforo, Vercelli, and the same painter's staggering *Cupola of S Maria dei Miracoli* in Saronno, laid down between 1534 and 1537. The Englishman championed photographs that were peerless in their day for singling out the disenfranchised—a blind fiddler, a boxed horse, a lame boy and old beggar. His *Old Priest* (1894) is as close to a Rembrandt as photography has ever come. And his nuns on a steamer, numerous sleeping people, and utterly inexplicable image of 12 sleeping pigs on the grass in Varallo, taken 24 years after his return from New Zealand, all reveal a man who had been somewhere for the first time in human history—though Marigold would have a hard time convincing his Squire of these suppositions. But Butler had known—the Commander paraphrased his writings—that some enormous range, snowy, descending at a near perpendicular angle into the vast ocean to the west, spewed forth thickening masses of timber, verified by few in years past, and that he— referring to Butler—had next to no faith in the enterprise, daunted by the rumors, but willing to test them.

"We will succeed in his shoes," Marigold exclaimed.

Butler's boots, spare buttons, matches and other supplies, gathered in Christchurch where he would later institute the first art exhibitions, had amounted to roughly 3,000 pounds in weight, by his own estimate. All the basics like tea and sugar and flour, oats and potatoes, utensils for the kitchen and garden, were drawn the 120 miles to his Mesopotamian V hut by six obstinate bullocks who staged their eventual mutiny in the middle of a river. It did not matter one jot whether he was nice to them, or unpleasant. They had very good reasoning to support their sit-down strikes, and no Englishman could change their minds. Eventually, as history proves, the poet/explorer reached his archeological homestead and subsequently launched towards his Upper Base of Operations.

"Camping out," wrote Butler in his *Forest Creek Manuscript*, "should be commenced if possible one hour before full dark—twilight is very short here."

"You can't possibly suppose that Erewhon was anything other than a fancy, a sort of hybridized William Jones in Asia, and Baudelaire in the Mauritius," Sannazaro objected, as it became clear that his companion truly intended an expedition that would amount to uphill drudgery, a species of constitutional for which Sannazaro (who could kneel for hours without wincing, no work involved) was otherwise unformed, with no inclination whatsoever to alter his body type or inhabit Everest. His habits were as ingrown as the Queen's nails.

"As a matter of fact, there was much truth to it. Goya's picture of a balloon soaring above the mountains, which Butler surely studied; the explorer's own later sketches of such sacred and vertiginous churches as those at Locarno and Varese reignite his New Zealand idyll and invest it with an unassailable realism. He walked to a hidden valley; he found a gigantic mystery. Scraped, pulsed and sweated against new dalmation granites. It was a tribe, and a bird, he hunted down. I know it in my gut. He found the path over a certain range where no white man had ever gone."

"Why don't we just leave it that way and call it a day?"

But Marigold would not listen to such wimpy retorts and subsequent weak chatter. He had already fathomed his route and rationale. Nothing could dissuade him.

Besides, the stakes had risen dramatically. By the time Commander and Squire had concluded their own peculiar preparations, a provocateur, a multi-millionaire bully named Spitzbergen, along with his macho medley of lackeys, were already underway on a rival expedition. The Norwegian team had come in quietly one late afternoon, ordered two dozen large pizzas and as many bottles of local beer from Toscano's, chartered a 125-foot cruising boat equipped with fancy satellite gear (which they surely added to), and disappeared across Lake Manapouri on their way into Doubtful, Dusky and Chalky Sounds. For months they had strung along the people of Te Anau and Manapouri over the western ranges. What was to have been a major filming extravaganza, with an armada of helicopters, local contracts for the 100-person endeavor, jobs for everyone, had been winnowed down to a guerrilla movement of almost no fanfare. The Norwegians' entire modus operandi was one of stealth. Comprising a half dozen trackers and abetted by two choppers previously employed in the brutal netting of deer for relocation to deer farms, these commandos were approaching the operation as if it were a military siege that relied upon a surprise attack for its greatest impact and sinister goal. Meanwhile, the reduction in expedition size had quashed local labor prospects and whole Southland towns that had been waiting for their winning lottery number were plunged into moribund aspect, their monetary mirages dried up.

No other details of Spitzbergen's efforts were known. His itinerary and moa-mimicking methods were shrouded in competitive secrecy, for the stakes were unimaginably high.

So, too, had Marigold fixed one desperate thought in his mind: that a single moa might yet be holding out in the furtive impossibilities of terrain, those ever-eroding seclusions of Fiordland, its fate now verily hinging upon the reconnaissance of those helicopters and the avarice of Spitz, internationally celebrated for his daredevil publicity stunts. His credo was that of the circus, his motto all brio and greed, a philosophy— if it can be dignified as such—of plunder. If he were to find the moa, he would capture it alive, transport it back to Oslo, and turn it into an exhibition; or, if he should find merely a corpse, he would take sample tissue for cells and viable strands of DNA, as had been provocatively attempted with the last of a long-haired Spanish goat, affectionately named Celia, felled by a tree, and an Indian gaur, its cells shipped off to a laboratory in Iowa, the offspring named Noah.

Mr Marigold, on the other hand, had spiritual communion in mind, and the creation of a preserve within a preserve. It was his intention to find the moa, via Samuel Butler's own path (the novelist had evidently sighted one in these rugged cordillera, though wasted few words identifying its whereabouts— those were the days when at least one local feather-hunter bragged about killing in one gory go more than 2,000 kiwi, now endangered to the brink themselves), learn its language and hence glean details of its 80 million-year-old history; and then contrive some manner of *in situ* protection, even if it meant enshrining the specific portion of lands surrounding Fiordland National Park as a private preserve and genetic corridor.

The Commander's sympathies with flightless avians were something of a mystery to his Squire, who would not comment on the erratic nature of Mr Marigold's affections. But there was no mistaking the tenor of their present expedition, steeped in the mystique of the Pliocene; of Diatryma and Phorarhacos, elephant birds, the large Cnemiornis goose, adzebill, and the greatest of them all, the moa.

More recently, emu, cassowary, ostriches and rheas had survived the ridgeless breastbone bloodline. Even the dodo, for a time, took its rightful place in this lineage of heavy-muscled long-distance runners, birds that had renounced the joys of soaring for a more shadowy existence amid dense fern clusters, savannas and cave environments. But only the moa was strictly herbivorous—a worthy companion, thought Marigold, and one in the most urgent need of rescue, now that Hong Kong's chicken population had been lost and Spitz had arrived.

As a beacon for the twenty-first century no other creature of the spirit—atua, as the Maori called her— was quite up to the moa. *Dinornis giganteus, D. torosus, D. novae zealandiae, Pachyornis elephantopus, P. australis, Euryapteryx gravis, Megalapteryx didinus* and *Anomalopteryx didiformis*: different members of the moa family. Twelve species in all, prior to the arrival of the first Polynesians. *Dinornis giganteus* stood—with her neck extended— possibly nine feet tall and could weigh 660 pounds. The tiniest of the moa, *Megalapteryx didinus*, was probably the size of a large eagle.

"Whereas its nasty contemporary, the South American Andalgalornis, or giant terror bird, lived by fearsome predation and a lust for killing," Marigold said, "here the moa adopted a—shall I say—Gandhian approach which paid off handsomely. Whereas Andalgalornis died out three million years ago, the moa, I am certain, lives to this day. Its lifestyle and metaphysic prevail, even if the bird itself does not."

Sannazaro peeled the skin off his head over that one—the consideration of a bird living, or not, by a philosophy which had some purchase over its evolution. But he knew his companion well enough to forego the obvious objections and let pass untested the one-track ululation that was the Commander's

Western wont.

"Can you imagine a more romantic, noble and noteworthy life than that of the moa?" the Count of Paradise Percussions sounded.

"No, your grace," mild-mannered Sannazaro replied.

"Chestnut-purple face, pure white body, vintage wine-red double-feathered collar, chest and ankles; purple eyes, brave bones tawny and bright, pellucidity all about. Their necks were similar to those of the most graceful of African giraffes, oriented to the consumption of fern roots. Can there be a greater dietary exemplar in the history of biology than that? Ferns. Bambi comes to mind. Some have claimed dimwittedness on account of nib and spike no larger than apples. But that is an insult to the legacy of St Francis. Imagine a Red Delicious with convolutions akin to any human cerebellum—yours, for example; the strength of intellect, aesthetic resonance and spiritual achievements reflected in its sonorous passion plays—Bach's *St Matthew* performed on wings—deeply pulsing throughout those damp primeval forests which were its home. Even along the sea dunes where, beside southern spotted kiwi, and in caves not too dark, it built sun-oriented nests. Altitude presented no problem for the birds, as the excavation of moa bones from Mt Owen, near Murchison, at over 5,500 feet attests. Their remains are everywhere in New Zealand, I have read, and it is supposed that the advent over millions of years ago of highland fruits was the result of a dietary preference and, hence, seed diffusion, of the avian emperors of these few islands. Indeed, given their multitudinous wanderings across the country, there is no reason to doubt that New Zealand's peculiar floral arrangements are, by nature, the result of a working relationship with the birds, who cultivated one enormous garden for themselves. Philosopher kings in the tradition of Pangloss. You, Iacobo, can surely appreciate that."

The Commander went on, discoursing on the sex life of moa atop specific ridges where an abundance of gizzard stones had been unearthed. He waxed on the subject of moa dreaming, quite certain of the fundaments that so many millions of years of pacifism would surely have invoked in any creature of such upright eminence and grace.

While ornithologists presumed the last moa to have been consumed by a Maori hunter 500 years ago, there had from time to time been sightings, suggestive quasi-glimpses more suspect than sound, granted. Several encounters in the last 125 years, gathered and analyzed by author Barney Brewster in *Te Moa* (one of the works commended to Marigold by Dr Ling), came recommended on the basis of details and circumstances too numerous, too uncannily smacking of truth, to be summarily dismissed.

"Consider, for example, the young homesteading girl with her family in that remote valley just north of Milford Sound," the Commander began. "Alice McKenzie was her name, and Martins Bay was as wild a place as one could reach. As she reported in a Radio New Zealand interview nearly 80 years later—and in spite of scholarly objections to her vagueness of detail, and suspect re-characterizing of her story—she had, in fact, discovered a huge bird sunning itself on a sandy beach in the winter of 1880. She even stroked the bird's back, and the enormous animal took no care in that. When the girl returned with her father, he measured the bird's footprints and from the heel to the middle of the middle toe was an eleven-inch span. Nine years later, the 16-year-old Alice saw the same bird again. It could only have been the moa."

"Alice in Wonderland, you mean," Sannazaro said. "Anyway, that was a century ago." He, too, had read the Brewster book and interpreted its subtitle—*The life and death of New Zealand's unique bird*—to accord with the general opinion of scientists that there was no moa. That all sightings were, at best, clouded, misinterpreted, occasioned in darkness with faint flashlights or at a distance through dense bush, or, at worst, the product of honest fancies or deliberate hoaxes. "And for all that, I am presently in misery from the ill-effects of having crossed the international dateline," he went on. "What day is it? Shall we take breakfast or dinner? Should I sleep or complain? Are there grizzly bears in these woods?"

Mr Marigold was oblivious to his friend's plight. His mind was on the track of the moa, and he remonstrated with a vigor born of some ornithological acquaintance, as well as a sure enough grasp of paleontological probability theory.

He went on to cite three remarkable occurrences in recent years, the first in 1928 when a Danish prospector, Jules Berg, saw what he believed were three rather large moa on the east side of Lake Widgeon near the head of Preservation Inlet—"at the seaward end of the Long Burn, one of the most remote and seldom visited areas in Fiordland, a region long known for its inaccessible places," writes Brewster, who further quotes wildlife scientist Rhys Buckingham: "If the moa could have survived anywhere, it would have been in a valley like the Long Burn, with its extensive, impenetrable swamp forests."

The year 1940 brought about the second celebrated sighting by one Miss L.E. Chell who, in company with her driver, allegedly discovered a moa in the vicinity of the Buller River, near Murchison. The bird was digging at a stump near the side of the road. Said Ms Chell, "The eyes, exceedingly large, resembled those of a horse, but completely round, dreadfully afraid and liquidly beautiful to look at. Around the eyes, the feathers were like long eyelashes..."

"No poet could have invented so precise, so lamentable a verisimilitude," Mr Marigold bespoke, on Ms Chell's behalf. "What's more, on a January night in 1963 a scientist on a research trip near Boulder Lake, not so very far from the town of Nelson, on a very steep track of *dracophyllum*, heard an avian screech the likes of which had never before plumbed the nocturnal air—a call so loud and desperate for attention, vocally plying the last of heaven for a mate that was no more, as to incite a fever pitch of anticipation. He raced with a lit torch in the direction of the noise and, aiming the beam, saw rightly an enormous bird "about a yard long and a yard high..." Another investigator later followed the scientist's itinerary. Brewster reports that "the man did not doubt the veracity of the scientist's explanation, that the creature must have been a moa (small variety)."

While it was true that fishermen, trampers, hunters and flyers had coursed most of Fiordland, as the National Park was called, it was equally true there remained vast tracts of land yet unaccessed. Aerial reconnaissance had no means of penetrating beneath the dense forests.

Thousands of hectares—luxuriant swamplands and granite escarpment, sinking bog, brant and scrape, pillowy mist and treacherous steep—were left to the imagination.

A totem pole of nostalgic embrace, ague moistening his exclamations, the Commander carried on: "They lived, easily, 40 years, and by comparative analysis with the parrots, I must conclude that it would not be unlikely to find a centenarian moa about. If, as their numerous nesting sites suggest, the moa preferred deep rocky enclaves where the young would be assured of avoiding the scrutiny of predatory eagles above and native hunters below, then all the more reasonable this recent history of elusiveness. Their hideouts were deliberate. The last frantic haunts of tormented beings. They were, but for their final wits, defenseless against the Maori and early pakeha settlers who must have slaughtered the last ones without having the slightest clue of what was happening. No larger picture in mind of what had occurred. And when the last of them vanished, there was no funereal conscience, no candles lit or recriminations. Bones piled along the sides of farmsteads. Jewelry crafted, feathers traded, and the myth began. The myth of the largest bird that had ever graced the planet. Consider the ancient site at Ohawe, along the South Taranaki coast—I have the map: there, see for yourself how the moa were discarded by the dozen simply for a taste of their calf muscles. These atrocities must be atoned for. And if, god willing, a single, lone survivor is to be found, he or she must rightfully rule as a Prince Among Human Thieves in this woeful world of ours, and be dutifully knighted."

Replied Sannazaro, "By all these verbal ejecta"—said avalanche quite overpowering already his famished sides—"I sadly gather you are up to self-mutilation in the jungle outbacks and, moreover, expect Yours Truly to grovel beside you?"

"Think of it, Señor, as your duty to this wretched world."

"My duties were executed and finished more than half a century ago, friend. Since that time, I warn you, my only duty has been to leisure time and my appetite. There is no such thing as duty to bullies, obligations to madmen, a burden to act, or responsibility to become someone other than yourself. "

"Your modesty does not flatter you. I think of you simply as a closed flower, waiting to blossom. And when it does, the purity of its scent will surprise you."

Marigold and his aide-de-camp were near vertically scrambling, or so it seemed to the heaving Italian, who found himself constantly whacked by branches the Commander had pushed aside. As he peered through the undergrowth that surrounded him, Sannazaro saw only a profusion of lizards and glow-worms populating the mud caves, and a severe world where nothing could be counted on; each step breaking away, the stability, barriers, and fortress-like thinking appropriate to the horizontal world, utterly upended and on trial. He was out of breath, while his craving companion honed in upon their singular mission, where free-for-all flight and prolix confusion had previously usurped the ages.

"Let us tramp delicately through the night," Marigold said, "and in stealth by day, giving all the ideas away, making sure they're stolen and put into place. Let every thief and plagiarist, moreover, take credit for the conservation, go ahead and claim the fame, such as it may be. Just let the acts be done. We need universal kleptomaniacs, break-ins at every level. Let all practical concepts be purloined, every formula philandered."

"You are burning up my provost, venting my vanguard, destroying my mental dominions," Sannazaro pleaded.

"I merely make the point that this summital travail has about it the sense of opera in motion: the simultaneity worthy of the name, that such ideas as a bird hanging on be buttressed as the last hope; an audience freely given to the performance, so that all might enjoy, take stock, ruminate and feel... feel the same endangerment... take full responsibility for the drama, insert themselves and their children and their children's children into the outcome, master the denouement, own up to the libretto. I call it experimental biology: that physical point whereby science turns to compassion."

"And we are the guinea pigs, I gather, in homage to this bird of yours?"

"Precisely. Now you've staked your rightful linguistic, it is method I speak of. Rationality inserted into a spiritual samovar. Though I warn you, it will be no summer's repast."

Few are they to withstand such picnickery, or constituted of a necessary stamina to feel such pain for so long ago. To actively lament the passing of a previous century, or harbor mental anguish where none need exist. Without protocol to dive unsheltered into the fray of unexamined causes and consequences with nothing more than a damp candle wick of hope guiding them. Yet, that was precisely Mr Marigold's unquenchable penchant. Neither verbs nor adverbs can quite catch the nuances of his indefatigability. Ill advised is he who would risk characterizing such emphatic behavior. Sannazaro's efforts to calm the Marigold were fruitless. Far less energy, though certainly not less risk, was expended in quietly succumbing to those eternal enthusiasms.

Thus it was that the twosome headed over and beyond Mesopotamia, in line with the coordinates of Samuel Butler's own madcap romp 140 years before, clambering beyond each successive ridge, where eventually, as the author had put it, he "felt a foreshadowing as though my attention were arrested by something more than the dream ... a succession of rugged precipices", where "grass there was none" and "each moment I felt increasing upon me that dreadful doubt as to my own identity—as to the continuity of my past and present existence—which is the first sign of that distraction which comes on those who have lost themselves in the bush ... and I felt that my power of collecting myself was beginning to be impaired."

For two days they bushwhacked in a southwesterly direction, duly hampered, philosophy held hostage, camping under the cold stars, filling up the forests with complaints alternating with exaltations.

Suddenly, after 60 hours of humiliating misery, scrambling on all fours through the underbrush, Sannazaro heard the unmistakable sound of an automobile. On further investigation, they staggered out onto the road that descended, just miles away, toward the eastern shores of Lake Manapouri. It was not quite six in the morning.

Before them was a coffee house, whose attendant was just beginning her day, collecting dead sandflies in a cup. Fearing the truth, Sannazaro nevertheless mounted the courage to inquire, "Is there no road directly from Christchurch to the lake?"

"'Course there is," she replied. "The scenic route, a few hours by car—good paved highway and excellent pit-stops all along the way. Just stay to the left. We always have to remind the tourists. Been some real crack-ups."

"I know never to trust you again," Sannazaro told Marigold, smoldering.

They sat silently over coffee, Sannazaro deeply stewing. A TV set at the rear of the café relayed a strange report from what might be described as the front trenches of New Zealand's predator wars. Possums, three species of rat, mice, ferrets, weasels and cats, in particular. This was all news to the duo. The "Special Report" brought with it the grisly particulars, all proclaimed with a vindictiveness that to the Commander's ears, seemed impossible to comprehend. A country's benumbed embrace of wholesale mammalian slaughter? The numbers—tens of millions of dead—were staggering.

"Do you believe them?" Sannazaro mused aloud. "It sounds like a snow job."

Marigold did not have the answers, not yet. He loved possums, fed them organic pizza, but did not doubt the tragedy their species had unleashed upon native plants in New Zealand, which had never developed bitter-tasting chemicals to ward them off, as in Australia. It was estimated that within ten years most of the country's forests, as well as the lower canopies and undergrowth where white-tailed and red deer added insult to injury by the omnivorous browsing, would be gone. Which spelled disaster for so many of the birds and insects, as well. Possums were often described as cute, wide-eyed chainsaws. The Commander could not deal with it.

"Let's get out of here," he said.

With a modicum of supplies, they were transported across the enormous body of lakewater by a local boat-owner who'd prepared a fine tea and smoked a large cigar to keep herself warm. There was little conversation during the one-hour journey, as above them rose an ozone-thin sun and with it a merciless swarm of sandflies.

From there, a vehicle took them past a power station, over the pass, and down to the put-in spot of Doubtful Sound. Two large sea-going kayaks awaited them.

Any bird knew that Fiordland was not for sissies. But to witness two grown men gesticulating traumatically in their long underwear, swatting at the impossible hordes of swarming insects which feasted on them in unfair quantitudes, protesting destiny with every known four-letter word, gave little reassurance that they had one chance in millions of ever succeeding over the 20 paces to their boats at cold-water's edge, let alone staging a proper put-in. And as far as attaining that rarified quadrant of unknowns heretofore reserved for spirits, the two bravos would first need to figure out how to get along with one another: a doubtful proposition, at best.

CHAPTER 53
Tracking the Final Moa of the Millennium

"WHERE WAS ALL your world-loving philosophy back there?" Señor Squire ridiculed his fuming companion, noting the sudden proliferation of swatting behavior, the two of them having managed only barely to escape the blood-sucking hordes of female Simuliidae. The venal mobs, newly emerged from their submerged cocoons where they had lain glued to various rocks and vegetation, gave fitting and fanatical justice to claims that they were the scourge that had inhibited most permanent Maori cohabitation in these fiords. A blessing, possibly, for those last remaining species everywhere else extinct across New Zealand. "Sandfly" or "black fly" scarcely calibrated for the silent greed, sinister stealth and capillary-crazed dexterity of these airborne cannibalisms.

Now, in fast-flowing open Fiordland water, the two naval officers commandeered their sturdy kayaks like anything but long-time operants. Indeed, their graduated hysterias—oars, voices, heads and arms flailing spastically towards any and all direction—suggested a rapid series of coming catastrophes. The ghost, rendered ridiculous, of Lord Nelson and his ilk. And in water so cold, they would be protected, at least, by their hastily stuffed 11mm wetsuits, when and if their boats overturned. But the very thickness of those black body coverlets now produced a sweat intolerable to either gentleman, given an ambient air temperature exceeding 20 degrees Centigrade. Between the unprofessional frenzy of their canoeing, the build-up of internal body heat, the trail of sandflies and the unexpected difficulty of maintaining balance—a sensation not unakin to panic—both men sensed a premature doom, though Mr Marigold outwardly made light of it. He was secure in his dumb confidence. Reduced from dualities of one kind or other (the sum effect resembling a new form of inorganic madness) to the greatest *idée fixe* in recent annals—an obsession as large as a masthead, the goal of all homing pigeons, salmon, braces of pheasants, a bird's roost covered in guano, some football field of concentration—his ball of a psyche kicked hither and flounced.

"I blame you entirely for this disaster. This time my gullibility has gone too far!" Sannazaro spluttered, befuddled, though so perplexed and pathetic a voice was muted by the enormity of the deep water through which they endeavored like fools to paddle. The fiord itself, one mile across, was invested by 5,000-foot canyon walls cloaked in tropical vegetation, or bared by land slips exposing adamantine rock surfaces polished to the color and consistency of jade by 800 inches of annual rainfall and a multiplicity of downrushing mineral-laden cascades. The winds were picking up, a blessing on the one hand, as such breezes annoyed and stymied the gymnastics of the sandflies, demotivating their bloodsucking. But the winds were also diagonaling at cross-purposes to both oarsmen.

"It's useless shouting! I can't hear you!" Mr Marigold hollered in return. He was casting his infirm musculature about, and throwing his arms around somewhere vaguely in the lead, the frightening currents of the 2500-foot deep sound in every sense controlling his lean, unduly burdened vessel.

A thousand times Sannazaro cursed his bad luck for having ever met Mr Marigold, and 900 times the Commander smiled blissfully back at his companion, never once acknowledging the perilous clutches to which they had, by sheer stupidity, entrusted themselves. One might be prompted to dote upon the purple physiognomies of this unravelling pair, but let posterity note that nothing of any additional value would be gained by it.

As unseemly as their ill-tempered responses and spastic shenanigans might appear to the naked eye, one point should always stand out, far above the battlemented crests of their ludicrosity: this was a real survival epic.

The winds were getting angry and a sea change was aboard, the hazards making for tremendous work in maneuvering the boats up-current, although not denting at least one of their paddlers' stubborn confidence.

"What, ho? Mermaids?" the Commander hailed, as his kayak angled by its own intentions towards an island in the center of the fiord.

Soon, both men arrived amid the clashing rocks of the shoreline. Surf and columnar barnacles, sea slugs and cucumbers, red and jewel anemones, sponges, brittle, cushioned and sand starfish, black twisting snails, carnivorous date mussels and piddock molluscs populated the tide pools. Colorful limpets, tubeworms with furry tentacles, Neptune's Necklace, chitons and isopods, sea mice and prawns, spectacled triplefin, bull and bladder kelps, even the odd pregnant male sea horse glowing gold were swept up in the crashing waves that tormented the tree-lined shore. To the two explorers, it was all a gelid blur.

"Where are your mermaids?" Sannazaro cried out, trying inexpertly to keep from being dashed against the sharp, boulder-sized rocks.

"There!" the Commander reared.

Along a suspect trail, parallel to the sea, three upright prancers waddled towards the men, expectant and, seemingly, interested: *Eudyptes pachyrhynchus*, more commonly known as Fiordland crested penguins, distinguished by a striking gold streak bifurcating their head and leading cleanly to the beak. The three wandered as close as prudence permitted, stared at the two newcomers, remarked in a language foreign, then dived into the water, swimming deep and out of view.

"Penguinos!" Sannazaro exclaimed. "Incredible! It is cold, yes. Yet the forests appear tropical. Am I confused? My geography is failing me. My head is light—no, it is heavy. God help us! Surely we are dreaming, or will be killed, and if the latter, pray to the Lord that it be swift and merciful."

He murmured airs of the *23rd Psalm*: "The Lord Is My Shepherd ..."

Both kayaks were now sidelong and threatened to topple. The waves were rising against their bows. All around them, banded dotterels and tomtits hurried to and fro on various errands.

"Will you stop your bumbling! Just watch what you're doing. That should not be too much to ask," the Commander appealed.

"I need to rest," Sannazaro insisted. "Let's stash the boats, and take some fruit and chocolates into the forest, out of the wind."

"A fine plan. Agreed."

They were able to protect the boats in a rocky cove and avoid (to their knowledge) intruding on any penguin areas. They found a magnificent promontory, then threw themselves down. In the cold wind, the sandflies had now taken total leave. The men's body temperatures stabilized in the wetsuits. They took off their rubber gloves, though left on the 11mm socks.

As Sannazaro devoured a Mars bar and tangerine, Mr Marigold took up more important navigational inquiries by way of his (admittedly antique) spyglass. For, in addition to his many other predilections, astronomy had always been his calling, though he never could distinguish one planet from another.

"What do you see? Where can we possibly be heading?" a now less agitated Sannazaro inquired.

"Wait—"

Marigold was studying the coastline and required absolute motionlessness.

"Let me use your shoulder," he said. "Sit perfectly still. Stop chewing."

"I can't sit still."

"Don't talk! Hold the tree. Don't even breathe for a while."

In this manner Marigold fixed on the causeway of fiordland tributaries and side canyons heading due north, up which he intended to progress. Inlets formed a maze of little-known backwaters, Cézanne islands, Matisse mangers of infested tropic, micro-archipelagos and bewildering alpines, all spanning the northern half of the national park, between Doubtful Sound and Martins Bay. Only one fiord, Milford, just south of Martins, attracted a significant burden of tourists. Nonetheless, so remote were these parts that adjacent to Milford, beneath Mitre Peak, the rare kakapo, the largest parrot in the world, had—years prior to its forced relocation—managed to elude extinction. Marigold studied a detailed map and fixed their course into a nameless middle turf lost within the fringes of other topographic frenzies. It would require technical scrambling of a sort neither gentleman had contemplated. Nor were they trained, equipped or in anything like sufficient physical condition to undertake such a journey. But since neither appreciated the odds against them, their ignorance held the day, and with a roaring enthusiasm the Commander embarked into his kayak, his Squire grudgingly behind. No other choice.

The water was a whipped froth of truly treacherous proportions but the winds had changed course and now pummeled the two adventurers in the direction of the Commander's anointed nightspot. Their journey was marked by the sudden emergence of marine mammals: Hooker's sea lions lounging on distant crags, and a large pod of bottlenose dolphins porpoising all around them. Newborns were among the frolickers, who numbered in the dozens, tracking the kayakers, swimming under their boats in deep diagonals and leading the way towards some known habitat suitable, our gentlemen hoped, for primates such as themselves.

Not once, in hours upon hours, did either kayak topple over—a fact which testifies to the fickleness of good luck, for it had nothing to do with exhibited skill. It may be that the number of contradictory movements applied by each skipper neutralized their ill-effects and miraculously balanced otherwise berserk boating techniques. By whatever means the addled arithmetic, early evening saw the two exhausted captains making for a beach that jutted out at the mouth of an indefinable canyon. There were sandflies in plenty, but the men had total body cover now, as well as netting over their faces. They dragged their kayaks ashore.

"I calculate we have covered 20 miles this day," Marigold elucidated.

"And I feel every inch of it," bemoaned the singularly miserable Italian.

"Let us work on restoring some sense of calm. A no-nonsense demeanor is just what's needed, for I have a hunch this is only the beginning.

And I did not plan for heroism in a vacuum."

They set up camp, erecting a North Face domed tent, firing up a Bluet stove, cooking dried potato-leek soup, munching on carrots, and plastering slices of sour dough with mustard and goat cheese, tomatoes and scallions. In addition, they nibbled on tofu provender. It had been many days since Sannazaro had displayed his affection for fish and meat, knowing the vehemence with which his Commander discouraged such blatant indulgences.

It was later on, and darkness had fallen at last: "What was that?" Sannazaro said. "Like a dinga-ding-ding?"

"I heard more of the ping than ding," Marigold applied.

"Wait!" Sannazaro's senses were keen. "That's some other sound."

Confusion reigned. Both men put their ears to the breeze. During subsequent seconds, there was a frightful groan—a kind of subdued screech—that repeated itself.

"Low down, east off," Marigold averred, pointing to the direction. The moon had dissipated, as it were, and the firmament was all aclutter with constellations and wafting cloud. With a flashlight Marigold examined the peripheries of the camp. There was nothing to be seen. Sannazaro, exhausted by the day's exertions and the after-effects of his meal, opted for bed, and fell immediately asleep. Marigold remained wide awake. The occasional screech was enough to keep him enthralled, but by midnight he was able to fix the beam of that light on the source of the noise: "Lo! Flightless bird four degrees South! While Sannazaro slept, 50 yards away, the Commander got down on all fours and crawled right up to *Apteryx haastii*, or roa, as the Maori called it: the great spotted kiwi, family name Apterygidae. It must have weighed eight pounds, Marigold determined, and seemed poor of eyesight but rich in olfactory capabilities. The Hermit of Tesuque could just make out the feline-like whiskers abase its long tawny beak as it sniffed the ground and quietly strode about feeding on the cornucopia of the earth: a feast of woodlice and waking slugs, of millipedes and crickets, ants and cicada nymphs. Everywhere about were the sleeping pupae of moon-infected moths, the chaos of shrubs and beetles. It was a female, this much the Commander understood, because not 20 feet away he discovered a second kiwi sitting on three eggs, and knew from his readings that this had to be the male who would plump down thus atop its clutch for up to 145 days.

Mr Marigold returned unnoticed to his sleeping bag inside the tent, ensuring that no disturbance would be conveyed to the birds. He was exuberant with the auspicious encounter, as well he should have been.

The morning shone variously bright. Seven or eight seasons poured through the camp before they'd even taken tea, and this tended to become a pattern of meteorological tumult—wind, snow, hail, rain, heat, calm, mist, fog, autumn lights, spring showers, ephemeral white-out, followed by perfectly mellow summertime as gloriously spread as rape flower. The uncanny dynamics had all the invigoration of a car wash.

For now, the men had no further need of their kayaks, and presently secreted them amid the dense forest cover: dark gray-born rimu, with olive-green leaves; the grayish-brown totara sporting yellowish catkins and oblong nuts; luscious southern rata glens fully enlivened by their crimson flowers and dark green leaves; there were miro and kowhai, the brilliant brown mountain cedar, clustering in pyramids 75 feet high; purple and red kotukutuku, or tree fuchsia, distinguished by edible berries.

"Taste it," the Commander suggested, plucking two of the alluring fruits.

With their large backpacks fitted for movement, and all supplies accounted for—their tent and sleeping bags, foodstuffs and rope, pickaxes, spare habiliments, medicaments and a radio telephone—they ventured off along what appeared to be an old foot-wide pathway into the dripping rain forest.

The luxuriant thickness of the lower canopy masked the men's purpose, and obscured their direction almost at once. Kahikatea rose 150 feet into the sky above the perdurable twilight that now confronted the adventurers. Carpets of spider orchids, berries and bushes of rice grass, thick in eternal damp, flooded their boots, making each step a tentative and unpleasant search for solidity. Dead matter and decomposing life transformed the entire canyon into one vast biochemical laboratory. Such human peregrinations *ad terram sanctum* were irreverent, meant the inadvertent upturning of fungi, billions of bacteria, flocks of caterpillars and vast hordes of insects. The men clung to the climbing vines, the labyrinth of epiphytes, as they crashed through hidden holes in the rotted-out floor. Everywhere astelias, mistletoe and collospermums caught water in their leafy rosettes, while 100 types of clematis, supplejack and weeping lycopodium gathered force in large clumps, impenetrable nets and piercing foliage, which collectively conspired to impede movement. Lavender wineberry, black pittosporums, miro seeds and hook grasses provided food for unseen creatures—fantails, riflemen and kaka—whose wings fluttered in silence throughout the forest. Magnificent fungi, like the beech strawberry or navy-blue *Thaxterogaster porphyreum*, spread out in colorful array.

The effect of all this was not lost on Mr Marigold and Sannazaro who, after some struggle, sat down on a fallen log amid the industrious goings-on of several huhu beetles, the odd foraging wasp, teams of mites and stick insects, sapsuckers and scalers, and contemplated the miracle of their whereabouts. Both of them did. In a country that boasted nearly 18 million hectares of land given over for purposes of sheep, cattle, pig, goat, deer, horticulture and plantation farming, and just barely six million hectares to natural forest, these fiordland ecosystems with their nearly 88,000 different species (if one estimated most life forms, including their own microbial tag-alongs) were rarer than one might imagine whilst seated in their midst.

"I had no idea, from the water's edge," Mr Marigold gasped. "Why, it's simply indescribable."

"Yes, but impossible going. I repeat: I cannot last much longer. Hear my breath. I exaggerate not. How far do you hazard us to continue through this biological maze?" Sannazaro asked.

"A week's worth, I reckon."

"Oh my God. Where will we sleep? I can't go on."

"You must."

"I won't go on."

"Patience, peasant. We'll find outcrops. It is my belief that the last moa must have moved on high to avoid the aerial poisons and the deer trappers."

"What poisons?"

"The whole region was covered, I believe, with rat and possum pellets to eradicate them."

"Would that not kill the other animals?"

"There is, yes, some controversy about that. My researches show a miniscule non-target margin of error."

"And the water?"

"What I have read indicates little risk to ourselves."

"I'm tired and it's only been 15 minutes," Sannazaro bleated, returning to his main theme. "I'm also soaked to the bone and brim."

"Get used to it," Marigold chirped. "This is what constitutes the oldest thing in the world worth speaking of—namely, adventure."

"I have never seen you so roused, Commander," Sannazaro observed. "That's because I have never—and I'm sure I speak for both of us—been in so majestic a setting. It is without doubt what is meant by wilderness. You might favor an apartment in Delft, near the Old Church where lies buried a Vermeer and his mother-in-law, or a garret upon the Left Bank of Paris, in a constant plane of conviviality. A life spent musing over coffee with friends. But I will always prefer this alternative burial, neck-deep in eternity, to meandering even through Rome."

He fell silent a moment, musing upon a certain ancient Maori saying: "Whatu ngarongaro he tangata, toitu he whenua", meaning, Man perishes but the land remains.

Then he revived. "If this does not renew the blood, freshen the complexion, restore hope and reinvigorate every life force in the man, nothing can!" he declared, standing up abruptly, before tripping and falling flat upon his head in a mud dip of quicksand proportions, so that he was entirely engulfed by loving ferns and sucking goos of the holy earth.

"I will not venture a dispute on that point," Sannazaro conceded. "But I would hasten you to reconsider this expedition, based upon the evidence of our current situation—yours particularly."

"Help me out of here!" Marigold shrieked.

Age and exhaustion notwithstanding, Sannazaro effected an entirely heroic rescue operation, and felt himself entitled to a wry observation, totally à propos of everything: "I am not eager to die, to molder unseen amid worlds within worlds, my body the stuff of beetle food and wasp pickings."

"I suppose you imagine a burial in New Mexico to be more appealing? Prey to vultures and the occasional red wolf tearing your corpse to shreds just for the sport of it? But why, in any case, this gruesome prognosis when, in truth, we sit amidst paradise to the left, to the right, underfoot and overhead? Have you not grasped the purpose of our outing? Or read the auspicious signs of our progress? Was not my fateful encounter with the great flightless kiwi sign enough that my hunches are rooted not merely to the logic but to the very destiny of the last living moa? So calm yourself, friend; we will go easy, step by step, with natural resting places and a pacing that befits your elder's status. I want you, I need you to succeed with me. I cannot do this alone. So I shall follow your circulation and heart rate, embryonics and pulmonary physiology accordingly, and check on you from time to time. Be certain of that. We will not go so fast. I am naturally sensitive to your profound limitations."

"Such as?"

"Your age, of course. For though you are a handsome, clever, well-musculated figure of a man—" (Mr Marigold knew how vain his Squire could be and calculated this bit of flattery for purposes of cajolery. It would succeed)—"you are also of a venerable time in life that demands that certain impulses and old acrobatics be checked lest the blood flow revolt and an all-purpose embolism result."

"Enough of my diagnosis. Shall we move on?"

Sannazaro opined. "Certainly."

It was some hours later, after Marigold's cajoling praises of his partner's ruinous pace, horrific hallelujahs (read: early nineteenth-century English travelers out on their Grand Tour supplicating before the high Alps), and rigorous throat-catching tantrums in the back forest, that they attained higher ground, as the Commander had predicted.

Mr Marigold climbed *au cheval* along a rocky promontory some 200 feet above the lowest canopy, reaching a point of no return that provided both a vantage over the distant fiord from where they'd come and a direct view up the side canyon they were now poised to enter. His heart sank, slightly, for he had assumed that they would have entered the canyon long before. The tortured time through such impenetrable forest had not registered properly. Now he measured by compass for a precise reading, noted the position on his map which he kept secure in a plastic coverlet, and backed up their positioning with a GPS device tracking off three satellites far over Australasia, from inside a clearing.

"We are here." He showed Sannazaro. The map resolved to 1-in-5,000.

"Which means what, relative to our destination?"

"There." The Commander pointed to the hidden escarpment which he believed to be a Pleistocene island populated by at least one moa.

"Thirty-seven kilometers from here," Sannazaro computed. "Whether in miles or meters, it's all the same to me."

"Misery, you mean. Notice, we have come, in six hours, a mere 1,200 feet. I am bloody and ruined. My spirits dimmed, every last ounce of thinking capacity damped. My hunger enflamed, as much as my hypothermic feet. My hands are shaking—you see!—And, honestly, I think I am going to die."

"Then do it over there, not on our trail, please."

"Trail? *What* trail?"

With that, both men laughed and cried, or wept and chortled, groaned, grimaced and howled with sundry revelations.

And the howling was returned.

"...Hey!???" the Commander whispered, his tensed hand upon his Squire's lips, a sudden silence enforced between them. "Did you hear that?"

CHAPTER 54

How the Commander Penetrated the Veil of Eternity

BOTH MEN LISTENED intently.

"A helicopter?" Sannazaro's senses suggested.

"I think you've qualified it, all right. Spitzbergen. Damn him!"

"You don't suppose he's seen our kayaks and is following our progress?"

"By such shade diffuse, the umbrage sequesters. How could they see us, why would they try?" Oh my, the complications, his head spumed. The chopper circled twice, then flew a distance from the two men's plateau of inextricability, finally veering to the left, which was southward.

"He's heading towards Preservation Inlet." Marigold showed Sannazaro the position on the map. "But he'll be 100 miles off, " he calculated. "They have nothing to fear." He was referring, of course, to the moa, whose vacancy his own imaginings would never concede.

"I say we leave this madness at once. I have been saying so all along, and you are my terrible stubborn foolhardy witness. Your teeth might be whitened, your lenses corrected, an arch strengthened, a mole removed. But no such meddling will help these mythic beasts of yours. With our human eyes, others, invariably, would follow. If, as you say, this Norwegian creep has staked his beeline on an incorrect vector, I say hoop-jug, leave it be, whatever's out there can rest in peace."

But Marigold, as should be well known, was no mere recess of reveries. His legs had mercenary genes, the toes were unusually altruistic. His thigh bones, such as they were, wickedly stubborn. Every joint creaked with the effort, but the effort was no less the worst for all the noise. Entangled in 50 different vines, each of which excited more of the Crusoe in his behavior, this throwback to those ages of devotion that demanded imprudence in the face of death now exclaimed, "That is premature giddiness, Señor. Surely you realize that the near extinction of this mighty bird is the result of tens of thousands of Spitzbergens who, over millennia, saw to it that not a single one remained. It is our duty to mark well our word and send a message of supreme conservation to those who would too easily write off the world's most peaceful modern denizen. Look around you. There has never been, or shall ever be again, a more primeval, perfect territory for the planet's largest avian. This heaven of ferns belongs to her."

"It is a national park. Hunting is prohibited, need you be reminded?"

"I understand. But I also know that this is a nation, like all other nations, of humans, not of laws. Without constant vigilance, the coordinated secrecy of best-laid rubrics and compulsions, there is chaos. No moa is an island."

And so, with a burst of near-comic certitudes, figureheads of animation, they made forward a pledge to find out that bird and ensure her absolute protection. The motives hinged upon the Commander's deep despair at being a human, at being himself—a man whose ambiguous nature outweighed any stature. Whatever remote faith he might have harbored in even his own sanity, he countered with impulses which were, themselves, ambassadors of all those other surges of volition he mistrusted. He was, in other words, an emissary of his own species, with its breakdowns and schizophrenias, fully aware of the double jeopardy his dreams and behavior posed for the world. He flew in airplanes, yet he condemned all such behemoths of consumption. He used kerosene, but despised everything about it. He chewed his food, while detesting the sharpness of his own teeth. Nothing suited him save for these very wilds, where no testing or trying or futile improving by human nature had been essayed. A world without cities and towns, buildings and gatherings. No suit of chainmail, no sweater of mohair. Not a tennis shoe or dime. Nothing to suggest a synthetic chemical or four-legged chair, a volleyball or chocolate chip. Not one scrap of paper on the entire earth. No garage, no motorcycle, no billboard, suited worker, polyurethane duct, high-tension wire, politic, tax collector, tarmac, garret, borrower or lender, cement truck, ruler, basement or museum. He would throw it all out and start over. Naked eyes peering out across the fruited plains.

Knowing how such musings were doomed, in a practical sense, Marigold had conciliated, giving in to a certain universal compromise. Initially his vision had been easily coined in the City Beneath the Hill, and to that end he'd gone searching after Mr Butler's own variant of it. With its Regency-steeped pediments of marble, Doric entablatures, enfilades of ordered grandeur, all coated in wilderness. Marigold's vision was deeply coffered in acanthus foliage, palmette-and-anthemion bas-reliefs; an ideal smoothed down by linseed, blooming above treetops; music rooms motifed in all the outfittings and echoes of St Thomas's Church in Leipzig, or R. W. Emerson's house. But these were not perfect embodiments of an ideal. Rather, they grudgingly endorsed serial diminution. By so many calibers, inches, notches and layers he had built up, and torn away, the sheaves of an unwieldy rhubarb only to discover that there was no essence down under; that human civilization was built on empty air. No revision of settlement, no alternation of humankind would ever be entirely satisfactory. We were condemned. And Mr Marigold, who bothered to think about these things incessantly, doubly so.

Yet, why couldn't it be perfect?, he wondered. Why not the New Human Nature he had so insistently encapsulated in the crystalline verbiage of his personal academy? The Sorbonne of ecological purebreds?

"Here is the dilemma," he spelled out for his barely breathing companion. "We are what we are. But we have the power to change at any moment. I believe that."

"And New York? With its dark wintry canyonlands, homeless people, murders and noise, 100-story buildings of marmoreal steel, iron frames, vaults, and the appearance of an order that will never go away. Here to stay. Like it or not. How would you change New York?" Sannazaro mused, huffing and puffing to keep up.

"I don't know," the Commander somberly stated.

In the crepuscular dusk of the oppressive canopy, waning light found the two gentlemen fixing their bivouac along a rocky ledge not one mile from their previous night's campsite. The glacial topography, combined with exotic forests of pahautea and tanekaha, the riot of chlorophylls, looming sidewalls caught out in alpenglows of no earthly description, made mute whatever protestations would otherwise have arisen in the dumbfounded Squire. He might have been hideously uncomfortable but found the strength and motivation to sit up atop the ledge in his warm bag, munching on dinner, silent and grateful to be alive.

"Tomorrow will be an easier day," Mr Marigold forswore. Sannazaro said nothing.

"I know you're distressed, but you shouldn't be. You handled yourself deftly. Saved my life. By God, I thought I was in the presence of a veteran."

"That you are: a veteran ignoramus, to have been driven like a mule all these days. I assure you, Samuel Butler never journeyed so far."

"We don't know that."

"He lived to a ripe old age. Proof enough."

"Look up there. See you not the cliff rounding off where passage, presumably, should be simplified?"

Sannazaro cast a pained glance in the direction indicated, observing nothing so much as sheer wall and even denser jungle. "At least today's suicidal antics were on the ground. Now you're planning nothing less than acrobatics. Look up there, you ask. I am doing so now and claim authority by one word: Impossible."

"You're just being dramatic."

"I'm sure my plunging a mile to my death will appear as nothing less. A pathetic play on the absurdist stage of vertigo."

"Step by step. We will take it slowly. Inexorably. Plenty to cling to. Just like the epiphytes. There's a way in. Every heart has its aortas and ventricles."

"At least there are no sandflies."

"Well, there you have it. Alleviation. Presto. A good omen."

Mr Marigold had not the slightest doubt about his plans. He lay in his bag as if its every baffle and downfeather were some portion of the equation for supreme happiness. And he knew from experience that Sannazaro was all talk. He was strong and stubborn as the best of the Renaissance squires and would never quit an expedition so bizarre. Moreover, he'd never be so foolish as to attempt to return home alone. He was too familiar with some of the more celebrated precedents of doom, like those men who parted ways with John Wesley Powell part-way down the Colorado River in the mid-nineteenth century. The ones never heard from again. Of course, it's always possible they made it out of the Grand Canyon and headed west to California, settling down eventually, raising children beside an apple orchard and white picket fence. But it's more likely that one of 100 catastrophes befell those sorry journeymen before they reached the rim, be it north or south. The Commander had in his library the first illustrated edition of Powell's epic and had happened to share it with Sannazaro, so the analogy was fresh in his mind, and frighteningly analogous to the whims currently wafting through their campsite. After all, Marigold was not indifferent to the fact Sannazaro more or less qualified as an elderly person; his resumé hardly recommended him for this space walk among hazards little tried by man on planet Earth.

Yet, the Italian gardener was a true wit, of good faith, a Catholic in his stomach, a simpleton to the core, a sceptic to the heavens, a philosopher in the end, a sensualist before all else, a man of the turf, a nobleman of fine drink, a solid, thorough, premeditating essayist on short and active legs. All these lent him the requisite oxymorons by which to live a carefree existence, even in such chasms of unrelenting hell.

Marigold looked over at him. "You all right?"

"Get some sleep," the Squire suggested, basking in a moment's diffusion of angst.

At some later point during the night, there was a rumbling that grew in intensity, though remained distant. Sannazaro lay awake listening, while his master snored oblivious to all acoustical threats.

An avalanche, the Señor registered, before passing out from fatigue several minutes later.

In the morning, both men were surprised to read 9.30 on their watches when they awoke. Feeling splendidly rejuvenated, Mr Marigold, needing in the worst way to pee, leaped up out of his bag, only to plunge off the ledge towards certain death.

Fortunately for him, he smashed into a pool of submerged fungus, a mat the color of Monet's flamboyant water lilies that stretched 12 miles in every direction, and thus suffered only minimally from gouges and wounds. (He did not know that he had just made intimate contact with one of the largest life forms in the southern hemisphere.) His long underwear was spoiled, but he had a spare pair. And the gash on his right arm was preferable to any break, so he considered himself extremely lucky, given the speed of his descent.

"Are you all right?" Sannazaro shouted from above.

"Quite," the Commander replied, slightly comatose but otherwise grand.

Suddenly, the fungus started to move, and then a hole in some portion of its floor opened wide, and a frothy, gurgling stream of vocables nonsensical issued forthwith: "Blub blub blub," it seemed to Marigold, as if the whole nation of humus and duff were fertilizing the air with rude cadence.

Kneeling within earshot of the tangled web of ground, he listened again.

"Who are you?" the tendrils collectively asked.

"Huh? Excuse me? Did somebody say something?"

"A moa you are not," the fungus declared. "A new species?"

"My goodness, is that you speaking to me?" whispered the Commander, now on all fours and peering into the moist, microsmic whorls of fungal spore and thread-sized evergreen.

"'Tis I indeed," the voice, a monstrous puffball, replied.

"But—but who, how, from where, by what means, and ... and..." He was at a loss, having never spoken so directly with a plant, let alone a fungus, and one so large. Upon first scrutiny the Commander could see it combined the very best of organic matter, a sterling skyline of yeast, mammoth mildews, mesmerizing mold. In one fell creature, arms of amanita, legs of laetiporus, a gorgeous acre's-worth of ganoderma, a spasm here and there of sparassis. The pearly white purity of Agaricus, and the delightful resonance— emanating from the pit of its punctuated cap—of the morel family. From the looks and no-nonsense sound of it, a hitherto unknown relative of the famed *Pongchambinnibophilos Kakokreasopheros*, first described by a cat named Foss in a letter to the musicologist, Sir George Grove, and dated 1860. That species, along with *Multifunglia Upsidownia* and *Topsy Turvia*, had been discovered by the cat's manservant, Edward Lear, near the Oatlands Hotel, but little generic or specific information could be divined of the creature's peripheries, volumetrics or attitude. Such dearth of scientific knowledge greatly enthralled the Commander in his present circumstances. Foss, all paws, had seen fit to render the monster in pastel pinks, purples and golds, based upon Lear's observations—a sketch hastily composed, and of minimal value to the Commander, who had never seen it, as it was housed in the Archdiocese Rare Books Room at Mount Sinai. But he had heard of it, sure enough, including its delightful color scheme, and always assumed the Kakokreasopheros to correspond with his knowledge of other fungi—namely, of dainty little fudges with shaggy manes and cauliflower precepts, of edible sulfur shelves and golden chanterelle. Of King Boletus himself, whose sunny season, August through October, gave him—and all his admirers—a vision of the world that was sticky and green, spongy and clean.

"You are a—bird?" asked the fungus in a voice strangely reminiscent of the Dungeness crab endemic to Dundee.

"Reticence, shame, dictate distrust of myself, who is a man, *Homo sapiens*, ordinarily given to mischief but, in this instance, meaning no harm—of that you may be entirely assured," volunteered the Commander, leery of admitting too much.

"Ahh," the fungus puzzled reflectively. "I am not familiar with that."

"Umm, you are luckier for it, then," the Commander went on. "Why is that?" perplexed the velvety voice with its hexagonal eyes and striped bass-like contours.

"The short of it, as our philosopher Frederich Nietzsche once remarked: we are a sick species."

"Sickly how?" pressed the creature. "No spots visible, neither a stump nor blight. You seem well aerated. Is there more to a constitution?"

"Think of us as your common multiradiata but deprived of the flower, the bloom, the upper leaves. Left only with basal lobes that aspire to more than winter storm. We dream of spring showers and a time of ripeness that will never come, not for us."

"That's dreadful," reflected the monster. "You don't appear so bereft as all that?"

"Because I dream." And then—"Do you dream?"

"All the time," his new acquaintance avowed. "That is what we live to do, of course. It is the very circulation of all those fluids within, which (I should add) quaintly mirror the passing stars overhead. To languish in a hollow, spread out across a jungle fallow, ripening and siphoning, flabby without remorse, thoughtful without end, with neither contest nor aspiration to debunk the esteem in which the royal *we* holds itself, is a sanctity, a very paradise unlike any other in the forest. A fungus leads a charmed life, how else to put it. Reciprocity times electricosity divided by the complete negation of ferocity equals the exact opposite of monstrosity, for which—in the case of myself—there is, as you can see, no paucity, as we are approximately 33,000 cubic mushrooms in size."

"That's marvelous, but who is this royal *we*?"

"Well, while I am a single fungus, certainly (unmarried that is), I include my parents and their parents and their parents, going back several thousand fungal generations."

"When will you marry?"

"When I find the right appendage. It may take time, but I have plenty of it. Meanwhile I keep growing: no shortage of moss or basin damp to worry 'bout. Bogs and estuaries wild, sink holes galore, pit-stops teeming with bacterial buzz—in all there is a mold manifest, giving every turf to fungal possibility. This is what we love: the knowledge we have no enemies, no jealous rivals. Our friendly symbiosis is the very revolution that mud-sloshed terrain such as this has long touted. A fungus is a friend for life.

All the ferns say so. You see, the whole story of the forest is our story; the weather, this continent, everywhere you might call home. I may not have traveled to faraway places, such as Lake Manapouri or Liechtenstein, but have certainly tasted their rain clouds, supped upon every microbe that saw fit to pass this way, and imbibed the earth forces underneath, to the sides, and above. I could tell you stories ..."

"Please do," the Commander implored.

And the fungus launched into some of the strangest tales recorded in the annals of forest slang. News from the hybrid zone of an all-knowing Z-chromosomal vole ten million years ahead of the rest of mammalian evolution; of a certain tree, somewhere, rumored to stand as tall as Everest; of a jumping spider that had never landed on earth; of an aphid and its pet ants; of rain drops whose sub-atomic satire was simply "too hilarious for words", according to the fungus.

"How do different funguses recognize each other? You all look alike," the Commander ventured.

Which triggered a rigorous and somewhat defensive exposition on the part of the green monster, whose analysis of facial characteristics and fungal personality was no less articulate and wise than Leonardo's very own *Treatise on Painting*, an exquisitely versed lexicon on the ins-and-outs of being a true fungus, true to oneself, and on the nature of the soul, the Self, fungal eroticism and other sundry philosophical divagations.

They carried on in this manner for hour after hour, it seemed, until an avuncular, concerned-sounding voice from above went off like an alarm, and Marigold bid the enormous fungus farewell.

"Will we meet again?" inquired the sleepy-eyed giant.

"Of course we will," replied Marigold. "In fact, I shall send you letters from time to time."

Marigold had fallen off the far right side of the promontory and now struggled to find a way back up. It required a delicate spreadeagling maneuver between slimy-bark trees. Shimmying up a Nothofagus, or beech tree, as some prefer, that grew alongside the lichen-oozing wall of shale and magnetite, he relied on the clustered nests of mistletoe, scraping along past a host of harsh-leaved ferns and coprosmas. This was not especially easy-going terrain. Birds' nest fungus jutted out from the bark, and a giant Powelliphanta snail the size of the Commander's hand crawled over an erupting Lycoperdon fungal ball. All of these flukes of nature contributed to Mr Marigold's change of plans. He slid back down the tree, determined to injure no living being, and instead made a longer, more arduous land-based assault back up to the ledge.

Within 20 minutes he had returned, a sorry sight, but grinning head to toe from the proud non-violence of his methodology, and something more.

"And the day has not even begun," the shining Squire advised him with a tenor of irony.

Marigold expatiated on his Gandhian trekking techniques—a point of systematic scrambling, he said, and of minimizing one's impact on the surroundings; a ballet under milkwood, of movement with religious observance at every step. "Beware," he went on, "God is counting every penny."

"If that is true," replied the weary Squire, "all this talk, these sojourns to nowhere, are truly terrifying, or penny dreadful."

But Marigold was in little hurry to regain his full composure, content to idle in awe, full of shivery buffaloes and silver-stained memories, paralyzed by the sheer joy of making contact with the Before Now and After Hours, as if Lewis Carroll himself had been jettisoned in a rocket ship for the view of the stars, but right here at home, in the heart of the greenest woods. Nonplussed, Sannazaro was at a loss to know what to do. He kept close to the dreamer, himself a victim of every turn, of each wild animal noise (particularly the wood pigeons flying off from hidden branches, their wingspans asserting a considerable air-foil of cacophanies), of all the hidden minefields of the wilderness about which he had next to no clue. Truly a case of the blind embarrassing the blind, a panic rising somewhere between a howl and a moo.

A stoat raced hither, a chamois cried yon. Mice scampered promiscuously through the canopy; the ruby peering eyes of mustelids, brightening the night. Fresh rata flowers exuding mellifluosities to the four dark winds.

Compassing in a dark tunnel of wilderness, by their waning wits they managed almost entirely to disappear. Apprehensions unsuited to known vowels. Faculties lacking elbows. Tongues with no mouths.

They went the entire day. Only that following evening did Marigold inform Sannazaro of his remarkable encounter with the fungus. Time was playing tricks on them both. Urgencies were delayed. Tales spalled. In their blood, some span separated verb from direct object. This wilderness drug.

The Squire checked the bruise on the Commander's head, which was the emphatic blueblack abuse and abduction of Niccolo Abbate's Persephone, and informed him kindly that he would be better by morning, and not to worry, and that all such talk of chattering funguses would seem like nothing more than a reverie the size of a spore, a hazy meteorology, a theory of crescent moons, a nervous scatter of sandtraps and false roots with no approximation in the real world.

"But that's just it," the Commander appealed, rather desperate to hold on to the miracle. "He said that this was a dream. If you had only seen it down there, in that perfect caesura of worshipful green ooze, 10 million trickles of pure water, 100 billion diamond-bright nuances of light, a gentleness I cannot describe—you would surely understand. A living, breathing, speaking laboratory. And one of these days he will marry, and then the fungus will be twice as large."

Sannazaro looked at him with a mournful tolerance, for who else but the Commander of Picaresque would expect anybody to believe that a fungus had spoken of sweet matrimony? He decided, under the circumstances, that he should simply be tactful and polite about it. Said he, "I believe you."

But the Commander had not done with his rendition, chaffering, plying and huckstering the fungus ideology until gray in the face in the tradition of the great poets Lorenzo Portobello and Sylvester Shitaki. "I made intimate connection with a plant. A giant of compassion. I spoke on a first-name basis with an extraterrestrial. I penetrated the veil of all eternity, landed literally in a metaphysic, founded my own transcendental beanstalk, perceived the wizard of wizards, attained the carnival of creations, the millennium of heavens, sampled Eden unimpeded, understudied from all the ages at once, explored the last unction of unknowns—can you imagine, 33,000 cubic yards of mushroom in extant? In sum, I have acquired a radically novel appreciation for fungus and, by implication, for every root rot, vine mold, bacterium and athlete's foot. I now know without doubt that atoms and every molecule are capable of speech, intelligence, personality, attitude, sophistication, sensitivity and much, much more. And you downplay it? Surely, better than most mortals, an Italian gardener can appreciate my journey to Paradise? What the master, W. H. Auden himself, described when he wrote, 'And children swarmed to him like settlers: He became a land.' I was there, upon those very shores."

"I won't doubt you. No questions asked. Now go to sleep, I'm tired."

"If you're tired, *you* go to sleep. There, well defined, Auriga and Capella, shining brightly. Your cue."

In this manner, for the next four days and nights, the two gentlemen bantered, argued and persevered, Schnaken & Schnurren, struck constantly by rocks, taking many a roll, making lugubrious movement through the bean house of mountain misery. Falling forwards and backward into burrows, crashing through cave ceilings, thrashing through tussock over their heads, trapped and tangled in vines that would not let them pass, stalked persistently by wood ferns with ulterior motives, bored silly by dull purple bird's foot, tantalized by aromatic teases—two-lipped, irregular panicles and composite brats, elongating catkins that seemed to take especial pleasure in harassing the duo unmercifully. Pinated, ovated and needled. A dreadful odyssey of stigmas and spikelets, to put it mildly. Even pursued by an owl, a rat, and a kiwi.

Their quarrels had escalated in direct proportion to their bruises and out-of-body travails. Then, one day, Sannazaro became as quiet as a pot of clay. He was too tired to argue any more. And so they realigned their wildly divergent attitudes, and it was possible, somehow, to keep going as a singular team. Much like a lonely jar of horseradish.

By the fifth night, according to the Commander's reckoning, the twosome had traversed ten terrible miles, were approximately halfway to their destination, and had broken out in 40 rashes, collectively.

They were in view of both glacier and fiord, and this was the cause of their suddenly stopping at 4.15 in the afternoon of that fifth day and gazing out with wonder. For, in truth, Mr Marigold was confused, and the satellite positioning did little to reconcile his perplexity. Before them was what appeared by azimuth and other counterings to be a 7,000-foot wall of rock, off which a single stream flowed. That would make it the largest waterfall, by far, in this known world. As for the fiord, the cliff, those glaciers: the map did not indicate that they should be there at all.

"I am truly puzzled," Mr Marigold confessed.

"At last, a moment of modesty from Zorro. What, no flourish of the sword? No single boast to breach the ramparts?"

"Sorry. I just don't get it. Do you?"

Sannazaro perused the map, but had no incentive to make heads or tails of minute lines in parallel—troughs, declivities, dense clusters, a variety of cartographic shades indicating verticality, canopy, rock, glacier and water. These elements were admittedly alien to his reading of nature. He preferred direct contact, even if—as was often the case—it meant a terror as opposed to a reason.

"So, jolly wonderful. We're lost!" the muleteer rejoiced.

"Not lost, just—" and Marigold paused, considering their philosophical situation—"between worlds."

"Let us sleep here then, and fathom our predicament in the morning. Anyway, it is gorgeous, I'll grant you that."

They set up camp, it being an unusually large plateau, large enough to take a tent. The grass was soft and, though moist, no bog as they had slept in some previous nights.

Dinner was divine. They went all out on the preparations. Sleep came easily to both men, whose thighs, calves, ankles, stomachs, arms and legs smacked of fatal fatigue.

In the morning they set off early. They could both smell the change. "Alpines," bespoke Marigold.

Within an hour they were crossing a pass between forests, a weirdly untouched open space after all their days of bushwhacking. Again, there was no sign of humans, only endless fields, dense with edelweiss and ranunculus. To either side, snow leading over talus and rearing up against the rock walls, down which hanging glaciers gave every evidence of coming off. And the gentlest of all wekas, improbably at ease amid the steeps.

The day's sun was penetrating and both men knew their hours beneath such ice were numbered. They'd been hearing the rumbling avalanches for days, and now the truth of those natural phenomena was before them: muddied spillways of titanic effluvia, burst from the frozen compactness of centuries across the slopes on which they now trod.

"We must move quickly," Mr Marigold urged.

"Agreed," Sannazaro replied "And, for the first time in my life, I must say I have the motivation and the means to do so."

Up high there was a telltale thunder. Sannazaro caught it first, stopping instantly to gauge the extent of immediate danger.

Then they both glimpsed Armageddon rushing down in the form of thousands of tons of ice. The roar increased. The whole pass became shadowed, then a tunnel, with a squall of winds and blown snow flying everywhere. The Commander and Sannazaro ducked for cover, as running was out of the question.

It took forever and a minute to pass over them. Both men were screaming in the blind blizzard of snow winds that catapulted them like tumbleweeds. The sound of punches wracking packs, of twisted steel and horrible shrieking, of sulfurous, atom-smashing rocks all added to the terrible price of adventure which might have seen the end of their days had the avalanche not been of a superficial nature.

In fact, by Fiordland standards, it was not enormous, and the center was nearly a mile in front of them. They had received only the mildest of fringe effects, and it had done no damage to life or property. What they had heard, and how they had vociferated, was evidence enough of the power that inheres in the mountains, but it had gained no true purchase on their passage. Yet Marigold could not hold back an equal flood of memories which, for the first time, he presently shared with his Squire. The death of his father, the days trapped in the concrete outhouse, and the whole extravagant loss which he had suppressed during those many decades since Ecuador. Sannazaro was rooted to the facts, and the near-enough analogy. More appalling, as he considered their true whereabouts and the power that had lurked beyond, was the horizon line, ever inclining into 1,000-hectare ice fields up ahead. A time bomb awaited them, and every particular of Marigold's remarkable youthful tragedy added terror to Sannazaro's imaginings and present prospects.

Nonetheless, when they had righted themselves and dusted off the powdery aftermath, both men shared a shivered laugh, acknowledging their pertinacity and watching the final throes of distant white thunder that clouded a column of air 1,000 feet high for the next half-hour. Then they trekked straight for the disheveled cul-de-sac of hanging snow cloud, certain that the same natural catastrophe would not strike in the same place for at least another century.

"My goodness," Mr Marigold exclaimed an hour or so later.

When Sannazaro caught up with him, he found the kneeling Commander examining an artifact in his hand.

"What is it?"

"I don't know. But it looks to be a human byproduct, dislodged from its tomb by the action of the avalanche."

Both men studied the fragment. It was the size of a fist, had plaited material—cordage of vine, bark, perching lily and grass tree.

"Maori?" Sannazaro wondered aloud.

"Most definitely," accorded Mr Marigold. "I'm astonished."

They left the item where they'd found it and proceeded past the devastated area of the avalanche, too anxious about the looming mountain wall—notwithstanding the Commander's assurances about rules of geological repetition—to stick around and search for other archeological relics. From there they made directly towards the upper slope of another podocarp forest, attempting to stay near to the base of the rock walls rather than be mired again in high thickets, and sickly beech.

The day drew to a rapid close, perhaps on account of their having lost all sense of time, or because of their height, or the lesser oxygen, or the ordeal of the avalanche, or because the high mountain walls created cool shadows by two in the afternoon.

They found a suitable bivouac, went through their routine of petty comforts, and settled in for the night, untroubled by the mountain above or the forest below. There was plentiful wood beneath a rock shelter, and it was dry—a rare occurrence amid these ever-moistened wilds. They burned it for fire, and sat under starlight admitting, both of them, to their exquisite good luck, thus far.

Around one in the morning, both men awoke to a deep rumble. They dived for additional cover, clinging fast to the rock wall.

The tumult dissipated. Then, two minutes later, they heard it again. Then again.

"Interesting..." Mr Marigold whispered. "That is no avalanche."

"You're right. But what, then? I would think it some dinosaur."

They looked at one another. Sometimes dizziness, or mutual revelation, precludes all other facilities. In this instance, both men knew that something was very, very odd about that sound.

"It's an animal, all right. But there are no polar bears or elephants in New Zealand," said the Commander. "The last local kakapo?"

"A whale from some distant fiord?"

"The tone or frequency is no whale. It is too meager for the feminine cry of the sooty albatross. Nor that of a wolf, for there are none in this country to my knowledge. More like the shofar of ancient Hebrews, or bone horns of the yellow-robed Tibetan peoples." Puzzled and alive, Mr Marigold listened intently. "Definitely no kakapo," he added.

Of the 27,000 new species to New Zealand, such as the tomato caterpillar, the codlin moth, the humble house fly, the Norwegian *Rattus rattus*, the pig and possum, bunny rabbit and pocket mouse, the wild deer and crazy cow, a humanized horse and vindictive stoat, there were two plausible candidates, though Marigold had never heard their bugle-like bellowing: the thar, brought from the Himalayas in 1904, and the chamois, shipped from the French Alps three years later.

The deep undulating plaint emanated from far away, echoing across the entire canyon. The tonality was hollow, Inuit-like and grave, a certain wisdom fallen unto hard times, instinct with foreboding. Could it have been the wind, one spirit calling to another? Or the very giant of a bird they'd come searching for?

It was a poignant call, in any case. Far away and wrapped in mystery.

Then the sound was no more, as if it had never been, a candle burned out where no eyes of the child ever were.

CHAPTER 55
Dead Man of Notornis Cleft

MR MARIGOLD TOOK a GPS reading of their position and marked it in his Venetian-bound notebook after the famed style of Zeno the Navigator. Then he tried to get some shut-eye, despite the increasing drizzle and one particular water node that traversed the upward veins of the rock, periodically plopping atop the Commander's nose. A hedgehog (its ancestors first introduced at Lyttelton Harbor in 1869 by Mr Cunningham) scoured the cave bottom for delectable invertebrates late in the night, having a go at the Commander's ear, and then thinking the better of it.

By morning the rain was ferocious—bushels and whole loaves of it—and both men thought it prudent to remain within their spookily prehistoric cave with its millipedes and grubs, slaters, litterhoppers and hedgehogs. A gale swept the mountains with hurricane force, bending forests 47 degrees, uprooting any lightness of being, even nudging antediluvian boulders of magnetite otherwise unshakable. The Commander, in his R.L. Stevenson attire—the knitted spencer, pilot-coat and velveteen—looked every bit the beleaguered merchant marine, holding fast to a bridge of rock between halfpenny candles and a lantern.

All through the day a terrible thunder of avalanches could be heard, though both men were now attuned to that melancholy howl of the ghost they had detected the night before, and thought might well have returned. It was difficult to distinguish one haunting thunder from another.

They spent a second night in the cave. Just before the following dawn, a quarter moon shone in the cloudless sky. An omen, alleged Marigold. Everywhere cascades plunged from higher sources, there having been, easily, 50 inches of water come down during the 36-hour storm. Every mountainous cranny vented explosive waterfalls. No alpine wall was left unsplashed; no gully little ambushed but with cataracts. The Commander had slept better, and was more disposed to think of this fanfare as a joy, whereas his Squire, having fared less salubriously for two consecutive nights, looked out upon what he could only describe as an international disaster, follies perpetrated deliberately by a vindictive god.

As sunrise burned through the carpet of fog, the plaintive howl of their spirit guide, as they now thought of the alluring source, pierced the cavalcades of water

"It knows we're here," the Squire reckoned ominously.

"Possibly," Mr Marigold affirmed, taking his boots out of his sleeping bag and preparing for the day. "I confess to an ache here or there."

"My heaven, the man admits to being human!"

"It will be good to move, in spite of the checkerboard of blood blisters that once were my feet."

"Not before fresh pastries, espresso and an olive, cheese, green pepper, avocado, scallion and mushroom omelet," Sannazaro phantasmed.

But Marigold had already broken camp, leapt into the native bush beside the interminable wall, and begun his sprightly tramp, cooeeting, pitching and whistling merrily, as if telescoped into a canvas by Roelant Savery: "*I went to the fungus's lair. His cysts and bird droppings were there. The lichens were drunk, his algae in a funk, but nobody else seemed to care, to care, to care. One night the fungus sneezed. Caused commotion among the trees. The algae prayed, the lichens swayed, while I got up from my knees my knees my knees...*"

Sannazaro struggled to keep up. Presently, they were seizing and grasping, clinging to damnable wet things and sloshing through mud that weighed dangerously loose atop slate and ornate slab. Ice mingled with broken rocky scree. Far off was visible the mist-engorged terminus of a fiord, which Mr Marigold believed to be the northeastern spur of Charles Sound. At length, they were tenuously inching their way upon a slippery cleft of impossible steeps, the far northern end of the Murchison Mountains. Twenty-five miles directly behind them were the western inlets of Lake Te Anau. On either side, waterfalls narrowed their orbit of movement to a razor-thin passage. A single misstep would usher in a doom like no other.

A fog shrouded the men as they moved up amid a forest of kamahi. The trees' thick verdant limbs convoluted the nearby steam as sun broke through the uppers, much like a Scottish burn. So much water was evapotranspiring that each leaf seemed to explode in prisms of light, transubstantiated hues scattering 1,000 rainbows. In the photon-laden air, motes of water registered luminosity, assemblages of iridescence, lambency fluorescent, luster electrified.

Rattlebrained, unsteady, vertiginous, the two gentlemen were suddenly stopped in their path by a deepening sonance that clamored, now, like some close-by chorus of altos and basses. It was the spirit.

A bird, no doubting its shape, sauntered before them.

"Look at that ... Shhh!"

"Moa?" Sannazaro hastened.

"No, nothing of the sort. But flightless nevertheless. Lay low. Not a word."

They studied the slow foraging of the indigo-blue beauty. It was the rare takahe, olive-green wings, a white tail, and red bill and legs. Magnificent.

Mr Marigold whispered to his aroused partner, describing how the takahe had been considered extinct until 1948 when a man called Orbell discovered a cozy little colony of the birds somewhere just south of there, behind Doubtful Sound.

"They've grown in number and expanded their range, by all appearances, then."

"Very likely, and lucky for us," Marigold judged.

The plump Notornis, as it used to be classified, had nearly died out as a result of feather and food-gathering Maori, and predators introduced by the Europeans. Its comeback was regarded with anxiousness and extreme care. These days, only people with scientific permits were allowed to get anywhere near them, marching in from Lake Te Anau. It was thought not to be possible to come in from the other side, where the two gentlemen now sat, legs akimbo across the mammoth underpinnings of a 150-year-old kamahi tree, in what was probably the most far-flung interior corner of all of Fiordland. Semi-wild ones, however, had been translocated to other parts of New Zealand, such as the picnic grounds beneath a lighthouse at Tiritiri Matangi, an island near Auckland. This was the jigsaw of New Zealand's fast-dwindling biological heritage.

The bird ambled out of sight into some hidden cranny that forbade larger visitation.

"Where to?" Sannazaro ventured, comfortable just where he sat, but seeing no obvious exit.

"I will scout our next moves. No point us both braving it," Marigold offered, unburdening himself of his 62-pound pack. "I'll leave this here."

And with that, he headed lightasafeather up the scrambling escarpment amid the trees.

As he climbed into a gnarled cavernous place, where rock and rotting trees had trunked the vertical, scoured the soil, hewn forth a condominium of hidden hiding places and roosts, each teeming with obscurant foliage, his eye fixed on something in the half-light. He shifted his weight and lowered himself into a kind of partial cave. There, unmistakably, was an implement sitting upright. He stretched from his perch until his fingers touched what appeared to be an ax. Straining to grab the device, his upper body lost adhesion to the rock, and with an utterly absurd contortion and by the lazy laws of a twisted gravity, he plunged sideways. An Arabian, in sporting parlance.

The fall jammed him rather astutely between two sides of a granitic chimney. Now he could reach the tool, but could not move the bottom half of his legs. Both feet were lodged in a fissure that, with every gesticulation, pinched him more tightly.

"What is this?" he muttered, handling the object. It was wooden, very old, and clearly a club intended for harm, fashioned from adjurite.

Then came the burning sensation in his right ankle. "Sannazaro! Help! Help me, for God's sake!"

"Coming!" came the far-off cry. "But where are you?"

"Look for the rock chimney above the doodles."

"The what?"

"Doodles. A canopy bed of ferns, traces on the rockside, a penmanship that is deceptive; upside down and to the side, 41 feet deep, to left, then to right. Lo, on a cave wall, inside the corner-most portion, I think. Oh damnit, it hurts! Hurry!"

The Squire minced no movements, slipping and slopping with utter single-mindedness in the soft downrushing grooves of mud towards the source of his companion's excitement. Within a few minutes he had reached the point from where the view down to Mr Marigold yielded a somewhat comical presentiment.

"Why are you wincing, and upside down, of sorts? And what's that?" he called.

"I make it to be a Maori hunting club, perhaps hundreds of years old. But forget about the club. I'm stuck. My feet won't budge and my ankles are breaking, slowly, which adds to the annoyance."

But now Mr Marigold was taken by yet another turn of events. For his Squire was no longer staring at him but at something that elicited a freakish aspect behind him.

"What is it? I'm not able to turn around. My neck has none of a bird's capacity."

"You don't want to know," Sannazaro said with a horrified expression, lingering in fascination.

"What, damn it!"

"A man!"

"What?" With that, Mr Marigold forced himself to twist around sufficiently to see what it was Sannazaro beheld.

"Ahhhh!" he hollered, on account not just of the pain in his neck and his left knee and his right ankle, but also of the vision before him: a figure, its brain cavity decorated with takahe feathers, lodged miserably behind the Notornis Cleft, as he would subsequently come to think of the precise spot, with all that it intimated: a private hell on the map of felicities—a man's death on this route through Paradise.

He turned back round and stared with unraveling fixity at his companion.

"A dead man!"

CHAPTER 56
The Shadow of Harpagornis moorei Streaks the Sky

IT WAS, OF COURSE, the man who had wielded the club.

"A hunter. But help me get out," Marigold croaked. "I'm feeling faint. I might throw up!"

As Sannazaro headed towards him, that's precisely what Marigold did, but without sufficient strength or flexibility to jettison his vomit at an appropriate trajectory. Remains of partial meal, seasoned with sandfly, ended up on his chest and down his legs. Before the Squire even reached him, Marigold had quite slipped clear of the rocky entrapment, coated as he was in his own lubricant.

They stared into the eye holes of the skeleton. "There was a moment," conjectured Marigold, "when his starvation nearly liberated him, the flesh on his legs shriveling down to the bone, but still he had not the energy to extricate himself. See there how his ankle and shin are fixed permanently, his wrist jammed unforgivingly? Perhaps an earthquake narrowed the fissure, cementing his doom. Think of the mother who lost her son, the children forever wondering. Or was he a lone personage, traversing these quarters with no other thought than the bird entrails he might consume by nightfall? Like others of his kind who together routinely succeeded in feeding upon some 300,000 newborn sooty shearwaters in one season. In his exhausted state, in the end, did he welcome his death? Were his reflections a necessary part of the universe? Was there some embryology of influence, a time-sequence-necessity, upon which men such as Merleau-Ponty, Martin Heidegger and Edmund Husserl have speculated, that informs our present course? Is there a god to have permitted so slow and agonizing a death? If so, was it the same god who, by killing off the hunter, saved the prey? Much like the Spanish, German and British production of animal meat and bonemeal for lifestock that—in the form of Creutzfeldt-Jakob disease—will eventually strike down millions of humans, inflicting dementia on half the people of Europe."

"I fail to grasp your analogy. Somewhere, perhaps, between ecology and anthropological melancholy."

"My point is whether each sequence of events has separate gods? This hunter got what he deserved. He carried a club, and meant to kill another. Conversely, one slain cow, according to the European Commission, reaches in the form of meat as many as 400,000 people. What is the worth of one prehistoric man's life, versus a bird's or cow's? And if not his, what about yours and mine? Should not both the cow and the bird live, as well as the person? Why must anyone die? If killing is wrong, how should we think about the culprit? As a consumer, or evil bastard? You know my sympathies. History adds romance to the confusion. All these half-hashed queries, poorly baked synopses, impartially sautéed conundrums would ordinarily plague my mind at such a moment of encounter, were I not myself anxious to leave this place and wash off the stink of my own vomit."

"Good plan," Sannazaro replied, "I pity the poor man."

"On the other hand," bespoke the liberated Commander, "there is about his noble predicament something of the 1773 William Hodges portraiture of a fur-clad hunter poised at sunset in Dusky Sound."

"Do I know it?"

"Any self-respecting follower of the human saga must have subsumed its unparalleled poignancy, if not the awesome palette," Marigold expounded. "It's in the Auckland City Art Gallery, apparently. And a second such hunter, beneath a waterfall, is at the museum in Invercargill. But never mind. We've work to do."

Once the Commander was away from the terrible crevice, he and Sannazaro went back for their packs, marked their spot with a GPS sighting, saved in memory, and continued upwards by way of circumventing Notornis Cleft, or The Hunter's Damnation.

But their troubles were only beginning. For directly above, more cliff presented itself, and above that ice. Farther on, peaks of insurmountable intricacy. The only possible route was through the forest lower down, which would mean a new element in their journey: descent, upon so much mud and ice-like slope. Every jutting trunk presented the equivalent of a colossal banana peel; no inch of soil was steady, no single spot on the mountain was capable of guaranteeing a toehold. Large chunks of soil, acres wide, had literally peeled off the matterhorn on which they trod. Nothing was secure; there was not an eyelash of clemency; and it now appeared that down-climbing was far more difficult, and hence dangerous, than ascending—a factor little appreciated until one has oneself been thus predicamented. The world of Tom Sawyer.

Still, they managed by dimwitted holding-of-breath to work their way down around the butte, with its mini-cordilleras and unleavened cirques, until they were safe beyond and well into the snarling kamahi forest.

The mists had evaporated, a tiny glimpse of sun, of foggy brilliantine. Within 20 minutes the two men were rightly appointed on puzzling but tenable track. Still, there was no evidence of other large mammals nearby. The doomed hunter had been their first human encounter in nearly a week.

At last the waters of Charles Sound were visible. They sat for lunch. "How's your ankle?" Sannazaro inquired.

"I'll live ... I've been thinking— about that hunter."

"What of ?"

"His quarry."

"Go on—"

"Methinks if we search for those most inaccessible tree lines, where the roots are most exposed, we will be in moa country. The hunter obviously knew that."

"But that's where we sit, more or less."

"Precisely." The Commander took out his navigational devices to mark their location and log in on GPS. "We find a suitable base camp in the immediate area and work from here."

"What kind of work? What else should we be doing?"

"Search for scat, bones, talon prints, tracks; follow the spirit calls. Use your instinct."

"I left instinct and good sense in New Mexico. They might as well be in formaldehyde," Sannazaro observed. But he did not complain further.

After some time they found what might well have been the most perfect vantage point in all of Fiordland, with a clear view to Mount Cook and the outer peripheries of Bligh, George and Charles Sounds, regions first spotted from an equidistant point out at sea by Captain James Cook and the crew of his *Resolution* in 1773. Cook, and the first European settlers to New Zealand, made Dusky Sound, way to the south, their temporary home. Sealers from England were holing up there as late as the mid-1800s, their backs perpetually to the east, which held no interest for them. The discovery of gold at Preservation Inlet also brought a small coterie of aspirants to Fiordland. But then the hubbub died down, and the region was again sealed from the outside for 150 years. As late as 1999, and despite the 34-mile-long Milford Track being one of the most popular controlled treks in the world, and the number of tourists to Milford exceeding 400,000 in some years, there must, Marigold reasoned, remain undiminished subdivisions of unexplored national soil within the fiords.

At the place where Mr Marigold and Sannazaro had established their cantonment, and now sat peacefully roasting a stew of dried yam, tomato, ginger, corn, onion and paprika, the chances of anyone having ventured there before were next to zero.

Still, the air was strange; something about the ventilation, sacks of moisture scudding over alp. Constable in Newfoundland. Whitman on electromagnetism. Mr Marigold, who sat back reflectively against the foot of an anciently stunted kamahi tree, tasted the bivalved capsule of a blood-red fruit plucked from a white flower, and gazed out across lower forests of competing silver pine, miro, matai and rimu. Birds chattered in kahikatea, respondents making merry aboard totara. Mountain beech of half-dozen copper- and plum-colored varieties mingled with the famed southern rata, whose dense clusters of crimson flowers now shone from above like Mars seen from a handstand.

The ice further away still gave off glints of a novel variety to the Commander, whose thought processes were seizing upon those inklings and nuances of nature with a child's greediness. Every physical property meant something, each ray of light bespoke a miracle, and he was willing to attest to it with all his muscle. The noodles were outfitted to receive such impressions, he knew—a theory advanced by Giorgione, Raphael, and Inness. Every nerve was ready to enlist. Axons agitating for input. There was immanence in every spherule of dew, aboard each little snowdrop flower. Now, having conversed with the fungus (which by and by had imparted important commentary on animal angiogenesis and the ID3 protein byproduct theory), Marigold had no doubt that everything—absolutely everything—was possible in this world. That each sentient being and unbeing proffered a wonderful intelligence. If the fungus were that spirited and imaginative whilst still a bachelor, what powers of perception awaited him once he'd shacked up with another fungus? The pantheist in Marigold mumbled, remarked and assayed. He too, after all, was a single gentleman. He let his mind wander, though none shall ever hear of its unorthodox peculiarities. His whole body hemorrhaged with incantatory purpose and projection.

The entire shed of First Principles, lean-to of Epistemologies, storehouse of Great Ideas was instantaneously overhauled and reworked. In a veritable satori of inward viewing, the Commander broke apart into 10 million flashes of illumination; his percipience spun out into ether, eyes rolling adulcently, fingers quaking, nose twitching, elbows relaxing, face flushing, shoulders thrusting. A profile in malaria turned thoughtful. Oddly, he reckoned, all these flashes were rather outflanked by something dark in nature.

There was an explanation, and it floated overhead, blotting out the sun: a gigantic darkening of bird-swooping proportions, perilously close to the stunted tops of the trees.

"Did you *see that*?" he whispered loudly to his companion.

But Sannazaro had his face in the stew pot. First things first.

Mr Marigold lunged for his binoculars. The bird again appeared. He focused the lens.

"It's an eagle," he breathed, exalted vibrato.

But it was the largest eagle he'd ever seen, with a wingspan perhaps ten feet across. He knew the bird had to be rare, and he conferred with a text in which the image of a skeleton could be read well enough.

"*Harpagornis moorei*," he declared with certainty. "Sannazaro, forget the carrots—*look*! Confirmation of our whole journey, right there before you!"

But by the time the Squire turned from his bucket of beans and mash, and got hold of the binoculars, it was too late. The supposedly extinct predator had vanished.

"What? What?"

"Give me those!" Mr Marigold grabbed hold of the spyglasses. "Damn it! It was there. An eagle, an extinct fabulous beast, the largest that ever lived. I'm telling you."

"What about the moa? And next, I suppose, you'll claim it was a Brontosaurus."

The Commander waited, watched, but the eagle was gone.

"It was incredible, I assure you. And what, tell, did the eagle feed upon? What else! The moa! We are, friend, seated atop an island, as I'd speculated—an island in the relic sea of Gondwanaland."

"Gone where?"

"Moron. The supercontinent of 200 million years ago that comprised all of the southern continents in one. And then, 120 million years later, the Tasman Sea had separated New Zealand from the mass. The evidence is not lacking. Look!" He pointed to a particular section of mountain aboard which sprung various *Nothofagus* trees. "The seeds are not carried aloft by birds, nor can they survive salt water. Rather, they are original members of that giant ecosystem long ago. Similarly, dear friend, the Podocarpaceae, or members of the cone-bearing trees, all gymnosperms, are also part of that larger, primeval family. As well as Hamilton's frog, an amphibian that is silent. And peripatus, half-worm, half-insect, half a billion years old. It walks, its feet are clawed, its throat air-conditioned. And tuatara, a Sphenodontidan reptile that stalks on land like a fish and fertilizes its mate according to a tradition spanning 230 million years."

"What are all these gyrations, numbers, dates, mating traditions? You are maiming me by the compulsory use of my mental faculties which, please trust, are at the moment more devoted to culinary feats, and an ample supply of oxygen, than to Hamilton's frog and things I can't even pronounce, thank you very much. Two hundred thirty million years, or even days, goes beyond my present circumstances or furthest intention. I have no room left for more than a few decades, and would rather not confuse the remaining years with cerebral hemorrhaging and circumambulatory abstractions."

"Are you so bored with the magnificence of the Creation?"

"No, but your enthusiasms are killing me."

"The meek shall not go hungry."

"Maybe not, but that is little consolation."

"Have you absolutely no acquaintance with the greatest musician in history?"

"That depends."

"I am referring to Bach, whose 'First Cantata' hails topdrawer with a sorrowing that ne'er shall venture empty but be satisfied."

"That is a contradiction. If I am scared, pissed off, up to my navel in troubles, who is Bach to say I'm satisfied?"

"Think of it as a Lutheran hymn."

"Why would I do that? I was raised a good Catholic."

"Where in all of Catholicism is it ever once admitted that what God has accomplished is actually well done, eh?"

"That is the common understanding of all religions."

"Yes, but it was the maestro whose four singers first declared it so, in their legendary performance at the Church of Nikolai, the day before the composer was ordained as cantor at Leipzig."

Bach?, wondered the little Italian, screwing up his eyes to fathom the *non sequitur*. "Now I understand how you manage to stay afloat in this sea that is your dogpatch of a compass and compressed contradictions and ardent trivia, so that you never once stop and admit to the insanity of your overall situation. Your perspicuity is equal to zero; your sapience the multiplication of one academic times another, which equals zero times zero minus zero; your politics a parade of naked ninnies; and all else a faint tactic guaranteed to show up at the battlefield on the wrong weekend. The grand illusion that is your life is simply stunning. But I can't say that I'm even a millimeter or imperial gallon envious."

"Hush—There! *See*! *That* is no illusion!"

It was the eagle again. Both men dropped down. Sannazaro yanked the binocle and studied the passing behemoth, his mouth slashed open.

He crossed himself.

"Santa Maria and heaven help us," he squeaked. "Quick, cover the stew!"

The eagle this time soared down past a rocky knoll where the treeline was attenuated—a final pass on the edge of the alpine island. Mr Marigold reclaimed the opera-glass and followed its flight to a bushy gazebo.

"I think I see the nest," he said.

"I'm not going anywhere near that thing. Did you see the *size* of its—"

"I must leave at once. You guard your stew."

"Gladly. But please, take every precaution, and watch your back—and your ankles, too."

With his nocars, GPS device and ungainly sized 110mm ice ax, the taskmaster set off in a state of heightened foment: a skinny, bumbling fantasmagorical ode to sureality clambering toward the unsheltered sky. Like a moth born to be burned in the searing carnival lights of its own dreamscape. That's how Sannazaro thought of him.

The Commander had less than 1,000 feet to cover, but the route was unclear. He scrambled, climbed, slid down on his behind, crawled, skulked and tiptoed with the stealth of the Cenozoic. He meant only to study the giant eagle from a safe distance. For he knew there were distinct dangers involved, not least of which the fact that paleontologists believed the eagle to be the only predator, other than man, of the moa. If that were the case, it probably had the ability to drag a moa—weighing possibly 600 or more pounds—into the upper canopy of atmospheres. That would make the *Harpagornis* as powerful as a Pterodactyl.

He reached an outcrop; stood alone. Watched. Waited. There was wind; his long hair covered his eyes. Then, suddenly—

CHAPTER 57
The Eagle and the Marionette

FROM NOWHERE, the dive-bombing commenced.

It came first as a shadow traveling 132 aeronautical knots, passing like a meteorite. Lucky for the Commander that it struck at the very instant he had raised his ice ax to surmount a cleft. The creature hit the wooden mantle, just below the adze, splintering it into fragments that were jettisoned like an explosive out of his right hand.

The strike came so fast the crowned head of this misadventure was left toppling down the mountainside in a clownish state of discombobulation. At least he was possibly yet alive.

He dived for cover under the nearest rock, gamboling betwixt the moss campion and granicule. Twice the monster swept by, its wingspan now visible to Marigold who calculated it to be more like twelve feet. He caught a glimpse of the eyes—acuity 14 times that of a human—and the talons the size of a large Quattro Stagione calzone, mechanisms of such apparent enormity and strength that, in combination with a beak as menacing as a rhino's horn, would certainly convert a Marigold who lacked most body fats to flaccid, leathery remains: an Incan mummified atop Ambato, shaky knees and bone marrow powder in an instant.

The Commander shouted for his relaxing valet. No sound fired back, and it became quickly apparent that Sannazaro was either sleeping or had, himself, been eaten up entire.

What do I do? Marigold, in panic, ruminated aloud. Think. Action. Rebuttal. Buddhism. Non-violence. Gentleness, came the reply. Psycho-linguistics. The language of the fungus, he reckoned, crawling across the slope on his belly (a landing at Normandy), moving twelve inches per breath. He kept to the inside edge of the forest, where the trees touched the bare tundra-like upper slope. From a suitable vantage, protected by an alcove of white quartzite, he removed his camera, mounted it upon a portable extendable monopole, and started firing off images with a telephoto. It took him no more than a few minutes to prepare the gadgetry, and the rewards were astonishing.

It was *Harpagornis moorei*, definitely so. Library bright. Archival clarity. The nineteenth-century Harvard ichthyologist Agassiz himself, discovering a gar in Lake Superior, could not have come up with a more logical conclusion. A living fossil that nobody could deny though thought to have disappeared from the face of the earth hundreds of years before. Its flight feathers were black; its face lavender white; profile remonstrating (if he was not mistaken); eyes cobalt blue, bearing down, ground to a laser polish, their focal plane deadly accurate. The talons were metallic. A soft hue of Velásquez greens streaked the black body which looked to weigh that of an airborn sumo wrestler, though Marigold could not be sure. In his confusion, perhaps the size had blurred beyond its actual boundaries. And there, far off, was a second and a third: two bobbing beaks and whining appeals. A nest fashioned of collarbones, rib cages, remains of rimu and rata. The eagle had given birth to twins.

All this abundantly good news made for certain difficulties, however, in rounding that crest and continuing the search for the moa. There was no escaping the purview of those raptors. They commanded the ultimate pinnacle of vision from a promontory without rival anywhere for 100 square miles. They could see a worm scratch its nose two miles away, or hear a mouse fart on an adjoining mountaintop, and enjoyed a dive-bombing speed that exceeded all visuals. The bird's fantastic weight, combined with such momentum, enabled her to carry anything that moved far away with no effort.

It would have been wiser immediately to abandon all future plans in the area, make expeditious haste back to the kayaks, and never mention this splendid moment to anyone. Sannazaro would thrice bless his master for so prudent a determination.

Mr Marigold was weighing in that direction, aware that he had threatened the eagle's young—that she could have easily killed him but chose, instead, to proffer a peace gesture, though he was not sure what. But such thoughts were cut short by the emergence, suddenly, of a helicopter.

It was Spitzbergen. He had tracked Marigold and Sannazaro through the Commander's periodic GPS log-ons.

Marigold made out several suntanned soldiers in the Sikorsky 1,000 feet overhead. All were dressed in battle fatigues and carrying rifles. They circled the immediate region.

Now Mr Marigold could see his Squire hurrying through the boulder field below the forest cover. He was waving his arms. He wanted to be rescued. But before the Commander could warn him, the eagle swept past his own clearing and headed directly towards the Italian. A disaster of crossfires was unfolding.

"*No!*" Marigold hollered, standing now so that he could be seen.

At that moment an entirely unexpected occurrence took place. The eagle did not attack Sannazaro. Instead, she alighted deftly beside him, perching on a boulder, preening herself. When Sannazaro saw the bird, he tumbled for cover, or fainted—Marigold, as he watched the subsequent events through his binoculars, was not sure which. A fabled eastern force spraying the normally good-natured Italian's face with downwinded urine and mire, a pitiful trajectory spicy beyond detail, the very bowels of a damnation, nature's vast assemblage, threat the Squire shouted horribly like the report of cannon, no less than three musket-balls, directed at all the sovereigns of the world, decrying having ever met the Commander, laying disgrace to any further adventure and shame to the likes of Captain Lemuel, Dr Johnson, the Cossack from *Mazeppa* or even the legendary Baron Munchausen himself.

In truth, the bird was not interested in Sannazaro, but focused on the circling helicopter, whose occupants could be seen aiming tranquilizer rifles. Mr Marigold yelled frantically to jar the raptor's attention and induce it to lift off.

Move it did, with a beeline defying human monitoring. In a single launch it went right for the side door, puncturing a clothes closet-sized cavern into the craft, before retreating to its nest.

With few seconds left before certain ruin, the chopper's pilot evacuated the vehicle, winging down in a sharp plunge towards Doubtful Sound, which—as the eagle flies—was only five minutes away.

Now Mr Marigold could see the great bird tending to its young. The vast avian's prowess was concentrated into the delicate cutting of vegetal matter. Here was the triple weight of a Steinway Grand and the ornate style of a *Moonlight Sonata* focused upon the simple task of conveying a cruelty-free meal to its young. Was there a lesson in this? He would test it.

"Sannazaro, come forward," the Commander declared to all the mountains around. His voice carried.

"Did you not see the monster?" came the frenzied reply.

"Of course I saw it. She's not 50 yards away. Sitting on her nest. She saved your life."

"What? What are you talking about?"

"She could have killed us both, and chose not to."

"So far."

"I assure you she means no harm, as long as we avoid her nest."

"No problem. Where's the helicopter? I want a ride out of here."

"Didn't you see—"

But Sannazaro had buried his head and missed out on the show up in the air.

"They were attacked by the bird," the Commander shouted. "The eagle protected us. But Spitzbergen has seen the delicate creature. He knows what we know. There's little time. Tend to the camp. Be careful. I'm going on."

"What? Going on? But where? Why? Enough, I say."

All of this conversation occurred across 800 feet of mountain slope, neither man aware that thousands of other ears were listening to their unfathomable talk. Weasels, reddeer, chamois, winter hares, tiny bats and mountain goats, ferrets and rats, wild cats and lizards, mice, and the odd giant beetle, *Deinacrida pluviaris*, less than half an ounce of sweet alpine demeanor. As well as birds of a hundred varieties.

Defeated, again, by his companion's stubbornness, Sannazaro crawled back to the tent site and zipped himself in, unwilling to take any more chances. He was petrified by everything.

The Superintendent of Tesuque would of course hear nothing of turning around, enlivened, instead, by his present SuperFungus Ethologique. Without further adieu, using his monopole for balance, he skirted the nest site, giving it a wide berth and staying to the dense upper canopy of forest. Time was a factor now. Spitzbergen would be back: there was no point denying it, or analyzing the hows and wherefores of that Norwegian's mind. What mattered was that an eagle which must neither have seen nor heard any evidence of human beings in its entire life, and probably in the fullest duration of its genetic predecessors, was suddenly confronted by a helicopter and two screaming men. Marigold felt horrible about that. Now he must go forth to finish the humanitarian deed. Excite compassion, invent extreme and instant remediation.

But conflict resolution like this was not his forte. Situations so grave had escaped his prior capacity. A crest bearing the imprimatur *Ridet favonio flante* (It smiles when the west wind blows), a sluggish bicycle, the reasoning faculties, and a wealth of book learning were his only defenses. Now he was called upon to act. Every futile analogy and factoid streamed from his recondition. There was a sea storm off the coast of Antwerp; a flagellation by Cimabue; Hendrick van Balen and his Four Elements; Hercules at the court of Omphale.

He coursed below the backside of the nest point, perhaps 500 feet away into the high forests and well out of view, and there stared down 8,000 vertical feet towards a short-ended valley that was boxed in. There was no access. Walls and glaciers protected it. Waterfalls flooded it. Twenty miles beyond, over several convoluting ice flutes the size of nine Empire State Buildings or eleven vertical *Titanics,* was what appeared to be the Darran Mountains on the rear of Milford Sound. The icy summit of Mitre Peak was visible. It was one of those lucky freaks of topography that the valley had not yet been discovered by trekkers. Getting down to it from where Marigold stood, or from any other point on the compass, appeared impossible—an alpine climb of Himalayan proportions. Attaining the eagle's perch for purposes of conference and a handshake was equally unthinkable.

At that moment clarity escalated into spirit.

The call undulated like summer thunder on a horizon by the late Courbet—rumbles that must in every era instill confidence in the cycles of rain and fertility, of autumn harvest and spring shower on all those painterly horizons that are timed sensitively to the synapses of the air that verily carry the sound, vibrating the very earth. An approaching storm. La Tempesta. A flash of lightning. Singed, hair upended, a towering truth as wide as Westminster, the same flash bearing naked reality in the sparkle of the unknown.

The thunder was near. Frequencies tense and ululating. It was upon him.

He turned.

There, before his palpating heart and heaving chest, as if she had been following him all along, was a creature of unimaginable beauty and grace, digging dexterously at an enormous art gallery of flaming green truffles sequestered beneath a cluster of furrowed *Podocarpus totara* in flower. The Heaven-sent vision vexed all ratiocination, swerved clear of the slightest cosmic preconception, lay into the Commander with that which has been ordained in the spiritual literature as Final Wants, Extreme Unctions, Born Again Ambitions. He stood paralyzingly still, then collapsed in a medley of muzzled emotion.

CHAPTER 58

Passions on a Pleistocene Island

MR MARIGOLD DIDN'T breathe. His fingers grappled stealthily, in slow motion, after his camera.

The bird was the size of ... he struggled to find an analogy. Taller by several feet than a champion stallion, twice the width of a silver-back gorilla, three times the size of the largest African ostrich, thigh muscles at least twice as big as those of a Kodiak grizzly (which would weigh in, guessing, at 100 pounds per tissue), talons as large or larger than the eagle's, and a beak with the length and steeliness of the biggest butcher knives manufactured at the meccas of Araby. A down blanket seemed to carpet the whole potential killing machine in a luxuriant ease, the feather-fostering sheens of Watteau. These were the world's original feathers, not unlike those carpeting the 200 million-year-old *Longisquama insignis,* that reptilian Archosaur. A lavender throat extended ten feet, at least. Striations, granulai and speculai of the painter's palette. And legs that could carry it 100 yards in six seconds, or 100 million years. All this maximal strength, endurance and aplomb were at the command of—a quiet, gentle, grazing herbivore. A connoisseur, no less, as could be divined at once by the particular luncheon tray of nibbles he, or she, had selected.

The eyes were winsome zephyrs of wisdom, dark ochre pools of innocence: the festive sobrieties of Salomon Van Ruysdael, tints of happy time from Fragonard's *The Swing*. So many cubic yards of equivalent humanity in a bird, watched over by another bird. For there was no doubting Mr Marigold's theory. The moa was foraging too unconcerned and way too close to the eagle for this all to be a terrible coincidence. Somehow, biologists had gotten it wrong. Their assumptions were misplaced. The eagle did not prey upon the moa.

Then there was proof, for just as the Commander was preparing to snap his first photograph, the shadow alighted. Between him and the moa the eagle had landed. It walked on its massive phalanx of claw right over to the equally enormous wingless bird. The moa, in a gesture of profound affiliation, shared some of the truffles with the raptor. Feeding quietly side by side, a John Crome and John Constable; two tenors; Cézanne and Pissarro. They spoke to one another in a language far, far beyond Marigold's abilities. A biophilia as dazzling as some beast, appropriately perceived by her prey, suddenly taken to extreme, unflinching tenderness in the mothering of her brood.

No logic to the prosody of the Commander's perceptions, or translation of wants. Exuberance unleashed upon the scene. Heaven-throwing party, consolidated in a man, truant, gravitational, embedded, seizing up. A gigantic event, heralding from within, like Swedenborg's spiritual light, a super-immanence. The bird and all that she implied struck Marigold in 100 dappled, hybridized golds. Spectacular revelation. The essence of religion.

The Commander recorded it all on film, burning two unselfconscious rolls. Better he should have paid attention. In the throes of a petrified astonishment, he witnessed nothing less than an exchange, feathers, grass, a talisman, and overheard words more like a tune shared in the canopy of secret slangs that dated to the origins of the pharynx, three vowels. Then the eagle lifted off and returned to its nest, talons clinging to truffles that would be fed to her young. Vegetarian eagles?

But none of this could compare with the leap from one energy field to the next which now occurred. The moa approached Marigold. She was speaking to him, of this there was no doubt, in sophisticated rumbles and gasps, muted roars, crazy clicks and silly-sounding burps. Deep sleep of bells from every limb and chapel lawn layered in astonishing chime. Vibrations from the bog, spekynge not to be believed, of physics musicked and nature insurrected. A mighty sinew of sonance, brimming to the bottom, plummeted and reflecting, soundings ashore, lutes spawning in the sky. Blithe their rolling words, as if orator, priest, angel and parliament—all with harp in hand—didst render flesh from miscellany archeology and the odd Fra Angelico.

But what? Sopite? Sonnet? To a skylark? Love-labor'd song. Animal rejoicing. Exceedingly rare.

Now the two creatures—the towering avian, tall as a 30-year-old live oak tree, and the shriveled six-foot-two-inch man—stood three feet apart.

"Good day," Marigold ventured, helplessly struck down by the beauty before him.

The bird extended her agile beak with an offering of truffles. "Good as gold," she implied with a Kiwi's distinct accent.

Mr Marigold accepted the gift with great pomp, then chewed down on the delicious white meats.

"I am a man," the Commander declared.

The bird replied in soft pianissimos whilst dispatching with her meal. A chunk got lodged in her throat and she reared back, doubled over, reared again to pass the obstruction while the Commander watched on fecklessly. There was no way to slap her back to aid in the extrication, as she stood twice his height.

Marigold was not new to inter-species gossip. Amigo, Rodriguez, Anastasia, Ebert, Monsieur Fungus, many others, had elicited in him a conversation, imagined or otherwise. The distinctive screeches of the stellar jay grateful for a tofu party. The butterfly, silently twirling in the breeze, emitting ultra-violet consonants. The samba of the cricket twitching its antennae. Ginevra's dogs comporting themselves like veterans of the Academy. A recently arrived weasel revealing within hours of the friendship his nasal neologisms and sylvan syllogisms; a barking bear whose linguistics mostly lounged in the adipose position; the itinerant mountain lion who cried like a baby and roared wickedly because she was so spoiled. Gabbing grouse, loquacious quail, chattering pigeons, multitudinous others. But none, no tongue, no dialect or evocation so importunate, motivated, magnanimous and primeval as the gorgeous occupant of the paradise before him.

So that presently he pursued contact, attuned to every opportunity of nuance and conveyance, taking the slightest hint, delicate tinge or foreign trace as a sign, reading all the domestic manuscript pages of nature that were laid out before him in the guise of avian ecopsychology.

All was new, exhilarating territory about which no human had ever traipsed. The bird by now was evidently more interested in returning to her nest, but the Commander had some queries to pursue.

"Ahh, it is a wise avis, whether feathered fowl or naked chick, keeps her collective counsel. I won't pursue the obvious things—whether, for example, you are alone up here? None of my business. Quite so. Or what's your surname? Absolutely not my school. Where you live? No. Such demands on your time would be a Franco-Prussian war beside your Giverny. I won't even question. By what extraordinary means have you survived in such extra-satellitic isolation? Quotidian unquotables. I'm quite sure you have your reasons for withdrawal. One taciturn deserves another. Closed-beak, I. Shyness whose demeanor is the Reserve Bank of all the Bird World's Withholdings. Let's keep it that way. I have no intention of imposing. You'll find no intruder in this carriage of old bones and reckless illogics. Frankly speaking, beside your noble lineage, with its imperial posture, radiant eyes and aristocratic bearing, I must seem a trifle Neanderthal, of ghastly visage, long of tooth, ugly and ungainly. My nails are stuffed with a month's dirt. If ever a Dickens character lived, it is this unbathed masquerade. All the sins I acknowledge."

"Hmmm ... You're not so bad," the bird allowed, having patiently endured the Commander's solid five minutes of expostulations.

Not as surprised as he might have been had not Monsieur Fungus first introduced him to the forest's enchantments, the Commander stated his thanks, without pressing for any other insight.

In its own time the glamor of their dialogue now constellated to both man and bird a dam-burst of aboriginal densities. An inland road, secret and giving, that led directly to the manger of hawthorne. All was well. A New Nature embedded in the old one that would surprise even the stoutest naturalist. Marigold had read hundreds of biologists, the 'Experts' and 'Number Crunchers'. Had come across redundant, incessant, unabashed intrusiveness. It was his opinion that animals and plants themselves were little consulted with regard to textbook definitions and descriptions. Proofs abounding without so much as a discussion across species boundaries; legal caveats, levies, bounties, quotas, qualities and parliamentary posturings all endeavored without so much as a single sit-down with a pea-pod, or congressional pastime in the company of a seagull. While in rare instances of historical jurisprudence a flea, a pig, a mosquito and a dog, a Siberian goat and race horse had been given their day in court, Marigold knew from his own historical rummagings that these celebrated exceptions were largely treated as farces, underscoring the bias of centuries which flaunted vivisection and deified torture.

The Commander had his reasons for depression in days past; the scores of centuries before any law in any land had made even the slightest concession in favor of another species. All the more astonishing, he reckoned, that it should be New Zealand herself which first nationalized full legal rights for primates, relying upon testimony of the animals' full range of emotional and psychological needs. While officials in the German state of Westphalia had endeavored to impart constitutional rights to pigs in the form of 20 seconds per day of human intimacy (a few kind words conveyed, by law), no other country rallied to the same appeal and no other species ever enjoyed anything like an equal footing. Perhaps the Namibian meerkat came closest, on account of its being cute, even-tempered towards researchers, and emphatically altruistic, a mammal with no apparent shortcomings whose evolutionary model, thought Marigold, might well make a suitable blueprint for humans.

These matters weighed heavily on the Commander. He knew that New Zealanders had agitated for world heritage protection of minke whales, only to be rebuffed by Japanese and Norwegians in the International Whaling Commission. And he had a mind to do something about that. It was on his save-the-world list. Others had tried for years and decades to grant rivers their legal due, trees their standing, rats their reverence. The dog particularly had been singled out for eons in some circles to be God's absolute reflection, and thus man's most natural companion. Yet Marigold had lifted the veil and seen through to the awful truth that dogs were destined to be caged, cooked, beaten, subverted or, conversely, pampered and sequestered. In China, boiling water was poured over the tangus, or 'calm dogs', who were plunged into shock, their throats slashed, the skin of their bodies completely peeled off. The boiling water made all the difference, said Chinese consumers, oblivious to their gruesomeness.

Sannazaro had questioned Marigold's resolve when they discussed this, a month or so earlier: "Would you save all the Chinese dogs, or save the water from being boiled? Would you prevent Chinese consumption of flesh in general, or just dogs? Where will you draw the line?"

"No lines," Marigold had spat back. "I draw no lines."

He knew that whatever fate awaited it, depending on the culture in question, a dog was rarely allowed by its stronger cousins to be itself, except on the plains of Africa, where a few remained wild and hardy. Human beings had all but turned their backs on any animal that was not a 'pet'. Science, too, had renounced egalitarian standing for non-humans, whether spider, *E. coli*, horses or hares, or any of the other 50-odd million disenfranchised species. In their rage to categorize the world, the naturalists, with no less zeal than the European bishops prior to the Reformation—small-minded men whose greedy connivance had involved protection of a sizably corrupt Church from the hoi polloi—had flocked to Latin with its frigid nomenclatures. Marigold knew his Latin and was the first to argue that it was the coldest, most logical of languages, and the one least suited to the Bible, let alone to an ecosystem or the month of April, when life began. Latin-trained biologists had rendered unpronounceable most living things; successfully isolating their fraternity so that no emotion, influence or nuance of the light would ever tarnish their test-tube existence, or carpenter ant get into their clean-room.

Marigold was no naturalist, no expert. In fact, he had no claim to any advanced degree of learning. All of his insights derived from sentimentality, the courage of a muttonbird, blind rage and daft determination. He knew about what he loved, and that was all. His passions constituted a serious artillery, high explosives one moment, drizzling in the echo-chamber of the last forest the next. The spike of a purloined flower out of season, breaking the air with sudden dew-point illumination. Bullfrogs scattering. Wet effervescence, the panther of a revolving star that will never become indifferent to those willing to peer directly into the light. The Commander's love of nature embraced every uncertainty and turmoil. His heart laid claim to each and every small detail, clockwork, intention. He loved goblins. He sleepwalked like a flame. A full moon. Illogical, hysterical, calm, perfect. These attitudes kept him trim, happy, undaunted.

But presently the Commander could well deserve an accolade of the highest merit, for by this time his intense involvement with the moa had exceeded all bounds of the cognitive world. In ten minutes he'd become the greatest expert on moa in the history of science, though his complete immersion in the scene would act imperceptibly upon his memory banks. In the event, he'd recall very little of the actual linguistic encounter. So fluent was their interpenetration. The observer falling in love. Some annals may well dismiss the yarn, preferring a version that saw Marigold badly bumping his head in that portion where the ability to discriminate between fact and fantasy is easily mixed up. All his basic faculties were tilted; the cranial nutshell, Broccoli's Region, his noodle-counting ability, the Hypopotamus, his funny bone and an index finger.

Whatever was said between them on that mountain has been lost for want of a translator or physiologic. Not even Sannazaro could get it out of him. But rest assured: something happened up there.

The moa lowered her head, threw her neck quaintly around Mr Marigold's waist and ushered him closer, like a Cameroons flamingo heating up to its mate. The Commander either feared not, or was entirely unaware of the advances enveloping him, and allowed himself to be urged in this way until absolute contact was unavoidable. Now he fondled the lower breast of the bird, marveling at the softness of the under-feathers, the quality of young down, the equipoise that enshrouded like a hearth or glove the entire carapace of tender-heartedness. This was the soft-spot in Dickens at Christmas. The guarded private truth of Hugh Lofting which lies buried at his tomb, a language unknown in most other living quarters.

The moa reciprocated with her own exploratory thrusts. To her, Marigold was a scrawny adolescent, obviously bereft of parentage and compass. A black sheep at serious sea. Her production of sound ushered from deep within her lungs and had the magnitude of bagpipes, the rolling thunder of approaching storms in the Black Hills; and the movement could be tracked with one's finger, for the bird had an Eve's apple the size of a pumpkin, which took to rapid gesticulations upon the arrival of her young. Her beak was puny, no larger than a vertebra, subservient to quiet curiosity and inquisitive eyes which bore down with diffidence and a coy disregard for the differences between species. Between them all, a close-knit family of birds, veritable celebration, and for no other reason (it appeared to the Commander) than that of a human in their midst, even after near extinction by the very same. *Go and figure it*, Marigold thought. During their séance, Mr Marigold was unaware of passing hours, or of hundreds of coalescing showers overhead, and completely forgot his earlier terror in the presence of the allegedly predatory eagle, which it was not.

He spoke now with the entire family. Frolicked in freeform with the juveniles. They discoursed about new worlds, about all those insider vegetative matters that swung across the whole gamut of simple cottages and pastel freedom from it all. Marigold believed anything was possible now.

That was the good part. There was the bad. For despite her height and immensity, the moa was too innocent for any other world, or encounter. She and her kind wouldn't stand a chance against Spitzbergen and his, Marigold realized. Unless the eagle came to the rescue in time.

But he had a plan, which he resolved to cement with the rest of his film. Over the coming two hours, Mr Marigold shot 20 rolls of 36. He managed to follow the bird and her offspring back to their luxurious abode, wherein he found yet three other families of moa. They all embraced him with such warmth as to shake up his bones and risk reshifting them. In the dark, regurgitations flowed with the consistency and smell of a bright sewer, and the five creatures snuggled together in the thick puddles that registered like afterbirth. Clearly, to the birds, Marigold was orphaned and without feathers and this certainly caused them alarm. But the group generated a sweat and the night was a clear one. Stars the Commander did not recognize were everywhere.

In the morning, well fed with hot gruel delivered pre-digested directly down his passageway, the once blue-blood bon viveur left the moa for the time being, and made for his aide-de-camp, skirting the eagle's trousseaux of fabricated limbs and mistletoes with a healthy respect.

By the time the Commander reached their bivouac, Sannazaro had already packed everything and was standing guard, waiting for the end. Upon discovering his master, he conveyed multiple hallelujahs, and threw himself down at Marigold's feet with a pitiful cry and a tormented plea for an end to this particular expedition.

"All night I thought I would be devoured at any time," he confessed. "Truly I believed you had already been killed. I did not know what to do, other than pray, which is precisely how I occupied myself for the past twelve hours. But, tell me, where on earth have you been? And what is that ecstatic smile which seems permanently fixed across your face? In other circumstances, it would guarantee your commitment—to an institution, I mean. Well, whatever the mischief, you are safe, that much is evident. But beyond that, I am in darkness. Please, explain everything."

"In due time, brave and manly Sannazaro. I am glad you have packed our things, for we are taken up, now, by a duty that is much grander than either one of us. We have an obligation to fulfill that must see us back to our kayaks at once. As for that Doctor Ling, he was mistaken. There are moa. This being eminently so, there is hope on 10,000 other fronts: prospects for the chickens of Hong Kong; expectancies for all those otherwise doomed Chinese piglets and dogs; solvency, perhaps, for the rattlesnakes in Texas and those many jackass penguins jeopardized in South Africa; there are implications even for the presidential elections in Greece, even the tennis players of Santa Fe. I believe I am not exaggerating when I tell you that this is the most important discovery of the last 13,000 years in terms of what it bodes and what we must do with two billion dollars and our time. Our course is set, dear friend, our destiny determined. If I am not mistaken, even the Canadian harp seals may yet be spared another season of slaughter. All it will take is persuasion, the gumption of this fantastical success. Mark you well; it has been a day like no other, this one. It will go down in history as a record of earned optimisms and biological tenacity."

"Fine. Excellent. But you mentioned kayaks. What, no helicopter to take us? When the Norwegians are so near? Let us make noise, smoke signals and save ourselves before that eagle has a change of mind about its dinner reservations. Then I will speak to you about destiny and all that."

Sannazaro was devastated by the thought of retracing their terrible journey. Past the Hunter's Damnation and the Sucking Fungus. Into Black Fly Hollow, Sand Worm Nowhereabouts, Supplejack Hell and the vertical Ooze of No Return.

"I can't go one step, I won't go on—"

"You will, we must."

By attenuated injunction, Mr Marigold seized his backpack, adjusted the fittings and started down. With a foul-mouthed string of whines and blasphemes, his attendant followed.

Their descent was surprisingly undistinguished and went far more quickly than either would have imagined possible. Now, with the added experience of so heinous an ascent, they were, in short, rather competent to return the same way. You can turn back the sky. They knew what to avoid, where not to walk, how to distinguish wet rotted tree bark from solidly rooted footholds. Sannazaro kept a lookout for those famous landmarks he'd come to hate, and the crossing of streams still presented awkward miscalculations and wartime terrors, but at least there were fewer questions about direction, compass, altitude, barometer, satellite reading and the severest of sallies. There is one word in every language—'down'— which, like the mechanics of subtraction, is an emphatic underpinning of the collective consciousness, leaving little to chance. Neither Dante nor Joyce could find a better word.

It took them a mere two days to reach their boats. For every five steps upwards, one step down would suffice. Several times, a helicopter flew within half a mile overhead. Meanwhile, the Commander explained everything to his foot soldier and tried to prepare him for what he believed would be the most important set of wildlife photographs ever taken. "The world will never be sane."

"But you've never, to my knowledge, taken a photograph that's in focus," Sannazaro reminded him.

"I was intimate with them. I have, in essence, become one of them. For the rest of my life I will prefer regurgitated meals, and speak a hollow drum. There was no problem with the focus."

"Perhaps you were too close. What about the flash? Depth of field? ASA?"

"What do you mean?"

"That's what I mean."

It was hailing heavily during their return kayak up Doubtful Sound, an ice storm exceeding 90 miles an hour, waves crashing over the laboring boats with hideous enormity, lightning devastating one tree after another along the shoreline, igniting a never-before-seen bioluminescent response from many of the sea drifters which, along with certain southern fur seals and squid, took to leaping into the twosome's vessels and creating some havoc there. The Hooker's sea lions were typically aggressive about the travelers who, they believed, posed threats to their harems. Neither man could paddle; they were victims of whatever was to become them.

"So much for your destiny," Sannazaro cried, his words muted in the hurricane. His sole consolation was that at least the weather provided a welcome reprieve from the sandflies.

Eventually, those nasty storms passed by, seals swam far, even the sex-changing eels, no longer attracted to loose bowsprit cords, went off towards wetlands far to the east. It was a bonny day, the water calm, ambient air even more so. For a time they could not have wished for a more even and unsurprising ride— until, suddenly, both kayaks were thrown 50 feet into the air, and came crashing back to the shimmering fiord's surface rather upside-down.

As both men struggled to save themselves and their fast-sinking supplies, they caught a glimpse of the unusual submarine which had surfaced beneath them (damaging its periscope in the process), then disappeared again, retreating no doubt to that elusive magnetic deep hole somewhere off the coast, where it would remain impervious to spy satellites and Marigolds.

The Commander—after some re-orienting—took agitated stock of their losses, then shrugged. Mounting a full-on offensive against the US military and a Trident nuclear sub at this time of day was beyond even his ken. Anyway, there were important things to do.

Later, having dried off and found no serious injuries between them, and few losses of equipment, even Sannazaro commented on the relative pleasures of the final return. No rueful memories. What had happened was behind them. The sub was gone. The storm had been swift, no harm done. A dozen seasons in six minutes. A world record, even for Doubtful Sound.

But upon reaching that same island where the penguins dwelt, just five miles from where they'd set out, they spied a 125-foot vessel, with its gaggle of wind-baked Japanese tourists, heading towards the mouth of the Sound, where it connected with the southern Pacific. Mr Marigold knew there was a conservation battle looming over the New Zealand Government's desire to increase the number of tour concessions operating in the area. In fact, a recent tally of paua, mussels, scallops, kina, fin fish, groper and lobsters taken from the Sounds showed, in all, a looming prospect of nearly 1.8 million dead animals per year, not including the decimated populations of organisms inhabiting the subaqueous cliffsides down which craypots were slid, gouging out the rare black coral and endangered brachiopod fauna. Here was one more element to factor into his desperate resolve to speak face to face with the Prime Minister about his most incredible discovery. That, and his plan to pressure the Government to revisit its 1979 transfer of Fiordland titles, deeds and designations which deliberately, or inadvertently (if one is generous), exempted the Sounds themselves from Scenic Reserve status. The land was protected, not the water. He intended to force a reversion to the earlier legal protection for the water—a ludicrous oversight, or perversion. In all, only a few miles of the Sounds were vouchsafed.

Add to that Marigold's desire to pump approximately 300 million dollars into immuno-contraceptive airdrops for possums, rats, dogs, cats and stoats, and that nearly summed up his modest plans for New Zealand.

He and Sannazaro were, however, met by an unexpected obstacle when they finally guided their respective kayaks to shore at the beach adjoining the docks of Deep Cove.

"You must be Mr Marigold then," a tall man observed with a deprecating air as he swatted at the flies that swarmed diabolically there.

"I am he. Let me introduce my faithful friend, gardener, Senator and Squire-to-most-Royalty, soon Governor of the Blessed Isles, Señor Sannazaro. And you are?"

"Fritz Spitzbergen. These are my associates." He extended his hand, which Marigold ignored. "You've seen it, haven't you?"

"Seen it?" The Commander's repetition was laced with design. "I've seen your hand."

"Where there is such an eagle, there is the moa. We both know it. What's that—a monopole? You got film? Excellent!"

"I have no idea what you're talking about. This is my ice ax."

"You'll need a ride over the pass," the Norwegian pointed out. "A boat to take you back to Manapouri. Then a ride to Te Anau. It's late in the day. The flies are hungry. A man could die in their midst. Then the ants eat the bones. I don't need to tell you. Your friend there looks particularly discomfitured, am I not correct? Alternatively, that air-conditioned Beaver there, it belongs to my buddy, Gordon, who is the smoothest pilot in the area and could deliver us to the bar in Te Anau in 20 minutes. Cold beers are on me. Eh?"

"Very kind of you. But I think we need the exercise. We'll walk."

"All right. I'll wait for you in Te Anau—with a medic on hand." Spitzbergen laughed. "We have to talk. I have a plan and there is a considerable amount of money involved. I would like to include the both of you, if you're still alive by then."

"Norwegians have a long history of wildlife in their blood," Marigold resolved cannily. "An attachment, if I'm not mistaken, to big, beautiful, intelligent animals."

"You have stated it precisely."

"In fact, the bigger the tastier."

"Come again?"

"You bastards kill whales. You eat them. Well, at least in New Zealand, national parks still mean something. They mostly love animals here. Impresarios who kill them, or showcase them like King Kong, are distinctly unwelcome."

The Norwegian shared a look of humor with his associates. He was not remotely interested in Mr Marigold's point of view. He'd already invested hundreds of thousands of dollars in his plan.

"You have a particular perspective on these issues, I see that," he said. "I respect it in a man. Perhaps you are unaware of the underwater marine observatory at the far end of Milford Sound?"

"I've not seen it yet."

"You should. It will help you to understand the future of conservation."

"Which is?"

"Zoos, animal amusements, byproducts, and gene technology of one sort or another. Education by any other name."

"That's not the school I'd send my kids too, sorry."

"The Government will back me on this."

"On what, the capture, relocation and forced slavery of the last moas?"

"There was more than one? My God!"

Marigold developed a lump in his throat, then measured more carefully his words: "Love it from afar. Leave it alone. No amount of education is worth a dissected frog."

"But we're hardly speaking of dissection. You've got it all wrong."

"Yes, you are. Ultimately, you are." He was so angry the regattas of flies no longer affected him. "We'll take our leave, if you don't mind."

The two men did not have long to wait. A service vehicle heading over the hill with supplies took them back to the power station on the far end of the lake where a commercial vessel came every 90 minutes.

Once in Manapouri, Marigold and Sannazaro hitchhiked to Te Anau where they were to catch the first private plane up to Wellington, the nation's capital. The agitated fumes emanating from the Commander's head remained palpable.

Weeks before, reflected Sannazaro, he was happily ensconced in Tesuque. Now they were heading towards riot, discord, impossible-sounding rural renewal. What had transpired to so involve his destiny in uncertain tidings? How had he allowed himself to be molested by the idea of adventure? Money? Fame? Boredom? He was plunged into what is generally thought of as soul searching, Cook's Worst Voyage, Sir Water Raleigh's Folly, and he did not like it one jot. His body was covered in welts, angry and blue, from all the sandfly bites. Itching them was insufficient. Lacking calamine lotion, he took to a fork and for the rest of the day jabbed, punctured and scraped himself with the madness of Flaubert's St Anthony, a canvas by Caravaggio.

CHAPTER 59
Mr Marigold Saves a Rat Overboard from the Government

"THE WEATHER," said Mark Twain, not long after returning from a visit to the Khumb Mela in Allahabad. And so it was that despite the adventurers' urgency to reach Wellington with news of monumental discovery, and to finger the nefarious collusions of the Norwegians, it was not possible. The squall that had gassed the heavens, harassing Doubtful Sound with breathtaking bad fray, now assaulted most of the country. Blusters of gall-sized hailstones gathered added force in what the locals called a screaming westerly, more appropriate to Latitude 50. Maori knew of 14 different winds, each one of which was now tormenting the nation's back country. No small planes were going anywhere. However, it was the advice of one grounded pilot that if it were really an emergency, they should drive down to Invercargill where larger, commercial aircraft might stand a better chance flying above the storm median.

The Commander seized the recommendation and away they flocked, to the airport in New Zealand's southernmost town, its population of around 52,000 shrinking every eleven months. But even there, amid larger-sized aircraft, the prognosis for a direct flight was not very good. The weather service predicted a three-day tempest. Even the landing strip was flooding out and planes had to be carted to safer ground. Why an airport had been built in a flood plain was part of New Zealand's charm. Once, in 1983, drowned animals piled up all around the airport as the estuaries flooded their banks. For weeks the carcasses emitted noxious trails into the city.

So, the weary Squire and his Commander checked into an historic hotel across from the train station. They indulged in hot showers, sampled the nearly local Dunedin dark ale, then strolled about the pancake-flat grid of second-hand, hardware, antique and general stores, stopping for pumpkin mash and chips at the Lone Star, and marveling at a machine guaranteed to suck one million sandflies per hour out of the air.

The town was bopping (despite the weather) in the wake of news of champion pet sheep and beef, prime lambs, Crossbreed, Poll Dorset, Romney and Suffolk; of yearling heifers and the well-publicized daily toll of Southland and South Otago blood money. Eleven kgs of lamb, including its 1kg pelt, $26.72 ; the pelt itself, shorn as they say, $4.98.

Twenty-one kgs of mutton, $23.14. Beef steer, $298. A modest-sized cow, $289. Venison at 60kgs, $382. Goat, 12kgs, $23.95. Wool, 37 microns, $382. Wheat per tonne, $266. Milksolids per kg, $3.35.

Butter, a whopping $2,350 per tonne. A fanfare surrounded wholemilk powder, casein, cheddar cheese. Venison schedules. Meat export return changes. And all this on top of the busy loading and unloading of containers—the *Sydney Express*; the *General Villa* from Gladstone with its load of alumina; a British ship carrying mixed uranium and plutonium oxide fuel on its way to Japan from Cherbourg, heading somewhere in the vicinity of the Tasman Sea; the *Seamaid* unloading coke; the *Crimson Forest* picking up logs; the *Rakiura Maru* from Japan dumping its pitch and taking meat; the *Pac Princess* from the West Coast of the US hauling on board fine New Zealand timber. And the *Golden Daisy* from Whangarei receiving huge loads of fertilizer. Even the Russian *Akademik Shokalskiy* unloading some South Polar scientists.

It was along that crowded promenade, plastered to a community bulletin board, that the Commander caught a notice from a local conservation trust proclaiming in no small measure a "country crisis" in keeping with the tenor of the nation's environmental aims, goals and hotlines. Evidently the Department of Conservation (Te Papa Atawhai, in Maori) feared a true disaster far more grievous than, say, the civil war in Indonesia, or nuclear proliferation in China. An all-points bulletin had been issued, special forces mobilized, and a joint session of Parliament convened in the middle of the night to address the pending situation, while a whole nation waited and listened to the hourly broadsides, tensed, ready to send its young men to war if need be. Not since the possum outbreak at Beer Can Beach on the North Island, or the invasion of bunny rabbits and spotted fawns outside Tulip Haven, had the people's steely will and staying power been so tested. DJs were quoting generously from Churchill's words during the period of Halifax and Herbert Asquith.

In sum, it was written, "A dreaded, stowaway black ship rat (*Rattus rattus*), possibly pregnant, was seen swimming to Whenua Hou (Codfish Island) as of zero fourteen hundred..." naming precise latitude such and such, day, month, year, etcetera etcetera. "Normally these rats cling to one another's tails, in long, unmistakable trains of waterlogged, beach-aspiring swimathons. But this rat is a super-rat, for it was acting alone in a most sinister premeditation, rat-paddling, according to the eyewitness, with an ease unheard of in the rat kingdom. Even if the sighting were mistaken, and it was a Polynesian kiore (*Rattus exulans*), or Norwegian grey (*R. norvegicus*), this fact of a rat overboard constitutes one of the gravest threats to New Zealand's, indeed the world's, most endangered parrot— the flightless kakapo (*Strigops habroptilus*). Its only other restricted habitat is the predator-free Little Barrier Island in the north, and the odd one, recently relocated, to Pearl Island. Equally threatened on Codfish are the Okarito brown kiwi (*Apteryx mantelli*) and the severely endangered lesser short-tailed bat (*Mystacina tuberculata*) which lives solely upon Codfish Island's 1,359 hectares, with their cornucopia of worms and fruit, insects and occasional parakeet babies."

The bulletin—three pages, pinned prominently to the wall— elaborated upon the manner in which the Polynesian rats had wiped out the greater short-tailed bat species from Rerewhakaupko, as well as the saddlebacks, snipe and bush wren from Big South Cape Island (Taukihepa) in the early 1960s. A wildlife expert by the name of Don Merton had achieved well-deserved international fame at that time for launching the first partially effective relocation effort of an endangered species. He was the same bright light in charge of the successful and all-poignant black robin restoration on Chatham Island. While the flightless snipe and bush wren did not survive the transfer process, and were today deemed extinct, the South Island saddleback population of wattlebirds seemed to be coming back across those few predator-free islands: areas, in other words, without rats, cats, possums, deer or bird-eating predators of the Mustelid family—ferrets, weasels and stoats. These creatures had been exterminated (shot or poisoned) or somehow removed, in order to ensure that the timid, all-vulnerable avians were able to court, mate, lay eggs and find food without the surrounding predatory influence wholly introduced to the otherwise remote islands by humans.

Rats were said to be among the worst of these killers. They could swim through high waves (unlike, say, the Norwegian lemming), climb trees, deliver large numbers of offspring in short order and, with startling efficiency, devour live hatchings and bird eggs while out-competing the avians for prime food sources. Their only two foes were humans and weka, a flightless bird equally efficient at stoking unbridled massacres.

Witnesses *en qui vive* had seen weka attacking other hatchlings, poking out their eyes, pulverizing their pates, just for the seeming sport of it. In short, the placid-looking Codfish concealed a biological war zone. The weka had been removed, or shot. But the rat ...

The dire communiqué, which was framed in the tenor of a "National Emergency", said this single adamant rat could wipe out years' worth of efforts, and millions of dollars spent by the country's wildlife division. It might even proliferate to the extent that several more species would go extinct as a result. Possibly even humans, if one based the conclusion on the sheer merits of the demographic comparison, or 25 rats per New Zealander.

How could a single rat wipe out the human race? Marigold wondered.

The rat was said to be swimming furiously in an attempt to outbid all those who might think of pursuing her. The creature had leapt off a dinghy that had come up from Mason Bay and was temporarily docked on the beach at West Ruggedy. The dinghy boy, awaiting his boss (who at the time was somewhere beneath the churning sea, outfitted in a 7mm wetsuit, snorkel in mouth, hunting for paua: his quota allowed for 15 tonnes throughout the year; he'd slice and grab some 200 kg a day, working mostly summers, earning after expenses $43 per kilo), was too late to impede the rodent, who scampered out into the water, and was last seen heading undaunted into the fierce winds, surmounting each whitecap with a verve and dedication rather frightening to contemplate, in an apparent all-out attempt to reach Sealers Bay on the scientifically protected Codfish, nearly two miles due west in the Pacific.

While it was considered unheard of for a rat to swim that far, it was possible. Countless others had swum to Breaksea, Ulva and any number of islands throughout New Zealand. All fishermen in the area were warned to inspect their boats carefully for future stowaways, and to keep a constant vigil for any rats, particularly this one.

"If you see one, for God's sake don't let it get away," declared the flyer, fanning a *Rattus rattus* panic.

"What are you thinking?" summoned Sannazaro, as he headed toward another pub.

" Of going there."

"Why on Earth?"

"To save the poor little fellow before the whole mob of a nation lynches her."

"But that's crazy. It's just a rat! Anyway, if they've posted alerts like this, I can assure you the Department of Conservation has the situation in hand. They'll be waiting for it, like the embunkered Japanese at Guadalcanal, machine-guns well positioned."

"You think that's fair? You must know that I have a special fondness for rats, though no less a fondness for parrots and bats. But the solution, if you ask me, is not the slaughter of a rat. My God, man, where is your humanity?"

"Mostly in my body, which is craving a warm glass of red wine to sustain it, if you must know."

But when Mr Marigold got an idea in his head, there was little likelihood of stopping him, even if he was confounded by the moral dilemma. The thought of a rat exterminating a parrot made him ferocious with pathos, and he did not know how to solve it. Perhaps the New Zealanders were absolutely right. The numbers themselves warranted getting rid of the rodents. They would survive elsewhere, while parrot populations were nearly extinct. On the mathematical surface, there should be no debate. Yet, Marigold could not help his soft spot for universal imperatives. All life is precious, and so on and so forth.

He bid adieu to his companion, asked a slightly demented-looking highschool kid with a mohawk haircut, baggy shorts halfway to his ankles, rings in every visible orifice and a skateboard under one arm for directions to Codfish Island. The boy had never heard of it, but a very old man walking his dog knew exactly where it was. In one of the many profound coincidences marking Marigold's journey throughout life, it turned out that the man had been a settler on Codfish—although in this case the 90-year-old's knowledge of the island served, at first, as an argument against Marigold even thinking about getting there.

The man explained to the duo how it was that the island had first been inhabited by ex-sealers from Europe in the early 1820s (the earliest, most southerly settlement of Europeans anywhere in the world— later, the English would attempt a short-lived experiment on Enderby, in the Aucklands, without success). Today it was out of bounds to all but the occasional researcher with permits in hand. Actually, the tradition of preservation had had an early start, according to the gentleman, for those former fishermen had taken to the island with the deliberate intent of separating themselves from the sea of slaughter happening everywhere else in New Zealand. The seals had done nothing wrong, after all, and their innocence was much remarked upon by the settlers there. In those days, the English thought nothing of taking a million seals and whales in a year, all thanks to the earlier discoveries of Captain Cook, a man whose profound celebrity, and thus the whole nature of exploration, thought Marigold, warranted more sober reconsideration in light of such disastrous consequences.

Marigold listened intently to the fellow, then replied enthusiastically, "A humanity conditioned by torchlight and the cave. No sailing ships or vacuum cleaners, neither matchlock nor chewing gum. What a time, what a place! That is the world I should embrace."

In the face of such enthusiasm, the gentleman was only too happy to continue reminiscing, so he proceeded to fill the travelers in on history which still shone brightly in his eyes.

"By the 1850s," he began, "whalers found Codfish of little use." And he continued by describing how most of the frontiersmen had moved back across the Foveaux Strait to Invercargill. This raconteur, little heralded, was one of the few whose family stayed on. He was born there, he said, and knew every crook and rat-cranny of that lovely place that the southern Maori called Whenuahou, or Newfoundland.

Today, Codfish hosted a population of no people, but some 1,500 fur seals, a rare skink and some 65 bird species, including 52 kakapo and a small colony of the very special Cook's petrel, elsewhere confined to the latitude of the low 40s. This kind fellow—Little Joe, he called himself, a descendant of James Spencer, possibly the earliest settler on Codfish— had continued to live at Codfish until his late middle age when the weka removal and possum killings started. He resettled first at Riverton, to the west, then found his way to Invercargill when his heart got a bit dodgy and he figured a lube job on his valves was a sensible idea.

The dog, Blackie, was furiously sniffing Marigold's shoes.

"What do you smell there?" Little Joe inquired.

"Moa," Marigold replied.

"Hmmm," said Little Joe, who seemed quite capable of reading a man, and certainly knew enough about the southlands to imagine any possibility. One of the great factors of the aging process, Marigold knew, was its faculty of outgrowing scepticism.

The Commander was utterly revved up, in a hurry to move out, scarcely had time even to ask, breathlessly, the question: "Little Joe?"

"Yes?"

"Any conceivable way to get out to Codfish?"

To his amazement, he found a shared conviction as he explained the situation.

"It's not so much my love of rats," Little Joe confessed, "because you can have them, far's I'm concerned. And nothing should ever interfere with those parrots; they have no neo-cortex, but they're as smart and as adorable as it gets. I should know. I lived 50 years with two of them. They lek, you know."

"Lek?"

"Only the male knows how. Fans his wings a kilometer a minute, leaves the nesting part to the gals. Quite a system. But I also stand up for the underdog."

By this time Sannazaro, having obtained his source of warm Pinot Noir just three blocks away, had come around and found the Marigold and Joe formulating their ludicrous plan. The exasperating details had already been laid out like fine print, and the brute force of their reasoning was only too clear. No time for an Italian's protest.

And so, tipsy and in spite of himself, Sannazaro was not surprisingly dragged into it, warmed to the well-honed fatalism of himself.

Little Joe threw Blackie in his Honda, and they all drove off along the New River Estuary to a private docksite on Barracouta Point, where Little Joe's grandson kept a 28-foot paua boat with snorkeling gear. Recreational and commercial paua fishermen were not allowed to go after the black and smaller yellowfoot (Queen) abalones with any diving equipment, but many of them did, including this fellow. The local police, and the judges, were not too exercised over minor infractions, though it spoiled it for the rest of the law-abiding fishermen—not to mention the paua themselves, who needed respites, as we all do, and perfect conditions for their sexual allures.

It was said that hidden pearls, placed in an anesthetized slit just behind the paua's brain, after two decades might grow into something worth 200,000 dollars, though the secret of their manufacture had been purloined. Paua's offspring required four years to reach 90mm, and another two to hit 125, amid the kinetic chaos of thunderous wave action, kina and topshell, scallops and brittlestar, a benthic bouillabaisse into which the rhizoidal *Haliotis* gathered its pink coraline cement, pustular slimes and algal clathrates, thereby clinging to the shattered rocks. These were the intimate whorls of the abalone, vastly underestimated intelligences that suffered mightily; creatures who might wander no more than 20 yards in their entire life, dodging starfish, but mostly human hunters like Little Joe and his grandson. Same story for oysters. Enormous consciousness.

These two knew these waters well enough, and Little Joe figured it would not be dangerous to steer the boat through the present westerlies. He'd done far worse things in his long career, before the days of GPS and GSM, when even a deadening fog presented only a modest challenge to navigation, for he still had his nose and good sense.

But Sannazaro declined to go along. He figured if he didn't put his foot down somewhere, they'd just get him wet. He'd float eternally in the damnation of another man's fickle-fated restlessness.

"I will not go out into that gale. No, sir. I am quite prone to seasickness, have no interest in seeing a place called Codfish, which I can imagine smells bad and is bleaker still, and will not have posterity remember me for dying in the attempt to save a rat from the ocean."

"What nobler memorial?" Marigold interjected.

"That eagle episode was proof positive of your medical hiatus. But what is all the more striking is the fact there are now three of you cultivating the gap in sanity. So enjoy the mental-case collaboration. I'll be in that cozy, coffee-undulating cafe just yonder. As the hours draw on, and your hypothermia sets in for good, you'll find me back at the hotel sleeping soundly, three pillows, flowers by the bed, dreaming of your torment."

But as he turned and secretly watched them sauntering out along the quay, Sannazaro noticed that the sun had pierced through that somber arc of nearly subantarctic luminescent sky. The ocean sparkled by turns an Antwerp blue, a leaden azure, a phosphorescent turquoise, a metallic lavender, and the Italian sourhead knew he'd be missing out on something just possibly grand. Yellow tin and ultramarine.

"*Wait for me!*" he hollered, furious with himself. He just couldn't help it.

Much will be said by historians of the peculiar psyche which was Sannazaro's. Like Mankind itself, he was the hallowed epicenter of indecisiveness, but with such ardent predictability as to be comical. To say it is one thing; to observe it, a real rash of mirthfulness—not that he hardly smiled, for he had little sense of self-belittlement. He was a serious mule of a man whose temper was saved by one essential quality: he had no difficulty changing his mind from hour to hour. In this, he and the Commander were plagued hand in hand. Each expelled confinement of an idea. Where one sought pleasantville, the other wasteland; at the moment of tranquillity, the opposite was also true; if true, false, false, true. No accounting could cover the excesses, so that together they nearly constituted the whole distance from Voltaire to Rousseau, but not quite, and this gap, or lag-time, or caesura of pure reason, amounted to the spark which gave their tandem flurries so much puzzlement and good fun in one another's company. In theory, theirs was the friction necessary for operating any mechanical device, and also that rare resin that lubricates the bowels of high spirits, avoiding all doldrums, excising inertia, routing complaisance. The end result was a Commander without the slightest military orientation, but one eager to weed a desert where not one weed had grown in 20 million years. And a Squire without portfolio, title or fabric to hold him in, keep him out, sort one preference from another for very long, or instill a common language. They were, in other words, a true team.

Together, they were not only lost at sea, but reunited with impassioned purpose, heading nowhere, everywhere, at all times. Finished, unfinished. In rags, in riches. Forlorn, ecstatic. Impossibly, possibly.

So that now the two of them, accompanied by Little Joe and his grandson, headed out towards Codfish, coursing beyond Smoky Beach north of Mount Anglem, which rose elegantly and alpine more than 3,000 feet into the cloudy sky, and then passed the Rugged Islands after only an hour's journey. Sealers Bay lay directly south-by-southwest, just six nautical miles or so away. The winds were not friendly, nor the six-foot swells. The temperature, however, was mild: the third consecutive summer of drought, said Little Joe, arguing for each and every restraint inculcated at the Kyoto Greenhouse Summit, and more. An end to all auto emissions. The needed demise of economics. The collapse of empire. Let us return to cave life. Consider the facts: farmers all over Southland had had to dispose of their sheep and cattle because there was no water for them; no grazing. The Government had had to step in with emergency bailouts.

"No rat could ever maneuver such waves," Sannazaro assured them, leaning weakly near the railing of the trawler. It was, by trawler standards, a tiny boat against so vast and churning a sea.

"I've seen it happen," declared Little Joe. "Keep a lookout."

They traversed back and forth before the island. Of course, this was needle&haystack business, for who was to say that the rat was intent upon Sealers Bay; that the rat even existed, or ever had.

"Philosophically speaking," Marigold began, "there was a rat, because somebody saw him, or her. But I would tend to agree with Señor Sannazaro: those are mighty telling waves." His voice rose and sank with the terrible trench warfare in which the trawler now found itself, combating each giant trough of sea swells with just enough structural determination.

Then the miracle occurred: Little Joe spotted something black floating in the water. It was no seal pup poking its nose into the ether, nor a porpoise nor bull kelp swaying and churning with each typhooned-size swell, no passive muttonbird meditating on the ocean's navel, or old tangle of fish netting harboring its toll of rotting catch. As he veered closer with the boat, all three men saw that it was the heroic, endlessly fertile ship rat, *Rattus rattus*. Teutonic, firm enough to crawl through any chink supial and fine, not 2,000 feet from shore, swimming with a valiant determination to astound the marine mother of all invention. It was a biological champion, possessed of some great *idée fixe* of which the four men on board could have no precise clue. What possessed a rat to attempt such an odyssey? It was not like the first woman to swim the English Channel, when much of the world was rooting for her, and following alongside in the event of an untoward current or great white. Here was a nearly universally despised rodent risking it all for freedom.

A kind of boat person, with no boat; a political refugee without hope of being granted asylum. She could not know that both she and her young (for she was big and clearly pregnant—a weight factor furthering the received impression of an astounding athletic performance bordering on the spiritual) were heading into a death-defying trap. Thesprotian, like a Phoenician merchant, nimble, hairpadded, haunted by zoological anomalies, sparkling, creeping, rhymed to death, given to night brawls. She was Shakespearian to the core. Hamlet, with better jaw articulation.

New Zealand's Second Fleet had been diverted from a detail in the Tasman Sea. The country's Navy SEALS were getting into position. No fewer than 20 high-powered rifle-toting conservation officers, five patrol helicopters, a dozen official motor boats, 200 rat traps, 50 gallons of chemical toxicants including the dreaded broudifacoum and metaldehyde, three beachcombing four-wheelies and a dozen straining Belgian Pit Brashers trained to smell a rat had been dispatched to annihilate that rodent should she dare to try a vacation on Codfish. Men with machine guns were hidden in bunkers on the beachhead. Snares, nets, spring-loaded cyanide canisters, four trained mongooses from the Auckland Zoo and an eerie silence awaited the poor waterlogged rodenta, whenever she should have the unprecedented audacity to drag herself up on that seemingly uninhabited oasis of dry land.

"Remarkable!" exclaimed the Commander.

"What's remarkable is the Commando Raid waiting to happen," said Little Joe, who had made out much of the above paratrooper and Navy SEAL activity with his binoculars from the heaving deck. "This is a blasphemous tragedy just waiting to happen."

"Do you have a net?" Marigold asked frantically.

"Yes, but it's not long enough, not in these waters," said Joe. "Ninety centimeters."

"What about a wetsuit?"

"Certainly. Seven or eleven mill?"

Within a few minutes the Commander was suited up and ready to enter the storm-tossed waters. He smelled of abalone.

"All right," Little Joe began. "I don't know how familiar you are with this kind of sea but don't worry. With no weight belt, and the thicker of the wetsuits, you're not going to sink. But whether anybody ever sees you again—" and here he looked directly at Sannazaro, whose 70-odd years meant that Little Joe was one generation his senior—"will depend upon you."

"What does that mean?"

"Take nothing for granted with that man," warned the Commander. "It means that from the moment your friend hits that unforgiving current, you absolutely must keep him in your sight. I've got boat matters to manage; my grandson, too. So it's up to you to maintain watch. Lose him for even three seconds in these waves and we've lost him forever."

As Marigold was putting the final touches to his suiting-up process (he looked unbelievably ridiculous, thought Sannazaro), then climbing down onto the rear platform which was just a foot above sea level, Little Joe shouted, "By the way, do you know how to swim?"

"Naturally," shouted Marigold above the din of the high idling engine.

"I mean in ocean waves."

"Don't know. Never tried, exactly," the Commander confessed.

But there was no time to quibble. Little Joe had espied the rat. "There he is! It's your show."

With that the Commander slipped into the infernal churning sea and began swimming towards *Rattus rattus*. She was indeed the pregnant black ship rat that had been reported, and she was dog-paddling at a rather remarkable speed, considering that the ratio of wave trench to her six-inch height was the equivalent of swimming up and down one 30-story building after another, whilst conveying up to ten blind naked young.

The rat saw Marigold pursuing her and started to cry out in a plaintive high squeak that transcended both the boat's engine and the roar of wicked waves all round.

"It's OK, little fellow," Marigold called out, preparing to net the superb rodent which was not but two waves away. "I'm a friend!" he shouted.

"What's your name?"

"Mimi," came the pitiful cry, this descendant from the Isle of Dogs back in the 13th century. And she had cousins from Yarmouth whose Asiatic accents could still be detected.

Suddenly, seemingly from out of nowhere, a helicopter appeared and a voice called through a loud speaker to the strange party 300 feet below. "You there! What the hell are you doing out here in such waves? Please signal if you're all right."

Little Joe, who of course knew all the proper international sailing gestures, lifted his right arm, bent it as if making a right turn in his car, and prayed that Mr Marigold—who knew nothing about such signals—did not do something stupid and wave either of his arms out of the water, which was the sign of distress.

Fortunately he did not, being occupied instead with the difficult task of netting Mimi, a fine exemplar of a family—Muridae—who came from the old country and today numbered over 400 species, not least of which, the chinese bandicoot-rats, African giants, and spiny mice of Crete.

He tried once: Mimi caterwauled. He tried again, proffering desperate blandishments, and missed. But on the third try, as the chopper circled away, Mr Marigold managed to capture the little lady, who could not be too careful among humans, lifting her out of the ocean in the net, then treading water while the trawler circled around to position the rear-end platform in a place where both the Commander and his quarry could be hauled out of the sea. Her tail, with its 212 rows of scales, slapped the water helplessly.

"Why can't you just leave us alone!" the rat cried out. And in that suffuse lamentation the Commander could detect the whole dastardly history of the rat world's immense suffering and concomitant pride.

A wave smashed into them, and they went under. Twenty seconds later a hand re-emerged, with the rat held high to save her. Then the Commander surfaced as well. He was out of breath, struggling hard against the incoming walls of salt lather, and doing his best to hold back his shrieks. (He had carelessly zippered part of his private region so that one testicle was not faring as well as the other: the pain was excruciating).

Once on board, Mimi, with her sizable tits and inquisitive face, long-soaked whiskers and remarkably minute paws (given their surprising agility in water) was handed a warm blanket and a grilled cheese sandwich with mustard and tomatoes, which she consumed up on the deck with a tamed sense of considerable dignity and curiosity. She was exhausted and hypothermic, but would have made the island in another few hours.

Little Joe uncorked a fine Hawke's Bay Chardonnay to celebrate the rescue. "I think I'll take her home. I've got 20 acres of ruined pasture on the north end of town. She and her young'll do just fine. Good for you, sir! You're my kind of man."

The rat too sipped some of the wine, which warmed her bones.

"You're all crazy," Sannazaro mused aloud, "and I include the rat."

Then he could contain himself no longer: he puked overboard at the smell of the grilled cheese among such waves and trawler diesel. It would be a long trip back to dry land and Barracouta Point.

CHAPTER 60

The Causes and Consequences of Bureaucracy

THE 20 ROLLS OF photographs were being developed and would be ready in the late afternoon.

Winter winds and rain pummeled the city by the sea, known for having the least settled climate in the country. Within 45 minutes, however, spring had bored down with imposing entrance, and the green regal hills burst from the ramshackle arrays of soaked dwellings. The appearance of old San Francisco damask, Irish tackle, Belgian cobbleways emerging like Balinese beaded nets, a gallery of wet bogs, azurite clouds, prehistoric woods perfuming Wellington's waking citizenry as a Bonnington storm abated and John Callow seas out in the Strait calmed to but a few whitecaps.

It had taken a day and a night before a plane bound for the nation's capital would leave the water-sogged runway at Invercargill with the exhausted duo aboard.

"That's urban growth, for you," Marigold declared as he gazed out his hotel window. "Stresses on land use, the sound of a freeway, noisy mopeds, the early-morning grating of a logging mill somewhere out there in the maze, wood pulp and veneer production, plywoods and particle boards, of fabricated metal industries for sports utility vehicles, garages, trailers and urinals, toxic mineral fuels and 145-decibel jets overhead. Dreary shopping malls gorging on youths. Lead poisoning from handling so many house keys. Dioxins in the credit cards. Dyes in the hair. A dreadful adherence to the worst of man," he went on, his generalized laundry list of petty complaints bubbling like an acid vat, even amid a mere 190,000 people, a city voted the very best in all the country, all the world. Cosmopolitan sustainability.

Sannazaro remonstrated. "What's with you? Don't you realize that Wellington is rated Number 1? There's scarcely a factory, no whiff of smokestack or lead. A 600-acre city sanctuary with kiwi and, what's more, a fine literary tradition."

"How would you know?"

"I read all about it on the plane, in *North and South*."

"So that makes you the expert?"

"Yes, and I must honestly tell you it is the most beautiful city I have recently laid eyes on."

"I am propounding principles, perhaps not the facts as I know them."

"That's exactly right."

Indeed, the Commander had sensed that his critiques did not entirely ring true. Yet there was no denying the strong sense of contradiction that assailed him at that moment. Not since those traumatic boyhood moments beneath the Ecuadorian glacial giant of Chimborazo had he experienced so pure and unfettered a wilderness as the one down there in Doubtful. To spoil it with this city saga was a letdown. Easier to raise an extinct dinosaur from a tar pit than human consciousness.

"And aren't we pleasantly disposed this morning," the Squire needled. "You should be grateful to be alive."

For Sannazaro, by contrast, was in rare form, ecstatic to have returned to civilization, and was infuriated by his companion's dour mood. He was plainly tired of it and wanted no more. And no more rats.

"Select the one in a million for your sentimental journeys into the soul," he said, "but expect not the madding minions to follow you there, and be grateful they do not, for you would soon perish in such a multitude. As Kazantzakis so aptly put it, if everyone were St Francis, there could be no St Francis. It is true that there are nearly three million licensed vehicles in this country, many noisy exhaust manifolds, and I am positive as many commercial rubbish tips with hazardous contents. There are factories, and occasional murders, not to mention one of the largest meat and dairy industries in the world. Though the sheep have declined in number, you'll recall: no Common Agricultural Policy, not since 1983. And plenty of green hills to wander amongst."

"I don't recall," Marigold admitted.

"Well, I can tell you from what I've read that New Zealand's farmers have been weaned off subsidies, unlike the Americans. And that's probably a good thing. Certainly for Africans who must compete with a stacked deck. Pay a man to plant a rose and that rose cannot help but emanate false consciousness. Pay a man not to plant a rose, and it is an even greater sin. You cannot win your war beside money and men. There are paved roads, few maritime preserves, a sinking economy. Compared with sequestering your favorite moas from harm, that will take more than a few fences, waratahs or landfills. For all that, give me but one night of city ways—a performance of Donizetti's *Elixir of Love*, or any espresso house in this city, Maori love poems and the product of a fine New Zealand vineyard—and I will gladly accept a shopping mall to one side, rude cacophony of traffic the other."

"That's all right."

"Really?"

"Yes."

"You're serious? No regrets, no tricks? You're not holding back on me? If I wanted to call it curtains, here and now, you wouldn't stop me?"

"Um-huh." He measured the impact. He knew where he was going.

"Of course, it's all very sad."

"What's sad?"

"The Renaissance shepherd that once was Sannazaro. Just your whole legacy. Everything you supposedly stood for."

"There. Damn it. You're doing it again."

"It's obvious, my poor man. The simple sea, the untainted breeze, the perfect stars in the blue night of Perugia. And where are Ariosto and Dante?"

"He is here. Having a hot bath. Holding sunbeams delicately in the balance."

"No. I know that look. A posturing that neither confirms nor denies, but by its very steadfastness has committed to the true path of goodness and virtue. I don't doubt that you are weary. This wilderness demands all of a man, and sometimes he is not willing to hand it over. That is understandable. Our psyches need rest, too. Biorhythms are sporadic. A worsening of weather can affect an entire philosophy. Where Claude or Poussin remarked upon the sunlight as it glorified Hellenic half-columns in a verdant pasture, Altdorfer saw only murderous armies reflected in the clouds; and Brueghel threw up a mirror with his *Dark Day* that placed the treacherous Zugspitze in the center of Northern European affairs, as if to confirm the horrors of life among men. In all these instances, Nature served a cause that issued from the personality source behind the particular brush; it was remade in the guise of an attitude. For some, like the Maestricht Master of Despairs, life was to be avoided. For others, a Corot, *par exemple*, it was to be embraced. I am aware of these delicate discrepancies in the human animal whom you embody."

"I embody?"

"Absolutely. Unblushingly so. All the seething contraries that the Placido Domingo of Verdi's *La battagglia di Legnano* brings to life. But because the delineations are so steeped in the history of gray shades, I would rather err on the side of ethical conviction than arbitrary pessimism. Just because it can be built, the technology sound, the economy prepared, that does not mean we ought to build it."

"All of these grand edifices are just thoughts, my dear Murillo," Sannazaro reflected. "Step back to something I said, and something you said. I've got to get this out."

"Go ahead. Get it off your chest."

"Oh shut up."

"I'm listening."

"All right, then."

"Go ahead."

"Are you going to let me speak?"

"Did I say anything?"

He darted the Commander with a barb, then began; "That journey—through how many blocks, or sections, or whatever they call it—Mesopotamia? I noticed quite a few things, and who could forget those farmers we encountered? On the surface, a charming remnant of Samuel Butler's day. On the other hand, a terrible reminder of all that is wrong about such back-to-nature countries as New Zealand—you read the grim tallies of mutton and beef and hide and ruin, of metals and manure sprays browning the rivers, killing the shags. These primitive transitional capitalisms rely upon the ruthless and systematic exploitation of the natural world for their very existence, or that is what the first colonists set as an example. Those farmers each had, what?—1,600 ewes, subdivided into little grassy partitions to provide enough solid grass to raise their millions of lambkins: 35 million in this country each year, all of whom are slaughtered. For what? About 45 dollars in profit to the farmer per animal, minus the 15 percent who die within weeks or months of being born. Their fate is the more merciful. They perish from exposure, or thirst, or hunger. And when a farmer sees one of them face down in a bog, he passes it by with scarcely a thought. We have livestock, we have deadstock, says he. The lambs are brutally murdered, each one of them. There is indeed great cruelty on the farms, admit the farmers, with a cold, steely indifference. What is that indifference? Is it cold, or is it damp? Is it woolly, evil, obscure, tentative, procedural, inevitable, ambivalent, penitent, guilt-ridden, implacable, the genetic summation of the non-zero sum theory? I cannot separate my own rubbish from the ore, but I can tell you this: it is Auschwitz multiplied by 100,000 lambs each day. These farmers, of whom your prized Samuel Butler was an early example, are too arrogant to consider their indifference to the cruelty they inflict. That is the definition, in some resorts, of psychosis, is it not? How will you stop it? Those whole shiploads of innocent creatures headed to slaughter, rusty blades, middle-of-the-night horror? Is there any conceivable philosophy that can justify it? No, I think not. The system of thought that might encompass it is a rationalization. Again I would submit: these are all arbitrary ideas which we allow in defense of the chaos we embrace. I, for one, love a good lamb chop!

"What troubles me—troubles me something terrible—is that the brighter notions—my Arcadia, your Utopia—are just as arbitrary. Nothing is thinkable. And the same farmer who is a Hitler by his treatment of other animals will smile, raise a large family of decent-looking kids, walk a riverbank which he has endeavored to protect, citing with honest affection that hawthorn and matai, this hedgerow, brown teal, pingao and macrocarpa. He will crawl out of bed at 5 a.m. to go milk his beloved Sandra, but encourage his old bulldog to go after rabbits, curse the scoured and driven hemlock, or bring down the government on his property with a vengeance, taking out by ghoulish means every wild cat, stoat, weasel and possum. All of this defines a nation dependent on beef, milk, wood and wool. Loving little native birds, hating all non-natives. Proud of their one mammal, the bat, of which three species are known, but completely unaware that their mammaldom constitutes an exotic non-native to the country. And their beloved dogs, once unleashed, have been known to kill 52 yellow-eyed penguins at their nesting sites in a single evening. I am crestfallen. It is a historical pattern. I cannot share your blindness. Yet I must admit I love most New Zealanders we have met thus far—love them even more than my fellow Italians, and that is saying quite a lot. I would even consider moving to this country, if I thought about it. Its prettiness seems slightly arbitrary to me, however. Maybe because there's so much of it."

To this vast speech the Commander listened intently. Somehow or other, this Sannazaro of worldly coffees and laid-back tinkering, a gardener, after all, accustomed to weeding out, making choices driven by preferences that were largely aesthetic, had come clean. Offered an acute picture of human nature.

"By what you've said, I now know that we shall share everything in life. Are subject to all the same judgments. In fact, you have adopted my philosophy and you don't even know it. Your beliefs, footsteps, instincts—merged. We are a brotherhood. Though lamb chops are not my preference as you know."

"No," Sannazaro went on, "I shall be remembered for a laconic reticence akin to whispering. Whereas your lips will be likened to the wings of a confused hummingbird. You cannot utter the word restraint. Your genes will not have it. You would argue a 25-volume encyclopedia to explain the decaf in a poem, whereas I would simply enjoy the verse without a fuss. That is a huge gulf between us. Critics will forever ignore your excesses, which is too bad. Knowing you gives an added explanation when your actions in the minds of others may fail to account for your noble intentions. Whereas I present no quandary or questions. To my posthumous friends, a pure simpleton was I. Posterity might say that my mortar was all concision and firm grasp, however unspectacular my reality, a solitary troop formation of quiet shadows and a few demands; whereas you—you're a dinosaur at the natural history museum, a fantastic exoskeleton upon which passing tourists might gawk for a moment but then move on, forgetful in the aftermath. A crumbling adobe with no meaning. Sorry, boss, but that's how I read it this morning."

"But stop and envision it—a completion! No gulf whatsoever. Nothing shall sunder our perfect complementarity or come between us. We are the same glass of spirits. The same class of disenfranchisement. Identical curiosities, rancor, despair. All of the crazy discrepancies will become useful to us. Don't you see? What you think, what I think, on this day, or tomorrow—each one will necessarily have its place, and there will grow up, of this I am sure, a basis for understanding pain in the world. In the meantime, we have work to do."

"You have, I've noticed, a habit irritating in proportion to its straying from the subject at hand. A near mathematical certainty, I would add, that for every sum of the parts most take to be quite human and normal, you dash to pieces with subtractions, divisions, and multiplications. Maybe that is what they call psychology. But I find it unclad and counter-productive. Your caveman with his club is not somebody I admire. I favor the infrastructure of a cappuccino; you force instead a recognition of the sewage system underpinning it. It is a mask you wear when your passion for critique obscures the fact that man is weak, mischievous and miserable. No one doubts that. It has never been entirely hidden. It can't be. The truth resounds, in spite of ourselves. A little happiness is all we ask. You'd be happier, too, if with all your good fortune and thoughtful airs you respected more the modesty that is us; neutralized your acid, forswore this tiresome bitterness and lightened up. There is a distinct advantage in cultivating calm weather within oneself. In short, my dear Marigold, you are too hard on yourself and, by endless implication, the rest of your fellow humans. We are just frail organisms. Some with super-egos, granted. But it is useless to expect pure gravy, or greatness."

"Sometimes you speak like a true statesman, Iacobo. I will not dispute your wisdom, for it is obvious. Have I not sought the compromise of the ages in attempting to divine some utopic plateau where all might live with a decent wage and back yard? An average height, its favors spread out in equal proportions, pro rata, without benefit to one quadrant over any other? I know that capitalism has stripped bare the world in real time, allowing the marketplace to trample and stampede with the nervous tic of the frightened herd; that communism has done so in advance, topdown; and that socialism has only moderated the free market to the extent of depressing its players. The end result in any political economy is the loss of Nature. What do you think we've been doing these militating days and nights, if not searching for that very alternative key? I am no fool to overlook a ripe strawberry. Show me a door and I will unlock it. I cannot promise that I will prefer the interior design on the other side, but I am the first to grant a man his bad taste. It is just that I should rather see a world swept free of morons and evil bastards, and one where moa can roam in peace. If that is wrong, then vamoose. Get on your own mule and drive away, for I admit, declare and vouchsafe that I am who I am, what I am. I cannot change that. Gold is gold. A standard is a standard, after all."

"But yours is too high."

"Is Dhaulagiri too high? No, there are, I believe, five others that are higher. Still, I should be happy with Dhaulagiri. I may be an idealist, but am not above cleaning out the creosote. This has been quite an adventure. But if we should fail to come to closure—to save those fine birds—then all our efforts will have been a pretense. I will not tell a pretense."

"Do you ever listen to yourself ? The way you speak? It's not of this age. How do you expect to change the twenty-first century going on in that manure?"

"But you also speak thus and such," Marigold decried, grinning. "I do not."

"You do. We've been through that."

"When?"

"Five minutes ago. A veritable manure pile."

"You're making that up."

"I certainly am not ..."

"Are."

"Aren't."

Continuing in this manner, the two tireless talkers took a taxi to Parliament Building, greatly taxing their driver, for purposes of an unannounced state visit.

A guard at the entrance directed them to the ninth floor where they were met by a receptionist. She, in turn, buzzed an Important Person, who eventually meandered out into the corridor where our two gentlemen stood confidently—or one of them did.

"G'day. Americans, eh?"

"That's right."

"Well, your dollar's two-to-one, lucky you. I am the Deputy Assistant for Public Relations—Knowingsworth's the name. I have little time, but how can I help this fine morning?"

The Commander launched into an abbreviated summary of his requirements, concluding with a description of a theoretical plot of land, 100 square miles in extent, somewhere in the country, that must immediately be set aside forever as a Special Preserve, where no person may ever venture. That enigmatic, unmentionable quadrant between the zigzags of a National Trust boundary, the shades of a Park, squiggles of a Nature Reserve, dashes of a National Scenic Area, polkadots indicating a Candidate for Special Area of Conservation, tanned squares for Woodland Remnants. A place left completely undefiled.

The bureaucrat was not remotely surprised or taken aback by this outspoken stance. He was a mandarin at the zenith of his government commission, and so had qualities which commanded universal esteem.

An ability to work long hours with a team of mature plants. To be comfortable with the telephone. Communication skills that suggested speech and the added ability to process words. Liked a hands-on role. Was outgoing even when incoming. Flexible. Good backbone. Was self-motivated but careful never to be so in public.

"You may know," Knowingsworth began, "that New Zealand created the second national park in the world, in September, 1887. We have 13 now, covering nine percent of the nation, in addition to 21 conservation parks, and that's another seven percent of the land. Add to that nearly 1,000 special reserves, and what you're really seeing in New Zealand is a country more firmly convinced of the values of conservation than any other nation in history—and a fourteenth park in the works. Indeed— may I speak freely?"

Marigold certainly nodded.

"We think of ourselves as the most sensitive people in the history of conservation, not to be immodest about it. Something like 22 percent of our virgin forests are still intact, versus less than nine percent in your country. But we are a democracy. Even our most fragile ecosystems allow visitors of one sort or another. What's more, we were the first to give women the right to vote—a decision that some may still question—but as you must know, we have enjoyed the subtle benefits of a female in the highest office for many years. Though you'll permit me to add that we have a crisis in this country for want of male role models, though that, too, is changing."

"All of that is very interesting and most fine," Marigold replied impatiently. "But—"

"But wait," Knowingsworth added, "there is more. When I am finished you will want to live in New Zealand, trouble free, assured that all is being taken care of in a benign bubble fashion. Take, for example, our history of race relations. Why, the indigenous Maori are among the noblest of races. Stronger, brighter, more firmly rooted than any European visitor. We Anglos were at least wise and fortunate enough to intermarry with them as soon as they would permit us to do so, going back 150 years. Beautiful people, I might add. Whether they would say the same about us, I cannot tell. But from a conservationist perspective, let me remind you that it was the Ngati Tuwharetoa people whose chief—Te Heuheu Tukino—first deeded land to the country in the name of Tongariro National Park. All this simply itemizes, line by line, our staunch, unswerving commitment to preservation and tolerance. We have the largest Green Party in the world. The public is welcome to dive down to explore to the sunken *Rainbow Warrior*. So when you speak of a place undefiled, you're speaking the language of this office and of this country. Unyielding green in our eyes. Of course, prudence sometimes dictates colors other than green."

"Which colors?" Marigold inquired.

"You'll agree that nothing is completely undefiled. Ask anybody in the country these days, they'll tell you the same thing: an alarming disproportion of prison inmates are probably innocent, not unlike the Blacks in America. There are sociological reasons which I'm sure you'll detest as much as I do, coming from a backward, racist, historically genocidal America, where I have visited. In honesty, we Pakeha are to blame. But why fan the flames of a sad debate? We'll work it out. Treaties, foreshores, and so on."

"Sir, I value a man who cherishes his country. You have spoken like the uneasy relative of a prince, which is realistic. Yet, I must lay claim to a more fervent ideal than perhaps you have even considered. One that might be deemed radical in other lands, but which is essential if the greatest discovery of recent times is to remain unharmed."

"I see. What might that be?"

"I think, given the seriousness of the subject, it would be more diplomatically correct for me to announce the finding in the presence of your Minister of the Environment and Prime Minister. That is only fitting. One ambassador to another."

"Hmmm. That will be difficult. He's a busy man, and she's a busy woman."

"Busy, at a time like this? Sir, we come with news of the twenty-first century. Data recently uncovered that will shatter every preconception, arouse the nation to awe and incite a degree of reverence unheard of in modern times."

Sannazaro rolled his eyes.

"It will cost money, of course," the Commander continued, "and the good will of the people. A uniform decision must be taken which, in absence of a national consensus, must elicit the leadership of those two imperial individuals, man and woman, Adam and Eve, whom you describe as busy. Busy, I am sure. But too busy to save the most important symbols of wildlife in the world? I think not."

"Not to be abrupt, but why don't you just put it in writing? An old-fashioned letter, addressed to his Honorable Minister. Here is his card. Email him, if you like. That is the most efficient manner of obtaining a response."

"There is no time, not a minute, good sir. Obtaining responses, putting in writing, that is certainly not the expedient I had in mind. Let me come to the point then, and the burden is on you to keep your counsel. May we get out of this public place? An office would be a more prudent spot for divulgences such as these."

"Why not?" Knowingsworth led them into a conference room down the hall. "Please, have a seat, gentlemen. Tea? Blueberry muffins?"

"No thank you."

"Yes. Tea and muffins would be lovely," said Sannazaro.

Knowingsworth poked his head out into the hall and hailed a secretary, then ducked back in.

"All right then. Here it is, in brief," Marigold started. "We have found two rare species."

"Happens all the time in New Zealand."

"I mean two species thought extinct."

"No, you haven't. All due respects."

"We haven't?"

"Look, gents, we hear such claims from time to time. Many of our native flora and fauna bear a striking resemblance to one another. Only a trained eye can weed out one Myrsinaceae or petrel from another. People are always confusing Cook's with black-wingeds. Bitterns with shags. Tomtits with wrens. Tuis with blackbirds. Possums with Tasmanian devils, weka fledglings with a rat, and weasels, if you can imagine, with pythons. It happens: bad weather, deep forest, fog on one's glasses. Eels in fresh water. No offense. Even experts, like yourselves, I'm sure, make mistakes out in a bog."

"Sir, you are insulting us. There are enemies about. Mad poachers on the loose who make no mistakes."

"We do have our share of them, though nothing like in the States."

"Perhaps you have heard of one Mr Spitzbergen?"

"Ahh, him. Yes, there has been a good deal of interest in that fellow's expedition. New Zealanders are always eager to show off their mythology, especially if someone like him is willing to pay handsomely for it."

"And if I were to tell you it's not mythology any longer?"

"That's his contention, too. I'll tell you what we told him: the Japanese thought they could find a moa. Were certain of it. But the whole affair, in the end, was useful only to the extent it paid good wages to local bush pilots, and provided endless cartoons for our satirists. Others have mumbled about great discoveries from time to time, just like that fellow who insists he saw a dinosaur in the Congo, another who believes he found a unicorn in Vietnam. They speak of Big Foot in Washington and atop Mount Shasta—in California, I believe—and slimy people from Outer Space in your southern New Mexico."

"Those are Texans they're referring to."

"There, you see!"

"My good man, Spitzbergen is a menace."

"I doubt it. He's with one of the best helicopter pilots in the business and he's got very restricted flying patterns. He's not allowed anywhere near the kakapos or takahes. What's more, he paid the municipality of Te Anau a very substantial donation for wildlife conservation. Good man. Even if he does have a flair for publicity. Don't we all."

"And if I were to show you photographs which I took earlier this week of the two extinct species in question?"

"We should regard such images with great scrutiny and some suspicion."

"As I would expect. But I assure you, I have such photographs. If you would be so kind as to set up an appointment for us tomorrow morning, I shall bring 20 rolls of developed film. Then you will understand the gravity of the situation and extraordinary opportunity at hand."

"Photos of what?"

"Moas and a giant eagle."

His eyes dulled. "Found where, exactly?"

"I can't tell you that. Although I will at the right time."

His face became glassy and impatient. "Must be in Fiordland. But I don't believe you, even if I wanted to. Which, of course, I do."

"I don't blame you. But it's true."

Sannazaro nodded his assent, though had remained silent throughout all of this, preferring to concentrate on his tea.

"If it were true, this would constitute the biggest news in science –not just in New Zealand, but anywhere in the world. It would spell disaster."

"But what do you mean? This is a breakthrough. Hope for the future."

"I don't mean to shatter your illusions about New Zealand, but we are a bureaucracy, gentlemen; a Commonwealth bureaucracy, which is probably the most exasperating kind, because its laws and protocols date back 1,000 years and are smattered and goulashed with special interests in every quarter: quotas and surveys, polls and votes; the status quo, defense priorities, and every known notch, increment and conceit of inertia. We still speak of freeholds, leaseholds and peppercorns between Lord and Vassal. Hope for the future is all well and good, but in reality—well, you can't imagine."

"Sir, you can't imagine what he can imagine," Sannazaro applied in the Commander's defense.

"Shall I tell you what would happen if you actually had discovered the last living moa?"

"But we have, damn it!"

"OK. Fair enough. Maybe you have. So I go to the Minister, and he laughs at me. But let's say your evidence is persuasive. He, then, calendars the time and goes to the Prime Minister. She might well be atop Aconcagua or Kilimanjaro, though she checks in by satellite phone with her Deputy once a week. But the Minister is equally persuasive, and the PM has every reason to believe him. A special investigation is ordered."

"Perfect, and I am happy to pay for it."

"Well, that's good of you, but scarcely necessary. The real problem is that any special investigation is only the beginning of a long and tedious process. A way of avoiding doing anything or admitting to anything. Sorry to sound cynical. But the investigation doesn't just happen. It requires a working arrangement with other ministries, city, district, regional councilors, iwi, all scrambling on account of the RMA. What to do?"

"So?"

"So the Army has to work with Forests, and they with Commerce, whose only focus is the price of sawdust in Singapore and matchsticks in Japan and what that's doing to New Zealand enterprise. At some early stage the Directorate of Communications receives a memorandum. So does the Deputy Director of Public Hazards."

"But what do they have to do with it?" the frustrated Commander asked.

Knowingsworth raised a hand. "Worse still. The Office of Records, the Mining people, and the Ministries of Conservation, Agriculture all throw in their two cents' worth. Everyone wants to be on the committee.

There are meetings to decide such things, while the months go by."

"We do not have months."

"Precisely. But in government—any government, and I would cite you Americans particularly—there is always time for complications. Eventually the whole thing is put on hold, relegated to a numbered file in Central Accounting, along with hundreds of other cases. Because none of us likes to deal with complexity. You see, our Government has some very delicate inherent problems. Consider, for example, what happened here in 1986. The Constitution Act. Perhaps you are not aware of it, but our Parliament claimed, in essence, divine right, usurped the people's sovereignty, revoking the *Magna Carta* of 1215 and *Scottish Declaration of Arbroath* in 1320, both limiting the power of Kings. Now, the people of New Zealand have little power. It has been seized by the political process. Mongolians have more legislative clout than New Zealanders. Take the Ministry of Agriculture's recent decision not to eradicate the varroa mite, which will destroy all of our wild bees and much of our fruit. A disaster that can only result in the decimation of most flowers and birds, and that in spite of everyone who knows anything about the bush—farmers, horticulturalists, scientists—telling these damned stubborn politicians what's what. Acquiescence to a presumed *fait accompli*. Ignorance edified. And I work on behalf of it. And they're probably going to do the same thing with regards to platinum mining atop Mount Anglem. And we've spent a fortune trying to wipe out one of the most beautiful birds in the world—the Australian lorikeet—at a rate which computes to 10,000 dollars per immigrant bird, believing that she bothers the tui, when all the evidence shows that, if anything, our native bellbirds are falling in love with lorikeets. A morbid mindset, a ruinous economy, the rule of the dollar. A chance to tear up some land that nobody sees or much cares about—never mind it may be the last paradise in this whole country—and walk away with hundreds of millions of dollars. But it is a free country, we are all agreed.

"But say I were to put a bug in the Conservator's ear, one of our finer DOC reps for Westland. An ecologist, not a politician. She gets round to reading the Comptroller's Report, which could take two years to generate. Usually they get shelved in the National Archives where they are lost forever, alongside all those dreary photos of cows hauling out kauri in the days of the timber booms. But say she reads it and demands a hearing, an emergency session of Parliament, which she would—I know her, she's the best conservation ally we've ever had in office. Then what? Well, I can fairly predict. She is viewed by the Co-Venter Party, or Full Compliance, or some other covey of politicos, as a barefaced opportunist wanting to make a name for herself, or secure a second home in Fiji. Someone who is trying to use this moa of yours as the basis for catapulting, perhaps, a future election campaign. The PM quietly suggests woman to woman she resign. Tall poppy syndrome."

"But this is all absurd. I thought you said she was a good woman? And who cares about Fiji?"

"Oh, she is the woman for the job. But there are plenty of political aspirants who might be only too happy to showcase the creatures, or see them as the country's solution to the deficit. A New Deal for the unemployed, a breadcrumb for the indigenous peoples, a symbol for the Greenies, something to take the country's mind off the fact its kiwi is endangered, its financial markets in the dumps, our water filtration systems breaking down in many cities. I can already hear speeches being written, by the same people who would secretly cut deals with industry to exploit the moa. Meanwhile, the Maori contingents will claim the region of the discovery as an ancestral burial ground. There will be protests. The *Natural Resources Act* up against the 66 plus 22 chains minus the prohibitions of the Coastal Reserve, and Maori claims of taonga."

"I'm lost."

"Picture this: the Army moves in, followed by the scientists. Then the merchants. The Government will take it as an excuse to build a dam and a viaduct. And surely a bridge. Jobs. Contracts. Another hydroelectric plant. Phosphorus. More national debates about outflow and effluents and kilowatts. Then come the bungee jumpers. Restaurants. Fences, roads, tunnels, an airport, a sewage disposal plant. Shops merchandizing moa keyrings, T-shirts, posters, pamphlets, coffee cups. Not to mention a black market for moa feathers and bone. Maybe even the last eyeball. All the while the Ministry of Education is trying desperately to appropriate money just to buy a few dictionaries for the children of Milton or Ross; foreign engineering firms are putting in bids to use the electricity for aluminum smelting; members of New Zealand's own genome project are looking to engineer moa beef steaks, perhaps even extract moa genes for insertion in red deer (more meat), while the ecologists are lamenting the bird's discovery in the first place, declaring it would have been better were it truly dead, where it might remain suitably symbolic and ecologically mythical, immune to crass commercialism, or iwi prepossession."

"But this is positively preposterous, from every angle up, down, sideways. I am horrified, sickened, repulsed, incredulous," Marigold said, missing Sannazaro's "told you so" demeanor.

"Ahhh, but it gets worse," the panjandrum continued. "Say this huge eagle of yours is killed when it flies into the rotor blades of a helicopter, which causes an international uproar. We have new General Liability policies following that dreadful beekeeper tragedy, and politicians use it to embarrass the current administration. There will be site visitations by UNESCO officials. And what if the helicopter crashes and the explosion kills people, and starts a fire that burns uncontrolled? The trees of Fiordland have no evolutionary mechanisms—like your sequoia—to retard fire. We're already in the thick of one helicopter investigation—some alleged sabotage, hard to say, no answers as yet, or none I can divulge, but the upshot is, I lose my job. Why did you even talk to them? I'll be asked, drilled before Special Session, midnight oil, hell to pay. A rigorous mess. My son's at university—not cheap. What do I do? Double car payments to maintain. A man of my age—see the creeping gray? They notice that when you try to make a fresh start. What, a waiter in Nelson? Like that former Governor of yours from Arizona, working in a diner? Don't think so. I have a mind to throw you out of this office right now, before you do any more damage to the country, or to my own retirement."

"All I'm asking for is five minutes with the Minister. I'm a billionaire, you see. I can help this country. What's more, I bring news of a giant fungus that talks."

Knowingsworth hiccupped, reflecting a disqualified and disgraced canoe lost in the sea of important people. "Another jew's ear," he reflected.

"A what?" Marigold angrily replied. "Was that an ethnic slur or some botanical observation?"

"See here—" Knowingsworth showed them a work calendar with 100 anal lines, marginalia reputed by Tudor or Stewart penmanship, fancy numbers and illustrious names. "The Minister is busy all day tomorrow, and leaving on official doings in Malaysia tomorrow night. Nasty business up there. Gay protests and water sanctions against Singapore. It's just not going to happen. Why don't you do this: send copies of your photographs to me. You can be assured they'll be in safe hands. When the Minister gets back, I'll show him. If he wants to pursue it further, we'll be in touch."

"Damn it, man. This is a *moa* we're speaking of !"

"It's the best I can do," Knowingsworth concluded, heading towards the door. "Keep in mind, New Zealand has the highest suicide rate in the world amongst teenagers. So many things on our minds, these days."

That struck both Marigold and his Squire as bizarre, however true it might be. Sending shivers to the heart of the problem. A lack of history? The economic morbidezza? Peer pressure to conform? A social inertia that overpowers the horizon, undercutting impetus, willpower, strength of vision, dreams? None of it made too much sense, particularly in light of a moa. But Knowingsworth himself had been a teenager once. And all the Ministers, as well.

"I'll think about it," the Commander said gloomily.

They passed on a handshake, strode deflated from the circular parliamentary complex, and hailed a slow-moving taxi driven by a man of other dimensions, obsessions at the wheel. Was life easier for him? To be unencumbered by such despairs, debacles, hopes such as flagellated the Commander? He worked for dollars and hours, not for the whole planet; translated time into money into a new apartment and dishwasher for his wife; slept peacefully at night, gave himself to his work for the allotted hours, then could set his mind at rest. No such luck for Mr Marigold. Who slaved in the dredged shadows of his own holy-rollerings. Was condemned like few have ever been. Did he know how rough he was on himself ? Did his Squire ever break through with tender words, or the thought of slowing down? Could Marigold hear the silence which pleaded from his heart, or turn the river round so that he did not expend all of his days in short order? He had no sure idea as to what was happening to him; no way to gauge the process, since he was in the middle of it, without mirrors or foils. Could not step back and gain perspective.

Nor was Sannazaro entirely helpful to that end. Though they shared many of the identical sentiments, their styles and orientations were offset. Sannazaro truly desired to be left alone; to have meager adventures, risk free, and be quiescent. The country life was for him. Whereas his tossed-together companion, once a modest hermit, had become a storm-trooper of unassailable stampedes without lesson or recall. Nothing could slow down his runaway train. They were like unto the Khour Dubai: Deira to north, Bur to south—a creek, in other words, dividing a whole country that was the one endeavor, made of two men.

"At least he was honest," sighed Sannazaro.

"I can scarcely comprehend. Who would believe that right is construed as wrong, discovery a bad thing, salvation a nemesis. That a moa should be ignored, the perpetuation of all that rings as true denied!" Marigold was appalled, his Heaven-hoping plans disparaged out of existence. No money in the world could dispel the frustration. "George Orwell got it right," he concluded.

"As my people say," replied the Squire, "*dalla rapa non si cava sangue*. You cannot get blood from a turnip."

CHAPTER 61
Quae amissa salva

IN SPITE OF HIS NIHILISM, the Commander managed an idea. "Let's simply inform the Executive Director of the largest conservation group in the country. Surely he, or she, with all the appropriate contacts, clout, inner-system wiring, will want to seize these reins. Remember, this is a country where 600 primary and intermediate schools—18,000 students—rose to the challenge of creating art that would help save wildlife; where 12 percent of the nation belongs to Greenpeace. A country that, for all its Knowingsworths, mandated that its seas and exclusive economic zone constitute a nuclear-free region, and which was the first to advocate an Antarctic World Park. With such pedigrees, you will never convince me that a Save the Moa Campaign will not fly."

Sannazaro shook his head forebodingly while the Commander thumbed through a directory and placed a call to the Wildlife Forever Coalition.

"Hello? Please listen carefully," he began. "I am what you might describe as an ecological diplomat from the United States. Not one of those Rio types, mind you, who trails behind sustainability conferences like some rock band groupie ..."

What is he talking about? Sannazaro wondered.

Mr Marigold cleared his throat and proceeded in thumbnail to sketch his peculiar situation.

"Come on down, right away then," the pleasant-sounding chap suggested, intuiting a donor behind the incantatory voice.

They went out towards the wetlands reserve at the Pauatahanui Inlet near Plimmerton where the Coalition's offices were located beside a charming garden walk and the sea. On the wall of the Director's office was a placard with a quotation from some famed New Zealand ornithologist, which read:

We are slaughtering everything in this country. Is that the future we desire for our children?

"Is it true?" Mr Marigold asked the Director, Thomas Miller, after handshakes. "The poster, I mean."

"More and more, yes. New Zealand has nearly 10 percent of the world's total of endangered bird species. Not until 1977, with the 341,000 signatures of the *Maruia Declaration*, did the Government even begin to own up to the fact of its responsibilities environmentally. Yet, to this day, the country remains essentially uncritical of industrialism. We are one of the 34 hotspots designated, sadly, by Conservation International. In fact, we are one of the very few entire countries that ranks as a hotspot—a biologically imperilled place. Trout fishermen who come from Missouri never get that far. It's the frontier mentality. In all of the Pacific Rim, only the Tasmanian Green Party members have figured out a kind of tense, if imperfect alliance with the power elite, and that's the Green–Australian Labor Party Accord. And believe me, it is no Utopia. Just ask the *Eucalyptus regnans*, tallest flowering trees in the world which are being clear-felled. But then, I'd be happy if New Zealanders could agree to agree to examine what's happening right now, forget the unlimited future. It's these petulant little blinders who are ruining New Zealand. A bit like those sunglasses that wrap all the way round. New Zealanders all think of these little green islands as a paradise, ignoring a history of bloodshed and wanton destruction that is ongoing. It's as bad here as in the Amazon or Tongass in North America. And we should know better. We do know better. Nine percent of the country is preserved, 30 percent partly preserved, though not from hunters. Everything is about money. But enough of my rampage. I'm afraid I have you cornered, which isn't fair. How can I help you two unsuspecting blokes?"

The Commander relayed the pertinent highlights of their face-to-face encounter with Bureaucracy. He concluded by referring specifically to the discovery of the moa and the eagle. "I can't tell you where the encounter occurred but I assure you, it did take place."

"You're certain of it?"

"Yes."

Sannazaro nodded his assent.

"But that's—" Thomas Miller was faint, staggered, sat down, breathing deeply, held his chest—"absolutely astonishing."

"I was hoping your Environment Minister would think so, as well. But he won't even hear me out, not directly, which you can appreciate is essential."

Miller took notes, swirled in his chair, pondered, collected himself, laughed nervously, then exploded with a hoopjoy. "I simply can't believe it. This is the best news I've ever heard. In my life, I mean. I have a daughter. She's precious. But, I confess, there are daughters everywhere. Whereas this—this is better news than the day she was born. I mean it. Thank you. Thank you." He paused. "But you mustn't despair about our Government.

That was Knowingsworth. A name like Cinzano, in Morocco. He's a positive freak, the height of party lines. Take no offence. I know him very well. We fish together. But he is no risk-taker."

"I pet fish," Marigold countered. "Yes, well, we eat them over here."

"But you're a conservationist?"

"Yes? So?"

Marigold had nowhere to take this. His mind had seized up into a fissure of no holds, slimy shadow, seaweed worlds, silent consternation. Life was caving in all around, certitudes cracking, chimneys crumbling. And his Italian counterfeit was of no substantive assistance. Sannazaro loved white fish. What was to become of these people? More to the point, what of all the fish, believed by neurologists to be the most sensitive of creatures on the planet? And last question: what of the moa?

"There is another way to pull this off," Miller went on, releasing the top button of his shirt. "Stuffy in here. Wellington officialdom must be no different from the obstacle courses of London or Washington. You just have to work around it."

"But how?"

"We have precedents shared by few other countries: a mere 3.8 million people, all of whom think of themselves as conservationists. Show us the photographs. One image can save thousands of feathered friends. We'll raise the money for full-page ads in the newspapers, just like you Americans did when your Army Corps of Engineers was going to destroy the Grand Canyon."

"Did we take out ads?"

"Well somebody did, a bloke named David Brower I think, and it worked. A million people were outraged enough to write to their Congressmen. A compromise measure was worked out."

"You don't need to raise money. I have the money."

"I'm speaking of a lot of money."

"He has the money," Sannazaro chimed in.

"Truly? All the better, then."

Sannazaro was agitating in his chair, and the Commander noticed. "Speak up, man," he urged.

"Well, you'll pardon my saying, but do you really fancy a million people knowing that there are moa left? Won't that stir a craze? You'll have every redneck bounty hunter in the world coming here to find the birds. Japanese. Germans. Not to mention Norwegians."

"The point, Mr Sannazaro, is to set up a private guarded preserve, is it not?"

"Yes, but it's already in a national park."

"A national park? Fiordland, I imagine. That will add difficulties, though not insurmountable ones. We know from experience what to expect, but we also live here and have plenty of time on our hands, and some very good solicitors. Some of them used to work for the Department of Conservation. And of course, there's always the provisions of the *Resource Management Act*, or *RMA, Section 5*, which in essence demands mitigation of any adverse environmental consequences."

"The birds have no time," the Commander underscored.

"I may be cynical," said Miller, "with good reason. But we do have some impressive examples of direct action in this country—better than most. We managed to increase the black robin population on Chatham Island from five individuals in 1980 to nearly 40, following their careful relocation to South East Island. As for the owl parrot, or kakapo, there has been a concerted effort for well over a century to save it. First, when the nineteenth-century ornithologist Richard Henry removed dozens of the birds to Resolution Island. Unfortunately, a couple of sly stoats swam across and killed the refugees. Bastards. I hate stoats. I gather you're vegetarian. But I assure you, if you met one, you'd hate stoats. Later, when a small population of kakapo was discovered on a virtually subantarctic peninsula, the birds were moved to Maud Island, north of Nelson. Stoats eventually swam there, as well. So the Government provisioned that the survivors be moved to Little Barrier Island, following a clean sweep of all predators. By 1990, one chick had hatched. Other kakapo were taken to Codfish Island."

"Yes, I know about them. I was just there, swimming with a rat."

"I heard there was a rat. I didn't hear about you. We hate rats. Well, the point is, there are members of Government who do care. And our Parliamentary Commissioner for the Environment and our *Forest and Bird* people are brilliant. The system is a system. I am no apologist, but have come to know that a meadow has its cumbersome clods, imperfect bumps, but they are true dirt nonetheless. We have DOC, after all. And make no mistake: it is the finest environmental agency in the world. Top drawer. Great scientists. Amazing accomplishments. Moreover, this country is concerned to keep all that's ecologically precious about New Zealand intact. Let's face it: ecotourism is the only reliable source of revenue this nation's got left. That, and the very idea of New Zealand."

"Kiwifruit?"

"Minimal."

"Wool, meat?"

"Industries on the wane. Biological oxygen demand. Nitrogen and phosphorus. Get the photographs, let me see them, I'll wait all evening if I have to. In fact, I'll drive you myself. If the images are what you say they are, trust me, we will get a preserve. The Government created a sanctuary above Lake Te Anau, more or less, so they'll certainly do it for moa. My God, *moa!*" He could not fathom the news.

But the situation took a decided turn for the worse when Marigold and Sannazaro, escorted by Miller, went for the developed photographs.

"What's this?" Marigold said with a weakening voice. "They're all white?"

"Sorry," the salesperson muttered. "Hope there wasn't anything too important on that film."

"Important? You've made an error in the processing. I demand to see your manager."

"He's in Australia for two weeks. His grandmother was eaten by a crocodile."

"That's terrible!" Sannazaro inserted.

But Marigold was undiverted. "Who else is in charge, then?"

"Well, it's just me and the processor, Sam."

"Crocodile!" Sannazaro went on, mumbling to himself. The horror of it. A grandmother. She couldn't have had that much meat on her ...

They were led into the back room.

"Sam, why don't you explain to these customers what happened on those 20 NG rolls."

"Oh, are these the guys? Bummer. You shot everything overexposed by six stops, Mister. We can work with two, sometimes even three stops. But not more than that."

"What's he talking about?" the Commander appealed.

"Just as I figured," Sannazaro told him. "You don't know the first thing about cameras. Remember when I mentioned ASA and exposure settings?"

"But it's an expensive camera. It's automatic. It does everything itself !"

"Not if your basic settings are completely unmatched to the film stock, which they were. Sorry, mate," said Sam.

"But ...but..."

"How old was she?" Sannazaro wondered, still hung up on the notion of the crocodile eating a grandma. Nature was so unfair. Or was this all about culling the sick and infirm from the herd? Were there herds of grandmas in Australia? He'd never been and couldn't say for sure.

"We're not charging you, if that helps at all."

Mr Marigold sat down on a stool, hunched and mortified. "I don't know what to say."

"Too bad," Thomas Miller murmured.

"Were they wedding photographs, or a christening? I've seen this sort of thing happen before," Sam offered by way of meek condolence. "Even a divorce came of it once."

"Both," Sannazaro indicated.

"Oh well, if it's any help, you did get one partial image," Sam conceded. "Though I can't tell you what it is."

Marigold lurched to his feet.

"Where?"

"I marked it, just to show you what went wrong. It's the last shot on the sixteenth roll. You must have dropped the camera or something, because the setting parameters appeared totally different."

"I did drop the camera, as a matter of fact. Where is the image?"

"Here." Sam withdrew one of the rolls from a bag and showed the partial quarter inch of emulsion with its perforated edge. "This one was probably shot at F5.6, and a fifteenth of a second. But all the rest were definitely wide open, probably 1.2, and nothing but blue sky. You probably had it on B."

"What is that?"

"Read the manual, mate."

Ignoring the insufferable reality of his own ineptitude, Mr Marigold put the sole half-image up to the light. There was a looming shadow, out of focus, unrecognizable but for its size. It towered above the Commander like the shade of a kauri tree, curved and rounded, soft and fine. Mr Marigold knew exactly what it was, but would anyone else?

Outside, Miller offered to drop the two men off at their hotel. "I'm terribly sorry, guys," he said, "but the image is worthless. So much for full-page ads. I'm in the dark here, and I'm afraid there's nothing I can do. It's your word against the last 500 years. Really, you should learn how to use a camera and go back to the spot in question. Then we'd have something to work with."

"What do we do?" Mr Marigold asked Sannazaro over dinner later that evening.

"I don't know. Maybe you should join forces with the Government, and offer to finance some kind of conservation center. Before they totally cave in to Spitzbergen. Maybe they already have."

"Why is the world so inclement? Why can't people talk to people, animals be part of the parliament, and the whole system work amicably, without rancor, discord, hostility, pollution or effort? Wouldn't it be easy, wouldn't it be sweet! If I can see it, why can't others? No swords, this time. Just a photograph. What a disaster! Those magnificent birds. I'm smitten, do you understand? This is true love."

"Maybe if you committed a full billion to the country."

"You're right. I should. I will." And he started for the phone. "Wait!" Sannazaro shouted after him. "Not a billion. It's too much!"

But Marigold was already dialling the Prime Minister's office. "Hello," he began, before explaining the whole saga to a surprised-sounding secretary. But to no effect. It was just another version of the perennial UFO. A phantom hoax, hearsay, the paranormal. All that money counted for less than proper ASA and F stops.

That night the Commander lay awake in his bed, contemplating the world.

"I'll learn how to use the camera properly and go back, then," he told his room-mate.

"I'm not going."

"I wouldn't expect you to. I'll go it alone."

But within an hour the Commander had changed his mind. Maybe there was a better solution, after all.

Sannazaro, equally unable to sleep, caught his mood. "*Quae amissa salva,*" he concluded. "Things lost are safe."

CHAPTER 62
Philosophy in the Twenty-first Century

IT HAPPENED THAT the Commander had reached another bottomland, no less a nadir than the Hong Kong prison where, as he would later describe it, he endured tortures of every sort. It was not the jail itself, which at least blocked his view, but the indelible inward realization that he was the same flesh and blood as those Hong Kong butchers. They had let him out of the cell, but there was no one to let him out of his humanness. Presently, his wit had crashed again, this time in the wake of New Zealand's bureaucracy. With so much suffering in the world, he had hoped for easy concordance on all those tasks oriented to positive change. Delays? Debates? Disillusionment? No time for such luxuries. Having read the most recent findings on hunger from the UN Food and Agriculture Organization, particularly the data from North Korea, Laos and Ethiopia—the fact of nearly 800 million hungry children; aware of the latest global findings on the biosphere, which boded uniformly ill, Marigold was desperately impatient to make a difference. He knew, for example, that global warming would kill all the ferns of New Zealand. He had hoped, frankly, for an immediate embrace of the logic of conservation—for much more, in other words, than Government scepticism and disregard. He also knew that wasn't entirely fair. He could easily have withstood the odd buffoon, gone directly to a Regional Council, or the Environmental Court or choppered in for more photographs. But something in him resisted. Sannazaro was right.

And there were 10,000 other queasies and fiascos to further put his bathos in proper perspective. Every newspaper edition engendered grief; each newscast another day of mourning for victims throughout the world, whether lobster or leatherback, Liberian or London homeless. If Buddhism had set its sights on alleviating agony in the person, telecommunications had rendered personal salvation impossible. Now, one was forced to extend the olive branch—altruism traditionally reserved for kin—to the whole planet, and this made for stunning odds against accomplishing too much of anything.

His list of grievances had escalated since his financial windfall. Against each sordid Goliath he addressed himself, this architect of sustainable solitariness, this shaman of socially-challenged humanity, maverick of extreme chivalries, impossible flame-thrower of a generalized compassion, doubly naïve diplomat, healer-turned-hellraiser, peace-nut, vitamin vizier, emperor of new beginnings and no-guilt fabulist favoring all affairs of the heart. First a fungus, then the eagle and the moa had triggered in him a deep afternoon, morning and evening of the soul. Mornings he slept in, as a rule.

Whereas Sannazaro took nothing personally. He slept soundly, repudiating any semblance of agitation. Indeed, his sleep was that of angels in Fra Angelico, of dead lipstick set idly on the ranks of a beauty queen, or old brick walls faintly traced with graffiti bearing shredded layers of past love affairs, remote gardens, forgotten graves and sepia-colored empires. He was his own species of dreamer, and that moa country had unleashed a lifetime of sea drifts. In Marigold, by contrast, the great avians had incited dreaded ordeals and prayers. The Commander had consolidated those inclinations to save the world in a list of current affairs that weighed morosely on his mind. With his voracious aptitude for sniffing out mischief, even prior to the incident of the chicken and the well, and its subsequent mayhem, he had cut newspaper clippings, glued together notices, downloaded items of urgency. Now, all those emergencies fed his inconsolability. The dead end in Wellington had punctured his balloon, banished the champion. He was angry.

He sat propped up in bed, reflecting on all the melancholy madnesses, while Sannazaro, nearby, rested, sipping on a fine New Zealand 1996 private bin Te Motu Cabernet/Merlot, watching a game show and flipping through back issues of *New Zealand Gardener*. It was a 4-star hotel, with plentiful 50-gram Toblerones and salt & vinegar Pringles in the quietly lit alcove above the refrigerator.

Marigold's husk brimmed with causes and recollections. He contemplated the atrocious slaughter of dogs in Taiwan; and the continued carnage of children, roosters, and hamsters in the Sudan, women in New York City, young girls in China and a grandmother in Australia. He went on a mental tirade against motorcycles and recreational vehicles (which Sannazaro proclaimed were no different from the exoskeletons of beetles), AM radio, plastic grocery bags and canned soup. He exempted Sanitarium Marmite, which seemed to him an essential of civilization. He sought answers to the hideous paradoxes of our time—the fact that Rwanda's former Prime Minister, Jean Kambanda, could so calmly admit to masterminding the massacre of 800,000, mostly ethnic Tutsis; what, he wondered, had NATO been thinking, as it remained inert during the massacre? He enumerated in his mind the sickening scene of 4,000 neo-Nazis calling themselves the National Democratic Party of Germany, gathering in cities like Leipzig to declare that "radical problems require radical solutions" and threatening to expel by force all foreigners. And he considered the 30,000 Cambodians who had fled from the Khmer Rouge into Thailand, only to sell their youngest daughters into sexual slavery. He imagined all those countries where a free press did not hesitate to broadcast a live suicide—as in Los Angeles—and those which sent editors and writers to jail for the slightest outspokenness, as in Tunisia, China, Jordan, Belarus, Cuba, Nigeria, Myanmar and Turkmenistan. He mused over the hundreds of millions of hunters in the world, over ozone-depleting chemicals, red mercury—a powder capable of decimating whole cities—and the recent NASA data showing that rain forest destruction in the Amazon was 30 percent worse than at any previous time, despite all the years of supposed campaigning and consciousness-raising.

With all this dinginess of human affairs beneath the clouds, he understood—groping and blind—that such looming perils required the same white knights, shining armors and human verbs of diligence, selflessness and courage as in past eras. Regardless of where the forest fire was burning, Mr Marigold seriously believed that there were systematic ways to put out the flames and refurbish the soil. In every trouble spot of his beleaguered brainstem there was some mirror image of an alternative. Perhaps this was unique to his peculiar save-the-world complex. Whatever inclement weathers motivated him, the Commander was aflame with one abundant hope, a strategy, a personal avalanche of engagement. He would not submit to Never, or No, or Impossible.

True, he was a sick man, Sannazaro reckoned. Maimed with worry. But that was what he rather loved about him.

He would say, to whomever might suffer his pontifications, that theories of karma and reincarnation would not suffice as the first order of foundations. What foundations? Never mind. But be apprised: one could not hope to understand the nature of right and wrong unless one had truly struggled on behalf of another. He would not hear of the inner child, psychotherapy, meditation, achieving spiritual contentment or oneness. He had absolutely no patience with those New Age narcissists who believed the world could not be saved until one saved and purified oneself.

"Horseshit," he rebutted.

Such philosophical posturing, he believed, was an academic leisure of self, imposed by the luxury of free time and a disinclination to become part of something greater than oneself. Learning without action, said Marigold, was an extreme form of selfishness; study without involvement mere self-absorption; knowledge for knowledge sake a tragedy. And he was reminded, in discussing these weighty matters with his Squire, of the British philosopher Karl Popper who once remarked that not to believe in reality was a moral sin. Beliefs come through action, insisted the Commander. Small particulars of the everyday that one could seize with one's hands. The greatest manifestos fell short of that moment when one being assisted another, asserting a simple gesture of kindness. Academia without ethics: pure nonsense. What was it about benevolence—helping someone cross the street—that transcended words, unless, of course, it was a kind word itself? Words could be helping hands, certainly. But in the end, they usually beggared a hollow sound, like "United We Stand" or "Make Love, Not War". Words came too easily. Sentences and books, as well. What was difficult, thought Marigold, was setting aside the words, and standing up for the world, all this from a man who had spent the majority of his years doing absolutely nothing but reading old books.

So he'd drawn up a list of worldly quagmires on a given day: a timely chronicle of deep wounds and slow, gnawing wrongs that had urged him forward into battle during the last months of the millennium. They were testimony to the times in which he found himself, with its global forest fires and vast pain. And at the risk of getting burned, of perpetual chronic fatigue and failure, he threw himself, with not a few stumbles, into those flames.

Some would say that he had the money to do so.

The money had only taunted him, thus far. Yes, it had bought awareness. But that meant identification with victims and a corresponding personal pain for which no remedy was forthcoming. The more he knew, the less money he had, if he bothered to translate and transmute the awareness of particulars into any given budget, which he attempted. In the end, he knew that blood would easily drown all the available money in the world. With the increasing futility of his passions emerged a panic born of clarity and, finally, burning rage towards the unlistening human race. He could not bear the thought of interest, passive income streams, of waiting to clip coupons or cash checks. He was innocent of yields, even short-term bonds. There was no escaping it: Mr Marigold, newly awakened in middle age to the way of all things, had discovered that he was utterly outnumbered by savages, with no indemnification.

He had never considered himself a misanthrope but rather as a lover of ideas and their people. Now he was not sure. The words of Blau, Milliet and Hartmann came back to him from Jules Massenet's *Werther* in moments blood-red and flushed: "*Les larmes qu'on ne pleure pas, Dans notre ame retombent toutes...*" ("Tears unloosed plunge back into the soul...")

There he stood, transfixed.

He had only blind, fitful prayer to sustain his illustrious vision of a preserved Pleistocene habitat in southern Fiordland. It was impossible, said Sannazaro. A form of masochism, an incurable disease, even to hope for such things.

"How loud would I have had to scream to have changed that retrograde's way of thinking?" he asked, referring to the Greenie who had turned him away for lack of photographic evidence. And the other one, Knowingsworth, who didn't want to know.

"It is not the volume," replied Sannazaro. "And the awful part—even if you chose to commit a terrible act of violence against a jerk—"

"I would never!"

"I know that. But if you did, you would still not have the satisfaction of changing his mind."

Mr Marigold laughed at the absurdity of his predicament. Soon both men were rubbing tears from their eyes. Too much hot oil in the *tiella di carciofi com aglio e peperoncino* ordered in desperation from room service. The Commander's first inkling of a dangerous variable sugar disorder. Then they grew silent from overeating. Marigold lay plopped down in his bed, staring out the window towards the Cook Strait, still munching nervously on his frayed artichoke.

Sannazaro, however, knew the signs: all of Marigold's untowards were in actuality his forwards. If one were to draw an itinerary of his life and travels, it was beginning to have the look of a circumspect zigzag skewed upside down and in reverse. Every moment of enthusiasm belied a tragedy. Each minor scrape revealed a wound that was a mirror image of a calamity, which nurtured a success, only to be undermined by so-called humanity all over again and again and again.

Later, as a storm picked its way across the Strait, slamming into windows throughout Wellington, Sannazaro suggested an outing.

"Wind and rain against the cheeks will do us both good," he bargained. "I vote for an invigorating trek to the nearest pub. What do you say? And tomorrow we'll fly home to New Mexico."

It sounded too good to be true. And it was.

CHAPTER 63
Islands of Inexplicable Levity

THE COMMANDER FITTED himself in outdoor gear, still coated in the mud and debris of his South Island travails, and the two of them headed to a nearby drinking establishment situated on a hilly corner, lights aglow, the music of conviviality emanating from every chink in the aging exterior. DB beer and rum with L&P, a variety of local lemonade, flowed freely, as did the language of old New Zealand: old mates, the "shaggy-bearded rowdy-hatted and independent" sort whom Butler first perceived amid "ragged roods of scrubby ground", chins in hand, boiler groans, boiled spuds, free-range children, one a pecker, a mess of prates, hind legs of the Lamb of God, the roadless North, bull strong and pig tight, those fences surrounding that famous "little tree touched with scarlet—a clump of toi-toi waving in the wind—and looking for all the world like a family of little girls drying their hair". Things baked on ashes upon the ground, and Haeremai, haeremai, haeremai, a Maori greeting, all around. In this *ancien régime* of a pub where civilized men, ranked by their drinking capacity, spewed news of hauspicious hoccasions, the biggest rabbits, birds, mouths, tattoos, wooden bridges, concrete breakwaters, cabbages, artesian water supplies, and glory-hearted people all mingling in the exchange of loud college boasts and great truths.

To Sannazaro's eyes, this was a contemporary tavern, no different, no less than a Friday evening's merriment back in Santa Fe. Nose rings, bald heads, exposed belly buttons and good drink. Cappuccinos afloat on the heaven of the coffee-bean explosion. But to Marigold this was the pub of Samuel Butler's day, with its bulletins, hair restorers, those careless of money, brooding observers, visitors from abroad, parents from Lower Hutt, brute strength and calm repose. Pipes-of-pansy water lilies, moral cowardices, rates of profit and losses, rubbernecks and road maggots, milliners and billiard-markers, foot-warmers. He heard no word of the America's Cup or Helen Clark or the All Blacks, or talk of Wearable Arts, but rather of running streams, stink trees and sheep fast asleep, bees in July, black billy tea, the air of loneliness, scattered wooden boxes, the gospel of love, comfortable lawns hemmed in by roses and natural songs, counterbalancing drawbacks, the last bottle of gin, heaps of pennies and the fact these Wellington men were known by the mechanical way they screwed up their eyes and clapped their hands on their hats. In short, Marigold was Marigold, and heard a differing ethos.

And as strange fate would have it, Marigold seemed on target to manifest a man right out of Butler's time, sitting there among them at the bar. An old harbormaster—Jonathan Salkeld was his name—discerned a captive audience and regaled them with a tale most elusive and fair. "Pull up a stump," said he, "if you've even half the spine of a whitebait. It's the story of the last sane person in this or any other hemisphere—a man blown yon upon those mystic winds of the subantarctic who had chosen for his course in life the quiet felicities of lonely thought, a historian of ideas, a monk of philosophical deep tidings. But what evidently had most impressed his thinking processes were the various mysteries associated with wit."

"Wit, did you say?" Marigold seconded.

"That's right. He had become an anthropologist of that human capacity given over to humor; the pun and its therapeutic effects on those who would listen. He'd evidently selected for his terrain the remotest islands in the southern ocean, the ones that whisper at night, not unlike sand dunes groaning as their iron pilings stirred, for reasons not entirely clear, except to say that these were the heartiest of peoples down south—survivors—and that no task was greater than to crack a smile in granite, or burst a sunbeam and a moment's calm upon a gale. In fact, he's still living there, somewhere between the 1808-foot Ball's Pyramid, straight out of the water, and some other crazy cliff halfway to Antarctica. Nobody's sure where or if he lives or dies."

The details were sketchy, but, upon some questioning, the salty dog admitted that, once, he had actually met the hermit of hilarity amid the operatic seas.

"What did he look like?"

"An odd man. Neither tall nor short. Of stalky build. Dashing, in a way; studious, too. A sort of Mungo Man."

"Did he tell you any jokes worth repeating?"

"Allow me time to embroider. I'm getting to the situation."

"Go on, then, for you have more than stirred my impatience," the Commander wrested.

Sannazaro could see that he had. Out of such doldrums as the preceding days, a little levity could certainly do no wrong.

"As his steel ketch with its 30-foot mizzen was circled by mollymawks staring hard at what I would've taken to be cray pots with their store of sad and ancient gyrating giants, the ones that move 7 kms a day on ocean bottoms, I assumed, naturally, this man was another crayfisher. A tonne of them 60-year-old monsters will fetch a good 100 grand a year. But that wasn't his thing. Nothing of the sort."

"What then?"

"He was using the pots for rescuing lobsters, not catching them! Oh he was a strange old Jacky, he was, and chuckling inwardly. Not your normal guffaw, but the squeaking of a hyena. The philosopher's irony, in a word. One who'd seen it all, was the effect. A researcher, a dilettante, somewhere in between? Who knows. Last anybody'd heard, he'd sailed his boat from off Pyramid Rock, beyond Pitt Island, across the Chatham Straits, 860 kms due east from Christchurch. It's uninhabited. Just a cliff, as far as can be figured. Not a single place for peat, possum, even gorse. Just the eternal wind and spray, and a deadly sea larded with white pointers who would take your leg if you so much as batted an eyelid," the fisherman explained.

"And?" the Commander pressed, wanting nothing more this hour than to be immersed in an uncomplicated tale.

"Some ventured he must be of Norwegian makeup, others held him a true-blood Moriori. A couple of Tasmanians said they knew him as one of theirs; a Ukrainian chap alleged the same thing. Bugger of a zigzag. A'course, he might've been a mere hermit from an island unknown. Truth is, nobody ever asked him. Till I did, that is."

"Tell us."

"He was Basque, from a village called Guetaria. And he claimed to be a descendant—and I would have to believe it—of the first man to circumnavigate the world."

"Magellan?"

"No, no. Magellan was killed on the voyage in the Philippines. His second mate, Juan Sebastian del Cano, also from Guetaria, finished the mission at the helm of *Victoria*, after uncountable adventures. In the end, the ship, with her 85 tons and 18 Spanish sailors, landed at Seville on September 8th, 1522, three years after her launch. This descendant of Cano carries that in his eyes. His hair is tied back and reaches his waist, his skin is burned by the wind and too much sun—hell, might as well capitalize them both, sun, wind—his voice strident with philosophy that comes from deep within his chest. I mean this man is a survivor. He's been everywhere, it seems. I liked him, and I feared him. For there was something about his motives which eluded me. That and his unearthly laughter."

"Motives?"

"Yessir. This stark, howling punster lingering deep within his insanity. There had to be a pretty solid reason behind it. But it was a madness that put to shame all those of us who imagined we were on some common ground or even plane. We each carry this veneer that serves like daily bread or fitting currency to get around, keep us clean and attired and away from each other's throats. The decency, you might say, which gives us half a chance of living side by side or on the same end of a harbor. But this fellow, he'd seen through our meager put-ons, knew it to be one crock a' pig pokey in chutney, and wanted none of it. Hard to get a word out of this stump of a man, other than a crackle. Sort of a ghost, one might conclude; a tough old green sheep, or wrybill plover with his bill bent to the west like them in the Firth of Thames, or Isle Osea, going all the way back to the first oyster."

"But what was he laughing at?" Marigold inquired.

"Yes, recite a few of his comments," added Sannazaro, eager for some good cheer.

"Ahh, well, now that's a story. By no other means do men show themselves more poignantly than through their humor. Who was it who said that? Anyway, you had first to see this little book he had. I beheld it with my own hands. Edge-worn sketches of no seeming consequence, diary notes like a schoolboy's or homestead's, little class scripts from private lands. A magic tome with recipes and spells, he said. Full of surprise plays on a word perpetrated upon man by the gods which he'd collected from all over this world. He mentioned journeys to Africa, New Guinea, Russia, Trinidad, Japan and so many other out-of-the-way ports. There was bedevilment on every page, to be sure; and, according to him, the cure for any depression. He told me the answer to existence, he did. But I was so drunk I can't for the life of me remember it. Later, when I was more clear-headed and sobering up, whatever the hell he'd said was gone. And so was he. I could kick myself and always had a mind to go searching back."

"His name?" Marigold pressed (Sannazaro could already detect the telltale signs of an impending doom—that impulse in the Commander to go looking for something).

"Crowquill," the bluecoat ventured, before signaling the barman for beers for all who would listen.

"Just Crowquill? No good name?"

"That's right."

"How long ago did you meet him?"

"A year or so this month, in fact," the mariner replied. "I wouldn't a' forgot that day, never, on account of some strange concurrence. In all my years at sea I never saw such a thing. His boat was surrounded by dolphins, playful, breaching, laughing creatures of that type. I mean hundreds of them. Along with the dark little fur seals porpoising just as friskily. They seemed to know Crowquill on a first-name basis. It was uncanny." Then, changing topics: "You don't resemble sailing men."

"Too prone to seasickness."

"Well, if you should ever want to find this Crowquill—" he could gauge the Commander's level of interest in the enigma—"we have patches for that."

"It's a good thought."

"It's a singularly bad thought," added the Squire.

"No, no... hold on a minute," Marigold countered, puzzling over the notion of the meaning of life. How could he turn down so obvious a little canter? To girdle the earth with dauntless hoots and volunteer one's flag in search of land, even if the boat, the man, his island were an imagination. A bondage to nothing but the crystal in a morning moon, a fresh mint upon the sea, a lady's lips up close, in no hurry, so that the mystery might linger still.

"I might even be induced to help you, just for the fun of it," said Salkeld. "Frankly, I wouldn't mind having him repeat what it was he told me. This time I'd listen better."

Marigold toyed with his chin, then said, "Done."

"Done? What means that, 'Done'?"

But Sannazaro could not forcibly arrest his Commander's obsession in the coming night or days.

"What good will it do your moa?" the Squire, truly panicked, pushed later on. "This is no longer funny."

"Don't you see? That book, the location, it's got to be the elixir philosophers on all continents have been searching for. If we could but locate the original joke, or sense behind authentic humor, there might be a chance to mend the world, to contain it by the yoke of its mirth."

"Elixir? Yoke? My candlepower be fried. I can already tell you who this joke's upon."

"It is no joking matter, dear friend. Nothing could be more serious. What I have just sensed is a trickster in subtle wise; the first impulse towards irony; a man, if you can imagine him, somewhere out there—" he gestured across a Delaware or Golden Valley of fantastic hectares—"an authentic consciousness endowed with the purpose of our ancestors to plumb the sacred code of all complexity and exhume that simple quintessence. Call it a joke, if you will; or, my preference—the very first smile in human history. Name it however you wish, but I sense in it the course of reason, the fate of our honor, whatever method was used to fabricate the human spirit. A smile, I repeat and would submit, that countered all baloney, whose steadfastness earned it the first inward pleasure, grateful harbinger, gentle sea, country cornfields and fragrant bosom. The root of all philosophy."

"And I foresee a shipwreck," Sannazaro countered. "I cannot, will not, ascribe to your larval stage wherein what is too obvious becomes veiled: Hollands gin perverted with obscurity. That look of yours that I know so well even now veers: no jaunts from the easy path into the thickets of Schnebelite—chlorate of potash, explosive, misery-laden jail cells in Hong Kong and fiords teeming with biting flies. No, I must not."

Marigold was amused by this gushing fool of disclaimers. For all the Squire's noise, they were bound by laws of brotherhood, boyish ligature, equal season. Follies beguiled by shared principle, a Pillow Book of Blather brashly welcoming some mutual cause of action.

Marigold began, "Need I remind you of the great 'Essay on Man' by Pope, whose Bolingbroke remembers that, 'All nature is but art, unknown to thee; All chance, direction which thou canst not see; All discord, harmony not understood; All partial evil, universal good; And spite of pride, in erring reason's spite One truth is clear: whatever is, is right'.?"

Sannazaro, addled by his comrade's fanaticism, added a timely appeal of his own from Tennyson's 'Ulysses'—but in reverse: "'It may be we shall touch the Happy Isles, It may be that the gulfs will wash us down.' It is this latter I wish not upon myself, thank you very much."

"Fear not," Mr Marigold resolved, quoting Benjamin Casseres. "'Progress is nothing but the victory of laughter over dogma.' Imagine this Crowquill, noble scion of the Castile or Navarre sovereignties, out there alone among high seas and endless storm, spreading the noble truths of levity, the godly tears of glee and buoyancy. Can there be a greater motive than to lighten this load you and I have unsuccessfully borne?"

"You imagine him. I'm going home."

"Where is your sense of adventure, man?"

"Give me cakes and ale, and spare the good cheer. If ol' Crowquill has such a godly thing going, why spoil it? Leave well enough alone, I say."

"You are hard before your time; short, rude and bad luck even unto yourself. Anyway, you're halfway there already, so quit this rubbish."

"What if you should find this nonsensical book, and its enigmatic author? What then?" the exasperated little Italian asked.

"Eureka after eureka," replied the mesmerized Hermit of Tesuque, sensing mightily a kindred spirit. "A gold rush of possibilities."

With time and money on his hands, and an appetite for brash, impossible fixations, Mr Marigold hovered over a map of the region— speckled islands in the Roaring Forties and Screaming Fifties, as they were known. There, between 44 and 60, and Longitudes 159 and 175, were the mysterious isles— Macquarie, Campbell, Snares, the Western Chain, the Auckland group with Enderby and Disappointment, the Antipodes, Windward, the 13 Eastern and Western Bounty Groups, Points 124 and 2391, the ten Chathams, including Pitt, and Pyramid. So many alluring names with their vivid hold on the imagination— Remarkable Arch, and Ball's Pyramid, to name but a couple. Craggy points of interest along that storm-wracked maritime New Zealand plateau.

The following day Marigold had a second meeting with the mariner Jonathan Salkeld, and pressed him for more about the lore of the region. The mariner told him that most New Zealanders knew little about the history of the Chathams before the recent publication of a book by an historian, Michael King. He explained how English naval Commander William Broughton had first slipped into safe harbor at Kaingaroa on Chatham in November 1791. A dispute had broken out and the first Moriori were murdered. Wildlife were plundered—the huia with their golden beaks, rails and albatross, fur seals and pigeons; and then, in 1835, a Maori warring party of 908 from the mainland laid claim to the islands, killing 325 Moriori, and enslaving all others, nearly 2,000 of the indigenes. Such was the turbulent, only recently resolved history. The last of the full-blooded Moriori, Tommy Solomon, was laid to quiet rest in March of 1933 on a point sacred to the Moriori. Today, a mere 750 souls, mostly fishermen, their wives and children, congregated on the 38-mile-wide Chatham, and 50 on the much smaller Pitt.

He left off, drinking heavily and weighing all the details of the commission. They would fly out 72 hours hence, when the twice-weekly service was available. On Sannazaro's part, curiosity betrayed equal fear.

"Who is this old fart?" he asked Marigold. "What makes you think he's actually seaworthy?"

"He looks the part," Marigold hastened.

"So do you, which exposes the flagrant truth. Appearances have not once worked in our favor. We know nothing about him. Or his boat. Did you even ask?"

"Yes, of course I asked."

"Well, that's fine. But I am tired."

"We are always tired. It is no excuse."

Sannazaro turned away. Seething. Confused. But already returning to the Commander's side, another glass of wine in hand. His own human nature was a like sailing vessel whose response to the wind could be predicted. Marigold knew that by now. Even if Sannazaro wanted it kept a secret.

Within three days and 45 minutes, the Commander, Sannazaro and a beer-fuming Salkeld were in Waitangi negotiating for a boat with a cast of brooding, suspicious, bait-smeared, orange roughy-fishing locals. A southeaster, 40 knots at least, was forcing its way abreast Chatham amid diminished sun count, veils of water on the wind-shattered cliffs floating upwards,never dropping down.

These islands, it was rumored by travel writers, had five things in reliable profusion (more of them per inhabitant than any other spot on earth): fax machines, Harley-Davidsons, cray trawlers, guns and wind.

For all the island's wild beauty, explosive surf, inland bogs mired in bracken, the populace, to Marigold's thinking, seemed unaffected by aesthetics. They were, instead, hunting crazed (the guns were for the grey ducks, weka, wild pigs and pukeko), sullen and rarely speaking, and to an unwelcome outsider seemed among the most humorless people on Earth. Maori used to ride their horses around the island three times in the belief that this would rid their inner sanctum of Europeans. It nearly worked.

The Commander toured the precincts but was happy to get away from these demarcated sand traps in the frigid southern Pacific. Sannazaro was not surprised, having suffered for one more fantastic flight into oblivion of his own. He had his method, however. It served him well to see his Commander ransacked by such dour airs when what he'd fantasized was some perfect island retreat. Clearly, inaccessibility was no formula for Paradise.

The Squire was only too eager to have Marigold fail at this; to crash through the rotted ceiling of revelations. That way, at least, he could finally counter any more odysseys with a practical retort: that they bid farewell to this contradictory part of the world where all the trees resembled old men's beards, where people never took their clothes off, and every pub concealed an abuse. Where dogs were maltreated and a damp hut thought of as a villa. Sannazaro had allowed himself to be bent, like the damnable supplejack of upper Doubtful, whose black adamantine limbs, or vines—whichever they were, technically speaking— were unrelenting. Iacobo found himself easily forsworn to misadventure because he was weak, gentle, uninclined to fight. The Commander's feckless ways were bound to come to a head and land him back in his original bed. Sannazaro had, to some extent, bided his time in anticipation of that great day. It wasn't that he didn't admire Marigold's humanitarianism: who wouldn't? He was just no marathon runner himself; no fame claimer or mongerer of good deeds. His lottery had been won and he would always give charitably. But to consume his own flame in long-ago visions ... no, not for him. A few more hours at the Chathams and it would be over, and fittingly, given their maritime coordinates, which fairly spelled the last inch on earth.

Alas, as the poor Italian refugee was to discover, such logical endpoints were not so easily achieved. Marigold, after all, was a fanatic for turning over stones, trying picnics, forging reckless rivers—"Ka whawhai tonu ake! Ake! Ake! forever and ever," hailed the Maori chiefs.

Prior to such battle cries, the Moriori had whispered love nothings, which now the Commander embraced as his true pitch and hue. There were documents verifying some southern Garden of Eden as recently as the eighteenth century. It was said by the earliest English and New Zealand navigators that the Moriori were one of the most peaceable tribes ever encountered by white men. Between them they harbored no shred of ill will towards anyone. Their demeanor not unlike that remarked upon in the famed diaries of Henry Heuksen, assistant to Townsend Harris, first US ambassador to Japan, in which he observed the members of the Imperial Palace: "Not one diamond sparkled among the crowd of courtiers. A small gold ornament on the handles of their swords was hardly visible... The simplicity of the Court of Edo, the noble and dignified bearing of the courtiers, their polished manners which would do honor to the most illustrious court, cast a more dazzling splendor than all the diamonds of the Indies ... Not one bayonet follows them; they carry no other weapon than two swords ... I fear, Oh, my God, that this scene of happiness is coming to an end and that the Occidental people will bring here their fatal vices."

The Japanese picked their noses, not with a thumb, like Europeans, but with a little finger. The Moriori didn't pick their noses either, said Marigold. How would you know? Sannazaro upbraided him. You've never even met one of them. And anyway, it would be impossible to be a person and never pick your nose.

Another argument that would never be settled between them.

Of course, no philosophy of human nature was possible in a vacuum, and later voyagers to the Chathams upset the pre-existing balance, importing their loud show of human imperfectibility. An anthropological perversion, played out in the psyche of the collective. But whatever insults were conveyed here in times past, settlements disrupted, harmony strewn (as it was in the Meiji Japan that followed the arrival in Tokyo Bay of Commodore Perry), the Commander was only too eager to embrace the notion of a Moriori legacy free of darkness and ruin, of a time in human evolution when fairy tales and mirthfulness prevailed. And to his way of thinking, this extraordinary period of innocence was not entirely lost. Indeed, survivors of the culture, were now enjoying a modest renaissance. The country had finally acknowledged that the Moriori were, in fact, the first to settle New Zealand, as early, possibly, as the seventh, though more likely between the tenth and thirteenth centuries. Either atop the Chatham or on Pitt Island. Crowquill was himself fascinated by them, according to all that Salkeld had heard and presently conveyed to the two naifs in his company. They were, in truth, Voltaire's "three blind men who grope after a fleeing donkey", as the scholar Theodore Besterman had once translated the rare passage from *Le Philosophe ignorant*, published in 1766.

CHAPTER 64
Captain Oguh Heads the Search for Crowquill

SALKELD HAD MADE inquiries in the local tavern, where domestic Black Robin beer was served up in considerable quantities. Yes, Crowquill had been spotted, though engaged in no ship-to-shore communications. He was last seen loitering about Glory Bay on the south end of Pitt. With him were a small coterie of giggling local girls and one adult, a woman, who was seen to be laughing for no reason. A pathetic sight, volunteered the observer, a shore fisherman who dared not speak with any of them. Good sense. But it was enough to inspire confidence in Crowquill's would-be followers.

Marigold hired a well-equipped schooner, the *Harbinger*, from Captain Oguh (whose blood, said he, was approximately one-third French, a third Maori, a third Moriori, and an extra couple of percent he wasn't divulging) and second mate Ti Iwi. Both appeared to be professional eccentrics: cynical, burnt-out, been-there-done-that attitude. They knew these waters, that was clear, and made no joke therefore of the hazards. Sannazaro would ordinarily have trusted Oguh, but knew deep down that this captain was not up to the Commander. He sensed trouble, naturally.

There were kayaks and an inflatable zodiac on board the *Harbinger*. And according to Oguh, the schooner had been all the way to 62 degrees South, acquitting herself admirably amid 70-foot swells and the treacherous labyrinths of ice known as polynyas. She came equipped with all due modern technology— satellite feeds, sonar scans, redundant systems, global positioning software and a laundry line. She was some 94 feet long, with her eight sails in 'OK' condition. Her flying jib, main topmast stay and fore gaff-topsails had been resewn by a Maori woman skilled in making traditional cloaks and baskets. When the light hit the foresail center ship, the whole boat seemed buoyed by the glow of her tattoo-patterns, warrior billows, beneath the churned-up southern skies.

Oguh was not one of those sea tyrants who insisted on everyone doing his share. In fact, upon sizing up Marigold and Sannazaro, *genu verum* the first, *genu valgum* the other, he laid down an aft-to-stern mandate that they stay out of the way, mind their heads, avoid the engine room and, in short, do nothing at all. He grasped scrawny ineptitude when he saw it.

The team—Salkeld managing the operation, Oguh and boy in charge of the boat itself—made its way out into strong weather, breaking into the rhythm of 20-foot surges, puking overboard (in the case of the Italian) and heading in a direct line to the harborage in question.

"When was he last seen there?" Marigold managed, between bouts of grip.

"Two months ago," the captain said. "No telling where he's abiding these days. But it's on your dime, so I don't mind at all us searching forever."

They reached Glory Bay late in the afternoon and for a time lay at anchor in a sandy bottom region of seven fathoms, out of the gale. Then a 90-horsepowered zodiac saw them to shore, where the Commander, Squire and Salkeld all shared a room in a but-and-ben conjoined with a muttonbirder's bower, while Oguh and Iwi slept on board the *Harbinger*.

It was no ordinary B&B, for tourists almost never came this way. Junked cars were piled in back, along with boar-hunting dogs unleashed and full of vinegar. They roamed wild, but their feistiness had been mollified through a careful regimen of food dependency. The two dozen families at Glory Bay—birders and fishers, the odd gout-ridden retiree— were connected to the rest of the world by radio beacons tuned into a faraway 2ZG signal at Gisborne in a northeastern corner of the North Island. They had a dirt track for off-road vehicles that ran north to the villages of Old Gaol and Kahiutara. Further south, the islet of Rangatira cast an ominous silhouette with its roughworn hills entangled flimsily in the flotsamed air. But south of that, Pyramid Island shone distinct and dark against the dazzling outlines of the perpetually stormy horizon. Nobody ever ventured there.

Almost as soon as the party landed on shore, amid festoons of green thallus and bladder, bull kelp, muttonbird scrub, jack vine and black swans defecating, their ears became aware of a peculiar set of chimes.

"Human gaiety, is it not?" the Commander ventured.

"Indeed, it sounds so," Sannazaro concluded, his own ear to the mistral.

They picked their way through tussock in an attempt to pinpoint the sound. On being admitted to the elevated hovel atop pylons that was to serve as their accommodation, it was clear that children were laughing, and several mothers as well.

"What's so funny?" the Commander demanded.

The children could not reply. The matron of the house—a woman of massive size, an edifice of ample adipose to absorb hunger, cold and all else—was not so prevented from a fair answer, as she appeared more immune to the hysterics of some previous prank. Her greater body fats apparently shielded her from comedy.

"It can't be something we said, or did, for we've said or done nothing, yet," the Commander thought aloud.

"It weren't," she bluntly told. "Fore yer time."

She gave them a key and a price: 20 dollars, including breakfast. The owner, who sat behind the reception area beyond the fat woman, was weak in her own right, and could not stand on her own two feet, but kept to a chair, with one hand to her side, for she too was ailing from lack of oxygen amid such a squall of joviality. Similar inconveniences and pain, to a greater extent on account of their youth, or added frailty, could be easily detected among the others, who frolicked in the ague of some terrific joke, but with little pulmonary or forced exhalation capacity to withstand such giggles.

"He's been here," the Commander speculated aloud. "Good Madam?" He turned to the glazed-looking innkeeper. "When? When was Crowquill here?"

"Can't rightly say, curse his name," she stammered between chuckles uttered as if in the shadow of some terrible Tourette's Syndrome variety.

"Oh it hurts, my ribs, my stomach, oh *God*! Ha-ha ho-ho—but please, if you see him, we need a cure, we do: we need one badly. Please!"

"A cure?"

"There, you heard her," Sannazaro declared. "She begs for a cure. So much for your praise of folly."

"I don't understand? Can you explain, dear friend? We're here to help."

"Frog spit and calm waters," the fisherwoman and innkeeper blurted.

"What's that?" he asked. A nervous tic? he wondered.

"Ha-ha, ho-ho. That's all we've been able to do. Ha-ha," the innkeeper yodeled with a metrical slavishness. "My ribs are aching from it. I've died 50 times. I can't breathe for all this wasted laughter. No fishing, no hunting, ha-ha, no activity worthy of the name. Sewing, candle-making, pickling, even the effort to devise and execute a chocolate cake—it's too much, I tell you. Break an egg I can do, bake it I cannot. Not since that devilish maeroero came round. Months ago, I would guess. The children and their mothers, too. God save us. Call the medics. Ha-ha, ho-ho."

"Maeroero? What is that?" Marigold questioned.

"A wild man of the woods. The first inhabitant of New Zealand. He may be the last one left," she cried.

"By what indications?"

"His way, his long shaggy hair." With that, she mumbled a Moriori hiri or invocation for those in need, spreading haphazard flicks of the finger to the four directions and proclaiming, "Moon, sun, brightness of heaven, calm pastures of Wairua-rangi. Go ye, spirit," and made a concerted effort to control her own chuckles with an inner battle of spastic gymnastics. "To the crown of Hiti in the east, Tonga in the west, Hui-te-rangiora—happy gathering of happy heavens—ha-ha ho-ho. Never mind, blast it. We'll be all right. There's a phone book in the room if you feel the need."

"For what?"

"For help."

It was as much as the demented woman could do to pour a cup of coffee for the guests and have them sign in the empty registry. Crowquill had not left his mark.

Observing the dozen other people in the house, it was clear to the Commander that all was not right. A debilitating fever possessed each one, without consideration of age or gender. One child was blue from so much laughter. It was as if some killer algae had released a neurotoxin, or they'd each stepped on the poisonous barb of the stingray.

"Was it a joke he conveyed?"

"For your own salvation I dare not repeat it," the afflicted one proclaimed. "But it was good. Oh yes. He knows a thing or two. It may look bad. It ain't that."

"Ain't what? I'm sorely confused. Are you in trouble? Are you not? Did you learn something, or did you not? Tell me. I can handle it," the Commander urged.

"No. We can't handle anything," Sannazaro rushed to add. "We don't want to hear, see, know!" And he tightly squashed his palms over his ears.

"Was there a book from which Crowquill read?"

"There was indeed," the keeper replied. "A sacred book, though sometimes I think it might be better burned, its ashes watered down and buried in a high tide, irradiated, mashed, plundered and disposed of deep in Hell's hole. There would be a dispute about that, and somebody might get shot. Fact is, nobody believes us. I've tried to alert the mainland, but my voice keeps breaking up and nobody will do a thing to relieve the terrible ha-ha, ha-ha that has gripped these parts. We have a dreadful dilemma on our hands. Then the panic recedes, and I must admit it is wonderful as the orgasm!"

"I can see it, dear Madam; your virtue shines beneath the gallows and gales of this strange humor. But you mean to tell me you've all been laughing ever since he departed?"

The poor blanched former figure of a woman nodded that it was terribly, blithely, weirdly so. "These fortunate isles have come under his dominion. I can't say whether it be good or bad. Only that all are crippled here with thought and strange cheer since Crowquill arrived and then departed. I used to cherish my depression. Now, damn it, I am truly happy. We all are. Glad to be alive. Wouldn't touch a flea in this state. It's the way of the world. I'm sure of it. Don't know if I can stand it, though," she carried on, obviously dreadfully confused.

"But you don't need help, in that case. You are to be marveled at. Admired."

"No," Sannazaro broke in. "Have you not heard a clip or wing of this poor woman's piercing cry for assistance?"

At that moment Salkeld entered the house. He'd been sniffing around a bit.

"Seems there's trouble here which is consistent with everything else I've been hearing and viewing," he said. "They've all gone mad, though I must confess they seem happier than most islanders you'll ever meet."

"Skinny, too," the Commander commented, noticing the evident emaciation which pervaded the cluster of laughing souls, save for the innkeeper herself. "They're prevented from eating. Their lungs are choking for air; their stomachs keeled over. They need medical attention," he concluded.

"What was the joke?" Salkeld asked.

"Damn you, don't!" Sannazaro pleaded. "You'll catch the plague. Close your ears, listen not."

"He's possibly right," the Commander seconded. But he could not walk away from it. "Go on, we'll cut to chase," he tried the woman. "Tell us. I fear no contagion, not when couched in mirth."

Sannazaro backed away. "No—I will not listen."

She began, but was taken far to the wind with a cry as galling and sorrowful as any. It came right from her roots, a plaintive appeal of the drowning sea, 100-foot swells liquidating her speech rudiments. Something was blocked in her lower chasms. She coughed up sputum the density and length of seagrass, then fell back into her rusty chair. The labor was too much.

"I can't," she gasped.

Marigold consoled her. "That's all right. You need to conserve strength for another day. Help is coming. Pulmonary physiologists. Head doctors. Pharynx doctors. X-rays and gamma rays. You will survive. And then you'll all look back at this episode as the saving grace in a human life. I am certain: these are beatitudes, special ordinations, the tiremarks leading to enlightenment. Fear not."

"And I say we get out, *now*!" uttered the Italian, escaping the mad looks, white hairs, damp jolts and high-energy pathos. "No good fun in any of it. Sickness only. Dire days behind, more in front. Now Jonathan Winters. Jack Benny. Bob Newhart. They are funny. And there is no illness involved, no risk of passing out. But this Crowquill business—I am against it. Something is obviously not right. I say we jettison. Now."

CHAPTER 65
A Mysterious Lighthouse Amid the Bounties

THEY WALKED UP A dirt road to several empty adjoining farmhouses. Down near the old fish processing plant, workers were fingering cigarettes that had gone out. Mr Marigold offered one chap a lighter, but the fellow's hands were lost to twitching. There were no explicit ha-ha-has issuing from this cabal, just a tetanus-like smile lockjawed upon each man's face.

It was the same everywhere they hiked. Women and female children who hadn't thought to smile in years—all were in the grip of side-splitting paroxysms; doubling over, tears. This among depressed fishing people accustomed to looking 60 at 30, and with the highest skin cancer and boredom rates in the world. People the most suited to a good laugh— which must have explained it.

"Did he state a purpose?" Marigold asked the eldest of the women.

She stared dreamily at the Commander with a perplexed sigh, enlightened, baleful titters, a mind lodged in mystery, like that Indian who emerged after 16 years of coma. Where had she been?

"He wanted to save the world," she finally allowed, mournful eyes distended, halfway to happiness. "'By reason, blest by faith: what we have loved, Others will love,'" she said. "William Wordsworth. He quoted him, he did. With some effect, I'd add."

"A learned man," Marigold declared, impressed equally by the woman's grasp of memory and her obvious familiarity with the Lake District poet. He'd underestimated these islanders.

"And by laughter he made his wisdom understandable, even for the children," she volunteered.

"We don't want to hear it," Sannazaro insisted.

"Are you sure?" the woman asked.

"Was it worth so many weeks, months of this exhaustion, this incapacity?"

"Yes," without pause. "Absolutely."

"My God, woman. You appear radiant with conviction. Are you able to fend for yourself? To carry on? Boil some cauliflower, replace a light bulb, clean up that infant's diapers, dispense some lollies?"

"You've missed the point," said she. "We don't need a thing any more. We've seen the light."

"Which light?"

"Some kind of laughing gas, ha-ha. He ran the island's one popsicle truck with it."

"Laughing gas! A popsicle truck?" Mr Marigold was more confused than ever. "Madam, help me out here. There is much bafflement in the air."

A dog, no pitbull but a poodle, disturbed by the constancy of daft-brained human companions, bit one of them, which resulted in more side-splitting. Someone else, in their bog boots, fell in the mud and slid down a hillside into a barn. Again, atrocious and unwitting merriment ensued among all those who witnessed the plunge. "They're brainwashed, that's what," Sannazaro exclaimed, the humor catching on.

"We're dealing with something supernatural, gentlemen. I need to call Civil Defense from the boat. This whole island, as far as I can tell, requires evacuation," observed Salkeld.

"We must find that book," Marigold hastened. "Those popsicles, as well. Maybe there's marijuana in them. Do what you will with the authorities, but I'm not leaving these waters until I know what Crowquill knows."

"You're tempting a new breed a' ghosts, Mister," Salkeld warned. "Remember: it's only one small step to lunacy."

"No fear of that," Sannazaro said. "For he's been in that state since I've known him."

"One can go blind by imperceptible stages in these parts. My father did," the old mariner relayed. "And I don't mean syphilis."

They found the popsicle truck parked against the side of a wool shed and turned it inside out.

"There's the real man," Salkeld noted. "He's been scavenging for spare parts from the looks of it."

There was no engine, but wires hanging freely where there had been an attachment. Of Crowquill there was no other trace.

Absent other leads as to his whereabouts, and without pursuing the old woman's confession, the trio quit the island, returning to the schooner anchored a quarter mile out in the harbor. Nothing made sense. Crowquill. The popsicles. Laughing gas. The people.

That night, the Commander puzzled in his bunk over the elusive Crowquill, this baritone of unknowns whose duty to humankind had flowered among the ladies of Pitt Island. None on board had been able to fathom him, though the captain had some ideas.

Captain Oguh had always thought of the Pittans as of a different breed, caliber and sensibility altogether. "You have to understand something," he began, upon hearing of the strange machinations on shore. "They're a mighty peculiar lot—always have been, even by Chatham standards. That's why they keep to Pitt Island. Insular and prone to haughtiness, they're better than the rest of us, or so they think. They can be crazy, too. What you're seeing may be the norm. Hell, they get a hold of something new, like a popsicle truck, and there's no telling what they'll do with it, or think of it. Sort of like that climbing tecomanthe, *Xeronema callistemon*, first found on Three Kings Islands at the end of World War II."

"What is so strange about it?" inquired the Commander.

"It's the most solitary plant in the world, that's what. Seems to like it that way. But these Pittans, they're goodly souls, don't get me wrong. And some of them quite wealthy, though you'd never know it. Father like son, mother daughter. Honed survivalists enshrined in modesty."

Oguh knew all the Moriori, as he was deeply enmeshed in local politics and working part time for the Moriori Trust on Chatham. There was no Crowquill in the island's tribal family tree. Moreover, said Oguh, Ti Iwi, who was normally given to absolute superstition and tree worship, had also heard nothing of any long-haired humor-mongrel among the locals, and certainly no *Book of Laughter*.

Nonetheless, Oguh agreed to call Civil Defense in Christchurch and filled them in on the strange situation, though he himself found the scenario slightly preposterous, as nobody in Chatham had yet been afflicted. The one local police officer whom Oguh called up, the nearly retired Witherspoon, had heard nothing of the disturbance but agreed to check up on those few families in Flower Pot at the north end, where he'd noted several phone calls had gone unanswered. Civil Defense, too, said they'd dispatch a medical team to investigate the following day or so, depending on the weather.

"What exactly are we inquiring after?" asked one of the officers. "Suspected foul play, is it?"

"Missing persons," Oguh estimated. "Whole town's gone wacko."

"Nothing new in that," the official poked.

But Marigold would have none of such cynicism. He thought it a downright shame to characterize the women's chuckles as in any way untoward. "It could be balance or imbalance, the release of pent-up energies, divine, subtle, cruel, even suicidal," he countered. "In a world which many are tempted to view as hopeless, ugly, increasingly oppressed, this small, elegant saga, one man's contagious philosophy of life—the willingness to smile, the ability to laugh at ourselves, and to take those overwrought moments we all encounter daily with, perhaps, a slightly more graceful balance of leavened mirth—can only be met with profound gratitude, don't you think? After all, was it not Bernard Shaw who said that the most serious things in life are funny?"

"Or doused in brandy," Oguh added, pouring himself, Salkeld and Sannazaro stiff shots from his own private cabinet.

They then, variously, retired.

The following day the *Harbinger* scoured the infernal coastlines of Pyramid, with its sheer walls, darting wild goats and deep caves. In a gigantic cove they found a kelp harvester, and for a moment believed that it might be Crowquill himself. Bedecked in bathyscopic headgear with an enormous oval-shaped coverlet of thick glass, and a wetsuit from the days of Jules Verne, the queer-looking stranger was covered in a thick red kelp forest, snorkeling through a dark grotto, pruning and collecting in his floating sack the largest of the succulent green bulbs traditionally used by Maori to hold the adolescent muttonbirds burned out of their nests. There was no boat in sight. He was out there in strange, perilous waters, all alone, no umbilical cord, no diving tanks, far from anyone or any anchor.

"Ahoy there!" called the Marigold. "We're looking for a man who goes by the name of Crowquill? Have you seen him?"

"What's that?" the diver called back through the choppy waters. "Crowquill, do you know about him?"

"Crowquill?"

"Yes, we're looking for Crowquill."

"Crowquill, wizard of the popsicle truck?"

"That's the one."

"Sure, I seen him, on his back. Showed me a thing or two about the giant squids, he did."

"Squids?"

"Yessir. Talks to them, he does. Damnest thing I ever seen in these waters. They came right up to him, and changed colors for him. Strange bugger. Only man alive, I reckon, who has seen the giants, *Architeuthis dux* and the flashers, the 175 pound *Taningia danae*."

"Did he tell you any jokes?" the Commander asked.

"No," the harvester stated—and ambiguously chose to leave go the subject, though he did provide one critical clue: "A lighthouse among the Bounties. That's where he called home."

"You're quite certain?" Oguh inquired. "For I know of no lighthouse among those islands."

"Those were his words," the snorkeler replied. "That's probably where he returned to. Three days, if the winds are on your side. Now I got business to attend. Good luck to you."

He disappeared beneath the sea.

"Humm," Marigold conjectured aloud. "Perhaps he knew better than to try laughing underwater. Or maybe the mask was so tight it constrained the veins to his pharynx, inhibiting the physiology attendant upon punch lines. But what did he mean about the giant squid? Are there giant squid in these parts?"

"Never seen one. Nobody has. Only the dead ones or the odd living larva."

"Three days to Bounty," Oguh repeated. "We have our wind, we'll go quietly, though the return against the same high pressure and north-easterlies will keep the engine busy. Diesel's a'plenty. No worries. I assume you want to go, Commander?"

"Absolutely not," Sannazaro cried out. "Of course we do," Marigold replied. "Which one?" Oguh pressed.

With that they headed southwest, only the vast sea and sky before and all around them. For Sannazaro, it was a time to reflect upon the strange quirks that had brought him to this end-of-the-world sailing expedition from his Italian Arcadia, via New York and New Mexico. As for the Commander, who can say what thoughts swished top and bottomside in his waterlogged cocoon of a sapiency?

On the third afternoon, Ti Iwi sounded the "Land ho!, sort of."

The winds and currents were powerful. The map showed a total of about 300 acres between all 19 of the twelve known granite islands and seven rock points, none of which was large enough to constitute even an islet. There wasn't much room, given that thousands of crested penguins stood on every available windswept nook of land. Salvin's mollymawks and Bounty shags circled in frenzied timothies, uplifted in the snowy white fogs, gentle swinging eyes in Chardin wine glasses, while erect-crested penguins, having cultivated their preening regimes to a fine art, screeched hilariously about who knows what from their steep granite slopes. Densities of life crowded out any obvious lighthouse.

They searched all afternoon, past Spider, Skua, Depot and Proclamation, along the impossible sidings of Ranfurly and Lion, Penguin and Ruatara. There was nothing but sheer void at Funnel, and it was nearly as bad upon Prion and Castle in the Center Group. Out at North Rock, a bleak nothingness on both spires, and to the south, at Molly Cap, waves 110 feet high, but no lighthouse.

"It is a ruse," said Sannazaro, happy to be rid of the legend. "May we go?"

It was then that Oguh spotted something on his navigational radar he had never noticed in the annals before. Twenty-five kms due west of Molly Cap was a rock that appeared to move with each wave. Oguh had been drinking as well as the next man, so asked for a second opinion. Salkeld gave it and now there was a consensus of two: this mysterious island moved with the currents, though stayed oddly centered atop what appeared to be a rare oceanic whirlpool thousands of feet deep.

"Thirty-nine thousand, by my estimates," Oguh acknowledged.

All three mariners knew what this meant: the deepest trench in all the oceans, never before discovered. And the first floating island of its kind. It had to be hollow, like a shell casing or granitic flagon; a monstrous agate geode with unimaginable quartz crystals lacing the interior emptiness. Its flotational abstrusities were unquantified; the speed, buoyancy or nautical depths unknown. Here was a freak of nature worthy of all speculation, like a seed bank moving slowly through the world's waters. A chrysalis harboring the laughing philosopher and other enigmas, but to what end?

After two hours of maneuvering through the rip tides, the dangerous breakers and labyrinths of other, newly discovered points of kelp that had accreted into more solid substance, they caught sight of it. There, looming in a stone battlement from a deep cranny on the backside of this utterly impossible island, the last southwesterly outcrop of the Bounty Archipelago. A Chilminar of granite obscurities.

Was it moving? Or merely the effects of the perpetual storm-lashing?

How to separate one motion from the other, when all induced a sickness of perceptual faculties? The ramming rock, a Gibraltar of misconducts eloping in high seas. Here in one were all the world's fossiliferous grit and millstone, clay and chalk, reprehensible hornblende and implacable feldspar, giving no quarter to even a landing. All was motion and ambiguity, marble Hades, voodoo-boring, fog-bound frowns, like a Nubian tomb the size of a city block, embosomed in a cloudy throne where roofs and ridges and grottoes of argillaceous sandstone made an impression of cork that bobbed in the garden of vast danger.

"We can't, we don't dare go near," cried Ti Iwi.

"We wait, noting the patterns," the astonished captain replied. The island surged with each breaker, a few yards, but enough to slice a ship in two.

For 30 minutes they kept to three miles' distance, careful to stay beyond the dire fringes of the oceanic sucking point. The island of osmium rose and sank the height of an Eiffel Tower every 48 seconds, forming a terrifying vortex of Niagaras plunging into the emerald hole from 360 degrees. When the island re-emerged, it was like some Victorian fairy world rising to the surface of thought; a visual palpitation bestrewn in all the glorious speckles of color known to the marine haze. Moreover, a vacuum in the air was formed with each descent of the land mass, a hole of nothingness whose physics portended of a weightless condition.

"That would explain the crazy happenings there, see!" Marigold alerted his comrades. For all of the animals thereupon were floating in air, though rooted to their rocks. A strange Apollo condition with no equal: anti-gravity matter and anti-anti-gravity matter consolidated in the same spot, defying every Einsteinian principle. One moment a flatland, the next a Karakoram. Now a jello, next a roustabout, then a granite. Ether, solid edges, mirage and maximum solidity; confinement, hologram, basal metabolism and frightful mist-of-no-substance. Miserable pain and heaven-defying unprinciples. Demeanour of Hell, contemptuous brow of slate, pendulous earth, unbalanced air. A punishing, headlong tumultuary.

"We'd be better off leaving this horrible dilemma of space and time," implored the Squire.

Ti Iwi, terrified by the grave commotion to the point of muteness, agreed.

But the Commander was positively enamored, amazed and dazzled by what lay before him, and Oguh was more than a little curious. Said he, "I would like to chart this island, and name it after these most bizarre occurrences. Three passes. If nothing emerges, I'll have made my numbers and charts—quickly sketching for now—and then I would suggest we get fast away from here."

Marigold agreed.

On the third pass, the weather had weakened even still, and it appeared hopeless. But suddenly, as these things can happen, just as they were turning away forever, a mist cleared and there she blew: a lighthouse!

Rising every 48 seconds, then disappearing again, the most strangely grave, darkly illuminated, provocative tower in any chronicle. A lighthouse that shone for the ghosts, removing any doubt from minds on board, however crippled by the sensation, that Crowquill was more than a man; he was, like Rubens, an entire workshop; or, in the manner of Michelangelo during his upside-down years in Rome, a tenacious acrobat. But unlike the author of the Sistine Chapel, Crowquill's purpose was as obscure as the thickening mists that once again occluded the sleeping hollow of dim and flashing lights—slow, silent, moaning lights, moored to a freak of mobility so far out in the cold, clear waters as to escape all detection.

That cold lent new definition to purity. Oguh had once sailed beneath the nearly 30 hectares of granite outcrop in Victoria at Wilsons Promontory National Park, the southernmost tip of Australia, where a lighthouse of stark domains had been refashioned in the early 1950s atop the vast cliff. Recorded in its ledgers, a history of nearly 40 shipwrecks. But that was a flat and gentrified Tahiti adjoining Dijon, by contrast to this extraterrestrial hazard.

It was unlike any lighthouse Oguh or Salkeld had ever seen, and that would be hundreds between them. Knowing the pattern, now, Oguh found a safe anchor point just outside the Circle of Sucking, and let out the winch on a fast-smoking chain. For Marigold had determined to put into a zodiac and make landing on the impossible island.

It would be no easy expedition, for there was no telling what might happen to him if he got improperly sucked down. The Commander was prepared to hold his breath for 48 seconds; but depending on how far he got slurped into the ocean's bowels, his ears, sageness and eyes would blow up under all the pressure.

"I am prepared to die to know what's out there," Marigold had resolved.

Salkeld had no such interest. Semi-retired, with three grandchildren somewhere in New Zealand, he was not ready to become smithereens. As for Sannazaro, he simply could not believe the Commander would do such a thing when he had the whole world before him, and so many new responsibilities of a serious sort.

"I can't let you," he cried, begging Marigold not to go. "Will you look at what that place is doing!" He pointed to the subsiding and rising. "It is a killer island, like a funnel cloud. Would you set sail into a tornado? For that is exactly what you are doing, but worse. This is not just air, but solid rock, and it will turn you into one more anonymity within the cold cosmos. Is that how all our days should end? A mitten of dust, inside the Qubth-ut-Allah, or Fist of God, as those who know describe it? I think not."

"It is the pursuit of knowledge that renders such fears and prognoses of little consequence," the Commander vowed. "Anyway, don't think I haven't considered the same hazards, shared similar trepidations? But let me point out one obvious and needed adjustment to all such apprehensions. Look there: am I mistaken, or are there millions of animals happily nesting on the turfless typha of cliff ?"

It was true.

"Well, then. How do you suppose they come and go? Hold their breaths?"

"Weddell seals can do so for over an hour," Salkeld explained. "They'll even mate 1,800 feet below the surface."

"A far cry from 39,000 feet. And what of those birds? Do you think they breathe under water?"

"The shags can stay under for four minutes," Oguh pointed out. "And they can fly away if they choose."

"Look again," Marigold pointed, sitting now beside the 800-horsepower Johnson motor on the back of the zodiac, ready to move away from the *Harbinger* and into the Sucking Hole.

It was true. The birds were not flying away but resting at ease, as they did on all the other islands, though it was more difficult to see for certain amid the dark cobalt turbulence that stayed to the cliff—an endemic meteorology of storm centers, hurricane eyes and bulwark of marmoreal tenacity blocking a perpetual tidal wave that would lash the granite walls. The winds howled, the waves burst, a new cloud formation unknown in the world lived atop the island. Rain, sleet, hail, ice fell in throe upon throe of violent kinetic activity. The harshest planetary epicenter: a throwback to the earliest weather, four billion years ago, Marigold suggested.

"Yet, for all that, note the tranquil mating habits of the birds; how the seals seem like the very philosophers of a Himalaya, at ease, introspective, a profile in imperturbability."

"Remarkable!" Oguh mulled, and Salkeld too.

Finally, Sannazaro decided it would be better if he went along, lest the Commander prove correct in his instincts and the Italian shown to be a coward. Salkeld also caved in.

Gingerly they lowered themselves into the zodiac, which spun round several times, the hyperlimneal water wracking the sides ... and killing the engine. Repeated attempts to coax the motor failed, so all the men were forced to start rowing. But neither Marigold nor Sannazaro was a born rower, or even born-again rower, and their counter-synchronicities augmented the vaudevillean collection, which now approached the Sucking Hole. Then some misfitted turbulence caught their eye: a breastwork of floating masses, heaving to and fro, and even more astonishing than the floating island before them.

"Mother of God help us!" Sannazaro's voice spasmed.

"Oh dear," Salkeld grumbled.

"What is that? That great cavorting of fins in the water before us?"

Mr Marigold exclaimed, his thinking processes enriched by all the Black Robin beer he had consumed in previous hours.

"Pointers? Seven-gilled tuatini! Leopards? Or be they pilot whales? I don't see teeth—do you?"

Then, from the confused deck of *Harbinger* they heard the terrible mother-of-god wails: "*Great whites!*" And saw Captain Oguh racing below deck for his guns and harpoon.

CHAPTER 66
Secrets of the Whale Shark

EIGHT-FOOT MOUTHS—mouths eight feet across— hundreds of them, lazily slurping up the glittering fishballs of luminescent, darting color above the spawning coral reef below the island. Billions of blackfooted abalone spore. Up aboard the cliffs, the methodically flashing umber light from the stone tower, twisting through mists and the cold steam of sunlight rising from the crashing flotsam. Below, svelte polkadotted monsters, Monet splashes of color, fulminating in the churned-up sea, their chocolate-colored dorsal fins thunderously slapping the water in an orgy of tea time ... And a lone zodiac carrying three flabbergasted men haplessly among them.

"We're going to die," Salkeld declared stoically, his lips, jawbones, tongue lashing the valiant ideal of every seaman, eyes tearing involuntarily from the sheer sensation of knowing he was about to go down clinging to the ten tons of teeth shredding him, slicing him, to bloody little bits. Only among blue whales had he seen such mouths.

With slack, dark, all-knowing nictitating eyes, able to retract from harm's way, and strange little barbels above their snouts, these colossi of the sea ambushed the frothing traffic jams of bait, advantaged by sensory organs known as lorenzini that were sensitive to electromagnetic information about their dinners—the precise food type and location of their prey—without having to rely on vision: a connoisseur's finesse that evolved at Richelieu Rock in the Andaman Sea, adjoining the Burma Ridge, 120 million years before.

"Move away! " Oguh screamed, trying to fix aim. He only prayed they were basking sharks, and not great whites, but conditions prevented his being sure. The sharks were flying upwards and downwards on the fringes of the great Sucking Hole, catching the small fries that were thrown upwards, then fell down again into the sharks' mouths.

It was useless, and he quit the effort. There were hundreds of the monsters, and the zodiac was lost amid their millions of pounds of dalliance.

Sannazaro was the first to topple overboard into the 39-degree waters as the boat lurched into a nearly vertical throw. (The other two men held on to the eyelets.) The fact Captain Oguh had insisted on their wearing heavy drysuits before heading out through the choppy waters was all that saved his life in the first ten seconds, or he would have lapsed unconscious in such frigid conditions. But the water was the least of his worries.

Sannazaro disappeared betwixt the Conveyance and Unconveyance, the Convergence and Divergence, a Fresh Water Mishmash and Salt Water Slimes, and no shouting from the briefly upended zodiac's remaining two occupants could do a thing about it. He was mired in the vast Sucky Suck.

He would only later remember the sensation: being vacuumed not once, but twice. First, into the vortex that went nearly to the center of the Earth, rushing past a million-odd spectacles he would never remember, but one: the vast mouth that caught him seconds into his journey downwards, along with oblivious shoals of munida and a zillion multistoried, supersaturated plankton, silvertip, mobulay, anchovies—what were they, guppies?—and 100 other moving things; and suffocating, momentarily, in the bilious hold of the leviathan's considerable interior, wherein no geography class had yet trod.

As Sannazaro's waning body frisked heavily to and fro, his mouth fast holding to the last seconds' worth of air allotted it this fateful moment, he noticed row after row of benign little pin pricks. What's this? he thought.

A shark with no teeth? Then again he was slurched into a gigantic radiator at the dark end of the hellish tunnel of a mouth, past the fan belt and carburetor, the spark plugs and hundred stokes, into the very velveteen gullet of beaks, orifice of orifices, engine at the beginning of time, where all further movement was uni-directional—down—though only for the tiny krill who bade farewell as they continued sluicing forth in a gusher of krilly soul evacuation towards the eternal belly of the monster, and the monster itself racing towards the bottom of the ocean.

"Goodbye," cried the tens of thousands of red martyrs, waving their tremulous cilia at the copipods and others.

Down there, inside the unfathomable monster, Sannazaro made the acquaintance of molluscs from the Antipodes and bull kelps who were normally residents of the Campbells. A pig accustomed to a more luxurious life among the Aucklands who'd been on his way to meet the Mayor of Invercargill, and several hundred Caspian terns lost at sea whilst venturing towards Namibia. There was a player piano gurgling Chopin, and several crate-loads of gold from 90 years before. And whole flocks of dancing spiders sucked in during Memorial Day who now sat around spinning tales of yesteryear in the dark cavernous wilds of their new abode. All in all, not such a terrifying place as one might assume, though there was little available light. Everyone inside squinted, paced the void, dared not speculate, but tried to buoy each other with high hopes of reaching the top, finding the vent, of evacuation in due time. This was no doubt a test of character on the high seas, said the elder tunas, who would not hear of pessimism. "Easy for you to say," lamented a cow fish, whose life expectancy was nothing to write home about, compared with the tuna. His 300 pounds were coddled by a most loving sea horse from Zanzibar, russet haze, spiral stripes, silver eyes, sliver-thin bangs, less than an ounce in weight. But she was in love and clung to the cow fish, knowing that sooner or later they'd both be extricated back into the open ocean. Until that day, she had no other care than this yellow giant who moped about in a deep funk, bottom dwelling on the monster's insides.

Fascinating as it was, all this had little soothing effect upon Sannazaro, who had precious few moments left amid the turmoil of oxygenless stomach fluids. Then suddenly—

A deafening roar. John Gully thunder coming from beyond the gullet, like some geyser of undigested clogs, coughing up from the inner sanctum of horror, that fish-processing plant of the ocean depths—and ejecting a wall of albacore and gurnards, of chitonous exoskeletons, squid remains, rubble shrimp and pelagic jacks, of molluscs, triggerfish, 100 species of invertebrate and nektonic larvae, rockfish, the odd pair of glasses, a black nully (poor thing), Lord Lytton's Witch Cavern and infernal fires of Aetna, and all on account of the inadvertent *tourista* who was distinctly unwanted by the Rhinocodon and from whose clutches he was now promptly expelled.

Again, science is instructive in describing these Jonah-and-the-Whale encounters: gastric eversion, in which the stomach is expelled, then re-consumed, the way a vacuum cleaner's sack is emptied and then refitted for further use.

In that colossal explosion of vomit was Señor Sannazaro, thrown, by coincidence, into the very boat, and no less the same seat, from which he'd been dislodged not a moment before.

All this was witnessed and later sworn to by his two astonished companions, who heaved ho against the oars, rowing hard to shore in the 48 seconds allowed them before the next suck. For a moment the engine puttered, and there was great hope for some mechanical certainty, until it was as quickly choked by the swarms of escaping little fish. A billion of them. All catapulted like their Squire by the force of upwards trajectory occasioned by the rising island, whose gravitational vortex had totally shaken out the insides of the monster with the energy equivalent of a flick of the wrist.

The threesome survived the siege, and staggered up past the oozing muddles of *Porphyra columbina* onto the slime-bearing sea stacks and a throng of magpie moths clambering upon cliff alongside the 1,000-thick crowds of inquisitive avians—more nesting Salvin's mollymawks in a glance than existed anywhere else in the world, and mammals that rummaged and lounged in the vast confusion of a coliseum.

"There must be 20,000 seals here," Salkeld declared, before finding himself distracted by erect-crested penguins walking by, along with some new subspecies of Bounty shag.

It was rare that a human ventured among the Bounties, which were so much more petite, fractured, than, say, the huge Aucklands, so that even the name *terra firma* hardly fitted these apiculate spires, gauzy monadnocks, ethereal granites floating just above the murky horizon of sea. No land birds ever came this way: a fitting commentary in itself. Even on the Antipodes, relatively nearby, two endemic parakeets— Reischek's and the Antipodes Island subspecies—fed happily upon sedge, tussock and other dead seabirds. But here, it was only ocean-going life that could withstand the utter complications of bitter wind and gravity-free chaos. Of perpetual black night; cliffs overhung, battered, boiling in the eternal flotsam of perdurable storm. Blue-black, oddly halfway between warm and frozen. A Paradise proffering coziness for all its pelagic mayhem. Sannazaro was still pulling strings of puke off his face, and out of his hair. He was invigorated to be alive, and smiling crazily.

"A moment of prayer," Salkeld called, "in honor of you, Mr Sannazaro. An amazing sight, that. A true survivor, you are, sir. Not in the maritime annals was there such a view, to be spat out forthwith from the bowels of a shark." He slapped his thigh in a mighty laugh, raw from all the alcohol he stowed away over the years. "But what did you do or eat to make him puke so?" he went on in magisterial satire.

Above them rose the eerie bastille with its revolving light.

"I never did see a lighthouse like it," Salkeld confessed, as they scrambled up the Jurassic, algae-infested granite towards the front portico, past subantarctic birds of every variety, and over guano knee-deep in corners and whole quadrants. The rock showed not a tree, a bush, only bare lichens encrusting the fertile gangplanks for life. Not even a scratch of any soil.

In his rambling and historical headstorm, Marigold knew exactly where they had come: Sir Thomas More had envisioned it—a Blessed Faroes, or Fortunate Isle. Butler's own Utopia which, for John Ruskin, whilst meditating on a certain seascape by Turner, described a similar scene as that strange, inhuman longing for infinity subsumed in no more than such a mere luminous distant point as may give to the feelings a species of escape from all the finite objects about them. That point was there before him. A garden of the senses whose history was the Commander's own pedigree. Many had speculated on that Garden, the *hortus botanica* of the Bible, and the Commander was fluent in their diatribes and heavy-handed moralizing (even to be an American constituted a moral situation, said Santayana; to be a Utopian, absolutely spiritual, alleged Marigold): these topographical incitements mirrored his own peculiar penchant for impossible spires and ocean-battered ramparts. He had spent many a drowsy evening immersed in Sir John de Mandeville's *Travels* of 1370, which had triggered so much speculation on the precise whereabouts of that alluring paradise. It was a question of geometry, said Bonaventura; of climatology, declared Aristotle; of culture, alleged Toscanelli. Sir Walter Raleigh sought the truth of it in Guiana, Willem Barents in Spitsbergen, Martin Frobisher in Labrador, and Luis de Torres in the New Hebrides. So compelling was the prospect that John II of Portugal had dispatched Alfonso de Parva and Pedro de Covilha to Abyssinia in search of that very Garden of Eden. Had the Commander and company now arrived?

"Is anybody there?" the Marigold shouted.

"My God, what a desperate place," Salkeld uttered, as they once again sank below the surface of the ocean. But no holding of breath was necessary. They were, of sorts, in a coal lamp with its own glass housing and oil wick, the kind carried by soldiers and seamasters. Nothing could explain what was happening to them; to the air pressures and volumes of salt wind; to the curvature of the sea as it rose and sank, or to the sun and moon which (too few theories to grapple with so diffuse a magnificence) spread out their glories in undefended generosity, so that the heavens above and dark sub-cellular seas below were without demand on the person or orientation, effected no challenge to the physiology or curse upon the fact of being biological amid inrushing H2O. The sun was where the moon should be; the moon in place of Mars—the Mars that aped a Northern Star, no larger than a mason jar, and just in time for tea. And all this chaos-turned-hilarity shone brilliantly off the furry coast, 900 miles to the lee. The hairy undermountains rose and sank, grew hairier by the second. Nothing made sense, of course. Which is how it should always be.

"Don't ask if you don't need to. Just accept that something unique has happened here, and now we are part of it," the Commander recommended to his two lieutenants.

"I won't ask. I won't say another thing, except to recommend an evacuation as soon as we are rested, for this is without any question the most god-awful place on the planet," Sannazaro concluded.

"With so many wonderful animals and animal heroes, I hardly think so," said Marigold, pointing straight away to a large bony spider well ensconced in a high corner of the outer stone eaves.

"*Rubrius nummosus*," declared Salkeld. "The loneliest invertebrate in the world. If it takes a liking to you, it will weave you a white bonnet which, in fairness, you must wear the rest of your life."

"We're doomed," the Squire bespake in raw seizures of wild-eyed surmise. He was counting the shark population below.

But suddenly, several seals washed up onto the lowest rocks, all rubbing their bottoms frantically upon little suction cups fitted there queerly. Others plopped down into the water, along with a newly arrived multitude of penguins caught up in the suck surges. Gassy bubbles rose in all directions. There was a genuine travel plan from rock to sea and back again, and not one creature took any notice of the sharks, of sucking crevasses, or vice versa.

"Well I'll be damned!" the Commander exclaimed.

"So, that explains it then," said Salkeld, peering intently at the unique spectacle.

"What?" Sannazaro was anxious to know. "Explains what?"

"Them be neither shark, purely speaking, nor whale, but whale sharks. I'd thought so, but couldn't be sure, having never seen one at first hand."

"What are whale sharks, then?" Sannazaro demanded, for he had the most personal stake in the outcome of the conversation. His pedigree, only recently stirred in his imagination—a survivor of legendary proportions, a governor who'd been dragged down to sea depths unknown, a modern-day Jonah—all that and more hung on Salkeld's every word.

"The largest of all fish, the largest of all sharks, and the most gentle of creatures in the sea, that's what. Vegetarians, every one of them. Why, they'd no more harm a man than a rock. Strictly filter feeders, and if my eyes are not deceiving me, I'd reckon this must be their secret mating spot in all the world."

"That's rubbish. I was nearly eaten alive," Sannazaro rudely insisted. "Swallowed viciously, moreover."

"No, you weren't," the mariner countered. "Only accidentally sucked up, that's all. Caught head on in a bit of shark breath. Look at 'em— they're not killing anything, and they won't. They're slurpers, and the oceans are one big milkshake, that's all. Whatever comes in with the slurp, if it's the size of crunched ice (you'll get my analogy), then it's fine by them. Anything larger, they spit out. You, for example. Had you even measured like a modest mackerel, or blue cod, then you'd have had a slight problem. Bigger than that, you're home free, as your standing here attests. Still, we'll give him a Purple Heart, eh Commander!"

"Va fan culo! You're just jealous," Sannazaro rasped. His glory was singularly wounded by all these pacifist assertions. "Because I might be the only man alive to have survived such a close call."

"You nut, it was a six-story guppy, Mother of earth having tested her hypothesis of non-violence after millions of years in a single creature of ultimate size. What would you guess, Salkeld? Thirty thousand pounds?"

"Or more."

"Thirty thousand pounds of cartilage and cunning, all to what end? Love and peace. Why, by comparison, such a creature makes the bunny rabbit out to be an Al Capone. You, my Iacobo, have tested the waters, literally, and they are free of enmity."

"Do not underestimate the rabbit," Sannazaro scowled. "Any gardener knows only too well their vicious and systematic attacks."

"Pout not. You are the victor. No scientist can dispute your bodily proof. It is in the nature of biology to be sweet and kind. The bigger, the gentler. That such enormity should equate with a diet of phytoplankton, and comport by a quiet browsing through the distant seas—they must live a century or more—why, it makes my heart skip a beat. All this and more. Bravo! Even their electromagnetism has rubbed off, for you are buzzing like a bumblebee that thinks itself a show stopper."

Sannazaro sat down, greatly disheartened. His valor had been socked in the stomach.

CHAPTER 67
The Last Existentialist

MARIGOLD POUNDED on the worn, elaborately carved wooden door between the uncommonly fitted stone walls built into the forbidding ravine. There was no response to these elemental queries, mankind's first primeval question mark—a fist pounding an entranceway—so he took his advantage and shoved it open.

The three men entered the ground floor of the acropolis—"Hello?"— which stood easily 50 feet. Not a large lighthouse, not by any standards. But an inviting one. Some might think it bleak, like the rock outcrop itself, part granite, part igneous. But Marigold at once swooned to the new-found larval stage of his fondest asseverations. A plankton life, drifting, cloud-borne; his idea filled with nutrients and time, upwelling beyond any such predicament or cover of darkness, but lost in a fantasy come home to welcome him. A man of 20 might have relished escape to such an outpost, the earth's equivalent of a space station. For a man of some 50 years to do so could be viewed as a commentary on the era. English travelers to New Zealand in the early 1900s would frequently comment on the rapid progress towards some semblance of civilization being acquired by the Kiwis, so that few men were any longer required to dwell more than a tui's cry from each other. Even then a domestic fraternity was deemed a prerequisite for all that was good and progressive. Farmers, of course, were exempted from this law of city breeding, but with the exemption came the bias of millennia; the prototypic low-brow.

His mark of cane, or butter, or corn. The farmer bore this stigma knowing secretly (or consoling himself at any rate) that he was the luckier of the two, and could, any time, venture into town and whoop it up. But the world was passing him by.

If so for the mainland farmer, ever more so the islanders who, obsessed with whale oil and seal blubber, made their desperate claims and fickle fortunes. The routine disaster left them frozen in home-thatched coracles, as on Disappointment Island, awaiting rescue that rarely arrived. Their gravestones, wind tormented, are testimony to an absolute solitude that defies all psychoanalysis. A backwards trend in the human organism that taunts evolution, throws out all handy theories of need and the gregarious, skewers sociology and argues for at least a single truant gene devoted to bedrock, stubborn silences, frigid wastelands.

Unless, it were a bird observer, whose enthusiasm never suffered for idleness, raw nerves or sadness, except in the case of an extinction; and for whom a single peeping harmonic at 4 a.m. was like a daily Christmas, melodiously drawing upon the Phrygian scales of the universal atoms and molecules, triggering the neural synapses which made for completion and happiness.

Here, inside the specter of such a man, were—all about them—signs of some extraordinary machinator: apparatuses bearing no common equivalent. Were they acoustic fog signals? Lighted buoys? Radar aids?

A spying cove for Nazis? Remnants from past sea towers populated this spire of spindrift dreams. Marigold recognized it at once: the perfect haven for the last man on earth. But the snugness aside, other indications of novelty struck them.

"There's no steel, no iron, no concrete," Salkeld noted. "Though there is a soft leucite surface, and that's the rock itself."

"Should there be steel?"

"Aye, I never seen a lighthouse without it. No caissons, no cylinders, no cement masonry. Nothing to indicate a formal situation."

"What does that mean?" Marigold inquired.

All was of granite and the igneous, cut, piled, joined and pieced together with an openwork frame of delicate dovetailing and superimpositions. The turret structure massaged gravity, the way some Himalayan punga and tree ferns have been known to jut from cliffs haphazardly like hovercraft, blowing sideways in the wind.

There was timber that gave itself to a delicately carved spiral stairwell, not unlike the old church in Santa Fe, the Commander noticed—in fact, there was a striking resemblance. And the steps led upwards toward the focal plane, so called, and an enormous fog bell and lantern gallery. The wood was bolted, fair enough, but with nails of stone, and the elevation cozified in granite arches that grew organically, if you will, like some heavy-breathing crystallization, all-purpose and philosophy, a troglodyte's Paradise that nothing, ever, could undermine.

They mounted to the summit of the home (for indeed it was a home like none other) with its view over the world, and all its children frolicking in so many nests of pearly white down and molt and blubber. White-faced storm petrels (St Peter's birds, thought by the ancient seamen to walk on water); sooty shearwaters (the titi, or muttonbirds, convening by the thousands of scores, darkening the sky in evening when, it was said, they'd come home); wandering and royal albatross, the ones with all-merciful, playful eyes, the world's conscience, looking out over the comings and goings with a calm knowledge that this too will pass. In addition to these lucky lookers, a medley of precious tomtits, snipe and spotted shag, azure teal, well-oriented pipit and banded dotterel. Wingless chafer beetles. Unknown bacterial eyes and ears. And others. All called Bounty home tens of millions of years before the first Polynesians even came close to the southern waters.

Inside, from the mattressworks, wedges, dowelling and dovetails of stone, Turkish carpet, bedsheets freshly pressed, a sink of laboriously polished brass, pockmarked smoky mirror, utensils of every odd variety and period, and the swinging distribution of light throughout—occulting, flashing, alternating— all was characteristic of one single metaphor: illumination. The earth had blended with the sea. The atmosphere had become radiant and indistinctive in the obscure construction leading to the god of the minaret, the reflecting mirror. It shone prismoidal, catadioptric, geometric, perfectly silvered; a *feux-éclairs*, or quick-flashing light amplified in a mirror of grand dimensions and hand-crafted details.

In its guts were rollers, lens panes, a wick burner and optical apparatus without tallow candle. There was a coal fire and incandescent oil burner, as well as a mercury float. No acetylene or obvious lamp—but something else, something unseen and unheralded. It was his own invention, this light. The product, somehow, of an unattended gas holder. But which gas?

The question lingered in Salkeld's mind alone, for his companions knew nothing of these lighthouse matters, nor were interested.

"Gorgeous," Salkeld said admiringly. "I can't imagine how in hell anybody could have figured it all out down here. I don't understand. It's not possible. And no such place on any map. If it's the same Crowquill I drank half a night with, why—he's giving me chilblains, he is. And the gas? What about that laughing gas the ladies spoke of?"

"But where is he? For I see no boat?" the Commander asked. Outside, spray mounted up the wall, as the full and ebb tides interacted with horrifying ferocity and sea sweeps pounded the lower ballasts. They were 100 feet above the terrible intersection and could see their zodiac lashed and tossed. It had been lassoed around a nubbin and secured with carabiners. It would hold, but the waves were mocking it now. Marigold stared into the old mirror above Crowquill's sink, aligning himself in his mind with this extraordinary mystery of a man, this mentor without portfolio, metaphysician beyond all known maps, but all he could see was his own image, floating up and down every 48 seconds at the summit of a granitic iceberg.

Suddenly, they all heard a munching, and noticed at once a little Norwegian rat, *Rattus norvegicus*. He'd made himself known, clearly missing the company of his human friend.

"A pet?" Sannazaro acknowledged.

"But why such neat and tidy things," Salkeld queried. "They hardly reflect the habits of a hermit, in absence of a woman. And there? His glasses case, empty, and all these clothes, neatly folded on the bed. What was he doing?"

"He left in no hurry, but with some calculation I would venture," the Commander inferred.

All were beginning to suspect the worst.

But who was this man, a half-life of impenetrable motives and zeal, lodged tenuously between the world of a shellfish and a rock? Everywhere, the crashing of ideas into the brant and scrape on the ocean's edge. The more cataclysmic, the better to see the stranger beneath the scene. Extraordinary energies without reference to human affairs. A diplomat desiring only minimal exchange. An ambassador from nowhere to nowhere. The normal understanding of a life thrown out the window. What rhythms made his heart beat? Those of the crashing surf, like some seguidilla of unprecedented loneliness and know-how.

It was then that Marigold saw the little volume under the spanking white Egyptian cotton pillows. This was no abbatial den of an ascetic, but the posh and perfect perimeter of every back-to-Nature fantasy.

Removing it, Salkeld immediately recognized the volume. "That's it! The one I told you about back in Wellington. My Lord. It's him, it is."

The Commander slowly began leafing through it.

"Careful, there's a powder keg 'tween those sentences. I caution you," went the Italian.

While the Commander began surveying the diary, taking a seat on the luxurious bed of the softest down comforters, checkered with old Moriori designs of delicate and handsomest handloom work, Salkeld investigated the upper galleries of the cupola. He was keen to examine the minute particulars of the technology that quietly percolated in every cranny of the structure. Crowquill's atelier suggested some kind of working laboratory, a pelagic Picasso's den, with few moving parts, but salient contraptions utterly strange and arresting to the mariner. A curious wafer-like mechanism gave off heat; tubes ran from it. A large hooded container of water bubbled, and two pipes of turquoise led to either side, one a seeming cathode, the other an anode—that much Salkeld could recognize. But what were the bubbles? Some kind of outgassing, with a faintly pungent odor that linked his nostrils to those seals' bottoms. The tubes ran into the wall and disappeared, but outside, they continued down to the guano-infested rocks. Above, the light kept flashing, and as late-night darkness magnified the scene around them, the luminescence of the chamber became increasingly clear, for it was a potent illumination that shone every 30 seconds on the *Harbinger*, waiting out beyond the flotilla of sharks who themselves were bioluminescent, reflecting glints from the southern lights, so that the entire crashing sea was on fire with a glow that could probably be detected from the lunar surface.

On his walkie talkie, Salkeld explained everything to Oguh. It was agreed that the three men would bunk up in the obelisk for the night, while the Capt'n and Ti Iwi rested easy on the schooner. They'd anchored far out enough to avoid the breakers caused by the Sucking Circle, and the winds had calmed somewhat. Even a calf moon showed herself.

Meanwhile, by a veritable department store of lighting, the interior of the campanile automatically lit up at 10 p.m., and dimmer switches on the eastern wall provided for an abundantly romantic ambiance that was wasted on the three male stragglers. Everything was automated. A computer, its programs rippling, clearly controlled the interior.

None of it made sense, and the book even less so. It was a diary, meant to be discovered, dating back two decades, from the marginalia of it. The Commander flipped through every page, mostly keeping to himself, but sometimes describing things out loud to Sannazaro, who was getting out of his hugely distressing drysuit (which tended to give him the first stages of the hives), peeling dried shark puke off his ears, and drying himself near an electrified heater built into the walls and fashioned, it appeared, of titanium. Even the marvelously crafted floors exuded warmth of a modern Scandinavian sort. Without any understood source of energy, the entire functioning edifice of a lighthouse remained an enigma. A lighthouse for whom? There had been no nearby shipping route since the days when the Sydney-to-London route ventured near to the Auckland Islands, far to the southwest, over a century before.

Salkeld reached the apex of the pagoda, and saw what looked like no lighthouse reflector he'd ever seen. In fact, it was no lighthouse at all, but a peculiar kind of belfry of observations, a pergola of mariner dreams. Then he divined a sudden insight. What if the pre-Newtonian light were not meant for argosies, but rather animals? A Euclidian concept, primordial in its raw reflections? A pure convex mirror image that concentrated distance for the purpose of guiding migrations, assisting optically in the homing of flying insects or long-faring albatross? A gospel of light in the world to convey comfort and precise coordinates inter-specially?

Downstairs 40 feet, in a dry set of borrowed, ill-fitting apparel, Sannazaro made himself at home by exploring a wine cellar, and bringing up strange bottles of no ascertainable origin or label. They were clearly manufactured by hand, and with their worldly itineraries and striking candle-lit translucences, reflected the implausibility of Crowquill himself.

Each bottle in the cellar was a kingdom whose story could be read. Sannazaro delved into one after another: the Portuguese and Pitcairn corks popped easily, assuring his unstinting consumption of countless samples. There were cobalts and fluorescent pinks, amber greens and ruby oranges—sand and salt cake, soda nitrates and arsenious oxides. Some were gilt, others mosaic. Here a Syrian mold-blown bottle; there one more etched in gold leaf; and there a beaker with colored threads. In corners, leaning weary and fine, black enamels and stipple-engraved sweetmeat glass; a decanter with facets; a finely cut calabash; violin types and 100 less recognizable forms. All had washed ashore, and each contained a precious liquid. Crowquill was a voluptuary of rarified tastes.

And there were messages. All of history—Patagonia, Alexandria, Carthage, Rosh Hanikra, the Solomons and Galapagos, Yapon and the Marquesas—seemed represented in this astounding cellar of stone and moss.

The spirits, as well. Where had they been appropriated from?, he wondered. There was an alembic for distilling, but no grapes, surely—not in the Bounties?

Imagine Sannazaro's stupefaction upon tasting the finest premiers crus supérieurs, pomerols, hock and Trockenbeerenauslese? He swam in heavy-bodied port and amber muscatel, and sniffed and sampled his way into a maze of well-seasoned sherries with no equal in his experience.

After dousing himself, so to speak, in Lacrima Cristi and Castelli Romani, he staggered to the icebox, where an equally astonishing array of freshly prepared cheeses was to be found.

"Who *is* this guy?" his smarts addled.

Among the piquant gallery of sapsagos and neufchatels, emmentalers and gorgonzolas, Sanazarro unwrapped one delectable bite after another— here a pecorino Tuscano, there a Trappist cheese from Banjaluka. The odors were sensational, salty, creamy, without precedent. Only later would it become clear, from the diary, that the cheeses had been fashioned from various lactating seal milks, some of it fed back to the seals themselves, who had acquired all their bad habits from this hermit of the Bounties. That was not all, for the wines, too, had come from the sea, in the form of those very green kelp bulbs that the alien in the bathyscope had been fishing for. The kelp forests were abundant in the Bounties, and Crowquill knew what he was doing. Other food types, though not a single piece of flesh, were there in the refrigerator, almost as if Crowquill were showcasing the spectacular possibilities for living alone in the twenty-first century.

"Goodness! Come take a look at this!" Sannazaro exclaimed, discovering a back greenhouse previously unobserved. Warm filtered stained-glass light, and heat coming from all sectors, allowed for enormous tomatoes, ginger, shallots, baby artichokes, medjools, huge avocados, nectarines, oranges, Belgian endives, butter lettuce and dozens of other delectables.

All seemed to flourish as a result of the island's eerie swooshing up and down. But the physics were one thing. Here was a gourmand with a dozen culinary PhDs, to have engineered so spectacular a system as this shaft of aspiring maritime space. In the parlance of science, it was a totally contained ecosystem of self-regeneration. Inputs were many, like the seal milk and kelp. But what fueled the elaborate, if subtle, technology beneath the heated floorboards? Hydraulic jacks fitted into the Suck Hole? A capturing device for the tidal swells?

The trio had their dinner, despite the fact their stomachs sank and rose, on average, one Eiffel Tower, or eight Taj Mahals, each dozen chews; then Salkeld and Sannazaro—burping and hiccuping their meal of pure molecular origins after half a lifetime of junk foods—found their own anointed sleeping quarters. There was only one bed, but it was huge and luxurious enough for four grown men—salacious even by Las Vegas honeymoon-suite standards. The two were soon snoring in their own heavens, but the sleepless Commander never quit the little diary for the entire night. As the stars came out, he continued reading by the dimmed candlepower of a sanctioned spotlight.

CHAPTER 68
The Book of Laughing Gas

MARIGOLD RELISHED the book. Who could have predicted such isolation? Or the conspicuous disappearance of its maker, a scientist, epicurean, poet, explorer, eremite; a bold visionary with no need of gossip or CNN, whose notebook began with a chemical analysis of laughing gas, annotated by a description of certain eccentricities of the upper atmosphere and its thin contagion of polar stratospheric clouds, as well as of the real magnetic poles. All was bolstered by re-engineering modifications to contraptions elegantly fitted to his tower, and leading—as if by pure literary license—to a rambling but readable tome that treated of the neurology, psychoanalysis, geopolitics, anthropology and metaphysics of laughter.

Translations in 100 languages. From ancient forms to every uncanny jest. The sound of white-fronted Scottish geese during wintry rounds, of tickling bells, laughing valleys, and shaking sides that make the weepeth smile. Here were foaming bowls, and soft lyres.

The handwritten meditations, conjurations, haikus and descriptions of countless personal voyages throughout the world seemed, at first blush, to evoke a singular story line: the mystery of laughter as a survival mechanism and—ultimately—chemical reaction to the way the world was. Hence, the nature of laughing gas—not the conventional nitrous oxide, but some other exiguous, heretofore unexamined substance floating about. Crowquill's laughing gas was the sum total of everything that man did and dreamed of doing: the air within his lungs, the scent within his nostrils, the vision, seen or unseen, within his head. Much like the original mysteries surrounding the whereabouts and whatabouts of oxygen. Hominid evolution, in one direction or the other, argued Crowquill, was altogether a function of its capacity to laugh at itself, or not. The laughter, and the substance, were one. Obtain either, and the other followed in strict adherence to the Law of Humorous Synchronicities. He was a profound theorist, that much was quickly clear. To relate what we breathed to why we smiled gave loft to the notion that earth was positioned in some fragile pocket of perfectly balanced and oriented cosmic as well as comic layers, so that the rate of oxygen and ozone formation, the kelp and iodine, the phosphorus and nitrogen and all those other bits and pieces, fitted precisely into the coordinates of a smile beneath a shining star we called our sun. More than the smile, the laugh, the games, a playful behavior was demonstrated throughout the plant, animal, insect and bacterial kingdoms.

It was all clear to the Commander, who detected the laughing of mews and glaucous-winged gulls out beyond; of Heermann's, ring-billeds and more. A cacophony every which way, as avians plumped down for the night. And thinking back—laughter at all times: in waterfalls and chipmunks; trees straining in the wind and all the humanities and audiences combined. The one universal quotient, it was.

Crowquill had evidently spent a good deal of his life searching for the first joke in prehistory, the way evolutionary microbiologists have traversed the far corners, from Isua to Shark's Bay, tracking down those original mutterings of DNA. Had he found it? From the evidence, he had, and it was dangerously infectious, possibly airborne, judging by the paralyzing impact upon those stricken denizens of Pitt Island. An aerosolized fraction that proved to be a cornerstone of all sustainability: that was his theory. Only in laughter do people exercise that sublime condition of reticence known as Treading Lightly. Not in orgasm, which merely induces overpopulation and all of its fundamental disasters; nor in sleep, which stokes nightmares turned into realities; neither in tears, that are the subject of themselves; nor even in love itself, which too frequently turns to ashes, or unrestrained desire. Walking—the sheer act itself—was the only other ecological coordinate that Crowquill had divined could be construed as a second order of sustainability, after laughter. But even walking, he imagined, frequently led to disaster. People had a habit of walking directly into a fire. Or stepping on ants.

But with laughter, there was nothing but spontaneous joy, without error, downfall or cumulative catastrophe. No energy to kill or maim, though one could laugh bitterly at another, true enough. Still, better that than lances. In laughter, no pollution. No crime, no conspiracies or consumptions. Pure reaction. An internal romp that led to nothing but good. He knew, of course, that some laughter was cruel. But the harm done was of little consequence to the earth. It was laughter, said Crowquill in his diary, that provided a biological baseline for estimating the worth and potential of the species.

Crowqill had not come upon these many insights without travail, and a life of obviously extreme seclusions. (Though there may well have been some genetic disposition towards merriment—Marigold was unsurprised to learn that one of the author's esteemed ancestors had co-founded *Punch*.) He might have inhabited the subterranean damps of the Paris Opera, writing missives from the edge of the known world.

Yet, he was all paradox: isolation competed with the packed concert hall; silence with gab; the hermit with the social butterfly. He had not held himself up in isolation without systematic recourse to his kind, traveling globally to research his theory, moving among people of all races and distinctions, sampling a true gourmet's palate of hysterics in order to truly grasp the miracle that was laughter, the importance of good cheer, and its translation into a Quantum Theory of Relative Humor that, he supposed, might change the world if it could be more generalized and evenly distributed. Might that primeval joke serve to lighten up the bureaucracy in Wellington and provide a means for the Commander to save the moa? The sewage system in Santa Fe? All the chickens in Hong Kong, monkeys in Vietnam, children in Sierra Leone?

Was he such a Mother Theresa, Marigold wondered, that he had put so much novel calculation and esoteric peregrinations together, in absence of collaborators or even any friends? How had he financed this remarkable endeavor? An inheritance? What strange motivations had brought him to a popsicle truck in the South Pacific, only to scavenge its engine? Or to the espresso machine in a stone fortress two-thirds of the way to Antarctica that had so endeared the stranger to all three present occupants who were badly in need of warming up and something tasty?

Whoever he was, Crowquill had carefully noted the dawn of laughter for reasons Marigold found utterly fantastic. He had pursued a train of inquiry that encompassed thinkers from Plato to Darwin to Piaget in the service of a humanitarian conviction. These men—all uniformly familiar to the Commander— had also sought to understand the origins of the giggle, to discern that magical instant when a human first smiled, laughed, cracked a joke, though it is unlikely any of them had made the extraordinary leap in thinking to an ecological principle of Kantian and imperative proportions. That amazing first pun contained the only known antidote to human violence, said Aristotle; a way to spawn hope in the face of utter nihilism, added Nietzsche; or entrance the manic depressive, the melancholic, the holder of every black mood with a vision of grace applicable to any habitat, however removed—and to every mindset, attitude, predilection and particulars of life, concluded Crowquill.

Laugh, and you will not bleed; smile, and God will cherish you; chuckle, and you will find your body immune to every untoward calling. The laugh renders its body untouchable. In mirth, never a harm is inflicted on another. Grin to defy history; giggle to soften tyrants. By jubilance, offer entertainment for all. A side-split, each species infected. With uproars and gasses, clowning and poppycock, cachinnations all, the world can't help but join in.

Marigold had devoted his weird irrelevant years to comprehending the breakdown of the earth's immune system at the hands of one species, but Crowquill—a hermit of even more dramatic stature—had sought humanity's resurrection in one of its oldest qualities: the gag. Understand laughter, said he, and all else will fall into ecological balance. That seemed to be his central finding.

To that end, Crowquill had examined most of the great minds of the last several thousand years in search of their own humorous bent, and to decipher, for example, whether William Caxton's discovery of moveable type affected the impression of the pun line; or if the real "bible of democracy", as Walter Lipmann had called the newspaper, was really the miraculous capacity of a joke to spread freely from mouth to mouth around a continent with greater speed than the flu. Did John Locke, Benjamin Franklin, Karl Marx, Guglielmo Marconi, Emily Dickinson, Sylvia Plath, Joan of Arc or Ibn Khaldun have a sense of humor, and if so, what good did it respectively accomplish?

Darwin's children were reported by him to have smiled for the first time on their forty-fifth and forty-sixth days of life, Crowquill noted. The question of whether laughter was innate had not yet been satisfactorily answered by behaviorists. But it was known that the laughter response could be elicited by the fifth week in children all over the world. Their breathing, correspondingly, was of seven times greater magnitude than adults'. Hence their ability to play more furiously, without cease; to delight in the world unconflicted; to accept the gift of air more graciously. Never a reason to choke on their own words or ambiguities, unless a chunk of toast went down the wrong pipe beside it.

In the nuclei of motor cells in a person's mastermind, Crowquill had drawn the very outflow of hysterics to the jaw, throat and lungs, to the diaphragm, chest, neck, back and limbs. He had medically analyzed the anatomical ecosystem as it responded to a good laugh. He had used the seals down on the rocks as his subjects, and tapped their resulting farts for fuel—a refinement which now seemed to explain the intricate wiring and energy source for the lighthouse.

His research among seals, birds and people had shown a pattern of convulsing facial nerves, intracranial pressure, a benign pain in the abdominal muscles (hence the name belly laughter), the feelings of breathlessness not unlike the first stirrings of an hallucinogen, of euphoria and orgasm—the expending, in other words, of about 150 calories, though in seals there was even more energy released. Even the tears of such laughter had a different salt content than tears of sadness, a discovery that had compelled Crowquill to consider the very biochemistry of humor, even of smiling. He noted that the act of laughing massaged vital organs, oxygenated the blood, released endorphins in the brain, stabilized blood pressure and served, in essence, as the body's own internal apothecary. Explosive laughter also freed and expelled discharges accumulated in the tracheobronchial tree. Hence its ability to heal patients in TB clinics from Houston to Tokyo. A little *Candid Camera* or *Monty Python* would have transformed the moribund residents of the sanitarium in Thomas Mann's *The Magic Mountain* into blooming begonias of health, according to Crowquill.

Indeed, laughter was nothing short of an inner marathon. It thwarted memory loss and senility, provoking enhanced alertness and stimulating a biological renewal up and down the body's cordillera. It made for great tea socials, and for the production of adrenalin so useful in bridge, bingo or mahjong games. A veritable miracle drug. Not surprisingly, Crowquill was not alone in his instincts, though none that Marigold was familiar with had ever dreamed of taking it so far. But humor had fairly become the preferred therapeutic technique for convalescent chronic-care patients. Amazingly, even artificial laughter was beneficial; a fabricated smile, just the gesture on the surface of the face, would trigger certain hormones, muscles and bodily chemicals that were life fostering and preservative. Crowquill had fixed upon these qualities.

Mr Marigold stared around the quietly lit interior of the heavenly stone stronghold with its four-foot walls and salt mustiness, this George De La Tour of citadels, and realized that he was sitting on the bed of the last existentialist; of a man who had quite obviously devoted himself to saving mankind by the most unlikely of methods. Was there a supreme joke not yet played out? And where was the player? Hiding? Watching? Waiting? Or was he a martyr to the cause?

Under the bed, Marigold discovered a stack of precious books, all in their original vellums and goatskins. James Magra's journal of a voyage round the world in his majesty's ship *Endeavour* during the years 1768–1771 in search of natural knowledge, along with a lexicon of Otahitee. A presentation copy of Jean de Man's *Souvenirs d'un voyage aux Iles Philippines*, published in Antwerp in 1875. There was Johann Adam Schall Von Bell's enormous hemispheric map of the stars, published in Peking in 1634, fitted in a splendid red morocco-backed cloth box; and a most strange broadside from January 6th, 1724 by one John James Heidegger on the art of Masquerade.

Crowquill possessed a copy of Percy Bysshe Shelley's *St. Irvyne; or, the Rosicrucian: a Romance. By a Gentleman of the University of Oxford*, printed in 1811, in which, flipping through its modest size, the Commander noticed the following couplets: "While yet a boy I sought for ghosts, and sped Thro' many a listening chamber, cave and ruin, And starlight wood, with fearful steps pursuing Hopes of high talk with the departed dead."

Such language shook him to his weary bone, for it seemed that art were modeling life too closely for any comfort just then. This uncannily lit sensation was enlarged when he discovered a book by one John Salkeld, dedicated to Sir Francis Bacon and published in London in the year 1617: *John Salkeld, Catholic renegade. A Treatise of Paradise, and the principall* (sic) *Contents thereof: especially of the Greatnesse, Situation, Beautie, and other Properties of that Place.*

Marigold grew faint; his head heaved beneath the laborious notion of a cosmic deceit in progress—some veil of uncertainty, a ploy on the part of all the chicaneries known to the four winds, to seduce him. Who was the old mariner? Were he and Crowquill the same? Or was this all some hallucination by which Marigold himself manifested his own ideals. Salkeld. *Their* Salkeld? Crowquill, Marigold's mirror image? The Commander closed his eyes and tried to breathe steadily, remembering back to the Castle of Lindabridis which flew magically through the air of Calderon; and the octogenarian's "Life is a Dream", with its own tower and later the famed words, "Never from that sleep profound, Wake, O Sigismund, or rise, To behold with wondering eyes All thy glorious life o'erthrown, Like a shadow that hath flown, Like a bright brief flame that dies!" In that purgatory of visualizations between high plateaus and desperate trenches, Crowquill himself had founded a School of Philosophy to which Marigold—little taken to laughter or smiling—now advented in full measure.

He made himself smile. "Ha ha ha!" he continued, much like the victims of Pitt Island.

As he "ha'ed", his purview of reading materials continued—there, for example, a very rare *Tristram Shandy* in full calf, gilt rules, morocco spine labels, black leaf, an engraved plate by Hogarth, half-morocco slipcase, and a quote from the esteemed bookseller, Bernard Quaritch of London, cited from a *London Magazine* review, February 1760, in which was stated, "Oh rare Tristram Shandy!—Thou very sensible—humorous—pathetick –humane—unaccountable!—what shall we call thee?—Rabelais, Cervantes, What?"

There was more. A copy of Søren Kierkegaard's doctoral dissertation, *On Irony*; Andrew Kippis's *The Life of Captain James Cook*, original boards, printed in 1788; and the incredibly rare account of Magellan's expedition by Maximilian of Transylvania, the son of the Archbishop of Salzburg, published in Rome in 1524, and containing reference to Crowquill's very own alleged ancestor who finished the voyage, thereby, in the words of one commentator, adding more "to the dimension of the world" than any previous expedition in history.

Crowquill's own journeys, combing the world in search not of gold or societies to conquer but of the smile, had most certainly added to those of his predecessors. Wilderness from continent to continent reduced to a grin from ear to ear. The Conquistador transformed into the enigmatic Cheshire cat. The ecology of the smile.

In Sri Lanka, he had attended an ancient Buddhist curing ritual known as the "Offering to the Vadi

Demons". Whatever eased pain and led the disciple towards nirvana was Buddha's primary goal: this was the secret key to the heaven of laughter. The surgeon (aka the ritual specialist) was accompanied by a dancer and a drummer. Together, they attempted to rid the tormented woman of the demons that had naughtily occupied her body. The cure was conducted in public, and the whole village had turned out to enjoy it. After bizarre transducenes and inexplicable orations (Buddha's own words being "stabbed" into the heart of the demons), the surgeon and his helpers then set out to make fools of themselves, a deliberate ploy to induce the woman, and everyone around her, to start laughing. Finally, the medical doctor himself pretended to be the sick woman, but what he did Crowquill would not say. Only that the woman was cured. Who was he keeping this information from? Did he expect someone to read the diary? If so, to what end?

In New Guinea, among the Kiwai Papuans, Crowquill partook of a secret cult of the dead in which survivors of a recently deceased child performed their burial rituals according to an ancient stand-up comedy routine. They did their acts atop the very coffin.

At Freud's home in Vienna, Crowquill paid pilgrimage to the couch where for many years puns were exchanged between the maestro and his many clients, mostly women. Freud evidently thought of laughter as the cure-all—a waking equivalent of dreaming, a release of excess energy that served to balance an individual, to make a person whole again.

Similarly, at Port-of-Spain in Trinidad, crowds poured into a large carnival tent for purposes of affirming the restoration of equilibrium and sanity to their entire community. For 150 years the calypso tradition of Trinidad—an absolutely irrepressible and unique form of Mardi Gras—had taken possession of the locals every January. Born in slavery as an antidote to misery, it had become a great art form. Hundreds of performers competed, according to Crowquill, in the realm of double entendre, comic storytelling, employing every fantastic nuance of the ribald. Performers adopted names, like Lord Monsieur Fake, Unstoppable Crayon and the transvestite supreme of all Carribea, the Menstruating Baboon. This latter maverick of mirth stood illuminated in the Canopy of Tears. There, a thunderous applause met his cascade of verbal antics: "You think the world is coming to an end? Let me tell you something—"

But Crowquill cut short his transliterations, leaving the Commander in limbo.

It was the same with every one-liner, whether among the obscene Sicilian women sporting their verbal cajones; the Chamula Indians of the enchanted Twilight Mountains of Mexico, who fought duels of wit, their very lives hanging in the balance; or the Anangs of Nigeria, allegedly the most eloquent humorists on earth. Their very name referred to an "ability to speak wittily yet meaningfully upon any occasion".

The Anang, reported Crowquill, were a people who took enormous pride in their fantastic jokes. The youths were trained from infancy. But, again, to what end, Mr Marigold wondered. Did they live longer? Were they happier? Were their communities any more sustainable, their energy production, their preservationist efforts? Did humor extend to an ecology of friendship, of love? Did laughter stave off all the agonies and turmoils of being human, of living with contradiction? Of famine and pollution, or the extinction of cheetahs? Did Crowquill know something the environmentalists had failed to decipher in their geographies of turmoil? Again, a murky veil obscured clarification.

Some time in the late 1980s, following a visit to the same shtetl where Sholem Alechem wrote his Hasidic witticisms (the basis for that very profound sense of drollery and esprit that had given Orthodox Jewry strength to perpetuate its belief in God, in spite of the Holocaust), certain of which were annotated by the adventurer, Crowquill had apparently journeyed among the Pygmies of Central Africa for whom uninhibited laughter was considered the highest virtue. He noted one occasion in particular when a tribe gave full physical vent to their laughter, convulsing on the ground, snapping their fingers, slapping their sides. These particular Pygmies never killed an animal, unlike their more moribund cousins who thought nothing of trapping and bringing down an elephant. Such a scene was in extraordinary contrast to the one he painted of his visit with a Senryu master at a Zen monastery in the Echizen Mountains of Japan. There the punster retraced the evolution of the punch line internally. Such humor was not about belly laughs but the enlightenment of shining chrysanthemums.

He described his journey into a headman's tent somewhere in South Asia (he called them the Paliyan tribe) and reported how the people appeared either so enlightened as to have gone beyond humor or simply catatonic. They were the most humorless people on earth, an entire society of deadly bores, among whom even speaking was regarded as too much trouble. Not surprisingly, all of their wells were poisoned, their children sick with rickets.

In France, however, Crowquill recorded an anomaly that threatened to challenge or set back his entire theory: a strange disorder characterized by the victim's inability to stop laughing—*le fou rire prodromique*. Marigold heard Sannazaro's own commentary on this ailment, which he found particularly apt, and he quoted from his beloved *Le Avventure di Pinocchio* of Carlo Collodi in which, seeing Pinocchio stuck upside down in the mud, a certain serpent "*...fu preso da una tal convulsione di risa, che ridi, ridi, ridi, alla fine, dallo sforzo del troppo ridere, gli si strappo una vena sul pette: e quella volta mori davvero.*" In other words, he laughed and laughed and laughed until a particularly important blood vessel exploded, and the creature died of his laughter, which gave Pinocchio time and opportunity to escape, and that was the important part. An escape from the madness of a great belly laugh. A true tempest of unstoppable laughter would not kill, but merely disable, and thus prevent injury to the world.

That is precisely what ensued during a remarkable period of some months in the early 1960s, said Crowquill, around Lake Victoria. There, the explorer found himself caught up in an outbreak of *enduara yokusheka*, Africa's most mysterious malady, translated as 'laughing sickness'. A young female student of a local mission had begun giggling over some joke. It would be discovered that the girl had taken her 'convulsive chuckles' home with her, unable to staunch the flood of outbursts. Others in her family came down with her snickering and tittering, then neighbors, soon after the entire village. The laughter was as contagious as the measles. After a week, hundreds were laughing, day and night. People started collapsing from exhaustion. More than 1,000 women and girls (men were mysteriously immune to the sickness) came down with it. Noted Crowquill, the children were laughing hysterically and could not be touched or they might break, for they were—in that condition—as fragile as Venetian glass. Millimeter-thin quartzite twists. Delicate diseases in the exalted throes of a divine and varicolored ague, the same one imported to the Chathams.

Crowquill was not the carrier, or not yet. He had been a mere observer, arrived by the bushy sides of Victoria only after the outbreak. However, it was his subsequent obsession to become infected himself. The epidemic lasted for two months. East African authorities were quick to blame it on US nuclear testing. Others claimed it was the work of a local witch doctor. No one died, though many were apotheosized in self-charm and group friendliness. A rare calm pervaded the villages afflicted. The contagion was contained by the authorities forcibly cutting off the region from visitors, but what no one ever explained, other than Crowquill, was the fact that during those two months, life around Lake Victoria became a paradise of tranquillity. The women and children with the disease, so called, had almost no needs—either of food, water, sleep or relief from restlessness. Content unto themselves. According to Crowquill, the ladies all exhibited that glow which is normally associated with pregnancy. None would say what they were laughing about, or what had transpired in their upstairs afterwards. There was no neurophysiological follow-up. Nobody wanted to speak of that fateful summer again, as if a group mind were protecting its secret treasure, some newly opened paradise gene of alpha dream-states in the human psyche. Utopia. Ecological perfection. The final point of bliss towards which philosophers from the time of the Late Paleolithic had looked nostalgically. Hesiod's Golden Age. Plato's Republic.

The same conspiracy of silence had been noticed by anthropologists in other cultures, whether among the Dani of Irian Jaya or the Kalash Kafir of the Hindu Kush—women, in each case, who kept a divine and covert shroud among those of their gender. But the concealment was breached, of course. Crowquill, by his own admission, was the only male to have heard the original one-liner, whatever it was. But he had not broken the compact until he came to Pitt Island where, as a scientist working in a fully protected laboratory, he had deliberately unleashed the virus of giggling. Marigold puzzled long and hard over this character of unremitting fascination, this baritone of unknowns whose duty to humankind had flowered in the most unlikely way. If he could actually discover the first joke ever told, would its dissemination possibly catapult humanity back in time to those days of ecological innocence? Or was all this busy work about nothing more profound than a Paleolithic squeak of flatulence, the first tumble on a banana peel? The original goof and gaff, with little to distinguish it from a crude primeval grunt? Did the subtle shift in nuance have the power to transform all subsequent 'punctuated' evolution, as Crowquill alleged? And if so, were we still so vulnerable to change?

All was a mystery, no less acute the next morning when Marigold and Salkeld compared notes. The Commander had come to the only possible conclusion: Crowquill knew he had an audience—this was the quintessence of a cosmological theory known as the anthropic principle— and it was his intention to demonstrate something that might enhance the richness of the world: the construction of a Utopia. If one succeeded, it would prove beyond any doubt the substance of a smile, and fix for all time the true location of laughter: there, in the soul's hideaway, where Marigold sensed he and Crowquill were one.

The diary referred repeatedly to specific coordinates that did not correspond to the Bounties. Rather, to some out-of-the-way glacier beneath Mount Welcome, in Oates Land, due south of the Balleny Islands—somewhere between a place called Yule and the Leningradskaya Base, precisely 71 degrees of latitude, 163 of longitude, in a bay called Cheetham, at the outer edge of Victoria Land, where the Transantarctic Mountains dipped into the ocean. Not 600 miles from McMurdo Base, though separated by an impassable cirque of icy inaccessibles. With unclear echoes of the likes of Fabian von Bellingshausen, J.S.C. Dumont d'Urville, Charles Wilkes and C.E. Borchgrevink, Crowquill bade those who would follow do so with little fanfare. A "modest proposal", the diary read, echoing George Kennan and Gorbachev.

That's it! Marigold reckoned, eliciting groans from his gluttonous Squire, who had only just removed himself from the wine cellar and cheese case.

To Salkeld, Marigold conveyed other remarkables that would be of keen interest to him: how, for example, the book had explained the operations of the lighthouse, which, said Crowquill, had proved beyond doubt that laughing gas—a rarefied mixture of seal flatulence and hydrogen, in conjunction with a little fuel cell—was the answer to future energy needs on earth. His bounteous empire was duly self-started.

A low-cost technology somewhere between an engine and a battery, was, he argued, the answer to an avant garde of solitude in Antarctica, where there was no acquiescence in the matter of rediscovering paradise, of protecting nature; all was without bias or personal qualm. A joke turned inward and solitary. The great white expanse was an empty canvas where human nature might begin anew, setting the ultimate example of self-preservation and sustainability. The Bounties would not do for more than one. They were already quite fully populated by birds and marine mammals. There were no places left for other people. Only Antarctica could satisfy the human expanse.

Marigold had found his mother lode, as improbable and inaccessible as it all seemed. In the joke which man had played on himself—over-population, the infliction of cruelty—there was, if one only looked for it, all the balance, instruction, point of view and objectivity that our species could ever hope for. "Submission to this wisdom was a precursor to the next millennium," wrote Crowquill.

These convoluted and weighty mentations were beyond Salkeld, who presently snored soundly. As for Sannazaro, ill at heart, clasping his belly, he continued to belch and groan, preferring to sleep in rather than face the trial of carrying their zodiac to the other end of the granite cliff, which Oguh, via radio, had suggested to Salkeld as a possibly safer pick-up point.

The miraculous tower was left as they had found it, nothing disturbed. But the Commander held on to the diary. He hoped that he might find Crowquill there, in the great yawning South, and return it to him.

It took them several hours of terrible labors getting round the island, dragging the 100-pound inflatable raft past one rookery after another. Salkeld and the Commander helped Sannazaro, who was utterly enfeebled by his wine-tasting binge, seasick, stomach mired, dizzy and very much afraid. At last, upon reaching the far side of the cliff, they took cover behind the upended boat, as the Sucking Circumference was creating sea foams a mile high, along with new pressure points of unexpected interest and peril. Few animals lounged on this end of the monolith.

At the precise instant—on the upwards cusp of a 48-second surge— they poured into the zodiac and powered out to meet the *Harbinger* through hugely undulating marine trenches, hurricane winds and mists thickening like peat. The steeple receded into a rumbling cloud, until even the island had vanished, as if it never were. Only the tonus of feverish sooty shearwaters screeching and hollering hysterically reminded them of Crowquill's perfect outcrop in the South Seas. The implausible horizon line, where mythology suggested an ancient ruin, bricks graffitied, embers scattered in warm reminder, the scant traces of some remarkable culture that had inhabited the recess—it was an imaginary point where the island soared, plunged and twisted in obfuscating tempest. No way to describe what had happened there—

the giant sharks, the little manifolds cupping gaseous outflow on all the seal bums; neither the geological phenomena nor ethology accounted for the community of several million animal residents, and their one human freak with his connoisseur's battlement, ensconced where no man should have ever laid anchor.

And now this, his incitement to kindred spirits, so as to raise the most philosophical question of all: did he even exist, or was he simply the Commander's way of coping with excess tragedy—the killing of chickens, the fatality of moa, and all those other extinctions throughout time which their plight described?

"What is this all about?" Sannazaro croaked, still seasick and weary, incapable of accepting the truth of that strange lighthouse at the fever pitch of horizon lines. "Where were we?" As their zodiac plunged.

"Still sampling public opinion," Marigold replied.

Later on, when he had time to recall the madness of their Lighthouse Escapade, Sannazaro asked, "Have you forgotten Santa Fe entirely? Or the fact of your riches? You are risking both our lives on these adventures, and I don't see the point. I have no energy to fight you, but mightn't we just go home?" It was a pitiful plea, an earnest call for help in the wilds, but in too weak a voice to matter.

"Not quite yet," Marigold replied in reassuring tones. "Be calm. I understand your frustration. But—how can I put this?—something in me has been awakened. I can't say where it's leading. I can't predict an easy path. But I'll understand if you want to quit when I tell you that we must follow Crowquill's cartographical trail all the way to the South Pole, if needs be."

"Quit? Are you kidding? Gladly. On the other hand, it's not all bad. I am, after all, a hero—" he invested the word with something like a sea veteran's ring of triumph, somewhere between Gog and Magog. "Who could fail to appreciate the infernal size and peril of that behemoth!"

"You nut. It was a guppy."

"It was a shark."

"A guppy."

"Damn you!"

"Gentlemen, one hell of a storm's moving this way," Oguh relayed, with detectable unease. "Just heard the details from a ship 300 miles east. Get your things bolted down. Hold your stomachs in. We're heading to rough water."

Marigold had already negotiated with Oguh for the ride further south. Nothing, he reasoned, could be more strange or forbidding than the Sea of Sucking Silences which they had already survived.

With the first imbalance in the swells, accumulating in size and ferocity, Sannazaro puked overboard. It stank of half-digested gorgonzola and attracted some storm petrels and wandering albatross who'd been diligently trailing the *Harbinger* as she steered in the direction of the South Pole.

CHAPTER 69
Mr Marigold's Second Utopia

FOR THREE DAYS the five deck swabbers traversed further and further into tale-telling ice waters, waiting with trepidation for the first of the great bergs. Each night the Commander stood outside watching anxiously. Sannazaro knew very little about the South Polar regions, less still the history of terrible adventures and worse plights that saw so many decorated heroes laid to waste amid the frozen sands and snowy dunes. He did not want to hear about it; no Shackleton, no Byrd, no Scott. His ears, mind, eyes were closed to the impending doom which he sensed in this latest moronic pilgrimage. Maritime alps, rosy sanctuaries, the shores of the Mediterranean and the Tuscan sun, a fine dry day in Tesuque—those were his tried tonics, but this, this unaccountable horror, ransacked his notion of what it was to be a human. The Bounties were insufferable enough. These frigidly encinctured dull charcoals-worth of swaying horizon were nothing more than trench warfare. Desperate petrels crying, he imagined, for relief, filled his lungs with hopeless air, his headparts with bile. But he said nothing. What was the point?

Until the third evening drew them within several nautical miles of an enormous iceberg, by satellite the size of ten Hopi mesas or five Santa Fes, large enough to conceal most of Liechtenstein and traveling 25 miles per hour through the super-chilled waters. Pieces of driftwood traveled beside it.

"That's a masthead!" Oguh exclaimed. "Allowing for direction of current, the fast-coursing waters of the Southern Convergence Ocean, it would appear that those are the remains of Crowquill's boat. The accident could have happened months ago, far to the south."

Only fate could have orchestrated the actual instant Crowquill's trawler of dreams would career and crumble upon the vast shore of an aquamarine icecap. The mesa of quicksilvered deep freeze lumbered several miles out from the eternal continent itself—the highest, driest landmass in the world.

The boat's masts had splintered as bow, port and starboard sides were obliterated by the traveling island of ice, its mauve undersides populated by miles of dense phytoplankton and red krill. There was no other force on earth to combat the power of an oncoming iceberg, one reason petroleum engineers had prudently advised against the building of any offshore oil rigs in the Antarctic ocean. Like a single derrick, a small boat was doomed. Crowquill's 80-foot yawl with its twelve-foot draft (as per his description of it in his diary) was no match for the monster of deep-freezing momentums. Indeed, against such mass, a boat simply counted for zero on the Richter scale of collisions. Nothing but decades of warm water would attenuate such an iceberg, upon which hundreds of dark little specks—penguins—took perpetual passage as the coriolis acceleration (as it is known) blew hurricane-force winds against the western sides of the continent, releasing surges of carbon dioxide, yellow lights, bromides and chlorines, and some heretofore unknown Syncretism of Terrible Consequences unique to contemporary Antarctic skies.

Crowquill must have grasped that this maelstrom of near twenty-first-century scientific beauty charged by compelling chaos multipliers was the destiny of his vessel and, presumably, of himself. Whereas Sannazaro, prompted by the unquiet memory of the pair of glasses thrown up with the other disgusting melange of gastric remnants, insisted that the monster of belly laughs was somewhere else entirely—in the burgeoning dark gullet of a whale shark. But there was no other proof, except to admit that Crowquill was not in his own bed within the tower, or anywhere else to be found. All signs suggested the obvious: his boat had been magnificently demolished.

Mr Marigold meditated on the unprecedented vista before him, that Bare Ice of Exile where Crowquill—who could easily have been the famed knight Amadis, aka Beltenebros—had done some miraculous form of penance, perhaps for his own Lady Oriana. Now firm in his resolution to rectify the unsolicited Pang of Being, to make right the injustice of one man's untimely disappearance, he avowed before his sailing men, "The boat's fragments are their own memorial, cast out in the luscious waves for all eternity. Now, I ask only to be put ashore, with all our trappings, and that you leave us to our final combat. I assure you, it will be funny. And our laughter will save us."

Nobody knew what he was talking about. Which combat, and why should it be final? What was funny about that? They knew what cold could do to a body, and it was not amusing.

Sannazaro was least enthused by the tone of his ridiculous colleague and hastened to apologize for it on account of the burdensome oxygen density of air; the unearthly penumbra and atmospheric phenomena all around them; the extreme magnetic confusion of so southerly a position on the globe; the recent agitation caused by such serious topographical isolation, with its known immuno-neurological and psychopathologic implications for Sensitives. The passage through the icebergs, strange, dangerous labyrinths and mazes, bergs upon which leopard seals lounged and around which killer whales preyed, had been disorienting for them all. The chill, the intermingling sea salts, the very scenes themselves, so blatantly given to hallucinogenic effect, posed enormous burdens for the frail aesthetic temperament of the Italian, notwithstanding the bravado of his Commander and the strangely unaffected attitude of their three seafaring guides who were collecting considerable fees each day for their vessel and services. Was Sannazaro the only rational intelligence left? The only one to fathom their deep and perilous immersion on the edge of the known world? It seemed so.

Once inside the eternal gallery of ice, which spread for twelve million square miles around the South Pole, there was no compass reading by which to take comfort: only wilderness and fear.

"Browsing constitutes a peril," Iwi reminded his captain, who sought the closest place possible for a landing.

"You have the technology," Salkeld explained to the unwary Marigold, "but the manual is sketchy. The temperatures, mate, spare no one. By midnight it will be far far below zero, and you'll be sitting on the ice with no cozy tower to call home. Only a few puns. But I fear the joke's on you."

"We're not leaving this boat," Sannazaro declared. "Nothing on earth could induce me to step foot from the safe quarters herewith. I swear I will see you for the last time if you insist on following that learned lunatic—" he was, of course, referring to Crowquill—"into useless oblivion. I shall sue for punitive damages."

"You'll be dead first," Iwi remarked, not simply sarcastically. From the looks of their position, insanity had been loosed upon the world. It was, for the Knight on board, the most errant of his days. It would be so for any other fool who might follow. This much was obvious. The continent lay before them, glittering, empty, the very meaning of doom, encased, on average, in ice nine miles deep.

"Then so be it," the Commander replied. "A man's honor is at stake here. But more than that, the untried Utopia which he has envisioned remains to be tested, and I too swear that it is my proper leaning in life to be the Chosen One in this matter of proof."

"Proof? Are you mad? Proof on whose behalf? The penguins'?" Sannazaro wailed.

Salkeld, Oguh and Iwi gazed on as the two sparring partners bickered boisterously about the wisdom of setting forth with no other plan than the instillation of a hydrogen fuel-cell apparatus and the erection of a quonset hut in which to hole up indefinitely. But how? In a day, alone? Actually, that was Sannazaro's characterization of the madcap scheme. The Commander had thought it out more thoroughly, of course. In fact, Oguh had already facilitated numerous satellite phone conversations between Marigold and equipment gadgetry in New Zealand and Japan. The Commander had summoned a considerable bevy of supplies to be flown in to Invercargill's charming little airfield and moved to the nearby harbor at Bluff. They included several dozen 40-foot containers' worth of raw building materials, the inventory of which he had studied carefully in the presence of Crowquill's beguiling diary.

The cost of these appurtenances was no object, naturally, and the Commander spared no nickel in acquiring every modern marvel of appropriate technology for the pyramidal-domed organic igloo he had in mind: a religious hyperspace, utterly self-sufficient, that got its energy kick from the operations of Crowquill's fuel cell. The primary AC-DC carrier for Marigold's Utopia would be laughing gas, laced with cow methane (seal farts were nowhere for sale) stored in hydrogen tanks and derived from four benign sources: photolysis (the liberation of hydrogen from the direct impact of the sunlight on an electrolytic solution), wind, wave action and a photovoltaic array. Of course, Marigold hoped to find penguin and seal volunteers for cupping their gas and, at least, generating heat for the stove. The end result was to be the most perfect human habitation in the world, a structure, sound of mind, latticed with Japanese ceramics, that could stand up to the perpetual gales and typhoons of dark winter. With endless power to fuel its quotidian mundanes, and zero emissions, the whole enterprise would confirm, according to Marigold, the human capacity for leaving no footprint—the great transition from materialism to fairyland, from abscesses of primordial slime to angel villages in shared sublime. Moreover, there would be a naturally induced heat. He had not a clue, in truth.

Might not such heat melt the ice on which they were to erect their Utopia? Salkeld mused aloud. But Marigold dismissed such heresies as flagrant conjecture.

The mechanical aspects of the construction had already been designed in Tokyo by Happy Homes, the largest prefab corporation in the world, the brainchild of Mr So and So, famed for his habit of belting out arias from the great literature of opera to his tomato plants. The robotic assembly lines punched out within 48 hours customized 3,000-to-6,000 square foot homes that combined the look of a teahouse with the cosmic durability of a space station, and that rotated on a revolving digital disc in order to remain oriented to the sun throughout the year. Each of the 300,000 homes constructed annually was lowered into place by helicopter.

Marigold had described his needs over the phone to So and So himself, who'd conferenced in the senior engineer within the company to transcribe the wish list onto computer. This was to be the first Happy Home in Antarctica. The 12-by-15-foot ceramic sections were shipped in the hull of a JAL 747 to Christchurch, lorried down to Bluff and set onto the launch which would carry the tonnage further south to the rendezvous with the *Harbinger*, just off the Antarctic coastline, in the shadows of the fateful iceberg against which Crowquill's boat, allegedly, had been wrecked.

The supply ship was on its way, with crates full of 1,000 widgets, shovels, canned goods, shingles, wedges, washers, o-rings, dowels, cogs, polyurethane ducting, blankets, appliances, bedding, furnishings, electric prime movers, hydraulic levers, nanosensors and spare parts, a computer mainframe running on SAP, and scores of manuals to go with it, and not a nail needed. All was pre-fitted to slip into habitable form with a minimum of effort. But these were simple details. The money and vision to engineer Utopia in a day.

No one had ever thought to attempt such a community in Antarctica. True, Admiral Richard Byrd had founded Little America 70-odd years before, and subsequently spent a winter more or less alone on the ice, but his community of one was miserably condemned to a sagging tent, frozen shoelaces, socks turned into wood, and constant 80-degrees below zero temperatures inside his half-sunken hole. His one energy source to keep him from freezing altogether was a vicious little stove that steadily leaked a flow of carbon monoxide that threatened to kill the headstrong explorer. Marigold was enamored of the adventure.

Captain Oguh had real scruples about leaving the emboldened Commander to his quest, for it was clear that his first and only lieutenant, Sannazaro, was truly frantic about their prospects, and confused (as many are at first sight of the Antarctic coastline) by the very nature of Existence. Are we dead, or alive? they are often heard to say. Is it night, or is it day? Does the world still exist? As a heaven or a hell? Such beauty is useless to their cause of survival, which threatens to smother them in an amphetamine of perceived causes, consequences, hazards and impossibilities, all of which turn out one way or other to be true.

In short, Sannazaro was imploding, and duly convinced that the Commander had a death wish, inspired by the splendid example of Crowquill, and that he was personally being sucked up in the whirlpool of self-destruction. Oguh, though paid beyond his wildest dreams (for the Commander was no businessman and thought nothing about dishing out the highest price—"The best deal is the one that transcends all negotiations," he'd oft repeated), was not eager to be thought of by his seafaring pals as one who'd callously forsaken the safety of his crew, even under these freak circumstances.

"There's nothing to do about it," he finally admitted, as all five of them watched the unquestioning stevedores of the supply vessel hurriedly downloading the mass of exotic hardware onto the ice, cowled in beaver-lined parkas, the air steamed and frothy from their hard-breathing industry.

By 9 p.m., the aurora australis was radiant, a spasm of rods and cones lighting up the gaseous night sky. The decks of the supply ship had been cleared, and all agreed that the Commander had best spend a final night on board *Harbinger*. They also hoped to talk him out of the madness upon which he was poised to embark.

"You will freeze to death. It's that simple," Salkeld advised. "It is not a pretty sight. I've seen it."

"He's seen it! Did you hear that?" Sannazaro reiterated. "Not a pretty sight. How hideous a sight?" he asked, hoping the grisly clinical truth would set his Commander straight.

"The face turns blue, then white. If there is a thaw, it goes green. The blood vessels pop beneath the skin, the eye sockets hemorrhage, while the penis, dried out, shrinks to one-fifth its size. I could go on."

But the Commander remained unmoved by these theatrics, miles away in thought, and his companions were stymied by his statesmanship. He then consumed three glasses of dark sherry whilst expatiating upon the fine points of fashioning a Utopia. His champion was Crowquill, who in turn counted among his predecessors a long and dazzling cavalcade of historical personalities and experiments. All these Marigold had thoroughly studied back in New Mexico. What an Eastern Gnostic Simeon Stylite born in 390, a pathologically inspired ascetic who stood for nearly four decades atop a pillar in the Sinai, had to do with a Happy Home in Antarctica, no one was quite certain. Nor, for that matter, were they sure of the many other mendicants, artists, philosophers, political and social idealists whom Marigold described. He knew them all—the pictorial renditions, celebrated essays, rumored hide-aways and cryptic topographies. He regaled his listeners with tales of Raphael's *School of Athens* and Lorenzetti's *The City of Good Government*. Went on about Giovanni Bellini's *St. Francis in the Wilderness*, echoing the famous translation by King Alfred the Great of Boethius' *Consolation of Philosophy*—"Men followed the path of nature in strict measure. They ate but once in the day. The fruits of trees they ate, and roots. They always slept out of doors in the shade of the trees; pure spring water was their drink." No fruit trees anywhere near Mount Welcome, nor roots, Sannazaro was quick to point out. As for the famed Sir Thomas More, despite his calls for clemency and abolition of capital punishment, as described in his bemusing little 1516 volume, *Utopia*, with its learned Greek clues (utopia = no place; its capital city, Amanote = dream town; and its narrator, Raphael Hythlodae = dispenser of nonsense), More did not intervene to halt executions during his regency as Lord Chancellor. Fittingly, he himself was beheaded, charged with treason after his dubious embroilment in the affairs of Henry VIII, Catherine of Aragon, Anne Boleyn and Elizabeth Barton.

The contradictions cascaded: the capital of Arcadia, in ancient Greece, was the heavily populated city of Megalopolis. So much for the intimations of pastoral calm. Whether in Antonio Doni's *Mondi* (1552), Tommaso Campanella's poetic dialogue, *La Citta del Sole* (1623), or Gerrard Winstanley's *The Law of Freedom* (1652), utopias—as he long perceived—were doomed, and the Commander was the first to admit it. No real flesh-and-blood, down-to-earth experiments, whether Father George Rapp's Community of Equality in Western Pennsylvania, or the Amana Society and its community of True Inspiration at Buffalo, New York, in the 1840s, ever managed to hold its center. Even the great *Court of Gayumarth*, a painting accomplished by Sultan Muhammed sometime between 1522 and 1527 in the Persian city of Tabriz, with its astonishing portrait of paradise, revealed upon closer scrutiny the true tragedy of its subtext: the rise of evil in the world during the realm of the legendary first Shah of Iran, and the eventual silencing of Muhammad himself by the royal court in Tabriz.

These were minor sidebars to the history of idealism, explained Marigold. While he was intimate with each, he was not troubled by the breakdown in internal politics which characteristically plagued all such picaresque endeavors. What interested him was the worship of nature, common to them all, which he plucked from a few lines of Campanella: "*e 'l mondo essere animal grande, e noi star intra lui, come I vermi nel nostro corpo...*" In other words, the perception of Mother Earth as a great beast, in which we all dwelt; the Gaia Principle, advanced hundreds of years before the advent of the twentieth-century British biochemical theories pertaining to kelp, methane and its importance to the regulation of oxygen content on earth. He didn't really understand the chemistry, any more than he understood Crowquill's philosophy of laughing gas. He didn't need to. The dreamer in him was satisfied by the underlying ideals of the utopian urging in man.

Nor was he exercised over the fragile social orchestrations of ancient monasteries and more recent sociological experiments. That he was proposing a paradise of two, with 50 percent of that population utterly unwilling to take part, did not seem to deter his visionary zeal. Nor did the fact of his having chosen for his Club Paradise the one continent utterly inhospitable to man seem to jolt his faith in the great haiku that was the vanished Crowquill. Quite simply, Mr Marigold was drawn irresistibly to the man: to everything about his person and impressive legacy; to that stark edifice from which silent eyes peered out over the stunning whitecaps of every Whistler and Constable, in earshot of the primeval jubilees of storm prion, arrayed like one more life form among the throngs of sentient beings—from cyanobacteria and golden lichen to Hooker's seal—whose fashionable behavior, unknowable thoughts, identifiable passions and patterns had not appreciably changed in millions of years.

All was a mere prelude to the even vaster infinities and enigmas incarnate across the gorgeous haunted landmass before them. A sculpted temple of every mint-condition horizon, surface, outcrop and square inch of earth; the color of prisms inverted, convexed, overarched and orgied; of insane azures and dusty ivory, metallic grays and devastating burgundies, pitched silver, unweened cobalt, sleek oranges and massive pinks; of ferrous striations blanketing the night, and a billion pores exhaling a billion colors only once voiced in the ongoing palettes of evolution. All enshrined upon a naked perimeter of origins, once a supercontinent—Gondwana—with all its crevasses, yawning riddles and Martian meteorites, and three times the size of the United States. Mountains unknown. Deserts larger than the Sahara, and as perfectly formed as Lalique crystal, without even a name. Ice crystals as large as an acre, as luminous as Louis XIV chandeliers in the Hermitage. A summation of geophysical art that was alive.

The Commander grasped all this in a fateful glance, and apologized to his friends for his sober testimony to Antarctica, which too clearly belied, even mocked all mental efforts at the superlative. But he was convincing enough. No one would say he was not of sound mind after his evening's aesthetic discourse. Even the esoteric science of the fuel cell and its operations had somehow percolated through that thick skull, so that Oguh himself, famed among his friends for a keen pragmatism, was sufficiently impressed.

"Maybe you have a chance, at least for the first summer," he opined, "assuming you can generate enough laughing gas. Your effort is certainly hysterical enough to induce a few giggles from saner men; and you've got that fancy satellite telephone, a good parka, earmuffs, and gourmet groceries of one sort or another. Hell, if that's how you want to spend Christmas, be my guest. Actually, a good tent, a dozen stakes to hold it down when the winds blow, a shovel to keep the snow from burying you, a little stove to melt it down for water—because your throat'll be parched—ahhh, you'll be fine. And I'll be more than happy to come and collect you when you're out of food. But don't wait too long. By early March, my little *Harbinger*'s out of business in these waters. The whole continent becomes a hurricane, if it hasn't already. And then, all the money in the world won't suffice to tempt a rescue."

To these rejoinders Sannazaro listened with pique and a flood of sweat pouring off his temples. The Commander had pulled the wool over their eyes. How could veteran mariners be so daft—to be persuaded by a madman? To let money rule their good citizenship? The issue was one of homicide.

"You cannot abandon him," the Squire finally managed. "This is my life we're talking about!"

"Then don't go," said Oguh.

"What, and leave him all alone to his foolishness? I am not that cruel."

CHAPTER 70
Angels in Antarctica

THAT NIGHT, SILENTLY in his bare bunk, Sannazaro thought long and hard, trembled and at times even broke out weeping with dry heaves, for he knew he had been swayed by the general opinion, and he hated himself for having so little strength of character. He was going to go along with the zany expedition. Still, he must have sensed that so much money as Marigold now possessed would never allow them to be marooned. With Oguh only a week away at Chatham, maybe it would be all right. Moreover, despite his having no clue how they would survive even a day, he could not fault the aesthetic logic of it. After all, he too had devoted most of his life to the nostalgia inherent to Arcadia. His own lineage recommended nothing less. It pained him, however, to think that times had gotten so bad on earth that one needed to resort to this extreme in order to engender a garden. In a place where there was not one ounce of real soil, scarcely a flower. To go to the moon to recover the earth.

Notwithstanding these details and moral complexities, by morning he knew that he was hooked. With a twit or jot of bounteous chance, Marigold would freak out after a day or two, call off the masquerade and return to his senses. They'd call in a flotilla of helicopters and all would be right. Within a fortnight, he should be safely re-ensconced at the Camp of the Spirits and sipping on a Martini. Moreover, a few days on the ice might not be so unutterable, making that Martini all the more remarkable. Something to impress Ginevra and anybody else who might listen to his tales of heroism and giant sharks.

The deeper truth was that Sannazaro felt more anxious for the Commander than for himself. Here was a man, after all, who was still a child in so many respects. A puppet guided by the strings of some tragic obsession. He really didn't have a clue how to live, not in this age. In that respect, he was an angel. But so was Sannazaro, and one with seniority. Angels needed to stay together. It was the least he could do, he figured, to look after the wayward misanthrope. There was more to it, of course, but time did not permit him the leisure to think about it. Few metaphors or semaphores survived in such cold. There was the landing craft to lower, the gloves and survival gear to worry about. Fixing the zippers, emergency flares, food caches; timing the arrival team who were to offload. A hundred details. It happened fast, as if in a war zone. Tarps flapping hard in the gale. Blasts of ice-laden mistral sweeping the edges of the ice shelf. A horror of winds, white dimensions, otherworldly skewerings.

By five in the morning, Captain Oguh, Ti Iwi and John Salkeld bade farewell to the intrepid Commander and his resigned Squire, who were deposited among a mountain of equipment. Three members of the supply ship had agreed to remain with the twosome, charging 5,000 dollars per day per man to assist in the erecting of the prefab. These were no builders, but strong longshoremen with a taste for income who reckoned the instruction manual from Happy Homes couldn't be that tricky, despite its being written in Japanese. Not a nail to be pounded, no actual construction required. Boxer, Winthrop and Maze stepped onto the ice with Marigold and Sannazaro, while their ship remained half a mile out at sea. The *Harbinger*, meanwhile, disappeared northwards, slipping through the passages in the ice with hardly a putter.

Said Sannazaro, peering out in all directions at white horror, "Once upon a time, there was snow. C'era una volta ..." And he whispered a jealous farewell to his former companions.

The three big New Zealanders set to work at once, while Marigold assumed the rank of Barker of Orders and Lord Chancellor of Unwrappings. Sannazaro assisted with the shoveling, for there was much ground to render even. A host of decisions were taken with little forethought, resolutions now consented to by both Commander and Squire, for Boxer, Winthrop and Maze were hired guns and did not fancy lending too much advice about matters utterly outside their ken. No master plan. No blueprint. A haphazard series of choices. Of course, there were some obvious things which Marigold had either overlooked or discounted: the proximity of the structure to the edge of the sea, for example. Winthrop had been many times to Antarctica and had seen whole sections of icy shoreline topple into the ocean, so it was only right for him to point this out, and the Commander accepted his advice gratefully.

All efforts were thus undertaken 1,000 feet away from the fracture line at which the glacial headlands presented a potentially dangerous declivity. That drop amounted to an enormous cliff of ice, hundreds of feet high, hundreds of miles long, that marked the tumultuous intersection of the continent and the ocean. The ice calved continuously, thundering into a tideless sea. There was no formal wave action other than that occasioned by the glacial explosions, on account of the density of ice which lent the Antarctic seas a freshwater taste.

They were racing against the onset of night, and cold. Daytime temperatures remained in the mellow 30s.

"We have a purpose supreme, dear friends," the Commander hailed, sweat pouring down his chest. "Aroma finer than prayer is how the great Walt Whitman likened it."

But his companions were not very interested. The task before them was great; the Happy Home a tangle, now, of instructions more incomprehensible than they had bargained on. They managed to lay the foundation which set down much like a traditional three-person dome tent, though 750 times its circumference. Raising the central pillars created a dilemma without a crane, or a dozen men. Selvedges were unclear. But two skidoos, brought in with the gear, were able to be worked like tow trucks, and eventually, with perlon ropes attached on pulleys, the group succeeded in accomplishing their nebulous task.

All these preliminaries were achieved beneath the ever-watchful gaze of Mr Marigold, a student of Feng Shui, with its precise choreographies of energy for every dwelling on the planet. He was lingering heavily over each task, mumbling on about metal and fire, earth and water, wood and horizontal rotations of the astronimbus mindset. Nobody had a clue what he was talking about: contours of time, trigrams and later heavens, tortoise markings and a dragon horse. He was so insistent on imposing the 64 hexagrams which, he argued, would be a real 'first' in the history of utopias, that he failed to notice a few important facts. Among his plans was not a single bedroom animal, tree or creeper; no garden energies to enhance the Wu Chi and Yin Yang. Instead: crevasses, which required maintaining ropes around the perimeters, so that if anybody disappeared there was a retrieval system for the corpse. Moreover, the Commander's grand scheme, his Happy Home, had no 'phoenix aspects' or low-intensity bounce-backs—essential facets of any I Ching-approved architecture. The toilet sat far too close to the front door, such as it was; there were no separate divining chambers. Thus, a dangerous situation had arisen whereby the astral energy flow constituted a rigid straight line, and this, in Feng Shui circles, was a colossal no-no.

"Bad luck, old chap," one of the hands commiserated.

But there was nothing to be done about it.

By two in the afternoon, the sun was still high above the 50-mile ridge of metamorphic mountains on two sides. The moon was also visible, and it was coming on three-quarters-to-full—a good omen, thought Marigold, in spite of the discouraging placement of the toilet in his Utopia.

The encampment sat at the narrow point where the escarpments pinched to an opening, looking out over the sea. Beyond, the glacial basin of sastrugi and incandescent barrier ice extended for thousands of miles.

"I name this place Behind the Moon Lane," the Commander said wearily, worn down from all the snow shoveling and nerves.

By nightfall, much had occurred. A huge ceramic freezer had risen before them. Reality had closed in, and with it gusts of light snow crystal whipping across the ice at 40 knots, stinging the face. The workers had finished their labors. The tanks of laughing gas had been placed, the house essentially completed, and all that was left were those countless small, needling, qualifying factors of unpacking personal effects, no special assistance required. Without much ceremony the men said good-bye, wished the Commander and his troubled companion the best of luck, and removed from the continent to their ship, which vanished in the twilight.

Now the two men sat alone indoors. The outdoor temperature was below zero, according to a thermometer hung from over a real-life sink. A flashlight died in Sannazaro's hand. He wore his parka, shivering beneath. It was colder by magnitudes than winter in Santa Fe. And this was the Antarctic summer.

"This is a ghastly situation," he reproved. "Fear not. Once we get the heat working."

"How will we do that?"

The Commander produced a manual. "It's in here," he said confidently. Until he noticed that it, too, was in Japanese. Without English translation.

With candles safely lit (flames will not go out atop a wick until the temperature reaches 55 below, he assured Sannazaro) the two men hunkered down around the dinner table and, in honor of Richard Byrd, divided a package of dried lima beans between them.

"Listen," Marigold pointed with a hushing fascination. "What?"

"Shhh!"

Sannazaro craned his ears, but heard only the howl of the wind and the creaking of the new structure. It was settling in. Or was the ice breaking up under them? He had no way of knowing, or of trusting anything.

"How do we know we're on safe ground?" he asked, struck by the fact nobody seemed to have asked that question previously.

"We're hundreds of yards from the ice wall," Marigold replied. "Winthrop had said it was OK, remember?"

"Winthrop? Like he's some renowned glaciologist? He wore earrings in every orifice."

"My dear Sannazaro, I fail to catch your meaning? Did you not see the enormity of those ice cliffs? Why, they are virtual skyscrapers of solidity."

"OK. Fine. Anyway, what's done is done. Here we are. Hopeless. And what I wouldn't give right now to be back in Crowquill's wine cellar. Safe from this unfathomable hazard in which we have, like absolute imbeciles, placed ourselves. Why do I listen to you?"

"Because you love me," the Commander said, evidencing a rakish humor, a clear sign of his recent inheritance.

"Either that," Sannazaro concluded, "or I hate myself with even more vigor. Adding the two neurological disorders, love and hate, together, I cannot but assume the hate transcends the love."

"Then work out some subtractions. Neutralize your imbalances," the Commander recommended.

"I am no mathematician. Nor do I possess the appropriate traits of self-analysis at this terrible point in time to undergo the seemingly impossible task. Friendship has driven me to an untenable edge."

"You don't exhibit any of the normal signs," Marigold assured him. "No hives, ugly rash, mop of sweat. Your demeanor, other than this moment's despair, seems utterly rational, blithe, even fair."

"We have to get out of here," Sannazaro cried painfully, oblivious to his companion's assurances. He was beginning now to panic, stricken with a mounting agoraphobic horror at their isolation. He had not counted on this reaction, but there it was, irrupting out of control. A veritable condition only now expressing itself. "Here."

"What is it?"

"A cookie."

The Squire munched upon the ginger snap, his face and lips freezing, hands shaking convulsively. He was terrified, at the point of death. Then he remembered the whale shark, and his extraordinary heroism. It seemed to effect the desired neutralization, at least for now.

At length, both men snuggled into their sleeping bags. Exhaustion catapulted the tranquil Commander deep into inner space, his savvy tick-tack-toeing into uncommon dreams of wet, mucousy masses of sea blubber riddled with pockmarks and areas of digestible slime. Of gastric sulfur eruption; white-blooded dragon, horse and snail, eel pout and left-eye flounder. His thoughts descended to the mesmerized wanderings of the *Pagothenia borchgrevinki*, with its exquisite serum anti-freeze; the lives of *Lecanora tephroeceta*, a lichen species inhabiting remote Marie Byrd Land, which could only survive if peed on by

Pagodroma nivea, a snow petrel that favored nesting on that very lichen. And the recent dinosaur discoveries from Mt Kirkpatrick set back upon the Beardmore Glacier of the Central cordillera—*Cryolophosaurus ellioti*, a crested reptile that shat mounds weighing 45 pounds, and the only Therapod known to exist in Antarctica. Sannazaro took four sleeping pills and eventually fell off soundly, far removed from all such dreams, impending terrors and katabatic nights.

CHAPTER 71
Compressed Natural Crowquill

MARIGOLD WAS awakened by a rumbling at 4.17 a.m. He sat up, peered across the ice through frosted glass, riveted to the astonishing light that enveloped their solitude, not a little overwhelmed by the sheer truth of their geographical segregation. What was the undertaking? What had he planned, really? He had bought their sovereignty—because he could—through artificial means of life support. Now he pondered the eerieality, unsure what next step to initiate. Marx and Engels in the first part of their manifesto had spoken of the "idiocy of rural life". Did Marigold mean to rebuke them forever more? To elevate the countryside into that Fragment by Euripides which suggested that "heaven assists the man that laboureth" into something more then a damp squib?

He thought he saw something on the ice, a finely chiseled Galatea, naked and pearly, animated by every early-morning glint, sailing across the drifts like an hallucinogen in a northeaster. She was the first woman, and this the first day. The first Greek, Mohican, Saxon, Troubadour. Presently, the first breakfast. Special Ks pulverized in soy milk. A hardened peach much bruised from its packing crate.

He and Sannazaro had spoken lightly of psychoanalysis. Lightness now turned to sobriety. In this living laboratory, the only real substance was their thought processes—how they might be altered to conform with some ideal, what rudiments of change could be manipulated, and whether these mental gyrations warranted extrapolation for the entire human condition. Such isolation tended to trap human time and make it palpable. You could caress it or be stabbed in the back, accordingly. It placed the mind in a vise, pressured all thought into self-appraisal on the edge of lunacy. No idea was unmirrored, so that the ecology of thinking became a real presence, crucial to working out each articulation and second. There could be no escaping the truth of one's heavy body or labored breathing, the color of urine on the ice, the rude leathery skin on a fingertip tracing a call for help on the frosted glass. How primitive the body, revealed for the first time under circumstances shorn of all cover-up or civilization. No more elegance. Weaned off the everyday, cast into the dried-out canals of another planet one billion years before. This was their condition, and Marigold was thrilled by the prospects.

"Don't you see what it has already facilitated?"

"What?" the Squire muttered as he tried fecklessly to hold on to the last of the one good night's sleep he'd had in many eons. He had not counted on such insane enthusiasm—day and night—for a room-mate.

"A true experiment in human happiness. If we succeed, for even 24 hours, then the rest of the human condition can be predicated."

"And if we fail? Then what?"

"Then we must let events take their course and know that it was for the best. I am of that frame of mind. I believe in our capacity to forge a new nature, but I will not insist upon new evolution. I am no biological braggart, nor fool."

"You are both, and this idea of yours is doomed," Sannazaro rashly replied. Then he set about completing his task: the consumption of a prune. In a matter of days they would be rescued, he repeated to himself.

Then all would be set right. Much remained to be unpacked: items Marigold had ordered by telephone, only to be rudely confronted with a certain ignorance, to put it politely, of their function and operations. An enforced policy of pinpricks.

"What are you doing?" the Squire asked some time later. He was dressed in all of his clothes, apart from footwear, and looking for water, for his throat was raw. "Shit!" he muttered under his breath. He had stubbed his bare baby toe on an ironing board left in the middle of the room. Space was going to be another of their problems.

"What is this?" the Commander asked, trying to gain some augmented prospect of the icy horizon by viewing it through an odd rubber attachment on a stick.

"That is no telescope, my dear pathetic person, but a plunger, usually employed in the service of unclogging toilets. Surely you are familiar with plungers?"

"Hmmm," Marigold said with some embarrassment. "What about this?" He was turning over and around a heavy object which he had just removed from a crate.

"It looks to me like a Cuisinart," Sannazaro said. "Ahh, right! Excellent. For dicing delectables."

All around them, the windows allowed the sunlight to heat up the interior quickly. Marigold drew the UV filters, a thin mylar drapery the color of burgundy. It worked like a polarizer so that the continent all around them acquired an even more fantastic visage—indescribable hues and coronas competing for effect on the mind's eye.

"Maybe it's not so bad," Sannazaro finally conceded, after quenching his thirst with homemade lemonade from a nearby Portland vase and helping himself to toast and marmalade. He sat down to admire the view.

"Warmer than I thought possible." The indoor air of the court registered a comfortable 55 degrees. Versailles in late autumn.

"You see? Cast thy bread upon the waters; for thou shalt find it after many days."

It was true. Now both men set to work, not to mention the plunger, according to Canonical Hours, to instill order out of chaos. The rule of Coss, of the Caterpillar and Goldfish Clubs, by which each additional tinkering within the dome of dim and drab multiplied their comforts exponentially, prevailed. It was agreed that Sannazaro should attend to the rough interior with its scores of redundant kitchen utensils and unspectacular provisions: sacks of grain, dried fruits, teas and coffees, sugar and salt, powdered milk and 100 other Canadian military-like rations. The bathroom and bedroom had their own equipments and detail work to be organized. Gumboots, pamphlets and penny-dreadfuls, down comforters, a wardrobe, biodegradable toilet paper, personal effects, tools, a CD player with pieces strewn across time and space, a sprouting jar, a Beanie Baby, a key chain and real mayonnaise. Absurdities were not obvious on the ice. What counted the most were familiar things, intimate memories enshrined in an object. Sannazaro managed to get their stove going using a temporary cache of butane and heated water. Within a day, he hoped and prayed, their espresso machine—DHL'ed from Rome to Invercargill at great expense—would be operational. After all, waxed the Italian in him, it was Mahatma Gandhi himself who frequently commented that the true worth of any society could be read in its espressos and hot chocolates. And Marx who cautioned whilst working one winter at the British Museum, woolen gloves affixed, that society would be reformed only when it embraced good tea and coffee as the predominant force in the mobilization of the proletariat. Sustainable dereliction, said George Washington during his first campaign. Coffee grounds—a necessary corollary to the birth of Democracy, Thomas Jefferson repeated throughout his life. Indeed, all those who signed the Declaration of Independence were coffee addicts. Those who failed to understand the impact of coffee upon civilization were doomed to repeat history, echoed George Santayana one morning in a Berkeley classroom at the turn of the twentieth century.

Outside, Marigold began the tedious struggle with the electrical device, based upon instructions from Crowquill's diary, Salkeld's description of their underworkings, and a detailed blueprint sent by the manufacturer. In Gortex windbreaker and parka, the snow blowing into his face, his thirst unquenchable, his hands stifled at every detail, he made little progress over the course of hours, and this was rather discouraging. Patience was unknown to the Great Commander. He retreated indoors, sat down and studied the book, periodically emptying his bowels in the low-flow toilet that came with the Happy Home.

"It is simply a question of appreciating that one gallon of water, in a fuel cell, has as much umph as a gallon of gasoline," he said, swimming through the manual.

"I just want to know when I can power my electric toothbrush," Sannazaro replied.

"Soon. If I could just figure out—" but he was lost in the instructions, silenced by the barrage of sustainable energy-carrier jargon: embrittlement inhibitors, hydride fuel storage with metal particles of titanium, vanadium and manganese, pounds per million BTU energy content, ultracapacitors, electric propulsion, the handling characteristics of liquefied laughing gas, alkaline electrolysis with its incomprehensible solutions of potassium hydroxide, flows of electrons and ions, bipolar cells and so forth—and all in Japanese! Marigold had a sinking feeling: things were not going well. Why couldn't they just explain how to put the damned thing together, rather than insisting he become a physicist or chemist or whatever the hell an energy expert was?

Finally, standing outside amid a row of portable tanks pre-filled with Crowquill potion, he figured out where the tubes should go into the proton-exchange fuel cell with its stack of membranes, each computed to produce 5 kilowatts of electrical capacity, which were channeled conventionally indoors as AC current. None of it meant anything to the Commander, except to say he was convinced it would work. Before long the electrolyte solution was bubbling beside the back entranceway, where it stood on a table, protected by a ceramic annex, inside a glass house that admitted direct sunlight. A tube ran from the electrolyzer directly into the tanks (as opposed to seals' bottoms). A gauge maintained pressure. It was a Rube Goldberg of miswirings, torsional variation, transverse vibration, of gyroscopic couples, conjugate teeth, four-bar mechanisms and compound trains. The Commander fumbled amid Hooke's joints and slide valves, idling the motor, checking each tooth of the spiral gears and cursing at the involute pinions. Until his axis of spin was more a reverse crank. But ahoy! Suddenly, amazingly, electrification was verified by Sannazaro, who toyed with a dimmer switch that ignited lights all over the place with sporadic flickering and frenzy.

He shrieked with joy. They were in business.

Each looked to the other. Marigold: "Do you smell that?"

"What?"

"It's very faint... Some sort of—like compressed natural... I can't quite make it out..."

"What are you laughing about?"

"What are *you* laughing about?"

"Idiot, I'm not laughing, you are!"

"Nonsense!"

And so on into the night.

CHAPTER 72
The Heroism of Daily Life

IT TOOK ANOTHER WEEK for the two slaves to get their house in order. To Sannazaro's fogged mind, it was amazing they were still alive. Time had transpired furtively, passing across the ice like so many afternoon shadows, fervently dispatched in absence of a single slack moment, so densely configured and urgently arrayed were the termite-thick tasks there to occupy them. Saga upon saga even in the pouring of a bowl of cereal, held hostage by heavy breathing and ever the survival quotient. To stew a tofu, a giant assay; make a bed, bewildering; stay out of the glare of the sunlight, frightful necessity. No single event of the day was wedded to the next; no pattern emerged, for every single thing was held captive in the glint of anomalous life. Blisters on the surface of existence; fantastic aeries, motes, barely manageable brimstones.

When the Utopia was completed, it looked like a meat locker in outer space, a joyless hull of frail abstinences and Samurai gardens stocked with nothing but metal canisters. Yet, for all its Bauhaus sterility, there was no angst therein, for the relief and pride exhibited by its two inhabitants was palpable—and a source of endless self-congratulation as they ate their first bona fide, hydrogen-cooked seitan patties smothered in the requisite garnishes, and christened the meal with two pints of Chatham Island Red Robin beer, a gift of Captain Oguh before he'd bid so-long.

Outside, while the two inhabitants of Behind the Moon Lane feasted, the wind was steadily picking up. The enameled siphons running between tanks whistled. Rusting chimes rattled, and the otherwise solid-looking Happy Home creaked and pined. Movements from every quarter kept both men wary.

"What was that?" Sannazaro ignited anxiously for the thousand-and-first time.

"What?"

There was a caesura, suddenly, a silence—and then—again—a rough lurch that threw both men from their chairs.

"*That!*" Sannazaro cried out, steeling himself for a crouch-blind beneath the dinner table.

"It's just an earthquake," the Commander vituperated stiffly, unwilling to concede fear, but nonetheless shaken to the roots.

The quake lasted for ten seconds—long enough time to terrorize both men. When it was over, and they saw that no damage had been done inside, the Commander raced out back to make sure the tubes had not been jarred; that the canisters containing the shrewd mixture of hydrogen and laughing gas, and the electrolyzer, were stable. He set about at once to hammer metal fittings, and do whatever he could to fashion a more solid housing for these two essentials of their existence. He was not worried about the explosive qualities of their gas storage, which had been wrongly accused following the famed Hindenberg explosion. In fact, said the company's president, one was safer sitting atop a tank of hydrogen than a tank of even low octane gasoline. With its cold flame, there was little likelihood of any trouble. But this earthquake business was an unexpected element of risk.

That night, neither man slept entirely, listening for the strange vast yawning sound that had preceded the quake—a distant boom, a revision in geography that ran counterclockwise across the ice like a locomotive bearing down from the interior towards the sea. Propped up against pillows in his double-King, Marigold read about Antarctic geology to see what the subterranean event might bode. To his relief, he discovered that it must have been what was called a barrier quake, the sinking of a vast amount of snow as a result of the cold. Nothing at all to worry about. He immediately reported these findings to Sannazaro, who lay curled up on a bed 50 feet away in an entirely other portion of the dome. He'd put up beaded curtains, in lieu of actual room dividers, to enlist some measure of privacy. Oddly, Marigold reflected, though they were best friends, and the only two humans anywhere for hundreds of miles, privacy had proved to be of utmost importance to their quality of life.

If this gave some currency to the notion that humans were, by nature, solitary, the Commander had no complaints, for it was his theory—and Crowquill's as well—that the twenty-first century would see more and more individuals reverting back tens of thousands of years to caves and prairies and ancient ruins and follies, to all those abandoned pastures of Kirghizia and Patagonia, to limestone fissures in Arkansas and vast tracts of Arctic taiga in Finland. To mountain strongholds in Nevada and Texas and deserts in Central Mauritania and Australia. All those back-to-nature addicts would take with them only the essentials, as he reckoned he too had done (ignoring the 40 million he'd probably laid out on his little experiment), to ensure a philosophical point of departure consistent with their simple schemes and solitary reversions.

In Marigold's case, a land purchase had not factored into the equation. Antarctica, under no flag or sovereign power, could still support homesteading, though it is likely that the Commander and Sannazaro were the first to undertake such a project.

"You still awake?" Sannazaro buzzed some time later. "Um-huh," the Commander mumbled.

The Italian got out of bed, walked over to Marigold's, then sat on the edge in his nighties. The heating elements were functioning, and the whole dome was indeed a Happy Home, a perfect 70 degrees.

"I was wondering."

"Umm?"

"What is the true purpose of a man, do you think?"

Marigold sat up in bed. "Good question, Señor. Why do you ask?"

"Well. Crowquill. There was a case in point. What do you suppose was going on with him? Extraordinary fellow."

Marigold paused, then embarked. "He was dying of cancer."

"What?"

"Yes. It was in the diary. Crowquill was dying of a rare, untreatable cancer, and was unwilling to seek conventional aid on the mainland. He resolved upon taking his own life before it was taken from him."

"Why didn't you say something before?"

"I just found out last night, reading the last few pages. There was no burial plot on his particular island, as there was no soil, you will recall. He had spent the last ten years of his life fighting the cancer alone. That's why, I am certain, he was so resolved to finding the antidote through laughter."

"But in the end, no joke was good enough and he threw himself to the whales. I saw his glasses among the shark puke."

"If he entered that water without a wetsuit he'd have died in less than a minute. It is possible he simply drowned among them, and the glasses were sucked up. You saw how timid those beasts were. He wanted their company during his final moments."

"What about the wood fragments from a hull against that first iceberg?"

"Somebody else, I imagine."

They were both silent. Then Marigold began, "That tower of his will remain a living testimonial to what Carl Jung termed 'the heroism of daily life'—not the life most people know, of course, furiously squirming after confirmation and success. But the solitary dignity which, in the end, is all a man has. That should answer your question."

Sannazaro reflected on all that. Then: "Dying of cancer. How very sad. Alone."

"He had the seals, the birds, etcetera."

"Yeah, but it's not the same."

"I suppose not."

"How long are you fixing to stay here, Murillo? Seriously."

They looked at one another, strength flexing beneath the lines of their haggard faces. "What would you say if I suggested the whole year?"

"I can't do that," Sannazaro immediately replied. "It's just not me."

"What is this 'me'? Are you so frightened by life?"

"Yes, if you must know. I was not made to live in Antarctica. Or Walden Pond, for that matter. I just want to go home. It is my right. It is every man's right. Please be reasonable. Am I not your friend?"

But Marigold didn't answer that. "Just go," he said, taking it too personally. "Call Captain Oguh and team. I'm sure they'd come back and fetch you. And frankly, I don't need you any longer. Now that my Happy Home has been built."

"You'd live entirely alone, here, when you have all the money in the world with which to enjoy yourself in places like Paris or Rome? The Dorchester in London? The Pierre in New York?"

"Meaningless to one who has been on the ice. Leaving no footprints. Mixing labor with nature, as John Locke said of it. The fellow behind Thomas Jefferson and Karl Marx, both. Creating a true economic revolution. Or, as Rousseau conceded at the conclusion of his second chapter of *An Inquiry into the Nature of the Social Contract or Principles of Political Right*," (the Commander had in his possession that strange anonymous translation, published in London in 1791), "'However it be, we can discover nothing but that Adam was sovereign of the world, as Robinson Crusoe was of his island, because he was its only inhabitant: and the happiest circumstance attending the empire was, that the monarch was secure in his throne; having nothing to apprehend from rebellions, wars, or conspiracies.'"[16]

"For one man. What's the point?"

"For everyone who seeks an alternative."

"No. For anyone who is crazy enough, and rich enough, as you are, to spend tens of millions of dollars to ship an entire house and all its provisions to the South Pole. I don't know about John Locke, or Rousseau."

"That is your simple agrarian charm."

"Which, I'll have you know, I am very proud of. We were an ancient and noble family."

"You've told me before."

They sat sullenly while the wind outside pummeled their enclosure.

A storm was brewing. It was not entirely dark out; the sky was blood red with fast-moving gases of hue, the aurora, transitional phases of stratospheric refraction that lit up the metallic surface of the last continent like a Mardi Gras. Suddenly, a blast of unusually heavy air struck the Happy Home, and the sound of the gale intensified. The windows were streaked with the arrival of an ice hurricane. The whole structure shivered and jarred and seemed to move a foot. "Jesus!" declared Sannazaro, ducking for cover.

Most of the wicks that had been arrayed like a semicircular Sea Henge, a shrine along the base of a cabinet leading to the sink, went out, as the wind, thick with particles of snow, blasted the interior.

The Commander raced to his feet, wrestled into his down booties and a sweater, and strode forthwith to the nearest window.

"A blizzard," he reported.

"Check the radio. Maybe there's some news."

"And what would you expect it to add?"

"I'll check it myself."

Sannazaro removed from the bed and reached for the radio in a cubicle known as the library, built according to the golden ratios for the finest acoustics: 1.6801339: 1. All was static, smothering a distant voice, Chinese or Indian, harried and emanating danger. The range of frequencies was harassed by forces of nature that struck terror in the listener. Faint thunder, useless hopes.

"You see," the Commander reaffirmed. "Enjoy the coziness of it all. From the looks of it, our first serious Antarctic storm. There's something to be said for sitting it out in such palatial quarters. Imagine the early explorers in their tents on a night like this. Or the Emperor penguins standing fully exposed on their eggs."

He then stepped into his mukluks and proceeded to open the front door.

"*What are you doing*?" Sannazaro shouted, as a wall of snow flurry flooded the entrance.

"The windmill. I didn't turn it off!" the Commander rallied, before stepping outside and slamming the vault of a door behind him.

Sannazaro made for the window, but could see nothing. It was a bona fide whiteout. He was feeling, for the first time ever, drastically claustrophobic, as if the blizzard were instinct, were doing its own perverse calculations in the manner of a swarm of angry yellow jackets that stung and bit, both. His psychological buffer of safety was rapidly shrinking. He went to the toilet and locked the door behind him, sat down, closed his eyes, stuffed Mack's pillow-soft silicone earplugs—the ear doctors' earplugs—into his ears, then additionally clasped his hands over them fully to block out the astringent, paralyzing dread of his situation. The whole Happy Home was ranting and caving in.

"Not happening, not happening, not happening," Sannazaro chanted.

CHAPTER 73
A Polar Blizzard Behind the Moon

OUTSIDE, THE COMMANDER HELD onto the perlon that had been strung as a protection line against everything—the lurking crevasses, serried dunes of ice, preternatural storm—and pulled himself hand over hand, naked fear, selfish struggle, until he reached the plastered, snow-mobbed mill-of-the-wind. His face was smothered in the hood of his nine-pound 100 percent down parka to avoid being stung by the wall of ice crystals. The blow must have exceeded 80 knots. The 20-foot-high device had been erected as an electricity generating backup system, 7 kilowatts, for he'd been advised of the constancy of high katabatic winds throughout Victoria Land.

Through the storm, he could not even see the blades which had evidently been fitted in accordance with the principle that were one to take into account the various mechanical, electrical and aerodynamic losses, the efficiency at output could reach a high level even when winds were moderate. But at high speeds, the so-called tip-speed ratio was actually diminished. In a hurricane, there was no point running a windmill. Never mind that the blades were several hundred yards away, having been ripped off moments before and hurtled out to sea. The storm had come from the interior, somewhere between Mt Welcome and the Point of Inaccessibility 1,000 miles closer to the center of the landmass.

Suddenly, Mr Marigold's feet shot out from under him. Having forgotten gloves, he clutched to the ice-hard rope with benumbed fingers, then lost his grip. He could not stand and rather crawled through the quickly rising drifts. Nor could he see through the disintegrating world, swimming to stay above the fast building snowfall.

"*Sannazaro!*" he shouted repeatedly, more exclamations than a Lord Lytton, but to no effect. The meager voice was snuffed out in the vast roar of storm that engulfed him. He crawled, an aimless, formless shape, in the direction he assumed would retrace his brief moments out-of-doors, but the house never appeared. It was like climbing Mt Everest ... Twice ... In the same hour.

Desperate, he crawled faster, tears freezing against his cheek, his eyes burning, no air getting to his lungs.

"*Sannazaro! Help!*" he screamed again and again, until his lack of breath made for a profound pain in his bronchial parts.

Continuing along the rope, tears freezing as quickly as they formed, he dimly recognized that he had gone in the opposite direction from the house, and was now at the rope's far end—200 feet from safety. He was failing. His sight was closing over, blood vessels breaking open, squeezing shut his frozen lids. The air in his lungs was on fire in winds exceeding those of Big South Cape or Cape Dennison—220 miles per hour. With no apparent way to return, he curled up, his back against the storm, and held on to the guideline, eyes tightly clasped, face buried in his chest, becoming crust, his extremities like wood. The malevolence of such wind was beyond compare. It was something almost personal in its antipathy to life. The ice hurtled in the form of a wall that knocked you down, kept you pinned and conspired in every microsecond to smother you with an unreal weight. Marigold's fading mind remembered back to the day of the avalanche that killed his father nearly 40 years before at Chimborazo. All those endless nights under concrete debris in the outhouse. He felt close to his father for the first time in years, dreamily submerged beneath the growing night-out.

By this time Sannazaro, clasping his own eyes and ears in the bathroom, had had a horrible premonition, and sensed the Commander's doom, for he'd been outside a good ten minutes. He lunged away from the toilet and out into the main room, threw on his parka, and raced for the outer vestibule adjoining the door, the place where mukluks and parkas were left to dry out. The storm was so intense now that he could open the door only with tremendous effort, for the wind was coming from the direction behind the toilet, pounding the interior, rattling every uncemented particle, hurtling objects through windows, covering the ceramic in verglass, blowing open the door as Sannazaro himself blew through. Upon which, he held himself, crucified, inside the mantle, as the hurricane force screamed clean through the white night.

"*Murillo!*" the panic-stricken Squire ululated. "*Murillo!*" bayed he in terrorized howls, squeezing himself between stays, holding on for dear life.

The distant yowl triggered a final life-saving reaction in the downed Commander, who woke convulsively from a dream that would shortly have turned him into his Galatea. Groveling back up onto numb knees, his gasping breath in tow, the wind picking his legs up into the air, which Marigold allowed to be blown horizontally along the rope, he then managed to twist his ankles around the cord, which enabled him to hold on, levitating at high speed in the shape of a Tyrolean traverse. He thereupon clawed along the thread-long hope in a reverse transmission, clutch gone, fingers chilled to the bone. It was the correct line of attack to the Happy Home.

By this extraordinary gymnastic, Mr Marigold managed to extricate himself from the 2,000-mile squall. If viewed from satellite, most of the continent would have appeared covered in a white swirling arabesque, almost indistinguishable from the patterns of the ice themselves.

For hours after falling into the vestibule, and discovering the painful truth of thawing fingers and nose, the roar of the blizzard continued ringing in his ears, a meteorological tinnitus that put both men on warning.

As if it weren't awful enough, some time in the middle of the night came more booms and jolts to the whole topography, echoing like bomb blasts in a state of siege. The entire inside of their abode was ransacked.

The men clung to tattered shelter beneath blown-open shutters, disgorged cabinets, their provisions strewn and frozen, their howls hovered in their lungs. All night. The bombing of Dresden.

Sannazaro pleaded. "We have to get out."

But Marigold recovered his composure and he began to behave more like the conquering hero than a man scarcely salvaged. Fate in the form of a vague holler had intervened to rescue the dreamer.

"It was *fantastic*, it was *real*," he bleated, thinking back over his near-death encounter.

"No thinking back. Stay here with me, in the present; no more, an *end*!" Sannazaro beseeched him, thinking him truly clinical, or giving in. It was a misread.

By morning, the drifts were higher than the door, and the electricity was out. The tubes connecting the canisters were blocked, or crushed beneath the weight of the fresh snowfall. There was no way out of the Happy Home, and the temperature had plummeted. The thermometer, cracked and dead, had stopped registering at an even 75 below. The windmill had been blown off its stanchions, 50-foot cartwheels of steel across the icy plateau into oblivion. The radio was no longer functioning. The GPS phone was blocked. Mr Marigold knew instinctively that the only solution was to wait it out. Eventually, the snow would melt. It was summer in the Antarctic. It wasn't supposed to be so cold.

"This was a freak storm," he explained.

"We're dead men," Sannazaro said resignedly, no longer angry about their plight. "You want to play a game of chess?"

"Sure, why not. Winner chooses."

"Chooses what?"

"Whatever seems important."

A stove flickered. The winds were no longer audible. Sunlight broke through the grey ventilator of dark morning. Fog dissipated. "Knight to Queen three," Sannazaro eventually declared. "Check."

Marigold rallied free. The game went on. At some point, the Commander got up to stretch and, noticing a large fan-shaped deposit of snow that had blown under the door, swept it aside before the dried crystals melted. As he did so, he tried the door, but to no avail. They were indeed trapped. In the darkness, the winds had shifted, slamming the door shut.

"How long do you suppose it will take for the drifts to melt back?" Sannazaro wondered, no longer even hopeful.

"Days, no more than that," instructed Marigold. "It'll do us both good. It's certainly more comfortable than that jail in Hong Kong."

"Yes, but not unlike the jail, I have to say this whole scheme puzzles me. If it is a miniature Utopia you want, why not simply continue the life you had worked out for yourself back home? You had everything. A maid thrown in. Use that to set your grandiose example of what a human being consists and is capable of."

"In time, friend, you will understand what compels the idealist in man; what role kin altruism plays in our destiny; and how a beautiful woman, an animal in need, a child that cries out, any of these three, will forever move me to move mountains. And no concern of yours, no fatalism of the world at large, let alone a little snow squall, is likely to stop me. My great ardor, you see, was inherited from ancestors who, themselves, remained devoted to similar causes for many centuries."

"Similar causes, and equally silly speeches."

"'Twas no speech."

"'Twas," he mocked. "A wooden, typically pontificating sputter of no meaning to anyone but yourself. Enough of your preaching. The world is disinterested, and you are perishing." Sannazaro was all huffed up, carping to himself as much as to his companion. "A dopey didactic moralizing man..."

"Am not."

"... Who would say with 10,000 silly words what most of us don't even bother thinking silently in less than two."

"Never mind." Marigold turned away. Closed his mental chess. Sannazaro gazed upon the shallow-breathing evangelist. "Look, Murillo. For some time I've been meaning to talk to you."

"Again? What about?"

"You're an anachronism in an age which can't possibly appreciate you.

'*Ti vertammo a veder sull tua croce, Tutti, e nessuno ti compiagnera,*' as we often say. They love to watch while you're being crucified, though not one will take any pity on you."

"That doesn't bother me. I know what a thoughtful, feeling person can achieve, in spite of the adversities. His foibles are predictable in the scheme of things. Nonetheless, I grant him his hope, his ephemeral gravies."

"Then I must be the bigger of two fools to worry about it. To have been coaxed not once, not even twice, but more times than I can count upon one absurd sally after another."

"Is that what you think they are?"

"Well I certainly don't think of this place as Utopia."

"But surely you would prefer this—this beauty all around, stretching into each seemingly infinite horizon—to the concrete hells of modern industrial life? Wouldn't you?"

"No. I wouldn't. Industry has its place. A man needs a daily routine. Labor is natural. Whether in a garden or some other workplace. I have my own Walker Evans theories about that. He never photographed a rose, as far as I know."

"His loss."

And with that resolute dividing point between them, Marigold retired to his tired bed within the igloo and tried, impossibly, to catch some shuteye.

As he lay there thinking—for his mind was a compulsive dealer, forever handing out cards, or strewing them, more precisely—he re-examined his own views regarding Utopia, perhaps as preparation for that inevitable day when his Squire would leave him; when all this talk of exile and the kingdom materialized, and he was left alone in the infinite frozen plains.

Was this the punch line Crowquill had been seeking? This confrontation with the Absolute? This submission to the extremes of weather, isolation, loneliness? Geophysical expatriotism?

In exile, with no compulsion of any note, his mind wandered freely across the great continent beneath the Southern Cross, out along the mighty barrier walls of ice that draped the South Polar seas. It coursed the glacial sprawl like the free-wheeling mollymawks of Bounty Island.

Sannazaro was worried about jobs, labor, routine. And understandably. A man's dignity was wrapped up in his work, or should be. But here, in these very quarters, was the original labor theory of value in practice, Marigold reckoned. What greater goal than the construction of a home, on one's own terms; a life without dependency; a daily bread that took from no man, exerted no willful dissolution of the commonweal even by slightest increment, and imposed no adversity upon the Earth. And all at a time when more than half the nations of the world were worse off than ever; when labor had become migratory against a context of industrial lowest-cost, highest-return production, resulting in chaos and imbalance. Six billion furiously competing Oblivios. The gulf between those with, and those without the proper amenities of life was growing every day, while so-called high-road corporate strategies were economically targeting those investment programs guaranteed to exploit the emergent disparities; to rape and pillage in the meaningless name of international trading agreements that further separated man from the soil, children from their parents, people from their community, and communities from nature. Rich or poor: both sorts were tearing the earth to shreds. No wonder those Africans and Pitt Islanders could not stop laughing, Marigold realized: the insanity of twentieth-century life offered no other alternative. Laugh because the world is insane. Laugh in order not to cry.

All the while men with crowns and women with silk hats strutted about with not even an ounce of conscience. Aristotle had suggested that no person should be allowed to accrue more than five times the wealth of the poorest person in any given community. Lord Buddha had suggested a similar strategy, but had expanded the mandate to the whole world, so that there could be no peace in one's heart if somewhere, anywhere, another individual—of any species—was suffering. That was the Commander's *modus operandi*. It had taken Crowquill to get him to this point, however: a stimulus of such coordinates to situate him at ground zero, on the ice of unforgiving clarity and reassessment.

For all that, the Commander couldn't help but wonder at the strangeness of his position, and how he had come to be there. After all, he might never have gone to Hong Kong, had Amigo not fallen down the well and thus increased his feelings for chickens. And were it not for that ornithologist with whom he had shared a jail cell, he'd never have heard the name of the moa and thus probably never have visited Wellington, where—again by random good luck—he happened to hear the mariner, Salkeld, telling those tall tales in a pub on a late rainy night. All these random accidents had brought him to a lonely perch on the last continent. There had to be a good reason for it. He had the feeling this was not the end of his journey, but was in no position to assess the future.

All through the next day there were strange jolts to the house; cracking pitch, gurgling noises, distant thunders like an array of approaching World War II Panzer tanks rolling across shattered debris, cranking up the volume in deafening shadows, which Marigold explained away as normal glacial digestion. Snowstorms came and went with a punishing force.

At one point, the two men heard what they thought was lightning. Marigold was immersed in a volume by Kipling and struck, particularly, by the following verse:

Till I make plain the meaning
Of all my thousand years—
Till I fill their hearts with knowledge,
While I fill their eyes with tears.

This was, for all the unknown natural forces around them, one of the most calming days in his memory. The low ebb and flow of a howling wind, the perfect loneliness and charmed companion, put him at Zen-like peace. He was not alone.

For Sannazaro, by contrast, such loneliness and so great an uninhabited landmass put him on the perpetual verge of unrelenting despondency. Not so much as a bird appeared to alleviate the degree of deprivation. No flower. Not even a mosquito for company. It was, truly, Mars.

That night another blizzard struck, worse than the first, it seemed. With all the power out, and the wafting pressure too great even to maintain candlelight anywhere in the interior, the men simply stayed in the dark, huddling inside sleeping bags, under blankets, on their respective beds. Thinking. Awaiting a terrible conclusion.

Several times throughout the night there were other booms, seismic events, a sense of sinking surreality. Both men repeatedly lunged upwards from sleep. In one instance the boom was more like a series of interconnected explosions, so that they believed the US at McMurdo Base, or the Russians at Leningradskaya, were conducting military tests, the horrible noise carrying 1,000 miles towards them.

"I swear to God it feels like we're moving," Sannazaro cried out.

"Only your stomach is moving," the Commander insisted. "I've had to listen to it for hours. What did you eat?"

A moment later: "Surely you felt that?" the Squire harkened. "Yes. Now go back to bed," Marigold pleaded.

"Damn it, I'm in my bed."

Whatever it was, something dreadful was happening, Sannazaro reasoned. He felt queasy with the imagined motions. His stomach was unsettled. At four in the morning he raced for the already-blocked toilet and churned up his insides, only to discover by flashlight that he had missed his target entirely. In his confusion, he had ventured into the wrong zone, puking all over the kitchen utensils. Disgusted by the hopelessness of it all, he went back to bed, drank several shots of brandy and passed out in his own wrath of vomit. He didn't care any more. Nothing mattered. He could hear the snow pouring down. Slapping against ceramic and titanium. Howling with fists of icy rage. As he dozed permanently off, he felt a gigantic lurch. The entire episode lasted a minute, and he could swear—without caring any longer—that all of Antarctica was shifting away. The sooner the better, he thought.

CHAPTER 74
How Their Happy Home Turned into a Disaster

BY DAWN, the continent shone brilliantly. Ten feet of snow had fallen and the Happy Home was completely covered, save for the apex of the structure, which was fitted with a sun roof and photovoltaic array. The winds, now completely died down, had blown any accumulation from the rounded summit of the ceramic mansion where the solar apparatus lay bolted to the roof. Adjoining it, however, all was deep in virgin powder snow.

The Commander smashed through the window, since it might be weeks before the ice melted around the doors, and more blizzards seemed likely. With the aid of a ladder he managed to haul himself out of the living room and into the outer world. Standing atop the home, Marigold—wearing thick glacier goggles, and covered in zinc oxide cream— gazed out. Was he dreaming?

There, not three feet before him, was a creature on its belly.

The Commander gasped, then—regaining calm—greeted it with a simple "Hello!"

The penguin ruffled its feathers, then closed its eyes. It had been sleeping and intended to do so again.

The Commander was awed, and gingerly extended a bare hand to stroke the bird, which permitted it, not even bothering to open its eyes for more than a second or so against the bright glare.

Marigold hastened back into the house, his painfully skinny legs dangling like a marionette's from the broken-open window.

"Sannazaro! Come. Quickly!"

"*What?*" the smelly man barked disparagingly, prepared for the absolute worst and exhausted from his night of a bad stomach.

"Just do as I say, and hold the ladder steady," the Commander shouted in a whisper.

Sannazaro applied himself, though sorely hung over from the miasmas of thought, climate and alcohol, and clung to the ladder with his whole body so that Marigold could safely return to ground level and explain what he had seen.

"There's a penguin on the roof!" he exclaimed.

"What?"

"Truly. Get your shoes on. But ever so quietly. Mustn't disturb the little fellow. It's astonishing."

"Do penguins fly? No, they don't fly. So where did it come from?"

"I don't know. Just hurry. It's sound asleep, I think."

Now the two men clambered topside. Sannazaro gasped upon seeing what Marigold—who went first—saw again. The same dozing bird, of considerable petiteness and sound resolve. But as the Commander kneeled down to better grasp the miracle of their new companion, Sannazaro turned in the other direction, which the Commander had not yet done.

Sannazaro gasped, then whimpered. He and his Commander were apparently no longer on terra firma. They were at sea.

Nor were they alone: hundreds of other penguins had joined them.

The waters were lashing at the mountain from which they commanded a horrifying view of open distances and oblivion. Their house had been covered entire, and frozen by the blizzards' worth of snowfall into a block of ice from which, by all sane appearances, there could be no escape. They had become an iceberg, dislodged from the continent which registered as only a faint, brilliantly white line on the horizon, and were floating nowhere, into disaster.

"Commander," Sannazaro said stoically.

"Whisper!" Marigold said, on his belly now, all eyes riveted to the magnificent avian.

"Commander, you need to look up," Sannazaro applied patiently, his voice brimming with that ironic bemusement sometimes witnessed in defendants moments before, or after, their sentencing.

"Can't you see it's sleeping, you idiot," the Commander again applied with a penetrating, paternal "*sssshhh*".

Sannazaro stared at the *Pygoscelis adeliae* and gasped.

"We're dead men," he repeated to the disinterested bird, who woke up, preened itself and stood gabbing with habitual gusto into the charmed sphere of the deepest south as its ancestors, the Sphenisciformes, had been doing for 50 million years since the time of the Eocene.

Their frozen rookery was on the move, its size incalculable in terms of normal measurements, for the sloping of the ice under the burning sun, the irregular convexities of time and space, were all bewildering to the naked eye. This was a mountain without analogues. The only relative index for appreciating the extremity of their situation was in calculating somehow the modest size of the penguins inhabiting the distant peripheries of the berg, and figuring on such and such a basis their distance. By that crude measurement, it seemed as if a chunk the size of eight square blocks of New York City had come off. They knew it had to be a fifth of a mile, at least, because that was the distance of their utopia from the water's edge. They also knew—and could see—that the height of those headwalls sheering off the edge of the continent into the ocean was easily 600 vertical feet—a tall skyscraper that leveled off in all directions along the circumference of Antarctica.

As if their having come unglued from the continent wasn't odd enough, a super-swarm of *Euphausia superba*, billions of pounds of living crustacean krill, were feeding for miles all around them, clouding the icy azure waters with their vermilion shimmer of densities. This color sensation had invited others, as well: sperm whales, *Physter macrocephalus*, twice the size of the whale shark that had devoured Sannazaro, patrolled the waters vacuuming up their breakfast.

Sannazaro tried to steady himself, took stock of their outrageous situation, and offered the following summary: "So much for your ideal state."

He was thinking back to all the tired rhetoric the Commander had lifted and cited from Plato's *Republic*.

"Ahh, well, nothing to prevent you from imagining yourself its citizen, and voting nonetheless," Marigold replied. "Unbutton yourself in this glorious morn. Fancy yourself free of those faithless, faceless, favorless hopes the rest of mankind clings to in lieu of the bolder truth. The brutal delightful dawn of our Being." He emphasized the capital Being, as if to rule out Becoming. "While the rest of the world, by my last count, has 11,984 unalterable problems," he went on, "we have only one. True to Señor Crowquill's own accounting, he who laughs last laughs best."

The Commander bowed to their penguin friend, who took very little notice.

The genius of this scene was too much for the poor Italian who, deciding it was all a bad dream, descended back into the icy vault of the Happy Home, crawled under his down comforter, dug into a bottle of rum, put on his eye mask, inserted his waxed earplugs, and clung tightly to his wit with two enormous pillows swathed in soft Egyptian white cotton, leaving the Commander to marvel at their strange predicament above.

But his isolation igloo—half deprived, scented with Sannazaro's own brand of samadhi—soon suffered a climatic intrusion, for within minutes the Señor started to sweat profusely. The temperature indoors was inexplicably rising.

It was worse all around them. The calving en masse of large chunks of the continental ice sheet. Stress magnitudes, snow-crystal sizes, basal silts, deformations and countless other culprits were to blame. But the single most plausible scenario centered around the indisputable fact that the oceans were nearly 5 degrees warmer than usual. The melting had originated at the bottom of the glacier, causing an entire square section, very nearly in accord with the New York quotient Sannazaro had calculated, to collapse into the sea. And two frail humans and their Happy Home, by improbable accident, happened to be there on that very scene. Or were they actually responsible? The Commander hurried back to the moments and days before the ungluing. Had he somehow mixed up the gas lines? Added too much heat to the contraption of hydrogen outgassing? Overloaded the fuel cells and thus superheated the entire land mass?

"My God! What have I done!" he mumbled.

CHAPTER 75

Two Madmen Are Rescued from the Ice

LANDSATS 4 AND 5 HAD sampled time intervals of the icy Armageddon with several thousand images whose co-registration and velocity vectors showed minimal error, down to a few pixels, each unit of resolution corresponding to 28.5 millimeters. The melting was part of a pattern which had first been detected 15 years before by a janitor at the Argentine base Paradise Bay, where the inhabitants later burned down their bunk beds and commissary as a result of the harmful psychological effects of living in unremitting darkness at noon. Since then, the Lambert Ice Shelf event, Pine Island collapse and dozens of other calvings had registered by satellite. In 1989, a chunk the size of Rhode Island, and containing the ruins of Admiral Byrd's Little America, was also jettisoned into the sea and had floated around, dissolving, ever since.

Oddly, there had been no reason to predict such calving in this particular region of the Marigold Happy Home. Something out of the ordinary had triggered it. The mass budget of ice boded catastrophe for the penguins, who were unable to withstand temperatures exceeding 45 degrees. The blizzards had entailed cold, yes, but also moisture far in excess of Antarctica's normal 1.5 inches of precipitation per year. The moisture meant cloud cover, which translated into warmer upper-atmospheric currents. These climatic and glaciological mundanities could mean only one thing: the Greenhouse Effect and its devastating consequences for Antarctica, and for the entire planet. If all the ice were to melt, the world's oceans would rise nearly 190 feet.

Had there been some central Antarctic headquarters which took account of anonymous people and their calamities—which there was not—the Commander and his Squire might have been remembered by scientists as the first individuals to experience firsthand the coming deluge, though, in truth, there were other contributing circumstances. The Commander's premonitions were correct, his sense of guilt well justified, for in fact the Laughing Gas had inordinately warmed their little bit of happy turf.

As the Commander lay upon his belly in the snow studying the exquisite avians all around him—to his ears their cacophony resembled an anthem of sweetest cajolery, multiplied in sufficient timbres and dimensions to define a veritable chorus, Handel's *Jupiter in Argos* or Vienna Boys' Choir—not 50 miles to the southwest was the polar vessel *Gandhi* making its way back from the Indian Base, Dakshin Gangotry, and bound for the harbor at Mumbai, India, thousands of miles to the north, via the Chagos and Maldive archipelagos. The vessel was nearly 300 feet in length, fueled by 10,000 kW diesel engines. A far cry from the days of Master James Cook, whose *Resolution* was only about 128 feet long and aided by nothing more than wind on a sail and the desperation of those with scurvy—some 30 percent of the crew.

The Commander stood up and wandered toward the denser congeries of birds atop the Happy Home. To his amazement, he thought he recognized Rodriguez the rooster and Amigo, Raquel's chicken, both eerily transmigrated from the Camp of the Spirits. Was he dreaming?

"*Sannazaro!*" he shouted in a whisper.

The Squire needed no coaxing to leave the claustrophobic confines below. For water was actually leaking in now; and the thermometer signaled a dangerous ascent of temperatures at upper body level, and a descent everywhere else.

"Can you believe it—visitors from home!" Marigold declared. Sannazaro shook out his head upon seeing the bizarre array of a chicken, a rooster and 100 or so penguins. The penguins thought it mighty strange, as well.

"Of course it can't be Amigo. That's ridiculous. Some version of a penguin."

"No, but it is. And that's Rodriguez." Overtaken by homesickness. "Damn it, you're hallucinating."

"Swear to God. I never forget a face. There's a reason they're here."

"There is no chicken, no rooster. And the house is filling up with water. We're going to sink, and unlike all of our newfound companions, we really will drown. Murillo, I'm frightened."

Marigold examined the situation and corroborated that there were three inches of water throughout the Happy Home, and the level was rapidly rising.

"Get the drysuits," the Commander calmly advised.

Both men raced down the ladder, unpacked the marine gear that they'd kept as part of their provisions from the *Harbinger*, and fitted themselves into their 11mm suits, neither of which exactly fit.

"Oh my god," Sannazaro cried upon probing with his finger the water which filled the whole surface of his bedroom in an even layer. The water was dark and metallic, and stung like electricity it was so cold to the touch.

"What else—what else do we need? Quickly!" Marigold roused. "Flares."

"What about food?"

"What about water? Get the gallon jugs."

"There's water everywhere. What about parkas? Mittens?"

"Wine."

"Pillows!"

Their bantering and hectoring continued as the water level rose. "My copy of Dante."

"A canoe."

"And Milton."

"Oars."

By the time they got out with all the necessary goods the water was three feet deep, and both Rodriguez and Amigo were gone, as were most of the penguins. Whether the Commander was hallucinating a chicken and a rooster among penguins would be satisfactorily resolved only many months later. Meantime, waves were lashing higher upon the ice mountain as the overall level of the Happy Home sank deeper into the sea. The two men stepped foppishly atop their sinking citadel not knowing what else to do. They had a zodiac, but it had been stored outdoors and was now sealed in ice, under the water.

Normally, a visual scan of a maritime horizon from sea level approximates the distance as twelve miles. But in polar regions, on account of the clarity of air and oblong crest of the earth, such a view could well constitute 200 miles. Such optics confirmed their predicament. There was no relief in sight: the shoreline was on the horizon, and growing fainter.

"We can't swim. What are we going to do?" the Squire ventured. "Die with dignity."

"I don't want to die with dignity," Sannazaro cried out. Visible tears stained his tired face. "Why did I ever follow you, believe in you? You've ruined my life."

"You say that every time something goes wrong."

"*Will you wake up!*"

"What for—especially at a time like this?"

"There's got to be a way..." Sannazaro sat down on the roof and tried to figure it out.

He watched as the last of the penguins one by one dived headfirst into the churned-up sea, which was now almost lapping at their toes. The birds would stand on their hind legs, aided by their steely tails which they used like an ice ax, and then leap existentially into the outgoing wave. Their porpoising and internal temperature management was expedited by the fact of a considerable complement of subdermal fat and twelve feathers matted per square inch of surface area. Now they dived after krill; and then returned back to the surface, bobbing in utter equanimity, impervious—presently—to matters concerning Greenhouse emissions.

But something about their bobbing—the way they seemed to float as if on a bed—struck the acutely observant Sannazaro.

"*The beds! Wood! Titanic!!* " he shouted exaltedly. He'd seen the movie at the Vargos Center in Santa Fe—who hadn't?

Both men raced back down the emergency ladder into the sinking chambers to unhinge their respective beds and somehow get them up onto the roof. An ax, stored wisely under the sink, was necessary to fragment the otherwise too-cumbersome pieces of framework. But in due course the largest possible sections of wood were removed to the fast dissimulating apex of the ice mansion.

The men practiced their grips as they heard pressure explosions beneath. A wall had caved in and the flow of sea depths crashing through another wall succeeded the blast within seconds, throwing the entire mountain onto a diagonal tilt that indicated very little remaining time.

Both men were half-breathless with a sudden and deepening awareness of their preposterous situation. And if this combined trembling soul may be maximized by their incredulity, distended by their fears, distorted by their rapid inventory of what would support life at sea, leave it be that panic now pervaded their hearts. Clearly there would be no luxuries—no wine, pillows, books. Only the bare rock of survival. Nonetheless, showing unshakable faith in the flotational qualities of their Japanese beds, the two mubble-fubble argonauts proceeded towards the far gangplanks off which the penguins had demonstrated a preference for leaping.

Their beds suddenly uplifted by the centrifugal nexus of outward wave action, they were launched horribly into the sea, sucked hither with the explosion of white water and ice hell as the monster berg disappeared beneath. Somehow, miraculously, their beds remained on the ocean surface.

Leopard seals immediately swam near, checking out the occupants of the beds. Two killer whales circled, their intentions all too clear.

Sannazaro whimpered. No more biological complexity for him. This was the beginning of a blank slate, or the end of one. As for the Commander, he was at once the harbor of a different occasion: an orientation of the strictest metaphysics. He gazed mistily upon the predators with that sympathetic agape that was his uniquely ill-suited naiveté. Some word or other escaped his lips, a final salutation, bearing in its vocable a long-lost greeting.

Twenty miles away from this scene of riot, an Indian logistics officer standing at the bridge of the *Gandhi* witnessed a bizarre freak of nature through his binoculars. Focusing precisely, there was no doubt about it. He handed the binoculars to his companion.

"Kya tum bhi wahi dekh raheho jo mein dekh raha hoon?" (Do you see what I see?) "Han! Agar mein thik hoon to mujhe kuch whale machliyan dikh rahi hain aur do aadimian apne bistaron pe lete huye bhi dikh rahi hain." (Yes. I see whales and two men in their beds, etcetera etcetera.)

Both men started laughing hysterically, for they had never seen such a thing in all their years plying the waters of the Antarctic and Indian Oceans.

"What is it?" the Master said, coming onto the bridge. He always preferred English, having studied his profession at the British Naval Academy in Greenwich. For him, and others like him throughout India, it was his way of verbally rejecting the Hindu fundamentalist politics of the BJP, the party that had officially changed the names of Bombay, Madras and Trivandrum to their traditional Hindu and Malayalam designations.

"Master—" The first mate handed him the binoculars.

Master Singh examined the horizon. "What is that? Kayakers? No, wait—" he fiddled with the focus.

"Am I dreaming? Two men in their beds?" He checked the radar and sonar sideways scanner, confirming the enormous section of iceberg before them, 83 fathoms deep, nearly a mile across, against whose daunting enormity any living creature on the ocean surface was now visible only to the naked eye. Radar could not pick it up.

Others arrived on the bridge, scientists and some of the ship's crewmen, and all could make out two men on wooden planks, surrounded by whales.

"Hame unhe bachana hoga!" (We have to save them!) voices resounded.

The *Gandhi* was there in 25 minutes, breaking through the polynyas of ice, circling and coming in safely beside the two wayfarers, who gazed upwards at these heavy metals of deliverance as through carbonated glass.

The water temperature was minus 1.2 degrees Centigrade, the cold that induced glycoproteins in Antarctic fish to keep their blood from freezing, but both men were snugly encapsulated in their drysuits.

Marigold's Utopia had vanished beneath the sea, twirling slowly around entangled in kelp, a favorite of barnacles and deep squids. It could not live without air—a fact often overlooked in the history of these matters. His hopes of fronting a revolution in individual behavior, ethics and purity—gobbled up in the meltdown of a continent and the zeal of his ingenious technological solitude. The platinum components, fuel cell stacks, compressed hydrogen/laughing gas hydrides, diary notes, best intentions were not equal to the task. How could he face so permanent a truth, explain his failure, acknowledge the folly of his ways? The colossal disappointment lay before him, across the churned-up sea. A thousand penguins frolicked in the intervening waters, adding insult to his numbness. If the Commander had touched a limit, there was nowhere else to go, no other place to dream freely. He was ruined. It was over.

"Now can we go home?" Sannazaro stated weakly, exhausted from terror, his voice lending finality to the epoch.

Marigold didn't answer.

A zodiac craft was lowered off the side of the vessel, two men descended ladders, and the Commander and Squire were quickly evacuated. Marigold saw at once that the ship was named *Gandhi*. In his troubled mind a whole new set of coordinates, injunctions and historical evolutions unfolded.

"*Gandhi*. But of course," he declared. "Every great mystery is fueled by some method. Reason works in mysterious ways. Unreason even more so."

"What are you talking about? Murillo! I insist that you answer me!"

"*Gandhi*!" he repeated dreamily, in the guise of an uncanny pledge.

CHAPTER 76
The Charge of the Coral Brigade

So when my nurse comes in for me
Home I return across the sea,
And go to bed with backward looks
At my dear land of Story-books.
—Robert Louis Stevenson, *The Land of Story-books*

FOR TEN DAYS and nights the *Gandhi* diagonaled north in a breezy bumptious sweep across the Indian Ocean, passing along the mysterious Indian Ridge due east of Amsterdam Island, into the Tropic of Capricorn, leaving the infernal cold of sub-Antarctica, and entering by tangible degrees the heat islands that blew fair winds back and forth across the 73rd meridian. By the time they'd reached the amorphous calms of the mid-Indian Basin, it was 75 degrees Fahrenheit. Amid such moist and delicious sea breezes, memory of the cold from whence they'd come no longer even lingered in Marigold's mind. He had privately resolved some ongoing difficulties, though said little to anybody. And Sannazaro had not divined any holding-on in him. The temper was mild, his attitude gravely softened. Both men were lucky to be alive. Nothing else mattered. No backward looks, supposedly.

They were a seafaring day from the US military base, Diego Garcia. This paradise was leased from the

British (in the late 1960s, early 1970s, its indigenous peoples had been forceably removed to Mauritius, 1,200 miles to the west, and were now suing for repatriation in a British court), and Ship Master Singh intended to anchor there for the night, a mile out from the horseshoe-shaped lagoon. From Diego Garcia, the *Gandhi* would continue through the Maldives, the equally lovely, coral-teeming Lacadives, and then, after a brief visit to the base at Cochi, in Kerala, on home to Navy Nagar near Coloba in South Mumbai.

For all of Mr Marigold's strange exclamations and occasional harangues, Singh was actually quite amused, even intrigued by this St John the Baptist of skinny brio. His father, Ezi, also an officer in the Navy, had disciplined his son like a rod of steel. He'd read all those sea sagas of Patty O'Brian, of Captain Aubrey and Stephen Maturin with their learned, blow-by-blow accounts of such battles as Lepanto, and that great day on the Nile when England demolished Napoleon's dream of conquering India. The muscles in the jaw were tight, and he in thrall with all that commended marine swells and great visions of sea light—Thomas Luny's *Bombardment of Algiers, August 1816*; the works which he had viewed at the Prince of Wales Museum in his hometown as a teenager: the blue-golds of John Brett, embattled whitecaps of Dominic Serres the Elder, John Moore of Ipswich's disturbing mauves, all the azure-greens, battle-rams and tranquil sails of Arthur Wellington Fowles, Pieter Cornelis Dommersen and so many others.

As Singh remembered, the artist in him was awakened, so that now nothing Mr Marigold said or did, neither strong opinion nor stupidity, could shake him. It could only expedite his own rise of metaphors. Not even the fact that within two hours of Marigold's very near death adjoining the so-called magnetic South Pole, after he had showered, gotten into fresh comfortable clothes and been served hot chocolate, he had for some reason taken to assaulting his rescuers with a slide rule of officious detail, attacking them with ecological diatribe, economic sanctions and demographic dementia. Whether entirely true or entirely false, there was—to Master Singh's way of thinking—something too terribly charming about this wily old fox's ravings for them to be written off as those of a mooncalf.

Singh admired the man's passion; his refusal to be deterred by anything so basic as preposterous overstatement or dangerously thin ice. To bumble without inhibition on unknown turf—this was a characteristic not easily dismissed in a stranger found floating about Antarctica in his bed. He was especially struck by Marigold's zeal; his insistent capacity for soaking up information; his ability to steal away into the ship's poorly lit library, devouring everything that pertained to their itinerary. In one week he had become the local expert on coral reefs. If he did not fully understand something, he'd pester Dr Chowdhury, the ship's science officer, for answers.

Marigold had acquainted himself with the coral lore of the Western Indian Ocean, navigating through a strange lexicon of patch and fringing reefs, limestone plateaus, islands scarcely touched by humankind–Tromelin, Europa, Iles Glorieuses, Bassas de India and Juan de Nova. He had learned the elementary language of seagrass beds, coralline algae, sediment traps, and nurseries in the Mozambique Channel. He'd memorized the legalese of the *Nairobi Convention*, which had instigated protocols to hopefully counter the looming threats to coral reef integrity, which now leaked into the Commander's thick skull and, as ever, got him all fired up to save not one but all the coral reefs, to swim not among one group but all groups.

Similar impulses had catapulted Singh into the Navy and then into polar reconnaissance. As a boy he had gazed out at the Indian Ocean as he wandered along the sea wall at Worli or Nariman Point, or gathered shells (when there still were shells) from Chowpatty Beach. Even then, of course, it had suffered from profuse excrement and garbage. But his boyish enthusiasms had led him into a Naval College which, in turn, introduced him to the Antarctic, where so much of the world's sea exploration culminated. Southern polar waters could not be further removed—in terms of purity—from India's sordid, deceptive coastline. When he finally became a civilian Master of a ship, there was no greater prize than that of sailing to Antarctica through the Indian Ocean; no more salubrious change of climates, terrain, flora and fauna.

These delectations he sensed in his strange refugee from America, who all day busied himself scanning the journals, and then, over group dinners in the evening, reported back wearily on the many threats to all these luscious volcanic life-fostering systems—oil spills, runoff from land, global warming. In that cursory exposure, Mr Marigold had resolved to effect some salutary difference, to somehow intervene to protect, literally, trillions of little things—polyps and pneumatophores, whatever those were. For, as he admitted, reading was not knowing, except that he had vaguely grasped that they were the crucial microscopic organs of the reefs, swamps and mangroves—one of the foremost preconditions for life, for oxygen on Earth. And they were all vulnerable to the depleted ozone, the warming of the oceans, global pollution and, particularly, the nearly 500 million tons of oil shipped across the Indian Ocean each year, much of which was discharged. In fact, of all the oil spills on Earth, almost half ended up in the Indian Ocean.

Thus, like an upwelling of adamantine verve and maritime devotion, emerged the coral genesis of Mr Marigold's latest motto: *I hope for everything, I desire everything, I am alive.* He said it with a glass of Eurasian Merlot in hand. All those seated round him aped the sentiment with a hearty "Hear, hear!"

Marigold's stubbornness to stay up reading all night, to miss no moment of study on the open sea, could not have contrasted more with Sannazaro's own style of sea-faring behavior. Passing out early, sleeping until noon, to hell with coral bleaching or sea urchin bio-erosion. This Squire was not one to trouble himself over holothurians or bilge tanks. All those causes of coral asphyxiation, of the reduction in calcification rates, the toxic contaminants which smothered growth and gave rise to algal mats and boring sponge infestations—Mr Marigold's current obsessions—were not relevant to a good night's sleep. Sannazaro was finished with saving the world. He'd done admirably well just saving himself. Now, he asked only to be left alone. No more adventures.

By the time they'd reached the outer ridge of the basin containing the 10,000 square miles of the Chagos Archipelago, Marigold had some idea of the waters they were entering. It was a bright, balmy morning, clouds dense with rain palpable to the tongue, mists that traveled singularly. As the ship approached Diego Garcia to the immediate north, Dr Chowdhury was leaning against the bowsprit shrouds, sucking on his pipe, watching as bottle-nose dolphins sported down below, leading the *Gandhi* into the maze of living atolls. "A bright morning to you, sir!" the Commander greeted the scientist.

"Namaste," replied he, nodding at the spectacle in the waters.

They stood silently, admiring the frolicsome mammals who seemed impervious to the wall of steel that cut through their world at perilous speeds.

"Over 700 species of fish down there," said Marigold.

"At the very least, I should think," Chowdhury conceded.

Suddenly, a high whistle from the ship's outpost signaled the first sight of land. The third mate had sounded the precious alarm. Diego Garcia emerged like a green phantasm, large birds swooping near, jetsam thick with seaweed parting as the *Gandhi* plied closer, and all 12 men aboard stood gazing towards the impressive ring of land with its exotic trees—guyoid and casa, and the hardwood takamaka. Even at 20 miles distance the famed lagoon rose up a few feet above the lolling waters, thrusting into the azure air a sinuous veil of coconut palms, primeval home to warrior crabs and geckos, feral cats and coconut rats. There were said to be some 300 feral donkeys on the Mauritian eastern side of the island where, traditionally, copra had been husked and manufactured. The 500 or so Americans occupied the western side. Jungle fowl also reconnoitered the lagoon, and insects that were endemic to the Chagos: spiders that lived nowhere else; true bugs, hemopterans, that had evolved separately on some minute sandy stretch of whispering shells, perhaps no larger than a dime store, only to make it home over thousands of years, a hospice that would transform the shape of their antennae, or abdominal wall, or give their exoskeletal features some metallic sheen that lit up in the dark as nowhere else.

It was on the western portion that the coral-flickering lagoon was dense with US military traffic. There was the base itself, with barracks, Olympic-sized swimming pool, squash courts, a nine-hole golf course, a bowling alley, a fuel pier, a hospital, and a large mobile pre-positioning naval force—the Sealift Command Unit with KC-10 Extenders, and jetfighters from the 60th Air Mobility Wing out of Travis Air Force Base.

In the water sat a fleet of ships that had been utilized during Desert Shield and Desert Storm. Squadron Two, as it was called, was part of the American Rapid Deployment Force, and comprised 19 ships with enough supplies to support 16,500 troops for 30 days, according to Master Singh, who'd been through Diego Garcia dozens of times.

He also described what could not be seen—the anti-submarine and surveillance support, tightly packed away in the dense thickets of warships and aircraft: the Patrol Wing One Detachment with its P-3 Orion aircraft for making secret reconnaissance missions over the Indian Ocean; Space Group known as '8750' which controlled a satellite array for doing sophisticated telemetry, tracking and command work, part of the United States Air Force. There was a Naval Criminal Investigative Service residing on the island, occupied with counterintelligence investigations between Africa and India. Even a unit of the Marine Corps was present, along with a special Camouflage Group. In addition, there were the British themselves—the 1,002 Royal Marines.

In short, said Marigold, upon hearing from Master Singh of this dense collaboration of warmongers, this tropical Paradise was a powder keg of oxymorons: a destructive arsenal flanked by coconut juice, defensive postures and heavy artillery masquerading as fishermen on wicker chairs. The offensive instinct in man—a bloodlust, red in tooth and nasty claw, and dating to the time of the first Australopithecines, as he put it—embroidered with transparent sunsets and ukuleles.

None of these bombs, none of this readiness and manpower was worth a damn when it came to protecting the coral reefs underfoot, however—a fact made poignantly clear when all hands on board the *Gandhi* spotted a gunboat of suspicious goings-on. It loitered five miles off the southwestern tip of the lagoon, sifting sluggishly through the water, with no flag or other indication of its origin.

Master Singh did not pay attention to it at first, but Mr Marigold did, for he thought he had detected a strange flash. Upon closer scrutiny of the vessel with high-powered binoculars, he saw what he believed to be a harpoonist.

"You're right," added Chowdhury, taking a look for himself.

"I insist we investigate," Marigold said. "They're pulling up coral and what appears to be a large fish."

"That's not our business," said the second mate, Haresh Deepak. "Fishing is allowed. It's rather a worldwide occupation."

"Well, wait. Not so," Marigold countered. He produced for Deepak a book containing the BIOT wildlife regulations, a manual of rules that made it very clear that endangering the coral reefs was illegal—and that included taking large predators.

Presently, the *Gandhi* had come to within 100 yards of the small trawler which was moving slowly over deep coral reefs. From the bow where Marigold had hastened, he could count the number of large chunks of coral that had been brought up in sections, hoisted by a mini-crane and gathered in nets. There were also massive heaps of dead fish. The back of the vessel was filled with the gutted remains of reef sharks, enormous black and white bat rays, silver barracuda, and wahoos, their colors already faded, and weighing, according to Chowdhury, up to 75 pounds. The sight of these heaps of death amid such splendid scenery—reefs visible to the eye from the deck, reefs he had metaphysically penetrated during days of study—made Marigold sick at heart.

Suddenly, a shot was fired.

"*Jesus!*" Chowdhury shouted.

"A warning shot!" Deepak yelled, sounding the general alarm.

All crew members, unaccustomed to hostilities at sea, converged on the bridge. Master Singh was already on the ship-to-shore radio with communication services at Diego Garcia.

Sannazaro, awakened from his first good night's sleep in many moons, for the waters were calmer near the reefs, was approaching the breakfast room when he heard the shot, which sounded so near as to have already killed him. He lunged for the nearest protection, which happened to be a steel pot. In a reflex reaction of some uncommon dexterity, he grabbed it and put it on his head, not knowing it was filled with hot porridge. His screams of horror only amplified the other hollerings on board.

Then came another gun blast, this one right over their heads.

Marigold saw a tool box, broke it open and, gesturing wildly to his attackers, brandished a sheath knife and marlinspike in each hand. Rather more threateningly, Chief Engineer Krishna aimed an M-16 at the mystery vessel, which remained in clear sight.

"Cease and desist or we will attack!" he screamed.

"Chiii! Vahapang! Amma Ta hukapang!" came the reply.

"They're speaking Sinhala," Chowdhury said. "I recognize the cuss words."

Master Singh emerged from the communications room: "I've just come off the phone with NCTS at Diego Garcia. I've explained our situation and provided details of the trawler. They said it's none of their business, unless the State Department gets involved and makes it their business. Which it won't. Apparently, they're Sri Lankan pirates, *kulahina karavas*, a low caste of coastal fishing people from the north of their country. Possibly Tamil militants among them, the saTankamiyas. They're working for a Big Man, a Dhanpatiya. The Sri Lankan authorities have been notified in the past. This isn't the first time."

"So what do we do?" asked the Chief Engineer.

"We back off. We're invited to anchor near the base if we want to put ashore. They've called in the one British boat that must patrol all of these waters. But it's north of here a full day and a night, I'm told."

The Master gave his chief mate new coordinates. A renewed chugging sound of engines, and the *Gandhi* started pulling away from the pirate vessel. The pirates, sensing they'd won, and that those aboard the intruder vessel were Indians, not British, merely continued their predatory activities. But at that moment, Mr Marigold, visualizing the worst, seized hold of the M-16 and a bayonet, and leapt from the starboard side of the ship into the ocean, screaming like a samurai.

"*Idiot overboard!*" blazed a clarion cry. It was Sannazaro, who had just cleaned the porridge off himself and was not entirely surprised to see the Commander again risking life and limb.

CHAPTER 77
A Marigold Routs Pirates Near Diego Garcia

MAKING EASY HEADWAY, the Commander—a true veteran now—began swimming towards the pirate boat, his machine-gun and bayonet flailing over his head in one shared hand, his convictions sufficiently buttressed by the warm salt waters to give him ample energy boost.

By this time Master Singh had turned back around, and several other crew members were also aiming weapons at the pirates. The pirates were firing into the water to warn Marigold away. They were shouting— "Bhayaanakay!"—and motioning him to go back.

He disappeared underwater, and even without a mask was able to witness the spectacle: the luminescent schools of mackerel and jacks, yellow fusiliers and parrot fish. A world like he had never seen. He did not want to come up, but was limited in each purview to 40 or 50 seconds.

Another shot, this time even closer, was fired to scare him off, the bullet smashing into the water. The *Gandhi*'s chief mate fired a warning exchange. Now there was screaming from both sides, a flopping Marigold caught in the cross-hairs.

In his struggles to gain hold of the lines dangling from the crane on the pirate ship, Marigold slapped at the sea, lunging in loud gulps, for he did not know if he'd been hit. Water poured into his lungs. Now his weapon fired—a full round right into the sides of an already expired 25-foot hammerhead shark that had been caught and lay strung up against the lower side of the pirate vessel. The bullets exploded large chunks the fish, which floated into the air like pillow feathers, then splattering across the water, and the Commander, inviting congeries of sheephead, red-tooth triggerfish and longfin bannerfish which now swept in for a feeding frenzy around him. In their exuberance, they mistook his legs for the meat of the shark, and this caused some further riot of gesticulations.

The Commander threw himself out of the water into the disheveled gullet of the monster.

Again, in his haphazard efforts, his weapon fired, the bullets smashing into the steel ribbings of the boat. The Sri Lankans now prepared to execute the intruder, aiming their weapons down at him, assailing him at the top of their lungs with the appropriate expletives—Rilapayiak vagee (You little monkey's penis), Elu enDeera (You piece of goat shit); Nariya (You jackal), and others: dull white cockroach, rat snake piss, coconut testicles ...

Similar reprimands issued from the rank and file aboard the *Gandhi* as Mr Marigold clung to the dead shark, grappling up the chains which held it in order to attempt an escape from the fanfare of little razor teeth slurping on the meat all around him.

Suddenly, two American military helicopters flew by overhead, circled, then hovered, and with loudspeakers told the pirates to bug off.

It was enough of a threat. Between the *Gandhi* and armed crew, the helicopters, and now the mad white man clinging to the dead shark with his weapon upside down—him they thought of as a witch, or ghost: he was too strange—the crewmen revved the boat's engines, and turned away.

"What do I do?" the Commander screamed.

It was an unnerving moment. There was no other choice but to dive back down into the water, letting go of the shark, to swim for it. A dozen little fish sunk their bicuspids—or whatever you called them—into his toes and thighs. Another got his neck. Puny chews all, but painful.

Mr Marigold made it back to the Indian ship and was hauled on to the lower deck. He stank of dead shark guts, mingling with the oozing blood of his own, and there were cheers from all quarters as he was escorted to the showers. From his lips came the unexpected words, "Neither life nor death, heights nor depths, bullets nor molars, or anything else you care to suggest, can deter the caring soul from its quest."

"Do you believe in God?" Chowdhury asked, surprised by both the sentiment and the way in which it was expressed. "For that rings a bell, what you just said. It's somewhere in the Bible, isn't it?"

"I have read both Testaments, and they are beautifully written. And it might be that I have borrowed from Romans, or Africans, Chinese or Tibetans, Greeks or Hebrews, I could not tell you. But God—yes, why not. We need someone to arbitrate, it might as well be him."

The Commander's wounds were of no more trivial sort that a little antiseptic cream couldn't mend. Later that day, while the commanding officer at Diego Garcia issued him and Sannazaro with temporary passports which Master Singh, in his own capacity, stamped with one-year diplomatic visas, Marigold and his friend were persuaded to try their hand at sports—first bowling, which was a no-go as the Commander got his thumb stuck in the ball and required something like surgery to have it liberated. Squash was little better as Sannazaro—who, it must be conceded had no proper shoes for such activity—succeeded only in smashing the side of his head with his racket during an ungainly return play off a wall.

This prompted the crew of the *Gandhi* to give the Squire a memorable gift—the steel pot (this time empty of porridge) which they suggested he wear on his head at all times for protection.

Many days later, as the ship neared the subcontinent, Marigold was still troubled by the image of himself as a white cockroach. There was more sense to it than his conscious mind was willing to examine. This, he realized, was the essence of a curse. His cogitations—borrowed probably from the Bible—reverberated in his head, though he had never paid much attention to God. Yet, in the past few months it seemed to him that some fairy godmother, at least, had been protecting him and Sannazaro. For what purpose were they being spared? Why so many skirmishes? He certainly had his own mandates, agendas with surprising staying power, given his personal history of staying in his pajamas most of the day; or was this titanic energy expenditure in row upon row simply a matter of his fulfilling some other master plan? Who could say? Who could he speak to? The two encounters with sharks in the space of three weeks, the sinking of his Utopia not one week after it was christened, the constant battle to effect good ... All these frightful near-death entanglements had begun to bore a message into his stubborn side. What raw nerve had been touched one cannot say, for man has a neurological management plan that does not admit an auditor. But whatever happened inside him, the Commander knew in his heart that something had taken root there.

It was night on the water. Within a few days, the palm-suffused Malabar coastline of Kerala would be visible. Marigold sat alone on the quarterdeck aft, wrapped in a loose-fitting shawl of Asiatic chevrons beneath the tall trail mill of Milky Way. He didn't know quite what to do. Time tormented him. Seventy percent of his life gone, according to the charts. And that if he was lucky, which he was surely pushing. Nothing to think about. To do. Salvation just another noun, lodged unheralded in the history bins. He was tired. Defeated. Ready to call it a day.

Then, on a sudden morning, hot, lambent and fair, lush coconut forests along the Arabian Sea splayed softly in the mellow blur of moisture-laden sunlight. As they entered the natural harbor, such woodlands resembled (at least to Sannazaro) all the fine hairs on a woman's thighs, spread out invitingly, ambiguously, undeniably. Dr Chowdhury, on the other hand, saw green turtle habitat. Singh, the accumulation of work awaiting him. As for Marigold, sheer joy: a new continent, new sky, new and untried possibilities.

When Portuguese merchant Vasco da Gama, having left the Lisbon port of Belem, reached this coast on May 20th, 1498, he is said to have wept, prior to his prayers and confession and conveyance of greetings from King Emanuel I to the local Hindu zamorin. He then proceeded to have carved a marble pillar, as was customary among the Portuguese, and to order the erection of a strikingly new monastery that fused the Gothic manner of S. Maria de Vitoria at Batalha, conceived by Alfonso Domingues, and the Monastery of the Hieronymites, after the Portuguese King's own style of suave flamboyance. The monastery, which would surely have been a Cistercian homage to the swaying of coconut trees and the thinly attired spice girls of Malabar, was never completed, though not for lack of enthusiasm. The pillar, too, disappeared, with its dolphin designs and fornicating nymphs. History records that da Gama's men generously gave out nougats and fondants, as well as pieces of boiled sap of the sapodilla tree, sweetened with guttah katiam, a novelty in the region, and befriended the natives with intimate charms. The soldiers' embraces annoyed the local Muslims who agitated for war. Ever the opportunist, da Gama evacuated the coast a year later for Belem, but within a short time he returned to southern India with a new title, Dom. Like so many before him, India had entered his veins and would not let go. Later, as Commander of the Empire, the great explorer took several mistresses and ensconced himself in the jungle.

As for da Gama's tears on that first vision of the Malabar Coast, they could have meant many things: the first fresh water in three months... a chance to relieve his sea sickness ... to be liberated from the continually chomping company of 1,000 rats or the cohabitative hell of rough men whose habits had grown wearisome. Or the almond eyes, cool plunder of coconut tits floating on the rim of his thoughts, and the golden complexion of a 14-year-old forest virgin, more likely.

He would die here 26 years later, after having swum naked in the warm Lakshadweep Sea with giant squids, watched meteorite showers beneath the cantilevered Chinese fishing nets, and fallen in love dozens of times with the stunning local nymphets who wandered beneath the cashew trees.

Portuguese, Dutch and eventually British, this one European stronghold on the subcontinent always seemed to Master Singh to be the most cosmopolitan of Indian cities, with the highest literacy rates for men and women, and a matriarchal tradition: an incense-rich density of free thinking that favored women's rights, Christianity, the Marxist-led Democratic Front, Socialist Republicans, money from the Persian Gulf, and a host of other intellectual and practical affiliations uncommon in the rest of the country.

The port of entry confused the perceptual hallway with its panoramic flotsam of goings-on: a congestion of ferryboats crammed with commuters, barges equally stuffed with black peppercorns or nutmeg, rice and coir fibre. Colorfully turbaned laborers hauled sacks along the weathered timber docks, depositing them in the long painted godowns which served as warehouses and swarmed, during monsoon, with rats seeking shelter. Descendants of the Portuguese rats five centuries before. Bridges linking Willingdon and Bolghatty Islands and the international airport fanned out on the way to the open sea.

After passing through Naval Customs, Master Singh and crew lent the Commander and Squire enough rupees to be able to do what they needed to set up wire transfers, for neither man had salvaged more than parts of his bed and his wetsuit from the Antarctic disaster. They thanked their Indian friends profusely, exchanged numbers and addresses, then bid farewell on the quay, from where Singh hired them a metered taxi bound for his favorite hotel in the Mattancherry district.

Later, from his room, which caught a view of the Periyar River and the famed 2,000-year-old Hindu temple, the oldest in Kerala, Mr Marigold immediately placed an STP 'super emergency' call to Santa Fe. It was eleven and a half hours earlier there.

That night both men experienced their first India, with its jigsaw of cultures and aromas, colors and inquisitive glances. It was the rude, delicious, desperate and unfathomable shock to the system that every other wayfarer before them had commented upon. A joyous, grievous, implacable and inexplicable India that, immune to change, had inhered from as far back as the days when St Thomas the Apostle arrived in Cranganore and established a religious colony there; and even before that, stretching into the blurred dim of prehistory as Phoenicians sailed up and down the Arabian Sea, sampling the local life and customs.

Amid the incessant harangues of fast-talking Malayalam merchants hocking their turmeric, red chilis, freshly caught prawns, cardamom, ginger, cinnamon and cloves, families traversed the narrow back lanes; Hindus and Christians and the rare Jew; ambling mellow cows; and little clusters of children in their freshly pressed school uniforms and blue knapsacks, coming home from school carrying metal lunch pails. From every corner, the shallot and coconut smoke permeated the crowds, through which Ambassador cars slowly crawled. In waning light, Sannazaro's nostrils were captured by the pervasive grill of scintillating basmatis, crispy fried pappadams in chutney, and a mélange of ever-distinct curried flavors. It was enough to drive a man absolutely mad.

Through all this came the savage drums of a Kata Kali performance in an open square. Torch-lit candlepower accented the shadows of the elaborately attired dancers.

"That is Krishna," a local bystander explained. The two foreigners nodded their thanks.

"No, but it really *is* Krishna," the man pointed out.

Two days later a package arrived, courtesy of Blue Dart Couriers, at the hotel. Therein were Marigold's requested credit cards and some telling messages: an election gone sour in Greece; an urgent request for money from somewhere in the Amazon; a pending lawsuit filed by an angry neighbor who was complaining about a certain bison that had taken to sleeping near her back porch and eating up her flower beds; good news from Norfolk, Virginia, about chickens in Hong Kong; greetings from Hidalgo and his wife, who were now permanently occupying a suite above the casino in Monte Carlo. And, the strangest thing of all, Ginevra wanting them to know that Rodriguez and Amigo had—according to the Hopi shaman, Thomas—just returned from the South Pole and seemed quite happy to be home.

CHAPTER 78
Marigold Touches Down on the Subcontinent

THE NEXT MORNING Sannazaro slept in with his customary disregard for this passing life. Who's to say that an extra moment or a whole fortnight enveloped in pillows, devoted to never-never-lands, is any less the poetic milestone than time spent alongside the bustle of merchants, the punctilious stride of workers everywhere, or the merrymaking of widows and widowers? In fact, the Squire's reticence to get up was no mere sloth but the result of serious fatigue that had plagued him ever since Hong Kong. Moreover, the previous night had proven to be a menace of anticipatory anxieties, a hotel room aswarm with rats. The profusion of turds, the incessant squeaking and scurrying throughout the long darkness, accompanied by a prodigious stench of pungent urine, did not make for heavenly sleep. The shower was scalding, the beds as hard as pavement. A dinner of week-old naan, a sauce the consistency of sputum, though it aspired to sweet and sour, globules of rice and Gobi Manchurian catacombed with eerie shavings of unbearable pepper, starched with wicked red nuggets, pre-masticated in an atrocious stew—all deadly impostors, in terms of actual cuisine. And the Queenhopper beers, meant to wash down the disaster, were fuzzy, warm and nauseating.

What's more, Sannazaro ripped his tongue on some unseemly granule of glass arrived uncannily on his plate. The shard should well have ulcerated his esophagus as so often happens. Yet, the Italian's poor protest fell on ears now more in tune with mystical communions than bleeding mouths.

This avalanche of annoyances, devastating though they were to Sannazaro, for whom the many weeks of nonstop travail across the planet had burdened him with a weight he could scarcely mention, did not seem to shake the Commander's rare enthusiasm one iota. He happily awoke, while Sannazaro snored; stretched athletically, yawned defiantly, put on the one pair of linen trousers left him after his near disastrous sea change, and took early flight to the streets in search of the real India.

Rain assaulted the day with biannual ferocity. Typhoons, hurricanes, low atmospheric depressions, floods and every other conceivable wet-weather calamity had been predicted, but no matter. By 6.30 a.m., an hour's browsing and his voracious curiosity had already hit head-on with 1,002 substantive, metaphysical, alluring, tragic, detestable, fantastic, mundane, bizarre, and ordinary events; chimeras of complexion, insignia and incense; tantalizing women of beauteous infinitude, exotic glances toward eternity; a three-legged beggar, a two-headed cobra. A morose woman pregnant with eight, to judge by her size; a depleted leper beseeching passers-by for ointment; two children chipping away furiously at tainted marble; a retired Inspector praying before the statue of a naked girl.

From a temple of gleaming white solitary towers issued the last choral japas of a Krishna Bhava, as they call it: the manifestation of Purusha, or Pure Being, that had continued all through the night, hundreds of hopefuls seated on stone floors belting their earnest devotionals from the greatest of poets, the ninth-century Manikkavachakar ... *Oh heaven, oh sweet heart, oh setting sun ...*

The bookseller with his moldering tomes by every conceivable author. Muhammad Iqbal's formulas for Muslim self-government, Mahatma Gandhi's *Communal Unity*, Mirza Ghalib on destiny, Gobind Singh hailing the sword, Shaikh Nizam Ud-Din Auliya on congregational prayer, Swami Vivekananda on Christ, Buddha's discourse from the Sutta Nipata—an inspired injunction to walk in solitude like the great rhinoceros. This the Commander attempted, with his horn sticking out into everybody's business, for his curiosity this day was like a demon. He desired all the philosophy he could get, and thought of it as so many goods to be hoarded and trundled off in a sack on one's back, then dumped in the tool shed like a cord of wood to be burned up when the temperature dropped, to heat the whole house all at once.

This zeal struck with the natural chorus of a lightning storm or Beethoven sonata, rising in the wake of so many strange and wonderful visions all around him. He at once thought he had grasped the miracle of India, as it is often described, shrouded in every veil of mythology and physiognomy, Vedas and Sutras, universality and simplicity. On every corner what the great Ramakrishna likened to a 'pillow case' (or was it 'mental case'?) containing the same cotton, regardless of tinge. Savages and conquerors, mendicants and rogues, dacoits and gurus. Some striving after material gain, others not. Counterfeit gods, emaciated yogis, men in cheap polyester suits, slaves and leisurely lords. Within an hour he harbored both profound and stupid ideas. Conceits and undertones. High-forging principles, ceremonial altruisms, and holy bathing waters on the brain. Under all their breaths, the same millennial chant: *Purab marey Pur Yapon tak, Pacchim marey Bind pahar, Dakhin marey garh Europa tak, Utter-sat khand Tibet.* This spiritual geography of each and every soul, a map of the world that is personal, élitist, intolerant, stubborn and desperate. A rage to satisfy the outermost boundary of the kingdom which is the Self. What is it you want? he asked a ghetto-woman in her tar shanty. A Taj Mahal? No, a toilet and a refrigerator, she replied without hesitating. How old are you? he inquired graciously. Twenty, maybe 40, 31 or 32, she puzzled. How many other children have you? he asked, noting the two in her arms. Eight or nine, replied she. And you, child, what do you want to be when you grow up? asked Marigold of the eight-year-old, for that was how old he appeared. A dung heaver, the lad proudly declared. Why dung? pressed the Commander. The boy looked at his mother, then started: My father was a heaver, and his father. Do you ever plan to stop having children? the Commander asked of the mother, who was on her way to market. She gestured to the sky and from her lips he read: God is good, God is great, God will provide.

Marigold meandered into the darkest deepest alleys, straying far from the hotel. The rain continued unrelentingly, but should he care? Out near a second harbor he found Lord Siva seated in a beedee house frequented by longshoremen. Further on, he noted the "reality of self" configured in the guise of a jackass panting after water with hundreds of pounds of cement on its back and a small whip at its heels. Still further down the rain-trodden road he encountered the ancient 'Laws of Manu' played out in the confinement of a wife to her house, where she leaned out a window, her face swathed in black muslin, dreaming of coupling with the handsome banker walking back to his office among scrounging Brahman bulls that shared the roadway with him. In every touch of the living brush that was India, Mr Marigold believed he beheld some secret slang, a grand insight, the blushing of history.

All these people would perish unmentioned in any annals; all these other animals too, he thought. It is a fallacy of wisdom, adrift in myriads of shades, where man—driven to distraction by reason, unreason, passion, austerity, brightness and darkness, conflicted over silk satin or softest wool, a pear or an apple, a kiss and a second kiss, wearing countless desires that have no end—a fallacy of longing, mired in so much hope for pleasure, and authority, in every passing instant of beauty—cannot resist, and thus plunges back into that state of unborn being, where the womb is no longer a seductive vagina, but an open sewer beneath a burning sky, so all things pass through phases, and man, despairing of change, eventually expires without so much as a single thought left in his waterlogged, burned-out and discombobulated head. "In this way," sing the long-dead poets of the *Bhagavad Gita*, or some other beast of world literature, "will Arjuna and Krishna debate for all time true piety and the meaning of life."

The Commander contemplated these exhortations on his way into a queue of stragglers and wealthy sorts, of women with children, and children on their best behavior, of elderly couples holding hands, and young men and women looking very smart. Of sickly ones and those in the bud of good health. Of brisk people without the capacity for a caress, those enchanted with monotony for whom complaisance is an art, some carefree, some constrained, yet others furious with hope, detained permanently in desire, once wicked, desirous of salvation, wanting only to be cleansed for one final day. Those for whom the sunset was pure joy, and those for whom even the sunrise was a signal to be forlorn. Others who felt nothing at all. No glory. No dreams. No path. More members of the human race, still, who never agitated, never exercised, awoke, brushed their teeth, tramped off to work on one train or another, had their lunch, computed their time, took home their monthly rupees, satisfied their daughter's dowry after a lifetime of squirreling away their 300 a month, and grew old in the shadows of their canopy. So many separate, insular universes all glued together like the greater and lesser Magellanic clouds in a starry night, in a distant unresolve, a far-off meaningless cohesion, a numeric fantasy that ultimately spelled the doom of all self-aggrandizement. The perplexing waxing palliative known as India. Arrayed in one boulevard of happenstance, of earnest fixations standing in the overflowing gutters, a soggy conviviality of expectations, before a red sandstone temple battered by the rain wherein something extraordinary appeared to be taking place.

"What's going on?" Marigold asked a bison of a man adorned in amulets, and a little girl riding his shoulders.

"Waiting to meet the she-lily, the rising moon, the honey bee that knows only love and compassion," said he. "We call her Sister Love."

How extraordinary, Mr Marigold thought. Such jasmine-haunted speech from so rough-looking a fellow, and a sweet little daughter clinging to his enormous shoulders.

"Stay," he added. "You, too, will receive a hug from the guru. Then your miserable life will be forever blissful."

Mr Marigold positioned himself in the feverish line of humanity. He could not decipher the many colored turbans, beards, feminine adornments; the morning half-darkness across weltered faces, bleating dialects, the multiguised clamor of small gods in the making. Lower India: descendants of 1,000 generations of weavers and farmers and emperors and the stream of time. Skirts, spring hearts, Persian poets, ripe bosoms, the dance and shiver of all that passes for the human dominion. The scent of canna, the ripple of sunlight through the chennar tree, the drowsy cloud, the moon behind the dawn. A chattering chataka bird overhead in a banyan filled to the brim with its wide net of weary, surviving limbs, carved out in the name of so many lovers and political slogans.

But this blush of compliant obsolescence was enlivened the moment the anxious 1,000 souls, one by one, crowded inside the temple mount, where timbrel and sarangi, voices of stained glass, manifested their freedom from bondage. A recitation of all the faithful replied in kind, one mighty undifferentiating glazed-twist of light conquering darkness, sugar despair, ends beginnings, mercifulness short-shrift. No more iniquity, unfairness, body. No weak seed nor powerless senses; no abject self arising nor despondency pertaining. Though Marigold could not understand a word she said, the meaning of the guru's rapt rollercoaster of injunctions was clear enough: the sanhita-mantra—all truth and quintessence, the firm fundamentals of *ahinsa*, or non-violence. She laughed, cried, wriggled, threw up her hands, and embraced each and every pilgrim who patiently scooted on their bums closer and closer to her mantle.

Sister Love sat on the floor as well, upon a ripe cushion, and every person who reached her—which they all did, said the bison man—would receive a huge manly hug, a sisterly embrace, that gave each to understand that they were the brother of God. People wept upon seeing her, collapsed upon touching her, trembled upon looking back at her when their moment was complete.

What am I doing here? the Commander thought.

What a silly man, Sannazaro—still in bed—dreamt.

Who is this poor sap-depleted foreigner? the bison man wondered.

Far from wherever he haileth, without cause or purpose, wizened, frail of mind, lacking in apparent relations or compass, wanting for friendship and guidance. So obviously bereft, so out of sorts and confused. All this, within a glance, the Keralan grasped of the Commander. Had he known of his billions of dollars it would not have altered his perception. To be without a solid plan, a child no clue in hand, a wad of stapled rupees and rueful countenance. Deficient in calories. A traveler who could not do it, find it, establish it, encompass it among his own kind, but sought instead the road of exile, expatriotism, lost loves, sadly neglected opinion.

Finally, the Commander neared his time, shuffling on his bottom towards the woman they all hailed as the One. She saw the Commander, all white, burnished with frayed nerves, waxy and squirming, silly of grin, long and skinny of front teeth, and evidently had already formed her strong opinion of him. Prosperity or adversity, grief or smarmy comfort, dusky feelings or the dawn of young nipples for ideas. It didn't matter which, he was there because his heart had formed a freeway to her, and there was no exit. He had arrived in India.

Part Three

The Immortality Trilogy

CHAPTER 79
Sister Love

SHE HAD BEEN RAISED a wild child in a fishing village somewhere in India's deep south, suckled by the family cow, straying from all community standards for little girls, her early years devoured by a devotion to Krishna. She would fall into trances, throw herself rhapsodically into the mud, always awash in the incantations to her beloved god. At school she would collapse like an epileptic, her seizures distancing her from all who came near. Nobody understood. Neither her parents who tended to scold her or beat her or think her mad and in need of a doctor, nor her brothers who all agreed their little sister was crazy. They tried to marry her off but each time she'd throw a tantrum, hurl blunt objects at the suitor, and further embarrass the family. One of her older brothers hired a cousin to kill her. But the knife attack backfired and the assailant died of a heart attack in the very act of aggression. Soon thereafter, the brother contracted elephantiasis, then hung himself in shame.

All the while the young girl increasingly drew attention to herself through her pure insistence upon the belief that God dwelled within each and every living being: that the slenderest sliver of cricket grass was a successful experiment in the divine; the mosquito manifested mercy, the molewort prayer, a crayfish compassion, whilst from its lair the mayfly mirrored every avenue to our fondest wish and holiness. She exemplified this absolute lust for life in each morsel of her breath, at all the possible junctures of human communion with nature. It was no surprise that dogs—ferocious with others—never left her side. Nor snakes and lizards, nor bustard birds. Sea eagles befriended her, but even eagles were no defense against a raging father who beat the girl unmercifully, lashing her to a tree and assaulting her until both legs flowed with feminine blood. She had taken a golden bangle from her mother's chest, sold it in the market and given the money to an old couple so that they would not starve. But her parents were enraged by such largesse and beat her again and again. Yet, not so much as a murmur issued from her pale and pretty lips—only the fallow, svelte and husky reverberations of the godchild Krishna, in so many beguiling, glorious guises.

Later, during prolonged trances, Devi Bhavas, she literally embodied the goddess, becoming Earth and Sky and Fire and Water. During these ecstatic periods, all those who came into contact with the peasant girl experienced her same trembling convulsions of joy. An opulence of simple song, transforming even the burliest oak of man or meanest bitch of mother-in-law into honey dew or mango juice.

But all this saintly business was a gigantic onus of shame to Sister's parents and they discussed killing themselves as the only way to save face in the community. Overhearing this conversation late one night, Sister resolved to take her own life in the sea, which she attempted to do, only a cousin saving her. Thereafter, the family dynamic evolved more reasonably, and mother and daughter were brought closer together. But it was the occasion of an actual miracle that totally altered the status of little Sister in the minds of everyone. It is recorded that one afternoon she was on her way home from the market, a basket filled with vegetables on her head, when she came upon a crowd of several thousand villagers who had gathered before their priest. He was reading from the great Marseillaise of India, Bande Mataram's "Hail to the Mother", with its cascade of jeweline metaphors, lotus thrones, ladies and queens, shore to shore, hundreds of millions of hands rising to greet the occasion of her muse, her wisdom, her dharma.

Sister went up to the priest, put down her basket and began chanting her own version of the love of god. Many in the crowd knew her to be the mad font of gibberish, the butt of ridicule, the embarrassment of her family, several of whom, including her mother, were present. They now demanded she show proof of her divine pretenses. Communists within the crowd agitated roughly for such a demonstration. They were members of the Society for Rationalist Thought and they detested Sister, wanted her banished, had earlier placed poison-tipped thorns before a temple where she danced barefoot by blue moon in one of her trances. They had tried everything to rid the village of her demonic presence, but all attempts had failed. Now, before the entire population, their denunciations had special relevance, for either Sister proved herself by performing a miracle or it would be clear even to her small band of followers that she was a fake.

Sister declared she was no pet monkey needing to perform tricks. God need not flip pennies nor make salt shakers move across tables to persuade the faithless of a divinity. But for purposes of silencing her detractors she agreed to a little handiwork on this one day. She asked that someone bring her a pitcher of water. She said a prayer and—lo!—the water turned to cream.

Then she splattered the adoring hands with the precious substance, but the pitcher did not lose its quantity. The milk continued to flow; and then it turned into five sweets, which also failed to be diminished despite consumption by tens of hundreds of worshippers. Old women collapsed in awe; the rowdies, as they were known, turned full corner and now embraced a god. Communism lost its toehold upon the subcontinent in her wake.

From that day forward, her parents had become her disciples. All her enemies melted away. Anonymous donors came forth with money for charities which she had established: cancer hospices, engineering colleges, houses for widows, special agricultural projects for indigenous peoples, and a gigantic hospital, the largest in Kerala, with intensive-care units second to none, free of charge. She created a school for the study of love, and all this without asking for so much as a dime. In her native Malayalam she had spread by word of mouth the message of non-violence and now millions of people believed in her, said the bison man, who sat beside the Commander whispering of these miraculous causes and consequences, the metaphysics of charity, as they approached the moment at hand. More importantly, he went on, in a society that oppressed its women, she had prevailed, ecumenically embracing all religions, claiming no one godhead over another. This Sister Love had built ashrams, institutes, a whole university devoted to compassion, and operated according to all the precepts, enigmas, adorations and prerogatives of love.

She had risen like a love psalm to the relentless calling to give equally to everyone, ceaselessly, tirelessly. No gulf of nature deterred her heart, which remained captive of that vast, simmering similitude in which every truth implied every other.

Here was the real thing, said the bison man: a ferocious eternal wild child, beginning with her miraculous birth, the blueness in her skin, the fact of her having learned to speak by six months, and her propensity for sleeping on beaches, under stars, beneath the deepest forests, beside mangers, in the huts of the poorest untouchables, always clinging to the wind and surf and never minding about herself. She preferred to grovel in the mud, to be utterly ravaged by the elements. Her celibacy was but another sign that she was destined to achieve the highest of the highs, the deepest of the deeps. She felt it all, knew the separation and eventual unison of mind and body which for 10,000 other philosophers and mystics was only a series of galling platitudes. She had penetrated to the core of that which is worth living and dying for, and while others might mouth the words, she had grown up in their luscious shadows. Had truly transcended every social adversity. A woman in India, born, according to the pundits, in the vagina of a jackal—for that is the scorn with which girls are typically admitted into a family. A burden, best sold off to any man as early as possible. All these insinuations and half-truths the Commander had only read about. All the more impressive, then, to see a female hugging male strangers. To witness such affection multiplied so massively, unselfconsciously, and with the full approbation of all those who came to her for nothing more than a touch, a kind word, a full embrace.

As for the message, it had to be contained in those very hugs and kisses, enshrined in those few balms which she muttered secretively. No one would know what she was saying, for the privacy of each exchange was the proof that she cared not in general but in specifics; that her hours and felicities were each woven of a name, a family history; that her encouragements were no idle gestures but intensely personal responses.

She seemed to recognize everyone, to know their names and whole histories in advance. Each hug was different—some light, mellifluous; others full-bodied strongholds of pertinacious support, headrests, bed pillows and down comforters, catalysts, bosoms, vast shrines of flesh-scented affiliation. Her touch was a cave of hope, a joy encompassing all four seasons, life insurance, confession without uttering a word, tears with no hourly fee, a telegram from the center of the earth. She tempered her behavior moment by moment in concert with a symphonic grasp of the personality, need, terror, hurt, ferocious hope before her.

How did she accomplish all this? Marigold wondered, waiting his turn. He learned from the bison man that these hugs of Sister Love, or Little Sister, or Love Sister, or just plain Sis, were conveyed 23 hours of every day. She rarely slept, never took for herself, focused only on one principle: that her home was in everyone else's heart. Where goodness abideth, there she would remain. Where pain exhibits, there she would flock. Where heartache mocks every hope, she would gladly suffer in its stead. The Commander was about to experience it for himself.

The bison man went first, and Marigold watched as he broke down weeping before Sister Love. For it turned out that his little girl was missing an arm, a fact not discernible to Marigold until now because of her clothing and the way her father had been holding her. But Sister tickled the child. She stroked the girl with unutterable kindness, murmuring what legend would later reveal to be a mantra of exquisite sonority: Lovelovelovelovelovelove ... And then something incomprehensible, impossible and unimaginable occurred: in the nanosecond of a gasp, without time even to quarter-blink or half-pee; before the cosmos, beyond the sunbeams of the rainbow, between heartbeats, in the twitch of a muscle, faster than the synapse; before language, cognition, pre-cognition; beyond all paradox, in the chime of a Wittgensteinian silence, alas, before any such mention, memory or scientific assessment; indeed, past all recourse to explication ... the girl's missing arm reassembled itself in Marigold's mesmerized mind.

The reconstitution was as radical and whole as anything could be. He thought back to the *Coscinasterias* brown morph, that lovely echinoderm that had graced the sides of weta-infested cliffs through which his expedition had travailed just weeks before in George Sound; a starfish that can regenerate an amputated arm within days; or a macrocystis bull kelp which may well grow three feet every 20 hours. The Commander had heard about these things, and seen for himself the fast-moving cold upper currents of the fiordlands, replete with pelagic tunicates, the bio-luminescent salps and billions of floating blue bits of imperial jellyfish among the Chagos corals. A purity given to reincarnation, multiplicity, eternal life. This was the essence, after all, of biology. If among starfish, why not an Indian child? If in a current of freezing Tasman Sea water larded with every particulate known to inaccessible biology, why not in the presence of a spiritual flow, the Earth goddess embodied in a woman? Those were the thoughts that swept over the Commander in that unlikely temple, before the unanswerable and charming aggregate of devotees all gesticulating in their convincing rapture as a little girl's arm strangely reappeared.

Here, then, was Crowquill's own aftermath, the Commander realized. Rebirth. Whether in a whale shark or a temple. The inconceivable lightness of the Sister's smile splashed across the room, inundating his every preconception. The whole teeming assembly roared with the stuff: guffaws, bellyaching screeches of maniacal mirth, tears of joy. The bison man was swept away by Sister who held him against her own weighty chest. For minutes they swayed together rhythmically, this 300-pound widower, his daughter and the genius of love. Then Sister gave the child some M&Ms, mumbled endearments into her ear, nodded with the wisdom of all the sages nestled into one, and chuckled mightily.

Marigold fell over backwards. Final proof that he'd been searching for. Or was he simply seeing things? Had the rain water gotten into his ears, clouded his eyes, flooded that quadrant otherwise devoted to clear-headedness?

The Sister winked at him. Marigold took a deep breath, then approached.

CHAPTER 80
The View Through a Crystal Ball

SO NOW THE COMMANDER emerged with every hope for a better world, as bland a championship as such a goal may seem. How did she know? He would never understand her prescience, but first she examined his weary eyes with an enormous scrutiny, then she asserted with a fine mixture of bemusement and sadness, "You want to save the world." To which the Commander replied, "I suppose I do. Yes, Ma'am. I am seeking an example, a model community that is as close to the ideal of love as can possibly exist. Call it my childhood fantasy, the tragic lost love of an aging idealist. But that's who I am." Towards which she bore into him with a penetrating "That is altogether possible, if you are up to it. But to do so you must understand both heaven and hell. So you will." Then, with jovial finality, she asked him, "Well, what's it going to be?" Marigold trembled. He could not say what had come over him—there was no time. Her embrace, the intensity of the exchange, was bound by some new and elusive physics of interaction. With trembling unresolve he whispered, "Tell me how?" So that she, a linguistic levity, happy as a holiday, as keyed in as the sharpest diamond, a voracious, vintage study of his perplexity, replied in one incomprehensible word: "Gundlepet."

"What is it?" he asked.

But she did not reply, looking, rather, to the large red-robed, long-bearded gentleman next to her—Kind Swami, as he was known. His eyes, like Sister's, twinkled, then fixed on to the Commander. "Ahh, Gundlepet," he repeated. "I have not been, nor do I know anybody who has." Gundlepet? perplexed the Commander. Where, what is it? Is the pronunciation right? Which language? What does it mean? Presently, the dam broke in him. He could not hold back the obvious discrepancies that swelled in his heart and seared his topmost parts. "It is a Hindu place, a temple, a village? What, what, what???? What am I to do with a word? Where is this leading to? There is poverty all around. Distress. Great gulfs between the rich and the poor. The slaughter of animals, the blowing up of bombs, the starvation of children. While you sit here on your thrones of adulation. This is India. You are gurus. You are supposed to be more specific."

"That which you seek, you already have within your heart. That is what Sister says," replied Kind Swami. "Beyond that, you need merely to study the map."

Mr Marigold should not have expected more than that—the vision of so many legions of hopeful souls lining up to take their moment and bask in the comfort of this woman and her colleagues. If it helped sorrowful lives to any extent, then, hoopjoy, hey, hallelujah, it was enough—a vanilla-scented psychotherapy, free of charge—and came after how many thousands of years of Indian metaphysical moments along Siddhartha's riverbank? Quite a few. Born of much agony in a land where triumph meant only survival against the grimmest of odds. Yet here, in the rifle-blast center of terrible evolution, was this villa of peaceful persuasions, an architectural placebo of unprepossessing calm, a vortex of love and patience. Those present could have been out in the hurlyburly streets, after all, angrily scurrying after burlap sacks of rice, wallet-brained, commuting to humiliating jobs of blood-stained brick and running mascara, of dock-ferrying, shoulder-harassing, loin-jolting labor; to the acrid smoke-infested warehouses and cracking overstuffed offices and predatory firms and garret cages; to the lines and cellars and fluorescent hells wherein bossmen and slave secretaries and orphaned interns and meddling middlemen, and morose full-of-themselves managers and burly bureaucrats and government assholes and killers and cobblers and menders and stone trundlers, and everywhere a lawyer greedily feasting on sorrow, all collaborated in the senseless ceaseless exploitation of one another, or of animals—innocent, desperate animals—in that age-old folly described by most as trying to make a living, to feed a family, to survive, oblivious to any higher callings.

This tabernacle, at least, was filled to the brim with non-paying jobs, with a conspicuous absence of machinations: a different kind of bricklaying, mortar by mortar, rudiments of the soul rising into a mighty edifice understood by one and all. Here, those higher callings, the poetry of faith, a symphony of worn-down tuning forks at its most lyrical, was concentrated—by whatever coincidences of personality and charisma—in this 130 pounds of empathetic flesh known as Sister Love and her gentle, most gracious and highly educated ascetical colleagues, who were referred to as sadhus and sadhvuis. Elegant, gorgeous people, refined PhDs, brilliant, eloquent spokespersons for the Indian outback, the heart, the ramparts, the history, the future. In their sparkling glances and generous poetry they shared the whole chateau of embraces, no matter who you were, or where you came from or were going to.

OK, Marigold thought. The sea is indeed bright before me in a sunrise of sufficiency and honesty. Nothing lost, a few notches gained.

He readied himself, upright on palms and kneecaps, to shuffle back away along the floor, when some final gratifying exchange burst from the confines of his meeting with Sister Love. Right there before him, with burgeoning almond eyes and marshmallow scent and a smile as wide as the whale shark that inadvertently devoured lucky Sannazaro, she enunciated with a mild pacific manner, "You will have a child!" With that she gave him a huge hug and in so doing he heard not one but two ribs crack, for in truth he'd eaten insufficiently since the Laughing Gas Utopia had misfired and he'd nearly raised the water levels throughout the world. His thin frame was no match for this bear-hugging saint.

With a groan he asked, "Sister, how can I have a child? I am a man." This one query he managed only barely as he clasped his ribcage in excruciating discomfort.

She laughed hysterically. He thought, this woman has broken my ribs, possibly punctured my lungs, cut off the blood flow to my greywacke, smothered my heart, tickled my personality out of its shell, made me question every last ounce of my existence, and now is amused in no less a manner than a naughty inmate of an asylum. So that he felt justified in saying quite frankly, "Sister, dear, I believe you have just broken two of my ribs, yet you are laughing, and I fear it is contagious."

To which she replied with an even greater, more magnanimous outburst of wit that signaled nothing at all. Was it the crazy wheel of life, with its sadistic appetite for confusion, disarray, mixed messages, theological paradox, the unknowable, unreachable avenue to the stars? Or was it all simply a word, the one word repeated down through the ages with as much frequency as that of God: the word of Love? Of love made flesh and manifested in her singularly affectionate Being?

Whatever the deep structure to these mysteries, Marigold himself could not help laughing, for in truth the whole setting now appeared positively silly, though this exertion added to the stinging pain down his weasly side. He held his breath, angst of a spiritual kind mingling with the asphyxiating out-of-breathness which comes from bone fractures.

Then, approvingly, she laid on his cheek the biggest slobber kiss he'd received from any woman in 30 years. It was wet, delicious, gooey, cryptic, full-bodied, mucilaginous and galvanizing. It was the kiss of eternity, the contact with himself through another that he had failed to know before this moment. The Platonic potion concocted from every vial of *agape*, eros and conscience. An altruism of teleology, born of a mother's breast, showing loyalty to one man, as if to the whole biosphere. In short, he was mightily awakened by it. The floodgates of the world's tears breaking over him from all peripheries.

Deeply devastated, in the most moving sense, Marigold got up to leave, thanking her profusely. Then, instead of handing him chocolates, as he'd seen her doing with all of the other pilgrims before him, she reached behind her, where 30 bramacharinis (the sadhvuis) sat in their splendiferous white vestments, and took a folded shawl of intricately woven lionels in her hand.

"Let him wear it in good health," she said as she gave it to him.

"Thank you, but who are you referring to?" Marigold inquired anxiously. "Who will wear it? The mysterious child I am supposed to have? Who?"

But Sister had other destinies to foretell and now ushered the very next in line. For there were 1,000 others waiting to be saved.

The bison man, a Roman Catholic professional big-time wrestler, smiled like a dolphin at the Commander and introduced him to his little girl, Alisa, the one Marigold had seen embraced by Sister. She, who was six years of olive-oil grace and cloud-eyed gratitude, hugged Marigold, whose smashed ribcage no longer effused in pain. But now, fantastically, she did so with two restless vital arms, arms of health, arms of restored use in this life. Arms defying science, reason, embryology, horticulture, vascular testimony, neurological order, mathematical system, anatomical chronology, and so on and so forth.

Miracle upon miracles. He touched the hand, the elbow, stroked the entire arm. It was real. The bison man was in tears.

Marigold was invited to visit Sister Love again the next day, when she would be holding court, as it were, at a different ashram 100 miles to the north, at a town called Calicut. Perhaps there, having exercised the requisite patience and sustained inquiry, the Commander would be granted the clarity he so longed for with regard to this Gundlepet, and the business of a child.

It was noon when the Commander made his way through the torrential rains back to the hotel, with so very much to divulge to his friend and Squire. A revelation of the ages. A breakthrough of irrefutable infectiousness. Lourdes. The Blarney Stone and Wailing Wall. Mecca. The Moonlight Sonata. Angel Falls. What blessings were these? How could such a one as Sister truly exist? If the entire morning were no dream, as he could easily have imagined, then why had she not replicated herself in some easily distributed pill? Salvation for the Hungry, Inc.? Why not proliferate her starfish amputee system, as it were, to every hospital across the wicked weary land of man? Why not save the world with a giggle and snap of her lovely fingers, and a few M&Ms to boot? One magic wand that could so easily cure the broken, the defeated, the washed up and devastated with a smile, a hug and a slobber kiss? It was so easy. Not even 1,000 million billionaires could compete with that. And he simply couldn't wait to tell Sannazaro about it.

But, according to the man at the front desk of the Snake Goddess Hotel, Sannazaro had checked out an hour before. Apparently he had called for a car to the airport, and left the Commander a message, which the desk attendant now handed over.

"My Imperturbable Friend," the Squire wrote. "You should not be surprised to learn that I have opted to return to Tesuque and cultivate my own garden before you can convince me otherwise. I am no Viking or rear guard; the Battle of Sekigahara or Normandy's not for me. I have no plans for saving every fish in the sea. In fact, as you well know, I like eating them. I have no words that will unburden your heart. I am a self-professed coward. I am neither a Greenie nor a politico; neither Spartan soldier nor crusader. I have no interest in the affairs of state, or even of Utopia. No amount of money or noble gestation could induce me to perpetuate this life of sinking icebergs, Sri Lankan pirates, seasickness, giant sharks, extinct eagles, and near death by every other means at your disposal, however exhilarating. So just let me say, take care of yourself, old chum, and come home soon. I shall await your return. You can find me at the Camp of the Spirits, which I trust—despite more addled insults to one cerebellum than any person has likely suffered in the history of addledness—you still remember. Do not forget me, nor your duties to Anastasia and Ebert and Alma and the others. You are a man with great responsibilities now.

"Moreover, I believe Ginevra genuinely loves you, so do not do anything stupid that would result in your obliteration, obfuscation or terminal laceration. I wouldn't want her to suffer on your account. If you cannot avoid doing something colossally stupid, which is certainly likely, then for god's sake, do not do something rash. If rash is also out of your control, at least be polite and restrained about it, so as to avoid instigating a hostile mob. If even politeness is not in the cards, either, then at least hold on to the good sense to hire a driver and keep him nearby at all times. If even that language barrier proves too much, seek out the nearest Embassy for consultation. But if your pride and obstinacy exceedeth even that, at least, I implore you for as long as you remain in this morbid country, put six drops of iodine in your water. That's what I have read. Two percent tincture. If even that simple advice is beyond you, then god help you, for there is nothing more I can do or say to protect you from yourself. I have diarrhea, I am hot, I have a yellowish fever, I am probably—no, certainly—dying of cholera, cranial encephalitis, typhoid and diphtheria, not to mention suspected malaria. And I have been exhausted from the day I met you. There is no air conditioning in this disgusting dive, nor does the fan work on account of an electrical short throughout the country, due to an alleged food riot or revolution in a neighboring city, as a result of the continued and total breakdown in international affairs which have, in any case, ignored India for 5,000 years. Nor are the rat turds something I can or will stomach. The food is dreadful, poisonous, tasteless, and there is no cup of espresso to be had for 3,000 miles. I miss the opera and I have not seen a single garden anywhere for months. Nobody speaks Italian, there are poor and legless people everywhere, child prostitutes sold by their own parents and living in cages, a government that I declare deplorable for its obvious disinterest in human welfare. This insipid country blatantly ignores filth, squalor, basic hygiene, and appears—after even a morning's notice—to be absolutely hostile to all that I cherish.

"I know you take these horrors as personally as I do. Somehow, you seem to ride with the punches. I on the other hand sink. You want to try and save the whole country? Be my guest. But I know my limits, and I'm fed up. I can be maligned, abused, humiliated and outraged only so far.

Then I break. I am too old for this. Hence, without further belaboring or expansive adieus, or self-deprecating thanks for nothing, and not without concerted fears for your general wellbeing, I bid you farewell. Until, I trust, and under more congenial times, we meet again. Your loving friend, advisedly, Señor Sannazaro. PS: Assuming this typhoon passes, I will be on the Cochi-Coimbotore flight, transferring to Madras and on to Tokyo. In due course, returning to New Mexico. God grant me a simple blooming lilac tree in spring, a warm breeze and a cup of tea. Therein. If you get this message, I pray you will come to your senses in time and join me."

CHAPTER 81
Mr Marigold Urgently Imparts the Miracle of Electromagnetic Neurotransmittable Embryogenesis to Sannazaro, Who is Not a Little Sceptical

"PRIMUM NON NOCERE—firstly, non-violence."

Mr Marigold set his course to the airport with great urgency. But speed was barely an option. The taxi crawled through three-foot-deep swamps that leveled entire streets— a consequence of all that squall-line business, as nightly weather satellites configured it. Those "solar energy temperature gradients" said to be inherent to the "extra-tropical regions" where heat lows, convection forces, cyclones and the convergence of dangerously dense cumulonimbus clouds together let loose those legendary raging downpours known as winter monsoon, accompanied by fantastic thunderclaps.

Accustomed though they were to this intrusive season, people nonetheless behaved like meteorological virgins, struggling dumbly to hold on to their umbrellas against the ghastly gusts, wading birds without proper apparatus. Hemp skirts floated to circumferential surfaces around the lovely teenage girls who occupied them scarcely. Dogs paddled along with the others through the watery mazes. Here a waterlogged cat struggled pitifully to live, grappling with waning facility beside the normally pampered wolfhound. Women held up their saris like tango dancers; men moved sluggishly near like-minded water buffaloes, all co-mingling with rats furiously swimming beneath the unexpectedly excited fusillade of raindrops. Every side lane rushed forth with the contaminants of city life, all gushing, oozing, sliming into the larger thoroughfares through which the city blunderbusses careened and floated. The lower-grade children who were too short, relative to the height of the water, could not venture to school. Those caught out swam home.

The Commander witnessed a crate filled with live chickens—at least 30 of them—bobbing down a wind-battered road, the animals crawling over each other, frantically trying to save themselves. They had been stuffed in a space unsuitable even for one chicken.

"*Stop the car!* " Marigold cried, leaping out into the rapids, swimming towards his destination, passing a woman floating by in the opposite direction in a wheelchair, and claiming a handhold on the top of the coop just as the owner also arrived via breaststroke. Together they managed to hold aloft the water-sogged pen, narrowly saving the chickens from certain drowning. The Commander then gave the man 4,000 rupees from his slimy wallet for all of the avians, but did not quite know what to do with them, especially given that the crate did not come with the price of the chickens, or at any price. There was no unflooded area anywhere around in which to deposit the birds, so he waded back with the loaded bin, emptied the chickens into the taxi, returned the wooden box to its owner, and promised the driver double his normal price because of the feathery mess in the back seat. People were screaming, the rain pummeling the roof of the taxi. It was noisy. Confusing. Heartbreaking. One might think the country would never pull through. Yet, this was normal.

Then, just as fast and furiously as the storm had dumped its 40 inches of rain, so the swirling purple clouds moved away from this particular epicenter. Lightning and dense cumuli gave way to silver sunlight. Such clouds are the least adulterated facets of the Indian landscape, from the Himalayas to the Nicobars. How many creatures looked to them as their one abiding symbol of hope and renewal?

Not far from the airport, past the moats and submerged paddies, the Commander discerned an elevated grassy oasis already warmed by the newly emergent sun. Free of human habitation, the pocket of land rose like a crystal of platinum from the rich black abyss of the storm.

"There," he decreed, alerting the driver and guiding him to the point of liberation.

The driver stopped, the Commander opened the door, and the 30-odd chickens poured from the back seat, running up into the bushes where, with any measure of luck, they might survive for a time longer than was guaranteed them back in that dismal pannier, though the driver volunteered that it would take less than a day for India—some part of India—to find and consume those birds. But for now they appeared delighted, pecking the mud for hopping insects.

"You are wasting your money," the driver reiterated, probably wondering to himself whether all Westerners were so stupid. Were not chickens born and bred for chicken masala?

They reached the airport, which had only just reopened. Already a swarm of hawkers was waiting. Marigold made no small talk and moved systematically through the hordes. Inside, a quick survey of departing flights revealed to him an auspicious delay of the carrier to Madras (Chennai), via Coimbatore. He raced to the lounge, and there found Sannazaro downing a cold Kingfisher beer and gorging on what, admittedly, were some of the finest French fries in the world, though drowned in a sordid-looking sauce.

The Señor spied his nemesis, believing that Marigold had come at last to brook no further folly but join him. "I am sorry if my letter shocked you," he said, "but the truth is mightier than catsup. I'm going home. I should have done so months ago. And I'm glad you've decided to return with me."

"My dear little man, sit down. I have something extraordinary to relate," the Commander began.

"I am sitting. And there is nothing that you can tell me, howl, screech or complain about that I haven't already suffered and endured."

"Psychoanalytically speaking, I follow your foibles, grant you your grievances, know your yellowtail, empathize fully with your reticence, but please bear with me on this one. Earlier today I experienced a phantasm which materialized like no ectoplasm. This was the real McCoy. We've all heard about miracles and metaphysical expeditions, shamans pulling ginseng from behind their ears. But this time, may sandflies suck me dry if I am exaggerating, I beheld transfiguration."

Sannazaro gazed upon him with a mixture of scorn and pathos. "Your eyes are tired."

"I mean to say my whole towering macho of observation, quid pro quo of professionalism, ballast of granite that is my blood—every petite protein and glob of cellular matter—quavered like Little Red Riding Hood at the sight of this emphatic, unsubtle, baffling, revelatory medical breakthrough: a biological proof that human beings are more than we had ever thought possible, each a little prince ..."

That was only the beginning of the sentence, but Sannazaro could withstand no more of the babble in one go. The onslaught was giving him sudden indigestion.

"That is certainly a truism in your case—what was thought possible, I mean," he replied instructively. He'd just noticed that his sauce was not red but green. It did not go with French fries.

Marigold continued, a font of fevers stoked like no other motor-mouth or incendiary: " ... That spirit can transcend body; that there is indeed a science of crystal ballography. That all that guru gunk is no gunk, no cream cheese, but magnificent reality. I tell you I have witnessed the impossible."

"And I many times: that I should have been induced to follow a maniac around the world!"

"Would you listen for once in your life," the Commander commanded.

"Yes, but why are you favoring one side over the other?" Sannazaro asked, referring to the fact that Murillo seemed crooked over to his left, and kept a firm palm fitted there, near the proverbial origins of Eve.

"A woman, Sister Love, accidentally broke my ribs—no matter, it was done with a generosity of spirit I cannot even translate; more to the point, she has restored a limb to a little girl, a gorgeous child named Alisa, whose father I have befriended; and 1,000 people saw Sister Love accomplish this uncanny transformation. Can you imagine? I am not speaking of artificial resuscitation, but the actual instantaneous telepathic pyschophysical emanation of kinetically discharged cellular and electromagnetic neurotransmittable embryogenesis, all concentrated into the reconstructed appendage that should enable dear Alisa to fly a kite like any normal child, to do a handspring, blow bubbles, chase butterflies, stroke the wavy coat of a Golden Retriever, fondle a frog, trace the outlines of a spider web, apply her first dab of little girl's lipstick, touch a cumulus cloud, or wipe away a tear at the loss of her first goldfish."

Sannazaro roared with such a hearty stupefaction at the stupidity of his traveling companion that others in the waiting area observed that he, not Mr Marigold, was the more berserk of the two. His cackles were of such an infectious nature that they, too, could not help but join in chorus with the nutty laughter— which is, of course, the sweetest kind. Indians are among the greatest laughers in the world, if given even a quarter the opportunity. Soon, half the airport's occupants were hardy-har-harring so that one would have thought that Crowquill had landed and worked his mischief.

"Poetaster in the face of a roof caving in," Sannazaro began amidst the floating sea foam of chuckling incredulities. "Idiot. This female quack has smashed your ribs! What sadist, bar-room bouncer, transvestite on crack—or was it you who ticked her off? A sexual affront perhaps? One of your obnoxious and incisive critiques? I've known the ghastly touch of gauche in you. That atrocious geriatric superbuzzard demeanor. How many ribs was it?"

"Will you just put a lid on it, damn it? She hugged me, very hard. I was not expecting so passionate, so spiritual, so ... so meaningful a connection. Whoever said my ribs were meant to be steel? But that is not the point. There was a girl with an amputated limb, the unfortunate victim of a bus plunging into a pothole, and suddenly, as if by magic wand, that missing link to the full-bodied child was restored. I swear it on this catsup bottle. On my velvet, perfect, honeyed mother's very memory: if there was no God, there is now."

"You are more the imbecile than ever. All that rancid incense has severely impaired your nostrils, destroyed your common sense, and burst forth with a dike of gibberish. You are like one of those Pacific

Northwest salmon fishes whose neurological sensors in a pea-sized brain, that homing instinct freely given to all but the most stubborn nomads, has been destroyed by a spirit spill. You have lost your way. Your greatest tragedy is that your childhood has never ended. Who loves you? Who have you loved? Add up your faults and attributes, the good and bad works, and ask yourself, who will be there at the end to bury you? The caretaker of an old-folk's asylum in some century or another where indifference reigns supreme, where nobody knows your name. Where alone you will enter the dust stream back into the star from which you came—no identity, no clue that you were ever here. Listen to one who is not unlike you in this respect, but has the sense to cling to friendship in familiar surroundings, to keep a low profile in the bastion provided and not to rock the boat. Life is difficult enough. So, please, Murillo, may I have the pleasure of knocking some sense into you. Come home with me and cease all further senseless wanderings *ad terrum terrible*."

"Señor, listen to me. Don't think I do not appreciate the wisdom of your advisories. For I have always noticed you could have been a successful weatherman on the evening news, standing before the satellite show of mighty typhoons with a calming voice of reason. An ability, which I admire, to anesthetize tumult with poetic tranquillity, much like Longfellow's translation of Dante. But, for all that, I can only assure you that our tandem destinies await us. Sister Love is giving what they call a Darshan later today, at an ashram in Calicut. We must go. This deserves further study."

"We are going to Tokyo. Then home to Tesuque, if you please." But Sannazaro was also a foolish bougainvillea of a dreamer. He, too, if given any incentive at all, could not help himself. "She really did that?" he asked, meekly. No need to analyze the instant he turned round from hostility to gullibility. The four ages of mankind reduced to but two. From the crib to the cane, in logic, was an easily achieved reach for this particular Squire. The whys and wherefores would be more difficult to unravel. Except to acknowledge that his own romantic sense of adventure was tangibly stoked, no matter how hard he tried to suppress it.

"Yes. I truly believe she may have found the key," Mr Marigold confirmed.

"All keys open a door," averred the Italian. "All doors lead to the same room, a finite floor, four constraining walls, a ceiling. For some, it is a claustrophobic lifetime of looking out, hoping, despairing, declining: a defeatism satisfied only by the artificial comforts of a warm hearth and a dream or two. For others, it is a launching pad—a window on the world that may lead to any number of futile avenues."

"Well spoken."

"Yet others fumble with their keys, and are unable to get into that room at all. Those are the lucky ones, left stranded in the hallway."

"Your point?"

"I don't remember."

"Then shut up and listen."

They both heard the announcement for Sannazaro's departing flight. He stood up to leave.

"Sit down," Marigold insisted. "I'm leaving. Goodbye."

"Please. What I'm telling you is that I have been given a rare gift and I want you to be my witness. After all we've been through together, finally, to share a little joy. I mean it. I need you. We can find the cure and donate its booty to the whole world. Everyone must know."

"My cure is boarding at the gate. Again, for the last time, adieu."

"Señor, I will pay you one million dollars to accompany me to see this extraordinary woman. Just for a day, that's all I ask of you. A million dollars."

Sannazaro promptly placed his buttocks on the chair.

"Why would you do that?" he said. "Because I can. Because I must. You have no idea how important this is."

It was an absurd offer, but a million dollars for a day was certainly tempting. Had those clouds not poured down upon Cochi, it wouldn't even have been an issue: he would have succeeded in getting out 40 minutes earlier and been on his way to the empire of sanity. He had vowed handsomely to himself that he would forever resist all future floods of the Commander's importunes; that to every new appeal he would turn away indignantly. Now, contrary to such vows, he felt the old suasion grabbing hold of him. Of course, it was probably just the money. But when Marigold again highlighted that little girl's restored use of her arm, why, it was genuinely moving an account, even to one who'd barely survived the Great South and resolved to end his days quietly at home, among familiar flowers and few remaining friends. Not in the clutches of a ludiological expedition. But even that firm, well-thought-out resolve was no match for these fantastic details, and a million bucks.

"Free and clear of all taxes."

"Done."

So that despite his finely conceived letter of farewell, he was again sucked into the liquidy logic of impossible schemes. Perhaps being older than Marigold he felt some patronly sentiment which expressed itself like the end of a rope, trusting to the tensile strength and durability of his own wisdom as the Commander's only chance of getting out of India alive, as if from a dark Platonic cave into which his impetuous middle age had driven him. A cave wherein he had slept for weeks, dreaming of crenelated Camelots in the air. There in the waiting lounge of the Cochi airport, crowded with steaming bodies eager to evacuate the flooded morass, these ironies swept over him.

Or just possibly Sannazaro felt sorry for Murillo Marigold at that moment. After all, who of a stable mind could believe in the miracle the Commander had described, other than the Commander himself? If this credulousness and blurred vision had metastasized to such magnitude, was it not, at the very least, his duty as a friend to see him safely home?

Just then a voice over the loudspeaker system announced the departure of a Jetstream Airways flight to Calicut, and Marigold seized the coincidental opportunity to drive his flock of two to the purchasing counter. Sannazaro was annoyingly won over by this great haste of logistics and enthusiasm. In a moment's flurry the appropriate details of the journey were spelled out. The Commander narrowly managed the acquisition of two boarding passes, for his American Express card, though Platinum, required a phone call for verification purposes. Did he remember his birth date, the maiden name of his mother, his address and phone number?—my God, such details—but all eventually came back to him; and on account of their traveling First Class, for neither Marigold nor the Squire was a consistent ascetic—never claimed to be, Sannazaro particularly worried about thrombosis—the authorities held the plane for them. They ran out onto the tarmac, splashing through puddles, and boarded the craft.

On the plane, the Squire did crossword puzzles—a girl can make this chalice, get ready for war, chemical got from peppermint oil—and listened to *Dil Le Gayee* and *O Meri Munni* to take his mind off the entire subcontinent.

The cowboy/fighter pilots landed fast and hard. These two passengers, who had no baggage, hailed a taxi and took it to the ashram, directions for which the Commander had obtained the previous day.

"Come," he beckoned his Squire, walking up to the Vegetarian Hotel, its painted front side coming off a wall, its portal, windows, wooden panels and aluminum sidings partly caving in. It looked like one of those famous tool sheds inhabited by a century of scrapped hand-me-downs and rusted ironmongery. They checked into a single 275-rupee-per-night room in order to save the seven dollars, a fact of some amusement to Sannazaro who no longer had the energy to continually battle the Commander about his fiduciary inconsistencies. For whenever he questioned such parsimony and asceticism, he got the same in-your-face windload of noble callings, simplicity and prudence. "Was my mother paid to give birth to me?" he always ended up ululating, though Sannazaro had no idea what he meant by that.

Once flimsily established in the facility, which was just down the street from the ashram where they next intended to journey, Marigold looked out the window of their third-story dive and at once witnessed a scene of peculiar frenzy. At some distance, crossing a dried and cracking dustbowl between fields of burnt-out hay pecked over by crow pheasants, peacocks, kites, cattle egrets and black-headed orioles, a vast cattle drive was making mournful progress, the thousands of hooves throwing up dust whose whorls occluded all sides of the horizon. Clearly the rains had not yet struck this area. The animals were moving with difficulty. Anybody could recognize the signs of weakness. Herders beat the bewildered beasts unmercifully, pounding their emaciated spines with long sticks.

The bones seeming to burst through the flayed skin, the bludgeoned hair of a dozen breeds standing on end beyond the gaunt ribcages: all was visible through Marigold's binoculars.

The twosome strode quickly from their room, hopped breezily down a flight of stairs, moving importantly through the hotel lobby and out the doors, and then approached the point of mass movement down the road, inhaling that uniquely Indian morning air, a pustular aroma of must and sod, the taint of excrement which had aerosolized into a virtual sandalwood of rural olfaction. Hundreds of crows cawed in the harsh light that pierced the canopy of pipal trees whose strands of liana descended from the bower above the road, an alley suggesting rusticated charm. In truth, this was merely a suggestion, for the forest was confined only to the sides of the one-and-a-half lane highway. Each tree was painted with a white stripe near its base. Beyond, past the odd laburnum and lantana hedge, to the left, a pair of red-rumped swallows fluttered into the bullion of skylight over the many squatting humans who were doing their morning business. Nearby, dozens of women bejeweled in every color of the mid-crepuscular daylight hours trundled pails, buckets, plastic jugs and ceramic vases under their arms, or atop their lovely long-haired heads, and were gathering to chat at the water pump while young men brought along for the purpose did the work of manipulating the hand mechanism.

"What is happening there?" the Commander asked a man walking along the road.

"Cattle drive," said he.

Suddenly, a herder began smashing his bitter hard cane switch against several of the animals' legs, screaming at them.

"But I thought you all worshipped cows in India," Marigold blurted.

The man looked at him crazily, turned and wandered off. He did not want to see. There was nothing to discuss.

CHAPTER 82
The Tears of Calicut

MARIGOLD CAME CLOSE on to the herders, who spoke not in words but biting curses, and all was haste to get the weary animals—cows, steers, goats, buffaloes and sheep— to their destination. But where? Why at such brutal speeds? More importantly, why the beatings? The Commander ran alongside the herds and at once saw more horror than he had beheld in all his many years on this Earth. The herders clearly wanted the two white men to bug off, and tried to outrun them. The animals were exhausted, their eyes weeping from the chili paste ground into them, their meatless bodies riddled with mange, warts, gaping wounds. Blood streamed down to their hooves, which were peppered with nails pounded into little metal shoes that allegedly enabled them to move faster. Many of the animals were tied by their nostrils and the ropes had gouged holes in their noses where the skin had been ripped. Foam was clouding the air passages and their panting was voluminous. More than a few seemed to be suffocating. The ropes lashed to their necks had tightened. Liquid pus mingling with tears ran in streams from their eyes—the result of malnutrition and growing blindness. All this was further complicated by extreme dehydration. Their tails were bloody and crooked, a clear sign that they had been broken. But why, and how? Their flanks were riddled with maggot-infested wounds, hair scalded, branded, matted, distended, leaving bald tracts of purple bruising where the bones had been struck and so often broken. The cows had had no water, or food, for days. Though oddly, the sheep's stomachs were bulging. Only later would the Commander learn that the animals had had bamboo tubes stuck down their throats and numerous pints of water forced into them so that they'd look fat at market. Animals continually collapsed and would not get up again.

Their bodies had somehow become the bane of the very monsters who apparently depended upon them for their livelihood. But how had such a cruel, mutated dependency arisen? By what heinous evolution within Indian society had brutality become the accepted norm? One writer, V.S. Naipaul, had called India "a wounded civilization". But it seemed to Marigold there was no civilization whatsoever. Only wounds weeping across the landscape of animal hell. Ten whys? Twenty what-fors? Thirty unbearables, all in the first minute.

The herders kicked at the cows, shouting furious expletives, as if something terrible had happened and it was each separate animal's fault. The overwhelmed creatures lay pathetically on their sides, wincing, tearing at the ropes that tightly entrapped them to deflect the repeated beatings, but without hope of any relief. The herders hated them with all their skinny, dark, odious, virulent might. Then, when it was clear the animals were no longer useful to them, the herders abandoned the nearly dead behemoths and continued forward down the road.

All this left an indescribable wrath in the Commander's veins. He tried to communicate with these horrible men, but unsuccessfully. He had no idea what kind of crude and criminal language their ignorance ejaculated.

"We must find out what's going on, and quickly," Marigold pleaded, his Sannazaro listening, and the two men raced back to their hotel to try to secure a translator, only to learn that the herders had come from Tamil- and Kanada-speaking locations, languages unfamiliar to the Malayalam rumor-mongers at the front desk of their hotel. It was hopeless.

Within five minutes the cattle drivers had vanished, leaving a dozen dying animals in their wake.

"So this is the miracle you wanted to show me?" Sannazaro's tone was sardonic.

The Commander, ignoring him, asked if there was a veterinarian anywhere nearby. He was desperate to find a means of putting the animals left on the road out of their misery, though had no complete notion, as yet, how that might be done.

"It is not for us to get involved," affirmed the hotel manager.

"It is their karma to be cows," his assistant added with a typically Indian lard.

"We all must die," declared a young, smartly dressed accountant type, a guest at the Vegetarian Hotel, who clutched a calculator upon which he was working out some mysterious principle regarding the purchase and resale of empty bottles.

"The local people will come and fetch them. That is the way it is done," allowed a fourth voice with the timbre of stern rationality. "You see, there is much poverty in these areas, as in all of India, and people must eat. Don't worry yourself about it. This has been the way for thousands of years and there is something very genuine about it."

"Genuinely what?" the Commander exploded.

"I told you so," Sannazaro decreed.

"You told me nothing," Marigold upbraided.

"What about that fancy theory—how does it work? Any insect, or cow, might be an Indian's reincarnated grandmother?"

But time was not on their side to debate the terrible mismatch of theory and reality, or to analyze this too obvious breakdown in Indian compassion.

Miraculously, a vet—Tariq was his name, a Muslim about 40 years old, casually dressed and perfectly athletic of build, with a tamed moustache and thick crop of black curly hair—did appear. It so happened he had been visiting the ashram for the purpose of obtaining a hug from Sister Love. He always traveled with his full supply kit the way a photojournalist documenting war zones is never without his camera and film, and was cut of an entirely different silk sash from nearly everyone around him. When Marigold pointed out the abuses occurring alongside the road, Tariq was only too familiar with the goings-on. He knew all the ropes of the 'system', as he referred to it, and agreed at once to go with them and see what could be done.

"Mind you, I am not optimistic. The real problem is that nobody around here cares," he lamented. "They always have the same lame excuse—my children are hungry. How can I afford to feed an animal?

Actually, this is the richest, most sophisticated region in the country. Yet one of the worst in terms of animal abuse. What does that tell you?"

The first thing Tariq did, and it was clear would have done whether he'd met Marigold or not, was to administer two grams of Phenlzone paste to those cows known as 'downers', as he put it—the ones that could no longer stand from all the torment they had endured. The medicine would ease their pain. In three cases, he had to euthanize the animals, and this sight put all to tears. Sannazaro could not watch. Mr Marigold suffered horribly, kneeling down and stroking the animals as they vanished from their misery into heaven by the gentle actions of this Tariq fellow.

"You see," the vet described, "we have a *Prevention of Cruelty to Animals Act* which dates back to around 1960—and many other laws pertaining to all the common cruelties. But nobody takes notice. It is, in fact, illegal to kill a cow in this country before the animal's sixteenth year. All of these animals are between three and nine."

"How do you know?" asked the Commander.

"Look at their teeth," said Tariq. He had opened up the mouths of several and pointed out the deep cusps erupting, the canines popping. "Only when these are worn down to half this height have they attained their approximately sixteenth year."

The Commander could not fathom the abdication of laws. He bristled with queries. "What man determined the age of 16? How did such an arbitrary adjudication justify the renunciation of thousands of years of alleged veneration of these most splendid of beings, and by what economic arguments? What parliamentary debates ensued at the time of the legislation? How could there be consensus in the matter of such basic abnegation? Your country's legacy, the rule of love, a history of compassion? I'm flabbergasted."

"I have no idea," Tariq replied, frustrated.

Marigold at that moment uttered out loud a resolution that this unforgivable practice would be stopped on this day. If his money was worth anything, at least he should be able to put a halt to the torment of cows, and he explained his situation and his vow to the veterinarian.

Tariq, as it turned out, was traveling back in his own Jeep to his clinic near one of the tribal areas. His vehicle was occupied by five goats he'd rescued earlier in the day and was relocating to a safe haven.

Marigold hired an Ambassador automobile and a driver who spoke many of the local languages (as did Tariq, who had grown up in the area). The driver was a young fellow in clean pressed trousers, and he smiled compliantly. The vehicle had the requisite round stickers in the lower left of the windshield to indicate a legitimate travel company, but there followed at least another half-hour of paperwork and negotiation, and then gassing up at a busy BP stop. Eventually they got underway.

What transcendentalist distortions and spiritual hocus-pocus had been adopted that people supposedly oriented to the more humble and humane sides of life—the manager, staff and guests of a Vegetarian Hotel—should be capable of so easily overlooking the reality of the cow horror? Was this a general truth about the country, or some ephemeral anomaly? How pervasive were these marches of pain? Their taxi driver feigned ignorance on all fronts, but Tariq was only too ready to show the visitors. In truth, he and his vet tech colleagues had become desperate, even contemplating an end to their mission in India given the unbelievable corruption and societal inertia they confronted at every turn. Yes, there were occasional journalists who seized upon stories with conviction, but what was a cover story today tended tomorrow to be newspaper wrapping around a veal chop.

The Ambassador followed the Jeep.

As always, the Commander looked set to follow this latest mission with an unquestioning inexhaustibility, and Sannazaro was not very happy about it. Another million would not mean much if he got himself killed on a roadside. As they drove towards the northeastern side of Calicut, the Squire repeatedly requested the driver to stop so that he could buy bananas, fried cutlets, Cadbury's chocolates, Darjeeling tea—anything to relieve the burden of that frightful drive, which saw their vehicle slavishly entrapped behind clouds of diesel smoke pouring forth from the lorries.

The pollution was atrocious—probably hundreds of times the World Health Organization maximal limits—and one had to cover all exposed orifices to avoid asphyxiation or burning eyes.

Everywhere, as anyone who has driven these roads well knows, the combination of people and animals and ruts in the road surface constitutes a paralyzing obstacle course of high-speed gymnastics. The driver narrowly missed colliding with dogs, children, motorcyclists, and other trucks which seemed intent upon playing Chicken. The taxi driver explained: "If they smash your side-view mirror with their own, they consider it a victory."

Every truck, painted with its garish pantheon of Hindu gods, spells out the one undying postulate of the roadways—"*Honk your horn!*"—so that these ancient pathways of the bullock cart (which still ply the same routes) have been transmogrified into transportation hells. The trucks race, screaming, in an out-of-control wobble, their horns manufactured to achieve the zenith of volumes. In every passing intersection or village plaza, megaphones broadcast 190-decibel radios, high female voices shrieking their own overtures, a musical version of housewife propaganda, a very far off-Broadway sociology intended evidently to animate the meandering stasis whereby rural India evidences its own unflexing testimony to historic inertia. Garbage upon garbage, the poverty of one generation turning a new leaf only to find an even more dismal disadvantage. With a labyrinth of foraging bovines, emaciated cats, dogs, goats and sheep, enormous pigs competing with crows in the high heaps of rotting cast-offs, children, some naked from the waist down, others in freshly pressed school uniforms and carrying their little totebags, old men and women with canes, disturbed people, begging people, bewildered people squatting, sitting and waiting, three-wheelies racing in and out of bicycle traffic—with all those possibilities for a collision, targets with unpredictable trajectories, the trucks nevertheless plow on, heeding no clue to the inevitable disaster.

Marigold and Sannazaro drove by two of them, head-ons in which trucks had exploded and dozens of people were still standing around taking stock of the death toll, more curious than appalled.

It got dark and the stakes were, if anything, magnified, because now the headlights shone blurred in their faces, thanks to the dust and smoke from tens of thousands of fires along the roadside and across the near country's interior, and from those same barreling lorries with their infernal diesel smoke. One gasped for oxygen, whilst shapes emerged out of the darkness and had to be suddenly avoided. It was better to close one's eyes than attempt to influence or divine the outcome of every near-fatality. Many trucks drove, mysteriously, without headlights.

They reached the far outskirts of Calicut, with its sprawling chaos, infernal by night. They had caught up with the cattle-bearing truck they'd been following, unaware of the actual conditions inside the back of the 40-foot container, which was covered with cloth. But Tariq knew for a fact that the truck was heading to a slaughterhouse. They stayed right on it.

Once at the crumbling factory, the truck disappeared inside a courtyard, but their taxi driver refused to follow it. He parked outside, as did Tariq. Marigold and Sannazaro told him to wait. With Tariq they walked up to the main entrance and surprised a worker who said nothing, unsure how to take the sudden appearance of two white strangers. They kept walking.

"I think this is a bad idea," volunteered the Squire.

"If it is, as they immodestly imagine, the destiny of those cows to be brought to this place of great evil, then I am certain, by an altogether different immodesty, that it is our humble and mortifying destiny to be witnesses," the Commander replied like a fortress of convictions.

"To what end?" asked Tariq. He'd been to such places before, and now very much wanted to know what these two innocents might do or say or show by their responses that could have the slightest impact. Of course, he didn't know who he was dealing with.

"We shall see what we shall see," Marigold stoically applied.

Not a second later, as they drew close, they began to hear the terrible cacophony that would continue throughout the night. A sound with no comparable timbre or meaning: the gigantic groaning of bovines as they watched their fellows slowly slaughtered before their big, all-knowing eyes. A sea of glaring cruelties awash in blood and entrails; all of the Rwandan, Algerian, Albanian, Cambodian and Kurdish massacres consolidated in the hands of 50 rusty-knife-wielding little Hitlers who spat at the terrified animals while they sloppily slit their throats.

Such a scene. The nightmare that would carry for the rest of any natural or unnatural life and condemn all those responsible in the court of heavenly law. The jugulars of blood gushed forth like broken water mains during an earthquake. Monsters hurried about their tasks, killing one bull after another. The animals did not just die, but struggled, howled, fought back despite tied legs, lurched and convulsed for five, ten, even 30 minutes in the blood and guts and excrement of their inexpressibly doomed community of vast, never-ending, never-vindicated tragedy.

Marigold collapsed ...

And there, in his mind's eye, Shakespeare, tormenting his lonely self that could no longer fall back on the slightest immunity,

...subversion of thy harmless life?
Thou never didst them wrong, nor no man wrong:
And as the butcher takes away the calf,
And binds the wretch, and beats it when it strays,
Bearing it to the bloody slaughter-house;
Even so, remorseless, have they borne him hence.
And as the dam runs lowing up and down,

Looking the way her harmless young one went,
And can do nought but wail her darling's loss;
Even so myself bewails good Gloster's case,
With sad unhelpful tears; and with dimm'd eyes
Look after him, and cannot do him good;
So mighty are his vowed enemies.
His fortunes I will weep. [17]

CHAPTER 83
Hell

FAINTED INTO the 20,000-square-foot pool of cow blood and offal that smothered the corroded cement floor beneath the dim 20-watt lights of Hell.

Sannazaro threw up, his heart pounding, then had the presence of mind to lift the Commander from the unspeakable horror at their feet, and to all sides, and somehow with the help of Tariq to remove him from those premises and back into the night, the Commander's arms slung over their shoulders, his legs dragging.

Still they could hear the screams.

"God help mankind," Marigold mumbled as he was ferried back to the taxi. Slaughterers were following the three men now, their messy cutlasses in hand. They were screaming in Malayalam, and both the driver and Tariq knew they'd better be off quickly or they too would end up steak tartare.

As they sped away they saw other lorries heading towards the same slaughterhouse.

"Where are they coming from?" groaned Marigold, regaining sufficient consciousness to question the origins of evil in this world, to attempt in theory to reverse its itinerary and confront the horror at the root of all madness. It was the "all", he reckoned. Because for a man, let alone a young man—half the killers looked to be teenagers—to slay a cow, among the most innocent and enchanting of creatures, required a full-bodied hatred of life, a loathing of self, that defied psychoanalysis. Herein lay The Great Despair which no philosopher or Marigold had ever quite captured. One could not imagine, thought the Commander, that scene of utter hopelessness. His mind flew in all directions as he sat slumped in his existentialism. Beyond pure or practical reason. Neither utilitarianism nor pragmatic ethics was up to the task of an Indian slaughterhouse—of any slaughterhouse anywhere in the world. All the academic debates. Great thinkers. Solemn colloquies. Religious parliaments. Messianic morals. Dulling statistics. Sermons, homilies and declarations. Speeches most grand before all the empirical gatherings. None had e'er so painfully peered into man's true Self, and neither Commander nor Squire nor a Shakespeare would ever be the same for it.

Tariq stared bathetically. There was little he could say. All his attempts to incite a consciousness, an avowal by the authorities for the laws already memorialized, had disappeared into the vaporous mists of paperwork and the adamant denials of those charged with enforcement. Local powermongers raped tribal girls, controlled every forest and district ranger, owned the police, poached with impunity, appropriated national park properties for their own private hunting preserves, and profiteered in the tens of millions of rupees on the slaughter of animals illegally transported and killed. Everyone was on the take. Everyone was owned, from the petty border guard to the head commissioners in Chennai and Delhi. All according to three irrefutable claims: poverty, hunger, survival. How many desperate years and nights had Tariq struggled with this curse upon the country, this inexorable hideous contagion of countrymen who thought nothing about the torture and killing? It was a reciprocal promise: violence by humans to animals and to themselves.

Through the mace and disgorge of night, along that insane eastern Nadgani route to Yedakera, on which was encountered an endless procession of cow- and steer-loading and -unloading trucks, they stopped repeatedly at guard crossings, gleaned direct evidence of 2,500-rupee bribes to countless middlemen by the truck drivers, and saw—within the manner of a few sleepless hours—the full implacability of a system formulated around the thorough conversion of cows into meat and leather.

But it only got worse. "At least"—in grotesquely inadequate quotation marks—the ones who "made it" to the slaughterhouse would die there. They were the lucky ones, though their deaths were endless, the duration of their agony a drastic variable. But out here on the roads, scores of calves and bulls and old, washed-up milk cows were tied together in dark hundred-fold huddles awaiting the trucks that would pick them up, then dump them off again at one auction ground or another. Between auctions they would be driven onwards, in detestably cramped quarters, or moved by hoof, as Marigold had witnessed near the ashram, beaten, beaten and beaten again. In all, explained Tariq, tens of thousands of animals were being moved each night, usually after midnight, when few if any locals would see what was actually going on.

They stopped with one group of the huddled masses, a crying, panting, suffocating collective. Some were as young as two, said Tariq. Their heads were lashed together. The blood and maggots and broken limbs and torn ligaments were profuse. The vet administered medicines to nearly all of them, for they were physical ruins, the end losers, amalgamations of all of India's centuries-old dolor. They were waiting, only, to be put out of their misery; wondering when, by what means, it would occur.

A truck suddenly arrived, and three shrieking men with hard teakwood canes began their work of unloading more cattle. These 1,000-pound gentle giants were tossed like luggage onto the road, some landing on their backs or upon one another. Thirty-five bulls in one truck, at least a dozen of them crushed by the weight of others who had been thrown atop the smaller animals during the three-hour journey from a place called Gundlepet where, according to Tariq, they had been auctioned off that morning. Some went to Yedakera direct; others were marched to halfway points. Others went to Sultan Batheri, or Manjeri, or, ultimately, to Calicut. Of course, there were probably a million family-run slaughter operations in the whole country. Children were often employed in the killing. Even five-year-olds who would first be given the task of blood collection, and later the knives.

There was the name, the answer to his tears: "We must go to this Gundlepet," Marigold intoned. "But first, we must stop this."

"You can't," said Tariq. "It would take a minimum of six months or a year of constant work with the locals, a team of a dozen of us. We don't have the manpower or the funds."

"Now you have the funds," Marigold decreed, straightening his back.

Suddenly, one of the herders at the rear of the truck began beating a recalcitrant bull to the point of death. Tariq shouted at him in Kanada but the man refused to stop. Now Marigold entered the fray and they came to fisticuffs. Sannazaro grabbed hold of the cane and started beating the herder. Two others leaped into the squabble from the front of the truck, until there was a standoff. Tariq, ever the diplomat, made peace between them, and Marigold had him translate his wish to buy each and every animal on that truck. At first, the driver would not hear of it, insisting that he had a contract to meet, that there were hotels in Cochi expecting the meat within two days. But when Marigold doubled, then tripled the price, the driver—counting out his own take in the process—was struck palpably by the windfall. His imagination was transparent as he did the arithmetic and finally agreed.

"How far are we from your clinic?" Marigold asked Tariq, who was thrilled but dubious about the prospect of buying every cow in India. Only a computer moghul had such resources, and this Marigold did not look like a computer moghul, but tonight he was not about to quibble.

They paid for the truck and had all the animals driven the 50 or so miles through the Kerala border crossing, where the drivers had already come; they took more money from Marigold to pay another tariff, then passed through the nearby national park, a terrible misnomer as Marigold would learn soon enough.

At four in the morning they reached Tariq's little clinic. Its white doors were wide open. Somebody had broken in: papers had been ransacked, drawers and shelves destroyed.

The many bulls were unloaded delicately. Tariq knew exactly how to cut their ropes and give them their freedom. Many fell to the ground, incredulous. Never in their lives had they been free of ropes. Their eyes wept. Those that could move at once set about licking each other, and the groaning was audible throughout the night air.

The goats, too, were placed in an adjoining yard to the rear, given blankets and bottles of warm milk. In another hour, the rising sun would warm all of them.

Then Tariq stood silently, looking for clues.

"I will rebuild you a much larger clinic. Have faith, young man," Marigold applied.

"This is not the first time," his gentle friend replied.

They set about cleaning up, sweeping the glass of shattered vials, picking through the debris for any antibiotics that might be salvaged. Tariq then made the visitors tea and they discussed tactics. There was no way, said the exhausted Muslim, that one could purchase all 115 million cows at between 1,000 and 10,000 rupees per cow. Marigold sampled an average, at 5,000 rupees, or at the black market rate (the one acceptable manipulation of Indian currency, he reckoned—poetic justice) of approximately 100 dollars per animal. Add all the goats, sheep and chickens in India, and Mr Marigold was looking at a zero balance sheet, as Sannazaro pointed out. Which meant no land to keep them; no fodder with which to feed them. A massive starvation. But the economics were more ridiculous than that, of course.

"Eighty percent of India is rural," Tariq explained. "People eat and drink their animals; they use their wastes for fuel and housing and fertilizer. You can't be so blind as to believe you could buy that which gives the human population its life?"

"And why not?"

He sighed. Then: "I have spent 20 years spaying and neutering dogs, cats and donkeys in the 12 neighboring tribal villages; have tried to manage outbreaks of mange, have given free veterinary care, administered vaccines for rabies, and tried to work the politically insidious system. Just maybe, I always believed, I might be able to convert some of the wardens and policemen into whistle-blowers. After all, everything you two have witnessed this night is illegal. If the police would only acknowledge, for example, *Article 51A* of India's *Constitution*. There you have a very straightforward maxim, long codified, that makes it the fundamental duty of every citizen to show kindness and compassion to animals and to take an active involvement in the prevention of cruelty to them. Hindu or Muslim, it doesn't matter. Moreover, the police were doubly entrusted with this responsibility, as outlined in the *Indian Penal Code 1860*, Sections 428 and 429, and, in terms of the local state situation, according to the very specific dictates of the *Tamil Nadu Animal and Bird Sacrifices Prohibition Act of 1950*."

"You seem to have the legal brief. Can't you drive home the message? What is the problem?"

Tariq shook his head. He had obviously been through this with strangers to the system before. Who could fathom the complexity of India's corruption? "Even if the police would work with me," said he, "as well as the Nilgiri Trust for Preventing Harm to Animals, the Collector of the Nilgiris, the SPCAs, the merchants, truck drivers, operators, farmers, wardens, forest employees, advocates and other veterinarians—if all of them could come together, which I believe would never happen in India, you would still have the added problem of how to control the foraging of the animals to prevent their destroying biodiversity."

"Put them on one gigantic animal farm, say—what?—a million acres?"

"Three hundred animals per acre? I don't think so," Tariq exclaimed. "You've obviously never lived on a farm, or with farm animals. Possibly 10 million acres would do it. But for those 10 million, you'd need another 10 million of grass-growing land. That's 20 million acres that does not exist in India. Your money is not going to solve the problem that way."

"Then what do you suggest?" an exasperated, brokenhearted Commander asked.

"As I said earlier. You cannot change the way Indians eat, or not overnight. But with tenderness and a huge infusion of rupees you just might be able to change their thinking, at least for a few years. And certainly that of the children. A western scientist working for some humane society produced a video of one of the slaughterhouses, and children in a school in Bangalore were roused to action by it. They've become ardent vegetarians and have vowed to volunteer their lives on behalf of animals. It was a spectacular revelation. That's where we must begin. Don't throw your money at impossible odds."

Sunrise saw the rescued cattle munching happily, untethered in the paradise-like confines of Tariq's clinic. But, as he explained, there was a practical finitude to his ability to accommodate too many more animals.

Marigold asked about neighboring properties. "Those 10,000 acres, for example. Might they be for sale?"

He then suggested they make for Gundlepet. He wanted to see the auction for himself.

Marigold, Sannazaro and Tariq headed off through Bandipur National Park in Karnataka State, passing countless gray langurs begging on the sides of the road, babies clinging to the mothers' undersides, three species of deer grazing in the misty clearings of early morning, male and female peacocks foraging in the middle of the single-laned road which had been burned on either side to extend the fire buffer, and dozens of bird species flitting about.

The town of Gundlepet announced itself well in advance as they passed hundreds of cattle marching to the selling grounds. These cows looked much better, and many of the bulls' horns were painted red or yellow or blue, even decorated. They seemed healthier, fatter. But this was a ruse, explained Tariq, like the preparations at a death camp prior to a visit by representatives of Amnesty International or the Red Cross. The idea, of course, was to make the animals appear healthy, and thus obtain the highest offers for them. Once sold, the cows were nothing but meat.

They parked along the fringes of the auction area, where thousands of cows, goats and sheep were being traded, wads of rupees passing back and forth between greedy fingers, fights erupting in angry nests of buyers and sellers, and trucks backing up to receive their 'commodities' which—in the case of goats and sheep—were thrown into the backs of the vehicles by gaowalas standing in a relay line. Mr Marigold and his two companions wandered through the melee of traders, catching all the seismic nuances of affliction that spread like a giant pool of blood, a tapestry of open canker sores, across that four-acre demon field scattered with pipal trees and crows who would drop down to feed on the abundant feces. In plain view of all the animals were the butchers—men and women, together with their scores of children—chopping meat, chopping off heads, which lay about their tent encampments like premonitory decor, lavish decrepitude, a scene reminiscent of the Belgian police camps in the Congo during the reign of Leopold, when human heads were placed ornamentally, according to at least two eyewitnesses, one of whom was Joseph Conrad writing in his *Heart of Darkness*.

The Commander, with his rudimentary command, asked the price from cluster to cluster by way of an introduction—Kitnai rupee?—and got the various ranges for the different breeds: those on their last legs, 1,000; those standing tall and beefed up, 10,000. None of the cows would have known, for certain, what lay in store for them that very evening. The goats, however, seemed to understand. They cried nonstop, could smell and see fallen cousins. There could be no doubt as to their mental anguish, thought Marigold.

But once the sales were transacted, and evening drawn long and dolorously upon the grassy clearings, whether cow, sheep, goat, or buffalo, there could be no more guesswork: the full assault had begun. It was the beginning of the death march for them, their reward for a quarter their natural lifetime of servitude. The cows had pulled bullock carts across fields, over endless roads, through teeming, polluted city streets, malignant tumors etched into their burdened necks rubbed raw by the heavy bars of the hauling carts. They had endured every weather, heat, monsoon, fly swarm, beating, poison; and for those milkless cows that had been abandoned to wander the city, had received acid thrown into their eyes when they dared take a lick of some old cabbage, apple or nibble on a cracker at a vending stall.

The cows to be auctioned stood in the direct heat, their nostrils tied down, not one bucket of water anywhere to be seen, though directly opposite the panting creatures a herder sat leaning against his whipping cane sucking on an orange popsicle. It was deliberate cruelty, of this the Commander had no doubt.

Marigold hauled himself into the back of a goat-bearing truck and groveled round beside each animal, communing there and demanding a price from the astonished traders to pre-ordain his interest as a possible, albeit bizarre buyer. He made his way on all fours through the feces and urine, for the animals were terrified to be crowded in the trucks, to have been thrown by their legs, wounded in both spirit and ligament, and now stared into Marigold's equally terrified eyes and shared all the grief which life forces in communion come to know under the duress of the end of the world. Tears flowed from all sides. Outside, baby goats and sheep were braying miserably. They knew, all right. At that moment, had Marigold possessed a machine-gun, he would surely have sprayed every person in the auction area, he told Sannazaro.

"Would that have included yourself?" replied the Squire.

"I am no longer a person," said Marigold.

"What, then?"

"An animal. An open wound. May I never see another human face. Speak a human word. May God grant that this whole planet be emptied of *Homo sapiens*, emptied for ever more. I shall gladly give myself up, turn to vapor, whatever it takes to stop what is happening to these animals."

He sat against a tree, holding a lamb, too angry and numb for any more tears.

In those eyes the fears that glisten as in pity for my pain
... on my lips the breath is fleeting—can it, will it long remain? [18]

CHAPTER 84
The Temporary Transmigration of Mr Marigold's Soul

THE DAY GATHERED in darkening layers of Hell for the animals, and for the three men who followed a group of particularly distressed buffalo. Thirty-eight of them dragged up a ramp and tethered into a dark, airless, 105-degree swarm of flies and excrement 40 feet by 12 feet: a truck adorned with all the useless Ganeshes and Sivas that some remote artisan had seen fit to doodle onto it.

The buffaloes were beaten to induce them to move, clubbed against their legs, upon their backs, red chilies ground into their blistering eyes, cattle prods jammed up their anuses. All to the sound of embittered barbs, half-caught by Marigold who could barely keep himself from killing someone—"Rodu kanakaye jelenge ... gardi me jaenge arke ... Kitar? Terk nambe? Nanjin kur ... Kerala chelege ... Calicut" and so on—hour after hour, a linguistic, bone-crunching, heaven-defying surreality charged with every torment known to the animal kingdom. And the perpetrators? Indian men, with children and mothers; Indians who had allegedly grown up in the cooling balms of Mahatma Gandhi, the shade trees of Lords Mahavira and Buddha, the luscious legacies of the *Vishnu Parana* with its beguiling injunctions to be kind to all living things, and, most recently, with Mother Teresa whose death had competed favorably in Indian media with the funeral of Princess Diana and the latest Sky-broadcast soccer match. It was a toss-up between the three for headlines.

Where had all the saints gone? Where had they gone wrong in their inability to disseminate so simple an incantation—compassion? How could these cow-killing bastards have so emphatically ignored all that India was supposed to stand for in a world that still aspired to at least a meager hope of poetry, love, kindness?

For Marigold, to witness this utter bankruptcy of the slightest virtue, of chivalry, of the most basic humanity, argued for nothing less than the rapid extinction of all people, or of all cows, whichever could come first in his personal quest to alleviate the unbearable torture now paramount in his universe. India was even worse than he had anticipated. Of course, these were knee-jerk reactions: in truth, he wished no ill to any man, only that they should be enlightened to the degree that they cease all harm to others. But how to accomplish it in a country of 900 million meat-eaters, 115 million cows, tens of millions of sheep, 60 million goats, for starters? Compounded by fast-disappearing grasslands, forest cover down to a few measly percent, nutrient-depleted soil laced with Green Revolution inorganic fertilizers that had poisoned the little remaining fresh water? It was a wasteland.

They followed this one particular truck with an idea of beginning somewhere. Once the lorry moved out in darkness it would dump the animals along the Tamil Nadu/Kerala border crossing. There, the customary bribe would be paid, the cows tied down in some narrow dark fringe of the canyon road, and, with sunlight, moved out towards the slaughterhouse 40, 60, even 200 miles away. The overland journey would take a few days. During that time the cows would get neither water nor food. It didn't matter any more, as far as the herders were concerned. Their job now was simply to deliver as many animals as could move. Their bosses had already calculated for downers, factoring into the economics of the truck haul, versus the overland, rupees and paisas down to every steak, which would be consumed, largely, by India's 175 million middle class, or shipped to the Middle East. Never mind the fact that according to Islamic law the meat had to be 'pure', hallal, which it was not, explained Tariq. Many of the leather by-products of these illegal tribulations would be exported to Europe, along with 60 percent of India's grain. The whole wretched scenario stank. This was an economic ferris wheel of cozy, seemingly unchangeable habits of consumption buttressed by a society which had convinced itself of the rules of the game: pleasure, profit, dietary self-destruction, and the total subversion of all ungulates. When the lorry was well out of town, past the dark, candle-lit Lakshmi temple built by the local Maharajato, the Goddess of Good Fortune 753 years before, Marigold got it into his head to document the conditions. Perhaps, via the Internet and international censure, it might be possible to bring pressure to bear on the Indian Government. Tariq was sceptical but willing to try anything.

The truck stopped in the blaring village of Masinagudi. It was early evening and the drivers were taking a tea break at a roadside stall. Marigold and Tariq climbed onto the back of the vehicle. Holding onto the wooden planks and dangling ropes, the Commander began photographing, using the flash on the borrowed camera to record the conditions inside. This time he would not mangle the ASA or F-stops. He'd learned his lesson in the Fiordlands.

Cows had crushed other cows. Limbs had been broken through the rough action of the animals having been dragged up the truck ramp. One 1,200-pound bull was standing on the ruptured belly of a smaller cow, which was still alive though its intestines were exposed and it was hemorrhaging. Others lay crooked and distended, legs propped into the reverse positions in which they had been thrown by the fast coursing of the vehicle. At least a third of the animals were down.

Suddenly Marigold and Tariq heard two doors slam—and the truck roared off. There was shouting. The driver had been alerted that strangers were on the back of the vehicle. They should not have been surprised by his reaction, which was murderous: he accelerated and began deliberately to swerve on the already circuitous highway. To their right was a deep ravine, to the left crumbling canyon wall. Oncoming lorries flashed their lights, whilst the Commander and Tariq struggled to hang on. They were dangling from the ropes, Tariq having thrown his bulk around the frail sides of his venerable companion for the simple reason that death seemed imminent. Marigold was not likely to remain dangling for more than another few seconds. It was simply impossible to hold on.

"Drop the camera!" Tariq cried. "Use both hands."

Marigold, frozen, said nothing, but he was not about to lose the evidence of those dozen or so pictures he had obtained.

They were probably traveling at 45 miles an hour, tunneling through the mountain. Tariq held his older companion. But his own hands were slipping. Coming around a blind corner, the driver swerved to avoid hitting a group of about 100 cows shackled alongside the road, awaiting some other lorry to pick them up. In narrowly missing a massive collision, the truck skidded sideways, swiped the painted edges of a neem grove, twisted, verging on a topple, then buckled back into the road and lurched to a halt, just as both Marigold and Tariq fell the six feet off the back.

Whiplash. Sheered skin. Crumpled limbs.

Marigold landed upon his head aboard a downed cow, Tariq on his feet to the side. The camera remained undamaged, but Marigold's head took a heavy hit and his neck was catapulted inches out of shape. The cow was thrown violently to one side, within the short latitude of its tether. Marigold, staring at it eye to eye, passed out.

The addled driver now revved his vehicle. The tires were in mud, and squealed and smoked under the strain. He tried to back up, but the truck would not move.

The vet collected himself and approached the driver. He was screaming in the native language, and brandishing a huge syringe which he had pulled from his vest.

At the sight of this demonic implement, the driver and his assistant fled into the forest.

Now Tariq took stock of their situation. Marigold was out cold. Tariq knelt down, applying all his medical skills to reviving him, but nothing worked. His breathing was irregular, his heart slowed down to half what it should have been. Tariq administered mouth-to-mouth, poured some water on Marigold's face, checked for abrasions or breaks, but could decipher no obvious hemorrhaging, only a serious bump on the head.

As far as the Commander was concerned, there appeared to be taking place all around him a kind of group cow mind. Some strange psychic interaction with he who lay among them, twisted and involved with the multitudinous injuries which were one and the same. A hundred cow eyes, and Marigold's, together resonated in the dark night of their respective transmigratory souls, collectively engaged in a commiseration that rhymed, winced and prayed.

Boeufs allant au labour... in their eyes and cries, the terror seizing them, despite all those bankrupt fables of Swiss chocolates, moo cows, religious and artistic pastures of happy communion. These *Bos primigenius taurie* were fully attuned to the soil and its link to the stars. Whether Brahman or Jersey, Aberdeen Angus or wild Indonesian buffalo, all were descended from those glorious free creatures depicted on the walls of Lascaux, rushing into Marigold's sagging sagacity, just as they were usurped by human history, the last wild ones destroyed in Poland in the 1620s.

It was during this eerie, silent séance—Tariq attempting to flag down any oncoming vehicles—that a word came to Marigold in his transmigratory state: *Amunawdr*, a word from the hearts of the beaten cattle waiting to die; a vision of some other time and place, a hope for deliverance. During those brief comatose minutes, Mr Marigold entered the minds of the cows, and saw written in blood and in flesh the full miracle of what it was to be a cow, and the unspeakable tragedy of their domination by this furious carnivorous stick-figure of a species.

Suddenly Sannazaro appeared in Tariq's Jeep. He was driving it himself, chanting the one and only mantra of any usefulness—"Left, stay left"—and as he slowed to a halt, Mr Marigold regained some consciousness, which was actually quite a lot by his normal standards. He remained foetally slumped upon the cow, however, not wishing to get up, but rather to feel the continuing power of the connection, for it seemed to him that he had slept 100 years in that ragged corner of cow flesh, cow panting, cow breath, cow smells, cow hell, cow passion. Had become a cow himself and did not look forward to returning to his human incarnation.

There was something more: a bovine's window, as it were, on that separate reality of cow existence, wherein the evolutionary end of the genetic line, whether cow, wild yak or buffalo, seemed to be focused on the same teleological conclusion—what Aristotle must have meant when he spoke of *eudemonia*, the natural outcome of a meaningful and happy life, a place that was indeed somewhere, rather than nowhere. If one could even imagine it, said David Hume in his *Treatise on Human Rights*, it must exist. *Amunawdr*. But what, where was it? All the cows spoke of it, emanated psychic attributes but no coordinates. How extraordinary that Sister Love would have urged Marigold to Gundlepet in the first place.

What was it to be a cow? Sunny pastures. Quiet mountainsides. Soft lounging, perpetual sustenance. They spoke the language of love, in no less a manner than the Sister; gave every birthright to their young, their neighbors, their endless stream of communing colleagues. These cows left no one out. There was never a stranger or alien among cows; no orphans. Their bodies embraced it all, connected directly with the source of all plant life. In the wild, they lived for three decades. Among men, a few years of torment, that was all.

This night, the Commander tasted their mythology, sharing tears, absorbing their terror. It nearly killed him. It broke his heart. Enlightenment that was nearly too late.

Tariq and Sannazaro, meanwhile, proceeded to ascertain that Marigold was not seriously injured. Only his neck would require some tender massage work, as well as a few stitches on his arm and some topical polymyxin B sulfate lidocaine cream applied to the wound on his forehead. His shawl, the one given him by Sister Love, was rather worse for wear: sheep blood, cow foam and goat feces shat in terror covered the precious garment. But otherwise, the Commander would live.

Tariq deliberated. Should he drive the fully loaded truck to the police station, thus presenting the evidence needed to convict the owners of the lorry? By law, no more than nine cows were meant to be transported in this size vehicle. Photographs might or might not be sufficient for evidentiary purposes. On the other hand, to press charges in that manner might be to condemn the cows.

Yet again ...

So with the help of Sannazaro, what he did was cut all the ropes binding the cows and liberate them, causing them to hear for the first time human words gently spoken, touches lovingly conveyed. Those needing medical care he thoroughly attended to. Using a large flashlight, and the headlights of the Jeep, he managed to direct each and every cow towards the river portion of the ravine where the blue eucalypts were thick and the under-canopy afforded good browsing and a degree of necessary stealth. Their destiny was uncertain, of course. But at least, for a time, they would be allowed a taste of that portion of the creation which should have been entirely theirs to begin with. This was the best of a dreadful situation. Unless they could become wild, avoiding people, their freedom would not be sustained for long, not in India.

As for the animals still stranded inside the truck, Tariq had decided to safely shepherd them as crucial evidence: a citizen's rescue, provided for under India's *Penal Code*. According to the *Prevention of Cruelty to Animals Act* he knew that, as a private person, he could intervene to "stop the cruelty", and that would imply the "citizen's arrest", including confiscation of the owner's vehicle and of the animals in no different a manner than if he were to rescue someone's child from a murderous parent. Under Article 51A he could press charges according to any number of his own direct observations of illegal activity, all expressly outlined by the Nilgiri Trust for Preventing Harm to Animals. These included all those malevolent physical acts they had witnessed throughout the day: the kicking, beating and overcrowding; the proliferation of inflictions; chains cutting into flesh; intentionally short cords restricting any measure of exercise; ropes tied to the animals' necks, hooves and nostrils; the evident starvation; the absence of medical attention; the sadistic pleasure shown by the owners, drivers, traders, middlemen and herders in mutilating the animals; the lack of any water or food; the way the animals were dragged into and thrown off the trucks, broken limbs, torn tendons and ruptured internal organs. And the resulting downed animals themselves.

All led to the abysmal transport conditions, and finally to the slaughter itself, with no provisions for first stunning or anesthetizing the animals; the abominable means by which children and others cut the animals' throats, allowing them to die slowly, to slice off legs, smash the animals with hammers, squirt acid in their faces, rub chilies in their eyes. All that and more.

So Tariq drove the lorry to the nearest Forest Service station where he could file a report and present the evidence. He then intended to continue with the animals to his clinic and there release them next door. Marigold, with poultices on his forehead and neck and right wrist, lay in the back of the Jeep driven by Sannazaro. The Commander had agreed to pay the neighbor for the browsing space. They'd work it out. The cows would go free.

Upon reaching the authorities, however, they were in for a very rude *uswakjan*, as the Goths, prior to the 12th century called it. Vomit rather than perfume; a shotgun in the face as opposed to a love letter, delivered in a bouquet of black roses.

"So much for all your brotherly and sisterly love," chimed Sannazaro.

"You might have witnessed the restoring of a little girl's arm in the atmospheric incense and vaporous bedlam of an ashram, but what about this?"

CHAPTER 85
The Makhna's Despair and the Shame of an Entire Nation

IN THE DARKNESS of a winding single-lane road, Tariq had slowed to a stop and Sannazaro come to rest as well. Tariq wanted to forewarn his two friends of the delicacy of dealing with the police. The headquarters, adjoining the Forest Station, was a mile away.

"It's not just cows that are doomed," he said. "It's any measure of justice in this country that is also fated to disappear. You don't even look these wardens in the eye or they'll arrest you. It's important you understand who we're dealing with before we enter their zone." He then went on to describe the recent debacle at the nearby National Park; how, the previous summer, a particular female elephant (Makhna) he had subsequently come to devote much of his life to had been dragged into the forest camp by five mahoots ("elephant tormentors" in the local parlance) riding their own kumki (elephants that had already been subverted to the perverse will of the mahoots) and dozens of game and forest wardens running alongside with rifles.

They had repeatedly and clumsily tranquilized the 40-year-old, 8,000-pound elephant, and when the hapless makhna woke up, she found herself bound by an inextricable mesh of fiercely cloven wires and barbed chains which cut into her throat and legs. The animal panicked and—as a video documenting the capture by the Forest Department revealed—could not stand up, despite repeated torture. One group was pulling her chained rear legs, another her forelegs, so that the poor creature was splayed, thrown, toppled, then gored by the kumki.

The video clearly showed the kumki massaging the makhna with their trunks, but upon the biting orders of the mahoots they would thrust a tusk into an eye, or gouge out an enormous hole in the makhna's throat. This they did from reflex, for they too had been caught in the wild, then tortured. That and starvation were the techniques used by many of India's Forest Department staff, game wardens and veterinarians to subdue the wildness in an Asian elephant.

Marigold had heard there were fewer than 5,000 wild Asian elephants left in India. But he did not know that this particular region was their final rampart, their last stand. The animals themselves, explained Tariq, knew that their days were numbered, and would frequently stare across open jungle, past several thousand years of history, and see their modernized cousins who had been captured and shackled, made to perform in roadside circuses or spend the remainder of their sorrowful years lifting logs, chained, confined during the day and the night to damp sheds with not even enough space to turn round. Their feet condemned to rot, their diet attenuated so that many of them lost a third or half their natural weight.

With India's runaway human population explosion, little habitat remained for elephants, and even less food or potable water. If the human demographic winter had usurped most space for cows, it had absolutely condemned elephants. The inevitability of their demise was written all over the forests. But the greatest tragedy of all was the fact that elephants had bigger brains than humans, and hugely softer hearts. They buried their dead, performed rituals, and like the cows were in touch with a depth of joy, a passion that was beyond human range. Tariq, who grew up around them, had sensed something of their special gifts. Moreover, he said, the elephants knew in no uncertain terms what was happening to their kind.

"They are called 'rogues' by authorities. In other words, to be 'wild' in this country is to be a criminal," he illuminated.

Eventually, said Tariq, the makhna was forced up by the tusks of the kumkis, as if on a razor-sharp hydraulic lift. Still bewildered by the tranquilizer, terrified and bleeding profusely, she was dragged 25 miles over a period of eight days from the tea plantations in the mountains above, where it was alleged she had killed 22 people who had tried to stop her from foraging in their gardens. Because the chains contained barbs on them, and were laced with wire, and tightened to the point of cutting off circulation in the makhna's legs, by the time the wasted creature was hauled into the Elephant Camp at the National Park, her injuries should, by most accounts, have killed her. Apologists within India insisted the authorities had every right to shoot the animal dead on sight, but instead, applied a "relatively merciful alternative" in order to rehabilitate the beast and allow it to join the many other chained-for-life wild elephants which did ritual pujas, ringing stupid little bells in their trunks for fat idiotic tourists, and posing for a plunder of photographs once a day.

The makhna had been confined in her fungus-infested kraal for many months, despite the warnings of a scientist from the US who managed to secure time to examine the poor animal. His report, widely circulated to the international animal rights community but ignored by Indian officials, described the elephant's hideous and improperly treated wounds in minute detail. His conclusion, backed up by Tariq, was that it was one of the worst cases of sustained animal cruelty ever documented, anywhere. The so-called "treatment" was derisory. Indian vets routinely stuck their ungloved, unsterilized fingers into the wounds, as if to deliberately taunt the doomed being. The Penicillin G so sporadically administered covered only a very narrow range of disease vectors. While some of the wounds had begun to heal, the general state of the elephant was disastrous, and had Tariq and his colleagues not wrung from her keepers permission to visit her every day, hand-feeding her nutritious foods and initiating antibiotic therapy, the makhna would surely have died.

The veterinarian had spent months nurturing the elephant and it had been one of his missions to free her. But now the forest staff seemed, at least in his mind, intent upon wreaking vengeance on her. They wanted to make the pain escalate hour by hour; to kill her slowly.

Tariq had fallen in love with the makhna, and she with Tariq. She even grew to recognize the sound of his Jeep as it came into the Elephant Camp each morning. These were her moments of hope, her respite from the hatred surrounding her. Then, one day, Tariq was informed that his services were no longer needed, that the Forest Department had the situation well in hand.

The veterinarian told the Commander and Sannazaro his unsettling story as they sat in the lorry. Then it was time to set off again. Tariq drove the truck with its load of suffering cows, Marigold sat beside him, and Sannazaro trailed behind in the Jeep.

Presently, both vehicles pulled to a stop beside the warden's house.

From afar came a forlorn trumpet blast. "What's that noise?" Marigold asked. "Jesus!" Tariq exclaimed.

It was the middle of the night, and the makhna was again being punished for some 'crime' or other—for too much obstinate wildness in her still. It was pure chance that her dear friend and his two world-weary passengers had shown up at this horrible instant. Thinking quickly, Tariq grabbed the tape recorder he always kept in his Jeep, checked the batteries, installed a new cassette and pushed the quiet little button.

"This way," Tariq whispered, racing up to the kraals where the elephants were kept.

What was recorded, and what they were condemned to seeing, they would never be able to banish from their thoughts. During the next 45 minutes two mahouts were busy 'training' the makhna by beating her legs with painful implements. The strikes were usually to the unhealed wounded areas that were still rank with pus, and left the desperate creature only one option, which was to lean against her kraal and cry out in agony again and again and again and again.

Every impulse in Tariq weighed in favor of decking the two mahouts, which he could easily have done. But he was also terribly torn. Without the evidence, nobody would ever know.

"I have to believe that the evil seeds are outnumbered by good Samaritans, both in and outside the Government of India," he cried, more by way of a pleading than any rational assertion. Certainly there was no evidence supporting his hopes.

But did he dare look the makhna in the eyes, which searched frantically to connect with his own? Was it better to turn his back? How much spiritual channeling could he convey to the elephant? Could the makhna understand? Or was this the ultimate cruelty—to love her, but stand by and do nothing? Tariq was paralyzed with uncertainty. How could the elephant understand his strategy?

Hidden from the mahouts, Marigold and Sannazaro stood by silently, raging inside.

"What if she dies?" the Commander whispered.

"She won't, not with me here," Tariq said. "It's horrible, but we absolutely must secure evidence of the torture."

As the secret tape recording later revealed, the makhna was struck nearly 400 times in just eleven minutes across her four legs, all in an insane effort to force her to lie down. That way, Tariq explained, the maniacs responsible could show their superior forest officers that they had heroically 'trained' the elephant and it was thus ready to be shackled outside its tiny 16-by-16-foot kraal and made to perform tricks, like King Kong, for the eco-tourist trade at the National Park.

The beatings escalated. Such anguish, coming just after the rash of calamities and tortures witnessed throughout the previous day and night, and across a region which Indian tourist brochures claimed to be one of the great natural wonders of the subcontinent—proof of India's remarkable biodiversity, her dedication to preserving the environment, her love of nature—served to push Marigold over the edge of himself.

That one word which he had imagined to have been uttered by the cows when he was thrown from the lorry—namely, *Amunawdr*, emerged again, but this time he sensed that it was emanating from the makhna herself.

Now the assaulted elephant uttered a new, even more strident howl, something Tariq had never heard, some deeper level of expressed agony.

"Oh my God," Tariq cried, unable to cope.

His beloved elephant was drowning in pain. And now other elephants in kraals throughout the encampment were crying out for their sister whose eyes, both Marigold and Tariq realized, were weeping. Sannazaro was weeping as well, too choked up to utter even a word, his body stiffened with the shame of being human beside so glorious, so maligned, so recognizably noble and sensitive a creature as an elephant. If only the world were inhabited by just elephants and cows and flowers, and Muslim saints like Tariq, he thought.

The veterinarian knew that violence would only get them all arrested, or killed. Besides, he was not out for vengeance. This region of southern India was too small a place for basic instincts. He had no desire to shame the authorities, for that technique—at least in India—might well backfire. He wanted only the liberation of the elephant. Of all the elephants.

But the billionaire hermit of Tesuque had no patience for strategy or tact. He knew only the torture before him. Sannazaro saw it coming. The Commander, screaming even louder than the mahouts, who had cursed the elephant each and every time they struck it with their sticks, seized the larger of the two men by the chest, ripped the whipping stick from his hand, and began beating him over the head with it.

"See how you like that, you sonofabitch!" Now the other mahout, astonished at this impertinence, called the guards who were in a shack down the greasy slope from the kraal, smoking cigarettes and flirting with tribal girls. But by the time these guards arrived, the accident had already occurred. The smaller mahoot, attempting to wrest the stick from Marigold, had slipped on elephant feces, fallen beneath one of the now hemorrhaging forelegs and been trampled by the crippled beast.

He appeared to have died. But then he started screaming, and before the makhna could step on his head, Tariq and the other mahoot dragged him away from further harm, an action witnessed by the arriving guards.

The mahoot was taken to a local doctor with a crushed right ankle. But he was lucky: elephant discharges, pus, excrement and vomit had served to cushion the mahoot's flattened bones. Some day he would walk again.

"She understood," Tariq uttered. "She told me so."

"Of course she did," Marigold added.

As for any charges, there were no witnesses to any crime. That's how it was left. And as far as lodging a complaint about the illegal transport of cattle, there was no point in doing so now—not now, not this night. So Tariq efficiently escorted the Commander—who had somehow badly broken a tooth in the scuffle—to the lorry, while Sannazaro returned to the Jeep and slowly followed Tariq and the cows to his clinic.

The bovines had obtained their eternal reprieve, but Tariq, upon replaying the secret recording of his makhna's torture, went into virtual convulsions. At three in the morning he was on the phone to journalist friends plotting a major protest march, with swamis and school children and as many members of the Indian press as could be marshaled. To listen to those eleven minutes of the elephant's protracted agony at the hands of sadists masquerading as government authorities was enough to change anyone for life, or so Tariq prayed.

Some time later, children did arrive with signs calling for the liberation of the elephant. They bypassed the beefed-up flotilla of elephant compound guards who had no means of interceding, for various saffron-robed gurus had also shown up, sadhus of one sort or other, including a famed swami from Mysore. To strike back at these pacifists, even in India, was too Anglo-like in its historical intimations.

The Commander tried, as Tariq and associates had tried before, to buy the elephant. To quietly let the episode pass. But the National Park people would hear nothing of it. They wanted that elephant to know she was being punished for life.

Many months later, Marigold would learn that the makhna had finally been 'tamed' by the equivalent of a massive lobotomy, but one in which there was no single midnight surgery, but a systematic, year-long regime of daily torture, beatings, forced infections, near starvation and perpetual hatred at the hands of authorities in Forest Department uniforms who attended to her eternal damnation. Forever in chains, forever in India.

Even now the Commander was lost. What had begun as a journey of love, a desire to know an ancient hegemony of beautiful cultures, had turned into a spectacle that was nothing less than a thorough indictment of humanity.

"I can bear no more. I give up. Let's go home," he said to his Squire. "Are you sure?"

"Yes. This time I mean it. Whatever we have heard about India, I now know it to be a thorough, calamitous fiction. These are desperate times because the people are desperate, hateful monsters."

"Not all of them, of course," the Commander recommended.

"Enough so to alter history's verdict. To change truth into useless, insulting mythology. I am furious, disgusted, heartbroken." And he turned away, dark tears staining his otherwise Arcadian complexion.

CHAPTER 86

The Journey to Toda Land

THE CLOSEST EVACUATION from the Indian subcontinent was via Coimbatore, many hard-going hours up, over and down through the Nilgiris. It had rained, and, as Tariq predicted, plentiful waterfalls poured off the mountains, wiping out parts of the treacherous road.

Marigold had promised to do what he could to change things, once he was back in the States. But he saw little point in continuing his expedition within the country. Too many avenues of corruption and attrition appeared closed to common sense, even to money. Changes would have to be political ones—of this Sannazaro had, at least for now, convinced him. That meant international ties, the forging of alliances between governments, not quixotic billionaires running around all five quarters attempting to save every rat and goat and elephant by peeing into a hurricane.

But Sannazaro also recognized the fragile thread of persuasion by which he had extracted the Commander's pledge to leave India.

"When you have to pee, you have to pee," Marigold reminded him. So the faster they got out of there, the better.

One stop was necessary, however. In Ootacamund, or Ooty as it was known, they were given the name of a local dentist who could fix Marigold's tooth, which had been nicked in the fight with the mahoot and was driving him bonkers. Tariq took them in his Jeep up the steep mountain pass above his clinic, a five-mile-an-hour road leading from one washout to another, eventually attaining the sub-alpine forests at nearly 8,000 feet altitude. Here Ooty, with its more than 100,000 people, lay like a ramshackle, much-tarnished jewel.

They said farewell to Tariq at the entrance to a commonplace motel where they had decided to spend the night. There could be no sleep, ever again, sighed Marigold. Not after what they'd seen. Then the Commander, in the company of his Squire, walked down the road to the dentist.

"Good day, gentlemen," the lean, white-aproned clinician cheerfully greeted them. It was rare that westerners came to him. "I am Barut. Dentist of Modest Distinction, Botanist in Exile, Would-be Soldier of Fortune. How can I help you? Oh, that shawl!"

Marigold had a sly manner of running into people who sounded just like him, thought Sannazaro. This coincidence of linguistic manias was almost a physic, or co-dependency, wherever in the universe the Commander happened to be—a curve in the reality of personalities that sent all vibrations down the same drain, into a centrally berserk sinkhole. Of course, it always meant trouble. No shade to buffer the glare; not a single quiet time to renew the senses. Every addled incident in the life of Marigold seemed to Sannazaro just another cracked mirror, multiplied in so many feckless distortions and ceaseless adventures. But where was the actual life? That freedom beyond the dreary Camp of Nomads? Some alternative form of breathing and eating, of sleeping and dreaming that did not condemn its creator to the same day-in day-out decoy of self-deception and endless introversion? Or was a man simply fated, from the moment of birth, to play out the repeating annals, cycles, delusions, tantalized by his own heartbeat, with no escape, except in death? What a terrible thought, he reckoned.

Now were somebody else to have been watching over these contemplations, he would have recognized at once the very nature of small-mindedness, of an itch—furiously scratched—on one's head. The Italian expected nothing less than comfort, homage paid him, a certain prestige in light of his former aristocracy, which was never lost or abandoned.

His comportion resided like a swan in the manor's loch, resident nobility that no longer enjoyed the master bedroom but was nonetheless served up the majority of relishes, flattered and appreciated. The new-found financial boom, compliments of his undigestible traveling companion, only added to his sense of righteousness, decorum, restraint. Sannazaro had been galvanized with dollar bills, given to imagine his own castle, then made unmercifully modest by the pain he had endured of late. Moreover, his few millions of dollars reared their spending power with faintness of breadth beside the Commander's billions, for even they now appeared ludicrously insufficient to accomplish anything of substance in this world. Doomed from almost the beginning, the gardener in Sannazaro had repaired to his previous quietude, where no extra-sensation was welcome: let habit be habit and custom custom. May the sun shine, the moon rise, and ask not for a baronage or lairdship. He had been content. Now he was shark-eaten, ice-ridden and greatly troubled. The cows and goats and elephants had percolated into his heart.

The Commander, after introductions, explained to the dentist their circumstances and described how Sister Love had mysteriously given him the garment—though, admittedly, it had seemed to bring little by way of luck.

"Well, friends, it *will* bring you luck. In fact, when you wear it I can assure you that it will prevent any serious harm from coming your way. It is called putxuty by the woman who spent four months fashioning it among her lady friends on the grassy knoll before her white adobe shelter," exclaimed Barut, as he led Marigold into the dental chair and proceeded to lower, then level him nearly horizontally. He then deftly seized the Commander's mouth, checked the extent of damage on the front tooth, and prepared a minor enamel cap with the assistance of a giggling nurse.

"Some beavers and aardvarks fall asleep when I do their teeth," he began.

Marigold wanted to protest but was unable, with so many metal implements reaching greedily down his throat.

Sannazaro sat snoozing by the partly draperied window, taking in the mottles of cool warmth and mellow shade that reminded his skin cells of Paris or Tuscany.

"I happen to know her personally," Barut went on. "A lovely old gal with braids to her waist and all her dentures intact, since I made them. Life throws wonderful coincidences at us, doesn't it."

"*Stop it!* " Marigold cried out, forcing his jaw to the antipodes.

But there was no escape. Some time later, after the sulfurous ordeal and long twining drills, the dentist beamed Marigold his most boyish smile. "All done," he exclaimed. "The chip has been replaced." Then: "And I happen to live not 20 miles from the village of Todas where that shawl was fashioned."

"Todas?"

Barut took the opportunity to explain who the Todas were, and how he'd become a dedicated student of their flowers, their language, their religion and especially their teeth. "I am also the President of the society to protect the Todas from the outside world. Here, wash all the blood out of your mouth."

"Flowers?" Sannazaro inquired, suddenly waking up.

"Good teeth?" Marigold added, spitting into the basin.

"Good teeth? My dear friend, I have examined all 1,495 mouths among the existing tribal people, and have never discovered an instance of decay, receding gums, root canal problems or any other ailment. The woman whose dentures I constructed had, like yourself, suffered an accident. She was struck by the horn of one of their buffalo which quite neatly knocked all of her teeth out. But, as a rule, they have perfect teeth, a world record.

A thousand years from now dentists will marvel at their diet."

"Which is?" the Commander pressed.

"A unique form of vegetarianism," the dentist replied. "Food choices, styles of consumption, emotional side-effects, charm and dignity characteristic of their entire society. For they are the original inhabitants of the Garden of Eden, if you ask me, and I'd implore you to spread the word, for a specific purpose. I judge by more than your teeth that the both of you are well favored under cosmopolitan heels of this life: true sophisticates. Just possibly—given your possession of that shawl—fate has had some hand in our acquaintance."

Sannazaro closed his eyes. He could see it coming.

The dentist continued. "The Todas need help, money, government intervention. As one who has stared into the throat of our species with a stern eye, I harbor few illusions. But I am not speaking of changing the ocean's tides, or rescuing the kelp forests, but saving one small community. Perhaps, you would care to check out the scene and see what I'm referring to?"

"Ola, we are going!" cried Murillo. "I have some money, too—"

"Not for long in this country," Sannazaro interjected. "A zealot and his billion are easily parted, as Samuel Johnson once remarked."

"Don't mind Iacobo," the Commander explained. "We are a case of the original odd couple. He is the cantankerous one. Bedeviled by every challenge, terrorized by his own shadow."

"And he the blithe idiot," Sannazaro added. "Place before him 10,000 hells, the worst experiences in human history—all of India, for that matter—and he will weep for five minutes, call it quits, then rise to the occasion with renewed enthusiasm. In other words, where others might take notice, learn from all their mistakes, he is incited, topples in reverse, strips his gear shift at every opportunity. There is nobody quite like him."

Marigold stared in the mirror at his tooth. "Good job," he said. And then, "If, as you describe, this tribe needs help, then I am on hand to deliver the goods, and fate may smile on this happy connection."

"Done. Marvelous. Perfect. Fantastic. You must stay with me. I have a guest cottage in Conoor," Barut exclaimed. "With a cow named Rosie grazing outside the door. My parents, with whom I share the abode, bless their hearts, will treat you like visiting sultans, for they have never ignored in their entire lives an opportunity to be hospitable, to sense virtue, elicit the best and most fragrant traits in mankind, and embrace them as true and vital members of the family. I would like to think you will actually find this quality well diffused throughout the Nilgiris. What's more, there are tea plantations in all directions: sights and scents to refresh a tired man, restore life to nihilists, vigor to the bedridden, and, by daily increment, renewed faith even in the mightiest sceptic. We can check you out of your motel when I'm finished here. But tell me," Barut asked Sannazaro, deferring to his seniority, "what is your purpose in India? And please excuse me for getting way ahead of myself. It's just so rare that a westerner wearing a Toda shawl should happen through my door. Are you here for business or simply traveling about on holiday?

Or was Sister Love your destination?"

"Ask him," the dejected though oddly reconciled Italian deferred.

"Given the eloquence of your own ebullience, and the ardor of your own ferments, you two might well be brothers."

"I would be honored were it so," Marigold applied. "The answers to all those questions which plague our fellow man and have condemned this world—that is why we're here."

"Excellent," cried Barut. "Are you averse to hiking?"

"Yes," the Italian began.

"We live for it," exhorted Marigold.

The dentist looked to the Commander, then to his Squire, and back to Marigold: "Then tomorrow and the next day we'll walk to a village. I think you will not be disappointed. If I may, some of the rarest flowers anywhere in the world are to be found on Toda lands. And animals, too.

Are you interested in nature?"

"Is my name no indication of my heritage?" the Commander asked proudly. "My God! Of course!" Barut cried out, a child of great gaiety in a professional's disguise.

Later he picked them up at their motel and they headed out over the mountain pass towards Conoor. Marigold tossed bananas to the monkeys that gathered in waiting phalanxes atop the short stone walls down the steep, winding roads. It was a marvelous airy day, cataracts and the smoke of small village stalls coalescing in the vertically differentiated ecosystems of tropic and transmontane. But even such beauty could not eclipse the recently experienced horrors that lay lodged in the Commander's heart, and he spoke of them to the dentist, who promised to see what he could do through his Forest Department connections. It was a bland assent, the Commander noticed; the dentist had wholly underestimated the seriousness of the request, or the gravity of the substratum. He did not know how to strengthen the impression. Clearly, he now realized, to ascertain the nightmare one had to live it.

Throughout their singularly rich ride from Ooty to Conoor, Barut expatiated on the wonders of the Ahl People, which is what the Toda called themselves in their own pre-Dravidian language, its origins more likely Australasian than Indic. He waxed upon many facets of their curious social underpinnings and heavenly overpinnings; how they lived, by what means and ideals, to what extent they were imperiled, and the forces coagulating around them: film-processing factories, chemical companies, uncontrolled building and tourism and water pollution, and the destruction of pastureland traditionally utilized by buffaloes, whom they worshipped—all these things, on top of the disastrous legacy of the British hill station occupation, with its syphilis in the days prior to penicillin, had nearly driven this remarkable people to extinction. So one dentist was trying to save them, along with a few others from around the world.

Barut related how an English anthropologist of the mid-nineteenth century, upon first discovering the Todas for himself, had described their way of life, indicting all those characteristics in a flourish of disdain utterly in keeping with an era accustomed to thinking of tribal peoples as brutish and stupid.

"The man was a product of his times," said Barut sympathetically, "but his stinging ignorance resounds to this day with an irony that is tragically instructive," and he handed the Commander an old book.

As they drove, Marigold paraphrased aloud from the work penned by the Englishman: "This bundle of wallflowers refuses agriculture, hunting, war, sports, aggression of any kind—the true marks of the more advanced classes. They will not harm a living creature, a sentiment befitting a little girl, perhaps, but surely no entire society of functioning adults. They resist the advance of civilization with a stubbornness that knows no bounds. While perfectly clothed, unlike some other savages along the subcontinent—among the Sentinel Islanders, for example—the Toda are utterly simple minded. They exhibit none of the professional aspirations which are the mark of a great nation; show no desire whatsoever to increase the spoils of their livelihood, or to embrace Jesus Christ. They will not harm a feather. They protest, even, at the killing of a wasp. They are intent upon resolving all differences. This they accomplish by way of a truly wishy-washy form of arbitration. They call it a *noyim*, certainly the most primitive form of politics I have ever witnessed. It involves the whole community in endless fraternizing that can take weeks, all for no other reason, evidently, than their love of socializing.

"By assiduously avoiding the clash of antlers they have, in short, renounced the civilized world. Such archaic and impractical norms might work on a pasture for a week or two, or among several honeymooning couples more or less confined to their berths on the Oriental Express. But it is clear to this observer that the Toda will not stay the tide of all those far more advanced northern races even now swarming down upon them with a motto that reads, 'Of tooth and claw'.

"Here, then, without doubt, is a primeval form of conscience doomed to be disappointed. While some might congratulate them, it is only too clear that they are of a weaker mental character, imbalanced according to the splendid organization of traits and biological possibilities about which Mr Darwin has recently addressed himself."

Barut shook his head. "Can you imagine a more formidable disdain? And these were men with power, money, influence." And he went on to describe how early visitors to the Todas, not just anthropologists, had also found the women to be beautiful—ironic considering the low esteem in which they were otherwise held—and how they impregnated them, passing along a variety of diseases unknown to these parts which would nearly doom the entire tribe.

Sannazaro had little interest in following the plight of yet another Indian minority. He'd already washed his hands, as they say, and was too tired to fixate on more bad news. Meanwhile, Marigold browsed through to the concluding chapter in the little volume in his hands, and read aloud, "In truth, they have embraced utter stagnation, plucking fruits from trees and wild beans from the stubble. That this should suffice for their diet. Yet all their neighbors of every color and persuasion are thorough meat eaters of high professional standing. There is simply no explaining the Toda's aversion to the more advanced dietary formulas and expediencies. They are a shadow passing from memory and we must not be seduced by the romance of their own fixations. For they cannot last, but on the canvas of a Claude or Poussin."

Marigold said nothing, contemplating the various conditions of humanity, or lack thereof.

At last the party arrived at Barut's family home. They settled in, and later that evening all three ate at the Gentlemen's Club, a throwback to British times. Ties and jackets were borrowed at the front desk. Whisky was served up amid that dying breed of pink-faced retirees, former prelates, comptrollers, hunters, import-exporters, suave expatriots, lechers with fat purple blotches under their eyes—those who had simply gone 'out' to India and never returned, bored, blanched, melancholic heavy-drinking men with nothing but a blurred, unreal and largely corrupt past to refer to. But one could get a decent grilled tempe hot salad and tomato soup, because Barut knew Ahmed, the chef, whose father, a Mason, and Barut's father, a Theosophist, had together founded the first dental clinic in Conoor two decades before. One pulled teeth, the other put them back, first in the form of gold, later in enamel. Barut had opened the second family clinic in Ooty.

In the morning, Barut, Marigold and a gravely disinclined Sannazaro headed out by foot towards the remote mountain villages of Inkblotty and Heerkittykitty, two adjoining Toda villages out of nearly 40 such clusters comprising half-dozen half-timbered sod houses, three times the denizens, and some 50 spoiled, picayunish buffaloes who feasted on the finest grasses and grains and would not let anyone other than the Todas approach them. Barut had been adopted by the tribal citizens after years of devotion, a dedication to understand these lofty residents, absorb protective speaking habits, delve deeply into the secrets of their societal glues, become one with them as much as it was possible for a modern, well-educated and wealthy Indian to do. He collected funds to protect them from the onslaught of that very modernity: city administrators, the surrounding Badaga tribe, 'superiors' who had managed to usurp much of Toda territory. Because Toda did not believe in possession of the earth, had no notion of surplus, capital and supply, no Marxist, capitalist or socialist doctrines of marketability, neither a labor theory of value nor money of any kind, no concept of exploitation, Alexander Hamilton or Max Weber, of profiting at the expense of another, no work ethic whatsoever, they were too innocent for this or possibly any era. A people that invited rape, pathos and inevitable extinction. Passenger pigeons.

Yet, in spite of all these attributes, and a profession that inclined him to back problems and a high actuarial probability of suicide, Barut was the most optimistic and far-seeing of dentists.

The laws of India, he affirmed, had classified the Todas as a Scheduled Tribe, a designation that afforded them legitimacy as aboriginals, heritage status and some protection from the tourist trade, but no legal standing or human rights assurances when it came down to the nitty-gritty of local politics and economic investiture. They were in trouble, he said. The pasturelands for their sacred buffalo were being taken over by planters more interested in eucalyptus nurseries and other fast-growing species.

"The world is doubly in trouble," Marigold reasoned. "Because if 1,400 beautiful people cannot be saved, how can the rest of the planet ever be salvaged?"

"Quite so!"

These thoughts weighed heavily upon the young enthusiast, and such were the discussions absorbing the three men, each in turn obeying paces of his own personality as they tramped through high stands of teak, silk cotton and jacaranda forest. Whitebreasted kingfishers threw calls to them, while magpie robins did their morning chorales, hidden from the golden-headed Brahmini kites that patrolled the upper skies. Flycatchers, racket-tailed drongos, Indian robins, azure sunbirds and darkly-construed munias all figured in the avian patchwork of their march. Along the way, the Commander and Barut shared their mosaic of preoccupations, the quest to discover that looming model of impossible sustainability. Barut believed he had found it. The Commander had not, not yet. Sannazaro knew he never would, but who could say anything to Mr Marigold? Such a goal was like the stubborn man himself, a tragi-comic throwback to every sheep commons, pure air molecule or futile moral fortress that ever was. But it was even worse than that, and Marigold himself knew them all. A billion Indians caving in on 1,400 Todas, just as they had upon the Nilgiri elephant.

Barut was mournfully tuned in to this collision course. But his youth had never once assented to the idea of failure.

"It is eleven miles and will take us a day and a half," Barut said. "But the walk is an easy one—too easy, I'm afraid."

"Why is that?" inquired the Italian.

"More and more strangers are walking in. Exposing the Toda to chewing gum, VCRs, pencils. The Todas deeply resent this invasion, but the police are doing nothing to prevent it."

Getting to this threatened Arcadia took the men through a foreshadowing of what Barut was referring to: habitat that had been invaded, trees hacked down, pastures burned. Signs of outside intervention everywhere.

Yet animal life was present all around them. The trampers witnessed a grazing elephant, quiet peahens foraging for nuts, two rare black Nilgiri langurs screeching and leaping between hardwoods, a leopard whose nonchalant traverse was signaled by an acoustical storm of hill mynas, mooning drongos, grunting chittals, Malabar giant squirrels fighting over a nesting site, barking deer, heartspotted woodpeckers, a whistling thrush and an all-watchful crested serpent eagle in search of such morsels as the bluebearded bee-eater. There were the tracks of sloth bears and tiger cubs, and the feverish-pitched squeak of an Indian pitta bird. In the distance, abase Mount Dodabetta, the rumblings of other elephants. Barut said they congregated in the Ketti Valley, at the drinking hole beneath the 130-foot Kalhatti Falls. To Marigold's mind, this was not an unhappy picture, despite what he knew of the threats to the people who called these forests home.

The men marched beyond the point known as Avalanche Top, past MacIvor's Bund, where Toda frequently had their noyim. Further abutting the cloud-soaked horizon could be detected the famed Mukerti Peak, far above the Mayar River. All these landmarks of the ancient Blue Mountains, east of the Western Ghats, had intuitive meaning for Marigold, who already felt at home amid their welter of wilds.

The dentist, with his perpetual bright gleam and impeccable courtesies, took the lead, a gusher of geographical fine points. Every plant astonished him, and though he knew them all by name his passion for describing their personality traits never suffered for excessive acquaintance. He felt compelled to divulge their genealogies to his new companions, as if introducing long-lost friends.

"Familiarity breeds gossip," he explained, by way of an apology for his barrage of excited commentary. He truly could not help himself.

"There, for example, the Nilgiri lily, *Lilium neilgherrense*," which he pronounced with all the relish appropriate to flowers of such wan and delicate disposition. He explained how the creamy flowers came alive no matter what in early fall, and had given the Toda people a certain security in the afterlife: the knowledge that no amount of sleet or adversity could diminish a deserving bulb its blossom.

Barut's botanical insights were themselves blossoming, for it was not long before the three trampers encountered that rarest of plant indicators, the odoriferous *Michelia nilagirica* which, Barut added, the Toda call *Mawrsh*. When it bloomed, the flower spelled the end of the southwest monsoon, the prelude to dry sunny weather. They trekked past whole mountainsides of *Satyrium nepalense*, a cure-all for Toda weariness. And the blue-faced conical clock tower, Katt, a striking plant which, according to Barut, flowered every six, twelve or 18 years depending on the subspecies.

The oldest of the Todas had witnessed multiple *Pyoof katt*, or 18-year flowerings, while those in middle age had seen only a few *Pelily katt*, or twelve-year flowerings.

Before long they were slogging through a vast stretch of crimson-colored Himalayan rhododendron trees named *Pershk* by the Todas. With some pride, Barut admitted that one particular discovery of his—a white rhododendron—had earned him his immortal moment in the sun. Thanks to Barut's keen detective work, the Royal Horticultural Society of Scotland, the international certification group, had officially registered it in the annals of botany as *Rhododendron arboreum* ssp. *nilagiricum Barut*. Nobody had believed that white rhododendrons existed outside the Himalayan ranges. His latest obsession, however, was the pale blue rhododendron, which his Toda informant, Kwatawdr Kuttan, had informed him indeed existed.

Pink-flowering mountain guava, wild strawberries and trees of white flowers smothered in honey bees—*Kwershntain*, to the Toda—graced their path. Such delightful environs gave both Marigold and Sannazaro a chance to contemplate the many spheres of their near undoing in previous days and weeks. Marigold had much thinking to realign; he needed to get some grip on his emotional cave-in. Sannazaro, too, had suffered.

They needed time to sort it all out. Why spare a penguin and molest the elephant? What good a billion sandflies but only a few moa? How did Sister Love triumph in a country so obviously inured to pain and indifference? By what means did she communicate to Marigold the genesis of that anguish, in a place forever known as Gundlepet, and what was implied by her gift of the Toda shawl? Or her cryptic reference to a boy? Something was yet to be accomplished.

"Tervary oy pooth kwehtin, Twoodrn tain oy kwes kwehtin!" yodelled the dentist on his merry way. It was an ancient Toda song about the lovely relationship that had persisted for thousands of years between the six-year katts, the honey bees and honey-collecting Todas themselves.

Wherever they moved there was something to celebrate: a nectar, a toxin, a medicinal bark or ground orchid. This one helped Todas with bronchial pneumonia, and this was good for perfume, nosegays, and weddings.

"That one—touch it. Go on," Barut urged.

Sannazaro did so. At once, his fingers began to tremble. The flower closed in upon itself. He let go.

"What is it?"

"How do you feel?"

"What do you mean?"

"They call it *Arkil poof*, meaning worry flower. Merely to touch it, as you have done, will alleviate any concerns you may have."

"Not likely."

"It takes time to set in. By nightfall, you will be feeling it."

They passed by red creepers to treat epilepsy, and flowering tidbits to inspire epic sonnets. This one for divining the best lyric, and that a premonition of a new girlfriend. Flowers that comment, collaborate, conspire and congratulate. Flowers of friendship and love, loyalty and solicitude. Nearly 80 varieties in all,

Barut mused, of species endemic to the Nilgiris.

"Imagine the colossal tragedy should these go extinct!"

Sannazaro, enchanted, sampled many of the seeds and collected them in a plastic zipper-lock baggy with the idea of introducing them back at the Camp of the Spirits.

"What's this one?" he asked.

"Ahhh. You see! That is *Oenothera tetraptera*, which the Todas refer to as the 6 p.m. flower. Regardless of season or weather conditions. Check your watch."

Sure enough, it was dinner time.

They bivouacked in a clearing on the shores of Pykara Lake. That night stars shone on the still waters. With a straw obtained from a Pepsi vendor on the road to Ooty, Barut drank of the firmament's reflections.

"What are you doing?" asked Marigold.

"I'm transplanting moonlight into my circulation system. An old Toda remedy."

"For what?"

"Everything."

CHAPTER 87
An Expedition to Amunawdr

NEXT DAY, THE TRIO AT LAST arrived at Inkblotty and Heerkittykitty.

The softly suffused medley of tribal people strolled into clearings beyond the rich canopy of forest and on into the deep grass to greet the threesome. Approbation. Independence. A festival of smiles. Beyond, in all directions, high hillocks gained steep assurance upon higher crests and Pre-Raphaelite escarpments of fir, woodpecker havens, langur mansions.

At once there was an obvious interest taken in the Commander, not because he was the oldest—that stature was guaranteed Sannazaro alone—but because of his height, shaggy beard, attenuated bearing and general character. He was an obvious veteran of unaccountable itineraries. Whereas Sannazaro had more the urbane demeanor: smooth skin, unruffled feathers, well-cropped hairstyle. A man who might be said to own property, or wear a watch, even drive an automobile. An educated Lord, in the British style. Such things were known to the Toda, of course, but largely without meaning, other than to those few younger ones who had made their way into the outer world and begun the long road towards assimilation. A few of them were 'weekend Todas', living new, non-tribal lives in Ooty and Conoor and coming home to their families on Friday night. They were the ones who let it be known that there were movies in Tamil, television sets, radios, bills of exchange. On Tuesdays, some of the Todas went to market, walking twelve miles to barter tea leaves, barley, radishes, bark and certain fruits in exchange for various necessities. Sometimes, they got lucky and hitched rides on the local buses. But these modern-day experiences had not altered their consciousness or lifestyle appreciably, even if a few of the outermost shanties had the odd television antenna jutting from the crudely fitted plaster.

Said the Toda elder to Barut, speaking about the strange visitors whom he had examined from dusty boots to tasseled head curls, "Wehzoshyaa!"

To which the dentist replied, "Wehtztoshbenie." Then, "Wood ud pawrsh ungya?"

Barut turned to his companions. "He asks if you will take some hot buffalo milk. It is quite clean, and most likely the finest milk in the world."

"I am a vegan, but, yes," replied Marigold. "Any animal that is loved, unexploited, is confirmed by my diet."

"Awn pawrsh ungin," Barut told the elder.

The man, in his magnificent shawl, who knew everything about the similar garment worn by Marigold but said not a word about it, sent one of his daughters for the milk, then asked Barut, "Eow kattvoof arstyaa?" "What did he say?"

"He asks, have you seen seven sightings of pyoof katt? Pyoof, as I mentioned, would mean the 18-year cycle."

After a moment's calculation the Commander summed up: "He is asking me if I'm 126 years old?"

"What he means, of course, is whether you are really as wise as you appear," Barut tactfully added. "It is,

I believe, a rare compliment."

"Tell him certainly not, but if he be pleased I can play the fool as well as another man," Marigold went on.

"Hear hear," chimed in Sannazaro.

At the sound of "hear hear" all the Todas burst out laughing, for it reminded them of their own village—Heerkittykitty—and they added nonsense to nonsense by repeating in unison, "Heer-heer kittykitty!"

Which signaled, and let no archivist doubt the subtle truth of the moment, two kitties who crept out from under some rain-washed logs and slunk around the developing party of humans to see if any food might be involved.

Every new Toda who arrived greeted the newcomers with "Wehtztoshyaa" (Hello, are you well?) and Barut and his two companions all replied with the identical (though wildly differently pronounced) "Wehtztoshbenie," meaning, I'm well. Buffalo milk was served up in teakwood jugs, and seven hours of courtesies and other exchanges initiated. Women arrived from other villages and knelt down before the men, who would raise a leg high and touch the sole of their bare, stained and crusted foot to the woman's head. By these highly original gymnastic affections, explained Barut, the men greeted the Toda women.

Despite the long day, and exhausted couplets of translated inquiry and social foreplay (in no other society, suggested Marigold, had one grown old and tired just from saying "Hello"), all was managed with an informality and purity. The evening mist of innocence dappled every glance; it permeated speech and gesture; it even infiltrated to the animals—a playful leopard cub watched over by a surrogate mother, a large, wild German shepherd. Hovering in the shola, or feebly entranced against their mothers' breasts, two infant Nilgiri langurs monitored others of their kind playing football. Here was the model of pastoral perfection the Commander had been seeking for so many months: a vision of harmonious aplomb, that island of true conscience in the sea of tumultuous evolution he'd so often pursued (though the smoke from the indoor stoves was as stinging as onion—Barut said the Todas were used to it). Even the wasps, hornets and horseflies were Viennese fairies, to the Commander's mind. All was couched in some perceived atmospheric indistinctnesses through which he fashioned his own Escorials from a compost heap. In truth, no man was more in need of a spell to substitute romantic snow blossoms for that collapsing drawbridge of previous horrors—goats, cows, elephants, sheep staring out from their dark confines—than Murillo Marigold.

The Commander took a deep breath and put a hand on Sannazaro's shoulder to steady himself. At length, he felt strong enough to continue the encounter.

In fact, among these Todas, it can be accurately chronicled that he was paralyzed with pleasure for want of the need of any other passion, convinced more than ever that this was the true course of the future, that all the human children would do well to end up in Toda Lands of their own. Did he dare draw a map?

He meditated on their vegetarianism, the more impressive considering that all other tribes around them, like the Badaga, were meat eaters. How did they come by such dietary non-violence? Barut had said that there was some evidence the Todas made a communal choice 1,200 years before, when certain species of flesh went extinct and they resolved to eat animals never again. But that data was extremely thin, Barut himself confirmed. Even if it were true, he said, the consensual forces that made it possible for an entire collective to decide to do the right thing—he was referring to the Todas—was of paramount importance.

Marigold chimed in. He believed that judicial revolutions in mindsets were possible. Lawyers in Marigold's own time had found ways to force car manufacturers to install catalytic converters, to file class-action suits against tobacco and gun manufacturers. State referenda, in America, had made it illegal to raise or kill horses for human consumption. The Kyoto and Buenos Aires conferences on greenhouse gas emissions had effectively addressed global warming, just as the Montreal Protocol on chlorofluorocarbons had succeeded, in the late 1980s, in stepping down the manufacture and release of CFCs. Such democratic breakthroughs were possible. Marigold had read that even as far back as the late seventh century the Japanese Fujiwara dynasty dictated that all animals be freed, and all criminals given amnesty. A thousand years later in Japan all guns were banned. Americans had enacted the *Lacey Act* in 1900, and later the *Animal Welfare* and *Endangered Species Acts*. Lincoln and Roosevelt had set aside the first National Parks. Clinton, Marigold had heard, had mandated nearly 50 million acres of national forest off-limits to lumber companies and roads. While none of these legal or societal triumphs was anywhere near close enough to solving the problem of violence, they were, he believed, certainly steps in the right direction. They proved that people *could* act unselfishly. Evidence in favor of tomorrow. A reinvigoration of an uncommon commons.

Most ecologists had all but given up hope, in spite of such meager gains, convinced that whole populations—species, genera, families—were doomed, and all that could be saved in the short term were individuals. Marigold frequently felt that way. But now he was heartened, for the fact remained—and it was there right before him—that the Todas had gone all the way. Had achieved one form of human perfectibility. Here was very likely one of the last, if only, vegetarian tribes in the world. They did not have access to healthfood supermarkets like Wild Oats of Santa Fe, where Alma was able to provision the hacienda to the Commander's requirements. The Toda had figured it out for themselves, like the nearly 100 million Hindus and Buddhists and Seventh Day Adventists, and quite a few others, who were also vegetarian. On a less sanguine note, Marigold knew that most Buddhists and Hindus consumed large quantities of meat without the slightest qualm. Yet, here was an entire society—granted, a small one—that defied the demographic odds, spurned all inconsistency, brooked no ethical ambiguity. Were there sudden winds and changes of heart in Toda society? It appeared not. Breakdowns in the inner clusters? None. Crime, recidivism, depression, adult-onset diabetes? Definitely not. Drugs, abandonment, loneliness? Never. Life expectancy? Well, the Todas seemed to live to an age that defied the norms all around them on the Indian subcontinent. They had no mythology of protein, or of vitamins; no obsession with B-12, or fighting colds, or obesity. Lean, blushing in health, they had lifted the burden of blood-lust that tainted the legacy of most *Homo sapiens*. The Todas were proof that humans had it in them to be virtuous. That we need not go out with an epitaph consigning us to hell. The result: perfect teeth, happy buffaloes, and a people who displayed a higher order of dignity than all others Marigold had encountered. The signs were all about, the lessons on the surface. Every exchange marked a great handshake; each twinkling eye a semiotic of some emerging paradigm. Love wove its magic spells without the slightest incantation. There was humor that eschewed the grave; daisies given out like party favors; carnal lightness and living legacy. All the flowers, forests and animals in the neighborhood shared in it. A Jan Brueghel the Elder.

It was in this spirit of high standards and universal love that the Commander proposed something like Platonic marriage to a hunched-over great-great-grandmother enfeebled by her more than 100 years. She was a guardian of female Todas, to whom he addressed the following sentiments, having succumbed to buffalo milk intoxication: "Oh Mother of Eternal Beauty, Windmill of all Windmills and Venus Mound of Mountain Tops, you Dandelion of Eternal Giants, you Nectar of Immortality, who has shouldered all burdens, consoled the disillusioned, triumphed over the mumps, served every evening's dinner of roasted garlic, kept the fire awake, and the milk curdling in your breasts—"

As he continued his goofy contrivance, the goddess to whom he was appealing stood up, spellbound by the bizarre attention. But Marigold was undeterred: "Sweet Lady, Sweetness of the Night, like a glow-worm stirring bright, incarnate are my vows to thee; a kangaroo no surer pouch beside its heart, nor a painter nearer to his art. Feverish with the bite of love..."

At which point Sannazaro finally broke the pathetic trance with a towering shriek: "Damn it, Murillo!"

There was an embarrassed silence, for the Todas never shouted at one another. This was the very zenith of Window Dressing, Fairy-, Never Never- and La La-Land all translated into one striking ethnography. The raising of a voice was considered extremely bad form. Unheard of. An impulse without etymology. In this society, guided by the ethical precepts of the noyim, all altercation was eradicated before it had a chance to arise. Had Gandhi known of the Toda he might well have fashioned an entirely different Home Scheme for the whole country, modeled on their psychoanalytic marvels.

Sannazaro, catching all this graceful censure, could not help but recognize the signs of it. He grew quiet. He was fed up with such human perfection.

Then, all were escorted indoors to view the interiors of the bungalows. They passed through the cramped smoky rooms, shorn of artifice, fitted neatly with the bare essentials of life at 7,000 feet altitude. They were, by Sannazaro's accounting, horrid. As idyllic as the habiliments were to Marigold's mind, Sannazaro saw only the prospect of eternal poverty: mangy mutts and babies wallowing in the mud. A people sadly convicted to the inertia of their ancestors, to the same old day-in and day-out routine. Cold mountain air, little food, no seasoning, no bathrooms or indoor heating. His response was an all-out grimace.

How different these two comrades were, the Squire and the Hermit.

For just as Sannazaro despaired at this remote mountain lair of mangers and demeaning straw-concocted shacks, and dreamed instead of the St Regis in Manhattan, so Mr Marigold thrilled to eavesdrop upon heaven itself. He felt himself slipping into that metaphysical bather's pool that takes all such reflection to be true creation. He knew these people would give the shawls off their backs, their last drops of buffalo milk, every lance of straw used in the construction of their marvelous domiciles.

In one such shelter beds of rolled clothcover, marked by antediluvian stains, baby's puke, dog and cat piss, octogenarian leakage, food spillage from earlier decades, was provided to both Sannazaro and the Commander so that they might take their rest. The Squire squirmed, certain that fleas and lice were at that very moment devouring his genitals and diseases spreading by mere touch. The Commander lay there staring at the ceiling in a daze of joy and tranquillity. To be immersed in the community: such a new, thrilling sensation.

Following the opening of the six o'clock flower, other Todas arrived, and around a large eucalyptus bonfire, tea leaf in the oiled air, beneath the Toda stars, there was talk of refurbishing the conical temple, their most sacred site, the center of the universe.

In the morning, a Toda sport dating back thousands of years involving the improbable lifting and thrusting of enormous granite spheres, each weighing hundreds of pounds, was played on a village green. Mr Marigold attempted but could no more budge one of those rocks than he could shove a building. A 15-year-old championed a 400-pound stone and hurled it ten feet.

Then all hiked to the 40-foot-high conical temple with its guarded buffalo sculpture and surrounding stonemasonry. This was the Toda Notre Dame, made of straw; the Colossus of Rhodes, fashioned from a few stones; the Tower of Babel, oriented to gentle concord. To the Toda, it was created by their Goddess Teikirshy and her father Aihn. All these huts and villages, two genders and the various buffalo clans, arose when the Goddess tapped her wand of cane beside a certain pool and yodeled her *ranz des vaches*. Inside the temple were the implements of the Buffalo Priest, including the sacred bell and *kwarsm*, the revered names, though none present was admitted to view or hear about them. Only the Priest obtained those rights.

The Priest stood to address them. There was urgency about his person, Marigold detected. He began, and Barut whispered a translation for the Commander and his weary Squire. The lands nearby were threatened with purchase by a movie studio in Mumbai, reported the Priest. The movie chief evidently had his eyes cast on the Nilgiris as a permanent site for moonglow and terraced rhododendron backdrops.

"But who owns the land?" Marigold inquired.

"We do, of course," said the Priest.

"Then what's the problem?" Marigold declared, revealing his innocence.

"There has been one trespass after another," Barut commented. "The authorities do nothing."

"Then I will simply make a financial offer that the government cannot refuse. Menacing minds are surprisingly cured by the sound of coinage. A bank note nullifies, where all the show of tears and distended bellies fails to ignite a note of sympathy. Fear not, ladies—"

Sannazaro could not help but notice how the Commander continued to address himself to the lanky females of the crowd. Indeed, he had witnessed with some trepidation the Commander's apparently increasing hankering—in some manner or other—for the opposite sex. The problem was the Commander did not differentiate between old crones and underage girls; middle-aged motherhood or great-grandmothers; remarkable beauties and remarkably plain trees. They were all the Great Eternal Feminine, as far as Marigold seemed concerned.

Barut translated the Commander's magnanimous offer, and all received these words with tremendous relief.

"Moy Irr Koreen Mow; Paridy Mokh foy Mow; Ton in Mow; Tarmaw Mow!" replied the eldest of the elders by way of summarizing the glorious moment.

Said Barut, "He answers by declaring, 'May the buffaloes bear calves; May the women bear children; May the God give blessings; May the God be compassionate.' In other words, I should safely think you have made their day."

There was a hushed discussion among the old men of the tribe. They took Barut aside and the earnest speaking continued.

Finally, the dentist returned to the spot where the Commander was sitting on the grass surrounded by adoring women who seemed intent upon teasing him into oblivion.

"They are ready to take us to Amunawdr now," he confided. "Assuming you both are up to the journey."

"No way, never!" Sannazaro mumbled, for he was quick to pick up the rhyme and reason of that injunction: another expedition; more peril; more work for an aging atheist.

"Holy cow," the Commander rallied, getting up from his privileged knoll of femininity. "That word!"

"What about it?" Barut asked excitedly.

"I heard the word, from a buffalo, just a few nights ago."

Barut was confused. "What do you mean?"

Sannazaro then rushed in to explain the bizarre comatose moment when the Commander had fallen from the truck onto the buffalo amid the dying heap of other cows and steers. All of which the greatly amazed Barut relayed to the Todas, who were themselves quite dumbfounded to learn of such treatment outside their universe, and more so to recognize in Mr Marigold a man of such shamanic depths. For only a fellow actually *capable* of reaching Amunawdr would be given the spiritual access by a buffalo itself. That it was a non-Toda buffalo confirmed their long-held suspicion that all cows, steers, bulls and buffaloes worldwide dreamt of this place, where their God Aihn had long ago journeyed in order to create an Afterlife known to them as Imunawdr.

All this Barut in turn explained to the Commander."Amunawdr is the Toda Otherworld, where that Afterlife—Imunawdr— takes place. They have made a most remarkable exception to the rule in offering to show you both the way, for normally only the dead Toda and buffaloes may journey there for purposes of catapulting the soul into final union with the soul of a deceased sacred buffalo."

"I'll wait here," Sannazaro quickly informed the bunch. "Amun, Imun doesn't matter to me. Have fun. I have no need, as yet, to get so intimate with a dead buffalo."

"It is a rare opportunity you'll be passing up," Barut warned.

"I can live without it, thank you."

"When do we leave, and how far will we walk?" the Commander asked

"Early tomorrow morning, before dawn, we will set out," Barut replied.

"You, me and a Toda priest you've not yet met. The journey, round trip, should require no more than 12 hours. The mountain we will climb has footsteps carved into the cliff. I have only heard about this place, of course."

"It is a round-trip journey?" Sannazaro asked, seeking all reassurances on behalf of his foolhardy friend. "Because if it is not, Murillo and I have last will and testament matters to attend to."

"We'll be back by tomorrow night. The priest, whom I know well, is as agile as that goat over there."

"All well and fine for the priest," Sannazaro stated. "But my friend here has a tendency to walk headlong into trees, and if not trees, every other trouble of substance—collapsing bridge, poison pothole, clever quicksand or hurricane. Just keep him on a short leash. His eyes are rusty. His instincts deplorable. He does not know the nature of heights or depths, of hot or cold. He cannot gauge a distance, or orient himself to a context. Times of trouble he brushes off, whilst he doesn't know how lucky he is. For your own good, let him not out of your sight; keep me informed, but do not wake me in the night when he screams suddenly, or hallucinates. He speaks to ghosts, imagines vocal facility in the slightest shadow play, intelligence where most men see only a rice paddy or manure pile. In short, he is easily spooked and has a reasoning illness most parts invention. I'd rather not hear about it."

CHAPTER 88
Mr Marigold's Third Utopia

SEÑOR SQUIRE SPENT ANOTHER squirming night convinced his body had been molested a dozen hundred times by jiggers, mites, ticks, noseeums and mosquitoes— which wasn't too far wrong. He'd been informed, not incorrectly, about the malaria mutations throughout southern India—even at this altitude, Barut had forwarned—and so had plenty of reason to be concerned. But there were no Primaquin or

Larium pills handy to combat the possibility, and this left Sannazaro all alone with his terror, the slapping of hands in a void. He struck gold upon flattening one such bugger squarely on his forehead, but, alas, seconds too late, for there was blood in the aftermath. The combat with the invisible carriers of deadly disease got so bad that he leapt from his bed, tripped in his efforts to reach the entrance to the hovel, and fell into another's lair—the one occupied by the old woman whom the Commander had rhapsodized. She had not had a man in her arms for many decades, perked up, and grasped on to the intruder even as he tried frantically to elude her amorous entanglements. Together, they formed a hot lantern.

In Toda Land, it would not have been right for him to leave her so quickly to the loneliness of her nest after provoking such fantastic flights of hope. He stayed on in her great blue rock cod clutches for a few heartbeats ... and the smile she proffered did him in, he could not deny it, even as the ghastly notion of anything more intimate struck him blind. But he was not about to proffer unkindness.

She murmured desperate endearments, he kissed her hand chivalrously, then parted her bony fingers and stepped outside for a cigarette, which the Todas were not averse to—hand-rolled, of course, and made of some rare and enduring highland mix of herbs. The smoke kept bugs away.

Sannazaro remained there until dawn. He fell asleep against the hut, and was still there when the priest arrived to facilitate Barut's and the Commander's expedition. Accompanying the priest was a sacred buffalo named Moszh which soon demonstrated a surpassing intelligence, for after a brief exchange in Ahl, the priest raised his arms, spoke to Moszh and bid farewell to the three of them.

"But what about the priest? Isn't he coming?" Marigold inquired, somewhat ill at ease at these marvelous rites of passage.

"No," Barut advised.

Then it was clear. It was the *buffalo* who would be leading them up the granite escarpment. Only the buffalo who knew the arcane way, had the real gumption. The Moszh whose view from above placed all else into proper perspective.

Mr Marigold was not a little amazed to be following a buffalo into Heaven, but Barut showed no surprise at such strange unfoldings. He had waited 20 years to visit Amunawdr. He would surely have been invited in times past had he requested it, for the Toda rightly loved their little dentist friend. After all, he never charged them for teeth examinations. But he was too shy to request such a favor and, he admitted, was slightly frightened by the prospect, for he feared heights, avoided cemeteries out of respect, and—like Señor Sannazaro—had no wish to leave this world as yet. Indeed, there were other aspects of the expedition, this tour of the Afterlife, which brought with them certain liabilities. A barking dog that attacked you on some border if, at any time in your life, you had committed sexual acts with a first or second cousin; the much-feared pied bushchat or karpulz bird that stood guardian over a drowning pool; countless lethal obstacles. Judgemental fever trees. A swamp worthy of the name. Tests of personality.

A visit such as they were now embarked upon was so rare a privilege as to happen but once in a lifetime, he said instructively, and presently they found themselves following the dexterous ungulate past the remains of funeral pyres—*Eugenia arnottiana*, "Nagapalam in Tamil, the Kairsh tree in Toda," Barut explained—where the ghostly utterances of some deceased's relatives could be heard saying, "Aah, howw howw howw!" No one could fail to hear these strange and distant perorations, or recognize the silver jewelry flashing brightly like dew drops all around them. The hallucination was setting in: the image of a diaphanous corpse floating in a cloth of black through the air; the slow-motion streaming of milk from a bamboo vessel, laden with insubstantialities of the Beyond, into a dead man's mouth. Into his or her cloak pockets went a steady stream of coins and snuff, millet and rice, combs and jaggery, even a knife. In a very important essay published in one of the Indian journals, Barut had first described these goings-on from his interviews of various Toda elders, but no social scientist had ever been allowed to make the trip. Nor did any outsider, not even the famed Toda grammarian/lexicologist M.B. Emeneau, speak such fluent Ahl as Barut. Now the dentist would see everything first hand.

Biers and processions, the ceremonious throwing of earth clods by each clansman, and the tossing of a stone (*Tifinykarsh*) far off into the Bellarambuhala Valley. A whole geography of spirit that was dense in sacred creepers, known to the Todas as Kaghwedry, evergreens, grasslands (Kojkocvilz), and the faraway delirious chime of bells harmoniously dulling the impact of an increasingly oxygenless ascent. A linguistic maze, higher and higher.

Barut pointed out that, traditionally, though seldom any more, when a Toda person died, a buffalo might be sacrificed with a single hit to the head by the back of an ax handle. Hardly consistent with a vegetarian non-violent tribe, Marigold pointed out, downright disappointed with the information. But he was put at some ease when Barut reiterated that it was a rarity and, in this century, almost unheard of.

The rituals accompanying their journey continued: the discovery of a piece of skull and lock of hair from some past corpse, or corpses; green and dry funereals; an earthen pot filled with magic water— "Never look back at ashes!" he warned. Monds or sacred mountain landmarks in all directions, secret companions, tree stumps covered in cloth, and then the famed Kinattulzy, a river that changed its mind from moment to moment, sending currents this way, then that way, up, down—eddies delirious and cursable, undercurrents of great danger, tides terrible, flows flamboyant, blow-holes merciless, wave action unlike a river, and all depending on the mind of the intrepid wanderer who was confronted with a crossing. Bad thoughts, bad deeds, and the water became vindictive.

All this Barut explained ... but then who should show up but Sannazaro himself, still somewhat intoxicated by the night's inhalations, shouting that they should "wait up" for him. He'd had a change of heart, unable to bear the possibility that he might be missing out on something important. It was his one weakness. The fast-drying glue that cemented his loyalty to the mad Marigold.

"Careful!" the Commander cried out. "The river has trick waters. Deep, shallow, vexatious, benign, lethal."

"What?" the Squire shouted, for the wind had made communication impossible, isolating the Italian on a fast-shrinking sandbank with no other choice but a direct traverse towards his companions.

But the Moszh was impatient and would not wait.

Thus it happened that Sannazaro began complaining aloud as he sank deeper and deeper with each step. Soon he was swimming, and cursing, and being dragged downstream, or upstream—for in Toda Land there is no difference. Now his screams were pointless for it was clear to his companions who watched that there was no hope of saving him. He had been caught in a whirlpool and was minutes away from disappearing under the Talus of Great Turmoil up ahead...

Then, quite suddenly, his watery grave attracted attention from below, turning silver, electric blue, metallic and fine, like some ether or emanating sheen. All around him tens of thousands of freshwater jellyfish—dime-sized, aquamarine, known as *Craspedacusta sowerbyi*—worked their magic, along with crayfish, water spiders, free-swimming medusas, a million polyps and vast swarms of blue dashers. This huge armada of curiosity-seeking river creatures lifted the Italian out of peril, depositing him on the far shore.

"Nothing surprises me any more," tried Sannazaro, spitting out barber-basins' worth of Kinattulzy water and removing stubborn jellyfish.

They carried on. At the Mittuny Karsh, a large cliff rose up before them. The buffalo proceeded first, remarkable given its weight and seemingly immovable prospects on so vertical an environment. Barut explained as best he could why this bovine ambassador to the dead was charged with taking the lead. But how a buffalo would manage the cliff, he could not say, though they would soon find out. Maybe the buffalo was already dead, and they just didn't realize it. Perhaps it was the priest, after all, and he'd adopted a different guise.

"If you allow yourself to believe in a land of wraiths, trees inhabited by bogeymen, barghests and kobolds in every slaphappy thicket, then no obstacle is overly daunting. Meaning occupies the ground underfoot, profundities parade across the horizon; each knot in the trunk, every face in the bark, the opening or closing of a flower, the way a sunbeam dances on the fern—it all has clairvoyant meaning to the cultivated one," Barut said with relish.

After all, nothing was as it should have appeared. A child's lock of hair, whitened with age; an umbrella left from 500 years before; a troop of howling jackals gazing up after them. Bumblebees escorting the foursome: the buffalo, the crazy Italian, the even dafter hermit, and the delicately jointed dentist. Each moved one foot, one hand, the other foot, the other hand—gesture by gesture—up the Charnockite wall, diagonaling along a 70-foot band of cliff with great and unprecedented nerve. The buffalo kept looking back to be sure his charges were all right.

"Don't look down, gentlemen," Barut quavered, his eyes as wide as a stereotype. But, "I figured there might be something like this," he said, upon reaching an exposed ledge.

Now, as they traversed the eeny-weeny teaspoonworth of slivering granite to better spy upon the upper requirements of the climb, the ascent took on new and noxious dimensions of some seriousness. A fall would mean no Scottish rhododendron garden. The only thing that was clear was that the buffalo would lead up the steep and serried wall in which had been cut great monumental steps for posterity—slightly too distanced one from the other to make movement either comfortable or secure. Somewhere between history and histrionics.

All was panic for the Italian, who had quickly come off herbal pipe and tonic and stared upwards to avoid any visual contact with the vertical below.

"I've done it again. Damn it on me," he mumbled, flinging upwards in the middle. "I would piss 1,000 times in my pants before doing this again."

Barut followed immediately behind the buffalo, whilst the Commander, altogether confident about their pilgrimage, headed up the rear.

"A marvelous day," he admonished all within earshot.

Neither companion said a word, for Barut was as terrified as Sannazaro, and each clung to every hold as if it were his last. Upon such ungiving granite, evolution itself trembled. All around them, from Silent Valley to the Upper Bhavani, the Nilgiri Biosphere Reserve, as it was known (a sad commentary, given what Marigold and Sannazaro knew to be the truth about the local governance of wildlife), was buttressed by immense outcrops rising in a semicircular ring thousands of feet above Bandipur, Mudumalai, Nagarhole—the three major National Parks—and the Kuppady, Wayanad, Moyar and Sigur forests. The air was exhilarating, but the drop-offs too close for compliments. Superlatives conspired to suffocate the explorers. They were stemming their own piece of dental floss between life and death. In truth, that is not unusual when caught out on the side of a precipice 1,400 vertical feet above the forest.

But Moszh showed no such fears or ponderability, lightly coursing upwards towards the final mond, as it was called by the Todas, likeaspore towards the stratosphere, a kiwi feather in an updraft, a ghostly cloud of metallic mauve rearing like a stallion, or the slow and even percolation of an icy crystal forming in the stunned air. Not the slightest sign of worry. Indeed, it was a magical mountain buffalo, and these cliffs made it most happy.

Scrapes, bloody knuckles, heaving breath; frantic lunges, last-ditch twists; overhangs and underclings, liebacks, loose flakes, off-sized cracks, pockmarks up the face, dihedrals and boiler plates—this was the physical and geological lexicon that now harassed the three amateurs in their desperate efforts to keep apace of Moszh. The summit was near.

A final crack led dead vertically, 50 feet, to an unknown conclusion. Light emanated from above, or that was the optical impression, as Moszh vanished, somehow astronomically propelling its buffalo body into the final ether, and disappearing. Its long tail twitched excitedly the entire distance. Who could say what was up there, or how they'd ever manage a descent. Was there another way down? Or any returning from the land of the dead? Sannazaro and Barut were almost beside themselves. Imunawdr and Amunawdr. Two separate realities. What if they were caught out betwixt and between? There had been no explication. No amends or latitude for error. Toda purgatories?

Barut went first, stabbing his fists sloppily into the weathered granite groove that shot headily into the highest spheres. The notches on the severe and stolid face, on either side of the crack, were scarcely suitable for a human form. How Moszh had managed it could not be described by any but those three who were present that day. No physiological protocols or physical methods could account for a buffalo of such freakish dexterity. What buffalo motivation, level of education, spiritual initiation could have compelled so spectacular a devotion, so knowing and soulful a diligence? Not to mention the acrobatics themselves, which defied every wild antelope, ox and bufaleau. Wallowing and plowing. A bullock jointed like a bird. Nitroglycerin without pause. Bones, cartilage and muscle everlasting. Such was the firepower that exuded from its nostrils and lungs, this behemoth leading the way upon the cliff.

It happened because it was meant to happen. Barut somehow reached the summit just after the Buffalo Priest; Marigold and Sannazaro after him. There, in the presence of certain bovine effigies, potholes filled with rainwater, cinquefoils that bloomed but one day a year, the whole summit flowered, the light piercing through the last of the winter monsoons. An undulating voice, or breath, or sonority of compulsive poetics, raised the ante of physical exertion to the level of pure transcendence. Was it thunder from above? Or the heavy lowing of Moszh? Until the soft light of the yawning cliff entered their veins. It was the beauty of the Earth.

A wild retinal embrace, threefold in its punctuation marks; three men, all their senses attuned far beyond the call of normal neurology, admitted to a prospect of the original world.

Moszh moved higher, to what appeared a final resting place. There he lay down on his gorgeous burnished haunches between granite knobs. The men, silent and obeisant to the moment, followed the animal. It sat beside a vent upon the summit where coins had been tossed. A chasm that appeared to have no bottom. The coins continued to float, as in a glycerine darkness, a greenstone and abalone kaleidoscope, never repeating the same fractals. From their promontory the threesome crawled to the cave's staggering edge and stared into its tornado stellar stairwell, a 2,004-foot cliff of fabulist Ernst, romance à la Miro, perspectives defined by Calder, Winslow Homer, wind that from below rushed up to drench their senses with Mondrians' vacant calm.

At that instant the light exploded in their faces: miles of glow-worms on the inner walls, their sexual bioluminescences shattering the dark like every constellation in the universe, all at once. Billions of minute bursts of pinhole laser light, flares of the divine concentrated in the cylindrical funnel. A vast, downward-reaching stained-glass cathedral, electron blizzards of every Chartres, brimming with incomprehensible photon shards. In each atom of that rejoicing, advancing and dissolving flame were the embodied souls of all those Todas who had come and gone, riding their buffaloes into the paradise of an eternal hearth at the center of the Earth, as seen from the dormer window at the summit of the world known as Iryoodh, not a single care or burthen.

The mountain was Teomuszhkwehln.

Adding to this blistering heaven, a double blue moon in whose lunar streams were voices echoing in the rising chorus, their souls descended from the beyond—the human beyond, a small clump of forest known as Awlvoodh. That cliff was the paramount meeting point, a vision as pellucid and inspiring as any terrestrial cornerstone could be.

Barut, Marigold, Sannazaro, Moszh: they stared as one mind into the infinite truth of reincarnation, their faces touching, tears falling, the easiness of being good, leaving light footprints, harming no living creature. Life could be lived in that way. It was obvious, now. They had stared into their future, seen all of its outlines and many of the more dramatic particulars, and they were challenged now to exercise the megatonnage available to the human conscience. In this eruptive fumarole of intimate connections with the souls of the dead they looked over the affairs of man, of other species, too, and detected how clearly incumbent upon each and every shepherd was the simple task to nurture and revere the world.

The ancient Greeks called it *synderesis*, that cathartic capability in the human heart to reach out, to reverse all those tragedies inflicted by our kind. In the airy citadel amid a confusion of so many unearthly lights, there was nothing to impede the direct impression. Now they knew there was no such thing as death.

"I am certain of it," Marigold declared. "Think how short are our fuses? Are we to be dashed and gotten ridden of just at the moment of our greatest gifts and wisdom? I think not." And he carried on with a weightless perspective, ever childlike. He now understood that while man's inner peace and blood pressure were prone to great fits, a little patience and altitude could easily reveal the truth of the full world and its timeframe. A truth that transcended the day-by-day vivisections.

For once in his life Mr Marigold was speechless. Now he had seen it for himself. He hugged his companions, and they hugged him, entering into that pact surpassing provocation. It was more interesting to face up to hell than give way to heaven, Marigold asserted, owning that Heaven was the state of Nature before man; but man had arrived and must be considered.

"Have we not a duty to deal with humanity, by honest implication? Such that we dote upon and spoil ourselves," Sannazaro vowed.

"But we cannot separate ourselves from six billion others," Marigold pointed out. "It is simply not in the best interests of the world for us to do so. I'll give no quarter to a selfish gene."

By nightfall, the all-knowing chameleon of a buffalo led them down a secret passage off the back of the mountain. It took them through a cave six miles in length, one of many systems girding the sacred alpines of the afterlife. There were enough potholes on the surface to throw continuous moonlight down the narrow limestone passageways. Throughout the cave complex, cataracts plunged, pug marks and feathers of hiding animal life punctuated their progress. Glow-worms covered the walls and their night lights were beacons to the wanderers. The geological forces which had fashioned this cave, millions of years ago, involved the flow of mighty rivers, the cleaving of enormous bulwarks of rock wall, calcium formations whose oozing remains had encrusted into coral forests hanging upside down, crumbling to dust if touched even gently by a finger; stalagmites of towering creamy white. Tannic acid glossed green the stones of the rushing creeks over which they traipsed, and giant spiders and herbivorous snails dotted the candescent subterranean cordillera.

They eventually re-emerged from the tunnels.

Sparks flowed from the heels of Moszh's centaurian hoofs. Slow-motion lightning strikes upon the abode of deities, moonglow abreast the birch copse. New species gracing the immediate landscape like diamonds. Moszh was no longer himself, but a seer, omniscient, enormous, beholding in his companions the miraculous change in man. The buffalo delivered this knowledge to his three human companions that night as they crossed the Keenyter, an expansive swampland in whose eerie center was located a kind of rusticated bivouac hut known as Kwershy, where one slept on cushions of Ter Borg-green moss and drank no-fat nectar which flowed from the center of the Earth through a small cranny into the domain, such that dreams turned into reality.

It was in this vicinity that the last Stone Age honey-bee collector was seen in the early 1990s, Barut told them. Twenty-five years earlier, four such mostly naked pygmies had been spotted by a Toda. Whether they had now become extinct was not known.

In the night cold, lungs partaking, head unwinded, nostrils keen, nose to the highs, heels to the lows, they drew at length upon a row of rare stone fireplaces known to the Toda as Kojkocbem. Heat was still emanating, even though it might have been years since a corpse's spirit traveled this route. Whatever the afterlife chemistry involved was not for them to glean.

Beyond, a certain rock swarmed with single-minded flies and maggots. Barut knew from his Toda informants that this was the place where diseases of this world were left behind.

By dawn, they were descending past the famed Kotyarrnvilz Maayn tree, part of Mukurti National Park, and into a valley of migrating Asiatic elephants, the ones with smaller toes. There were also fresh tiger tracks. They came upon a rushing stream known as Pufirkeen or Bhavanipuzha, where one's spirit was supposed to be cleansed of any remaining irritants or adulterants.

"But how?" asked the Commander, prepared to wade but finding it too deep.

"I'm not sure," said Barut, waiting for the buffalo to scope it out. The mighty animal moved upstream, though the men could see no better method in that. Suddenly, however, the Moszh leaped into the water and without too much trouble stood upon surface stones that provided a kind of causeway of solid ground straight across the shallows. "Follow on faith," Barut suggested. He knew from his informants that this was the famed 'thread bridge' invisible to mortals. No fears now, despite electric jellyfish. More blue dashers. The buffalo waited for each of the three men, extending its horns so that they could pull themselves across without difficulty, as to the grail.

Guts gaping, foreheads brimming, inner thighs pulsing, knuckles battered, toes tortured, heels burning from blood blisters and gouges grim, at last they completed the exhausting, night-enflamed, tendon-warping trek all the way back to Heerkittykitty and Inkblotty. There they were greeted by a slumber party of horny women (one of whom was particularly eager to resume her lascivious tryst with her Italian amore) bearing mugs of hot buffalo milk, curdled and disgusting, and some elusive weed that grew unexpectedly and which they worshipped. A Nilgiri marigold, Barut said with a smile at the coincidence of it, mashed into a delicious, life-affirming gruel.[19]

CHAPTER 89
Saving the World, Versus a Well-salted Tomato and Mozzarella Salad

IT WAS AN INORDINATE descent. From the ecstatic, glow-worm-infested Paradise of Buffalo Bonanzas and Heavenly Hereafters to Moribund Mumbai. A huge inevitability, somehow logical and on the way, no matter the come-down, like some snake charmer reeling them in, the potions of geography exerting all those inexpressible combinations of desire and depression, panic and perverse appetites, equal portions of altruism and alienation, humanity and homophobia that are grace and gravy on each birthright.

UNESCO, the World Health Organization, UNDP, read any journal, which Marigold certainly had: if you are serious about making a difference, then save the children. The same sentiment echoes down every gutter. In the picture gallery of slums. Then it must be India. The largest democracy in the world, a hackneyed cough. Over a billion people. The sheer smell of it. Change their minds, change the body politic. Alter an orbit. Upset the moonlight. Obscure the very sun. Reverse a history. Give them back water to drink, air to breathe, soil for planting, seeds they may call their own. A symbol for the rest of us. A shift, in other words, whereby one shapes the grand design in a particular. Mends the big picture by embracing an individual. It must be Mumbai, city of fortune tellers and bright marigolds.

And thus began a new day ...

"Dilli To Pagal Hai—ka masterpiece, abhi khareedo, kal khatam ho jaayeega!" the shoving boys cried out, jockeying at every crawling intersection in the city, tapping on car windows for attention. *Buy now, tomorrow gone.* In their hands, the pirated home videos of a recent classic Hindi love romp, a *Chorus Line* of suppressed passion in its most family-moving manner: pent-up romance released only after three hours of pillow fights and interminable intimation. At a dozen theaters across the city the throngs of movie-goers were tossing money at the screen in adoration of its masterful frolics, and the sultry, never to-be-kissed, star-crossed universal heart throb, Marjorie.

"Thik-hai," Mr Marigold said, paying 200 rupees for the cassette, rolling down his window, staring at the handsome worn eyes of the young vendor, a what-makes-swami-run. The boy coursed between the traffic jam occasioned by the closing of two roads on account of the forty-eighth anniversary of the death of Ambedkar, the great compatriot of Gandhi who turned Buddhist at the end of his life. Impoverished Dalits were lined up for miles to pay tribute to his cremation site, had queued for days to commemorate a fellow untouchable who had achieved literary and philosophical eminence. It was not impossible, but rare.

"But you'll never watch it," said Sannazaro.

Marigold noticed his Squire's eyes, tired and ringed from all their travels, a blue sack breathing markedly beneath the left, and a squeamish ocher sore on his right cheek.

"The boy's smile is the price of admission."

"To what?" Sannazaro fiddled, less discomforted than in previous days, acclimating now.

"The treasure chest of revelations," sighed the high-riding commodore, his head skirting the ceiling of their rented Maruti 800.

After countless new resolves and reconciliations, hopes uttered, frustrations put to rest, master plans conceptualized, others tossed, Marigold and Sannazaro had left the company of their new lifelong friend Barut, bid farewell to Toda Land, and managed to make their way northwest into Mumbai, home to Master Singh, of the *Gandhi*, as well as to 18 million or so for whom the day was like any other, as life lamented, celebrated, strutted, drowned and weathered on. Ignorance, cruelty, desire. Such pitfalls were everywhere manifest on any given street of the bewildering megalopolis. They represented the world, and Marigold knew he had to fight it. To remain in Amunawdr was not the solution: not for him, not for anybody. He could simply not abide the seizures all around him. In a matter of months he had changed from a hermit, happily to himself, to one who could not live without seeing others equally disposed.

"How can I be content to lounge in the Garden of Eden, when everybody else is peeing and coughing up blood?" he admonished his exhausted compatriot.

But Sannazaro insisted that the sacred buffalo had conveyed some other psychic directive entirely. "What I heard him remark upon was a Four Seasons pizza done alla Tuscany, a fine Chianti from Sienna, and a well-salted tomato and mozzarella salad the way my own ancestors prepared it in Positano."

Marigold expatiated on the dangers of consuming too much salt, and argued strenuously for a vegan appetite. As usual, he prevailed upon the dissembling Squire who had no will left to fight. They had philosophically entered the maelstrom, giving it meaning where possible, making their way by taxi in an effort to assimilate it all, traversing whole sections of the city, hour after hour, in search of that unknown trigger-effect of consciousness likely to galvanize their next move. Marigold relished this aimless peregrination. For purposes of assessing the overall condition of the locals, one street or neighborhood was just as good as another, he pointed out. He was counting bodies, pains, disturbances and opportunities, taking a close mental toll of all the ills and prayers that accosted him second by second.

Sannazaro was relieved by the size of the city, with its portion of gleaming high rises and the fact there was an international airport. The next stop would be London or Hong Kong, and then home to the United States. He counted the hours.

Wouldn't it be lovely, he kept thinking, to sit back, do nothing, mount a campaign of unprecedented hedonism, safeguard not Toda flowers but himself from all the turmoil and complications; to avoid work, risk, exposure, human contact. To pay no heed to the disastrous course of human self-destruction. To accept as destiny Nature's own unparalleled plight. Wouldn't it be swell to ignore suffering, disavow trouble, escape all comparisons, noise, squalor, subjugation and taxes. Shelter himself with every luxury, protect his funerary, hidden within tens of thousands of luscious acres, from tampering. In a shrine to himself, air conditioned, his precious belongings all around him. A lonely haiku by Ippen as his companion, his garden and a few sleeping pills in the end. This scenario was tempting. But then, with one look at the Commander, so laden with beliefs and hopes, a tired champion of the impossible, emerged a volley of guilts, profound sadness, nausea. What sort of man was Sannazaro, anyway? A monster of unfeeling? A man no different from a lorry driver or depraved mahoot?

Wherever they drove, the movie hoardings crowded out the sky. Escape from misery, if only for a few hours. Mythic heroes flashed guns and swords, painted heroines against emblazoned backdrops. The great names—Shyam Benegal, Shabana Azmi, M. Dixit. Another sequel to the 250-crore box-office smash, *Hum Aapke Kain Hoon*, a wedding video, of sorts, that had become a national institution. At an art house, revivals of the Om Puri classics, *Mandi*, *Jane Bhi Do Yaro*, and *City of Joy*, the poster describing that rickshaw driver in Calcutta as a man "who could not care more", as countered by a man, the American co-star "who could not care less". Such opposition, the fundamental breakdown of the psyche in Mumbai, caused juxtapositions of wealth and poverty to pour from every seam, out every cranny, down each alley and boulevard, through every single window and door, all the way to the horizonless gulf separating whosoever's heaven from everyone's hell.

You could try to fix it, someone had said (the very point of *City of Joy*), banging your head against every wall of every room of every house or hovel in every district of each city in all the nations. And your head would not even measure a bruise or a bump, in India.

Indeed, the country's problems were immeasurable, and—according to those purportedly universal ground rules of the perilous, dog-eat-dog African night—seemed reliably fixated on rebuffing any fool who might set out to fix them, or aspire after general principles of amelioration, or seek to model himself after the actions of any saintly behavior. All were drowned out in the urgency to get on with practical survival that was Mumbai, a city transported by sacred slums and escapist cinema.

Mr Marigold had come vast distances to reject this self-fulfilling mindset on the very day the newspapers were quoting a State Department official who had uttered a memorable bromide in reference to the mounting crisis between India and Pakistan: "Leaders must be extremely cautious about actually using nuclear weapons."

"Two rights do not mend a wrong, necessarily," Señor Sannazaro was quick to point out, "however much you may laud or, god spare us, emulate the wonderful actions and convictions of a Mother Teresa or rickshaw driver in a movie."

So far, this face-to-face with India had only substantiated Sannazaro's worst antipathies. Not everyone shared such bilious opinions of the place. One leading Indian expatriate female film director had groaned "Boring!" to reporters, insisting that India was not the one portrayed by Louis Malle in *Phantom India*; that it harbored no more of those much-touted extremes of indifference and poverty, but was, like any Western power, a nation of cellular phones and middle-aged housewives driven by ennui and lesbian proclivities. The Señor, however, was not impressed by the growing middle class (15 percent of the total, so he'd read), and saw nothing but unrelieved sorrow, a society of denials, blinders and karmic hypocrisy. This was his verdict after simply opening his eyes. No one of any sensitivity could fail to catch the too-obvious sense of futility that India inspired. "I know about India," he had insisted weeks before, having just been plucked from the Antarctic Ocean. "I don't need to go there."

"We'll go, and I'll finance the country's way out," Marigold offered.

"Why not renounce your own bacteria? Same thing," the Squire replied.

Now that he had been coaxed into coming (a refugee with little choice) Sannazaro was admittedly more shocked than he had anticipated. Stunned not merely by what he had witnessed of the unbelievable cruelty to animals but by the dreary haze of fatigue enshrouding all of it. The eternal war zone that was India. An impenetrable isolation evidencing no inner forces of correction; Plato's Cave enlarged to millions of square miles. Nine hundred walking people, Touchables and Untouchables, rub shoulders on their way to the mills, road after road. Squatting, tending, plucking, preening, pouring, swinging in circles, clapping hands, retrieving from the road, picking rice, plucking lice, talking of new times, twisting bidis. The cavalcade graced the Maruti, whose western occupants—the Commander and his Squire, and local driver—wobbled like an upended beetle, bared by so much density and inch-by-inch progress as part of the morning squadrons of rush-hour Mumbaians.

Sannazaro reminded the Commander of a story he'd heard of Mother Teresa. How a Swiss banker of some prestige had come to her in Calcutta and spoken of his intention to be associated with her by way of a charitable donation. Mother listened patiently, took the earnest financial trendsetter's hands and kindly, ever so gently, replied to the effect that Indians could take care of their own poor. Perhaps he should consider financing a home for the elderly in Zurich, instead. But was that true, or mere pride? Was there room for pride at such times? Marigold had his own ideas.

There was too much turmoil all around them—a guttered fanaticism drenched in despair. No chance of escape, no reason to go on. A boy, standing splayed before a tent, wept, while idle children, skulls shaven, sat waiting for nothing, ever, to happen. A dog, tied uselessly to one senseless corner of the war-torn world, furiously rubbed its mange. Amid the endless hammering of metal workers an old woman clutched at a pink door wrapped in drying saris. The huts sprawled everywhere, like cartwheels of geometric illogic.

The moment-by-moment traffic continued to crawl. Up above, and to most sides, upon wooden scaffolds (they used to be bamboo, but it was disappearing across Asia), skinny men in dhotis went about their construction work. The light changed and their driver, Mohammedbai, raced through the congeries of dust and smoke, outpacing the diesel lorries. He cut it within a camel's hair of colliding—a game of wily rooster that made no sense unless this was your only world, day in, day out. He took in a sign: ICICI Bonds, Rs.3,000 become Rs.100,000. A dream pulsating, from Servo and Exide to the hills of India where he was bored to tears.

A desperate dog nuzzled in a garbage pit. Requiring a new definition of garbage: the number of tons per square inch multiplied by 5,000 years, divided by zero.

A prolixity of films perpetrated their fancy heroic illusions down every corridor of the city—Shapath, Quahar, Dhaal—hoardings of curiously encrypted aesthetic purpose. To all sides placards of enterprise, and struggle. Everywhere Marigold's impressions were swept over by a barrage of signs. India hosted more signs than any country in the world. Laxmi Enterprise; Shankha Pushpi for Best Performance. Banana Vendor, Ltd. The prurient magazine stall; Vishwa and Thums Up competing with Pepsi, STD ISD PCD, Bristol; Shanti Teas; a stall of apricots like soggy bums; Jai Brake-O Oil and Grease; the lice picking in duplicate; the distended stomach syndrome; "May Your World Always be a MARVelous Place", the sign read in the hut, picturing a peacock at play near a pipal tree; and the scrubbing near the Maharashtra Beer Center and State Bank of India, all this.

Gold Flake, Dave Tobacco and Gopal Travels, too. Concentrated. The big Water Tanker, a gusher of leaks; the lucky ravens, kites scooping up their daily thirst quench; Mayur Jewellers, a parade of dowry dreams; Peppermint Room; Bhadshaw Wines (the latest Indian bid for international recognition, that) and Milan Stores; Marush Matai Paper Marts; women's coops in Gujarat famous for their hand-dyes in every pore, every inch of tissue permanently stamped with inks; Sri Labdhal Laundrments, the boys beside the steamers, wiping their eyes on their loin cloths, an image of steam that is the commemorative stamp of the whole country; S.L. Raheja HOSpita and Magna Sites; CHEMICALS, PLASTICS, SALTS, METALS, LYES; the rushing train with its flotillas of standing men and boys clinging to the outsides, heads bulging like distended gourds from inside, clustered in the impervious urgencies of getting to miserly paying jobs. These are the lucky ones. Pan Beedi, a girl getting whipped, no reason; Lottery Center, hopefuls queuing up for another go; Motor School—middle-class aspirants these, the female achieves her independence at last; Lime Depot; Jackpot Country Liquor Bar; Madania Kirana and Johnson House. A crowd of garlanded boys practicing for a wedding band, five children clinging to their sleeping father beside the tracks of the railway. Four hundred famished pigeons, scuttling under the whining brakes of a train just in.

Marigold saw through the huts, which sat directly beside the ten layers of tracks upon which trains squealed with strident high twines all day, all night. Some of the huts were favored by collages of scrap to conceal, if not one decibel, at least the sight of the ugly mechanical monsters screaming by. But most huts did not. Bengali paper thrashers searching through garbage to resurrect their own complex, cyclists careening past the 5,000 smoke fires of the rock cutters whose children squatted on the pavement floor in the 95-degree December sun, defecating, peeing, swarming, jammed, plagued and beset, wailing and beaming.

"The smiles are interesting," Marigold at last confessed. "Not," Sannazaro mumbled. He detested the country.

They paused beside a rowhouse, more ramshackle plating of scrap, with its hanging ornaments of green and red peppers to signify prayer and auspicious good tidings. A stocky woman with a child was kneeling to scrub, and smiled exuberantly upon seeing the two men, who smiled back. How did such a smile originate amid such deprivation? Their few personal belongings confined to the recycled, endlessly re-used essentials: a hand wire brush to do the ancient Indian swastikas; a grandmother who can hold the baby; a man peeling back bottle caps with an awkward tool that has been suited to the task for a century (the bottle caps can be sold at the recycling centers in Forlorn, Asia's largest slum); a string for hanging the soiled muslin; a teenager whose task is to shout "hello hello" to passers-by; another bandaged, unemployed grown son sitting akimbo on a palanquin of tar paper preparing his morning chula with its improvised mix of cannabis derivatives; a comb to partition the grease; a bucket for washing; a husband who sits near the dog whose two-foot chain keeps it shackled next to the broiled sun of the railroad track; and the mad woman wailing at the purposelessness of such misery.

"COKE COKE ENJOY COKE" plastered throughout the terrains of Tulsi. Or "GMC FOR A BETTER LIFE STYLE. And JAI MATA JI, and Natraj Traders, and Jolly Lunch Home, and BITS for those who might someday inconceivably take up computer trades in Marati, the local language of Mumbai. THEY'VE CLEANED UP CALCUTTA, reads the sign. And goes on: THAT'S THE PLACE TO BE.

A man wobbled on one leg, his foot in a sandal. Another dragged himself on a roller board, his legs reversed, truncated at the pelvis, his back nuanced like a coiled scorpion's tail, his bangs bristling with the sweat of endurance, the total effect an arc de triomphe of inward pertinacity. Where was he going so briskly in that manner, no more than 11 inches from the ground, such as it was (a choked pavement of injuries accumulated over centuries, razzle-dazzled with the importunate impurities of every species of phlegm and discard, gravel and oil drop, feces, crab, HIV residue and the froth of death undelayed, connected to every spice of life and caked in some disease of disorder that is solid to the touch)? Yet, a man nearby danced with a chicken, the latest step. At the Mud Gate before the mills, men furiously repaired taxis. People chopping corn, trundling burlap sacks of black salt, pulverizing small piles of coal; the sign said FINESSE INFOTECH, and on the corner a condom dispenser, a woman, who strung her dozen brands in the limelight of the morning glow of a neem tree.

Along Tulsi Road, near the Lokhi Marg Dispensary, across from Elphinstone's Textile Mill, its 190-foot smokestack reigning over the slum-dwelling aggregates with a dark infinitude of hopelessness for the 100,000 Bengalis living in tents there, Marigold noticed a wizened monkey tied to a stake at Gajjar's Roadside Metal Fabrications. It looked back at him. Like a mirror. Every monkey, every miserable creature that had ever lived, and died, was reflected in that very moment.

The Commander took hold of Sannazaro's shoulder. "See there!" he cried.

CHAPTER 90
Marigold Sees Himself in the Mirror of Monkeys

"MUHAMMEDBAI, BACK ... back *up ... stop!* " Marigold instructed feverishly, his forehead sweating profusely, the blood in his veins coming to boil for the ninety-ninth time that morning.

"What will you do?" the Squire asked.

"Just keep a lookout."

"What—what are you doing?"

But it was too late. Sannazaro crossed himself as the Commander skirted the anarchy, and ran headlong between cyclists and berserk diesel truck drivers who came within inches of creaming him.

A rhesus, the color of old rum, discerned Marigold by instinct, picking the one out of 1,000 wobbly objects all around him, a blur of purpose heading directly towards its prison. The nearest other human to the monkey sat intently upon a stool piercing a metal plate, hammering a rusted iron beam into a molded shape, recycling scrap in the eternal karmic metallurgy that was his destiny. No food, no water for the monkey. Only the squalid dirt floor, the heat, the incessant hammering, the added furor of the road. And that chain which held it within a lifeless arc of a semicircle, and three or so feet. A desert of desertions. Far in the distance was a rim of myrobalan and sal trees, enough to ruin the primate's nerves with nullifying nostalgia. Cool shadows of peepal, harada, jackfruit and neem, of keekar and babool, sami and banana that once harbored its infancy; green silences of the forest in which his family, for a moment, experienced one another, secured in the branches of Lord Vishnu. The succor of memory all that was left it. Before the rupture, more than a decade before: first the jhuming, shifting cultivators, plows and bullocks; then the road, and one night, by torchlight, a sudden gunblast. His mother plunged from the tree, his siblings falling with her. Only this one monkey survived, to be taken away in a net.

Now the monkey peed in anticipation. It divined the arriving hand before it was extended, glucose wafer in his fingers.

There, a moment between two species, utterly lost to the raucous hell surrounding it. No greater God reaching out for Adam's finger; no more memorable instant of translation and affinity in all the annals of touching.

The monkey swept up the offering, coveting it to his breast in astonished, nearly mournful realization of a hospitality that was unheard of in the land of taunts and terror. This Indian law of the jugular.

"It's all right, we love you, sweetheart," the Commander calmly murmured, stroking his ears, preening his fur, the sentimentality of Schweitzer in the midday candescence.

The metal worker laughed, gesturing, perhaps incredulous or embarrassed. Whatever the sentiments they at once turned hostile, and when Mr Marigold demanded, with all his bunched-up height and heavy-breathing Dragon Americanus, that he must have the monkey, the little man returned the attitude no less indignantly. His anger grew with the foment of those others nearby who rushed forward, as they always do in India, to throw in their combined huddle weight. But this was a battle Marigold intended to win. He had not stopped the beating of an elephant, or saved a million cows, steers, goats and sheep at Gundlepet, but he was truly worthless if he couldn't at least free this one monkey.

"God damn it!" he shouted at the top of his lungs. Now that was something.

Muhammedbai had managed to make a u-turn so as to park the Maruti directly before the metallurgist. He and Sannazaro stepped out and cleaved to their compatriot, though the Muslim from the hills was befuddled, for he had no idea what had inspired such nonsense. "Tell him I will pay any price for this monkey," Marigold said.

Muhammedbai conveyed the words.

"Nei," the metal worker laughed. "Pet."

"It is his pet," Muhammedbai translated.

"How much?" Marigold asked, exacerbated beyond any and all compliance, and Sannazaro feared for fisticuffs, as had happened so many times and always with unenviable results. Here, lacking even a sword, the odds were definitely stacked against them.

"Nei," the metal worker squelched, this time with a hotter temperature.

At which the Commander withdrew a fresh wad of 5,000 rupees, still stapled with the white slip around one end. He flipped the money cuff like a dealer a deck of cards, and there was no doubt about it: the money meant something. But this was a conniving, cunning bastard accustomed to every difficulty and hatred, to slow progress, to wielding an altercation of terms rigorously and patiently.

"Twenty-five thousand rupees," the man demanded in a tone that belied his own astonishment at so outrageous an asking price for a mere monkey, and one he'd acquired only a week before, from a cousin who had addicted it to amphetamines for purposes of invigorating the animal's performance for tourists along the ocean walk at Marine Drive. The cousin had died. The monkey was sick. There were probably but a few weeks of work left its life.

"No, boss," the driver pleaded, spitting at the sheer arrogance. "Way too much."

"Tell him 15,000, then," Marigold bargained, unhappy about negotiating over a life.

But to Muhammedbai, who netted that much in not less than four months, driving 18 hours a day through the oppressive swarm, sleeping on a concrete floor with a paper-thin mat beside the elevator of the building where he was full-time employed, 15,000 was an outrage. At 59, with no wife and only a younger, sickly brother to look after, his life was one of solitary and mysterious acceptance of such hard-going. But this asking price for a monkey was beyond his silence, and he protested vigorously, making as if to pummel the metal worker with a solid blow or two. It could easily have ignited another communal war in the city. That happened all the time. A single word could spark a conflagration, taking out miles of huts.

It did not come to that. They would settle on 14,000 rupees, approximately 320 dollars. "It's a good thing he came to his senses," declared the Commander.

"Or there would have been hell to pay."

Now the monkey was removed from his chain, a task of precarious engineering as he had been affixed with the idea of permanency. Moreover, there was always the possibility the primate would flee the instant of liberation into an almost certain death amid the traffic. But Mr Marigold comforted the haggard being in ways that seemed to touch everyone, even the awe-struck co-workers who remained gathered around the transaction. In India, no matter how cruel, such beneficence was, ultimately, remembered from some religious penumbra of the past.

In historic India, civil wars had been put on hold so that a sacred snake could be pacified, a leopard cured, a tiger honored. Gods had turned into crickets; Vishnu, the eagle, the boar, the fish and the turtle. Brahma, creator, the swan; Durga, goddess of fortune, a Brahminy kite. Even the princely rat had figured as the mount of Ganesh, god of wisdom, whose head was that of an elephant. These hypocritical associations in Indian prehistory mocked the reality: an India intent on cleaning the slate, killing every beast of the forest in exchange for calico and saltpeter, factories of indigo. The famed Mughal Jahangir boasted in his diary of personally killing 14,000 animals between 1580 and 1616. The Emperor Aurangzeb, much revered across the subcontinent, employed his entire army to flush out the game. All those 'Paradise scenes' in miniature: the lustily favored princess, aiming her rifle at the unsuspecting peacock, preparing to blow away the tiger and its mate on the water's edge.

Even as late as the early 1960s, a royal hunting expedition arrived from Great Britain. Picture the Queen herself standing with other 'dignitaries' beside the dead tiger her party had bagged at what is today Ranthambhore National Park. In 1900, there were an estimated 50,000 tigers in India. In Marigold's time, as few as 1,000.

They say that some monkeys in India speak 'Hindi' words fluently.

This, the Commander knew, had not stopped Indians from slaughtering the slender loris for its eyes that always appear so astonished in death; the lion-tailed macaques for their skins and meat, believed by locals to increase a man's potency, as if that were any problem in a country overrun by more than 600 million men; langurs taken from the wild for the blood and organs; and the rhesus, like this one, shipped off in agony to American biomedical laboratories, or forced to perform tricks for the odd rupee until it drops.

The animal, now clasped to the Commander's chest, had not felt the warmth of an affectionate soul since infancy. He was not about to give up the chest and shoulders of this sudden and amazing liberator, nor demonstrated the slightest sign of distress when the party returned to its waiting vehicle.

Muhammedbai spread out pages of the *Indian Express* across the back seat, where the monkey sat upright, beside the suzerain, to lessen the likelihood of any accidents, and they drove off in the direction of the nearest National Park. Never had the Commander seen such slums as those they passed through—

encrusted, archeological sinkholes whose populations had doubled every generation for 200 generations.

"What if he chooses not to leave?" Sannazaro remarked. "I'm talking about the monkey. Or if he's lost the ability to forage for himself?"

"I'll instruct him," Marigold replied, his face flushed with victory. "On my all fours if need be. And rest assured there is always a mate in the woods. Advice you too should one day consider."

CHAPTER 91
Bharat (India) Ek (One) Dhin (Day)

DEEPER AND DEEPER into the guts of the marginal metropolis they drove, hitting hard against December. The traffic came nearly to a halt. A lorry had jackknifed, roads congesting upon twelve catacombing corners, screaming drivers locked out like angry yellowjackets, smoke filling pinioned air. With persistence, Muhammedbai struck out along a lone, implausible course through tortuous alleyways, past mail-order houses and chili-pepper boutiques. Suddenly they emerged.

"Oh, look!" Sannazaro cried out. "Ice cream!"

They'd come out of oppressive quarters by destiny, and there was Arabesque 29, referring to Flavors.

They studied, they purchased, they devoured. The monkey received his own two cones—caramel triple fudge pecan, and butterscotch marshmallow—seized up with suppressed conviction. Then he had another, before he puked. Sannazaro got him a large bowl of water and some animal crackers, then helped himself to a cappuccino, adding iodine, and one for the driver.

Sitting indoors out of the petroleum haze, the Commander took the opportunity to scan the midday newspapers, always reading between the lines, forever on the lookout. He read a statement issued by pollution control authorities declaring that "at the moment, one can say that by and large, more or less, for all practical purposes or otherwise, no water from any stream, river, creek bed, or water faucet should be consumed by humans anywhere in the country. That goes for food grown in the ground, on account of pollutants in the soil; and air breathed within two hundred miles of any town with more than a million residents." Which fairly encompassed every square mile of India.

It was International Human Rights Day in Mumbai, but poor twelve-year-old Vijay stood tied by the ankle to a fence somewhere to prevent him from running away. His mother squatted nearby peeling potatoes. He'd been tied for years, said the report.

"FREE—One CALCULATOR—with every Lexus (briefcase)". The Sensex and BSE-index continued to plunge nearly 100 points as the selling pressure by those overseas investors and the taking of fast profits by all the local operators wreaked havoc in all quarters. The NSE-50 index was also fluctuating wildly, as world economists chided the country for not moving fast enough on reforms. The rupee hit an all-time low of 45 against the dollar.

Serious steps were undertaken to free pedestrian footpaths from illegal occupation. Eleven unions of hawkers took up arms. Twelve squadrons of pedestrians took up legs.

"Saudi Arabia—Free Recruitment—Fun in the Sun". "Executioners, guaranteed elimination of white ants".

Even rickshaw drivers hotly debated the Jain Commission Report's new allegation (without foundation, aired an immigrant mob) that a former Queen of Nepal's assistant had asked a nameless honorary aide-de-camp to a former King of Nepal to arrange for the assassination of a former Indian big-wig. Formers, assistants, nameless mystery figures.

"THE NATION IS PLUNGED IN CHAOS!"

"JAIPUR SCULPTORS IN TROUBLE: More takers for Gandhi idols in Paraguay than within all of India".

"CENTRAL RAILWAY AUTHORITY IN DESPERATE NEED OF RELIABLE PARTNER WITH GOOD TIES".

Two persons were killed in fresh police firing during communal clashes. Elsewhere, a woman was raped by six Sikkimese attendants and thrown off the top of the ten-story building to her death.

A conspiracy theory emerging in Dharmsala. Multiple Chinese assassinations of high-ranking Tibetan lamas.

The Rotarians of Churchgate had a luncheon comprising roti, bhaji, chawal and dal to discuss "Population Control: Yes, or No?" Meanwhile, the Government had abandoned any pretense to a Population Policy, after 45 years of debating its merits. Pundits predicted that within another 30 years the nation would number two billion, far outstripping China as the most crowded country in human history. Still, the newsbrief said consolingly, there would be enough cinnamon rolls, cherry-coated popsicles and fruit tarts for everyone.

On that day, the number of sub-castes in the country exceeded 4,000.

Superiority and inferiority remained "the basis of Indian society". Polio drops were distributed to eleven lakh children, while the country's fiscal deficit widened.

Tens of thousands of condoms were buried by family planning workers in a southern part of the state because, it was admitted, the men did not know how to use them. Smoking in public was banned in one section of the city. Rejoicing. Cotton manufacturers stunned the market. Bakery industries were scrambling. A hundred-plus years before, British forces were defeated at Stromberg, in South Africa, declared the conferees at a study group in Calcutta, which proceeded to draw all sorts of scintillating analogies to the "present crisis".

"DUBAI IS CHEAP".

Everywhere Gul Mohur trees were sprouting audacious red clusters of wilted flowers as two more Indian satellites were launched. In Juhu, residents of apartment buildings gathered to protest to the local authorities over the accumulation of garbage during the past five years, as well as the unchecked proliferation of "beedi and cycle shops, food and tea stalls, milk stands, an unsavory phone booth filled with pictures of naked harlots, a rickshaw repair center, scrap dealers, cobblers, garages, upholstery venues, grocery outlets and barbers" on the beach in front of them, thus obscuring the view. Eleven houses were set on fire and seven of those fleeing the conflagration were fired upon. Twenty-eight women jumped from a fast-moving train on the rumor that there was smoke. All died of complications. Several miles away, at 12.23 in the afternoon, a new high-rise apartment building collapsed, killing 168 people. All such high-rises (tens of thousands of them across the city) were put on notice for possible faulty construction. " 'Just leave,' advised the nearby constable.

'Migrate to the south, where there are fewer high-rises.'"

In *Navakal*, the popular Marathi daily, readers woke up to a headline telling of certain aliens that had recently conducted hybridization experiments on Mexicans. Soon, Indians could expect similar tests, it was widely feared.

A performance of the Bakavadham Kathakali at the Keli classical theater fest was interrupted by the arrest of certain Naxalites hiding out in the audience and carrying sticks of dynamite.

Cricketers and footballers continued to dominate public interest; the Bandra Packers and Royal Caterers all remaining neck-and-neck, while breaking turns in international squash were little followed.

A bulldog and shih tzu were successfully crossed for the first time.

A movie theatre burned down. The audience managed to escape, but every actor in the film died in the blaze. Rites were held later in the day, with verses sung by hundreds from the Rudradhyaya Mantras and thousands of bilva (woodapple tree) leaves burned as part of an arati offering.

In adjoining parts of Maharashtra, official promises were kept, and goals achieved. For example, 40 million rupees were earmarked for the Market Intervention Scheme; 12,000 bore wells dug; 100 backward villages lifted up by their bootstraps; employment potential for 300,000 jobs worked out; 2,900 new primary schools built; three Barge Mounted Power Generation Units set up; 199,000 hectares of irrigation potential envisioned; homes for the homeless designed; free textbooks, uniforms and midday meals readied; 3,743 Backward Castes put on notice of smallpox; 23,000 primary health centers commended; savings accounts opened by 19,222 new customers at the All State Bank; 6,433 women taught how to sign their name; 138 villages collectively agreed that all young women would delay first births by a year; biogas digesters for converting human excrement into methane balls, good for cooking stews, were acquired by 900 villages; 40,000 new second-hand soccer balls requisitioned for the state, thanks to the Japanese; and over 90 tonnes of food grains calculated by hand.

To some fanfare ("End to Energy Crisis Looms Near") an Indian daily had reported on the discovery that 40 lotus flowers (*Nelumbo nucifera*) generate the same amount of heat as a 40-watt bulb.

With equally cheerful disposition, firewalkers defied detractors by promenading barefoot across coals heated to 1,700 degrees. Scientists around the world were busy studying the "Leidenfrost effect" to make sense of such sampradaya, or traditional doctrine of knowledge. One heel was burned in the exercise, which experts were attributing to momentary lack of faith.

Everywhere the "sweet taste of sycophancy" was paraded.

Meanwhile, on a National Highway leading into Mumbai, a truck carrying heavy goods lost control at high speed and crushed a rickshaw taking six children to school. All but one of the kids was killed more or less instantly. The driver and other occupants of the truck, as is so often the case, fled the scene. At the precise moment, near the Taj Mahal, twelve foreigners died in a similar crash.

An Urdu scholar of renown spoke with a reporter in the "twilight language" of sandhyabhasha, and pointed out the play between "paroksha and pratyaksha, the unseen and the visible".

Personal trainers came into vogue. Sugar and oil trading ground to a halt.

Four hundred and fifty-three people were injured in a freak hailstorm in certain parts of the city. Many were crippled for life, it was said.

("Did you notice any hail?" the Commander asked his companions. They shrugged.) The Commander then chose to paraphrase the Sardinian revolutionary from Ghilarza, Antonio Gramsci, to more or less capture the day, "If I pose the conjecture, Who are we?, what I'm really asking is, What are we capable of? And this leads, by turns, to the ineluctable flurry of other formulations: Can we determine our destiny? How involved is evolution in our daily quest to master the Self? Is hope the province of idiots, as the Russian poet Lermontov believed? Is there a God? Salvation? And, if so, by what right does God abandon children to a slow death and the indifference of their elders?"

Of course, thought Sannazaro, the children were mere pawns in a much more embroidered web of chaos that swirled around the country, wafting from state to state like philosophical cigar smoke. He could envision its mad proliferations, like the movements of Kathakali, or the exaggerated expressions of the gods in the popular Pattachitra paintings and papier mâché masks. Throughout the vast land, a trillion small things were happening—some good, mostly bad.

Take, for example, the young Bhil, a tribal lad, sitting uproad from the town of Dungarpur, a thoroughfare used by pilgrims on their way to the famed sacred sites at Baneshwar. Would they stop and purchase a colorful scarf from him? The 14-year-old had dreamt of a different life. Dreams merging into grander schemes—that vague land peopled with nightclubs, a pretty girlfriend, money in his pocket, whatever he wanted to eat, new clothes, a moped, a Walkman, eventually money for college.

The dawn of hope? Forget hope, the dawn would do.

Fisher folk gathered for their noonday lunch on the island of Kalijai in Lake Chilka, near the Orissan city of Puri, feeding on rice and prawns (all with their right hands, of course) off plates of palm frond. Men and women who had seen most of their livelihood stolen by the commercial trawlers, powered by large-horsepower engines. They could not compete. To make matters worse, factories on all sides of the lake had so badly polluted the waters that the prawn catch was down 80 percent. The world was coming to an end for them, and for the prawns as well.

And on that day ... A man averts his eyes beneath the draped colorful ajarakh in the Gulf of Kutch, trying to avoid the dust storms brewing. He is a cattle herder and a Muslim and he is fasting early this month, as is his family's custom. In his solitude he, too, dreams the day away. Seeing himself decked out like a Maharana, with a large ranch, thousands of head of cattle, several young compliant wives who will not question what he wants to do to them, and an indoor toilet with real toilet paper. He is the sound sleep of a continent.

A woman mantled in high-priced pines burns on her own funeral pyre in Benares, a city where at least one person has been on fire every moment for 2,000 years. The cost of wood has made the traditional pyre prohibitive for many who are now dispatched in a crematorium. All the ashes are cast out into the stinking Ganga; small leaves with melted burning wax set out with them.

Another woman cloaked in vermilion with gold lace reaches for the rakh, a high pedestal of ashes at a Hindu mandir, or temple, in order to properly perform her puja for the dead sister. Sixty years together, a lifetime of memories ... No outsider can penetrate, yet who does not feel the musty image-bank of so much cloying culture around him ... Marigold peers back ... Remember, Sis, when father was promoted and all of us moved to the plantation in Assam? You were barely six then, but how well I recall your first impression of the elephants! Oh, and the orphaned tiger that you walked on a leash to St John's School in later years until the headmaster threw you both out. Then Father was shot in the back during a union dispute—he wanted to open the farm to the landless: remember his pride in being one with his village, how could he turn his back on them?—and he had to take early retirement, what was it, 1,200 rupees a month, and you used to read to him from that peculiar *Thorstein Dreams of a Daughter*: "I dreamed that I lay bleeding, Beauteous bride", and "Thirty thousand cranes arrived from Libya with foundation stones in their crops. Ten thousand storks carried the bricks, and the water was brought up by the plovers." He sat in the wicker chair, under the fan, the bullet still lodged somewhere in his L5. His chest was large, he had asthma. But he kept his wheezing confined and indistinct on our account. He loved you the best, Sis. He took you, his favorite, to the 77mm CinemaScope in town and how you raved about *The King and I* afterwards, and how you howled with merriment when a boy first glanced discerningly your way. Beauty of Assam that you were, in your stylishly butt-hugging salwar, negligent skameez and purple dupata scarf. You were the pretty one. Now I am over it. And you are dead. She circles the temple, tosses the ash into the river, recites the prayers: "Your body is only a stage for greater dreams in death, it too passes with the seasons; fear not, my Sister." Weeps for a year, does every imaginable penance. Into the heart of just one family from a remote corner of the country, dispersed by all these years, the one widow is all that's left, a locomotive of population conundrums, each human a beehive of memories that make the nation.

A young girl carries on her head a huge basket in which are to be found bunches of radish, bhindi and onion. She is walking five miles home, singing the filtered-down couplets and verse from Sri Aurobindo's life: "God be gracious, God be good. God see me through this neighborhood."

A fight erupts at a wedding among the Nishi in Arunachal Pradesh because the groom's family refuses to pay the bride's parents ten mitun, or bulls. They bargain instead for a price of 20 dighas, or hectares. Everyone settles back down, gets drunk and dances the night away. In the morning, the groom and bride shed their magnificent tribal apparel, the long leather jackets, boots, ribboned straps, wooden bowties in their waist-length hair, and don Levi jeans and Adidas and ride off on the back of his Vespa. In town he has a mobile phone and a small real-estate concession. They are the transformation of the country.

A sister of the Vinobaji Ashram stitches her white shawl, chanting vows of poverty, and reciting by heart a recipe for chocolate truffles that a traveling nun has secretly conveyed to her. She is the hidden smile of the Mother Land.

While an old man of 42 years worships a highly ornate manifestation of Shiva from a reckless promontory in the mountains above Manali, up near the Rotang Pass. In his dreams, a stone hut on the middle of a cliff, with a pillowy cot free of lice and a freshwater spigot, and a cabinet nearby, protected in the alcove, provides him his every need, centered around the ever-deferred Sabzi cutlet with coriander and coconut chilies. That's not all, for this Holy Man has probed beyond mere words and slokas and haikus and Hadith, into the imagined heart of turmeric, cumin, florets of cauliflower and black mustard seed. He has plumbed the spiritual quintessence of onions and fried chilies, added raisins to basmati rice, cardamoms to khichuri, grated radish and salt to cabbage soaked in vinegar, bay leaves to dal tarkari, and sugar to kela kofta. Every savory snack, lentil cake, omelet curry, deviled egg, soured chickpea, chopped tomato, heated ghee, red kidney bean and potato sautéed in tamarind has passed before his desiccated-coconut glance, his mustard-oil purview. From ascetic to culinary monster, he is the soul of India's emaciation. Dreaming of a full meal tomorrow, while today he and his dog will content themselves with meager scraps.

At the Bhavnagar train station in Gujarat, meanwhile, a leper woman cries for help, bread, chocolate, water, a few rupees, anything. Other women, coolies earning 30 cents a day, struggle with large luggage containers, ignoring the leper. They are carrying five suitcases, to be precise, for a Brahman lady whose husband has called for her. He is the newly appointed commissioner for all sanitation inquiries, and she will spend her time fixing up their flat, entertaining nearly 30 children and grandchildren, and mastering her Gujarati. He will play polo, visit the latrines regularly, and mark his time for eight years before retirement. They are the backbone of the country.

A cow gives birth outside the Prag Mahal in Bhuj as a little boy listens to his first radio 20 miles from the city of Amritsar. They are a verse couplet that signifies the path from the jungle to the jukebox which, in its latter-day context, is the very profile of land unsuited to abrupt juxtaposition, a soil weakened by familiarity, a commerce contaminated with indifference to consumers. He shows a way, though does not know it yet. That business is an opportunity to promulgate forgiveness. In 100 days he'll have the Internet, too, but it won't matter, because he has already reached beyond profit into mercy. A vast experiment in tolerance consolidated in this one individual. How did he arrive? All these jewels of thought, strung like laundry, or bright scarves leavening the sun. Will he dry up and die before anybody hears his name? Is he the lost cause of India? His wasted life? Her reason for pessimism? Only India knows.

Ladakhi laborers with the Himank Border Road Organization sweep away ice from the highest road in the world, at about 18,000 feet, as the broad expanse of the Himalayas suggest something like eternity all around them. They whistle and hum, oblivious to the 40-below-zero chill factor. In their happiness is the joy of the mountain king, a deeply abiding contentment in the face of salt on the roads, ice in the eyelashes, brutality in the wind. Their clean room of visual infinities knows only purity—purity of the Tibetan Buddhist canon that has entered the mainstream of a wild iris, an unlabored breath and a focused, selfless life. They are the pure sound of India.

A member of the Hizb-ul-Mujahedin prays for a relative shot dead in an ambush in Srinagar, where over 15,000 Hindus and Muslims have killed one another. His tears cannot wash away the too many sorrows. A river of unmercy welling up in flood waters of murder beyond redemptiveness, hatred before time or documentation. His kind would reunite with Pakistan, and in that volition one can read the fate of every empire. So that he is the echo of partition, the call to all those with memories who will come to the temple of doom in the dawn and sing of previous days. No potentate can pierce their cabal, nor make sense of the politics of despair, for the grave sites are more permanent than the proclamations, and the skeletal remains more fixed in the mind than any boundaries.

This, too, is the legacy of a man. Floral arrangements unsettled on the gravestones of India.

Far from the bloodshed, 12 million other Hindus gather at the Sangam near Allahabad, a point of convergence for the Ganga and Yamuna, where the Magh Mela is celebrated and baptismal dips into the muddy, sluggish waters are initiated by one and all. A priest of poignant gestures learned from his own father marks out the best times for immersion. A woman worn down by too many children, staring into a cracked mirror, her sari raised above her flea-bitten calf muscles, sinks in the dioxin-laden mud.

Together, calculating priest and sinking devotee, they register the central icon of India in their names.

A fashion queen greets visitors at the Bombay Turf Club, holding her pet peacock, Baraj, by a leash (such birds are going extinct in India), while a man bathes an elephant, Yog Josh; another dresses as a gold-painted demon; marches a chained bear, Harumph; races a cow, Amruda; walks a tightrope; taunts a cobra, Savita, from a basket; wrestles in a sandpit, or crashes on a motorcycle, somewhere, everywhere, throughout the country.

In Hyderabad puppeteers, practitioners of a dying art, perform at night for 35 children—Rakshi, Aloo, Kumbh, Naj, Ratee, Laia, Atish, Mohan, Bharat, Kera, James, Astee, Wilson, Avinash, Gajeshwar, S.P., Astrid, Ajaz, Benedicta, Peeti, Sachin, Kealdas, Sanjay, Mahavirprasad, Antony, Ninad, Baburam, Veerendra, Shyam, Vaibhav, Devaraj, Dhanesh, Sunil, Alpesh, Joharali—and the drama, *Mahabharata*, is drawn at length beneath oil lamps. For seven hours, the epic. This, the living eternity of the gods at play.

A family burns its fires beside its hut to roast another meal. Calories, conviviality, where all struggle commences.

A Bishnoi woman stamps her fingerprint at the Self Employed Women's Association offices in Rajasthan, praying to every god for a job, anything, that might provide her a rupee or two so that she can purchase rice for herself and her daughters who are starving.

Calories, where all gods forsake the multitude.

A riot breaks out among BJP opponents in a back street of Ahmedabad.

Sparks, fires, in whose burning clutches the wars of attrition and hatred egress. Another riot occasions the plunging stock market. The heat of greed transmogrifying the nation.

Take its parts, and India all adds up: calories, hard-earned little triumphs (a tasty breakfast), cyclical tragedy, hurricane, flood, monsoon, the sun anew, a transport of flute players, footballers, a lone bicyclist in a storm of sleet in Sikkim, a slightly mad goat herder resting in the Nilgiri Massif tossing nuts over a cliff, a young diamond polisher at Surat dreaming of the diamonds he works all day and will never afford, Gujjar nomads driving their cattle in Rajaji National Park, foraging for disappearing foodstuffs and fodder, and from midnight to midnight, another 50,000 children born into poverty.

"Let's go," Marigold urged, coming forward.

All of these thoughts pressed in on the sachem and his footboy as they made their way towards the forests with an all-wondering monkey seated proudly, inquisitively upright, in the back of the taxi, his lower lip covered in ice cream.

CHAPTER 92
The Most Fateful Day in the History of Potato Chips

"MUHAMMEDBAI," the monsignor from Toda Land commanded, his hands wavering like a feather, undecided, against the matted brow of the primate, "we must get it to a river. Is there a river in this park?"

"Dam, Sir. Sanjay Gandhi National Park has all water supply for. But dam is closed."

"No matter. We will go. But quickly."

They sped up the highway past the international airport, Sannazaro sighing, considering his options, only to be plunged into the largest of the slums, where six million slaves of impoverishment were said not to live, but to visibly scavenge on the margins of existence. Here before them was proof positive of the Apocalypse, borne upon the crusted lips, blurred gaze and unhurried retreat of all that once was human but that now descended infernally.

Lean-tos thrown together before dung fires, squalor multiplied in the onrush of smoke, congestion, filth, weariness. Babies squatting beside the road, venting their diarrheas in viscous throes. Young girls braiding each other's hair, the grease shiny in the burning sun. Their uncles or siblings or fathers hunched against poles, bundles, abandoned huts, staring absentmindedly as the women cleaned the families' pots, scratched for water or clarified butter in order to fry a chapatti for breakfast. Dogs, mostly ribcages, pilfering amidst the rubble. Refugees, millions of them, who had permanently settled on this strip of highway leading out of Mumbai. Jodhpattis, the name assigned to their hut communities, legal and encouraged in a democracy which had forsaken the lower castes, but at least with regard to the absolute underdogs, the adivasis, the tribals, the scheduled and backwards peoples, so-called, the untouchables, gave them the right to squat and claim land—some land. But once those people had established themselves within their particular huts, the Government could also on a whim wash its hands of them. No water, no sanitation, no food, no schools, no social welfare, no medical care, only the one atrocious right: to sleep on the street and fantasize that it belonged to them. A fantasy more and more abrogated by local hoods agitating to 'clean up their city'.

The foursome proceeded past this scene at dangerous speeds. The driver was insane. The monkey was appearing frightened, anxious and stressed.

Passing the entrance to the park, the guard looked in the car. "Video hai?" he uttered.

"Nei," the driver replied. Mr Marigold supplied the driver with the 40 rupees entrance fee and they moved on up the road, past the zoo, past a strange-looking temple with three sculptures—naked men standing 40 feet high, and peering towards the forest.

"That's curious," thought Marigold, who had no clue as to the religion being proffered there behind the effrontery of huge nudity. But something chimed. He looked back upon the three men as they drove by.

The dirt road led past a series of power lines at the base of which a cluster of rather established jodhpattis had been erected. The compound, as it were, had a water well, a giant shade-giving pipal tree, mud paths between huts, antennae for television in some of them. Everyone who lived in the village—perhaps 50 people—seemed to be working at the same tasks as they had for centuries.

"We don't want to stop," the Commander declared. "To the river. Where is the river?"

It was only another ten more minutes before they arrived at a small bridge crossing. Below lay something between a trickle and a rivulet: the monsoons had missed most of Maharashtra but there was water nonetheless, and several egrets had gathered there.

"Will this not do for the monkey?" Sannazaro asked.

"Better above," Muhammedbai suggested. "Where there are many monkeys. Otherwise lonely, this place."

"There's water?"

"Yes."

So they continued until the one lane of rough-going dirt dead-ended at the entrance to the walkway which led to ancient Buddhist caves, carved at the time of Christ. Vendors sold fruits. Local tourists went on outings. Dozens of wiry, leaping, studious rhesus monkeys foraged from the humans, their infants clinging to their mothers' necks, working out—or not—their own socialization of food sharing. Most of the food tossed at them was banana peels or milk biscuits, the odd sautéed potato and onions or half-consumed Coca Cola. Chocolates were never spared.

The monkey felt by every instinct known to his kind that he had come home. He had most likely been abducted from a similar place, and if not, his genes told him where it was. Frantic to escape, he swatted at the back of the Commander's neck, screeching a high-pitched howl for help. Sannazaro leapt out of his side of the back seat, leaving the door open. The monkey followed.

Within seconds, he raced to the largest tree, and continued upwards, eventually settling on a position high up in the canopy where he could take stock of his new-found freedom. Other monkeys ganged up on the same limb. Mr Marigold watched admiringly his handiwork of liberation.

Sannazaro bought some potato chips and sat down on the edge of a wall. He was at once converged upon by four monkeys vying for the food. The Squire backed away; the monkeys advanced. He was cornered and cried for help, though neither Muhammedbai nor the Commander took his plight seriously.

Until one of the monkeys took a more opportunistic approach, conditioning Sannazaro's response with a show of force that bade the Squire relinquish his nibbles. The rhesus had the seniority in these matters, having conned, intimidated and played for a fool tourists from 30 countries. He knew the ropes: snarl, hiss, show the bright teeth, flash the white-palmed hands, and thrust with frantic precision. It was all an act of course, but he mustn't fail to achieve a result because his peers were watching. It was a matter of pride. In the early days, this was only sport. Now there were heavy politics attached in the rhesus world. So he lunged, making sure to connect with the bag of wonderfully salted chips (you could smell them 60 yards away), but in the act inflicted a sizable flesh wound, not intended, not expected—and induced a flourish of hysterics: "Lord, I have been slain or something! *Help*!"

Sannazaro stumbled away, clutching his right arm with his left hand.

There was no blood, yet. But there was an impressive puncture wound. All the other monkeys shouted and jeered. This was good fun. But the offending primate knew he'd done something wrong, and felt awful about it, as if awaiting censure from Mr Darwin.

The monkey that had been liberated from the trio's taxi looked on, stunned by so much well-greased rhetoric and socializing. These were uncertain, indecipherable theatrics. He turned his back on all of them, more interested in the bark beetles underfoot, which he studied with dusty calm.

"Rabies!" cried the Italian meanwhile. "I don't want to die. Oh God..."

"You're not going to die yet," Marigold replied, trying to restore the earlier mood: a monkey had been given its life back, and all should have been jubilation and relief.

Upon closer scrutiny, however, both men saw how deep were the multiple puncture wounds in Sannazaro's arm.

"We're taking you to a hospital. Let's go," Mr Marigold declared. It was the first practical suggestion he had ever laid claim to. There was a reason.

They returned to the car, wrapped the injury with a towel which Muhammedbai used to clean off the insides of his windows, and clattered down the winding dirt road, passing the three naked Jain statues, then back onto the main highway, past the same slums, reaching at last the terrible almighty Mumbai, and an hour after that St Climacus Hospital downtown. Mr Marigold helped Sannazaro into the emergency room.

"*Dominus illuminato mea*," Sannazaro murmured, as the doctor approached with a very long needle.

"No worry," the doctor said calmly, rubbing alcohol on his patient's muscle. "This will hurt."

"What is it?"

"Penicillin, just in case."

The Commander, squeamish before needles in, and out of, Third World countries, couldn't watch. Instead he wandered the ward. Women waiting for tubal ligations, the excision of tumors; children queued up for polio drops; a fresh amputee recovering. Rickets. Elephantiasis. Anemia. Stomach disorders. Congenital ailments of a life-long nature. Beyond the ward, an intensive-care unit hummed and beeped and whirred with machines, IV attachments, oxygen tents, the normal life-sustaining equipment.

A dull sensation. Something paramount. Catch it if you can—the punctuation mark. A full stop on the evolution of our species—time enough to pick out a louse from a mop of hair. There—where a pair of bare olive wrinkled soles were hanging limp beyond the perimeters of a soiled white sheet. Mr Marigold stopped, taken with the gold paint on the toenails. He could not see any further, for a bevy of doctors and nurses, an anesthesiologist and a surgeon worked on the body. There were quick motions, and indifferent omens, the swift replacement of scalpels and the exigencies of various voices. Soon, all the shuffle was replaced by a flat line on a machine, and the strident high monotone of a light gone out.

The doctors parted, and before him lay the most loving embodiment of a human being he had ever witnessed. The girl, no more than 15, lay dead, framed magnificently by a crop of long black hair. Her eyes were swollen, her face purple and dimly bruised, the sheet just now returning her to final darkness.

"What happened to her?" Mr Marigold inquired of the surgeon, who had stepped out into the hallway to speak with someone.

"She was murdered," he replied matter-of-factly. "They hacked her arms off."

The Commander was stymied. "...But who? Why? Who did?", as if these afterthoughts could count for anything.

"The assailants have not been caught. The police are looking into it."

"Looking into it?" Marigold repeated, struck by the astonishing calm with which the surgeon related such affairs, the fact of so inconceivable, so barbarous an act.

At that moment, the Commander noticed in a corner a child—a boy, more exactly—shivering. A humid hot day, and here was a shivering lad.

Malaria? Marigold wondered. The kid was outfitted in his smart English school wear but was utterly unattended, barren of comfort on that hard casing of a bench.

"Who's the little boy?" he asked the surgeon, who had turned towards other particulars.

"Oh, I believe he is a family member," he said, turning back. "Apparently the only one. A nurse will break the news to him." He gave a sign with his eyes as if to indicate not to worry, this happens more than occasionally. Life.

The Commander nodded, acknowledging the confidentiality. That he, an utter stranger, should hear such news before the lad. But no nurse was there; the surgeon was busy; no administrator, not a single caregiver or official of any kind, was on hand. Finally Mr Marigold himself went over to the boy.

"May I sit down?"

The boy vaguely nodded.

After some time, "What's your name?"

"Rajibai," the boy said, his voice quavering.

"Rajibai. What a lovely name. My Christian, that is my given name, is Murillo, though most people simply call me by my surname, Marigold."

"Sir, as in the flower?"

"That's right."

"We have many such surnames in the fields of India."

There was a marked caesura in the chatter. Then, "I don't like hospitals," the Commander volunteered. And, worse for words: "My friend got bitten by a monkey. He'll be all right, though. The monkey, I mean."

The boy did not react. Suddenly, without warning, came a stretcher, rolled down the hall by an unwary attendant. There was the corpse, her golden toenails, the long hair, the cheek exposed ... and that same little voice, the boy's—the truth presently betrayed—started to crack, before exploding in a mob of groans.

The sheet unfurled by accident; a torso, mangled, lacking arms, drained of blood, was momentarily exposed. A hideous commotion. A volume of staunched paroxysms as wide as the entire corridor. Doctors, nurses converged upon the scene to stop the flood of the boy's horror.

Panic rising and subsiding. Then something about his bearing, noble and unspeaking, worked to silence his sobs. An internal mechanism of restraint enabled the boy to take charge, even of his own anguish.

Marigold took hold of him. Away from the awful sight, from all the people. Into a corner. The boy's tears splashed on the Commander's chest.

CHAPTER 93
Sunya and Rajibai

IT HAPPENED WITH THE perfunctory ease of a disinterested party: a man for whom all calamity, discord, revolution, was normal. Like the clean-up crews which attend upon the aftermath of a rock concert, sweeping clear the remains of unimaginable chaos that occurred the night before. Or the blasé elevator operator repeating the same moves and greetings. In this case, the man in question was a police inspector by the name of Abbas Nayar. He approached the Commander.

"Do you know this child?" he asked.

"No. I'm here with my friend who was injured, down the hall. A monkey bite. Not deliberate, I should add, in defense of the monkey."

"Your friend had a bag of potato chips in his hand, no doubt?"

"Yes. How did you—well, I suppose that's why you're entitled to a uniform. Such insight. That's marvelous. But tell me—" And Marigold stood up weakly to move a few paces in front of the bench, where their conversation might be extended into a sort of whisper, removed from Rajibai's ears. "About the boy—no family members? None?"

"Who told you that?"

"The surgeon on duty. I heard what happened."

"Yes. It was awful. One of our many sordid truths. Violence among the poor castes. We mustn't generalize, but some realities cannot be masked. We have to understand them, not duck for cover."

"What do you mean? Surely it's not just the poor?"

"Mostly, it is. You are from the West. America, by your accent."

"Yes."

"Where 80 percent of all violence is the result of poor Negroes driven to perpetual hostility, isn't it?"

"That is preposterous."

"Well, I don't have the exact numbers but I can assure you that here, in this wretched country, the poor are at the breaking point, and it's their fault, so yes, we blame them."

What was this imbecile talking about? The man was a racist, a bigot assembled in a brown uniform; Marigold noticed how his mouth contorted like an oboist's as he delivered his nonsense. But there was no point getting into it with him. Only to restate the obvious.

"But a young girl—to hack her arms off? How could your thesis account for such a barbarism?"

"It is not the first time. There are sociologists on staff. Psycho-therapists. Historians. Criminologists of every caliber. We in the profession have traversed the worst of the country. The truth cannot, should not be held back. The poor are testimony to karma. And they are more statistically likely to seek vengeance for their predicament. It is a known fact."

"A known fact?"

"Yes, of course. But how could you hope to understand? You Americans. Always apologizing after minorities. Wipe out all your Indians, then try to make it up to them, filled to the highest point in church with remorse."

"Yes," Marigold mulled, unwilling to go down that route.

But the inspector wasn't listening. "Still we know how to extract confessions. It is our job. Now, if you please, I must ask the boy some questions."

The inspector thought to take Rajibai to a room where he could conduct an interrogation without any distractions. But he could also see that Marigold was intent upon helping the lad, lending whatever measure of emotional support was possible. Perhaps this strange American's presence might bolster the boy's candor, or his memory, the inspector reckoned.

"Come along," Nayar said, motioning to the two of them. Marigold helped the boy down the washed-out blue corridor. Nayar did not touch the boy, but rather ushered him along with a procedural absence of contact, even kindness, that suggested to the boy that he was under arrest. They passed the nurses' station where files were kept in large stacks, held in place by rubber bands, between large black telephones, a haphazard bundle of wires and ancient jacks. Upon some quiet exchange between the inspector and the head nurse, the trio was shown into a room behind the administrative area. A dank place, in spite of overhead fans, open windows and a steady wind blowing in from the polluted quarters of chaos outside. Yet the hospital was impeccably well run, clean, orderly, the staff among the most professional and well trained in all of India. Compared with the street below, it was an oasis.

Abbas Nayar had not yet been to the site of the murder. He would get round to visiting it the next morning. If he went at night, he'd only get himself lost in the maze or stabbed in the back. Instead three local policemen were there at that very moment, had called in, but were vague on the evidence. Typical of the slums, and the cops who worked them.

"So, young man," he attempted. "You were the first little boy to take the helicopter ride, I imagine." The Med-Evac chopper had been recently donated to the St Climacus' Trauma Center, the first in Mumbai, and been in operation barely a month. It expedited transport of victims to the Center's surgical theatre, bypassing hours of gnarled traffic—though in the case of Sunya, it had no effect whatever.

Rajibai couldn't think what to say. The ride had been horrible. Blood all over the place.

The inspector caught his dissembling looks and sought to get back onto a firm track of questions and answers.

"How old are you?" he asked.

"I am ten. I will be eleven, sir, on July the ninth."

That was better. "Well, you are growing up very fast, and now you will have to grow even faster. So I'm going to ask you a few adult questions and I want you to answer them properly, you understand?" The inspector's voice was stern but began to soften. This was a mere lad, after all.

"Yes, sir."

"Did you see who killed your sister?"

"The butchers, sir."

Marigold interjected. "Butchers! I could have told you. Monsters!"

"Please sir," the inspector broke in. "I must insist you remain silent. Otherwise, the child has no chance of getting it right." Then, turning to the boy, Nayar began, "Son, try again. What makes you think these were butchers who did the terrible deed?"

"Everybody said so."

"Why would they do such a dreadful thing to your sister?"

"I don't know, sir."

"It's in their blood," the Commander rallied. He could not control himself. Then, seeing the crossfire with its exacting target aimed right at him, he apologized: "Sorry, it won't happen again. Silence is my name." Nayar regained his composure, but not without a look of final warning to the American. "Now, listen carefully. Can you tell me their names?"

"No, sir."

"Do you not know their names?"

"No, sir."

"You did not see them, then?"

"No, sir."

The inspector was impressed by not only the boy's fluency but also his restraint. "Where did you learn to speak such a fine English?" he asked. He was sure that for every word spoken, the little urchin was actually thinking whole paragraphs. One could decipher the holding-back in his intensely absent-minded drift. His manner was perfunctory, dismissive, obliging, but his powers were exercising just offshore.

"I was taught my ABCs at the School for the Blind in Forlorn, sir. It was a free service on account of my sister and I being orphans."

"But you're not blind?"

"No, sir. But my sister was blind in her left eye and so she qualified and went to school four days each week, and I filled in the other two days. We shared the week."

The police inspector cleared his throat and returned the child's strangely dreamy, almost indifferent gaze. Possibly his sister's death had not yet begun to sink in, not in the lasting sense.

"Orphans, you say. What happened to your parents?"

"My sister told me they had to go away but would come back."

"How along ago did they go away?"

"When I was born, sir."

"What about uncles, aunties?"

"None, sir."

"Brothers, other sisters?"

"None, sir."

"Grandparents, cousins?"

"I wouldn't know, sir."

Marigold looked at the poor youth in all his vulnerability and felt ... felt something new.

"Then who has raised you all these years?"

"My sister, sir."

"By what means?"

"Means? Means what, sir?"

"Uh, what job? Begging? Or did she sell herself at Kamatapura?"

"I should say not. Nothing like that. Sunya worked at the panjorapor. She loved to be near the orphaned animals. And to look after them. She didn't have to see so well to feed and pet them. And the Jains who operate the establishment—we are Jains, you see—gave her food and rupees. Very nice people, sir."

"Was Sunya at the panjorapor this morning?"

"I don't know, sir."

"Where were you?"

"At the circus. Mr Krishna is my friend and lets me ride the merry-go-round for free. No school today. I also ride the ferris wheel for free."

"But your sister was not with you?"

"Yes, but only to bring me to Mr Krishna. Then she went away. Later, she came back for me. And then she was in a great hurry and she made me stay in a chai shop and I was drinking my mango lassi and talking to Mr Joshibai, the owner, when I heard all the shouting from across the street at the butchers' corner."

"How do you suppose your sister came to be at the butchers' corner where they attacked her?" The inspector had learned that much from his colleagues on site.

"I couldn't say, for sure, sir. My sister had her own things to do. As I told you, she loved animals. All of them."

"The medics brought along the torn-up remains of a sign which read, 'Cows are God's creatures. It is hinsa to harm them.' Did your sister write that sign?"

"Yes, sir."

The inspector thought about that, aware of the years of heated disputes on the subject of meat eating. He remembered the famous protests years before when 20,000 people had staged a sit-in outside an abattoir to block the arriving cattle trucks. The demonstration lasted three days, and then business resumed as usual. The Municipal Commissioner had made certain promises that were not kept. How could they be? A billion people had to eat. Cows and steers, after all, were overpopulated. As were goats, which devoured the countryside and had to be controlled. And there was Muslim practice to uphold. Muslims ate meat. No Jain was going to alter 1,300 years of tradition.

This is life. This is India, Nayar told himself. God is good. God is great. The law is not particularly interested in animals in India. That is left for all the religious people, most of whom don't think twice about eating hamburgers and serving up fancy steaks at dinner parties, even if Mahatma Gandhi—who had often said that the inviolability of the cow was the essence of Hinduism—rolled over in his grave. That was the old days. Now the modern sophisticate, the upwardly mobile, the middle class, could not adhere to such superstitions. This was the era of nuclear weapons, freeways and mobile telephones. Fingerprints could now be checked on the computer. Even DNA analysis of blood and semen samples, though Nayar himself had not yet had the opportunity. But he had watched *LA Law* and *NYPD Blue* and knew all about it.

Nayar's father had been a poor farmer in Bihar, whose eight sons and daughters (Abbas being the youngest of them) grew up rarely tasting a braised lamb shank or rotisserie chicken. Today, Nayar and his wife Nina dined at least four times per week on meat. There was no more visible sign of success. To be able to consume meat without counting the cost. And there were other signs too that Abbas had escaped rural India. One of his five children had had a vasectomy from a doctor who could perform 100 surgeries a day. His son received 800 rupees as his incentive. But never mind. Nayar and Nina already had four adorable grandchildren. The whole family cut a modernist profile. The inspector had every intention of becoming Chief of Police some day and moving with his wife to the exclusive Malabar Hill Road, dining periodically at the Taj or Oerboi, and using a Diner's Club card to pay for it. He even fancied printing marriage invitations for his youngest daughter with pure silver threads, a new vogue among the elite of Mumbai society. One such set of invitations to 800 guests, along with the wedding, cost the bride's parents roughly 45 million rupees. A single lak (100,000) was more in line with a policeman's pay. Even that could take an entire lifetime to save up for, given Nayar's base salary of 24,000 per month, before exorbitant taxes. There were occasional perks, pay-offs in the silent margins, that covered the rare round-trip airfare to visit his in-laws up in Delhi, a new fax machine and expensive Mahot Brothers saris for his wife.

Nayar often dreamt of driving back along the dirt roads from Patna to his ancestral village of Nalanda and showing off his Ambassador, with his very own driver, to his old schoolmates who never made it out of that drought-stricken hellhole. That day was coming, and perhaps this case, which was already gaining notoriety, would expedite destiny. There wasn't a whole lot of time, either. His parents were old, the mother in throes from chronic bronchial complaints.

"And do you suppose your Mr Joshibai saw who did it?" he asked. "I don't know."

"We have hundreds of witnesses. Yet, so far, not one person is willing to come forward to identify the killers of your sister. Did they not like your sister?"

"Of course they liked my sister, sir."

"Well, we do know they were butchers. There aren't that many butchers in the area, but we can't arrest them all on suspicion. That wouldn't do. So, you see, my poor little friend, the police are somewhat stuck. Nobody wants to tell on anybody else, which I can understand."

Rajibai nodded guardedly, then looked to Mr Marigold, who looked back adoringly. The boy's hands were folded limply upon his lap. He sat low before the inspector in his matching navy-blue shorts and jacket, his one uniform from the School for the Blind.

"Will somebody be coming for you?"

"I can't say, sir. I don't know who would."

"Well perhaps—" Mr Marigold began.

"Please," the inspector hastened. He turned again to the boy. "Can somebody look after you from the school? Or how about this Mr Krishna?"

"It is altogether possible," Rajibai deftly considered. "He has a lot of children already, though. What use would I be to anyone?"

"Another child wouldn't matter, would it."

"No, sir."

The policeman paused, not exactly sure what further good to him the boy could be. According to the detectives on site, 100 witnesses had already declared their unanimous lack of cooperation in so many words and gestures. Even in the hideous murder of a beautiful young girl. What could she possibly have done to incur such apathy, or wrath, or both? She protested the slaughter of the cattle by herself, after all. There could not have been much of a commotion. It was puzzling. Such a gentle-looking girl, with a bad eye. Why a communal cover-up?

When he was younger, hungrier, he might have pursued the matter with fanatic zeal, questioning and re-questioning every single witness. Making a stink, and getting his promotion. But now that he was in great pain from persistent asthma and parasites, which tended to demotivate such earlier gusto, he had to go about it differently, using modern methods. Luncheons with the local headmen, politicians, lamb-chop cooperatives, mutton unions. He was in his early fifties, had another ten years to work out his goal of becoming chief. He had to be careful; he had to go about things in the right manner. These communal riots and rapes and murders were messy affairs. Police were instructed not to get involved in religious matters. Since the girl had not been raped, according to the doctor in charge, it was most likely a case of religious differences.

She had no parents to carry on the investigation, and by law Rajibai could file no charges, even if certain shreds of evidence might yield a suspect. There was no possibility of tort, no civil case, no winning testimony from eyewitnesses. That was the kicker, the great loss to humanity yet again. It happened several times a week, which was considerably better, as statistics go, than the death tallies in other places, like Los Angeles or Alexandria. The police were proud that fewer deaths occurred in their beloved Mumbai, a city of 20 million. Other, lesser crimes were more rampant, but a system of bribes, judges, fiduciaries, policemen, people of high standing, people with money, were collaborators in a splendid suppression. But in the case of a young girl, slain in the middle of the day, countless witnesses, there was no escaping the fanfare. Little possibility of a cover-up. This was Nayar's moment in the sun.

She'd been killed in a slum, whose residents had their own laws and ways of meting out justice. If everyone knew the killers, which naturally they did, then there would surely be some kind of repercussion, a karmic aftermath, whatever was required. The police were not inclined to interfere with cosmic necessity. Still, maybe there was a way to insinuate authority; to take hold of the handlebars and infuse some steam into the inevitable. It might even gain for him and his family a freezer full of free meats.

Nayar's whole demeanor had changed, from the oboe to the French horn.

"You must be hungry. Let's get you a nice snack, then," he told the boy. He left the room and asked the nurses to bring him food.

When he returned to the room, the boy and Marigold sat chatting. He ushered them out into the corridor, where Rajibai was given a cheese and cucumber sandwich and some cookies, along with a bottled Coca-Cola. Nayar turned to speak to the Commander and urged him down the hall slightly: there he could speak more privately.

"You said you were from America. From which place, exactly?"

"New Mexico."

It drew a blank. "You seem to have taken in an interest in this case?"

"Not the case, the child."

"Yes. It is easy to get attached. Indian children are lovely. But I'm afraid there are too many of them. Such a multitude of orphans."

"Really?"

"Oh yes. That little fellow is left absolutely alone now in this world. With his sister dead, and no parents."

"But what will happen to him?"

"Temporary custody of the state, then remitted to a government orphanage. Where he'll get two square meals a day."

"What about school?"

"No. He'll work."

"At what?"

"Hard to say."

"And adoption?"

"At his age? Frankly, after a year or so, the chances for an adoption are very slim. Past five, unheard of. He's nearly eleven."

"But what a tragedy."

"This is India, we don't think of it as tragedy. There are tens of millions like him. They'll be fine. In fact, one prominent researcher has proven that the harder their life, the better their immune system."

"By that logic, the poorest of the poor, the hungriest, the sickest, the ones in the slums, should be the healthiest, and happiest," Marigold reasoned with cynical aplomb.

The insight was apparently lost on the inspector.

"Yes. Precisely," Nayar continued. "I've been saying it for years. If you were to go into the slums—which you mustn't, of course, being a foreigner, it's very dangerous, they chop people up, as you've now discovered—you would find incredible happiness there. It's a kind of socialized world, where everyone knows everyone else and they help each other. That's the Indian way."

"I suppose this girl was merely an exception to that Indian way, then? A blip on the social register, a hiccup among pundits more apt to love-thy-neighbor?"

The inspector glanced precariously at the Commander. "There always are blips. That's what keeps my job interesting. It's densely crowded over there. The stress builds. Violence breaks out. It is human nature. A young couple cannot find a place to be alone, ever. They must settle for kissing in the presence of family, friends, perhaps four generations of lookerson. But, they get used to it. And to the filth—" He made a grimacing expression with his mouth. "But, you see, it's all part of the Great Indian Inoculation. Only the slum-dwellers really benefit. Sometimes I think I am envious."

"So move in."

The inspector laughed disdainfully. "That's all right, thank you." When Nayar and Marigold returned to where Rajibai sat on the bench, the boy instinctively grabbed hold at the Commander's waist with the fingers of his left hand, twisting at a loop on Marigold's belt and clasping it firmly.

"He seems to like you," the inspector said. "Now let go, child—" and he tried pulling the boy's hand away from the Commander, who was deeply moved.

But Rajibai didn't want to let go.

"It's all right, Inspector," Marigold said.

"Better be careful. You don't want to invite an attachment you're not prepared to satisfy."

"What makes you think I won't?"

"What, are you willing to give him a job and pay for his food and medicine?"

"Perhaps more than that."

"Perhaps. Perhaps not. Don't use words too freely around a boy, or the police. Just some friendly advice."

Marigold sat down on the bench and knelt Rajibai, who was small for his age, beside him.

"What is your full name, Son?"

"Without parents," the inspector interjected, "he'd have no Hindu family name to be identified with or fall back upon. That is common."

"Rajibai Jain," the boy stated. "I am not a Hindu. "

CHAPTER 94
A Boy's Life

"WHAT DO YOU want to be when you grow up, Rajibai?" Marigold inquired.

"I should very much favor astronomy, sir," he elocuted strikingly.

"Very good."

"But now, I just want to live, sir. Hard times, these."

The Commander marveled at the child's intuitive way. Here was a boy bereft, alone, yet so clear-headed. He set an example, though it was one the inspector appeared utterly blind to, jaded as he was by the doldrums of his police work. But Marigold could see clearly into the future: something had to be done, and the task at hand was obvious. He saw Nayar placing the autopsy report into his frayed yellowing briefcase. It was clear to the Commander that the inspector was eager to remove himself from the hospital. Even now he was bidding good-day to the attending nurses.

"Come, child," he said. "Say goodbye to the nice American gentleman. You have a new life awaiting you. I'm sure you will find the orphanage most congenial."

"Wait—" Marigold began. He wasn't exactly sure how it would all emerge—the words, the sentiments, the aftermath. But the words were now on automatic and his choice had been made. Events were irreversible.

"Might I have a word with you alone, Inspector?"

Nayar led the Commander to the same sterile room in which he had interviewed Rajibai.

"Tell me," Marigold began. "What if I agreed to take the boy?"

"You mean, adoption?"

"Yes."

"Highly irregular, at his age, as I mentioned."

"Nonetheless, I am serious." The Commander's heart was beating furiously. He had every idea what he was saying, and none. He was a man who had lived nearly 50 years with less responsibility than any person on earth, and he knew it.

The inspector pondered the remarkable idea. "Certainly, under the circumstances, a most generous gesture. Probably a knee-jerk reaction on your part, if I might be so bold. What happens in a week's time when your emotions are stayed, the sentiments cooled, the altruistic reflex dead?"

"You presume too much, Monsieur Inspector. But the truth is, I too had a sorrowful life at his age, bereft of parentage. I was that boy, though the manner of it was very different. I could care for him. On a permanent basis."

"There would be a burden of paperwork. This is India, where there are ten forms to sign when one should suffice. Character checks. Government red tape that even someone in my position finds exasperating. And before the ink is even dried, 100 other forms, stipulations and obstacles arise.

All the time foreigners are coming looking for children, but in any single year I think very few are actually given up. The law refers each case to a specialist. The specialist is duty-bound to find Indian parents, prior to any consideration of a foreigner. Are you married? Are there other children who might provide sibling comforts?"

"No."

"Hmmm. Even more difficult, then."

"Surely there must be as many exceptions to the rule as there are rules themselves? Another blip, perhaps?"

"May I speak frankly, Mr Marigold?"

"By all means."

"You don't want this boy. I don't know you, but I can assure you it would be a terrible bundle of problems. He is a poor boy."

"Ahh, but what of the immune system you spoke about so glowingly?"

"Quite. But still, problems of a mercurial, unpredictable sort. I am no psychiatrist, of course, but we know our Indian children. They need other children of their own skin color and experience, you understand?"

"I assure you, Inspector, I have a father's instinct about these matters. I have no other children, this is true, but the boy has no other family. This was made in heaven, as we say."

"Possibly. You have a loving heart, that much is obvious. And I have little doubt you can afford to keep the boy, eh?"

"Certainly. I suppose by most standards I would be considered quite wealthy."

"Wealthy enough to consider a small donation to the orphanage?" the inspector volunteered in a suddenly subdued voice, that version of corruption most suited to understatement.

"How about a large donation? What would you suggest?"

Nayar weighed his options. He had been going in that direction systematically. "Five thousand rupees would certainly be remembered."

"How about 5,000 dollars?"

The inspector eyed the Commander with that sharp awareness of hidden potential—opportunities in a land of plenty, and all for himself. He just didn't know how to broach it or get there.

"What about an additional donation for your own local police division?" Marigold went on. "Perhaps the annual policeman's ball, or some charity? Funds for updated vehicles? New Mercedes, perhaps?"

Nayar wasn't sure what to think. Mercedes? Was the man crazy? With import tax, a new Mercedes cost nearly half a crore—five million.

"Anything to help find the murderers of that girl," Marigold continued. "An additional 25,000 dollars towards your own personal investigation? You understand what I'm saying?" He was speaking in rather whispered tones now as well.

"I don't suppose you would have that kind of assistance in available paper—cash, I mean?" Nayar answered in kind. "No I'm sure not. But you see, checks, credit cards—well, there are difficulties using these in India. Bank records. As in Russia we are a system of *kompromat*. It is almost impossible to do business legally here."

"Say no more," Marigold said. "Cash it is. US greenbacks. No problem. I would be honored to help the police force of Mumbai."

"You are a sterling character! Will you excuse me a moment? I shall call the head of the orphanage to which the boy would be taken, and get a second opinion on this. To save time, mind you. Just two minutes."

The inspector removed himself to a private room and placed a call on his mobile phone. It gave the Commander a moment alone, a chance to sit tight, his heart exploding, and begin to comprehend the steps he had just initiated; to gauge, by emotional sonar and intellectual infra-red, how badly he wanted the child in his life.

What was this overwhelming sensation? This need that issued from a hitherto silent reservoir? How could he take on such a responsibility? The boy was bright, affectionate, a postcard to behold, well mannered in every perceivable way, with his school uniform and inquisitive eyes. Who were his parents? What were his genes? A useless conjecture. It did not matter. But could he ever fit in? Could anyone ever fit in, given the remorseless oppositions and tirades of human nature and the world? There were plenty of Asians in Santa Fe to make him feel at home. As for his darker complexion, so was Marigold's, and there were Hispanics and Native Americans in Santa Fe and across the whole Southwest. Anyway, Marigold had no immediate plans of returning to America, not until his work was done. Could the boy journey with him and Sannazaro? Why not? A third eye, a boy's point of view, would most certainly take the burden off Marigold's constant rub against the so frequently contrary rebuttals and cynicisms of his Squire. A ten-year-old's optimism was just what the two old veterans needed. Indeed, it was the ten-year-old heart that found such an adamantine response in the Commander's own nature.

He had to do it. The boy had no one else. Mr Marigold was there at the right moment. It would be a spectacular completion to his life. An opportunity to do something for a real live human being. He could retire in his child, give up activism, admit to his hermitage, profess no other duty, single out the chaos for its one summital achievement: an offspring. Nothing more was needed. He could refuse all future injunctions, give vent to his carefree years without exacerbation or guilt, much like the old days, months prior.

In this accelerated scheme of recent entrées into the world, Marigold had nearly forgotten who he was. So much consciousness-raising had elevated him into an ether of self-denial. Abnegation of all that he had lived for over the course of four decades had marooned him on a plateau of impossible convictions, culminating with India. Inscrutable, unsaveable India. The boy came into his life at the perfect instant. Would Rajibai change him, make him a better person? He was eager to find out.

Would the complications be beyond him? Not with two billion dollars plus change in his estate.

There was something else. The boy was special. The Commander had caught that about him right off. His grace amid such unspeakable tragedy. The marked equipoise, the dignity of his bearing. To lose a sister like that would drive most other people insane.

The inspector returned looking very solemn.

"Well?" Marigold hastened.

"It is difficult, but not impossible," said Nayar. "There is that business of paperwork. I believe, after speaking with my contact, that a slightly larger donation could hasten the ink-drying process."

"Fine. Just name the figure."

Gingerly, knowing he was on very tenuous ground, the inspector suggested a sum double the original in each case, both for the investigation and the orphanage.

The Commander requested twelve hours. For he would have to get hold of a banker who could pay out what was ostensibly a bribe— Marigold was under no illusion on that score—in US dollars.

"Two requests," he said. "First, I keep the boy for the night."

"Where are you staying?" asked Nayar.

"Oberoi."

"What room number?"

"The Rajasthani Suite."

"Good. And the second request?"

"That I be assured of the validity of all paperwork. Because I'll need a passport for the boy."

"All will be properly authenticated. Of course—" and he took the Commander aside, though the boy could see and hear everything—"these are not normal channels we're talking about. You understand?"

"Naturally."

"Good. I will come tomorrow to your hotel."

"And you will be accompanied by the head of the orphanage?"

"Yes. Miss Puna."

"Say, 1 p.m.?"

"Excellent."

They shook hands and wandered back together to where Rajibai had been seated finishing his lunch. The odd nurse had come round to console him, offer more Coca-Cola, flatter him on his school outfit. Small talk in the face of what everyone around the nurses' station knew to be an abysmal circumstance, the unclothed waif beneath a uniform.

Arriving at length, the inspector addressed the seated boy.

"Rajibai, Mr Marigold here will be seeing to your dinner and accommodations tonight. Is that all right?"

"Yes, sir. Thank you, sir," Rajibai bowed, his expression deeply convincing, though it could not be characterized as particularly beaming. His prospects, so far as he could fathom, were anything but bright.

"Goodbye, then. One o'clock." The Inspector took his officious leave.

"Well, here we are," Marigold ventured, looking tentatively at Rajibai, and wondering just how to proceed. Not even the depths of Antarctica were this remote. Feelings were emerging and they were as strange as any moa.

Yet he had to make it work. The decision had been made, and though there were no maps, itineraries, compass readings to give him an edge, the situation seemed to right itself of its own accord. Marigold simply trusted to fate. He realized that it felt good to do so. Submission to an ideal that sat before him, trusting little boy's eyes ablaze with the great unknown.

"Yes, sir."

"You needn't call me sir, young man. Murillo, remember?"

"Murillo." The boy pronounced it very slowly, carefully. "What does it mean?"

"It was the name of a famous painter from Spain. How does the name of Marigold suit you?"

"Suit me, sir?"

"Would you like to be called Rajibai Marigold?"

The boy was stunned, well aware of the implication, for from the moment the tall foreign gentleman had first appeared he had hoped that just such a scenario, however outrageous, might come about. He had long harbored the dream of a male to guide him, hold him, confirm his every wild-eyed intuition. But there had been no such figure, not ever. No hope of such a thing. It was too fantastic.

"So? What do you think about that?"

Rajibai nodded agreeably. If his response was tinged with the tentative, it was only because he was still puzzling through the multiple realities, fearing that his fantasy was just that—and that he would be cast into the grim shadow of Indian bureaucracy which reached absolute depths in an orphanage. He was desperate not to be silent, but to speak up—to speak of his needs, his desires, his rights. Rights? Did his solitude, his poverty, his absolute lack of connections grant him rights? Was he under arrest or some suspicion? Would the butchers come after him next? Who was this tall, leaning foreigner, anyway? This man being so kind, mumbling onwards in obvious awkwardness— "I rather like the ring of it. Sounds to me like a certain species of marigold flower. Perhaps, with a smattering of geography, one might think of it as hailing from the desert, where the colors are always livelier, more direct. Rajibai Marigold ..."

Rajibai feared the worst—that such solicitude would turn sour. To reinforce his will, he repeated: "Rajibai Marigold. Rajibai Jain Marigold. Take my family name and place it mid-center, if you please. I would like that very much, sir."

"Murillo."

"Mer–"

"Mer-riyo," he enunciated.

The boy got it right. Then, suddenly alarmed: "Where will they take Sunya?"

"Who is Sunya?"

"Sunya is my sister, si- " he started, then drew silently to himself.

It was a question Marigold could not answer, but it certainly conveyed the appropriate priority. He must oversee and pay for all funeral provisions.

"I will take care of everything, you needn't worry," the Commander said, holding the boy firmly. "Everything that can be done will be done. Is there some religious practice that would be most appropriate? I do not know the formalities."

"We are Jains," Rajibai explained. "Jains." Marigold knew nothing of Jains. "What is that? I'm sorry."

"Some parts are like Hindu, most parts are not," Rajibai told him. "Do Jains bury or cremate their dead? Or something else—leave them for vultures perhaps, or cast them into the Ganga?" Marigold knew that some other religions dealt with corpses in a variety of ways but did not want to elaborate.

"By fire," the boy said quickly, apparently distracted by some other importunate calling. "Where's the bathroom?"

"I must say, you're a very brave kid," Marigold said to him on his return. He did not know that Rajibai had just vomited.

Then the Commander remembered Messer Iacobo. It had been two hours since he'd left him in the emergency department having his monkey wound attended to.

"Come. I want you to meet somebody very comical."

"A clown?"

"Better than a clown."

They got up and went to the nurses' station to track Sannazaro down. From there they were led via stairwells, peeling plaster, dangling wires, an old elevator, to an outpatient hall where, betwixt every conceivable injury, oxygen tent, tube, wire, scanner, dim light, the lame, downed, limp or dying, the Squire was sitting up upon a mattress reading an old *Times of India*, complaining to the nurses, demanding fresh coffee, itching his arm where an angry rash had formed, shifting to and fro, just back to the living from his own bout with penicillin, twelve stitches and a patchwork of gauzes.

"Rajibai, meet Uncle," the Commander hailed with a flourish. "Uncle, meet Rajibai."

CHAPTER 95
Father and Son

Bless this little heart, this soul that has won the kiss
of heaven for our earth.
—Rabindranath Tagore's *Benediction*

MARIGOLD, SANNAZARO and Rajibai left the hospital together. But Sunya had to remain there, in a freezer. Cremation was put on hold, pending at least a month's investigation. "We need the evidence," the inspector had said greedily.

Marigold had gotten himself a boy. Sannazaro was astonished, though he and the Commander had spoken no words about any adoption as yet. Murillo himself was too intent upon the demands of the present, immersed in the total picture of his new compadre. The frame of that being kept enlarging until it boded of spectacular and awesome complications. From the moment they entered the cavalcade of streets, he was aware of the burden upon him to proffer every advantage to his new companion. But how? What were the rules of lending a hand, raising a son, nurturing a permanence? The Hermit of Tesuque could no longer elude or dull the vivid edges of any decision. All those contradictions of modernist life, with their reductionist antipathies to the life force itself, were no longer worth dwelling upon. That whole dreary evolution of human society, from the first moment of slavery and Sumerian surplus to the final sunrise; carved into the pockmarked pillars of wisdom before the last belching smokestacks; trails forgotten, and the hundred moldering bones in the human anatomical foot, strewn like so much anonymous calcium and phosphorus and density beneath an unknown gravestone. And over the ridge from the silent burial site, the only pub left to humanity, but emptied of celebrants, barren and forgotten, its timbers caving in, and the hugely aspiring slope of our history no more than a tedium of dead lichen. These were not appropriate subjects for conversation at this juncture, or ever again, Marigold realized. Now he must keep the effects of such world-weariness from the splendid boy. Not daunt him but awaken him, instead, from the burden of loneliness and pain that was his life.

His mind journeyed to his library back home and to the Gypsy Girl in that 952-page *Heir of Hazel Dell*, written by one Hannah Maria Jones and published some time in the mid-nineteenth century, with its steel engraved apotheosis of the "little bare-footed and bare-headed, sun-burnt girl"—an unforgettable saga of emotional affiliation whose very sentiments presently soared heavenward in Murillo. Only by such human connection, begotten in the unexpected furnace of frailties meeting head-on, could such knowledge and heeding of the heart be understood, he reckoned. It was a new day. Two souls, two paths, rather than a lonely one.

Even Monsieur Iacobo had begun rising to the avuncular challenge in the course of minutes. Which made for three of them all together. Three unlikely travelers tossed into the same gunny sack. A dragon, a cigar, a lily child; brazen buffoonery, eclectic coffees, a king in sprite's underwear; a holy roller, a watchmaker, the window on the world's soul.

An umbrella, ground creepers, the rain.

With no singular command of his train of thought, Marigold cogitated over the startling scope and particulars of his new-found fatherhood, absorbed by the ragamuffin countenance of this prince of a child who had nowhere else to turn. Such stateliness in so modest a covering. A twinkling eye over the dreaded pit. Economic speech, eloquently conveyed; dignity outclassing all others; grandeur emanating from each modest gesture and look. There was about Rajibai's gait the breath of open vistas. He had no ilk, no peer. Rajibai was entirely an original. A flagship of childhood endemism, not unlike the montane cloud forest. A cotton-top tamarin of wounded dignity, peering with all the inquisitive hope of Milne-Edwards' lemur. Eyes as broad and elegant as bunchgrass. He moved like a suni, the small forest antelope of Zululand, and in his heart were lodged too obvious for words the threats to every generation of being.

The boy was small for his age, and this could only have resulted from chronic malnutrition, vitamin deficiencies, the sheer absence of daily calories. An innocence arrayed in all its demure aspirations, hidden and silent beneath the gentle demeanor of courtesies learned by incalculable suffering.

"To the New Oberoi!" Sannazaro, with heavily bandaged hand and domineering tenor, called to the taxi driver, who wore an Indo-Burmese green turban. Swinging by a frayed party tassel off the dusty rearview mirror was a durable plastic figure, Durex sized, of his guru Nanak, a protective deity for the hurly-burly roads. In the mirror itself, a snapshot of the unlikely trio who had just stepped away from the hospital curb and crunched together on to the cracked vinyl back seat.

"On second thought, that's not necessary. We'll go the nearest youth hostel," the ever-prudent Commander amended, tapping Rajibai's knee for good measure and fatherly show. "A penny saved, a penny earned."

"No, the Oberoi," Sannazaro rasped. "You said you already informed the inspector. There is no other choice. A well-deserved suite, at that. I've been attacked and bitten, numbified and bloodcurdled, punctured by needles, thrown topsy by dastardly drugs, sewn up with stranger's hands, wheeled like an invalid down a corridor exuding viruses of every denomination. Now I want my modest corner of comfort, if you please."

"I tell you it is not right that we should spend that kind of money, just to sleep. Better for pigeon seed. For food for our new little Rajibai. What would you like to eat, Son?"

"Everything, please, Father."

Marigold glowed with the beam of that word. *Father*... How strangely wonderful it was. "Fine!" Sannazaro yelled. "You two sleep on the sidewalk with the birds and beggar children. I'll get a massage. Do you forget that, by your own admission, just since we've been away from Tesuque, Hidalgo's investments have earned your already considerable estate another 400 million?" He was referring to one of the documents included in the courier package that had arrived in Cochi identifying the rising market and Marigold's mushrooming portfolio of green-screened mutual funds. "I think you can afford the few hundred dollars a night we're talking about."

"Which Oberoi?" the taxi driver inquired, turning off the ignition to save gas and tiring of the improbable jabber behind him.

By night, all were safely sequestered in the New Oberoi. No sharing of a toilet area in a field, as Rajibai was accustomed to. Marble floors extending to the horizon. A man performing Henry Mancini at a piano, the music rising 100, 200, however many hundreds of feet towards the interior architecture of stars. Their very own Taj Mahal. Angels gliding in gold saris across the manicured landscape, wafting scents of every delicacy; men in perfectly fitted black suits and fluffy white shirts executing the visitors' slightest command with a grace that was utterly uncharacteristic of India, at least in Rajibai's ten years. There was a book store with lofty volumes filled with glossy color photographs, and newspapers from foreign lands hot off the press—how did they get to India so fast, the same day, even?—and a palm garden growing inside. It was all miraculous.

But the elevator was even more so, leading to a carpeted, air-conditioned hallway which allowed access to a Maharaja's chamber looking out over all of Nariman Point. A room, or rooms to be precise, that seemed larger to him than 100 huts. His very own room, with a king's bed, and famous paintings on the wall from Japan, or China, or ancient India herself, and fresh flowers next to the bed, and a bowl of fruit and—*My Go-od!* " exclaimed he, "my *very* own telephone! And *bathroom!*"

Two fancy-wrapped chocolates on the pillow with a message in an official envelope that read, 'The Management would like to take this opportunity to welcome you and invite you to a cocktail hour in the executive lounge between 5 p.m. and 7 p.m. Wishing you a most memorable stay!' The boy raced into the bathroom and gasped again—"*Another telephone!* "—turning on the shower, testing hot water, and letting it run and run to see if it ever ran out, which it did not. Another basket of fine soaps and shampoos— "What is conditioner?" So many questions and revelations.

"Are you OK?" asked Murillo from his adjoining room.

"Fine, Father. Thanking you enormously and handsomely," replied the child, bursting with happiness, as if all this were somehow a tribute to his sister. Her due share in heaven.

"Where did you learn to speak so—eloquently?" Marigold asked.

"Our headmaster was a learned man. *Tom Swift and his Flying Machine. The Song of Hiawatha. The Rise and Fall of the Roman Empire. Oliver Twist.* We were forced to memorize portions from each of them."

"But how extraordinary. In a slum?"

"Yes, but it was mostly Sunya who encouraged me."

The Commander took all this in. An orphan girl somehow responsible for raising so stellar a younger brother. A crumbling school out there in the thick of moribund and madding millions. Amid so much decay and death, Edward Gibbon. Charles Dickens ... It was astonishing. Yet, what better historic and literary mirrors?

Marigold began setting out on his bed some of his few possessions from his burlap shoulder bag. Next door, Sannazaro lay curled up in his own deserved bliss, watching a pay-for-view movie from America and drinking Scotch from the mini-bar. At length the Commander addressed the boy again.

"Neither I nor Uncle," he said, "can or would presume to fill in for your sister, who must have been a marvelous girl. You understand? But I will be a true father to you. I will tell you honestly, child, I have never been a father to anyone, so you will excuse my clumsiness sometimes. But I promise you this, together we will try. And it will be a success renowned throughout familyhood."

"Thank you, Father," the boy said, but his mind hadn't really heard what, to Marigold's way of thinking, was the most earnest, forthright speech of his life. Instead, the inquisitive beaver was gazing in all directions, mesmerized by the parlor of gizmos in his sudden favor. Three times he explored the world of the bathroom with its indoor toilets—the second one a total puzzle; immaculately fitted hardware of what appeared to him to be solid gold and silver, the wash basin free of debris, a vast mirror without competition for use, or grime, or cloud. Roll after roll of toilet paper, cotton bathrobes, slippers in endless array. And most astonishing of all, that bath tub, large enough for water sport. The sheer quantity of hot water, free hot water, streaming over his fingertips ... all epiphanies. Not to mention the whirlpool jets.

Marigold watched while the child took in his new domesticity.

A half hour later the three Mumbaiteers opportuned in the direction of victuals. Over a platter of tandoori sundries and thallis, peshwari naans, soy cucumber raitas, onion bhajees, other starters, midway soothers and finishers and post-finishers, biberons and tipples, they agreed to revisit next day the site of Rajibai's Forlorn slum, a morass of hutmen spreading for miles, and see about farewells before the grand journey that Rajibai already sensed awaited him. He knew instinctively that he was leaving forever all that was familiar: every festering cranny and hiding place beneath the pile of garbage, tanning and tie-dying heaps, tarshack bungalows and corrugated dumps. Away from those other orphans in rags with whom he had grown up fast along the mud alleys and gritty currents of life.

That night the boy dreamt of a Garafalo-like cherub amid an iconographical mishmash, a fever-pitch of fear, of the murder among garish gods, hoardings, burnished icons staring out from temple facades, gold plasters and silver foils fabricated from a surface of mythic altercations.

And his sister, now the little English match girl, staring into the frosted windows of the rich people who sat comfortably consuming their dinners beside warm hearths. Of some color illustration—by Rembrandt, perhaps—from one of his school books. Could it be Saint Luke, or Joseph? Or Simeon? Two turtle doves who had no idea what was coming. A knife. He rolled over, then suddenly was awake, his face smothered by the Egyptian cotton of his fancy sheets. It was very late in the night. He could hear the television from another room. The Commander was listening, softly, to a debate on BBC Human Rights Night: a round-table which included Mary Robinson from the UN and the new President of Rwanda. Suits and neckties, respectful outrage. As he drifted off, Rajibai thought about his strange new companions, whose religion, ancestry, place of origin, motives and true intentions he had not yet begun to fathom. But there was surely kindness all about them, and magic officially sealing his deliverance. But what was that knife? And the fate of the two turtle doves?

At one o'clock the next day, the police inspector showed up alone, saying that Miss so-and-so from the orphanage had given the clearance— "Nothing in writing, mind you"—and he had come in quite a hurry to collect the donations. The Commander handed him the money in new hundred-dollar bills, neatly stashed within a large envelope. The two men parted company with an exchange of every courtesy.

As he left, the inspector patted Rajibai on his head and reminded him to be a good little boy and do whatever his father asked.

Sannazaro was unimpressed—and aflame with nerves. Later, reflecting on the absence of any papers certifying the adoption, he warned, "You should have insisted upon documents. Who could possibly trust that basilisk of buffoonery?"

"He's just a self-important bureaucrat. The deed is done," Marigold said, unconcerned.

"Let's hope so, for his sake," Sannazaro aired, resolved that the boy might just solve all their problems and, somehow, the world's as well.

CHAPTER 96
Travels Through the Largest Slum in the World

IN THE MORNING, Sannazaro booked their British Air flight to London—first class—which was scheduled to depart late in the evening. There was time for a late checkout and a long, sumptuous dinner.

With time on their hands, Marigold, the Squire and Rajibai took a taxi to the fringe of Forlorn, Rajibai's former home, then trekked by foot into its very guts. The taxi driver urged them not to enter there. "It is not a place for guests of such a fine hotel," he argued. But their minds were quite clear. This was the infernal intestine of ogres' land that time dismissed, where the boy had made his weary way among a maelstrom of other victims of his kind, human entrails consumed in the bonfire of atrocities. Now he somehow or other imagined he could make peace, perhaps invite several million of them to the Oberoi for a farewell dinner, or even purchase, with his new-found infinity of rupees, a larger hut for himself and some of his friends. Buy new crutches for Dipti, dentures for Mr Salesh, a woolen blanket for Gauri, new shoes for Joshibat. Torn between so many worlds, a chaos flung itself at him. No landing, no visual, no sense of where he was going or what would happen. Only that he was now being powered into something like reincarnation.

In truth, he didn't know what he was going to do, where it was all leading, how to make amends with a life of drudgery, to come to closure on so much unforgiving.

Past 10,000 industrious naysayers, the trio scrambled through onrushing masses of the work day, arriving upon one of many epicenters: this was what it all meant to be a boy in the slum; here were the origins of one child's abuse and misery in this world, the sordid place where Sunya had perished—a nearly indistinguishable event amid so many other lost lives. A candle gone out in the tar pit.

Their shoes scummed with the odious accretions of every conceivable fecal matter and moisture-laden scrap; acrid slimes hovering archeologically over each square block of tied-together tunnels, domiciles, hut facades, rancid abutments of crumbling brick, cinder, glass, concrete shells, rusted pipes large enough to sleep in, like a paste holding together the decades of nullity and pain. Occasionally a real house, of four walls glued together, swept dirt, brass pots, a jerry-rigged black-and-white television, facing out over neighbors who dreamt of nothing else. Two hundred paces away, a communal space for going potty.

Their nostrils reeked, ears became attuned to the din made by the feeding frenzy of kites and vultures and crows which teemed aboard dung heaps and competed with pigs, goats and garbage-swiping children.

Two hundred thousand tons per day, it was said the birds (eyes lidded to mediate blue fumes arising from 10,000 kilns) managed to consume.

Rajibai, fast skipping, deft and gymnastical in his too-familiar setting, came upon his friends one by one, and tried to deliver his farewell speech, proffer introductions to the Commander and Uncle, invite them over to the hotel (a gesture Marigold was loath to discourage, despite Sannazaro's efforts to divert such offers), to cheerfully amalgamate his 'hellos!' and grant the hard-parting goodbyes. But invariably a crowd began to trail directly behind and to all sides of this Pied Piper of Indic millennia and his two silly-looking Western companions. Word of the murder had spread, after all, to all six million inhabitants. Some were calling it an 'assassination' with political or religious motives.

These were the lucky ones, Rajibai explained, who'd somehow, like himself, escaped from the masters and now scrounged in packs for themselves, no longer the victims of unrepayable debt.

"What masters, what debts?" asked Marigold.

It didn't take long for the two Westerners to decipher the signs. This deep into the catacombs of Forlorn, the slave shops could not be hidden. On the outskirts, where the occasional policeman might venture, teams of lookouts and artful dodgers relayed word back through the labyrinth. But no sane officer of the law ever patrolled the far interior of the slums. The hundreds of miles of tent paper, cavernous coveys, rambling lean-tos, never-ending quagmires, narrow passages hewn from the walls of poverty constituted a perilous landscape for any outsider. People simply vanished forever inside one concentric morass or another. Desperate sociologies, etched in the faces of 1,000 generations, convening for their brief durations in the sewage lines of fallen times and a disinterested government.

All these frail riddles of have-nothing were, in fact, a sorry litany of struggling industry, where bangles were fashioned from cheap silver, beedi cigarettes hand-rolled, carpets woven or leather worked. Shoe factories abutted up against one silk sari-dealer after another. Prostitutes marooned behind bars bared their still developing breasts with For Sale signs, while tea shops billowed in smoke and slaughterers hung their meats amid swarms of maggots and thousand-faced rabble. Wool fluff from the carpet factories filled the air, deforming the lungs of the hundreds of five-, six- and seven-year-olds who sat upon the concrete or dirt floors of the sweat shops working the looms. The dead sheep dust dampened all breathing space. Flotsams of stained wool splattered everywhere.

Rajibai knew many of the hunched, sickly workers by name, all boys and girls about his age, or slightly younger, or older, but dared not linger or dally in his greetings, for these were dangerous precincts best passed by hurriedly.

Outside, he tried to explain. "Child workers, Father. Because of the parents, mostly."

"How so?" asked the Commander, an itch amplifying in his gut of worries.

"There is no money."

Rajibai knew everything about it, for he had been born into that hopeless realm, and only through the courage of his sister managed mostly to escape. Mostly, on account of the lingering web of friendships and connections that he would never lose sight of. The slum stayed with a person always, fashioned the angle of contemplation, the color of light, swayed one's incidence and furloughs. Now, at last, in company of his new-found father and uncle, he believed it might just be possible to accomplish what he had meditated on persistently for years: the liberation of his young peers—millions of them.

He could not actually see the picture of such freedom, only trace its outlines in vague dashes towards an opening. Like a fire escape through the ceiling of an elevator, a rumored pathway never previously attempted. Ducts leading up and away, where nobody had gone, a perimeter beyond all tangles and trouble that evinced in his heart some defiant cry that it must be so. All the eyes of all the children forever looked towards this one final resting place: freedom.

Marigold, too, felt an opening, but this was not admitting the free air of sunlight. Rather, it bore down upon him with nearly hopeless weights. Sannazaro at once caught signs of the onus shadowing his partner. What the previous night had appeared to Marigold's mind a ticket toward tranquillity—his sequestration to the happily interrupted down-time, no cause for further regret, a child in tow to take up the slack—would now reconfirm J.P. Sartre's belief that existentialism made it no longer necessary to judge our fellow man. Give in to passion, catch the thermals: save *every* little Rajibai! Stave off dissolution, reverse the slums, jettison the tyrants.

In this way towards folly he thrust his generosities wholesale at every outstretched finger. A gusher of faith. Ardor prevailing. Canvassers of freemen. Seamless their strained strength of character. A choir of thousands. To comfort them. Wavespeech. Untonsured locks. Like father, like son.

Thus began the day, a shocking tour of the camp of bonded child laborers. No one asked questions of the trio, for the rulers of this kingdom had the arrogance to know that they would never be put out of business. In 5,000 years they and their kind had obtained every sinecure and immunity, congealing the forces of deprivation around a highly profitable system of child servitude. No other concept had arisen in this nation of masters and slaves, or, if it had, was of so little purchase on the poetic imagination as to be conceptually bankrupt before it reached the state of discussed cognition. Here, among such ancient and codified graft, there were no saints or revolutions. No Morelly to envision a Basiliade, after the dreamscape of charity first taken up by Gregory Nazianzen. Western social philosophies that would produce various Codes of Nature and Social Contracts; Cabet's benevolence, Chambers of Invention, Universal Associations, Phalanstères, Winkelblech's Co-operative Societies, and Lassalle's Labour League. All these innovations—pillars, however chipped and eaten away—of the working man's rights; of true socialism and fair play, had long ago been banished from places like Forlorn.

Stable after stable, noxious sheds, parlous pods, barbed-wired pogroms. From cremation to cremation. Kids in holding tanks who had been sold by their knowing or unwittingly coerced parents and cousins to middlemen, to become camel jockeys to the Gulf States or heavy laborers of 1,000 varieties right here in Forlorn, for 60 or 70 dollars a child. Even now, the illnesses were apparent—the rashes from scabies, the bronchial distress, the swollen joints. Deformities from being tortured and twisted into industrial crouches. For mile after mile, factory after factory spread throughout the slums: carpet-weaving looms, chemical dyes, razors and knives and children looking ancient even in their first dozen years of life. Marigold was to discover the many ways in which Rajibai's friends had been lured from villages all over India, Nepal, Pakistan, Bangladesh, and parts of southeast Asia. Eight-year-old boy and girl prostitutes working 20 hours or more a day. Gang raped for pennies which went to the middlemen and women. Chained, branded with hot irons, ragged, their eyes burned with squirts of acid if they complained, a technique practiced all over India on cows.

A glass factory. Splinters slowly burrowing into the hands, bare feet, cheeks, legs of the child workers, who were charged with positioning the glassy bangles on trays, then placing them in furnaces where the temperatures exceeded 1,600 degrees C. They would dip the iron rods into the molten glass, then pass on the products to the molders and blowers, moving quickly with the rods in their torn-gloved hands, tripping over electric wires dangling every which way, breathing in air heavy with glass particles. Burned, tubercular, anemic, genetically fried. All in the service of a voracious world market for chandeliers and wine glasses and the beakers purchased by pharmacies and hospitals. The irony.

A pit where the digging out of stone, the chipping away at granite, the detonation of boulders occupied the entire world of ten-year-olds working throughout the night. Here they were trundling stones along the abyss, one child Sisyphus after another, with pneumatic drills, housed in huts of straw and of mud, earning the odd rupee with which to pay back a debt of some ancestor three generations removed. The children would be dead by 20. The Bonded Labour Commission had yet to find a means to stop the practice. The hundreds of millions of dollars earned each year from exports made it too important in the eyes of those officials who benefited from the payoffs. These bribes were illegal, of course, but that was a sordid detail left to piles of paper at the government blocs hundreds of miles away, amid the present armada of luxury vehicles and long lunches for the owners.

Down the lane, four children were busy at silk hand-looms. Breaking off the silk threads in their chipped, corroding teeth, they consumed the chemical dyes, fingered every taint, and this, learned Marigold, caused every nuance of peptic ulcer, never treated.

"How much are they paying you?" the Commander asked one child. Rajibai translated the question, and the answer, which came in a dialect of Marati.

"Fifty paises per hour, she says."

"How's your math?" the billionaire pressed his son and translator.

"How much a day?"

"In American money, I think about 20 cents," replied he. "That's if they work 20 hours."

Marigold asked, "In this economy, what will 20 cents a day buy you?"

Rajibai thought carefully about the answer, calculating: "One banana, or handful of rice. Two lollies, though not of chocolate—that would cost more. A glass of water."

But the extrapolations were further compromised by the one undeviating truth of this economy: the children never got the 20 cents. That was debt repayment.

The trio continued surveying the drama before them. Marigold was determined he would make it his business to exhume all those legal codes on reams of crumbling paper in New Delhi, their sorry applications, and the multiple interpretations between Hindu and Muslim law that had a lockjaw on status quos.

Past lawmakers had, in truth, attempted by various means to put a halt to certain of the more grotesque abuses. There had been parliamentary grumbling for years from some concerned corners; Congress Party lawyers had filed dockets, called for state-mandated injunctions, boycotts, charges and levies, or the equivalent of class actions. These initiatives had collapsed for lack of support, been downgraded to mere whimpers on a wish-list of murmurings in every state assembly. At least, it was argued, the children had employment. It was always that flimsy, indecent 'at least' which prevented any constitutional amendments from gaining headway; gave precedent to obscenity, concretized national indifference.

But these successive generations of nihilists and conspirators had not anticipated a rabble-rouser of such adamantine verve and gesticulating fury as the Marigold. A man of dangerous genuflections who knew by now that high ideals were the only way to stir up mental mischief and rabid debate, to fathom outcomes and forge fantastic fibrillations.

There was a book store, a jumble of kindling and stained papers which was thought of by the slum-dwellers as a library. Marigold searched the pitiful tiers of leaning volumes in order to find any tome on Indian law. There was one. He purchased the book for 400 rupees, then sat at a tea stall with his son and Squire and studied those relevant rulings.

"Listen to this," he began. "As early as 1933, the British had passed the *Children (Pledging of Labour) Act* and, five years later, an *Employment of Children Act*. In 1948, when the Constitution was barely in the making, India had enacted the *Factories Act* prohibiting the employment of children under the age of 14. Within the Constitution, there were mandates making education compulsory, a means of keeping children out of the workplace until they were ready."

This mandate was fortified, Marigold discovered, not only by the *Factories Act of 1948*, but also by the *Plantation Labour* and *Merchant Shipping Acts of 1951*, the *Mines Act of 1952*, a *Motor Transport Workers Act* and *Apprentices Act*, and the *Beedi and Cigar Workers Act*, passed in 1966. *The Bonded Labour System (Abolition) Act of 1976* outlawed bondage of any kind.

"I fail to understand any of it," the Commander puzzled, helpless before so mammoth a contradiction, the vast slave fields around them undermining India's reputation as a safe and vibrant democracy. "The laws are clear. It's not the lawmakers who have abandoned the country."

Who then? he struggled to fathom. Clearly, nobody was paying attention to these Delhi-based right-minded principles. The country had dive-bombed into poverty; her debt load was soaring, food and resources waning, and her population doubling every 20 years. Children were the only fuel that enabled the country to keep on.

From time to time politicians gathered in their hallowed English parliamentary style, all pomp and formality, to demonstrate their good intentions. Of course, their own children had nothing to worry about. Most were in private schools, and would go off to England or America for college. They were the ruling class, which meant that all this talk of 'saving the children' was taken no more seriously than saving the cow or protecting the peacock. Acts of Parliament meant to prohibit all employment of children under "hazardous" circumstances suffered from deliberate obfuscation. If the work could be characterized as "family based", the laws simply did not apply. But the definition of family was a deliberate legal ambiguity aimed at absolving all slave labor. Distinctions were altogether blurred in a society that lived by densities of little hands. Families were easily invented where the rupee was involved.

The first *Factories Act* in India had been pressured into passage in 1881, following a similar measure in England three years earlier, and outlawed child labor in the Indian textiles industry. But the reasoning for that proscription had nothing to do with the welfare of children, but rather with the global competitiveness of the mills of Lancashire, which believed themselves to be at severe disadvantage by the cheap labor wielded in the guise of Indian children. Such sordid jungle logic was repeated more than a century later at the *1986 General Agreement on Tariffs and Trade*, the Uruguay (8th) Round of *GATT*. Under that rubric, Marigold learned, the push for greater market access by countries like India and Indonesia would condemn children to ever-increased labor conditions. The new Indonesian administration, under President Wahid, suggested some hope, but India's fundamentalist government, in power over a decade, showed no signs of softening. Structural Adjustment regimes imposed on India by the IMF furthered the country's false dependency upon its child workers. Despite the earnest outcries of Senator Tom Harkin, a Democrat from Iowa, in conjunction with several notable South Asian NGOs and coalitions to end child slavery, the upshot in Washington, as in New Delhi, was depressing. No alteration in status. The US continued to import hundreds of millions of dollars worth of such products, like carpets.

An old friend of Rajibai's, eleven years old, arthritic, blind in one eye, dying of pneumonia, Lakshmi, who for years had worked late into the night inhaling paint with toxic thinner. She and her younger brother Darshan had been abducted in Moradabad, in Uttar Pradesh, brought to Forlorn and sexually molested repeatedly. Anybody could see that Lakshmi was dying. Marigold noted that her brother Darshan fared only slightly better. Another of Rajibai's friends, the frail seven-year-old Adjai, had been sold by his parents to a landlord for one penny a day.

"He was the lucky one," explained Rajibai. "You see, Father, his jobs are many. He gets out. Most never get out. Not even for a single minute."

Upon closer investigation, what that meant was that early in the morning Adjai would massage his master and perform oral sex before going out to collect cow dung for fuel. Then he'd come back for more sex and to work in the monster's fireworks factory, mixing a noxious batch of liquid substances for use in making match tips. He had AIDS, tuberculosis, persistent diarrhea, and burns over much of his body—for his master 'treated' his wounds by breaking up match heads, scrubbing the lacerations with the sulfur, and igniting the chemical as a way of stopping the bleeding. Adjai had been sodomized a dozen times before his sixth birthday by the master and all his master's cronies.

"How was that known?" Marigold asked. Rajibai knew: other children had been indentured for the orgies. The word spread as quickly as the resulting diseases.

It was the same with nearly all of them, hundreds of thousands of slaves stooped over one galling industry or another, whether the fabrication of auto parts or leather, iron or yarn balls, terracotta or slate, coir or walnut furniture, brassware and dishware, tea servers, ornamental pieces of tin, the working of diamonds, rubies, lapis lazuli and topaz. Girls at dangerous drilling machines; an old man, bonded since childhood, still stringing amethysts and garnets; a little transvestite prostitute cutting tiger stone; a four-year-old wrapping beedis in newspaper at high speed—1,000 boxes a day for two cents; dozens of children, watched over by men, chipping eucalyptus and pine for firing kilns that produced charcoal; others struggling with wheelbarrows filled with gravel; some using mercury in their bare hands to help in the separation of gold.

How could India permit this? Marigold speculated. What about the rest of the world? Sannazaro wondered. Which had dumbly nurtured the notion of Indian spirituality, citing her nationhood as the largest, most tolerant of free states. It was a country hailed for its pacifism, its love of animals and worship of Nature. Not since Hitler rallied his people, Sannazaro decided, had so many lies, such mammoth treachery and heinous crimes been consolidated under a single flag.

Just then, the visitors were shaken from these dark jolts by a joyous shout whose animation was the other side, the brilliant India.

"Budjo!" Rajibai cried. It was his old buddy alongside whom he'd once worked at the candle factory, where no light shone—or not for them.

"Rajibai!" Budjo sang out, collapsing with emotion.

CHAPTER 97
The Escape from Forlorn

A GUARD SHOUTED at the boys and tried to force them apart with his stick. Sannazaro was the first to intervene, slapping the man hard across the face. Then others joined in the fray. "Dekko!" came the barbs from all directions. Children kidnapped from far-off towns like Mirzapur and Zaipur hooted and cheered, and a skirmish ensued. But the tall, powering Commander put an end to it by knocking the guard over the head with a box of salt that set him floundering for aid.

A gang of masters returned from their assorted repasts—lunch? Snooze? Sexual trysts? Who knows, but upon their arrival at the work pits they were to discover that dozens of Budjo's comrades had risen from their sacks, boxes, jute machines and joined the trio in what was now the beginnings of a march across the largest slum in all the world. Their fast-collecting size guaranteed their immunity, for there was absolute strength in numbers. Who could resist the impulse to join a towering nimbostratus of children taking flight, embracing their freedom for the first time?

"Iacobo, I am proud of you," Marigold hailed.

"I have limits," Sannazaro replied, out of breath but more emboldened than the Commander had ever seen.

"*De l'audace, encore de l'audace, et toujours de l'audace!*" both men sang.

As they passed by furnaces booming, and dark interiors where metal dust saturated the air and minute slivers of metal went ricocheting in all directions, the assemblage grew in direct proportion to the furore that arose from the slave masters.

"We're heading into trouble," Sannazaro pointed out.

The number of marchers had increased exponentially, until mob met mob, the horde and throng jockeying for advantage.

An enveloping mob that must make a great man or destroy him. In this surge of unknown forces and arising combat, Marigold was no sparrow, nor Sannazaro the morning dove. They saw the lines of fire clearly, and could only marvel at the fast-surfacing heroism of their new little friend. For Rajibai had seized his destiny, and Marigold discerned the crusade to end all crusades. There were fisticuffs, bruises and bloody noses. But then the masters, gravely outnumbered, fled before the onslaught of so many. A march of the children was now in force.

In their forward advance, they saw a firecracker explode in a girl's hand, a child smothered in the mud of a cave-in at a quartzite factory. They found 100 girls confined behind bars in a sex shop, children from the hinterlands across Asia. It just got worse and worse as the day slipped by and the trio, moving in the front guard of the crowd, strode from one scene of damnation to another.

Sixty million child slaves in India, according to the International Labor Organization. A number equal to one of the largest nations in the world. All that sadness measured by the absence of song, the trill of cicada, or the trees and willow clumps in which they thronged. Not even a flower for square miles and miles. No bumblebee or blossom. This multitude of pangs confirmed in all of its endless depravities the spiritual emptiness of a continent, and the biological caveats of Thomas Malthus some 200 years before. Those who would doubt that so-called civilization (what Nikos Kazantzakis had instructively renamed "syphilization") was not an utter failure were simply and conveniently blinded to the most salient fact of the twentieth century. This. Forlorns, all their child slaves. Multiplied in omnivorous pursuit of profit at the expense, in country after country, of every human affirmation, hope and tenderness. No Bible seemed capable of standing up to the mad rush of such hell, first levied against animals and then human children. A cycle perdurable. Here was poisonous, psychotic greed displayed for all to see atop a funereal ziggurat of young corpses. In Forlorn, the survivors were hailed by government epidemiologists as impressive evidence that stress and adversity gave rise to a surprising immunity to all common diseases, just as Nayar had echoed. This was India's way of elevating their greatest shame to a New Science, not by way of apology or resolve to rectify, but in retreat from the heavy improbability of change.

As Marigold and Sannazaro too clearly realized, no morning's trek through such slums could yield any other truth than that of total horror, and the condemnation of a country and every conspirator in it.

How then to explain this bubbly child, Rajibai? Despite unfathomable tragedy, there was no more chirpy saint, a blushing, larkish and fair-cheeked parakeet, his morning electric with hope and every anticipation. Here in the presence of his former inmates of ruin, his own liberation burned and the light could be seen by all. Though only a child, he understood down to the marrow that for every cruelty there was an antidote. His sister was not coming back, but her martyred body—in the spirit of the Jain tradition from whence she and her younger brother evidently sprang—would enjoy a meritorious rebirth.

Murillo took Rajibai aside, away from the raucous horde. He as much searched for meaning as described it, because this little kid, his newly adopted son, acted on his sense the way filaments define the light bulb, or leaves a tree. The Commander firmly believed that life was nothing but guesswork, the future no more solid than passing clouds. Our determinations, for all their vigor, were, in the end, unprepossessing. Yet, storms could be predicted, and death was always there. Somehow, somewhere, the inner confines supported a miraculous moment. For the Commander this long, eternal day was that moment, and he tried, albeit gropingly, to commend it to the boy; to commend the purpose, and to entertain as vivid and charged an alliance as humanly possible. He wanted this new connection to work. With all his heart.

And to the Commander's astonishment, his son was right there, proffering an eloquence of thought that gave no precise clues to its origins. His diction, the complexity of thinking, no, the sophistication, were without peer. On the other hand, Marigold posited that just possibly this level of understanding was consistent with suffering, and the sudden release of all that had preceded. Rajibai's many friends and acquaintances might not sound off with the philosophical bent, but all shared the same fire and years of pain in their eyes.

Said the boy, "We are all the same, you know? Everybody wants the same thing."

"A Taj Mahal?" the Commander asked.

"No. Just a house, clean sheets, a solid meal. Water."

"That's all?"

"Freedom."

The idea emerged in Marigold's head as the crowd around them grew ferocious. His dialogue with the boy carried over. Somebody handed him a megaphone and the words just popped right into his mouth: "Children, you are as of this moment *free! Liberated!* You heard me? *Free!* No more work. No more Forlorn. No more beatings or torment or hunger or fear.

"Life will be very different from now on. All who join me and my son, Rajibai Jain, and Uncle Sannazaro, in the march to the nation's capital; all who pledge to have no more than one child of their own, who promise to be kind and take no revenge on those bastards that have persecuted you, and who vow to never harm a living being, whether a cow, a dog, a bird, or an insect—you will all be given 2,500 rupees. Spread the word to your friends across every street and byway and village in this whole blasted country. Children, your time has come! Tell them Mister Marigold, Uncle Sannazaro and Rajibai Jain have joined forces with you!"

The man who'd placed the megaphone in the Commander's hands translated. There ensued a vast stillness, incredulity followed by euphoric pandemonium. Tears flooded the muddy backroads of Demonville like a sea of deliverance, which it was. Except that neither Marigold nor Sannazaro quite knew what to do with their new-found celebrity, or where they could find the number of rupees the Commander had just promised. Of course he had no idea what he was unleashing, or the speed with which his message would spread. A wildfire of panic, commingling with news of the earlier backstreet brawl with the masters. The way (in India, at least) 200,000 people show up for a milk miracle, shoving their way towards God. Like wasps imbued with pheromones, the alacrity of hummingbirds, the scent of a rodent's corpse measured in parts per billion of olfactory sensors.

Time stood on his ears. Word of mouth erupted. Infernos of great domestic and international cause. A day became two out on the road, and two four. There was no more accounting for the hours, which rushed by in the head of engagement. Before long, hundreds of dailies across the country were carrying the news of the American's offer. And reports that insurrections by children were occurring throughout the land. The moment was irresistible to a nation of repressed children, particularly the girls. And Rajibai found himself squarely in the lead, with Marigold and Sannazaro trying to keep up.

From the deep blue corner of a hospital corridor to a champion of human rights. The Commander quietly paid witness to the transformation of a boy. He had known him for only a week, or less—he could no longer even say—but already his pride exceeded all peripheries. In Rajibai Marigold perceived the country's salvation. He wasn't overreaching, for all around him were the arriving multitudes, in the boy's image.

They came from Surat, where diamond-working children had rioted as recently as 1993; they joined the march with rotted teeth and white hair, with dysentery and the plague, from slave camps as far off as Firozabad, Bhadohi and Sivakasi. They emerged from pit mines and blast furnaces, from glass factories and sex cages. They came shouting a chorus of "Bachpan Bachao Andolan!" (Save Childhood!), with their hands extended to the white men who'd made the big promise. Twenty-five hundred rupees, roughly 55 dollars, was a fortune to these kids. The chance to walk away, to run, and for those who were willing to forgive those who had abandoned them, the chance to search for their mothers and fathers and older brothers.

"What have you gotten us into," Sannazaro worried. "You started it," replied the Commander with a grin.

As the phalanx advanced, as activists who'd been working to end child slavery for years joined the ranks, a barrage of camera-snapping photojournalists also descended, along with dozens of television and Internet reporters. Across the nation, news flashed of Murillo Marigold's offer. In 912 languages and dialects, from Nagaland to Kerala: "American Billionaire Puts Money Where Are His Teeth"; "Wacko Flower Child From US Embarrasses BJP"; "Imperialist Poses Challenge to Congress Party—Troops Called Out"; "The Great White Hope: For Shame!"; "Government Must Extradite Marigold or Admit Defeat on Child Slavery Issue". The Government was beset. Who the hell *was* this guy? It remembered only too well the havoc and international fray unleashed when a small boy by the name of Iqbal Masih, a twelve-year old former carpet weaver turned activist from Pakistan, had been murdered in April 1995. Troops were put on alert. US ambassadors were notified. An incident of global scope had begun.

But the several hundred thousand who now stampeded through Mumbai, bound for the Ministry of Labor in New Delhi many hundreds of miles to the north, was only a trickle in terms of what was coming. Like a flood whose main course is swollen by the conjunction of tributaries, children from all over India were screaming like locomotives in the night, racing to claim their 2,500 rupees, escaping every conceivable thralldom in the knowledge that their masters were now powerless to stop them. Similar zeal had avalanched before in India: food riots in Calcutta, rice hoarding during the Emergency years; sterilization circuses in Tamil Nadu in the early 1970s when performers on stilts at carnivals lured tens of thousands into the camps for entertainment 24 hours a day, a 50-rupee prize for all those willing to undergo a quick, almost do-it-yourself vasectomy or tubal ligation.

The country always relished a parade, anything to distract its minions from the dreary nuts and bolts of getting through the day. But as the arriving swarms blocked the road leading out of Mumbai, the first serious confrontation with the Indian military occurred. Five large Army helicopters circled what was, by now, a crowd of a million-plus marchers. Soldiers dressed in SWAT-team fatigues, carrying batons and rifles, raced into position. But the melee overwhelmed their segregated number, convincing the men to change their attitude. It was a no-brainer. Join in or be trampled.

"You've done it again," Sannazaro mused that night, where all were encamped beneath the stars in some vast congeries of mustard fields that stretched for miles, redolent with water buffalo dung, the slippery outlines of green mambas and cobras.

"Done what?" Marigold wondered.

"Pulled me in. To be here, instead of nicely encamped in a First Class seat on a plane to London."

"What? Stuffing yourself with chocolates? What about your figure? And anyway, that was eons ago. You've lived several lives since then."

"No, that was earlier this week." In fact, the train of events had become a colossal fog in the Squire's brain. First the arrival in Kerala; all the subsequent mysteries, hells and miracles. Then the monkey bite, followed by the boy. Until there was no stopping the logic. Now, two or three or possibly five million children were camped to all sides, and there he was sleeping out in a bedroll, his head upon a rock, a cactus fire keeping him warm... and a ten-year-old was calling him "Uncle".

Now the battleground faded from importance, and what remained was the actual *cause célèbre*: to save all those children who laughed and shouted, played tag, tossed marbles of stone, regaled each other with urgent tales, saturated whispers, stories of white nights—in sum, admitted every unceasing energy expenditure known to the young adult. Sannazaro looked out at this spectacular multiplication of millions of eager hearts and minds, a wonderland never previously beheld. So much compressed joy, such fellowships, fevers, revolutions, all on one colorful umbilicality of upbeat pasture. Spreading to every horizon of the night. Speaking to the very source of the Squire's humanity.

"Children are an excellent idea," he concluded.

By dawnlight the procession moved on, adding multitudes throughout each village. The army of children was imperturbable. They foraged, finding crafty ways to feed, water and secure their numbers. There were no longer orphans; no disputes; ample provisions were culled from the secret crannies which only children know.

They came upon the Ellora Caves, such was the northern zigzag of their itinerary, and here the gaping roar of youngsters ran riot over the intriguing configuration, igneous extrusions that had been metamorphosed into 100 or so chambers for the gods and goddesses. Jain, Hindu, Buddhist. A profusion of sculptural edifices that played host to the merry squadrons, the arty crags hundreds of feet high, amphitheaters and football fields of statuary. Bahubali, the son of an ancient king, his naked legs entwined in vines, sculpted 1,000 years before, sedimentary ants forming processions upon his unmoving toes—a potent, larger-than-life carving of profound tranquillity that had come to symbolize the country's predilections, gone awry. Where was that moderation today? What energies of restraint were left to temper a nation's maddening trespass upon its spiritual roots? The children clambered over the friezes and stonework, held court in the large outdoor temple surrounded by chiseled fragments from the first Indus Valley civilization.

Among these tempestuous ghosts they pretended to rule over their own imaginary empire, addressing the hard problems of their time, stationed proudly on every sandstone outcropping, braying aboard the spacious courtyards, following pomp and protocol, answering the challenge of 100 practical discords, policies and disagreements, whether rationing candy bars or providing ramps at the ruins for the handicapped.

In tune with the historical proceedings, Marigold called for silence. Like Joshua commanding the sun to stand still, he silenced the entire chorus of little children. One flourish of his arms instilled an unprecedented sobriety; buzzing fever dissolved into the art of listening, charging youth became one humble reticence. Practicing for the time when the real moments would come, when all this foment and energy must appear before a judicial proceeding of adults, the Commander called upon the young bandmasters and small fry, superiors and headmen, pacesetters and motivators, ringleaders and trail blazers, athletic teams and splinter groups, co-equals and syndicates. Each fellowship, trade block, Bund and Diet was summoned forward to make some serious decisions. And not just for fun, he warned them.

"Children, let me challenge you with the following. Pose before your mind's eye the most terrible of dilemmas. A city has run out of clean water. There are too many people. No attention paid to birth control, women's rights, the abuse of animals, garbage littering the canals. Residential zones. Heavy industries churning out chemical toxins. Everything's related and you've all seen it. But not a single water tap remains to be tried. Out of luck. My question to you, you captains of the next century: what will you do? How will you ensure water to drink? Animals to rescue? Your grandmothers and grandfathers to be looked after? Now think carefully."

A disorganized confusion fanned out, one boy looking to the next, each girl pawing her forehead for answers. Quizzical defaults, speechless riddle-weaving, threads of ambiguity slicing through ignorance.

A tough teenage lieutenant sort, gleaming naked chest, eyes twinkling, pride pushing his bravura heart, stepped forward from a high columnar tower of Shiva's mount and replied for the several million: "We shall form a long parade, each with his bucket, and move out like soldiers to all the adjoining creeks across the land, returning in due course with new water supplies."

"And if the creeks are dry?" Marigold retorted.

"But, sir, why would they be dry?" inquired the lieutenant with slight hesitation.

"Global warming, too many people in adjoining villages, a dry spell, no monsoon, any number of reasons."

The boy looked to the others around him; no one was quite accustomed to such pressure where life and limb hung in the balance.

"Then, sir, we should all die."

"Not good enough," an adult cried out. "No one needs to die. India has had its droughts and famines. Now we know something about it. We shall build cisterns, plant shade trees and hedgerows, dig irrigation channels, search for springs, cultivate dewdrops. Itcanbedone. Wewill help them find the water, no worry."

The speaker came from the ranks of the military. For by this time the SWAT team had sworn to the children's defense. This, Marigold knew, would aid them when they reached the nation's headquarters. "You men will be handsomely rewarded," he had earlier assured the 75 or so paratroopers, heavily armed and camouflaged. "And I don't mean in Heaven." He had secretly paid each of them a 'perk' amounting to 10,000 rupees apiece. The soldiers had moved out so that they were partitioned equally throughout the heaving crowd. They would protect and spare. It was a brilliantly conceived strategy, and it seemed to be working. Even Sannazaro was impressed.

Excitement galvanized the youth corps, a confederation among generations amounting to absolute glee. Here were garbed, armed military joining the ranks of rebel children. In Indian history no such alliances came to be. The moment was memorable. Nothing, now, could stop this rampage of inexhaustible hope sheltered by bullet casings, the enthusiasm of idealists buttressed by seasoned ground troops. It was precisely what the world needed.

Two days later, the motley milieu neared the edge of the city of Bhopal. By now Rajibai's flood of little friends numbered well over 12 million, all of them chanting one vast mantra, "*Rajibai, Rajibai, Rajibai...*"

"It's downright embarrassing," the Commander confided.

"You both deserve each refrain," replied Sannazaro with not a shred of scepticism.

CHAPTER 98
Rajibai Leads the Rebellion of Twelve Million Orphans

"ICH BIN AUFGEFLINK," buzzed the Messer Sannazaro's notochord, chiming and spellbound by so many whorls of voracious volts, amphetamized amps, young children. "Methinks this confederacy of tomboys and ragamuffins is leading us into a trench from which there will be no escape. Not ever," he reasoned, an array of jail cells, backlashes, retributions and glories inkling his nerves. He knew they were beyond the point of return, and it didn't matter. The actions had already spoken.

"That, or we shall found a new nation," said the Marigold, "or die trying, as any knight-errantry must do."

"Nothing appears more plausible at first sight, nor more ill-founded upon close inspection than such a scheme," the Squire concluded, paraphrasing legislative powers, citizens at large, the duties of a man, and all those plots against governments and declarations of war described by the three authors of the Federalist. The two carried on, in one breath Murat's ostrich plumes and French and Russian battalions at the *tête-de-pont*. In another the lost "*Engano a los ojos.*" What could have possessed these two idiots to prattle and preach so?

For Rajibai, this was the only fun he had ever known. To be the ringleader of a parade stretching across the Milky Way. Indians specialized in parades and celebrations, most notably the Khumb Mela, that Hindu mass pilgrimage to ecstatic dunking pools at the northern city of Allahabad, where the Ganga and Yamuna rivers converged, and where dedicated devotees of the gods ceremoniously stooped into the gravy-thick rivers. Such rites of passage related to those immortal drops of nectar rained down across the land from a khumb, or goblet, stolen in haste by one god from another in a mad cosmic relay race. This silly sport, upon which so much of Indian spirituality had laid claim, ensured that those who basked in the holy waters would enjoy a long life, rich in bacteria. There were several different melas, and by confusing coincidence one of them happened to be occurring that very day. Across India, people were on the makeshift move. Ten hundred thousand bullock carts were going left, another 59,000 heading to the right. Throngs of families walking to the north, equal bunches of massed wayfarers weaving south, trundling gourds of tepid water, sacks of wheat flour and lentils, the trident spears of Lord Siva. Naked yogis splattered in mud, children frolicking in all measure and proportion. The whole country was in disarray, torn between religious faith, money-grubbing hysteria and social uprising.

And there stood Marigold, a tramp in Thuringen, caught out not blind but struggling to assist, wafted and bestowed like a flowering hawthorn in the drift of the majority, with its intellectual diffusions and sorrows of everyone, young and old.

Long life, doubtful life, short life, whichever it was going to be. Both the Commander and his Squire were quite certain that this rebellion was beyond comprehension. No multi-billionaire's largesse could keep up with the outstretched hands streaming forth to claim their rupees—an additional half million every day, or was it by the hour?

"You've stirred up the whole country," Sannazaro figured, calculating on the palm of his hand a mathematics out of control, a siege upon the Bank of Santa Fe, revolt among the Trustees of Tesuque. "You haven't the brain cells of a Gates, the capillaries of an Annenberg; neither Buffet's business sense nor Turner's uncanny collaterals," he kept reminding him.

"Now *they've* got real dough and yeast to spare. Cattle-baron brio versus your pipsqueak of fickle modesties and fiduciary stumps." He was referring to the fact that Gates, the richest man in 1,000 golden moon bears, had bestowed over 25 billion dollars to his foundation and various causes. While Turner, in one senatorial gesture, had turned over a cool billion to the United Nations. For all of his aspirations, Marigold just didn't have the necessary clout of resources. A few billion might seem like a goodly sum. But in the relative world of wealth accumulation, it was a trifle, a few earth clods.

On the other hand, he knew, only three percent of all American charitable donations were dispensed in favor of the environment. And a mere one percent for international affairs. Nearly 50 percent of all 'giving' was religious in nature—tithing, the passing round of church envelopes. Of the 41,750 independent foundations in the US, one could count the minuscule numbers devoted to other species.

Whatever the odds against and percentages in favor of charity and inter-species largesse, Marigold carried on like the richest man in the world. This was a serious fallacy, a personality defect (in this, father and son were alike), and Sannazaro was the first to appreciate a liability when he smelled one. He truly was afraid for all of them, having stirred up madness in absence of do-able method.

If there were an approach, it was that of the apiarist providing a house of dreams to Indianized bees. These millions of heaven-hopefuls had much to be angered about, and Sannazaro did not see how such soft-core mantras as "a shovel for every hovel"—one of the Commander's visions for revising the country—could possibly guarantee hygiene for 800 million poor.

Ever the anthropologist, Marigold made much of his commonsense fraternizing, keeping apace of the multitude, asking questions, listening to the lore of the gutter, sensitive to the street languages of urchins accustomed to the barest minimums, to every hostility, austerity and hopelessness.

"There is no greater font of wisdom," Marigold explained, "than these children, with their tales of gray lice and philosophies of pudding."

Sannazaro could see the changes coming over the Commander by the hour.

"Moreover," said Marigold, "I intend to master the art of bio-gas digestion—" he had seen it employed in numerous households—"and I will learn the fine art of preparing chapattis, bathing along roadsides, making my toilet in the black mustard fields, becoming one with the people ..."

As Sannazaro observed, and not without astonishment, Mr Marigold had become, in other words, an Indian.

But for all this assimilation, his wearing of a dhoti, his atrocious accent, he was likely to get them into deep water, the Squire feared. He recognized the signs of addled adolescent turnabout; knew how stellar hope could easily verge upon dungeon despair, then turn to hostility when thwarted. And with so many self-jettisoned child slaves arriving by the minute, posturing with the hubris of imagined wealth in their possession, their pursuers not far behind, the situation appeared quite volatile. Ethics could easily be ransacked, guttersnipes suddenly parade as viscounts. Marigold, this one-time misanthrope whose forearms broke out in hives whenever he was in the proximity of too many people, was surely not himself. He had spent his life eschewing nearly all those of his species. Ever since Sannazaro had known him, he had displayed profound discomfort around people, yet now he revealed none of that temperament. Indeed, he seemed to embrace each individual with an aptitude that was nothing short of warmhearted and abiding. It was surely the influence upon him of that woman who broke his ribs.

"You will squander every last penny," he warned, his empathy and excitement losing their previous focus under the sensation of a panic attack.

"I intend to. Let the money be spent, and not fast enough. Let every good idea be plagiarized and re-plagiarized."

"The sea will still be stormy, the waves incessant. These children will devour us, ending up no better off once their money is spent. The system is 5,000 years old, Murillo. They will return to it."

"How dare you! Stay that sordid tongue!" Marigold chided, tossing his arms upwards, fingers and wild eyes ignited. He was tired of having to defend the obvious to his fraternal sceptic. Tired out. To sleep, perchance to dream, better still to sleep in, he thought. His day would come. In the meantime, stay the course, his futile headstrong westerlies reiterated, suffice under pressure, fear not the tirades of your opponents, ignore the cynics. "Do you not see the accomplishment to date? Even now there is a new inner government, I should declare, a child's kingdom of fairy values and the bulwark of a whole generation to defend its principles. But for the admittedly base temptation of a few dollars, this revolution could not have swept so vast a landmass with such effortless allure."

But Sannazaro had his own point. It was clear that there was no way to equally distribute the cash, which was like air-dropping M&Ms or tossing kernels of rice from the backs of trucks to those who had not eaten in months; no way to prevent a stampede; no time to calculate the rate by which the Commander's money was now flowing freely into the desperate hands of all who had flocked to join the fanfare, goaded on by the strength of fabulous rumors across the subcontinent. The gabfest not only of money but of a young saint, Rajibai, who had become, within days, a mythic figure in the minds of other children. Rajibai was on an unreal rebound following the death of his sister; he stood at the center of the media's adulation, from Goa to Calcutta. He had ignited a flurry of interest, as had the unsolved murder of his sister, whose benighted corpse had also made it to the headlines. Indians are not shy about exposing their dead, even drenched in the blood red of malevolence surrounding them. She too was a saint, a growing refrain indicated. Both she and her brother.

Lofty ideals were being tossed around at campsite after campsite. Firelight infusing task forces and revolutionary brigades. Speeches, encores, the formulations of a new charter that would be conveyed without compromise at New Delhi. But dignity perishes amid so much money. The 150 bankers who'd taken Marigold's credit-card imprints were unprepared for the drain upon the wheelbarrows of rupees which came in stapled wads of 10,000. The system was collapsing, as if soccer fans in a sports stadium were toppling the whole edifice. This further amplified Sannazaro's belief that it would all turn rotten; that every high-minded message and messenger would be undermined by the sight of a few thousand rupees, and panic would result when the money ran out—which it had to.

Indian rupees are a mirror image of the vast labyrinth of hands that have passed them from one to another. Hands that have sweated in the heat of every conceivable dream, anticipatory anxiety and noon-day fixation. The money deteriorates like no other currency—it has seen and done it all for over 50 years—soon becoming mealy, the consistency of molded cottage cheese. Eventually the bills simply break in half, or quarters, particularly the one- and two-rupee notes, those which have been handled most frequently, by the poorest of the poor, salvaged with glue, or scotch tape but, in the end, useless, for in India a torn bill will normally not be accepted by merchants. The new 100-rupee notes—the largest of them, worth less than $2.25—corrode more slowly, for they tend to be traded by higher castes, people more likely to manhandle them with less tension, the bills flattened more securely in large quantities of other 100-rupee notes. It is a mystery and a mistake, money, thought Marigold, a sad tuning fork for human evolution and class disparity. He gazed out over the hundreds of entrusted strangers now charged with passing out a fortune to each young person who had joined the march.

Organizing this effort well was simply impossible, for there was no real plan, only the frantic news of free money, of freedom, of 5,000 years of slavery about to be broken with nothing more complicated than one man willing to part the Red Sea by paying the bill, and 100 million children desperate enough to believe in him. A skinny, devout, insane-looking cockroach (he still had not gotten over the verbal assault of the Sri Lankan pirates), photographed at the height of a yawn, presently exploded with the frequency of a Marilyn Monroe across the nation's tabloids.

There was no way to gauge anything about the process, except to say that Visa and American Express executives in such remote corners as Carol Stream Illinois, Boulder Colorado, Sioux Falls South Dakota and Henderson Nevada had set 300-million-dollar limits per card with the Reserve Bank of India—sums unheard of across the subcontinent.

By now, every young person in the country, along with interested cows, ravens, kites, dogs, burros, sheep and goats, was flocking forth for a handout, or to see what it was all about (one of the country's exquisite traits), and the Commander—much to Sannazaro's exasperation—was complying 24 hours of every day.

Among those who saw the American's photograph in the papers was Inspector Abbas Nayar who, until now, had not lifted a finger to find the killers of Sunya. But presently the pressure had mounted.

"So!" he contemplated, well aware that he had quietly fixed things beneath the dusty table with respect to the so-called adoption proceeding. There had been no signature; Miss Puna had not done the paperwork, nor he. In fact, the adoption was a hoax that would not amount to anything until the border crossing. Customs would demand a proper passport—which the child, of course, lacked. Should the Commander ever attempt to bring authorities back to the source, Nayar was fully in a position to claim that the Americans had abducted the child, exploiting the tragedy for their own ends.

Yet he also considered the alternative scenario, though it meant extending his own risk. That 30,000 dollars (nearly 12 lakh), which, at the time, he thought to be an absolute fortune, was enough to secure an apartment on Malabar Hill, or Bandra, the dreamt-of upscale sides of town. But now, this new information: a man throwing money at the masses? Perhaps the 12 lakh could become 15 or 50 lakh? Why not? Nayar had the power, in truth; he knew how to exert panic in a civilian.

With a foreigner, in fact, the possibilities were endless. What could this Murillo Marigold know about India? Nothing.

Nayar left his post early that afternoon. Parul, his wife, suffered from a peptic ulcer which her doctor needed to examine. He would drive her.

He got into his government-owned 1982 Maruti, watched over by an attendant who took home 80 rupees a week in tips, and drove slowly towards Churchgate, calculating his next move with respect to the American and how he could extort another 75 lakh.

On the outskirts of Bhopal, news reached the throng of tent people now staying with Marigold—journalists had stopped estimating after 12 million—that, in addition to the Mela, another enormous protest march was brewing that very day within the city proper to commemorate the fifteenth anniversary of the explosion at the Cooties plant. Mr Marigold had remembered the Cooties incident, but failed to associate the year with the fact he was now within sight of the very factory where the explosion had happened. What to do amid this sudden confusion of priorities?

Twelve million people fanned out across the Indian plains. It was a sight of apocalyptic, painterly proportions, like that famed scene by Albrecht Altdorfer of the battlefield from the life of Alexander the Great, or the rush of humanity before John Martin's *Day of His Great Wrath*. In fact, the closest analogy was the Khumb Mela itself, which every twelve years ignited along the Ganga, bringing pilgrims from all over India to bathe in the sacred water.

Twelve million people can actually live in harmony for a few days. Such a population is equivalent to 24 times that density which once arrived on the grassy confines of a place called Woodstock, or 200 packed Rolling Stones concerts in stadiums bursting with energy. Many had come from places like Palamu and along the Narmada, where the Koyal Karo and Sardar Sarovar Pariyojana dams had forced millions of rural farmers, already living on the edge, into the unsurvivable hinterlands. Others had swarmed in from towns along the slow-moving itinerary of the marchers. Still others had arrived like trumpeter swans, sooty shearwaters, African flamingos, alpine lady bugs, swooping down in the hundreds of thousands to find that one source of salvation for their kind, a watering hole, a safe oasis. A rainbow whose ephemeral promise from biblical times was now poignantly seizing this untamable democracy. *Mujhe Bacha Le Amma! Save Me my Mother.* They were referring to Mother India, but none could fail to recognize, in that upwelling of patriotism, the Hermit of Tesuque. He stood like the hermaphroditic Tree of Life beside his little androgynous Joan of Arc.

It was a lot of people, with little or no food or water to support their contagion. But with so magical a conjunction of forces, this proud, elated 12 million were models of excellence. They were free. And little Rajibai and his nutty father were the center of it all. Rajibai was "the boy who had triggered the conscience of the world", reported the *Hindustan Express*. "The little fellow who worked his way into the heart of the American", went the ritornello, from mouth to mouth, ear to ear, until America, and its President, could do no wrong.

"You see! Could you possibly have negated it?" said Marigold to his doubting Squire. "There is a method," he kept uttering. "With enough people—all these millions, I mean—there is no way the Government can fail to do right by them. They will find the means—here, you can see it in action!—to shake off the yoke that torments them."

"What will you have the Government do?" Sannazaro replied. "You will not be around for the next generation or monitoring every session of Parliament in New Delhi for the next 20 years."

"Well..." and the Commander gave this some serious thought, just as he had done on countless occasions back home, for he had not actually figured out anything other than the end result which, of course, must be the typical liberation of all beings. A cliché without much mustard. But some ideas did come to him with surprising ease. For example, said he, "Sociologists one and all will agree that love perpetuates more love.

That freedom will never even consider defeat. Those now freed will pass along their passion, of that you can be sure. An Olympic torch that will illuminate the very sky, putting an end to all dictators, warlords and inhumanities. The world shall then revert, as my beloved John Ruskin once suggested, to a contemplative Florence, and there relax amid art, and beauty and tranquillity."

"And for the 100 million who have not made it here today, and have even less a chance of visiting Florence in this lifetime?"

The Commander, amid the colossal din and hue, his throat getting hoarse, for he'd come down with a bronchitis, reflected quietly. "All right. Forget Florence. Concentrate on this very place. That cactus bush. Those flowers. We are setting an example. The road we're traveling is chosen by the will of the people. I have no idea what will happen, in truth. I believe that India's legal department has in place the necessary safeguards. We have talked, you and I, about those labor laws. It is the political staying power, the courage to put them in place, that have been forlornly lacking. Now, politicians will see that they have the constituency. The ruling élite with their nationalist rhetoric will not be able to ignore this show of strength by the people. Look at the marches by millions of children across Columbia. The insistence of all those kids spoke reams' worth of Constitutional revision. Here a similar revolution can be effected. Nor can the tyrants attribute ulterior motives to this pandemonium, placing the blame on the two of us. You will recall that the former Prime Minister agreed by next year to liberate two million of his country's children. Three percent of the total mass of victims. We are simply keeping the country to its timetable, and more so. How can Delhi deny *Article 45* of the Indian Constitution? Free and compulsory reading and arithmetic for all. Committees must be formed to ensure some statutory vigor of compliance in these matters.

"I swear, Sannazaro, I have faith in this country. I have seen enough to know that, despite the great sadness in so many quarters, there is a Rajibai within every living being. I have read the Supreme Court's documentation in *Neeraja Chaudhary versus State of Madhya Pradesh*, 1984 and I must tell you—"

But Sannazaro broke in. "Are you making that up?"

"Of course not. How dare you."

"But when the hell did you have time to read a Supreme Court of India document?"

The Commander's expression lightened as a flame in a benighted winter corner. Bemused, barely the same man who started out that day or the day before. Who once asked only to be left alone.

"Take my word on it," he said. "It's added proof that the country can—it must—reform its own officials. There is a *Juvenile Justice Act*, an *Indian Penal Code* with quite specific provisions ..." Marigold, equipped even beneath the roasting sun to opine on matters he should not by any right know anything about, went on and on in his usual old-fashioned evangelical manner. He paraphrased from the vagaries of his memory that famed little printed card Alfred Stieglitz had issued in December 1929 when his gallery, An American Place, was born at Madison Avenue and Fifty-third Street. "It was his very Constitution, and might best be thought of as a rubric for India's own Parliament. No more games or expensive cocktail parties; no devious advertisements or ill-lit corridors; not one ism or special privilege; no esoteric theories to explain what it's all about; no quarter given to the media or special interests doted over; no institution whatsoever, or needless explanations for that which should be clear to the average person. The halls should be open to everybody; information, rights, guarantees. That is the government I see—an art gallery of human and environmental rights that lives not just upon the walls, or in the Penal Codes, but in the hearts of all who see it and feel it and breathe it. In every community. In every forest. Along the seacoasts, leaves of grass, high in the mountains where the mother nestles her child, the birds sleep, the panther strolls, the monkey sighs."

"Don't talk to me about monkeys."

Sannazaro was dealing with his own sobering up. For here he was, by no other rationale than to serve in the one way he could. No grand edifice to imaginary governments, certainly not in Asia. But to have a child. To be a father. To have a friend. To have woken up, as the English say, aboard a patch of greensward, beneath the live oak on a windy afternoon, and seen a buffalo become a god, a hermit a savior. These were real occurrences. He had to give them their due. They had taken life in him. No matter his patter, he avowed loyalty to these truths and was prepared to undergo certain hardships in their service. He had a choice, after all. Loads of money now. Yet, he stayed along for the ride.

And Marigold kept talking. "In addition," he went on, "a fully ordained *Convention on the Rights of the Child*. This march will remind the Government that it has ratified one; that the *Trade Union Act* must be extended to allow children the right to form associations in the matter of their own working conditions. Already there is a 'Kaleen' label on some carpets, meaning that they are child-labor free. Already over 1,000 mobsters have been prosecuted under the existing laws. It is a beginning, Sannazaro. This will push the envelope. Have faith. The United Nations, countless news organizations around the world, are watching."

The speech echoed across the cracked slip of tarmac leading to the fringes of the most despairing town in recent decades. There galvanized populations pressed in from every corridor and corner, heaving towards that blind alley of confrontation; they were given microphones, set up like rock stars upon the proscenium of nightly news; cameras shoved wildly, the paratroopers hung tough, providing protection, and all interwoven was like a rare design on the wings of a butterfly.

CHAPTER 99
The March Continues, Befuddled by the Campaign Against Cooties

THE SCENE got clouded.

"If I am not mistaken," the Commander declared as he studied his map, "we are less than three miles away from Bhopal."

"Bhopal?" Sannazaro muttered. He, like the Commander, remembered the name. Which could only conjure added grief.

Presently, 200,000 Bhopal residents were staging a peace march in the opposite direction, directly towards the tidal wave of Rajibai and his followers. It would be only another hour before the two groups converged in the middle of the city at the site of the Cooties Corporation, a vast sprawl of a chemical plant adjoining Bhopal's own densely configured slum, where, one night a decade and a half before, there had been a methyl isocyanate (MIC) gas leak from the Cooties pesticide division.

Marigold was not familiar with the details, but he would soon discover that since the disaster the company had been decommissioned, then sold off, its shares traded at profit, despite the loss to humanity of at least 12,000 dead and as many as 600,000 injured. Tallies varied: some estimates suggested a million victims in the first decade, and double that in the later years if one counted the trauma in so many emotional nuances and physical forms passed along from one gutted generation to the next.

One of the journalists who had been tagging along nearby Marigold took the opportunity to fill him and Sannazaro in on many of the particulars. It seemed appropriate, since Marigold would no doubt be questioned about his motives, whether there were politics enflaming the itinerary that encompassed the legacy of the Bhopal disaster. He had best know what went on there. And so he listened, inquiring about the intervening 15 years, only to learn of all the infernal, ferocious, hairsplitting spleen and blame, *sturm und drang* volleyed back and forth like a carcass on a playing field between the US mother company and its Indian subsidiary; between the Indian Supreme Court, a New York Federal judge and a Texas civil action. Betwixt secret diplomats in the night acting on behalf of the American and Indian regimes. Moneybags changing hands. Nuclear spare parts in the offing. The manipulation of loyalties to offset international tensions in China and Pakistan. Pressures at the highest levels of government, East and West.

Cooties executives argued that the whole sorry affair had resulted not from their own shoddy maintenance, their having ignored internal memos and local whistle-blowing journalist investigators, but from one disgruntled Indian saboteur, a low-level technician employed at the plant who alone was responsible for the mundane spare-parts juggling that quickly, in the chipped time-frame of a few hours, delivered a large amount of water into the MIC tanks, thereby precipitating one of the worst industrial disasters in human history.

But, as Marigold pointed out, even Bhopal paled by comparison with the downside of the industrial revolution itself. He was not one to be hemmed in, even by so monstrous a calamity as Bhopal, but rather expatiated upon its myriad other ramifications and innovations: tyrannical technology and emotionless engineering in generic form, whether automatic whale and seal harpoons, or the original ice-making apparatus developed by a fellow named Perkins and indispensable to all future transport and consumption of meat. That, in turn, had served as a hideous precursor of the factory farm revolution. Then there was the packing of meat, instigated by one William Pynchon in 1662; Mrs Wilmer Steele's manner of breeding boiler chickens in the 1920s using artificial lights; the internal combustion engine, whose incarnation in the automobile was the second largest unnatural contributor to the death of animals, after human consumption of flesh. Ironically, even those celebrated humanitarian breakthroughs in the history of medicine which had succeeded in lowering infant and child mortality, and extending life expectancy, had laid the groundwork for the population explosion, and—over time—billions of additional hungry and dying individuals of all species.

He had actually computed the pain index, and it was uglier than could possibly be imagined. His equation came together in this manner.

"Consider," he told Sannazaro, "the estimated 100 million species on Earth, about which science knows fewer than 1.5 million. Of those, only some 40,000 are more than a passing reference in an academic tome. Over the next century, given the long-time trends of human behavior, as much as 70 percent of those 100 million species will go extinct, slowly, horribly. But what does that really mean?"

"I haven't the faintest idea."

"I'm speaking of the vast quantities of individuals who will perish. Now we can roughly gauge the mean average of individuals per species for the entire vertebrate and invertebrate worlds. Several trillion ants, 22,300 known species. That works out to, say, 300 million individuals per insect, give or take. Once, during the time of James Audubon, there were three billion passenger pigeons, before the last one—Martha was her name, confined in the Cincinnati Zoo—died out in 1914. Among parrots, camels, and giant sloths, North America has seen each one vanish. My point is that whether tiny insect or huge mammal, there are going to be at least 50 to 100 million individuals, and probably many more, for each species. But even if we maintain a conservative estimate, say 100 million. Times 100 million species. That equals— let's see?" He tried to figure it out but got stuck at the level of thousands of quadrillions. "I can't tell exactly—I don't know what comes after quadrillion. But it is something like one billion times 10 million, or a million hundred billions, or a hundred thousand quadrillions. Or a zillion New Yorks. Yes. That's what it is: 100,000 quadrillions. I'm speaking of individuals who will be slaughtered one way or another by people just like you and me over the coming century. That's exactly what I'm talking about. Think of it like 10 billion Auschwitzes, every day, every night. And much of it occurring in just 34 biological collision points that take up less than 2.3 percent of the earth's terrestrial surface. Add the marine hotspots, and the numbers are multiplied by over 80 percent. And then add another 50 to 60 billion farm animals consumed each year, or four trillion since 1900. Computed differently, every 1,000 dollars spent on consumer goods translates into something like 10,000 to 15,000 dead animals. That's how it works."

Sannazaro shook his head. He wasn't following, or didn't care, or was thinking, *How could anybody be expected to care for quadrillions of things?*

"May I say something?" he said.

"Certainly."

"Your numbers aren't relevant."

"What?" The Commander was stunned.

"No, I mean it. Do I worry whether a supernova detonates a galaxy, or whatever they do? Do I shed tears for all those planets that are every other day obliterated? Some of them no doubt harbor life. OK, so?"

"We're not speaking about other planets."

"But you might as well be. I won't hesitate to weed out the lice from my hair. Why should I care about a few million other invertebrates."

"That's a form of blasphemy. If life is not precious, if these vast tragedies are not relevant, then everything is lost."

"Not so. Is Rajibai lost? Look at him—" They could see him in his element, 75 yards away, in the thick of a robust discussion with a few hundred friends. Laughing, jousting, hoping. Full of all that mattered.

"I would say he's been found, regenerated in a way that proves there is life on Earth, and there is humanity in man."

They carried on in this way for some time. Sannazaro speaking to the point, Marigold to an entire mountain range, or out along the horizon. But no matter how vague and general his indictments, Sannazaro accepted the fact that the Commander packed a terrible punch, both in his expectations of himself, a Lord and Executioner over his every move, and in his idealism. Given the circumstances of his unflexing intellectual and moral demands, how could he even live with himself? Sannazaro often wondered. But this was not the time or place to suggest he lighten up. The sad truth was all around them: nothing light at all.

But what mattered most this day was the convergence of a perplexing confusion of priorities in Mr Marigold's fragile ball of a brain, more mica than crystal, on the site of Cooties. Just imagine, if you will, the striking scene, the horrid confluence of imperatives, crying out for resolution. As if the Israelites, fleeing from Pharaoh, came upon millions of Cambodian refugees streaming in the opposite direction away from certain genocide. Human history compounding itself in a palpable enclosure, the size of one man's vision, spread chaotically across the nexus of flatlands of Madhya Pradesh. But it must have proven even more perplexing to an observer, for in all the excitement of millions of marchers, dozens of bands joined in with their jazzy trumpets, squeaky clarinets and undulating trombones, their drummer boys and baton-twirling cheerleaders. Frenzy after frenzy.

"The senselessness," Marigold exclaimed, sitting down in the dust to quiet his heart. He was bewildered; even he, daunted by the sheer magnitude of the chaos. People as far as the eye could see. A combustion of the gravest environmental crises and calamities known to man adjoining five, ten million smiling children.

Here was a company—the manufacturing zenith of that esteemed science known as chemistry—that had betrayed the trust placed in it. For every death, a different version of the downfall of civilization; for every widow and widower, a new face for Hell; another unresolved mire left to the annals of clutching, anguished fists slamming into private walls, and newspapers spilling no ink for every child erased in the mass burial grounds. Only the bastard memory, scarcely a name, perishing in the heartland which no one, outside of India, even knew existed. Embers gone out in the melodrama decried as 'The Third World'.

The same with all the child slaves. Not enough compassion in any Den Hague or UN building; no amnesty enough, or presidential decree; no volunteer army with sufficient swords to stir a transformation with the same glee as a beauty pageant or soccer game. Was all this melee about social transformation, or greed? Had he unleashed the worst in these children, or the best? Did it even matter, now that so many of them had escaped from their pits? Marigold finally consoled himself with the notion that the history of human transgressions would never catch up with the future. It provided some solace—the ability to start anew each day, undimmed by the sins of our ancestors—though the analogy with pain killers for bone cancer patients struck him as too close for comfort. Such drugs could not work fast enough to soften the terrible blow to the marrow. He'd known someone in Santa Fe for whom, in the end, the only solution was a deliberate overdose of morphine. The future might well be that patient. History his tragedy. Oblivion and forgetfulness his only hope.

After the disaster in Bhopal, Cooties Corporation had been re-invented, with all the brilliant disinformation convenient to the goal of revivifying a multinational in the spirit of stockholders, charitable donations, a new hospital, a few million here and there in the immediate aftermath. The company went so far as to launch its own massive investigation, with an accompanying film documentary allowing for lawyers and experts to debate the many scenarios, ultimately exonerating Cooties of any wrong-doing. Although a team of lawyers for the victims filed suits totaling 150 billion dollars, the Indian Supreme Court imposed a fine of just less than 500 million. Approximately the same amount the company was insured for. The case was closed, though criminal charges against certain Cooties executives were still, in theory, active.

In its most recent guise, the Cooties complex had been technically transformed for purposes of manufacturing benign helium balloons for children's birthdays and parades. A welcome change from pesticides. Even now, from his contemplative perch on the edge of town, Marigold, through his binoculars, could see workers on company grounds blowing up the balloons to somehow mark the occasion.

The Commander's lips were parched. Sannazaro offered him a warm Limka. Rajibai, meantime, conferred with 100 little senior friends who had joined him from the shitholes of Forlorn. Thrown into the fantastic fray of protest and quicksilvered forward motion, none of them had the slightest clue what to do with their freedom; all were comparing the bundles of rupees in their hands, scheming every revenge, plotting itineraries that would see them safely home again. It was a political struggle, but nobody knew who was listening—or listening to what. There was no unified approach to objections, only a mass of frightened youths, trembling before the uncertainty of their rebellion and what might happen to them as a result. But the psychology of strength in numbers held sway and granted a rare deliverance that no other set of circumstances could touch or engender.

Rajibai, catapulted into the forefront of the marchers, felt only joy this day, aware that his life had changed forever; that he was somehow appointed by dharma, or destiny, to help his friends in this way. His gusto served as a rallying cry for barefooted five-year-olds. This one carried a bag of bread, and this one a Coke bottle he hoped to sell for two paisees along the way. Their only shared knowledge was that they had hit the road for the first time in their tired lives, escaping the desperate darkness of that life into which they had been born, or sold.

Whereas a profoundly separate agenda, articulated with excruciating precision, rigor and rancor, issued from the hundreds of thousands who had gathered before the Cooties plant, furiously throwing their arms into the air, hurling their demands at the executives, at the Government, at all who would listen. Was anybody even out there?

Despite all the rulings in the 15-year case, the masses volubly appealed to the High Court of the State of Madhya Pradesh for a new protocol that would provide for proper compensation to survivors—over one million of them. The September 14th, 1989 decision by the Supreme Court of India directing a final settlement to the tune of 470 million dollars was rightly considered a joke wrapped in an insult by Bhopal residents. A major blow to justice for all mankind, said Marigold. Adding further sting to the humiliation was the lengthy opinion from the jurists on the bench in Delhi which suggested that 470 million dollars was actually far more than an Indian court would ordinarily have awarded. In 1990 a new Government in India prepared to consider overturning the easy settlement. It did not happen. Instead, experts argued into the night, hairsplitting over fragmentary data, abstracted actuarial tables determining compensation flow, flimsy determinations of victims partially disabled, permanently disabled, dead or asymptomatic. It was a mockery, furthered by a court decision prohibiting victims from seeking damages in US courts, despite the fact Cooties was an American-based company.

Mr Marigold asked questions of those emissaries from the adjoining marchers who had come to discuss the fast-evolving situation of two separate protests and how to handle the chaos. They described to him in some detail the vexatious truth of that ruinous night in Bhopal which had burst upon the consciousness of the world the day after. The grisly legacy of storage tank number 610 into which water had poured with the disastrous consequences; the runaway reaction, increased temperature and pressure, and the unstoppable four-hour breach of methyl isocyanate, hydrogen cyanide and other reactive gasses that steamed into the quiet starry-laden night; the plant's fail-safe system either unworkable or unsuited to such a situation while a million people slept nearby. How it took a full hour for any siren to alarm, as about 30 square miles of city were covered in a dense deadly cloud which made breathing next to impossible, that seemed to gouge out the eyes with molecular knives, sent hundreds of thousands of vomiting victims fleeing into an agonizing nowhereland from which they'd never return, as they awoke to screams, and unbelievable pain, and foaming mouths, and suffocation, and animals squealing, then dropping dead where they lay chained, or caged, or sleeping.

A train filled with unwary late-night travelers had pulled into Bhopal at that very moment.

There had been no advance protocols for dealing with an MIC release; no dissemination of information whatsoever (the fact that the gas was heavy and tends to kill more people on ground-level floors, not second- and third-story floors); that there was, indeed, an antidote that could retard long-term tissue damage, if only it were promptly administered, which it was not, and so forth.

Listening to all this melancholia, Sannazaro found his voice, and addressed his friend. "There is only one trustworthy source they are going to turn to for cash now. Not the Government, which has admitted to its legal naivety; not the company, that succeeded in abdicating responsibility, tossing one legal curve ball after another at the wall of human woes; no assortment of outraged NGOs whose cries are mere stick figures representing Western guilt, gesticulating wanly in the wind outside the fences. But yourself. You will be stuck with every single bill, I promise you. Because it's there."

"I will pay," Mr Marigold said. "After all, are we not Americans, responsible for our fellow Americans, and in the privileged position of being able to do so?"

"You are that ideal of biology you always speak about—the ultimate kin altruist," Sannazaro replied. "But I see a few hundred thousand victims to the right, millions to the left, and nearly one billion elsewhere in the country, not to mention the rest of South Asia. Another billion in China while you're at it. You're no General Motors or Sultan of Brunei with all the money in the world to spend. In fact, you're not even on the *Fortune* magazine list. Yes, Bill Gates donated a hundred million to child immunization causes and to fighting AIDS in Botswana. But you didn't see him providing another 17 billion a year for secondary school education for girls around the world. Why not? Well, he'd probably say—and rightly so—that he simply can't afford to do everything. And he's worth 50 times what you are. We've been over this. How effective will you be once your money's gone? A nobody. You need to recall your master plan. Ease up, put the brakes on. You are not going to assuage the trauma, mend the wrongs, clean up all of the Cooties in the world. Not here, not this day, not ever. I'm not saying, Give Up. I'm saying, Be Smart."

Marigold was far too distracted to give much sensible consideration to such calculations.

"Are you listening to me?" Sannazaro said, annoyed by the Commander's apparent indifference to his views. "What were all those think-tank sessions about back home? All that lip service devoted to spreading your wealth intelligently, not blowing it on the first great cause that comes along. You are a fiscal virgin, and that is a huge liability. What about Santa Fe National Park? Have you forgotten?"

Marigold now started to listen more carefully to what his Squire had to say, and suddenly looked hunkered and sobered, the whole sweep of his many endeavors, the illogic of their diffusion, the depth of his amorphous international thrusts hitting him over the head with as much ferocity as an apple.

A dozen reporters tried to push their way into his face. The Dragoons, as he likened his paratroopers, buffered him effectively, but still the questions rang out: Will you apply your financial leverage towards re-opening the Bhopal investigation in the courts? Will you pay for medical needs, clean up the existing toxins, apply your army of children towards some conservation corps here in Madhya Pradesh? What is your next move? Which is your priority? Don't you find it strange that it should be an American who frees our children? When did you first fall in love with India? What do your parents think of you?

My parents? His heart quickened. For a moment he turned, somewhere along the road to a pause, where memory became relevant. And then he let it go, unable to remain there in the never-never realm of his heart's recollections. A stranger to it all. Back outside, where he faced the day, a frenzy surrounded him, the words coalescing into a pan-pidgin English that garbled his insides, left him linguistically bereft, on the side of a cliff. He held his son, unspeaking.

Chapter 100
The Chemistry of Sleepless Nights

THE COMMANDER WATCHED wearily as the march of children hit like thunderclaps the unnerving riot of Bhopal victims. So many marooned men, shipwrecked children, mothers chewed up, all the basics collapsed. Eyes blinded. Faces, genes, whole generations, every plan, presumption, pleasure blighted. Seniority severed, childhood deleted, that hazy hope for deliverance decapitated. All this waiting for impossible redemption, and without that, insisting upon deaf justice. In the long welter of Bhopal days, nights, set out against illimitable odds of dried-up alkaline flats, demolished farms, poison in the bird's beak, one billion other woes and private grievances, what was there for the Bhopalis but this day—a fifteenth anniversary, a few angry speeches—to mark their horrible experience.

Marigold knew he had to act presidentially in these heated circumstances. But how? A 300-mile-per-hour typhoon could not have done more to eviscerate the community and undermine confidence. On the one hand, 12 million disenfranchised children. On the other, a million victims of greed. Surrounding the circle of indignity and pain, a celebration. Too much contradiction for any one human. Nonetheless, he was now in the limelight. His every action counted for several columns, front page, of the Indian dailies. He had to measure his words, stand up straight and tall, set an example, suggest policy changes. In short, he had to become political, which was a terrible joke. Marigold was as much a politician as an aardvark a bookmark. No abracadabra could change that.

Imagine the scene: an inferno of pissed-off hopefuls advancing with their bloody placards towards the site of devastation. Who was there to greet them? A new generation of company sympathizers who had renounced the past and proffered a new spin on the future. Local ombudsmen and panchayat aspirants vying for re-election. Outside NGOs competing over loudspeakers, reminding the throngs of all the misdeeds committed by the status quo. Above these John Martin plains of chaos, no single voice was audible, no message clear. Just a white noise of benumbing nullification. It was the same everywhere. If all humanity were assembled in one playing field, nothing could possibly happen: no judgment, no final awakening, no consensus. The vote, the show of hands—a genuflection of denials, anger, ignorance, half-bred regrets. If even half the mass of our kind gathered to hold a candlelight vigil, they would give insufficient illumination to heal a single wound. Comfort in numbers? Not on their life. The mass, all our multitudes, meant nothing.

The only guarantee, more chaos. Hatred. Repudiation. No evidence for a convergence of individuals and governments. No hand-woven, home-crafted compromises, not where 12 million people were concerned. The Tom, Dick and Harry. Icon of a restless species. Even 100,000 defied the odds. A Superbowl, or rock concert, should easily exceed the carrying capacity of measured tones and providential grace. Among two, a possible conclusion. By lover's rule. But three spoiled it. Invariably. Hence, a mathematics of the threshold, turning on the fact of a specific capacity. The town forum was its original conceit, with a few hundred quiescent Quakers, no more. A graspable coherence allowing for participation. But redemption—impossible.

Consider once again this present scenery, all the reminders of human folly surfacing in Marigold's nonquiddle of a brain: the goats of Chernobyl, the red robins of Love Canal, his firm belief that creosote and copper-coated 78-inch fence posts surrounding white wine vineyards in the vicinity of Mendocino, California, were responsible for the melting of Greenland, that the use of drugs to curb fleas was killing humpback whales. American suicide rates among teenagers on the rise. Male sperm counts plummeting. Humanity in fear and illness. That was the landscape—augmented globally—before him.

The Commander could not fail to do what was right. He was there, the man of the moment. But what could so bumbling a diehard pull off? What foundations might his erratic behavior build? Was there any consistent application, the growth of a legacy, remains that could be excavated, a message remembered, files kept, documents passed down? Hope laid its claims to a fiefdom of idiots; desire, the sovereignty of fools. Somewhere between these two earnest spectra was the beast in the petticoat, that altruistic kingdom of Marigold.

Or was his whole crusade nothing more than an abominable lack of humor, dimwitted and unsure; more focused upon unfathomable wholeness and mystical murmurs, deep breaths and nauseating truisms?

This was what concerned Sannazaro. He was going to be an old man one of these days, had not a moment to waste, and would prefer to leave some handprint, at least, of his having touched and been touched by the Earth. But not necessarily like this—these sporadic rounds of gunfire to no end, these volleys of impulses that could only dissipate like the mists of a waterfall in the harsh glare and abrupt winds of daytime reality: a cellular tower's voltage vanishing in air. Or, as the rare Konkani dialect might describe the syndrome, *Alle khalele oondravari, ranne pedyeri kaan sarailele mazravari.* Like a mouse who's eaten ginger and a cat that's rubbed its ears against the kitchen hearth.

Marigold's eyes began to weep, but he did not know how to answer to the practical injunctions of Sannazaro's indictments. It was true, he could not doubt the wisdom of it: he was not rich enough to eradicate all mayhem.

This nettle of remorse worked its way into his few remaining cognitive faculties, stymied his wanderlust, encroached upon his dream of a separate Paradise for each and every being. His compulsions spun out of control as they had so many times before. The manic depressive in him dipped low, slumbered in darkness, turned away from what was calling at his doormat, burned inside with fevers that only those similarly afflicted (and with no diagnosis or willingness to take medicine) can describe. It was an hysterium bound by the same laws as those affecting someone very seriously high on drugs. A combination, in other words, that galvanized and emboldened whilst enfeebling and shrinking. A frisson which is the starburst at the heart of creativity, self-destruction, undirected high-energy vibrations and ultimate silence.

All those years of book learning had somehow kept this demon of change under lock and key, confined to a dusty hacienda, without incentive or instruction on the ways of the outer world. It was the sheer volume of his reading, the weight of straining ideas and counter-intuitive injunctions that paralyzed him and kept him from doing anything. An inertia engineered from the time of his youth, in absence of parental demands, friends, responsibilities, schooling, performance exams, requirements, necessary signatures, worldly guides, or want of any basic goods. In the days prior to attention-deficit drugs, such inertia served to protect him from himself. He never had to put away his socks: that was the brightest undoing that gave him the capacity, in middle age, to explode with earth-shattering goals and head-bashing ideals. He never had to clean his drawers, wash out his sink, take a bath, endure dancing lessons or weed the lawn— Heaven forbid it with his surname! No discipline beyond that of his own inner rule. Pecos Marigold had insisted his son become his own man at an early age. Even before the momentous foray to Ecuador, young Murillo had championed only those causes guaranteed to relieve him of all chores, be it Latin, Greek or Tolstoy. Now, his time had come.

A turn of adamant conviction presently laid in to him. "Have you not learned?" he barked at Sannazaro. "Would you penny-pinch amid such blatant need? Look at our son." He turned to Rajibai, who stood at his side. "His freedom, and that of his many friends, is the result not of calculations and parsimony but of compassion and clear thinking. First Bhopal, then Santa Fe National Park. The thread should be obvious to any dunderhead."

"Fine. Blow your wad. What do I know? Or care? It's your money, and guess what? You're absolutely right! One cause, one truth, is as righteous as another; one life equal to the rest of the them. Do I begrudge you any degree of madness? Do it. Make us paupers so that we can finally beg a ride home in steerage and end this. End it here, now. I'm all for it. In fact, I insist!"

The squall of protesters who had formed a half-mile-long band around the Cooties perimeter were holding hands, chanting, "Down with Cooties. Justice for Bhopal!" and other plaintive cries. The little Italian began campaigning among them on behalf of his loose stool of a benefactor. Anybody who would listen was entitled, said he, to gobs of free money. "There he is, that's the one, grab him while the money's good, buy yourself some food, medicine, some condoms, even a television. He'll throw in free cable."

But with millions of cadres from Rajibai's Rebellion joining in, the Bhopal protest was becoming an overwhelming showdown of humanitarian shadow play and panic. The cavalcade of unrest was continuing to attract a turmoil of news reporters. They made for the makeshift camp erected hastily by the marchers, and occupied dozens of buildings. There several of the former slaves—all friends of Rajibai—answered direct and heated questions regarding the conditions of their forced labor, the details of their sexual molestation. It was a *tour de force* of confessional outpouring highly unusual in India, where such lurid details are usually withheld.

They gave the names of all the bosses who had captured, starved, raped them; of conspirators—the ones they knew firsthand—who'd maintained the silence: bankers, traders, drivers, onlookers, buyers, sellers, gurus, solicitors, teachers, policemen, merchants, politicians, religious people, magistrates, parliamentarians who had visited the slums and were never heard from again, parents and siblings who had sold them. In short, they pinpointed the entire mesh and fiber of India's back streets and inner communities.

Meanwhile, the Bhopali protesters were hysterical. For sheer numbers of aggrieved, this onrush of child slaves far outdid the numbers on their own commemorative march.

Competing screams, questions, an absence of answers. Petitioners reminded the reporters that, in America, the courts valued a dead person at 225 million rupees, but an Indian at only 25,000. How could such discrepancies be sanctioned by the World Court? How could a chemical industry such as Cooties sell off its shares to a European company at a profit, while hundreds of thousands of Bhopali victims and their families remained unreimbursed? In every home, people were still dying, women still cloaked in black. Who would pay? Who would remember? Reporters put down their pens. Boils on bodies, cornea opacity, reproductive ailments, defective nucleotides, TB, fevers and neurological disorders, the fact that—according to the Indian Council of Medical Research—nearly 25 percent of all those who had survived the exposure remained "chronically ill" or were slowly dying off ... it was too much to digest. The fifteenth anniversary induced tears that smudged diaries and waterlogged the news columns.

Marigold heard how contaminated sludge from the disaster had been buried and hidden to avoid future scrutiny by chemists; how Cooties' CEO hid out in his cozy Florida beach condo, safe from extradition despite criminal charges that he had absconded while on bail; that an ongoing inquiry by India's Central Bureau of Investigation had pressed "culpable homicide" charges against ten Cooties fugitives from justice, all residing in the US. But such allegations had been met with impatient indifference. Shifting blame, muddled memos, a multinational with a portable home base, skittish officials, covenants between the US, India, Hong Kong and other Cooties-based locations that simply mocked any pretense of justice. No young reporter seemed capable of disentangling such a travesty. Cooties, in the end, was a publicly held corporation, which meant that stock owners were not held to any standards of consensus.

They had no motivation whatsoever to pay out awards, to be good Samaritans.

"Write, damn it!" Marigold raged before the journalists. "This is your story, your doing, your responsibility. Must I bash my brains against the company's perimeter, spill my guts, expose my naked flesh so all of you can recall that we are but human, vulnerable, in a state of innocence from the time of our birth? That we grow up as children trusting to the supposed wisdom and care of our adults? Believing with all our hearts that life is good, that our parents will protect us, that the government is for the people, by the people? Do these truisms not devolve to the human condition and warrant reappraisal in light of what you see here today? Would you shirk the glare of so much abnegation?"

His questions continued in a blaze of steady cannonades; the gathered enclave of journalists and politicians were silenced before the evident shame cast upon their nation. There was no way to excuse or mask the truth. He and various spokespersons for NGOs present had laid it bare, and it was the ugliest thing in a century of Indian politics and social aspirations. Their entire society had been leveled in one day by two tandem outbursts. The adult world had denied its children a future.

On the other hand, grumbled the local politicians assembled for damage control, these grievances were not unique to India. Two American judges had all but denied the Bhopal suits on home turf, while the US State Department had warmly embraced the Cooties fugitives. Americans massacred their Indians, lynched their blacks, filled their prisons with Latinos. England, in its day, had conquered half the world, subjugating hundreds of millions of natives to Commonwealth tyranny while approving the trade in slaves out in its colonies. Chinese, Mongolian, Soviet and most Middle Eastern potentates, South American dictators and North African fundamentalists had also turned their countries, people and history into rubbish bins and killing fields. No, India was a democracy amid a world of fascists. India had its problems, but they were fixable. In a free country, everything was fixable.

Disagreements flourished. "Where are the solutions? The money?" Outspoken representatives of the Bhopal NGOs from New York, London, New Delhi and Bhopal itself referred angrily to the fact that the number of beds at the city's major primary hospitals and health clinics was nowhere near large enough to accommodate all the remaining victims. There were reasons militating against the construction of more hospitals, according to the various superintendents charged with the city's building codes: the escalating market price for steel chips, not to mention the ever-rising costs for syringes and such. Medical records were fading. There was not enough money for intravenous sets. The present Government could not be held accountable for decisions taken years ago. Moreover, said one particularly defensive local administrator, the Bhopal People's Health and Documentation Clinic was successfully continuing to help the chronically ill with free medical assistance, weren't they? Did not the European Community, on occasion, donate milk powder? Had not women's sewing opportunities been instituted, several new schools built for children of the victims? Wasn't that enough? Never mind the absence of safe drinking water or sanitation: those were luxuries the Bhopali people should not consider their right, given that most communities throughout India were lacking such things.

"There are strange vibrations and conjurations today," Sannazaro pointed out. Then he grabbed the Commander, who was about to stand atop the highest podium and mint some patriotic speechifications about pivotal power. "If you intend to make a difference, I suggest you do so from abroad," he said. "You promise any more money today, and we will surely be mobbed to death."

But it seemed inconceivable to the Commander that there was no basic unison here at Bhopal. Had not a million victims the right to expect vindication? Could there be any question about their plight, their cause, the blame of a nation? The truth of stillbirths, tumors, blindness?

Despairing social activists held up charts to the news cameras, showing how at least a third of the death claims had been rejected; that most of the 470 million dollars of insurance money had never reached any of the claimants; that Cooties' lawyers, local judges and government tribunals had collectively promulgated perhaps the gravest judicial miscarriage in modern times.

"Yes, yes it is terrible," proclaimed everyone. The politicians soft-pedaled, the scores of Indian reporters nodded sympathetically, women wiped their weeping eyes, fathers held up their deformed babies, those dispatched from foreign press agencies scrawled their outrage in short-hand. Their readers back home had never heard of Bhopal. But it was the number of protesters that was the real news.

Amid these revelations and the carnival atmosphere of mixed metaphors, cries for justice, the tears of widows, 10,000 miscarriages, 20 marriages, 14 marching bands, and 12 million youngsters feverishly wondering what they were doing, where they were headed and whether there was any more money in it, a great clamor issued from inside the Cooties plant itself. There, thousands of colorful balloons and hundreds of white doves were jettisoned all at once, rising triumphantly into the heavens, winging and drifting over the polluted fields towards a new dawn; and a strident voice carried by a loudspeaker shrieked across the airs above Bhopal in an ungodly voice: "Responsible Science for India. Hope for the Future. Let us all come together as a Family. No more Ill-will. Let Bygones be Bygones."

But the words were difficult to make out, for they were uttered in an impossibly high-pitched voice that broke the somber sound barrier of chaos with irrepressible humor.

"What is that?" Marigold winced. Sannazaro and Rajibai listened intently.

Again the voice repeated itself: "... Bygones be Bygones ..." But the tenor was absurd, riddled with hiccups, a high-twined, helium-induced squeak that had only one universally recognized equivalent: the fanatically falsetto choral concoction of Alfred, Theodore and Simon, lovingly remembered as 'The Chipmunks'.

Other balloon-men, unaware of the leaking helium and the inevitability of their inhaling the stuff, declared their banalities in great stride, hoping to calm down the protesters. But absurdist capriccios had engulfed their comedic vocal chords. The auditory emanations were phantasmagorically ridiculous. Cooties Corporation had long anticipated this day but, like its predecessor, was incapable of assuring a leak-free factory ground. The machinery, built on Indian soil, had minor kinks, of no great liability factor, but was consistent with the history of such fizzles and chemical breakdowns. Helium got out in volumetric liters as the attendants charged with filling the balloons inhaled the gaseous outflows.

A vast amphitheater of guffaws and chortling ignited among the children, and adults too, as if the spirit of Crowquill hung above the site of disaster. Tragedy mingling with mirth; environmentalists and human rights activists slipping on the peels of human comedy. Politicians giggling where perdurable penance was more appropriate.

"Can helium really make us forget our pains?" Marigold wondered. "I doubt it, or not for very long."

"This is terrible ... A travesty ... Explode the balloons! ... They're sabotaging our protest!" came a wide refrain.

Sannazaro stared balefully in all the berserk directions. "This is insane," he concluded.

"What's happening?" asked Rajibai, who could not contain his own laughter.

"Time to move on," said Marigold, who spat on the ground, made the sign of the cross, and thereby endeavored in his own peculiar fashion to exorcise the contradictions assailing him. "Rally your forces, Son!"

CHAPTER 101
Marigold Contemplates an End to Nuclear War

AFTER THE EPISODE of escaped helium momentarily suppressing the wellspring of so many modern tears, the 12 million marchers left Bhopal by delicate dawnlight, restless to reach ever-sprawling, fuming New Delhi and press home their demands on the Government of India. No more obfuscations of the truth. An end to the betrayal of every upcoming generation in the name of a poor country and income generation. For those in Bhopal, their day in court would come again. Mr Marigold, without fanfare or self-promotion, signed a check for 100 million dollars (US) to be spent on a number of well-conceived avenues: 25 million dollars for hiring the best team of lawyers in the world to try to have the Cooties' corporate charter revoked by a US Attorney General, and to press for civil charges of wrongful deaths against all those identified by the Indian Central Bureau of Investigation; and 75 million dollars for the various NGOs responsible for conveying appropriate medical attention and social services to victims.

Caught up in the unusual ether of international good will and paternal patriotism, Sannazaro threw in 25,000 dollars of his own new-found riches. Some of those in Bhopal would remember the Commander as a great inspiration for the future—an enigmatic example of self-effacement, a prince of peace amid a slew of imperatives. They hailed all three of them as true blues. The boy a Jack of Beanstalk, the little kid who could from Forlorn Slum; Marigold a biblical-style saint fabricated on the Golgothas of edifice-building, San Sebastio riddled with golden-tipped arrows; and his Squire they named Sannazaro Baba. He produced monetary miracles between his thumb and index finger, was the spry voice of reason, the one who kept it all together, and along the route never ceased complaining about white ants, the heat, lack of water, and raising profound questions as to the ill-smelling campsites and the thousands of births each day to teenage girls.

Others, however, doubted their motives; made Marigold out to be an impresario, a spy for a Western multinational or a virulent egomaniac sweeping innocent lives along in his own parade. Some thought he was really out to develop India and ruin her homespun rural character. To finance beach hotels and bring in busloads of tourists. To replace the country's arranged marriages, camel fairs and innocence with computers and overpasses. That Sannazaro was attached to the Mafia, and the orphan Rajibai their unwitting puppet. That the two men were stalking vulnerable Indian families in order to buy off their children for foreign adoption agencies or prostitution rings. Or that was what somebody had overheard from a plain-clothes policeman amid the throngs, a stalking voice of fastidious and quiet persistence, asking questions, zeroing in on his prey.

But these were minority voices. The vast seething majority of those who would be helped by so much concentrated largesse harbored no doubts that Mr Marigold was putting his personal fortune on the line for causes that had been ignored by their own Government. Such virtue was automatically idolized in India. To have spent 100 million dollars (4.5 billion rupees) on the Bhopal victims placed the Commander in a unique position of fame and adoration. To have spent more than that towards the liberation of child slaves across India made him a serious threat to the Indian military/industrial establishment; even qualified him to run for the highest office. After all, a Gandhi of Italian birth had done so.

The march advanced, the trio in the lead. Arguments erupted at every village. Left? Right? Straight? Back? Are we almost there? Papadams! A black mamba! Taxi? They're out of water. A cholera outbreak. A hundred dead from hepatitis. The Imams are objecting, as there are Muslim girls among those boys. Help us, please Sab! Pens? Penssab? Are we almost there, Father? Communist infiltrators, local labor unions, upholsterers, barbers roving through the sea of children, shaving cream-and-razor dispensers, chain-link fence manufacturers, a boycott of the whole wheat bread distribution system, puppeteers and coir fabricators, 1,200 cotton weavers, all children—"They say they are staying, they're tired, fed up, and a wealthy merchant has offered them more rupees." Hour after hour, as the 29 miles of marchers proceeded north into Rajasthan's Tar Desert.

People in white turbans roved out to greet them—a community immune to the drought that ravished the area. (Elsewhere in Rajasthan were hundreds of funeral pyres, thousands of dead cattle, food for vultures who stood defiant in their proud social hierarchies, pecking at the eyes and preening one another. A surprising cleanliness amid carnage).

There were desert refugees streaming in all directions, but the Bishnoi were not among the dispossessed. Rather, they were on hand to assist, offering curd cakes, lentil pudding and opening their wells to the myriad of thirsty ones. The Bishnoi—nearly one million distant relatives of the Hindu, who dated their spiritual lineage to the medieval saint Jangeshwar Baghwan, or Jamboje, born in 1452 in the Rajasthani village of Pipasar. That happened to be extremely close to where the 12 million marchers had presently arrived and were camped out in preparation for their staging of a demonstration at the nuclear cave site of Pokhran-II, a former artillery range some 40 miles from the Pakistani border. Marigold had been on the loudspeaker trying to explain how freedom entailed certain responsibilities. "Speak up!" came the raucous surge.

He cleared his sinuses, not a pleasant vibration, aiming his ad hoc remarks at a makeshift boom mike: "Now that you are liberated, you must educate yourself. Get involved, speak out, take an interest, make a difference." Amid disturbances and interruptions, reading from his ill-prepared note cards, the Commander struggled through a cursory rehash of the terrible events of 11th and 13th May 1998, when the Indian Government had detonated five nuclear devices, and what that had meant to the children, why it was so terribly wrong. Of course, this dissertation in the desert night proved hard competition for heightened campfire lore, 100,000 card games, rolls of the dice, frisbees and marbles. Girl-chasing and general rabble-rousing that surely out-competed strategic analyses, comparisons with the US, France, Yemen, Iraq and North Korea, and a microphone that echoed and twanged.

But some did listen. It so happened that the Bishnoi farmers who had wandered out across the desert floor to observe the incoming avalanche of marchers had been the first to witness those most recent discords of the South Asian arms race. Seconds later, a seismic station at Nihlore, not far from the Pakistani capital, Islamabad, had recorded the shock waves.

But the ethereal explosions of white and gray gradation fanning out in rings of expanding pulses, electrons fashioning their own clouds, were all the more horrifying for the Bishnoi because of their religion, which an old shepherd presently explained to the trio. They were strict vegetarians, and tended to revere every plant and animal. They wisely cultivated the morning dew, storing it in cisterns; they ensured that their animals did not over-browse, and maintained strict legal codes that were enforceable against any and all who transgressed the rights of other species. Hence, when a famous Indian movie star joined an illegal hunting party and killed a svelte-hoofed creature on Bishnoi territory, they were the first to turn him over to the police.

Said the shepherd, through his child translator (a little fireball of maverick skills, a cardsharp and hula-hoop champion of Rajasthan): "We Bishnoi worship the khejare tree, one of the highest protein-bearing plants in the world, and prune its upper twigs carefully." The Commander's perception of an uncommon presence was strengthened as the steward went on to share most surprising details. He described a centuries-old process of drip irrigation to effect their bonanza of lucerne, millet, radishes, carrots, garlic and onions. Every Bishnoi child, he said, looked to the wildlife for instruction, and the result, in so many words, was sustainable consumption millions of years old. For Marigold, this was a dream tribe: a people like the Toda, or Bhutanese, who added enormous weight to the logic of hope for Asia. One more beacon in his crossword puzzle of global possibilities. A people who listened to ants and conversed with the clouds.

The shepherd then demonstrated how his people alone had been spared the drought whose ravages were apparent everywhere else in the desert. He pulled from a hidden pocket in his long frock the hard-seeded leaves and berries of the Ziziphus jujuba bush and of the sweet-fruited *Capparis aphylla* tree. These, he explained, were the preferred taste treats of the local chinkara and nilgara antelope.

"Try it!"

The trio sampled the sweets.

"Yuck!" exclaimed Rajibai. He spat out the seeds and rubbed his stained mouth with his arm.

"Son, where are your manners?" Marigold said.

But the shepherd grinned. An acquired taste, he indicated.

More Bishnoi children, Rajasthani speaking, drew close upon the fire where the famous threesome and their venerable shepherd remained in deep digest. Other curious ranks now swelled all about them. An atmosphere of profound Nature observation flooded the ambient conversation. Wild peahens strolled near, full of questions; an eagle swooped in the darkness, its bright eyes stern with conjecture. Golden orbs in the guise of magical black buck, panting jackal and stealthly desert fox scoped out the city-of-perimeters. The shepherd extolled the virtues of the blackbird, who knew a good lentil from a bad one, and of the desert bobcat, with its marked distaste for sorghum and distinct delectation in peanuts and sesame oil.

The legendary saint Jamboje, said the animated shepherd, his skin like crinkled paper by the firelight, had counseled all the Bishnoi through the treasure of his pen. A book, *Jamsagar* (literally, "Show the people light"), had been formulated as a series of commonsense codes of behavior linked explicitly to Nature: decrees covering every salient and subtle detail pertaining to the Tar Desert's indigenous bean tree, the acidic contents of dung, the nature of cyclical droughts and fluctuating food supply.

He sang a contagious strain, throwing his arms in webs and wanes, rising to the power of thrall, a step of muses, a fandango bedeviled by dervish charm enchanting one and all, so that the children in attendance laughed hysterically, slapping their thighs, pushing one another over and off their logs. But Marigold saw through the humor to a penetrating message: by tying religion to ecology, Jamboje's revelations had obviously given the Bishnoi a unique purpose in living. The little boy, who continued agilely to translate, more than demonstrated the distinctive zeal. All viewed themselves as shepherds who would never dream of harming a living being, and had every motivation to intervene to prevent others from doing so.

Later, this pilot of moral plateaux described how in 1730, when outsiders tried to take a large quantity of wood from their lands, 363 Bishnoi laid down their lives hugging those same trees. They did not stop the butchers, and in 1988 the Government of India commemorated these desert martyrs—the men in their glorious white turbans, the women adorned in sensuous magenta and lime-green apparels—as the first ecological heroes of the country.

"What a find," Marigold marvelled, thinking himself their veritable discoverer. In fact, he had an idea germinating faster than Sannazaro's spray repellent.

"I don't like your brainstorms," his friend, seeing the signs, reminded him. "They invariably get us into trouble."

"Just think a moment, if your brain has that potential, which I seriously doubt. Here are one million fighters for nature. Add 12 million children in our financial debt, and 100 paratroopers. We are a force larger than India's standing military, are we not?"

The idea was truly inspired, Sannazaro reckoned. "Except for one small detail."

"What is that?"

"They have guns. Bombs. Tanks. Jet fighters."

"And we have 120 million deft little fingers, hearts 20 paces ahead of any armored tank or barking general, ammunition to last for generations, in terms of spunk. Not to mention the speed and stealth of swallows. And you see how fast they reproduce? The next generation is already well on its way, sorry to say."

"I repeat: they have bombs, nuclear weapons. You did the analysis."

"That's why we're here."

"What is that supposed to mean? Murillo, talk to me."

But before any such elucidation could occur, there arrived a second reason for a fighting chance: tens of thousands of Jains, whose own contribution to the growing appeal for human rights and non-violence was an ancient one, though presently organized by a guru from Calcutta who also lived part time in Nairobi—a former Jain monk, now in his 90s, known lovingly as Paramatman, or Highest Soul, by millions of his followers around the world.

Whether the issue was the abuse of cows for dairy products or nuclear proliferation, Paramatman could be counted on to strive for moderation, gentleness, compassion and clarity. Clad in his own pure-white flowing garments and dashing long black hair, with his many thousands of friends in tow, he could be seen walking across the desert towards the satellite-detectable array of campfires. An enveloping mirage of nectar stride and primeval purity amid the many illuminati sparking into the gathering twilight.

Others were arriving as well, activists from every quarter: secessionist Punjabis intent on restoring their homeland, Khalistan; nearby Haryanans; hundreds of thousands of Bishnoi armed with peace offerings of millet cakes and sweets which they passed out to as many children as possible; and an Indian military convoy of darkening proportions—dozens of tanks—that did not bode well. The battlefield was growing. A million congeries of bedrolls lay scattered across the waning red of desert and giant glowing cactus.

"You're courting World War III," Sannazaro pointed out. "It appears we're taking on not one but every issue in the country. Is that wise? Will it not cancel out the fine energy of the original campaign or break the camel's back?"

"It makes every sense to amortize our compassion," Marigold replied. "That way, the damsel fly can ride on the shoulders of the gorilla and fatigue becomes a non-starter."

"I've known only fatigue from the moment I met you."

Marigold took that as a compliment.

Then Sannazaro adumbrated in a more serious vein: "You've noticed, I presume, that our son"—he was now accustomed to calling him "our"— "has stowed a pair of wire cutters in his satchel. He can only be up to no good."

"Let us pray it be so."

"I overheard him talking about eco-sabotage. Where the hell did he hear that phrase?"

"He's a good boy, and a fast learner."

"Yes, and I think I know who's instructing him."

"A pair of wire cutters is unlikely to have much impact on anything," the Commander pointed out.

"That's what they told Archimedes when he mentioned a lever. Who knows what's possible in the hands of a child?" Sannazaro waxed, or warned, though he was little surprised by anything, or any possibility. "You need to calm down. Anyway, in a day or so we're off to South Block in New Delhi. Lots of five-star restaurants in that town, you can be certain. Probably 20 minutes to the British Airways terminal." Actually, for the first time in months, certainly since his miraculous deliverance from the stomach of the whale shark, Sannazaro wasn't feeling so bad. This was a man who balanced the crystallography of his brain between internalizing and externalizing, whose stomach contained all the elements, whose hands could coddle the soil and a fine bottle of wine with equal expertise. A man of the world, he was not the servile packbrain his Commander too frequently took him for. Indeed, so much of their adventure had struck the tower bells at noon in his heart.

For he, too, remembered that awful morning when the news was filled with the first details of the Bhopal disaster. He had felt something profound for the victims, put down the newspaper in disgust at the human condition. But what good was it to dwell on the fatal particulars?

He was no General MacArthur.

Similarly, in 1976 when his own countrymen and gentle women, in the little town of Seveso, north of Milan, suffered the worst chemical affront in European history, his chest had burned with outrage, but there was nowhere to take it. Tens of thousands of birds had fallen dead out of the sky. Children were stillborn, and so hideous was the onset of other medical catastrophes that Italian authorities secretly adopted a resolution allowing, for the first time, medical termination of pregnancy. Ultimately, after many denials, lawsuits and deaths, the whole chemical plant was buried deep beneath concrete. But the toxic legacy remained, and what had anybody learned? Just outside Milan, the largest garbage dump in all of Europe continued to discharge effluents larded with trace metals into Milan's drinking water. Mesmerized by its own economic stardom, the Italian Government ignored all the warnings. A think-tank in Washington had likened much of Italy's soils to the waste lands of Somalia, unrecoverable at any price. Sannazaro had abandoned his homeland for all of these reasons, and more.

India was no different. Except that while Italians ignored the monstrosity they were creating, and instead focused on end-of-the-week faviolas, the fermenting of their Cinzano grapes, sautéeing their arrabiatas, making fashion statements for suitably gorgeous people, shouting at one another and arresting their leaders fortnightly for tax evasion while letting Venice sink, here clustered mightily across the dark desert floor was proof, thought Sannazaro, that Indians, particularly the next generation of them, however wounded by their parents' history of indifference, had exactly what it took to transform a nation. Oh, call him an infertile ass, but he would be the first to stand up, to insist, that Mr Marigold should not be faulted for his idealism. Italy was lost. India had hope. The Messer heard himself saying so. By firelight the ever-restless Commander read up on the Pokhran-II situation, while Sannazaro, clutching his poche tabac and a warm bottle of Cabernet acquired at the fancy hotel in Mumbai and carried along for just this sort of hardship, lay in his sleeping bag, newly acquired, safely snuggled out of harm's way of the bitter windy night. The excited Rajibai played hopscotch in the dust with his friends. There were sizable bets at large among them, like who would go first. First? Neither the Squire nor Commander understood the wager, because it was passed back and forth in the cipher of Marati, the children's native language.

The situation: the threat of nuclear war. The details were all new to Marigold, who read from a document given to him by a Bishnoi priest. The Commander agitated and perplexed: how to stop the madness that transpired between India and Pakistan—their "graveyard spin", as one journalist called it. For those who attempted to follow it—and he could now claim to be one of them—there was no more volatile hostility on the planet.

In his mental upstairs, still fresh from the memory of lingering funeral pyres in Bhopal, of the network of slavery in Forlorn, was the chain of events that less than 18 months before had ignited the desert all around him with rumbles and flashes reminiscent of that fateful morning long ago, when he returned with Hidalgo from Albuquerque to Tesuque following the death of his father in Ecuador. Ill-boding smoke signals from continent to continent.

A flash that could easily happen again, any day now, lighting up the southern horizon as 'Mike', the first thermonuclear device, once did upon the white sands of New Mexico. It had been beautiful to him, then; mysteriously, almost religiously linked in his mind to the avalanche on Chimborazo. A signature that some great event was unfolding. Forty years later he had come to stand up to the insidious armies responsible for such evil.

The details had begun forming their own master plan of stupidity as early as Indian-Pakistani partition, when at least a million Muslims and Hindus killed one another. The British had left over 570 principalities, ruled by Maharajas and Maharanas, to decide for themselves with whom they would align. The Maharaja of Kashmir was Hindu, and he chose to go with India, despite the fact the majority of Kashmiris were Islamic. In 1971, India and Pakistan went to war over East Pakistan, which wanted its own independence, and India helped her achieve it, at the cost of more millions of lives. Islamic Bangladesh, though grateful to the Sikhs who were the predominant guns of the Indian military, became testimony to the long-standing enmity between Pakistan and India.

Then, in 1974, the Government of India detonated its first nuclear weapon beneath the sands of Rajasthan, triggering Pakistan's own race to join the nuclear club. Throughout the coming two decades the two militaries fired rounds at each other up on the glaciers of the southern Karakoram. International diplomatic efforts resulted in a ceasefire, and a "no first strike on nuclear installations" memorandum at an Islamabad Summit at the end of 1989. A curious document: spare the plutonium, incinerate the people.

Then suddenly, in the early spring of 1990, 200,000 Indian troops amassed in Kashmir. The Pakistani President and his army general were ready. Aboard American-made F-16 fighters they had stashed a half-dozen nuclear weapons. A BJP member of Parliament in Delhi said bluntly, "If there is a war, we will wipe out Pakistan."

Meanwhile in Kashmir, terrorist bombings, the kidnapping and execution of tourists and journalists continued. A nuclear war was brewing. India vowed that she would never give Kashmir to Pakistan.

Pakistan vowed to take her back by whatever means. The Congress Party—deemed moderate—lost in the most recent elections. The Hindu fundamentalist BJP came sweeping into power, just as India's population approached one billion.

Marigold knew that the BJP was not easily dissuaded. After all, in the wake of their May 1998 nuclear detonations, they appeared to have the popular backing of 95 percent of their rabidly chauvinistic constituents. Needless to say, none of those polled were children, yet children constituted the overwhelming majority of India.

There was international pressure on India, to be sure. And similar appeals to sign the Comprehensive Test Ban Treaty were directed at Nawaz Sharif, then Prime Minister of Pakistan, whose own country had ignited five bombs, each between two and 18 kilotons, just days following the blasts at Pokhran-II. According to Pakistani specialists, their technology of mass destruction was "safer" and "more sophisticated" than that of the Indians, a doublespeak playing upon the supposed differences between the plutonium from spent fuel and enriched uranium.

Despite all this, India's Union Finance Minister declared that his country would not be browbeaten. Yes, both countries were all for total disarmament, but not while the superpowers maintained their own strangleholds on such weapons of mass destruction. And as both countries pushed to be fruitful and multiply—Hindus making more Hindu babies, to fight Muslims making more of their own kind—scientists within India challenged the official claims by both countries that no gamma radiation had been emitted during their weapons tests. Indeed, a cloud of radioactivity was said to have spread across Rajasthan and there were plentiful medical casualties to prove it, according to those at ground level.

But the "stranglehold" allegation was true, and Mr Marigold knew it as well as anybody who paid attention to such things. While the UN General Assembly, comprising 149 signatory nations, had passed a test ban treaty on 10th September 1996, it did not require disarmament by existing nuclear powers. This was the catch which infuriated the Indians and Pakistanis: that they should be held to a double standard. For all their talk, powers like the US and Russia between them had conducted thousands of nuclear tests, killed countless down-winders and continued to maintain arsenals of thousands of weapons.

Beneath the desert sky, Mr Marigold dozed off, trying ineffectually to apply the logic of Kant or Henry George or a simple Bishnoi flockherder to the crisis of looming war. But there appeared no way out. The Third World had the option to avoid the pitfalls of the Industrial and post-Industrial Revolutions, wisdom obtained at great price by countries like Germany and France. India had chosen to go down that same flawed path, producing identical pollutants, poverty, social injustice and weapons manufacture. What was that idiotic obstinacy which demanded redundant self-destruction in the face of clear alternatives and the salient lessons of history? He was too tired to figure it all out. And there was sand in his underwear.

In the morning, the Commander awoke to a variety of commotions. Firstly, the gentleman they called Paramatman had come to pay his respects, and with him several thousand Jain disciples, as well as numerous Bishnoi elders.

"Who are you?" Marigold asked, rubbing dust from his eyes.

"I saw you in my dreams," replied the Jain holy man. "Perhaps I can be of some assistance."

"You're certain it was no nightmare?" the groggy gnat-infested Squire mumbled. He'd been struck by three shooting stars during the night, one after another, leaving him in less than an enthusiastic embrace of the freezing sunrise.

CHAPTER 102
A Jain Ascetic in the Desert

"A JAIN? MY SON IS A JAIN," Marigold explained to the eminent visitor, though Rajibai was nowhere to be found.

Sannazaro, adjusting a half-dozen crooks in his back, for he had slept upon a slab of marble covered by gravel, his pillow nothing more than a bottle of port (part of his secret stash) wrapped in burlap, had not seen him either.

Twelve million children were up and about, roused to action, squatting on the desert floor, gobbling down a multitude of porridges and chapattis, searching for water, awaiting the 'word' from above. A restless energy careened over the morning in the form of a most purple and rare thunderstorm. High in the troposphere, traveling horizontally at 50,000 miles a second between clouds, could be faintly made out a form of lightning known as elves. The Jain guru looked up and smiled. He seemed to understand that this electrical display of tau neutrinos, so unusual for Rajasthan on a winter's morning, was somehow a good omen. But of what? Marigold wondered.

The two men bowed before each other and discussed the day's mission as the thunderheads and electromagnetic pulse sources turned into rain clouds, and a dry squall sent sand cyclones twisting along the gorgeously detailed, Maynard Dixon horizon. Red-spotted cows— Rajasthani Angus—steamed towards the magenta peripheries of light. Cactus transformed marvelously into monarch butterflies. Paramatman explained that he had come simply to show support, on behalf of Jains everywhere, for what was rumored to be a new mass movement within India. The news had reached the furthest corners of the country and had been characterized in hundreds of ways. Journalists had tracked the broad swathe of the marchers, filing reports to which the public tuned in during dawn, siesta and starlight. When the guru had learned that Pokhran-II was on the itinerary, he knew he might be needed, for there was no way that the Indian military would permit a demonstration of such size—of any size, for that matter—in a restricted zone.

"You see," he said, "we Jains have long debated the tactical points of intervention according to our foremost principle, *ahimsa*, which means, simply, non-violence."

The Sanskrit word also was translated as 'non-interference', a linguistic and conceptual framework that might be construed as inherently contradictory, Paramatman added, citing the most revered sage in Jain history, Lord Mahavira, an elder contemporary of Buddha who spent most of his life naked. What an uncomfortable prospect, Marigold imagined, tweezering acacia thorns from his soles.

But the gathering glints in the guru's eye said it all. This was no pomposity in formal attire, no saintly cover, but the same Crowquillian hindsight in the present: a twenty-first-century trail, unfettered by doubt or compromise, all bespoken of with lighttraveling mirthministering balancingact propriety.

It was not quite 7 a.m. Water was scarce, but Marigold—awake, vigorous, eager to embrace whatever the day presented—excused himself momentarily, then returned, all ears, with three cups of steaming Starbucks—double white mocha, 60 percent decaf, no whipcream, with silk soy—in two hands. How had he accomplished the miracle? Nobody would ever know, but in a desert where sages manifested air conditioning and flamingoes recited John Dryden, all was possible.

"Mahavira lived from 599 to 527 BCE," Paramatman began. "Buddha actually studied with him for several years, and Jainism is credited today as the originator of Buddhist tradition."

"They were different religions?" inquired the Commander, never one to conceal his ignorance.

"Oh yes. Buddhism was a much less strict discipline, which stemmed from a basic difference in theology. Buddhists were not and are not universally opposed to killing, though many are, of course. But Jains are so universally. That is the cornerstone of our beliefs. This divergence, you should try to understand, represents a profound discrepancy with respect to one's choices and behavior. It was said that Buddha did not believe the people were ready for Jainism. Perhaps he was right. We are absolute idealists, turning vivid hopes into daily practice. Few have shown the stamina for it: the Bishnoi—or Vishnoi, as we say—are exceptions to the rule. Today, there are several hundred million Buddhists, but fewer than 20 million Jains. While countless Buddhists dine on chicken or steak, and have fought repeated wars, killed one another over issues of owning a monastery, or securing the privileges of an Emperor or Shogun—exhibiting, in other words, many of the same schizophrenic hypocrisies of Christianity, and nearly every other religion—the Jains have never fought a war, showed virtually no incidence of crime within their communities, and remain almost entirely vegetarian. Not vegans, sadly, though that too is changing."

Paramatman's profuseness could not have been some random act of general assistance. There was the trickster in his eyes, a prophet written into his hands, firm resolve planted in his staff. His striking demeanor and patient guise were targeted at the Commander and hundreds of children who were now seated around them listening.

But where was Rajibai?

Marigold felt as if he had come home. To a new Avalon or Forest of Arden, in his back yard, in the legacy of his very son. Sir Thomas More, Campanella, Emerald Cities of the Sun and Moon, and Annabel Lee, the New Lanark and Cézanne's *Mont St Victoire*, right in his very lap.

In this first mention of one Mahavira were all of the Commander's very own obsessions, a mirror confirming his fondest ideals and making them breathe in the guise of another. What the Greeks knew as agape. The way one discovers an author and must devour every work, massage each detail, incorporate the personality for oneself until a biography has been born in the form of an autobiography. Marigold's stray nimbus of a brain grew faint and chalky with all the reasonings behind the Renaissance, the outbreak of beatitudes in Brugge ...

Looking about him, the eyes of a guru bearing down lightly, he saw—vertiginously—Guercino's *Aurora* on the ceiling of his parting eyes; the bright face of Geertgen Tot Saint Jans' *Nativity*, that woman of perfect light gazing into the heaven of an infant cradled eternally in the safe darkness. He imagined a frisky dog beneath the greatest of alpine summits in Watteau's *Pilgrimage to Cythera*, and that vast nineteenth-century canvas by unknown hands of a waterfall somewhere in North Carolina. An impressionist river in Florida by Moran, and the unprecedented joy in Matthias Grünewald's *Isenheim* altarpiece. All this and more. Starry nights. Swaying Siberian wheatfields replete with stormy history and the romance of forgotten love affairs hidden under icicles— Dizzy, he closed his eyes and reached out for a helping hand.

"Are you all right, good sir?" inquired the guru.

"Quite," exclaimed Marigold, and he requested of several children that they go and find Rajibai. "On the double!"

That was no easy task, considering the size of the crowd. What did 15 million children (the numbers were still growing) do and sound like at 7 a.m.? A circus of unbelievably noisy antics; an amphitheater of would-be gladiators making mischief, throwing up, peeing upon one another, running, grabbing, gamboling, darting, flitting, starting fires, chasing antelopes, throwing stones at the clouds, taking decisions with no due process, banishing the lame, exercising every tyranny, gathering into gangs, and— by rapid involuntary musculature and principles of political economy—replicating the very mistakes of the adult generation, until Rajibai's Rebellion looked more like a prison turned inside-out. Children just the other day liberated were now enslaving the weak among them, inflicting every imaginable cruelty, behaving like morons.

"Lord of the Hobbeses," Paramatman said with a knowing grin. "All of our most curious foibles. Ahh ... but the children are good. They are fine. They will grow up to be conscientious sceptics, no flag-wavers, no blind leading the blind, not in the next century. Mr Hobbes and all his fellow Republicans, the ones taking such a dim view of freedom, and intelligence, and art, all those glorious things simple people can do when given half a chance, they will in coming years be dismissed outright for their stinginess, mean-spiritedness, their ignorance and foolishness. All the evil men of Serbia, Iraq, Texas, Beijing—they will simply die out. Yes, it's true. Nature has her own tactful methods of dispensing with germs. Meanwhile, these children will grow up to become able-minded citizens, cadres of a universal heart."

Marigold liked him enormously, this spear-swallowing poet of gracious depths. Golden hearted, he could catch intractability in one hand, and throw three strikes with the other, whilst reciting the History of the World.

Nonetheless, thought Sannazaro, no less astonished, the children were racing about churning up a sandstorm of troubles. Confrontations. Military might amassing to all sides. A barbarism seemed truly in the making.

Paramatman caught the little Italian's reading of the situation and smiled. "That's all right. They are children who have been abused. Let them course the ages in a morning, traverse the seas of argument, decipher the system of castes and castaways; let them be shipwrecked and rescued among their own, figure out the balance of power, the truth of powerlessness and of turning the other cheek, and the beauty of thinking for themselves. By the looks of it, you have given them every advantage by which to embark on that adventure. They'll get it right."

"We adults never did."

"Some did. Which is not to say that we Jains think of ourselves as anything but normal people and proud members of the world scene," Paramatman stressed. "But to point out that there is the capacity within people—children most readily so—to live firmly by their beliefs. We Jains have a Sutra, or Book, known as the *Acaranga*, a biography of Mahavira that recounts many of his sayings. Like Christ, he himself never wrote down a word. His close companions, men like Indrabhuti, did so around 400 BCE. And such words! For example, 'A wise man should not act sinfully towards Earth, nor cause others to act so, nor allow others to act so.'"

"Mahavira said that?"

"We believe so, yes."

"But that—that's exquisite," Marigold protested.

"Yes, isn't it? We have a tradition that holds up the motto 'Live and Let Live' as the emblem of ultimate compassion. But it must never be mistaken for that Dutch tendency during World War II—the saving of little Anne Frank aside—best described as, 'Don't bother me and I won't bother you.' Jains try not to bother anybody, unless it is perceived that they need to be bothered." He laughed.

Marigold grinned too. "How does that work?"

"You see, we have no missionary tradition. The monks do not go around converting people. In fact, the Jain community has remained small because of two very important tendencies. First, small families. We instinctively understand the perils of overpopulation. Even the Chernobyl Exclusion Zone, ravaged by radioactive cesium, flourishes with 270 species of bird, dozens of other internationally endangered species—and why? Because the officials of Belarus and the Ukraine have not allowed people to live there, though a few do so illegally. The point is, overpopulation is far more destructive to other species than even radiation. Second, we believe that preaching, proselytizing, are forms of interference. Even worship is intrusive. Live and let live stems from our vegetarianism—not to look slim, or be healthier, but because we love life. That is why few Jains will ever profiteer at the expense of a tree, a four-leafed clover, a sea shell or a buffalo."

All this settled quite well with the Commander. But he also picked up on his Squire's mounting scepticism which, duly considering the weight of contraries which had gathered like a crown of thorns molded into theory, he now took for his own. There were just too many pockets of reversion. History had rarely allowed for absolutes, least of all absolute good.

He took a deep breath, spinning the reticulation of hypocrisies in his spider web, pretenses and bad faith, and began, "You're telling me that not one Jain has ever picked his nose, trimmed his moustache, stepped on the grass, kicked dust off his heels, ridden a bicycle along a dirt path, thus causing havoc among ants, thrown a rock into a creek and terrorized polywogs, feared a snake, purchased a canned good, implied a threat, masturbated, acquired a possession, converted water into steam, or worse ice, wiped away tears irrespective of their desired itinerary, disturbed air molecules with speech or a basketball? That no Jain has ever driven, been driven by or sold an automobile with leather seats, or written upon a piece of paper, the result of cutting down a tree? That it is unheard of among your kind to kill bacteria by washing under the arms? That no Jains use any drug derived from animal research, or soap that was tested on animals? Or stayed in a hotel that has been built at the expense of the earthworms underneath, or lived in his own house that supplanted flowers and weeds and bushes, or worn a pair of jeans manufactured from cloth taken from Mother Nature, or invested in the stock market where one's own hard-earned rupees are going towards the perpetuation of a company that might be employing these very children, once slaves, or made money in general? That not one of you has ever toppled the equality of tribal barter systems with a disenfranchising egotism? Or plopped down for a picnic in the grass, terminated a rose, carved the first stirrings of love for another in the innocent bark of an aspen tree, closed your eyes to the headlines, stepped off the pavement into the dirt teeming with its own microbiota, flown in a CO_2-spewing airplane, thought ill of an infestation, consumed in some fashion an antibiotic, swatted at a mosquito, feared the rattlesnake, shunned the cave, cornered the fly, plucked an eyelash, picked a scab, wasted the dark side of a banana, cursed the traffic jam and people in it, fibbed, lied, gossiped and carried on, acted in bad faith, schemed, plotted, badgered and berated? Assure me that not one Jain has ever turned down a tribute, ignored praise, renounced flattery and adulation? That in your history not one of you has eaten meat or struck down a corn stalk? That there has never been an intention beneath the highest dignity, or even a glint of revenge? No corpse ever held back from the activities of the soil, no sweat wiped off ? That nobody within your faith has ever—I repeat, ever—competed, usurped, eschewed or manipulated? That exploitation exists not in the Jain vocabulary; nor abuse, perversion, degeneration or betrayal, profanation or subjugation? That no businessman has ever profited upon another; no soldier worn arms; no mother scolded her child; no father berated his son, or spoken ill of another, or characterized an opponent, formulated an enemy and spread this malice throughout a household or workplace? That not one of you has contributed to a sewage problem, or unnaturally heated a house, indulged in an ice cream, relied on fuel oil, killed amoebas in a frying pan or suffocated a daddy-long-legs in a warm bath? That no monk has ever caused pain to his parents, no nun exasperated a would-be suitor? Tell me there is perfection and I shall gladly go to my grave this instant."

"You do me great honor by your wind, which is as perceptive as it is long," Paramatman replied with jovial embrace. "Truly, sir, nobody can fulfill the mandates of absolute inactivity, other than in death, whose trappings, even, are beyond our control. You are right to list the litany of proneness, the accidents and routes of customary human nature. No doubt. No doubt. We are on a path. Much work to be done. Far from the end. There is scarcely a moment that is not an injury, however removed. A Jain monk recently fasted for 208 days in Mumbai to prove the exception. He sat still. Prayed silently. One sip of water per 24 hours was all he consumed. Yet, to his surprise, and that of his disciples, he lost not one pound of body weight. Nor did he succumb to either illness or despair. Yet, all around him, a dustbowl of inequities persisted. AIDS patients multiplied, more children sacrificed; there were more wife burnings and castings-out of old widows. More wars and natural disasters. How to properly assess these perverse twists on the idea of justice, cause and effect? Why did he do it? To challenge the status quo. Did it succeed? The evidence would suggest his Herculean fast accomplished nothing more than a line in the book of world records. After which, the following day— 209—he helped himself to a modest meal, and resumed his previous life. What have we gained by his attempt at human purity, his nearly seven months of ecological perfection, of total absence of contradiction, in one man? Nothing. Because unless the entire population is engaged in similar practice, the malaise of our malignancy cannot help but spread, fleas in the night, laying millions of eggs a week. But at least we know that if it is possible for one man, it is possible for everyone."

"It may be possible, but I do not quite see the incentive for doing anything against such odds—all those millions of eggs being laid every week," Sannazaro expostulated, greatly emboldened by the obvious fallacies in human nature which he had seen for himself in plentiful dose—a too obvious web of rich dichotomies that argued for his Cappuccino Theory of Human Existence.

"We all have a long distance to travel in pursuit of some perfect harmony, which in any case might be colossally boring or, worse, quite impossible, and hence—as Mr Shakespeare evidenced by his wit—much ado about nothing: lives wasted, a useless passion. Unless, of course, you are among the 24 honored Tirtankaras of our faith—those saints (23 men, one woman) who have forded the stream and become, for lack of a better word, omniscient."

"A word that must strike irreverence and scepticism into all who hear it," the Squire intoned, Marigold remaining silent, for now.

"Understood. But note that each one of these Conquerors of Self, as we describe them, was once mortal. They had love interests; in some cases—like Mahavira—a wife and daughter. They had ambition, riches, poverty, profound doubts, frustrations, problems. All that is important to realize. They made themselves. Nobody did it for them. In no different a manner, say, than your titans of industry, the Andrew Carnegies or Henry Clay Fricks, who began from humble origins. In addition, I am honored to report that at least a few of our monks—like the one I just referred to—come as close as any humans I've ever seen or heard about to this quality of an absolute harmony. We have a sect of Jains, known as Digambara, or Skyclad, who go naked; who have only two possessions—"

"What are those—wait, let me guess, a credit card and dental floss?" The guru launched upwards with a squeak and slapped Marigold on the back. "Oh, that is a jolly good one!"

"Well? Which two possessions," the Commander pressed.

"A pinchi, or broom of peacock feathers taken from the ground— feathers that have naturally been shed—and a kamandalu, or gourd, for carrying boiled water."

"What is the use of the feathers?"

"To carefully brush away any insects likely to get in the monk's path."

"Which path is that?"

"He walks his whole life, you see, as I did, from village to village, spreading the message of ahimsa. At each opportunity he will sit down and discuss with villagers he meets ways for translating need and daily toil into gentleness and love. To champion resolution for all those insightful contradictions you have hit upon."

"That's very good. But boiled water? Wouldn't that hurt the water?"

"Ummm. A more complicated scenario involving the belief that unboiled water fosters germs which spoil and die, or can kill. Whereas boiled water kills fewer."

"But what do the monks eat? What do all Jains eat, for that matter?" Paramatman went on to describe the Jain theory of five-sensed organisms. Lettuce is one sensed; a vertebrate five sensed. In between are countless gradations. A traditional Jain diet is restricted to one-sensed organisms. Yet, even these are carefully delineated. The goal, Paramatman said, is to achieve a minimum of consumption, to inflict no harm on any creatures with neurological organizations that might be said to be susceptible to pain—much like hitting a hole-in-one every day. He described some of the food types which most Jains consumed regularly, your normal Santa Fe cooperative-type diet: wheatflour breads, spinach, cabbage, soy products, chilies, peppers, papaya, mangoes, oranges and ground nuts, lentils and varieties of basmati rice, countless other vegetables and spices.

"Of course, the best thing would be for the monks to eat only what has fallen off a tree and already been nibbled at by a squirrel or a bird or a worm. That is the ideal, but most of us—myself included—are not there yet. I came here in a car. I fly back and forth from country to country. I am a modern, no doubt about it, with an apartment in Nairobi and a lovely little abode in Calcutta. Yes, once I was a monk, and I walked barefooted throughout India. But then I fell in love with my wife, and we bore children of whom I am very proud."

"Where is she?"

"Heading up an environmental campaign back home. She has more energy than I do. But my point is, a true ascetic would never bear children, not because he doesn't love the woman, and love the children, but because— how to say it delicately?—to bring a child into this world is to court a mathematical certainty: that child will suffer. What's more, for every one sperm that fertilizes its egg, tens of millions also suffer and perish.

What to do? You see at once the paradox. Without the householder, the nightly rituals of love and biological sacrifice, there could be no Jainism. No Mahavira, no reason for generosity, penance, modesty or restraint. No acknowledgment of suffering or the needy. The sacrifice truly serves the future whilst honoring those who have passed before us with a pledge that we shall try to be better."

Marigold's eyes widened. These were concepts altogether new to him, yet fully graspable: it was not the sex, the lust, the passions, that violated any precept, as he commonly understood it, but the killing of sperm. Nor were saints worth their one piece of cloth, or show of nudity, without observers to pay their own obeisance. The links were paramount. The saint was a goal, much like those elusive acrostics in the *Book of Kells*, or the idea of religious passion as understood by Bach. An ideal. A society without ideals was unthinkable.

"What a lemonade of philosophy," the Commander mused aloud.

"And two little children giving it away, in glasses with pure ice, on a street corner in the summertime, for free, beneath the broadleafed trees afloat in gossamer and 17-year cicada. I see it all."

"It is much more than a vision. I have to assume that you, too, are no mere philosopher, or you wouldn't be walking across our country this way. Both of you. Of course, you know what they say about two philosophers? One writes the book, the other reads it. Who is closer to the truth?"

"Trust me," Sannazaro broke in, "he is a philosopher all right. And a rich one. But to be honest with you, I'm not sure which came first—the money or the contemplation. And as for book learning, no worries there.

The whole world is his oven. Nothing I can do to stop it. We both get burned all the time. Does that hamper his idealism? Not a chance. Quite the philanthropist with every cause. So philosophy and Wall Street end up in the same Mixmaster; a blind ram—stubborn beyond definition—and a donkey suffering from an undeserved nervous condition, are condemned to the same rollercoaster ride, the same seat, even. No seat belts. And no breaks. If I had my way, we would proceed more slowly. But I don't."

"Yes, I have heard that you've both been quite generous," Paramatman acknowledged. "It is a wonderful thing you're doing, though I doubt our Government sees it that way. They have never been fond of foreign donors. They distrust them. And rightly so, I suppose. To be on the dole is a tricky business. Like welfare that perpetuates a dependency, a mindset. But I think in your case there is no question about it: you have set off a wonderful time-bomb within our country. People feel ashamed; you have touched their social conscience. In a country like India, that is a supreme accomplishment."

"I've only reacted to what I've seen and felt," Marigold said. "I have no other goals than what should be obvious to everybody—the alleviation of unnecessary cruelty."

"Quite so," Paramatman confirmed. "Bravo for you, sir. No organism wants to suffer. You don't want to suffer; these millions of children don't want to suffer; I don't want to suffer. Even this ladybug—" and he carefully pointed to a ladybug crawling up his white robe, now dazzling beneath the stormy sky—"knows well the difference between pain and happiness. So it is our responsibility to ensure that every creature enjoy its life and is allowed to evolve in its own way, undeterred by our clumsiness and misconceptions of self-importance."

"You would much relish our new Toda friends, bemused by their buffalo milk and flower songs, their noyim and granite boulders. Add to the club one highly refined Bishnoi shepherd who joined us around the campfire last night and drew at length a picture of Paradise in their desert."

Paramatman knew very little about the Todas, but was altogether familiar with the Bishnoi, many of whom were his friends. But this multiplicity of little utopian communities merely reminded the Commander, and Sannazaro, how large India was, what a patchwork of diverse tribal collectives, and how easy it might be to bring those clusters of ethnic groups and venerable traditions together to combat the mindless inflictions of a monolithic bureaucracy and unfeeling corporations. On the other hand, maybe that convergence was impossible. What did the guru think about it?

Began Paramatman: "Mahavira, born into a princely clan, gave up all of his possessions while still a young man and spent most of his life walking naked throughout India, spreading the message of peace. Why? Because he loved his fellow man; he loved every grain of sand, in which he imputed a soul. He was a biologist, describing thousands of life forms at a time when Western science, embodied in the works of Aristotle, had categorized no more than 600 species. He intervened when he noticed that a young couple about to be married were to serve their cherished guests hundreds of animals waiting in cages to be slaughtered. 'How can you celebrate your love union by killing others?' he asked them. The newlyweds were instantly enlightened. It's that easy, if you open your heart. One can change one's bad habits overnight."

The guru's eyes were earnest pools.

"We call that the capacity for *anekantavada*," he went on, "the relativity of thinking. It is a form of compassionate reasoning that extends to every facet of human behavior, which is why Jains have been so obsessive— down through recorded history—about psychoanalyzing violence and pain. We mean to put an end to those things, to replace violence with love, to substitute liberation, or *moksha*, for pain."

"But, as I pointed out and you confirmed, it is impossible to stop all violence," Marigold said.

"Agreed. Forget about our own missteps. What of natural calamity? Even that lightning blast, hundreds of millions of volts if I'm not mistaken, heats up the surrounding air by tens of thousands of degrees.

That will surely kill nigodas, little creatures the size of atoms. Lightning strikes the Earth millions of times each day, burning up trees, destroying nests, killing people on the golf course."

"The komodo dragon devours a goat, hyenas a sick wildebeest, red ants a grasshopper. But what about men who enslave and strike their children or beat their spouses?"

"There is a profound difference," Paramatman assured the Commander. "We have the knowledge to act differently according to the dictates of our conscience."

"You assume all people possess a conscience?" Sannazaro injected. "I do," the Jain guru hastened. "But it must be nurtured, molded, encouraged. *Kshayika samyak darshana*—true insight through the destruction of karma or karmic impediments. You've heard of karma?"

"I have heard—I have seen—that some Indians use karma as an excuse for maintaining the status quo. Those who are poor and in shock, in other words, deserve to suffer. I find the whole thing pathetic."

"Yes, if it is merely the means to apathy, you are right. But according to Jains, we build up dirt on the window, obscuring our ability to see and to feel clearly. Clean the window, and you have a new slate. You understand?"

"Yes. But how? It can't be as simple as a car wash or everybody would have done it by now."

"Well—" and Paramatman grew pensive and patient, his phrasing parsed like a man handling a newborn. "This is a new process in evolution, I believe. And a crucial one. But the process has clearly begun. That is where we Jains have striven to make a difference: along the *dharma tirtha*—what we call the holy path. It is a wending of human nature, each according to his own, without preaching or bombast, without pointing fingers or shaming opponents, through tenderness and discipline, through a labyrinth of charities, through forgiveness, universal friendliness and affirmation; a road towards equal rights for all of Nature; the practice of meditation or critical self-examination for at least 48 minutes each morning; a life lived according to certain behavioral restraints, or *vratas*, as we call them; this road leading higher and higher, filled with fitting renunciation, starting small—the everyday things so given to obsolescence—and leading by increments to bigger things—an automobile, a new house, new shoes—until, eventually, one has renounced it all and walks the earth like a Digambara ascetic, naked. That is the great rejoicing, the living, breathing realization that all souls, all jivas as we call them, are interdependent—*parasparopagraho jivanam*. This is the sacred ecology my Bishnoi friends speak of, as I would interpret it. This was precisely Mahavira's message to the villagers and the other animals during the occasion of his wondrous Samavasarana in what is today Bihar state: a moment in time very similar, if you think back, to your Saint Francis speaking to pigeons and wolves and people alike. We call it *mettim bhavehi*, universal love through ahimsa. Gandhi, even up to the moment of his assassination, acknowledged that non-violence limps, but that it is the only way. Non-violence and love. You see?"

"I don't see," Sannazaro insisted, not merely to bait or throw a wrench. He truly didn't like the situation. Had his cohorts forgotten their surroundings, the looming circumstances? They were on a battlefield, all right, and this gentlemanly discourse—as removed from the burning moment, or the exigencies of Rajasthan, as the *Meditations* of Marcus Aurelius—appeared to him as hopeless chatter, idle convictions with no usefulness at all.

But the Commander did see, and he was greatly impressed with this new-found tradition shouldered by the Jains. These monks and house-holders had been around for thousands of years, but their revelations were as striking and contemporary as any could be—hummingbirds and water ousels of invigorated flight. An entire society of 20 million souls had somehow managed successfully to integrate ancient ethical standards into the hardboiled realities of the most brutal capitalism the world has known, India.

They were, said Paramatman, the first 'Greenies', and today their portfolios and corporate practices ranked as high as any on the report cards of environmental watchdog organizations.

"My fellow Jains, for the most part, simply refuse to engage in any practice that harms other life forms. Hence mining, agriculture, pharmaceuticals, most chemicals are out. Anything involving leather— no way. Food, other than vegetarian cuisine, forget it. Twice daily Jains recite the ritual *pratikramana*—imagine, 8,400,000 sentient beings, all biologically classified according to the highest taxonomical insights and utterly, unendingly, revered. Nine hundred years ago the Svetambara philosopher Santisuri wrote 50 verses commending even the life force of rock, which he determined was alive for 22,000 years. Don't ask me how he arrived at that particular quantification. But he didn't stop with rocks. He went on, in the phenomenological spirit of Mahavira, to elaborate at great length upon the so-called *prthivi-kayika jivas*, the earth-bodied souls. Such analytic and instinctive attributions are at the heart of Jain activism and emotional conditioning. I could go on and on, but you get the point."

"What about the military? Do Jains ever join up?" asked the Commander.

"Yes, on occasion," Paramatman replied. "We are not pacifists. We believe, at last resort, in self-defense, and in defending those we love. That includes Mother India. Hence the contradiction I referred to earlier with respect to the very definition of the term ahimsa, or non-violence. It also means non-interference. Yet Mahavira himself declared that we must not permit others to commit violence. Well, the injunction is bound to create problems. Even self-defense might be construed as interference. Then so be it. But the Jains originated the concept of no first strike. We will give an adversary every chance to redeem himself."

Sannazaro was sceptical as ever, for the more precious the philosophy and tremulous the tidings his ears interpreted, the more maimed dogs and children, oppressed women and disillusioned old men he encountered. Now, staring directly at the site of five recent nuclear detonations, as armies of the morning converged to engage in—what? more violence? a massacre of innocents?—what could 15 million children or the memory of a man named Mahavira do to stop adamantine army tanks? In Beijing 3,000 students were shot down. It could happen here.

Which led the Squire, pointing wildly, to exclaim: "My God! Over there, look!"

CHAPTER 103
How Rajibai Defeats the Indian Military with a Pair of Wire Cutters

ALL EYES WERE diverted to a dreadful prospect a quarter mile away. Beneath the flurries of wind and sand storm, and the fleeting droplets of cold rain, the children were swarming, and the army had engaged them.

"Oh my Lord!" Paramatman exclaimed, between Gujarati utterances of prayer and bad omens.

The Bishnoi were hollering hysterically, running like antelope towards the scene of evident contest. The Jains all looked to their guru, who motioned that they too must hurry. A square-off was inevitable. Now Sannazaro and Marigold leapt to their feet, remonstrating at the top of their dusty lungs amid the bedlam.

Beside them, a confusion of refugees rolled like a cyclone towards the perimeters of the military area. Remarkably, nobody was trampled. A path was cleared for Marigold and Sannazaro, along with the Bishnoi and some Jain elders and Paramatman to come forward. The Commander at once noticed that whole sections of the security fencing had been cut, and that children had entered the Pokhran-II site.

Thousands of little bodies had amassed atop army tanks. Soldiers were shouting at them, their large guns turned down; helicopters circled overhead and military commanders directed serious-sounding threats at the protesters through scratchy loudspeakers.

"It is a game to the children," Paramatman volunteered. "They have not seen what men in fatigues, when outnumbered and frightened, are capable of. I myself have been shot in the leg. I can tell you, it is unpleasant." M-16 rounds, a hail of warning shots, were ignited into the sky. The guru strode towards the general-in-charge. He meant to seek reconciliation, to apply all those wonderful principles he nurtured in the hothouse of his heart.

But what posed the greatest threat, thought Marigold, was the radio-activity. The Government had denied it, but contamination was almost a certainty, and millions of kids were there—though still no Rajibai. Marigold surveyed the madding frenzy from an evacuated watch tower that leaned along the edge of the barbwire. Tanks surrounded his position. Sannazaro knelt beside him. Both scanned the chaos in search of their companion, but the boy had positively vanished. Poof! "There's going to be a massacre," the Italian opined. "Impossible," declared the Commander.

Paramatman was handed his own loudspeaker by a military leader, who was irked by the presence all around him of turncoats, the paratroopers who had banded around the marchers for days and weeks, and were now adding to their cadre other deserters from the nuclear battlement. From above, Marigold could perceive the impact of Paramatman's pre-Raphaelite gracefulness as he wandered betwixt and between, his white robes flowing through the mottled sunburst of agitators. Like a ghost of gleaming promise, manifesting so much sutra-enflamed beneficence, he swayed like a pianissimo performing a softening of the massive phalanxes. Asking each and every dissident nerve, trigger-finger and venom to be seated and silent in prayer. It took an hour, for 15 million children are not easily tranquilized, 2,000 troops rather hard to pacify at such moments, but finally the delicate task was deftly accomplished.

From the air, the sight must have been spectacular. One Indian commander seated in the front of a chopper said to another, "This is beautiful."

Marigold and Sannazaro climbed down. They were gravely concerned about their missing sprite. A sense of foreboding hovered over their crowded purview.

The photographs would dominate the news for days to come. A mela at Pokhran-II to signal the real voice of the country; a poll of the children that was unambiguous. They wanted an end to nuclear war. Children who had been slaves to a system that perpetuated the supposed strength of a nation only by sapping its truest laborers (a principle described by Marx and Engels), denying childhood to one generation after another, accumulating great wealth at the expense of the infants, taxing the hollow fruits of that labor by nearly 70 percent so as to sustain India's enormous military expenditures, and then using its weapons of mass destruction to scare off the rest of the world and prove itself a nation among nations. Idiots among idiots. Deformed twins.

"We have the bomb, and we will have the Internet," went the refrain among strongmen in Delhi.

Yet here was something else in addition: proof positive that the new generation of Indian children had what it took to hit the baseball into the rear bleachers. Mr Marigold looked out upon the miles of seated marchers, a magnificent vigil silently paying tribute to—to what? Some children gossiped and giggled; others threw little stones at the girls, or stealthily tied up their braids in knots behind their backs. Two million boys saluted the army tanks. Two million others said they wished they could see the bombs go off. Another two million girls said that was wrong. Fourteen-year-olds lectured to 13-year-olds who scolded 12-year-olds who told those junior to themselves to get lost.

But the children with seniority—those 15 and above—knew very well what this was about. A well-groomed youth, perhaps 17, took hold of the megaphone and addressed his peers: "We're quite repulsed by the politics of adults, and altogether willing, thank you, to take over the country and rule it properly!"

"And what would you suggest?" Marigold pressed.

"Free ice cream, tap-dancing lessons, tennis shoes and soccer balls for all children. No more work. No more dowries. College scholarships. No more beatings. No more bribes or policemen. Safe food and water for everybody. Basketball courts on every corner. Mandatory garbage collection. Free spigots. Free television. No more rules for children. Free doctors and condoms. Free motorcycles. IBM Thinkpads. CD players. Mandatory tours of India by Aztec, Madonna and Metallica."

The list of demands kept escalating.

"Free movies!" roared 800,000 children of Western Indian descent. "Free cigarettes!" roared a million others.

"Free military uniforms for all the boys!" cried hundreds of thousands more.

"No more school!" shouted the multitudes. "No more adults!" went another gigantic refrain.

The army tanks just sat there, dumb worked-steel hulks. The soldiers, who at first shouted and threatened, then aimed their weapons—only to have the rifle holes stuffed with scores of Cadbury's chocolates—had crawled out of their tank holes, finally, and joined the children, saluting them. It was a mighty reunion. Nobody knew what anybody else was there for. Fifteen million innocents; the thousands of crack troops. An uninhabited conflict sprinkled with anodynes and merrymaking. And a fantastic show of lightning that seemed to confirm the concord of the gods. But to what end?

And where was Rajibai and the inner creche of Forlorn exiles? Sannazaro, it was agreed, should go off to search for them.

"I fear little was accomplished this day," Marigold confided in Paramatman. "It was silly, by any definition. Chaos furthering chaos.

The near-sighted leading the far-sighted on the roof of hell."

"No, no. It was good," the Jain guru countered. "Never before have I seen soldiers play with children. And with nuclear weapons stationed just around the corner."

"Yes, but now the children all want to become soldiers," Marigold declared. "That's the history of America."

"Look again—there, see that? This is India. Soldiers wishing to recapture their childhood. It's just a question of which passing fancy comes first."

"So the weasel becomes the prairie dog, and the prairie dog the weasel. Nothing changes."

But that wasn't entirely true. Many things seemed to be in flux— change marked by the number of smiles and chuckles pervading the desert. There a shepherd did his dance; here a general's heart was surely softened; there 1,000 rifles were laid to rest, and magazines and sleeves stuffed with hand grenades piled high near an altar to the Bishnoi patriarch flamboyantly painted after an aboriginal Vishnu. Army tanks were abandoned. Positions de-commissioned. Fifty soldiers in a circle, clapping hands, singing innocent ballads, roused to joviality by a clown no more than seven years old who performed his silly stunts to the admiring onlookers. Old veterans of the Karakoram skirmishes against Pakistan reduced to hopscotch. Highly skilled marksmen playing marbles with the slum children. A colonel debating the fine points of Tagore with the *New York Times* Delhi correspondent; another reciting *Shakuntala* by heart for the benefit of the ladies.

What had Paramatman said to effect such sanguine evolution on the battlefield? What biological arbitrage? To have seized upon the age-old chink in the machismo muscle fiber with a tiger balm of philosophy, and married musclemen to nursery rhymes—that was some accomplishment. Usurping red in tooth and claw with green in joy and splendor.

"It was not I," insisted he, "but—" and he embraced with both arms the vision of a vista before them: of youth instituted, unguents becoming ground swell, emollients a mass movement. Add up this salvo of petite compassions, figured Paramatman, and you have a world turned sweet.

Only after some time did Rajibai and his mates show up, covered in mud. Brimming across the boy's face, a naughty smile. Behind him, Sannazaro, quizzical, who gestured by his hand signal some stunning victory yet to be revealed.

By late afternoon, the fanfare was thinning out, as marchers two by two headed towards Delhi. Paramatman walked beside the Commander, the Italian, and their son and son's friends. Later that night, as they camped on the eastern fringes of Rajasthan, Rajibai explained how he and his buddies had managed to smash their way into some concrete bunker, spring open the trap door, slide down a series of waterlogged tunnels, and break through a ventilator. At that point, Rajibai alone dropped down into a sizable chamber that, he said, looked like those pictures you see of the inside of an airplane cockpit, but a hundred times larger.

"There was nobody inside?" asked Marigold. "Nobody."

"Then what did you do?" the guru questioned.

Rajibai withdrew the wire clippers and held them up gallantly. "I won the poker game," he said with pride.

"Yes, so, go on?"

"Which entitled me to do the honors."

"The honors? Don't be so secretive, lad. What are you saying?"

Marigold could see the boy was holding back, titillating all with the suspense of some mightily conceived artifice, a veneer holding back great sadness.

"Well," explained the boy, "I used the wire cutters on everything. I cut all the cables in there, hundreds of them. Bent the switches, snapped the controls, squeezed out the sensors, disassembled the wires, destroyed the keyboards, zeroed down the power and—" he thought back, carefully searching his step-by-step and move-by-move—"and then I left a note taped to a computer screen."

"A note? That you wrote?"

"Yes."

"What did it say, child?" his father asked, only too aware that a note constituted evidence which could be used against all of them. "Something my sister had taught me as an infant," he confided solemnly. "A prayer she recited even as the butchers were cutting and chopping off her arms. I know, because somebody saw, somebody who was there—" and the boy began to tremble and cry, and Paramatman put his arm around him ("It will be all right, I know, I know.") and the lad continued, shaking violently now—"he was right there, and he told me that these were her dying words, uttered in plain sight of everybody who watched while she was killed, as she lay dying." Courageously he recited, "Khamemi sabbajive, sabbe jive khamantu me, metti me sabbabhuyesu, veram majjha na kenavi."

"But what does it mean?" the Commander implored, his watery eyes welling in shared grief with his son.

His boy, around whom Marigold placed the Toda shawl given to him by Sister Love, squatted near an open fire. Paramatman, tears streaming down his face as well, translated what was one of the most ancient of prayers known to the Jains: "I forgive all beings, may all beings forgive me. I have friendship toward all, malice toward none."

Marigold hugged his little boy, the eco-terrorist.

Sannazaro closed his eyes in deep amazement. He was certain retribution was awaiting them in due course.

CHAPTER 104
Rajibai's Rebellion Enters New Delhi

IT TOOK THE MARCHERS a dizzying week to reach the nation's capital, and lawmakers were ready for them, having rolled out every red carpet, unfurled all the whimsical rhetorical flags, proposed eye-glazing face-saving legislation to fortify the existing statutes prohibiting child labor—each one more vacuous and unenforceable than the next—and called upon 250,000 ace fighter troops to stand on the ready.

The soldiers were nervous, of course, and fidgeted with their batons and M-16s. Their brown starched uniforms merged into a dark leavening of ill-wind as they spread out around the inordinately large number of national monuments and set up barricades to close off special MP roads. The National Airport highway was lined with canvas-covered patrol trucks crammed full of artillery soldiers, who sat upon sunken benches in the rear, awaiting their hopeless orders. In the scudding sky, aging choppers fitted with impact canisters of corroded mace and millions of pepper-spray pellets swirled like spotlights back and forth over the dense sprawls of the infernal city where 15 million citizens waited tensed for the unimaginable. If violence erupted with this overnight and agitated doubling of population, it could be an unprecedented catastrophe, even in a country accustomed to disasters.

Amid all these armored preparations, what the Government failed to anticipate was whether this moving federation of 15, 16—17?—million zealous children might be put to wheedling use by protest groups for other causes. From the perspective of those seizing the opportunity, it obviously made excellent sense to flesh out a meager cry in the wilderness with the bulwark of so massive a Punch & Judy show. So it was that countless others from those lowest Varnas classes of dispossessed, abused, disparaged and disenfranchised Hindus arrived on the scene. Millions of tribals and untouchable Dalits merged with that tidal wave of yearlings, many of whom were new to the rebellion and desperately seeking out the famous American billionaire from whom they had every expectation of receiving their 2,500 rupees—a sum which had grown in magnitude like biblical fish. ("It's not 2,500, it's 25,000," spread the miracle phrase. "Or even more, depending.")

"Depending on what?"

"He'll tell us," came the cacophany of expectations. So that many arrived in the nation's capital prepared to take a seat in Parliament, or possession of a Mercedes, Swedish amplifiers, or their own private toilet.) Latrine cleaners born to do nothing else flocked to him too, along with neighborhood crones ready to crucify the dog catchers, Sikh militia demanding pay rises, grass cutters hoping for automatic clippers, sanitation officials on sit-down strike, water authorities outraged over the number of corpses found floating in the mains, 90 disgruntled polo players in search of live horses (most were eaten), 90,000 school teachers demanding a school lunch for their children. Hundreds of protest groups that had taken this grand opportunity to show their face and be heard were merging into a mathematical wobble wherein human numbers were transmogrified into physics; gravity elaborated, every force associated with the curvature of Earth—ratio, proportion, cause and effect—becoming an eerie nausea encompassing 200 square miles.

Said Marigold, "I think never in history have so many hopes been concentrated in such a confined show of human fever. It makes one proud to be alive; to pay witness and take part in the greatest rally since the Israelites escaped Egypt and nomads fled the Ice Age."

"There were maybe 1,000 nomads, Murillo, and 10,000 Israelites," Sannazaro opined. "If I am not mistaken, all of India has crowded this shaking doorway. From the looks of it, there is going to be a war. We're all going to die."

"Nonsense. Take my hands and don't let go," the Commander instructed his companions. "The three of us must form a chain-link. There, that's it." And they were ushered forward into the mad rush towards nowhere.

Marigold rendered the commentary—"Do not fall down whatever happens!"—though his words were muffled by the seething hysteria all around them. The surge of the crowds was terrifying. There was no way to stop it. If somebody went down, they would be trampled, obliterated. An *Ode to Joy* or *Ode to Despair*?

"Will you make a speech, Father?" the boy bayed, trying to be heard above the roar of 30 million protesters.

"Let us see. First we must get our orientation. Determine what's what and where we're going."

"Where are we going?" Sannazaro exclaimed, ruffled in every direction, ready to take flight on the heads and shoulders of the frenzy.

"I would think to the Prime Minister's office," Marigold reckoned. "I presume that's what this is about. He and his cabinet must give the revolution a hearing."

"Forget it. Nobody can hear anything! This is an asteriod slamming into five French Revolutions."

That wasn't entirely true, however. The crowds conformed to the shape of the city, with its winding back alleys, intestinally cubbyholish neighborhoods and vast open dustbowls; they occupied temples, the Red Fort, soccer fields, stadiums, huge intersections, lawns, parks and building fronts. They fanned out like lava down every avenue and boulevard. Loudspeakers detonated their potshots and punctuation marks. A thousand verbal skirmishes were set off simultaneously.

For example, there was the Society to Ensure Proper Wiring for Cable, several thousand in number, untouchables who were furious that they could not get HBO on their street. Fifty thousand other adivasis were in despair at not having had fresh water for eleven years. The Charles Dickens Club, money lenders, vacuum cleaner salesmen, and union leaders of the National Transport Authority were all setting up booths.

The hordes screamed in from the Nehru Slum, a thicket of despair encompassing hundreds of thousands of crammed hutmen and named, of course, after the country's first President, a venerable gentleman who would have curdled in his tomb to discover that despite the billions of rupees lavished by subsequent leaders on the beauty-parlorization of the city, and more than half a century since Independence, so many residents of the nation's capital remained without access to clean food or water, sanitation, health care, human rights or schooling.

As the trio, hands locked, were urged towards South Block, seat of the politicians, they passed by one makeshift rally after another. Highlights: 30 elderly women holding their ground, banners proudly proclaiming protection for and the inalienable rights of rats. These were the Wildlife Welfare Women of West Bengal, putting their lives on the line. Rats crawled all over their bodies, clung chirpily to their shoulders, rode in their shawls and skirts, panties beholden.

The Grand Dame among them described their urban life: the brutality, shortness of breath, difficulty of feeding their young in a city shorn of compassion, and teeming—however contradictory it may seem—with slim pickings. In Mozambique only rats can detect the minefields.

"Fascinating," Marigold embarked. "Bravo, ladies!" And he handed them 100 dollars before being rushed on in the throes of the human glacier.

There was the Society of Car Dealers protesting the fact only Brahmins were hired by foreign manufacturers. "In India it is possible to show profits only if upper-caste salesmen and managers are exclusively employed" was the corporate argument in Europe.

There were congeries of committed lawn bowlers upset at the disappearing opportunities for open space. "Down with shopping malls!" they shouted. Yet others were busy spray-painting streamers and pennants with angry phrases of protest over the Government's refusal to regulate the flamboyant colors of saris. An ardent assemblage of librarians was campaigning against crumbling paper and the fact they had not been given money to acquire a single new book in 12 years. There was a gaggle of retired military generals dismayed by their dwindling purse-sized penchants; a flock of young soccer players marching to demand that their game scores be given greater prominence in the national newspapers; a flummoxed concatenation of obstetrician gynecologists angered by the Government's refusal to allow them to legally cite the gender of a child following ultrasound; scores of disgruntled rickshaw drivers wringing their tired hands over the Marxist infiltrators; pantyhose manufacturers arguing for higher tax exemptions and citing statistics which proved Indian women's legs were getting hairier as a result of air pollution, a truism that had forced them to recalibrate their machinery, at great cost; condom distributors upset over the post-GATT favors shown competing latex from Hong Kong; the Union of Powdered Milk Societies staging a sit-down strike until the Soy Importers Congress agreed to postpone their national campaign; a peace demonstration by the All India Rag Pickers in favor of open garbage dumps which had been increasingly eradicated from downtown areas; the expected multitudinous show of hutmen and their families appealing to God for their having been routed from their most recent squatters' camp in order to make way for a video arcade; a noisy rally of psychiatrists opposed to the recent Government decree that incest not be openly discussed; a call to arms by the Friends of the Common Sparrow Coalition of Andhya Pradesh, the Ridley's Turtle Fund of Orissa, and the Association to Save the Nicobar Islands from the Introduction of Bowling Alleys; the Theatre Association of India demanding tolerance for homosexual themes; a march of 10,000 praying for the release of movie heart-throb Gugal Gosh, arrested on charges of obscene dancing; the Hoardings Institute of Mumbai appealing to the Government to eliminate quotas on the number of movie billboards per city block; the Indian Society of Astrologers announcing Armageddon; devout, white-clad nuns of the Monsoon Mission of Bihar protesting India's continued reliance on a fossil fuels regimen; the Urine Foundation of Calcutta seeking to revisit a celebrated court case involving damages awarded plaintiffs whose records showed that drinking eight glasses of urine a day had triggered an outbreak of hepatitis A throughout West Bengal; 500,000 lawyers throwing eggs at each other, on strike; and a huge rally of outraged television producers determined to reinstate heavy petting and kissing on the lips over the airwaves.

In each instance, Marigold—to his Squire's admiration—handed out 100-rupee bills.

By the time Rajibai's Rebellion reached the center of Delhi, the stampede numbered well over 20 million, not including the additional 15 to 20 million locals, most of whom appeared to have joined their own protest march of one form or other. Marigold noted the Society to Save Silk Worms; the Sludge Reformers of Madras; the National Feminist Fellowship seeking to ban all male doctors from practicing on women; the Trustees of the Ironing Board Collectives from Uttar Pradesh seeking damages for poor labeling regarding the dangers of steam; a sizable medley of outspoken lower-echelon bureaucrats rejecting the Jain Commission's findings on matters pertaining to Rajiv Gandhi's assassination; a chlorine manufacturer's band harrying an anti-paper-pulping coalition and announcing its lawsuit against all nine million so-called environmentalists in India; the All Indian Bhindi Growers demanding pay hikes in tune with those afforded eggplant and radish farmers; a gathering of spinsters calling itself the Indian Match Makers' Union seeking to legalize video dating; a patchwork of frustrated entrepreneurs asking for 800, 888 and 900 telephone numbers; a Tournament of Turbans in full force; the Associated Chambers of Commerce calling for a Government protocol to mandate robots in Indian manufacturing; a fat persons' commission from Maharashtra asking for an end of discrimination by skinny people; a delegation of lobbyists from Japan quietly seeking Government promotion of sex tours to India; and a Euthanasia Committee—devoted to ending the human race—that was systematically promoting AIDS in South Asia.

Angry antagonists were ejecting discord from every camp: societies favoring water wheels, bicycles, phut-phuts, diesel, ethnic cleansing, a third monsoon, papier mâché toys, tie-and-dye ajarakhs, canopies of appliqué, large-scale agriculture, small-scale agriculture, a new color scheme for the Indian Tricolour; hostile bands demanding better store fronts, more mangroves, an end to brackish water in city parks, more time for pujas, government funding for old men's homes, a dramatic increase in the minimum wage for agriculture workers. Cabbage growers were raising hell; Ezhava and Nair Hindus taking up arms against Union Muslims; copra manufacturers in disarray alongside coir transporters; Project Tiger volunteers calling for an end to gravel pits and power lines in National Parks.

In truth, commented the Commander, there was no more interesting city in the world. Delhi was up to its goiter and arm bands with disaffection, grandstanding and tirades of every timbre. All those luxurious estates with demarcated yards meant to keep out the have-nots were now overrun with the vagrants; particulate matter was spewed in dense whorls along the tree-lined roundabouts as traffic ground to a mobbing, bewildering standstill. Tourists stayed in their high-rise hotels, gazing out upon the inconceivably vast surge of humanity who mowed down wide avenue after avenue, past Embassy Row, around Connaught Circle, up Janpath past the British gardens of the Imperial, surrounding Red Fort, Humayun's Tomb, crowding every square inch of Chowdni Chok. There were surges in a nine-state area. Electricity went out. Even the uninterrupted power supplies in the five-star hotels were down. Water and gas dribbled in surcease. Turbines and generators slowed to a halt. Fans stopped turning. From all sides of the city the mobs converged, overtaking the Prime Minister's whitewashed manse where 10,000 chapattis were thrown at his windows, laying siege upon the President's low-lying fortress, heading like maddened army ants through the great Arc, past the tomb of the unknown soldier and on to the Government Buildings.

It was a remarkable sight. Where the painter Marsden Hartley once complained upon his first visit that Paris was not made of mother-of-pearl, New Delhi suffered from no misunderstanding, understatement or confusion. It was the rumored graveyard of excitations; that exponential haze of possibilities forever in rotation; some fabulous cave-in of foibles, dreams, disillusionment, set against the effect of doves taking to flight, brown kites eyeing the goings-on, black ravens and green parrots chattering above, having staked out their dense positions on every available branch. Rhesus monkeys fled the profusion of three-wheeled fart-farts which drove along grass, finding no pavement left anywhere. The city was all but paralyzed. From minarets the graven-voiced muezzins called out to the faithful. Loudspeakers boomed in Hindi, Urdu, Gujarati and Punjabi. F-16As streaked the skies at the speed of sound. Armed militia gathered to encircle the unsurveyable swarms. Hundreds of army tanks positioned themselves to protect South Block. It was a royal mess.

Sannazaro eyed his colleague's grave erratic enthusiasm, which had alternately despaired and rejoiced during their 1,200-mile march together. But this situation could not be more given to danger: there an implosion, here a discharge. Ballistics to all sides. Foment. Anarchy. A near civil war. It was one thing for Marigold to pontificate at the La Casa Sena over a bottle of fine Bordeaux. Now he had 30 million missiles ready to go off all around him.

CHAPTER 105
Mr Marigold Delivers a Speech to Half a Million Farmers

AMID SO MANY curious paroxysms of the South Asian moment, several hundred farmers were on hand bearing placards to protest the Government's recent joint venture with a Russian pharmaceutical company, a contract little noted in the press, what with tens of millions of children on the loose. These were angry landholders, mostly absentee *zamindars*, exploiters of the poor, businessmen whose ability to continue to grow healthy cereals, to hybridize their live seeds and thus maintain vital gene pools, was imperiled because the intellectual property rights to those germ plasms had been transferred by the Government of India without any public debate or constitutional license. It was a scandal with serious implications, but the Delhi politicians responsible justified it on the basis of a generous profit-sharing scheme worked out by both parties to the deal. A percentage of such moneys would presumably flow back to the native seed holders in the form of biological royalties managed by the Government, as suggested by the *Agenda 21* convention of the Rio Summit years before.

The children inadvertently added force by numbers to the seed protest. "They too are our seedlings," shouted one lobbyist at the windows of the Agricultural Ministry.

Amid the 150-decibel din of protesters, bystanders, the jetsam of every race and denomination jockeying for the dissident limelight, it took much restraint to prevent Army rifle blasts from sending 30 million people into a panic. No Chief of Staff was interested in being remembered for a massacre, not with hundreds of journalists and television reporters among the throngs which had gathered for the biggest rally of the millennium, as they were hailing it. This was the place to be: bigger than the 850th birthday celebration in Moscow; vaster than the Great March in China, or the Fourth Crusade, or New Year's Eve in Times Square. Coupled with its live coverage, and a billion viewers, this was the Oscars, four Super Bowls, the Beatles' first appearance on *The Ed Sullivan Show*, the last episode of *Seinfeld*, Clinton's televised confession, the O.J. Simpson verdict, the Beastie Boys performing live at Central Park to Free Tibet, and the Khumb Mela, all in one gigantic miscellany of noise, civilization and its discontents.

But to Mr Marigold it was obvious that this day would pass, that the multitudes would slowly vanish back into the disheveled crannies of the subcontinent from whence they'd arrived, a billion others would flip the channel, and business would resume as usual. The 20 million children would fend for themselves after this hike halfway across the country, and nearly 60 million others would probably remain slaves. Even many of those 20 million might well fall prey to the same syndrome of abuse and working incarceration. Sannazaro had as much figured it out.

Young girls would return to their cages, their hand looms, to HIV-ridden truck stops and red-light districts, boys to their blast furnaces and mining pits. Parents would sell off more of their children; there would be more dowry deaths and wife burnings, and vast waves of chronic malnutrition, especially among girls. The US Congress would again fail to pass measures boycotting the importation of Indian textiles. India and Pakistan would continue to expand their nuclear capability, and South Asia would remain friendly to any multinational chemical companies wishing to exploit native labor, to dump their toxic wastes for a price, and to revisit the preconditions for another Bhopal across the land. All the Sister Love, Toda, Jain and Bishnoi spirituality in the world would not curtail a frenzy of consumerist digging, usurping, exploiting, extracting, exhuming, cutting, dynamiting, sundering, severing, trespassing, displacing and 1,000 other destructive participles, each bent upon serving the 150 million middle- and upper-class Indians at any price. Indian tigers and Asiatic lions would soon disappear from the wild. That was the first clue to what was really going on. No amount of protest or lip service was going to change it. There were just too many target audiences across India. Nearly 1,000 languages. Customs as different as Neptune and Saturn. No one message was wide or narrow enough to enact a transformation; no language sufficiently broad to be understood by enough people who could make a difference. No politician with the balls or time in office to initiate a reform. No appeal for change so strident as to clamber beyond the ethnic blur of a neighborhood. Nobody would take a chance, stick his neck out, risk the nullification of a personal retirement fund.

"Was all this hope and labor in vain, then? Have I truly played the fool?" Marigold repeatedly queried his Squire-at-Arms.

"No. You've given these children a dream, some a new life. You said it yourself, up on the cliff above Inkblotty and Herekittykitty: don't look back, don't look down, just do what comes naturally. Surely our new friend Paramatman has corroborated and escalated the wisdom in that."

"I suppose so," Marigold acknowledged glumly. "But now, lo! Another crusade, quietly insinuated among many, but one that I believe may touch a chord of grave complexity and pervasiveness: cries of thievery, the very rice strains of a nation at stake. Talk of a Russian deal that will undermine Mother India and her genetic future. How can we help the farmers? Redress the wrongs of that parade of western hubris, the Rio Summit? Ensure that no foreign corporations lay title to indigenous seed banks? I'm tired. I'm still recovering from wounds received in moa territory, and from the hurricane in Antarctica. From bruises inflicted along the way in Toda Land, and from my fall atop the cows of Tamil Nadu. There are needles in the soles of my feet, fever blisters on the underside of my tongue, and my right shoulder blade and left ear lobe have been numb for a month following my bout with pirates."

"That was a dumb thing to do!"

"Which one?"

Sannazaro showed a tall facade of absolute, unshakable resolve. "You've done your share. It's just one country. There are nearly 200 others, remember? And you don't need an old sway-backed mare to rummage between villages. We can fly First Class, stay at a Ritz or two, soothe our wounds in a bubble bath, and delight in the company of our new and well-deserved next of kin, for whom I willfully confess to strong avuncular, even fatherly, regards. Don't be so hard on yourself. Just because you're rich, don't assume you can change human nature with a wad of dollar signs. I've told you that countless times. That's like saying 2,000 US marines could have changed 2,000 years of history in Lebanon. How many democratically elected leaders has the US Government wiped out? How many billions to petty madmen like Osama bin Laden?"

"You see, even you are reduced at times to numeric thinking. It is an easy temptation."

The two old veterans took hold of their Rajibai and separated, as much as was possible, from the fringes of the heaving crowds, trying to escape the reporters. In their scuttling this way and that, the Commander found himself led by well-meaning dignitaries on to one of the many bully pulpits, this one hastily erected by the farmers, and there he was cajoled into making some kind of official statement on behalf of the nearly half-million gathered below. Whatever he had thought to himself, or expressed calmly to Sannazaro, now passed from his brain like a badly fashioned paper airplane thrown out of a window, the merging of a heat island with perfumed language.

Among so many millions of others stretched out to every horizon of the city, these half-million angry, pitchfork-carrying men constituted a mere postage stamp of disaffection. Peering out over their many-colored turbans, Marigold made a remarkable speech, thought Sannazaro, one filled with every angle on "We shall overcome" and delivered with all the bombast, strong verbs and circumstance due the subject matter.

"Rice ... rice ... rice! ..." the Commander pondered aloud, and the crowd leaned forward, spellbound by the pale philosopher grappling for the precise words. Eventually he found them—something to the effect of: "We cannot, we will not, we must not"—to which a roar of approbation issued from the listeners' mighty jugular.

He then went on about being the commander and chief of one's own soul, belonging to the soil, loving one's wife and children as if they were the land. Plowing one's wife, tilling one's children, digging up and turning every clod in Congress, all for the pleasure and dignity of a rice pudding.

From there he proceeded in the grandest of hortatories to address the issue of seedlings and who should own them, presenting his own son to the mob as an example. But an example of what? He could not remember, having fully lost track of his train of thought, if there was any to begin with. For he was not all that accustomed to speaking before 500,000—or 30 million—people, and frankly, he didn't know what he was talking about. Hadn't a clue about genes. Or genomes. Or agriculture. Or how to plant corn, or what rice was—protein? A pulse? A vibration? A grain, to be sure. But then he recalled that a banana was an herb, not a fruit, and this had always made him quite nervous on the subject of food and vegetables and pancakes. Now that uncertainty truly haunted him. He ended his speech with comments after Aristotle's *Politics,* Book Eight. What, wondered Sannazaro, did Aristotle have to do with rice? Who cared about Greek democracy, the somber tales of a Spartan shoemaker or the Athenian mechanic's lament?

Cheers of grandiose thanks rose up to each queer expression: "cheese wads of history", "the soy-paddy hypothesis", "erogenous fertilizer". Never mind that his magnificent speech—which somehow got on to the spirituality of watermelons and the grave crisis amongst pecans— was directed to the wrong Ministry, for they were standing before the front entrance to the Governmental Agency for Big Brass Bands, newly appointed, with its unemployed trombone players from Goa forming a line here, French hornists of Hyderabad there.

The speeches from those gathered at the forefront of the 30 million were still ringing out well into the afternoon when the trio, who had conveyed their fond farewells to Paramatman and the others, managed to elude the intrepid posse of reporters that had clung to them. The Commander had made statements, some more provocative than others: "I've considered funding our own party here in India," he explained. "The Children's Party. It will be a veritable picnic, run by children, the poorest, most neglected sector of the human race, but the one, obviously, closest to our natural origins, at the front end of untainted wisdom. All adults will need special permits to carry on, and those visas, if you like, shall be obtainable only at the cost of total re-construction, re-sensitization, and re-education."

But what sort of re-re-re? asked the journalists. Was he serious, some mumbled, or just screwing with them?

"A steady diet of jacks, jumping beans, marbles and hopscotch," Marigold went on. "Of bunny rabbits, sunny bonnets, meadows and red ponies; of innocence and guilelessness; of German chocolate cake and lack of stress; no big-city ways, no matriculations or fancy articulations; frisbees and looking glasses, hula-hoops and gunny sacks, slinkies, grape slushies, olive pits, carnivals, animal-free circuses and county fairs, Harry Potter, pen pals, try-outs, swings on porches in late summer nights, skinny dipping and first loves"—and he tried to put his thinking in line, assort his thoughts alphabetically, so that tofu resided beside Toda, and Jain meditation near John Dolittle, who rested near enough to Edward Lear to lend them both some posthumous comfort in their deserved eternities.

"For starters," he mused, "let me add the following sentiments. I have no doubt that tomorrow's papers will be unrecognizable to me, but I do not hold a grudge. You are, after all, confused, self-defeating adults, who are precisely the target audience for these aforementioned visa applications..." And he launched into a verbose paean upon the history of all those famed exploits and escapades whose mischievous shenanigans and precious twinkles, Sylvies and Brunos, untiring dignity and bright eyes, constituted the very passage so urgently required of humanity if, in his opinion, it was to regroup and save itself. It was the history of the grown-up into the child; of thralldom into open space, tiredness into waking, wrinkled into pressed, has-been into unborn.

"I would include in that regimen a tutelage containing all the wisdom of Haji Baba, Ferdinand Count Fathom, Grandfather Frog, and Castruccio, Prince of Lucca. Not to forget Santa Claus or Amos & Andy, Professor Challenger, Hank the Cowdog or Roderick Random, heroisms all around them, Henry & Mudge and Robinson Crusoe. I would add, of course, Huckleberry Finn and the venerable Robin Hood. And what good re-education without a thorough recollection of Alice, Nicholas Nickleby, Gooroo Simple and Old Mother Hubbard? Not to mention Captain Popanilla or Peter Rabbit?"

While the *Daily News* man was frantically writing down these enormously weighty recommendations, a television news crew from Bangalore pestered the trio with an assault of tracking shots, tight shots, full shots and zoom-ins, while the persistent on-camera host tried to pin the Commander down on all fronts. "How do you define adult?" she asked.

"Now that is an interesting question you raise, young lady," replied Marigold. He looked to Sannazaro, then to Rajibai, frowned some, scratched his head, then chose his words with utmost peculiarity: "By the light of the green lagoon swam in reverse a wealthy baboon. He peeked to the left and glanced to his right, then secretly lifted his spoon, his spoon, his silver spoon."

The journalist was poised attentively, awaiting further illumination. The Commander grew silent.

"I don't follow," she said, looking to her comrades who suffered equally on account of the ideological density. Was it the "silver spoon" that should translate into a telling irony? Or the fact of a wealthy baboon to begin with? Was wealth treading water—a comment on India's elite? The country's foreign policy? The BJP hard line on the riots in Bombay in the early 1990s? Was the baboon watching his back? If so, was this a point taken with respect to the endangered lion-tailed macaques of Kerala? Or Pakistan? All these questions addled her over-intellectualizing brain.

"You, Madam, are indeed an adult, and that is the definition I was looking for," the Commander offered.

"But I don't understand."

"Excellent! Ignorance is a wonderful thing, when the opportunity exists to begin all over again. You have every reason to be optimistic."

"I'm sorry. That's bullshit."

"Please, Madam, there is a boy among us."

She had interned at CNN; expected candor, objectivity and reality-tinged charisma, based upon all she'd heard about this character. But presently, having spent no more than a few moments with him, she was all but exhausted. He had resisted not only the logic of 30-second sound bites but logic in general. The reporter did not want to be unkind by portraying him as an utter lunatic, but he left her few alternatives. One moment he was speaking about his Theory of Deconstructing, Decommissioning and Deactivating Adults Worldwide, and the Teleology of Pinocchio, and a moment later about the oppression of Dickie Harding. His stupidity, as she perceived it, favored connections. The subjects were even more absurd. It was one thing to rhapsodize about cows, but to insist upon their own country in the heart of India? With their own cow constitution and elected officials? The same with Malabar flying squirrels, Hansel and Gretel, and all those depauperate classes. He was all fired up to abolish Parliament, burn all government documents, lose all pensions, tenure, terms of office, possessions, tenancies, chattels, incumbencies, sinecures, bonuses, dividends, yields, perquisites, bounties, schemes, industrial complexes, business arrangements, the military, garage doors, high fences, automobiles, buses, officials, experts, authority, barbwire, guns, bullets, bayonets, steel, plastic, convolutions, iron, trucks, airplanes, packaging, pavement, railroad ties, levers, fulcrums, dowels, ball bearings, microchips, oilfield equipment, trucking, cosmetics, forest products, aerospace and defense, securities brokers, air freight, semiconductors, attorneys, savings and loans, tires and rubber, Brent crude, pipelines, auto parts, precious metals, chemical commodities, soft drinks, most—not all—footwear, tobacco, explanatory notes, commodity indexes, bleachable tallow, lard, grease, and anything else that had the slightest remnant of 'adult' written into it.

"There are 400 million adults in India. What will become of them?" she fired away.

"A new beginning," he went on.

"Translate?" pressed she.

"Clubs, tea parties, social organizations, volunteerism. The children will determine what is best for them. But I can assure you that the talents of adulthood will not be wasted. Where there are valid skills, know-how, expert systems, wisdom: all will be secured for re-integration. And with so many volunteers, no animals or children will be homeless again; no gardens left untended; no poachers able to sneak into forests. I see this vast population of retirees becoming, in essence, an Indian Conservation Corps."

"What is a retirement age?"

"Probably 50. The age Plato commended as the year of the philosopher king."

"OK, I see a few hundred million specific problems, but what then?" She was particularly befuddled and exasperated—for the Commander had just made obsolete her own parents, who were very much at the height of their careers and earning power.

He went on to describe his newly dreamt-of political confederation of childhood states across the subcontinent: childhood stamps, money, housing benefits, laws, unicycles, parliamentarians, journalists, co-ops— all the same partitions of responsibility he had witnessed in previous days and weeks among 12 million of the little critters. Moreover, he would provide for skateboard ramps on all public buildings.

The journalists filled their notebooks. The foolishness crescendoed. Sannazaro checked every impulse. Eventually, the reporters dispersed. The Commander had managed to utterly undermine their stories. How could anybody possibly summarize what he had said? There was no credibility or through-line, no catchwords or phrases that stuck in the mind. Well, perhaps there was one, and it would certainly show up: "An end to all economic activity." That's what the billionaire had called for.

Hours elapsed. The three wanderers found themselves before a medical building in the grounds of some research complex a few miles from the epicenter of the Rebellion. They had followed the path least traveled by, and stood amid the mass of red sandstone government halls. Most appeared to have been abandoned by civil servants, who had fled or joined the protests. Security had been discombobulated, and the high-tech blinds before them admitted to a partial view. Marigold peeked inside and there beheld an array of laptops and chemistry sets. The interior caught his eye especially because the occupants—all wearing white laboratory smocks—seemed oddly distracted, so focused as to have overlooked historic events occurring right outside and all across the sovereign plains.

This appeared to be the one building alive with bustling bodies amid a conspicuous void of bureaucratic presence.

"Look at that: a fairy tale of tranquillity. Science at its calm, rational and dispassionate best," said Marigold.

"I need to pee," Sannazaro added. "Rather earnestly, in fact."

"Come to think of it, I feel an even less civilized urging," replied the Commander. "That dubious roadside stall upon whose interesting cuisine we dined earlier, using all available fingers, did not quite set well beside my overworked stomach lining."

"And I shall simply die out if I don't get a cold drink soon," Rajibai declared, deftly adopting the ways of his new peerage.

CHAPTER 106
Secrets of the Gene Cannibals

THE MILLIONS OF protesters had nowhere better to go than onto their butts beside enough bonfires to illuminate northern India's Moghul history—a task of ponderously vast candle power—and raise substantially the pollution index, already exacerbated by dust storms from Rajasthan, the heavy canopy of carbon and nitrogen puttering out the rear of every phut-phut (pronounced fart-fart), and a dense cold fog setting in. One could not breathe without some protective covering over the mouth. The nation's administrative center had the look and feel of a burst appendix. An eviscerated liver. Canvas tents, lit from within, gleamed like decoys or magic lanterns. A gaming impression, copper-hued and spacious, tents haphazardly thrown throughout the amphitheater of dusty light. Enough to brighten or annihilate. The protests had transmogrified into the largest sit-down strike in human history, with its associated jamboree of crows and eagles swooping upon the infinite prospect of leftover suets, morsels, dietary loose ends and stools which birds know best.

Hundreds of thousands of farmers had by now gathered, many emboldened by Mr Marigold's rousing call-to-arms, demanding genetic copyrights and an end to their Government's easy compliance with the multinationals. They were blandishing broadsides and bulletins, and one of many South Korean-made farm tractors driven onto the manicured grass had dumped 1,000 pounds of fresh manure within the ministers' entranceway. Further blocking their way were several thousand bulls marched in for the occasion. Rifle-toting guards knew better than to try to stop these amateurish gestures. In fact, amid so many other protest rallies, and the vast siege of Rajibai's Rebellion, there was really nobody listening inside South Block, where Indian and Russian officials had in previous hours toasted to their smooth sailing. The deal had been signed six months before, though the press had gotten no wind of it. Research had been proceeding at a wondrous pace, fueled by the international pizzazz attendant on the race to map the genome.

Fending off the swarm of Delhi's dementia, the frantic diaspora of social causes, bidding adieu—with all great expectations—to the galluptious emancipation of children for which (as history shall record) they were largely responsible, the trio pursued their mundane calls of nature that late-winter afternoon in New Delhi, on the cusp of a new millennium.

Sannazaro had every reasonable hope, finally, of returning to Tesuque. He was tired of India and its many willful woes. Battle fatigue had left him feeling his age, his eyes drowning, heart wounded. If he saw any more canine skeletons scavenging for food along a roadside, a shackled elephant carrying freshly lumbered hardwoods, or a chained bear tormented by his circus trainer, or another defanged cobra trapped in a basket, or a naked baby with bloated belly, more melées of malaise demanding change—incessant imperatives here and priorities there, hundreds of millions of little emergencies, bureaucratic logjams, yet another cruel slice of life—he thought he'd go mad, or already had. How, he wondered, had little Rajibai withstood a life of such assaults? Had it built a more solid character in him? The boy seemed impervious, a perpetual pitcher of milk, endlessly intrigued, adaptable without short-change or fuse, fending for himself, no rancor or recriminations. It was not as if the Italian had not also suffered in his time, but nothing like this. These bloated carcasses upon the soul. This many-colored carnage. These broken lenses, crushed leaves, wind so hollowed out that no shell dared contain. A countryside better off in its austere despair and furthest desolation than these multiplying cities, whose crumbling stairwells were crowded to the final rung, and without exit, inside the famished, cloud-hidden ceilings of doomsday, or *samvartaka*, as the Hindu forever thought of it.

In this cosmology the boy had grown up and prospered as a human being, despite appearances to every visual and emotional contrary. But how? The question weighed on Sannazaro, who could not factor the irreconcilable hell with the youngster's heaven. A demeanor so calm, mature, ripe. Ears perked, not to survive the predator but hear the concert; a nose fitted by eons to be sensitive but not rapacious; eyes that lit whole mountainsides ablaze, yet without wrath or heat or any destruction. These qualities were not found in bastions of good fortune, he decided. It was an old theory, of course, right out of Henry Murger's novel *Scenes de la vie de bohème*. But unlike that author's chronicle of Rodolfo and Marcello, indulgent bores at the conclusion of their early turmoils, or Puccini's Mimi, a sacrificial lamb on the altar of ephemeral youth, Rajibai had transcended every predictable outcome, or so it appeared to Sannazaro. Where could such an escape artist, a boy of such equanimity, flare, dramatic penchants and foundations, go from here?

They turned into a separate wing of the government complex. Odd security officials were there taking black tea beside the reception desk, self-involved and unobservant.

"Yes?" inquired the receptionist.

"I am the Commander, and these are my colleagues. We need a Coke machine and a restroom, if you would be so kind."

"Certainly." She pointed down the hall, no other questions asked. He was white, he was a Commander, he belonged—though the woman looked hard at Rajibai.

They passed dozens of laboratories, a hubbub of busy lab technicians rushing trays of samples, slides, test tubes from one important experiment to another. The men's bathroom adjoined the largest of the labs on the ground floor. Marigold detected the signs of extreme animation, and caught a glimpse through a slightly open door of several scientists huddled over a computer screen.

The air was heavy with anticipation, a palpable excitement. Gigantic anatomical conundrums were coming to light inside that inner sanctum. Somewhere mid-point among the welter of monitors, electronic microscopes, computer models and medical paraphernalia, an email of spectacular implications, and garnished with chemical mumbo-jumbo, flashed its way into the imaginations of all those equipped to interpret it.

From inside the unusually cleansed white ceramic urinals, Marigold's eyes were glued to the crack in the open-door cattycorner of the loo. He was struck by a partial sentence: "...chemical deterioration time of the corpse".

"What do you think that means?" he whispered to his two companions, both of whom shrugged.

Out on the grass a large military helicopter touched down. Guards swung into motion, rifles lifted attentively, salutes brimming across each forehead. The outpouring contingent, headed by a shaved muscleman of sinister-looking strength, made straight for the laboratory.

Of the visiting Russians, this one, Alexi Malevich, was a breed unto himself, the receptionist noted. He was the brute who stood out from the rest of us, she thought; that barren ugly scar on his left cheek could be interpreted to mean the worst in man in general. The characterization was only too obvious to her. A trail, consolidated within his bristling musculature, of pain and ruination. His hair was shaggy, but trimmed around the neck. In his Brioni suit and Swiss shoes and watch, his air was abrupt, uneven, and reflected an obscure personal past. He was the lead executive in the co-venture deal with the Indian Government. Unlike their counterparts among Western pharmaceutical giants, Russian firms doing business abroad, their own in particular, were altogether content with royalties, rather than copyright, a key point of earlier contract negotiations, as it turned out.

Most importantly, Russians paid in cash, street money which, with nearly 1.8 rupees trading for every ruble, represented a substantial infusion at a time when the Asian recession and lingering IMF and World Bank sanctions following Pokhran-II had left the Reserve Bank of India in a crisis mode. It was not just the money, but the supercomputers the deal brought with it, and the very real prospect of converting heretofore unexamined weeds, insects and the last few unexplored Indian floral gardens into money.

Speaking to his awaiting colleagues, Malevich said, "You will find that we have taken the best of capitalism and left the worst. Furthermore, we make better vodka."

Inside the research facility three dozen Russian gene hunters worked alongside Indian colleagues, most of whom had trained in the West, at places like Cal Tech or MIT, before being seduced back to the Third World with high salaries and extensive perks. (The new imperative: Stop the Brain Drain.) On this day the researchers had been continuing their wide-ranging biological survey of specimens taken from India's diverse back country, searching for new drugs that could be gotten to market quickly. The next yew tree, or super-aspirin. India used to tout one of the most mega-diverse sets of ecosystems on Earth, equivalent to those of Indonesia, Brazil and East Africa. Her species possibly once numbered in the millions, if one included insects. But that was long ago, before the conquering Moghuls, who enjoyed shooting anything that moved; and the Portuguese, who were obsessed with cutting down native forests and replacing them with coconuts; and then the British, who—as one historian commented—simply backed their trucks up to the nation and drove off with the goods.

At the Rio Summit, India's Minister of Environment and Forests had declared that India had managed to save 19 percent of her primary forest canopies, a highly disputable assertion. Most Western nations had saved no more than 5 percent, and much of the West's wildlife had been driven to the brink of extinction. In most G-7 countries there was terrestrial and aquatic ruin, despite per capita incomes exceeding 20,000 US dollars per year. In these rich countries, and even the newly developed nations, there was a common belief that when people reached the 4,000 dollars per capita income benchmark, there would be a wave of trickle-down largesse earmarked for the environment. But such moneys had disappeared. Wealth did not translate into ecological resolutions. Moreover, the rich were notorious for giving the smallest amounts to environmental causes.

But if the G-7 revealed atrocious ecological selfishness, what about a country whose economy was marred and pockmarked, the majority of her people desperate? The rupee had remained devalued and at historical lows for years, the 150 million rich and middle classes obtaining their livelihoods at the expense of 850 million brothers and sisters in absolute destitution, whose annual per capita incomes averaged just 8,200 rupees, or approximately 180 dollars. Marigold had heard numerous theories that the Minister of Environment's own experts in India had sold him a bill of goods, and written the deception into his speech at the 1992 Rio Summit. The displayed satellite images of Indian forests were bogus, revealing not primary forest but mature sugar-cane crops. In reality, there were fewer than 4 percent of remaining forests across India.

Two billion human consumers were predicted for India's late twenty-first century, yet already the majority of children were hungry. In the early 1980s, the UN Food and Agriculture Agency declared that India would have no problem feeding its masses because 90 percent were vegetarian, and the Gangetic plains were among the greatest grasslands in the world. Both assumptions had proved to be false. First off, Indians were chagrined when the nation's largest sociological poll showed conclusively that 90 percent of the population were meat-eaters, not vegetarians. Secondly, the overwhelming majority of the grass species in those aforementioned plains had gone extinct. The River Ganga was so polluted that most of its water was not even industrial grade, by American standards. So the Ministry of Agriculture and Chemicals had good reason to be panic-stricken about its gene pools, and eager to adopt whatever strategies were necessary to get a financial grip on any genetic heritage that might be left.

The Environmental Ministry was in no way up to the task. It had sold off mining rights in National Parks; turned the other cheek on tiger poachers; made no attempt to stop the trade in live peacocks; and could do nothing to halt the tide of lumber industries from consuming the last primary tracts of tree canopy. Even the Government's own Tree Patta Scheme allowed each family in many states one acre of loppings—fruit, leaves, flowers, deadwood. Multiplied by the country's population, this represented a complete denuding of the preconditions for soil renewal and biodiversity. But the affront by people against Nature went further: amphibians and reptiles were nearly gone, along with the tigers, Asian lions and mangroves. Every vertebrate species of any possible use for food, aphrodisiac, leather or feather was killed on sight, whether hoolock gibbon, clouded leopard, pygmy hog or rhinoceros.

Given hundreds of millions of impoverished Indians who, every night, provided warmth for themselves by whatever means, that usually meant pulling branches off trees, shaving limbs for toothpicks and hiding bundles of wood that could be used during the colder winter months (the least studied contributor of all to Global Warming). The laws themselves allowed for one bundle of twigs per person per day, pulled wild (that usually translated into about one acre of allotted scavenging). By such democratic largesse, it was calculated there would be no more forests left in India within ten years.

All this spelled disaster for wild genes in the subcontinent. Of the more than 8,000 species of rice that once were known to exist throughout India, at the moment that Marigold, Rajibai and Sannazaro stood eavesdropping in a bathroom, there were fewer than a dozen breeds. One pest, one massive blight, and there were few hybrids to prevent total famine. During Rajiv Gandhi's brief administration, the Prime Minister acknowledged that over 70 percent of the nation was best described as "wasteland". Wherever the more than one billion Indians lived, most exotic plants didn't have a chance. Only the northeastern corners of the country and a few pocket regions in the far south offered any hope for plant and animal preservation.

The northeast was India's last expansive wilderness, where population density was one-thousandth of the rest of the country, and the largest quadrants of truly unexplored, untouched lands anywhere in the world remained. When the Russians first proposed a joint venture that would channel hundreds of millions of rubles into the Ministry of Agriculture and Chemicals for the stated purpose of Indian gene preservation, under equitable conditions, it was a no-brainer in New Delhi. The northeast (what used to be called NEFA, the Northeast Frontier Agency) was the prime target for bioassays.

Mr Marigold could hear the excitement in the adjoining lab. Then he caught sight of the ventilator shaft above. Intuitively he knew that something was wrong; sniffed the scope of perilous discovery vocalized by the visiting Russians.

"I think we should leave," Sannazaro whispered anxiously, seeing that both Marigold and Rajibai seemed stoked by the same fast-evolving scheme, whatever it might be. He dared not speculate, but had, ringing in his mind, and for no predictable reason, an image, fixed, unsettling, premonitory of the famed corner of the poet Thomas Gray's tomb, yew trees and elm in the shade of Buckinghamshire's most famous church,

Stoke Poges. And the somber poet's elegy itself, haunting the moment. The Squire's palms were sweating. His fingers trembling. He knew there was big trouble coming.

CHAPTER 107
A Body in the Brahmaputra

SEVERAL DAYS PRIOR to the rallies in New Delhi, the continued dust and heat squalls in the northeastern quadrant had given rise to massive lightning storms that pounded the arid forests, some say from below. There was the scent of sulfur in the air, a prelude to unseasonable monsoon rains which started dumping their warm acidic waters on the scorched earth.

In the high mountains to the north, fresh snow plastered the harried canyons, added foment to glacial descent, dislodged avalanches down every unstable wall. Forecasters were at a loss to predict the movement of the rain curtain, for it had come so unexpectedly. All animal life took refuge. In the frontier town of Sadiya, in the state of Arunachal Pradesh, 100 miles south of the disputed Chinese border, the rains had within hours swollen the southern tributaries of the Tsangpo River, known as the Brahmaputra on the Indian side of the border. It flowed a mile wide past the town. Whole sections of forest, along with the occasional animal, had been mowed down by the floodwaters and moved swiftly like so many chopsticks. The river was muddy, and had traveled 2,500 miles across Tibet before making an abrupt 90-degree turn somewhere north in the Himalayas and heading due south towards the Indian jungles. By the time it had reached towns like Sadiya and Dibrugarh, it was a wall of fast-coursing debris.

Distinguished by a heavy Indian military presence, given its proximity to the disputed McMahon Line with China, Sadiya also supported a state-run hospital and medical research facility wholly disproportionate to the size of the community. It was a poor town in the jungle, with its share of satellite dishes, a movie theater, police station, a proliferation of small shops, wood cutting, tea distribution and cottage tie-dyeing industries. The latter operations produced purple and orange oils which were emptied uncurtailed from 1,000 sources into the vast river system.

Through torrential sheet rain and wind, Indra Rakshee, a physician, was driving to his office in his beloved 1957 Studebaker. His window wipers had been stolen, and palm trees had crashed into the country road. A thin layer of mud covered everything, making this day's commute particularly unnerving. He passed several military vehicles heading in the opposite direction. To one side of the road a water buffalo stood utterly at peace in the middle of a swamp. Two white and ruffled egrets, looking the worse for the rains, rode his gleaming back. Turning a bend, Rakshee noticed three boys dragging something from the punishing river where the lips of the rapids lapped the tortuous highway. Water spilled over. Sandbars were eroding, three-foot waves pumping across the storm-tossed surface. One slip off the bank, certain death.

Coming closer, he saw that the boys were hauling a human body. Rakshee ducked down out of his car and raced over to assist. Quickly drenched, speaking Assamese, he helped them lug the badly mutilated corpse up on to the embankment, and at once noticed its physical peculiarities. He said nothing about that. All then lent their strength to managing the cadaver on to the back seat of his car. Then he turned to the others.

"Was he a friend or relative?"

The boys shook their heads and explained that they had only just seen the body and had no idea who it belonged to.

The grossly bloated stiff was that of a young man, probably late teens or early twenties. It was otherwise emaciated, with huge contusions that had distorted the bone structure. The boys had spotted what looked like a kind of mane bobbing above the ghostly white remains, so logically thought it was an animal, maybe a dead tiger—something bearing a saleable pelt.

At the hospital where he worked, Rakshee put other tasks aside and got the body into pathology where, with assistance from a colleague, he examined it in minute detail. It seemed to him something was definitely odd about the deceased's morphology, and an autopsy should set the record straight. Certainly the river had not been kind. The young man had been struck by heavy objects. His neck and head were badly bashed. His clothes had obviously been ripped from his body. He was like no person Rakshee had ever examined. He wasa white male, with waist-length hair— but something else was really quite amazing: the fellow's grotesque facial structure was not merely a result of injuries, multiple collisions during his unguessable river journey, but an actual racial type. Rakshee remembered hearing about a tribe of supposedly Caucasian Pygmies who lived in trees somewhere in Arunachal Pradesh and went extinct in the 1930s. This lad was Caucasian, but lanky. He stood about six feet. His musculature was Australasian—strong—but his eyes, toes, fingers, mouth, teeth, earlobes, buttocks, and uncircumcised, odd-looking penis (a very long penis with three distinct testicles) all came from some unknown tribal corner of the human species.

More bizarre, and clearly significant, thought Rakshee, was the young man's blood type, which results showed differed substantially from that of any person he had examined. In fact, the blood chemistry defied everything Rakshee knew about medicine. He was no specialist in hemodynamics. But it was clear that this was a new type of hemoglobin that displayed properties more akin to the action of chlorophyllose ($C_{55}H_{72}MgN_4O_5$) than blood, and that was an observation he based upon the rich number of white blood cells, and—strangest of all—the fact that those cells appeared to be alive, despite his estimating the boy's time of death as two months prior.

The platelets, normally activated for purposes of clotting during injury, had instead begun reproducing. Loss of blood was extreme, oxygen starvation was there. But the organs should have been totally dried, festooned with vast, busy colonies of anaerobic clostridia that normally oxidize the fat left on a corpse. There should have been ample evidence of the breakdown of all the carbohydrates remaining in the body. In death, a person's muscles give off a chemical known as inosine monophosphate, which marks the beginning of the cellular implosion. The lysosome organelles within every cell will start feeding on themselves, decimating every last carbon bond that has provided the fuel, the structure, the logic of life. In the end—and it happens within a day or two of death—all that remains is a minute amount of heat energy trailing off into the biosphere.

But none of that normal post-mortem physiology was observable in the Sadiya pathology lab. Instead, the cells of this freakish corpse appeared hungry, somehow confused, unwilling to accept death, and meeting it with an equally audacious response. A jump start, thought Rakshee, might even bring this mysterious boy back to life, as was being tried with the recently recovered Siberian mastodon. The good doctor was baffled and enthused, and put in the paperwork to have the body frozen immediately.

Then he called a local anthropologist friend to come have a look. The fellow taught at Dibrugarh University and had made the only, albeit fragmentary, survey of tribes in Arunachal. The coordinates of his research were geographically precise. There were two large areas outside the perimeters of his survey: one far to the west, adjoining the northeastern corner of Bhutan; the other, a few hundred square miles in extent, along the river, just beyond a particular mountain ridge, past the last village leading to the Chinese border, where neither he nor anybody else—to his knowledge—had ever been. Secretly he had always believed that site of worrisome inaccessibility to be inhabited by the world's last Stone Age peoples. This corpse had been flushed down that river, and the anthropologist had never seen anything, or anyone, even closely resembling him. The body must have come from Quadrant X, as he called it: the last unexplored— and, he hastened to imply, probably unexplorable—region of Arunachal.

Rakshee subsequently emailed the interesting highlights of this discovery to a colleague in New Delhi, who happened to specialize in blood chemistry and was currently working on some joint Indian-Russian research task force to identify new proteins and Cytochrome C molecules from plants and animals that might have commercial prospects. Maybe, Rakshee explained in his message, there was a publishable article in all this.

That colleague received the peculiar data, and entered it into a molecular models program on his computer. It took only a few moments for him to recognize that something amazing had happened. A glitch, suggested others, including a group of Russian businessmen touring the facility with their in-country hosts. Everyone crowded around the monitor. But after they had examined the report more thoroughly, it was clear that the pathology data were no technical aberration or joke.

The molecular program into which the data were downloaded had been developed only that year at the Mendelyev Institute at Moscow Medical School. It was the best software in the world for positing and extrapolating new genotypes.

All this—the discovery of the corpse, the location of Rakshee, the body's remarkable properties, the notion of 'immortal cells' and Quadrant X—was overheard by Mr Marigold et al as they huddled in the laboratory's toilets. This information could not be ignored. Sannazaro caught that old glint in Marigold's lisping eye, all too reflecting, now, the ceramic glaze of fire in Rajibai's own. Having displayed such great dexterity in sabotaging Pokhran-II and dropping down through a ventilator shaft, Rajibai again evidenced his superior gymnastic capabilities. Helped up by Marigold and Sannazaro to the vent above the toilets, the lad assisted them in turn, whereupon all three peeled back a thin veneer of fiberboard which allowed for an uninhibited prospect of the adjoining lab.

What they learned was that Quadrant X was precisely the area the Russians had intended to scour for new gene plasms. Two advanced military choppers had been appropriated for the mission.

The timing of this discovery could not have been more fortuitous. At the Indian National Security Bureau, an analyst making routine checks of domestic emails from government facilities had picked up the transmission from Sadiya, and taken note of its destination. She copied it to her superior.

This transmission, in turn, was intercepted by the CIA in a new program designed to prevent the agency from being caught with its pants down when a Third World nation detonated a nuclear weapon, and America's brightest intelligence learned about it only the day after, from the *International Herald Tribune*, an embarrassment in the highest diplomatic circles in recent years.

Seeking precise data on the geographical site in question, the CIA conferred with the Defense Mapping Agency inside the Department of Defense. Across the Beltway in Washington DC, one voice to another: "Where the hell is Arunachal Pradesh? And what's this Quadrant X all about? Who do we have near there?"

By that time, the trio had already slipped out of their precarious hiding place beside the men's latrine, exiting the research labs with great stealth, to make their way unnoticed across the back lawns of the building, falling into even step with the fanfare of the common man. Millions of people were leaving South Block; the roads were opening up again. The protests were winding down, save for one: "No, no and again no!" Sannazaro exclaimed.

"I'm going," the Commander said, with a steadfastness his Squire only too clearly recognized as useless to contest. "You take Rajibai to the Embassy, get him his passport, and you two go home. I'll meet you there in due course."

"I'm not leaving without you."

"I'll only be a week or so."

"You heard me."

"Son, what is your preference?" the Commander asked the boy. "Adventure!" replied Rajibai.

"It could be dangerous," Marigold said. But Rajibai had his own brand of stubbornness and mocked all peril.

"You two were made for each other," Sannazaro applied. "And I am the greatest of fools."

"I swear this will be our last outing," the Commander volunteered. "And I herewith promise you a governorship, a kingdom, another cool million dollars for your troubles."

"You might flatter and persuade some people with your pampering and greenbacks, but you can't buy me," the long-sufferer impugned. "I'll commit a senseless act on my own, independently. You need not multiply my stupidity by your own shamelessness."

It took them little time to reach the airport and catch the first flight to Calcutta. They slept conveniently nearby. At dawn, the Commander chartered a small aircraft which got them to Sadiya, where Marigold flashed his temporary diplomatic visa, the one obtained following his arrival in India on the ship *Gandhi*. That unorthodox document was not sufficiently confusing, however, to convince the military guards at the landing strip at Sadiya, where an Inner Line Permit was absolutely necessary for all entry, even for Indian citizens. A permit, or considerable baksheesh, whichever came first.

"Do you take credit cards?" Marigold asked.

"No, but there is a Lambretta I've been wanting to purchase as a dowry present—my daughter is to be married soon, you see—and they take credit cards," the airport guard quietly explained.

From the Sadiya landing strip it took them only an hour to locate Dr Rakshee, who was at home, and for Mr Marigold to explain their purpose in coming here.

"I swear to you they are of a criminal disposition," the Commander explained, recounting his eavesdrop on the Russians and their Mafia-style purpose wholly devoted to exploiting natural resources, and people—whatever it took to commercialize India's last untouched places. "I believe your friend in the lab"—for by now Marigold understood the connection—"and his other Indian colleagues are pawns in a Government venture, which is the whole reason for hundreds of thousands of farmers coming to New Delhi in protest. It should come as no surprise. Conversely, there may be a way to stop it; to nurture whatever it is; to protect Quadrant X. But you must tell us how to get there."

Raskshee was hopelessly perplexed. Before him stood a child and two old eccentrics from America. What was he to do? There were national security issues involved. He could get into great trouble. Yet something inside him chimed with a disturbing sense that Mr Marigold knew what he was talking about. Moreover, he recognized the Commander from the newspapers. You're that rich American, he thought to himself. The one who thinks he can single-handedly save all the children ... Perhaps you are a man of your word. But Rakshee could also see that Marigold and his unlikely companions were no Tarzans.

"Even if I put you in touch with my anthropologist friend, there is no way you'd be able to manage an expedition of that kind. You'd need help, resources, a helicopter. The military control all helicopters. There is the issue of air space. China. The disputed border. Even if you were able somehow to work all that out, there's ground travel which is utterly out of the question. You have no idea what it's like in there. Few do. You'd need mountain-climbing equipment, kayaks. More importantly, you'd need youth, experience, expertise. And a month or two of provisions. It's impossible. I have lived here all my life. I know enough about the northern fringes. You'd never make it. Not one day out there."

Sannazaro listened and trembled and knew that this would be the costliest error of all their ways. But he said nothing. One look at the Commander was enough to convey the worst apprehension. The more Rakshee spoke of peril and adversity, the less likely Marigold was to back off. How to account for that stubborn streak of hara-kiri? Could it be he felt immune after surviving the avalanche as a child? Was it some strange genetic debt-repayment to the memory of his father? Whatever it was, the Commander's courage and headstrong forward motion put all who were near him in jeopardy, but he didn't care. He saw only the battlefield; believed in *Oklahoma, Girl of the Golden West*, every movie and stage performance he'd ever seen. Marigold was Peter Pan; lived in Fantasia; thought Santa Claus was real. These were not mere delusions of middle age or tired sentimentality. They were the lens through which he viewed all decisions; the gravity field of his antics; the name of his family tree. Marigold feared only that he should not have enough time to complete his mission statement.

Rakshee took the trio to the hospital, down into Pathology, and into the deep freeze.

Marigold stared in wonder at the remains. He knew at once that this was a miracle. He asked Rakshee, "What is it you want most out of life, Doctor?"

Rakshee told him.

"Good. I will triple your pension in one lump of sugar—no need for you to wait for monthly checks— and I'll throw in a lucrative bonus for your troubles. We can go to the bank right now."

Sannazaro marveled at the Commander's unflinching style. One had to admire it.

They went directly to the bank manager. Marigold extended a line of credit on his American Express card. Rakshee got on the phone to the anthropologist who, in the event, and after some discussion, took his own little bonus from the intercourse, providing precise enough instructions on river entry to Quadrant X.

The same airport guard who now proudly displayed his new motorcycle was only too willing to secure a helicopter ride for this madcap trilogy of easy expenditures. There were several people to be paid off: a control tower director-general, the pilot and co-pilot, the field maintenance manager, the odd lieutenant and an ordnance officer. The guard also threw in some army provisions, Spam, battle fatigues, a rope and fid, backpacks, a few loaded semi-automatics for good measure—whatever the "Commander" wanted. Finding hiking boots for Rajibai was the most serious of their difficulties.

All these frantic machinations occurred just two hours before the Russians arrived. Had their timing been any different, the situation might have gone very badly for Mr Marigold and team—although from Sannazaro's perspective, as the chopper angled fast and precipitously up the wild river canyon, through tropical storm, past sheer cliff face, searching for the first clearing in which to drop, things could not be any worse.

The weather was a frenzy of change. Every minute saw a different rainbow, or bolt of lightning, a hailstorm or the advance of summer: seasons stolen out of turn and aggregated in a strange force field of winds that buffeted the chopper violently.

"There!" the plain-English-speaking pilot announced in his headset. "Please get your gear together, we're going down. You'll have to be quick, with these winds, and mind your heads. Out the front, not the back.

Tell the boy."

Its rotors spinning, the chopper hovering inches above the first lonely clearing of rocky terrain, it was time. The threesome hopped down with their provisions, ducked away and fanned out around the front of the helicopter. Each held down his parka hood as the chopper pulled off.

The plan? There was no plan. A pickup point or time? There was none. Only a radio beacon that, when properly activated, would provide coordinates and signal the party's desire to be retrieved. The batteries were good for several hours, or—spread out with prudent parsimony—several weeks. But if the signal was missed at Sadiya, they were on their own.

"Alternate your beacon when you're ready," the pilot had cautioned. "Thirty seconds every five minutes. Keep track of that battery. Keep the spare one dry." The chopper disappeared. All was a chaos of jungle and mountain and raging river.

Sannazaro was seized by the most terrible fear he had ever known, at least since the sinking iceberg. "Now what do we do?" he asked, though he started by taking off his parka, for the ambient temperature had suddenly risen. It was uncomfortably warm.

"It is no more rugged than our Fiordland adventure," Mr Marigold reminded him. "And no black flies."

"Eeeuuww!" Rajibai exclaimed (or somesuch), shaking his hands wildly and jumping in a circle of panicked starts.

"What it is, Son?" the Commander shouted.

Suddenly the grievance was too clear, for all three were feeling the same sensation up their legs, down their jackets, everywhere. "What's that?"

"Something crawling ..."

A moving crease in his trousers. A silly slimy submarine burrowing into underwear, seeking novel cuisine.

A head emerged, inflated with red blood cells and the first inkling of a smile in days.

All looked, amazed. Then: "Leeches!" screamed the horrified Italian.

CHAPTER 108
A Weathered Little Book at the Eastern Gate of Paradise

IT HAS OFTEN been remarked that time erects barriers in certain asymmetrical locales and lopsided personalities, spurning the aging process, smoothing out the edges of discord or discontinuity, overturning any and all notions of evolution. Subantarctic Brachiopods, 60 million years old, adhere to this possibility. Where the life sciences admit to no predictable path; where neither form nor function leaves a notch, not one hieroglyph to mark the impact of biological anomalies. By miracles without a name, flightless birds, for example, are able to propel themselves up 90-degree slopes; or some new potion of youthfulness is elevated to the extremes of the land or the person advancing either a new vista of enduring grace or some tonic or muscle tone heretofore unknown among gallants.

It happened in a Dead Zone of biological oxygen demand, off the coast of Louisiana, for example. The same effect was cited by a lonely officer of the Canadian Entomology Caucus amid the pulverized, volcanic breccia and frozen cinders of Haughton Crater on Devon Island in the Northwest Territories. An agrarian reformer, wandering lost for 12 years with his family of farmers, saw the same, though could not name it, along the desert shales and sands in the region of Santa Ana de Chipaya, in Bolivia. Where wind and weather fashion nothing, and life makes no imprint. Where geology has given rise to no monument but loneliness. It is a striking sight.

Or, conversely, at the heart of a teeming sinkhole in the jungles of Borneo, where the famed ornithologist who discovered it deciphered so much life and threatening shade having converged for over a billion years as to render indistinguishable all gradations or hierarchies. A biological implosion of carnivorous satisfactions, cellular metabolisms, a free-for-all of life sciences out of which no individual or purpose and no goal is discernible. The smooth sides of the Trango Tower, for example, shadowing the Baltoro Glacier; the walls of the Ruth Gorge, nicely smothered in verglass; or the granite draperies down Chamonix's paramount Dru.

Leeches of the Eastern Himalayas similarly challenge a philosopher to assemble a chronology, or comment on the ways of community, defying the reasoning powers of paleozoology with a steadfast evolution that will not reveal the slightest deviation from one millennium to the next. Here is the relentless stream of an underworld where time, truly, has been banished. All seconds merge seamlessly in the jungle of unregistered appetites and chaos. Bloodsuckers feasting on the groin, the thundering of rivers, the daily downpour from above. The infinite palette of reflections in its impenetrable mind, the cartwheels of air molecules and spores, the passing clouds no historian could ever track.

Such inaccessible and native territories gain immortality to the extent they are far removed from human contact, from all those measures and counters, scales and formalities by which any civilization, or far-flung community of humans, marks its passage, buries its dead, leaves traces of a clambake here, a wishbone there. Beyond such 'truths', a wilderness has no cares or caveats, engendering illimitable neurons for fancy, populating that quadrant of the imagination with all the settings of infinity suited to an endless stream of sentience and omen that is at the heart of the hermit. The eremite, whose monastery is the land, whose thought process takes flight with the wind, marks every moment by the filter of cool breeze through the creek bed, through dense forest where little light can strike, rolling in the fever of mud. Nothing bothers, changes or signals. No cuneiform to capture the play of dramatic abandon. All is as it was a million years or more before.

In this prehistoric veil of outermost fringes, the trio swatted non-violently at midges, plucked leeches from their ankles and private parts, screamed at ghosts and hamadryads, and bushwhacked with amateurish theatrics towards an end that had quickly become confused with nothing more than survival. With little effort, they had entered the realm of outer oblivions, and Sannazaro, for one, was cursing his gullibility. No amount of rupees, dollars, promises, governorships or rose gardens was worth such misery, he thought, as they scrambled in awful circles. To tarry in the Himalayas was imprudent. To be finicky, preposterous. To demand safety, comfort, compliance, sheer arrogance. Just as Rakshee had predicted, Sannazaro emanated their fast-enshrouding, collective defeat.

He sat down, stubbornly refusing to advance another step until some certainty could be evinced in his colleagues as to their destination and purpose. No such conclusion was forthcoming, so the Italian resorted to compounding the misery by citing a stream of yearned-for confections: rinktumditty, baked macaroni with piquant sauce, mock turtle in anchovy garnish, breaded leg of mutton and St Julian with capers, cabbage and lobster salad. His attitude was not helpful.

"I might be able to withstand it, but don't you go speaking such evils around the boy," the Commander scolded him.

Rajibai, of course, proffered a wholly different opinion throughout all these travails. Nothing bothered him. Sheer heights added to his brewery and thrust; nor could any regrets by the mule thwart his throttle. Neither lament nor reproach affected him. In fact, the more frantic the third member of this trio became, the more high-spirited went Rajibai, a little infinitude of indefatigability. Until Sannazaro was convinced that idiocy worked in twos, that father and son were even more emboldened to be alike when genes had no say over the dictation. For neither was the Commander set back by these continually disappointing threats to their existence. Each insult, looming disaster and darkening bowery simply heightened his sincerity. He had singularly committed himself to saving India, all indigenous wilderness, endemic genes, for purposes of a grand ideal, an edifice whose altruism was not of this Earth. He could not stop thinking about Paramatman's notion of a 'new nature', whatever it might mean. Like an author obsessed with erecting an Eiffel Tower.

Thus, in this place that can scarcely be described, the trio edged their way forward, or backward, at the mercies of a tireless dreamer and child of inexhaustible fantasy life. Neither could hear the cracked voice of reason that was fading in the throat of their venerable older companion, the Squire of Many Heartbreaks. But by nightfall their collective predicament defined the full range of peril, discomfort, dissolution and what it meant to be lost.

Marigold was busy clearing a section of forest floor for three sleeping bags, his headlight affixed clumsily to one side of his mosquito-taunted head, when the light ignited the most remarkable of all discoveries in a very long time—a metal box upon which two bright yellow banana slugs were copulating.

"Look!" he exclaimed, removing the two innocent creatures to a cirque of teeming aloes, and lifting the tantalizing container into his hands.

All gathered round to examine the miniature treasure chest.

"May they, praise be, be cigaritos," said Sannazaro. "I would wager circa 1900, by the amount of rust."

"Gold coins," offered the boy expectantly.

"It is old, and that is English," Mr Marigold pointed out, touching the unintelligibly encrusted words printed there.

They huddled around the box in the glow of their headlights. "Open it!" agitated Rajibai.

The Commander pried the upper from lower lids with a Swiss army knife, gouging out the rusty layers of demarcation, then lifted the contents. "A book," he declared.

"A diary," Sannazaro volunteered (thinking, 'Oh shit, not another diary! ') "Never mind that. It is handwritten. Carefully."

Marigold undid the faded ribbon that was tied around the crushed red Morocco-bound pages. "A woman's hand," he surmised from its finery. The heartswept filigree, care woven like Pre-Columbian yucca—no drought, but evidence of well-watered recollections. Some 53 pages of damp yet legible confession. Marginalia enshrined atop a worm-scrawl of memorabilia. Epistolary passages here, a page of luminous commentary there. All edging toward unknowns.

"Read it, Father!" the boy urged him.

"From the beginning," added the Messer. "And do not spare the slightest detail, for this icon of the night might well constitute a road map, our deliverance from this mess you've once again gotten us into."

"Shhh!" the Commander insisted. "You're foiling my powers of concentration."

Marigold fitted his spectacles and began to read aloud, following the sure hand. The writing was sometimes stiff, slanting left, slanting right; red ink, black ink, blue ink; a pen of minute steel, another of thick dimensions. Penmanship that seemed frantic, at times, though the sign of a woman's touch was also paramount throughout. Hence, the odd impression from the very first page of a collective effort by one person, an odyssey of situations and reminiscence without much recourse to normal settings, propositions or expectations. Duration seemed wholly absent from the unsteady confluence.

The three sat huddled with their book as darkness encroached. Rajibai was in heaven. His sister used to read bedtime stories to him—a fact the Commander recognized, and which added to his flourish of delivery, not least his efforts to get some of the Russian words right. For his part, Sannazaro listened intently, praying for some clue to their position and the means of escape. "'It was winter in Gorki, near Moscow, 1923,'" the Commander read. "'The streets were gloomy and ice-laden. By three in the afternoon it was nearly dark. Vladimir Ilyich Ulyanov Lenin, leader of the Soviet Revolution, aged 53—' Goodness gracious, Lenin! This book is nearly 80 years old!"

"Just keep reading," Rajibai urged.

Marigold scanned ahead. "It continues with the following diagnosis: 'He was dying in a hospital from two strokes and sclerosis of the cerebral arteries, a condition greatly complicated by the assassination attempt five years prior by one Fanny Kaplan in which the bullet casings had been doused with strychnine.'"

"I didn't know that. Is that true—about Lenin, I mean?" the Squire asked.

"It goes on: 'Although the injuries from the wound had healed, the trauma and poison had weakened his immune system. The great visionary had little energy left to fight for his own life.'"

"Maybe we don't want to hear it," Sannazaro volunteered. "Maybe this whole thing is bad luck. Lose the book. It's clearly an omen. We Italians are superstitious and never wrong." He had not forgotten Antarctica.

"Shhhh!" both father and son hastened.

"'Lenin's guards sat resignedly beside him. One flirted with a nurse, while the other read from the latest

Communist Daily. All this I was told later."'

"There—an I. Who is the voice? Somebody's speaking." Sannazaro looked over his shoulder, confused by the tenses, perspectives, first, second and third persons. It was late, his feet were aching, and he was not at all up to this complicated series of literary chicanery.

"If you'd shut up and let me read."

"So read already." The Squire put his head on his pillow. "I have a headache."

"'Outside, a Model-T Ford, escorted by soldiers on horseback, chugged to a halt against a snowdrift. The horses were clothed in woolen blankets. The temperature was minus 12 degrees. From the vehicle stepped a general in the Red Army. He entered the hospital and made straight for Lenin's room. In his gloved hands he carried a satchel containing striking news.

"'Lenin, now paralyzed, could speak only with great difficulty. He wanly gestured for the general to read the document, whatever it was. A message from Uli Stuchka, in charge of all Red Brigades. Stuchka would have come himself but duties of state demanded he remain at the Kremlin. The general went on to summarize the letter's contents: the remarkable discovery of a diary—this very one, freely annotated—that had arrived from somewhere in the mountainous hinterlands, sent by a Soviet scout on the far fringes of the empire, and received two months prior. The pages of that diary, in turn, revealed the scout's obscure journey into the Himalayas where he encountered several tribes.'"

"Tribes. Oh dear," Sannazaro moaned. "That's bad. But wait." He sat up. "Am I not confused? Or am I the only one who senses a glitch?"

"What do you mean?"

"How can we be holding the diary if said diary ended up in Lenin's hospital room?"

"Don't be so analytical. How should I know? Am I Einstein? Houdini? Just listen, there's bound to be an explanation."

The Commander continued reading. "'It was rumored that one of those groups, living high in the mountains, was naked, never knew illness among its kind. "Never is not a word to use loosely," Lenin sighed, then turned his head away: his normal display of impatience and cynicism.'"

"Then there's a continuous smattering of hard-to-distinguish dialogue," Marigold said.

"Read it," Rajibai prompted.

"Well, it begins, 'Why are you disturbing me with such gibberish,' the leader said, amid a coughing spell.

"'I'm sorry, Comrade Lenin. But Stuchka felt this was significant.'"

"Wait," interjected Sannazaro. "Are you reading the real dialogue or making it up? The author, your mystery woman, is elaborating, using hindsight, as if she had written it up in a fiction."

"I suppose so," conceded Marigold. One theory was as good as another. Clearly the little volume had traveled, in no less a manner, one might adduce, than the corpse plucked from the river. For there had been no obvious ceremony of burial. The book had been carried along; had arrived in a mush of hurried weather, haphazardly deposited by Himalayan hydrology and meteorology. Its original intent defied analysis. To have happened upon it, in that thickness of jungle, intercepting a literary destiny otherwise cemented in oblivion, had about it the odds of coming face to face with a meteorite. As for clarity, only Lenin gave a compass reading, but he lay in the Kremlin, thousands of miles and countless decades away. What could it mean? Who was the author? What purpose enshrouded its uncanny tale?

"Let me see that—" Sannazaro grabbed hold of the book from the Commander, and for a moment the two tugged back and forth, spouting angry denunciations—"I am no ornamentalist" ... "How dare you"...

"You're ruining the story" ... and so forth—until prudence demanded a clean resolve. The Commander gave it over to his persistent Squire, lest the frail manuscript be damaged, and watched as his comrade peered confusedly into the same handwritten reminiscences. Page after page were, indeed, a synopsis of events past and present, commentary and blow-by-blow account. Most was in English, some in Russian and French, both languages known to the Commander.

"All right then. I just wanted to see for myself. You'll forgive me. These days have been dreadful and, frankly, I should rather be home sleeping, dining, dreaming I had stepped foot in the Himalayas, if you must, than enduring another waking moment of this ... this ...never mind!" Flustered, ready for sleep, Sannazaro handed the book back to Marigold, who carried on:

"'What is significant is the fact I am dying and there is no one with any nerve or even a single ball to replace me,' he evinced, exasperated, too tired to actually scold the general for this tiring waste of his time, trying to get up, but lacking the energy.

"'That is the whole point,' the General declared. 'Stuchka is doing everything he can. You are a young man. Russia needs you.' "'It's hopeless,' Lenin summarized, his head collapsing back against the pillows.

"'He's been very depressed,' one of his Preobrazhensky guards whispered.

"'I heard that,' Lenin mumbled.

"There is a break in the writing, then it says: 'These were the precise words relayed to me by General Gromsky.' "But this is all wholly remarkable," the Commander said, looking to his son and uncle. "These are the very words of Lenin, if the transcription is to be believed. How, why are they in this diary, in this place, and in English, mostly?"

The trio shrugged, looked about in the darkness, where the banks of a nearby creek bed flowed wildly through a forest of gigantic deodars and eastern chestnut. Enormous boulders of gneiss and feldspar were covered in debris, broken hulls of wood, the whelped remains of countless storms, tendriled mesh, tangled skeins of moss and mistletoe. It was clear they were in some sort of spillway from torrential floods that had passed this way year after year.

"The book was obviously driven considerable distances, safeguarded in its metal box. But where has it come from?"

"Is there any more? Yes? Then keep reading," Sannazaro now insisted, caught up in the genesis of the yarn, and sitting propped upright against a rock.

The Commander continued: "'The general realized it was no use going through the other materials that Stuchka had sent to the leader. Lenin would have no patience to withstand such learned nonsense. Even the general himself, who would soon be leaving the safe, comfortable confines of the capital, had little interest in the fabulist rash of anecdotes or fine details of the coming expedition. Stuchka had given the task to research assistants in the Moscow archives. Their job: to uncover any and all historical references to the alleged tribe. To find any other possible sources of corroboration of the remarkable story. One frizzy-haired kitten had uncovered a bonanza of intriguing myth and lore. Grastina, a lover of Stuchka years before, had lost a leg beneath a toppled troika on the ice. She'd aged ten years in two, permanent purple rings (the result of pain killers) under her weary eyes, and no longer held much allure for the men who used to favor her. Feeling some pity, Stuchka had compensated her with a good-paying job in the library. What she discovered was of marginal use, but it served, at least, to further Stuchka's resolve to dispatch an army expedition in search of the tribe. How much could it cost the Government? Lenin was a shrewd businessman. After all, he'd kept open the Marinski Theatre, courted New York businessmen, and had even created a Ministry of Enlightenment (Narkompros). There were one million priceless objects in the Hermitage, and fabulous riches for the taking at the Alexandrovsky Market, at the Cathedral of St Basil the Blessed, the Cathedral of the Assumption, and, of course, throughout the Kremlin itself. With the imperial family out of the picture, venture communism was now in vogue. Lenin was a greedy sonofabitch. He wanted it all.

"'Grastina's notes, now in the general's satchel, referred to the ancient Greek map-maker and mathematician, Ptolemy, who had heard of such a tribe. Plato, too, had referred to them. There was, in addition, the famed Marco Polo who relied on classical sources, including the historians Pliny and Herodotus, to chart his own trek through the Karakoram mountain range, just west of the Himalayas, during the thirteenth century. He, too, had detected mention of the clan's existence, even whereabouts, lodged between clouds and cliff. A steady stream of medieval explorers set off in search of the tribe after Marco Polo's *Book* became a runaway bestseller. It enjoyed over 130 editions in countless languages. Across Europe, people believed that somewhere far away in Asia there was a pocket of humanity that lived beyond the pale. Jesuits were convinced that these must be the same backpackers alluded to in the Bible, and that they inhabited the original Garden of Eden. Most notably, Marmaduke Carver, whose *Discourse Of The Terrestrial Paradise, Aiming At a More Probable Discovery Of The True Situation of that Happy Place of Our First Parents Habitation*, issued in London in 1666, cited zoological sources in learned Greek, Latin, Hebrew, Chaldean and Aramaic to prove the existence of this plateau among monoliths, this ledge amid mongrels. From Drake to Pindarus, Sir Isaac Newton to Pliny, Addison to Pausanias, from Aethopia to south of the Tigris, claims of originality, wonder tales and likenesses, zealous topography, lionizing latitude and zebra-colored zeniths cascaded. Butterflies the size of Harrod's whose naked and elongated caterpillar form stretched the distance from London to Norwich; a black-faced Heath-breed of ram with nostrils 17 feet wide; a Tscherkessian sheep, *Ovis dolichura*, that shed the true golden fleece, and more.'"

Marigold continued reading: "'Much later, British spies and envoys in Tibet, European botanists and mountain climbers had also sought out these peoples and their pets. The famed Sir John Mandeville claimed to have actually found them, and established a Christian empire somewhere in the Himalayas, or Sri Lanka. John Milton wrote of them in Book Four of his *Paradise Lost*: 'Against the eastern gate of Paradise, a rock of alabaster, piled up to the clouds, conspicuous far, winding with one ascent, accessible from earth one entrance high. The rest was craggy cliff, that overhung, impossible to climb.'"

"So learned a diarist," said Sannazaro, baffled by all these arcane allusions.

Marigold turned the page, had trouble deciphering something. "There are water stains and foxing. Lines have intermingled, the spine is deteriorating," he pointed out.

"Just keep reading," Rajibai insisted.

The Commander held the book sideways. He read on: "'The scout who'd written the diary did not know about such obscure quotations and references. Instead, he was one of that breed of late nineteenth-century explorers who exhausted whole lives searching for lost treasures; men (and the rare woman) who thought nothing of disappearing for years at a time, living out of tents, surviving on weeds, thistle, the fruit of Darwin's barberry and rations, disinterested in comfort. They could be valuable assets to a government, because they were not in it for promotion, high salary or power. It was the sheer lust for adventure that motivated them. This particular scout's last whereabouts were more or less known—the latitude and longitude, at least—and the diary concluded with a fantastic description (albeit hearsay) of some kind of alleged drug, or plant or animal food which evidently sustained the snow people. They were believed to live naked up on high, never evidencing the least medical ailment. Which, in theory, could mean but one thing. Nothing else was known about them.'"

"Blast it. One diary that speaks of another. It is all too confusing," Sannazaro complained. "And what is the one thing? And who is asking about it? And for what purpose?"

"And and and. Just wait, won't you. Patience must yield some meaning, trust give rise to completion, an addled brain to revelation. Parity, plausibility, explanation, these are the universal rules." The Commander went on: "'The scout had managed to dispatch the weathered little book back to Moscow on a yak caravan crossing Tibet, before heading out himself in search of these people. That was eight months before and nothing had been heard from him since.

"'Lenin, who did not share Stuchka's optimism for any such elixir, let fly a witticism to brighten up the fatal gloom shadowing his hospital room. The general heard a very sick man wheezing down the hall. Another, closer by, spat up blood and phlegm. He could read Lenin's mood easily: no diary or intimations of immortality were going to alter the irrevocable truth of the leader's slow demise. It was only a matter of time before the heinous Stalin, with his insane letters in green ink to all the party apparatchiks, would have his chance. Already there was political scrimmage behind the scenes: dozens of top officials knew their days were numbered, that Stalin might even go so far as to try to have them arrested, or worse. Many had already immigrated to France or Austria. Stuchka himself had prepared himself for evacuation in the night to Paris the moment Lenin died. He kept gold, official documents, his traveling papers, in a prepared suitcase near his bed. His children had already been placed in a boarding school near Brussels. Two of his colleagues had followed their intuitions and gone to Mexico.

"'You might remind our Stuchka that Tibet is even colder than Moscow,' Lenin finally managed. 'Nurse,' he cried, 'get me my pain killers.' "But the wheels had already been set in motion, an expedition planned, elaborate care taken in every minute singularity. This much I knew. Several days later a young assistant in Stuchka's quarters was finishing a photographic session. She had filmed every page of the diary, and handed over the plates to Stuchka, who placed them in a vault.

"'Later that day, General Grotsky surveyed the line-up of military explorers standing in full regalia in the snowy courtyard of the Moscow Military Academy. Stuchka was there and reminded them all of the significance of the expedition Grotsky was to command: nothing less than the salvation of Communism (same old pomposity)—a medicinal cure for Lenin, if this rumored tribe and the substance they consumed could be found. As Stuchka moved through the snow, he stopped before me and my fiancé, the ranking

Lieutenant Vladimir Charnoff.

"'I know you will make your father proud,' he said to me. Stuchka had personally guaranteed my qualifications, as I was the only female attached to the dangerous expedition, and an American at that, though I had lived in Russia since the age of 12.'"

"An American!" Sannazaro exclaimed. "How remarkable. But then, again I must submit: to whom is she writing this strange reminiscence, with its asides and insights and oddly flamboyant characterizations? It is no letter home, by the style of it, no missive to a brother. And we can safely discount a correspondence with her lover, since, by her own telling of it, the two of them are now together—in a snowy courtyard of the Moscow Military Academy. While I lie here fair game for leeches and monsters in the dark. It doesn't make much sense. There have been far too many Russian-related matters in my life of late. I do not cotton to the coincidence. They are proving mightily uncomfortable. Moreover, I do not even remember what we're doing here." Addressing himself to the Commander, he continued: "First you spawned a revolution in India, the collapse of New Delhi, sowing high hopes that can only be dashed.

Then it is on to the next emergency—medical matters, gene sciences, Himalayan phantoms. Am I not the greatest fool on Earth to accompany this madness with no resistance?"

"Yes."

"Thank you. I wanted to be sure."

"Now that we've reached an understanding on that point, may I proceed?"

"By all means. Do not be alarmed, however, if I sleep through it. Or am gone by the morrow. I am calling for a taxi."

Marigold smiled, took a sip of water from their canteen, then, ignoring his companion's routine whining, continued, his eyes wider.

"She goes on: 'More importantly, my work in the new field of genetics had given Stuchka confidence that if the tribe was discovered I would have the proper know-how to obtain and analyze blood and tissue samples, or whatever else might be required, to insure acquisition of the mythical substance.

"'I was 19 years old at the time, having arrived from Boston seven years before. My father was the famed Proctor of the Moscow Medical School, formerly Chairman of Biochemistry at Harvard. My mother was a poet of some distinction, after the style of Longfellow. I had worked under Mendelyev, following early studies in my teens at Harvard. My fiancé, Vladimir Charnoff, was also assigned to the expedition. A brilliant engineer and disciple of Jules Verne, he had built an elegant contraption named after his mentor that was intended to float above anticipated dangerous obstacles in the Brahmaputra River. The river was believed to be the third largest in the world, but much of its course, particularly those regions that twisted through the narrow ramparts of the eastern Himalayas, was totally unknown to my generation. The obstacles referred to in the scout's letter were also unclear. Adding further challenge to the madcap exploit, the *Jules Verne* had never actually seen one moment of action in real white water.

"'Stuchka examined up close the enormous river craft, with its demi-bateaux, which was to be hauled on a large open carriage, pulled along by army mules, the hapless offspring of donkeys forced into the front trenches of World War I. Stuchka was assisted into the passenger seat of the boat, which presently sat on wide wooden planks atop snow in the courtyard. A demonstration had been prepared. Gas jets surrounding the helium-inflated bladders of thickly stitched leather and metal baffles were ignited. As the enormous balloon rose up, thus alleviating weight on the ground, an engine with a propeller jettisoned the troika-like iron behemoth across the snowy fields, Vladimir in the driver's seat. As they approached a large brick wall, Vladimir pulled down a lever and the *Jules Verne* rose, narrowly skirting the 20-foot-high barracks before them, grazing off a smoking chimney, before touching down again, this time on Pushkin Avenue before the Academy.

"Astonished Muscovites dispersed to all sides. Young boys and girls on skates converged upon the strange mechanical monster as Stuchka congratulated Vladimir. It was a wonderful vindication of an exotic contraption, and of its creator, whom I must say in those days I thought I loved.

"'That night Vladimir and I were packing our things. In the morning, before dawn, we were to head out by train for a two-week journey to the south, whereupon we would commence the more serious overland migration by horseback. I remember how sentimental I was about some family photographs that were in frames and insisted on bringing them. I had, in addition, probably packed way too much medical equipment.

Vladimir scolded me. It was essential, he said, that we travel light. I was always stubborn. My mother used to say I was born overdressed.

"'I remember Vladimir asked me what I would do if this alleged elixir for immortality were actually discovered, and I remember saying, Nothing different. Our plan was to be married when we returned to Moscow several months later. I would have a job awaiting me at the medical school, and his prospects in the military were assured, even under a Stalin administration. In time, we hoped to have a son and a daughter. Eventually, I made clear, I had every intention of returning to Cambridge, Massachusetts.

"'I later returned to my own flat, which I shared with two medical students. I remember everything as if it were yesterday; how I undressed, neatly folding my Red Army uniform and placing it on the floor, then got into bed naked. I never wore a nightgown to bed, something Vladimir found extremely bold and unconventional for a woman. Upon my reading table were stacked a pile of research materials on Central Asia, and the new science of genetics: H. T. Colebrooke's *On the Height of the Himalaya Mountains*, published in Calcutta in 1817, and a fine illustrated first edition of Darwin's *Origin of the Species*. I turned off the two oil lamps, and stared out the window at the stars above the city that was cowled in fresh deep snow. I could hear the quaint chimes of troika taxis delivering partygoers to and from the many theaters and cafes up and down the busy, frozen avenues. Ballet. Opera. Symphony. Jazz. Cabaret. Galas. Art openings. And a mile away, lines of starving poor. Such contrasts. Frozen birds. Squirrels that had dropped dead from the cold. Dogs with parvo. Children, widows suffering from influenza, their fathers and husbands having died in the war. I whispered a prayer to myself and fell off to sleep. I remember every detail. What a different world it was, then. From who I am, now.'"

"What does that mean?" Sannazaro inquired, curious and assuredly awake—his being on the lookout for leeches ensured it. "When is now? By what means? And where is it? Damn it, there is a contagion of unknowing out there, and we are, I fear, caught in its midst. There is too much coincidence surrounding us. I don't like it. Not one jot."

"I cannot disagree," Marigold said. "I have no idea, no shred of any notion, no proof one way or other, nothing to go on nor back away from; all is some Aladdin's lamp minus the illumination, a magic carpet with no floor to start from. Not even a semblance of what she is talking about or where headed. But there are many more pages and I glean some distant glimmer of advantage by reading them, even if until daylight." He glanced down at Rajibai, who had fallen asleep—Colebrooke's *Himalayas*, no matter how high, were no match against a boy's sandman. He covered him completely with his sleeping bag, then resumed reading the diary by headlight, enthralled with the idea of this emergent Bostonian beauty, as he already had her pegged, and so many other things—qualities of mind that took him from himself, gave off the sparks of freedom—fully unconscious of the fact he was using up their beacon battery.

CHAPTER 109
An Himalayan Expedition, March 1923

MARIGOLD NOTICED that the ink had changed color, the width of the quill was different from before, even the hand less steady and controlled. In the writing style was discernible an evident haste, or agitation. Tenses freely altered. Temporality skewed by unknown forces. No reference points— sunset, passing month, full moon; all was disturbed, lacking the normal demarcations to suggest a command of passing time. She was writing, usually, from the moment, with no distance or means of dispassion. Perspective had been fractured, a Cubistical slide across the jungle floor. Many of the words were indecipherable where water had transformed proper English into ink blots of jungle maroon.

"'We've been out in the wilds for over two months presently—or three, there is no way to be certain. Three dozen soldiers and I, heading through Tibet. The terrain is spectacular, difficult. The cold is infernal, as Lenin predicted. Grotsky rides atop his Lippizaner, a frustrated stud who seems to miss the Viennese ring, with an impractical show of authority over his men, while the others carry on by foot, their leather leggings swathed in yak fur, their bodies hunched over, labors made treacherous by deep slush, unbreachable cliff walls, dusty narrow chasms, and local Tibetans who insist on sticking their tongues out at us at every opportunity. This has resulted in more than a few drawn weapons. I learned only much later that such gestures were the normal signal for "Hello!" among Tibetans.

"'Earlier today, mules struggled to drag the *Jules Verne*, as well as large ammunition caissons along the frightful path. Kropotkin, Vladimir's second, studied the horizon lines, triangulating the height of the rocky ridge before us, as well as the distance to the river, where the expedition intended, any day now, to launch the craft. Our food supplies are severely depleted, and there are no other caches to be had. The Tibetan villagers have only tea and potato cutlets to share with us, for their life is anything but luxurious. Tibetan children are malnourished, and the life expectancy among adults extremely short. I confess to being somewhat amazed by the squalor and turmoil of their lives, even by rural Russian standards, but heartened to witness such openness and generosity. Coziness and friendship combat their every ill. No obvious truism, but in these harrowing Himalayas there is often no other succor. Life reduced to the elemental stronghold of the sheer family intimacies whose caress and understanding seem to anesthetize all other rigors and tragedy. Whatever the Tibetans have, we are free to sample. Grotsky has demoted several of the men for their having taken advantage of the women, I'm pleased to note.

"'At the village of Lodhu, with its many deteriorated mud huts, we advanced upon a scene of devastation. There had been an enormous rock slide and at least 100 shacks and lodgments had been smothered.

Villagers were wailing, bewildered, trying to dig out those buried. I will not attempt to illuminate the heartbreak or horror of such riot. This settlement was the last of human enclaves before entering the gorge, as it was referred to: those enigmatic canyon lands through which the Brahmaputra snakes its way towards the edge of the Tibetan plateau. From there, very sketchy maps describe a vertical descent where the river falls off into terra incognita in northern India. The gorge. It would change my life, the life I now lead.'"

"Again this cryptic atemporality," Sannazaro noted. "My bafflement, even at this late hour, will give me no rest until we solve the riddle."

"Spoken like a true aficionado," Marigold relayed. "I, too, am unsure what to make of it. The rust on the box confounds my clairvoyance. I cannot divine the mystery."

"Read on, then."

Marigold proceeded: "'We moved quickly to aid the villagers. I searched frantically for the medical kit that had been lashed to one of the mules. Grotsky dismounted from his horse and ordered all shovels out. Troops began removing fallen walls and digging out the victims. An old woman was found alive, buried in a pool beneath rubble, along with her Tibetan mastiff whose healthy, liberated bark elicited the first weary smiles from all survivors. I set the smashed arm of an old Tibetan gentleman—the elbow was shattered, three crushed fingers, a fractured wrist, very ugly—and applied the tools of my trade, but when it came to an injection, the Tibetan steadfastly refused, preferring chang—Tibetan tea laced with rancid dee—to any western pain killer.'"

"What is dee?" Sannazaro wondered aloud.

"I have no idea," the Commander muttered, undeterred, his speech slurred from lack of sleep. "'In gratitude for their help, the Tibetans turned over all of their remaining storehouses to us. While the men ate, bodies from the mud slide were chopped up by Tibetan untouchables, and left for vultures atop a cliff nearby. I must say I was both horrified and fascinated.'"

For 20 minutes Marigold read on, conveying delicately observed customs and preparations. Finally: "'After three days making various geographical calculations from our tented encampment on the outskirts of Lodhu, trying to decipher any last references, notes and measurements from the copy of the diary in Grotsky's possession—'"

"Wait a minute," Marigold exclaimed, calculating. "What?" the groggying Italian mumbled.

"Are you awake? Did you hear what I said?"

"Of course I'm listening."

"There are two books, Grotsky's and our Lady of Boston's."

"OK, so?"

"I'm just remarking upon the fact. I don't know what it means. Or are there three books? An initial diary, a copy, one left in the archives, another—somewhere? I don't know. Do you?"

"Stop, I say. You are mightily confusing me. I cannot count that high, not at this time of night, in this condition. Even a library of one is more than I am able to profitably stomach. I cannot think past the fabled lands of half-sleep. I don't want to be reminded of anything real. We are not here. This earth is not hard, these sleeping bags are actually beds. I have a bottle of Chianti by my side. There is a warm hearth. Sliding doors. A Japanese waterfall. Stones. A pool with slowly doting carp. Linen sheets.

All fine. Safe. Leave me alone. There is no tomorrow."

"'The men packed away a sizable reserve of barley meal and vegetables in burlap sacks,'" Marigold continued. "'We all then proceeded onwards to the dramatic entrance of the river gorge. The Tibetans had never heard the river called Brahmaputra. To them, it was the Tsangpo. It was here that the real rigors began, for the soldiers were now directly below the northern Himalayas at their easternmost extreme. The heretofore sluggish, mile-wide waters of the Tsangpo came together from dozens of parallel tributaries. The confluence disappeared round a maze of bends and high glacial palisades, and the force of all that water was death defying.

"'After many agonizing circumlocutions, we finally put into the river. The remaining mules—those that had not died from exhaustion and pneumonia, and been served up in one borscht or another—were left in safekeeping with the local yak people. Several of the herders were given special material incentives to come along as porters since they supposedly knew where to expect the coming dangers in the river. These Tibetan porters were snugly clad in huge yak- and goral-skin boots and triple-quilted jackets of snow lion, swaddled in earmuffs of Asiatic ocelot and a species unknown to us they named clouded leopard. They carried their own teakwood-frame packs filled to the brim with the beef jerky of Asian blue bear and takin—a distinctive Himalayan bull—and herbal medicines culled from tea trees and broadleaf oils. I was unfamiliar with most of them. I personally tried each one in boiled water, but could find nothing particularly special to medically recommend their use, except in the case of one dark leaf that seemed to have calmed the hysteria and sickness displayed by some of the men since reaching the higher altitudes. It effectively combated migraine headaches in a majority of the soldiers and must quell the frisson of nerve endings, I surmised.

"'After some hours we found ourselves moving more seriously and directly downriver. The altitude was approximately 14,000 feet. Light snow flurries enveloped the desert-like environs. A glint of fogged sun filtered through the freezing mist. The *Jules Verne*, which housed 12 of us, was accompanied in the water by a floating flotilla of four inflated goat- and yak-skin rafts. All eyes looked upwards as two lammergeiers with seven-foot wingspans attacked a herd of wild mountain sheep on the slopes falling into the river. A lamb was picked off. The bird flew 200 feet up into the snowy mists, then released the prey from its talons. The infant crashed with a thud into the rocks below. The raptors then flew in to feed on the hot entrails. "Tool users," hailed Vladimir, though I could not bring myself to share his ornithological enthusiasm.

"'The map from the diary was no longer yielding information. Wherever that scout had gone, he left no further record. We floated beyond the remnants of a wooden suspension bridge, and the remains of a cliff monastery, most of which had collapsed into the river like a sunken ship, its elaborately painted beams protruding from between boulders in the strong current.

"'Just past these clues of prior habitation, a wicked thundering within the river could be heard. We were approaching it at breakneck speed. Turn! Turn!, Grotsky ordered, to no avail. The first rapids created havoc for all, as the canyon narrowed to less than 100 feet in width. The men in the rafts were trapped. Go with it! Stay to the center!, Grotsky shouted above the infernal roar of the waves. But the situation evolved far too rapidly for precautions to be taken. Recollection fails to catch the horrified nuances of difficulty that burst upon us. It was only now obvious that they'd never been down the river. Under present circumstances, disciplinary actions were out of the question. The whole expedition was in jeopardy. The smallest of the rafts were immediately capsized, and the Tibetan herders vanished. None of them had said they couldn't swim. But it was clear they could not, as they drowned, one by one, before our eyes. Nothing could be done to save them.

"'Grotsky was furious. "Inept bastards! Serves them right," he exploded.

But now all the others were imperiled. The four large rafts carrying troops had neither the maneuverability nor the proper oars for such walls of water—ten-foot waves of fast-moving mud atop glacial current without warning. Blatant bedrock. Horrifying scour. We were swept through the narrows at an astonishing 40 miles an hour—that was the sense of it. The water was dense with the remains of red mud slides, whole slopes iron rich, that had been pulverized, and the undercurrent a veritable gallery of shifting boulder fields and manganese shards. The river bottom, punctuated by hints of pyrite—fool's gold—was literally being carried and crushed beneath us. Those in the rafts were doomed, sucked sickeningly into the explosive funnels that vented the nearly 300,000 cubic meters per second of white water, the approximate volume of the river, according to Vladimir, who somehow assessed it. I am in no trustworthy mood to figure imperial conversions of such enormity.

"'This was the deepest, narrowest gorge in the world, and the waters of the Tsangpo entered it like a razor-thin hurricane, sucking energy off the adjacent walls, creating thunder and lightning within. No one who has not seen this phenomenon can imagine it, nor the terror that engulfed us: electrical fields ricocheting in the infernal floodwaters. The swirling blight also engulfed the large metallic river craft, which received the lightning blasts and heated up, shone brilliantly in the underworld. But for all that, it withstood the creaks and yaws and 10 million volts.

Thrown like a toy by the thunderous tumult, it slammed into building-sized granite boulders, but did not rupture or go down.

"'However, all of us aboard were flung like ragamuffin dolls within. Bodies cracked, bones broke, in our last-ditch efforts to ignite the gas jets. It was an ill-fated attempt to rescue the men aboard the rafts. The craft fought the winds and roar of 100-foot waves. Slammed through the narrows. Electrified in the cut-throat chasm of impossible forces. No defense. All was blind in this horror of unexplored river. The *Jules Verne* rose 150 feet, careening off a side wall, leaving multiple punctures in the plating. We were struck by the lightning and turned blue. We shimmered in a haze of physics, hair standing up, then flattened by the inundation of a billion gallons of water each second. It was the misery of miseries. From our elevated position, we were exposed and ruptured. I cannot describe it.

The winds throwing us up the canyon. Noting that the *Jules Verne* weighed six tons. Yet, it was a wing of falcon feathers in such a storm.

"''I can't hold it!" Vladimir screamed, as the vehicle's engine twined and strained, and the smell of diesel indicated a ruptured tank. "We're going to blow up!"

"'My fiancé struggled at the wheel, turning off the fuel jets, as ropes were lowered with baskets into the impossible tumult of battering river below. We were smashed first on one side of the canyon, then another. The vehicle tilted 30, 40 degrees, before flipping upside down against an overhang to the other side wall. There was no hope. The rope baskets dangled free, hurled from one side to the other or dragged down into the funnels of water and snapped like matchsticks. Not one survivor. And this was only the first of countless rearing obstacles ahead.

"'The size of the troop was now down to eleven. An officer inside the *Jules Verne* had broken his neck against a metal pipe during the rough ride. I tried, so help me, but could not save him. He had fried in that millisecond. His body was dumped without the slightest protocol into the river. Our defenses were down. Hierarchy demolished. Officers, soldiers—all were equal in their desperate struggle.

"'The *Jules Verne* crash-landed on a gravel bar, inundated with black smoke by the time it set down. Everyone on board evacuated. But there was no fire, as it turned out. The vehicle could be restored.

"'We discovered a way off the water, battening down the gunwales and tying the vessel to enormous uprooted trees with soggy two-inch hanks of hemp. With buckets we all chipped in, pouring water over the heated oil casings, which, said Vladimir, had caused the leaking fuels to overheat and smoke. We all planned to return to the vessel. But the dull realization of our peril had now set in. Taking stock of our losses, the revelation surfaced that there was no way back.'"

The Commander eyed Sannazaro. "You don't think—"

"It would certainly appear that way," replied he, contemplating the likely death of the young medic and her fiancé, which would mean, of course, that this book, rescued many decades later by a hand in the night from the vicissitudes of Nature, was the only record of the disaster. "You must read on," the Squire urged Marigold, having wakened to his full senses despite it being sometime after 3 a.m. Gone were his sleepy tirades and ill tempers. Now he actually felt a certain stay-of-execution in the storytelling. It took his mind off their own unbelievable whereabouts, and the weird noises everywhere about in the darkness. The oldest known story—such misadventure—and surely the best worth telling, staying up for, keeping the eyes wide open. It was upon such mishaps, amid just such unexplored territory, that the earliest campfire discussions in primate prehistory no doubt hinged, he firmly reckoned.

Marigold continued: "'With all the porters dead, and more than half the troops drowned, it appeared hopeless. Nonetheless, I made a stubborn point of sampling the various flower species. I plucked the plants from along cliff walls and the undersides of boulders about the river's edge, as our diminished little army continued towards the glacial peaks before us. There were new plant species, to be sure. But none that offered any unusual genetic characteristics. The odd Chinese redwood, Christmasberry, *Ailanthus altissima*. A never-before-encountered golden chinquapin and some sub-species of virgin's bower growing tropically with no puffballs or hair. Of course, the conditions in the field were not suited to conclusions. The process was tedious; the precision work greatly compromised by the ordeal of travel, the constant sleet, the winds. We were being pushed to the limits of what strength remained in us. With the loss of so many men, there was a feeling of desperation mounting.

"'After dark, strong gale-force winds up the gorge physically abused and marooned the remaining eleven members of our expedition. We bivouacked in a blizzard by the river. The wind was deafening, the cold beyond what any were prepared for. Most of our remaining food had been lost, or waterlogged and subsequently frozen solid.

"'One morning, between the ferocious up-and-down swings of weather, there appeared a window of foreboding calm. As if in the center of a hurricane. It allowed for our frightened and miserable assemblage of soldiers to continue down towards what had admittedly become a blurred goal. The solemn phalanx advanced at a snail's pace along the river into ever wilder glacial canyon. The men were, by turns, trigger-happy, moody and superstitious. A pall of terror permeated them all. One day we were attacked by a fantastic swarm of bees that slept concealed in the crook of an 800-year-old rhododendron. The injuries were perpetual by now. Exhausted, we attempted to climb above the frenzied river, along a wall of crumbling rock. We used large metal spikes called pitons for this purpose. Rope ladders were then affixed along the cliff wall. This groping, labor-intensive process was terrifying, as the bees were most certain to return. We had to hurry. At length the troops managed a precarious evacuation from the river, which was now socked in with narrow overhanging walls preventing all further travel along its banks.

"'We ascended several hundred feet. A soldier headed out in the dark to answer Nature's call. In the morning his skeleton was found, 30 feet above the ground, hanging upside down. All the meat on his bones had been consumed. There was no trace of the attack or the attacker(s). Later that same day, an arrow, its bright feathers drenched in blood, was found protruding from the bark of a tree at eye level directly in our path. Now we would do anything to move higher, away from the demented mists and blind corners of the gorge bottom. The men fired their weapons at the slightest cause.'"

"Question," Sannazaro spake. "Have you obtained any sense of where these descriptions pertain, geographically speaking, in terms of our own present position? Or dare I not ask?"

"To be honest with you, friend," Marigold replied, "I haven't a clue."

"That's what I figured. I just wanted to make certain we were absolutely, positively screwed. But do read on."

"Your fears are unfounded, brother mine. This all happened nearly 80 years ago."

"Yes. Of course. Silly me."

Marigold averted his eyes from Sannazaro, and continued with the saga.

"'Reaching the rim of a middling band of cliff, beyond a dense stretch of forest that afforded views far down the gorge, we were confronted by two large totems—ancient sentinels—with gaping mouths and eyes. The wood was petrified. But protecting what? We saw nothing above. All was frozen in mist. Huge snow drifts—60, 80 feet high—abutted up against the cliffs all around us. The roar of wind higher still suggested enormous mountain peaks. But we were in a blind, and could see nothing on account of the endlessly stormy weather.

"'Eventually, we reached the lowest portion of a glacier, where the moraines crashed into the last vestiges of forest. Leprechaun back country, haunted, misty, a bedeviling labyrinth of icy pinnacles, sudden drop-offs and frozen rock. A city of crevasses spanned miles in all directions beneath the imposing mountain walls—the largest Himalayan peaks we'd yet seen—drifting in and out of the dense cloud cover surrounding our now terrified band of stragglers. There was no more military discipline. Only stupid, clumsy antics of survival. For days we struggled towards the mountain wall, up the fringes of this glacier. We had no idea, of course, where we were headed. For where was there to go? We were lost in Tibet, with no way back. Like drunken misfits of Nature, we moved just to keep moving. The alternative was to freeze, or starve to death, or both. It was just a question of which came first.

"'One of the men killed himself. Another tried. My relationship with Vladimir was surely strained by all this. I believe my youth served me well. I held up better than the others, and made no fuss about having to squat behind a rock to do my business. For Vladimir, this misadventure was not about saving Lenin's life. He dreamt only of great flying machines, huge bridges, 100-story buildings which he had designed. As interested as I was in the biology flourishing all around us (tropics converging in the alpine zone), he had espied engineering principles in every 500-foot granite wall. But even these passions died now. He could think only of food, which we did not have; of warmth, which even my body could no longer provide. This death march had not inspired in him great passion or chivalry. Whereas I know for a fact that the sickness of the men had elicited in me all that I was trained for, and capable of.'"

"A remarkable woman," Sannazaro noted. "Isn't she!"

And he continued, "'Unfortunately, there was little more I could do to help any of them. The situation was certainly made even worse when three men—including Grotsky—plunged to their deaths in a crevasse which appeared to be bottomless. A rescue was attempted and my Vladimir volunteered to rappel down into the guts of the ice. His weathered rope was held by three other men. I watched it slipping through their cold, bloody fingers. Everyone held on to stomachs and arms, but there wasn't time enough to hammer a wedge, which they had with them, into the ice.

"'And then the worst happened: Vladimir fell while searching the upper crevasse. The rope had snapped. I thought for sure he was dead. The remaining soldiers managed to haul him back up on to the glacier with another rope, however. But there was not enough rope or incentive in the world to find the three victims. Nobody had the strength left even to consider the prospect of a continued search. Grotsky was gone, and with him his pack in which he'd kept the diary. Not that it mattered any longer.'"

"Now we're getting somewhere," Marigold hastened. "Subtract one diary. And if it was the same that had been brought to Lenin, we may assume the diary—the original diary—is gone forever. What's left is this commentary by our Bostonian. It's beginning to make sense."

"Sense? There is no sense. We are—I cannot say where we are. How many more pages?"

"Ummm. Forty or so."

"I think I need to sleep."

"Let me at least conclude this section. There are sections, you see."

"Fine. Do as you like."

Marigold wrapped up: "'Days went by. The weather got warmer, and this lightened the mood somewhat. But a curtain of rain and sleet created flood conditions in the open runnels of ice. Yet, it was rain, after all, not snow; and that meant that spring was coming to the Himalayas. But with rain came mud slides and rock fall. We seven remaining survivors were continually ambushed by what was now without doubt a total death trap. I told my wounded Vladimir that I didn't mind dying in such a grand place, with the man I was to marry. But he was far less romantic about it, and ailing from his adventure in the crevasse—a twisted ankle and shattered rib. He was now preoccupied with getting the remaining troops safely into the middle of the glacier. At least that way we were all free of the torrent of loose mud and rock roaring down in streams from unknowable heights above. It was this incessant unknown that gripped all of us, for the heavy rainfall had not permitted us to actually see the tops of the mountains surrounding our base camp. We had no idea where we were, and it appeared certain there was no way out.'" The Commander put down the book and sighed heavily, for he easily visualized this heroic young woman and her poignant desperation to survive. An American scientist, obviously a prodigy of her age, who had moved to Russia during the heart of the Revolution. That was a gutsy thing for her father to have done, leaving an undoubtedly cushy professorship at Harvard for the battleground that was Moscow. And then to permit this young woman, whatever her name was, to go off to Tibet, in winter no less, with a group of hardened, now doomed soldiers.

Marigold noticed that Sannazaro—still awake and listening, though his eyes were closed—was gnashing his jaw, chewing over deep thoughts.

"What is it?"

The Squire spoke, his eyes remaining closed as if he could no longer bear to acknowledge their own situation: "If we're smart we'll imbibe the lessons of history. Let this little tragedy in two parts be our guide and get the hell out of here while we, unlike her, still have a chance."

"But there is more to her tale," Marigold protested instructively. "Who's to say how it will end—for them, or for us?"

He flipped over the book and began reading from the remaining pages.

CHAPTER 110
An Avalanche

"THERE'S NO WAY. Every last breath has been extinguished," Sannazaro declared with the mood of an encomium. He had sensed a closeness to the anonymous diarist, this female out of another time, and now intimated a pang at her inevitable loss that likewise touched Mr Marigold—who was not so quick to give up.

"Every *tour de force* has its hazards," opined the Commander, "but no fortuity lacks for a hidden trail or lost valley. No gamble earns the name without a flier, while even the most hostile mountain wall conceals its angling ledge, like that which saw us safely to the summit of Toda Land. Don't give up on them so easily."

"I really don't want to hear the grisly details," Sannazaro insisted. "She seems too pretty and dignified to go out in a mudslide or whatever awaits her." And suddenly: "Tweezers, hurry!"

The Commander grabbed hold of the pair each of them had applied earlier that night and passed them over to the stricken Squire, who launched down beneath his trousers and plucked the invader from the vein along his calf muscle. The leech was over two inches long, and grossly inflated with the Italian's own hemoglobin.

"Damn it!" he declared, flinging the poor brute far off into the jungle. He then stood up, shook out his sleeping bag, then re-situated himself, moving rocks, clearing a new space, trying, albeit impossibly, to get comfortable.

"Are you quite finished making all that ruckus?"

In spite of Sannazaro's reticence to hear any more of the historical suicide mission, the Commander proceeded to read on, his headlight— aswarm with moths and jumping fleas—illuminating the little book that aspired to describe Paradise, only to intimate each striking shudder and seizure of hell. Throughout it all, he kept seeing its author, gripped by her dilemma, unwilling to cede her demise.

"She begins by commenting upon the cloud level, which, she says, was down to a mere 100 feet ... 'The claustrophobia at night—with sounds of avalanches all around us—was unnerving. We camped miles up the glacier, as measured from the point at which we had first entered the river of ice, having used torches at twilight to circumvent a bewildering mass of crevasses. We could hear the thunder of streams below the cavernous surface, the churning of the glacier deep down in its ancient bowels.

Against this din, in our tent Vladimir and I plotted a retreat—'"

"I knew it!" Marigold interjected. "You see?"

Sannazaro lay with his eyes closed, his head bunched up on a sweater for a pillow. The Italian knew he would be awake all night, and every other night, as long as their travails in leech country must continue. Just to his right, Rajibai slept like an exhausted angel, without a care in the world.

Marigold noticed his friend's discomfiture and appealed to good cheer: "Listen to what she writes: 'Maybe, with this arrival of spring, there is a way out, after all, a way back to the *Jules Verne*. If we can just avoid floodwaters and rock falls and the winds, and whatever else this ungodly canyon is likely to throw at us. Vladimir has calculated the amount of fuel left in the tanks and believes it is enough to see us free of the gorge and down into the northernmost tea plantations of India which, being British, would be almost like going home. We have had no intimacy since the beginning of the expedition. But now, buoyed by this new-found enthusiasm—'"

The Commander stopped reading. Sannazaro opened his eyes. "Why did you stop?"

"Something interrupted their passion. I'm trying to make it out." He traced a line with his fingertip through the circumlocutions of ink stains and disorder. Two pages had stuck together. He tried delicately to pry them apart, but the outcome was not beneficial to the task of decipherment. Finally, he came upon a clean section of writing where the narrative resumed in past tense.

"'...by a commotion outside, as a huge white light passed over our tent, across the whole vast expanse of glacier, like a sunburst, or ghost the size of a city. It was the moon, full and frightening, after weeks of winter and spring monsoons. The last of the survivors were awake beneath a night sky crisp and clear. The weather had finally been shaken. A warm breeze passed its hand across the ice. Tam! Bosha moi. Shto eto? the soldiers cried out, pointing to—something? We got dressed, emerged from our tent, and stared with the others at this phenomenon. It was as ghastly and terrifying as it was enchanting.

"'We were all drawn to the sight, emboldened by the radical change in weather. We moved forward with ropes, ice axes and torches. For nearly a mile we trekked across the melting glacier surface, held in thrall by what had risen before us. It was not just the mountain wall that served as a magnet, but the pillar of white ice. It stood like a frozen sword, narrow, jagged; a spear aimed at the cosmos—the highest thing ever seen by man or woman. So tired were we that no free association could possibly divine the truth of what rose before us.

"'Finally, Vladimir hit upon an extraordinary idea: what if it were an icicle? The others joined in unanimously. Of course it was an icicle. For some reason, now inconceivable to me, there was levity, rather than fear, among them. The warm winds had prompted the men to rid themselves of their heavy overcoats. By Vladimir's reckoning, this 1,000-foot-wide icicle must have been three miles high, higher than any building he had imagined, enlarged optically by a cannonade of fogbows encircling it, and leading into astral ether, higher than any Everest, or so it seemed at that moment. It reared like a deity encased in a ziggurat whose most austere extensions intruded on the stars, beckoning. And it was alive, for there was grating emanating from within, cracks, yawns, sounds of something coming. It was speaking to us—or such was the extent of our distressed perceptions, keeping in mind we'd had little food between us for days, and had been moving steadily for months.

"'I had a sick feeling in my gut, alert to the instinctive nuances of looming disaster. For how else to characterize so mammoth a thing before us? A moon whose very size taunted us by revealing the vastness in which we were lost; stars that only added to the predicament of our loneliness at the edge of the world, notwithstanding Vladimir's earlier optimism about recovering his *Jules Verne* and escaping to northern India. As far as I was concerned, that contraption only mocked us now: a heavy, obsolete freak of iron dumbly cast upon the shores of eternity. No trace on the Rhodean shore. It had nothing to say to the sight before us: the mountain that was adamantine, unimpeachable, and seemed to go forever.

"'But I kept my counsel at that moment, as the temperature rose and I smelled my own perspiration. How could I have been so passive before the obvious calamity, except to cite the powers of that magnetic icicle, which brainwashed and hypnotized throughout the starry night? By dawn we had reached the base of this magnificent structure. As the sun rose across Asia, the moment gave pause to us all. Exhaustion commingling with prayer. A silence before the end.

"'Vladimir was the first to realize the error of this midnight escapade as he stared along the strange basin of melting ice in which we stood like innocents before the day of wrath. It was a frozen river, cracking inch by inch like a wintry tale, suddenly warmed. If one had machine-gunned the mirrors in the Hermitage, the effect could not be more obvious. The full moon should have been our dead giveaway. The moon meant a hot sun. And the sun was now upon us.

"'All of us gazed with horror upon the unfolding cataclysm, and there was absolutely nothing we could do to hide or protect ourselves. We were right below it, out in the middle of a wasteland.

"'"This is no icicle, but a frozen waterfall," my poor Vladimir asserted with the finality of unreason. And it was beginning to melt, as the full brunt of the hot sunrise made its tragic presence felt. It happened quickly, though as I remember them now, the events occurred in nauseating slow motion.

"'I drew attention to a cave which I spied lying to the distant edge of the ice, but the words were no more than a heartsickening rasp, my voice already inundated with terror as the glimmering vertical wall above began to collapse. Shards of green glaze, shiny coal black, pear-shaped diamond.'"

"My God!" Sannazaro panged. "That's it then. Horrible, horrible!" But Marigold did not stop: "'The final deadly crack was like a sonic burst that exceeded the limits of the inner ear. We were all wearing army boots fitted with heavy metal crampons. Such footwear was not made for quick escapes over a glacier. We had little dexterity, the cave was 200 yards away, and the men were too dazzled by what was coming. I grabbed Vladimir and we started running. Every man chose his own path, fumbling before the unearthly assault. The three-mile pillar of ice came down quietly at first, slowly, and then with a deafening roar. The explosion occurred in the middle, as the entire spire buckled, then burst. Hundreds of chunks the size of railway cars hurtled to earth, the entire spire disintegrating in a volley of cosmic occasions. Star fields colliding, planets in flux, the orbit of earth shifting. The sheets of ice slammed into the glacier, each erupting like deadly cannon fire. Some of the men were killed instantly, disappearing in the vast clouds of icy debris. The few still alive had only seconds left—for now there was the waterfall itself, which also exploded beneath the ice, a volume of water that was nearly as powerful and unstoppable as the Tsangpo into which it flowed.'"

"Unbelievable," Marigold mumbled.

Both men stared at one another. The obvious question loomed: how did she survive to write these events down in her little book? How did the book survive?

The Commander continued reading of the terrible devastation, a purge that was total—or nearly so, according to the diarist. She described her final seconds with Vladimir, who proclaimed his love for her. And how that final declaration was severed, literally, as the roaring whiteout overtook him like two trains blurred and passing at high speed in the night.

She went on to illuminate in terrible detail how, by fickle fortunes of the deluge—only much later would she understand its exquisite periodicity, she said—she was thrown to safety by the very ferocity of wind which was one with the avalanche. Smashed against the cave, and out of harm's way, she was knocked unconscious, severed clean from her lover.

Later on, though there were no given number of days or weeks reconciled by the text—all was cleaved and sheer, the permanence of words suffused in the dampness of rotting weather, the congealed forces of ink cloying to paper, paper to a leather binder, the binder chemically coalesced with the tin box, rust insinuating a catalyst that transmogrified the whole into a slowly deteriorating time capsule—she reminisced upon the fate of the others and described for the first time the highest waterfall in the world which had poured down over the glacier. As she put it, no Noah's Ark could withstand such geological chaos. Nothing could survive. All was lost beneath the vertical tidal wave that kept coming and coming from far, far above. And she alone, by mute illogic, was testimony to it.

"I knew it," Marigold rejoiced. "I knew she'd survive."

"That was nearly 80 years ago, boss. She's long dead. Sad to say."

"I know. It's almost at the end. But she continues, 'Sometime late that afternoon, I awoke from an unconscious state. My body was wracked with pain, my head bruised and spinning. I remember putting a finger to my temple. Blood. And a pool of it on my chest. I was dizzy and nauseous. My left hand had been smashed. Several fingers were broken. Probable muscle, tendon and nerve damage, ruptured internal organs. Hemorrhaging. I could not open one of my eyes. Before me, where once stood the man I'd intended to spend my life with, was a huge broiling cavity filled with chalky gray water, icebergs, boulders, the limbs of trees, mud and spume.'"

Marigold scanned the painfully written words ahead, lured by a drawing of this extraordinary scene of ruin, and summarized for Sannazaro.

"She describes the continuous roar of the liberated waterfall above and to all sides which wiped out every other sound. And listen to this: 'So great was the colossal force of the down-crushing waters that a rebound in the form of a vertical hurricane had emerged. The air had gone mad, swirling below, forming before me a vast upthrust, or syndrome of microclimate gone berserk, like a cyclone rearing upon itself in circles, flinging every particle of dust and snow and ice thousands of feet aloft. A tornado arising from the glacier. The system, oddly enough, was warm, so that the recirculation acted as a heater across thousands of acres, lugging in its wild squall all the humid tropics up from South Asia.

"'I edged further back into the cave, away from this insane meteorology. In my mental labors, I remembered my schooldays at Harvard, in Cambridge, and saw back to Mother Russia, as well. I figured

Lenin had probably died and been buried in Red Square, his tomb a monument—to what? The absurdity of our expedition? I hated him, and all those military morons, for killing my fiancé. Along the imperial walls of the Kremlin. Lenin's tomb. A perverse dream, as it turned out. Obsolete and finished. And yet, in my heart of hearts, I reveled at the fact of my peculiar pertinacity. Nothing would take that away from me. As Lord Byron, one of my mother's favorite poets, had so rightly stated, this moment in that cave was my fatality to live. Here was the perfect pedigree for any young Russian romantic who yearned after pale moons, tuberculosis and magic mountains. To die alone in a faraway mountain cave—that sensation of exile and isolation, a change of worlds. Even for Anna Christov—all science and facts and Hippocratic Oaths; bereft of the man by whom she would have had two children—even for me, this moment was too wild and free for despondency, mourning, or cold calculus.'"

"Anna Christov..." Marigold repeated. "That was her name."

"Anna ..." Sannazaro repeated. "Of course. It had to be something like that. Simply incredible. Lovely. Go on, then. Read to the end. Why are you stopping? Now I must know what happened to her."

Marigold scanned the final paragraphs, whose penmanship had grown indifferent to appearance or the rectilinear discipline of earlier days, obviously undermined by anatomical ruin, her broken fingers, head blurred, a tragedy affixed in the impermanence of vowels vexed in their final articulations, nouns, verbs vying for air: "'I tried to stand, but my injuries would not permit it. Pain shot into my brain. My head burned, my body was broken. I vomited, but was sufficiently conscious to recognize that I'd probably suffered a serious concussion. Resigned to whatever fate intended, I remember sitting back down, all was blurred, and resting my body against the cold rock of the cave. Relief, at least.

"'Sometime later, I thought I heard music. A strange advance of death? I wondered. What kind of music? Strings. Flamenco? Monteverdi? I had to have been dreaming. I knew it was the end. These odes and airs, a prelude to all that myth and religion had underscored since time immemorial. The notes that led Dante after Arnaut Daniel, famous for his weeping, was it? A spiral staircase, a column of gold-flanged incorporeality. Halos abounding, senses dissimulating. Christ throwing open his arms to true believers from the pedestal of cloud-consuming aureoles ...

"'But then the music appeared in physical form.

"'I took a deep breath.

"'Emerging out of the darkness of the cave, from the very heart of the waterfall, was a little girl, naked save for a loincloth, and with a musical harp at her waist which she plucked with agile little fingers in an obvious attempt to communicate.'"

Marigold and Sannazaro sat up in their sleeping bags. It was as if the world would never be the same.

"She writes, 'The little one was Caucasian, her hair platinum, with streaks of red and dark, falling long and luscious beneath her waist. She was the wildest creature I had ever seen.'"

Marigold closed the slim volume and stared outwards.

"And that's it?" Sannazaro asked. "There's no more? Who was the little girl? A tribal?"

"I don't know. The diary has concluded."

Both men gazed upon the book in mystery. "What time is it?" Sannazaro pressed. "Nearly five."

Marigold and Sannazaro examined the spot where the book had been recovered, looking for any other clue. But there was none.

"Eighty years is a long time," the Commander reflected. "This very place could once have been covered by the glacier of which she speaks."

"Her spirit is out there somewhere," said Sannazaro, spooked and enthralled.

"Go to sleep. We'll figure out what to do in the morning."

The men turned over, covered themselves completely with their bags and tried to indulge in some shuteye.

Suddenly, Sannazaro sat up, fidgeting. "What?" Marigold asked.

The Señor couldn't help himself. "What if that little girl is still alive? I mean, it's possible!"

CHAPTER 111
The Pursuit of the Creatures

IT WAS AN HOUR BEFORE DAWN in the eastern Himalayas. Rain had started to pour. From still silence to thunderous fury within a single moment. Himalayan rains burst from the dark and angry nimbostratus with the ferocity of nitromethane. The engine for such moisture can only be explained by accounting for the nearly 10,000 peaks over 23,000 feet, which gather their own weather, socked in thousands of valleys with types of clouds seen nowhere else on earth. Such cumuli are chemical reactions that explode without warning. Cumulatively abetted by the molecular ferocity of each successive basin and depression; by the density of updrafts arising from every canyonland. All the evapotranspiration condensing from the broadleaves of every high-standing tree, swelling vertically in pantheons of restless humidity. An angry flexing of current. Harbingers in every low casing of thunder, and then the fire dance, ecstatic blasts ruining 1,000 years of chlorophyll in a femtosecond. Swathes of charred ruin, washed out within an instant of floodtide sweeping the downrushing pendulars. All this chaos ruptured in the hellbent barriers, heavy weather, seas of inland river carrying their urgency to the Indian Ocean far away. The gravity that is grace, if seen from far enough above. Particularly in the eastern corners of these mountains, where the valleys are the deepest, and the towering lenticulars and anvil-thick cirrus most dangerous and unfair. Not only the insanely vehement rain, but the Kansas-style winds signaled something altogether different. Eastern Himalayan blusters are notorious for bringing down planes, choppers, even eagles.

Many years ago, one eagle, in particular, was found by climbers at 25,000 feet, with its wings mysteriously shredded. It had been hit by a cross-current that must have thrown it 90 miles, like hot ash from a gastric caldera. Climbers had also discerned whole slabs of rock plastered with thousands of insects, also caught in cross-tumults. It could happen to people just as easily. Eight hundred miles to the northwest, one whole tribe, the darlings of an Austrian anthropologist, had gone extinct all at once; had been splattered, rumor circulates. It was all about hot air entering the realm of cold air.

Miles away from the trio, through a pair of binoculars, someone was monitoring a team of high-level Indian military Green Beret types tracking something through the dense coniferous forests of the transmontane, a region between 5,000 and 9,000 feet in altitude. The trackers were orienteering with heat-seeking laser lenses that fed infrared scanning signals into their headsets. These, in turn, yielded micro-imagery of thermal and chemical body changes and movements within their purview. Old technology, new software.

A sharpshooter whispered to another—"There!"—pointing his rifle through the dense mists. Racing frantically over rocks, dropping plants which it had been gathering in a pouch affixed like a loincloth, was their quarry: some kind of bipedal animal. But this was no Yeti. Or Big Foot. The trackers could hear a female's voice shouting in some bizarre language. She seemed to be screeching in cipher, frequencies that defied tonal comfort. The trackers could not quite make out the creature, only a shape, dashes of a dark, lissome beast, desperate. They could hear its panting, and faint cries of terror, and see quicksilver, unblemished feet and hands grappling, trapped, then shimmying effortlessly up a massive podocarp.

"That's it. We got him," said the Russian military officer attendant upon the Indian command. It was Alexi Malevich. There was no anger in his voice, not even a touch of hostility. He was being systematic. This was business.

Two days before he had received confirmation from the Russian Ministry of External Affairs. Permits were in place for him and his team to join Indian military exercises to ensure the successful outcome of the enterprise. Exercises, they called them. In a memo to the Russian Ambassador in Washington, a similar phrasing had been applied, and this was to serve as the model for long-drawn-out diplomatic discussions, were they to become necessary.

The saber-wielding trackers rapidly laid nets and prepared to climb up the tree after the creature, using grappling hooks and seat straps like those employed by telephone company workers. A helicopter was approaching, and there was the loud static of back-and-forth communications between the pilot and ground forces.

Just then the Indians saw several additional creatures moving along a nearby cliff rim. Only their bare feet appeared—feet that would seem human, except that they were so fast, elegant, so honed and crafted to this landscape of vernal steeps. Their ease amid such dense difficulties suggested mountain goat or gazelle. Below the cliffs, the team was working its way up a gigantic 200-foot sequoiadendron. Suddenly the moist air was shattered by the plaintive scream of a woman. Malevich placed his eyes against his spotting scope. He followed the line of embreakment towards that place closest to the top of the tree where the other creature had been confined. He saw a boot, then canvas pants.

"Huh?"

It was a strikingly defiant-looking Caucasian woman clad in queer military regalia.

Malevich cleared beads of sweat from his purview, then blew up the woman's freeze frame on his tracking device.

"Who is she?" he whispered to Jomsom, a backwoodsman extraordinaire assigned to the team from Nepal. Accustomed to hunting down Maoist insurgents up the Kali Gandaki, even across Mustang.

"Don't know."

"Any ideas, anyone?" Malevich asked, turning the monitor so that the Indian lieutenant Singh and others nearby could see the woman's image on digital freeze frame.

Singh, in turn, reported into his walkie-talkie: "We have a complication here. There's a Western woman among them."

The Indians monitoring from Sadiya were baffled

"We're checking in Delhi for the last year of inner-line permits. Don't hurt her, whatever you do." It was the best the mission officer there could suggest.

The individual in the tree was terrified and made strange noises: a combination of music—stringed, harmonic sounds—and powerful shrieks. He was trying to communicate with his friends. The noises were like frantic chimes, or plucked nuances from a small harp worn at the waist, fingers deft and rhythmical. The melodious cadenza was clearly a form of advanced semiotics, language-speak submerged in gutterals unknown to the Indo-European stratum of loquacity. A partly hidden male standing beside the woman threw a long hemp rope to their stranded compatriot from the cliff. The man grabbed hold, paused in panic, but then—encouraged and goaded in the heat of the moment—swung free of the high-standing trunk across the airy gap, managing to pull himself up the rock wall, where he disappeared with the others.

Hidden behind an abutment, the woman shouted down: "Go away! Leave them alone!" Her English was heavily accented. Then they all vanished above.

At the Indian military installation at Sadiya, officials were following the audio via live microwave relay. A certain lieutenant concealed great agitation with a linen handkerchief. The fact he'd been paid off by the Americans to gain access just hours in advance of the Indian assault was potentially problematic.

An operator stroked a key on the computer. The woman's words again: "Go away!"

It was now clear to Malevich that she was Russian, or Russian/American. He grabbed a loudspeaker. "Dobre dyin!" he called. Then tried again: "Who are you? With what university? Which company? What is your name?"

But there was only silence from up above. The woman heard the words and they sank in like nettles of confusion: a language she had nearly forgotten, a man's voice, absolutely startling.

She was panting—too much oxygen. Sweat dripped down her blouse. The clothes were unfamiliar to her, heavy, thick, uncomfortable.

At the cliff location, the incoming chopper set down, picked up Malevich, Jomsom and a half dozen others in their team, and took off in pursuit of their apparent genetic jackpot. Malevich scanned with his spotting scope, Jomsom the same. As the chopper swept across the upper cliffs, which were interspersed with sections of deep forest clinging to the last turf-bits of gravity, the woman and her dozen companions, absolutely at home among the slippery lichen- and fern-washed slopes, dived down. She, too, Malevich noted, wore the strange musical instrument at her waist, the way some tourists carry a Velcro wallet. Motionless now, like tensed rabbits, they hid themselves beneath a cloak of dripping verdance. The chopper circled alongside the cliff over a river. But the winds were now making it dangerous for the Sikorsky to move in any closer. The pilot couldn't control the craft.

Then several of the tribals emerged, running for a new position—and Malevich and team had their first fleeting full-bodied glimpses of their prey.

"Bingo!" Malevich mumbled. "The creatures," as he called them. "My God: will you look at that!"

This was the news Malevich had hoped to report back to his corporate colleagues in New Delhi and Moscow who were following the action. They were the same proto-humans as the corpse recovered from the river.

Seeing them alive gave him a 60-volt charge: not merely because they meant, potentially, enormous profits. Undeniably, these Caucasian freaks were the most gorgeous, erotic, sinewy bipedals he'd ever seen in books, in movies, in cartoons, in life. If the computer model from Mendelyev was correct, they ate something which, from all chemical appearances, made them essentially ageless. He figured he might be gazing upon the most fantastically adapted *Homo sapiens* ever. The ultimate survivors. These were no aliens or primitive beings, but somehow, inconceivably, the future. If their genes could be duplicated—and he was sure they could—they would set the new standard for customized drug therapy, targeted delivery of a substance that could fight any disease, even aging. He scanned in his mind's eye the possibilities—for fashion, advertising, cryogenics, gene selection. If what his firm believed was true, then Malevich was staring eye to eye with some kind of freakish cellular edifice. Immortals, by any other name.

To acquire even a remote glint of their truth, their speed, their grace and athletic prowess, their unbelievable sexiness, anyone who could afford it would pay a fortune for a pill, a vial, a nasal spray, drink, cotton swab, subcutaneous insertion, behind-the-ear patch, any minute fragment of these beings.

But who the hell was *she*? This imaginative link, a flesh-and-blood woman? Malevich conjured possible explanations: moles within the company who'd leaked the project to competitors; the Indians themselves, using a westerner as a front to get an edge on their own partners? Anything was possible.

The Indians fired empty shells at the creatures' feet. It was a typically idiotic response. But one of the bullets ricocheted off the cliff wall, and made a direct hit upon the chopper's fuel tank. A leak burst, started to smoke, and the vehicle veered into a dive. The crew managed to evacuate in the forest below. One of them tossed his cigarette away, a dumb reflex. Seconds later, the vehicle exploded.

The Indians called in backup and reloaded their M-16s—this time with real ammo. But the tribe had again vanished into the upper labyrinth of mountain wall.

"Did you hear something?" Rajibai whispered, the first to awake, turning his ear towards the higher jungle. Groggily, the Commander and Sannazaro roused themselves from troubled sleep. It was not a pleasant awakening, for they were covered in an active patchwork of slimy crawly creatures and the stinging nettles of mala-mujer, known locally as 'bad thing'. Rajibai lay still, not breathing, his head hot with anticipation.

CHAPTER 112
Quadrant X

AT THE DEFENSE Mapping Agency's war room, lodged somewhere beneath the Pentagon, a team of experts had assembled. Days before they'd intercepted Rakshee's email from Sadiya to the laboratory in New Delhi. Data transparency, a corpse gurgling in the afterlife, inexplicabilities. Now the Agency had picked up the flash of the chopper explosion from a remote sensing satellite that surveyed Quadrant X, in northern Arunachal Pradesh, from a KH-12 out of the base at Guam, eight hours' flying time from the Himalayas. Heavy-thinking men sat listening to the recorded gunfire over static, in real time, and viewed detailed images recorded from 55,000 feet off military monitors in the jungle. A zoom that could pick out candlelight on the moon.

Richard Bradley from the Department of Agriculture was certain that a high-stakes commercial taskforce—Indian, and four days ahead of any possible Western intervention—was involved.

"If we don't move fast we'll be out of the running," Bradley advised.

The images scanned across by the KH-12 flyby, then bumped via satellite, revealed bodies matching that of the corpse whose autopsy data had found their way to the Pentagon and on to this assemblage.

Now the debate ensued.

"We believe it to be the first bona fide case of immortal cells working together to accomplish something after the death of a host," said Dr Fenton, a Nobel Laureate in biochemistry from Einstein Medical College in New York, occasional consultant to the Department of Defense. "For how long after?" asked Jacob Riley, Deputy Director of the CIA.

"Without a live sample, no way to know," Fenton replied. "Long enough, possibly, to keep tomatoes and lettuce from spoiling. Which certainly bodes of one more agricultural revolution worldwide. But maybe even longer."

"We hoped you'd say something to that effect."

Bob Nash, head of DMA, introduced field operative Jigme Namgyal. A Tibetan Khampa, 37 years old, he'd gone to Dartmouth as a result of a Ford Foundation grant in China, which was how the CIA recruited him. Jigme was an Olympic athlete, one of the great runners in the world, and a brilliant mountaineer (he had soloed Nuptse). With his Tibetan physique, his lungs larger than most, he had a distinct advantage: he never tired. And he was not remotely conflicted about his strange, frequently violent double-life. He was a Buddhist, and he was smart; he harbored no illusions about the world, self-defense, or right and wrong.

Also present in the group was 74-year-old Dr Catherine Wouverman, the elder stateswoman of Himalayan anthropology, who had been delivered to the war room in her wheelchair. Surrounding them, other permanent DMA staff members manned the monitors and remote sensing apparatuses.

Nash asked that the most recent audio/video be replayed on the large monitor before them. It showed the pursuit by Indian troops of Himalayan natives. But not just any natives. Accompanying that aggressive force were a Russian and a Nepalese.

Catherine Wouverman stared at the intercepted satellite blow-up, its pixels distorted, flattened and elongated. "Who's the woman?" she asked.

Said Nash, "We don't know."

"We've run every search imaginable," Riley added. "As far as our friends in Russian intelligence can tell us—and I must say they've been very friendly since Yeltsin's bail-out by the IMF—she doesn't exist. There is absolutely no record of her anywhere. But that one certainly exists. His name is Alexi Malevich, a former KGB field bully turned capitalist."

"He runs MWPH, a leading pharmaceutical company in the country,"

Bradley said. "They pay their taxes. Very chummy with the Kremlin." Riley went on, "For the record, ten years ago he was also an assassin. Our people tried to apprehend him. Mr Namgyal here knows all about it. He—in fairness, we—missed."

Namgyal sat silently. It had been one of his first operations out of college. He had stared face to face with Alexi Malevich.

Wouverman rolled her chair up to the screen and squinted into the glaring image. "Can you freeze on that scene and blow it up?" she asked, then added what was only too obvious: "The aboriginal is naked."

All eyes blanched upon the staggering visage on the screen. Wouverman continued. "Gentlemen, in 1982 there occurred a chance encounter between four Indo-Tibetan military scouts and a dozen members of some tribe in a region not more than 100 miles due west of that area presently before us on the monitor—all part of a zone known to anthropologists as Quadrant X, for Unexplored. The encounter occurred during a reconnaissance by the Indians to better establish proprietary data for their country in its ongoing dispute over the border area with China. The two nations have never actually resolved their differences regarding the eastern Himalayas, and engaged in limited combat there in 1962. It was a stalemate. I'm sure you all know about that in much greater detail than I. It was January 1982, and these four Indo-Tibetan scouts happened to observe the tribal people eating with their hands in a cave, evidencing no knowledge of fire. The tribals, both men and women, were naked—and this somewhere above 15,000 feet, well past the snowline. It occurred at a place called the Chetak Pass in Arunachal Pradesh."

"How could they live without fire in the snow?" Riley asked, his tone one of an objection, for it defied logic. "Don't all humans know about fire?"

"We thought they did. At least since 1.5 million years ago. That's the earliest known record of a fireplace, and it comes from Chesowanja, in Kenya. But a US Naval officer named Charles Wilkes led a survey of the South Seas in 1836, an expedition financed by the US Congress, and at a place called Fakaafo Island he reported an encounter with aboriginals who also had no knowledge of fire. Nor did they exhibit any sign of illness, or even cavities. The nudity doesn't altogether surprise me. Other tribes are naked in many parts of the world, particularly India. In the Andaman Islands, for example, the Onge, Jarawa and Sentinelese peoples wear no clothes. But they have fire, and they live near the Equator.

"After the Chetak Pass incident, I was invited to India and met with Prime Minister Indira Gandhi and her top military aides. Madame Gandhi herself claimed the discovery to be—and I quote our private discussions—'stunning'. She had studied anthropology as a student in London and knew how significant these people were to the world's cultural map. But the tribe managed to disappear. That was in 1982. Two years later, a naked tree tribe was discovered close to Bhutan's border. We call them the Sulung. But they were quite adept at starting fire—they were probably the reason 20,000 acres burned down in the summer of '88. They were quite comfortable in the Stone Age, and looked nothing like these people here. The problem is, we just can't do follow-up research in Quadrant X."

"Why not?" somebody asked.

Nash, with the expertise of one who'd examined and produced satellite maps of almost every square inch of the planet, said, "We're talking about the last unexplored corner of the Himalayas."

"Probably the most rugged mountain region in the world," Namgyal threw in. "I know about the area," he went on. "All Tibetans do. I've never been there, but I have relatives who passed near during their forced exile from China."

"Even our satellites flake out on us," Nash went on. "Too much rain. Wettest place on Earth. Look at the image. Audio we can pick up, if we have a beacon—in this case, their own transmissions. But visuals are rare. Only when we have a momentary break in the weather and a dedicated satellite tracking the precise region at the exact moment of that window. That might mean ten seconds, or ten minutes. There's just too much cloud cover. This is what we've been able to get so far."

"The fact is, even the Indians won't permit their top people to go anywhere near this region," Wouverman explained. "To my knowledge, no anthropologists have ever gotten into the northernmost sector of Arunachal."

"Then what's she doing there? How did she manage it?" a senior National Security Agency official aired aloud.

"I haven't a clue," replied Wouverman. "I thought we knew just about everyone doing this kind of analysis in the Himalayas. Evidently not."

"We know the Indians have formed a major joint venture with MWPH," said Bradley. "The deal was signed half a year ago, though the news only broke last week amid all those huge protest rallies in Delhi. The country's coming unglued. Half a million Indian farmers staged a sit-down strike for fear of the loss of seed copyright, mostly mustard and maize species."

Wouverman looked to Bob Nash. "Mr Nash, you called me away from a meeting. You called everyone here away from something. Why are we really here?"

Nash looked to Fenton, who helped himself to some fresh early-morning coffee, then summarized. "If they should manage to capture a live tribal member before we do, the implications in terms of genetic research are staggering."

"This is about famine, world famine," Bradley concluded.

"Let's get real, Mr Bradley," said Wouverman, fixing her dour and penetrating gaze at everyone present, forcing discomfort. "This is about money."

Nobody spoke.

Finally Bradley took the helm. "Doctor, at the Department of Agriculture we make no pretenses about what's at stake in world agriculture. I'm sure you can appreciate our dilemma. Most of us in this room have probably rippled the numbers at one time or other, or some coefficients thereof. There's going to be 11 to 12 billion people on the planet. That we know for a fact. What we can't predict—not at all—is whether there will be enough food to go around. And that might be decided by ownership. Who will control growth hormones, genetic assembly lines, seed patents, soil micro-organisms. Rights to the columns of air, moisture, cloud cover. The very genes that make the food, most of which, you can be sure, will be new ones. The very worms in the soil. The genes in those worms. There will be a scrimmage. Trying times. Famine. Somalia is only a distant glimmer of the violence likely to occur as those without the power will go to war, regionally, globally, to feed themselves.

That's human nature."

But Wouverman was focused on something else entirely. The feet, as they appeared on the video screen. A dangling physiological modifier that belied another dimension to her fears. Unspoken, as yet, and well nigh unimaginable.

CHAPTER 113
A Question of Paleontology Beneath the Pentagon

FIRST LIGHT HAD penetrated the eastern Himalayas, where three weary travelers lay frightened in their bags. Rajibai stared motionless at something in the jungle. Its eyes peered back at him. Sannazaro, meanwhile, scratched at countless bites on his head, wrists and ankles—a mid-lice crisis—and the Commander remained curled up, wanting to dream of a million senseless things that had no connection to his present tense. He fixated on—well, for one, Andrea del Verrochio's *Bust of a Young Woman*. On palaces in St Petersburg and picture books by Ludwig Bemelmans. Adolf Dygasinski's *Animal Stories* and soda pop at the Tesuque Market. *The River Book for Boys*, and Jan van Eyck, particularly the landscape looming perfectly behind *The Madonna With Chancellor Rolin*. All this and more, to impede the truth of the hard jungle floor which, only days before, he had yearned for. Now, flat out on his smarting sides, the Crillon in Paris seemed a whole lot more sensible for a sensitive Marigold. And he tried to picture Anna.

Not far away, the Indian military maneuvered to cut off their escaping prey.

"What is it?" the Italian, fully open-eyed, now asked the boy.

"It sounded like an explosion, and gunfire ... Father, wake up!"

Far away, beneath the Pentagon, reconnaissance data flashed intermittently on the large screen before the gathered experts, who continued to formulate a strategy amid the heated rebuttals of Catherine Wouverman. In response to her outrage and cries for restraint and human rights, Dr Fenton mustered an argument that took into account the inevitable trail of moral triage they must all confront, with its conundrums written into the fact of disappearing species and human mortality. He reminded them that America once boasted of 6,000 species of apples and pears. Today, fewer than two dozen. In the 1970s, 80 percent of the domestic corn harvest was wiped out by a corn blight. The cause: lack of hybrid species to rejuvenate the ailing gene pool. Hence, the CIA and Department of Agriculture, along with the National Security Agency, had taken considerable interest in the disposition of the Environmental Protection Agency, and the Federal court system with regard to bioengineering. The CIA had been chiefly responsible for the bulk of genetic data, and the Agency had calculated some very grim scenarios, using the recent food shortages across the African Sahel as a model.

Agriculture was one side of the coin. Disease control, an aging population and the resulting impact on social security were the other.

"It's not just the money, the power and the ownership," said Bradford. "It's American security interests. Our grain supplies, and those of China, are competing on the open market. But people don't just eat grain. It's a fallacy of the Old Order to predicate caloric minimums on staples. There's more to it. When we speak of intellectual copyright we're talking of biological software, and that includes those fragile six inches of topsoil that will make or break the human species in this coming century. Forget oil. Forget SAT, DOS and other computer operating systems. Whoever owns the patents to the genes will have the ability to survive, to propagate, to be remembered, assuming we still have fresh water. The three fundamentals of being human." He then looked to the screen and waxed more like a ruminant: "Simmering in these creatures there is a gene, or multiples of genes, that bode of something extraordinary, something never seen in other people. It may hold the answer to all our problems. It is a soil of its own tenth power."

"There are no easy fixes, Mr Bradford," Wouverman declared. "Human nature being what it is. The sad truth is, that tribe is probably going extinct on the very day we discover it. And all your futurist filigree, philosophical gas and White House shenanigans can only hasten its demise."

"What would you have us do about it?" Bradford pleaded, for show.

Wouverman had no real power. The US Government had already formed its conclusions.

"I don't know. Leave them alone."

"Can't do that," Riley replied."Oh hell, of course you can," Wouverman exploded.

"If a Russian or Indian firm should end up controlling the most important medical or agricultural breakthrough in human history, well, I'd say we might have a problem."

"It would end up on the Internet. And even if they managed to conceal the data, what—you think you're just going to fly in there, walk up to these people and ask them for a blood sample?"

"That's why Jigme is here. He knows mountain tribes," Nash said confidently. "He's one of them."

"Look, I know mountain people," said Wouverman. "I have no doubt that a Tibetan, sensitive to the situation, would stand a far greater chance of, one, getting in, and two, presenting a slightly more gracious introduction. But a Tibetan is no closer to this tribe than the rest of us in terms of culture, genes, mindset or perception. It just can't be done."

"It must, and it will," said Nash. "He's going in. He's going to make contact, get some live samples and get out. Before foreign powers discover the elixir for eternal life and the US is left out in the cold. Get on the same page, Ms Wouverman."

That was a curve ball Wouverman had not expected.

"What we're talking about," declared Fenton, "is who should have the privilege to live forever: them or us."

That took a while to set in. But eventually Wouverman responded.

"Sir, in absence of mortality, we who are the mightiest consumers the planet has ever known are as good as dead. We'll strip bare every last leaf. Gouge out the planet's resources with covetous rage. If we can't die, I have no doubt everything else will. And furthermore, what gave you the right to play God?"

Fenton was not new to such ire. "If you want to speak of medical ethics, fine. I would argue strenuously that if those cells could be cultivated, what do you think we're talking about here? Tomatoes the size of pumpkins—"

"They'll spoil."

"Heifers whose milk production can be quadrupled."

"They'll die."

"We're looking at saving human life. Stopping pain. Inhibiting the aging process. It will be an expensive series of drugs initially. Yes. But, ultimately, it might be the very promise of a second chance for humanity to vindicate itself."

"Or invite the final Holocaust," she inveighed.

"That's not up to scientists to decide. What do you want me to say? That certain cures, and the most revolutionary drugs—penicillin, malarial suppressants, smallpox vaccines—were ethically wrong? I don't believe that. Yes, more people fight more wars; more people go hungry than ever before. That's not my fault, or Jonas Salk's fault. Science is never free of politics or bloodshed or money. You've heard the speech. Study the history of science and you'll discover an equal history of patrons who were kings and senators and bankers. Whether one speaks of Aristotle or Madame Curie. Without them, there would be no iron or glass, no Notre Dame Cathedral or National Park, no microscope, no steam engine, no antibiotic, no rocket ship. Think about it."

"I'm no medical doctor. But I think I have a fairly clear idea why you're all really here," Wouverman snapped angrily. "Securing wheat harvests, my ass. You're all seeing the dollar signs of the century, aren't you?"

"That's not true," Fenton ignited. "Whatever it is these people have, it would be medically irresponsible to ignore it. There are too many hundreds of millions of sick people—and other animals—that might benefit from whatever it is gives them their adaptive edge." He meant to cut off the rancor emergent. "We all want the best for these tribal people, however many there may be of them. But their quantity is trivial, versus six billion of the rest of us. Bottom line: we need a live sample. Computer analysis won't cut it for us."

"These are people," Wouverman reminded them. "They are true innocents. Look at them! They are not commodities. I've seen this happen in country after country." She was incredulous.

Said Riley, "Nobody's talking about exploiting—"

"That's exactly what you're talking about. When freelance oil engineers working for a joint Dutch/Australian firm bushwhacked into the remote Strickland Gorge of Papua New Guinea in the early 1960s, they found a tribe that worshipped the oil. It was their god, known to them as Afek, and they rubbed the oil on their bodies for health and fertility. The explorers sampled the pools, found them too high in sulfur content to be marketable, and promptly trekked back to where they came from. But the trauma to the tribe—the fear of outsiders, and what they might do; the very fact that strangers dipped their vials into the black pools of their god ... Well, that spelled disaster. For the Bimin-Kuskumin, as history remembers them, this was a veritable rape of Afek. Their plants withered thereafter; bees, wasps and bats failed to pollinate; worms in the soil dried out; children died of hunger. Call it hogwash, name it some mythology, but the fact remains the sacred cassowary birds flew off; old people perished from a variety of immune-system breakdowns ... And the 200 members of the tribe were extinct by 1984."

"I'm sure we're all terribly touched," said Nash. "But what's the point?"

"The point," said Wouverman, bristling, "is that there is not one elected official in this room. As I see it, that's a formula for zero accountability to the American public, the European Union, the international community."

"Madame, all due respects," Riley interjected. "But we all have specific marching orders here."

"Which are?"

"National security."

"I would really like to know how our security is threatened by these gentle mountain people."

"Call them gentle, call them whatever you like. It's not their fault, but they are part of something bigger than themselves. They've got genes, and the world is going to sample them sooner or later. It's just a question of who gets there first."

On the screen before them was the skirmish captured in harrowing fragments.

"The twenty-first century is closing in fast," Nash concluded. "None of us can stop it. Emails get sent. Scientists get curious. Corporations get greedy. Consumers have always ignored the source of their products, the back stories, the contexts. Governments have to intercede. Adam Smith, remember? A visible hand."

"Adam Smith was not speaking of armed military touching down by helicopter."

"Helicopters are inevitable," Nash decreed. "I remember when President and Mrs Marcos stepped out of a helicopter on a ridge in Mindanao in 1968 to shake hands with the Stone Age Tasaday."

"We in the anthropological community remember it quite well, thank you," Wouverman charged. "Chewing gum was passed out. That was the trade: their spirit, their dignity, their history, their whole world for a stick of gum. Like giving wampum in exchange for New York. Then the pictures flashed and the wire services did their number. The cave people became instant international celebrities. They went culturally extinct, in other words."

"I see no way around the syndrome," Bob Nash opined.

"Perhaps you're right, Mr Nash," Wouverman replied. "But I'm sure as hell going to try to prevent it."

"You're too late," Dr Fenton observed. "As leery as I may be of mixing science and politics, I must agree with our friend from the CIA." Appealing to her reason, he went on, "Look, in the past decade there have been over 6,000 patented organisms loosed upon Nature. From bacteria to lettuce, from rats to sheep cells. Six thousand newly created beings brought into this world solely for the use of people; whole species owned and operated by corporations that work in secrecy, and who may well be mucking up Mother Nature. The courts haven't seen fit to stop this rampant experimentation in the name of progress, though environmentalists have tried. They lost out to big business, and to scientists like ourselves. I confess: I actually own the patents to nearly a dozen such genes."

"Congratulations. You too are a whore," Wouverman shot back. Fenton took no offense, pausing to offer calm reflection. "It may be. But we've prevented peach mosaic disease in Colorado, and saved hundreds of thousands of acres of hardwoods in Indonesia—where, by the way, the orangutan and several indigenous tribes, as I understand it, are still able to live because of our efforts. Not so bad. Maybe we're not all monsters."

"I'm not arguing with you, Dr Fenton. I'm only asking for empathy.

I've spent a lifetime looking for these people, and now I'm listening to Indian military troops and some Russian assholes shooting at them in order to cash in on their blood type, or proteins, or whatever runs pure as gold in their body. That is any anthropologist's worst nightmare."

"Genetically speaking," Fenton declared, "what makes you so certain they're even people? *Homo sapiens*, I mean?"

A million-odd miles away: "We've got to get out of here!" Sannazaro mumbled frantically. Night, with its escape into storytelling, had vanished. He could not open his eyes but that his urbane sensitivities populated each cranny and the 360 directions with dread.

"Foolish man," Marigold replied, coming around to the awesome miracle of their predicament. The Crillon, he reasoned, would still be there, waiting for them upon their return. But this day was the proverbial butterfly dreaming he was a man; a special day indeed, more like a fitting tribute to his insane sense of invulnerability. All was well. All was good. The best of all possible worlds, and so on and so forth. "This is wilderness! Wonderful, forgiving country, rural roads. Hanging arbor. Haunted jasmine and the sing-along of bumblebees. Never before has my spirit soared so. Look at those cliffs! Hear that river! Are you not in thrall to be so removed? Even New Zealand could not manage such inaccessibility. We are lost, yes. But on Earth, no worry. We have arrived, not gone; been reconstructed, not dissembled. Our bodies belong to the greater good now. And what we think and feel is but one measure of the reciprocity all about us. We are part of this—these Himalayas, these weather changes. Be not spiteful or ashamed; hide no sensation; rule nothing out. Be a prince, give thanks, be kind to yourself. A child here knows best— see his equanimity before the onslaught? The gleam on his temples, a brightness in his eyes? Is that the look of fear or consternation? Of course not. That is the very thing we have sought out. A nimbus whose ring of light contains all salutations. Place yourself in the heart of the Renaissance devotional, with its streaming rays of prayer. At the seat of a French Cistercian monastery, in its architecture of silence. The tranquil comforts at the center of benison, as imagined in the forces of creation whose laying-on of hands has gotten us this far. I swear: nothing can go wrong when man and Nature are one. The outback is my witness—and yours, too. Paris, Normandy, Languedoc comes later."

"Are you quite finished?"

"I suppose so."

"Fine, then I suggest we get the hell out of here. Many a good soul was killed despite such prayer, and countless are the woes that resulted from any laying-on of hands, in case you didn't know. The Hundred Years War, for one."

"No, we must proceed as planned, higher and higher, further and farther, or farther and further— whichever comes first, I never can remember."

Sannazaro shook out this nonsense, refused to listen. Instead, he stirred his aching bones, defused his cramping gut, awakened his rallying cry, ready to move out. But where? And by what means? Leg power? In this backswamp of infernal steeps? He stared in horror at their predicament. It all made sense now: his gullible gumption, the night of little sleep, with its tale of Anna Christov and the predicament of predicaments. His fascination now came back to torment him, for daylight had arrived and the scope of their errors made monstrously manifest. Though neither Rajibai nor Marigold seemed capable of seeing it.

"Am I the only one here who knows when enough is enough? Who sees clearly? Who harbors the normal inventory of human nerve endings? Have you both gone completely mad? You are walking into myth. You will disappear and none of us will be heard from again."

CHAPTER 114
The Anatomy of the Future

CATHERINE WOUVERMAN was enraged but not entirely surprised by Fenton's sinister challenge, his transparent effort to acquit his conscience, and that of those seated around the table with him. If these were 'animals', as he had implied with the royal 'merely', then no discussion of human rights or ethics was necessary, in their minds. There was ample historical precedent for the supposition that some people were less than human, when it suited the oppressor to think so. The most enlightened Greeks were blinded by their own practice of keeping slaves. Two thousand years later, the Pope and his minions would not allow that the Indians of South America were 'human', which meant they could be freely massacred during the years of Catholic expansion in those woods. The policies of genocide and eugenics which characterized much of the nineteenth and twentieth centuries did not give much quarter to those peoples deemed by dictators to be something less than White Male, or Educated, or Citizens, or Aryan, or English Speaking, or Han, or True Blood, or Upper Caste.

"Their morphology is subtly different," Wouverman reluctantly agreed. In fact, the differences were more striking than even she was willing to concede. But she did not want to linger there, for it was obvious fuel for military mongers who would use such differences of physiology to bolster their case for intervention. "But it is their behavior and culture, their dreams, that are important, and about these we have no clue."

"I'm not interested in their dreams. I'm speaking of their blood chemistry, which does not exist among the human race," Fenton said. "It's all a genetic blank. A map without any reference points. This is where we're all on the edge of something unknown, and until we learn more we can only work with a blurred image. I would say that until we can obtain greater clarification, any discussion of ethics should be held in abeyance."

"It will be too late by then," Wouverman decreed, acknowledging what in her mind was painfully obvious. "This just goes to show what little meaning a Nobel Prize has."

Fenton withstood the dig. He didn't disagree with her convictions. But he also saw wisdom in percentages. A small cluster of tribals versus the rest of humankind. The odds, the logic, favored securing that blood type to aid the overwhelming majority. Whether one argued non-violence, ethical protocol or humanitarian principles, this was the wrong time for heroism. Besides, the medical precedents were already well established.

A rabbit's kidneys inserted into a sick child, a dog's bone implanted into a Russian nobleman, transgenic pigs with a gene for human anti-clotting protein, a bull named Herman who carried a gene for lactoferrin, the creation of Dolly from the cell of a ewe's udder, and the first tests on monkey cloning—all were tried and known uses of the technology. Moreover, the first human cloning was on its way and infertile couples were lining up to be among the lucky ones. Governments were in chaos.

There were no ethical protocols, or none universally ascribed to. South Korea and China went left, America veered to the right.

Of course, Fenton also knew that the closest *Homo erectus* discovery thus far had come from a cave near the village of Yuanmou between Chengdu and Kunming—teeth and toes dating to between 500,000 and 600,000 BC. The DNA was dead. It had been tested. Even if it had remained alive, scientists wouldn't have had a clue as to whether the alleles were mixing in a manner that might retain characteristics and mutations from *Homo erectus* as opposed to other, subsequently contaminated DNA. Step it up half a million years. With all the bone fragments in the world, science still didn't know much of anything about the sequence of ancient bases in Neanderthal DNA: whether there had been the slightest preservation of mitochondrial chromosomes even over a period of a few thousand years. That was the technical fact. There were difficulties, to be sure, but Fenton wasn't about to dwell on them.

Bob Nash looked around the room. "We have a mission here. It is in our nation's interest to control the game, rather than be controlled by it. I have orders that supersede consensus in this room. Frankly, Dr Wouverman, you are the only detractor. Now I respect your views as a paleontologist, I'm sure we all do, but the fact is, we are going to get a man in there."

"We can blow that up, sir," a computer operator called, taking as his cue an incoming video signal from the high-altitude aircraft. "We have a video window."

The image was enhanced, five times, 25 times, all the way to 600 times in magnitude ... until the eyes of a terrified being, stranded high in a tree, stared back at those in the darkened war room.

"Can you cut out the wobble?"

The operator evened out the picture, cleansing it of much grain, enhancing contrasts, trying different backdrops and shadowing. Finally, it was there, feebly peering across the fragments and ouija board of bizarre probabilities, of a civilization without precedent gazing directly at them. Wouverman put her glasses back on, resolved to cutting her losses and making the best of an impossible situation. She examined the details— facts that were, to her, no different from the discovery of a new galaxy, or prime number, or primate species. But of a magnitude that infiltrated the emotions. Her entire career was devoted to this moment. As a young paleontologist she had specialized in all the bones of Choukoutien Man, and earlier *Australopithecines*, making a name for herself by her ability to instantly recognize million-year-old distinguishing characteristics, however imperceptible or ambiguous, that would take others in her field weeks, even months, to sort out.

"The jaw is different, and the forehead. But it is not prognathic. The brain is large, perhaps 3,000 cubic centimeters. But fully in proportion with the body."

"Translation?" Bradford asked.

"Your brain, Mr Bradford, I would guess to be around 1,600 ccs, normal for inside the Beltway. Neanderthals were two thousanders, and were, no doubt, more crafty than us. Smart in directions we don't understand."

"What do you mean?" asked another.

"I suspect they suffered from no depression whatsoever, until the very end, when they knew they were going out as a species. There is a remnant gene of the Neanderthal that survives among a few hundred descendants living on the Canary Islands, and they still show statistically high IQs as a population."

"The size of the cranium is no indication of IQ , is it?" asked Riley. "One usually impacts upon the other."

"The brontosaurus had a pea-sized brain," Fenton admonished. "Relative to its size, yes. But the brontosaurus was also extremely advanced neurologically, as can be inferred from its dietary habits and behavior. Similarly, the ants, sea slugs, parrots, pigeons, crows, bees and yellow jackets have small brains relative to their weight, but are among the most sensitive creatures we know anything about. Short- and long-term memories, the ability to formulate mirror images of the surrounding terrain in their minds—images that are crisscrossed with information, time and space coordinates. Mind. That is the key, even in a gnat, based upon observations of their flocking behavior. But the point is more emphatic when we're speaking of a human brain that is 3,000 cubic centimeters. That's a complicated organ, a hologram within a hologram. Blue whales and Aristotle, Bach and Beethoven, elephants and Picasso, Leonardo da Vinci and Queen Elizabeth I: they were all 1,850 cc'ers.

You figure it out."

"If they're so smart, and they're the same tribe you referred to from that 1982 encounter, why haven't they discovered fire yet? Or clothes?" Bradford asked.

"That's not a function of intelligence, but of need. I would reverse the question if I were you. What do they know that we don't know which has allowed them to dispense with fire and with clothes? I believe that is a question of lasting relevance." She moved even closer to the monitor.

"Look at their feet. Can you blow it up any more?"

The feet were extended 700 times.

Wouverman gazed at the blue toenails. Impossible to tell whether they'd been painted or were that color naturally, which would suggest little if any blood at their extremities—a bodily response, perhaps, to the altitude; a means of regulating core temperature without necessarily sacrificing the fingers and toes. She'd never seen such adaptation. But the feet themselves were even more astonishing.

"Remind you of anything?" she challenged. The image could not have yielded a more uncommon resemblance. "Cloven hoof. Mountain goat. Mountain sheep. Count the toes."

"One, two, three ... twelve. Twelve toes."

"Connected at the middle joint. Now look at their waists—there, stop the image."

"Freeze frame," Nash ordered. "Blow it up."

"If I'm not mistaken, that man has three testicles," Wouverman said, gazing intently, not a little excited by the implications.

"Yes. That was in the report from the Indians," Fenton admitted. "What about those instruments?"

"Culture. Advanced culture. The only other example of wearing an instrument at the waist, that I know of, comes from the Namibian Mesolithic, about 5,000 years ago—a single cave painting, the quality and sophistication of the ancient Greek sculptor Praxiteles. And look at the length of the appendages. I have seen such proportions only in Burundi."

But there were 100 such pronounced details, a bewildering grammar of new body unconnected to any known or equivalent physiognomy.

"My team back at Yale would need time to study them," Wouverman said. "But we already know quite a few things about human evolution in the Himalayas."

Namgyal, who had sensed the magnitude of what lay in store for him, listened carefully as Wouverman detailed certain other recent findings. Nobody around the table seemed eager to cut her off, even with a live skirmish occurring on the monitor right before them, demanding other immediate discussion and determinations. Perhaps it was because she was the only female in the party, or the only person physically challenged. Or perhaps it was because what she had to say was so remarkable that not even the hardest, most stubborn bureaucrat could deny the power over the imagination of the region, the tribe, the unique geographical and environmental aura surrounding them. And she knew more about them than anyone else in the world.

She went on, hurried, angry, frightened. Her voice quavered, for this was the one obsession in her life; she was seeing something she believed to be the consummation of her dreams. Possibly the most remarkable scientific discovery of the century. And it threatened to be wiped out by any number of military and commercial prospects. It did not take a scientist to pick up on the bold-faced agendas jockeying in the darkly demonic room. Unquestioning egos vying for power, money, influence or fame.

She began: "Four mandibular fragments were found some years ago in the Pondaung Hills of northern Burma—Myanmar. They belonged to a form of monkey very similar to today's Burmese gibbon. This region—which pilots, I believe, refer to as the Golden Triangle—has recently been hailed as the birthplace of human beings, not Africa, not Australia. Two colleagues of mine at the University of Maryland have delineated the genetics. While their conclusions are still debated, there is no doubting the genetic tree in Asia which includes baboons, orangutans and *Homo sapiens*. Gorillas and chimpanzees originated in Africa—not East Africa, but northern Mali, the sub-Sahara, where eight chimps still walk bipedally. They may already be gone. The locals were killing them for food. But it's quite possible that our direct ancestors came from the eastern Himalayas. You can see why from that video. Look how dense the foliage is. Can you imagine the number of edible fruit species?

"While older *Australopithecines*—some of the earliest hominids—have been found throughout Africa, they were not in the main lineage to man, but probably unsuccessful evolutionary attempts. None of their descendants survived. But those that grew up among the Himalayas suggest a direct line. In 1981 an upper molar of *Ramapithecus punjabicus*, 11 million years old, was discovered in a cave of south central Nepal. Very likely a direct descendant. A year later, research in the Siwalik Hills of Pakistan confirmed the existence of orangutans 14 million years ago—*Sivapithecus*, once again our very ancestors. And of course the recent findings from China of 800,000-year-old tools also suggest the Asian connection."

"What about Arunachal Pradesh?" Fenton queried.

"The data just isn't there. As has already been pointed out, such environments are tough on members of my profession, not to mention fossils. I know. Before my accident, I spent ten years in the trenches. The oldest known remains from the area come from northern Assam, a bit to the south, and date to the third millennium BC."

"Half the cities of India are more ancient," said Nash, who had been regularly to the subcontinent.

"Of course. Rain accelerates bone degradation. Add a few floods, or avalanches, and there's no trace. Further compounding our ignorance is the fact that there has been but one paleontological survey of Arunachal, and that was in the late 1970s, carried out by the Calcutta Government Survey and an anthropologist at Dibrugarh University. The research was confined to the lowlands and mid-latitudes. No work was done at higher elevations. If I'm not mistaken, the highest points in northern Arunachal exceed 23,000 feet."

"If you include Namche Barwa and Gyala Peri, two of the highest unclimbed mountains in the world, the altitudes exceed 25,000 feet," Namgyal pointed out.

"One begins to grasp the difficulties," Wouverman said, trying hard to impress those seated around the table with the extraordinary importance of this discovery. "As I indicated, nobody has gotten in. Those two mountains are separated by the deepest canyon in the world, and to my knowledge it remains unexplored. Perhaps Mr Namgyal knows differently?"

"It is incredibly wild in there," Namgyal confirmed. "But not beyond reach. A kayak team with *National Geographic* has been down part of the gorge. But none of the tributaries. And by no means the entire canyon. Most remains a mystery. A parachute and the appropriate survival provisions, a good lay of the land, boots that breathe, a week of wolf's sleep, a large bottle boasting of John Barleycorn and the odd mantra—"

He eyed Nash, who nodded a general confirmation before pulling images for his file.

CHAPTER 115
A History of Inaccessibility

JIGME NAMGYAL would be dropped into Arunachal Pradesh, and Wouverman knew that nothing she could say or do would prevent the transgression. Her heart, her enormous expertise, could not impede the menace of big business and geopolitics. But neither was she defeated. Now she countered the inevitable with frantic strategy: how best to affect the thinking of those around her; to overwhelm bureaucrats with the urgent music of delicate cultural nuances. She was appalled by what she had seen, returning to viewing its distorted freeze-frame time and again. And she was puzzled by the tribe's geographical position.

If they were the same group that had been confronted from a distance in 1982 (the observers at the Chetak Pass were, by their own admission, 400 feet away), why were they at so low an altitude now? Had they been chased from above? At what altitudes did they dwell? How many were left? Were they in trouble, perhaps nutritionally? What international instruments of law could be used to force the Indian military to cease harassing them?

But Wouverman was also conflicted. In spite of her objections, she too wanted—desperately so—to learn more about the tribe. A piece of that corpse or, better yet, live body specimens might enable her to examine nucleic acid sequences in the cellular DNA, which, in turn, could offer proof of lineage in much the manner of a leopard seal's tooth, or a silver spruce's rings: biological imprints that offered up to the knowing eye a genetic timeline. With blood and tissue samples, even hair follicles, from a live individual, her team might well be able to positively age the tribe, and to determine whether they constituted a new line, a new species of human.

For years there had been speculation that a new kind of being existed. Recent Yeti data from various regions certainly argued for some such species. The Mongolians termed him al-mass, the Kazaks ksy-gyik, the Chinese Yeh ren. And the Tibetans had a host of names for what they knew to be real: mu rgod, lung-gum, gangs-mi, or mi bom po. It was the Nepalese Sherpa who called him Yeti, meaning 'naked glacier man', or lord of the mountain. Chinese scientists from Wu Han University, with whom Wouverman had been in touch, had been searching for him in Hubei Province along the nearly 1,500-mile-long Shen Nong escarpment where Yeh ren footprints had been found leading into caves more than half a mile deep.

But in her opinion it was northern Arunachal Pradesh, and the lap of the bend of the Brahmaputra, or Tsangpo, on the Chinese side, that offered the most remarkable possibilities for discovering a new primate species. A careful profile of genetic data in the Himalayas suggested that there was but one vicinity capable of harboring this last unknown human—and it was there before them. Quadrant X had eluded not only most satellite scrutiny but exploration as well. Only five known expeditions had ever attempted the gorge, three of them around the turn of the century, two of those British, one Russian. The Russians disappeared, all presumed dead. The British subsequently sent a local guide, Kintup, traveling as a Buddhist pilgrim, into those portions of the upper gorge never before reached. Kintup found a high waterfall up one of countless tributaries. He did not specify just how high it was, or in which side canyon. British botanist Francis Kingdon-Ward and his Scottish photographer friend Lord Cawdor explored all but four miles of the gorge proper, before they too were turned back by the steepness of the canyon walls and the bad weather. Cawdor's images were archived at the Royal Geographic Society in London. They revealed glimpses of porters in loincloths hanging upside down on ropes over raging tributaries or scrambling across artificial ladders affixed to the cliffs. But the explorers never found what they were looking for.

Eighty years later, a small Italian group attempted to retrace Ward and Cawdor's expedition, and published a glossy photographic book of their travails, but they too found a complete negotiation of the gorge impossible.

Then, in November 1998, a team of Tibetan scholars from the US and Nepal, helped along by eight Sherpas and porters, completed a partial descent of the canyon from a starting point in China. During their 17-day expedition they found a 100-foot waterfall, which they measured with laser range-finders, and 4,000-foot cliffs. But there was no way they could penetrate the countless side canyons that were cloaked in impassable hemlock and rhododendron, and teeming with tens of thousands of other species, many probably unknown to science. The exploration community thought that was the end of it, and the world press exploded with the flash: "The Discovery of Shangri-La". But that was a broad term, and meaningless:

30 seconds of nightly news, a headline that glossed over thousands of square miles of impossible terrain as yet unseen by human eyes.

Tibetans had always thought of the entire region as Shangri-La, or Pemakod. Namgyal described to the group how a former Canadian Ambassador to Nepal had reported that he had been approached by a middle-aged Tibetan refugee in Paris who confirmed that parts of Pemakod had provided an escape route for Tibetans fleeing the Chinese throughout the 1950s. But the region comprised literally hundreds of canyons. There was no way to know where individual parties of refugees actually went. Most sought refuge elsewhere, via lower passes into Nepal, and then down into northwestern India.

In the early 1980s, a satellite intelligence group confirmed with high resolution part of the area in question, possibly the canyon Kintup had found in 1911. It showed remarkable cliff formations 15,000 feet high—three Grand Canyons stacked one atop the other—perpetually covered in shadow because of the narrowness of the gaps and the huge amount of precipitation. With over 1,000 inches of rain per year, and abundant snowfall, this inner sanctum harbored a bewildering congestion of declinations. All this in an area known, since the work in the 1930s and '40s of German anthropologists, to support at least 20 major tribes and 70 sub-tribes spread out across the Himalayan jungles. Other than such quasi-assimilated groups as the Nishi, Adi, Mishmi, Abhors and Dafla, most of the smaller tribes were just suppositions by anthropologists. Extrapolations of normal demographic diffusion coefficients.

As for the Indian scientist who had made a partial survey of the region, his work was confined far to the south. Every square inch of territory to its north was described on Indian maps as "Unexplored".

And as for the river which wound its thunderous way through that gorge, fragmentary satellite images—picking up the head and tail, though little in between—showed it to descend from nearly 20,000 feet to 2,000 feet in less than 100 miles, making it the sheerest, most voluminous cascade in the world. No other major river was even close to matching its ferocity. Energy experts had speculated that the mouths of the Yangtze and Amazon put out less electrical potential per square cubic meter of flow than the Brahmaputra—and that was on a level playing field. Add a descent rate of nearly 180 vertical feet per mile of flow, then multiply that conundrum by the incalculable force inherent to the explosive pressure from the narrowness of the canyon walls—electrons in water heating up other electrons, the mass colliding with the inertia of granite, an alchemy that triggered unknown molecular reactions—and you were speaking of a river that behaved more like a continuous detonation. Enough pressure in that thunder to squeeze sunlight into darkness. To reshape the physics of nature in a chasm a mere 40 feet across. To splinter shadow, and lay encumbering night upon the mountain wall.

"Overlay a map," said Nash.

All observed several French SPOT and Landsat resolutions superimposed on the monitor. Adjoining the mainframe screen were other, smaller monitors carrying the live KH-12 data and the video intercepts from the now obscured live action on the ground. Audible were augmented snippets of the strange and terrible encounter—the Russian's voice, the whispering Indians, post-modernist rifle fire, weird pangs punctuating distorted glances, distress signals, creatures on the run, a woman's frantic voice—"Go away!"—and the screams of the occupants of the chopper as it went down, then the explosion.

Wouverman was anxious to leave the claustrophobia of the Pentagon and this room where horrible men toyed with lives. She summarized her concerns: "Gentlemen, it is my longtime conviction, and that of many colleagues, that there is a species in the eastern Himalayas—and we may be looking at them—that are new to the human bloodline. They belong to no known evolutionary path. Forget the missing link. These people show no precursor whatsoever, no family tree, no genetic markers. None of the earlier peoples, be they *Homo erectus*, Choukoutien, Cro-Magnon, Neanderthal or even Stone Age, offers us any insight. For these tribals of Quadrant X are neither the present nor past."

"Then what are they?"

"Some formidable successor species," she said quietly. Then, turning to direct her conclusions smack into the burning azure eyes of the Tibetan, she declared, "The most magnificently adapted species ever known to primate evolution. The future, if we will permit it. That is your choice, young man. If they die out, we may all die out."

The words, the concept, affected them all—how could they not? But almost instantly their impatience, a fever to be in on the action, triumphed, superseding any mystical ruminations.

Suddenly, there was a break in the static on the screen. The sound of engines. Over the intercom, the co-pilot of the KH-12 could be heard: "Are you getting that? It's an Indian military convoy. We read about 30 vehicles."

The convoy, seen days earlier leaving Sadiya, had grown in size, and had moved 80 miles to the north on monsoon-demolished mud roads. There was no question that the Indian Government was providing backup for an all-out attempt to capture one of the creatures.

Just as suddenly as it had appeared, the audio and video signal blanked.

The broadband window, as it was called, had gone out. An image as faded as the impression of Christ on St Veronica's sudarium, its meaning, haloed in darkened devotion, so obscured that to Wouverman it seemed nothing short of the spiritual—although to the others it was simply an injunction to conquer and get in there. The KH-12, traveling at 547 mph in circles over the rain-socked Asiatic mountain range, had lost its visual window of time, a duration defined by the density and type of cloud cover, except for one odd electronic beacon, a universal frequency used in the manner of an SOS or aerial reconnaissance rescue signal. It was coming in 30-second spurts from a dark spot on the electronic map, 12 and a half miles due north of the last identified position of the Indian convoy.

"We're picking up a separate signal," the co-pilot said. "Somebody else is in there too."

This nobody expected. Nash looked at Namgyal. "Get your gear together. On the double, soldier."

CHAPTER 116
Goldfinch in a Lilac Tree

NAMGYAL'S PACK was outfitted with the bioassay equipment necessary to sample plants in the immediate vicinity of the tribe—as many and as diverse as possible, using syringes to extract fluids. He was also to make a similar withdrawal of blood, hair, urine and epidermal samples from a male and female of the tribe itself.

He'd have an open channel to a dedicated satellite, with additional relay capacity to and from the KH-12 overhead, from which he was to be ejected. Wherever the Russians moved, he would know it, and it was thus hoped that he might second-guess their travel plans and reach the tribe before them, within a few days. The time sensitivity of his mission was critical. For Namgyal to get in, find the tribe, take the samples and get out over the northern passes, via Lhasa, where exit logistics would be handled by an agent in place—and all before the Russians could pull off their own handiwork—was terribly ambitious, and Nash reminded Namgyal, in the most delicate of terms, that if there was a hostile encounter with the Indians, or Russians, or Chinese, or the tribe itself, he was to use his discretion and weapons appropriately. But he'd be on his own. That might sound terribly dated, but some things didn't change.

Namgyal reassured Nash, and tried to appease Wouverman.

"I'm Tibetan, remember. Buddhism teaches non-violence."

"I know," Wouverman replied. But she also knew that the Khampas, the traditional protectors of the Dalai Lama, were deemed the bravest but most dangerous fighters in all of the Himalayas.

Late in the night Namgyal arrived by chopper at an Air Force base outside Washington, and packed his 60 pounds or so of gear—North Face big wall polyester stretch pants; a woolen plaid Pendleton shirt beneath a Gortex coverlet to ward off wind and rain; Italian single boots; a Primus, snowsealed and fitted with mini-crampons; dried fruit and protein bars, and all the medical sampling gear; a 200-foot 9mm Perlon rope; slings; carabiners; an electric hand-sized pulley; and a sizable contingent of miniaturized weapons, explosives, even a rocket launcher, as well as the latest satellite gear. He helped himself to a mercury-laced bath, then suited up in triple-mylar flight leggings and jacket.

The flight would take about ten hours. The KH-12 flew with a 3,200-mile range, extended by an added wing tank, which slowed it down, of course. It also had a midair refueling cap, but that would not come into play in this mission. It was an all-purpose EW (electronic warfare) bird, modified after the best of the Lockheed C-140 JetStars, with three feet resolution, an improvement over that of the KH-8. During his approach time Namgyal drank plenty of high-protein water and ate a considerable flood of fruit. An hour before the drop point, he injected his thigh muscle with an epinephrine compound.

It was night time in Arunachal when the Tibetan's unmarked aircraft flew over at 59,000 feet. Up there, of course, the stars were always shining, even through the thin veil of stratospheric cirronimbus. The co-pilot announced that they were now ready to slow down to Mach 1.18, and then to 200 nautical miles. Namgyal would have a 45-second window. He was seated in a stealth capsule, known as HAHO (High Altitude High Opening), which kept the rest of the aircraft from depressurizing. HAHOs were undetectable, and totally protected against the minus 55 temperatures at that altitude. Once out, the speed would hit him like a locomotive. In army terms, he'd be hauling-assing.

Twenty minutes before the drop, he affixed his oxygen mask and started breathing the 100 percent pure O2. Slowly, easily, steadily. He checked his helmet, goggles and harness, making sure to keep his crotch free of any wrinkles and the metal buckle.

"Get ready," the co-pilot announced into his headset.

The overhead UV-protected hatches were opened. The high twine of the engines—160 decibels—ground like a diamond bit into Namgyal's ears, and the wind roared grotesquely all around him.

"You'll be heading through a storm at 28,000 feet. Some gnarly clouds.

Watch out for lightning. The night is yours, sir," the co-pilot shouted over the din, signing off.

Namgyal felt the detonation as his seat exploded, and he was out into the cosmos, flying upwards at 33 feet per second, the equivalent to the senses of a million miles an hour. He was alone in space, a solitary flying object somewhere between convective energy forces, Coriolis deflection, horizontal and angular velocities, and the earth's rotation as experienced in the jet stream. The brain that time forgot. His eyes were closed. He hung not limp but firm, fighting off the pressures assaulting him of a high-altitude free fall of nearly 35,000 feet. The normal skydive was around 4,000 feet from an altitude of 9,000. Namgyal, however, would dive for five miles—nearly five minutes' worth. The parachute was blue/gray in color, square cut, containing computer chips in the box that—in the event he lost the wherewithal to open the chute himself—automatically triggered its opening at 2,000 feet above the highest, radar-detected point on earth.

At terminal velocity, Namgyal was a mere 100 seconds from the summit of Mount Everest, 66 seconds from the summit of Namche Barwa. As he hurtled downwards, he stared dead ahead at the storm. Lightning bolts were streaking the sky two miles below, and the tops of the electrical discharges were like neon squiggles, blurred one-million-volt signatures of cobalt amperage, and he was heading right into it.

The Tibetan sucked in his stomach and twisted his upper torso to guide his body clear of the storm to any extent possible. He was sliding through space horizontally now. At 115 miles per hour (his true speed), any wind foil was directional. He extended both arms towards the left and oriented his body accordingly. Now he flashed past the black swirling cumulus storm clouds, borne along the very cusp of electrical discharges. The largest number of lightning flashes on Earth occur in Arunachal Pradesh. He hurtled through walls of 10 million watts, turned shimmering hue of platinum, a bullet traveling encased in aureoles, hazarding no thought, leaving no clue. Adroit gyrations of the birth of a star, fighting gravity with blackout speed.

Within 20 seconds he was below the meteorological turmoil, safely plunging towards the eerie patchwork of glacier and jungle arrayed like so many somber hints of a puzzle on the fast-approaching surface of the Earth.

There, somewhere, in the utter confusion of dense cover, three world-wandering misfits, by turns miserable, excited, argumentative, unquenchable, lay adrift in their wet sleeping bags, too exhausted to scratch any longer at bugs. Their one consolation was Sannazaro's cologne, which tended by some inadvertent miracle to repel the leeches, though not the fire ants. They had wandered upwards for an entire day, struggling like old, arthritic pieces of driftwood through the ferocious back country. At every turn one complaint led to another. Sannazaro insisted he saw a tiger. Marigold a python. Rajibai a ghost. First it was too cold, then too hot. Sannazaro had a broken back, Marigold the flu. Then one insisted on going left, the other right. Every one step forward resulted in three in the other direction. They quarreled, insulted and mocked each other. Under these circumstances any shred of manly dignity was the first thing to disintegrate. Rajibai marveled at the untold depths of the adults' cantankerousness, which merely served to bring his laughter to the surface when, for example, his father walked headlong into a tree, and Sannazaro fell off a slope and rolled 100 hard-going yards into a bear burrow filled with enormous scat.

At a certain point the party came to a standstill. The Commander and his Squire were not speaking to each other. The world had ended for them. Darkness prevailed. There was no longer any point going forward, backward, up, down, sideways or in a semicircular manner. Nothing could calm their madly pumping hearts or addled brains. No compass could revive their good behavior or self-confidence.

And so the boy carried on for all three of them, setting a noble example of poetry and delight. For Rajibai, these were first-time encounters with real mountains, jungle, wildness. After the life he'd led in the galling slums, every sight and sound was to him a revelation. To the Italian, such pleasure simply seemed to mirror his own colossal penchant for -ities—gullibility, stupidity, masochisity and insanity. But for the Commander, whose only intent was the natural integrity of the world, Rajibai's good humor was a lesson. He had gotten them into this mess without the slightest hesitation. Now he must not dither or falter any longer. No more angry fluctuations in response to his silly Squire. No more overheated dialogue or wavering footsteps. He had once made a commitment in a jail cell, based upon nothing more than the sole mention of a moa. Now they stood in the dire vortex of the Himalayas because he had overheard some Russians from a bathroom. This was how Mr Marigold operated. Replies of impulse.

Actions devoted to split-second decisions. An entire philosophy built over the course of reactions. Spurning calm consideration and restraint, he must now commit to a no-first-hesitate policy, a strikeline as big as his mouth and bountiful as his purse. Enough of this bickering and barking. Fears were senseless, accomplished nothing. His son proved that. Around each blind corner he showed the way. Now he must simply follow the boy's scampering footsteps and give not an inch to that whining back-pedaling yelp which emanated from his lackey.

Of course, he had no idea how to pull off whatever it was he planned to accomplish; he had no sense of the geography, the tribal complexity, his older companion's infirmity. Everything he trusted to fate, which was showing a complicated face. They were lost, tired and—in spite of appearances—depressed.

Far above, ice gathered on Namgyal's mylar suit as he hurtled through the high thin air towards earth. He plummeted into the final cloud layer, 2,000 feet above forest, then slowed to float down like Tinkerbell. His helmet was outfitted with an infrared computerized topography program which enabled him to guide himself out of harm's way. He landed in a high fir tree on a mountain ridge, dangled amid spiders' webs and astonished baby birds, cut his cords with a knife fitted in a sleeve in his leggings, and climbed down. Then he pulled in his chute and buried the lot. He took a compass reading; his altimeter showed 8,400 feet, the temperature was a balmy 42 degrees. Barometer reading, moisture content, distance to the nearest microwave station, current alien satellites within range likely to pick up transmissions—all this data was at his disposal on his wrist. A low pressure cell was building.

Namgyal tightened his pack, plucked a leech off himself with his knife, put it into his mouth with the platinum tip of the dazzlingly sharp implement, and ate it alive. He quite fancied the taste of leeches, which were like candied caramel. As a Buddhist, he believed his consumption of the leech insured that the little creature would be reborn into a better life.

Then he started into the deeper woods for cover. Almost at once, with his red-beamed headlight and lightning-rod senses, he knelt down and recognized the signs of a tribe. He heard the howls of the hoolock gibbons in the high canopy of banyan, peepal, asoka and bela. A huge Indian bustard flew overhead with its noisy seven-foot wingspan. Somewhere within a few miles a lesser florican cried for its mate. He moved on the alert for wild mithun or buffalo, pygmy hogs, rhinos and clouded leopards, all inhabitants of this zone. He studied the sky and heard faintly the sound of a passing jet making slow invisible circles until refueling time.

He checked for ants or snake nests, then made a bivouac. Blood vessels had burst near his groin. His chest was in pain. The upper air temperature was minus 120 degrees, if you included the wind-chill factor. He would sleep for a few hours. He set his watch for a 4 a.m. wake-up call.

Elsewhere, in a forest primeval, millions of years removed from silly points of view in places called Washington, Moscow and Beijing, Mr Marigold lurched up, alert to an untoward sound. It was not clear. A mussy contagion of half-sleep mentored by confusion and sautéed with apprehension. Motionless, the Commander was alert to the tangible sense of approaching footsteps and whispers. No time to take a decision.

They were under attack.

The assailants were all males, dark-skinned and naked, though one wore a Nike-emblazoned baseball cap that lent a certain charm to the assault. They prodded him with sharp points, motioned all three to rise up, and began rifling through their packs with their long spears. To Marigold it was as if a marvelous dream was overtaking them.

Now he stood. "Pack your bags quickly, Son," he whispered to Rajibai. "Get your pack on." But Rajibai was transfixed, unable to move, staring with his puckish wide-open mouth. For all of his quickly established sophistications, he was, after all, a little boy, and he'd never seen people like this in Forlorn, or anywhere else. The tribals gawked back at the boy with a mixture of amazement and appetite.

"Bon giorno!" Sannazaro clumsily declared, smiling. "Croissant?" With a sudden turn of whimsy, of aggression moderated by surprise, the assailants seemed to be motioning the trio to leave, and quickly. There was no way to be absolutely certain. The turns of event—malice that signaled pleasure, curiosity whose outer expression was more akin to hatred, joy meaning sadness, anger not unlike the solace of raindrops ... These people conveyed opposites, and the clock was ticking: one wrong gesture and all would explode.

"I think they're telling us to run," the Commander advised weakly. "All the way to Detroit."

"What makes you think that?" Sannazaro asked.

"I just have a feeling."

"Then run!" the Italian erupted, able to decipher one part of particular trouble out of a million maelstroms.

Now Marigold grabbed the boy's hand, and the three of them blasted off. As they fumbled and sped, Mr Marigold was reaching for his semi-automatic, a weapon he'd never used but whose cold galvanized grip felt suddenly comforting. The feeling was short-lived. The last thing he remembered as the mechanism fired was his own flight; a sense of fleeing from those strong gleaming bodies, of strange beautifully painted faces, bellies decorated with stripes and dots, gold dabbed on the tips of their penises.

But it was not the gun that had gone off.

Instantly he, then Sannazaro, were swept up at least 22 feet into the air. The boy kept running, however, somehow spared the randomness of the trap. He hid in the jungle, eyes indistinguishable from so many millions of ripe berries—salal, spiny hopsage, red osier, golden currant—and bright leaves—black mustard, stinging nettle—illuminated in the early-morning light. He found himself in a tall lilac bush, as big as a tree, not inches from a gossipy goldfinch. The two of them spoke about the weather. "That's good, but no egg roll," Marigold muttered.

His leg was injured, the pain shooting up and down the veins and muscle. The sudden lurch had strained tendons, pulled other fibers, left him a wiggling cripple. Upside down, he stared into the eyes of a tiger, similarly trapped and upside down. It had been caught by its rear right paw. The feline, with waning energy, lashed out spastically at Marigold, then at Sannazaro, its tired claws narrowly missing the Italian's face.

"Once I was happily retired, cultivating my garden, good memories behind me, wonderful hopes ahead. Nothing to disrupt my contentment. Then I met my neighbor, and now look at me," lamented the lowly Squire.

The force of the strike pushed the tiger in a direct pendulum swing into Marigold, who braced the gun in his trembling hand. Sannazaro saw what had to be done: he deliberately threw himself towards the haggard feline—"Good kitty kitty"—pushing off the chest of the beast and preventing the inevitable head strike to the Commander. The cat lashed out at Sannazaro's left forearm, narrowly missing the bone but leaving a swathe of ripped flesh. The force of it threw the benumbed Governor, as Marigold still sometimes referred to him to keep up his good humor, into the path of a suspended musk deer caught like a dozen others that hung kicking in a pitiful gallery of slow writhing death and forest cries. All this dangling lamentation and peril the poor Rajibai watched in horror from his hiding place beside the sweetly preening goldfinch.

The tribals were approaching. This had been their strategy: to rope them into the traps. But with the missing boy—their cannibal fantasy—there would be more trouble. In such generous circumstances there was no subtlety, only stabs in the back; pugilism played out in the inferno of gestures and rows. Hostility which looked like laughter. Laughter, tears. Tears, the doom to all that moved. Reflected backwards.

CHAPTER 117
At the Entrance to the Gorge of No Return

WITH HIS FINAL STROKE of good sense, waning breath blearing into ether, depleted strength and bankrupt thought, Sannazaro clung to the deer's belly. His arms, aspiring to be pincers, were but poor jelly; his legs dangled Harold Lloyd-like. It was either make the move, or swing right back into the tiger. The deer's legs, too, struck out furiously in order to keep clear of the cat, auguring less than a pretty sight once the Italian was hanging on to him.

"Move away!" Marigold screamed, trying to avoid contact with a Himalayan wolverine caught in an adjacent dangling snare. His situation was as grim as at any moment in the whole history of inter-species relationships.

With blood pouring into his beaver-dam eyes, the Commander could dimly make out the approaching hunters, their spears and blowguns at the ready. His semi-automatic was partly raised, though untrained on any one recipient because his left hand was holding the right hand in an effort to control the shakes. Sannazaro's eyes were running, his facial muscles in a spasm. Marigold took flimsy aim: there were eight hunters to contend with. Or was it eleven? Or should he shoot the tiger? With only 1,000 left in India? Not on his life. On the other hand, there was only one Sannazaro. Dilemma. The wolverine, an endangered species in Delaware? Never. The hunters? How many bullets did he have? He had no idea. How many did guns contain? Was the safety released? Where was the cross-hair? Did he have the right trigger? Was he upside down, was the gun rightside up? Where did his dreams end and the day begin? Should he laugh, cry, be aggressive, or do nothing? Was he supposed to set an example? Where was his son? What if these hunters *were* cannibals? Would it not be better to let them have their way with two adults, and thus quench their appetites? Or was the tribe looking to the boy for dessert? All these awful unclinched pearls of candor shot through the hole in his dike.

"How many bullets are in here?" he cried out to the Governor.

"Five? A hundred? I don't know. But watch where you're pointing it, for godsakes!"

As the tribals tiptoed through the underbrush, and Marigold's molasses-drenched pancake for a cranium spun further and further out of control, seizing upon one option, then another, only to realize that none of them were truly options at all, he suddenly caught the movement of a strange shadow, then swiveled to his right just in time to catch the source of a discharged round of fire power that instantly put the tiger and wolverine out of their respective miseries. With equal speed, both the Commander and Governor then flew headfirst to the ground, bullets having ripped through the vines that held the both of them. Someone here had expert aim.

"My neck's broken!" the Governor wailed.

"If it was, you couldn't carry on a conversation, intelligent or otherwise," the Commander suggested above the spray of bullets smashing every which way.

All this fire power certainly impressed the hunters, who made a riot of confused screeches as they retreated back into the forest. Little darkling stag beetles swarming like massed maggots in the shady primevals. Butts bouncing back into thicket.

"Who are you?" Namgyal said by way of introduction, arriving in urgent stride from under cover and pointing his gun at the fallen figures of the Commander and Sannazaro.

"Leave them alone!" shouted Rajibai, now running out of the jungle to protect them.

"And who are you!" Namgyal returned, irked and ill-humored. He whipped around, gun aimed dead-on to meet the boy, and his face fell.

"We're Americans. I am Mr Marigold, this is Governor Sannazaro. And that is my son, Rajibai. Now if you wouldn't mind putting down your weapon."

Namgyal slowly did so.

Some (not all) explanations were conveyed to everybody's satisfaction after Namgyal had led them with efficient dispatch to a nearby river. There, the Tibetan had stashed an inflatable raft, blown up from a mere one pound of mylar. It was anchored to a tree and bobbing in a smooth eddy beside a raging torrent. With

Rajibai sitting on his father's lap, it would just carry the four of them.

"What makes you think this thing is safe?" Sannazaro worried. "I'm not the best swimmer, in fact I detest cold water, and we have no wetsuits and—"

Namgyal ignored him, scanning for electronic transmissions in the area, and positioned the second microwave station. He had placed the first such station the previous night, enabling the electronic cartographers at the war room to locate his position. The apparatus was 'hot', which meant he enjoyed a continuous live transmission that also allowed him to talk with the two-man crew of the KH-12 which continued to circle the northern subcontinent. But he thought better of revealing just yet the added complication of these bizarre and feckless newcomers whose motives, it seemed to him, were nothing less than insane.

"They can actually hear you, right now?" the boy asked, as they put into the tributary and moved away from the sheltered cove.

Namgyal nodded, and attended to Sannazaro's arm: lotions, topical creams, four antibiotic pills, an injection of penicillin and another of codeine. Then he applied a hot poultice heated by nanotechnology—solar cells in the fabric. Finally he wrapped the Italian's arm in a sling thickened with a chemical that maintained the optimal curative temperature. He then sprayed a strong dose up his nostrils, squirted drops in his eyes, had him roll up his shirt, and injected his spine with a painkiller.

"Thank you, thank you very much, but it's just a scratch," Sannazaro said, grateful and bewildered by all these goings-on.

"It could lead to gangrene."

"Gangrene!"

"It won't. Just a precaution."

"Don't get him too used to such ministrations," the Commander warned. "He's already badly spoiled."

"That's not true," Sannazaro argued. "By the way, I hope you have more of that codeine." His eyes were starting to fade.

"You're going to make an addict out of him," Marigold reasoned. Then he looked around him. "Do you have any idea where we are? This is obviously not the Brahmaputra. Too small."

"A tributary. No name. There are many tributaries this far down. They all start to come together a little higher. How do you know about the Brahmaputra?"

"He doesn't," Sannazaro explained. "Not a clue."

They maneuvered into a calm central portion of the current.

"Oh it hurts, oh it hurts..." the Governor went on and on, and Rajibai giggled. He thought Uncle was joking.

Then they reached a mysterious island that merged with the shore on the western side. It was a blind trap of sinking sands and mangrove swamps, buffeted by boisterous waters, shackled by tenebrous jungle and desperate cliff. But it was their only way out of the rapids.

"Do you think we've lost them?" Sannazaro implored. He was strapped in, panicking and pale, hunched over, eyes closed, absorbing all the drugs in his body and fighting off the pain. The tiger had salvaged half of his arm. His right fist was tight, carbuncles white, his teeth clenched.

"Yes," Namgyal reassured him. "But that's not who I'm worried about."

"The Russians," Marigold declared. Namgyal displayed agitation.

The Commander explained what they'd overheard in New Delhi and their reasons for being this far into the jungle. This young man had saved his life and, by his fine English and astonishing paraphernalia, it was clear was some kind of American spy. Probably CIA. Marigold felt at relative ease in his company. But he said nothing about the astonishing diary of Anna Christov, and his Governor kept his own peace on that score as well.

At that moment their raft was torpedoed by a muddy explosion in the river, a boulder that had dislodged and been catapulted downstream. It grazed their boat, and sent them hurtling into the falls just past the ledge on which they'd taken respite.

Too fast for anyone to say a word. One moment they were safe, the next lost in a thunder of white water.

Namgyal clutched Sannazaro by his uninjured arm, lunging for a portion of the white trunk jutting out from between two boulders in the river as their boat plunged over the 15-foot falls. Now Marigold let go, separated in a sweeping lunge from the dogwood limb. With his son in tow, he crashed over the slime-baked walls and disappeared from Namgyal's view into a keeper hole.

Namgyal got Sannazaro ashore, and the Señor promptly passed out. His rescuer leapt back in after the two Marigolds who were caught in the numbingly cold undercurrents. He deliberately sailed over the tumbling torrent, his body diving like a lovesick trout between the massive rock walls. Again his skills proved unequaled, for he saved not only the Commander and his boy, but also the insulated polyurethane food bags which had been severed from the O-rings holding them to the inflatable. They had been flushed up into a pinch-hole between river boulders beside a smooth eddy area adjoining a beachhead.

When the havoc-strewn foursome awoke, they were drifting quietly into the shadows of some mighty chasm which was formed by the convergence of two parallel ridges descending from inescapable alpines all around them. The trigonometry of their situation was baffling, right out of Anna's diary. Implacable forces were sucking them along. There was no escaping the dark storm front of mountain wall and tortuous hydrology directly before them: the unknown terror of a canyon that disappeared forever.

To make matters even less sensible, Sannazaro was laboring under the powerful influence of the drugs Namgyal had administered. His lungs were still swimming in white water. Rajibai had a bloody nose, the result of banging headlong into a tree, and Marigold seemed to have fractured his right funny bone so that he made the queerest antics each time he tried to say anything. If he asked for the time, his left leg flopped. Or if he dared contemplate the universe, he peed in his pants. His arm behaved badly, pockmarked with spasms which flared up every eleven minutes and induced him to slap himself, or whoever was standing closest to him, in the face.

Worst of all, as a peculiar function of his handicapped elbow—some heretofore unknown process in the circulatory system, touching upon matters of the psyche—whenever Marigold got a good idea, or had some inspiration or other, the opposite effect seemed most likely to emanate.

All in all, they were a mess: adrift on a raft in the twilight of the unknown Himalayas, entering the famed Gorge of No Return; in over their heads by years, centuries, and mile after mile; goaded on by a young zealot whose purposes were unclear to them; faced with unearthly waters; too committed to complain, too exhausted to whine, too frightened to turn back.

Water that was a fever of motion one could not successfully contemplate. It came from glaciers, that was certain, up there, off in the mist: a whole Tibetan outback stretching thousands of miles of dense run-off. In its volume and ferocity, there was every reason to die. Water that was silver and bejeweled, an animal of seismic company; liquidy and chaunceable, elastic, drop by drop, conduit, fear and conviction, unto wine bewitched and liquor-like. Into whose undiluted veins the four of them—like a phrase jettisoned in greater speech—went wonderfully scorched into unknown consequences and whole paragraphs.

"Hold on!" somebody screamed, floating pell-mell through parish after parish of wild constellation, stream and quantity. Discharges through tub and glass, skin and sheet, bucket and gourd, jar and channel, barrow and bellows. This grist-mill of motion, motorizing the senses with no equal. Strange pottage, tansey of gruel, prospects fenced in snow fame that fronted counted leagues and water life. By moisture their faith, by slang their tower. Smoke tathed and vaporized in monarch pieces globe and farm.

Until occluded, their vertical cell, through windows precious, like a nectarized Christ siding along the stream. Hence were they shaken and stomaed, silled with rime and rate, twisted like the ouzel and the water spider, limpid and clear, mercurial, supplied at every extremity. Loaming, ratting, worshipping, to-wit the crake that swims hind legs first; the insect found at bottom-pond; the lizard leaping above stones for drops to drink. All marshy and obscure, these latter-day madcaps engendered in the wind of mountain spray with little balance of hope this day. Fleeting through meadow fairest toward that end capricious wherein each had his own element, and purpose. A barge filled with dreams, no chance to parse them out—one farthing per port—or to center on the practical. In their rush towards final oblivion, only one cogency adhered: wet spray in the face, mouth agape, eyes wild, half-closed, before each oncoming battlement of white water, through which the travelers dared to fathom, no thought for the morrow—and just as well. Through eyes of the child, synapses working 224 miles per second.

CHAPTER 118
The Hanging Gardens of the Tsangpo

FOR MOST OF A DAY the beleaguered foursome continued along the central river bank, in and out of the water depending on the negotiability of the cliffs which convexed forward. The tributary crossed this country diagonally, from east to west, working at times against the gravity of the south. It was swollen with rains from the north, which came and went with pulsating regularity, shifting with the huge curtain of clouds that spun off the vast mountain chain in their midst. Mountains made their own weather. Such microclimates also induced unusual ecological niches, and Namgyal sampled a large variety of the plant species using an infrared beam generated by a 100-gigabite hand-operated computer device that scanned for plant chloroplasts, carbohydrate molecules and other photosynthetic markers. The autotrophic-sensitive light beam provided a read-out in kilocalories, and stored data pertaining to 1,000 files.

Sheet lightning engulfed the sky for hours, every burst occasioning after-rumbles of thunder which ululated for hundreds of square miles, shaking the forest, reverberating in the bones. A triumph of melancholy.

Later, the watercourse simmered down, white water replaced by calm eddies and slow, suspenseful currents. They drifted by an entire cliff covered in bright blue Sikkimensis plants. One hanging garden after another dense with flowers Sannazaro himself had never seen. The air was haunted with the taste of jasmine.

"Listen!" Rajibai buzzed.

They all put their ears to the passing wall. "Hear that?"

Echoes faintly etched—the slightest sense of talkative tulips and garrulous ginger. The whole jungle seemed to be carrying on, and bumblebees no less vociferously, whilst 10,000 varieties of birds and other insects added their commentary, mused aloud, remarked, incited, whispered or coughed. Even the skittish mayfly could be detected making a magnificent speech, such were the theatrical acoustics of the canyon: an Epidaurus of eligible bachelors calling for a mate or signaling by way of secret slang the dissipating storm front.

It came about just after their tea time that the spellbound foursome found themselves confronted by a dubious drop-off ahead. Namgyal got onto the cliff that fell into steepest white water and peered around the corner. The choices were unpleasant: either take the drop into the falls, or attempt an ascent of sheer rock.

At that moment, they heard the distant rumble of an approaching chopper above the din of the river. There was no time now to deliberate or mount effective strategic analysis. A confrontation was inevitable, and that meant possible weapons fire—a situation greatly complicated for the Tibetan by the unexpected civilians in his company.

The falls gave no indication of their height or intensity. They might be a man-eater. But there was no alternative.

"We have to," Namgyal said. "You ready?"

"I can't," Sannazaro pleaded. "Not again."

Inside the chopper, the pilot seated next to Malevich spotted the inflatable raft held by its 9mm rope from the ledge where the foursome now stood precariously. The Russian was not surprised: "They're the Americans." He was fully aware by now of the KH-12 circling high above. The invading troop had learned of it from the Indian Embassy, which had already lodged its diplomatic protest in Washington, to no avail. "I can see them," said Lieutenant Singh, binoculars glued upon the distance. Singh, of course, was Sikh, one of a class of military strategists from Punjab State. The Sikhs all but controlled the military in India, and their sabers and rifles had become symbols of their religion: force, self-defense, national pride. They were hardened soldiers, good at what they did, and a crack regiment from Delhi had been assigned to work with the local Sadiya militia. "One of them looks Tibetan," he said.

This information weighed heavily on Malevich, who remembered only too well a Tibetan double-agent from his days in Afghanistan.

Sitting behind Malevich was Gurab Jomsom, the Nepalese tracker working with the troops, a legend among the military in New Delhi. He had found the CIA satellite dish secretly placed on the slopes of

Nanda Devi in 1995.

Jomsom too knew of one Tibetan CIA agent. "If it's him, we may have a problem," he thought to himself.

But it was Malevich who put the possibility into words. "I know who he is," he said.

The Russian, now in his early 50s, had his own very private reasons for being in India. It began with the loss of two brothers in the fighting in Afghanistan. When he returned to his family home in Tbilisi, his mother had been turned into a beggar, and his friends were agitating for independence. His father would be killed in that struggle against Moscow, blown up in an old castle, turned tragically into living theater, during a performance of *Titus Andronicus*. Then his own son had lost his legs when he stepped onto a mine. Malevich had worked for the KGB as a freelance assassin, but, by his own admission, had killed only people who really deserved it: an Iranian fundamentalist who had tortured women who had dared to sleep with their lovers out of wedlock; a madman in the Ukraine who had brokered plutonium to German agents and was preparing to detonate a small nuclear device in St Petersburg. That would have destroyed the Marensky Theatre, which was unacceptable.

A few others.

Malevich had harbored strong opinions—most of them favorable— about Glasnost. But he knew there would be economic reality checks, as when a secretary in his own branch headquarters was not earning enough money to feed her son, who actually starved to death, or when the state-run gas company was unable to pay two billion dollars in back taxes but rather paid in gas to those who used electric ranges. He had been a strong believer in Gorbachev's reforms, but he was in the minority. With the collapse of the KGB, private enterprise—the free-market miracle that gave birth to the new oligarchy, clumsy privatization, street traders, oil and nickel monopolists in the Arctic, aluminum, energy, media, foreign automobile and real-estate moguls—was the only option, and a good one, as it turned out, for Malevich.

Now the economics were crumbling, Yeltsin's administration succumbing, a man of his own ranks named Putin waiting to emerge, and only pharmaceuticals, free of regulations—because Russia had no FDA, no protracted legal hurdles prior to the release of new products—offered great promise. With his paramilitary background, Malevich was an obvious candidate for MWPH, which needed a strongman of liberal convictions and security training. He was now in an ownership position within the company, and he and his wife drove a sleek black BMW. He had a daughter studying Japanese literature at a university in Riga.

These were all unthinkable achievements in life ten years before. He was not about to lose them. He had his priorities straight. Seventy years of Communism had demystified the romance of Nature. They all carried on in spite of heavy pollution, and carnage, and had no illusions about rustic country life. Russians were not hamstrung by the ethical delicacies of forcing progress down people's throats. The mountain people of the former Soviet Union—the Chechen of the Central Caucasus, and the Ingush—had been given outhouses, schools built of corrugated aluminum and houses made of concrete. Yurts were no longer fashionable. Herding mountain goats for their dairy products was less profitable than doing public works, like the building of new highways through the Urals that would lead convoys to the oil fields.

Malevich's Indian collaborators exhibited a similarly low esteem for the primitive peoples of the Himalayas. Such tribes were even beneath the contempt ordinarily reserved for Untouchables. But their lives could be 'improved' and this justification provided the motive for all exploitation, greed, development. One look at a town such as Dibrugarh, on the southern fringes of Arunachal Pradesh State, said it all. Former mountain people had moved to the urban shanties, left their thatched huts and ancient traditions behind, and become cloth or spice merchants. Their lands were no good any more, for they had overpopulated, overfarmed, and been forced away as a result of watershed destruction. Now, the more successful ones ran businesses of their own. They still kept up the practice of keeping numerous wives, and cattle. The herds foraged along garbage-strewn highways on the outskirts of villages. The wives worked 20-hour days in the various shops.

The chopper swung low to get a better fix on the occupants of the raft, but it was too late. The Americans had vanished and the tributary was too closed in by walls and forest for the chopper to make pursuit. Namgyal, who clung to a tree jutting out from the cliff, while the others hid more comfortably on a narrow rocky passage around the falls, knew that this encounter was an excellent harbinger. If the combatants (the Russians and Indians) had captured one of the tribals, they would not still be in the area.

The chopper circled back and headed further to the east.

"They're going to put down," Namgyal foretold. "They're looking for a safe place."

And then the tree snapped, and all four fellows and their nearly weightless mylar craft plunged into the falls below. "This will kill me," the Italian bellowed.

But they stayed together as they were spat out of the hole. From there they swam 100 feet to reach a sandbar, Rajibai helping his feckless father, Señor Sannazaro pulled roughly by Namgyal.

Later, they left the deciduous rain forests and entered a deep gully which led to snow, larger cliffs and then an even deeper canyon which continued all the way into the high peaks. The temperature was dropping with each 100 feet of elevation gain. The winds were starting to pick up. This was more like Namgyal's territory. The no-nonsense survivalist could fetch anything for dinner: snakes, edible rhododendron. And he had a long-winded prayer for each endeavor. Always the first mouthful necessitated the tossing over his right shoulder of something—a pinch of dirt, a piece of skin.

"What happens it you throw it over the left shoulder?" Rajibai wondered aloud.

"Don't ever do that!" Namgyal said, without breaking his solemnity. He then winked at the elder Marigold.

The Commander and Sannazaro had warmed quickly to Namgyal. Despite his Ivy League education, his English still skipped off the lips with a Mandarin inflection, and he exhibited qualities that you just didn't find on the streets of Santa Fe. It was this so-called primitive acumen which had attracted city dwellers for centuries, ever since a great eighteenth-century German philosopher, Herder, described Tibetans as "the most civilized" of people—a fact the Swiss social critic, Jean Jacques Rousseau, had picked up when he proposed his radical theory of the "noble savage". There, before them, was such a man, Sannazaro reckoned. These men inherited the Earth. Namgyal's family still endured in Lhasa. He detested the Chinese, who had systematically murdered several million of his people. But his anger—like that of most Tibetans—could be assuaged with a counter-offer. He was a reasonable person, with a great capacity for laughter, and a bit of a prankster. Even the Dalai Lama's fury over the genocide waged against Tibetans by China had been somehow softened by his audacious capacity for mirth. One could see a drunken Buddha smiling beneath every adversity in such men.

Generous, wild without knowing it, Namgyal bowed to the spirit of mountain, river and forest, but did not expect his three companions to do so. He loved regaling both Americans with tales of Uncle Thompa, the legendary rascal (read: sex fiend) of Tibet. The same one who seduced all the virgins to his cave of enlightenment and could become a snow leopard at will, just like Milarepa, the saintly poet in Tibetan medieval history, best known for his "hundred thousand songs".

Now, said Namgyal, he was in his prime. The higher the altitude, the better he felt. But it was his unstoppable stride that most impressed Marigold. His knees had the strength of well-fit ball bearings. His hands were similar. His buck teeth were ivory and strong from his habit of rubbing salt on them. A scar on his neck, he related, came from a bear which he accidentally stumbled into one night, when drunk. The poor bear happened to be relieving itself beside a tree at the time.

Across the tapestry of mountain wall the young man was absolutely adroit. The Tibetan's First Rule of Thermodynamics, as he described it with a piercing vision, was: the further you go, the faster you should go.

The further you go, the less air you should need. The further you go, the easier it should become. If any of these three proved less than accurate, you were an invalid. The way he alighted over wet stones and gnarly root while the others struggled—his pace was mesmerizing. Unstoppable, except when he prayed, which was frequently. He solemnized everything: trees, plants, mountains, the clouds, the rain.

They climbed on all fours up a steep embankment above the river, their mylar boat folded neatly into a bundle which Namgyal kept in his pack.

Trees had been smashed, uprooted, carried pell-mell into the broil of white water below or flung back to shore where they lay pummeled and beyond botanical identification. Slabs of white granite had spilled from cliff sides, careening downslope in detonations that had left scoured bedrock. White apartment-sized boulders, unbalanced in the deadly thunder of river, stood ready to tumble. Namgyal was leading them into the main canyon.

"Are you sure about this?" Marigold asked.

Namgyal simply shrugged his shoulders. "Just a hunch," replied he.

They cottoned to and liked the Tibetan, but could not trust his motives. Satellites, CIA involvement, assassins and military might: to the Commander's mind it was all a bureaucratic fog that perverted the truth of their whereabouts and threatened to puncture the bubble of his exquisite dream of a tribe that had never experienced evil. Namgyal was part of that offensive, despite his native looks and generous nature. Both he and Sannazaro knew there would come a moment of decision.

There had been much rain, and no contact with the satellite for hours. In the mist and impenetrable country, their intended ascent was a huge gamble, because it was much more work, climbing into higher altitude, particularly given his three companions' total lack of acclimation. But Namgyal knew that the tribe was on the run, and they'd be moving to the highest ground possible. The way bears relieve threats, leaving them behind and below.

In spite of his invidious position as both informant and guide, he had deeply personal hopes and intuitions concerning these people: who they were, where they came from and what, potentially, they represented. There were motives and long-suppressed hopes which none of his colleagues could have reckoned on. The dream of a yak herder long ago, lodged in the purgatory of his own nostalgic return, in which no geopolitics confused the first order of significance in a man's life; in which livelihood might be eked from a giving soil, a family churned up in the dust and drench of reincarnations. A life, in other words, shorn of guns and wars and wicked men.

As they tacked exhaustively north, parallel with the river, towards Namgyal's homeland of Tibet, anchor to windward, hove to in the lee, all set a clear course, no dangling modifiers. Ascent like a straight arrow, northward.

CHAPTER 119
Flash Flood

"LOWER IT," Malevich shouted at the winch operator.

The door of the Sikorsky was open and a half dozen Indians were ready to rappel out. Guided by a rope, Jomsom slid out first, stabilizing an inflatable zodiac raft into the river. Now the others glided down the ropes from 100 feet above, just past the falls over which the foursome had earlier plunged. Five other military men remained in the chopper, which now veered off south. They had circled the area for nearly two hours, trying to find a way in. Finally, discerning no landing site for miles round—not one foot that wasn't taken up with the vertical—they opted for the more dangerous maneuver directly over the cataract. Jomsom knew they were close. The wind was fighting the machine, the narrows treacherously upon them. He read it in the broken branch above the falls, and the human hair which he retrieved from a Hottentot fig, detected just as the sunlight hit it so. Malevich was impressed. To find a single hair in the Himalayas—the man was good. Jomsom could even kneel down upon a footprint and tell you precisely when the print had been made. In fact, he was able to determine whether a clouded leopard's toe prints revealed a male or female cat; whether, if female, she was pregnant, and how pregnant. He could tell you to the day—even to the hour, in the case of those they were presently pursuing—when the print was made.

The Americans had an advantage, decried Jomsom, because they had a Tibetan with them and they were unburdened by so many essentially inexperienced Indians, whom he loathed for their soft city ways, starched uniforms, aristocratic airs. But Jomsom and team had the heavy weapons, more bullets, and massive back-up.

Half a mile further north from Jomsom and company, the foursome found themselves perched betwixt run-off and loose scree, angling across a precarious slope high above the river.

"Don't look down," Marigold quavered.

"I need to rest," Sannazaro appealed frantically, dozens of watts coming out of his armpits, off his forehead.

"Not here," said Namgyal.

"I'm stopping," the Italian insisted.

"It's too dangerous. There's rock fall."

"I don't care." The Governor plumped down, his head sunk beneath his off-kiltering knees, mumbling Latin cuss words. The others conceded, and rested with him.

Suddenly, half the wall above started down in a massive shift. "Move move move!" Namgyal cried out, making a 100-joules-per-second dash, dragging Sannazaro, Marigold and the boy with him across the pitch.

The debris plunged past them, pulverizing their resting place of seconds before, exploding into the river.

"You were right," Sannazaro conceded when at last he'd regained his breath.

But Namgyal uttered no word. Instead he ushered them onwards until, amid a wilderness of instability, in the concavity of a huge boulder that seemed stable, the foursome plopped down at last.

"What?" Marigold asked. "Shhh!" Namgyal gestured. "What?"

"Shhh!"

Then suddenly he came down with his cutlass on something dangling from above. A poisonous snake which he deftly cut in half.

"Gross!" Rajibai screamed.

"What was it?" his father exclaimed. "Bad news. Two seconds to die."

The Tibetan then proceeded to wash off the deadly juices and tug at the skin as if it was beef jerky.

"I thought Buddhists didn't kill," Marigold said.

Namgyal smiled. "We don't, as a rule, unless it's snake jerky, tuna fish, chicken salad blessed by His Holiness, or the occasional New York T-bone."

Marigold didn't know if he was being screwed with. Probably not, he decided, given the enthusiasm with which the Tibetan actually devoured his portion of the snake's head.

"You'd better eat, friends," Namgyal advised. "You need your strength."

"I'm a vegetarian," the Commander declared resolutely.

"What about you?" Namgyal asked, offering some to Rajibai, who shriveled up his nose and looked away.

"He's a Jain," Marigold advised.

"Suit yourself. But what about you, sir?" Namgyal asked, extending the nastiest of the entrails to Sannazaro. He, too, rejected the provender.

"What's with you guys? I thought you were hungry?"

"I'm Italian. Raised in the lap of gastronomic subtlety. My stomach is accustomed only to the finest penne al dente and olives cured in vintage liqueur."

"So, pasta noodles—they look like snakes, no?"

"If you believe that, then a rooster resembles a sardine."

Their sparring would have continued uninterrupted and unabated had not the Tibetan, with his eagle eyes, seen a flash of light down river about two miles.

"It's them. Let's bolt!"

They moved haphazardly throughout the afternoon, goaded on by the Tibetan taskmaster who knew too well the persistence of their predators and seemed to take the most consistently harrowing path in an attempt to lose them. The three amateurs were catching on to the survival game very quickly—no choice at this point. Rajibai was particularly adept. His own uncanny abilities went hand in hand with climbing down ventilator shafts at nuclear test sites in the desert. As for Marigold, it was amazing that he didn't trip and kill himself and everybody around him, for his bowlegged comportment had all the finesse of a stringless puppet, or stripper with a jammed zipper. A one-legged ostrich. Sannazaro, partly crippled in one arm, enfeebled first by age, then by fear, hunger, drug overdoses and terrible seizures that expressed themselves in sudden overwhelming cravings for Turkish coffee, or a bottle of wine, or a down comforter, did little to help sustain the necessary momentum of the expedition. But at least, stammering and stumbling, he maintained the ability to put one foot in front of the other, although it was his perpetual complaining that truly made the Tibetan's own rapid progress miserable.

Rajibai, by contrast, was the life of the party. Not two minutes elapsed when he did not discover something of interest: a fossil trilobite, wild carrots, a dead mongoose and—most telling—a boot.

Namgyal examined it in detail. "It's Russian," he declared. "Turn of the century."

They came to a long abandoned hut. There were animal droppings before the bamboo entranceway.

"Panda," Namgyal said, stooping down to examine them.

"Should we stay here for the night?" Marigold inquired. "No," the Tibetan replied. "We have to keep going or they'll catch up with us for sure." He scanned the enormous wall of misty giants drenched in downpour, snowstorm and wind before them. Huge drop-offs in every direction, sinuous trails that were not real trails, leading into disappearing cul-de-sacs. It was clear that Namgyal intended to continue north. "What makes you think we'll find the tribe that way?" the Governor pressed.

"Fifteen thousand feet is my prediction. We're now at 10,500."

"But that's nearly a vertical mile!" the Commander groaned.

"I can't. I'm telling you it won't work. I'm done." And Sannazaro stuffed himself into his bag, turned over, and reiterated his resolve. "I'm not going another step. Tell the world to pick me up in a few weeks."

Namgyal started to say something but the Commander urged him to think the better of it. "Don't bother. He can get that way. Now that he thinks himself rich, anything is all right. He will sleep in a subway or the arms of a tiger. Fears no charge or authority. Is his own man. Just needs some pasta to give him a boost."

In time, the Italian had to give up his privileged if ephemeral snooze, and the foursome moved on. Then night swallowed both teams in the gorge. The trio and Namgyal were lodged on a narrow island of ridge, sheltered by a stand of cypresses. The winds were howling. Far up in the skies, thunder and lightning continued, dulling the air with a soothing sensation, for the storm was far away. For Rajibai, who lay awake in great joy, warmed by his polyurethane bag down to his last little bone, this adventure was simply the best.

Somewhere, not far away, coming from inside an enormous pinkly blooming rhododendron, a strange musical composition was emanating. It merged with the wise croaking of frogs and crazy-chorused cricket song. It was the tribe, all squatting dexterously on various limbs of the tree like a troop of baboons. Ten thousand years ago, there were more baboons in the world than people. These particular luminaries knelt poised somewhere between evolutionary branches; they were wearing only loincloths which held little stringed instruments upon which they communicated in rapid crescendos and chords. This was their language, its far-reaching modulations—adagios and pizzicatos, melodious intricacies played out across the whole harmonic scale of Asiatic tones, animal cries, more familiar thirds and fourths—were all of a precisely syncopated staccato nature. Did the melody come first, or the meaning?

With them was the mysterious woman in Red Army fatigues. It was none other than Anna Christov, a member of their family, fluent in their language. For 76 years Anna had lived among them.

"We cannot sleep here for the whole night. We must keep moving. They are bad people."

Tribal member, a young man: "We saw a big bird fall and flash like a star."

Several others: "Yes. We all saw the bird flash."

Anna: "Not a bird, but some kind of flying machine. An airplane.

That's what they were named where I came from, over the mountains. Made of something harder than rock. People like us sitting inside. A liquid which—" she wanted to say, like a fuel that burns, like fire, but there were no sounds for such things, and no meaning for fire, or fuel—"is inside the machine, which gives it the energy to fly. You saw the men inside. They will have a special sound for it. And there will be more where that one was built. They will search for us and try to find us."

Tribal member, an older male, not entirely comprehending: "Then we must go back. But we must bring food."

There was general agreement. Anna was visibly frightened, an emotion that did not altogether register with those around her. It had been a problem for her from the beginning, whenever that was, for she could not remember how long it had been—no idea; no obvious benchmarks, not since she lost her diary and was unable to keep track of the passing days, years. The tribe did not know about needing protection. There was no danger in their world. How could they imagine that perils did exist in the form of other people? Now, confronted with her own kind, a deep, unsettling yearning absorbed her. She was running away from it, but part of her wanted to do something like the opposite.

The men and women, dozen in all, were youthful, ageless. Together, they descended the tree with agile abandon and moved rapidly on along the rocky underpinnings of the high mountain canopy. For the third time in one day the storm had closed in. Now the rain started, giving a hiding to the pounded earth.

For the foursome, Sannazaro especially, the night was long. They wore woolen undergarments and

Gortex shells. Rajibai lay curled up beside his father, who snored like a two-engine Cessna. In front of them, Namgyal kept watch, seated in his bag, a machine-gun in his arms. Sannazaro could not find a position that worked, grumpily cursing every rock under his back, the slightest hint of a midge or grain of sand in his shirt.

"You wouldn't ever shoot anybody, would you?" the boy asked the Tibetan.

"Not unless I had to," Namgyal replied.

"Why would you ever have to?"

"What if somebody tried to hurt you first?"

"In my religion there's no first or second or third. It's all the same," Rajibai alleged.

"Then I guess it comes down to him or me. You want to live or die?"

"That's also the same," Rajibai said. "No beginning, no end."

"Those are just words. You're avoiding the question. Him or me. I'll go with me."

Rajibai turned. Something caught his kid's innocent ear. He listened: "Do you hear that?"

Namgyal paused, waited, but there was nothing. "Just the rain." But two seconds later it was there, everywhere.

"Oh shit!" he screamed.

Without warning a flash flood exploded out of the dense forest above, and carried four bodies with it.

Anna and the tribe had been moving all night above the same tributary, an offshoot of the mighty Brahmaputra three miles away, and heard the distant clash of English and Tibetan curses as they crouched low beneath the shrubs. Already frantic from a world closing in all around her, Anna tried to imagine who they were. Below, a struggle for survival was taking place. In the dark chaos, Namgyal was smashed against rocks and knocked out cold. Luckily, Marigold was right there with him. Otherwise, the Tibetan, the trio's only real hope, would have died. In the darkness, it was impossible to make out anything ahead of them. Boulders. Logs.

Walls of gray caulk jutting into the river.

"Protect your face!" Marigold screamed. "I've got hold of a branch.

Can you see me! There, grab it!" He kept Namgyal's head above water, quite the hero for the moment.

"What was that?"

"Hold on!"

"Rajibai?"

The words were muted in the grip of drenching, miserable night, until dawn, when the weary foursome, worn down to multiple breaking points, gratefully and in tandem acknowledged that it could be worse. They could be dead, after all.

Chapter 120
The Spider, a Monkey and Their Mule

THE WILD ASS, a member of the genus *Equus*, originated it is believed in Asia Minor. More petite than an ordinary horse, everything about it is shorter, verging on mystery. The creature is absolutely intolerant of anyone on its back. Over years, and certainly generations, it may come upon or be seduced by certain foods (though cannot digest much in the way of protein) or by watering holes frequented by less skittish members of its kind. Only fools know to approach it with extended hand.

Yet at times it will lick such a hand—soften, in other words—the result being its domestic cousin, the donkey (*E. asinus*), who is known for her more gregarious, patient nature and is willing to carry an occupant if properly pampered, though most compliance is the result of her being duped into a desperate donkey dream, occasioned by the characteristic squeal—half bagpipe, half the cry of a baby.

Both in the wild and on the ranch, the hybrid offspring of a male ass (or donkey, as the case may be) and a female horse, or mare, typically results in a sterile, long-eared burro, so called: small-hoofed but big-brained, historically exploited for its broad musculature as a pack or draft animal. The smallest of these biologically tortured creatures are found in parts of South and North America.

Taken together, the world has lumped all such equine hybrids into one oppressed category, the mule, or hinny, depending upon whether its mother or father was the donkey. Such was Sannazaro's fate by this time. He was depressed and in pain, and with his cagoule covering his already rain-soaked pack he resembled the most oppressed of all, which perfectly fitted his gait and demeanor. Rajibai thought him the mule, while Marigold a hinny. Namgyal saw through these bizarre dynamics and simply reckoned all three of them crazy and cut from the same buttered popcorn.

For all Sannazaro's braying and naysaying, Marigold, on the other hand, was feeling a certain empowerment. Consider his likely frame of mind. They had been out in the wilds for three days now, surviving the most remarkable grist for storytelling, as he preferred to think of all their trials. He shared none of Sannazaro's superstitions, or Namgyal's ticking clock. His were merely the literary travails of one bent upon transforming duels into learned fireside chat; foreign legions into illustrated books; danger into the aroma of a freshly laundered petticoat.

Rajibai was no less affected by these great perturbations under a Milky Way; his moment in time had arrived and it just seemed to get better and better. The boy's freedom had been assured. A caged animal suddenly released to the world, every flower a new nectar. He could do anything: squelch military might, win out upon every landslide. Though this expedition was taxing even his scrawny endurance or physical strength, he might yet rout certain demons.

The party climbed up into a vertical fissure of rock that had allowed them to gain a 30-foot advantage above the rumbling tributary. The flood was over in five minutes. Fortunately, their packs, though drenched, had been strapped on tightly and not been separated. None of their provisions were lost. Marigold had learned his lesson: always sleep wearing the essentials. Sannazaro's arm was bleeding again. A goodly chunk of flesh had been shaved whole, though not cleanly. He took up the tatters like the painter Vuillard's seamstress, and fitted them back in place without so much as a murmur of complaint.

"Now I'm actually worried about him," Marigold exclaimed, and Namgyal gave him another injection and applied his fine stitching expertise.

Namgyal's own head was bleeding. Rajibai diligently wiped leeches from the wound with Uncle's cologne. The Tibetan administered antiseptic creams upon himself, took doses of Hydrocodeine and Roxicet, and taped a poultice on his forehead. It was heated by an electrolytic surface area of three square inches. He cut up some leaves he found along the creek bed, mashed and chewed them to relieve pain.

Even the blithe Rajibai could not conceal the odd groan to accompany a trickle of blood from a gash in his head. Excited hornets had discovered the spot. Only the Commander had come away from this most recent disaster relatively in one piece, and feeling downright napoleonic for having saved their Tibetan guide.

A weather window opened, a circuitry of sporadic cloud compression, fickle winds. Almost at once a voice sounded in Namgyal's headset above the static: the mainframe operator back at DMA was updating his status. The KH-12 had located him through the audio pickup and the aircraft had also detected a half-dozen Indian choppers within ten miles of their position. Namgyal planted a third beacon for transmitting signals in the fissure.

The weather held, long enough.

Like clockwork: "Jigme—" (referring to Namgyal) "—the bird is directly overhead. Look up. Right. We've got you. But we're also seeing three other life forms nearby, has to be within 25 feet. Their heads are down. One looks like a spider—"

"That would be a Marigold."

"Come again?"

"No matter."

"We're also picking up a monkey."

"That would be his son."

"Whose son?"

"Never mind."

"What about the mule?"

"That would be their Squire."

The electronic cartographer looked over at Nash. "Is he speaking in cipher, sir?"

"They may have got him. He can't talk." Nash took the transmitter in his hands: "Jigme, it's Bob." And he continued with some "Delta delta alpha beta" gibberish.

"Bob, Bob, I'm fine. No sign of the tribe, or not yet. But we've established a two-hour lead over the Indians and I can verify that they haven't found them either."

"You said, 'We'. Who is we?"

"Don't ask. You wouldn't believe it if I told you."

"Tell me."

"Bob, I repeat, don't ask. It's inconsequential."

"Whatever you say. Now listen, we've spotted a village. You should be able to see it. You're over it, in fact."

"There's nothing there," Namgyal replied, speaking in low tones into his headset.

"It's there. Trust me."

Suddenly, Namgyal smelled the smoke of a slow-burning fire, which would never read on satellite, was too easily confused with mist.

"I got it," the Tibetan said. "Over."

As they were climbing down, Namgyal saw something leap in the forest. "Don't move!" he whispered to the others.

But it was too late. They'd been spotted.

This was some new tribe in a region laced with divergent aboriginal cultures: not hunters but curious, even excited farmers. They led the newcomers peacefully in the direction they had planned to go in any case: higher. The tribesmen (no women) wore coverings over their genitals, but otherwise were naked. The oldest one, probably Namgyal's age, exuded a broad welcoming smile minus even a single tooth, and uttered his one significant phrase to commemorate the occasion: "Really cool!"

"Might I take that to mean they've been assimilated," Marigold commented.

This impression was strengthened by the appearance of a visor on another of the young braves.

The foursome were marched half a mile to the remnants of a village. Some genetic variant of the Staffordshire bull terrier announced the arrival of the procession of nine with a chorus of howls. Faintly the low villagedom of leprechaun lean-tos emerged out of the misty morning. Regal cock, no corporate municipals or Porcion or Candrede. A sleepy low-born land, unkempt and startled, muting all echo, its borough made of commingling. An infant with tired eyes reached out and touched Marigold's face. Namgyal counted two dozen huts constructed from scraps of the forest. He was unfamiliar with the tribe per se, but it was clear they were nomads, embodying the modern definition of sustainability. Total low-impact consumers. Fleeting as perennials, old growth, humus in the wash, the cyclical duff of no traces. Satellite reconnaissance followed Namgyal's every move, at least while the weather held, and the Tibetan was able to convey a blow-by-blow commentary, whispered aloud, as if he were talking to himself, the mouthpiece from his headset neatly fitted beneath his chin, the battlefield become an intimate adagio, uplinked from the trenches.

Up above, from a distance, Anna and her people watched these goings-on warily. She did not know what to make of the feelings aroused in her by the sight of westerners, nor of other tribals 1,000 years away. Alarm, curiosity. An urgent caveat converging in the flow of her memories.

The women in the village prepared food for the newcomers, a gruel of unwashed mushy little balls, greasy and hot and larded with sautéed insect parts. Sannazaro looked to Namgyal, who dabbled unconcerned by whatever he put in his mouth. Marigold was not about to stand on vegetarian protocol at a time like this, and followed his lead. As did Rajibai, who pointed out that they tasted like celery. No more ceremony.

They ate, and drank, whatever it was. This was no capture, but a celebration of inquiry all around them. Gawks and ogles, amid varicolored cloth, gourds, necklaces, headdresses and stuffed animals. The children were grimy, ragamuffin, with cold chill marks under their eyes, across their ruby cheeks, blood unwiped from their noses. They clawed and slid around in the mud, feverishly but not hungrily. They seemed to be healthy. Sannazaro gave one of them a bright handkerchief on which was printed "I Love New York". Three mottled boars grunted sadly, confined to a cramped and sweating pen. Even out here, on the far edge. Abuse inherent in humanity. Old women, untroubled, were busy tying sticks into disorderly bundles with a kind of twine Namgyal had never seen. A new plant? Two young girls, their nipples the size of bug bites, sat peeling pimply breadfruit of some kind—again a new species. Across the river, gigantic yews leaned nearly horizontal, so oppressive and overhung were the cliffs. Flowering dogwood writhed violently in the whorls of what was, according to Namgyal, alluvial run-off from nearby glaciers.

The scope of their surroundings was of concern to the Tibetan, whose natural inclination was to search for a quick exit. A river on one side, mountain walls on the other. Mud from the downpour blocking escape to the south. One obvious route, passing by a clearing suitable for choppers. More to the point, he could hear a gigantic roar up beyond the first layer of canyon. He knew it was the Brahmaputra. Its ire and thunder, so fissured and dissimulated until that moment, were only now egressing audibly— the reverberations of distant cannonades, a mighty river marking its course through alpine tropic as yet unseen.

The Commander was focused on another facet of the morning. All around him he saw glimpses of a past world, the headwaters of some mythic opportunity. But his body hurt. He detected easily enough Namgyal's worries. The wrinkles in his shattered forehead said it all.

Rajibai had other concerns. "Father, look!" the boy squealed, pointing to a fenced-in area filled with a dozen little sand boxes protected by more fencing. Peering closer, he saw tawny centipedes, dozens of them.

"Ouch!" he emitted. "We can't stay," Namgyal said. "We're setting them up. They're innocents. If the Indians come, these people could be harmed."

But the tribals were intent on fraternizing. They had a very ancient game in mind, and their guests were not leaving until they had sported with them. Soon, the awesome stupidity of the merrymaking became apparent. It involved sitting round a circle and letting one of the pet centipedes have a go at whoever it selected. Great fun. And the stakes were soon apparent.

All were seated. Placed in the middle, the centipede was free to choose its victim. This contest was presaged by the predaceous arthropod's intelligent stare, first at one, then at another human. Whoever it selected could be sure of an attack.

The 100-legged monster, confused and annoyed, went right for its first victim, stinging his crotch with a rapid, vicious jab of its poison dagger. The man's fingernails bored holes into his own palms until blood flowed, as he contained his (amused?!) agony. Cheers rose up and he was pushed into the mob of waiting females at the entrance to the play room. Now it was his choice to consummate his lust with any one of them before he passed out. He was dragged to an adjoining hut.

A new centipede was readied, and the foursome took their horrified positions.

Namgyal figured these people had probably been playing this sadistic little prank for centuries. Survival of the fittest translated into consensual sport: the children of the village were, then, all offspring of the game of the centipede. Did the poison ensure a higher survival quotient? Maybe.

Namgyal, a would-be victim, did not hesitate to chop the chilopoda in half with his own hand, karate being second nature to him. His three immediate companions were mightily impressed, but it clearly pissed off their hosts. That was the chief's pet centipede. There was probably no greater insult to the family tree. He had just destroyed the crux of their genealogy. Had he burned down the Mormon Tabernacle in Salt Lake City, detonated the Kaaba Stone, the response of the centipede disciples could not have been more distraught. But they all had bigger problems just then.

Three Indian choppers were swinging in low and moving fast up the tributary. "Get out, get out!" cried the voice in Namgyal's headset.

CHAPTER 121
The Waterfall

MALEVICH AND JOMSOM had seen the rising smoke of village fires which, on account of all the rain, were soggy, a gathering haze dark and lingering.

Three men and the boy made their break, fleeing into the upper forests. They raced for nearly a mile— 45 minutes in such country—up the one possible avenue of escape, while the tribe necessarily focused its attention on the arriving helicopters.

Namgyal and team attained a position that provided a view of the village and of the adjoining, larger canyon. There was ice in the lower reaches, and the Tibetan (scarcely a trace of hard breathing, though his companions gasped) informed them that, probably a century ago, there was a glacier there that had since receded. Through Namgyal's high-powered spotting scope, and Marigold's binoculars—compliments of the airfield manager at Sadiya—they were able to see the Indian choppers land just outside the tribal enclave.

The villagers confronted the mighty flying machines with evident angst. They already possessed the charm of angered yellowjackets following the death of their centipede god, and were in no mood to be humored by these cargo conveyors. The military were rough with the people. One of them pushed the old chief down and pressed his face into the mud with his boot. Then Malevich discovered Sannazaro's bandana. The village was ransacked, huts razed in a rapid inferno.

When a young brave threw his spear through the throat of one of the Indians, war erupted.

"They're killing them!" Namgyal whispered into his headset.

Half the tribe had been machine-gunned down before an Indian general had the afterthought to halt the massacre.

At DMA, Catherine Wouverman demanded that Nash, or Riley, or somebody with the authority to do so call the President, get the Indian Ambassador to the US on the phone—do something!

"It's none of our business," said Riley. "Informally, of course, we'll lodge a complaint."

"Then the same will befall the very people whose genes you seek to replicate," she admonished. "I'll go to the *New York Times*. They've written about me in the past."

Riley reminded her that this was a national security operation, and any breach on her part would have the severest legal ramifications.

"Mr Riley, I'm older than you, probably by 20 years. I've survived revolutions, been laid by Himalayan hunks as part of an initiation ritual, trekked across Mongolia in winter. My books have been translated into 40 languages, I've won two Pulitzer Prizes, and I'm a citizen of the world.

You have no idea who you're dealing with, you little piece of shit! All of you—" She peered round the room. "I'm South African. There was a time, not too many years ago, when I thought about becoming an American citizen. That would have been a colossal mistake."

She wheeled herself away towards the elevator, brushing off the assistance of dark-suited goons.

Back on the troubled ground, Malevich knew there was nothing more to be had from these people. They were not the ones. He felt badly about what had happened, but was comfortable, at least, in the knowledge that the tribespeople, followed by his Indian military cohorts, had started the conflict. He reported back to his colleagues in New Delhi. They, in turn, would prepare the embassy staff. There would be some, though not serious, fallout from the killings. Self-defense, most assuredly, would be offered as the justifiable excuse.

It was Jomsom, attempting to clear the site, who detected the footprints leading upwards. His instincts led his nose in a beeline towards that promontory where Marigold was staring at him.

"Get down!" Namgyal yelped.

But it was too late. The Nepalese had detected them. "Let's move, boys," the Tibetan incited.

Spider, monkey, mule and CIA agent raced upwards, but progress was treacherous, for huge avalanches had clouded their path in the recent past. The remains were fresh, observed Namgyal.

Malevich and Jomsom, along with their half-dozen armed Indian cohorts, went by foot, while the three choppers provided overhead surveillance. Malevich now knew he was in a dead heat with the Americans. Indian satellites had picked up the presence and repeated flight patterns of the KH-12 high above the region. It was clear to him what was happening.

The Americans, probably a combination of government and big business, were trying to get the jump on MWPH.

Running for their lives, Namgyal and companions turned a corner above the tributary, only to find the larger river off which it spun.

"Tsangpo!" the Tibetan said. It was the lower run-out of the Brahmaputra, half a mile wide, encased in gigantic mountain walls three, four times the size of those sheer granite monoliths in the Baltoro Cathedral region of the Karakoram, with water streaming down thousands of enameled cracks, and enormous trees hanging like Oriental gardens off sloped ledges. Every shade of verdure, whiteness of foam and darkness of cavern. The 10,000 and 15,000-foot walls were saturated with whirling mists, as if nature had been fitted to time-lapse photography. Five-hundred-foot-high chunks of ice lay half buried beneath 100-acre mummies of chalky dust and granite resin in the moraines adjoining the river junction below. It was a scene of spectacular ongoing devastation. Black, green, cobalt, ivory. Wave after wave of insects—hundreds of thousands of ladybugs, wasps and flying beetles—plummeted from one canyon over to another. Wild primroses—were they primroses?—in large, colorful assemblages dotted the walls of wet slate. There were thousands of square acres of blooming begonia. Furious river waters, counter-turbulences informing a new physic—magnitudes off any chart—were hurling riot at stone, scraggly schist bristling atop muddied spillways from the higher glaciers, titanic forces down-hurtling in every direction. A paradise, but not one in which a human could remain for very long.

Still blinded by the incoming abrupt angle of mountain wall on their side, the little party could hear something wonderful: a thunder other than the river. But the men couldn't yet see what it was.

"A waterfall!" Namgyal shouted above the din. The choppers were coming.

"What?" Marigold yelled back.

"A waterfall!"

"See!" Rajibai cried. "Nigodas! Jivas! A zillion water molecules floating about, each one with a wonderful idea inside its head." He reached up his hands into the mist, exalted by the millions of drifting prisms, hundreds of rainbows, all the first butterflies. He threw his face into the downcoming siege of glorious spray.

"What's he talking about?" Namgyal asked. "Like I told you, he's a Jain," Marigold explained.

But there was no time to ponder the child's universe. A more pressing injunction was their precarious situation. They were considerably outnumbered, and they'd seen only too clearly the etiquette of their opponents. But Namgyal had discovered a razor-sharp trail, quasi-human and used, it appeared, by mountain goat as well: toe-prints of centuries and unimpeded agility led round the mountain corner towards the fulmination. The foursome moved by stealth, inching along the outer bulge of cliff. For ten minutes, without pausing, traversing the steep slimy ledges, grasping delicately for purchase, they continued.

"One slip—" Marigold whispered.

"Shut up!" answered Sannazaro, nervously testing a toe-hold, absolutely deathstill in his movement, dynamite between his teeth.

They executed the turn, and all appeared before them.

A vast, vertical cul-de-sac. And more. The winds were violent, 60, 70 knots. Gale force. It was difficult to stand, particularly with the added weight of all the diffused spray in the air.

"Tighten your packs, gentlemen," Namgyal advised.

The entire Earth was seething, as if in constant seismic uncertainty. It was indeed a waterfall—a mile away at its base, though the side wall, to the east, was right upon them. It was the largest thing any of them had ever seen, imagined. It fell out of the clouds in slow motion, from miles above, whites, emerald mauves, azure golds, 10,000 phase shifts, 100,000 songs, a million colors, 14 mathematical dimensions, all of the inner Himalayas, layered into the last days of Monet, and plunging towards tornado blackness below, where the vast Moebius column of water collided with the Tesla earth; and higher still, above the saturated clouds, glimpses of glaciers spidering Escher-like across Namche Barwa, Gyala Peri and Sanglung.

"Mountains too high even for birds to fly over," Namgyal prayed aloud, though nobody could hear him.

A creamy hurricane, probably 120 knots, streamed over the summits, detectable by the ventricular clouds it formed and the powdery snow flying 50,000 feet up into the stratosphere.

In pools before them that had collected over thousands of years, hordes of little insects, hydrocorises, tettigones, coleopterae, or water-fleas, all feeding on yet smaller creatures, Namgyal knelt down and kissed the earth, obeisance to his gods, a microscopic waltzing of life lapping upon rocky shores.

"It's got to be 20,000 feet high!" proclaimed Marigold in staggered breath.

"I'll tell you exactly," said the Tibetan, standing back up. He withdrew from his pack an electronic sensing device, marked a coordinate, placed a beacon, and communicated with the KH-12. Together, they triangulated the height of the falls in a matter of moments.

"That was good," Marigold commended. "A true surveyor."

"You were very close: 17,897 feet. Twenty Eiffel Towers. And on the other side is Pemakod," Namgyal confirmed with a reverential quietude.

"Shangri-La. And the ancient village of Tumbatse."

"How far?" Marigold asked.

"I'm not certain. It was abandoned 500 years ago. But 200 miles further is the Mandalting Monastery, on the Nam La. Nobody's living there, I'm pretty sure. The Chinese destroyed it during the invasion. Beyond, the Dashang La, the pass over which most traders journey for collecting salt in Tibet. That, too, has probably been unused in a century. But this way, no one has probably ever gone. There was a rope bridge 100, 150 miles to the north, but that was 300 years ago. A monk crossed it between day and night, hatred and love. Much poetry has been written about him. Was he real? Nobody knows. Two armies, ready to clash, lay down their arms, took off their armor, sat and meditated in the snow.

The world was set aright. But then the bridge was burned. Darkness fell across the land, and a mighty dragon came, finally settling over Bhutan. This place—abandoned, feared, inaccessible. It is unexplored. That much I remember of the story."

After ten more minutes of mistwhacking, the foursome arrived at a small clearing that harbored a half-dozen dolmens of crocidolite—tiger's eye—overgrown with masses of white mushroom. They were set in a triangular configuration, and in the center were two larger-than-life totem poles. Their faces looked Aleutian, eyes slanted out and up, a Paleolithic warning: No Trespassing. Two intertwining spirals were faintly etched across the elongated torsos. Together, the two humorless guardians of mahogany were appointed with colored banners that had been weathered down to mere traces of the original effect. The spot marked a periphery, the limit of someone's world. Not even the silver tread marks of a slug, nor a bay leaf, nor one strand of gossamer; not so much as an ant's toehold or spider's breath could be detected beyond it.

Namgyal had been watching for any signs of tribal life—the Lopa or Aka, the Mishmi or Monba— different tribes said to inhabit the highlands of the Indo/Tibetan border area. On occasion, they traded with Tibetans on the other side. But this was altogether new territory. The two tribes they had encountered were thousands of years behind the times, and without name. Namgyal knew exactly where he was electronically, as measured from the sky by instruments which, ten years ago, even in the technological world, did not exist. But the cultural and psychic landscapes were now a total blank on his inner map. The mystery was unnerving. But one thing he did know: this had to be that secret entrance to Pemakod he'd heard about as a child. This was the waterfall; no other cliff anywhere in the Himalayas was so high and mighty. That meant one thing, as foretold by his great-grandfather: there had to be a way to the top, and at the top, the place every Tibetan Buddhist dared not hope for. He was sure of it now.

Namgyal shrank from further discussion. He felt another presence. They were being watched. That, too, he was certain of.

CHAPTER 122
Hidden Chest-widths of Fair Weather Within the Cyclone

SANNAZARO STUMBLED, laboring beneath the roaring winds. Marigold and Rajibai helped him to his feet.

"I'm not feeling myself," the Italian moaned.

"You look terrible," Marigold confirmed, eyes wild.

Namgyal tightened the band holding his sunglasses, attempting to batten down his companions' rucksacks as they stood with their backs to the brunt of spray while also attending to the crackling voice of Bob Nash at DMA. The team there had gotten corroboration of the three incoming choppers.

"Say that again. The wind is berserk here. Again?" Pressing the headset to his right ear, Namgyal picked it up at last: "Got that, over."

"Jigme ..." Marigold mumbled. "Jigme!"

Turning away from the dumbfounding vantage before him, the highest waterfall in the world, he found himself staring into the barrel of a gun. A very old gun.

Anna Christov, standing on the water-enshrouded slope, shouted something in a broken, panic-stricken Russian. She seemed to stutter. "Presteetya, kto vwee?"

The party stared back at her.

"Kto vwee? Tsel'vashevo veezeeta?"

Again an awkward silence. Finally, desperate, "Zachem vwee proshlee? Kak vas zavoot?"

In truth, of course, she had not spoken her second language for a very long time, longer than she could possibly realize.

The three men, and then the boy, raised their arms and stood, facing her. She was alone. Marigold could only grasp part of her Russian. Again, this time in French, but one that was not comprehensible, not in the blizzard of wind.

The Commander had a rudimentary grasp of croissant and Gallois jargon, and used it to good effect. "Je m'appelle Monsieur Marigold. I'm an American. Do you speak English?"

"Americanskee? Wha—wwwwhat you doing here?" said Anna in her flustered, tragic English from so long ago. "He—" she pointed her gun at Namgyal "—is no American. Tibetan," she affirmed.

"That is correct. His name Jigme Namgyal. You speak Tibetan?"

"A mirror. Do you have ... a mirror?"

"Mirror? Yes. Yes, I have a mirror. One minute, but if you please, put down the gun," Sannazaro pleaded, scrounging through his pack for his small shaving mirror.

"Folks, we've got to get going," said Namgyal, as he gazed upon the gorgeous woman before him. He knew this was the rogue anthropologist whose existence had so shocked Dr Wouverman. But there was no time to get into that now—not yet. "Nash is giving an ETA on the choppers of two minutes. We have got to move, now!"

"No move!" shouted Anna, still holding her gun which Namgyal could see to be authentic. Rusted, 100 years old, a .455 double-action Webley-Fosbery. He was certainly perplexed by that. But their situation was urgent.

"Ma'am, I don't know who you are, but we are not the enemy. And if we don't get you to cover, and I mean now—" and he tried to put his hands down to get things moving, but she was adamant.

"No!"

Training the gun on all of them, despite the shaking in her hand, she took the mirror from Sannazaro with her other hand. In nearly 77 years she'd not seen one image of herself. Pre-benumbed to possibilities, she examined herself. Yes, she'd known certainly that her hair had never lost its dark luster, shown a single strand of gray; that her hands and arms and breasts and all the other parts of her had never wrinkled, only gained in tone and golden glow. But she never had had an opportunity to see her face, the real proof, for the water up high was milky white from the glacial minerals. It held no reflections. But now ... her astonishment! And the way the fingers of her gun-holding hand tried feebly to explore the untarnished skin, gave away something of her extraordinarily emotional confrontation with herself.

"You've been out here a long time, haven't you?" said Sannazaro.

"You are the one!" Marigold cried out. "The one who wrote the diary?"

"What diary?" Namgyal importuned.

"Anna Christov!" the Commander declared. "But—but so many years? Look at you! How is that possible?"

Sannazaro stared at her lovingly, perplexed, her story flushing over his memory from two nights before, when Marigold had read her little book, which he now produced from his rucksack and gave to her.

She took it in her hands. A rhapsody of tears left her powerless. To hear her name uttered. To find that one remnant of the day her life changed forever. She crumpled to the ground in desperate confusion. Relief. Terror. She dropped her gun, which Namgyal seized. There were no bullets.

"Please, we must go," he implored them all. "Before it's too late."

Marigold and Rajibai helped Anna to her feet and they moved towards cover. Anna heard the choppers before the others, and she was attuned enough to recognize that these three men, with the innocent boy, were surely different from those who had attacked her and the tribe many days before. She proceeded to lead them at an astonishing dash towards a cave, the very one from so long ago, bounding behind boulders which would ensure their concealment and protect them from the down-rushing hurricane. Even Namgyal found her pace exhausting.

The choppers came in low and fast, circling over the broad basin, but they could not move closer to the waterfall because of the pounding winds. But as they were radioing this fact to Malevich and team, who were trekking a mile behind on foot, one of the co-pilots saw the two wooden sentinels. He knew these primitive towers presaged another village somewhere nearby. He reported this in his radio exchange.

"They're up there," the co-pilot acknowledged.

The Americans had no more than an hour or two's lead over the Russian/Indian team. Anna's path led directly into the peripheries of the gigantic concavity of the waterfall. Wild sprays, miles of water, formed an unearthly vertical wall, prehistoric drapery brushing the insides of a sculpted amphitheater the size of Delphi. From within the funnel clouds emanated a nightmare of cyclone thunder, continuous explosions ripping through other explosions, water detonating typhoons underlying hurricanes. No words.

But Anna showed absolute faith in the one knife-edge path, leading by blind corner after corner towards—what? Then all became clear. It was an enormous recess, like a ground squirrel's underground burrow, although nobody could muster such foolhardiness as to approach it, for it was concealed completely by the watery mayhem all around it. Even 500 feet from the apparent center of the falls, the winds and force of pounding spray were deadly. Anna led them towards the concealing zone of narrow calms, hidden caesuras, a miraculous three-foot wide razor's edge, like a crescent moon leading to Abraxa, *in lunae speciem cujus cornua*, through which one narrowed down one's bulk to remain strictly within the chest-widths of fair weather, precisely memorized, that was miraculously immune to even a breeze. One step to either side, and it would be the end; a person would be shredded by the gusts, flung a mile off into oblivion.

"Follow me, every step. Precisely," she cautioned, her English coming back as if riding a bicycle, waiting to pee, going to sleep—some things never forgotten. She took Rajibai by the hand.

Once inside the cave, a series of dubious, conflicting, self-contradictory tunnels led into deepening shades of darkness, hues that defied the color scheme, that seemed to suggest an inward journey, with all its turns and starts. Human nature itself—dreams, nightmares, assaults, restraints, trepidations, fears, glories, mysteries. The whole evolution of our kind in the very architecture and passageways of a cave. Every germ of a thought, each nuance of hope and despair, the circumlocutions of biological history made manifest with each crawl space, revolutions and yawning schisms favored from ledge to ledge. Century after century, displayed into the eternal night of our wanderings, exiles, expatriotisms, cafés in Paris and flights from Egypt. Question marks laid out for all eternity in the cosmic darkness of animal beginnings, and the illumined premonitions of the future. Alfred Wallace in Java; traces from the Paleolithic; cuneiform and cosmic background radiation: all was there, in the stellar depths which rolled further and further away from the outside air.

Anna paused, trying to decide something crucial.

"But which one?" Namgyal asked. He could see she was terrified. "We won't hurt you. We would never hurt you."

Only Anna was able to see in the darkness. Namgyal switched on his headlamp, and affixed the nicad-fueled device to his forehead. He had one spare, which the boy held directionally, moving in front of his father and Sannazaro, shining a path, still holding on to Anna.

"May I ask, where's the tribe?" Namgyal queried.

"What do you want from us?" Anna proclaimed, repeating herself, to be sure they understood her English. She was still utterly shaken by what she had seen in the mirror. Joy mixed with unspeakable fear. A very private confirmation, lacking dates, a yearling before so much duration, and these strange yeomen, vestiges of her forgotten long ago.

"I work for the American Government," the Tibetan volunteered. "I know there is some substance here, and the tribe consumes it ... don't they? They eat it, or drink it? I must find out. It could help the world. If the Russians and their Indian collaborators obtain it, however—"

She looked upon him. He was rather beautiful, if one ignored the fact that he looked like hell. And the others, so pale, so utterly unmuscular, like infirm children who'd been sick since birth, kept indoors, anemic-looking, muscle meant for sewing or carrying groceries, not life—or not the kind of life she knew.

She stared in the darkness at Marigold, who reminded her of her own father. Caught between two worlds. Finally, she uttered, "I am American."

"It said so in the diary, which we took the liberty of reading," Marigold admitted. "We found it a few days ago. You'll pardon our curiosity, Anna—may I call you Anna? You see, we could have had no idea... the metal box was so old and ... I don't even know what to ask you about all this."

"That's all right. You didn't know anything. Where was it?"

"Ten miles downriver. Lodged in a thicket. Amazing that it emerged."

"Yes. It is."

Namgyal was at a disadvantage, knowing nothing about the contents of that little book, though he would learn soon enough.

"The others. You've seen what they're capable of doing," he began.

"You won't hurt me?"

"Never."

She nodded, confirming for herself her own inner resolve. Then, she pointed the way.

"How far does it go?" Namgyal inquired.

But her thoughts were racing beyond the moment. She countered with a sudden idea: "What year is this?"

"Year? Why, it's 1999," replied Rajibai.

"One nine nine nine?" she asked, working out the numeric visual in her mind. "Almost 2000?" she cried, her throat choking up, slowly making the mental translation into her world, frying her brain cells with exponential wonder. "Is it possible?"

"Please, where does the tunnel lead?" Namgyal again asked, bypassing Anna's terrible moment.

But the beautiful woman was too devastated to speak. She leaned against a rock, then sat down with her head in her hands.

There was an awkward exchange of looks, first by Marigold, then his son, each trying to determine how best to offer her assistance, chivalrous respect, warm comfort. Who could understand her perplexity. Rajibai stood before her with the eyes and inarticulate support of a younger brother. Sannazaro felt her pain, but didn't know how to assuage it either. Namgyal was the one actually to sit down with her and lightly take her hand. He looked into her utterly self-absorbed quandary. Noting the barely visible blonde hairs on her neck, like the soft fuzz of a human fetus, softly suffused hues of quince, the color of Monchinel apple, lanugo and pappous plant untouched by time. Her face appeared unblemished by every modern want.

"My name is Jigme."

"Jigme," she whispered, grasping after any reality.

"Jigme Namgyal." He pronounced the two words slowly.

"And I am Anna Christov."

Finally, as the three men and the boy hung on her every word, she said in a removed, disinterested way, "I was born in the year of our Lord 1897, in Boston. I graduated from Harvard at the age of 15. My father had a great opportunity for research. The family moved to Moscow. There was a Revolution. Perhaps you heard about it?"

CHAPTER 123
The Time Tunnel

NOBODY DOUBTED HER for a moment, but still, the truth of this dimension without precedent, her personal transcendence, was stunning beyond any conceivable computation, and they all felt the weight of her coming-of-age, this timetable of eternities which gave her every logical and evident succor. A situation of the mind larger, more complicated, supporting greater potential than anything that could be voiced. All was wild surmise. The song of the whales, recommending Gilgamesh, Enkidu, at the very least. A condition as remote from understanding as the spider's eight eyes or flame-skimmer's aerodynamics.

The conversation, haggard and moist, continued for some moments, providing enough information for Namgyal and the other two men to make a reasonable deduction: the genetic monster was real. Moreover, it was not merely genetic. The substance was out there, either plant, animal or possibly some mineral combination in the water they drank, perhaps even the microbiota on the rock surfaces, that gave them, and apparently Anna too, this arrested aging process. Or was it some other elixir? Could it be the caddis flies or mosquitoes, or some water-borne insect agent of transmission? Possibly the excretion of gastropods in the water they drank? *Ariolimax columbianus*, or *Arion ater*? As for Anna, she looked to the men to be in her late teens, or early twenties, at the most. If she had aged, it was only a year or two from the time she said she first arrived in this place in 1923.

Her staggering beauty and innocence, and the pounding waterfalls around them triggered in Namgyal an unexpected hailstorm of incoming visuals. Vulnerable to the cumulative truth of his wild heritage, his family Buddhism, an aura as grand as the Ra Sa, or land of gods enclosed by walls, which once protected all that he had known prior to the Chinese invasion. In the sanctuary of Jo k'an, the Jobo, a Buddha 1,300 years old, smiling at the little boy. His weekly visits with his father to Ramoche, Sera and Ganden temples, each spectacularly lit by lanterns known as *mar mes*, and frescoed in the spectacular paintings from the legendary hands of Pad ma mk'ar pa and sLeu c'un, images of the realized masters—Rin po c'e, Padmasambhava and Tson k'a pa. Four arms swooping down to cuddle the child, eleven heads, 1,000 hands all offering kindness. A profusion of personal divinities, or *yi dam*, protecting him from harm. *Gser t'ani*, golden figures against black, floated down in the many mistrals of wind and spray, alabaster eyes, rock-crystal lips, soft stone fingertips. Sheets of silver paper drifted by, engraved with lapis lazuli renditions of the pratimalaksana sacred literature—the threefold basket, the five *suttas* or discourses known as *Nikayas*, the *Khuddakanikaya*, the long suttas and middling-long suttas each conversing on yoga, meditation, the Eightfold Path, five stages of attainment and personal trances. There the genius of goodness, and there Samantabhadra Bodhisattva riding on his elephant. Diadems of five Dhyani Buddhas, reliquaries opening the way to the eight-leafed lotus flower path, petals bright and wide, incense burners at full pungency, and Siddhartha himself coming forward, followed by naked heretics, patrons in the form of thunderbolts, jeweline reformers, aureoles in the night. All this and more.

In his mind, the bells and cupolas and stepped terraces of eternity; sPyan ras gzigs chanting hymns on the nature of thirst or *tanha*—said to lead to rebirth; the many apostles and masters following in the trails of water, a meteorology of supreme beings. For a few brief moments he was transfixed, ambulatory in Heaven, wandering through his homeland in the days prior to the ruins; to the front gates, into the monk's secret beer cellar of the very Castle of Leh, built by the glorious King Sen ge rnam rgyal, about whom legends had infiltrated every household for subsequent centuries. Until he was delivered back again, having reached Buddha's throne, and made his peace. He had arrived. All wet, to be sure. But he was there, more alive than at any time in his life.

He opened his eyes—and there before him, the remarkable fact of Anna Christov and the awesomely beautiful falls surrounding them at that moment. He took a deep breath.

"Where did you go?" asked Rajibai.

"Home," said Anna. She knew. She'd been there with him. This much even Marigold could divine. In the way her own eyes became that lapis; her fingers those soft sandstones; her ruby lips the very crystal.

Coming down with a lurch from his sudden aerie, Namgyal could reckon on the magnitudes before him in the guise of this remarkable woman. There was, easily, a Nobel Prize or two fermenting in the blood of Anna Christov. But as he presently set about to situate a microwave relay dish at the inside entrance to the cave, he hoped that it might be a prize for peace, not medicine or chemistry. This was a change that had come over him; as he dared meet her probing gaze, borne upon aqua velveteen and sumptuous surreality—just like that, he wanted to love this woman. Desperately. She brought him back to the vitality of the mountains, and to that soft quiet eternal life that had been taken from his family by the Chinese bastards. Peering fixated into her eyes, he knew he had returned.

Anna presently urged the group onward. Namgyal's transmitter was useless inside the tunnel. They were cut off from the frequency world. As they started up one of the underground cross-traps, Marigold tried to explain their own purpose in coming. He made a meringue of it, philosophizing blue in the face, citing various defunct utopians, Stuarts and Bourbons, pontificating on the question of pantheism, his funny bone acting up between unrelenting meditations on *Ephiphanius in Anchoret*, number 58. But

Anna was in no mood for learned philology nor the politics of the end-of-the-world. She was too shaken to contemplate the whys and wherefores. But she was clear with her ingenues about a few salient facts: everyone who belonged to her life back in Russia, and in America, was dead. She had a new family now, 21 members, that was all. They saved her life once; and since that time, they had saved her for all time.

She had not imagined that the outside temper of humanity would ever find them out. Now that it had happened, she could not grasp the real-timing of it, the links to escape. Her thoughts were burdened by the survival of her family; each precious personal destiny she harbored upon her shoulders. All the military might of the early twentieth century rushed into her thoughts, clouded her hopes and prospects which had already suffered from changes up high—revisions affecting the very livelihood of the clan and accounting for their forced descent.

Moreover, something else had occurred in her life, and it had been two months of pain, with no explanation forthcoming.

She referred among other things to her having been a doctor back in Russia. How she felt the same ethical responsibilities to this, her family. They were innocents. The modern world was unknown to them. And if, indeed, the year was nearly 2000, the modern world was unknown to her too.

Namgyal carefully explained to her what was at stake. She listened studiously, asked questions, nodded compliantly. The years had in no way dulled her survival instincts—quite the contrary. In the end, she made them promise absolute confidence, gentleness, love. They all pledged fidelity to her cause, her tribe, her secret.

Namgyal didn't know what he was doing any more, for he had, in essence, just thrown away his career. The desire he felt for her was overpowering. Nothing else mattered. Her sobering situation, more confusing than anything Wouverman had intimated, her plush physical appearance, ripened him. A magnanimous grape of a man, coerced back to what nature had intended for all of us, that signal cliff of reverberating electron desires, proton demons. It was the cosmic handshake, the Rings of Saturn dance, of fairies fairly foolish, a daze that only perfect chemistry can ensure, and it was blushing all over him. Ripples of longing were hewing his gut. Anna knew his desire, saw it written all over the senses around them, but she refused to acknowledge it. There were other conditionals, priorities, caution flags.

As for Marigold, who found Anna no less ravishing, he felt—as he had been governed towards his boy—a new father's protective instinct, nothing more or less.

They started up the right tunnel. Swallowed into knots, hurdling through shallow waters socked in by turtle crawls, tank spongers, worm-knees, short-limbed and 100-year-old inches. Picking round hedges of rock, creeping past the silent trails left by unknown insects, unraveled in the plying, loitering dark. By Braille along ancient pockmarked passages, the way of sluggish reptiles.

The other two tunnels, Anna explained, led miles into the center of the wall, eventually coming to dead ends, but not before spinning off into dozens of similar cul-de-sacs. If one did not know the way, there could be serious consequences. Lost forever. In trenches embanked by bloody undoing. Black holes of somber space, lopped off from guard, or daylight. Nightness eternal. A narrowing of hand and eyes, where the soul in deepest misery went hither to the ditch of self-finalities. In certain instances, she said, the tubular passage did not admit to paths back. There was no way to gain a 180-degree turn; the roundabouts were as slender as the pick-axe. No wheelbarrow to plant the reverse; no method of excavation; denuded salt-stone harassed the visitor; forces of magnetism so confusing as to render the traveler helpless amid the cave-in of darkness and claustrophobia. A Yeti had gotten trapped centuries before. Its skeleton remained locked in ambivalence, three miles into the center of the wall.

She led them through an amazing world of stalactites, stalagmites, calcareous waters that had left millions of years of color saturating the inner walls. It reminded both the Commander and Governor of their descent from the Toda Land of the Dead. As they went deeper, higher, they passed pools larded with reflecting chunks of pure gold, and the little light coming from three miles above reflected off the crystalline surfaces of the interior to create—in concert with the fine mists and tiny rivulets of streaming water—a vertical amphitheater of prisms. Star sapphires of a glitter scarcely before observed by human eyes protruded promiscuously from the inner walls. A phosphorescent lake, perhaps 200 feet across, teemed with biology—thriving freshwater fishes elsewhere extinct, a Tibetan cisco, schools of golden *Moxostoma lacerum*, magnificent lampreys and downy sculpins, even the Asiatic chub, thick tailed, whistling to the travelers from underwater, the sound carrying across the vertical Tiffany's whose sulfurous walls dripped with transparent nematodes. Each worm a dangling chime, transacting sound frequencies that echoed perdurably across the countless chambers. A music of infinite spheres within the hollow world. Inflammable vapors, green sparks a mile or more, whirling upon themselves like fairy spells, zephyrs that weep, or glittering hands of a mightier intelligence at rosy dawn. Creatures that did not exist elsewhere in the known world. Any one of them, Namgyal realized, might hold the substance they'd come looking for. The array of possibilities was enormous, bewildering, and he understood how hopeless his task had been. To individually bioassay so large a sampling pool was ridiculous. What were they thinking?

"Does the tribe eat any of these?" he asked. "We kill nothing," she said.

Marigold radiated. "You're all vegetarian, then? You eat no meat?"

"Watch what say you, thank you," applied she, indignant at the very idea of killing.

"Pardon me, Madame. Trust that I, too, would never harm a living being."

All around them were structures new to geology, and with no geologist present to burden them with explanation. All was sheer, uncompromised wonderment amid Tarzan country, suspension bridges of hemp, drop-offs around the barest margins, a path just wide enough to squeeze by. A climb that invited terror—or would have had they not been in the company of an expert like Anna, whose every move through heavy oxygen wedded to night was measured, providential, safely conforming to the ease of the path, once you knew it. The entire interior world of the waterfall was honeycombed with the action of mineral deposition and scouring, holes going nowhere, trails that were not trails at all but fossilized rivulets, caked over with the impacted purple strands left by giant Himalayan elephant snails.

"The snails speak," commented she, expatiating no further.

They continued in silence for a time, then Anna spoke again. She explained that the tribe had gone ahead, and would be back at the village by nightfall. It would take several hours to reach there. The foursome grasped this news with joyous relief. A village. Normality. But then Anna continued. Did they notice how the time tunnels were alive with musical droplets of water echoing at different timbres throughout the labyrinthine complex? Her people, she said, had studied the music and adopted it as their language.

This was too much to grasp at once. Marigold, bedazzled by the implications, had difficulty holding on to the pathway. Monsieur Governor simply gasped for breath. Rajibai, racing ahead, tripped o'er a dangerous gallery of new things, animate and otherwise.

Moving past an epidemic of bottled earth, tunnel-anemia gripping their slow prowl through catacomb paste burrow, glacier foot, evaporating fires. Heavy *Aphonopelma*-like cutylenums (a new species of tarantula), silk lined, finest brocade, weighing two pounds, holding fast to their nests in the glittering sparkle of headlamp. Silver voice and not dangerous, Anna said.

As they ascended, Anna tried to explain what happened to her people in the preceding months, and why the tribe had to seek food down below the waterfall, where they had never been before. How some mysterious phenomenon had been killing off their plants along the rim—something in the sun, she believed. Marigold reasoned it might be ozone depletion, about which, of course, she knew nothing. Or global warming. It was the tribe's descent beyond their known world which had first put them in contact with the hunters, people very like an entirely different species. Such natives must have gotten word out to other tribes, until, eventually, the information of their existence reached the Indian military.

Marigold then informed her of the recovered corpse that had triggered the whole subsequent sequence of events. Namgyal confirmed that he, too, had heard all about it.

Anna stopped. Her face reflected everything. She was shattered. If her speaking was carefully articulated before, impeded from lack of exercise, now it was all she could do to make sense in a human language. Implosion holding back tears, she questioned them intensely about how old the body was. What he looked like—questions that neither Marigold nor Namgyal could possibly answer for reasons they would later explain.

"Only that he was young and badly injured. Long dark hair. Caucasian, tall. His body was shown to us in a pathology lab. Could you have known him?" asked the Commander.

"Yes," she managed.

It seemed clear enough to all that the 'corpse' was that of her lover, or husband, or whatever they called a spouse in this society. "How was he buried?" she asked.

But Marigold only reiterated details of their brief and moribund encounter with the body at the laboratory. He did not go on about the freezer room, the fact that scientists were studying the corpse, or that its discovery had spawned an international paroxysm of corporate and government greed that might well spell the demise of her people unless some draconian strategy could be enacted.

"What was his name?" the Commander asked.

Pausing, then ... Anna played a sound on her mini-harp. There was no way to translate it. A cadence of flight feathers in bliss, or airy lovely cloud with no concerns. The passing overhead in a single flock of a million Sara orangetips, hindwings dangling in the bright sulfur air, sunny canyons in their brain, mustard plants on the nerve endings of their tongues. Of passion beyond reference. Day and night, night and day, forever. Nectar drooling down fuchsia-flowered gooseberry.

Namgyal raised the obvious issue of longevity, and how it worked. He wondered how it was that this person could have been killed, and if others of the tribe, in her experience with them, had died.

Anna divulged a few intimations of what she knew. The fact of a magic plant, a pure cobalt poppy, but nothing like the common dicentra or eschscholtzia, not even close to papavers and romneyas; more akin, an outsider might observe, to *Meconopsis baileyi*. In any event, very few remained, halfway down the wall. And hence, every member of the tribe was reared from earliest age to be a jumper.

"A jumper?" hazarded Sannazaro, always the first to catch the scent of personal risk or injury. "What is that?"

But she would not explain, or not at that moment. Rather, she described how the plants and the tribals had co-existed for a very long time and seemed to depend upon each other. Without the plants, the people of the waterfall would not be who they were, and without the people, the plant population would never be sustained. The symbiosis—a primordial dialogue between the tribe and the plants—was accented by her own joyous and obvious nostalgia. To have known such unique plenitude, total absence of harm's way, or the ghosts of prior injury, left the Commander dazzled by implications he could not follow, resonance unrivaled. He gaped at the wound of his own mortality, contemplating the alternative who stood before him in the guise of a perfect woman. She was bound to the purgatory of her unique experience, had managed to go beyond shade or hesitation; and he longed for all of it. "Jumpers?" Namgyal reiterated.

Anna was steadfastly withheld from saying more.

But if the plant possessed a rare gene for longevity, why did that man die? Marigold was intrigued but wary of pressing too hard, given what they now divined of Anna's relationship to him.

She pointed out that, based on her own knowledge as a medical doctor, it appeared the poppy totally inhibited the aging process past a certain point. The ceiling appeared to be approximately 500 full moons, the age of the oldest member of the tribe, the shaman. But it could not prevent death from injury or starvation. Anna then confirmed that the temperatures had been heating up for years in the eastern Himalayas and the gigantic hanging glacier on Namche Barwa above had been showing signs of weakening. Sizable pieces had come off, not the least of which was the 20,000-foot icicle that had killed her fiancé and other members of the expedition all those years ago. There had been increasing numbers of earthquakes. The whole mountain could go at any time.

"I understand," Marigold said.

"That's the reason the tribe hoped to resettle below the wall for a while, out of the way of coming catastrophe. But the lower altitude was hard on them. Too much oxygen," she went on.

"Well, how high do you call home?" Namgyal asked.

"We all live above 20,000 feet," she estimated.

"But that can't be," the Tibetan replied. He knew that the highest known village in Tibet was at 17,800 feet. There was another, similarly, in the Bolivian Andes. For most, 18,000 feet was considered the death zone, where human habitation was impossible beyond a few months, as during a major mountaineering ascent. Usually, such climbs were aided by bottles of oxygen. Most high-altitude mountain people developed overall lung capacity exceeding that of lowlanders by 30 percent. But it did not guarantee immunity to rampant adult-onset diabetes, heart and lung disease, ulcers, depression, occasional suicide. In fact, scholars had shown that Tibetans during the Middle Ages died by the hundreds of thousands from stomach cancer. Tibetan and Andean life expectancy was nothing to brag about. In fact, Namgyal had always believed that mountain people were condemned in most respects. Acclimatization did not correspondingly ensure happiness, or living past 60.

Anna had no explanation, except to say that the people were used to it. They'd always lived there.

They continued moving steadily higher and higher through the mesmerizing maze of tunnels. Every three steps caused Marigold and Sannazaro to stop and take ten breaths. With every inhalation, some aroma infiltrated their minds, passed them from the present to the next step, as if by some alchemical twist, bottles of wine in a tango between glasses. Anna held Rajibai's hand, while he continued to use his headlamp to light the path. A sinuous trek beneath glittering stars in a boy's eye—pendants in the cavern pave-set, platinum hoops, naturally blue diamond clusters, pearl tassels and briolette-baguette. Bezel and foliate, white gold en suite, rosecuts and cabochon secrets.

"What time is it?" Marigold muttered, out of breath.

"No idea," his Squire remarked. "Nor day. Nor month."

"Well, wait a minute—" Marigold tried putting back the pieces of their previous 48 hours, but could not. "Jigme, uh, when did we first meet up with you? How many days ago?"

"Why that was—uh—" And Jigme, too, was stymied.

"Come to think of it—" But Rajibai was also unsure.

"But how is it that none of us can remember such a simple thing?" Sannazaro asked. There was no explanation.

"Surely it's Monday," Marigold proclaimed.

"I thought certainly Thursday," replied his Squire.

"More like Sunday, isn't it?" Namgyal conjectured.

"The year is more troublesome," thought Rajibai.

"I thought you said 1999?" Anna interjected. "Is it?" the foursome rejoined, one perplexity more taxing than the next. "Isn't it?"

Rajibai's brain was reeling now. He hadn't said anything about the year, only thought it.

Outside the wall, Malevich, Jomsom and team were nearing the wooden obelisks, guided by the chopper surveillance overhead. The trail had ended. All marveled at the waterfall, at least for a moment or two. For there were other distractions. Malevich had brought something in his arsenal Namgyal hadn't counted on: a metal detector. With it, he could easily locate the presence of the microwave relay the Tibetan had hidden just inside the cave entrance.

"We've got them," the Russian exclaimed confidently.

The half-dozen soldiers each had flashlights, far weaker than headlamps, and their ability to move quickly inside, or gauge the context of multiple tunnels, was hampered. One misstep led to another, and—after the first false start—Jomsom realized this was no easy proposition. He could not 'read' a trail with his normal facility. But he was tenacious.

As for Malevich, there was no question of turning back. He knew that this plant, this elixir as alchemists for millennia had thought of it, would earn him a fortune. MWPH would become the Microsoft of pharmaceuticals in the twenty-first century.

"Faster!" he urged the troops, who moved maniacally, a phalanx in the glowing dark.

CHAPTER 124
Anna's World Above the Falls

THE COMMANDER, Sannazaro and Rajibai were sick. Maggots seemed to be eating out their intestines, hornets their brains. The extreme altitude compounded perceptions with queasily filtered, heavily burdened eyesight. Namgyal, for all his genes, fared only slightly better, at first.

High in the rock-wending funnel, where pyres of granite might have greeted Gustave Doré, and the likes of Zadak's final wilderness, figures of some other Testament heretofore unwritten emerged to meet Anna. They were mostly naked, their purity at once astounding. Only a portion of their sex organs were concealed beneath the little mini-harps at their waists. What sorts of instruments, Marigold pondered, flashing weakly between striations of altitude demoralization, kneeling in his stomach, his lungs collapsing, cave-ins along every artery?

Triple-action sixteenth-note transpositions, no fixed tones, no pillar or board, no neck, no comb, no hollow or mechanism. It was a different instrument entirely, melded to the bodies of those who played them, with strings of dried chlorophyll (no cat gut for 1,000 miles) stretched without analogy from their origins to the future of all vibration. A column of air, piped through perforations like those seen painted on walls at a burying ground by the archeologist Bruce in Thebes; not so different from a Greek trigonon, as much lyre as lute. Filled with sudden outbursts of rustic, musical greeting, curves from ancient Ireland, Lude harp diatonics, Asiatic semitones, the effect, somehow, of pedals in the upper stratosphere where all stood. Vegetal matter made the minor scales, a combination of air and water the lily-pond upper notes. Half-tones that seemed chromatically to fly upon some invisible disc, like the revolutionary pillar rods of Cousineaus or Erard—angels doting on G, clustering about D, avoiding A, purely striking F sharp, somewhere between B and E a quip, a candle, touch as soft as down, never close to C sharp. Passages of scale akin to pianoforte, or claviharp. Sixty octaves, or more—could it be!—colored by invisible tuning pins and nodes of intangible melody caught at altitude, as if a wind itself played the instruments, helped along by fingers accustomed over eons to the Aeolian storms that gripped these mountains high. All this Marigold deciphered in his reckless state of final abandon. Such harmony...

Emotional symphonies accompanied their surprise upon seeing Anna's companions in the crepuscular glow of the summital half light. Chords rapidly articulated. Hearts mirrored in the river of their language that had become such chanson. Like the quietest of Schumann aretta. Marigold recalled that shifting center of triple pianissimos in the great romantic's *Davidsbundlertanze*: silhouetted notes, or beings, penumbraed in waning twilight, that appeared to the four outsiders as creatures from another time and place—embraced by both human joy and angelic dispassion, plainsong and lyric, whose every courtesy bespoke appreciation beyond formality. Such as Dante commemorated in his 26th Canto. The Occitan and Poitevin lyrics of the twelfth-century troubadors of Languedoc. Bernart de Ventadorn's women bringing their lovers to despair flooded Marigold's inert mind. Concinnity achieved through the sheer power of fascination which their bodies and gestures necessarily elicited in all those present. An imaginative transport, in other words. Dulcet strengths of foot, finger, wrist-action and wing. Euphony without regard to theme or particulars. That spiritual handmaiden's table of participles and simulacrums, a quality known during the Renaissance as *venustas*, or inner radiance.

Such evident internalized character was as some contagion, pheromones ministering to the uninitiated. Just to look at them, thought Marigold, was to be supremely privileged, vouchsafed in the ultimate secret of biological design. Their beauty, he believed, was the essence of beauty, as only the great Greek and Italian sculptors had once captured it. Strong aquiline men; curvaceous, bronzed women. Erotic fires beneath their perfect proportions; bodies that defied the normal sense of having come from some racial region but rather held a mélange of world-dispersed physiognomies, as if the very best of the planet's genes originated with them. These were not aliens, or prehistoric brutes, but graceful beings, the aristocracy of evolutionary success. Artful, sexy, vulnerable, innocent— and Anna appeared right at home with them.

Even young Rajibai could not help but take note of Anna's own tight body, the movement of her breasts beneath the Red Army attire, her long velvet hair, shockingly chartreuse beneath the last light, the stride, the hips—everything that can be gleaned about a woman's physique had propelled massive attraction in her male admirers. Rajibai recalled that little slum girl he once loved, and who disappeared the night he had mustered the strength to speak with her. For the Commander, Anna embodied the Medieval ideal of a princess. She was a Platonic Form in Sannazaro's mind, the Quintessence of Beauty. To Namgyal's eyes, there was no more desirable female on earth. He was stricken. He had had a few girlfriends, and his parents had always hoped he would find a Tibetan companion. But that had not happened. Now he thought he understood why. Destiny had saved him.

The newcomers were led along a hidden series of notches over an interminably dark surface of quartzite. Sunlight was nearly away as they removed from the last of the tunnels, coming out—with four gasps which no machismo could suppress—onto the wall itself, where a series of granite switchbacks wended tenuously across the sheer, down-sloping edges. There, just after sunset, they reached the summit, and saw everything. The evening lights of the lunar sky. First glimpses of oddly inflated Corona Borealis, Delphinus, Antares. The gigantic river pouring off the glaciers above, booming over the rim of the cliff, an unexpected tonic of sonata dimensions, literally erupting into the troposphere at 20,000 feet. Impossible glories and phantasie all around them, plunging forth in millions of yards of ice water per second. Like a Beethoven song cycle, disappearing wonders, lost memories and *les adieux*, before all time, where the clouds go to be alone.

Namgyal, moving with amphetamized caution behind the object of his stupefaction, held back his frenzy of hormones in an effort to meticulously take his satellite readings. Gauging by their whereabouts, with the glaciers above and cliff below, he at once recognized the signs of a serious dilemma: they might never make it over the cirque of Namche Barwa behind them.

Amid half a dozen other absolutely spectacular lasses hovering around him, all naked, with very small patches of light, almost auburn pubic hair, the genitals of paradise. Perfect breasts. He was aroused to the vanishing point of adolescent urges. He hadn't felt this way around women—ever! Was he dreaming—a Peter Pan in Kensington, a Pinocchio in the Sahara—or did they all seem to offer themselves?

The other three newcomers were no less awestruck. Female nudity that was painfully, deliriously inviting. A genuine, unaffected taintlessness that could not be readily assimilated by those who had come from the land of deodorants and distilleries. All the women appeared to be around 13, 14, 20, who could say? As erotic and mature as any bodies in the history of womanhood. Perhaps what excited Marigold most was the realization that they were not quite human, but something more. Little Rajibai's feelings were similarly confused; he trembled on an emotional abyss. As for Sannazaro, 100 sex changes a minute in his mind: to make love with any of them would be to enter a wild, perfect female. Paradise multiplied by each touch. Namgyal, too, was dying for that. The women's sexuality catapulted absolutely new sensations in his imagination. New thirst. New air. New sight. As if he'd never before seen a female. The waterfall, one vast salivation. They all seemed to come to a zenith in the countenance of lovely Anna, a hybrid of both worlds which he could relate to.

But Namgyal was also deeply agitated. The unfallenness of these people, these marvelous pedigrees of undiluted light and never-ending andantes, were an open invitation to disaster. Anna could not fail to sense it as well. The pastorale was endangered, the serenades striking out into passages and nocturnes too close to the barbwire of modernity.

They shared that knowing look. How could he even broach the subject of medical extracts, a notion utterly demonic to his mind at this point? Now the fears of Catherine Wouverman haunted him in a way he had not entirely grasped at that night-long session beneath the Pentagon.

Yes, he understood it with regard to the destruction by the Chinese of his homeland. But, at least, against so genocidal an assault, there was a remaining civilization of several million people, and the Dalai Lama to help front the flame of Tibetan durability, however restricted and cruel the circumstances. Here, there was only Anna to hold firm and represent the people's plight. Anna, in all her personal tragic dimensions which Namgyal could scarcely fathom.

His decision was instantaneous, and he shared it with Marigold and Sannazaro. Whatever happened, he would not be a part of these people's destruction, and if that meant renouncing the CIA, so be it. He'd already undergone the moves in his head. The one thing he would guarantee, with all his expertise and might, was that nobody else should discover them. He would find a way to steer the Indians and the Russians back where they came from. Or kill them, if he had to.

"You won't be alone," Marigold said, seizing the moment. "Chivalry and derring-do are the codes by which I have always lived, thought and behaved. While I would never choose to employ a weapon—and we happen to have two semi-automatics—I assure you I am no faint-hearted cherub. I have studied the petard, wielded a lance, would not stand by any attempted assault upon these heavenly Dulcineas. Of course, there is one slight problem, notwithstanding all the fortitude, backbone, courtliness and gallantry one might hope for an entire artillery."

"His aim," Sannazaro volunteered.

"That, and the basic operations beyond the safety. But I trust you can teach us?"

"I think so," the Tibetan said, grinning broadly, before sitting down on the rock. He was dizzy with love.

And there was another, equally powerful motivation seizing Namgyal's instincts, as he and the others were led along the cliff rim. This was the place the sacred books of his upbringing had always referred to. No question about it. He remembered the stories; how, in 1911, a Tibetan monk by the name of Jedrung Rinpoche had explored Pemakod on his own, staying just to the north of the Tsangpo Gorge. He had written a small, cryptic volume entitled *The Bright Torch Guide to the Path to the Secret Land of Pemakod*, published in Paris the year World War I broke out. In it, he warned would-be explorers of the perils of paradise, and of an "inner land without time". The ambiguities of the text remained in Namgyal's mind, a fitting warning about following one's dreams, begging several old Asiatic aphorisms—terrible truths that most people might not be prepared to swallow.

He recalled how in 1954 a famed Ningmapa Rinpoche, along with his family and servant, sought out Pemakod with the help of Jedrung's guide as a means of escaping to India. The roar of 1,000 fighting dragons they kept burning within their hearts as they passed through the Delhung Mhe forest, the nomadic encampments of the Nagchu region, Yagnado and Adrak Zamar. Riding wild stallions across the open meadows, through deepening mountains, repeatedly crossing the Martsang Tsangpo, all of them survived the journey, though none would ever speak of the events that transpired during their exodus. Only the servant, blind since birth, later intimated that something unexpected had occurred. As an old man, living out his days on a government pension in the town of Kalimpong, helped along by a companion all-seeing monkey, he at last broke his silence by speaking with a journalist. He described his adventure 40 years before as "the most important thing that ever happened to anybody; proof, absolute, without direction, beginning, middle or end, with no clue, no roads, signs, evidence, traces, aftermath, mention, material goods, spiritual remains, relics, transfers, transmissions or words; no communications, letters, telegrams or signs; not even a whisper. In short, nothing to validate or verify, the Other World. But Buddha himself."

The summit rim was a complex of utterly heart-stopping drop-offs. There was only one way into the village, and it was altogether concealing. No angle yielded a view; a maze of airways pelted the habitat, which lay ensconced in Heaven's lounge within the absolute privacy of the cliff's vertiginous shadows. An edge of granite 19,000 feet sheer. Hanging free. Children pranced about like parnassian swallowtails, oblivious to the danger all around them. As if there really were no danger, rare birds, these kids. Cloudless sulfur, tailed copper—gossamer-wing hairstreaks and coronis fritillaries, children who could fly on a spotted blue or elfin gray, plucking their little harps with eager fingers. The entire outrageous locale was rhythmically energized by the arrival, for the first time in 76 years, of outsiders. In company with a child, no less.

By the time the foursome had all but reached the huts, three of them were down with delirium. The altitude had laid waste to their brains, midsections, bicuspids, every appendage, and especially their knees. Marigold's broken crazy bone was still driving him potatoes, and Governor Sannazaro was going through a strange erotic conversion, from Platonic love, to multiple epiphanies forged on the loincloth of each and every individual who appeared in waning light before his tired, oxygenless eyes.

In short, each newcomer was a one-man bowling alley of sentiment and near-death hypoxia—that strange queasy converse terror of gravity that excites outward momentum, otherwise known as grand mal skipomania, of tilting migraine, leaning stomach, a pit in his bowels, the sensation of a turnip in his lungs, blood in his eyeballs, cotton candy cloying his nostrils so that he could not breathe, and, overall, an informed wish to die. Not even the seasickness north of Antarctica could compare with this. How strange a contrast, to witness the Tibetan in his prime, and the many children of the waterfall so immune, beside this lowlander epidemic of total body disaster.

Namgyal dispensed certain medicines—Diamox tablets, nasal sprays, PM Tylenols—and made certain they drank plenty of fluids. And as soon as possible he got them indoors so that they could occupy their sleeping bags and not move.

"You might possibly be ill from some form of edema, pulmonary or cerebral, which could prove quickly fatal if not dealt with," he explained.

"How exciting," the Commander mumbled.

The tribals, grasping the state of their fast-declining visitors, also gave them something—a plant, which Anna vouched for. Namgyal did not even consider sampling it for the data it might yield. He had made his decision.

The Tibetan knelt down and touched his lips to the smooth granite rim of the cliff, uttering prayers from the ancient Tibetan texts of *Do* and *Vinaya*, the merits of which were said to confer relief from any accumulations of bad karma. He stood up, knelt again, stood up, knelt again, several times, chanting from the famed *Sadakshapa*, known to Westerners as *Om Mani Padme Hum*, but in his translation, "I invoke the path of truth and universality of experience, so that the jeweline luminosity of immortal mind be unfolded within the depths of lotus-centered consciousness and I be wafted by the ecstasy of breaking through all bonds and horizons." *Om Mani Padme Hum, Om Mani Padme Hum* ... Namgyal chanted repeatedly.

He was already homesick for this place, even at the moment of first arriving, because he had no idea whether, in this world, it could last, or whether he was the very agent of its destruction. Shangri-la. Shambala.

As a child in a monastery, this is all he'd heard about; what all the Buddhist poetry of his upbringing had described. The place of Buddhahood. Nirvana. Absolute enlightenment. "Thus shall you think of this fleeting world: A star at dawn, a bubble in a stream; A flash of lightning in a summer cloud; A flickering lamp, a phantom, and a dream," were the lines he remembered from *The Diamond Sutra*.

Before them was a cluster of three connected hanging long-houses, suspended on the very cliff, far, far above the two guardian sentinels. The huts were tied with thick cordage, hammocks like those used by big wall rock climbers, but 60 feet long, 20 feet wide, engineering feats of the imagination. There, in the strange concavities of the summit walls, where the physics of sound were magically jolted, all was silent. The pounding madness of so much water stopped short, against the blank ferocity of granite that absorbed every wavelength.

Only music—ravishing cross-accents, an opus of mysterious coloring, whose conversations on feisty levels struck a chord between scherzo, ballade, a telegram and mazurka—echoed across the pleated interiors. In the huts, only a distant hiss from the waterfall could be heard. Who would know that a cascade five times larger than the largest known waterfall on the planet, and with perhaps 30 times the energy coefficient, was flowing right there? If one were to place Angel Falls atop Yosemite and Ribbon Falls, and throw in Iguassu, Tugela, Skjaeggedalsfoss and Roraima for good measure, one would begin to grasp the picture. A funnel of freezing white water that plunged free and fortissimo out over the hanging huts, coming from the gigantic, unclimbed pyramid of Namche Barwa, and dozens of other glacial monsters all around it, to the extreme north.

The huts were completely, forever hidden behind the explosive arc of waters pouring off the rim. No one would ever find them, unless they knew for certain they were there. Moreover, reverse cyclones—winds that came from below with the velocity and force of a missile—seemed to roar back upwards, missing by a very few yards the far edge of the structures. That was something entirely new, but the newcomers were too exhausted to think about it.

The peace of this village of 22 souls could not strike a more dramatic contradiction, given Nature's absolute and ultimate chaos all around it. "We are in Tibet," Namgyal explained to the Commander and Sannazaro. "Then those bastards down below have got no jurisdiction," Marigold reasoned.

"You saw what they did to those villagers."

"But the Indian military cannot simply go around killing people."

"Is that a question?"

"A verity, my good man. There are still laws, international treaties, universal obligations."

"Not really. The event we witnessed will be covered up."

"Then I shall go straight away to the Indian Prime Minister and let it be known in no uncertain terms. I have the means to do so. I am a force to be reckoned with."

"That he is," Sannazaro groaned, feeling the full weight of the worst illness in his life.

Namgyal had not enjoyed a moment's respite from the instant he first laid eyes on these two weirdos hanging upside down. Where had they originated, and by what means, purpose and convictions? He had no way of knowing that the Commander had been at the forefront of the Delhi protests, or that he could damn near buy out the Russian pharmaceutical giant with a single gesture. Namgyal recognized something of the American's quixotic nature, though could hardly imagine the extent of his mental complex.

Suddenly, two Chinese jet fighters in formation screeched over the cloudy ribbons of Himalayan twilight. Somewhere not too far away, the KH-12 coursed the storm clouds overhead, plowing through 300 miles of high-pressure sheet lightning, transmitting the sighting of the fighters back to Washington.

Over satellite shortwave from DMA, Nash warned Namgyal of possible Chinese interference, and requested a mission status report. Namgyal paused for a moment, seeming to brace himself. Even

Marigold, in his pitifully weakened state, could see that the Tibetan was going through some kind of crisis. It was indeed the moment Namgyal had been dreading. The merging of ultimate disparates: political tyranny, thousands of years of hatred, greed and military demonology, with true Paradise. Namgyal was hopelessly caught out in the no-man's land. A terrible contradiction on a burning fence.

He began at last. "The Chinese are on to us. It's a mess. Four nationalities. Nobody is going to take a shot at this one." It was of course a devout lie.

Mercifully, static was intruding upon the signal.

"Jigme?" Nash fired back, annoyed.

"There's no time to explain," Namgyal rasped. "We're breaking up.

I'll do the best I can, but there are some complications. I'm sorry I can't be more conclusive. Much ground between here and Lhasa. I'll be back in touch shortly."

And that was it. Nash was discomfited by the deliberate haste of the conversation. He tried in measured tones to inform the others of the ambiguous situation. Nash also knew that Namgyal wasn't being straightforward. Something was terribly wrong, a delicacy hinging on the berserk, beyond all borders of reason or unreason.

Riley, the Deputy Director of the CIA, got the Russian Ambassador on the horn. "Sergei, you've lost, we've all lost. Call off your goons. The tribe has disappeared into China."

He then called up Dr Mehta, the Indian Ambassador, and explained the situation in a most tactful manner. Mehta, in turn, said he'd need to discuss it with Delhi, and that that would take some time.

On the cliff, this state-of-the-art communication system baffled the tribe, as did the mostly cloud-obscured aircraft in the sky. But Anna's reaction was particularly acute. Namgyal picked up on it at once. She had missed out on nearly a century of progress. She had acquired the wildness of mind of the tribe, but also paid a price: she knew nothing about the last 76 years beyond the waterfall. He sensed that she was not entirely at home here in this impossible setting.

They entered the main long hut. Anna introduced the foursome to the shaman, and everyone else, strumming her mini-harp with ease. Marigold, normally the one to bow ceremoniously before such refined assemblages, could barely manage a smile. He was out of breath and needed to sit down. The maggots had eaten their way through his bowels and were now in his throat, it seemed. Sannazaro and the child were already on their backs, panting, by the time Anna began trying to translate everything that had happened, all that these strangers represented. She was clearly agitated, even overwhelmed. Namgyal could easily glean a deep terror in Anna Christov. The future, suddenly, was totally before her, upsetting every achieved wisdom and balance. There was no pomp or celebration in any of this.

"There is so much to ask you. All of you," Namgyal began. "There's time," Anna replied. "This is where you'll sleep."

She showed them an area of thick blankets. A cozy nest at the edge of the world.

"The tribe made these? And built these huts?" Namgyal asked. "Those before them," Anna said.

The children watched her in amazement as she uttered words, conversing with the strangers. Words to them were like soap bubbles, to be played with. They giggled but did not emulate the speech. Or could not.

"What about the cold?"

"What cold?"

True enough, there was no cold. All around them a warmth emanated mysteriously from far below. A perpetual Chinook vertically rising.

"The winds carry the tropical air upwards," she explained.

"So it does," he said. "I can feel it." Then, "Your friends never wear clothes?"

"No," she said, voicing the obvious.

"What about you?"

Anna started to reply, but was conveniently interrupted by colossal snores coming from the direction of Mr Marigold's and Sannazaro's four nostrils. Both men lay sprawled upon the blankets, mouths wide open, dead to the world. From Rajibai came twin snores higher in pitch, yet softer in emanation, like a romaunt.

She and Namgyal both had a good laugh, and it was the first light moment since they'd met.

"You're incredibly beautiful," he said, clumsily trying to salvage some sense of restraint amid enamored bewilderment. But it was too late.

She turned away, shyly, and busied herself.

CHAPTER 125
The Originals

THAT NIGHT, the tribe settled in as it had for millennia; and as 300 million other so-called indigenous peoples throughout the world also confined themselves to the elemental comforts of modest dwellings and close-knit families and communities. The phrases had different meanings; a biological protocol could not be standardized. All people were born, suffered, died, dreaming themselves connected, or confronting the inescapable fact of their aloneness. Death was the organizing principle. Beyond these certitudes, the remainder of a thinking life was veiled, far from view. Some, like the Todas, had their inward contracts, that mythology which centered upon the buffalo. Others, like the Bishnoi, were bound by the same zealous conviction of a stewardship, the devotion to protect every shrub out to the horizon. This gave them identity, purpose and, conceivably, some comfort at the slow or rapid moments of their demise.

The same could presumably be said for the many others who clustered around campfires, in tents, yurts, out in the open, in earthworks of adobe and straw and rock face. But here, atop lost worlds, the tribe of naked snow people seemed absolutely unafraid of anything. No necessary protection or punctuation marks, principles or allegories. No single oral folklore, fiction or fact that could be distinguished to give them an edge in the struggle for existence. Did they struggle? Was there gravity to their thinking, apprehensions, swings in destiny? Was it even possible to lack frustration, goals, chimeras?

At a certain inexplicable moment in the night, the Commander opened his eyes, just like that, and declared, "I had a dream." And he proceeded to recite all that had happened during the last three days, only to be reminded by Sannazaro, also awake now, that it was no dream. Marigold was mightily perplexed. He felt himself to be hovering on a diving board of accelerated consciousness, much like that spectacular convergence of science and emotion worked out anonymously by Erasmus Darwin, Charles's grandfather, and the true founder—never truly credited—of the principles of Evolution, presumably because he had had the courage to outline its merits and rationales in the form of a whimsical botanical poem of epic proportions. Marigold was in that place, at one with the entire cliff; nature's launching pad for reflection, that one lonely spot on Earth where the grandest dreams were collected for posterity or jettisoned out into the world, like seedlings. And he wondered why did all this happen here? What was it about the cliff, the waterfall and these people who inhabited it that spawned such contemplation? Such an aerial immunity to the lower, mundane trials of life. They had, by their very circumstance, renounced all those temporal transfixions, allowed for no obfuscation, maintained pellucidity at all costs, even to the extent that they had lost the need of speech among themselves and knew no other category of human with whom to seek correspondence. Was there no sense of loss, of absence? None that Marigold could yet determine. Indeed, there seemed to be no longing for that which was unknown, unimagined. If they had always inhabited this place, as had truly been the case, for example, among denizens in certain hamlets and hollers of western Tennessee who never left their birthplace by more than a few miles, then there could be no other explanation than that the geography beyond was irrelevant. A condition not unlike most people's lack of concourse with, or concern for, the situation on the moon or on Venus. So, too, these people of the waterfall had no reason to look beyond their cliff and all that it boded.

Sannazaro was not indifferent to these noisy contemplations, attempting to assemble in his collapsing mind's eye a plan, closure. Pondering aloud from a very different angle. So that the two contemplations were like an odd couple of bad duets crying for a venue Off-Off-Off Broadway, somewhere so far Off as to define their cliff of misfortunes. A Mozart might have made good fun of their final late-night reckonings, but to those afflicted with elevation malaise, it was no picnic. Some people, the nauseated Sannazaro reckoned, might ordinarily express thanks for transcending the supposed ennui of our ancestors: the presumption that they were slow of mind, barbaric at some level, and lacking in toothbrushes and Café Vienna. That their cultures were nothing more than dim-witted reactions to Orion's Belt and the Big Dipper; ululations accorded the way a chicken's disemboweled gall bladder might reflect light, give off a sign, presage an omen; that their women gave birth beginning from the age of nine and did not stop manufacturing babies until they died. That the extent of their artistic gifts could be measured by so many tiresome proliferations of similarly painted ceramic shards and pointed if pointless ziggurats to dead gods. That their diet reeked of uniform, tasteless entrails, and, finally, that war was their only diversion from the deadly sameness of 30 or 40 years, the maximum span of their miserable lives.

This, certainly, was the favored mindset of most advanced cultures which continued to marginalize and annihilate the last indigenes on earth. Sannazaro had only the highest regard for these oppressed spirits; indeed, after his days in Toda Land, he found them truly noble and magnificent compared with most others who called themselves human. But in his current, disintegrating physical condition, he harbored few illusions about the demanding rigors of their daily toil. Their languages, wisdom and way of life were vanishing beneath the onslaught of one world culture, one language, one hamburger, one high-rise, the Top Ten, a pair of pre-washed jeans, a new land cruiser. But he was vanishing even faster. They might be ostracized and mowed down by global technological homogenization, the quest for dollars, but every part of his body was feeling downright minced, chopped and diced. True distinctions of cultural significance were possible among these last tribes only out on the fringes, and among the very poorest of people. But as far as Sannazaro was concerned, they could have their distinctions, their poverty, their nobility ... Just give him a warm bed and enough sleeping pills to disappear.

In other words, while he altogether sympathized with the primitive condition, he wanted none of it himself.

As for Rajibai, checking it all out, nosing around—a fever pitch of giggles and other unexpected blood flows associated with altitude—he, too, was deeply immersed, alert to the swaying buttocks before him, tanned and febrile, smooth like glacial granite. He had escaped the past, his past, with its unfortunate truths and terrible calamities. Like a bird removed for the first time from its cage, placed on a wild branch in a stormy gale to feel the forces, every thousandth leaf shimmying against the brunt of cold free air. That sanguine rush of bodily fluids and volumes of excited vegetal primacy within his bones bespeaking great liberation, all went to his head, which presently lay stilled, some solemn weight upon the pillow of his sleeping bag, his little frame, so jubilant and tired, spinning circles, crunched beside others his own age in the oxygenless canopy of stellar night.

Namgyal. The shock of first love. Head awry, heart having come home. That stratum of religious expression that preceded his own Buddhism by 100,000 years. The world seemed totally complete to him at that moment. It all made sense. Though he'd gone to school in Hanover, New Hampshire, and earned 80,000 dollars a year with the Agency, Namgyal, unlike his two elderly traveling companions, instantly fell into step with this altogether different survival stratagem. He was ready to embrace it for life.

And on this night, lacking the fruits that might have been gathered down below had their foraging expedition not been aborted, the tribe made do with a rather modest repast of cold roots, tubers, and berries from on high. Soft clumps of golden barberry and *Primula tibetica*.

The Commander gazed in utter amazement at everyone around him, causing considerable shows of gaiety among the girls, who had never seen such a strange-looking creature as he. With his busy nervous fingers and bushy long hair turning prematurely silver in frizzy patchworks, his grizzled face that sported the unmistakable signs of a red beard that was not exactly a beard but perhaps some kind of algal bloom or fungus, and that long narrow Tony Johannot face, a rapid pen and ink that blotted beneath the eyes—he was a vivid study in purloined misadventures, madcap intrigues, late-night huddling beside the stream, renegade absentias, every love's torment. He embodied misty, historical things hidden in the garden, an expression of romantically haggard incompletion from so many months of unexpected travail to all the ends of the Earth. He bore the look of an emaciated bear, or scarecrow down on its luck. They blushed, and Marigold teased them, and then partook of their meager stock of foodstuffs, and fell in quite comfortably with it all. Particularly with the shaman, whom he supposed wasn't that much younger than himself.

The Commander contemplated his new friends eking out their fortunes in a world of chance. But this tribe, with no name, had one strange advantage, of course. The average human life span, all countries combined, was something like 70, give or take a few years—a decade more in heavy-carousing, Aryan Iceland; three decades less in places like Guinea-Bissau. At the time of Joseph and Mary, life expectancy was a mere 30 years. Did Roman soldiers, their many wives, slaves and babies know what they were missing? Probably not.

But such comparisons were meaningless in the face of the scenario that had arrayed itself before the Commander at 20,000 feet: nearly two dozen beings whose cells would never age, according to what they had learned from Dr Rakshee in Sadiya. What consequences for human civilization, if that bloodline should be duplicated among the six billion people on the planet? Oh, to live forever, imagined the Commander. To have time to read and memorize every book, and still more time to forget everything all over again. Time to make friends with everyone. To turn over every stone of an idea, to sample all sweets. Or to sit absolutely still, doing nothing, without regrets, knowing that someday you'd have the time to change your mind. To live for a century in every country. Flirt with every maiden, champion every cause, collaborate on every project, speak from every podium, carry every torch, never losing sight of the flame; to be fickle, fabulist, precise or sloppy; pursue the picaresque, plaster the world with petitions, swim naked across the Pacific, solo Rakaposhi's South Face during monsoon, walk around the world, live in a tree, study the language of every species, spend ten months on every island, run for President, disparage all the disparagers, manifest a world of equity, justice, tenderness; eradicate all evil, convert the world to veganism, and—in short—presume everything in the secure knowledge that, eventually, you would prevail. To know absolutely that the odds were with you; that, in the end, you would win, because your blood, your genes, your situation had already conquered the only true fear—death. Happy in the common company of immortal souls. Paradise? Or ecological disaster?

He was not sure, not at all. Yet, it had to be admitted outright that with this windfall of longevity the hut inhabitants did not evidence any obvious impact on their surroundings: no class consciousness or self-congratulations. They seemed, in fact, unaware of their special gift. The way, conversely, a mayfly, here for one day, seems utterly satisfied for its 24 hours, as if that were a lifetime—which it is. Their staying power was the lightness of their touch. They left no footprints, exceeded no environmental carrying capacity (the phrase used by scientists to indicate the extent to which any given community stays within the limits of its natural resources). For them, there were no resources. Nothing—ever—to exploit. Earth had given herself without arithmetic. Drama. Tension. No conflict—until now. Though not of their making.

Indeed, they seemed hardly to affect the world at all. When they were gone—but gone where?—no one would ever know that they had lived. Was this a quality to emulate? This world without even so much as an ember? Mr Marigold thought so. Crowquill would surely have ascribed to this manner.

As for their ascertainable culture, what particular gifts, other than the art of living itself, did they demonstrate? Was that enough? True, their engineering capabilities were bold, full of emotion—to have chosen such a location for their hanging huts. They displayed no obvious artistic penchants, other than their music. But that music! How even to describe the octaves, tetrachords, modes and semitones? Mandolins and lutes, lyres and bowstrings in every air. But was it not the case of form following function? Their music was their language, as Thomas More (whom Marigold knew with utmost vigilance) himself once described under the category of Religion: "For all their music... doth so resemble and express natural affections—the sound and tune is so applied and made agreeable to the thing—that whether it be a prayer, or else a duty of gladness, of patience, of trouble, of mourning, or of anger, the fashion of the melody doth so represent the meaning of the thing, that it doth wonderfully move, stir, pierce, and enflame the hearers' minds." As far as he could determine, they either refused to speak, or could not, other than the emitting of occasional strange groans, or grunts—vocables suited to the basics. Why no speech? What evolutionary tricks of the trade had conditioned their vocal chords for this abnegation of all rumor-mongering and verbal snooping? There was no doubt that their lack of lip motion constituted some transcendent capacity. To have outgrown the detestable clutter of airwaves, gossip and useless blather. The twaddle of politics, the gibber-jabber of boredom, all those drivels and mutterings, chit-chats and sputterings. Idle palaver, loquacious horsefeathers. Jargon and small talk, spouthing and mouthing ... Yet nothing good to be said.

He knew that some key to these people could be explained by those little harps. Some wore them on the right, some on the left. All appeared ambidextrous.

And it was in this environment of perceivable cultural bliss that Rajibai played unceasingly with the children, who began instructing him in the ways of the harps, and they cajoled him to take off his clothes, which he did—no objections from his father—so that he was naked. The girls all giggled at his dark little dick and touched it to see if it moved and so forth. Anna looked to the Commander, who thought better of saying anything, for his son was clearly at home and enjoying himself.

"Is there no mother?" Anna asked.

"You're looking at him," Marigold said. "At least for the time being. We were both orphans. But I know that I'm getting the better part of the deal."

Unusually, the Commander was at a loss for words to describe the emotional Utopia little Rajibai had stirred up in him. What a sensationally good boy he was, with that font of electrons streaming from his little heart, directed towards all virtuous things: a genuine fondness for people, a clairvoyance with other creatures, sentience before trees, compassion in the company of bugs, an overflowing loft that enabled him to transcend all fears, regulations, conventions, and strike out on his own. A boy strictly oriented towards cheerful courtesies of every kind. How had the slums, the many privations, and the gruesome murder of his sister resulted in so sterling and well-choreographed a human being? That was a mystery which would take many years for the Commander to better understand, and which no number of socio-biological textbooks could answer. Sannazaro launched into a coughing fit, clinging to his blanket.

Namgyal administered some more drugs. He knew, logistically, that the Italian was in trouble, serious trouble. There was no exit, not from here. Reversing their way in was not fathomable even to the Tibetan, not in the grip of this crazy encumbrance of a trio. Their predicament was strange indeed. Amplified by the as yet unspoken sense that nobody wanted to leave.

The shaman offered Sannazaro some mashed-up berries. The Messer, who no longer felt like any kind of Governor, consumed them with a grimacing resistance. His aches were everywhere manifest.

Anna translated an outpouring of sentiment from the tribe, who could not avoid witnessing the Italian's sorrows: "They say your eyes and thoughts are afraid. But what are you afraid of?"

Said the Commander's Squire, "Nothing. Everything. Think about it."

"I don't know," she said. "You've come here with a purpose. They—all of us—would like to know what it is."

Marigold leapt in: "We came here, honestly, to save you from—"

"People just like you?"

"No, nothing like us. Big companies, governments, greedy bastards searching for medical cures, genetic anomalies they can exploit for profit. That's not us."

"And you thought, by coming here, you could stop it?"

"Yes."

She looked directly at Namgyal. "And you?"

He looked down and started to speak—but she stopped him: "Look into my eyes."

The Tibetan did so. "I am with the US Government," he said. "I told you that. This device—" he rummaged through his pack and brought out the satellite phone with its headset "—I was talking to them. It works like a radio. You're familiar with the technology of the radio?" She nodded. "But I've totally altered my opinion about everything. I've changed my mind."

"Tell me. What are you thinking? I must know."

She already knew, but did not have the heart, not yet, to give away one of their more compelling secrets.

"I didn't expect to meet you. Your people. Now I understand. I apologize. I'm going to make it right."

There was musical discussion: Anna and 21 tribals conversing, a kind of group mind in action.

Finally, Anna looked at him and said, "You're not telling everything."

"What do you mean?"

"There's more to it, isn't there? They're still coming up the caves. They followed you. And those airplanes. They'll be coming, won't they?"

"Not if I can stop it."

"Who is Bob Nash?"

Namgyal nearly fell over. "How ... I don't understand ... Where did you get that name?"

"You were thinking the name. Who is it?"

"Oh my—"

"They can read thoughts," declared Mr Marigold with a revelatory grin. "That's simply marvelous!" He was old enough, and wise enough, to read some of those thoughts, as well, and could surely recognize the flourish of feelings between these two.

"It is true," Anna volunteered.

"But how?"

"Because they're not like—" and she paused.

"Us?" the Tibetan pressed.

"I don't know. The plant effects a change. I don't know what I am. But they are surely different from other humans."

"They are humans, aren't they?"

"You see what they are."

"I don't know what I see."

"Then look more closely." She paused. "They are, I believe, the originals."

CHAPTER 126
The Tower of Babel

THIS WAS ALL a stunning mystery of mental precipices— uncanny genetics that could divine all those heretofore impenetrable synapses, ideas, inner silences—like a cliff of its own, off which Anna's own levitations of mind extended. The whole tribe, she volunteered easily, without any to-do or cutting emphasis, could 'read thoughts'.

No discipline was more exact, immediate and enforceable than that their thinking processes and points should so ruthlessly be denuded, exposed like trees without bark.

"What am I thinking, then?" asked Marigold, keen to test its limits.

"Rhinoceros," she replied.

"That's extraordinary. What now?"

She twisted her lips, a funny spin: "A royal society bull beetle, curious."

"What else?"

"Hmm. An animacula, sampled in Semine Masculino, as well as the last state of the large gnat. You are a strange fellow."

"More."

"All right, you're thinking of a yellow centipede from West Indies and a Monoculus found exclusively in the Thames. What is all that about?"

"My God. I am thunder soddered. Iacobo, did you hear that? A complete crystal ball on every last word. Amazing! But discommodious at best." Marigold scratched his temple, was vexed, irked and utterly scattered in undigested premonitions. "The point is well proven. Now what do we do?"

"Wait!" the Squire ventured in. "Let me try... Now then, go ahead: read my mind!"

She stared easily at him: "Cappuccino. Double."

"Yes. Yes, by Jove. I am humbled, Madam."

"What is a cappuccino?"

"A form of coffee."

"Then you best stop thinking about it."

"My sentiments," Marigold threw in. "He delights in tormenting himself and all those in his company."

For all his levity, the Commander was thrilled and appalled by the possibilities of such mind-reading should they be generalized to the human race. Would it mean a new era of absolute restraint, each individual retreating to a mental blush of silence, some sudden tincture of wonderful breeding, or would it signal the eruption of all-out conflagration, the final war, hostilities raging across the land from neighbor to neighbor? The parade of insults and slights, all the jealousies and dark designs bursting out into the open for all to see and hear. Battlefields lit up in the night. Endless strife, a world of mean-spirited solitaires hidden behind leaden walls. Or, conversely, the nudity of absolute communal calms, no secret left, all spelled out for everyone to think about. Little Brother in every household. A nightmare of eavesdropping fever.

But Sannazaro wasn't done, could not believe it. "I want to try it again. None of these easy-to-read one-liners. That's no different from trained horses and wanna nuts. Now, what am I thinking?"

Anna peered at his balding pate, screwed up her eyes, wriggled her nose, made as if to minister a limerick, then recited Sannazaro's own inner reflection.

"An Italian poet. I do not know Italian, however."

"Aha! A catch surfaces! But in translation?"

She continued to bore straight through to some amalgamation of Dante, involving the general form of paradise, close at her side in the happy world, angelic bees, the lustrous moon, beatitudes and blessed virgins, the confession of Hope to Saint James and the waters of Lethe.

All came through.

"You know your poets," she applied.

"But you have at your fingertips poetry of poetry," the Señor concluded, utterly ravished by her subtle penetration.

But Anna was gazing over at Namgyal. "There's something else I'd like to point out," she said.

Namgyal tried, but could not avert her eye. "Who is this Bob Nash?"

Marigold could see the name impact her person, and was greatly moved by the poignancy of her fears. They showed all over her face. She was demanding truth on behalf of the tribe; her sense of hurt, betrayal, and her accent, which was luscious, contained all that imagined drama of the Russian Revolution, heavy with Anna's purity of purpose and awesome beauty. But this! This absolute gaze into the bottom phases, lowest ages and highest echelons of the gray matter. It put all else to shame, made the brightest seem lame, was, without debate, the final breakthrough. IQ at once obsolete. The reason parrots lacked the need of a neo-cortex perhaps: richer imagination, more complex feelings.

Or that's how the Commander thought of it.

Namgyal again made clear his change of heart, explained how he had been dispatched on a certain mission by his Government, by people like Bob Nash, his boss, to prevent those with odious intentions from capturing the tribe. But he could not conceal his country's sinister goals, gibbeted in his own unconcealable light of internal expression.

She pondered these untoward motivations. He knew that she knew. She knew that he knew that she knew. But Marigold knew something neither of them probably recognized, and warned, "Friends, there are so many cerebral mirrors, open books, mental marbles and glass-bottom knowhows flying around this hut, somebody's going to get hurt. Those aren't ping-pong balls, after all."

Meanwhile, the children of the tribe were nudging up against the silly-looking Commander, demanding to be tickled. He obliged them. Others insisted on exploring the contents of Namgyal's backpack, with a little computer, those strange little gadgets, the Commander's watch.

The Tibetan moved his weapons out of reach, but Anna saw them and gasped.

"Don't worry," said Namgyal. "That's to keep your former Russian classmates and any would-be Indian misadventurers away."

Within minutes, one of the young men was deftly typing on the computer. Sad fiendish strokes.

"What did he write?" Anna asked, coming over to the spot. "Nothing," Namgyal said.

"I wouldn't be too sure," Anna added. "I don't understand these devices you've brought, but I know the typewriter, of course. We had, I think it was called, an Olivetti, at the hospital where I worked. I wouldn't be looking at the words, or letters, so much as the shapes of the letters. A 't' to them might mean a tree, a 'y' the fork in a twig, perhaps broken by a deer foraging for bark. That 's' a bend in the river. That 'shhh' the wind. For all you can tell, he's just described this location with scientific precision."

"Why would he bother doing that?"

"Curiosity. Play."

Namgyal looked around. The women wore no jewelry. Not even the diamonds strewn across the walls of the tunnels held any interest to them for purposes of self-decoration. How rare was that? Very rare. Nor was there any use of body paint, like that so in evidence among tribes elsewhere in the world and four miles below. There was no metal of any kind, save for the oxidized buttons on Anna's Red Army uniform, and that old rusted gun which had been packed beneath a boldly patterned blanket, one of many woven from local grass species for most of the century. No buckets, shovels or poster-beds that might be used to enhance their quality of life. Had they never traded with outsiders? Their implements for drinking had been hand-hewn from wood—he assumed they collected it from the tree line thousands of feet down past the cliffs—and they served their food on leaves, also presumably gathered below, the way many cultures in South and Southeast Asia served dollops of rice. But here, without a hint of style, elaborate ritual, custom or vanity, one would be hard pressed to know what these people actually did all day long. There was nothing hot to eat. No fire. Yet, he had never seen such crimson health in human bodies before. But to be without fire! The humility of it constituted a revolution of staggering proportions.

"No fire," Namgyal ruminated out loud. "Is it even possible?"

"They have no fire," Anna reiterated.

"No fire?" Marigold hazarded, suddenly awakened. He had been reclining in his sleeping bag beside Rajibai and Sannazaro, his eyes half closed, his body trying to cope with the four-mile altitude, which weighed on him like an additional 200 heavy bones, another 160 pounds.

"But how?"

Anna simply said, "Not necessary."

"Not necessary," Mr Marigold repeated. "No necessity, no invention. And there you have a whole new unwritten history of our species." He remembered how the great French anthropologist Claude Levi-Strauss had thought of fire as a key ingredient to being human. Without it, he inferred, we were something else. What culture did not have its stories of the origins of fire? Myths regarding the Creation that were fire and ice oriented? Religions, like Zoroastrianism and Christianity, which pitted good against evil in the guise of the cooling balms of heaven opposing horrid fires of hell? From ancient Egypt to Greece, from tribes in the Amazon and Australia's wild Arnhem Land to Tibet, fire was key to so much. Without it, what chance was there? How could people survive? Even the ecology of fire was crucial to the growth of culture, to agriculture in the ancient Middle East, he reflected, to the renewal of pastures and forests from Yosemite to Bavaria, from the Nile to the Tigris-Euphrates, and to the animals that grazed there, and the people who grazed upon the animals. Burn out the forest, and evolution selected for young plants, which in turn invited foragers. It was the way the world worked. Was there not lightning atop the waterfall? Could a tribe without fire have culture?

Recalling all that she had left behind, Anna began, "To narrow minds, culture is the sole recovery of a human being: his psychic repository, permanence and, ironically, his gravestone, as well as those descendants who can air nostalgically upon the epitaph. Now, observe more closely.

You tell me if it is culture that makes a girl slip into her alter-ego by the full moon, or instructs on the techniques needed to convert a piece of old wood into a useful bowl. How to laugh, by what injunctions to make love. Culture is not instinct, music, impulse, and certainly not passion. I recall only that culture perpetuated exclusions and anxieties; ordained a society of machine addicts, disassociation from basics; enflamed ideologies, hatreds, soldiers, and their idiotic, horrible wars. Culture is the vainglory of the collective. It imposes a severe price on the world. One you would not pay, if only you had discovered the alternative. That's what I remember. Those who function outside the culture are carefree, benign, beloved by nature, and loving in return."

"But what of Westminster Abbey? Bach's *St Matthew Passion*, Dante's *Paradiso*? Is not culture the sum of both good and bad?" the Commander suggested.

"But who does the arithmetic? Those same architects of the Tower of Babel, the ones who found all the ways to separate people."

"Surely you would concede that there were other forces of separation as well—geography, mountain ranges, inaccessible gorges which you surely must recognize. I know a few good souls. I would always cherish the name of the child, who is inherently good."

"Of course. My point precisely. Culture is what distorts their personalities and destinies. Just like the politics which swirled around Lenin. Geography is one thing, and climate, and available food resources. I am speaking of power and its effects on the average person who goes about her business and has no interest whatsoever in being a Lenin, or Woodrow Wilson. I remember Wilson's peace proposals at Versailles one week, and a world war the next. No, I'm sorry. Culture is a perilous fall into time, a great hoax that has dumbly been accepted, like religion, and language and customs in general, as methods for obtaining an advantage and for justifying a sense of superiority. Fire, language, culture—all can be left behind in the future. The future which is right here, right now. These people would show you the way, if they had the slightest interest in doing so—which, by the way, they do not. They are not missionaries. They are innocent of all that. To paraphrase Benjamin Disraeli, remember him? Nature has not endowed this place with all the civilizing pleasantries of London. Rather—and for this we must be terribly grateful—she has, in her primitive ways, seen fit to lavish other blessings not enjoyed by countries of a more Christian and chemical disposition. They would just like to be left alone."

"Aristotle wrote somewhere that spoken language was the dividing line between humans and all other species. Are they a new species?" Marigold finally pondered, exhaling with a degree of concern. He did not mean in any way to suggest an insult, but rather spectacular augury.

"Does it matter? What is a species? Another one of those obnoxious, silly words, like culture. It is a word encoded by humans," she said, thinking aloud. "I studied the great eighteenth-century Swedish taxonomist Carolus Linnaeus when I was in medical school. The father of biological nomenclature. But his idea of dividing up the organic world—kingdom, phylum, class and so forth—was the product of some strange, useless rage to separate life into neat little compartments that could then be manipulated—hybridizing plants, getting rid of so-called pests and weeds (there are no pests or weeds on this Earth!) and for segregating beasts of burden into pens where they could be then tortured and fed to the higher, meat-eating classes of superior beings, all-lordly man. Don't you see? I believe that may be what was bugging Mr Darwin. You no doubt recall why he pointed out so forcefully that there is no true test for determining a species or attributing exclusive characteristics. Thus his theory of polymorphic variants."

"Did not Darwin describe the ability to sexually reproduce among one's own kind as the absolute truth of a species?" Marigold asked.

"Maybe, maybe not. If I recall, he spoke of differences in degree, not kind. He also cited strange physiological aspects of marsupials, of nostrils, of dermal covering in vertebrata, even the way some insects fold their wings versus the way some others do, or the variation in color among algae—all were equal to sex in manifesting a view towards diversity. But the discovery of unity within diversity is a far greater achievement of the mind. It may prove tempting to point to a blemish, a gnarl in a tree, a dimple on a beautiful woman's face; but let him be more excited by the beauty of the woman, the grandeur of the tree, than the color of a person's skin. My father had a collection of Korean pottery. The blemish was deliberate, it made it more valuable. When I was a doctor, the assertion of a new species would have been a great moment. Now, to me, it suggests nothing more than that a bored and boring person with no vision, grace or compassion, and nothing better to do, has once again been poking round tormenting the state of Being. Men might patent machines and methods that can extract silver. But let no man believe for a moment that he can patent silver itself. Or the human gene."

"What are you really saying, dear wondrous Anna?" the Commander implored.

"Dear wondrous Marigold," she smiled patiently, "the concept of species is useless to all but the political animal. Which is how Aristotle defined man. Poneemayesh?"

She went on to show—quite conclusively in the Commander's mind— how the invention of the concept of the human species had been the work of capitalists and philosophers who kept slaves, who killed other animals, who thought of themselves as indispensable and superior to all other life forms.

"She sounds just like you," Sannazaro indicated. "How ironic. Go to the ends of the Earth only to find your mirror image."

"You flatter me, Señor. If only I might look, feel, think like her. Could there be a greater happiness?"

Anna was impervious to the compliment. Marigold realised she would be over 100 years old, by all that they had read and heard and seen. An absolute command of English had come back to her within minutes of first speaking it. Her fluency had never left her, which argued for some quarter of the brain that loved words. Certainly Marigold did. He was not all that comfortable with the tribe's musical refrains. To embrace it exclusively would be to eradicate his precious library of lifelong companions. That would never do. He thought about her extraordinary situation, the obvious forcefulness of her views, which had been formed in the cauldron of such intensive changes, to judge by her diary. To have begun as a young, obviously brilliant scientist, and then to have three-quarters of a century to re-examine everything from the loftiest Mt Olympus in the world. He supposed that must be the equation for creating an Anna Christov. Everything about her left the Commander mesmerized, though not a little sad that he was, even in his early 50s, an old man who had missed out on raising that only daughter.

"Biologically speaking, all life is equal," Anna rallied, having clearly divined his inner turmoil.

"I know that. That's why I'm here."

"Well, most scientists certainly don't know that," she said. "I have not renounced the curiosity of science and the arts. What I have turned my back on are those scientists and engineers and politicians who stick pins and needles into the world—spoiled brats who insist on knowing everything, when there is nothing to know. There is only the world.

They call it a cure, a breakthrough, an invention. Ridiculous pretenses for power-hungry egomaniacs. Without science there would never have been bombs or famine. Only balance. Science favors scientists. Lacking humility, contentment, joy in simple nature, much of science—the science I knew in my time—was utterly, hopelessly sidetracked by vanity and greed. Species favoritism. I was among them. I came here to champion a breakthrough. Earn a name for myself. I was broken in the process. Thank God. And then reborn. This is the new Anna Christov you're seeing."

She smiled flirtatiously, clearly enjoying an excuse to speak, after so many decades. Gazing back at that complex colloquy of human affairs with every dispassion. Her thinking emanated utter loft, the wings which other comprehensive thinkers—Plato, Aquinas and Kant came to Marigold's mind—had utilized to passionately ply their considerable insights and render systematic commentary beyond the foibles of the everyday. This was why the Commander was himself so lost in thought: to be able to shy clear of the mundane impediments, old habits and nauseating truths of human reality by erecting new worlds to inhabit— this was, by itself, an epistemology turned into flesh. By the process of immersion into the abstract, he had escaped all that might intrude. Now, ironically, he was the intruder.

To this paradox he added further insult in terms of the considerable, and possibly fatal, complications he and the others had caused Anna and her people. He had prompted a crisis. What a fool, he thought, to have been so easily led by his desires. But who could have predicted, and what could be done about it now? Namgyal had made the changeover. Had the Commander himself? What would it require? That he go down at once? Or stay to protect them?

Anna looked out upon Marigold, humored by his twitching crazybone and silly chivalries. She was aware of the man's inner struggles that oriented both vertically and horizontally, confusion oblong, bafflement egg-shaped, so many agitated pointillist touches lacking finish, cohesion. His turmoils were as palpable as a peach ready to roll off the canvas on the edge of a still life, a man without his parasol beneath the burning sun, a lone shoe beside a roadway. What did she know of this terribly strange middle-aged wanderer who bore striking physical similarities to what she remembered of her own father? His own intensity had driven him and his family halfway around the world in search of something as well. Marigold was no dogmatist, but the sort of fellow her father—back in the last century—would have had over to the house for a sherry: a thoughtful person, steeped in quaint, old-fashioned biology, history, ethics. Could his motives be as innocent as they appeared? What had he spoken of—the goodness of children, Dante, Bach ...? Something about him rang true. This was a man, she reckoned, who was eternally restless, whether for knowledge or simply to escape the unthinkable trap of domesticity and its repetitions.

And the Italian, what to make of him? So dapper and unpredictable. A nervous wreck in fine haberdashery; stylized, aristocratic, saved from pedantry by a wry and trenchant manner. He and Marigold together were pure Vaudeville, she reckoned. But what of the Indian child? And how could so unlikely a trio have arrived at the waterfall in the company of a Tibetan military spy, no less?

There was no sense to any of it.

On the other hand, time was running out for her and the tribe. Perhaps these newcomers had come just in time. That thought did pass her mind.

CHAPTER 127
The Love that had Replaced Fire

LATER, ANNA AND Marigold spoke quietly together while the others slept. Eventually Anna herself called it a day, leaving Marigold alone with all his thoughts and Tintern Abbeys. His head upon a pillow of bunched-up clothes, and turned away from the others, the Commander reflected upon many truths, ambiguities and unknowns. He was not one to dwell on has-beens, but Anna's version of human folly ever since the Tower of Babel certainly resonated with his own sense of history. Of course, one could make a case that the tribe's uniqueness derived from the special coordinates of their habitat. They were one with the land. It was that simple. But simplicity and isolation also harbored concealed perils. A general latitude ensured greater survival. But extreme adaptation was a liability.

Mr Marigold recalled the remarkable study by the late Colin Turnbull, who had analyzed the extinction of the Ik on Mt Morungule in Uganda. They were totally dependent on the plants that grew on the mountain. When the plants withered during a prolonged period of drought, the tribe was incapable of resettling on the plains below. They died out, one by one. The final survivors took to cannibalism. It was one of the worst cases of environmental symbiosis gone awry in the annals of anthropology. Dependency on so narrow a margin of life had proved disastrous.

At first glance, this tribe, which numbered so few, seemed to be going extinct. One adverse winter, one avalanche, and they'd be gone. Forever.

Then again, if they were immortal, who needed any back-up plan? If one individual had been blessed in his or her veins with all the redundancy necessary to ensure the continuation of the tribe, then there was no reason for lots of them when a few would do.

Anna was herself unsure about this issue of their borrowed seasons. For she had spent only 76 years with them, after all. She could not prove anything, despite what they had indicated to her. Much more time was needed. Even those 76 years, she explained, were so much blur. Once she had lost her diary, it was impossible to keep track, in absence of a writing pen, or paper, or the custom of speaking. Days and nights began very soon to merge without variance until, at some point, she simply forgot everything and started to become like them.

That's when she took off her clothes, she admitted, bathed in the upper pools towards the glacial terminus (where, she added, there were remarkable hot springs) and then was initiated into the falls. That, she said, changed everything.

It was the first time she'd mentioned these new elements to the equation, but gave no details. She reminded the Commander of the equally remarkable Madame Vignette, and for a sudden moment he was safely back home in Tesuque, nestled snugly in his canopy bed, like a dragonfly, beneath his favorite painting by an anonymous artist of the Renaissance, of Paradise. Animals arrayed in resplendent conviviality, surrounding the Tree of Life. The painting had been in the family for centuries. Darkness pervaded the Zen-like interior of the hut, save for reflections of the moonlight off the water and higher glaciers, and the added light source of Namgyal's headlamp, which had caused something just short of havoc among the children, as it would among most beings, whether squirrel or gorilla, whose rhythms were oriented to the sun and the dark. Their excitement had, for a brief while, prevented their biological clocks from setting in. They now wanted to stay up and play. Their game was similar to marbles, a frolic spread out across the woven floor of the hut—marbles which, if Namgyal was not mistaken, were perfect, spherical rubies. Priceless. But how old were the children? Five years or five centuries?

"Has anyone been born into the tribe since you arrived?" Namgyal asked Anna.

"Twins. Those. But I can't tell you how many years or decades ago. I've truly lost track."

Namgyal recognized the signs that distinguished them. Their fingers and toes were shorter than those of the others. Their hair was flaxen. Where did these genes come from? The others were all dark haired. Would the flaxen turn dark? Was it sunlight? Or some genetic change beginning to occur, a reaction to ozone depletion, perhaps? For how long did they suckle? Years, decades?

Again, Anna couldn't recall. Normally, Anna informed him, members of the tribe fell asleep just after dark, and were awake with the first light of dawn. A farmer's life. But to have no access to light at night, not one match between them! No knowledge—or knowledge renounced? —of rubbing sticks or slate. Wasn't it the first campfire that enhanced the very brain power of our ancestors? Marigold was familiar with studies relating the size and weight of the cerebellum of *Homo erectus* to the advent of fire. For three million years the size and grip of our ancestors' brains had evolved slowly and ploddingly. But with the coming of fire some million and a half years ago, 700 cubic centimeters of gray matter were acquired in a matter of millennia. In fact, paleontologists had shown that *Homo erectus* brains were packed over the course of a few hundred thousand years with 40 million new neurons per cubic centimeter—20,000 neurons added per hour during the *Homo erectus* baby's first three years—for a total of 10 billion neurons and 100 trillion neural connections, all in the service of new ideas that propelled human evolution forward. Did this tribe have different neural connections? Were they, in fact, something other than *Homo*? Had their brains evolved according to a different set of rules and priorities? Did they know more, or less, than the rest of us?

"What do you think?" he asked Sannazaro, waking him up from a deep sleep only to get a grumpy, incoherent and well-deserved tongue lashing, the linguistic summation of all those hundreds of thousands of years of supposedly forward evolution.

That was the answer he'd suspected. Their love had replaced such fire, and all the woeful sparks attendant upon it. This was a tribe that had thus avoided the pitfalls which led, inexorably, to a Sannazaro, or himself.

Whatever the answers, now, a million years later, 21 proto-humans survived with no knowledge of fire, at 20,000 feet, naked, in the snow. They were of the sweetest disposition, as gentle as an aged wine, and vegetarian without even a name for such blessed behavior. Answers enough for all the questions which plagued Marigold's hyperactive mind.

They played infectious music and displayed what both Namgyal and Marigold took to be a reverence for life that was absolute. The Buddhist in Namgyal, the surveyor in Marigold, recognized the signs almost at once. No compromise. From an ecological point of view, they were the ultimate form of benign humanity. Like those Toda, those Bishnoi, those naked Jain monks Paramatman had described, Paramatman himself, wandering the backroads of India their whole lives with no possessions, and causing no impact whatsoever on the environment, here too was another aspect of the perfect human possibility. A beacon in the night. More extreme, by dint of their location, but no more anxious to sustain harmony than these other assimilated peoples.

Of course, the monks spent their time devoted to teaching and setting an example of non-violence for others. Whereas these tribals, lacking awareness of conflict, seemed to have no cares beyond the fringes of their isolated mountain kingdom. Who were they? How long had they been here? Where did they come from?

"Maybe we all started here. That's what you meant, isn't it?" Marigold asked Anna.

"I think it's possible," she said.

Rajibai, meanwhile, was flat out, and Sannazaro had settled back down into nausea-land, altitude-sick but relieved to be free of his Commander's excited pestering for the time being.

"I think they're sitting ducks," Marigold finally mustered, harnessing the totality of sensations, examining the obvious vulnerability of the individuals around him, seeing a near daughter in Anna, and recognizing so clearly Namgyal's truthful turnaround and his obvious feelings for this refugee who herself had heroically made the leap from one culture, one time, one way of being, to something altogether different.

"They don't even know how to ask for help," Marigold finally exclaimed. "That's what I think. The modern world isn't ready for this. Nor could they possibly cope with the outside."

"You're absolutely right," Namgyal said, joined at the hip to a whole new Milky Way.

He was no philosopher, but this hut, and its occupants, were as close to the heart of the matter, the source of all spiritual truth and happiness, as he could imagine. They might be the hope for the twenty-first century. But he had every intention of preventing that collision from happening.

The rest of the world would just have to get along without the jump-start of this sacred cluster of humanity.

He started to get up, and to take his machine-gun with him, to stand watch atop the tunnels. Just then a naked woman, her eyes porcelain and delicate, came to him and knelt down. She then offered him something in her mouth.

"What is she doing?" Namgyal asked, astonished. "Take it," said Anna.

"But what is it?"

"She's regurgitating for you."

"Regurgitating what?"

"Does it matter? What she had for lunch. I don't know, don't ask. Just accept the offering like a gentleman. It is a form of love."

"Love?"

He put down his weapon and took the offering in his mouth. It was hot and gross. Then she lay next to him; her lips tumid and blue upon the oval expressiveness of her face. Her breasts were large, recently suckled from. Her stomach was taut. She plucked a few suggestive strings of her harp in accordance with her mood. This was a jazz of seduction. She spread her legs and tried to take hold of his hand to advance her cause.

"She wants you," Anna told him.

"I gathered. But just like that?" At such altitude, blushing went quickly from one's cheeks to one's head. He stumbled.

"Yes."

Anna knew, of course, but did not elaborate. The women of the tribe were totally in tune with their cycles. When the moon was full, as it was this night, they were ovulating and nothing could hold them back.

"Please, I can't," said Namgyal, and he tried to stand up. "Tell her I think she's beautiful, but I just ... I wouldn't."

"Why not?" Anna asked. "Is there another woman in your life, not that it should matter?"

"If you can read thoughts, then you can decipher her name, for I'm thinking it right now."

He turned and staggered out of the hut.

Marigold, it appeared, was next on the woman's list.

"No. No. I could be her father. Tell her I'm too tired, tell her anything," he begged Anna.

She laughed. "She's much older than you are. Are you so shy?"

"I guess I am," he said, summoning all his inner reserves to fend off the most powerful sexual allure he'd ever experienced. (Maybe that was saying something, maybe not.) "You tell her." He was desperate. Should he have sex? Would there be anything morally wrong with it? By jingo—he told himself, mustard-brained and emboldened—just embrace the moment.

But there were people in the hut! What sort of example would that set for a newly adopted son? Terrible, horrible, impossible.

On the other hand, Rajibai was fast asleep.

Yet the lad would surely wake up, attuned to every cricket's breath.

On the other hand, so what if he did wake up? An education.

No, bad idea. He suddenly recalled the distant echo of startling his own father en flagrante so many years ago in Ecuador. An unpleasant memory. *Lord I know not. Help me, he whispered.*

This was a terrible problem.

He carried on this way, ruminating with fretful contortions, his crazybone reacting with the gymnastics of an awful rash, gesticulations compounded by the exhaustion of so much mental trial, further stressed by the effects of altitude on his libido, a twitch, a stutter, profuse sweat and the sheer stamina of his resistance, a monster of abstinence, until the woman lost interest, or grew justifiably frightened.

Later, two of the women tried Sannazaro, musically feverish, primevally moaning, but utterly confounded by the zipper of the sleeping bag. They'd never seen one and had no idea how to open it. In any case, it appeared from the looks of him that the Italian was never going to wake up, no matter what incentives. They swatted at his nose, thinking a bumblebee had nested in one of his nostrils. No one in the tribe had heard snoring before.

CHAPTER 128
The Waters of Immortality

OUTSIDE, NAMGYAL sat alone inside the top of the tunnel, restless and agitated.

Like the Commander, though with slightly more experience, he'd never encountered such complex desires, overwhelming freedom, a woman fully prepared to take inordinate pleasure in pleasing and being pleased. These were all intimations, an opening into his heart. No female's eyes had stared at him quite like those of the women among the tribe. Wild iris, optic calm, retinal fruit of a wholly different expectation. Their bodies gleamed between hormones and music, this sweetest of dreams.

Jigme Namgyal knew exactly what he would do: he had to protect her, all of them, from people just like himself. From flying machines and loaded guns, and the menace of stockholders who would think nothing of condemning the people of the waterfall to scientific cages, and test tubes, or of splattering their fragmented pictures on the covers of newspapers. Like a lamb. Dolly.

The Tibetan searched, measured, walked the boundaries, felt the rock formations, deciphered blocked passages, large boulders, hidden shelves and cubic volumes. With these rudimentary observations he formulated a bold plan. He intended to detonate the primary tunnel, which should effectively block anyone from getting in. These men and women, and their perfect children, none of them would stand a chance otherwise. He already knew that the tribe had at least two alternative approaches within the tunnel complex, and these would guarantee their ability to go foraging down below the waterfall, if need be, after the destruction of any interlopers.

Anna was also restless that night.

The stars were inconceivably bright, in and out of the fast-moving clouds.

Later, as Namgyal sat at the top of the tunnel staring out, keeping watch, his machine-gun in his arms, Anna emerged.

"It's me," she whispered.

She took his hand and led him to a secret place above. The hot pools.

They were several hundred yards beyond the rim. Just over the crest, from where it was possible to gaze upon 1,000 square miles of moonlight splashed across the unsteady glaciers of Namche Barwa and adjoining peaks. The light source was immense. But even more astonishing was the presence of trees—a fact of no little significance, for by Namgyal's reckoning they were easily 8,000 feet above the timberline. What kind of trees were they? What were those large Moreton Bay Fig-like creations shining in the night?

They reached the pools and Namgyal tested the temperature with his fingertip. Steaming, far too hot for bathing. Probably 160 degrees. Yet, Anna slipped out of her clothes without hesitating and stepped in.

For a brief instant her body lit up like a flare, a phosphorescent mirage.

"What are you doing?"

"Try," she encouraged him. "It will heal that wound on your head."

"It's a superficial laceration."

"Just try."

Slowly, toe by toe, he got in until, after ten minutes of tentative holding back, he was fully immersed in the near-bubbling water, naked, with Anna Christov. Her body, undulating in the pool, her breasts rippling reflections onto his skin, boggled his senses. Anna was aware of his gaze and felt, for the first time in most of a century, self-conscious. Their bodies touched in the stellar bright of the indigo darkness. She clung to him, smelling his neck, tasting his tongue, floating among the lotuses.

"I want you," she declared forthrightly.

Namgyal knew, as he felt her pounding heart, and the erect nipples, that Anna Christov, for all of her remarkable transformation since 1923, was still a woman of the twentieth century. A woman who once studied Liszt, read Dostoevsky and Flaubert. She had basic needs, too.

On the slimy granitic edge of the pools, she wrapped her legs around his waist and said, "I'm quite fertile tonight."

Hours later, she walked away demurely, and put back on her Red Army uniform.

Namgyal's head felt better already. Scabs were beginning to form. He examined the wild kingdom of bacterial mats, invisible biological champions quite obviously charmed by the steamy water. By their color and odor he knew enough, from college biology and from what Fenton had prepared him to look for, that these pools were home to thermophiles, heat-loving blue-green algae, the stewards of life responsible for the most primordial photosynthesis on earth. He smelled the streaking of acid sulfate, neutral chloride and calcium carbonite across the rock surfaces, the very chemical conglomerates from which such byproducts as insulin and penicillin were first created. Enzymes like *Thermos aquaticus*, which had already reaped some scientists nearly half a billion in profits elsewhere in the world, were there too. Such curative baths, if discovered by the outside world, would only add fuel to the destruction of the tribe.

Anna informed Namgyal that these resinous seaweed-like grasses thriving in the hot baths were the mainstay of the tribe's diet. They had the taste of scrub mints and yellow balms, like those reputed to have been found along the Lake Wales Ridge in central Florida. She urged him to try some, and Namgyal did so, foraging across the whole range of bacteria.

"What was that?" he mumbled, aware of flitting shadows glinting cobalt in the dark.

"Birds," she replied.

He examined the shapes at length, and by starlight verily gleaned a kind of jay feasting on the same food sources. And there, high in a tree, a Tibetan spotted owl.

Namgyal took Anna in his arms.

Back at the long house, everyone was asleep, save for the shaman, who used thousands of rainbows coalescing in the waterfall which hung right outside his 'window' to prepare what turned out, upon Namgyal's questioning of Anna, to be the last of the tribe's supply of poppies. No one had gone in search of them for more than two months, ever since Anna's lover—the corpse recovered in the river—had vanished. Namgyal took out the portable bioassay kit, and microcomputer which, in their waterproof kit, had survived the many travails earlier on.

"What are you doing?" Anna asked."Aren't you curious at least to understand what's in the plant? I suspect they're no ordinary poppies. I would like to know—wouldn't you?" She grew anxious.

Namgyal scanned a fragment of the flower into his computer, though the electricity was beginning to wane.

"I can't believe it's still working", he puzzled—then blew up the image 50,000 times, for he had the latest laser/microscopic component. He showed her the results of his handiwork: a cell from a dead petal, still undergoing mitosis at a rate hundreds, possibly thousands of times faster than should be occurring in a live culture.

Now it was Anna, utterly contradicting her emblazoned tirade before the Commander, who fell swoon to this sudden *déjà vu* of science, for though the scientist in her had always speculated, this was the first time she'd ever seen it. She'd known the hereditary traits described by the Austrian monk Gregor Mendel, German embryologist Walther Fleming's discovery of chromosomes in salamander larvae, and the American biologist Thomas Morgan's studies of sexual heredity in fruit flies. But she had never seen DNA, with its primordial and simplistic double helix. She had no idea there was such a thing as a genetic code that could be created from scratch, that there were nucleotides in DNA corresponding to amino acid sequences in proteins. How could she have imagined that a sheep would provide a dozen identical offspring, all manufactured with human intervention from a single cell of an adult ewe?

This was even more astonishing to her eyes, however: palpable proof that the poppy extract permeated the cell walls—every type of cell that she was capable of seeing under these conditions—and it entered the nucleus, forming its own gene-splicing industry. It affected every gene known to be related to the immune system, to embryology, to brain-stem chemistry. And she began to describe how the plant was to be taken in combination with the bacterial grasses in the hot pools: "Once consumed, held inside the bladder for at least an hour, you pee into a little bowl and then drink your own urine. Sometimes the whole tribe collectively drinks. The urine contains the metabolized essence of the substance," she said. "But none of this means anything without a rather serious leap of faith. I am speaking literally."

But she also felt a certain revulsion before this onslaught of insights.

"No, *no!*" she said angrily, pushing the microscope and computer apparatus away. "I don't want to see any more. It's wrong."

Suddenly, the long hut started swinging with violent throes.

Mr Marigold, roused from sleep, shrieked. "Earthquake!" Namgyal said calmly, holding fast to Anna.

Everyone was now awake, clinging to the wooden stays of the hut. "What's going on?" the sleepy Rajibai moaned. His head was heaving from the altitude.

Marigold took him in his arms. "Everybody just grab on!" Another temblor, and another. All were gripped, sitting up.

Swinging.

Namgyal's gadgets flew across the room. The computer hit a rock used for grinding tubers into mush, and smashed into pieces of glass and circuit board. Just like that, the end of science.

And the lustrous night grew still again. Namgyal sat beside Anna. Eventually, she began to speak more of her tribe with no name. She had taken a position next to the parents of the youth who had died, the man she'd loved.

Anna was certain, based upon what Mr Marigold related about the corpse, that he had been hit hard by a rock avalanche, and thrown out of the recirculation system, as she referred to the still mysterious waterfall.

Presently she taught Rajibai basic greetings on the mini-harp, which ignited a fantastic musical séance from the others.

Namgyal withdrew a match from his pack and without pausing to discuss the ramifications of it with Anna, he ignited it.

There was a stunned silence, every single member of the tribe staring hypnotized into the flame. The shaman hid his eyes, plucking urgently on the musical instrument melded to his waist.

"What did he say?" the Tibetan asked.

"Don't touch it, it will hurt you; don't look at it, it will blind you. Forget about it, or the memory will taunt you," Anna translated.

"What's the big deal?" Namgyal innocently conjectured.

"I wouldn't be so glib about it," she scolded. "You have no idea what harm you might have inflicted by that." She was stunned by his indifference, or stupidity. But it was too late, now. He blew out the flame.

Then apologized.

They had no wheel, either, though it was possible, in times past, that at least two of the elders met Tibetans on the Namche Barwa side (which Anna claimed to be much wilder than the waterfall side— she could never handle its difficult terrain, she said) and visited a Buddhist cliff monastery where they probably saw prayer wheels. Again, there would be no need for a wheel on the cliff. The tribe's tools were of wood or stone, no steel or iron, and there were no weapons either, or none ever conceived. Since the people never died—or none in 76 years, until Anna's very own lover—there were no customs associated with burial; no skeletons; no cosmology that should account for an afterlife; and no notion whatsoever of heaven.

Anna decided against telling the parents that their son had perished. It could serve no useful purpose. They were in Paradise, here and now. Why spoil it, she reckoned, wary of showing tears.

Namgyal knew she was thinking about him, the corpse; and he began to understand the depth of loss she felt for one so young who might otherwise have lived forever.

Eventually, the Tibetan asked, "Do you marry?"

"They are all married," she replied.

Later, Anna recounted particulars of the tribe's diet, which extended only modestly beyond the confines of bacterial blooms and high-altitude plantain. They also consumed innumerable vaccinium family edibles, principally blueberries. While she did not use such words as vegetarian, Anna described the tribe's view of the soul, which for them would never perish precisely because it had never killed, harmed, exploited, inconvenienced or prevailed upon another animal. The proof was their own longevity. Rajibai remained glued to her every explanation.

"They would never dream of harming so much as an ant," she reiterated.

"You might describe their value system as given over completely to a biotopia."

"My boy is the same way," said Marigold. "I would add that it is no less my sovereign disposition."

"What about sex?" Namgyal finally inquired. "Is it always preceded by regurgitations?"

She laughed. "They certainly know about sex. And are totally at peace with it. But it is unselfconscious with them, unlike my student days in Boston."

"I went to Dartmouth," the Tibetan informed her.

"And I have been to Hanover," she recalled. "For ice skating and a Winter Carnival. I remember the huge snowman."

And she went on to recall some of her interests then; a little-known group of painters—they called them Cubists and Post-Impressionists, she believed. One artist in particular. She couldn't remember his name.

Namgyal ran through the usual suspects—Picasso, Braque, Monet, until he hit upon Gauguin.

"That's the one. But how are you so familiar with the obscure French painters?" she asked.

Namgyal proceeded to tell her a few things of his own about the last 76 years. He mentioned James Joyce, Susan B. Anthony, Margaret Sanger, antibiotics, the Stalin purges, nuclear weapons, World War II, Auschwitz, Hiroshima, Mahatma Gandhi, I Love Lucy, Martin Luther King, Jr and desegregation, fast food, jazz, the Beatles, a birth control pill, *Roe v. Wade*, President Kennedy and men dancing on the moon, the Vietnam War, Pol Pot, CDs, PCs, the destruction of Tibet by the Chinese, Federal Express, the Viking mission to Mars, Voyager to Saturn, the Internet, the rise of labor unions, the average per capita income in the United States, the global human population and what it boded, the crisis of biodiversity loss and a host of other ecological problems, cloning, medical ethics, and a free Russia.

But of all the craziest things, this last notion—that of a Russia free of dictators—was the hardest for her to imagine. Cruelty she saw plenty of in Mother Russia, though nothing like Namgyal's description of the Jewish and Tibetan Holocausts. Pollution was omnipresent during her youth, when most home heating came from coal. Abortions were also common in her day. She performed many, even in medical school. The moon, especially a full moon from their perch above the waterfall, seemed not so very far away from earth that it should prove difficult to walk upon. She was amused by the idea of Federal Express, and the ease of communication, but it also made her a trifle nervous, she admitted. She liked peace and quiet and the ability to tune out, as was now fairly obvious.

Anna, in turn, answered plenty of burning questions from both Namgyal and Mr Marigold regarding her 76 years. Did she yearn to return to Moscow or Boston? No. How did she cope, in the beginning? Coping was not an issue. Her injuries were remedied within hours of the hot baths. As far as she was concerned, she had died and gone to heaven. Had anyone else ever visited? Not in this century. Who, what, were the jumpers? To this last question she promised to show them next day. That was, at least, a breakthrough. But no more matches, she warned.

Throughout the night, however, there were more earthquakes, swarms of temblors. Anna told the newcomers that such violent shocks had always preceded an avalanche. She was greatly concerned. The tribe had been closely monitoring the main glaciers on Namche Barwa and they knew that it was only a matter of time. The tribe had registered this foreboding.

"How do they monitor such things?" Namgyal asked. "Do they climb onto the glaciers?"

"Yes," replied Anna. "Some of them have climbed the mountain."

"To the top?" he asked, astonished.

"Yes. Why not? For fun."

For *fun*! Namgyal was incredulous. Namche Barwa, an overhanging monster of ice walls nearly 26,000 feet high, was said by the mountaineering community to be the highest unclimbed peak left on earth, the one that might never be climbed because of its inaccessibility and the sheerness of its walls on every side. Now his world view was truly being turned around. Or maybe Anna was just pulling his leg?

None of this talk had any impact on Rajibai whose late night in the long hut he would remember for the rest of his life because of one great truth revealed to him: sex. He had spied openly upon a young-looking woman who had played for her lover a melancholic love psalm on her harp, then ravished him without the slightest embarrassment. The two of them made considerable noise, to the merriment of others. At one point, the woman farted with wild abandonment, and it was the odor, thought Rajibai, of licorice (which he loved). Sex was on his brain, sex with the girls all around him. Mr Marigold detected the signs, all right, but signaled no parental point of view on the matter. Remaining neutral, even nostalgic, he allowed without the slightest concern Rajibai's own experimentation late that night, amid the other outside temblors, though he exercised paternal decorum by hiding his head beneath his blankets, having only hours before rejected a similar amorous opportunity.

At first light next morning, the zealous little squirt was sound asleep in a cradle of affection with the three rambunctious, utterly curious girls who had introduced him to whatever it was they did. What a lucky boy, the Commander thought.

Mr Marigold was relieved to see that Sannazaro was also feeling better.

"What year is it?" the Italian asked, not a little silly and drunk from so much of 20,000 feet.

"I think the more appropriate question is whether you are still alive, for we had our doubts."

"Couldn't feel better," the Squire expostulated with renewed vigor, droit du seigneur, this being the great day of his yawn. He was ready to embrace the New World, whatever it had in store.

CHAPTER 129
Free Fall

NAMGYAL HAD SPENT THE remainder of the night keeping watch over the summit exit from the tunnels, and now returned to the long hut with urgent news. He informed Anna and the others that he'd heard the intruders, deep down in the upwinding caverns, but could not be sure how far away they were. The noises were deceptive.

Anna translated. Several of the tribal males, and the shaman, followed him back along the summit, Marigold and Anna in tow. Once at the entrance, they could all make out the rough scraping and bitching of the soldiers below. An Indian was shouting to someone. The echoes were not definable, in terms of distance, but it was clear that they were systematically making their way higher and higher.

Malevich, Jomsom and Lieutenant Singh had had no communication with their colleagues at Sadiya for nearly a day. For them, too, of course, the tunnel blocked all electronic transmissions. Malevich knew that the Americans had beat them, at least for now. He was furious that this could have happened—blamed clumsiness in numbers, an expedition no match for a lone agent—but confident that the spoils would, at the very least, be shared. Namgyal and the tribe were cornered.

Another temblor shook the tunnel. The quakes were increasing in frequency, Anna confirmed.

"The point is, we've got to get you all out of here for the time being," the Tibetan aired gravely.

More earthquakes shook the entire wall. Five-pointers in rapid succession. They heard a distant rumble. Everyone crouched down low to the ground.

"The mountain," Anna's voice weakly admitted.

They looked up at the glacier, whose terminus was less than half a mile away.

"If there's an avalanche we won't have much time," she allowed.

Namgyal knew mountains, and this was going to be the biggest avalanche he'd ever seen. When he was a child, a neighboring Tibetan village had been hit by an avalanche. He didn't like to think about it. Everyone was killed. Limbs flayed, protruding from the dark rims of ice, which formed the consistency of concrete, entombing its victims within seconds. Nor was Marigold a stranger to the scenario.

"There are three tunnels," Namgyal calculated.

"Yes but—"

"So if I blow up the one the Russians and Indians are climbing, you can all take cover in your choice of the others. Get the children. Now."

"No," Anna reacted. "That won't work. Water flows through all of them. Mud. Rockfall."

"I don't see any other way. We'll take our chances. Please, just do it."

She looked to the shaman, her dark blue eyes, her mental choreography laying out what, to the tribe, was already obvious. They had seen the work of the Russian and Indian invaders. Death visited upon their senses for the first time. Now it was the shaman who enacted the only possible response. Motioning to his cohorts, he made his decision.

Namgyal was frantic. "What's he going to do?"

Soon, the plan was clear. Everyone was following the shaman back along the rim, down to the long houses and continuing beneath.

Namgyal watched from his position, confused, as were his three companions. "Anna? What are they doing?"

Marigold intervened. "We'll fight them in the tunnel. We have three distinct advantages: my money, which exerts the most surprising turnarounds in people; our height, since we can see them coming and drop rocks on their heads; and diplomacy. Keep in mind, despite what we have seen, they must answer to higher authorities. I have a direct link to the politicians in New Delhi."

"Since when?" Sannazaro rebutted.

But Namgyal was engrossed in observing as the tribe moved onto a precarious ladder of twine suspended beneath the long house and leading to a narrow ledge under the wide arc of the falls.

"The jump," Anna said cryptically, intending to encompass all meaning. She motioned to Rajibai, Marigold and Sannazaro to join the others in this.

"You must all come," she said gently to Namgyal. "The waterfall is their salvation. It always has been."

"I don't understand."

Who could have had a clue to this ritual beyond logic or physiology?

A myth that had become flesh, usually with only the best repercussions. The Tibetan didn't have the slightest notion what Anna was talking about. But he had set his own agenda and knew well enough there was no time for debate.

"Go, then. Do what you have to. Save yourself," he said. He took her hand. "Just know that I love you." Then he raced to the entrance of the tunnels and disappeared inside.

Marigold, Sannazaro and Rajibai followed Anna back to the long house, then, pausing, each voiced his own respective horror—or two of them did.

The 300-foot walls of Bandelier or the cliffs of Toda Land were low-falutin stepladders compared with the prospect that now presented itself to the horrified crusader and his senator-turned-mule. Rajibai, however, was a very brave boy who trusted implicitly. Despite the many rampages in his brief life, he had not lost that playful and unsullied purity which invested faith where it belonged. He climbed down the ladders with his eyes open.

"This is not the first time we've been on vertical walls," Marigold stuttered, hoping to stir support from his Governor, his voice rising on an arpeggio of insubstantial airs, false confidences and all-out panic.

Sannazaro couldn't form words; his mouth was a dry and trembling overflow of frantic nonsense and babbling brook; every conceivable utterance collapsed in absolute resistance to inevitable death. Finally, a glazed-over prayer issued from his frozen lips and flattering tongue: "*Vires acquirit eundo*": It gains strength as it advances.

The entire tribe reached the ledge. Winds, spray, thunder were everywhere exploding, funneling, conspiring. No exposure on earth was more dramatic, no cliff higher, no panic more vertiginous and confusing. Sweat trickled down the Commander's palms, blood vessels quietly burst in the Governor's temples, terror swarmed over both of them. Marigold's ulnar nerve was flopping like a captured fish. His knees had collapsed. Sannazaro's lungs were heaving. Marigold started hiccuping from nerves— that and his hyperactive crazybone.

"I can't breathe! Sannazaro feebly cried. "I die, I die, I am dying!"

"I promise you," Anna cajoled, almost bemused by this Neapolitan paralysis. "Do as the rest of us, and you will be fine."

"You heard the woman," Marigold stated with shivering resolve, defying his own certainty of the end.

Deep in the tunnels, 20 men were approaching, Malevich and Jomsom in the lead, their M-16s drawn. Racing to head them off was Namgyal, a walking explosive. He carried several sizable chunks of C-4. Normally you could, with impunity, do anything to C-4, unless it was otherwise modified—even burn it to heat your food, stuff it between cracks in a rock, slam it hard with a sledgehammer without risk of detonation.

But with the present chemical primer the plastic explosive acted very differently: it was timed to the least disturbance.

With steady and systematic machinations, Namgyal lay the delicate trap for the assailants, working out the placements behind enormous boulders ready to topple within the natural catacombs. He laid snares, and a long fuse leading to a touch pad. No dynamite poles or complicated ignitions. Just a digital read-out, and the concerted pressure of a single finger, to bring half the tunnel complex down. All this he executed downwind from where he planned to position himself squarely between two cantilevered walls, which he figured provided the best hope of surviving the blast.

At DMA, Nash tried unsuccessfully to warn Namgyal. Several Chinese Migs were coming in fast. Satellite had spotted the Indian choppers and intercepted their own transmissions. There was going to be engagement right over the area. But Namgyal was out of satellite contact now. In fact, since his last disheartening exchange of words with Namgyal, Nash was totally in the dark about him. He had no idea what was going on.

Standing on a large ledge 30 feet below the long house, a wooden calabash was passed around for all to sip from. It contained the combined urine of everyone present, in addition to a concoction of pulverized cobalt poppy, thermal bacteria and silky long grass stems. The shaman was watching, waiting. The Commander and Governor, their eyes closed in revulsion, drank the urine, coughing like wretches.

The humiliation, thought Sannazaro. Not only to die, when Paradise was at his fingertips, but that his last drink should be this unspeakably odious juice.

Anna stood beside Rajibai and his elder companions, whose backs inched precariously up against the granite wall, miles of space touching their stupefied noses.

"Remember the spot," she uttered.

What did she mean?

Far far below, hovering near the base of the waterfall, the 12,000-pound choppers were prevented from moving any closer by the colossal Venturi effect, which tossed them around like toys. The mountain wall was unapproachable. They swung diagonally, then rose in parallel formation with the deafening chutes. But they could get no closer to the column of water than a mile or so.

Among those on the ledge, the potion had begun to take effect. The shaman knew well these signs.

"This is where you'll return to. Don't worry, gentlemen," Anna reiterated. "We've all done it, hundreds of times. And they, since time immemorial. But there are risks. Stay close together. Hold on. You'll understand." Her voice faded away, as everyone took their cue from the shaman with his Quetzalcoatl gape, wild nerve and tilting finesse.

The drug had entered their collective veins. The shaman turned around, so that his back was to the waterfall, lissome flesh flashing all of Asia.

"He will take a deep breath, strike himself three times just so, to stimulate the blood flow, I believe," Anna explained.

"And and ... then?" a unison of squeaky incredulity escaped from *les misérables*.

"And then the leap into the heart of the waterfall. The upward drafts will moderate your fall. The shaman goes first, literally testing the water. That is his responsibility to the tribe. He knows. You must trust him."

"*Then* what!" Marigold gasped.

"Then you will see," she replied. "You will love it!"

Love it? All of Marigold's brain cells had already escaped out his ears in the form of final sobs and desperate doubts.

Anna held little Rajibai, who was trembling but stoic about it all. There was no way he was going to reveal an ounce of fear beside all the other absolutely tranquil denizens on the ledge, especially the girls. They showed no cowardice, only glee. They *loved* to jump!

The shaman closed his eyes, and fell off the ledge. All present watched him drop backwards with a long roll and sobering smile, disappearing immediately into the tumult of thundering emerald- and amethyst-glinting vertical sprays.

Overhead, the sound of two more Chinese Migs flashed by, shooting right out over the top of the falls. They were unable to see the 24 people left standing there, all hidden beneath. At DMA, Nash and his colleagues were tracking the large number of choppers from the north, as well as from China. They also picked up radio-telephoned Hindi and Mandarin altercations from the Indian Army down in the gorge, who were following the incoming troops on their radar.

"They're going to fight," Nash relayed. He still couldn't reach Namgyal. "Where the hell *is* that man?"

Inside the tunnels, Jomsom smelled a trap. Namgyal was well hidden, his high-powered weapons aimed straight at the combatants. The Indian General, Chadhuri, totally out of breath, laboring in pain at such altitude, loudly informed his quarry (he had no idea how many were there) that they were in Indian territory illegally and must lay down their weapons.

"This is Chinese territory, friend. You're completely out of your element," Namgyal replied from above. "By the way, from the sound of it, you haven't taken your Diamox."

"Not so, I did take it. It's just not working very well."

"I'm sorry to hear that. What's the color of your urine?"

"White."

"Not good. You need to get down."

"Soon, soon."

Malevich was humored by all this repartee between the General and—from his accent—the Tibetan.

"Hello Jigme," the Russian said. "Malevich," Namgyal replied. "Long time."

They could not see one another. Flashlights were no match for the thick darkness.

Suddenly, from outside, they heard an explosion. One of the Migs had fired a missile at the Indian choppers. It was a miss, but blew up a large section of cliff along the gorge. Those back at DMA watched the action unfold on their monitor. A wide window had opened in the weather, the full Himalayan sky breaking out into a magnificent day. The KH-12 had circled lower, and armed its own missiles. The Indian choppers fired back, missing their targets. These were heat-seeking missiles which followed the Migs' trails of exhaust. But the winds at 24,000 feet, which was the level of the aircraft, were fierce, and the hot emissions were separated from the aircraft more quickly than the warhead algorithms could correct for. The missiles exploded high upon the glacial pyramid above.

Four minutes had transpired. Suddenly, the shaman re-emerged, tossed hither like a feather. He grabbed hold of a crack, slightly off his mark, and pulled himself onto the ledge where the whole tribe waited.

"How in the hell?" The Commander was astounded.

"You just have to know how to work with the winds," said Anna. The explosions from the combat were audible to those on the ledge.

Then a distant thunder. For Anna, it was a *déjà vu*. An avalanche had been set off by the missiles, in concert with another earthquake swarm. The combination had finally triggered what had been waiting to happen for eons. The tribe had all but a few moments left before the mountain would sweep the entire rim. They knew this. Down in the tunnel Namgyal heard and felt the coming calamity. All his montagnard senses could gauge precisely what it would be like. And his slim chances of survival. The whole mountain was shaking. He braced himself for the end. Malevich ducked into his own position.

Along the ledge, there was no trepidation as one by one the tribals, then Marigold and a gaping Sannazaro, all went through the same ritual of tapping themselves, before leaping out into the falls. Anna and Rajibai were the last to go, holding hands—just as the avalanche exploded over the top of the cliff, sweeping tens of millions of tons of black rock and boiling ice.

In the tunnel, Namgyal was slammed into a fissure as the C-4 explosives detonated all around him, triggering an ear-numbing hell inside the claustrophobic world of cliff. Walls collapsed, whole galleries of precious, sparkling surface area with their crystals and raw diamonds. The force of the coming ice literally plowed through the rim, gouging out a 100-foot cave, detonating walls from sheer heat. The rock burned. The ice flash steamed, such that the heat exceeded several hundred degrees where it careened. Phosphorescent pools and rivers exploded from hidden runnels across the whole labyrinth of mountain face as it all began to cave in, liquefy, with mud and water pouring down every crevice.

Namgyal was able to throw himself into a corner adjoining the V-shaped opening, sheltered from the mayhem above. Ice water poured in all directions, and the steam from the colliding forces turned the dark labyrinth into a living fire. He closed his eyes and prayed to Buddha. As for those beneath him—Malevich, Jomsom and all the Indian troops— death must have been molten and instant.

And in the waterfall ...

So fast as to touch god in the first microsecond. When Rajibai opened his eyes, the world was foam, his speed undifferentiated from the roaring. The speed collided with his muted brain, against his little rolling corpse of a body. In its deepest recesses his mind mumbled an ancient Jain mystic's refrain, *Ab hum amar bhaye na marenge...* Now I am immortal, as spray flashed at his eyes, which stared into Anna's. She fell serene, haloed in a multitude of bright illuminations and blinding comfort at the beginning of time. Now they were in a wormhole of cosmic darkness, no breathing, no need. Contractions of the free fall down through the thundering. Chaos. The end of grammar, of words or thoughts that could even hope to make sense of the sensation, or reconcile it with everything that had occurred in his little life before now. A breakthrough. His eyes landed on the vision of Anna, whose hand was still in his, and of this immortal tribe, choreographed in mid-air, the light of ice crystals forming hundreds of prisms. Surreal sweeps of time passing before him. In the hurricane of perfection.

The tribe fell 8,000 feet through the falls. And then, strangely, they started to slow down, gracefully, according to some inner law of the wind's proportions, like a floating troop of Peter Pans alighting. At length, their free fall was cushioned mid-air.

Until they quite literally hung suspended. They were frozen in time, transfigured in the flight of their salvation. The lingering of naked bodies, clasped hands, closed eyes, poised aerial gods, withstood opposing forces of darkness and wind, the fantastic walls of water plunging to all sides...

When, suddenly, a rock—or a chunk of tree, or ice, dragged from above in the falls—crashed into the boy's shoulder. It happened too quickly. No reaction. His hand was severed from Anna's, and for a split second he saw her frantic expression, the explosion of a single utterance— "Rajibai!"—as she vanished above.

Outside the normal system of recirculating winds that held the others, his consciousness fast disappearing, he hurtled like a stone downwards, away from the tribe, from the Commander and Sannazaro, from all that was left of the world he knew.

Anna tried to throw herself after him. But there was no fighting the forces of the wind. Blackness covered the entire wall, a shadow screaming in the outer limits of mayhem: the avalanche! Anna pirouetted with the others in space, as all around them sections of granite wall, stewing mud, steaming ice and molten air—chunks the size of stadiums and skyscrapers, quadrillions of molecules on fire— poured off the rim, half the mountain collapsing and coursing over the giant arc of cliff amid the vertical, down-rushing Amazon of white water.

The single, continuing explosion was the equivalent of a thermonuclear reaction. Its noise was of such a magnitude as to silence even the waterfall through which Rajibai continued to drop. Now, with the light wholly obscured, and the freezing ice gale entrapping him, the Indian child was lost within himself, and took a journey—in a split second, or over the course of long moments—that seemed to carry him back in time, through the entire saga of human history.

An illumined veil of stormy tungsten emanating from within. He saw glints of it all: faces, animals, plants—that alleged flashback to the beginning when one is on the cusp of death. Some wisdom, or great revelation? Or nothingness, the purity of Being itself? For who could ever say, if he could not? And there was no speaking in that waterfall. He had no idea what was happening. The forces around him—physics bereft of any certainty—could not be scrutinized, for they were hidden, sheltered even from the known universe.

The avalanche had exceeded terminal velocity by over 200 miles, so that the trillions of pounds were coming down at a speed of nearly 325 miles per hour, heating thousands of cubic yards of air, creating yet additional winds, winds unknown on earth, which triggered an indescribable event within the lower reaches of the waterfall. Winds fighting winds. Galled and hovered. Haloed and windfallen, Rajibai was scattered, torn, vex't, by vertical line propelled from coast to coast, a mariner eaten raw, by eight borias and nine inclement fortunes. At his mouth, in his nose, sapped strength, blowing members. That temple of vibrations unrestrainable and swollen, playing his body like an orchestra full, percussion, wandering alone down beaten blasts. An insect fertilised. Reason gone, a passionate shower clapp'd, air bladder'd, fragmented harp, chimney self. Through every hood and washing, by every turn and breeze. Floating to the poles, musically an alloy, wind-fast, wind-tight, a wind-furnace wherein the riggings, the apparatus, the support, the valve had all deserted him. No angle between God and the violins accompanying his plunge. Until the succession of curves and quick steerage contracted into a superstition, cutting the halse, mothered o'er the grave, by necessity his whole life before him in a flying spindle, a compact of wet conviction. Fully and finally exposed. All. Forever.

Rajibai's eyes were shut tightly, his mind numbed. And then, after an eternity through space and time, he smashed into a pool of water, a deep wondrous pool. Windless now. The lee calms amid exquisite insanities.

The smashing was slow, his mind enveloped around his earliest memories—of his sister Sunya on the edge of the Sanjay Gandhi National Park inside a burned-out hollow in a tree filled with flowers, honey bees, cozy places to perch, hiding from the world. The two of them. Forever safe.

For a moment his eyes opened and he felt himself being pulled by waves to that shore of deliverance. He dragged himself into a clearing, vaguely aware of the arc of cave all around him and the volitional articulation of his limbs. It was the same Mother Earth where he was born. He could breathe.

And there he passed out ...

Nearly two miles above, Anna reached with the others through the seemingly impenetrable wall of water, touching rock. Wedded to the group mind, they all knew what to do, and the timing was familiar. She pulled herself by her fingers and saw that Marigold and Sannazaro were doing the same. The gales were holding them all in mistral suspension.

Directly before them were the last few dozen cobalt poppies, quavering in the updrafts, protected by a rock shelter. The tribal members each took a single petal and placed it between their teeth. Like marionettes waiting for all of the after-debris of the avalanche to settle, they continued to dangle in mid-air.

The shaman studied the situation, extending his hand. There were no more chunks of rock or ice, it seemed, and he gave the signal, or thought it.

A force dragged them all upwards. The shaman nodded to everyone around him, pushing himself by example away from the rocky ledge, only to be caught in the updraft. Anna and the others followed right behind, Marigold and Sannazaro obeying by sheer group physics. There was nothing else to do. They were sucked cleanly back into the falls and shot upwards.

The sight of the tidal wave of frost exploding over the rim had been translated from the KH-12 back to the Defense Mapping Agency war room. It took 16 minutes for the blizzard of powder, crystallized water and sulfurous dust to subside sufficiently for any resolution of imagery to be yielded up by the high-altitude remote sensing cameras. The aftermath of a gigantic cumulous cloud, spindrift from the blow-out, lingered in the air, and would do so for days. The video surveillance was replayed because Nash wanted to be sure.

The second time there was no doubting it. Whatever had been there—a person, a tribe, the Russians and Indians inside the tunnel—was no more. Nothing could have survived the obliterating forces that had come off that mountain. There was no sign of anyone. No transmissions. Only static. And a cloud of white debris rising 33,000 feet towards the stratosphere. The size of the avalanche was staggering. Like a hurricane viewed by satellite. They could only hope that Namgyal was nowhere near that mountain.

The Indian choppers had barely managed to remain outside the ring of devastation, 400-mile-per-hour winds ignited by the frontal throw-weight of the avalanche, the atmospheric effects of which extended easily for 100 miles down the Tsangpo Gorge.

After some minutes, Nash admitted aloud, "It's over."

CHAPTER 130
The Aftermath

THE VAST CAVALCADE of sulfurous ice, rended granite slab and smoking slush choked off the raging Brahmaputra, or Tsangpo, depending upon which side of the devastated debris—that in its frenzy of frenzies continued to avalanche from millions of crannies, rumbling off the cirque of four-mile-high escarpments—one happened to be standing. The cumulous cloud of smoke and dust rose higher and higher, like a billowing sail with dreams of adventure. The flummoxed scene, a sky island of perturbations, as witnessed by those pilots of the Chinese Migs and choppers now returning to their base of operations at Chengdu, back across Southeastern Tibet, and the Indian squadron attempting one last aerial sortie in search of any survivors beneath the falls two hours later, was one of stunning chaos.

Add, for that matter subtract, all the words from all the contending human languages and still there'd be no way to make sense of, or do poetic justice to, this riot.

"There is no cave, Captain," the chopper pilot reported. "The whole area has been destroyed, sir. I have never seen anything like it."

From the Indian military's new vantage, it was obvious there could be no survivors. No single oasis in a radius of howeversomany miles that had not been turned to elemental mineral. Not even a copse that wasn't reduced to its subatomic particles or cinder. The base of the falls had become a new glacier, 1,000 feet high, that spanned miles of gorge where previously there had been a tropical river. Ten Mt Saint Helens, ruptured. Ten million flowers, dimpled specklewort, soft fronds of every shaggy moss, bracken and polypody fern, pepper trees and northern mockingbirds, rainbow trout and hermit birds, pocket mice and night herons, yeti and cucumber beetles, all turned to alluvial sludge and loam of regur.

As the heavy-grinding choppers made their final buffeted swings around, there occurred amid seismic lurches in the wind some ghastly explosion, as if 1,000 oil refineries had blown, sending incinerated pulse waves out as far as the Bay of Bengal, even beyond. There, those happy islanders knitting, carousing, sleeping the day away in hammockville among the easy Andamans, might well have caught some ominous sign of this glacial Krakatoa 1,500 miles to the north, as part of the new ice formation erupted, and a geyser of superheated compressed water and mud detonated tropospherically into the surprised heavens. It was the river, once trapped, finally bursting from its confining dark.

The river's transmogrification out of frozen jumble sent water three miles into the Himalayan skies, steam half way to the moon, a flood bursting vertically, like lava, then arcing down towards the conspiring earth. This anomaly of nature spanned the distance of rainbows that started and ended in a kind of hydrological infinity. Something not seen in recorded history. A purple pottied tuningbird turned tremulously into an O3 molecule; a Tibetan blue bear and her two dainty cubs were now nothing more than sand illustrated by the odd tuft of hair. Where once a flock of gallant egrets strode proudly up the banks of the mighty river, picking off their day's quota of common silverfish and cutthroats, now 14 diamonds in the rough sparkled on an icy shore, such was the unusual astringent of so much physics all at once.

The last visual transmissions from the KH-12, prior to its leaving the region, also confirmed the extent of the calamity. The Indians had given up, and admitted to having lost their entire team. The Russian Ambassador and economic attaché were advised of the disaster.

The choppers vanished from whence they had come, and the obscure area on the northwestern fringes of the Golden Triangle, a little white blank on a Pentagon map of India and China which designated this disputed labyrinth of geopolitical mountain turf as Quadrant X, was once again returned to its primeval wildness, only more so by fathoms of calamitous fulmination whose beauty remained like unto a star.

Yet, just mid-point betwixt a geological porridge and mind-boggling maelstrom, there were unscathed survivors. The tribe had made it back to its jumping point, a ledge that remained without blemish or even a bounce; an eternal return for those fairies caught in the updraft.

But the sonance of the shaman's harp was different this time, a melancholic strum like that of the Welsh cittern. For Rajibai was gone. Mr Marigold, mesmerized by every one of the preceding seconds, and Sannazaro, stammering in a madman's flophouse but whose one salvation was his ability still to breathe, to see, to feel, were not yet able to process any of it. They groveled back to the hanging huts, which had survived the avalanche, apparently sheltered from all ferocity by express orders of some hidden evolutionary guidance system.

Each member of the tribe, aware of Rajibai's loss, bowed before Mr Marigold and Sannazaro, and touched a single finger to his or her forehead. It said everything.

Anna raced across the rim towards the tunnels. But the scoured summit slabs were unrecognizable. Boulders, which once provided shade in the afternoons, were now air bubbles of bruised emptiness. Smoking ice, steaming pools that had been displaced entirely, huge slimy cavernous depressions that were new and made progress along the granite track all but impossible. Hundreds of feet of debris blocked all entrances to the collapsed tunnels; below, fires jettisoned additional somber masses of smoke into the burdened atmosphere. Billows of particulate mayhem rained down soot and droplets of glowing embers upon the virgin snow, while the healing bacteria trickled aboard every crevice from the ruptured hot pools. Knowing that Namgyal, too, had vanished in the wrathful fray, Anna crossed the apocalyptic chaos and returned to the long hut.

No one slept that night. The hermit of Tesuque and his friend, the gardener, wept, and there were no hankies at 20,000 feet to check their sobbing. Rajibai was so young, so fresh and new to the world. Everything was before him. Doubly immortal. The Commander was desolated, Sannazaro punctured in every emotional quadrant.

A fury of unfairness rose up in Anna. How could she have let go of Rajibai, or allowed the stubborn Tibetan with that joyful, marvelous grin his warrior indulgence? But there was nothing to be done about any of it now. An emptiness of profound dimensions left her weak and disinterested in living any longer. Her physical distribution seemed to have run out. She was a lost cause entire. She had taken to the Tibetan on the rebound, after the loss of her previous lover. But it was more than that. In Namgyal she had seen herself 76 years before. Her heart loved him wildly. Her body, too. And in Rajibai she had seen atop the falls that little girl, now a young teen by standards of time, who had rescued her in that cave during a similar moment of devastation and loss long ago.

That was the idea that seized her. It rocked in her chest as her fingers clutched to the still-warm idea. Perhaps there was hope? She waited restlessly for the first glint of sunrise. She knew what had to be.

A child squatted nearby, pissing out the pee hole at the far end of the hut, as Anna again climbed onto the rim. The others all slept. But this child followed, running ahead, playful in the aftermath. Hundreds of fragments of exposed tree limb and ice lay strewn and ravaged along the half-mile perimeter of the cliff.

In her frolic, the child gained speed. Anna saw it coming, but no music could reach the ears of the little one, who ran enthralled atop the stubborn contusions of uplift, before slipping. Anna screamed. Those in the hut woke from their sleep at the sound. They came running. The child was toppling down towards the edge. The end was near. When— From out of subterranean depths a bludgeoned, weary pair of arms caught her.

"Namgyal!" Anna hollered.

The exhausted Tibetan had saved himself, Lord knows how, enduring only the odd wee bit of bodily damage, and had spent the entire night digging out from behind a boulder in the top of the tunnel. Now he held the child, whose life he had saved. Anna hugged them both, ecstatic with tears.

Then she explained what had happened to Rajibai.

Mr Marigold insisted on coming along with the other males of the tribe, as well as Namgyal. It was a treacherous descent as they clambered down the one secret passage that was still relatively free of the smoking chaos and collapsed walls. It was a circuitous route, made longer and more arduous by the inundation of mud. Throughout the night and the subsequent day they proceeded. It was late in the second afternoon when they reached bottom and beheld the full extent of Nature's violence. Not the least of which was a 100-story wall of ice seracs, leaning in dangerously unstable, charred edifices. Small waterfalls poured like emerald wash from 9,000 runnels; steam rose in colorful ellipses. Acres of ice and mud were still settling, the front walls calving every 20 seconds or so. Thunder emanated from subterranean gushers, and geysers belched forth a sweet-smelling gust.

But that vision of calamity was transformed and silenced when Anna and Namgyal and Marigold, and all the others of the rescue team, came upon the crumpled body of Rajibai. He lay against the rock on his right side; on his left, the skin had literally been shaved off. Blood seeped across the pink inflammations. He was unconscious, his core temperature having plummeted, but—amazingly! —he was alive.

Anna surveyed his injuries as the group carefully evacuated him from further harm's way. His shoulder was broken, his wrist dislocated, both ankles shattered, purple and twice their normal size. The skin on his buttocks had been sliced off; there were facial, neck and chest lacerations, and his spine had suffered a serious jolt. There was internal hemorrhaging and a head injury. Blood still oozed out his nostrils. His head was bashed. One eye nearly ruptured. It was more than a miracle that he was alive.

The group remained at the bottom of the tunnel that night, taking in the warm tropical air, giving Rajibai a chance to lie still. Sometime in the early morning, Rajibai opened his one good eye, saw Mr Marigold, and murmured half-consciously a word: "Father!" There were tears aplenty, and no one held back.

Later, they began the difficult ascent back up through the secret passage. There were continuous cave-ins to all sides, sudden breaks in the tunnel floor, explosions of water. Rajibai was carried by the largest of the tribal males. Anna knew that as soon as they could get him to the source of the hot pools, the more quickly he would be restored and out of his misery. However much the little boy groaned, she felt he would not die. He had, after all, consumed the urine, and with it the metabolized poppy. Still, there were no certainties.

Somewhere near the top, one of the young men heard something that sounded peculiar and went searching through a section of tunnel that had been opened by the after-shocks. Presently, the frantic vibrations of his harp-plucking permeated the inner maze of the wall. Other males went searching for the source of the music. They attained a small crawl space, shimmied along a ledge the size of slug dust, and finally found their companion. He was kneeling over a small bioluminescent pool in which a man— Malevich—lay mangled but still conscious, with all but four inches left for him to breathe beneath the shallow wall of ceiling. A whistling frog floated dead nearby. Large red cockroaches clustered along the rocky escarpment where a meager file of oxygen remained. Water from countless crevices was percolating along the ribbons of cliff, quickly filling the pool in which Malevich's legs were jammed and broken. He had little time left.

Anna arrived, and Malevich seemed to recognize her. "Pomeegayetue mne, pazhaleste," he pleaded. "Help me, please."

Namgyal and two of the strongest males tried to free him. But it was no use. Boulders had trapped him under water.

"They mustn't see him die. They have never seen death," Anna insisted.

It was true that the tribal men had witnessed the attack on the village by the military. But from a mile above. There was no way they could have understood what was truly going on. But here, now, up close—no, she mustn't let it happen. They had no reason to be exposed to the outside world, not in this way. She asked the others to leave.

The scene was terrible. Malevich was struggling for every last breath. He started praying in Russian, which touched off an emotional outpouring in poor Anna, who returned his desperation with whatever words she could muster in their common language, holding his head above water.

"I was a doctor. It is my duty to save him," she protested.

"It's too late," Namgyal said, stepping back. He took out a pill from a little plastic bottle in his side pocket. Both Malevich and Anna understood.

"I meant no harm," Malevich muttered.

Water was getting into his mouth, and nostrils. There was no more time. Namgyal placed the pill in Malevich's mouth. He swallowed, and within a second his head vibrated, his eyes closed. He was dead. His body sank. Namgyal blessed the corpse, as is customary among Tibetans.

Many hours later, the tribals reached the summit and delivered Rajibai to a safe corner of thick blankets. Anna gave him large doses of the plant, and other staples. He slept. It seemed to him like many days. In fact, within an hour of getting him to the safety of the long house, the tribe had delivered the indefatigable kid up to the remaining baths. Already the spring-fed lotus pools had repopulated the devastated moraines of Namche Barwa. The falls had resumed their normal course. Nature was restoring her own circulatory system. Rajibai's friends slowly immersed him in the water. His broken body needed time to heal. But he was young, malleable, resilient. He returned to the living, and within a few weeks was able to receive the nightly visitations of the precocious Aphrodites who cloyed and cottoned to his every whim.

"They've created a monster," Sannazaro observed whimsically. "A little voluptuary true to my own heart."

It was sometime later—no way to know the exact number of days— when Namgyal declared his desire to stay with Anna, and with the tribe, for as long as they'd have him. Anna was happy with his decision, as were the others. No more matches, no more headlamp. His pack, nearly everything he'd brought—weapons, cellular phone, supplies—were gone. The hut again regained its natural composure. It was a blue moon, and the cliff, the waterfall, the world was cloaked in quiet candescence and ultramarine glow.

Then came a second decision, and this was more difficult. Rajibai had recovered remarkably from his injuries with the help of the plant and the bacteria. Both the Commander and Sannazaro were well acclimated and feeling strong. They tacitly shared the urgings of a coming decision. But neither man was certain what the boy wanted to do. Anna read their anxieties and suggested it was best simply to confront him.

"What's it going to be, sport?" Mr Marigold asked him one morning. "Do you want to go to America, where life is pretty tough, uncertain, crowded and weird, sometimes ugly, painful, dangerous—basically like Mumbai, though with one or two happy times?"

"Such as?"

"An adventure in Disneyland, if you like," Uncle threw in. "Shopping at the mall. Movies. Popcorn."

"Or you could spend the rest of your life—and a very long life, indeed—here, with all these lovely naked girls, doing nothing but playing all day."

"Wait a minute," Sannazaro repealed, revising their common agreement. "What the hell was I thinking? I'm staying."

"Never a single espresso for the rest of your life?"

"Hmmm."

"Or book, or conversation with a friend at a coffee house?"

"Twice you mention caffeine, knowing my terrible weakness. That's unfair."

"You wouldn't last a year."

"*Disneyland!*" Rajibai suddenly blurted. He had contemplated his options. Now, without the slightest doubt, he exclaimed, "*Adventure!*"

"He's right," the Italian admitted.

"Are you sure, son?" the Commander asked.

"I'm going wherever you're going."

"Forget the Tibetan side," Namgyal explained, when it came to strategizing a way out. He was prepared to lead them, but it was no good attempting to cross the horrific pass over Namche Barwa, and down into the Tibetan plateau, in winter, where temperatures were 65 below, plus wind chill. Their only chance was a descent by the way they came. That would mean circumventing the walls of the river, snakes, leeches, hostile tribes, the Indian military.

"The Indians we can deal with," the Commander said. "Money is an unsinkable raft, a flower that never loses its scent, ice cream that never melts, a love letter that will turn even the harshest heart around."

"He keeps saying that, but not once has it ever worked," Sannazaro pointed out. "His money is a big dud."

The day came, and the four men prepared to leave just as they had arrived, except this time Namgyal had a woman waiting for him. He promised her he would be back within a week.

As they started down the one remaining open tunnel, the shaman hugged all of them. Then, apparently quite casually, he spoke. "Namaste," he said. It was the Tibetan equivalent of "Shalom".

Everyone, particularly Namgyal, was astonished.

"They're picking up your bad habits," Anna told her lover with a chuckle.

What none of the Westerners, including Anna, knew was that hundreds of years before the shaman had met a lonely Tibetan monk who had by himself slowly descended the gorge between Gyala Peri and Namche Barwa, discovered the tunnels and made his way up through the darkness to the rim. No footprint. No record. A Vasco Da Gama without a ship, its crew or any navigational equipment. Like the wind itself, twisted into a human curiosity, whose wingspan and colorful design enjoyed no admirer or posthumous historian to exhume his solitary heroism. Imagination his sole symbiont. A thousand sutras recited in the depths of a canyon, nobody to hear them. A Buddha whose monastery was the mist. A saint whose deeds were those of exploration. Whose wildly beating heart, it could now be reasonably deduced, had never tired. For he had likely sampled the poppy, and forever after vowed, by his own immortality, to keep Buddhism alive. There upon that rim two great sachems had connected. The only word ever uttered between them was that, which the shaman practiced for months. It constituted a great anatomical challenge, for his vocal chords were not human, after all, and required a tremendous act of will to be molded, even evanescently, for purposes of enunciating that one flying fish of a courtesy. It was the first and only word spoken by any member of the tribe.

The trio vowed to Anna that they would forever keep secret all those marvels that had transpired in Quadrant X. Her glorious life was secure. She knew that. The twenty-first century would just have to survive without any elixirs of immortality.

The Commander would always believe in Anna's world, the way the poet Percy Shelley had entrusted Mont Blanc to the enameled locket against his heart: a place free and untrammeled, where only the imagination lived. Shelley had spent all of three days beneath Mont Blanc, in July of 1816. By then the mountain had been climbed eleven times, but the poet chose to ignore such trespasses (said Marigold, rooted in the mundane minutiae of cramponed boots and ice axes) when he wrote of "some unknown omnipotence", of the "veil of life and death", "a homeless cloud from steep to steep that vanishes among the viewless gales" and that mountain itself, "Far, far above, piercing the infinite sky ..."

For days the trio and Namgyal renegotiated the terrain, with a bit more wisdom this time around.

"Never look up at the sun," Namgyal kept reminding them. He had his own cautions about the future, knowing full well that neither the Commander, Rajibai nor Sannazaro would enjoy a night of peace again if Nash learned that they had had physical contact with the tribe. The boy's sexual coming-of-age. The calabash of shared urine. The food, the touching of hands, the hot pools. Not to mention the cobalt poppy itself.

"Satellites can only identify you if they see your face. Keep your heads down and you three will always be remembered as nothing more than a spider, a monkey and a mule."

They had no idea what he was talking about.

Besides, it was not always that simple. Rajibai frequently stretched his neck to look up, and Marigold as well, what with his ongoing spasticities and funny bone-itis.

By now, even the grudging Sannazaro could read the landscape with the benefit of having nearly lost his life around each turn. They had interned under all the signs of hunting nets and panda trails; been tutored by the sickly sweet odor of death and reincarnation in a roasted banana and smoked plantain; been mentored, as it were, under the precarious tutelage of the centipede tribe; and could claim to be veterans of the hidden white waters of the lower gorge.

They traveled light and fast, much galvanized by the relative warmth and moist density of oxygen available to their lungs after the raw, attenuated turmoils of 20,000 feet had begun to feel like home. Now, they swam in an excess of breathable air, and the oxygenized blood gave a boost of energy to their veins and muscles. Marigold seemed to fly down trackless slopes of 71 degrees, where—just weeks before—he had desperately crawled and caterwauled.

They divided company with Namgyal on the far fringes of Sadiya. It was a parting woven of tears, enormous hugs and emotional stoicism. All knew that, for the young Tibetan, this was a vast beginning. He had not yet truly been initiated; the jump still awaited him. And the physical truth of what the jump actually triggered within the body: not merely faith in the unknown—a quantum of willing suspension of disbelief, of absolute love rare in these times—but the embryological miracle of eternal life with which they too would now have to grapple. Like a Fra Angelico, not hanging on a wall, but in their blood.

For the trio had consumed the plant, and would no longer fear for growing old and dying. Their only concerns need be the many, unpredictable accidents of life. All Mr Marigold needed to do (and his son by his very example) was resume that life he had once known. Days preoccupied with nothing more dangerous than the voracious consumption of books and articles and scraps of outdated news; nights amid the towering totems of manuscripts from ancient times, sonnets and epigrams, diaries and encyclopedias, the many dusty accounts of knights in knickerbockers, gentlemen farmers and cappuccino-addicted ascetics, love-struck heroes and petticoat heroines, purple poets and lyrically dissolving troubadors. To spend their days beside the Governor Sannazaro, picking wild strawberries and tilling the soil for sweet Maui onions. To feed the chicken, the bison and squirrel. To manage the affairs of state, such as they were, which Hidalgo had wisely entrusted to somebody happy to take on such burdens. To let go the rest: no more saving of the world. The end of the millennium was upon them, and—if they played their cards right—they might well live to see the next 1,000 years out.

Maybe in the year 3000 they would return to visit their dear friends atop the waterfall.

Marigold, his son and Squire crossed the sluggish Brahmaputra by ferry, and made for the nearest bus station. From there, they continued solemnly and incognito across Northeastern India, until, many days later, they were in Calcutta. Marigold took Rajibai to the American Consulate, for all their documents had long ago disappeared in the jungle, or some protest camp. Who could say where, exactly? A few phone calls and emails and faxes straightened everything out, though there was still the difficulty of Rajibai and the legality of his adoption. Money.

With their 'official' papers in hand, they made one final pilgrimage to the ghats, where the Commander, needing glasses but refusing to acknowledge his impairment, inadvertently tripped over a burning body and fell headlong into the flames. His palms were scorched but otherwise he was all right, though the family in mourning considered this intrusion—sudden and preposterous—more disturbing than the death itself.

As he washed himself off in the Hooghly, a dead cow floated by, its corpse bloated and weeping. Up above, a million commuters streamed across the 1,500-foot-long cantilevered and pylon-free Howrah Bridge, built back at the time of World War II. It was one of the most crowded bridges in the world. The whole city was a fitting site of farewell to Asia. Calcutta's sewage system had been engineered to withstand the contributions of 600,000 people, no more. On this day, 15 million people excreted their wastes, but the sewage system had never been expanded. The crowding, the noise, odors, sludge, fumes, smog and illimitable signs of soiled and toxic putrescence could not have encompassed a more tangible heartache of contrasts to those now fully accustomed to the wilderness. Nothing could change Calcutta, in Mr Marigold's mind. There was no longer any use even thinking about it.

They headed for the airport, and got on the first available flight out, which happened to be bound for London. It was two days before Christmas, 1999.

A CODA—LONG AFTERWARDS

An eagle flies high above the newly situated glacier.

If you were anywhere within the thunderous reign of the plunging waterfall, or hidden behind some geophysically freakish sound barrier, the distant but familiar music in the wind might become audible. A ghostly improvisation, half real, half remembered from childhood. Just the faintest of suggestions ... Listening more closely, you might even detect the rhythmical, fluting air of a melancholic mantra, tinged with all the sweetness of shamanic light. Again, a fantasy.

But were you somehow over a period of, say, many backwoods scrambling impossible terrifying months, to manage the vertical steeps higher still, climbing beyond logic or technique, without fear or hope, and peer behind the eternal mists, those socked-in, satellite-free, meteorological congestions of air pressures and temperature variants rising up from the Assamese plains hundreds of miles to the south, colliding with these still unknown colossal jungle and canyon lands of Himalayan incline, you might catch a glimpse of two slowly moving lovers bathing in the waters of immortality. Concealed by hovering butterflies. Behind the veil. Never certain it isn't just a perfect, desperate mirage. A million densities of vaporous glint and evaporating philosophy.

There, Anna and Namgyal, along with other members of the unabashed tribe, are lounging unconcerned for all eternity, naked, in the perfect hot pools above the ever-toppling rim over which the glacier streams converge into one mighty cataract, still undocumented, unknown, by the outside world. Golden scarabaeuses in silver lotuses; dragonflies Ghentish-green working the crimson thermal grasses.

For how many years, decades and centuries the aboriginals had enjoyed this scene, every morning and every night, and at other times of the day as well, if the spirit moved them, is hard to calculate.

Half submerged, Anna places Namgyal's hand upon her bountiful belly, hidden just beneath the watery balm, and remarks, "Can you feel her? There... She just moved!"

Part Four

Millennium Madness

CHAPTER 131
Communion with Mr Freud in London

MR MARIGOLD DOZED WITH something seizing up, sovereign and drugged in his veins; an historic intersection of silliness and sophistication, of goosegirls and deglamorization, where brain cells brigadooned and hopes hallelujahed together in an aura of stupefaction all the way to London. His brain was a fern twisting counterclockwise, a yarn shop ransacked by spool-crazed kittens. His head was the plumbing of a busy bar, copper, invulnerable, like weather-impervious Japanese ceramics. But the hammering of storms, and colossal splurge of so much tumult, could be read in his eyes.

New stars and skies, a pervasive dawn; best of all, a novel child nestled in his tender blue lambswool blanket and pillows of Egyptian cotton beside him. The lad watched movies, sampled seconds, thirds and fourths on the meal service, snapping half a dozen Belgian chocolates off a tray, helping himself to Bailey's with ice, to red and white wines, to champagne, and listening to 15 channels of audio with his very own headsets. Did he by now compute that he was the true and only son of a somewhat infamous billionaire? Had he begun picking up bad habits from Uncle, now fetchingly free of his own sordid travails out in the jungle, unabashedly evidencing all those contagious trappings of an aristocracy? After he'd sneaked a peek behind the pulled curtain at all those poor, cranky, disheveled sods stuffed together in farty Coach Class with their single bags of peanuts and screaming babies, Rajibai was certainly astute enough to grasp that from here on life would be a honeymoon.

He also most assuredly recognized the importance of girls. What would they be like in America? How many could he have for himself?

He took a full body bath in cologne in the little bathroom and helped himself to a roll of toilet paper for his own private stash—he had never possessed such soft, user-friendly tissue in Forlorn, where thrice-stained foolscap, bludgeoned butcher paper or the daily news was as good as a diploma. He helped himself, in addition, to three of the little bathroom towels, systematically charmed the stewardesses, and harassed the co-pilot with questions of a nautical and aerodynamical bent as, heading west, they soared silently above all those southern fringes of the Himalayas. It was a clear pellucid afternoon. One could discern Pumori from Lhotse, and that entire testament of geological time which encompassed Chomolungma to the right, Nanga Parbat to the left.

"There I leapt across a mile-wide river!" he cried ecstatically. "Oh, and there we fought the cannibals!" A few moments later: "That was where Uncle's arm was eaten by a tiger, and he would have been devoured entire if not for Master Jigme, who owns the CIA! And there! And there!" he added on and on. Until, finally: "In the end, I jumped naked from 20,000 feet with three of my girlfriends and broke every bone in my body."

"And throughout all of these exciting adventures I bet you weren't even scared?" the pilot declared.

"Naturally not," Rajibai attested—before promptly passing out from all the alcohol.

Two stewards assisted the lump of foaming diablo clay back to his security blanket beside his father, who at that moment was deep in undisturbed, ecstatic melancholia, thinking vaguely that if one aspired in relative terms, all things were possible. Place those dreams beside an absolute, and the whole endeavor was doomed to failure.

By this modest crystal ball of forebodings, Marigold had made a decision, taken between chance and lucky stars, those peculiar bylaws of his nature that recommended no more campaigning or risk of limb, an end to all such days previously devoted to the likes of Sinbad, or Aladdin, or even Gulliver, so as to retire, instead, from public life, such as it was a life, and thus regain hold of his solitude. He wished only to become once again an eremite, allowing, of course, for a son, a Squire, companion animals and plants and well-nestled neighbors, so that he might live out his anonymous days dining in absence of any clamor, reading leisurely the printed tomes with their generous typefaces, steel engravings, and sterling aquatints of dead men and women, without pressure to perform, revive or revolutionize: no more electronic gadgetry, Ipv4, satellite uplinks or corporate equity-related remonstrations.

But also, it must be admitted, the Commander's own circumstances had taken an abrupt about-face after such debilitating and frankly depressing tête-à-têtes with Calcutta. Who, upon any border or back lane of that stifling megalopolis, has not felt his dreams demoralized and valley of flowers flattened? Reason enough, surely, to have questioned the whole outward enterprise, thinking it might be better, after all, to have stayed with the tribe? What mighty chasm in his character was so blind as to have renounced that which he had won? Sibyl's soothsayings foolishly scattered upon leaves left to the four winds? What ill-conditioned, spiteful happenings—when one really thinks about it—would have prompted any reasonable person to give up a life among Mazaruni daisies, wasps of the painted nests, scarlet-thighed leaf walkers, a glittering rose eternal, and foliaged wood beyond the latticed world? Had he imagined his life could get any better than that? Lined with licorice?

Whatever phantasms and cricket lullabies he envisioned, a brief transit through Calcutta, hell sprinkled with literary told-you-so's, brought him swiftly back to conspicuous consciousness, the face of mortal tyrants and inimical disequilibriums; to countenances grave and alphabets devised for purposes of cruelty; to shattered children, quarrels as complicated as spider webs, and momentary murders muffled by the density of squalid ligaments. Not a single eminence or calm, every human connection tainted by motives, each shopkeeper concealing a slingshot.

Was it that vision of human degradation, so augmented on the streets of Calcutta just days after the other world, that provoked his inner crisis? Or the scent of scintillating sex upon those aerial ramparts which threw his studied torpor into torment?

Whatever it might be, now the Nawab of Oude's subtle paean evolved into a full-blown point of concentration on the life of Mr Sigmund Freud, for reasons of a pressing compunction.

Freud's legacy, which Marigold presently consumed in one handy volume, was not out of tow with these persistent distractions. The Moravian Jew had, at a tender 41, pruned the lowliest of subterranean screws, and these plopped down into Marigold's thinking bowl with striking coincidence, like a hailstorm upon pansies. The Commander had seized a potpourri of the morbid analyst, arrayed in a first spine-cracking, page-foxing, edge-wilting edition, one of only 70 copies, from a banana vendor in Calcutta's worst district for 211 rupees. Never mind that it had been poorly translated into Bengali. The handwritten marginalia were of an English spelling that yielded those strange conjurations of a century: phantasmagorias, flamboyant fixations, crises of the soul. Who could not fall prey to the irresistibility of such profound gibberish? They went to the rotting root of Marigold's confusion.

He well knew, of course, that Freud had expounded upon all matters of the human mind, those arias of the brain that resembled seas of milk, islands of cheese or hissing rivers. From his Viennese love seat he had confronted the same deep-shadowed clefts and countless mirages as the Himalayan interloper: a landscape of halos on high, terrible sucking things, and the fragile Self as it struggled to surmount each obstacle in the odd aspiring, repressed or, by turns, ecstatic guises of the personality. Marigold felt at home in this terrain of unease, despair and social hope.

The conflict of a Spinoza and John Dewey: a spiritual thinker, concerned with ethics, versus the ruthless pragmatist who wanted to know how to fix the clock, the steam engine, the economy. On the one hand, he wanted to go home again, retiring amid his familiarities. On the other, he wanted never to do so. Freud was the one who'd counted all the discrepancies and disparities and made a splendid senselessness of them, which suited well the Commander's topsy-turvy mood. The mathematics of human folly compounded by homesickness.

Like Freud, Marigold had always espied demons in the psyche, and marveled at mankind's insistence on marrying them. With 15 hours of flying time, the Commander (who was tired of Commanding) had time to read, and to fall asleep reflecting upon the author's *Civilization and Its Discontents*, published in 1930, wherein Freud laid the groundwork for assessing the perceived death of nature in the context of the human capacity for barbarism and sexual frustration. But none of his investigations prepared Freud for the horrors of the Nazis. From his refuge in London, he could not believe that human beings could embrace such nullity, burrow beneath the last gutter, elevate depravity to a deity. Marigold, for his part, could not fathom Auschwitz in one hand, ouzo in the other. Adam and Eve did not help one bit. In fact, the two of them had created utter chaos for later psychoanalysts like Freud and Marigold.

When the stewardess awakened the Commander, his son and their Squire—the plane was an hour out of Heathrow and they needed to fill out their landing cards—Rajibai puked all over his blanket.

"Perhaps next time your little boy should go easy on the drinking," she cautioned the boy's father.

Marigold felt little gratitude in such instruction, for it was his most vouchsafed principle that his son should have no discipline other than that which Nature wisely provided in her clamor of fascinations and allures. Hence, to vomit was a valuable lesson.

As they stepped off the plane and went through customs, Marigold was still thinking of Freud, of Marx, of Dickens and Shakespeare; of all those great minds that had tried to save the world in one form or other, despite every lampoon and ridicule: those who would mock a phrase like, "The forest is in pain, the birds are crying out", and speak of all sentiment as "stultifying". There were as many intellectual and aesthetic blinders as there were techniques, personages and forms for ignoring one's age. Yet, it was the age, and no less the history that made it, which was quite responsible for the mess things were in, and that was the point. You had to do something about neighbors, power lines, garbage, polluted streams, war criminals, the global economy, the rich and the poor. You could not simply retire in the face of orphans, or walk away from scoundrels. How could any human being turn away from a puppy, or cub or fledgling? Had not all of evolution worked towards the creation of a lamb? What were the biological sciences but a chronicle of larvae and aspiration, cocoons and noble purpose? What was man but that evolving capacity to shepherd others? And woman to nurture the shepherds? And children to confirm and substantiate the women? Thus it had gone, bestrode, was written and still writing, recycling every opportunity to reshape destiny in the guise of a tightknit confederacy of same-minded genes, generous hearts, survival of those who loved most. From generation to generation. But where did a Marigold fit in? He loved, but not other people, particularly. Or not previously.

This, then, was his most terrifying realization: that he was responsible for another human being, all in the absence of a mother—like Anna— whom he might adore, and who would help share in the baffling burden of raising such a handful. This thought gave the Commander greater pause than at any time in his life. That he was alone in this. A cliff much higher than 20,000 feet.

What was expected of him? To guide the child down dark corridors, or intimate their existence? Forcefully ensure he elude all adversity, or insist upon his full tutelage in that regard? Prepare him like a regular student, a soldier, a monk, a king? Or provide the opportunities for him to do so on his own, should he choose to? Those were the logical dualisms. But then, there were illogical ones as well. The rebellion and waterfall had been cases in point. What other boy had mustered such obvious dexterity in the face of quintessential hardship? Who else but a product of the worst slums could have apotheosized degradation into nobility?

The boy had more watershed experience than others in ten lifetimes. Was he lacking for a school drilling or a conversation with drug addicts on the corner? Did he suffer for want of television or science fairs? Did he need religious education, or instruction on the birds and bees? Drugs, alcohol, disrespect of elders, peer pressure ...

Was there anything in Rajibai's life that could have been improved upon? Yes, that his sister should be alive, and his original parents, too. Otherwise, not a thing. The Commander had quite literally become overseer to a little saint. A boy whose wits allowed that he should bargain with the stars, who had the ability to eschew common sense, dance brilliantine on the lip of disaster, face every hostile encounter with exuberance. His courage was that of an insect, his breath as sweet as cinnamon. No impediment disturbed him. Equanimity was his password, assured strength his name. In character, conviction, irrepressibility and the advantage of surprise, none approached Rajibai's strength. His only weakness, if one were to judge against the brutality of the world, was his innocence. But even this quality played in his favor: it provided him with enough naiveté to fear no evil.

Marigold had grown up, for the most part, without mother, father or siblings. He'd never had a girlfriend. He didn't really have a clue what to do, or how to behave—heavy or light, obsessive or disregarding; how to hold his hand or wipe away tears. He knew nothing about discipline, school, orthodontists or football, and had no intention of starting now.

As a creature of habits, the notion of actually steering the course of another person was horrifying to him.

Moreover, they were no longer in the wilderness, where the rules of life were easy; where child and adult were equals before death and the mountain wall, and no other tasks were required than getting up the trail, and down again, without killing oneself. But London was something else.

This very night happened to be a Christmas Eve. He didn't even have a present for his son.

There was, besides, even more to induce a panic attack. For the first time in Marigold's life, he was unable to shake a certain gigantic lust—the memory of that regurgitating naked beauty, with her feline body and glimmering breasts. Freud only aggravated his sense of angst.

Of course, there were women in Santa Fe, and elsewhere, but the Commander was certain that none of them would exhibit the same natural proclivities—how to phrase it? Now that he had observed the absolute harmony of unselfconscious eros, could he ever settle for anything less?

On the fatherhood front, these Freudian issues were bound to resonate. After all, the boy had already lost his virginity, not in some awkward 30 seconds of incoherence, and accompanying loathing and guilt, but with three adoring beauties throughout the night and into the next day. This boy had become a sexual savant of unique dimensions, having learned patience and gratefulness without even knowing how different most sexual experiences probably were. Anything like those three female extraterrestrials was unlikely to be found in any part of northern New Mexico. But now a precedent had been set, for the Commander had allowed his boy his own freedom without so much as a murmur of commentary or caution. Their complicity was set in the veil of mists they would never forget. The child needed no trainer, no preceptor. To be tutored in the truth of himself, allowed for latitude to go there, afforded the security that should he fail, or digress, no lack of love or money, of pride or certainty, would follow him. In the Commander's and Uncle Sannazaro's hearts, there was permanence. A home that Rajibai could now claim without the slightest hesitation.

Of course, Rajibai was a very special child, as emotionally mature as he was stunted in physical attributions, or most. Apparently, he made up in stamina what he lacked in height. In addition, he was the most courageous, clever little character one was likely to meet. No affect. An attitude of grace before abomination. How he had survived his dreadful life up until this time was a testament to human adaptation and faith. His Jainism had saved him, in ways Marigold had begun to comprehend. His ability to take charge and lead a massive rebellion upon New Delhi's insensate bureaucracy was nothing short of spectacular. In two more years or so, amazing as the concept seemed, he'd be an American teenager. What problems might that bring down upon the otherwise elaborate silence of the hermit's hacienda in Tesuque? Not to mention America in general? What revolutions might this child of mixed fanfare unleash on the history of a nation, especially in light of his wealth? Collectively, these mighty miasmas of ghastly wants and sudden responsibilities precipitated a certain ungluing. Marigold staggered momentarily and held on to the Governor, who hailed a taxi and specified the Ritz. They had not a shred of luggage between them, other than hand particulars, like Marigold's binoculars which somehow had clung to him throughout their epic adventures. Enroute, they passed Trafalgar Square, where snow lay in shadowed depths.

"Look at all those pigeons!" Rajibai exclaimed.

"We'll get out here," Marigold signaled.

Sannazaro rolled his eyes with quiet obedience to a new taskmaster.

But it was a stop he would long remember.

Within minutes the boy had dragged Uncle off to commune with all the birds, whilst Marigold found himself immersed in conversation with a woman eager to speak her mind. She took the wizened Commander aside, sprinkled birdseed on his head—a magnet for several hordes of avians—and unburdened her soul as they sat down.

CHAPTER 132
A Stranger at Trafalgar

TWO DAYS AGO," she began, "I was here feeding pigeons, a ritual of mine for nearly 70 years."

"But you don't look a day older than 50," the Commander conceded, lying heavily.

She pinched him on the cheek—"What a charmer"—and continued: "My three daughters have always alleged I'm more concerned about the plight of these birds than the homeless teenagers populating the dark crannies to all sides of Trafalgar Square. Which isn't true. It's just that the birds make me feel good about myself. I'm dying of cancer, you see, and the only ones that know are the birds and my doctor. And now you. I don't know why I'm telling you all this. You clearly have a way with women, sly fox that you are. Anyway, for six months, since I first heard, I've spared my children, and their children, the annoying news."

"You needn't worry, friend," Marigold replied. "My ears are lock-boxes, like Social Security."

"The fact is," she went on, "I have lived my life deliberately, no regrets. The birds stand on my head, just like that, see! Make me act silly, cluster along my outstretched arms, where I have stood since childhood all dressed up, in bliss, covered in pigeon poop. That, and seeing the wild ponies of Dartmoor as a little girl, spring meadows draped in colorful ranunculus, are among my greatest childhood memories. They allow me to forget that one of my granddaughters has had two abortions, is unmarried, unemployed and I'm certain quite miserable. Another is married to a despicable low-brow whose dot.com is on the verge of bankruptcy. The third, born with polio just one week before vaccines were available—it was either a peremptory C-section or her demise, though she's never accepted that version—is shuffling around with crutches and has great difficulty across the street there at the National Gallery, where she specializes in the restoration of frames. Sidney, her husband, is a policeman. A life that would suffocate her grandmother. The birds are grateful for the seed, as you can see, which I purchase each morning from the vendors over there. That is enough, at my age. No long-winded discourses. No regrets. If I have tuned out of the world, so be it. I am reconciled. My late husband, Morris, has been dead a decade. My pension covers most necessities. I have no complaints. Convent Garden, the symphony, occasional lunch with the few friends still among the living. All is well.

"That was my philosophy, if you will, until two days ago, when I met a man, a boy, really—although he seems like a man. The strangest fellow I have ever encountered in all my years. I could describe him in 100 ways, but let me just say that he was clad in a pair of cut-off jeans, no shirt or socks, despite the fact it is wintry cold in London, isn't it? He travels barefoot, says a skateboard harms ants. I estimated him to be no more than 15. He was sitting right over there, all alone. Biding his time. Definitely not feeling sorry for himself. No way to tell what he was feeling, or thinking. Damned strange, even from the beginning. But wait— "I would have passed him by with a parental scowl. I didn't, on account of something in his eyes, all about his person, that struck me the way I am overwhelmed in a great cathedral, gazing through the light of a finely wrought wall of stained glass. I am not given to outright wonder, celebration or mysticism, but believe me when I tell you this kid is, well, out of this world, or, conversely, more down to earth than anyone in my experience. A freak of nature, an ideal embodied in flesh, a mystery I cannot shake. I said a few words to him, asked a few questions. One word led to another. Now, I shall never be the same.

"Yesterday morning I paid some bills, then took the bus back to Trafalgar Square here. I avoid the tubes, at my age. The birds are desperately in need of help during these cold winter days, as you can see. Here, take some more. I fill a little rucksack with loaves of bread which I break up. The boy was there. Sitting in the snow. Foolishly half-naked.

A radiance all about him as he spoke with the birds, the way I do. But—and you may not believe this—I swear the birds were speaking back to him! Me they ignore, the minute the seeds are gone.

"Now, the important point is this: there were quite a few things the boy said to me as well, and I believe destiny had a hand in all these events. I can quite make out that you are a fine listener. That fact, as well, somehow enters into the equation, though I am not the one to work it through. My memory is not memorable, and I can't read my own handwriting too well—arthritis does that—but when I came here yesterday I brought a notepad and tried diligently to write down as much of what he said as possible. Oddly, as if granted to the occasion, my hand stopped shaking, had no difficulty whatsoever in committing to paper the few things he conveyed to me."

Marigold listened intently, certain that the destiny of which the woman spoke was at hand.

"'Suvrata, that was the day, or time of month,' the boy begins.

"'Is that Spanish, or Portuguese?' I ask him. 'Where do you live? Why don't you get up off your butt, if you'll excuse my French? Get a job, go to school, return home to the cozy nook and guidance of your family? You seem like a nice kid,' I started. That's called ragging on me, according to one of my granddaughters.

"'He who does no acts has ceased from works; he who has ceased from them is called houseless. He who clings to his home is turned round in the whirl of pains,' he replies.

"'OK,' says I. 'It's obvious you're no neo-Nazi, but maybe a Hare Krishna. Or Born Again? I bet you're hooked on drugs, and you're broke, right?' "'No Ma'am,' says he.

"'Well you're going to freeze to death at this rate.' He actually was blue, or gold, or some combination thereof. I can't explain it, except to harken back to that image of a cathedral—Notre Dame or Chartres. You see, there was this strange light emanating from the ragamuffin youth.

"'Ruth,' he starts, 'all the complaints of the world I would inhabit.'

"Of course my first reaction was to wonder how on earth this boy knew my name.

"'Ruth,' he continues in absolute calm, 'every bird here in the square has over time touched every human connection. A smattering of generations separates the human family and non-human family. The air each pigeon breathes, the human heads of hair they have stood upon, the seed and bread that has been fed to them—all grown in the earth, attached to bacteria, nigoda, molecules, interconnected. A planetary consciousness struggling to become true conscience. Trafalgar Square is one epicenter of the world. A window on the spirit. Like Mt Everest or the Grand Canyon. Spread the word among the pigeons, and the Earth shall listen.' "'Maybe I agree with that,' I reply, still unnerved by the fact this stranger knew my name. 'But what word? What does a teenager who sits half-naked in the snow have to say to an old woman, let alone to a bird that has half a chance of even surviving the winter? Listen up, I've been around, young man, I've seen the idealists thwarted, and crazy or inspired people barking at Hyde Park ignored or laughed at. And while you and I might spend a few moments in idle chatter, a billion other kids your age and younger are starving to death. The world is hemorrhaging.

The price of a good bottle of wine, of lentils and whipped cream is rising. Pain and cruelty such as I cannot begin to describe. This world's an awful place.' "'Ma'am,' he goes on gently, 'this world is in transition. Be patient. Have hope. Love and non-violence are everything. One must not harm a living being, and must prevent others from doing so, to the extent possible. We are all one.' "'Words, words. I feed the birds, that is enough,' I tell him.

"'Quite enough,' he replies. 'The birds are the salvation. Each her part, but no less than that.' "'What's your name?' I ask.

"'Once I was called Vardhamana. In those days Kundapura was a tiny village. And my hair was long, combed with various herbs gathered in the surrounding forest. Rather like the St Martin's fields which once covered the spot on which we sit. I had a pet cobra. Now, I have no name, and every place I call home. Every living being is my mother, my father, my son, my daughter, my friend...' and his thoughts trailed off.

"'But how did you get here?' I said, breaking into his reverie.

"'Birth, and re-birth. From village to village. One day at Vaisali, Nalanda, Pava-puri, the next day in Yosemite, Paris, Trafalgar Square.' "'Frankly, I didn't understand. Vaisali, Nalanda—no clue where they are. Not that it matters. But there was no denying the power of this lad's presence. He exuded the unexpected. This was no two-bit con vying for favors to get him to his next fix. That much was clear. Quite brilliant, I have to conclude. A prodigy whose emotional depth I can't begin to ascertain, except to say his heart went instantly to my heart. I knew him like I knew myself. He provided a door, a way in. And oh, how he had suffered. I could see it in his eyes. In his supreme humility, his compassion, even in that wry sense of humor lurking beneath that near-naked truth of himself. A maturity that surpasses all commentary or analogy.

"'Jiva-daya,' he repeats. 'Take care in everything, every step, every action. Seek moments whereby all can be soothed, liberated, made to feel the same joy you felt as a little girl when you first came to Trafalgar Square and thrilled to the sensation of feeding the birds, communicating with them, loving them and being loved. Keep that sense of profound enthrallment, balance, of ecological mission, and the whole world will be relieved of its pain. Nothing else matters...' "'Well, that's about it. We spoke at length for most of the morning. But in the end, I was hungry and not a little restless. From the sublime transport and ethereal clouds, I craved some hot beet Borscht and a scone. Maybe a chicken salad sandwich.

"'Go vegan,' he says beguilingly. 'If you truly love the pigeons of Trafalgar Square, then you know that chickens are their most loyal friends and colleagues. And they suffer just like you.' "'What is that? Vegan, I mean?' I ask. And he explains. And suddenly it makes a lot of sense, with mad cow and so on, but he did not make me feel shame for my ignorance. Or afraid. His smile absolved me.

"And then the most idiotic and predictable turn of phrase issued from my too-human lips: 'Show me a miracle,' I pleaded. 'If all you say is really true. Something that will leave its mark on an elderly cynic.

Change the world for a dying woman, son. Do it, and I shall then believe. I'll even forego chicken salad sandwiches.' "'I'm no circus animal performing tricks,' he shudders. 'But perhaps I will do a small thing for you.'

"'And what would that be?'

"'Wish you a long life.'

"'Shows how much you know,' I muttered. Enchanted, but sad for him.

Sad for myself. Sad for all of us. I had, for an instant, imagined that he was some Christ-like figure who had returned to save us. My private senility. My unrequited dream.

"So it's getting late and I have to go. He kisses the bony fingers of an old woman's hand, then utters the words, if I can pronounce them: 'Michchhami Dukkadam'.

"'Take care of yourself,' I said, absorbed by his lonely chivalry. And then I headed home."

"What a remarkable story," Marigold declared.

"Oh, but you haven't heard the best of it," she went on. "That was last night, just after dark. I felt strange leaving him there. Turning, peering back through the smoke and London's rush-hour traffic, I thought I saw him get up and leave, tramping through the snow, a wind of pure crystals, a light trailing behind him."

"And?" the Commander inquired impatiently.

"I was feeling most unsettled, turned on the TV, made some supper. Read through my notes. And then—well, how can I describe it? I felt ... different ... good. *Really* good. I got scared and called Joyce, my doctor.

'Something strange is happening, I'm spooked,' I told her. So she agreed to meet me at Brompton Hospital, and took a few X-rays.

"'But that's impossible! Your cancer—it's gone!' she exclaimed. "Just like that! A miracle!"

"But that's unbelievable!" the Commander howled.

He knew then who this extraordinary teenager really was, and looked over at his own son, fully immersed in the life of the birds. The connection Ruth had triggered was unequivocal, he thought, reflecting back upon the very tales told by Paramatman, and the fitting coincidence that his own son should embody all that same sentience.

"This morning," Ruth went on, "I raced back here, desperate to find the stranger with no name."

"And?" Marigold pursued ardently.

"And what greeted me instead were the birds, thousands of them. Just as you see them now. Except this time, I swear it, they were all bathed in his very light. There? Do you perceive it?"

Marigold stared hard across the gray moisture-laden haze of the square into the filtered sun. "Yes, by Jove! I think so!" he exclaimed.

"Each and every bird was speaking to me," Ruth carried on. "Not enough notebooks in the world to tell you what they're saying. But this is where you'll find me now. You may tell my children, and my grandchildren. Grandma's at Trafalgar Square, conversing with the birds."

And with those words she bid farewell to the Commander and walked away, covered in pigeons.

CHAPTER 133

A Relatively Calm Christmas Eve in Henry the Seventh's Chapel

IT WAS A TIME out of time, an encounter that—most unusually for a Marigold—left him speechless. Eventually he rejoined his son and Squire and the 500 birds that attended to their hand-outs.

"Where were you? Did you see her?"

"See who?"

Anxiously, he attempted to convey highlights of what had just happened, badly translating the strange language part so that it sounded like ykcowrebbaj backwards and upside down.

"You'd disappeared. And what a pity. The coincidence was remarkable. You have to meet her," he bowled stridently.

But Rajibai had read the situation without flinching. "Of course, that was Mahavira she was speaking of," he said. "He shows up from age to age."

"But here, yesterday. In the guise of a homeless teenager? It's too incredible. If only Paramatman. Anna ... everybody ... had met him! A day away. I'm losing my mind."

"No loss there."

"Come then, meet Ruth," the Commander said, urging them back to the bench where he had sat with her.

"Well, where is she?" asked Sannazaro, ever the wiseacred tarmac.

The Commander searched high and wide across Trafalgar Square. But in the dark his eyes scarcely defined even an inch. He shouted out her name, but all such plaints were useless against the crescendo of evening traffic, mobs crossing 24 intersections. Christmas bells, the rumble of undergrounds, the blaring horns of restless commuters and heavy swoosh of dozens of buses. Ruth had vanished as sure as the stranger, their identities and verity gobbled up in the rush of humanity. St Martin in the Fields. Carolers. A snowman. Cider. Frozen tears.

"I suggest we hail a taxi and get to our hotel," Sannazaro said. "Exhaustion is now added to by bird shit. I have no more reserves."

That is what they did, but en route Rajibai saw too sterling an edifice.

"We have to take a picture!" he cried.

"That's Westminster Abbey," the taxi driver explained. "Nine hundred years old."

"Give us a minute," Marigold asked, the group removing themselves from the vehicle.

"Sorry, I can't park here," the driver explained.

"Of course you can," the Commander aired, placing 100 pounds in the driver's hand to bolster his confidence.

The twilight, larkish and fair, was swathed in wintry mist and the chill of the North Wind. As they admired the complex, the Commander was suddenly addressed by name.

"Marigold?" an elderly woman's voice rang out. Turning, he saw a familiar face but could not place it.

"That's, uh, what's her name ..." Sannazaro hazarded, applying himself to a bankrupt memory.

"Catherine Champion," she exhorted, taking hold of the Commander's hand in a warm and long lost embrace. It had been ages since their community meeting in Santa Fe. "My God," she went on. "It seems as if the whole world's been looking for you. Where have you been all these many months?"

"Months? Has it? Is something wrong?" he blundered.

"Wrong? Only a war or two brewing since you disappeared. It's been plastered across all the newspapers. But, look, I'm late for a very special gathering. Why don't you and Señor Sannazaro join me? Who's this?" she finally came round to asking.

"My son, Rajibai Marigold."

"Your son? I didn't know—"

"He's new."

"He looks pretty old to me," she laughed in a manner the Commander now remembered.

"We've only just arrived and were on our way to the hotel," Sannazaro said, exasperated. If he didn't get a bath soon, there would be real war. "Never mind that. This is a once-in-a-lifetime-opportunity, and come to think of it, no one is better suited to joining the fray than yourself. You'll particularly appreciate that it is a gathering of the great spiritual thinkers and theologians from all over the world, by invitation only, for a Christmas Eve group prayer, tea and discussion in Henry the Seventh's Chapel. But we must hurry."

"What makes you think we'll get in?"

"I know Tony."

"Tony? Who's Tony?"

"Why none other than the big cheese."

"The big cheese?" Marigold repeated dully.

"That's right. The PM. His Deputy is hosting the gathering. And Tony himself may drop by. Now come along."

They paid the taxi driver, who by this time had earned a clear warning from a bobby, and hastened into the main Abbey entrance, past security, through the magnetometers. Many were arriving—long-bearded men in ashen surplice or scapular mantle, others swaddled in saffron, still more in sweeping colorful African djellabah. Portentous priests, rabbis, gooroos, imams, predicants, an archbishop, sirs, lords, professors, deans and deacons, His Holinesses and Her Eminences, Munificences, brothers and sisters, preachers and Highnesses were all elegantly arriving at the same kimono moment. The great bells in the Abbey rang out, and all strolled magnificently in concert down the long Gothic corridor towards Pompous Corner. They moved into the perfectly perpendicular-styled chapel with its early sixteenth-century stone umbrellas dangling from the intricately manicured ceiling, the architectural poetry of France, wherein Chartres had exerted the greatest influence.

A huge Christmas tree with 1,000 illumined crystal ornaments graced the nave. Rajibai, the only boy in the entire sculptural Eden, stared in wonder, waking up to the odors of Christmas cake that wafted across the marble gallery with its hundreds of perfumed wax candles burning in diamond-shaped hand-cut Regency and George IV flint-glass holders. Whilst the numerous religious leaders and observers mingled for cocktails, the boy strolled up to the tree as if in trance. It was a standing chandelier of spirit, canopied and caparisoned in faceted lusters all molded from pot metals of a dozen hues: amber, cobalt, ruby red, ochre. Heavy Venetian glass ornaments, salt-glazed stoneware, Rouen porcelain and floriated silver: all had been fashioned into a pantheon of theological symbols. A Moslem Comb and Turkish Star of Bethlehem; a Maltese and St Andrew's Cross; a Star of David, a Chinese Swastika and Solomon's Signet. Each served as a refracted prism whose light originated from the maze of oil lamps strung along wire bands encircling the great tree—a flaming revelation altogether new to the boy. The effect silenced him.

Everyone took seats and the Father of Parliament welcomed all present and introduced various individuals from the many illustrious corners of the world, thanking them for their selfless zeal in putting aside any differences of opinion, and coming to embrace global dialogue on this most impressive of times, Christmas Eve, 1999.

Not far away, the House of Commons and PM had convened to conduct an emergency inquiry into the grounding of an English super-tanker carrying seven million gallons of oil off the southwestern beaches of County Kerry, in Ireland. The double hull had apparently withstood impact on an elevated sandbar, but two of the compartments had cracked; dog whelks and polymerus barnacles clinging to the ship's iron bolts had expired in multitudes; a gale was threatening the region; and a flotilla of helicopters had been dispatched to drop inflatable petroleum-absorbent buoys, and oil-eating bacteria if need be.

Along the many miles of coastline with its whorls of giant feather dusters, sandcastle worms, moon jellyfish and red sponges, volunteers were filling sand bags, and vets arriving with antibiotics, syringes and warm towels. The last time a tanker had collided with a cliff in bad weather, off a nature preserve in Scotland, tens of thousands of animals and untold numbers of fish had been asphyxiated.

In yet another chamber, the Great Committee Room, a meeting of high-flown parliamentarians was underway amid superior bunkum to contend with other Irish-based turmoil—a spate of terrorist bombings in Derry at a most indelicate time of year, century and millennium. But none of these sordid truths had yet infiltrated to the concatenation of hortatory unfolding before the trio's weary souls. Sannazaro was still driven to hopeless distraction by the prospect of a sauna and massage at the Ritz. The Commander, however, was steadfast, perhaps too tired to be discourteous or attempt an escape amid so much hot air. Stuck headlong in the morass of the moment, it was easier simply to sit still and suffer in silence, as Schiller recommended.

The first speaker recited 12 teachings by Baha Ullah and Abdul-Baha, calling for an independent investigation of the truth. Which truth? Marigold wondered. And what was that concerning a universal language and a spiritual solution to all money-related matters? Who was the All Wise, the Ordainer?

Came a second speaker, a lovely yogic nun who had spawned more than 1.3 billion minutes of prayer for peace among people in more than 80 countries. She went on about a jeweler who had once been inhabited by a Luminous Self in 1936 and entrusted the awakening to single women, all clothed in white robes, and all using only the finest dry cleaners. Their task was to exhume the latent qualities of Shakti—Hindu love, purity and celibacy—in every human being. These were trying times, said the sister, whose methodology for eliciting this universal love relied heavily upon volunteers, which was a good thing. For if one attempted the love revolution according to the Earth's diameter, utilizing the good will of a million complicit love-volunteers, it should be an easier task than going via the circumference, which would necessitate numerous equatorial island-hoppings, finding the last savages and so forth. However, with enough disciples (and here, Marigold thought, Sister Love's own ranks and minions might help multiply the effort) each could seize upon a portion of the radius—say, Detroit to the Bahamas—or, conversely, attempt latitudes one by one: hit up the meridians, stake claims to longitudes, add up the time zones. Never was spirituality more tiring.

A Sri Lankan Buddhist spoke of shramadana, the giving of human labor to the community according to Buddha's Blindfold Path for Little Travelers, Nickel Hopefuls, Ballet Shoes, Child Whispers, Early Lessons, Wild Livelihood, Blurred Belly Laughs, Right Of Way, Keen Gait, Restful Understanding.

But by this time the Commander could neither concentrate nor think; Sannazaro was losing his capacity for effort, and no livelihood or mindfulness seemed capable of drawing any action from Rajibai, who was fully focused on that Christmas tree and all the presents and food tables beneath it. Food for Rajibai was a cumulative, compelling necessity, born of many thin years. Prey unwarily gathered at the watering hole. Whereas for Marigold cuisine was a necessary annoyance, a bodily intrusion that could have no lasting significance for the True Knight or Absolute Ascetic. Sannazaro took a different approach again: for him, food was a sublime derivative, the perfect aftermath to a good pre-prandial port or curative cappuccino.

The prayers, meditations and well-meanings for the next century buzzed around the chapel. Normally Mr Marigold would have cherished any sensible invocations for global peace of mind. But he was simply too exhausted to keep his head up. So that what he heard was more like a Holbein cross-stitch, every other knot missing its mark: the "eradication of minute people or temperaments", "as great ideals spark in the minds of little spiders" and "all noble souls descend from the frying pan into the fire of global inamoratos". He detected great theologians waxing wildly about inter-faith telethons to raise rubles and lira for the search for God; African Synods and Memphis Conventions warning of the Y2K; an ambiguous commentary on population control in *Acts 17:28*—"For we too are his offspring"; a story in Luke about the lamentations of a man on his way to Jericho whose underwear was stolen; and something about St Francis saying to hell with furs, I'd rather go naked.

But all this adult chatter sounded even more nonsensical to the boy who sat utterly hypnotized by the twinkling lights of the Christmas tree, his stomach wambling, his face plastered to the ginger cookies and victualage of cakes. From his place beneath tables on the hard stone floor, he made out only the vaguest rim of adult murmurs: an eye for a Thou; an arm and a leg. Strange-sounding utterances by heavy-voiced nuns and soothsayers; names like Adi Grand; the Confusing Analects, and Zorro something or other. "Desire not for anybody else", "never do to others" and "do not impose" or "what is hateful to you" and "that which pains yourself" and "regard your neighbor's gain" and "what the hell are you doing under that table" and "don't you dare touch that pie!" and so on and so forth.

"If we all simply became a Christ on a Cross, there would be no possibility of additional turmoil or altercation," regaled a high-standing Blackcoat. He was probably right, thought Sannazaro. But what a horribly bloody world that would be, littered with nails and lamentations.

Catherine Champion, who sat beside her Tesuque friends, was beset by the smoldering Commander's head against her shoulder. Jet-lagged, exhausted in proportion to the degree of pontifications from the many wise men and gentle women, he too had crossed over the fateful transpontine of sleep, issuing a voluble snort through his stuffed nose.

"The truth has set him free," Sannazaro whispered into Catherine's ear. Then he noticed Rajibai out cold on the floor, surrounded by crumbs. The little mouse had managed, remarkably, to consume nearly half the desserts for all the superluminaries.

"I think we really must be off," the Squire went on, waking the Commander and then gathering up the boy in his arms, unconcerned by the abrupt halt his interruption had caused to the proceedings.

Everyone looked at them.

"Excuse us, your Reverences and Highnesses, but the little fella literally just flew in from Tibet and had way too much whiskey on the plane." With that he snatched a huge piece of treacle tart and placed it against Rajibai's nose, knowing it would work the same miraculous powers as smelling salts, which it certainly did. The trio then walked calmly past security, and out the royal entrance.

Darkness streaked by London's nightlife, electric lights as sharp as cacti, and a gentle snow coming down as if signed by Samuel Beckett. Hundreds of protesters were there, though none that the revived Rajibai, pie crumbs confusing his mouth, would have recognized. But their fervent calls to "END THE BRITISH OIL INDUSTRY" and "STOP KILLING THE WILDLIFE OF IRELAND" had its natural effect.

With no table of sweets or twinkling tree to distract his thoughts, Rajibai immediately ran off into the thick of the agitators and gathered up whatever information he could. Then, much to the chagrin of the crowd, he returned to his parents, as he sometimes called them, and suggested they skip the Ritz and make a beeline for Ire Land—such a nice-sounding place, he said, to save seagulls.

Mr Marigold gazed upon his son admiringly, for the two of them were unquestionably hewn from the same liniment of camphor, cut from a similar citrate of Lithia, precipitated by the exact pepsine powder of Seltzogene.

They hailed a jaunting car. Lo! —this was to be its jarvey's special night. She was pregnant, and en route to the airport an escalated series of contractions, bursting water and all the other radical transformations a woman must endure assailed her at once. Marigold, closest at hand, assumed the wheel, which was a mistake on four counts: one, there was a reason he was never granted a driver's license; two, he especially could not navigate a country of roundabouts and left-handed preferences; three, he hadn't a clue where they were, or how to get anywhere else; four, it was snowing, sleeting and in general downpouring, and the Commander had lost his pantoscopic tinted bispectacles, and neither he nor Sannazaro could find the button for the window wipers. So that they ended up backwards, turned around, lost and confused at a place called Fish Pond Road in the otherwise beguiling village of Saint Albans, from whose ancient and ecumenical cathedral issued a melodious enchantment.

Marigold and Sannazaro helped Destina—the cabperson's good name—into the church, where Henry Purcell's *Fantasias for Viol and Cello* were being performed *dolcissimo* by a string quartet beneath the 800-year-old stained-glass windows before a crowd of reformed ears. Purcell had written these marvelous airs in his early twenties, just after he had obtained an assistant choirmaster's job at the little church at Windsor, a fact of no small importance to the history of beauty.

Destina cried out with a piercing joy whose vernacular and four-letter plaints ricocheted off each window above. Before he knew what was happening, exactly, the Commander, with sweat pouring off his considerable temples and nose, found himself pulling forth a perfectly slimy little human—a female by most accounts. Rajibai then knew exactly what to do, for he'd seen birth 1,000 times in his old neighborhood. It was not a matter for open-sesames or googols of zeros. Any sharp object would suffice for cutting an umbilical cord, said he: broken Coke bottles, tree bark. Nothing to it. Noticing 100 glass candle holders from the era of Cromwell, he did the most sensible thing under the circumstances, which was to smash one upon the stone floor, where a Roman martyr long ago sacrificed himself to the cause of Catholicism.

He cleanly severed the cord and exclaimed, "There! What a fine little baby."

The mother named her child Alba after the occasion, then, upon all due congratulations and a hearty farewell to the chaplain, the trio made their exit into the night, leaving Destina, Alba and all the others in a flurry of unrecognizable excitement. The baby nursed about her taxi-driving mother's teat, beside an ancient resting pew.

Finding their way to Heathrow, having commandeered another taxi, Marigold was consumed by the extraordinary contagion of events that seemed relentlessly to have taken hold of their little company. It all came down to one strange notion, elucidated he: the existentialism of a sweet tooth in the modern world.

"What do you mean, Father?" asked the boy, always keenly interested in anything connected to sweets, whether sweet lassis or home-baked pies, as they proceeded through Customs, all three chewing gum.

"You see, son," Marigold explained, "there was once a cross-eyed philosopher of lasting fame, from France, of course, who used to sit around in cafés smoking Gauloise cigarettes, talking with pretty Russian girls about the soul of Paris, the bitter-sweet life of the mind, the nausea attendant upon that moment in which the many veils of this world were parted, and one saw clear through to the insubstantiality of it all."

"He means tooth decay," Sannazaro added smartly. "Too much chocolate."

"Well, naturally, that is the point in the ultimate sense."

"You're confusing the poor lad. Don't go spoiling a good brownie."

"What on earth are the two of you yapping on about?" the wise little one embarked, patient only up to a point.

"From recent observations, my son, it is clear that all these confusions—whether existence, essence, subjective, objective, before, after—can be easily transcended when one's mind is focused; and what better focus, what more comprehensive diet, natural process, benign agent, than those occasions calling upon the sweet tooth. Never mind what sort of sweet—lemon tart, cherry, apple or pumpkin—even artificial sweetener. Doesn't matter. The flash of desire, call it the one universal epiphany: it is the perfect case study in existentialism, which refers to the complete person in his or her exquisite, sweet-tasting calm. That imperturbable tranquil weather. Think of it as the embodiment of companionship, afterlife, alter ego, tragedy, happiness, birth and death. It both accompanies and precedes his every adventure. It succeeds him where no other principle has a chance. It is the heart of all wisdom. Neither rationalism nor naturalism quite depicts the state of nature which is this will-waiting-to-be-activated. That newborn in the cathedral—"

"Alba?"

"Alba. Her eyes were closed. Her life lay before her. We, who were absolute strangers, facilitated her coming into existence. Strangers, mind you. Does that not tell you that this world itself is sweet? That what we thought was bland, commonplace, is really not? That great change is possible? One day, you were a child in an Indian slum. Now, you are my son, bound for Ireland. I was once a lonely man, now a breathless father. Uncle, too, has undergone countless translations, transmigrations and tribulations. We all do. It is this bonbon of experience—"

"Toffee, brittle, scented like a mint-tree," Sannazaro added.

"—this patisserie we call a life that never fluctuates, and allows us to forget our troubles and focus attention on our taste buds. Think of the lollipop as the bottom line, the canary in the mineshaft, poor thing. It regulates everything else we do: preempts our sadness with our nougats; gives us to remember pleasure and negate pain. The pie ordains that our lives be this eternal sweet tooth, maximized for delectation, minimized for rough going. Which is why a good baker is always in demand, by friend or by foe, during both peace and wartime.

"Yet, the pie is a weird mixture—elements strange and unknown to us. A cherry or apple from a tree—but which particular tree? How old, whose land? Crust that has been prepared according to a recipe, but whose recipe? Burnt, soft, sugar-coated? All these things, you see, we depend upon without control. Yet, the end result is a happy man. A lyric little boy. A family well-disposed to every misery that shall inevitably befall them." But the Commander was on one of his own cinnamon rolls, never mind that other people, standing in the customs line were trying hard to ignore the trio.

"These are all metaphors, you understand? Poetic allusions to the way the world is. That is not to say that we are whatever creampuff we eat. But rather to acknowledge that even a panic can be softened with a little chocolate in whose sweet kernel is found enshrined the most important argument on earth: that this too will pass. That is existentialism. A philosophy of hope which actually appears to be desperate. It is not desperate. In spite of the fact that all the books in the world attempt to mask the inevitable, there is no greater comfort than this underlying principle."

"Is Anna an existentialist, Father?" the boy concluded.

"Yes. I would say that Anna is the definition of existentialism."

"But if that is so, why did we leave?" he inquired, suddenly confronted by his own dilemma. After all, he was the one who had expressed such an abiding interest in Disneyland, in America, in travel plans far, narrow and wide. Even cotton candy started to dull.

"Son, who is to say that someday we will not, again, find ourselves atop a mountain in the company of Anna or others of her kind? That is what's so wonderful about existentialism."

"And those Paris cafés where philosophy really owes its origins, not Athens," ruminated their Squire. With all this existential nonsense, his mind had fallen in with two legendary disputants, Irma and Robert, at the opening of Jean Paul Sartre's play, *Nekrassov*, on the bank of the moonlit Seine, waiting anxiously for a man to kill himself, however unlikely, by leaping from a low nearby bridge. Not a very impressive final splash. And why would anyone wish to kill himself in the greatest of all cities, where the more impoverished, ill, or bereaved one might be, the more romantically it all translated, á la Pucini's *Mi chiamano Mimi*.

The boy mumbled, nodding distracted, 10,000 miles from Paris, or Tibet, or existentialism in general. Then said, "Gentlemen, a butterscotch sundae sounds like the best solution of all."

Chapter 134
The Journey to Port Maggie

THE FACT THAT Sabine's gulls, little ringed plovers and puffins were threatened by millions of barrels of oil; that the legendary coast of old Ireland, its smiling dolphins and misty shores was endangered: all gave currency to the Commander's existentialism. Little sweetness about an oil-spill after all. An oil-spill rank with philosophy gone awry, human nature at its worst. But nothing the Gentilissimo Signore, His Excellency the Newly Tasked Governor-General of Some As Yet To Be Determined Independent Commonwealth might argue would change his two companions' overall mind or gumption. Now, of course, Marigold had the added voting power of a son who was proving to be even more passionately the fire hydrant than Marigold himself—which meant that Sannazaro was from here on outnumbered in every decision involving travel itineraries, delicate matters of state or fever blisters of the heart.

Sannazaro recognized this new parity and seemed, if only from sheer enervation, to accept gracefully his status as but one more board member, as it were. Notwithstanding his having been rewarded with no foam bath at the Ritz, he felt—strange to say it—no compelling force urging him back to Tesuque. He rather liked the UK, the pure sense of Tories (minus any political agenda) and Holm Oaks. Relished the sound of manor, mew, Lords and Ladies; even 'cottage' and 'lawn' had a different skew in England. He favored Border Collies and castles, oak panelling and Cotswold style, and even the Churchill cigar, once manufactured by Bock, seven inches long by 47-ring gauge. Yes, Sannazaro could easily take up the life of an English gentleman, he reckoned, since Italy had failed him. Surrounded by magenta corncockles and perennial composites, Victorian grottos, beautifully proportioned rooms, Grade II-listed Georgian village houses, the Domesday Book, post & railed paddocks, former mills, snooker rooms, Elizabethan origins, the sound of Devonshire, Howardian Hills, Royal yachts, Goat-and-Welter Land, Cornwall and Kent, Old Rogue ale, dukes and Acts of Parliament. He especially fancied the thought of Ireland. It was Christmas Day, yet not one jot of homesickness infected his demeanor; if anything, only a queasy feeling in his gut about the state of affairs in New Mexico, amplified by the heightened stakes and unknowns of the end of the year, century and millennium. These were strange times, the Commander reminded him. Harrowing moments. After all they'd been through, the near year, 2000, boded of some weird triage. Existential—certainly. A good reason to be committed to the sorrows of birds, than the too easy contentment of oneself.

"Muy Señor mio ..." Marigold began, reminding the Messer early next morning that he was, of course, free to return home. He'd done more than his share towards furthering the world's salvation, and if he wanted to cash in on merits in the next life, this was as good a time as any to do so. On the other hand, the cajoler added, what greater innocence than that of little terns, already down on their luck as a result of stubborn winter storms across the Atlantic, only now to be hit hard by a toxic weather of benzine and other chemicals.

If a flotilla of pontoons, or salaries for volunteer clean-up workers was needed to stave off devastation, the Commander rallied, he would gladly pay for them assuming the British Government failed to do so, or if the usual time-consuming quagmire of blame and finger-pointing should erupt between the oil company, the Coast Guard, the navigator, the shipping firm, the local Lord Mayor and his constituents, the Prime Minister and Irish Uachtaran na hEireann, the insurance companies, barristers, magistrates, international navy seals and so forth. A similar outbreak of incompetence, a babble of legalese and the shirking of moral and financial responsibility, had left southeastern Alaska bereft of millions of precious animals more than a decade before. To this day, officials in Valdez and the oil clean-up business were still fecklessly debating "when clean is clean".

Sannazaro had never been to Ireland, and for that matter, neither had the Commander. Both felt pulled by the island, an allure made more compelling by the bardic legends of *The Interrogation of the Old Men* and *Annals of the Four Masters*, by Irish malts served at the right temperature, by native crosanacht and spiritual fabliau. Who had not wondered, from time to time, about Lady Wilde and Holinshed's *Chronicles*; about Bishop Cloyne, Jonathan Swift and the great modern *Ulysees*? Marigold had read Elizabeth Bowen and Liam O'Flaherty, knew the *Knocknagow* and followed Melmoth the Wanderer across his many-multiples of misadventure. In addition, of course, there was the power of Irish countryside, with its abbeys and thatched roofs, and rousing folkloric melodies of the Chieftains.

Rain. Shannon. Early afternoon. A hired Toyota Land Cruiser with a driver named Hardiman to whisk them over bumpy mountain passes, down narrow lanes, cross-country into Co. Kerry, to a region 25 miles north of the Dingle Peninsula. Out to a remote spit, beyond the grass-engorged hills.

Hundreds of people were there. Helicopters hovered in the air. The tanker had held. No containers or baffles breached; no oil spilled. The storm had died down. A Christmas gift to the coastal life of Ireland. The tide was already coming in, eight yards by 4 p.m.: sufficient, said the group of experts present, to give the ship a second chance. Dozens of tugboats were already connected to tow the vessel back out to sea. But, lest anything be taken for granted, pontoons, buoys and biodegradable chemicals from Germany had been generously dispersed around the threatened areas.

All this pluck, plus that break in the weather, permitted the Commander, with his binoculars, a far-distant glimpse of some pyramidal shape out in the ocean. It was maybe 40 miles to the south and cloaked in haze, gigantic in its intimations and sovereignty. An isolated rock island.

Marigold handed the binoculars to one of the workers on the beach. "What is it?" he asked her.

"That would be Sceilg Mhichil," the rosy-cheeked matron exclaimed.

"What's that?"

"Sceilg Mhichil," she repeated.

"Again?" the Commander tried.

"Sceilg Mhichil," she reiterated with a chuckle. "'Course that'd be the Gaelic. Skellig Michael's fine. Whatever your mouth can manage. Not to worry."

"My, how beautiful and mysterious it is," the Commander intoned. "Anybody live there?"

"Ghosts," replied she. "Of the oldest hermits in the world. Why it's the loneliest, purest, finest place in all Europe and the Isles. But a damned difficult one to set foot upon, I can tell you that. A diamond of slipperiness. I've never been, though I've resided in these parts all my life."

"How would one attempt it?"

"Ask down in Port Maggie, somebody'll know. But not this time of year, surely not. The ghosts crave companionship in winter. So watch yourself, lad. It's a whole different crowd at the moment. Perhaps you'd best come back in the summer. Good luck, then."

She winked at him weirdly-like, and was off in her gumboots and woolen cape, wading out with the hundreds of others to stand vigil over the grounded monster and make sure it went away and no taffy or mousse escaped.

The driver made a few inquiries and the trio were soon back in the van, heading out past lonely or abandoned farmsteads and the occasional spurt of forest towards the Iveragh Peninsula and Port Maggie. Mostly the land was bare of anything but grass, like so much of the country. Grass and fences and sheep— *who knows what be their destiny!* he thought—and clichéed red hair floating atop freckled shepherds with their flocks.

They stayed that night in a B&B in Dingle, for not even a single room was to be had at Port Maggie at Christmas for any price. For that matter, hardly a phone was answered upon inquiries.

An Irish rhythm and blues band kept little Rajibai in thrall for many an hour. Again he consumed an inordinate quantity of alcohols, but Mr Marigold, so fully unaccustomed to the responsibility and stewardship of another, made no comment to the effect that he should stop or was too young. Nor did Sannazaro, who was drinking even more heavily than the boy. After all, it was Christmas. And Ireland.

Every sight and sound was a miracle to Rajibai, whose bag of possessions now included British Airways socks, along with more rolls of toilet paper, a box of perfumed Kleenex and plentiful Christmas cookies. The sheer sensation of clean things, of possessions to be had, was for him an experience of awesome liberation. Every face and expression of interest in his well-being and origins was the true theophany his father had blathered on about; that strangers should be kind to him in their silly, sweet-garbled English was incomprehensible. And of course he had never heard anything like the harmonious melancholy of Irish flutes, haunting fiddles and Celtic love songs.

Certainly he had experienced more than this atop the waterfall. Stuff and deeds and sexual acts he could not say. But this was back in the other world of towns and men and automobiles.

The next morning they continued into Port Maggie. Rajibai and Uncle, both, were hung-over and heavy with jet-lag. The drowsiness before time. There was weather again, a heaving sea, no rock island to be seen through the windy fog and downpour. Sleet added to the general inclemency, waves crashing violently acrest the harbor brants and slates. There was no talk in any quarter of a boat-for-hire. Hardly a person to be seen. The storm closed down upon them like a giant New Guinea bat, so that scarcely any light got in or out, and even the calendar on the wall at Maggie's Café & Grill was near impossible to read—the date, that is. That's where Sannazaro, Rajibai and the driver chose to pass their time, as the waffles were fresh-soaked in honey and sweet butter, and the home-grown coffee quite grand. Nobody else was about.

Rajibai had never tasted waffles. The sensation did him good. As for Sannazaro, he found himself mesmerized by the clock on the wall—no reason why. His gray-wolfish eyes peered over at the time every few minutes, and he grew sleepy in direct proportion to the extent of his consuming one Guinness after another for breakfast.

Rajibai flirted with his knife and spoon, until, magically, he got them both to stand erect at the table without support. The driver spoke softly into his cellphone—without much luck. The signal was queerly down, he said.

Soon, other signals seemed to go out as well, no doubt in response to the foul storm. The clock on the wall slowed to a halt, though Sannazaro didn't notice; the shades on the store front fell down; imperceptibly the shadows grew, a reversion without whistle, reinforcement or logic; the proprietor vanished, stepped aside did she, or simply got up and disappeared; the grill turned to solid gold; their beer ran out, spilling on the floor, dripping through the timber, which seemed to rot at their heels with no understanding—a weathering underfoot whose time had come and gone, or gone and come; and even the scent of waffles wafted far off, so that all the nostrils in the café seemed to recede into a tunnel where nothing made any sense any more.

The knife and spoon remained standing.

CHAPTER 135
Anno Domini 999

MARIGOLD'S RESTLESS NATURE, meanwhile, had prompted a ramble along the loom of the land. He wanted no waffles, and was happy to go alone—consumed by all his exhausted thoughts, he told the other two. With his windbreaker and gloves and newly acquired galoshes, he strode out crazily into the open, wind-gutted country, brazenly ascending a road of muddied edges that soon did vanish abreast a nameless sweeping swale. Auxiliary inclines. No countering, no nameable sections. Land spun topsy-turvy in the geometry of ancient pathways. All was soon enshrouded in a curlicue of bogs, fast asleep in moss and brine, hammered by the gale, the whole heath breaking out in ferns most certainly peculiar, twisting neither right nor left but in a new direction altogether.

Beyond, deeper into the muck of unreality, solitary and without register, was a primeval oratory, its layers of stone collapsed in the center top; adjoining it were the rectangular remains of a church damliac, its doorways, lintel, enormous jambs, gable and bargeboards still intact, crossworded in ivy and lichen.

Hoary stone fences led the Commander by turn and dale to the strangest of junctures yet. Here, miles from anywhere, on the obscurest apex of a hill, six faint trails—could be bear or oxen—converged in a soup of spoor. The surroundings entire were a reverie, laced in pungent fennel, Fuller's earth and lung tonic.

Where am I and where is this? Marigold perplexed, absorbed and slightly ill at ease. He made to turn back towards the café. Maybe some waffles would do him good, after all. Then he thought better of it. Something was urging him forward.

The rapid fogs cleaved only deeper, and there before the lone wanderer was an unmistakably inviting stone crannog, a path meandering through piles of peat moss and ponderous confines of cow pasture, much as a lavish, bluebell-infested Crimonmogate, the last of its kind. A charcoal fire was visible beneath such a cauldron as one might expect to find in ancient Grecian days. The six trails merged at this cottage, its doors and windows ajar, despite the gathering tussle of opposing drafts, where richly chased brass lanterns in colored glass shone in each of six windows facing out upon the world. Around the farm were easily 100 grazing ox, wether and hog, who not a sound between them made.

Heartily stirring inside were cheerful voices, and the music of pipe and harp, the reading of a poem, the stolid, unmistakable sounds of checkers being smacked down strategically upon a board, and the gaiety of food and drink preparation. The Commander hauled himself in, past several sacks of malt, the fresh odor of wheat and salt everywhere about.

A young woman greeted him, her vermilion strands of hair plaited and held bare by a diadem of gold. A vision into Irish lore. He was cold and needed warming up; dizzy and wanting for a comfortable seat near the open fire; lost but didn't care.

"Good'ay, me Lord," she applied, bowing slightly to honor this guest, distinct tones of Old Norse and madly wonderful Gaelic.

"Indeed it is, before the sight of one as lovely as yourself," he replied, with a flourish of gestured gallantry.

"That accent? It's no' an English I did ever hear."

"New Mexico," the Commander explained. "America, of course."

Vacant stares.

Seeing how there were steaming jugs of scented wine, and drinking horns, bronze flagons and silver goblets, and food laid out in abundance on fine linen—wheat meal and omelets, pies of various delectations (just the thing, the Sartre in him began openly, to more confusion) and wonderful freshly baked breads—he asked, "And what roadside inn is this?"

"'Tis the local breen," averred the secretary attending to the coire ainsec.

He was a man of enormous size and stature, hair wild and disheveled, in a mantle of sea otter and woolen kilts.

"May I ask what is it you're boiling there?" the Commander inquired, unable to place the queer odor rising from the cauldron.

"Badger meat, seal, ox horn and good other tripes," conferred the monster of a man with foremost smile.

"Might I have a drink, instead?"

"Of course you can. The brughaid'll take your order," the friendly ogre volunteered.

"What is your pleasure?" she obliged. At that a boisterous laugh exploded from some roughs imbibing their ales at a low table of blunted oak. "Take it stingily, would sayest a Capuchin; Neh, with prayer, please, begs the Benedictine; Forget that, lads—I'll swig the caig, stomps the thirsty Dominican; Until not a drop can be found in all the land, promises the Franciscan!" They laughed hysterically, but Marigold missed out on the punch line, if there was one.

"Do you have any lemonade?" he asked.

All stared at one another. Finally, the bejeweled hostess volunteered, "Lemons are hard to come by this time of year, sir. Surely you be knowing that."

"Then ale, please."

"Which county you be coming from?" the lady inquired, serving him up with dispatch. "Not Kerry, I suppose, looking such and speaking that."

"More likely a Dublin Dane," a voice more harshly declared, by way of a suspicion or a threat.

"I just flew in from London actually," Marigold offered, to clear the record.

All around was silence. Even the stirrer of the ale looked up with a start. The checkers flatly halted, the toughs backing around threateningly, the princess a hand to her stomach as if her period had just begun, and such a sudden strangeness in the air, you'd think the Commander had insulted them all with a word.

"You *flew*?" the ogre fellow demanded. "I did hear that, or did I not?"

"Yes. Aer Lingus. The shuttle. To Shannon. Why?"

All looked at one another in utter fear, then a cowherd-type, who'd not a word yet elaborated, stood up and suggested: "I think he should leave. Quit the custom, breen and all. This wizard brings bad luck to these premises."

"Excuse me?" Mr Marigold started.

"He's right," the ogre began. "It's the week, isn't it?"

"It's the day," another speculated. "I aren't drink that much not to know such a day as this."

"All the signs have been true, then?" the princess allowed.

"God grant us our innocence!" they cried one after the other in a bizarre show of—*what*? the Commander puzzled.

"What signs? What day? The day after Christmas? The oil spill—it didn't spill, you didn't hear?" the Commander tried to say, attempting to assuage these strangers' fears.

"You came from Rome, didn't you? To tell us the news. Tell us, then, damn you!"

"Rome? No, I told you, from London. Yesterday morning. And last night we slept—me boy and I—" 'Me'? He stopped himself, what was that? —"and driver and the Governor, a friend that is—in Dingle, at the B&B."

"Dingle? What Dingle? What is that? BB? What is B and B? And you say London, yesterday morning, was it? Of course he flew! He said so himself! The proof!"

The Commander, utterly fagged out, sat down. Shook his head. Looked around. Then made out what he hadn't seen before: in their eyes, bone structure, actually, everything about them. How could he have missed such obvious evocations? The make-up. The relics. Attire. Food. Language. It was a dream. Or a museum devoted to a dream, to ancient artifacts and recreation. Or perhaps the rehearsal for a play. He had somehow stepped into the middle of it and caused some disruption.

But this consolation lasted only a few seconds.

They were speaking amongst themselves, as if he didn't exist, or couldn't hear. Indeed, his eyes were tearing, for there was considerable smoke in there, a score of chopped onions too, and the voices faded in and out, here one moment, gone the next, like a fable. So that the Commander wasn't even sure any more what he heard, or what he only thought he heard and repeated to himself. Two differing theories of reality: one heading to the left, the other right; one marked by seconds, the other by centuries; two separate instincts, diverted by a prolixity of postulations, imitating a central theorem by which assumptions had to be discounted, imputations reversed, hypothetical situations abridged and pandect crossed over; no thesis bore up under such scrutiny, no ascription could be described as sound. First principles becoming last. Every picture of reality reduced to a mere proposition—Der Satz. No truth following another. Laws of inference bungled by tavernkeepers. Peculiarities wobbling on the table. Normal conclusions, simple relations, adjectives, accidents, symbols, superstitions, justifications, internal properties—all outside logic. No right, no left hand. Guesswork shot through with surmise; conjecture riddled by divination. Premonitions so alike in their evolution that sometimes one gained purchase over the other, one possibility taking precedence in his mind—not that their differences were so extreme that he might not prefer the first to the second, or the other to the one. Both admitted to an obscurity that upset the balance, leaving the Commander greatly confused, disoriented, ever frightened for his life, or at least sanity, such was left of it.

The storm did not let up. Darkness came early. But hadn't he just left his companions with their waffles? For how long had he hiked, and what distance? No idea.

Then came a fear, rising with a provocation unlike any he'd yet experienced. There was no doubt about it: they were afraid of him, or had mistaken him for someone, some thing, of a loathsome and terrifying aspect. Everything he proceeded to say only worsened the situation.

It was that business about Aer Lingus which seemed, most of all, to upset them. What could it mean? Perhaps they were more loyal to British Airways—but surely no harm was done? Both airlines served decent enough meals, provided ample leg room, were sensitive to thrombosis issues, sustained dependable service and mileage plus. Superb captains. Equally lovely stewardesses, and terrific punctuality and service, as a rule, notwithstanding a recent case in which a man's underwear and two rolls of exposed film were stolen by baggage attendants.

Then the name of Pope Sylvester crossed one of their lips.

"Now *he* was taught to fly," ejaculated the misfit (by his forlorn and mussed-up breeches). "Aye, by a witch in the southern deserts, where the storms originated. It is known she be his mistress, and I for one are to believe it, I would."

"What? What are you all talking about?" Marigold agitated. Now he was losing his demeanor.

"The Last Judgement, that's what we're talkin' about, sir! We are no fools out here, see!"

The hostess thrice made the sign, and blessed all present, spitting on the floor, a dark guber, thrusting a cross of silver 'gainst her pounding heart. Covering her face with a fringe of her veil by the other hand, she turned away in panic.

Jesus ... Mr Marigold muttered, staggering backwards out the door, slipping on the ram shit and falling on his arse into the mud.

No laughter accompanied this gaffe, but only the slamming and bolting of the door, otherwise left open for all strangers. Because in Ireland—unlike England—in these times all wayfarers were assured of free food, drink, lodgings and good cheer, lest they be a wise man, or Christ in disguise. But the Devil, he was not welcome.

And so it went, had become, was certainly the case ... For over one year, throughout the known world, terrestrial denizens had been keenly on the lookout for signs, omens, supernatural occurrences and all other freak phantoms such as Mr Marigold, whose wraith-like demeanor was fairly convincing. And they were plentiful.

In India, for example, just north of the Garden of Eden, Hindus everywhere were thinking—though none dared utter the words which stood for the Kalpa—of Doomsday. Famines had scoured the countryside, with its 70 million inhabitants; dust storms had caked the croplands, asphyxiating the tender shoots of maize and rice, rendering the rivers undrinkable. Parents ate their children, and children their parents.

Along the entire Trans-Himalaya, earthquakes—9 pointers—shuddered; they spalled whole cliffsides down, altered the course of rivers, made valleys where none had been before.

A month of December rains in China had so swollen the Yangtze that an estimated 80 billion tons of topsoil, and an equal weight of uprooted trees and corpses, were spat out into the China Sea, 1,500 miles downstream. Amid this chaos, a young monk whose name has been lost managed to save a single painting, and himself, from ruin, trekking 100 miles across a collapsing mountain range, its watershed having been demolished by charcoal merchants eager to supply the calligraphy market. Through hurricane-force gales, the 17-year-old Buddhist gathered up the scroll—*Ch'ing-luan hsaio-ssu* ("A Solitary Temple Amid The Clearing Of Storm Among Peaks")—which had been painted 33 years earlier by the greatest of the Northern Sung masters, Li Ch'eng. A fact of major significance to the aesthetic history of China, but of little consolation to the millions who died during those final weeks of 999, when there was no clearing.

It was the same everywhere. In Outer Scandinavia, all the ill-winds of the wretched, end-of-the-world Götterdämmerung had blown through town, a teleology of damnation that had become personal for every living creature who stood to gain, or lose, according to which gods or demons prevailed. Fearing the worst, the Kings of Norway, Denmark and Sweden all had themselves baptized, clutching the crucifix, in the odd chance that their old god Thor should prove incapable of combating Odin, Fenris and that giant Hound from Hell, Gram. While all still hoped for Ragnarök, the famed twilight time of divine grace, no one dared predict what darkness might permanently envelop the Earth beginning New Year's Day, 1000, particularly in light of the sad fate of Olaf Trygvasson, the Norwegian pagan monarch.

Olaf and his weary men had found themselves trapped on the Dragon Vessel. It was the greatest Viking craft ever fashioned, at nearly 6,000 square feet of timber, hardwoods hewn from the steep forests along Hardanger Fjord. The vessel was equipped with rowing stations suitable for three dozen he-men. Pursued by his arch rival Jarl Eirik, who was seeking the throne, and revenge for the beheading of Hakon, his father, they soon engaged in a furious bloodbath along the chalky escarpments of the Isle Rugen in the Baltic Sea. Olaf fought bravely, taking aim, and plunging his spears one by one into the shield of his adversary. None penetrated the chainmail; nor was hand-to-hand combat any more profitable. Unwilling to be taken alive by his opponent, which would have meant long and drawn-out days of torture, he threw himself overboard into the freezing waters. All of Europe was talking about it. Puppet-masters redramatizing the events in village squares.

Further east, in the Principality of Russia, the temperature that last week of 999 dropped to 99 below zero, if one allowed for the chill factor. Piss actually froze in the urinary canals of men and women, badger and horse. And vodka in the throat. Eyes were locked open, or shut. Snow drifts 60 feet high effectively isolated the country. There was silence that week. Nobody moved, nobody spoke, nobody breathed. In Poland, temperatures were even less forgiving. All the birds and squirrels perished, and the wild dogs, whose night-time cries across the Polish steppes were heard clear to the frontiers of the German Empire. A great pity penetrating every knot of the alder forests, sad groans creaking in the frozen ponds.

In the Principality of Lombard a woman gave birth to ten infants, each with two heads and tongues 15 inches long. These were not the seven-headed monsters from the *Revelation of St John*, but close enough, and all were duly hacked to death by onlookers, and the woman who delivered them as well. Their body parts were then fed to boars, who in turn were burned alive, and the ashes peed upon, then buried deep in a salt cavern.

Billions of locusts swarmed over the Fatimid Caliphate, and locals burned tons of poppy heads, carbolic and mustard oils to try to stop them, to no avail.

In England, King Alfred the Great spent his time sequestered in his castle, entering into world literature the first bona fide descriptions of the Midnight Sun, the color of blood. Blood in his royal eyes. In his bath. Looking into the mirror, he saw only the blood of his fellow countrymen, Celts and Anglo-Saxon serfs who were being slaughtered in their beds by indescribable creatures that had risen up each night from the megalithic stone circles, crawling out of the snow-sodden earth with torches and pitchforks of iron in their talons. None could stop them.

In Byzantium, children were afflicted with boils such that the high priests reckoned the plagues brought down upon the Egyptians by the God of the Israelites had again descended upon the earth. Throughout Constantinople, the Eastern Orthodoxy hastened to the synagogues to be converted back to Judaism. But the Jews were having it no better. Their children were dying of pneumonia, coughing up worms.

Across the Duchy of Hungary there was turmoil in the land. Crops had withered, madness had broken out; witches were burned, traders in human flesh populated the market places. Stephen, successor to King Geza of Hungary, had defeated Koppany at Lake Balaton, chopping his body into quarters and posting them on a castle's gates as fair warning to all would-be dissenters.

In a single flash, the night sky was lit up for 7,000 miles. Bulgars, Patzinaks, Ghuzz and Karakhanids all witnessed the meteorite shower, whose cannonball-sized chunks of molten Martian rock exploded erratically across a third of the known world, killing randomly over a period of three days—from the Emirates of Buwayhid, Baghdad and Hamadan, to those of Sheddadid, Samanid and Shirvan. Fires broke out across the West Bulgarian Empire, while freak cyclones killed most Serbs and Croats. The ones who survived blamed each other for the devastation and vowed to get even.

Throughout 999, the Welsh recorded a series of spontaneous fires along dozens of coal veins near the sea. These quickly spread to most villages, where the conflagrations roared out of control the last week of December. The entire country was rendered homeless. Cockroaches perished in the millions.

Among the people residing under the tutelage of the Dukes of Normandy, hemorrhoids, gangrene, stomach cancer and chronic diarrhea wiped out infants and the very old. In Brittany, underground methane explosions laid waste to the land. Lakes and rivers burned for months.

The Kings of Leon and Burgundy noted an outbreak of St Anthony's fire—possibly a fungal infestation of rye—causing a horrible slow death. Tens of thousands of locals fled into neighboring Navarre, where a great healer was rumored to live with three child whores. The exodus occasioned fighting on all the roads, for there was insufficient food or drinking water for so many scores of enflamed refugees. Packs of wolves fed on the human corpses, it was written, though later disproved.

Across the North African territories of the Umayyad Caliphate, a sand storm lasted the entire year. Two-thousand-foot high dunes traveled two miles a day, and winds exceeding 400 miles per hour resulted in the disappearance of, well, everybody. The sun did not shine for months.

Those who could dived into the sea and headed for the Kingdom of Barcelona, but there vipers descended from the hills, and fire ants egressed from underground and went on the rampage, exploiting so much pink human flesh.

A similar phenomenon befell the Gobi Desert, where a deadly black sand storm, 1,400 feet high, shaved to the bone some two million herdsmen and their families, horses and yaks, dogs and wolves. Nothing lived for 3,000 miles. Pools of flesh, some miles dense, became home to new colonies of hornets, attracted to it like cat food.

Some theologians, had they known, might have recognized this Mongolian horror to be the beginning of the end. In Roman terms, the storm rose up in the year 996, exactly 1,000 years after the Nativity, the same year King Herod went to his tomb.

The Venetians—uniquely noble in countenance and race, normally immune to the tribulations of the rest of Europe and Asia, their women content to parade among their male adulators in colorful silks, strumming lyres, enchanted by everything—were not unscathed either. A masked ball and week-long orgy went on in the various palaces where those of the upper classes ate, drank and fornicated furiously, since this might well be their last. Outside, across every swamp and Campo, dust from the year-long storms in the Sahara had made breathing impossible. Mario Polo, who only of late had established the first gondola concession (paving the way, of sorts, for his adventuresome descendant, who would bring honor and distinction to the family name) declared bankruptcy. Nobody dared enter the lagoons, for the fish had lost their flesh to some carnivorous algal bloom; thousands of little white exoskeletons floated through the canals, whose water had turned to blood.

On Baffin Island, the Emperor of all Eskimos, his name unpronounceable, was eaten by a polar bear. This was considered an inauspicious sign, prompting a mass suicide. People simply took off all their clothes and sat down.

In Patagonia a mudslide pretty much wiped out all of the Sea Otter Skin People.

In New Guinea, where penis sheaths had just come into vogue and the first mascaras and cross-dressing introduced—life, generally speaking, was quite pleasant—a series of calamities befell communities across the entire length of the island, all the more surprising since they knew nothing of the year 999, of Christ, or Dionysius Exiguus's sixth-century calculations pertaining to the alleged date of the Savior's birth. Nevertheless, the forest spirits grew restless. Little microscopic carnivorous worms entered all the men's penises; tree ferns and casuarina, marsupials and bamboo, coniferous saplings, lizards, insects and all of the undergrowth started to perish. Streams dried up. Lightning flashes—one every five seconds— struck the land, shredding the very skin and feathers off the cassowary's back, as they say, and causing huge blazes through the wilted forests. Then came the onslaught of killer bees whose vast numbers covered the sky for miles, creating a deadly shadow over the land.

In Bangladesh, there was no 999, because of a typhoon that basically erased the country.

Along the ancient riverine basins of what are today Idaho and Wyoming, 10,000 thermal vents ignited on the same weekend, one geyser catapulting hot water and burning lava 2,500 feet into the air, freaking out millions of grizzly bears who had been napping in the middle of the night. A lake boiled over; a volcano erupted.

In the Seychelles, nobody knew anything about the eruption of deadly scorpions across the highlands of Ethiopia, the Mayan drought, or the blood which poured out of the sky over Aquitaine. They had their own problems: The Last Tidal Wave.

Throughout most of France, tens of thousands of pilgrims were selling everything they owned to finance their pilgrimages to the Sepulchre of Our Savior in Jerusalem, flocking to the tune of the hoped-for Second Coming. Others across Europe were heading towards Rome.

In Germany, the mythic Muspilli—a rain of hot embers—fell upon the faithful and unfaithful alike.

And in Ireland itself, 19 years before, Maelsechlainn II, surnamed Mor the Great, King of Meath, had become the Emperor following his massacre of the Danes at the Battle of Tara. A man named Brian had contested the throne long and hard, and his efforts had resulted in a truce, signed in 998, that gave Brian the southern half of the country. This bifurcation was of little appeal to the Dublin Danes and Leinstermen, who fought both Kings in 999 at a place called Glenmama, near Dunlavin, in County Wicklow. As if the killing of 7,000 men was not enough, the Irish force moved on to Dublin, raped, pillaged, did all the normal things men crave in war, broke savagely through the barricades along the River Liffey, went on to Leinster, and killed King Sitric there.

But, like elsewhere in Europe and the world, Brian and Mor could not hold their truce, and further outbreaks of sedition and riot ensued, so predictably characteristic of the year, even the month. As in all other quarters of the human maze, there was havoc, and absolutely nothing that such heavy, imperial monarchs as Otto the Third, Basil the Second, Robert the Pious—or Brian—could do to contain the apocalyptic ravings of one frightened constituency after another.

So it was that all of Christendom placed its final hopes in the singular lap of the most eccentric scholar in Papal history, Gerbert de Aurillac, Pope Sylvester II, Gerbi, for short.

How could this giant of learning reconcile these berserk, unlettered minions and their irrational fears with what he knew to be true about the universe? After all, had he not delved passionately into the literature of his greatest predecessors—Aristotle, Cicero and Porphyry? Stayed up late nights contemplating the tragic fate of Boethius? He had been a famed professor, conveying the nuances of poetry and logic. He adored mathematics, music and astronomy. An author, philosopher in his own right, this uncommon

Pope had dispensed with most biblical commentary and built his own observatory, with high-sailing globes that recreated the known planets. He'd also constructed a sundial, tinkered deftly with an Oriental abacus. On top of all that, he personally owned one of the finest libraries in the world. Imagine, then, his dilemma, upon being looked to as God's sole mouthpiece. Better the Devil's brassiere. There could be no more embarrassing situation for a man of science. To have to weigh the future of the world, puzzle through its warring tumbles and too human foibles, whilst all of Rome stood shivering throughout the night in St Peter's Square waiting for some divine embrace. Was redemption possible in a world of doubt? The stakes were ultimate. One man of science, wearing the highest robes of the Vatican, against the unknown.

All day Gerbi had been contemplating his fateful options, starting with a bubble bath and cherry-scented brandy. What could he possibly say to instill courage among the hundreds of thousands of *penitente* who for weeks had been gathering in the rain-soaked palazzo for the Midnight Mass? Across Italy people knew that Vesuvius had lately been belching large stones, that the Great Day of His Wrath was near, the long night of the winter solstice, the final battle between Gog and Magog. Any moment the Antichrist would emerge from the Tribe of Dan, hissing like an adder, looking up to greet the deadly conjunction of Venus (desire) and Mercury (avarice).

Should he endeavor to elicit a mass genuflection, or let the multitudes squirm a little? After all, not everyone agreed on the meaning of the moment. Some took it as a license to rape and plunder and be rowdy. Just a few miles away, women prostrated themselves before the erect bronze penis of Priapus, rubbing themselves into frenzies, howling like wolves; others engaged in unspeakable acts in deference to the ancient wild heathens, Cybele and Agdistis, playing out the Dionysian frenzies of Tobias's Night. Lust, drunkenness, the joy of the final party, was unleashed upon the seven hills.

Who was the wiser? To ascend somberly, in prayer, embracing Christ, assuming he really was on the move? Or riding down to Hell atop the olive-skinned pile of young slithering naked bodies, oil steaming off their breasts, love juices dripping down their virginal thighs? For all his fame and reputation, Gerbi was not entirely certain. What if he were wrong about this? What if tomorrow he were to wake up and it was business as usual? The corruption of monarchs, another day in the fields and libraries, another sunrise and sunset? More Books of Hours to be illustrated? Could it be that all this wringing of hands in the service of one vast hunch was nothing more than the delusions of old men fearful of losing their congregations, their posts, their marginal sinecures?

There had been a rush to the pew by those sinners who'd never stepped inside a church. Was such sudden devotion not transparent to God? Or did He care? Was this whole event calculated by Him to evoke a panic? A second great passion play in which all of humanity had a role, was sacrificed and resurrected?

A great anvil cry roused him from his deep meditation, rising up from the restless hordes outside: "*Veni, Domine Jesu! Veni, Domine Jesu!*"

"Jesus," Mr Marigold said aloud, struggling to get back up onto his feet in the pelting storm. He'd had a dream. So many discordant images, out of time. Now four rams were chasing him to his senses down the muddy hill.

Above, the crazed inn remained brightly lit, but its heavy doors had been locked, and the occupants gathered in prayer and preparedness near the openings, ready with pitchforks and swords to drive through the Devil lest he attempt a second visit.

CHAPTER 136
The Day of the Barbarians

SHEEP, AN OLD EWE'S FLEECE trailing on the ground, had taken cover beneath the moldering overhangs of a shed. A long-haired pony, broken from its tether, galloped past, slipping in the mud and toppling over. It lay still, shocked and breathing hard. The Commander went to the animal, which suddenly sprang to its feet, unharmed, and ran off into the encincturing mist, neighing forebodingly.

Marigold clambered down the hill, away from that vanished vortex of Gaelic hallucinations. Who were they? What had happened? His head spun with visions of disaster everywhere, eucharistic dementia, fugitive apparitions, ubiquitous countertempers. A battle between ration and irration, between the polished linear finesse that aspires to external permanency, and the jaunty construals that are the exclusive domain of an interior fancy, without particular finish or want of conclusion.

It was dark, and Mr Marigold's only hope of finding his way back was by heading toward the distant thunderclaps of the sea wall.

The storm had only intensified. It was freezing rain, and the Commander suffered for it, groveling with clenched fists and teeth for many a mile into the unrelenting winter blackness of the wee morning hours. Fraise de confusion. Dismantling the hurdles along the philosophical track towards a homogeny of living presence. To make sense of those masked tronies, somewhere between hypothetica and Bohemia, transcending time but contemplatively inescapable, and this contradiction a poetic monumentality as unclear as anything could be to the Commander, all emotional fluster and physical brouhaha.

Nowhere even a candle light, a hanging lantern, a human admission or squeak to shelter his exposure, or guide the inexplicable terror.

Only in the dawn did he discover, far to the side and down below, the harbor at Port Maggie, though the town still concealed beneath a weather of vaporous pea soup. Perhaps it was his being above it now, in relative light, that he saw it differently. But entirely rusticated. No car, no paved road, no antenna. Where was that café? *Amicitia et familia*? His Squire, his dear child, their driver Hardiman? What of that leaning brick-lined gas station, painted white, or charming single-roomed post office marked by perforations and cancellations of an earlier era, or the stiff scent even of fishing trawlers moored just yesterday beyond the loading docks where he'd noticed a forklift or two, and pallets of pine bearing crates of some kind? Mackerel and smelt. Whiskey, sautéed cauliflower, fresh carrots, copper plumbing supplies, 100-pound burlap sacks of coal chunk and acrid lime?

He struggled down into the village and would swear there was a profound difference—he could not say exactly. The cliff-shanks were the same, but without a quay, or gas station, nor one manifestation of the previous day. Some inexcusable muse?

He breathed hard. Scooted into the first domicile, another ancient one at that, to find his way back, for there could be no doubt about it now: all was mightily unwinding in his head.

"I'm looking for my boy. Also, a man, in his sixties, Italian of descent, and our driver? A burgundy taxi, limo more like, four doors—excuse my wet look—have you seen them?"

A family of 12 stared at him, mouths agape. Not a peep from their unstoried lips. Marigold's entry was as startling as an ill-timed fart in a solemn opera moment.

Desperate, the Commander raced outside again, and down through the muddy lane which paralleled the sea, where the waves exploded thunderously and the storm would not let up. Still no pyramid out in the frightening waters. Only dark and craven clouds, scleraed, low and racing with desperado energy, the furies themselves hovering just off shore.

Into another chalet he emptied himself, explaining the particulars to a more light-headed-appearing couple, farmers clearly, though of such a complexion as to stoke other worries in the Commander about their mental fitness for the task. They too stared in obvious perplexity at this newcomer.

"Ehh?" the man of the house announced.

"A boy, dark skinned, and—" But it was useless.

"A boy, you say?"

"Yes! Eleven years old, and his uncle, so high, both speaking English, like myself. Have you seen them?"

The man escorted the Commander back out into the rain, and pointed far off.

"Thank you, thank you."

Marigold hurried, his heart hammering in his chest. Even on that ledge with Anna, ready to jump, he had not felt such fears and uncertainty.

For 30 more minutes he wandered face into the wind, accosting the occasional hunched figure but achieving no results other than an added inducement to panic. Acoustical slippage into the outermost zone, a pounding in his chest, a thud coursing the inner ear.

Finally, he saw a boy, and threw himself after him, scaring the lad something awful.

"*Stop, please!* I beg you to stop!" The boy waited, looking around for any possible assistance. When the Commander arrived before him, he withdrew a dagger and screamed. Marigold jumped back, and the boy, not much older than Rajibai, threatened him with the weapon, no mistaking his seriousness, and the Commander pleadingly spoke his mind, his hands raised in a gesture of peace and supplication.

"I am looking for my son. Do you speak English? Where is Port Maggie? Where am I? Please!"

"You've been to the breen?"

"The breen? Yes. The breen. I was there."

"And?"

"And? And—and nothing. I'm lost."

"You speak strange. Are you a Catholic?"

"Uhh, yes. I am, a Catholic. Where is everybody?"

"At damliac, those that can. The end is near, man. Don't you see? Now I've got to be moving on. You shouldn't be here in those clothes."

"What is damliac?"

"Damliac? Church, of course. What's wrong with you?"

"But where is it?"

"Why, up the hill, see there?"

He pointed to a large and mournful crucifixion site, and mother of God, if there wasn't the body of a heretic hanging there, her hair long and streaked with blood, her naked, bottle-blue and waxy lead body savaged by pikes and other implements, one-inch nails, a Roman incursion of horrible strokes.

"You best be careful," added the Slavic-looking lad, moving off, keeping his bright Indonesian dagger by his side. "With only two days to go, things aren't exactly the same around here."

"Two days? To what?" Marigold shouted up at him. The boy had now distanced himself 30 paces or more.

"He's coming!" the freaky kid hollered back. "Beware!"

Then he too was lost in the fog, head deep, winter laced, bred by the furthest bog.

Marigold raced in the direction of the church, a huge rectangular building of old stone, and as he approached he heard the cacophony of prayer issuing from within.

"Rajibai, Sannazaro!" he cried out at the entranceway, fearing now to enter. "Are you in there?"

A desperate cry came from within: "*Father!*"

It was Rajibai, throwing himself out the door, and Sannazaro scattering not two paces behind him.

"Thank God!" And they all three hugged and the boy wept. "Where is Hardiman?"

"We don't know," Sannazaro gulped, out of breath and terrified. "It all happened so fast. One moment, waffles, a phone call on the cellular, and ... and ... turning round, a crowd, staring, jeering, yelling—"

"Worse than the tribals!" the boy broke in. "Touching my face. *Brown boy*, they screamed at me."

"Hardiman panicked and ran for the car, we were too late, he shouted back to say he'd go for help, they tried to stop him, said he was the Devil, like they'd never seen anything like it—the car, I mean—and Hardiman drove away amid a flurry of stones thrown at him. He disappeared up the road, and when I looked again it was no paved road, orderly and such, but this—this mud primeval nightmare. These barbarians. Jesus, we're screwed. What is *happening!* "We need to figure this out," the Governor advised in a panic. "There's a grotto on the beach, I saw it. Free of people."

"Right. What are we waiting for then?" the Commander declared. So the three of them raced away down the hill from the church, back towards the sea wall, and there took awful refuge within a sort of rumbling cave lashed by waves and teeming with black widow spiders dangling long.

"I don't have a clue what it all means, or even a desire to find out," Sannazaro cried in muffled hue, rain drenching his hair.

Even the boy, once the laureate perpetually on cloud nine, now had only one urgency: to question gravity, to make sense of their strange predicament, which he felt as soberly as his two companions.

For hours they sat stumped in the cave of unforgiving damp and incoming tides. Sannazaro's head was bursting, assailed from within by a volley of serious irritants, each one hard to distinguish from the other, a cumulative arithmetic he could no longer shoulder.

"Fat lot I care," he suddenly exclaimed. "I'm getting out of here." But it was only talk. Where could he go, with the sea having trapped them for another night?

CHAPTER 137
Shipwrecked on a Dark Pyramid

THE BEACHED COMBERS BORE lottery lashings, the serpentine sandstone gouged out by thundering explosions 'gainst the peninsular coves. One hundred feet, vertical. That, in addition to the radium-glow thicket of biting spiders, made their night in the grimy grotto less than pleasant, heads hung-over like waxy balloons, and no escape for hundreds of miles.

Yet, just as it appeared that all was hopeless and beyond moribund, the weather began to clear. A cold wind blew down from the north, and the midday candescence of a December sun magically re-invented the entire landscape. For a moment, nothing seemed wrong. The glistening greensward of Ireland touted its finest hour; mists burned off the lenticular meadows, ablaze in every columbine and flowering thistle. Yellow-faced bumblebees hurled through the lambent dawn, dallying above the hairy honeysuckles and golden ear-drops. The village seemed no less the globe gilia, blue-violet innocence, balled up into a village fine, certainly not inflictive, blunderbussing or sociopathic. In fact, there was no one about—neither on a road, nor at a table, not even the distant scent of tobacco—though from somewhere amid the clustering hills, cloying church bells clanged to greet the miasmic morn along the pier.

The trio rambled with inconspicuous intent along the inland side of the sea wall, out of harm's way of the furious wave action, following the trail of a donkey cart, until in one high-voltage jolt they staggered to a standstill.

There before them, not more than eight nautical miles away, was the resplendent, otherworldly pyramid of Skellig Michael. From that distance, its triangular base appeared to be of basalt, a cubist's unresolve of forbidding black buttresses. With his 100x binoculars the Commander could make out a footpath angling ever more steeply past domed huts in several vertiginous sectors of the 700-foot sacred mountain.

The totem pole of Himalayan rock rose out of the churned-up purple ocean, a fierce apex of unknowable spirits—nothing like Codfish, which was a safe harborage, the color green, by comparison. Giant whitecaps smashed every square inch of lower rock wall, and massive numbers of birds lazily circled the high slopes, catching the sudden warm thermals, delighting in the change of weather which would give them some time to dry out their matted bodies. Even eight miles away their midair gabbing was audible.

It was of alabaster, by the glint of silver sky brushing off the cloud tops. Rock impressionistic. Childe Hassam dappling the inaccessibility. Before- and aftershocks of steep, divesting, leafless skewered air. No pledge sufficient. No hold too firm. A catchment of final reality that was not for human hands. Mineral tufa speckled and fine. Borax and sulfide, feldspar and silver. Rich pastellines concentrated in a swirling sediment the color of coffee stain and suffused wine, of Muscovite and Bonnard. It rose Homeric and primordial, a Goddess Fortuna of paragons that knew no office or trespass, had never suffered the passage of human affairs or investiture. The stairs were for dreamers. The birds at home there.

This unabating terra firma had for 10,000 years bordered the confines of the imagination. Situated between the mellifluous zephyrs of the Western Isles and the awful sorceries of Gog and Magog, heaven-high its Cybelline prophecies invited; no quarrel with the blank map, an infinity positioned precisely upon the tip of that delicate nerve ending in the eye given to an obsession with Paradise. Especially as the break in weather admitted to an opening no less suggestive than the parted curtains of Rembrandt's Danae, and the rain of golden light upon her human form.

The air currents palpably died down, and with the coming caesura a noticeable increase in temperature. So that there was no denying the fine day. Almost to the cue, what ten minutes before had been a kinetic frenzy of dismaying tidal surge was now no more than murmuring pleasantries along a sandy walking beach. Crabs festooned the still pools, raising their mitts like vying prize fighters in the midday glow. Electric nudibranches, elegant and slow, undulated in the low tides. Sea lemons, their six white gills passively processing the dead organic matter of the food chain, carried on in phalanxes, scouring the 270 million-year-old untrawled barnacle-laden calcium carbonate-rich bottoms, whilst peri- and dogwinkles weighed in and sported upon the upwellings of zooplankton. All this dense eyestalk and flared lip gave nutrient-rich projections to the day. Marigold himself got the religion of bryozoans, encrusted plant life, whorls of conical hope and intertidal poetry. By razor-clam degree, like an opalescent squid, he and his harried team searched the harbor area for a plan. Scanning all available outlets, phone booths or passenger cars. Nothing. No exit.

But there was one wee sight welcome enough to melt the heart of any displaced person. Tied down not 37 feet away was a large rowing boat.

Knowing his friend's hearty appetite for just such escapades, and deciphering that certain look the Commander sometimes assumed at moments of intense scrutinizing—unbashful, tilted, the distant wandering gaze of a clinical imbecile— Sannazaro declared, "I suppose you'd have us borrow the vessel and row across?"

"Why not? The Vikings clad in mere baum marten did it, and Norsemen, too. Or would you prefer to take our chances here, where all the locals have gone stark raving loony and, from the looks of things, would not hesitate to run us through with pitchforks on an end-of-the-millennium whim. Or, worse, crucify us?"

"And once we're away—out there! —then what?"

"There's got to be a radio tower, some kind of beacon or relay. Surely the Irish military has a station on the top—broad-band or microwave sensors, whatever they're called. Wouldn't you think? I mean, it is a strategic point. We'll call for help out there, safely separated from—" he tried to fit a characterization to the surreality of his experience—"from this village of the damned."

"Do you realize how far that is? If the currents are against us, the next stop is the North Pole."

"That would make sense, surely, in terms of symmetry for the year."

"We can do it," the boy rallied.

"Don't you encourage him now!" chaffed the Governor.

"The votes are in. Excellent!" culminated the Commander.

"You are neither relations nor friends, but four-letter agitators who have ganged up deliberately to ruin my life."

Rajibai suppressed his grin. Uncle gave the boy a timid Dutch rub that betrayed only his love. "Damn it!" the Italian carped, caving in predictably.

With that sum of cyclical incitements, they got into the rowboat, took a roll call, went over basic procedures, adopted two oars in hand, and started out towards the unknown mountain of God where scurvied ascetics were once said to have ... what? Played ping-pong and roasted marshmallows? ... as they struggled, the three of them, to hold a straight line betwixt their six spastic arms, flailing against the recalcitrant sea and fulminating troughs. Not far below, only a few yards, gathered *A. dux*, the near-transparent larvae of giant squid, who would soon join their 36-foot-long brethren down in the 700-fathom depths beneath, and sojourn in quiet, dangling company, with nerve endings 100 times thicker than Sannazaro's and eyes the size of Marigold's head. Unlike the Commander, however, the squid used all 20 grams of his brain, whereas Marigold was presently reduced to the use of but four grams of his own mental propriety, so unoccasioned was he to the stress of their dinghy, which was no ocean liner.

It took many hours, and the day was not long. They hadn't counted on the transverse tides, the grumbling undertows, or the current mutating towards the Canaries, if not headlong into Gibraltar's steely clefts.

"Naturally. Snow!" Sannazaro determined, hazarding a summary of all that was presently happening around them, meteorologically speaking. Perversely, the temperature had plummeted by degree with each yard of separation from the shore, the winds reacting in kind, waves growing thick and fast, and a grouchy jetstream fighting them at every move. Panic seized all on board.

"Harder *harder—pull pull pull!!!*"

The three battled for what historians will remember as their miserable, waterlogged lives. Chroniclers will note that a blizzard had massacred the skies, hurling down snows atop wrackweed. For every foot advanced towards the pyramid, their dwarfed little boat was thrown three feet to the left, due south—in other words, towards that Spanish Sahara of malaria and lymph-flukes.

"We're going to miss it!" the Governor cried. "Not if we pull *harder, harder!*"

Which they did, and by massive luck came within 27 yards of the southwestern tip of the mountain ... only to be sucked back away.

"Jump!" the Commander pleaded with his mates. "It's our only chance."

No truer words were ever shrieked.

As all captains, caliphs, khanates, Royals and postilions must, he ventured first, holding his nose, squeezing his toes one to the other in their dark socks, clenching shut his eyes, squirming overboard in one manic leap, leaving his soggy journal and binoculars on board, and freestyling with all his maverick might while holding the traces that had moored the boat back on the shore in one hand. The sea crashed over him where he muttered in distress, but he would be taken for no mad coward.

Rajibai leapt bravely after him, faintly aware that no harm could possibly come—after all, they were veterans now, having won the Himalayas and nearly brought down an entire government—and Sannazaro, not wishing to die alone, though nothing if not palsied with rictus and horror, all dromomane, joined in.

The water was ice cold, of course: perhaps not Antarctic cold, but the Atlantic in winter nonetheless. Under any other circumstances, 27 yards might not countermand the senses, nor usurp the staying power of mortals, no matter how dulled by pain and panic. Nor should such distance require more than a minute or two of hard, saltblasted swimming. But there were other complications. Not only did they have the shock and colic of the ice water and a strong outward gust to contend with, but also crashing sea squall, 15-footers, slimy guano-covered slabs of basalt rising near vertically, with only narrow fissures allowing for purchase under the best of times. Marigold was hurtled and bashed, somehow managing to maintain a handhold. He clung to a sharp ledge, ripping open all five fingers of his right hand, and tossed the halyard with his other. Rajibai grabbed hold the line, was imperfectly dragged, partly thrown on to the same perch.

Sannazaro was less fortunate. They could not get the rope to him, so that he was scabbered like a helpless sack of weightless croissants, trajected hither, strewn yon, pulverized up, down and sideways, then swept back out towards infinity, only to be engulfed and slammed by the body-rupturing thunder of monstrous, infernal killer waves.

He could easily have died, and by all rights should have—they all should have—but on the third horrible detonation, a fur seal resembling a bull kelp resembling a tumor, bloodied to a pulp—none other than Sannazaro—landed on the same perch as the others, and his hand connected with the hand of somebody who would not let go.

"We have to climb, are you able?"

"Blub blub blub..." came the salt froth from the Italian's sobbing lips. "I'm hurt, real bad I think. If not my body, my pride."

"Try. Have to try. Heave. Pull. Hold. Or die."

Rajibai and Marigold frantically worked to help him surmount the first series of overhangs and crack systems. Sleet was pouring down, but at least that water was warmer than the sea. Soon they were above the breakers, upon a perilous wall whose ascent was made nearly impossible by the accumulated layers of slicked-down avian turds. Rajibai led, and his agile abilities saved the day, which was fast turning to night. He attained the trail. From there, he found a way to tie off the remnants of clothesline and toss it down. The hawser length was barely sufficient, but by dangerous means, and addled gymnastics, somehow Sannazaro was hauled upwards to more safety. His hands—his whole body—streamed blood. And now Marigold's own lacerations became clear.

A harpy eagle soared free, issuing a warning.

"You're both losing blood," the boy pointed out.

"Wait—a light! There's a shelter!"

"Check it out first," Marigold demanded, ogling aslant.

Rajibai scrambled up the trail, then disappeared. They were long occupied minutes.

"My God, what's he doing?" Sannazaro mumbled despairingly. He thought he'd faint.

"Should I go see?"

"Please."

Marigold stumbled up the crooked, gnarly path, a foot-wide series of palimpsests, just as Rajibai, adroit as a turkey, could be seen topflight, descending.

At length: "Well?"

"Amazing," he stammered.

"What? Is there anybody?" Marigold cried.

"Not that I saw. But food, and candle light, I can't explain it," garbled he, trembling, hypothermic.

"Marvelous. Home free. A gift."

"Yes."

The three reached the hut, which was the shape of a beehive, made of stone, painted white like one would see on most islands of the Cyclades. It was as if they'd been expected, so generous the table setting, the burning scented beeswax tallow and wicks of fir illuminating a spread of humble but altogether edible sea cucumber, roasted garlic, slabs of butter and wheat bread, even sheep cheese nicely aged. That and more, for a boiling kettle atop a metal cookie sheet, of sorts, and heated by a configuration of oil lamps, had been readied and left for the newcomers. In it, a brew of herbal delicacies.

Nearby, a stash of woolen blankets, and three beds, like gold nuggets.

"They must have seen us fighting the storm," figured Rajibai, wolfing down his portion of bread and cheese, and wassailing their unknown benefactors.

"*Date et dabitur vobis,*" Sannazaro conjectured, the Vulgate ever at hand for such occasions. "Give and it shall be given unto you. Surely the monks are nearby."

The Commander speculated silently, gratefully as he attended to Sannazaro's and his own wounds, achieved just short of the price of their lives, wherein the novelty of danger was no less piquant.

"I suggest we eat and sleep. Tomorrow should illuminate our situation," he said.

It took little cajoling to effect the stated goal. Sannazaro was in such pain from having been sliced like some sushi upon the razor-sharp rocks that it was all he could manage to crawl beneath the blankets and pass out, whining quietly as his unpomaded wounds enflamed. Rajibai was not far behind, and then the Commander himself.

Wind pounded the hut. Sea affronted beneath. Peculiarly, no calmer, safer, gentler reunion in all the seven seas, he dreamed. Or thought he did.

CHAPTER 138

The Ghosts of Scelig Mhichil

IT WAS SOME TIME around midnight that the boy opened his eyes with a start. In the distance were muffled ting-a-lings of chimes and carillon. Tintinnabulations muted and frail, uphill, fragmented, like bells breaking the spell of curfew in an ossuary. Looking outside, he saw a full moon haunted the entire pyramid. A week ago, atop the waterfall, there had also been a full moon. He did not voice the question but let it reside. Waves gently coddled the cliff bottoms, and a mellowing Humboldt current graced the nocturnal ambience with temperate good tidings. His clothes were wet and cold, his tennis shoes frozen and hard, but he found a pair of sandals, wrapped himself in his blanket, and tested the situation, silently exiting the hut to explore the angelus ringing upstairs.

Lightheaded in the evening's orchidaceous air, he ascended towards the eerie peals. Star depths twinkling, intermittent raucous from nesting gulls and guillemots, and somewhere along the dark bands of cliff and higher clumps of deep red mountain tussock, a pungent incense wafting over the slopes of fragrant primrose coming out as he scrambled upwards. Sweet woodruff, angel's trumpet and chocolate cosmos, aswarm with hawkmoths.

There, far off upslope ... He approached a cluster of huts, honeycombs of white-painted stone, with galleries of burning oil lamps to light the way. Ducking beneath a carved lintel of natural slates, along the bristling sea drop, he observed an astonishing duo of burnished shadow-play—human goings-on inside. Two figures, only their heads visible—a venerable saintly sort, tousled, features both kittyish and retroussé, beside a callow youth, each absorbed in prayer. By the silhouetted angle of their lowered faces they appeared to be kneeling on a primitive floor, reciting unrecognizable words from some large open book. *The Second Epistle to the Thessalonians,* as it turned out.

Rajibai moved closer in. Tripping on his oversized sandals, he dislodged a crucial rock in the puzzle of the laid-out trail, and this in turn triggered a small avalanche over the cliff. He dropped, unable to hold himself, smashed into a ledge and continued rolling towards the end-of-his-life. One last lunge saved him, for a palm-sized jagged edge was there, and his fingers would never let go. His legs dangled over the 500-foot overhanging wall, his sandals and woolen cape dropping far into the waves. Naked now, grasping and clawing, yammering hysterically, he managed desperately to reattain the slippery, sinuous groove of a path.

Confusion in the night. A flurry of footsteps down the steep passage, staff, cloak, rummaging somnambulances.

"Father!" a boy's voice called out. The young monk was now standing directly over Rajibai, who had gathered himself back up, the moonlight burning his dark nudity into a platinum vision atop a slope of glistening true sedge.

The old man materialized, his face its own cloister of chiaroscuros. Both monks, old and new, fell to their knees to welcome little Jesus, who had arrived in their minds' eyes.

"Your arrival, Lord, has been eagerly awaited for 1,000 years. We trust your journey was pleasant," the old monk proclaimed, though he was afraid to look Rajibai in the eyes, his face pressed down to the very surface of the frozen runnel of rock.

"Well, sir, we nearly ate the bullet," Rajibai replied.

"We?"

"What did he mean 'ate the bullet', Father?" the young monk whispered.

"Don't know, don't question, shhh!"

"There are three of us," Rajibai continued.

The old monk, who was the Abbot, and his oblate gasped, showing deference to this astounding news by plastering multiple signs of the cross against themselves.

"And believe you me, that rowboat wasn't much against the storm."

"We are sorry for that, oh Lord. Happily, you have arrived in all your splendor." *Never mind you are much younger and of a different race and color than I might have expected*, thought the old man. And, continuing out loud: "But, as your last devoted inhabitants of this, your sacred mount, named in honor of your Archangel Michael, and upon whose bountiful precipices we have communed our entire lives, we heartily welcome you, and stand ready to be delivered whereforever you dost deem it appropriate."

"Hopefully Paradise," the oblate burst out, only to receive a hard knock to the head from the old man's burnished hand for daring to speak to the Lord so willfully out of turn.

The much-aged eremite had debated the possibilities of the Lord showing up for decades. Some years his cynicism had won out, and he humiliated all those who sought comfort in the Second Coming. 'Not on your miserable life,' he would declare. 'He'd have to be a fool to show his face around here!' But other years he was far more sanguine, feeling duly deserving of salvation. After all, he had sacrificed most of his life. He could have sired freckly wee ones, established himself in iron blasting or tin trading. Or mined a peat bog up north. Instead, forsaking all that was once dear to him, he had embarked on the loneliest of pursuits—that of an ascetic, always on the verge of starvation, benighted by temptation. Ragged with recriminations and fear. Seeing the despondency in the weary eyes of his young disciples whose lives he had ruined.

The scabrous front-runner of theological design collected himself anew, bowing again before his God, gently patting the boy monk on the head where he had nearly toppled him seconds before.

"He means well. In our enthusiasm ... the new dawn, imagine! A new millennium, *Te Deum Laudamus*—" the boy monk started humming the tune—"and you have come! I'm not crazy. Ohh my ..." And the old man started weeping.

"There now, there now, it's all right, you'll be fine, everything is going to work out," Rajibai coddled them, thinking, *They're as crazy as Assamese woodpeckers!* and bringing them up to their feet after they had each tried to kiss his toes, which rather tickled. "And say, is there any kind of Navy radio transmitter or satellite telephone on the island?" which rather sailed right over their heads.

The two monks escorted the young Jesus back down the bypath in eager anticipation of his two fellow wanderers. Who might they be? God himself ? Mary? Joseph? The Holy Ghost? St Paul? St Peter? Two of the three wise men? St Simeon? The possibilities were frightening. To think that they had chosen Scelig Mhichil, not Jerusalem or Rome, as their point of earthly communion for the most important night in history: the springboard for the few remaining faithful to be ushered up to Heaven on Jacob's Ladder, and the gangplank for all sinners to be damned. Was it any wonder? Had the rock not been dedicated to St Michael, patron saint of high places, of those myriad elevated waystations on the way to Heaven? Was it not that same Michael who was deemed by Emperor Otto to be the Captain at Judgment Day, his image enshrined upon banners in a recent crusade across Europe? The very same saint who ensured the campaigns up and down the Danube where the Magyar Infidels, Lehel and Bulczuk, were finally subdued?

As they descended the harrowing catwalk, the Abbot pinched himself at his good fortune. For 80 long years he had eaten dust in his cave; demons had tormented him every night of his life, offering him sweet little girls and whiskeys of every variety from the mainland. But he had resisted, combating an erect member with the words, "*Nosce te ipsum.*"

Well, mostly resisted. Long, long ago there had been one 13-year-old beauty, disguised as a boy, since no women were allowed on the rock, and none of the monks could say "No" to him once it was learned that he was a she. Finally, it was decided that Nelly—that was her name— was a descendant of Mary herself, come to remind the monks of the ephemerality of lust, and nothing they did to her mattered, because she was always going to remain a Virgin, always going to remind them of their true purpose. For one glorious night, legs, tongue, lips, 20 years of anticipation. And then he was plunged anew into that realm of the desiccated, miserable wretch that was the quintessence of his piety. As Nelly was rowed back to the Dunbeg Fort on the Kerry headlands, the old monk watched from his upland cave, banishing her mile by mile across the waves and from his thoughts. Such sexual tergiversations were worth it, though, he would remember.

They reached the beehive hut.

"Father, Uncle!" Rajibai asseverated.

The two drowsy, aching itinerants glanced up from their respective ill-covered fetal positions upon their cold bedplanks and were warmed by the sight of the two visitors.

"Humanity!" the Commander declared, gazing upon the face of the old man, unclear of its authority— much like a Jan de Rousseaux, or Isaac Jouderville, even Jan Joris van Vliet. Then, upon seeing his naked boy, he said, "Son, out of respect to our hosts—monks, I can fairly recognize— why not clothe yourself? This is not Anna's world, after all."

"No no!" hastened the frazzled ascetic, who had again knelt down obeisantly, motioning the neophyte to do so as well. "For verily you brought us into this world naked, and have decided to take us from here in the same manner."

Cueing the oblate, both monks then dropped their horsehair attire and waited, vestments draped over their waists, bare of chest, before their maker, or makers, for nothing about these visitors was obvious.

"Get up, for God's sake," Marigold urged them, countering such rule-abiding, bootlicking. "And please—" He waved his arms to indicate they should not freeze on his account.

"As You bid," the Abbot replied.

"Oh dear," Sannazaro expelled, getting some measure of the picture here. He whispered to the Commander: "You don't suppose they're harboring grand illusions about us, do you? What day is it?"

"I've lost track. Surely it must be close to New Year's Eve?" Continuing in a whisper, up against the Commander's ear: "Well then, you see, that perfectly explains it. What do we do? They think we're emissaries of the Lord, or the Lord himself."

"Go along with it. Be kind. Why spoil the dream? They've probably lived their whole lives awaiting this moment—certainly the old one." He smiled at the monks encouragingly. "My children," he asked. "What day is it?"

"Why, Lord, the last day of the millennium, of course."

"Which millennium is that?" Marigold continued.

"But Lord, You jest?"

"I'm testing your knowledge, oh humble one."

"Well then, my Lord, it is the year 999. Ten centuries ago to the day, more or less, according to our astrologers and Church Fathers, the earth was blessed with Your birth. Or was it His?" He looked to Rajibai. "For, truly Lord, I am, sorry to say, unsure who's who among You. You see, our collective memory of Christ, the countless icons of our faith, all portrayed a man much like yourself: long shaggy hair, mustache, and— pardon me, Lord—sallow, white skin. Not an African Negro lad."

"In due course all shall be explained," Marigold exclaimed between coughing fits.

The trio shared in surreptitious seance and looks of incredulity. Sannazaro rather collapsed back upon his bed with the sorrows of philosophy, bewildered first by the startling aftermath of his Asian leap of faith, that 20,000-foot idyll with its numbing promise of the ever after. Now this, madness multiplied by so many centuries backward. What could it mean? Had their ingestion of the poppies anything to do with it? Time travel? Nonsense. Impossible. Yet, there was no denying the strangeness of their situation. These two surviving monks were convinced of their time and place. Had the rock pyramid escaped the fraternity of seconds and hours, days and years? If so, by what physics? Could the monks have somehow escaped time, outlived their century, arrived in the twentieth? Or, was the effect reversed somehow by the mammoth escarpment alone in the sea, catapulting the trio backwards? All of the Irish peninsula doing so, for verily this disturbing trend had clearly begun on the mainland. Like one Japanese soldier hiding to this day in a Pacific Island jungle unaware WWII had ended; or the famed hermit ewe of Mou Tapu Island in Lake Wanaka.

Rajibai took a blanket, covered himself and, to dispel his own rising confusion, began piling some cheese on a crusty end slab of unleavened loaf, not entirely distraught but not sure what it really meant. Would 1,000 years really change anything? Were they pulling a fast one? The Commander adopted a stupefied look, deeply existential, after Crowquill. This was dry-as-dust confirmation of what he and the others had already suspected but dared not believe. But how? And now what?

He and Sannazaro looked at one another, trying to filter out some answer, neither fully grasping the question, both holding back the nervous laughter of the queerest deliverance.

"So then, I presume, it is time to rectify everything, Lord?" the vicar of encrusted saps went on.

"Yes. And the first thing it should pleasure me to know is whether you two are the only ones upon this splendid piece of real estate?"

"Real estate, Lord?"

"This island of perdurable stone."

"Indeed, Lord. The boy, Finian, and myself—they call me Stephanos— are the last, save for the she-goat, Melissa, who wanders the hill. The other monks lost their faith years ago."

"I'm sorry to hear that. What we need first is a good night's sleep. Let us billet, then reconvene with the sun."

"Not before 9 a.m., please," Sannazaro insisted.

This brought the first makings of a grin to the cloud-carrying prelate, who began, "As of course You already know, we rise at midnight for our Matins and Lauds, are back to bed, then up at six for Prime, an early Mass up the hill at the summit clochan—"

"Clochan?"

"Ahh, of course, You wouldn't bother with such a linguistic trifle! Clochan, it's Irish for hut—the beehive huts, an architectural form derived from a small cave inhabited hundreds of years ago by our revered Kevin of Glendalough, Ireland's first naked hermit. A true ecstatic around whom gathered other naked ones, thus establishing our first monasteries. But I don't mean to bore You with facts You know far better than Your humble servant, Lord."

"Yes, thank you. Go on, then."

"The Mass, then tea and saltless crackers, followed by my labors in the scriptorium—I've been writing out a copy of our six precious manuscripts for ten years—and Finian's efforts in the garden, then off for High Mass, a simple meal, then back to bed. That has been our life. We have, thanks to You, more inner resources than we perhaps know what to do with."

Marigold had no intention of scotching the program. "Tomorrow I should be most interested in touring the mountain, and seeing the manuscripts you refer to," he said. "Whenever it is convenient between your prayers."

"Tomorrow is the last day, Lord. What about ..." He feared to say it.

"What?"

"The Great Day of Your Wrath." And he proceeded to remind the Lord from verse one of *Revelations*: "I saw an angel come down from heaven, having the key of the bottomless pit, and a great chain in his hand, and he laid hold on the dragon, the old serpent which is the devil, and satan, and bound him one thousand years, and cast him into the bottomless pit, and shut him up, and set a seal on him."

"Oh no, no, you misunderstand! There will be no wrath, no, absolutely not. None at all. Nor dry deserts. No quicksand or tortures. No excess heat or cold. I can't stomach it."

"But what about all the sinners, Lord?"

The Commander winked at him. "Forgive and forget."

"Ahhh!" the grizzled anchorite gasped, the power of the notion entering his veins like a dozen amphetamines. "That's marvelous!" He paused, then hazarded an even stickier thorn: "But what about the rest of us? Your faithful, I mean. Won't we be going somewhere fancy, Lord?"

"That depends. Where would you like to go? No, wait. I'll tell you what: you sleep on it, give it some thought, and we'll talk tomorrow. How's that?"

"Oh, thank You, Lord. And I presume there will be enough time to dispatch Your humble servants by whatever means are peculiar to Thineself, all powerful?"

"Of course. Don't mention it."

The boys, meantime, had been sitting side by side. Rajibai had shown the oblate the game of slap-the-hands, kick-up-your-heels. Next might come marbles, thumbs, then dreidels, and after that tic-tac-toe. In time, devil-may-care roulettes. Their friendship was struck up almost immediately. They seemed to speak the same language, despite everything. Among youth, no self-abasing or prostration.

"Good night, then," the Commander said cheerfully, and the trio saw their hosts out into the radiant perpendicular darkness.

CHAPTER 139
How the Threesome Escaped to the Twenty-first Century

THE MORNING FANNED out by faint dissimulation, soft and pensively; cerulean sea, celadon mist, an auric star. The temperate rumblings of rocky blowholes squirming angrily abase those perimeters of the pyramid, spume salting the air. The cries of the petrel skewing to the foam-lines encircling the cliffs, where so much gristly brine of cracked mussel and shrimp arose in aromatic half-shells.

For centuries Scelig Mhichil, like other monk-inhabited Irish islands—Iniscealtra, Monaincha, Lough Currane and Inishmurray—had preserved the best of European civilization: ideal communities, dreams of the perfect sheep pasturage, hopes for a merciful Day of Judgment, warmed loaves of softly buttered cow bread fresh from a clay oven, and a vintage shot of some curdled port cured by one's grandfather. Modest technology, stern organization, spiritual idealism—these were the civilizing components that made for a pot of flowers, a loaf of bread, a pillow. No shotgun, no elevator, no territorial imperative.

These lone self-mortifying beacons of men who once, as ordinary dimwits, walked deep in manure across cow commons and swales of swine had now by stubbled cheek and solemned psalm become like stubborn stone—rolling heath and four-letter barrens dipping into prayer. The names of Saint Kevin, Molaise and Patrick, and the glorious sites of Clonmacnoise, Tuamgraney, Armagh and Glendalough, all recalled this desire for a better world. The churches and monasteries had been hewn first in mortar, then rock: walled complexes of round towers, canoe-shaped oratories, jutting stones, grand lintels, firm jambs and, most elegant of all, the small, intimate, dome-shaped clochans of Scelig Mhichil, about whose stylishness the great Sayid Ibn Ahmed of Toledo had analogized to the effect, "Even the shrewdest architect must envy the hexagonal ingenuity of the honey bee or mountain ascetic." Here were stones, after the shrewd, milk-giving St Clare of Montefalco, in which each of three weighed the sum total of the other two—an enigma in keeping with the spirit of the nimbus, the annals of miracles and prodigious hosannas.

All five sauntered along the jutting terrace, with Melissa, a creamy white Nubian who browsed upon the clusters of sweet alyssum and bouncing bet that grew 550 feet above sparkling sea on the western portion of the pronounced pyramid. There were six huts in all, whose main construction, said the Abbot, had occurred about 14 years earlier, when a dozen monks still inhabited the rocky peak. Just below the summit, a small hermitage greeted them, and a rectangular oratory, dated to around 800—the loneliest nook in all of Europe. A meditation chamber and library were to be found there, and a table of imported cedar all the way from Jerusalem, upon whose worn surface the Abbot Stephanos had spent many sang-froid years copying the sacred texts in his possession.

"Each Chronicon is Yours, my Lord. We slave over them only to better understand Your ways and prepare ourselves for—well, in fact, for this very day, which we have long anticipated."

Marigold examined the Merovingian-looking ciphers, and employed the piece of glassy quartz on hand to study in some detail the finely wrought illuminations. Cryptic texts hiding other texts beneath yet other layers of conveyance. The whole effect was one of obfuscation and concealment, a secret language meant for very few eyes. Here, obscurantism was prized above all else.

"That is the *Lebor na hUidre*, or *Book of the Dun Cow*," the Abbot proudly stated.

"And this one?" asked the Commander.

"*Codex of the Flummoxed Testicles*," replied the Abbot with some trepidation.

"Titles most rare and uncommon. What about this one?" Marigold inquired, pulling from the worm-eaten case a slim volume embroidered in most unusual silver wire.

"Ahhh... *The Book of the Holy Mountain*... Beloved to us all. Its tormented scribe certainly shared that most apt passage from the fourth-century *Life of St Gregory of Nyssa*: 'He who makes the true ascent must ascend forever.' A miniature illustrating that sentiment revealed St Gregory, along with St John Climacus, both falling to their deaths—a sad commentary on your *Genesis 28:12*, Lord," volunteered the Abbot: "'And he dreamed, and beheld a ladder set up on the earth and the top of it reached to heaven; and beheld the angels of God ascending and descending on it.' Those that suffered temptation, or lost heart, also lost their footing. Here, on so steep a mountain, such words are the more meaningful." The wizened renunciate grinned, wide of gum, and belched a gas most unpleasant, even to the Lord who'd presumably smelled it all.

Sannazaro stuck his nose more deeply into the pages of colorful diagrams. "Now these are quite interesting," he pointed out.

"That is an image of our beloved Acepsimas who remained in his cell for 60 years. That one is Sisoes standing on a ledge for 50 years. And he is none other than Stylites, of course, one of Your greatest servants, Lord, chained atop his mountain pillar for 37 years. We always think of him as the most holy martyr of the air."

"Who's that one?" inquired the Commander.

"Why Lord, that is St Anthony. Surely You recognize him?"

"I left my spectacles on the rowboat," Marigold replied. Which brought a great coughing fit of hilarity from both monks.

"... Left His spectacles on a rowboat!"... It was, possibly, the best joke they'd heard, ever!

When the raucous mirth simmered, and the monk had wiped away his tears and apologized to the Lord, he began: "In the *Vita Antonii* by Athanasius, our great predecessor lived, as You better than the rest of us well know, atop Mount Colzim by the Red Sea at the far eastern edge of the Gebel-el-Galaza, and there he remained at the height of his meditation, and at the summit of the mountain, for his final years, before passing away in 366. There is not a day that we don't remember him with love and gratitude."

"How nice," the Commander mused.

"Such impressive memories," Sannazaro averred.

"What about this one?" Rajibai petitioned, taking an equal interest in everything.

"*The Martyrology of the Famished Boatman*," tendered the self-mortifier, taking an especial interest in the leathery manuscript, "possibly a Canary Islander who lost his way and therein describes a sea journey very reminiscent of the letters of St Brandon, written from the sacred isles."

"To his mistress," the bushy-haired and freckle-faced oblate obliged. The Abbot shuddered and heaved at this blasphemy, yanking from his cape an osier branch and whacking the youth across the head. "Now now," Sannazaro stepped forward. "Leave the boy be."

"It is true," the old Abbot admitted, "that there are some questions concerning Brandon's home life. But that is no reason to taint a venerable memory that shall hallow posterity and give for all time the season of paradise its due weather."

"This one, at the end of the shelf? *Vade mecum*, is it not? Moroccan binder, gold bracket—" for Marigold knew his books. "But lo, what's this? Dirt caked upon the binding, and a different script, I believe?"

The Abbot was by now growing more comfortable with the astonishing fact of his engaging in dialogue with his divine guests. "Indeed," he said, "with such built-in spectacles is it any wonder You're the Lord? That is Ogam. From the Greek Ogmios, god of eloquence ... well—" he was suddenly aware of his misuse of the nominative—"a Greek god, which means a charming fiction. I would never stand before You and presume to justify the etymological origins of our most learned, secretive, but troublesome of scripts—"

"Why troublesome?" Marigold urged him patiently.

"May I?" The Abbot took the manuscript from the Lord's hands to better explain its unique stature among all other codices.

"Note its five notches, arranged in triple confusion, amplified by diphthongs, to indicate the whole letter and vowel combination. This reference, for example—" he pointed with his long, bony index finger.

"In Gaelic translation, Cormac Ua Cillin, of the Ui Fiachrach Aidhne, comarb—the Abbot—of such and such, has died at such and such."

"What is the name of the book?"

"*Grammatology of Grandfather Worm*," the covener of antiquities declared with some pride. "Or that is our admittedly peculiar translation, as there is much ancient Greek and prehistoric Irish between the lines that conflicts with the subsequent emendations."

"Odd, isn't it?"

The Abbot looked at Finian, and then lowered his head towards the ground. The Lord was testing him, he could sense it. "Twelve hundred pages in all. Devoted entirely, Lord, to Your sublime Creation. A text for which we have no reliable origins, no date of original inscription. A work almost entirely of science, Your Omnipotence."

"Don't get too used to such flattery," Sannazaro mumbled out one corner. He feared such praise would shoot straight to the rudiments of the Commander's head.

"Do go on," Marigold purveyed.

"Yes, by all means continue," Finian added with a goading spout. "Not a word from your lips, you ungrateful—"

"Now, now—" Marigold appealed, but he could put two and two together in a glance. How many desperate lonely seasons had the boy sat hunched over that manuscript of inscrutable details, engaged in what to his handlebars was useless transcription? Morosely confined to the cramped, cold scriptorium for purposes of studying not angels playing harps, or good deeds rewarded with a permanent place-setting on a cumulonimbus, but lowly, incomprehensible dirt, and all its worms. How humiliating such scholarship. It was the revered St Augustine who had written, 600 years before to the day, in his *Confessions*, Book Two: "The world is drunk with the invisible wine of its own perverted earthbound will; an intoxication which gives it great happiness but causes it to forget you, Oh Creator!" Was not the study of dirt, then, a retrograde task akin to groveling? figured the lad. Some great hoax perpetrated by the Lord as a specific punishment, a form of penance? But why not persecute the old one, instead? What had Finian done to deserve such low esteem? What boy could be expected to exhaust his youth transcribing a book devoted to worms, and rudimentary earth science?

Finian's recalcitrance had been met with repeated beatings in the name of God from the old ascetic. The trio needed no special sensitivity training to detect the legacy of tears, washed away by the persistent wind that battered the beehives. They could well imagine all those ghastly twilights, in full view of the mainland with its many signs of a warm hearth and soft bed. And knowing that Nelly, and other redheads just like her, were showering their glorious favors upon other undeserving lads from one breen to the next, while he remained condemned to an island prison of shackling faith with ever-fresh flatulence.

Not to mention all those other endless chores which fell upon Finian's shoulders. The tilling of the scrappy garden atop pebbled cleft and sheer slopes, sandwiched between the mocking colonies of black terns and herring gulls. A routine of desperate tedium as his youth vanished, sacrificed for what? The copying and study of that obese tome.

As a child Finian had arrived on the obscure beetling cliffs, delivered to the salivating monks by parents with twelve others to feed. He being the thirteenth, there was no question but that he should be shipped off to the pyramid. By five years of age, at the price of a herniated anus, he had learned his *ars dictandi* in more ways than one. But to whom might he dispatch an SOS? Or dash off a confession? To his mother, whom he sorely missed, despite her having abandoned him? To the invisible Lord? But what Lord would permit a young boy to be tormented so? Later on, he was enslaved to the quadrivium and trivium, to Grobar and Cassiodorus, Ptolemy's astrolabe and Alcandreus' astrogeophysics. But he never learned to swim, which would have served him best.

"My Lord," said the Abbot, "this book of dirt provides a complete enumeration of all the creatures saved from the Great Flood in Noah's Ark. We have pored over certain difficult theories intimated therein, one of which is particularly troubling."

"What might that be?" the Commander generously volunteered. "Lord, forgive me, but it is blasphemous."

"He can handle it," Sannazaro laid claim.

Marigold noticed how the monk's hands trembled, how sweat poured down his bald pate and gathered under his much-worked eyes and blue-veined nostrils. He had palsy, that was clear, and arthritis, and gout, and probably a host of other ailments, and he smelled of rotting bouillabaisse.

This collective hardship in one man, and his desperate charge, went to Marigold's heart; bespoke of the entire Middle Ages, not in some glib footnote, but as a labored, suspiring hell.

"It says, Lord, You'll forgive me, that You created the earth not several thousand, but several billion years ago; that we are evolved from stars and monkeys and black men; that Adam and Eve never existed. And, worst of all, that Paradise is here and now, and that this is as good as it gets."

Sannazaro looked bright-eyed to the Commander. There was nothing he could say to advise him, and nothing he was going to say himself. His relish was the size of a hot dog. Do they dare muck with history? Would it be wrong to spill kidney beans a little early? Could it possibly matter?

After all, Stephanos' days were numbered. And the boy? What could he possibly do with such information?

Marigold contemplated what to do. It was nearly midnight, New Year's Eve.

"Tell us, Lord?" the Abbot beseeched. "Give us a sign. Anything. We await Your Judgment."

"It's all true," the Commander finally exhaled, dramatic sensifics animating his blush of ambiguities. These people had to know the truth.

"Furthermore, look closely at this word. Ring a bell?"

The Abbot studied it under a magnifying glass of alkali feldspar. "I cannot read it," replied he.

"See this—" and the Commander worked through the letters, one by one. "Aristotle, no question about it. The single surviving work by his own hand. A relic as rare and as telling as the Shroud. I thus declare all subsequent interpretations to be in error and henceforth struck from the record. Let it be freely admitted, therefore, that the earth revolves around the sun. That sex is fine and women have the same rights as men. That the earth was formed 4.5 billion years ago, maybe even a few hundred thousand more, from cosmic dust, except for Kansas, which came much later and still has trouble figuring it out. And let no man put words into the mouth of another, or of his son. Finally, be it official that all ghosts are holy, and it is OK to worship spirits in the trees."

The monk's eyes grew large and ovaltine. Blue, cold, clammy red spots. Finian smiled with miasmas of relief.

"I knew it!" the boy exclaimed. He took hold of Rajibai's hands and, laughing hysterically, the two did an Irish jig, a Virginia reel—one step, two steps, repeating caper and a leap, senseless all—on the side of the mountain. Young boys in the fresh air. Timeless.

Stephanos clung to his heart, kneeling down, hyperventilating. He tried to speak, but only squeaks gurgled forth. His entire Universe was shifting. Anti-matter taking over, gravity escaping. He collapsed.

"Now now, not to worry," the Commander hastened. "Rajibai, Finian, help Stephanos to bed. On the double."

But even a rumpled Marigold could catch the obvious: here was a likely medieval blood cholesterol problem, atherosclerotic arteries compounded by all the signs that didn't change over time—loneliness, isolation, a low arterial dilation grappling with so much excitement. In other words, a heart attack, or stroke.

They all pitched in and delivered the ailing abbot back to his beehive hut, carrying the bag of bones down the smooth stones through the moonlight.

"The candles have burned out!" Finian whispered to Rajibai.

"True," the Indian lad replied. "So, get a match, I'll light them again."

"You don't understand. They were timed. It's *time*! See the hour glass?"

"Time for what?"

"It's *after midnight!*" the oblate explained. "The *new year!* And we're still *alive!*"

"Take it easy, kid. *Salute Garibaldi!* " Sannazaro rejoiced. "Happy New Year everybody. Who has any whiskey?"

Finian slipped a jug out from behind the Abbot's chest. His secret stash. He'd seen the monk stealing swigs now and then thinking himself unobserved. The precious stock was 30 years old. Stephanos was too agitated and lifeless to do more than accept a humble cup of the precious spirits and drink with the rest, knowing that this Lord and his bizarre accomplices were strange, and nothing at all like he had expected. That a century of religious observances was for the birds.

Everyone toasted, their assorted exaltations and caveats, pleadings and vested hopes, musings, follies, pearly wisdoms and wisecracks all pivoting upon one shared sentiment in the silence and among the ghosts of Scelig Mhichíl: relief. Relief aided by prayer for the next 1,000 years.

That it should be better than the last. That we should somehow manage to learn from our numerously grave mistakes and foibles.

It was, indeed, a curious admixture of sentiments for the trio, who knew only too well how much would happen in the coming millennium, such that this lonely pyramid of rock out in the Atlantic actually seemed quite homey and appealing, benign by any standard, the coziest place in Europe, by comparison with the teeming tragedies that would define the coming 1,000 years.

In Rome, the bell signaling the new millennium could be heard for 100 miles around. One village echoing the next throughout adjoining dioceses and eparchies. Tears of joy forming rivers of salt. All hailed the new age with desperate gratefulness—thanks that they were still standing and the fires of hell had not devoured them.

Their equally mystified Pope, Gerbi, declared anxiously, "Everybody OK?"

A little tern near the summit scriptorium looked at its neighbor and threw up some arrow squid.

On a cliff somewhere in the Echizen mountains of Japan, a Shugen-do yamabushi priest lowered himself by rope down the precipice, and hung there until he had passed out for lack of oxygen and got some revelation or other, a rebirthing, direct from the long-deceased lips of his spiritual master, En-no Gyoja. But at the end of a rope, mankind's destiny was all too clear, and spiritual secrets of a long life easily confused, for example, with the top ten IPOs for January.

Further south, in Tokyo, 25 million people celebrated, watching their 1200-resolution NHK special in Shinjuku on an 800-foot high video screen, whose image was broadcast in a montage of similar euphorias from Rio to Manhattan. Denizens of Caracas abstained from the festivities in honor of the tens of thousands of their brethren killed just weeks before in disastrous flooding. WGBH-Boston and the BBC World Service simulcast their live transmissions from 100 locations—tribal drummers in Burundi, step dancing from a red barn in Burlington, a sensation of fireworks off the Eiffel Tower. Locals banging drums and recreating the original seduction on Easter Island, Maori greeting the first sunrise waist deep in the pale Sauvignon-Blanc waters of the Pacific.

At the Sanctuario de Chimayo, a line of pilgrims waited to collect their pinch of sacred dirt.

In a sandy grotto along the Mediterranean, in the Kingdom of Amalfi, 30,000 monk seals slept soundly. Out in the sea, blond mermaids glided effortlessly through the haloed dark, foraging for phytoplankton.

A tragic fire in a Korean nightclub, the second in four months. The threat of anthrax in a Moscow subway. A Y2K scare across Belgium that amounted to nothing. The capture of an international terrorist in Afghanistan. More good news from the World Health Organization. A lowering of the prime and a rally on Wall Street.

Atop the waterfall, Namgyal and Anna sat in the hot tubs, contemplating their eternity.

In Dusky Sound, somewhere up high, the last moa dreamt of the last 65 million years.

All across the Ross Ice Plateau, winds blew 220 miles per hour as a storm headed north from the South Pole towards the Indian Ocean, skimming over the heads of 14 billion little red crustaceans, each one a living being filled with desires and great plans for the coming day.

That clear day arrived in the form of a pure sunrise. Melissa was the first to detect the light, her eyes opening to it, and then the sound, a twitching in her ears.

Rajibai leapt up and ran outside the hut where all five had passed out several hours before.

"*Helicopters!* " he shouted, running back inside to wake the others. There was a disoriented scramble of hangovers. Stephanos was too weak to stand. His left arm was paralyzed. He sat up and looked out the open door to catch a glimpse of the huge birds hovering over the cliffs. He prayed for his personal salvation, and for that of the world.

Finian stood near the door, unsure what to do.

Rajibai and Sannazaro jumped up and down, throwing their arms into the air and shouting their hallelujahs.

"*Presto! Andiamo!*" the Squire frenzied.

The Commander handed to the weakened abnegate a cup of cool water, recognizing what was happening to him. He was giving up to the inevitable. Dehydrated. Shrunken. Blood vessels paying their farewells.

"Bless you, Father," said Marigold, gently stroking the old man's grizzled face. Then he stepped outside.

There were two Irish Navy choppers. Sleek metal baskets were lowered, as there was no way to land on the pyramid.

"You can come!" Rajibai urged Finian. "I can't leave him, he needs me," the boy finally resolved, however much he was ready to get out.

"The old man is dying," Marigold said. "It could be forever before another rowboat arrives."

"I know," the boy admitted, unable to hold back his tears. "I have a shovel, though. To bury him with. And enough bull kelp to fashion a coracle. Nelly'll still be a young lassie."

"Go to her then, and fear not," sayethed the Lord.

"Praise be," Sannazaro cried aloft.

Rajibai saluted Finian, then got into the basket and was hauled up into the open door of the hovering helicopter. Sannazaro went next.

"Are you sure?" the Commander asked a final time.

"I will live, if You will permit it," Finian declared with a noble air.

And one last dangling uncertainty: "Wait ... Are all the birds in Heaven that big and noisy?"

"They're not birds, lad. But machines. Like windmills."

"Windmills?" He drew a breath of supreme confusion.

"That's right. Those are blades, built by mortal men like you and like me. They suck energy out of the air, just like water from the earth. And as for Heaven, lad, I assure you—such a place exists only in your heart."

Finian evidenced shell shock, his eyes slipping left, sloping right, turning inward, then bearing directly upon the Lord, unmincing, fearless. Ready to change course for the rest of his life.

In a glance Marigold recognized a radical shift in the youth's whole orientation. He would work it out.

"Goodbye, then. Take care of yourself."

The Commander patted the boy on the head, stepped into the waiting basket and was raised by pulley into the chopper.

Rajibai winked at his friend, whom he would never see again. Finian tried, but could not wink.

"Happy New Year, gentlemen," said the Navy co-pilot. "Nice way to start it. We found the rowboat about 80 miles out, and the diary. I presume these are yours?" And he handed over the pair of spectacles and the binoculars.

As they glided out over the sea, thousands of disturbed birds were swinging wide arcs all around the pyramid.

"Nobody else down there?" the co-pilot presumed aloud, incapable of penetrating whatever veils of time and mists of magical geophysics so obscured the summital point.

"Definitely not," Marigold assured him.

Heading inland, inhaling the day, they crossed Ireland's heartbreaking hills, swathed in the morning mists of a new century.

Some time later, Marigold would learn that Irish history records no sign whatsoever of human habitation on Scelig Mhichil after the first few years of the eleventh century.

CHAPTER 140
The Homecoming

ENDURING FEW wrinkles at Customs, the trio returned to the United States, no clue that anybody was following them. They spent two well-tempered nights at the Pierre. Rajibai went up to the observation deck of the Empire State Building (scarcely a drop-off, he insisted), had lunch at the Plaza (rather relished the sorbet), visited the Cloisters, the Metropolitan Museum (African masks, minute Scythian gold horses, the period of Fra Angelico—that's what he'd remember), saw *Tosca* (mesmerized by Domingo), dined afterwards at Nirvana overlooking Central Park ("Much better than the greasy spoons at Forlorn"), was limoed to JFK by a most eloquent Eritrean, and flew to Albuquerque via Chicago.

Sannazaro returned to the Camp of the Spirits. The compound was wintry, of course; no lush cottonwoods, tulips, wisteria or apple trees in bloom. Gone were the snapdragons, hollyhocks and poppies, the violet Indian paintbrush and scarlet penstemons, the bluebonnets and cadmium-yellow sage. Instead, spread out in the cold sun, the equally elegant bare spines of cedar and juniper, of salmon earth and the smoky valley inhabited by farmers, whose tenacious lineage dated to the ninth century, or earlier. Cold road, dirt as hard and ungiving as cement. Not a flower, other than those indoors.

But the ever-cheerful Ginevra was on hand, along with Father Alvaro, back from Brazil. All had 1,000 burning queries for the Italian, who collapsed in his bed, his gray matter overflowing with the net worth of inexpressible adventures. Raquel and Amigo were also there, and several conspiring canines. There prevailed at large news abundant to last for many days and feverish nights.

Next door, however, Marigold's hacienda was moribund and run down to an extent previously unachieved. It was not served well by emptiness, and presently languished in that air of abandonment which begins to sag in the thinner sections of roof. The odd window had been broken, graffiti sprayed annoyingly at the gate.

There was a single notice in the mail box. A yellow slip from the post office, advising him of overflow.

The car had four flat tires.

Warily, the Commander led Rajibai inside. He took a deep breath, knowing it to be both a superstitious sign to himself and a kind of prayer. He must now introduce a real boy to his new life in America.

"Welcome home, my son. This—" he pointed to the large sunroom off the study "—my favorite chamber, shall be yours, all yours if you like. How does that suit you?"

"It's as large as a whole slum!" the boy waxed happily, wiser than that by now. It was no Oberoi or Pierre—but it was his! After the jubilation of opening that famously carved front door had passed, a panic swarmed over the Commander. His appendages bespoke an uncoordination. All appeared strange. The clocks had stopped, every one of them: no cathedral gongs, no alarm, pendulum or striking movements. A dead barometer, a silent metronome. The ABC Dinner Stove was filled with cobwebs. He scooped up the odd recluse in a jar and relocated her 100 yards up the mountain. The screen door out the back had been demolished, as if someone had walked right through it. Debris and large mounds of feces littered the frozen garden.

It took some effort to get the earthenware oil stove and Aga heated. Badly peeling, its concentrated draught was malfunctioning.

His lean-to vinery had collapsed, all the organics curled over dead. Rat turds abounded. That was not surprising, but the scene bespoke more of aggravated assault than a mere winter's desiccation; of *Tiny's Picture Book of Dead Souls* with its charnel house of vegetal matter dispersed by the unknown, like some miniature Gettysburg of caked and cracking earth, the exoskeletons of forget-me-nots, sweet peas, pumpkins and butter lettuce wilted and rotting. It was all in the perception, and spoke to the Commander's unsettling distemper. He was not happy to be home; his veins tingled with unease.

His cushion carpet broom was dismembered (something you notice); the Scotch and Nottingham lace curtains moth-eaten. Most shapeless and contumacious was his bathroom, its chandelier twisted, encrusted and pathetic. The floor was in ruins: feathers suggested that a barn owl had flown welter and skelter about, been attacked by a muskrat, saving itself at the expense of knocking everything over. Imagine the riot on that tiled floor: a strewn pound of black antimony, chloride of lime tins, spilled boxes of Cascara Sagrada; cocaine pastilles, a shattered bottle of tannin and toppled vase of dill-seed water, mangled musk and a catastrophe of Homburg salts; acid phosphates simmering on the peed floor, Iceland moss poultices molding beside a ruined Rooke's elixir. Embrocations, ointments, extracts, emulsions, electricities, tonics, powders, lozenges, oils, creams, acids, syrups, crystals, capsules, fluids, soaps, essences and sundries (mostly the feminine remains of Alma's tenure), such was the cabinet of constituencies bolstering his body and subset of shadowy cavities that lay scattered like the aftermath of some great confusion or haste to leave this place. Exodus venting wrath upon the medicinals.

The kitchen, study and bedrooms were no better off. Who had used the saucepans, steamers, seasoning boxes, salad washers and ironmongery with such indifference? Or recklessly left the feather beds, Belgian linens, French mattresses in disarray? Down had been stolen from the comforters, dragged across the floor. These thieves had neither patience nor morals.

The Persian, Turkish and Indian rugs were curled up, stained and in shoddy repair; Kurd, Scinde, Velvet Pile and Axminster all saturated with the odor and color of animal urine. Utrecht velvets were falling off walls; damasks, chintzes, plushettes and trimmings all utterly malfactored, dusty, a mess.

Rajibai had nowhere to sit; there were few routes through the labyrinth of toppled books, the piles of paperwork, stacks and tiers of articles, clippings, yellowing marginalia of a life which struck him as lonely and insane, made manifest by ransack.

Books everywhere on the floor: *Tilden's Chemical Analysis, Chambers' New Series of Expressive Readers, Pitman's Phonographic Teacher*; the complete works of Twain, Buffon, Scott, Thackeray; a primer of astronomy, *Mackay's Manual of Modern Geography, Cassell's Complete Latin-English, Kirby's Elementary Textbook of Entolomogy*, and so on. All with pages notoriously ripped out, the binders—stained with linseed oil or uric acid?

If anything had been stolen there would be no way to tell. The Commander was not much accustomed to keeping track. But one possession, handed down by Pecos Marigold, did catch his eye: the Turner, a painter he greatly admired in every respect. The work, which had suffered only the odd tooth mark, was fashioned in October 1819; it described a gondola at sunset in Venice, enhanced by fiery mists that were the painter's stock-in-trade, of course.

The masterpiece seemed to elicit the dilapidated splendor of a visionary city-state which had been occupied by the Austrians and might well have been Marigold's own hacienda, certainly his mind, in the sense of its ruins and piazzas, and the atmospheric obscurities tantalizing each atom with the prospect of a home-life in the beauteous hereafter. Turner had caught the fever of a disheveled aesthetic era with his energetic nomadic eye; had utilized a technique of fast, elegant pencil-work beneath a gauze of oily admiration.

It was the Italy of Pope Pius VII, whom Sir Thomas Lawrence was painting in Rome at the time; of Sir Humphry Davy employing the latest scientific wizardry to salvage the treasures on papyrus from Pompeii. It intimated in deft strokework the women promenading before poets of Byron's caliber who, having taken up residence in Ravenna, had made much of the Venetian female allure. Turner captured these passions, and its culmination—between the four small borders of its frame—surely enlivened an otherwise sobering Marigold household. The riveting perspective, he explained to Rajibai, was really the artist's attempt to discover in the world a place like Arunachal Pradesh, or a pyramid in the Irish sea: a horizon instinct with all that was beyond normal human understanding. Spectral hues, golds and cobalts; or Schubert at age 18— that rush to fruition of imagined string quartets and sonatas amid the pageantry of passing clouds, sinking, rising, biding time for all eternity.

To make such wonders familiar enough to call home.

He remembered precisely those lines written by Turner's greatest admirer, John Ruskin, who had said of him: "... Turner's mind was, in two great instincts, at variance with itself. The affections of it clung ... to humble scenery, and [the] gentle wildness of [a] pastoral life. But the admiration of it was, more than any other artist's whatsoever, fastened on largeness of scale ... he was continually endeavoring to reconcile old fondnesses with new sublimities."

Every artist, Marigold went on, rhapsodized that access to revelation which was the natural world, and the Venices of the heart were the only cities, so called, to incite such feelings. Paris, another. Tesuque could not be ranked among them, he furnished, but still, as a village it excelled at the upper tiers.

"With patience you will discover this to be true," he applied in his sincerest, most hopeful Tesuquois.

"And you have all the time in the world to make it yours, to engage new friendships, to discover what I personally love about it. One day we'll visit Venice, too," he said. "Joseph Mallard Turner—that lonesome wanderer who maintained his modesty to the end, always staying hidden from view, a hermit of monumental proportions—will be our guide. How does that sound?"

"That sounds very confusing, Father."

Marigold handed Rajibai the painting. "It's yours. Allow it to enter your veins, as any great work should."

Alma was gone; she'd left no note. Anastasia and Ebert, too, though the squirrel was most likely hibernating somewhere on the mountain. But what of that dear old bison? Despairing of Marigold's absence, she might well have gone seeking members of her own kind. What if she discovered and mingled with the embroiled herd whose ownership was being disputed on alleged misdeeds by the Forest Service? He knew from months before that requests for a review of the records sent to the Office of General Counsel under the *Freedom of Information Act* had been belligerently refused by the Forest Service for reasons, they claimed, involving a said lack of public interest. Absurd! The upshot: Mr Marigold feared several possible consequences. First, that five-foot-high fence would prevent bison migration. Second, and most unbearable to contemplate, that bison would be slaughtered. When the New Mexico Department of Game and Fish had sold off the state's only bison herd the previous year, one rancher who purchased many of them stated he planned to both breed and slaughter the animals. A bison bull was worth 5,000 dollars to a buyer, a female like Anastasia probably 4,000 dollars.

She loved fresh-baked goods. What if she had wandered into a shopping mall, DeVargas, and been shot after trampling a few automobiles or pedestrians? If she'd gotten through the doors of Albertson's, things would have gone very sour indeed.

"In retrospect," averred Sannazaro, who had ambled over to check in on the boy and his mad eccentric father, and then survey the damage, "we were both utterly irresponsible."

Suddenly, a loud raucousness issued from under the sink. The trio raced to the kitchen, opened the cedar door panels and discovered a miscellany of cotton balls, newspaper clippings, book pages and Russian down—aha!, a regal pompadour of pine needles and other forest duff. It was Ebert only just awakened from a long winter sleep by the sudden sound of familiar voices. He had chosen most wisely to hibernate in the best of all possible worlds, which now revealed their well-indulged remains: a battlefield of cans forced open by some unimaginable forceof desire and Sciuridae dexterity; of lacerated boxes and disemboweled jars. Ebert had fairly eviscerated all carbon-based delectables—raisin bran cereal,

Graham crackers, pure butter assorted shortbreads, spécialité Suisse pralinettes with chocolate and hazelnut creme, peeled straw mushrooms, rice parmesan (soy free), lemongrass and artichoke hearts, Bac'n Bits (no cholesterol or meat), Tom Yum soup, papaya preserves, licorice chews, Maranatha almond butter, Comet sugar cones, cut baby corn, Hormel vegetarian chili and so on.

The Commander knelt down to pet his old friend. "How are you, Ebert? Need I ask? Meet Rajibai."

The boy extended his hand, Ebert his paw.

"He likes you."

"Hey, Ebert," Sannazaro threw in. "What's been happening?"

"He's really a pet squirrel?" Rajibai asked.

"Yes, and I'm happy to see that he looked after things while we were gone."

That brought a roar of the jollies from the boy and the Governor as they hung around the devastated kitchen, taking stock of the vibrations, so novel in their way, and such a come-down after the endless plateaux of adrenaline during their expeditions to the outer edge of social causes, kingdoms of sunshine, gushers of love, and faint sorties into terrifying antiquity in previous days and months.

CHAPTER 141
The Disappearance of a Lonely Bison

A NOMAD'S LIFE, the general tenor of humanity's first 110,000 years, is given to a delirium of constant distraction, and had become surely the preferred mode of being for both Marigold and his esteemed Squire-in-misery. But now that Monsieur Odysseus and immediate colleagues were home, that edifice deep within the body's endocrine system towards which all endeavors are by nature said to be bound, oriented and healed—the idea of renewed dissociation and radical flight—seemed remote and exhausting.

On the other hand, within all of a day, the hacienda spoke to the Commander of dreary clean-up, of has-beens and stasis, an inertia altogether disorienting, and he was none too thrilled about it. Such a clunker of onerous burdens inspired only restlessness and apprehension. Where was his deserved double cabin? All the trials of the previous weeks and months took on a luster, even if it was a lie: the worst ordeals seemed like Cockaignes; cesspools had become, in his mind, Golden Bays and Ecbatanes in Media; ant-infested tents, Dorothy Wordsworth's filigreed cottage. What responsibilities to make good the floor, replace the books in their proper spots, fuss about replacement drapes, order carpets (Ebert had greedily marked 100 territories indoors) and so many other time-disrupting chores? Of course, he would hire a cleaning crew, steam out closets and turd-infested drawers, contract a new housekeeper with a three-month trial tenancy, work 'at will'—whatever it took to re-establish some livable semblance. But he already missed the simplicity of the hanging huts, the free air of Scelig Mhichil, Crowquill's tower, the great whiteout of the last continent, bewitched by chimes, wind and time out of time. He yearned for few possessions, no cares, no duties whatsoever. He could afford those things now. Had the money to acquire nothing—and the time to think, or write, forever, to paraphrase a Twainism.

"Where's Anastasia?" Marigold wondered aloud, hoping somehow that Ebert might lend insight.

Nobody seemed at all perplexed by this upstart of inter-species gab, so normal in such a household. But that was asking too much, as it turned out. That, or Marigold's own ears were not yet sufficiently evolved, in spite of their ungainly size and form, to appreciate the particulars which he elicited from the loquacious squirrel.

The water and electricity were functioning. Marigold still had clothes in a closet. There remained some unmolested pillows to soften the night, and beds remaining upright.

"No television?" asked the boy.

"Alma had one in the sewing room. I see it's gone. She got married to Sam," he went on. "You'll meet her, though I have no idea where she is. They'll know next door."

"Surely," Sannazaro agreed.

"She raised me almost from the time of my mother's death," the Commander explained to Rajibai. "She came all the way from Mongolia, far to the northeast of the Himalayas. And looked after me."

He pulled out an ancient oak traveling trunk, the Scarboro, with its brass patent fastener and wrought-iron clips and japanned blue interior, and withdrew his little school uniform which he wore when he was nearly Rajibai's age. Calf-galoshed button boots, a Galatea maritime suit, velveteen single kilt, Chester tweed overcoat, and a gent's extra-quality silk hat of the finest plush.

"That was me," he mused, showing the boy a photo from his traveler's holdall. "Not bad, huh?"

He looked grand, but considering that was the era of young Elvis Presley, it was clear that Murillo had grown up in a time warp. No wonder he had so few friends, no way to break out of those hundreds of years of solitude. So your mom died the same day you were born?

Yes. Then your father? A bit later. When I was your age. Zapped in his prime. You didn't even have a brother or sister, an Uncle, a bison, not even a pet squirrel, nobody?

Rajibai thought about all this, and all the other things not yet discussed, though well intimated. They'd been on the road since day one, having so many adventures and fun. Girls. A rhapsody of feeling colored by all the wild animals in the bush, a life of roaming free and nibbling.

There had been no time, no reason, to discuss family histories until this moment.

"I say, let's go on a foraging expedition next door, introduce you to our neighbors, have some taco chips smothered in pineapple salsa and get some sleep, eh?"

Mr Marigold put back his mementos; Sannazaro led them up the hill, then made the introductions. Ginevra gave the boy a huge welcoming hug. The Commander noticed the tears welling in her. She hugged Marigold, as well, scolded him for not writing even a postcard.

"That would have been impossible, under the circumstances," he said.

She started, "Alma and Sam had a little girl, even named her after you. Mariah. Seven pounds exactly."

Murillo contemplated the news. Ginevra saw how it made its mark. The full circle, after so many years.

"That's wonderful," he said. "But where are they?"

"That's the strange thing. They were staying at your hacienda until just last week. It happened in the middle of the afternoon."

"What happened?"

"Alvaro saw a white government vehicle pull up. I was getting a facial in town. Two men stepped out. They were deputies of some sort. Alvaro will tell you."

"Where is he, by the way?"

"Sleeping."

"Is he all right?"

"Sleeping with somebody."

"Oh."

"Raquel."

"You're kidding?"

"Hmmm. That's another story. Anyway, we thought Sam had gone and done something stupid, or that you two were in trouble. There were any number of possible scenarios, what with all the news from Hidalgo."

"What news?"

"You haven't been in touch with him?"

"Ginevra, you have no idea where we've been."

"Oh. Well, the good news I guess is that your money has doubled in value."

"The whole town must know of it, then. And the bad?"

"Well, there's a few folks—quite a few, actually ... Remember those news articles before you left, the ones that tried basically to assassinate your character because of the debt-for-nature swap scheme?"

"That was no scheme, but a most legitimate and elegant and, I dare say, practical concept."

"Well, now there's a whole movement against you, and there's been a class action. Poor Hidalgo had to fly back from Europe."

"Hidalgo's in town? By the way, he loves litigation."

"No. He settled the suit and rejoined his wife back in Monaco."

"Settled, how?"

"He counter-sued for frivolous allegations. It went to appeal, all very quickly. A writ mandamus, I believe he called it, 100,000-dollar-a-day fines. Your opponents caved in, lacking a legal fund. Now they thoroughly despise you."

"I have no stomach for this. What shall I do?"

"Relax. Hidalgo says you're now worth even more. Who could ever keep track? And there are no known suits against you. Nobody has the money to launch such legal battles. Except you. Amid the current Internet IPO euphorias. Ups and downs. Additional properties. Fifty subsidiaries, I heard him mumble. What's more, some people don't even believe you exist. Hidalgo wouldn't divulge the details. But I can tell you this: I saw him in action one day and I really think he enjoys making a myth out of you. He wants people to think you're a shell, a dummy corporation of straw based in the Caymans, not a real person. Even the judge was sceptical, evidently. Is that good?"

"Absolutely. He's just trying to protect me. Always has. For that I'm grateful. Has he seen the house? Surely *he* knows where Alma is?"

"That happened after he returned to Europe."

"Tell me more."

"Well, after a while, the men departed, I'm afraid with some documents. You better have a close look around. That night, Alma and Sam left with their baby. We haven't seen or heard from them since."

"Have you been to the house?" the Commander asked.

"Oh yes, in fact I made an attempt to clean things up after they ransacked the place. But it didn't last. I'm very sorry."

"Did Alvaro hear anything? A commotion? I mean, Christ, there's broken white china, luncheon trays, crumb scoops, half the history of Tesuque on that floor, not to mention my mother's pale pink toilet trinket service, smashed in the bathroom. And my father's Alaska household cabinet refrigerator—over a century old—demolished. There's glass everywhere. Did those creeps do it?"

"No. It was Anastasia. Once the house was abandoned, she must have gotten lonely. Your squirrel's inside."

"So we discovered."

"And you've seen how those two love each other."

"Of course. But—"

"Anastasia couldn't find her, probably."

"Ebert has taken up winter residency under the kitchen sink. He carried all the linen, down comforters and pillows with him, after carefully chewing everything into bite-sized dollops for sleeping on. Rather a mess. But you've got to love him for his little industriousness. Quite a clever chap. Voluptuary, I dare say."

"Well, poor you. I was not about to discuss it with Anastasia. She throws her weight around. I do believe she slept one night in your bedroom, another in the kitchen. She was cold, hungry, horny and forlorn. She rubbed herself against every solid post, walked through doors, toppled the books, marked her territory—must have had Yellowstone on her mind—masticated whole rugs, micturated vases' worth, somehow got the radio to work and it annoyed her big time. She tried drinking from the toilet, then managed to lie down on your canopy bed, with the disastrous results you've already discovered. What does she weigh?"

"Five, ten thousand pounds, or is it tons?"

"Well, three days ago she walked off."

"Where?"

"North."

"Could you follow her?"

"Murillo, no, we didn't follow her. She went into the hills. I believe in the direction of Espanola, possibly Chimayo."

"Chimayo?" Marigold mulled aloud. "That would make sense."

"Why's that?" she wondered.

"How big is Anastasia?" Rajibai interjected.

"One and a half times your average Indian water buffalo," Sannazaro pointed out with the bitter grin of a cornerstone anxiety. He well remembered their time together at Chaco Canyon.

"Why Chimayo?" Ginevra repeated.

"I'm not sure," said the Commander. "Just a feeling." He did not elaborate.

"Where's Chimayo?" inquired Rajibai.

"Twenty miles from here, as the New Zealand fantail flies. Pilgrims walk there in a day. You would love it. So would Anastasia, I suspect."

"But what is it?"

"A place of great miracles, lad," Sannazaro began. "I would have to say it is my favorite spot in all of New Mexico, the birthplace of mystical Christianity in North America."

Ginevra's Corsican dog, Negrescu, sat at Rajibai's feet, taking an immeasurable interest in the new kid on the block. After all, the clever canine, forever gaining sympathies, must have elicited a majority of Rajibai's spinach soufflé and hot buttered sourdough by now.

"Please don't feed him any more," Ginevra begged. "He lives to eat. But at night he'll do it on the carpets."

Later, slouching around the fireplace, Ginevra asked casually, "So where have you all been? We were worried."

Sannazaro enumerated the countries with calm disinterest, not about to go there. Why risk a lukewarm response to unimaginably vast events? There was no way, or reason, to expose those transforming moments that had, each one, altered his entire nervous system, uprooted his kneecaps, singularly flattened his wish ever to hold a passport in hands again. The particle physics of his untouchable memory, still fresh, a live-wire of the unthinkable, the inexpressible, the ineffable, were best sequestered in the private pincushions of his own mental monastery, he figured.

Rajibai went for the wine, and it was Sannazaro who suggested he not do that.

"But why, Uncle? You're drinking it."

"Because, Son," Marigold broke in, "here in America alcohol makes people very sick and stupid. It kills babies, causes car wrecks, and anyway, Ginevra probably has lemonade, doesn't she?"

It felt good to exercise the first fatherly prerogative, and he eventually sent the boy home, next door, to get his bed ready. He'd be along soon.

"Are there bears?" Rajibai asked. "And snakes? Or tigers?"

"The bears and snakes are asleep. We have no tigers in America."

"OK." With that he raced out, his new buddy Negrescu by his side. "It's six in the morning in Ireland. I'm turning in as well," exhaled the Squire.

Ginevra and the Commander were now alone near the fire.

"It's wonderful to see you," she applied softly.

"You too."

"You've changed."

"Oh?"

"You're even more handsome."

"Now I know there's something terribly wrong in Tesuque. You're lying."

"It's true. Something about you, Murillo. In your eyes. The long wild hair. Your attempt at a beard."

"That's not my doing."

"And a son! Tell me—how did it happen?"

But before he could begin, there was a huge entanglement outside, Negrescu throwing a major tantrum, and Rajibai screaming with his last ounce of vocal chords.

"*Tiger!*"

CHAPTER 142
El Christo Negro

THEY ALL RAN outside, casting the light of one Eveready on the cornered mountain lion, *Felis concolor*. Its ribcage was visible, the animal staggering. Negrescu was ready to attack, but knew better.

"Oh dear," Ginevra groaned, acutely conscious of northern New Mexico's drought. If it was hard on people, it had stressed a mountain lion to near extinction, or into highways, where it was easy road kill. America had no equivalent of Islamic *haq-i shurb* or "right of thirst" laws, instituted in the *Qur'an* and granting the fundamental acknowledgment (and at least some needed concessions) that all creatures required water, the same as humans, making water holes the responsibility of every land owner.

"The poor thing."

"Father—is it a tiger?"

"Lion."

It probably weighed 70 pounds. It was young and starving.

"Stay back, Son." The Commander turned to Ginevra. "What do you have we can give it? Quickly."

"A bowl of milk. Spaghetti with marinara. Day-old pizza. Two minutes in the microwave."

"What about soy milk and vegan pizza—non-dairy cheese?"

"Oh shut up!"

"All right, just hurry!"

They dimmed the light; Rajibai held tight to Negrescu and backed up. Ginevra raced off, then returned, placing the milk bowl in the middle of the clearing, the food adjacent to it.

"Move away," Marigold urged.

She did so.

Now the weary feline, dizzy, beyond care of additional hazards, staggered up to the cold milk and threw its face into it. Then came pizza, before which it reclined on its trammeled haunches, digging in for good. The onlookers watched, 30 feet away, as it gasped and retched its way through the meal. Dry heaving. Even Negrescu seemed to understand the situation, and sat patiently.

Later came baked tofu. Melted cheese on wholegrain bread.

"It needs a lamb shank, I hate to say it," Sannazaro applied.

Ginevra marched to the downstairs freezer and brought out a 3.5-ounce, 85 milligrams of cholesterol T-bone from Alvaro's stash. The good Father had always devoured his share of blood meal, unconcerned by any rumors of self-destruction or its moral equivalency. Ten minutes in the microwave brought it to pink. But the big cat would have none of it.

"You see! Obviously a Jain monk in an earlier life. All the proof one requires of reincarnation." Marigold went for a pillow, tiptoeing into his hacienda (though the cat did not even bother to watch), and returned with one of the few comforters the squirrel had not pulverized.

"Careful ..." the others whispered.

The Commander showed no fear, no common sense, only urgency to make the cat comfortable. He placed the pillow right under her heavy head.

"We'll call her—for it is a she—'Tiger'. How's that?"

"Lovely," Rajibai exclaimed. "So there *are* tigers in America!"

The next morning, the Commander awoke just before noon to little paws digging into his nightshirt. It was Ebert sleepwalking on his chest and taken to some dopamine-driven dream of a treadmill. Marigold managed to slip from under the covers, putting the little nocturne of fur on his own pillowy platform without waking him, and went to the sun room to check up on Rajibai. But the boy had disappeared. Outside, Tiger was not to be seen, either.

He went next door. Father Alvaro and Raquel were in their pajamas in the kitchen, concocting a breakfast of scrambled eggs and hash browns. Amigo was catching scraps along the floor.

"Allo allo allo!" the champion of salutations hurrah'ed upon seeing his long-lost neighbor. "My God, look who's back from the Sahara, or was it Teebet?"

"Amigo," Raquel ignited warmly, hugging the savior of her chicken. "Look who's back. He always clucks about you, Murillo."

"Listen, you two look marvelous, and very chummy, but have you seen Rajibai?"

"Who?"

"My son. Oh, that's right—you don't know. He's an Indian—East Indian. Eleven. I adopted him in Mumbai."

"Where?" said both.

"Bombay. India. Have you seen him?"

"Have you looked in Bombay?"

"He and the lion are gone."

"Lion?" Alvaro and Raquel threw each other glances, then focused back upon the source of so much nonsense.

"No, Murillo. Haven't seen the lion, the squirrel, your bison, Alma, Sam, their new baby, or your son from Bombay. But otherwise, how are you? Sit, have some ginger tea. Tell us everything. We're madly in love, by the way. I'm giving up the cloth. It's not big enough for me and my erection."

Raquel admitted a naughty grin.

"Later. I need to borrow your car."

"Sure." Alvaro retrieved his keys. "The tank was just filled yesterday."

As Marigold headed to their garage, garage-door opener in hand, Sannazaro walked in from his gardener's chambers in his colorful woolen Santa Fe bathrobe, the kind that kills, as they say in town. "Where's he going?"

"I don't know. He's borrowing my Porsche."

"But he can't drive."

The Commander had already backed out of the compound over an entire bed of narcissus and tulip bulbs being nurtured for spring, and entered Bishop's Lodge Road. They watched as he drove away, beginning an erratic reconnaissance of every dirt side road where his son might be.

In fact, Rajibai had been up for hours, exploring the neighborhood in search not just of Tiger, but also of the legendary Anastasia and a place called Chimayo for good measure. He was still on Asian time.

He'd stolen away from the hacienda just after 7 a.m. Tiger had wandered off earlier in the pre-dawn. The 18-month-old lion, recovering from a hunter's bullet lodged in his hip which made normal predation all but impossible, had moved up the hill to a newly fashioned lair behind a boulder on Camp of the Spirits property. Now he'd be back every night for the remainder of the winter for warm milk and pizza and the company of Negrescu, who had dreamt that night of the blonde bombshell.

Rajibai had gone straight to Marigold's trunk and put on his old school clothes. They rather fit him. He also took a large cluster of bills out of the handbag his father had acquired from a bank. It had been viewed and utilized as communal property by the trio. In fact, Rajibai had never had more than 20 rupees in his pocket at any one time in his life. Money didn't mean anything to him because he'd never had enough to buy more than a soda, or a meager lunch served up along the open trenches of Forlorn. So he had little if any respect for rupees, and none at all for dollars, which to him were play money. The whole culture was play, with its fineries and fancy-spun estates, cars in excess, cleanliness to spare, open, uncrowded thoroughfares, spotless avenues, attention paid to facades. Neither garbage nor the poor. No bullock carts or legless beggars dragging themselves on hand-fashioned dollies. Skyscrapers, well-clad individuals, everybody proffering riches beyond compare.

Yet, for all that, Rajibai sought, but could not find, an animal sociology.

By the time he got out onto the Bishop's Lodge Road which ran past the entrance to the hacienda, the local school bus was chugging around the corner on its way to Espanola for repairs. It being the holiday season, school did not resume for another three days, but when the driver saw Rajibai standing perplexed in his dashing uniform she stopped and opened the door.

"Eager beaver, huh? You're new on the block."

"Yes Ma'am."

"Well, you're in luck. No school till Monday."

"I was wanting to go to a place called Chimayo."

"Chimayo, huh? Half-hour up the road. Your folks know where you're headed?"

"Yes Ma'am."

"Hmm. Well, I can get you to the turn-off, that's pretty close. There's pilgrims all over the place today. It's the new millennium. Lot'a religious stuff goin' on. My name's Bunny, by the way. Hop on."

Bunny had to stop at the Chevron station that adjoined a casino on Indian lands along Highway 68. While she was gassing up, Rajibai thought to wander into the gambling hall and see what all the fuss was about, for there were hundreds of cars parked in the lot. He cashed in a dollar. Played the nickels. Had a windfall, before a reservation cop grabbed him by the collar. But by that time a television above the cash registers inside the Convenience Store had drawn his attention. It was playing a rock video featuring some beautiful naked girl who reminded Rajibai of Anna. Her long hair covered her breasts and she walked towards the camera along a big city street, then cut to her seated upon a screaming subway barreling through the metropolitan bowels, singing in a full-bodied, lilting howl, "Thank You India". Ironies welled up. He stood gawking at this princess whose name he never did catch because Bunny called him back to the bus, apologizing to the policeman for her naughty ward.

Twenty minutes later, she let him off at a junction, following a customary scolding.

Several families were inching aboard the high desert floor, passionate pilgrims—Phineas Foggs and Wandering Jews, some confined to wheelchairs advanced by zealous assistants, an old junketeer handling deftly his dusty cane, another roamer hauling a mahogany cross on his donkey-wide shoulders. The sun warmed their over-burdened backs. It had not snowed in many days.

Rajibai inquired about the destination of the Bedouins, or globetrotters, or whatever they were, roused by the scenery and hobo stream which so suggested to his beady-eyed brain an expedition. Fun. An Hispanic adolescent, probably 16, wearing thick-rimmed glasses, the son of one of the carriers of the 200-pound cross, introduced himself as Hernando and explained how just a couple of miles over the hill in front of them was the Chimayo Valley, where two churches rose up from ancient fields that Indians and later Spanish settlers used to cultivate. Seizing an opportunity to summarize a recent school report, the young man described how the dirt was sacred and healed people of every conceivable disease. How so many men and women and even children—the Tewa Indians, the Hispanic people following de Vargas' reconquest of New Mexico, even the more recent Anglos—had all come to this place for *haber cumplido con el deber*, the fulfilling of one's obligation to Our Lord of Esquipulas, the annual sacred duty of one's own family.

"Who's that?" asked Rajibai, referring to this figure of Esquipulas. "He's from Guatemala," explained Hernando.

"Where's that?" asked Rajibai.

"Central America."

"Oh," Rajibai declared, thinking he must have flown over it on the way from New York. "Is that your Dad?"

"Yes."

"Why's he carrying that statue of a dead guy?" He'd seen them at St Albans, and atop the Irish pyramid.

Hernando, who lived at nearby Nambé, described the legends of el Cristo Negro. Then added, "You're sort of black, too. More and more Negroes have been coming here each year."

"I'm not a Negro," declared Rajibai. "Or I don't think so. I'm from India."

"Well," began Hernando as they continued their walk. "There was a Mayan Indian chief named Esquipulas and he refused to fight with the conquistadors. So in celebration they made this Christ out of a dark wood, and all the Indians now had a Christ that looked like them. That's why in Chimayo they say that the next Christ who comes will be black. Maybe you're the one?"

Rajibai shrugged his shoulders, thinking, *Not again!* "What are conquistadors? Who is Christ?" Other questions flowed from his greenhorn lips.

Hernando patiently instructed this new arrival, then: "Anyway, they had these little cakes of mud at Esquipulas, the town where these Indians and their black Christ lived, you see. We call them *tierra bendita del Santo*: you dissolve the stuff in water, drink them and—Holy Mother! —you're cured. Anything: broken arm, depression, I don't know."

"Rheumatism!" Hernando's grandmother said. She was walking robustly in the front.

"Infertility and heartache," another relative added.

"Bad back, hepatitis C, tinnitus."

"Quadruple bypass," explained Hernando's great-grandfather, Don Diego, who helped shoulder one of the heaviest crosses. "Just look at me. This sucker weighs a couple hundred pounds, I'm 85 years old. A retired physicist from Los Alamos. Every year I come with this same cross: no problem since 40 years ago when my doctor he says, 'Don Diego, you either cut out alcohol, coffee, animal fat and cholesterol, spicy fast food, or your heart it's going to explode and you gonna leave a lot of orphans around New Mexico.' I say I can't live without certain things. Physics, I can live without. But cheese quesadillas, a few tablespoons of superfine sugar, Mexican lime juice, two ounces of gold tequila and a touch of Marie Brizard triple sec, that I shalln't forgo. Gotta shake your life with ice. I should be dead because I'm so stubborn. But guess what?"

"What?" Rajibai stared at him with conviction.

"Hell, just look at these muscles, boy! That dirt over at Chimayo, it's got something. Does it ever. 'Course, the blessings are a corollary. And that Father Coca, a saint, I tell you. Every word from his mouth, listen carefully. I never went to see my doctor again. Eat all the queso fundidos and frescos I want. Wash 'um down with sweet Margaritas, no problem. I'm a happy man. Two acres. Nice house. Cable TV. A good pension. Lots of kids. Too many, if you ask me. Right, Hernando? A fine wife, best potter on the pueblo. My mother, God bless her soul, was a good woman. Now, I was a scientist, and that person may ask: is it really the dirt, or is it faith? Well, it really doesn't matter, does it? Because now I'm a believer. But mark my word, boy: that dirt has got something."

They passed by the remains of dozens of New Year's Eve bonfires, some still smoking: you could smell the pitchwood across the pink granite on Tsi Mayoh hill, the most wild and sacred of the Tewa mountains. Scientists at Yale had analyzed the rocks and the dirt back in the early 1950s.

The Chimayo historian, Borhegyi, had related their findings: some 65 percent of the mud was comprised of silica, another 16 percent alumina, 6 percent iron oxide, and parts thereof magnesia, sodium, potassium and calcium. It was the very same mud that had been utilized for healing purposes and pottery since the twelfth century by the local Indians of the Tesuque, Isleta and Picuris Pueblos. Scientifically speaking, it offered, at best, a moderating influence against indigestion, nothing more. No unique medical properties. But it didn't matter in the least. This was the epicenter of believers. To believe was to substantiate the edifice, a monumentality of the ages, all oriented towards the susceptibility of truth—any truth—to the confines of habit. Habit that was personal, took roots in the community, grew by custom and then tradition, tradition becoming the rule, the rule implacable. Until out of this system of faith emerged the facts that guided whole cultures. Add a dollop of struggle and oppression, spice it with poverty, and one was ripe for a miracle, which could be easily accommodated in such a structure of believing.

Hernando picked up a piece of dirt. It was the pure mud found all over the area. He put it in his mouth and started to eat it. Rajibai did the same.

At that moment Negrescu, who had stubbornly chased the school bus mile after mile, came running up exhausted after his new friend, hoping to find Tiger. It was an inopportune dash up the center median, for a low-rider—for which New Mexico is famed—came screaming over the hill from the opposite direction of Taos, and seemed to strike the poor animal broadside. Negrescu was thrown 20 feet and howled its death knells.

The car skidded to an ugly halt and two heroin junkies, notorious in the area, jumped out and stammered their apologies, but they were in the throes of a high and hardly knew what had happened. They were both packing handguns, and withdrew and aimed them at any would-be critics. But Rajibai's full attention was focused upon the dog, and he was so hopelessly distressed that he vomited the mud he'd been eating all over the animal. He immediately took off his jacket and wrapped the poor canine. Negrescu began to shake violently.

Desperately, failing to hold back a flood of tears, the boy proclaimed a Jain prayer—*Ahinsa Paramo Dharmah*—inciting the way of peace and happiness for the animal which he held in his arms. Twenty people stood around watching as his tears mingled freely with all the blood on his naked chest.

Then something never before seen by anybody happened. The dog, nearly limp by now, its eyes closed, shook itself off, wagged its tail and jumped out of Rajibai's arms as if from a freshwater lake in the Caucasus.

People staggered. The retired physicist and three colleagues dropped their cross and collapsed onto their knees, hands marveling in the numinous air. All proclaimed the supernatural occurrence, hysterically invested in the portent. Here was consummation at last of that which they had always conceptualized and dreamt, in spite of little succor or confirmation, as their way of life. Jesus, come to save them. And such timing! "Dios Mio!" sounded the desert refrain. "Este muchachito es milagroso. Celebremos la segunda llegada de Jesucristo!" All were astounded and ecstatic.

An old woman made the sign of the cross, kissed Rajibai's toes, then invoked the name of Saint Niño de Atocha.

Rajibai himself remained calm. He knew the power of Jain prayer. But Jains did not ascribe to miracles. "It's not a miracle," Rajibai tried to explain. "It's merely the dog's own good deeds."

But nobody paid attention to that, only to the boy's perfect modesty and the fact that he—in concert with the magical mud he'd been ingesting at the time he vomited—brought a dead dog back to life. They surrounded Rajibai, and hailed him for his wondrous doings.

Then Hernando got it in his mind to call him "el Cristo Negro", a refrain all seemed eager to chant.

"El Cristo Negro! El Cristo Negro!"

Don Diego pulled out a bottle of tequila and offered a salutation to the miracle child. Rajibai took hold and proceeded in the heat of the moment to imbibe its total remaining content. His eyes turned to hot coals.

"Wow!" said Don Diego. "A boy who can hold his liquor. That's pretty good!"

Now that striking video he'd seen of a naked girl, along with the uncharacteristically hot winter weather, went to Rajibai's head. And his head, charged with a quart of raw tequila, went to his heels. Add to that the memory of all those girls atop the waterfall, and one could understand why he suddenly took it upon himself to slip out of the Commander's school clothes (they hadn't been washed in 40 years and were definitely festooned with fleas, sidetracked with larvae, aswarm with irritated mites—reason enough to remove them rather quickly; even his boots were filled with mouse droppings) so that he, too, was as naked as any Jain Digambara monk.

Not only did the pilgrims not object, but this show of nudity only encouraged their awe and adulation even more. Hernando folded the suit with the reverence normally reserved for Christ's shroud, and carried the bundle in his extended hands as he and the crusaders—Negrescu and the junkies in tow—continued over the hill towards Chimayo.

CHAPTER 143
The Miracles at Tsimajopokwi

THAT GLEAMING olive-skinned boy, naked as a French fry, whom all assumed to have come *laissez-passer* from Esquipulas, or mystically from Heaven, smeared in blood, his now fully revived dog exuberating beside him, trailed by a happy band of four dozen other transmigrants burning with "el Cristo Negro", their wits juiced up, brain cells astronautolized, every emotion on tap, fickle fanfare flaming the fires, was an uncommon sight. Even the two drug addicts appeared to have instantly gotten religion. They ditched their car by the side of the road, to embrace the little traveling toad as their staunchest ally. Muscles, guns, switchblades in defense of Him. There was Manuel fervently carting an old goosebump of a witch in her painted wheelchair ("Not too fast, Son," applied her elderly husband) and Galegos taking a heavy cross singly on to his own back, Venice Beach style. Shrugs, agonizing peals, the contagion of martyrdom before its divinity.

The procession moved through the stunted juniper, low piñon, with the wide arc of the land thrusting down its glories upon them—the many pronounced peaks of Sandia, Canjilon Tsikomo and the Truchas. As they proceeded into the two-mile-long, quarter-mile-wide Chimayo Valley, watered by the Río Quemado and Santa Cruz Rivers, they passed by caves in which the Tewa Towa'e underworld spirits were rumored to dwell. They continued to the original sacred site known by the local Tewa-speaking Indiansas Tsimajopokwi, the place of the hotpools, with its sacred mud, *nam po'uare*, scattered with ancient black and cream tuffs, biscuit shards, mineral deposits—an entire open-air museum devoted to some sanctity or other. Cynics might bridle, but some things never changed.

An oratorio in honor of San Buenaventura had been constructed nearby in 1751 in the Plaza del Cerro. Visions like those experienced at Lourdes in France (though many years before Lourdes became known) had fired up passers-by for generations, though the Catholic Church of the Santa Cruz parish that controlled Chimayo was never compelled to investigate any of the outlandish tales, in spite of their remarkable frequency. That was before the smallpox epidemic of 1780, which killed hundreds of *paisonos* and preconditioned a miracle or two.

Even in the earliest days, the community and the land were dense with revelation. According to the Isleta pueblo peoples, a sheep farmer one day chanced upon a mysterious figure of a man jutting upright from the quick of a slope. It was none other than a life-like sculpture of Esquipulas. The farmer carried the object home, but his spouse was superstitious about the effigy and wanted it incinerated. Her husband, conversely, wanted it revered. They argued, she took sick, nearly died. Only by supplicating before the image did she recover. Thus originated a pattern.

Among the Picuris pueblo Indians a different narrative arose, but the end result was a shrine to house the image. Scholars like Borhegyi, Kay, Chavez and some of the priests of the Sons of The Holy Family had all tracked the historical accumulation of such occurrences in their respective books. Hundreds of thousands of pilgrims had come from all over the world. There could be no doubting the power of the place.

In 1813 one Father Alvarez had written a letter to the esteemed Vicar General of the Diocese, referring to the fact that for three years a "miraculous Image of Our Lord of Esquipulas" had been situated in a private chapel in Potrero (the region encompassing Chimayo) adjoining the home of Mr Bernardo Abeyta, a *penitente* of Jesus Nazareno. Abeyta had experienced his own shocking epiphany during Holy Week; had witnessed a brilliant display of fireworks, or sheet lightning, emanating from a hole near the Santa Cruz River. Rushing to this pot at the end of the rainbow, he found not gold but the very crucifix of Esquipulas, and a source of sacred mud. The crucifix, which he dug out of the hole, kept shirking all human habitation, preferring instead to remain where the penitent had found it.

Thus it was that permission was granted for the construction of a public chapel on that site. Twenty-seven hundred square feet of continuous nave filled with simple but evocatively painted santos, bultos and reredos.

Above the altar, the Black Christ as originally enshrined in the jungles of Guatemala, embracing all the myriad rainbows of skin color, racial origin and ethnic diversity of His universal flock.

At least one later nineteenth-century cleric, Bishop Lamy of Tesuque, objected. He found the art too primitive. Much of it was created al fresco, on old wooden doors. Pigeons roosted in the spire, shat on the floor.

The wind blew in, snow too. Fortunately, the chapel and metaphysics of Chimayo were outside Lamy's control.

A host of other private chapels sprang up, including the Capilla del Santo Niño de Atocha adjoining the Sanctuario of Chimayo. In this instance, the Holy Child who was worshipped, and whose mud was believed particularly beneficial to children, wandered throughout the valley assisting those in need, wearing out His shoes.

"A little child shall lead them," said the Prophet Isaiah (11:6), and these words were taken to heart. Traversing the ground of such history, their stranger in bare skin and his canine leading the way, the procession grew in size, picking up stragglers and tourists to all sides. Hundreds of visitors had come to spend a few hours at the Sanctuario during the first week of the new millennium, and they were not entirely surprised to see the "little child", el Cristo Negro, walking naked into town. In Chimayo, anything can happen, and usually has.

Rajibai, who was enjoying the occasion, had not yet reached the church, where something else was also going on. There, the resident Fathers were debating what to do about the gigantic bison who had entered the Sanctuario, crossing over the small cemetery courtyard, past the narthex where the beaverboard was stuffed with offerings—pictures, graffiti, the odd driver's license revoked for drunkenness, love letters to the Lord, diaries: a kind of Wailing Wall of local obeisance. Now, the beast had taken up a position inside the main nave and sacristy. A hundred people sat paralyzed with the beauteous sensation of the bison in their midst. It stood, four hooves planted firmly on the old wood, between the two rows of pews, and had arrived for reasons no one disputed: after all, it, too, was black, and its animal nature somehow fitted right in among the many mythical animals rendered by the three great artisans of Chimayo—Jose and Miguel Aragon, and Molleno, the chili painter.

Imagine the scene: a huge buffalo standing in the center of the 184-year-old chapel, observing all the Mexican woodcarvings gilded in gold, studiously peering at each red-on-white reredo, sniffing the florals, and gazing upon the many provocative bultos while the growing surge of faithful looked on. There was San Antonio, and nearby, the Virgin. On one panel a depiction of baby shoes, on another San Rafael holding a fish, or Señor de Santiago dressed as a Mexican *caballero*; other wooden banners with tin decorations; an embroidered sun; the crucifix of Our Lord Esquipulas directly behind the altar, done in Champagne green and adorned with golden leaves; a statue representing the Holy Child of Prague; San Miguel on a dragon; San Geronimo with trumpet and lion; and San Francisco de Asis carrying the cross of Jerusalem.

Looking down at the great furry behemoth, with her ochre-tinged mane of the softest mohair, her enormous darkly scanning eyes, the strange beguiling crook in her head, feminine nostrils exhaling the palpable mist of a massive churning neurology—mental images, instincts, impulses aswarm—was a reredo by Molleno of Jesus with his five wounds, an arm of Christ crossing that of St Francis, the Cross of the Holy Sepulchre in Jerusalem, bunches of grapes, stalks of wheat (the bread of the Last Supper), and Miguel Aragon's white dove (the Holy Ghost) adjoining a Santa Teresa. All these constellations of art greatly appealed to the animal, or so it seemed to the multitude who uttered not a word, watching her every tentative move. She was a charmed beast, and the church was most assuredly the better for her presence, even though a sign on the door read: "No Animals Allowed Inside". From her nostrils issued a tranquillity that kept the entire mass of visitors in thrall.

Then, something went dreadfully awry. Anastasia caught sight of a painting done on buffalo hide! Digging her horns into the wooden panel, and with mighty snorts and fearful frissons, like a steam monster she ignited, stirring considerable consternation among the worshipful. The Fathers called the police, and people fled the church. Sirens blazed. Those presently in the sacristy, a back room adjoining the main nave where the custom was to stand in the ankle-deep pit and take away a bag or two of the dirt, were trapped.

At that moment, the huge procession arrived from over the hill. The Sanctuario, which had become a National Historic Landmark in 1970, after its purchase for 6,000 dollars 41 years earlier, was now the site of the greatest show of chaos in recent New Mexico history. Not since the *Treaty of Cordova* on August 24, 1821 that freed Mexico from Spain, and thus opened up the Santa Fe Trail for trade, or the annexation as an American Territory of all of New Mexico in 1850, which saturated an ancient cultural hegemony with an explosion of sardines, tomato soup and sewing machines, had there been such confusion consolidated in one place, at the same moment.

Don Diego and his great-grandson Hernando, as well as dozens of others, were proclaiming the miracle of el Cristo Negro, and the frisky Negrescu was living proof. There was nothing the Fathers could do to prevent the naked boy from entering church, and they were all the more impressed to see Manuel and Galegos, the town hoodlums, following him. For Rajibai, this was all part of the New World, a grand drama that had begun the moment Mr Marigold comforted him at Climacus Hospital in Mumbai. His friends Stephanos and Finian would have loved Chimayo, he thought.

Then he saw the buffalo. There was only one word that came to him: "Anastasia!" which he uttered in so kindly and inviting a manner as to impact the great beast's enormous ears with the gentlest of reminders.

She turned and faced the boy. "Anastasia!" he repeated.

All watched the Second Miracle, for the justifiably maddened bison now walked up to the naked boy, whom she had never seen in her life, and—recognizing her own name with all its wonderful associations and the countless taste treats that always accompanied its utterance—sat down with huge effort at his feet. Rajibai could not have been more delighted. Father was right, he thought aloud; "You *are* bigger than our water buffaloes back home." He sat on the bison's back and lay his face in the mane, luxuriating in the jungle of soft fur, stroking her with a pent-up affection that now burst, and feeding her M&Ms which he had obtained back at the gas station. Chocolate hit the love-in spot. The two creatures stared into each other's incredibly doting eyes. Love such as has rarely swept this Earth flowed between them, and people wept to see it. The boy and the bison beneath an image of Blaise, patron saint of all wild animals, where Anastasia had wisely chosen to seat herself after her one outburst—27 pounds of manure, 45 quarts of expelled methane gas.

Even the policemen, arriving with their guns unholstered, were deeply moved, and all looked up in that direction normally associated with the Lord and blessed Him for this deliverance. It was a day to remember.

Finally, Father Coca dispatched his tidings before Rajibai and begged forgiveness for his own sins, and those of all the Faithful, and asked with trembling resolution whether His arrival on this day was, in fact, the Second Coming of the Lord.

Rajibai, who had been all through this a week before, began to have serious doubts as to the mental stability of Christians worldwide. What was this Second Coming? Was it like a Second Chance? Second helpings at dinner time? Or Second Place? And what about Thirds, Fourths and Fifths? Was it just for Christians, or could Jains, Hindus, Moslems, Buddhists and Jews also have seconds?

Hearing something about the damage done to Saint Santiago, Rajibai immediately knew what would get Anastasia off the hook on that one. He asked Hernando, who still held his clothes, to look inside one of the pockets and remove whatever money was there. Hernando did as he was told and handed the large wad of 100 dollar bills to Rajibai, who in turn gave all the money to Father Coca.

The Father counted it. "Holy Jesus!" he muttered. "Twenty-five thousand dollars!"

"Take it. My donation," el Cristo Negro replied.

Father Coca passed out, or acted out an equivalent melodrama such that he fell onto the floor. The two bullies who'd seen the light helped him onto a bench. He winked at them.

Now there was more weeping, mostly among those connected with the parish who'd been pressing for a new roof. It had not been repaired since 1873.

An hour or so prior to this spouting jugular of marvelous mayhems, Sannazaro had gone after the Commander in a second vehicle, caught up with him just off Bouquet Lane in Pojoaque, and the two had proceeded together in Alvaro's Porsche. Presently the two of them had arrived, both in their pajamas.

"Anastasia! Rajibai!" the cries poured forth. "Son, you're bleeding! What have they done to you?"

"I'm jolly good, and having a really excellent day. And what a *wonderful* buffalo, Father. You were right again!"

It was at this peculiar junction of emotional outpourings and even stranger phenomena that—from high above, their silhouetted shapes blinding to the eye against the harsh winter sun—five large choppers descended, setting down behind the church where parish lands were farmed for more than 100 varieties of chilies, apricots and corn. The local policemen got onto their radios. They had no idea what was going on, or who had called in the big boys. The last time anything like this had happened a low-flying flotilla of Army choppers had been scanning (ineffectively) for drugs—a coordinated effort by Joint Task Force Six from Fort Bliss at El Paso, the Army surveillance team from Fort Polk, Louisiana, and a local Indian Law Enforcement Agency.

Two of the cops worked to control the crowd, which had turned into a seething cauldron of perhaps 500 holy rollers. Anastasia gymnasticated in dangerous circles, leapt airborne à la Picasso, so excited was she to be reunited with the Commander. Her tongue was wagging, her hind legs kicking as in Chaucer springtime. The other officer ran off towards the choppers, gun raised. He knew something very heavy had to be going down. A heroin bust, he figured. But why the dozen individuals, unarmed, covered in large white space suits, some in helmets, others mylar nets, their hands in gloves and holding devices of some sort—Geiger counters?

A new manner of handling evidence? They were rushing towards the church from their choppers whose rotors continued to turn, kicking up considerable dust. Anastasia winced and made to panic.

At the same moment, a dozen unmarked vehicles with makeshift flashing lights came squealing into the crowded parking lot. Now the great wild oxen, *B. bonasus*, revered in Pliny, once hailed as the Urus of Caesar, roaming from Lithuania's forests to the rocky British Isles, even into the tropical scrub of Florida, reached its boiling point. Sweat poured off its brow. All this commotion was really too much for any buffalo to bear. Amid the bedlam the cross-eyed Anastasia raced off towards the adjoining cliffs of Tsi Mayoh Hill, in whose mysterious escarpment were several caves sacred to the local Indians. On her back, but facing the wrong way, was the naked East Indian, and making svelte pursuit was the healthily barking Corsican hound, Negrescu, no behavioral indication to suggest that an hour before it had been creamed by an ultramarine '55 Thunderbird.

There, further behind and panting to catch up, two old geezers of indomitable Italian and Spanish inheritance, shambling in their wrinkled PJs just catty-corner to that crazy canine and berserk bison.

CHAPTER 144
Corn Hard Boy and the Bad People

Oremus, oremus
Angelitos somos
A pedir aguinaldos.
(We pray thee
Know that we are but angels
And from heaven we've just come)

IN THE VENERABLE village of Chimayo, thousands of stirred-up Catholic faithful watched these frenzied gambols. Devotees were rightly convinced that el Cristo Negro had conferred on them ordinations without precedent—this, his most timely visitation given the hoopla of the millennium. Contrary to the television images of a few nights before, so many monotonous glees suggesting that the human species was good only for dancing, fireworks and mass pandemonium, here was proof that our demeanor might collectively enshrine some other capacity, born of faith in God.

All fables lead to the same moral, sway to a similar tune, press equally delicate crown ferns and hooded orchids between identical pages of verse, are remembered for all comparable reasons, remarked the good Father Coca, upon regaining his composure after the high emotions of the morning. For some, it is a moral dilemma he went on, for others, a categorical imperative. "Our grandchildren will speak of this day," he imagined, already reminiscing about the boy and his buffalo by early afternoon. A sprawling crowd— hemmed in by dozens of patrol cars and helicopters, assault forces, spacemen, an expectant and confused cacophony of raised rifles, flashing lights, cell and radio telephones— heard the Father reiterate blessings which, he declared, should fairly change the very fiber of American civilization. All those paramilitary added grist to the logic of a Pontius Pilate in their midst.

"I foresee a great canonization," Father Coca went on, referring both to the darkling boy and his heaving beast. Before long, the events in question had occurred a century before, to hear him mythologize the occasion. The miracle, the healing of the dog, had been viewed by dozens of people. Now many of the paintings inside the Sanctuario appeared to be weeping milk. No more suburban cynicism; an end to violence, break-ups among families, vices and sins. This was the moment all of southwestern spirituality had hung its hopes upon: that articulation of the unseen and ineffable. A UFO-caliber event in the very matrix of the church. For the faithful of Chimayo, it was the windfall they had never dared dream. Coca, who had presided over the Sanctuario for nearly 55 years (five generations of roosting pigeons—he knew them all), had achieved much fame in his day, but nothing to match this ... this culmination! His speech completed, he sat on the bench in the front courtyard, reflective, his wide eyes weeping. His slate had been wiped clean, given to an ensemble of hallelujahs. "I am reborn unto you, Lord," he cried exhaustively, then took a great swig of Merlot from a coveted bottle nearby.

"Who are you people?" shouted two local policemen standing on the field of choppers.

A man flashed a badge indicating some National Security Agency affiliation. "We need you to help us contain that mob," he asserted above the din of the rotors. "It's them we're after—" and he gestured up on the mountain to Marigold and company.

To come anywhere near that mountain, Tsi Mayoh, with its lethal escarpments and the one legendary cave in particular where no mortal dared venture, was to enter the pure and forbidding world of Tewa spirit, a pantheon of living attributions, talismans and razzle-dazzle deities, all arrayed in a tenebrous confine of Dalmation granite scalloped with feldspar, mica and quartz. A place remote enough and unknowable. Dwelling mysteriously therein, chimed local Tewa elders, was their ow'a, or priest, whom they named *agoyonohusendbie*, a "star-dark old man-his-child" who was a reincarnation of himself, century after century. How these quantum physics worked, only the oldest of the old apparently knew. And their dark-blue quivering lips were sealed. Such dimensions were even more obscure than those motivating the churchgoers down below.

Not even the most reckless of local teenagers risked the wrath of the toothless crones, stepping nowhere upon that great hill of ancestors. Hence, no graffiti had ever been smeared on the cave walls, or condoms left in any of the suitably lubricious hideaways abase the cliffs. No off-road motor trails or raucous bonfires. While warlords sold cocaine down in the village square and late-night bars boasted of a steady clientele of gang members, Tsi Mayoh was forever blacked out, rising unquestioned above. Had shaped up centuries before, inviolate bounty in its granitic bowels.

But to what ends were such caves and shamans disposed in this modernizing era when belief in trickster coyote who became a governor, or little prairie dog transformed into python girl, had so waned? What ancient insights or remedies might be counted on to deliver the same punch in an age of N' Sync, CISCO, Time Warner and BMG? a teenager might ask. Could the new enemies be combated, or neighbors reasoned with, when they no longer spoke the language of the dream? mused an old Indian along the willowed sandbanks of the Rîo Quemado. When their heads were filled with AM/FM noise, internet icons, the diesel-infested roar of pickup trucks, the alternating current of Bingo parlor lights, of low-riders angling towards their game of Chicken, and vengeance easily spelled out in the form of a gun in one's hand? voiced a school teacher at a nearby pueblo.

He shouldered the community's coming-of-age, without the slightest show of it. Unheralded, holding down the fort, he was the rampart of Indian culture. The glue and the aroma. Every tribe depended upon him, in one guise or other, for its pedigree. Without the rituals and wisdom of the shaman, Indians could claim no lasting distinction from white men. All descended from Siberia, moved southwest, or southeast—didn't matter—10,000 or 40,000 years ago—also of little consequence. What mattered was the fateful fork in the migration 7,000 years before: one path led to unadorned Tsi Mayoh; the other to Anatolian Catal Huyuk. Many moons following these primordial itineraries, say historians, the world witnessed the collapse of matriarchy, of Ice Age spirituality and wildness in mind, ingredients of the human spirit soon replaced by an anonymous rampage through time that led directly to the florid debaucheries of the massively male Vatican, and in the East to the 90-story towers of Shanghai and the megalomaniacal palaces of Saddam Hussein.

And spoiled brats glued to their computers. And corporate farming devastating the bovines, the soil, the rivers and air. To 140,000 rapes per year in the United States. Nearly two million Americans in jail. Hundreds of global civil wars. To Armageddon in all forms. And not a single Earth Disparaging Law to protect against the death of Nature herself.

For many months ago yonohusendbie had been somberly discussing this sordid state of affairs with a nine-inch-wide black beetle sporting rhinoceros-sized pincers, who resided deep in tsin gwake, the sheer cliff. While most people in North America were looking to see how the Dow and Nasdaq and the presidential primaries would shape up, and whether *American Beauty* would steal the Oscars, the ow'a and the beetle were deeply concerned about this looming 'thing' that actually mattered: whether the moon cheese storm was coming.

"You mean, of course, the *hawinwemba t'owa*, or bad people?" reflected the beetle.

"Precisely," replied the priest, who had dug his fingers in the poshu, that miraculous black dirt of Tsaewa'unge (his name for Chimayo, which black beetle called home, as well), and looked into the fibrous dark to divine the horizon, with its two angles of option: the one, a massive destruction; the other, a hand of deliverance.

On this day, ow'a was especially anxious: beetle had opined a third possibility, beetling itself into a rapid spin within the center of a circle of bones, and uttering a faint cry, as slight to human ears, or altogether inaudible, as a wan sigh from the sullen somnambulance of Earth. And what was it? A supernal reverberation signaling a coming conspiracy of denials, a rush towards disintegration, a series of humiliating masquerades by the power élite, dangerous falsehoods and flashfloods. In other words, a great evil coming up the mountain.

A circle of bones. Which bones? In this case camels, fragments from 14 southwestern Miocene species, over 20 million years old, which littered the Tesuque Formation of the Rîo Grande rift, as well as other bones of kae, ke, kuyo (mountain lion, bear, wolf) and of old men and women who had come to the cave—a kind of rocket ship—by which to move on. A faint cry? The sound of alarm seasoned with prophetic powers, honed over hundreds of millions of soil-browsing beetle years, requiring in man only the patience and cultivated sensitivity to pick up the frequencies and detect the clear-as-day expressions in the beetle's animated face. Morning, noon and night ow'a had stared with all his own considerable powers into that face until a microscopic width of tarsal hair appeared to him as wide as a phone book, its eyes as large and compassionate as a whale's, its language as percussive and evocative as any Tewa lullaby.

What the beetle—this grandfather worm—harkened was a foreboding, meticulously presented by the grandest prosecutorial eloquence of all: vibrations in the central web of cause-and-effect, monads and billiard balls (to coin an astrogeophysics) of biodiverse purposes, actions, peril and resurrections whose medium, of course, was the soil, with its quadrillions of micro-organisms and larvae conducting the varied messages, heartbeats and caveats. These diverse injunctions were anatomically consolidated in the beetle, and the priest was able to translate. That's how it appeared to work.

So that the priest was not entirely surprised by the sight of that two-headed *kopo/pinangkwa* (buffalo/boy), or *potseyi seno* (Yellow Water Old Man), or *potsa'we seno* (Blue Water Old Man), or for that matter Running Dog (Negrescu).

They arrived together at the foot of the cave amid a swarm of fireflies, whose bodies were busily oxidizing luciferin to produce an uncharacteristically bright glow for this time of day, and the presentiments of thunder in the darkening sky.

"*Stop!*" Marigold cried, his lungs clawing at available oxygen.

The indigo-eyed ow'a, clad in a manta and man's skirt shortly-wrapped, and adorned in beads of jaclaw, living in his premonitory mosaic of earth-moving thoughts and traces, nodded agreeably at his visitors, the first humans in many years. He then carefully removed a withe of spindled parrot feathers from a 'killed' olla before him. The ceramic pot, known as Sakona, was what archeologists call a red slip, black-on-cream polychrome. The priest had drilled a hole in the pot's bottom, thus killing it. But this was altogether ordained in that it allowed, evidently, for the transmigration of souls. Ow'a shook the feathers. The beetle had already told him that these visitors were *hiwanin t'owa*, good people, but that they would soon be followed by the bad.

Rajibai slid off Anastasia, who walked up to the priest and licked his hand with his massive tongue. The ow'a venerably squeaked, a quarter-giggle, and blessed the bison by shaking the parrot feathers three times upon her colossal head—a kind of knighthood, Marigold reckoned; then he did the same with the quiet and compliant dog as well as each of three humans. He then motioned them to come into the cave, where a small fire was smoking, and to sit round the circle of bones. The cave was large enough even for the buffalo.

They sat in the quiet measure of their palpitating heart muscles. Agoyonohusendbie stared hard at Rajibai, then declared, "Kupishare!" As he at first spoke no English, and none of the trio Tewa, they could not know that he had said "Corn Hard Boy" or w hat it boded. To Sannazaro, ow'a said appreciatively, "T'a sendo," meaning "Sun Old Man"; and to Marigold he whispered, "Hewemboharahi!", which translated as "Elder Brother". The priest's calmly configured intrigue with his guests countered their sudden terror, as a dozen spacemen surrounded the cave entrance. They had climbed after Marigold and company with frightening resolve, and now stood in vast juxtaposition to the cave and its innocent inhabitants. Their leader held a megaphone. Half a dozen others raised Geiger counters into the shadows.

"Mr Murillo Marigold?" the lead spaceman inquired in a voice of oblique authority.

"Yes?" the Commander replied in kind.

"Sorry to spoil your day, and I hope we haven't scared you—these suits tend to make eyebrows incline a little. We're with the National Security Agency, sir, and have strict orders from Washington to get you, the boy there—I presume that's Rajibai Jain—and you sir, Mr Sannazaro—we don't have a first name for you: all of you are to come with us for your own protection. We have helicopters waiting." He looked at the priest. "Who's that?" he said.

"He's a local. He lives in this grotto."

"That's all right. Nice to meet you, sir," the spaceman said with an almost believable humility. "You can call me Bob. Now then, if you'd all be so kind—" and he gestured away.

"Kindness comes in many forms, friend. Perhaps you could tell us what you propose? I would hope it's a good one because you've certainty created a disruption here."

"Sir—" Spaceman Bob withdrew from a pocket under the billowing sleeves of his cumbersome suit some sort of official-looking document, which he presented to Mr Marigold. His badge was already out and pinned to his suit. "I have instructions to take the three of you in that helicopter and to get you post-haste to a laboratory at Los Alamos for questioning."

"Questioning? At Los Alamos? City of the Damned? How thrilling. I've always wanted to tour that legendary facility. Questioning about what?"

"I'm not at liberty to say."

"Well you better say, especially dressed like that, or I'll tell you what: you can take a hike, take a piss and pass Go, whichever comes first," Sannazaro declared, emboldened. He never did take kindly to bureaucrats.

At that moment Anastasia emitted a big one in front of the spaceman. In a buffalo, flatus is almost visible. It gets inside you, like bitter almond, or cyanide potassium gas, even through a spacesuit, and remains for hours. Similarly, buffalo patties can wipe out red tussock, sitting there impervious to weather for a century.

"Damn!" the priest said in recognizable English, clearly impressed.

"That's our pet buffalo, and that's our dog, and I don't care who you are, or what this is all about, we're not leaving them," the Commander advised one and all.

"Sir, I'm afraid you don't grasp the legal protocol here. Your constitutional rights are essentially nullified under security circumstances, as draconian as that may seem. I didn't make the rules. One way or the other, you're coming with us."

The Commander was not intimidated. "I know that if you take another step in the direction of Anastasia, you and your pals will certainly learn a thing or two about gravity. When she passes gas like that it means she's nervous and getting ready to stand up and make her move. Trust me: you don't want Anastasia losing her temper in confined quarters like this. I believe you probably witnessed the speed of which she is capable."

"Mr Marigold, we know where you live on Bishop's Lodge Road in Tesuque. I can arrange for the state troopers down there to escort them back along the highway. The dog can ride in the car."

"Where do they train you people? You think you can walk a buffalo like it's some French poodle?"

"If you prefer, I'm sure we could get it into one of the choppers and set it down right in your back yard.

How's that?"

"She's not an *it*, and I don't think so. Listen, fellows, if this is about my boy being naked, and everyone thinking he's Christ, let me assure you such things are all in the minds of the believers."

"Sir, we have not come for religious reasons. Here's a blanket for the boy. Where are his shoes?"

"Not until you tell me what is going on."

Seeing the rising blood pressures all around, the priest started chanting in a melodious voice, a flute-playing timbre of elusive and atavistic origins, while he pushed the smoke of the pinion fire towards the good people with his fingers ... "P'in pinu oving sokhuwa," he began. Then he continued in perfect English, so that all the bad men could hear it: "Learn the lesson of the tame animals and children who have come here, all those little people loved by the gods and great mothers. The ones that come as gently as the fog, their sound-breath reaching to the heart."

"We have to go," Bob decreed.

"They told you they don't want to go. Now you're on Indian land," adamantized the priest in persuasive English, his own heart marching to a drumbeat. "I have legal responsibility for this hill and all who dwell upon it. The equivalent of your Fire Marshal, or State Senator, or Chief of Police, whichever you prefer. Now it's part of our pueblo, which makes you dudes trespassers. So I think you better leave. I got a cell phone here—" and from the thick of all those skeletal memorabilia he brought forth his little satellite device "—and I could bring 20 tribal police here before you'd even have time to shit in those pantaloons of yours. What's it going to be, fellas?"

"Sir, we mean no disrespect, but Indian lands are legally irrelevant when national security is involved."

"Yeah, my people have only heard that line for about 500 years. It don't hold water no more. You're in our nation now. And we got our own security."

Rajibai took in the verbal ballistics with his unflappable sense of impending excitement—another 'international situation', as he'd become accustomed to thinking of them.

"The truth is, we didn't intend to come up here, but it don't rightly matter where we conduct our business. You go ahead and call whomever you like. In the meantime, I will advise you that we are armed. I just did not think it prudent to reveal our guns in the presence of the boy. I can assure you, we mean you no harm whatsoever. In fact, Mr Marigold, it is the opinion of the Agency that you, the boy and your colleague there may well be national heroes of sorts."

"Heroes, huh. And you're still not going to tell us what this is all about?"

"I'll bet it has to do with the time travel stuff," Rajibai inferred. "Quiet, lad." Marigold was thinking.

"Time travel? Now what might he be referring to?" asked Bob the spaceman. "Perhaps your whereabouts the week prior to that daring rescue by the Irish Navy? Because, frankly speaking, our satellites lost you for 48 of those hours."

That's not good, Sannazaro mused to himself, keeping up the silly facade of a grin but mightily disturbed inside. He stared at the Commander with a conspiratorial question-mark of a face.

Mr Marigold considered all of the above, and knew that this was not about the enthusiastic crowd below or their belief in Rajibai's Second Coming.

Anticipating his train of thought, the head spaceman declared, "We had you in our surveillance cameras over India, sir. Now perhaps you understand the situation a little more clearly."

"India, huh?" the priest conjectured, off on his own speculations. "If we refuse to come with you, what, you're going to shoot us?"

"No, sir, there would be too much paperwork to fill out, in that instance." Bob smiled. "But I might then have to point out that the Central Bureau of Investigations, the CBI—India's equivalent of the FBI—has lodged a complaint regarding your ... how best to put it—" And thinking twice about saying it out loud, he whispered into Marigold's ear: "The Indian Government believes you have kidnapped the boy there."

"That is an outrageous lie!" the Commander apoplexed. "I went through the proper channels, and made the appropriate donations."

"You have the receipt and certified stamps of approval to prove it?"

"The receipt, sir, was lost in the jungles."

"But you could surely have a notarized copy sent to you?"

"Yes. There was an officer of the law in charge of the proceeding."

"Hmmm." He mulled that over for a moment, then continued, "My sources, which are pretty good ones, including the CBI, the State Department, the FBI, and the officer I believe you're referring to, all say sorry, Charlie."

"This is outrageous."

"What is it, Father?" Rajibai asked, beginning to get spooked.

"It's all right, Son."

Now Sannazaro got the drift of these exchanges as well, and concluded, "Maybe it would be a good idea to talk over these matters with Hidalgo, and to go along with them to Los Alamos, Murillo? It's just over there."

"Ten minutes' flying time, gentlemen."

The Commander was furious. He felt the incendiary longing to use his good fortune—his money, that is—to demolish the corrupt and inveigling system which seemed to him to have eyes and to have invaded their privacy all along. Not just theirs: for now he understood that Namgyal and Anna, and Anna's tribe, could not be long for this world under such all-invasive scrutiny from above. At least the young Finian was safe, 1,000 years before them. To be back there again ... Already the Commander was daydreaming of his return to the isolated pyramid, or to the waterfall, or a mountaintop in Toda Land, not unaware of the odd paradox that his reverse timepiece of a personality, this Corot among cows, had unleashed a most frustrating perpetuity of ever-unfulfilled yearnings, the grass always greener far behind him, with every forward step.

He knew what these bastards wanted. They were no different from their Russian and Indian counterparts, the gene cannibals. If he did not go along with them, for the time being, all those blessings which had showered the trio in recent weeks and months might be reversed, and much worse.

"How long will this questioning take?" Marigold asked, ready to resign to their dilemma but flip the logic, if only he could figure out how.

"A day, a night, perhaps a few days, no more."

"What about that CBI nonsense?"

"I'm sure all can be forgiven and forgotten, in the group spirit of cooperation."

"I am here," said the priest in a resolving tone, and he recited another chant: "Life long, now, we ask to be loved; we children people grow up, good fate to us given."[20] The priest nodded at the trio, their dog and buffalo. Anastasia, remaining calm, clearly understood. It would be all right.

Mr Marigold realized wisely that he had no other options at the moment. Anastasia was seduced by extraordinary means (sugar cubes which the cops always kept on hand) into the cargo hull of a chopper, and flown back to the hacienda where she was left with a considerable stash of goodies and the companionship of her long-time buddy Ebert. Negrescu was similarly coaxed and given to his devices at the Camp of the Spirits, where he would sit up all night waiting for Tiger.

Corn Hard Boy, Father and Uncle were escorted down the slopes from the cave by the spacemen. They circumvented the waiting multitude of churchgoers, many of whom were now convinced that an Area 52 Government cover-up was in full swing. Some got into their cars or recreational vehicles and attempted to track the choppers, which lifted off in formation from the wintry fields beneath the Sanctuario, heading north, then circling left towards the western fringes of the Los Alamos complex across the valley.

Hernando, Don Diego, Manuel and Galegos all looked with sad, frustrated wonder at the disappearing choppers. They knew, along with the holy father of Chimayo, that the Christ of Esquipulas had come into their midst for an afternoon and was now probably being subjected to horrible dissections by the Government. Typical. But there would be an agreeable outcome: apostles fanning the flames, a revival across northern New Mexico even now shaping up to be the best reason for another church, more donations, sinecures, the commission of a few more frescos, and an order from Rome confirming the miracle. There was nothing like an ordination to increase the number of pilgrims. And martyrdom was the best thing a religion could ask for, guaranteeing membership, votes, money, adherence.

An icon painter would render the sacred bison upon which the magical boy had ridden up that wild mountain.

And in the cave abase Tsi Mayoh, a fire would continue to burn for the spirits of those five unlikely visitors for all time, watched over—like the rest of the world—by the ow'a.

CHAPTER 145
City of the Damned

LOS ALAMOS—"the poplars" in Spanish—is a town that for years had tried hard to deny its true purpose; to fit neatly, at least from the illusion of a safe distance, along that legendary ridge down below which the Indians of Bandelier had made their sovereign homes in the cliffs for so many centuries, and where the Commander and his Squire and Madame Vignette had once reveled in the Cave of the Dragonflies and seen to the heart of all Essences. It was among these mountains that peoples propelled by nothing more complicated than the desire for sage, or flax, made migratory journeys out along the wide windy rims in search of new friendships and trading partners, a spouse and far horizon, season after season.

Animals cavorted with a telling density of biological glee up amid these 8,000-foot peaks, mountains of endless germination. Forests blushing with 10,000 berries, roots and tubers; deep sylvan enclaves of fir glistening beneath a million snowfalls; meadows adrift in all the hues of the mountain bluebird, common whitetail and stink beetle; carpenter and honeybees wafting across the table mesas with prolific freedom, pollinating pods of every Epicurean description.

Wandering freely with an equal equipoise, the human ones who left their record of enthralled ramblings upon each square inch of sandstone down every canyon wall.

The flute-playing anthropomorph inscriptions upon cliff were modeled, in White Rock Canyon, for example, after the vast flocks of sandhill cranes which make these alpine ranges their stopping grounds. Tewa gods of countless varieties populated the crannies—Rabbit Prince, Lizard King, Coyote Regent. In hundreds of thousands of lazy doodles and informed descriptions; encoded with the alphabet of Nature by Indians hundreds of years before, where every page could be read and transcribed from generation to generation, was a petroglyphic renaissance.

The pictorial ease of expression which dominated these nameless societies, peoples in touch century after century with the southwestern breezes and the ripening dogwood, with tallow and kaolinite in their tea and the humility to know when and how to die, would have no impact on the successor species, which preferred to forget they ever lived, no Mormon genealogies on microfiche.

But all that brilliant evolution, whether in the porcupine's slow doddle or the insistent punctuation marks of a woodpecker, would be transmogrified into the application of Lord Science in the twenty-first century as the one bogus mouthpiece for the myriad phenomena of Mother Earth. Here, where the flotillas of helicopters presently circled their landing pad, science had been catapulted into a net of powerful atom-smashing perversions destined to shatter the innocence of all previous times. Fires out of control. Nuclear weapons. Stealing of secrets, hiding of computer discs. Espionage and disaster. The world never the same.

That this alteration in the space/time continuum of the human psyche should have occurred within the same square mileage atop that ridge overlooking Bandelier, and within so short a period as a century bodes of the very worst in a species' devolution. Separating the world-loving sentience of the last resident Indians from those sinister soldiers who flocked to this remote outpost under the secret covenants of the Manhattan Project was a mere 100 years of hubris and conflagration. In terms of duration, the life of one parrot, the childhood of a sturgeon, the mere inception of a sequoia seedling. But here, in the space of a few decades, Hell had masqueraded in the name of 'national security'.

A town of some 20,000, with more PhDs and rifle-toting militia per capita than any other human community on the planet.

The trio and their armed escorts landed in an obscure field beside a series of underground laboratories never talked about, near the heavily contaminated TA-55 area, the most notorious of Los Alamos National Laboratory's toxic legacies. A contingent of suited scientists was there to greet them. Security was unabashed, even by LANL standards.

"This way, please, gentlemen," the awaiting head administrator, Dr Rush Limborn, volunteered with a demeanor of utmost courtesy and bloviation. "Remember people, no touching. No handshaking."

The Commander whispered an innocuous exchange with Rajibai, "Everything'll be fine. Just do as I say," he said. And he issued thumbnail instructions: "Tell them nothing."

"What should I say?"

"You tell them the jungle was filled with buggers. No mention of a tribe. Tigers and centipedes, that is all, got it?"

They winked at each other. It was lovely to think that conspiracies could pass that simply and unnoticed in so monolithic a surveillance chamber. One could have been muttering Chinese, and they wouldn't have caught it.

They breezed past the Corridor of Zombies, where the conventional physicist's den and stuffed academician's covey of stacked research papers and rows of fat incomprehensible books gave way to a far more rigid defense posture of architecture, sealed rooms, bland shiny vaults that could be opened only by voice and fingerprint recognition, and an elevator leading into a marvelous mine shaft of isolation. All decorated with foremost Institutionalism.

Rajibai found the whole journey immensely entertaining. Metallic causeways, secret passages, skinny dickheads in black jumpsuits bearing arms... They passed the bizarre entranceway to the X-2 Group's clean room, devoted to the mathematics of thermonuclear reactions. Here was the vaunted citadel of many of the lasting names associated with The Bomb—Meitner, Hahn, Strassman, Fermi, Wigner, Oppenheimer, and their Major General, Leslie Groves. Therein lay the operations center for such notorious research experiments as 'The Sunshine Project' of the 1950s in which tons of animal corpses and children's skeletons from countries all over the world were secretly imported for purposes of studying the effects of radiation on life forms. Only recently had the full brunt of such research come to the attention of the American public, when Energy Secretary Hazel O'Leary demanded that all 32 million previously classified documents scattered throughout the US Government laboratories—much of it at Los Alamos—be brought out into the open.

Since that time, scientists at LANL had been scurrying to discover ways to decommission the world's 1,200 tons of plutonium, an atrocious burden of bad news accumulating at a rate of 75 more tons each year. The problem with recovery and integrated extraction—such responsible-sounding words—was that nobody had even an eighth of a snot of understanding as to the precise fate of plutonium once it was ceremoniously buried, no matter what wicker basket of containment. Ten million garbage pails-worth of plaster. Yes, there were Los Alamos robots capable of trundling the restive radioactivity, exposing it to ingeniously concocted aggregates of nitrogen to help purify it of the americium, melting down the denuded plutonium into turd-sized metal pearls that could then be sequestered in safety deposit boxes and buried. But no storage of such ruins, given enough time and geological intrusiveness, would be sufficient to protect future fawns from drinking those adjacent streams, or local children riding their mountain bikes nearby.

These Heisenberg riddles were all loaded question marks lingering in the sordid air of Los Alamos, a grim reaper of irresponsibility almost palpable on people's lips as they played racquet ball, or hung out at the corner healthfood store, or blew their diets at TA-31, the local ice-cream parlor.

Not all of Los Alamos was devoted to The Bomb or its sinister aftermath. Hundreds of scientists did other things non-lethal in nature, though no less smelly, and were loathe to speak of the weapons aspects of LANL, mostly from cowardice. These were the boys and girls who, under a 1994 Department of Energy Task Force on Alternatives, pursued new antioxidants, health benefits, transportation fuels and ozone replenishers like lemonade, soybean genisteins, vegetable saponins and diet cranberry juice. Under the *Stevenson-Wydler Technology Innovation Act of 1980*, LANL had begun joint research ventures into such highfalutin fields as super-duper-conductivity and grease-ball recovery. Under so-called CRADA defense funds the University of Eastern Winnemucca had collaborated with a major rickshaw manufacturer on the plasma-source ion implantation process for reducing fungal rot on gaskets, and on fashioning rollerblades, badminton rackets and pogo sticks that were impervious to rust.

But perhaps the most thrilling aspect of the laboratory's most recent work concerned its unabashedly invasive bioengineering—an assembly-line vision of a new and massively selective monoculture. This effort had been designed to throw off the yoke of all previous eons of biodiversity and replace them with an Aryan orchestration at unassailable odds with each and every untoward gene fragment, lackluster vegetable, modestly sized sheep or boisterous bacterium that might be deemed to underachieve, linger inefficiently or outright interfere with The Agenda.

Located atop these otherwise pastoral forests, with their barbwire perimeters and deadly soil and water, was the fundamentalist epicenter for genetic meddling. The last precious touch in the long history of human tampering with nature; the Great Injection, or Pill, or Surgical Procedural Protocol that would ensure the Superiority and Immunity of Our Kind above all other creatures, no matter the demographic winter of longevities.

The pension fund of implausibilities. Or, as the Pope once willy-nilly promised, 40 billion people sharing bread over a dinner table.

This was the first national laboratory assigned to the *Genome Project*, in 1988, under DOE imperatives, along with Lawrence Livermore Laboratory and Lawrence-Berkeley. Part of that effort consisted, once again, of robotic cataloguing of DNA fragments within a host of bacterial colonies, and this was the area into which the trio was now escorted. A corridor of scum-green cubicles in which every last hidden closet of human evolution was being charted on wall hangings with magic markers, in test tubes and in supercomputers. The odd Playmate of the Month centerpage also discernable here and there.

"What is this place?" the Commander demanded.

"The Annex," said Limborn. "I thought you'd appreciate knowing that your Government is actually doing something; working towards the accomplishment of saving lives, not just inventing ways to incinerate billions of people. We're biologists in this sector, Mr Marigold." Blinking modestly, with a nearly partisan pose, he went on, "We don't really have much in common with the thermonuclear types, though I do appreciate the dilemma they find themselves in."

They passed by the actual genome labs, able to catch only 8-by-12-inch window-framed glimpses of the white suits and white gloves carefully doing their thing inside, not unlike the joint Russian-Indian lab which had yielded a similar glimpse back in New Delhi.

"We got nowhere, and no further," the Commander now whispered to Sannazaro.

"What were we doing there?"

"Searching for the source of the Yellow River," replied he. "Understand," began Limborn, hoping to impress his captives with the nobility of the *National Genome Project*, "each of our 46 chromosomes contains 3,125 fragments, with 40,000 nucleotide base pairs per fragment." He went on rather high above their heads, launching into nuclear transfer and xenotransplants, culling from the arcane lexicon of 30—80,000 genes (the same number as mice, and roughly 1.5 times that of nematodes and other invertebrates) and the fact each human is susceptible to something like 4,000 diseases. "We want to save lives and soon, as an added boon, we'll be creating the perfect turkeys, cows, goats and chickens."

"More like boondoggle. I think they're pretty good already. Of course, there's probably some money in it, isn't there?"

Limborn paused. "The genetic map of the fly, and of an entire human, will be made freely accessible to everyone over the internet. No secrets."

"Then what are we doing here? It looks pretty secretive to me?"

"Well, friend, we have reason to believe that what you three have experienced is likely to catapult the process beyond what any of us in this line of research could ever have anticipated. Until we understand it, we feel it essential to move quietly and under secure circumstances. I know for a fact that you have had some dealings with the Russians lately. So I believe you among men can appreciate that there are indeed corporations out there who would kill for the data."

"We experienced only a walk through the jungle. You've got the wrong idea about us."

"Well, you've done nothing wrong, so there's no reason to be defensive or evasive. This is an honor, a national duty. A thrilling opportunity. That's how you should view this little diversion. Your walk through the jungle may have exposed the three of you to some very potent pollen from the flowers, or to pieces of spider web, cytospora, or even algae on your boots. Did you ever consider that? Spoondrifts of crowded spook yeast on your lips, amebic crypts in your eyebrows, migratory bacteria up your nostrils, crazy carpetweed between your toes, a single airborne fragment of rhinoceros dandruff mingling in your hair?"

"I'm highly allergic to pollen, rhinoceros dandruff, and certainly any and all spooks. I'd have known about any sneezing fits," said Marigold.

"He never sneezed once," Sannazaro added. "I would have heard."

"Not a single cough," Rajibai went on. The boy's eyes darted devilishly to his father. "He farted once or twice around the campfire. Does that count?"

Sannazaro was utterly unimpressed with the sci-fi world into which they'd been kidnapped. "Where are we going?" he asked. He held back a verbal avalanche of hostilities for the sake of that one solid future both he and the Commander now fervently believed in; the one thing in their lives which seemed, truly, to matter: Rajibai.

"To a hotel room, in essence," Limborn replied. "A place where we want to ask the three of you questions, and then do some samples."

"No samples," the Commander hastened.

"I'm afraid that's part of the deal," Limborn said. "Simple outpatient procedures. It won't hurt," he added for the benefit of Rajibai. "Not one bit. Now I'd like to introduce you to Dr Susan Wayford. She'll be questioning the boy. This is Ruth Landesman, a psychologist, who will be briefing you, Mr Sannazaro."

"You can call me Iacobo," he said. "I don't like strangers using the family name."

"Iacobo is it? Very good." He then turned to Marigold. "Meet John Helstrom. He'll be your handler. Three rooms, three sets of questions. It's important they be conducted separately—for the different points of view, you understand."

"Father?"

Marigold again winked, and his son showed the sure sign of knowledge with which Sannazaro, witnessing the same signal, was equally complicit.

Said Limborn, "Hopefully you'll be out of here and back home with your companion animals in no time." He smiled with an apologetic grace which utterly belied the nature of the trio's capture and manner of delivery into this demonic outhouse of scientific arrogance—a dung-heap of ulterior motives anybody with a nose for mischief could rightly detect.

CHAPTER 146
The Interrogation

THEY WERE ESCORTED into separate quarters, stupidly appointed with all the big clichés of police work. A French cigarette on the steel table, testicle squeezer, mix-master, head brace, ray gun, a syringe, polygraph paraphernalia, xenon candle-power.

"Have a seat, young man," Dr Wayford began, tapping the dimmer switch to lessen the severity of the light source. "I understand you are quite fluent in English?"

"That is true, Ma'am." Rajibai looked around with a shudder. "So what do you want from me?"

"Well, firstly, to apologize. I'm awfully sorry about all this." She had her own daughter, at school just then. The logical chain of substitutions was a human need, no matter how jaded the players. "You must be exhausted from your recent journey. Am I correct that this is your first trip to America?"

"Yes, Ma'am. I think so." Then: "What wonderful caves they have in America," he waxed, mindful of the sticks, piles, white fluxions and snares being carefully laid for him. He was ever the observer, having learned well from his father, taking note of the chart of the constellations overhead (the Big Dipper paramount), a poster on the wall from a film titled Doctor Strangelove, and the Lady Doctor's falsely apologetic tone.

As she began to work him for effects, she could see all the signs of stress and evasion: his eyes dilated, face fecklessly flushed. He was lying.

Which, she deduced, suggested he had picked up every contagion of the slum from whence he came, all of its imposed survival stratagem. He was still out there, far away, in the trenches of evolution, searching for his next meal, a runaway. She'd heard the highlights of his epic tale. Yet, there was more to this queer little personality. A fancy-free flamboyance, entertaining divagations like a divaricating ground creeper, devoir that was really ribald and rebellious, had been well trained in the art of deception, the picaresque, tall tales. That much was obvious.

She knew from the start—his manner of describing deodar shade and sunny twinkling canopies in northern India, his scented fingertips, the slender brown eyes, his posture that gave way to a sense of testimonial superimmanence—that he would not be easy to corner. A tough walnut to chew open. A candleflame touch-me-not, majolica surfaced, a flypaper of instincts, his eyes a windowsill filled with all the chimeras of East and West. A contra of linguistic highs, masquerading as a little immigrant. So that she was at once on guard, only too aware of the diminutive imp's combined skills. While there could be no precise genealogy, it was clear that a shyster had a hand in his composition and trained him in the art of invention and recreation. She must be on the look-out for the slummary of half-truths. But there was a danger in her acuities: he would surely sense her scrimmage and react accordingly. A true Cruikshank.

Just like him, she would have to manufacture a style in real time that somehow circumvented this gully of self-fulfilling obsequies and evasions. She teased, prompted and seduced for answers with the faintly yellow sputter of a lightskirt. Her method was as subtle as a suppository.

The doctor switched on a tape recorder and began without pretense or formality.

"So how is it you came to this country?"

Rajibai relayed his considerable saga of tragic bombshells and eccentric deliverance. She was utterly unprepared for the sobering Gestalt of trauma sitting before her: beyond the self-contradictory nuances of his terrified rattle, there was a poignant person there, a truly twice-orphaned soul of noble demeanor and forgiving happiness. Her aggrieved impressions clouded the task at hand. To have lost one's only relation in the world to a mob of butchers. It was too ghastly. Yet, he seemed to have dealt with the calamity with remarkable maturity for an eleven-year-old, for anybody. He had repressed the incident through his own version of grand guignol, inflating the circumstances of his journeys to cast a mighty shadow.

"And your business in the jungles of northeast India?" she finally got around to inquiring. "What was that all about?"

"Just your normal holiday tour," he understated, thrilled by his newfound capacity for stretching verisimilitudes, plumbing new depths to the meaning of fabulous fibbing. In short, he'd become a little con, and she was not unwise to him, but there was nothing to be done. One minute a water spout, the next a suspicious cloud over cactus. These were not merely prevarications and taradiddles, but outright, barefaced and stunning reconstructions. He had been, in a former life, to Leeds, and seen the Mayor and all the emus and ducklings in town hiding under saucers and coffee cups.

Where had he learned to boast and enlarge? To feint with cock-and-bull, concoct through his own hat, color, fence, equivocate and forge? He had not spent near enough time in the deft company of a father to have picked up such a magnificent vocabulary of falsifications. Yet, there was the gild and varnish, the gloss and magnification of only the greatest fiction. From his lips issued pure moonshine—shameless, sycophantic, spectacular. No stranger to St James of the Sword, or the Order of the Norwegian Lion, he had, as a child, read no less than the Commander of Dames Grand Cross and the Order of Bath. He could speak unrelentingly on the ceremony occasioning the conferring of knighthood, with its treble strikes and cryptic formulas; knew all the subtleties—the fact Marigold must possess a golden spur, Sannazaro a white one, of inferior metal. Had memorized the Battle of Pinkie in 1547 and, most applicable, the theory among knights of orphans and wardships.

So that when she calmly asked him to describe his most recent adventures, she had no idea what monster she was unleashing. Not even Marigold could have grasped the extent of his good fortune in finding one of such rare similarity to himself. True asymptotes separated only by age and the number of battles they had fought.

"Oh, well—let's see, who could ever forget the Cliff of Cannibal Leeches, parasitic bucket-mouth flowers that dripped poisonous goo onto your nose, cartwheeling spiders—Pisauridae, Uncle calls them—that ran up your pants and bit your dick, scorpions playing little accordions on their hind legs. An eruption of methane gas laced with bumblebee urine. Our lungs were scorched. Our eyes gouged out by fiery broccoli balls flying through the air. We made in haste for the raging riverside, awfully cold, fiercely flowing, and after that, oh yes, there was that poor Bengal tiger, upside down—" Whoops!, his little cerebellum vesicles exclaimed like a buzzsaw, but too late to reverse the blunder. Inductions hovering over him now. Svabhavakripana—follies of his own making.

She pressed to know everything about the trap which had evidently caught the tiger but Rajibai was navigating deftly now, like a kid on a skateboard, and agilely self-corrected for his wrong turn. Never had his language abilities so soared across unknown boundaries: a fever of whackoland and paradise coves; a speaking disorder (as Sannazaro had likened it—thinking of the Commander himself) born of gigantic talent, enthusiasm, rebellion, but linguistically well trained, pathologically unbridled, whose sole orientation was the spark of the imagination, seconds of nonsense faraway; a stunning brainpower well beyond what it meant, in most societies, to be a boy. He was now fully at the helm of the control panel, a runaway mouth guided by Marigoldean instinct, and a surprising number of adventure sorties well stored in his razor-sharp eyes. The English of Little Byron during his most radical, untutored, uncontrollable best, and add to that the seasoning of countless other continents and hair-raising diversions, Chaplin's 'Circus'.

"Scared away by so many ants, we hiked out 20 kadams, then had dinner with the Nabob of Trichinopoly at the Green Goose Fair. A very foolish old chitty."

Suavely, with all of his schoolbrat ringlets and Fulbright and look of weary enchantment, he sampled her cognitive net worth: "We never knew. Never saw. Heard nothing. Just crawled day after day around that jungle. My father, you see, is a great and mighty explorer. A knight who once slew the Giant of Hildeberg."

"How can you be sure?" she said, holding back her smile. "He has a diploma in his bedroom that says so."

"Ahhh!"

"And that's not all. A frightening dagger smeared in gold blood rests there beside his cabinet of armor. There are little plaques describing each and every one—I remember all the names, as I have been boning up on my English. Breastplates and sollerets, jambeaus and gauntlets, all of which he used to good quotient in Hong Kong when confronted by the Maoist Chicken Shits. I know because he has patiently explained the whole urinary calculus to me."

Her eyes broadened. He continued: "Beside his skirt of tasses and pallette is a medal from the Duke of Moravia that honors him for saving the Dwarf Queen from the Babesiidae of Bohemia and the Malignant Jaundice of Jooboomontane. There are teeming telegrams of congratulations posted in his bathroom from the Duchess of Fenwick and the Archbishop of Brigadoon, not to mention Indira Gandhi who was, after all, my mother-in-law."

"So you were married, then?" inquired she.

"Ages ago," replied the high-speed page. "Remember, we are of the race that reincarnates without blinking. How many lives do you have time to listen to?"

She could not help but fall helplessly for this sprite of graduated charm; invention amplified by every alloy of fiction.

He went on to describe his father who had received countless bronze awards from Suzerains in Macedonia, landgraves in Bohemia and paramount lords in Lapland. He had tamed the Mountain of Metamorphosis, fought bravely the brambles in Madras to rout the green lizards, dodging all the Cydonian darts and Cobra de Capellos—the evil muses; and when carabineried, bestewed and lassoed, lampooned with an equal fury right back at them. He made mention of caparisoned wheelbarrows right up to the Circassian frontier; of giving alms to every Ma-jee; liberating all the cows from their Gaowalas. He entertained that Marigold had subdued the entire Libyan fleet in the Gulf of Sirte, even neutralized the Myriarch's Legwork in the Deserts of Samothrace, and xeroxed a million and one dollars to the homeless kitty-cat shelter in Santa Fe.

"Quite a personality, I'd say," intoned the psychiatrist.

"I tell you, Madam, my father is the greatest of ringleaders. A four-leaf clover, six-leaved nutmeg, twelve-leafed cinnabar. As straight as an arrow from Dungapur, as soft as the smoke from a Persian pipe, as sweet as the Calcutta sugar-plum. His whole life a civil message made of light, thatched roofs, wild beasts, baskets of almonds and lime, castle hills and inlaid trappings."

She could not begin to fathom what he was talking about, and dimly suspected that was the point, the "say's law" of psychoanalysis, whereby the questioner unwittingly triggers an untamed assembly line of inventions by the patient. He was proving impossible, and since this was no therapy session, she decided to try another tack.

"You really love him, don't you?" she said.

"Wouldn't you? He saved my butt. I was just another slum urchin. Doomed before I met him."

That was no invention, but now Rajibai shrank back slightly. After all, he'd spilled more lima beans than he'd intended. His father had given him due license to fabricate a darning needle, but he was rendering a veritable machine shop. Yet, there was a gusher of devotion, a council of turkeys, that no restraint could stem. The esteem and licorice lace in which he held Mr Marigold only now avalanched before her, somewhere between a farthing rushlight and Bokhara purple. This way, she had evidently afforded the first opportunity for his heart to burst. But what Dr Wayford did not anticipate was Rajibai's need, more than anything, to express his thanks. She was elevated by his loft of a confession, moved nearly to tears by the obvious veneration the boy had for one who'd taken on fatherly responsibilities only within past months, as could be determined by the report from the Indian Criminal Bureau of Investigations. This diversion into a regaling of gratitude, of his admiration for all things American, his great pride to be a real son, with a real father, clearly granted his struggling soul the much-needed possibility of vindicating his sister through the sheer power of holding fast memory and collaborative commemoration. These telling revelations were of psychological interest but did not lead Wayford down the expected garden path. In fact, she had nothing to show for three hours of pleasantly bizarre, but unproductive conversation.

"A tiger was hanging upside, you said earlier," she repeated after wiping away some tears with a Zuni handkerchief. "That would mean that a tribe had set a trap, wouldn't it?"

It was, of course, the tribe she was after. Not a knee-jerking history of little boys and their various troubles and fantasy life.

"A tribe?"

"Certainly."

"Oh no," Rajibai rejoined, thinking fast on his little bum. "It is the topsy-turvy tree, known in my language as Achedanamoorti. All those who come in contact with it go Jala-Jala, or plop-plop. Very dangerous, and slippery too."

The psychiatrist took notes, but to little avail. It was hopeless. Sannazaro, in an adjoining soundproof room, was even less forthcoming, his replies to questioning as smooth as the most expensive face cream, smarm whose humectant combined the finest cornflower oil with a free hydration, verbs skimming the surface of dimethicone, adjectives stringing along the listener with a mist of sodium: a dancing glass of silicon shivers as ridiculous as the crazy grin he had permanently assumed for purposes, obviously, of throwing off would-be assailants. His style was all of holes-in-the-pocket, sieves and litigants, prussic acid and copper gilt. He spoke in cursory English, breaking off annoyingly into the Italian of his ancestors.

"Sir, we know from satellite imagery that you were at a much higher altitude than you are admitting to," Ruth Landesman alleged with a sharpened bite. "That you were in the company of a Tibetan CIA agent named Namgyal. Ring any bells?"

"Dinner bells, luncheon bells, et belle cuisine. All of which underscores the importance of a good diet. Which reminds me, I'm starving. *Vivo bibere, bibo vivere!*"

"Come now, where is he, and how did you all link up?"

"Who?" the senile old apostle of the arts stuttered. "*Le donne, i cavalier, l'armi e l'amori*," he fashioned his reply, calculated to infuriate the beady eyes before him.

"I'm sorry, Mr Sannazaro. I do not speak Italian."

"Food is a universal word."

"When you answer at least one question with a straight face, and take this session more seriously than not, perhaps we can talk about dinner."

"*Si, si*... You ask where he is? I'll tell you: somewhere between Calabria and Monopotapa."

"Where is that?"

He replied scornfully. "Your face is ashen. I believe this building has not been sufficiently checked out for radon contamination. Am I right?"

She removed her glasses, rubbed her eyes and rang her buzzer. It was time out. These proceedings were pointless, she'd explain to Limborn.

In Marigold's room, John Helstrom was experiencing an equally appalling endurance race—what the Navajos call a 'chicken pull'.

"Just answer, Yes, or No, if that would simplify it," he resorted, losing his cool.

"Shades of clarification rebuke a simple Yes or No," the Commander quietly replied. "This is tricky business, after all. I would always err on the side of prudence. Imagine your distress were I to exaggerate, or convey a misimpression. Why, there's no telling the adverse consequences. I want this to be a memorable conversation, really. For both of us to look back years from now and think, That was a wonderful repartee. No borderline truths, not in this mouth. I would give you precision, when possible, and when it is not, I shall be frank. No point raising false hopes. Optimism is a disease, not a cure. So let me start by declaring, it was an empty quadrant."

"Empty—what is that?"

"I say, you are the scientist. Empty means bare, absolved, uninhabited, vacant and clear; without, absent, as in no catsup or mustard."

"You mean to tell me that you saw no other people in the jungle?"

"Hard to say," the Commander speculated aloud.

"Surely you recognize a human when you see one?"

"That presupposes a clear view, but keep in mind a jungle such as that interminable one across northeast India comprises 14,324 trees per square kilometer, on average. The human eye can delineate two million nuances of green. Multiply that by edge effects—wind brushing the leaves, eyes leaping to and fro, movement of an infinity of sorts ... caterpillars, jumping frogs, harpy eagles—and one is confronted by a confusion. Did I chance upon a human being in this outer woods? Was I a centipede dreaming that I was a pair of human hands? Or a pair of human hands dreaming I was a centipede? Did I see a moth lay open to the burning sun, a wild beast from the gardens of Arabia, a flesh-eating Coleopterae? Or was it the face, instead, of some damsel in exile? To my knowledge," he went on, "there was no damsel, or I should have done the chivalrous thing and escorted her to safety at once."

Thus did he successfully exhaust his interrogator, who was additionally stressed by the fact that mobs of rallying protesters had gotten wind of the "capture of el Cristo Negro" and were gathering in an angry cloud outside the triple barbwires and electric towers of the laboratory. Millennial fevers had broken through the hand-to-hand chain of living security guards.

Realizing that the questioning of the trio was not getting them anywhere too soon, Limborn had them returned to their hospitality suites where they could shower and clean up before dinner.

As it turned out, none of the trio cared to shower, though dinner was very much on all of their minds: four veggie burgers, mushroom barley soup and mixed salads would lead to a dark boy's stool, an old Marigold's urine, and one single strand of particularly potent dental floss tossed into a waste basket by the Italian (Sannazaro suffered from a receding gum problem, resulting in some blood). All these fragments should constitute a viable pool of metabolized cellular samples from whatever it was these weirdos had been exposed to in the Himalayas.

The trio was released and Marigold assured in writing that the CBI, India's Criminal Bureau, was now off his back with regard to that question of improper adoption, though the riots in Bhopal and Delhi, the embarrassment of the cow rescue, not to mention a certain question of breaking and entry at Pokhran-II still lingered around the name of Marigold, such that he was not welcome back in India. This last piece of wisdom was conveyed to him as a sort of favor by Limborn as the threesome got into an unmarked chopper parked some distance from the thousands of zealots converging outside LANL, and were secreted away to Tesuque.

There, a very agitated bison lay waiting in the tall unkempt grasses of the Hacienda Marigold. A squirrel slept in her furry mane.

In a cave 20 miles away, a shaman sang his song, a lullaby composed 1,200 years before: "Put all distractions to rest, let your eyelids collapse, before the bad people steal your dreams."

CHAPTER 147
The Madness of Altruisms

WITHIN A DAY of the trio's visit, the top brass at Los Alamos were enmeshed in some other crisis—radioactive copying machines in the secretarial pool—that all but eclipsed their Himalayan idyll. The genetic mystery would remain ambiguously couched in angstroms of plaque and tartar, contaminated by the cinnamon flavoring of the dental floss from which Sannazaro's blood sample had been surreptitiously extracted. After 72 hours of feverish reconstructive work, the scientists at LANL were unable to glean anything definite to say about the supposed substance in his veins. Nor were the urine and fecal samples adequate to the task of marking a definitive substrate. By some means as yet undescribed in the annals of food science, the veggie burgers, upon alimentation, defied all trace analysis. Tofu appeared to wipe out gene markers; mushroom barley soup co-opted DNA strands; sweet potato French fries negated all phenotypes, made folly with every scientific aspiration. The meals were a biochemical disaster.

World-weary, back in the lordly confines of his Tesuque, the Commander slept for three.point.seven days amid the venerable comforts of his hacienda—steam shower, cherry woods, and slate and mahogany floors, albeit trashed by a lovelorn bison and sleepwalking squirrel—and imagined in his unhurried dreams that none of the fantastic foregoing, starting with the seasickness, vertigo and savior complex, had actually involved him. There had been no financial windfall months before, nor airfare to Hong Kong. No notion of moa or Sri Lankan pirates, of disappearing icebergs or ozone depletion over Tibet. No legendary master of mirth nor Irish ghosts.

Yet, a moment later, awakened to the awesome responsibility that was his by nothing more humble than a ringing telephone, a newspaper slapping the door, the squeal of brakes somewhere on Bishop's Lodge Road, the Commander got himself together, sat himself by a log fire and reflected on his present status. Simplicity was not his best suit, nor understatedness. Nothing came easily, he thought. Better one wildebeest than 10,000 bankers, one vegan than 10 million meat-eaters; sooner a world of Tinkerbell, manatees, Democrats and white asparagus than all the cities and carousels combined. He was developing a theorem, all right, however unequipped he was to account for the way the world was. Gradations and nuances that favored old-time evolution while allowing for radical punctuation marks, if that was what was needed to alter the human animal in real time. Eskimos, for example, should be able to change their diet when the wisdom of environmental degradation exceeded the carrying capacity of their habits. While the Commander did not presume to dictate human nature under adverse circumstances, where four billion years of survival instincts were bound to kick in, with more predictable turns of events, the human beast—however hobbled by imperfections—should be malleable, or could learn to be. Even if it must turn somersaults and effect handsprings to render a balance sheet.

Marigold had thus far enjoyed some success as metallurgist, and rubber band, no doubting that. Had stirred up an impressive share of debacles; inspired, confused, outraged and enflamed countless witnesses to history. He'd also managed to make an obscene sum of money, despite his frenzy to bankrupt himself. Yet, there was darkness outlining his largesse. Even Rajibai had understood the makings of a tragi-comedy that was his father. And Sannazaro knew that something could go wrong at any time, as evidenced by their previous itinerary and circle of friends.

But, on the other side of these dire premonitions, he was home. Safe. Secure. With no immediate plans to alter this recovered stasis. Apathy with no envy of the stars. He reclined very still and alone. Bach's *Mass in B Minor* resounded throughout the hacienda. It was the Maestro's 250th anniversary. Only in the attic of Marigold's cerebrum were disquieting glimmers of gigantic moss carpets spouting Elizabethan English, of green typhoon and violet iceberg; of slums the size of Connecticut and sharks more docile than bunnies. He dimly perceived a dizzying train of monks and mountains, monkeys and deserts, Gaelic and Gujarati. But none of it was real, as he lay in bed and surmised the gray dawn of contradictions on a Friday morning, prepared to embrace the new and crazy millennium with an altogether dispassionate mode of being.

A rare deliverance from guilt had saturated every fiber, muscle, brain cell and molecule of Professor Marigold, as Senator Sannazaro now occasionally referred to the master of deplorable distractions, the guru of agile circumlocutions. He had come to a potent resolve: no more crusades.

"I'm bed-ridden, and I like it." Yet, even as he mouthed the words he felt the tingle of a looming disaster, some newly awakened hippogriff that refused to give up, that took no quarter with the easy way. There was no relief in sight, though he would claim it vociferously.

"I'm not going anywhere," he repeated exaltedly.

To that pitiful heap of a survivor who was his accomplice, such words were a fresh breeze loosening the bronchials, a suite-en-suite in Paris. Señor Sannazaro, home at last, wealthy enough to buy Borneo, was untroubled of mind, poised for spring planting—a pepper tree, some lemons. No more saving the world. Yippee-yi-o! Then again, he knew that Marigold might be overstating the truth, for even now the Commander commented on the sensation of some dim pressure within his subconscious. A leak in his caverns. His glue was deteriorating, a restless itch without name.

"If, after six weeks, you're still here, only then will I truly believe it," the lounging petite pomme of an Italian intoned heartily, while indulging Ginevra's bloated kitchen. True to her former ways, this hausfrau of unstoppable demeanors had provisioned every shelf, counter and refrigerated cranny with a cornucopia of foodstuffs to delight the returning mavericks. This was her style, a generosity indifferent to excess, expense or even waste. But her shopping expedition to Wild Oats and Alfalfa's was especially serious in light of the new addition to the family, Rajibai, whose future prospects had already excited in her a certain proprietary curiosity inseparable —Sannazaro divined—from her interest in Marigold himself.

"You must weigh heavily the task before you," she declared to the Commander. (She and his Squire had now wandered over to the Commander's hacienda, carrying assorted nibbles from which to fashion a meal.) "Which one?"

"That of the boy's schooling. He needs friends his own age, a healthy distance from shopping malls, from all those seedy alleyways where Ecstasy and alcohol are exchanged; he needs a baseball glove, a tennis racket, a reliable placement exam. And you must explain to him the thing about girls."

"No need, trust me."

"Of course there is. He needs a father; wisdom; love; discipline. And he must somehow come by that love of America that might animate his understanding of his miraculous deliverance. Which is not to argue for a dismemberment of his homeland in his memory, but from what I understand, there is not a whole lot to recommend where he came from. In other words, my good man, he needs all those parental forms of support that money cannot alone acquire. Are you up to it?"

"Have I ever implied otherwise?"

"No, you have not. So let me recommend the following: the purchase of a basketball hoop affixed to the old coach house."

"I must protest. We do not want the sound of a basketball in these monastic wilds."

"You see! Since when were children forbidden from natural exclamations, punctuations and shouts of jollity?"

"Tesuque transcends such mundanities."

They pattered on this way for some time while Rajibai outfitted his bedroom, puttering around the citadels of junk, corners populated with amalgams of strange Marigold memorabilia, esoteric trinkets, paleontological artifacts, doubtful documents, baubles bearing a mechanical origin, gimcracks of some antiquity or gewgaws of strange illegibility.

The whole magical chamber was teeming with one unique quotient that made it bloom: its sole occupant had an enormous appreciation of the fact it was his. Objects that now gathered weight of meaning, acquired custodial prominence in his imagination; a utility compensating every gap; facilitating the great leap forward, even an orbit of a few feet, gaining ground on arcane jumbles until he forged a system of identification whereby it all came into spiritual focus; possessions representing a history entire of the family name.

He fondled the cracked bronze Philoctetes churned out by a factory in Antwerp in the eighteenth century, the inward smile suggesting more than two continents and two dozen centuries. A set of old pens, still ink ridden. Glass jars suffuse with colored powders of unknown aesthetic or medicinal purpose. Others stuffed with notes. He forced open the first rubber gasket and withdrew a message, yellowing and crinkled, on which were the delicate words extolling the suggestive beauty of a half-eaten fig. A samovar, circa 1840, reflected the floating brushstroke of an olive tree rustling in a Chinook breeze outside the linen-laced leaded glass. Molds, mildews, warps and foxes had gathered abreast many of the volumes of Diderot's *Encyclopedia* which sat leaning in an unused sprawl on the teakwood bookcase. A white plaster mask atop a Moroccan throw rug thwarted interpretation; Spanish leather chairs with golden lionels hovered in tousled corners; other disarrayed shelves were weighed down tohu-bohu with myriad contents and haphazard clusters. A suit of armor from Poland; camelhair paintbrushes and Ducal jars for mixing turpentine. A worm-eaten George III desk crowded with unfiled letters.

So many strange attractors lay in the lap of this enthusiast who stood on the edge of a new continent he could claim as his own. A carpet from 1539, woven with Karabagh geometrical patterns, almond-tree motifs; a line engraving in the Raimondi tradition of Frans Floris de Vriendt; a statue of the patron saint of ecology from the Church of S. Francesco in Montefalco; a capital with the Adoration of the Magi from the Cathedral of St-Lazare in Autun; black and white etchings of Piranesi's "sublime dreams" and Alexander Cozens' *New Method of Assisting the Invention in Drawing Original Composition of Landscape* (1785)—a first edition. There was an oversized volume on the fifth-century rock paintings from the slave pits of Zimbabwe; a framed floor plan of the Escorial; 28 pounds of green chilies from Chimayo; an unopened letter from Umbria; and an iconography of saints in one pretty volume much resembling those manuscripts atop the pyramid.

He thumbed through the hand-wrought watercolors detailing the good works of Agatha (patroness of children's nurses), Agnes (patroness of gardeners), Ambrose (domestic animals and wax refiners), Andrew (patron of sailors, healer of stiff necks), Anne (Christ's grandmother), Anthony Abbot (basketmakers), Augustine (of the flaming heart), Barbara (invoked against thunderstorms, patroness of architects), and so on. Rajibai was fascinated by all these saintly pragmatists, men and women adept not only at prayer, which he thoroughly ascribed to (he had prayed that day benumbed upon the infirmary bench outside the terrible Mumbai operating theatre) but also at such other eminently useful tasks as combating nettle rash and twitching, walking on water, the keeping of wasp nests, wool weaving, candle and rope works, entertaining with the viol and harp, sewing gray tunics, the use of mortars and pestles, the treatment of headaches, baking of Jewish rye, curbing toothaches, sweeping chimneys, childbirth, charming dragons, walking through fire, etiquette while on pilgrimage, mad hatting, infantry pointers, pencil manufacture, holy wedlock, raven feeders, linen-drapers, and tolerating other children his own age. All these facets of life, in the person of the saints, the history of the Marigold hacienda, spoke infinite worlds to him, one unified expedition right in his room, whose depths were now multi-storied.

But there was more: his very own trapdoor, with indecipherable notations carved into its armor. His father said it had been locked for a century and the key was lost three generations before. He had no idea what was down there.

"All our hidden secrets," the Commander figured.

Rajibai stayed close to his room, intent upon excavating its ruins, getting into that trapdoor and shaping his own destiny in New Mexico.

Meanwhile, Marigold began the tedious process of sifting through the canyons of paperwork that had piled up in his absence, with no executor to stamp sense upon the chaos: to pay bills, restore utilities to the house, fix the iron-wrought plumbing, replace 40-year-old electrical wiring, take up the cause of a massive green mouse, Macedonian moth and white-fly infestation; to aerate the soil, pull out ruined beds, trim the arbor, prune the orchards, mend the decks undermined by swarms of *Zootermopsis angusticollis* (dampwood termites by any other name), clear away trees that had fallen to the European earwig, and a barn collapsed from the activities of the carnivorous long-horn and ten-lined June beetles.

These latter tasks might go to Sannazaro, he imagined. After all, hadn't he been well paid, in the millions of dollars?

Think again, the horrified Squire informed him. He was not remotely interested in work. In fact, he felt a rush of self-righteous laziness coming over him.

"Leave me out of all involvement," he protested, not about to enter the realms of domestic refurbishment, let alone set foot into trouble or controversy. "My time in the trenches is finished. I will not again risk life or limb on anybody's count, not even yours. No hard labor, global monkey business, no protests or cries in the dark. My days as a worker and revolutionary are finished." He could not have been more emphatic about it. "Murillo, you're on your own now, old man."

Marigold was not listening. Other more pressing reality checks were crowding his dim skull, like those many initiatives he had launched prior to departing American shores and that had now come back to fleece him. He would have liked to resolve every conflict across Africa, the Balkans and all the other trouble spots by throwing chunks of gold, pouches of T-Bills, wads of rupees, whatever bonds, notes, securities and hard cash might elicit the original world, as he thought of it. A time and place of tranquil cohabitation, of Poussin's classical landscapes and gently treading shepherds. Of beautiful women who, as Ingres noted, were simply impossible to paint. Of poets who spent their days pining; of honest laborers; a lost civilization of benign tree pruning; of white pilasters, gracious Caryatids and Platonic portals to the heavens. Under olive groves. Atop Alps. In shadowed creek beds, in pergolas, before natural dioramas of rare solace season by season. This is how, he thought, our evolution should be guided, instead of by all these other intruders, intolerable hatreds and the upwelling of one massacre after another by high-school students or nation states.

The Commander had learned much that should help him resolve that turmoil shadowing his insides and, by dual impression, resolve the paralyzing negations and twists that tortured every community, in every city, state and country. He sincerely believed that what he felt, all people must feel. If we were all of the same genes, flesh and blood, then how could the simulacra be any different? Each of us aspired similarly; hoped for our children, and their children, with equal ardor and fixation. So that he was not only convinced (lacking any evidence, it must be noted) but galvanized by the belief that if he led the way, others would follow. Even though he had vowed to give up the frontlines, he still held out these mammoth hopes for humanity, based upon nothing other than his faith in himself. On topics as wide ranging as universal health care for pet parakeets; a social security net for abandoned individuals of all species, even the ants; an end to unfair corporate privilege; inducements to every kindness; a rethinking of profit; a closing down of the mints and eventual abolition of money; a deconstruction of the idea of taxes, of computers and speedboats; a decommissioning of nation states, human patterns of all kinds. He was no longer willing to abide by concrete, inorganic metals, architectural hullabaloos. The Commander was tarmac weary, sidewalk despairing, at a loss to find greenery again. Automobiles be banned. Buildings removed. Whoever ordained that he should be electronically conditioned, forced to hear planes overhead, trains out beyond, cellphones at every juncture. Tired of the talk, nauseated by the walk. Disgusted with empire building, product lines, factories, work ethics and superiorities. Burdened by everything that was Western. He wanted Toda land back. The waterfall. The simplicity of a Bishnoi shepherd camping beside his orange cactus. No more quarterly reports or cash-flow charts, derivatives or defensive compromises.

At first he had thought to set an example for his son to follow. But how to do so when the kid knew more than his father? Had embodied the primitive survival instincts with grace that surely defined what it was to be human more than all the billions of dollars or marks of success normally associated with the twenty-first century? If anything, Marigold might better to study under the aegis of the boy. Let the child reign over the continuing devolution, just as he had tried to explain to the reporters at New Delhi. The young man's uncanny dominion had never been tainted by doubt, paradox or indolence, whereas the Commander could not survey a situation without replacing it with the Ideal; was incapable of judging something on its own terms. For Rajibai, every word was original. Conversely, Marigold could not utter a sentence without recourse to the encyclopedia, or history, or some sweeping generalization. Prince Charles on sustainability, quoting St Matthew's lilies of the field and the *Brundtland Report*. Or Nietzsche, who once declared something to the same effect, "He must have utter, unrelenting chaos within who would give birth to an evening madrigal." Where Rajibai knew how to have fun, the Commander knew only the arid *history* of having fun, the *teleology* of taking pleasure, the *metaphysics* of the smile and *algebra* of delectation. But he did not know, himself, how to let go. Had never thrown his face into cotton candy.

He was, in short, stricken with comparisons, analogies, metaphors. Nothing was good enough; nothing was itself. A bridge resembled another bridge, a range of glaciers, some other cirque of icefalls. No grassy plot quite measured up to the silken aesthetics of Soji; no milkshake was as yummy as the ones from the local drugstore of youth. Nothing was good enough for Mr Marigold, in other words. And all because he hinged every action of mankind upon the greater needs of the vegetable kingdom. His proposition that the world be nonviolent undermined all natural predators, whether cheetah or dragonfly. The Commander could forebear no trials of life. The reality of nature's brutal extremes set him off. He rejected them. Replacing tooth and claw with—well, marigolds themselves. He was in a topspin, unable to accept things the way they were, or vouchsafe himself, and unclear how to steer the day differently. He had sacrificed most of his life to thinking about the alternatives to a cruel world. Evaluating, sampling, probing to the extremes, he'd uncovered by way of an antidote small, deliberate communities that isolated themselves from everyone else. No predator control. No meat or fish. But how could that actually work, as a general principle? And how much would it all cost? In possum-infested southern rata forest, for instance, wherein all non-natives would be lured out by a mandolin player, properly clothed, given spending money, then shipped First Class to Australia, provided a good pension and mostly sterilized. The Todas and Bishnoi had certainly spelled out the methodology by their example. But would it catch on in North America? And if so, what would it look like? Was he up to the propagation? Would it require him to get out of bed, which—at present—he had no intention of doing?

These imponderables were not easily assimilated by the Commander, or by anyone else for that matter. For all his wild scheming, no Hesperides, no Broceliande seemed realizable, not anywhere west, north, south or east of the Indus. His net physical energy was simply not up to the multiplication table of taskmasters. He tried, in fact, to put it all out of his head, to let go of the details, to somehow delegate. This was the essence of his great revelation on the plane trip across India, all the way to London.

But, in closer truth, he could not. He simply did not have the focus to follow through, or not well; he had no capacity for even the slightest due diligence over those idealistic flights of fancy which, with little or no deliberation, he had funded in the immediate aftermath of so much financial euphoria. He could not live the real whilst sighing in his arcadia; the temptation to exist was undermined by the great allure of the unreal. And this perfect paradox left him without the slightest road map or capacity. The larger the individual's dream, the less likelihood of community consensus on any matter of significance. So that democracy could not exist in company with a person of integrity. And all that talk of progress and hope for the next generation was merely the aftershock—like mumbling down the hall in a home for the aged—of an impossible dream.

Nor did he anticipate the assault upon his person—the recent lawsuit which Hidalgo had handled, the spate of angry phone calls, jealous threats, ire and wrath, of unsolicited mails and public debate.

He should not have been surprised by all the fanfare. Not after word got out in town, throughout the state, and over the internet, that he had consigned 50,000 dollars to the Save the Marmot Campaign on Vancouver Island, and 150,000 dollars to the Muriqui Society of Eastern Brazil, again in hopes of staving off the oblivion of the most threatened primate. And ten million dollars to the Kakapo Hall of Fame, in an effort to safeguard the few dozen remaining birds, those "mountain gorillas among parrots", who were waiting desperately for the rimu trees to burst with fruit lest the avians perish. But no amount of financial incentive could coax a rimu mast, as it was called.

Or what about the 5,000 dollars he laid out for the Worm Protection Society of Delaware, an anti-anglers coalition whose website spelled all the grisly particulars of the worm's nervous system and what fishermen did to it, and to the fish (nothing like the predation of worms by kiwi, but bad enough)? Or the 15,000 dollars to the Espanola Nonviolence to Cockroaches Club, with its special program for restraining exterminators and turning them into Born Agains. That caused quite a stir. While some computer mogul was funding inoculations for children, the Commander had financed an entire rat rehabilitation and mouse trauma program in Baltimore; a Portuguese NGO that had pledged to ban flea circuses worldwide; an anti-bear referendum in Pakistan and Texas; a Save the St Bernards campaign in Santorini (his presidential candidate had lost and was in litigation in Athens); a vegetarian fast-food chain that had opened its doors in all the heavy meat-eating capitals, as well as some 200 other impassioned endeavors around the world. A hundred million dollars worth of spur-of-the-moment madcap altruisms.

Sannazaro laid out what he believed to be the problem.

"You are a father now. You have years of catching up. Ease down. Become light on you toes. Hang out. Lose yourself. Be a kid again. Do you even know how?"

"I have never hung out!"

"Well, my point precisely. Maybe you should. You've earned the right to."

Marigold considered the provocations, then righted the equation. "I really appreciate your thoughtful advice, Señor Squire. Truly I do. But I must protest, and you among people can appreciate what needs to be done in this world."

"I thought you said you were giving up all that! That you were troubled by what seemed impossible odds, decks stacked high against the ordinary man, that what was needed was finally and unalterably beyond your tired, singular command. Isn't that what you said?"

"I am troubled, no doubt. I cannot be who I am not. Nor do I know who I am. I used to know. But that was a different me."

"But if that different person is not you, and you are not you, who is he, what am I, if I know you and you, in turn, recognize me, which makes two of us who know neither of us, which sounds ridiculous to me, but then I am not the one seeking to know myself. You are."

"Stop it at once, I say. I have no idea what you're trying to do, but my brain is addled enough. That's the problem."

"Well, may I?"

"By all means, but only if you promise to heed a rational disquisition. Your babble does me foul."

"You're right back where you started. Except a hell of a lot richer, and with a boy to look after. Those are two enormous differences of which you have every reason to be thrilled. What's more, your squirrel's returned, your buffalo is home, you've got a new pet mountain lion, a grateful rooster and hen, and a rich enough vein of experiences to last anyone a lifetime. I suggest you calm down, rid yourself of the demands upon your purse, and regain that hermit I first met in PJs."

"What was I doing?"

"Peeing against the side of that cottonwood one morning, whistling Beethoven."

"My goodness, why was I doing that?"

"I believe you said that Alma had locked you out of the house and your bladder demanded evacuation."

"Ahh. Yes. That would be Alma."

Eventually, their conversation came back to Marigold's self-proclaimed philosophical emergency, his inward confusion, the fact he had set in motion countless worthy expenditures that needed caretaking. None were closer to home than the operations of a certain animal sanctuary, the Oasis, two hours or so from Tesuque, whose aegis he had assumed in sober hopes of providing some relief to at least a few meager populations of both wild and domestic refugees in the state. (He wasted no time delineating or separating out: domestic and wild were the same, as far as he was concerned.) These poor souls were otherwise prey to multitudinous hunters who thought nothing of using cows for target practice, or of dismembering coyotes, poisoning eagles, and blowing the brains out of grey and red wolves. The Commander figured there were plenty of animal rights aficionados who needed work and could manage such a ranch. But now he'd learned of numerous and grave problems threatening its continuation.

He had purchased the Oasis thinking: Animal Farm for the Twenty-first Century. But he'd never actually read the original *Animal Farm*; had miscalculated, underestimated, over-reached and, the truth be known, knew nothing about the great out-of-doors, the common-day biochemistry of manure piles, a sheep's deteriorating bicuspids, or stubborn gopher holes. How could he have anticipated swarms of *Strongilis vulgaris* eating up the horses, cows, pigs and goats, or bots feasting on their legs and stomachs, burrowing into their tongues, working their way down each esophagus, entering bloodstreams prior to departing through the mouths as fully grown butterflies. Pink eye, cancer eye, leptospirosis, vitamin B deficiency, unthriftness, strangles, bluetongue, rabies, and animals plain dropping dead or bashing their brains in during a moment of rut. The Commander was not prepared for the ordeals of normal Nature. Hectares of misunderstanding; acres deep in Riband, Pastoral, Consort and Regina—to him one big setaside of seed potatoes and winter wheat. A veil of idle dreams cloaked in permanent pasture, where he took leave of his senses, confusing arable with oxygen, spring with fall, oilseed rape, barley and Golden Promise with the corncrake. He mistook the impoopo for a black-faced ram, thought the bearded argali a large gopher, the European ibex a kind of wolf. Cinereous hair, bluish in hue, seen blurred at sunset across the hills beyond, he swore up and down was *A. temmamazama*, otherwise known as chichiltic, a wool-bearing antelope endemic to New Mexico. In fact, as Rajibai pointed out, it was a flock of bluebirds, silhouetted.

"An easy mistake," Marigold plied, checking his spectacles. He never wore them with any discipline. Moreover, they were 40 years old. Not once since his childhood had his eyes been checked.

"Not really," Senator threw in, eager to thwart the slightest genesis of an ideal. He was not about to see his colleague stirred to any new misadventure. He'd endured enough of the syndrome to recognize the pot prior to its boiling temperature: every time the Commander had got a little information, it grew by systematic distortion and keen distemper into a leviathan of impulses. Once the monster was fully formed, nothing could stop it. Only ignorance, chained to its sleeping pill, might stave off utter self-destruction.

He knew that Marigold needed a woman, a chair and strong drink, a reason to settle in. These anodynes were available in a city the size of Santa Fe. Surely there was hope for a return to the old days?

Then again, he had hardly known the man prior to their setting forth, before so much Fool's Progress. Maybe he would not have cared for his neighbor back then. A book reader beside a gardener. That was a configuration open to possibility. One spoke, the other dug; a dissertation in one's fingers on the bulbs and berries of geography beside a storyteller who loved to hear himself go on. Had they been man and woman, husband and wife, there might have been a commerce to recommend the scholar at his bench, the green-thumb pruning her blue-creeping lawyer. Side by side. Humming and ministering all day long. But a bully Commandant and retiring mule, these two were not made for each other in heaven.

Ahh well, thought he. His nature is his own problem now. I shall not trouble about it or interfere any more.

So that just when the Verecund Marigold had curled up in the remains of his bed, retrogressive, obscure, sequestered all, and eager to take up his backwoods superannuation, fed up with so many sordid, insoluble problems, the blind and groping phrases towards a better world, that same planet was gasping for air all around him. None of his household companions—the bison, the squirrel, et cetera—with whom he might collaborate to turn desolation and confusion into cohesive action were anywhere to be seen. Instead the old fading Champion of Miseries and Unresolve had to confront his long-pent-up moment on his own.

Finally, he went into Rajibai's room.

"What are you doing?" Marigold asked.

"Figuring everything out."

"Good luck. It's a mess. I apologize."

"No, it's great." Then the boy looked at Marigold more sternly. "Are you OK, Father? You look sort of—dead."

"That bad?"

"Ummm."

Marigold didn't feel right about involving so pure and inquiring a spirit. What was the point? So he said, "No big deal."

Oddly, the more they spoke, albeit in short and tentative sentences, the more easily Rajibai stoked the inverse of the obverse, the positive of the negative, multiplied by its reckless reverse of the inward times the outward, minus the minor, drab and drear. In other words, he would hear of none of the darkness or complaining, and was ready to embark on more of the same globetrotting dares, which was not exactly what Marigold had in mind. Rather, he wished a formula for living that would give him inner peace and quiet days. Whereas Rajibai was just warming up. It was his turn to be wild, so that Marigold thought it best to bring the boy back to Earth.

"Perhaps Ginevra would bake some chocolate chip cookies," he suggested. "What do you say?"

"Yum."

Ginevra was only too glad to make cookies, and to offer advice. Marigold saw in her pure alabaster poise an untroubled Aphrodite. She stood arrayed like an Empress in all her splendor. Yet, for so much country of Queens and Czarinas atop pedestaled confidence, he could not see her for a real woman who had suffered her own scores of injuries. Nor had he yet taken the time to decipher the fact that every insult to her soul she had made into a great poem. So that her excellent advice fell upon ears already pointed, convoluted and steadfast. And her chocolate chip cookies were sumptuous.

Finally there was his trusted Squire, as tradition dictated. He went to him later that night, deeply troubled. Sannazaro, having taken flight repeatedly, was not surprised to hear added imprecations and appeals. Now he came up with a plan, one situated not far from home but worthy of their previous forays.

"You need a project to keep you occupied," he suggested. "Clearly you are of a mind to seek solace from the animals. And let no man say there be any better tonic than in concourse with those outside our total reference. Clean perspective. Raw reason. Facility undiluted."

But Marigold did not want to hear of projects. Rather, he envisioned the animal in him, be it the moa or the buffalo. In the rarest of form, he proceeded to expatiate upon his pent-up animal feelings.

"To be outside the fence, beyond all conversation, without the slightest human reference point or possibility for discourse."

"But blast it, here we are, speaking with one another. What is so wrong with that?" the Italian asked.

Marigold's eyes were radiant with higher powers. He began: "To nullify and disqualify all person speech and plunge instead to the heart of beatitudes."

"Which is where exactly?" Sannazaro inquired.

"Which is the best in her quietest quintessence. No more lawn bowling or Workingmen's Clubs. No ties, dancing lessons, Internal Revenue, motorcycles, paved road, obesity, postage stamps, unnatural mortality, gravel embankments, petroleum products, ringing telephones and wax museums. Not one more electric fence or antenna. Not a single country club or rifle. Hurray, I say!" And then he continued: "I would part company with that to embrace, instead, the wings, fleet-footed fairies, palpating breasts, soft their look, keen their senses, every newborn a miracle that looks to my eyes more lovely than its human counterpart, who is, for comparison, often alien and wrinkled. Whereas the animal comes perfectly sculpted, damseline and velvetine, with fur only a master of the Renaissance could have painted, and with panoramic intellects, abundant musculatures. Cubs—black panther, polar bear, ant eater; fledglings—the sooty shearwater, the wandering albatross, the bald eagle; the newborn spotted deer, or dorcas gazelle—I mean really. Can our hearts survive so much adoration? Animals, I dare say, build character in the rest of us. They are smarter, we know that by now. And far more liberal in every respect. Not a political shred among them. The ultimate pragmatists, yet their generosity cannot be doubted. They do not conceal a sneeze or an affection. Their love is a blueprint for the rest of us. Their homes, modest; their possessions even more so. No greed or outlandish consumption among them. One large predator in 4,000 herbivores—a ratio I know you admire. Neither taxes nor the end of the world troubles their heart, only lack of shade, or putrid water. They are the angels. We are their students, or should be, or you should be, to put it precisely. And if I am not mistaken, having by now browsed once or twice in your own peripatetic library, it was Señor Kant who suggested a transcendental aesthetic by way of the animal mind. So I would not be any surprised were you to say unto me, 'Sir, I have observed of late that you have become some avifauna giraffe.' To which I would reply, 'It's true. I have gone dashing about with the foxes, leaping over fences with the white-tailed deer, boxing like the kangaroo, foraging with the giraffe. I am no more of human character, shape or form. And am to be recognized henceforth as some new, albeit ungainly vertebrate. Even a whale shark would to me be an orgy of greatest justice, should I turn into one.' Truly, it would be a blessing—for all of us, I dare say. To lose yourself, I mean. Therapy second to none. That is what the wilderness has done for some. Perhaps the Oasis is just the thing, after all."

And so it was settled. The Commander had managed to talk himself into doing something, despite all those impossible dreams.

CHAPTER 148
How Ebert Helps the Commander Effect a Revolution at the Oasis

THE OASIS, A PRIVATE TRUST, comprised roughly 3,000 acres of lush alpine valley in northern New Mexico, where gophers and ground squirrels had left a labyrinth of dangerous holes in which the rescued cows and steers were at risk of tripping, which might mean breaking a hoof or fracturing a bone. Local ranchers, enraged by the sanctuary's openly animal liberationist outreach programs, had slipped poison to several of the animals at the Oasis, hoping to see them turned into collagen, animal feed or children's toys. The staff, alleged a local newspaper, had infected children with perverse ideologies and turned them against their own parents, most being hunters and ranchers. In fact, nefarious misdemeanor charges had been anonymously filed under New Mexico's arcane Article 30-10-2 of the criminal code, or unlawful cohabitation, in this case, people and animals.

The trust had managed to outbid all other competing interests, enabling the Oasis to lease adjacent public lands otherwise earmarked for heavy cattle growing, and with those leases (costing 49 cents per acre per year) do nothing but provide silent genetic corridors and buffers, a form of conservation leasing that had previously been contested in places like Oregon and Idaho. There were over nine million acres of state trust lands in New Mexico, and 90 percent of them had been grabbed at fire-sale prices by ranchers. The Oasis initiated a new trend, and neighboring ranchers were furious. They had long reaped inordinate public tax benefits and were now appalled by the notion of somebody doing 'nothing' with the land, and seeing it pulled out from under them.

Neighboring ranchers were at war. "Better to destroy it, in the interests of the economy, than nothing at all," one cowboy was heard to say in an angry town hall meeting. Placards proclaiming "Tierra or Muerte" were plastered on the sides of a nearby gas station, where impoverished locals wove 35-micron cross-wool from churro sheep, and where, back in the late 1960s, a pro-logging group started a war against the district forest rangers over the rights to ponderosa timber and grazing lands which had been fundamental to the way of doing things in the regional community for 300 years. Four sheriffs were shot, though not killed, and several of the outlaws hid in the mountains for months before being captured.

Where natural resources were concerned, sentiments ran high. In 1997, a federal judge ruled that the home team could cut down a million board-feet of old-growth timber, fueling outrage from out-of-state environmentalists whose appeals came too late. It was the same tenor of warfare surrounding the salt beds in the New Mexico desert 25 miles from Carlsbad, where the first nuclear dump in the United States was officially sanctioned in March of 1999 after 25 years of legal wrangling. The Waste Isolation Pilot Plant comprised deep tunnels a half mile beneath the earth's surface. There, more than six million cubic feet of materials contaminated with radiation from the country's 23 weapons installations would be stored during the coming 30 years. Protesters tried to block the roadway to the 1.8 billion dollar repository, but in the end, the plutonium-rich flatbed truck arrived and its cargo was deftly unloaded to the ruby-cheeked cheers of a few dozen Carlsbad patriots whose paychecks started flowing at that historic moment of national garbage collection.

Amid this wealth of hazy, haphazard, hazardous contraries, in a state notorious for them, the Oasis arose as a concept in the beleaguered mind of one woman, Wisteria Serena, the tenacious descendent of a massive food-manufacturing family. She'd been won over to the cause of horses whose long journey to the glue factory had given her brief life little rest.

The horse scandals in America were dreadful. Well over 300,000 of them turned into glue annually. Glue for envelopes, dolls, quaint little family matters, for sealing toys and other broken things back together.

Among racing horses, a known 7,000 were retired each year. After earning billions for their owners and fans, they were turned out not to rolling pasture but to slaughter.

"If one horse is in pain, anywhere, I am in pain," she had frequently Buddhacized to the Mexican laborers who helped her out 70 hours a week.

She not only helped the animals, but might suddenly give a worker and his wife a goodly sum, pay every dime of a heart transplant, or send their kids to college.

"No coffee breaks," reported one of her staff. "Time's better spent brushing pig bellies."

Wisteria's marriage to the Irish Poet Laureate of Trinity College served only to delay her eventual return to the New Mexico of her upbringing, and to the very mountain range where as a little girl she'd experienced her first epiphany in nature. The unexpected inheritance from a great-grandmother of 200,000 Common B unrestricted shares of vegetable bisque soup, prunes and artichoke hearts set her free. They were trading at the time of her inheritance at nearly ten dollars a share. Enough for her to cash out and acquire the Oasis, a mountain of old-growth forest with century-old barns, a creek, a river gorge, and paddock cleared in the nineteenth century for a lumber mill.

Wisteria rescued show and race horses of every variety, particularly the Tennessee Walkers, the most abused of all equines. Each day was spent combating diseases like strangles, eastern, western and Venezuelan encephalitis, and various *strept equi*. Her passion soon encompassed goats and cows and sheep and burros as well. Every cow she saved meant fewer taco fillings in Mexico; fewer gallstones for jewelry and less liver for Heparin. No more hide for footwear and upholstery, nor tallow allocated to candles and floor wax. And no more steer bone for bonemeal or dried blood at $4.35 a pound.

Several hundred wild turkeys cruised the property, taking advantage of the many hay and alfalfa cube depots for the other animals. Let the turkey defy Democracy. Spurn the White House. Reject every other US household. A mountain lion, some coyotes and bobcats and a few reintroduced wolves also inhabited the uplands, which now connected Wisteria's ranch to 2,000 acres of surrounding green belt she had leased for 99 years from the US Government. Let ranchers perish in their acrid jealousy. And the range they had destroyed come back, and the ghosts of all those dickless cowboys toss and turn in the mythology of their wicked graves.

She had a special love for goats. Goats that were massacred by Mussolini, who believed that a Fascist Italy was too good for goats. A third of the Italian hollow-horned and ruminating Capra had been wiped out during the Dictator's time. Wisteria had a reputation for remembering every such insult, too numerous for any one human to enumerate, even in ten lifetimes.

A staff of seven, in addition to her gardening team, saw to it that the more than 400 animals were abundantly doted upon. Wisteria spent several hundred thousand dollars each year to cater to the animals' every whim. The single largest expense went for the hay, oats and alfalfa, and supplementary foods. The grasslands were insufficient to accommodate so unnatural a consolidation of large animals. Grain hay was the practical, if imperfect, alternative: wheat, alfalfa, corn, soy—organically grown, the mixtures usually ready to be tested by late May. Bales would be brought to the ranch, the animals introduced to the crop for the year, and if they spat it out, it was back to the drawing board. The cows particularly were finicky about their hay. It had to be free of chaff, of course, with just the right amount of moisture, green fodder content, and creamy heads. Wisteria had been sued twice by laborers who'd injured their backs bringing down bales, so one of her last expenditures was for a used squeeze, a hydraulic forklift which cost her loads.

She got all teary-eyed when they died. Like elephants, whales, parrots and ants, cows wept, mourned the dead for several years, composed eloquent verses on the subject of their bereavement, left clues to their rituals in cow-patty circles high upon ridges. These Wisteria had evidently deciphered.

At one point the local utilities company planned to expand power in the area and had obtained approval from the state to put up miles of line and poles across land which included Wisteria's. The power was unnecessary, she argued. She was no energy authority. Instead, she fought the proposal on the basis of the threat to intrinsic beauty. For five hours Wisteria testified as an expert witness to the value of scenery before lawyers for the Public Service Commission. The resulting 108 pages of transcript constituted a legally defensible definition of the love of nature and the rights of animals, forests, valleys and mountaintops. The attorneys for the Commission struck a deal with her: they'd go elsewhere with their power poles if she agreed to keep her testimony private.

"She was trapped," said Louise, one of her assistants, with whom Marigold dealt upon purchase of the ranch. "Of course we all would have liked to see her testimony disseminated, at least on the Web. But she had a stronger imperative—only one, really: the care of all animals. New Shore. Baby Face. Leonardo. General O'Brien. The Rainbow Mare. Valley Girl. Whiskey Voice. Hundreds of others."

Marigold had paid three million for the Oasis. It was to be a think tank for compassion, a place where steers could be free and roam as on the Serengeti—a strange notion in North America (or anywhere for that matter), a vision that had obviously poured into him at Gundlepet. He would not rest until every cage, bifurcation and name tag was extirpated. No barbwire, rules, zones, ordinances. Nothing to prevent the grand scheme of animal socialization which he had in mind. For the Commander, this intermingling was a picture passed down by Savery and Jan Brueghel the Elder, eschewing all practical side effects. For he had risen to that plateau of parables and startling nuances whereby ideals far exceeded reality, and one could simply go there.

Still, certain annoying details begged his attention, no matter how deeply he strode or how intellectual his high-minded pursuits. The old house needed a complete overhaul, and an insurance binder. The stairs were caving in, the roof sinking; it was home to several screech owls and their young. Wisteria had refused to bother them. She also feared Western doctors. Failing to look after herself properly, or to take her radiation pills, vulnerable to all those who were after her money, including accountants, book-keepers, lawyers, executors and bank officers, she died sad and probably angry, but not alone, Marigold was to discover. There were hundreds of animals to console her.

Her ashes were tossed into a storm, wind and hail, 70 miles per hour the day the Oasis went up for tender, causing quite a stir among locals, who took up a collection to try to appropriate the acreage, topple the sanctuary, and have all the animals put down.

By the time Marigold stepped up to the plate and acquired the properties, the Oasis sign had been riddled with shotgun blasts, the gopher holes and watering trenches poisoned. He'd been hit by notices from federal agencies regarding imposed responsibilities upon said owner for the investigation and clean up of any hazardous waste sites and the provisions under which he might be granted "safe harbor" status, as it was termed. The Army Corps had determined that during heavy rains endangered red fairy shrimp might theoretically be holding up in two sinkholes near to the Oasis. They had mitigation problems of their own and so filed an injunction for a Biological Opinion and the removal of all ungulates. Marigold fought back. The case was being developed. None of which he quite understood. How binding judgments could be toppled by spineless judges, or other judges bought outright. He was to learn that this was standard practice in the United States.

What began as a simple enough "think tank for compassion," a steady supply of alfalfa cubes, carrots and grain hay for the animals, a summer resort for wild turkeys, an oasis for cows and goats, a reprieve for race horses otherwise condemned to a life of torture and burros earmarked for destruction by the government, was now mired in paperwork concerning liability under the Department of Defense *Appropriations Act* and the *H.R. 3610 Comprehensive Environmental Response, Compensation and Liability Act of 1980*. It gave Marigold a major migraine and he simply could not cope. He longed for the old days of poor anonymity. And that was just after a fortnight of efforts.

That yearning was amplified amid the present stampede of soil and water experts descending on the ranch in search of toxic wastes, trace metals, improperly disposed-of manures, leaking diesel drums and watershed liabilities. Flood controls had been abandoned. The animal chalets were leaning, the water hydrants inoperative, and the two-ply fencing around the perimeters utterly inadequate. Because Wisteria was partial to termites, she never touched woods but insisted on providing safe haven for them all, as well as the seven known species of sapsucker, woodpecker and flicker inhabiting the property—Nuttall's, Williamson's, white-headed, red-naped. A hundred problems assailed the exhausted Commander. Ten thousand cries.

Ranch terms, alone, were enough to throw him, for he was completely unfamiliar with the speech, cellular details and tacking concerns of real or working people. In fact, he knew nothing about his own species. He was a stranger even to himself, acting out impulses with no real compass, register or ledger. Lost to any firm control of his senses, a victim of involuntary accords, nervous twitches, a crazy bone that refused to heal, physiological affiliations uncharacteristic of most males, gut reactions and six senses crudely choreographed. A reaction time unbeholden to gravity or common logic.

His aspirations were as peculiar and convoluted as the 108 pagodas built between 1885 and 1895, by hand, one stone at a time, atop Mount Maisan in Chollabuk Province by the Korean monk Yi Kap-Ryog to help end the world's agonies. And he was afflicted by what Karl Marx described, in his *Theses on Feuerbach*, as that tendency of philosophers to render historical commentary without ever once considering the possibilities of present or future social responsibility.

How to do so? his irascible heartbreak confided. One task at a time, or by voluminous pontificating? Empower people, or scold them? Raise the issue, or let it sink the human race silently and in their sleep, thus sparing Mother Earth any future indignity?

He marveled at and gobbled up the litany of woeful flashpoints in John McNeill's stunning work of history, *Something New Under The Sun*, a meditation upon turmoil. Marigold asked, Did one really need to know so many uncountable griefs? Superphosphate mining in Kazakhstan; devastating nickel production in New Caledonia; land clearance in Cebu; smog epidemics in Glasgow? Were we as a species destined to pour metals into the Rhine, raw sewage into Puget Sound? Was our rape of the Ogallala Aquifer, the Amazon and Aral Sea a fact of our very genes, and if so, might some Three Gorges Dam-type fiasco effectively serve to waterlog and ultimately destroy the agent of destruction? As of the 1980s, McNeill pointed out, following a drought that had exposed sediments at Russia's Lake Karachay, a person standing out in the open air nearby for a merely an hour would receive a lethal dose, 3,000 times more radiation, in fact, than was released at Hiroshima. Not only that, the breast milk and tissue of many Inuit could be described as hazardous waste, while all of the Arctic was melting.

All these contemplations fairly mired the Commander. Who am I? What have we done? What can I do? Can I go on, I can't go on. You must go on... over and over again. Between the harried hue of Samuel Beckett and unheard plaints of Gauguin.

"You need to hire a manager or two," Sannazaro explained with his flair for easy simplicity and coolness of mind.

"Then who will manage the managers?" replied the Commander. "More managers. You can afford thousands of them if need be."

The notion had not escaped Marigold, nor the idea of expanding upon the land's biological carrying capacity, saving more downers, tracking the hateful activities of the Animal Damage Control, and ferreting away the doomed predators and non-target victims before the US Department of Agriculture bounty hunters could get to them with their cyanide-laced spring-loaded traps, their snares and shotguns. One more emergency shadowing the Oasis: armed mercenaries converging on his land.

But he was no ecologist, or biologist, or conservation manager. In fact, Mr Marigold knew very little about how anything in the natural world worked. Why the sky was blue, or why stars twinkled; what prompted a potato to sprout buds, or a spider to eat its mate. Lacking any grounding in even elementary science, his no-holds, no-grasp, no-knowledge, no-experience, all-intuition approach to resolving ranch crises put him even deeper into a pit. He had no credibility. No common sense, no desire to become too well acquainted with anything practical beyond his antiquated knowledge of surveying trig points, delineating east from north (when he was lucky), subtracting 21 percent or so on a compass reading to establish true North—or was it the magnetic North? Long before the US military had fiddled with GPS waypoints to confuse the Soviets, thus further confounding the surveying world, Mr Marigold had—with absolute conviction—totally retired from the slightest practicality or point of fact. Every detail was to him a tyranny. His very breath a fiction. So far out of his depth was the Oasis that it appeared likely he would have to spend the rest of his woeful history mopping up manures, sweeping termite droppings, sweet-talking rats and flees, and neutering gophers.

"The cost of doing nothing in a sadly indifferent world," he told his faithful Squire. "Or conversely, stepping into the river."

"How can you speak of costs? A glib word, hewn from the meaningless argot of intangibles. Furthermore, there are strong interests in every quadrant—people passionate about causes. But yes, it is sad, until somebody like yourself comes along and steps, in truth plunges into that river."

"We're just quibbling over words," the Commander said in a huff. "That's how it works, idiot."

"No, that's how it melts down."

"You take pleasure in torturing yourself. Still. After all we've been through. What's more, you will concede we are a species helplessly addicted to quibbling. Nothing can be done about it."

"We could stop entirely. No more speaking. No more patois. Adopt a new methodology."

"Walk around like zombies, you mean?" Sannazaro was tiring of the Commander's self-inflictions. They could lead nowhere.

"No, there's the music of the tribe, for example."

"And you're the one who decided to leave. To give in to the silly ideal of Disneyland."

"That was only a metaphor."

"But Rajibai took it seriously."

"He'll get over it. We're not going. No way."

"What you apparently fail to understand is that your whole Being inhabits Disneyland!"

The Commander thought for a while, greatly confused. Finally he said, "I imagine somebody once built a boat of rushes, tens of thousands of years ago. For what reason? One may speculate. But having reached the opposite shore, the boat sitting there undamaged on the beach, all was possible. The future had been writ, full of shrilling, fossicking and skimming, alive with honey-eating, hut-building, expenditures in every direction. It took thousands of years to build up this huge edifice of pathos, my dear man. And now we sit on the shore, full of self-doubt and the onus of responsibility. I am lost. I admit it."

But what he did know, and knew quite well, was what constituted suffering. The cat that had been burned; the three-year-old pit bull who'd nearly bled to death after his ears had been sliced through with scissors; the mountain lion in a conibear trap, eating its own paw off and starving to death. Sometime before Marigold's acquisition of the Oasis, the Governor had signed into law SB 339, making extreme animal cruelty a fourth-degree felony across New Mexico, punishable by up to 18 months in jail. But it did not account for wild animals, or birds or rodents, stock animals or research animals, hunting, fishing, trapping or pest control, and these glaring gaps in the law brought droves of animal rights supporters down to the state capital rotunda in Santa Fe to protest the discrepancies.

And, as the Commander now began to realize, the "Land of Enchantment," as the state was labeled, suffered from a raft of human dysfunction. Of all the states, it was said to be the cruelest to animals in the entire nation, and the Oasis seemed, to him at least, a last chance, a crucial sanctuary where sanity and distributive justice for all beings might prevail.

So there he stood: virtue surrounded by gravediggers piling up all around him. And, to make it worse, the utter chaos unleashed by an over-zealous resident gardener at the Oasis—an Australian who had proposed a pattern of floristic shade that would lend itself to the clime and zoology of northern New Mexico (he thought). With the best interests in mind, he had planted adaptable ornamentals, wind breaks, and sun-reflective, drought-resistant species from South Africa and New South Wales. It all sounded elegant and breezy on paper. In reality, the whole ranch was unraveling. Cows had started belching inordinate volumesworth consuming Cape honeysuckle and asparagus fern; horses were spitting up the red-centered hibiscus. Donkeys had destroyed acres of bracelet honey myrtle, creating a tinderbox ready to detonate. Sheep had lost their balance consuming Swan River daisy and pincushion hakea, and were walking into each other, utterly drunk; and the entire property was overrun with sexually aroused quail taking refuge in the cat's claw. A rare form of sea urchin hakea had invited tens of thousands of nectar-feeding birds that were now multiplying at a fantastic rate, while all the goats were getting stoned on the seeds of little kurrajong trees (a favorite of Australian aborigines). If that weren't trouble enough, the *Grevillea* Ivanhoe had engendered a never-before-seen outbreak of Hummingbirditis—a highly contagious infection causing Vietnamese pot-bellied and Yorkshire pigs to attempt flight, as they had done in the West Indies, it was rumored. A few of them actually achieved lift-off. At the same time, Spanish-speaking bees were swarming round the fern-leafed banksia and producing not honey, but salza that was inducing a whole new rhythm among frogs and crickets, and altering nearly overnight the evolution of the ecosystem in the immediate vicinity. And there were additional problems attending the widespread planting of the gorgeous gray Cootamondra wattle, non-native frangipani and coral pea. All the plants were swaying to undetectable tunes; their pollinators growing little headpieces, like sombreros. It was bizarre. And could not be good for the poor little creatures, whose confusion was palpable to the Commander.

But worst of all, feeling the heat from so many other temporarily deranged species, the gophers and squirrels at the Oasis were frantically digging multitudes of burrows and holes to escape the shambles overhead, causing cows to injure themselves. And now two of the ranch boys had taken to making dinner stew out of the rodents.

And then came an unexpected fanfare of bombshells: Rajibai declared his intention of enrolling in public school. Alma re-emerged, or, more exactly, her lawyer, demanding half the Commander's estate. There were other emergent claims as well, not least of which that Marigold was not of his right mind, could not even manage his socks drawer—according to his embittered housekeeper—let alone all … that … money! The Commander was hurt and flabbergasted by these and many other preposterous half-truths. Especially in light of all those years couped up with the unprotesting Mongolian. But Marigold still thought of her as family. It normally took the Commander three seconds to forgive and forget. But Alma was not his only distraction.

So entangled were Marigold's sudden problems that he actually considered one extreme solution which, according to Sannazaro who was quickly drawn into the labyrinth of woes, was no resolution at all. Marigold intended to leave the United States for good, and retire somewhere near Erewhon Flats, to live a life of near utter solitude, far from America and from people in general. To renounce all responsibilities, connections, goals, hopes and dreams. To raise his son as a wild child, and remake himself in similar guise.

"It will be a profound experiment," the Commander concluded.

"No. Nothing profound about it. Hundreds of millions of people live in rural solitude. Tribals throughout the Third World, weirdos holed up in log cabins in Idaho and Montana, hunters in southern Missouri, homesteaders in Alaska. All you'd be accomplishing is your own defeat, and a sad day in American history that would be. I won't bother dignifying it more than that. It does not warrant discussion."

Fortunately, within a matter of days, the one practical step had been taken to fully scratch that Erewhon Flats scenario and ensure Marigold's relative peace of mind: Hidalgo cut short his round-the-world odyssey and flew directly home to tackle the monstrous pall of legal fiascoes. Sannazaro had been the one to track him down and convey the dire state of mind of their mutually beloved friend. And Hidalgo had immediately applied a salve. No matter how serious the allegations, Hidalgo explained, these murmurs of fiscal lynching were nothing more than hold-ups, slow-moving cogs that would amount to naught.

"Indeed, we'll counter-sue and recover court costs from all of the bastards," he went on, confident his client was untouchable.

Moreover, the money manager in whose hands Hidalgo had placed a considerable portion of the Commander's funds now reported that in spite of rampant and diverse expenditures on nearly every continent, the Marigold estate was nearing five billion in value. His 15 million shares of Cisco, Microsoft and Oracle had enjoyed numerous splits, accounting for a 400 percent increase in value. The market knew no limits. Wall Street analysts were speculating on a Dow over 40,000. Other Marigold investments, like those on the Isle of Jersey, had achieved even more spectacular returns—a 2,800 percent increase in 12 months. His wealth was now generating five million a day, with little or no tax liability given his various depreciating assets. By the time he was 60, he might well be worth 50 billion, said the money man. Moreover, the bulk of investments were eco-targeted, socially responsible. All were vastly outperforming the S&P 500.

None of this money talk alleviated the Commander's anxieties about the squirrel and gopher holes, however.

The first thing he did was fire the ranch hands who'd been sautéing the critters and putting chewing gum or mustard gas canisters in their burrows. But while he might fill in all the holes, the squirrels would just keep making them. Marigold was no disciplinarian and hadn't a clue what to do. So he went to the source, seeking advice from little Ebert.

Now that might seem nonsensical to some, but in fact Ebert and the Commander had always loved one another and had a way of communicating which neither thought out of the ordinary. Their familiarity was half the method. For all the little fellow's mooning atop the rich furry mane of Anastasia, he needed a bona fide mate, and Marigold was at least slightly more his size. But Ebert was no ordinary squirrel. He had grown up on the South Rim of the Grand Canyon; was an Epicurean accustomed to truffles that grew in the moist underpockets of high-country ponderosa pine, and sleeping until noon atop down comforters. He'd newly taken to snozoling under the covers with Rajibai, and it was the Commander's hope that Ebert might impart his unusual sleeping habits to all the other rodents of the Oasis.

Hence, while the financial citadel was assailed on all sides and Hidalgo held down the fort, off went Rajibai, Sannazaro, Marigold and Ebert to the Oasis. They drove in Sannazaro's brand-new cobalt Bentley.

"A little ostentatious, is it not?" the Commander pointed out.

"It's a safe car, and a nice color," replied the Senator. "But Iacobo, what's gotten into you? That's 350,000 dollars you could have spent rescuing kiwi, or saving mangroves."

Sannazaro, more taken with the incredible paint job and full service bar in back (including teak holders for coffee cups), was scarcely apologetic. "I couldn't control myself," he said.

They dragged behind them a large U-Haul loaded with hundreds of down pillows and blankets, and several hundred pounds of nesting material of every variety—mohair and cashmere, straw, chintz, rolls of velvet, serge, and thousands of cotton balls.

The next day, the Commander assembled all the ranch hands like an Army general. It was a heavenly New Mexico morning.

"Friends, I know we've got this problem of squirrel holes, so I'd like you all to meet one of my dearest associates. His name is Ebert. That's both his good name, and his family or genus, or whatever."

Ebert came out almost on cue from inside one of the pillows. A grand entry. There was applause from all present company. Shuffling to and fro, his little snout to the ground, he made his way to the Commander's trousers, then leapt almost effortlessly to his high shoulder and there sat perched like a navigator, chirping loudly at his astonished admirers. Rajibai laughed hysterically, for he'd never seen a squirrel act so presidentially and with such a flair for celebrity. All were charmed.

"Now, to work," hailed the Commander, and he led the way, demonstrating the plan. He placed a sweater from the new Saks in Santa Fe in the lowest limbs of a large pine, then fixed it up with seductive cotton balls, shredded newspaper and—best of all—a granola bar, chopped avocado and bag of unsalted peanuts. Ebert dived headlong into the nest, thumbs up.

Ebert then figured out how many other squirrels and gophers inhabited the territory. Like prairie dogs, squirrels have the intuitive means of taking inventory on the basis of scent and sound, and all those on the property knew that an outsider had arrived. The communications had zipped back and forth like energy beams between stones at Royan-ji. As the staff outfitted hundreds of other trees with pillows and goodies, the squirrels and gophers came forth from their holes and began exploring the new food- and pillow-rich niches. Soon the forest was swarming with like-minded voluptuaries, all staking out their own mohair sweaters and down comforters. A mighty commotion transpired between one and all, red furry *Sciurus vulgaris* and the larger gray *S. carolinensis* all communing together in their new evolutionary Paradise.

Forget parsimony, was their maxim.

"No more holes for them," said Ebert to the Commander in a language Marigold alone understood.

True to their Rodenta rituals, merrymaking continued well into the night. Normally, squirrels sleep quietly after dark. But not this bunch. Their evenings would never be the same. In time, a new arboreal sub-species would materialize. Meanwhile, the cows, burros and horses of the Oasis could resume their meanderings across unsullied paddock, worry-free as long as the peanuts and avocado slices lasted up in the trees where neither rattlesnake nor coyote could get them. It was all that simple.

"There is a great truth to be had in all this," exclaimed Marigold to his son when the day's tasks were done and they were dozing off in the back seat of the Señor's Bentley. But he could not remember what it was.

CHAPTER 149
The Liberation of All Roosters

NOT LONG AFTER THE nearly 4,800 ground and tree squirrels had checked into the Oasis, Rajibai was coming home from his first mixed bag of a Tesuque school day, tripping in the sunlight, sauntering lightly in no less a manner than an Ebert, coursing the gathering allée of Bishop's Lodge Road, a little rucksack slung over his relaxed shoulders, when he caught sight of the most ghastly occurrence. A hunter, prowling from the doorstep of his ranch-style house, shot dead-on an elk—or wapiti, as it was called—that was gingerly feeding along hay fringes left for a palomino in his yard. The animal collapsed, hemorrhaging. Rajibai, no more than 100 feet away, stood frozen with fear. Overhead, from the forested couverte, a brain-fever bird began commenting frantically.

Rajibai ran across the road. His heart was pounding. Inside the animal, no clot forming, but salt, running in rivers towards the sad source of all gravity.

The boy scrambled beneath the fence, where coyotes had dug, sweat pouring off his brow. He raced towards the aid of the cow elk. Tears were welling inside.

He screamed. Everything was moving too fast.

Cries, eyes, nostrils, the approach of Heaven. His veins flooding. His flesh hearing every collapsing inside. Every joint detonating. The light of reason going out. Gnashing in fury. Rajibai's throat a torrent of boy pain that was more a cannonmouth striking out at the sole culprit: the casual, killing adult world.

Directed squarely at the adult himself, who stood there impervious to the horrific deed, unrepentant, Rajibai jettisoned a bomb blast of rage. Then sank down beside the gentle giant, whose sublime, unsurpassable body had been brought to the ground by a brute silver bullet no more than an inch long; every duct, tissue, gland, hormone, vessel, artery, muscle, cell, trembling on its final abyss, staring into the soul of the boy for final unctions, then passing away for the last time. For it is said by the elk that a human kill will not support a reincarnation, because such folly—the madness of people—holds hostage all of Nature, perverts down to the last detail, puts buckeye in albatross from sheer sadism, reveres the credo of the Nazis where the rest of the animal kingdom is involved—no doubt about it. It harangues, heckles and systematically disrupts the natural chain of being. For what? A few straws of hay?

Rajibai, paralyzed, looked up as the rancher arrived, aimed and put the animal out of further misery, which wasn't necessary. The elk was already gone.

The boy screamed again, lunging at the monster.

A Marati furnace erupting at the unfair universe.

A boy pounding on the big ugly cowboy's chest.

The cowboy slapping back, for that's how violence works.

Rajibai leapt away, fraught with the tantrum that was incredulity paying witness to atrocity.

"I'm going straight away to my father and uncle, and their lawyer, and then you'll see what'll happen, you foul shitbrain! Rapist! Murderer! You'll go to jail. The electric chair. They've shave off your beard! They'll burn your chest hairs. I will personally have you skinned alive. *Bastard*!"

"He was eating my horse's hay, you little asshole. Killin'ums within my right. Now get off my property before you get on my nerves, kid," shouted the man, reddened by antipathy, a loathing of self, one might adduce, though no annals of psychoanalysis had ever truly revealed the sickness inherent to killing. "Or before you piss off my dogs, and they have a go a' your liver just for sport."

By this time the rancher's dogs had indeed converged upon the scene and were howling in a carnal amusement that elicited canine pop-appetite from some atavistic human emulation. Not all of them shared in this bloodline, the boy noticed. One of the dogs, the youngest of them, paced in the rear, crying out, obviously disturbed by death, hateful of the entire ranch thing.

Rajibai ran away from that juncture of madness, and headed straight home. Breathless, he tried to explain to his father everything that had happened. The kid was sobbing, and each tear, every wail stabbed the Commander's heart like never before. Marigold felt these things, identified comprehensively with every animal's pain, and could almost not bear to hear of them.

Nonetheless, he was able to ascertain who the responsible party was. But what to do about it? The Governor, before his stroke, had passed a law allowing for ranchers to kill as many elk as they liked on their own property if they could prove reasonable damage to stock-animal provisions. Here was an obvious case in point, however inane and verminous. But to see his son sobbing from the shock of so horrible an experience did little to support the fact of any law that made it possible for murderers to commingle with arrogant immunity just down the country lane. For blood to gush in codified circumstances. Nor was that particular killer the only such offender exploiting the weakness of the state's moral code. This was not the first time. This was a Republican thing, a Democratic thing, the standard to which all states, denizens, officials, teachers, religious folk, Presidents, Mayors, parents, scholars, merchants, the white-collar workers, the blue-collar workers—everyone—paid their respects; this was the American way. Killing animals.

Marigold had not yet explained this facet of the nation to his son. Now he proceeded to do so, illuminating the relationship which Rajibai would have no difficulty understanding. As a Jain, he did not distinguish between life forms. An apricot, a rabbit, the venerable Al Gore. All were equal under the code of reverence for living beings. And hence, to take the life of a rabbit was to kill an honorable man as well. To strike a woman, step on an ant; smash a fly, abuse a child. Eat a steak, consume one's grandmother.

Later, after all his tears had washed away and Rajibai had had time to reflect more soberly on the horrors of the afternoon, Marigold attempted to expound upon the escalating crisis in the United States. He wanted the innocent to have as complete a picture as possible. Maybe here, too, Rajibai could work his magic with wirecutters.

"You see, Son, in America, as in most of India, an animal's life is valuable only to the extent it can provide a person with a quick material fix—money or food. The animal is rarely considered in its own right. All animals are said to be owned by the state, however ludicrous and vindictive a notion. But most ownership terminates when the animal is murdered, at which time it becomes the property of the killer, unless it is an endangered species, and then the pelt is confiscated. In some cases, the local Indians may keep eagle feathers for religious purposes, or bear claws."

"The truth is too horrible. There are over 400,000 known hunters and anglers in New Mexico, and all of them consume their grandmothers. You believe in reincarnation. You understand exactly what I'm talking about."

The boy nodded. He simply hadn't counted on the richest nation in the world stooping to this. Eating all the grandmothers, and grandfathers.

Marigold went on to describe how these unrepentant assassins had all been issued official licenses to engage in free-for-all slaughter by the State Game Commission, a group of insiders selected by the Governor for four-year terms. Their job, on the surface, might be deemed laudable by the unwary: to carry out the provisions of the *Wildlife Conservation Act*, with specific reference to endangered species. Endangered. This was the one designation behind which all other acts of barbarism were concealed or justified. The Act assumed that some species should live, others could die, a distinction based upon nothing more than economic tabulations. An entire population was perceived in terms of the sustainable harvest it could yield for human satisfaction.

Moreover, countless endangered animals could themselves be murdered under certain conditions. A person could easily and legally claim self-defense if, for example, a river otter, gently meandering muskrat, pike, redfish or white bass could be shown to have threatened the man's property, or his other domestic animals; if a rainbow trout, leaping high, should scare his children or—crazy though it sounds—a mockingbird disturb his pet hamsters.

"Children your own age, Son, are also free to kill. And you kids don't even need a license. There are many other exceptions as well. You can kill one fur-bearing animal every week for an entire year, again with no license, for the sheer sadism of it, if you like."

"But what's the difference whether you have a license or not? Isn't murder murder, no matter the circumstances, Father?"

Marigold replied with great pride in his little wisdom-getter, "That's right. Governments have OKed murder when it's called a state of war, or capital punishment, or against an animal. The license is nothing more than another form of taxation, just like a surcharge on alcohol and tobacco. The state, and countless bond issues, are in part funded by murder. That's the way it works in America."

Rajibai was stunned. So far, his experiences in the United States had convinced him this was the worst country in the world and New Mexico the worst state of all. A place where life was not worthy of consideration and death upon everyone's lips.

Yet, some species were listed as protected: rails, weasels and kudu. Others, definitely not. What did it all mean to the javalina pursued with headlights and shotguns? Or ibex chased to exhaustion; aoudads, francoli cranes and oryx which didn't stand a chance before the gaggle of high school hunters out on a Friday night; or the timid nutria fallen prey to punks high on smack? The law conceded privilege to jovial masked ferrets; the deep Grunt Family sargos with their silver bellies and first dorsal bars; the crazy spotted whiting (known as corvinas); and the soft-furred pine marten shimmering in the autumn leaves. But it could not monitor the mayhem which had reduced each of these species to fewer than 1,000 individuals. Special notice was made of the delicate coatimundi, spectral, haunting the night, barely hanging on; the light-footed avocets or phalaropes—buffy and silvery members of the sandpiper family; and American pronghorn, so few as to give rise to doubts whether they any longer existed. New Mexican curlews had suffered 98 percent loss, while minx were formally credited with their nonexistence in the state. The poetry of nomenclature was all that could be laid claim to; the actual creatures themselves were gone, mere memory, each one a sorrowful tale of transgression, hatred and stupidity. Nature education reduced to history lessons.

Fines for killing an endangered species, if such penalties were ever adjudicated, amounted to no more than 50 to 1,000 dollars. Ranchers, putting poisons in their own stock animals, killing the human consumers, were equally immune to monitoring or legislation—at worst, a letter from the US Department of Agriculture scolding them. The travesty was ingrained, Marigold explained, in the 'ole boys' club', a distinctly American form of bullying injustice that rewarded big business and bloodlust at the expense of the consumer and all of Nature. These concepts were entirely new to Rajibai.

It was true that some of New Mexico's fishermen were catch-and-release sorts, small sadists, but most were not satisfied short of bagging a 45-pound *Morone saxatilis*, or striped bass, smashing in its head once on the boat. With their arsenal of horsehead jigs, rat-L-traps and rattling spots, streamer hooks and saddle hackles, these dumb slobs, said Marigold, were undifferentiated in their cruelty from the gaggle of muzzle-loaders, archery hunters, trappers and handgun enthusiasts all devoted to blowing away whatever came into their gunsights. Such crimes—and the colossal grief encincturing the animal kingdom—were somehow missed on most residents of the Land of Enchantment.

The Governor had additionally declared that hunters were entitled to slaughter any and all "nuisance wildlife". To that end he cited elk in alfalfa fields, coyotes, lambs and beavers in back yards. Never mind that the cows and sheep were destined to be slaughtered, or that the alfalfa, fed to beef cattle, was usurping the overwhelming proportion of the state's scarce water supplies. Even a lovesick ram that had taken to spending winters with a flock of mustangs, attempting on occasion to mate with them, was deemed a negative influence on New Mexico by the Governor's forum, and forcibly relocated to the lonely Manzano Mountains where its days wandering amid declining herds of Coue's white-tailed deer were surely numbered. These were the panic grass, fourwing saltbush, spurge and western ragweed-covered hills where trackers came in search of cougar sign and Gambel's quail, and a ram was anybody's trophy.

The point: it was hopeless. Most New Mexican wildlife was doomed. The boy had experienced it first hand this day, blood splattered on his hands, a droplet dried upon his cheek. They had left Tibet for this?

"You may change the minds of a few, but certainly not all of the millions upon millions of hunters in the United States," Sannazaro reminded the Commander. "Any more than your tirades and some silly swordplay could have made the slightest possible difference to the chicken farmers of Hong Kong. I'm no fatalist, but we've been through all this. Three days ago you insisted upon long-term intentions quite officially, I thought: No More Crusades. Only to oversee the Oasis. Or did I miss something?"

"Damn it, Iacobo, can't you see my son has been hurt? Are you so insensitive at a time like this?"

"I know what he's feeling. What we're all feeling."

"Then admit that times have changed," replied the indomitable dreamer.

"Since three days ago?"

"Since two minutes ago. Now consider: perhaps with the force of the law, in addition to my money ..." He was pioneering a new possibility.

"What? What are you doing? I know that look."

"I'm not sure, yet. But I must confess to feeling more political than ever before. All has become extremely personal. In the weeks since our return, you know as well I that all these situations have borne down upon me with a kind of terrible ferocity."

Sannazaro knew that serious eventualities were afoot.

Over the coming days the Commander, inspired by his son as well as by that much-noted 83-year-old British Viscount's campaign for re-election to the House of Lords, presently in the news, began to formulate a plan. That gentleman had called for an end to fishing by rod, and for the muzzling of all cats when out of doors to prevent what he rightly described as "the agonizing torture of mice and small birds". Marigold's kind of man.

Now the Governor of New Mexico pushed Marigold over the mountaintops by upholding a vote that allowed cockfighting in some parts of the state. The notion was appalling to the Commander, and he decided to take his son to see first-hand what could be done about it.

Bringing Rajibai had its own strategic logic, because throughout southeastern New Mexico children routinely frequented the killing pits, despite at least one legislator's attempts to ban youngsters from witnessing what went on. While nine New Mexico counties banned cockfighting, it was legal throughout the rest of the state, as it was in Oklahoma and Louisiana. (Strange, considering that in Oklahoma it was illegal to maim fruit but not to slaughter animals.) But New Mexico was considered the real 'sanctuary' for breeders and gamblers, the number one hotbed for rooster killing in America.

"I don't know how big a deal it is here, really," the Governor had weighed in.

In 45 states elsewhere in America, cockfighting was a felony or misdemeanor. Accordingly, most of the more than half-million cockers took their disingenuous atavism to those few remaining hide-outs, where killing was encouraged and legally sanctioned, and New Mexico was a major source of income for these assholes, as Marigold called them.

Squired by Sannazaro in his new Bentley, the Commander and his son arrived in the small town where the mob was coming and going. Jeers and hollers permeated the dusty bleachers above the pit, which was set in the confines of an antiquated drive-in movie theater. There were, easily, 700 spectators, each of whom had paid their 20-dollar admission ticket. The cockers were busy down on the floor preparing their roosters with secret concoctions, incantations from Thailand, Mexico, the Philippines and the Creole bayous, and sharpening the razor spurs which had been kept bayonet-like from the time of the birds' adolescence. The men (and some women and teens) were rubbing down their feathery little killers with sulfur and rum and gunpowder.

All at once, to the whiskey-throated exclaiming of the referee, two tortured birds were freed from their cages in the rings and went at each other, clawing with desperate rapidity, each one shredding the other. Within ten seconds both birds were down, panting, spurting blood. The orgy of infliction was greatly augmented by the howls of abominable stupidity from the spectators' gallery.

"But *why* are they doing that?" asked Rajibai.

"Because they are insane," replied the Commander, thinking back to the strange description of a barnyard cockfight by St Augustine, who had somewhere written, "We chose to watch."

Bets were waged, won and lost, and a good deal of cash exchanged. Families ate their picnics, enjoying the repetition of the scene: two birds, genetically tracing their language, and probably their genetic customization, to 10,000 years ago, killing one another with impossibly fast thrusts of their talons, each of which was outfitted with a three-inch-long razor. The blood and guts splattered everywhere, and the birds wobbled in the purgatory of inevitable death, opining no other ounce of willpower than the struggle to remain standing during their last few breaths. The whole drama was an order of barbarism that no sane human could abide. But the worst was yet to come.

"Rodriguez?" Marigold muttered.

He was certain he saw Rodriguez being readied in a cage. Someone had come into the Camp of the Spirits and stolen the bird! Defying the crowd and a chorus of jeers, the Commander raced onto the floor and demanded to gain a closer inspection. Sure enough, upon calling the bird, Rodriguez let out the most dreadful cry imaginable. It remembered the Commander from Antarctica, and from that day at the well, long ago, when Rodriguez had been present during the aftermath of Amigo's deliverance. Who could guess the horrors of his present status? How had this proud avian of superior intelligence and feelings been separated from his loving Raquel?

"That is my bird!" Marigold shouted as the rooster clawed furiously at his cage to be freed.

"Like hell it is!" exclaimed the burly redneck who towered over both the Commander and the rooster.

"We'll see about that!"

"But you can't permit it!" cried Rajibai.

"Fear not, lad. I've got a plan."

With the opening of the cages, as loud as their lungs permitted Marigold and Rajibai cried out the proud name "Rodriguez!" The inducement was complete. The rooster turned on its slave trader with the righteous venom of all roosters oppressed and tortured throughout history. His so-called opponents, other roosters of every variety, size and color, little feather-beaten gladiators who had been forced into the ring to kill each other when all they had hoped for in life was to greet the dawn and strut like first love through the high grass and belt arias to the den mothers of Chickentown, did the same. Galvanized by their comrade's rallying cry, they struck out at the humans, slashing cheeks and wrists, and clawing out eyes before anyone could stop it, flying into the bleachers and slicing dozens of throats, arms, foreheads in a confusion masterminded by the singularly brilliant and world-renowned Rodriguez.

Once settled in Marigold's arms, the bird simpered, pleaded, professed every adoration, and passed out, allowing the three of them to make their hasty departure. And 29 other roosters raced free into the desert. The commotion in the pit and up in the bleachers was so great that nobody exactly caught their exit.

With the bird safely in his arms, and the boy by his side, the Commander made it back to their vehicle, where Sannazaro was waiting.

For a while, all of them remained silent. Then Mr Marigold roused himself from his revery. "I'm running for Governor," he said. "And you, Rodriguez, will be my running mate."

CHAPTER 150
Mr Marigold Runs for Governor

BY THE TIME they'd reached Tesuque four hours later, his resolve was adamantine, despite every argument opposing it. Sannazaro mustered memories of Ross Perot, Donald Trump, Steve Forbes and other political wannabes who'd learned that money wasn't everything.

But the Commander was undaunted. He had already begun to configure his team. With his novel Lieutenant Governor Rodriguez confirmed, he chose Sannazaro to become Chief of All Approximations, Inquiries and Public Opinion; Rajibai as the Superintendent of Schools and State Waterfalls; Alvaro would be in charge of Sex Education in the Classrooms, based upon the MexFam exemplar (demonstrations of condom use, et cetera); Lady Champion could run the Animal Leisure Time Development Board; and Ginevra would take charge of New Mexico's image, a brand new department he named Division of Enchantment. He asked Madame Vignette to head the State Lands Preservation Commission; chose Hidalgo for Attorney Spectacular, and Raquel to head up the Poachers' Punishment Office. He pegged a motley crew to spearhead the Small Business Advocacy Council; selected every local environmentalist to take up the reigns of hundreds of other workforces, spheres of council, tenures and jurisdiction. Greenies arrived by droves from thin air.

One of his first acts in office, he proclaimed, in addition to liberating all roosters and hens, and banning all animal-related sport, exploitation, consumption and presumption, would be the total dismantling of Los Alamos. Never mind it was a federal laboratory—he was dying to fight the good fight under so-called *42 U.S. 1983*, the Civil Rights statute that had been expanded over time to include all federally protected life, liberty and property. He would piggyback upon his Los Alamos assault a volley of other rapid-fire endeavors, including (but not limited to) the debarring of two out of three lawyers in the state; the dismantling of nearly every unclean judge, bank and trust, using the Disciplinary Committees and Ethics sections of the New Mexico Bar Association, as well as the banking regulatory environment, to do so. He would stay out of the state courts, and keep everything tied up in federal jurisdiction. That way, there was no bail. Justice was swift. His reforms would be sweeping.

He had worked out his strategies for abolishing the Livestock Bureau, the Poultry Office, the Dairy Association and the Realtors Confederacy of New Mexico. He would make tennis illegal within state lines because of the bad influence bouncing balls evidently had on sensitives like Elizabeth Herbert Buzzard-Breath, who he had decided to place in charge of his new Neighborhood Revitalization Committee. That would include trailer court and Indian Reservation beautification schemes. All nuclear wastes would be shipped out of state COD to Washington DC; a 20 percent tax would be placed on all video, massage and beauty parlors, as well as drinking establishments, such proceeds earmarked for services benefiting Native Americans, children and mothers. A strict quota system would be placed on visitors from Texas, New York and California.

"I will mandate that 51 percent of the 42 state senators be women, rather than the existing ten, and that a greater than equal share of the 70 representatives be allotted to those of the fairer sex. Most importantly, I intend to outlaw all hunting. Concomitant with that shall come an edict to conclude the mournful era of cages, jails, pens, traps, snares, blinds, pitfalls, forced domestications, hybridizations and genetic modification. I intend to make cockfighting a mandatory 59-year public-service sentence. Guns will be illegal in the state of New Mexico. Neither civilians nor lawmen will ever be allowed to have them, under any circumstances. Every day shall be proclaimed a state holiday in honor of a different species, and a lottery held for which all proceeds will go towards improving the life and habitat of that species and the community which shares the niche with it. Moreover, those eight percent of Americans—or nearly 20 million—who see fit to live in mobile homes and trailer parks shall be commended. By their example, the soil is afforded a reprieve. There will be fairness in my Administration. No creature singled out. Man and beast alike. Simple, no?"

Aside from such 'executive decisions', Marigold was resolved that most other orders and mandates of his administration would be weighed in consideration of a single gold standard.

"What would that be?" the bemused Squire inquired.

"Simply put, each judgment and resolution must cut the mustard in Jain, Bishnoi and Toda society. And it should pass the test of compassion and wisdom which, you can be sure, Anna, Crowquill, Paramatman and of course Rodriguez and friends would collectively demand of any amendment or adjudication."

"But New Mexico is not Toda Land," Sannazaro reminded him. "Ahh, but you forget the universal seduction of the Ideal."

"If I forget it's only because I am somewhat preoccupied. Ever since the Marshall Plan, and the end of the Cold War, the ideal you're speaking of has lost most of its punch. Most generations have forgotten."

"That's entirely ridiculous. Who would not be spellbound by the vision of a Utopic Poictesme, her children perpetually skipping stones, sucking on lollipops, resolved to be silent and good, white edible sculptures by Maillol; or the Paradise of Antan, its jeweline Isles of Wonder somewhere behind El Dorado, with air conditioning, ruled softly by the Queen of Faery—all in our back yards!"

"As Chief of all Approximations, I must confess to serious scepticism. Who do you expect to be spellbound? First of all, nobody, myself included, has ever heard of half the places you refer to. Most Americans can't even tell you whether Milano is east or west of Roma. Eighty percent of the public had no qualms about our sending troops to the Persian Gulf, but the vast majority had no idea where it was or even in which continent. How do you expect them to get all fired up about Poictesme? However you pronounce it. We've been through every rhetoric, sampled public opinion, and, frankly speaking, in one city, town and country after another have discovered only uneducated, dour, selfish, violent, cruel, indifferent, gun-, God-, shopping mall- and money-crazed individuals whose idea of Utopia is a beer, a bag of popcorn and a B-movie. If that sounds cynical, you know me well enough to understand it's even worse than that. I am not a misanthrope, I simply have my standards. Unlike you, I do not impose them on others. That's the big difference between us."

"It's a new century, man; let bygones be bygones. Do not forget that New Mexico played a pivotal role in this country's first *Wilderness Act*, signed by President Johnson 35 years ago but, in truth, secured years before by such mystics as Aldo Leopold, Elliot Barker and New Mexico Congressman Clinton Anderson. These three truly hatched the wilderness scheme. It was Leopold, just out from Iowa, who managed to have the Gila—up in the Mogollon Mountains—designated as America's first wilderness going back 70 years; who called for a half-million acres of similar preservation in every western state; conducted something like poetry readings by horseback in the Carson National Forest; shamed hunters and fishermen and other trophy-believing sportsmen; made solemn our oath to preserve a future—an "anchor to windward", as Anderson later put it before all those dastardly oil and lumber lobbyists in Washington. All this fine and lasting sentiment ushered from the guts of New Mexico. Don't you see how easy this will be? To reinvoke all the chimes and precursors that were struck and laid down right here, in our own home turf, before us? Why, my running for Governor is as easy as pruning the roses, for the roses have already been planted. No bone meal in this Administration."

But Sannazaro's mind was fairly made up. Despite his fellow historian of idealisms, nothing seemed likely to alter humankind's record of abusing the world, of economic caste systems and power mongering. Sannazaro could deal with all those shortcomings by simply retreating to his garden and taking no care or involvement with the American public.

After all, he could rightly claim a more elevated, Italian lineage. He was an immigrant; better to keep cushioned, hide out, lay low, make not a wave or even intimate the surf. Marigold, too, might be immune, if he cared to be, to the failings of the American persona, having grown up in a more or less European household. Why bother? Let "fatigue press its seal on your eyelids", as the Danish advise. "Hear the nightingales, smell the dandelions."

But now the Commander was harking to an entirely different tune, ready to throw himself into the inferno of public scrutiny. He'd gotten the balls of Macgilliannore, the wisdom of the Elfin-King, Knight in Green, St Clair and Trefoil, too; he'd obtained Schwafurlama's magic sword, Hervardur's charms, Guido Cavalcanti's heaven's decree, the Dryad's hail and Triton's swarm. His bulk had grown immense, his pike and javelin were now shivering, till grisly texture grow, and by the Danube's banks, his prancing steed to go, or some such gibberish.

"Call me an old monk, or baron. Name me Oluf the Sir, Gaundul or Skogul—no matter. I'm ready!"

"Jesus," Sannazaro winced, fearing the outcome.

"Don't name me Jesus, though. Not in this state," Marigold appended.

"What makes you think you're able to run for Governor? What if there is some law preventing lunatics, not to mention roosters, from holding office?"

Marigold pinched his cheek. "Don't you wish! But calm yourself, dear friend. When Monsieur John Q Public understands what wonders I have in store for his community, why, he'll embrace me as if it were Sunday and we were all in church together."

"When did you ever step foot in a church, and why, speaking of God, with all the turmoils engulfing you just now, would you undertake to cause a veritable rain of sorrows voluntarily?"

"Only a Governor can effect those decisions a billionaire cannot."

"Such as?"

"There are countless executive orders that require no consensus by a state assembly. A Governor can mandate state monuments, thus tying up land under conservation rubrics, but without the damnable process of winning votes for preservation."

"Your money can do the same thing."

"But my money, after all, is limited. Whereas the only restraints upon the Governor are the boundaries of his state. Why, if he so chooses, he could declare all of New Mexico sacred, inviolate, a conservation sector.

Which is more or less my intention. Hence, the wisdom of getting into politics. And surely you've figured out that a billion dollars is good for some things and not for others?"

"Precisely. With a billion dollars I can buy every happiness and never again think about the rest."

"You cannot buy love."

"Sure you can. There was the case of the fabulously wealthy eighteenth-century Moroccan caliph with a harem of 900 of the most beautiful virgins in all the Sahara."

"Do your arithmetic. How could any one man service 900 a night?"

"I'm not here to argue the anatomical computations. Only to sigh with some remorse at my solitude."

"My dear Chief, it is true that money can convert an empty field into ripe tomatoes, under suitable meteorological conditions—120,000 pounds of fruits, herbs and vegetables per acre, if I'm not mistaken. But it cannot change a man's mind about drinking, or slitting the throat of his hog, or maligning his wife."

"Very true, but then neither can the Governor, nor the President, nor even God, assuming they wanted to, which it is clear from our entire history they never did."

"But the Governor has one preeminent advantage over both the President and God."

Sannazaro waited with curious stillness.

"He can delegate more effectively than anyone else in office. Because a state is a manageable size. It is surveyable. He knows all the alleys, the players, those forces for him and against him. Whereas a President, for example, is surrounded by 8,000 scheming advisers, prevaricating, diverting, warning and scaring, praying, confusing and braying, laying legal traps, snooping and recording, contorting any direct line of expression, policy intention or willpower emanating from the Oval Office. I don't know why I never thought of it before."

"Well your timing is certainly candid. The primaries are in less than two weeks. But what will your campaign consist of ? Do you have a real plan? And how on earth do you expect your constituency to understand Rodriguez? Will you make speeches on his behalf ?"

"If need be. First I will call for legal standing for all roosters and, by implication, all other critters. We need to convince the citizenry that a rooster is canny, filled with brain power, capable of deep thought, emotional complexity, moral fiber, historical connections, biological brio, literary sophistication; is noble as Aesop first insinuated, and solutions-driven. Just what New Mexico needs. But let's develop our strategy as the seconds unwind. No point embracing flypaper if we don't need to. I am confident, for starters, that we will find unanimous support for our community relations agenda from the Dumb Friends' League, the local Astronomy Club, the Green Party, the Federation of Animal Shelters, the Lion's Club and the Jaycees."

"Presumably, you will buy broadcast time?"

"No. I don't trust television. The future is radio. By my calculations, it will cost us no more than $6.37 per citizen to disseminate my candidacy and secure their vote. In a state as politely populated as New Mexico, that sum turns out to be less than I paid to save marsh grass along the Tigris-Euphrates."

"Us. You said 'us.'"

"We are running together."

"No, sir. The only place I am running is far, far away. In the other direction." And Sannazaro continued, "It's one thing to fantasize whilst driving on the open road in a Bentley with the wind in your face, Vivaldi on the CD, a bottle of signed and numbered Cave Girl Tequila in the back seat, and a tank full of gasoline. But quite another to carry on in that fashion once you have arrived back home. You cannot possibly imagine that the same demons of local origin who delight in slaughtering wolf pups returned to the wild will just turn over their weapons because the Hermit of Tesuque has asked them to? Will you pay them to do so?"

"If necessary. I tested that very formula once, on Alma. But moral suasion would be my preferred methodology."

"What would you do with all their shotguns and M-16s? Their metal snares and cannon fodder?"

To which question the Commander had long considered his response: "Once, during the reign of the Shogun Ieyasu during the early seventeenth century in Japan, all guns were confiscated from the general populace, gunmakers put out of business, and the tens of thousands of rifles melted down into an enormous bronze Buddha. That's not all: prisoners were released, housekeepers and serfs of every kind emancipated."

But Sannazaro was not so easily impressed. "Once the guns were gone, they killed each other with swords. That was the Way of the Samurai."

"And I say there is ample historic precedent for coping with all those stubborn, moronic throwbacks to the days of the samurai."

"Go on?"

"The great Greek playwright Aristophanes has provided the means for pacifying them. Consider: there are 380,015 women of childbearing age in New Mexico. Let each of them refuse to be impregnated unless the male reforms himself according to the Governor's Code of Utopia, as I shall title it. A fair trade: sex for weapons."

"I'm going to go home and make myself some pasta," the Chief of All Approximations admonished. Then, "Oh," he added, "I suppose you will be a Third Party candidate?"

"The Greens are already the Third Party. I shall be unnumbered. We shall call ourselves the Utopian Party. No contributions accepted. I shall live my platform."

"Good God, friend, why on Earth would you heap such obvious pitfalls, perils and outright diseases of the commonweal upon yourself and all who know and love you? I thought you cherished your privacy, the silence of Iceland, the poetry of birds? And have you already forgotten what a mess your Children's Party in India turned into?"

But Murillo would hear none of these appeals.

During the coming days he set about to do his homework in his inimitable manner, preparing to meet the people and the press. He followed the state's unemployment trends which, to his surprise, were down from 7.5 percent to 6.3 percent. Nearly 20,000 new jobs had been created each year since 1993. The minimum wage had risen to $5.25 per hour, and a 500 dollar child tax credit for children under 17 had helped 177,000 families. Head Start funding had increased greatly, 247 new public school teachers were being hired, and other benefits for Technology, Literacy and Pell Grants for low-income college students were flooding in, all on account of the Democrats. Naturally, the Commander supported all of these benefits and trends. But he questioned the type of education being foisted on the students. The sorts of jobs being created. Did they promote compassion, love, tolerance, ecological sustainability? Or simply more paved roads, income? Who, if anybody, was watchdogging these things?

The Commander immersed himself in the Clinton Administration's AmeriCorps programs in New Mexico, hoping to expand their field of endeavor from hospitals and parks and schools to forests, gardens and mountains. He studied the various Tuition Tax Credit initiatives and thought of 100 other ways, working for Mother Nature, that students might apply themselves. He examined the budget for the Safe & Drug Free Schools Program with an eye towards full legalization of marijuana. He would increase the Welfare-to-Work Grants from 9.7 million dollars to 30 million dollars, vastly upgrade the Health Care for Uninsured Children and the Special Nutrition Program for Women, Infants and Children, providing a special state-wide budget for birth-control bills and abortion services. He wanted a full agenda developed that would encourage adoption, rather than pregnancy—tax incentives, even public land giveaways. He intended to ensure that all RU-486, Norplant and male abortifacients be legal over the counter. He would model incentives on those of the Indonesian and Chinese Governments, providing more lucrative employment packages to those who volunteered to be sterilized. Not a dime in tax abatement for large families.

He weighed the Childhood Immunization Initiative, with its emphasis on two-year-olds, diphtheria, tetanus, pertussis, polio and Haemophilus influenzae B, and decided to pay equal attention to young birds, orphaned squirrels and puppies, ailing deer, troubled coyote, morose mountain lions, and all farm animals, so called. He would donate outright, from his personal funds, 100 million dollars to AIDS victims in New Mexico, and another 100 million dollars to AIDS research, and he would challenge every other Governor in America to do the same, even offering—again from his personal checking accounts—a matching grant in every instance. Never mind that he would be broke ten times over, according to Sannazaro. Such details no longer mattered: Marigold was a contender! He schooled himself on the Superfund, and its clean-up efforts throughout the state, such as they were, and was resolved to more than triple the budget in this domain. Much of New Mexico was a toxic waste dump and he intended to transform Los Alamos into a clean-room of wilderness; to retrain all parking-lot attendants and bowling alley and tennis club employees into ecological waste collectors; to abolish prisons and prisoners by converting their remaining behind-bars sentences into Superfund clean-up time. Prisons would become ashrams. Monasteries. Every inmate would be enshrouded in the same aura and practical regimen of dignity by which monks are perceived and treated. Punishment, thought Marigold, was a bad idea from the beginning of time.

"No more punishment. Rather, enlightenment. Choir practice. Hymnals. Shakespeare and Cervantes served up intermittently with vegan barbecues. That will soften the hearts of America's two million prisoners, and all the callous administrators and wardens who watch over them."

He ruminated on the Safe Drinking Water Fund, knowing that there was virtually no safe groundwater anywhere in the state, and within hours developed a blueprint for developing pollution-free corridors between point- and non-point pollution sources, using mystical quartzes and Tibetan chants instead of chlorine. And as far as illegal immigrants went, he had what he thought to be an ingenious plan. Once in office, he would work with other Governors to establish a US Refugee Corridor stretching from northwestern Texas up the eastern spines of New Mexico, Colorado, Wyoming and Montana where, according to the Environmental Protection Agency's Environmental Monitoring and Assessment Program, there were no endangered, threatened or imperilled species.

"What does that have to do with anything?" Sannazaro inquired.

"Simply put, a new policy of invitations. We will ask those governments abroad, where biodiversity is threatened and the human populations expanding out of control, to send their people to this corridor. And we will ensure that those specific states bypass federal legislation in order to admit them. In other words, an open-door program whereby regions of rich biological endemism are relieved of the human burden. Bring half of Mexico to Texas. Let them struggle in a land where they won't be killing jaguars. Let dot coms replace tacos. And the motel business outstrip life in the jungle!"

"It will never work," his Squire promptly informed him. "It will, because the idea is so logical and attractive."

In every sector of government he attempted to decipher the indecipherable system of accountabilities. Who was held responsible for institutional performance, whether in elementary schools or at the Rotunda in Santa Fe? Lacking leadership, he would take on the role himself.

The Commander embarked upon his campaign with abundant seriousness, all the more remarkable considering how, in days recently past, he had sat slumped in moribund reclusion, fed up with humanity, resolved on leaving it, or dreaming anew. Until days just prior, he had thought of nothing but escape; of leaving behind all that even faintly smelled of man. Eager to adopt the forest as his mentor, and wilderness as his hair spray. But now, in contradistinguishment to himself, he was ready to save the world once again. The syndrome was a fallacy, but a great fallacy, and Marigold had it, like some rampant influenza.

Rajibai helped him write his press releases. It was a new millennium, a new opportunity for humanity solemnly to rectify wrongs against nature, and to do so in a microcosm called New Mexico. Sannazaro marveled at the Commander's cheeriness, his inexhaustibility. With so much money, how much easier to have simply avoided the fray, indulged himself without fanfare, a different Grasmere or Schoenbrunn (as the case may be) in every port, with liveried staffs to wait on him and endless pushcarts filled with doubloons to satisfy his every idyll. Neither his son, nor closest few friends would want for anything, and the world—which, in any case, would forever be the same world—would never know the difference.

Instead, the Commander spent his hours contemplating a federal law that forced every state to demand of its welfare recipients that they find jobs within 30 days. He studied race relations, garbage disposal, utilities deregulation, the role of natural gas for heavy-farting Americans, and 1,000 other matters which, months before, would have meant absolutely nothing to him. Now he was voracious, and no talk more appealed to him than that concerning kilovolt power lines, land trust boards and extraterritorial zoning commissions. In short, he had become, to Sannazaro's way of thinking, a colossal bore. What had happened to the man who once thought nothing of scrambling up a blind cliffside in search of a prehistoric bird? He had acquired a calculator and a tie, rode elevators and talked in 30-second sound bites ready made for radio.

The elections got off to a nasty beginning, mudslinging in every gubernatorial quadrant. The three other candidates were thrilled by the function the Commander fulfilled, for they each could cast their aspersions in a manner that would not backfire because, for all his eleventh-hour research, Marigold had not bothered to inquire of his opponents.

All candidates were the same, by his reckoning and he was not about to stoop to the gutter where they did their bidding, muckraking, lying to people, throwing obscene sums of money at television commercials. His aspirations were eternal truths. He was prepared to remake human nature by the very political latitude allowed a singular leader. If it could happen in New Mexico, it could happen everywhere. He suddenly had national inclinations.

On the campaign trail, he always carried Rodriguez in his arms or (a leash reminiscent of that connecting the late Gerard de Nerval to his lobster), walked hand in hand with the remarkable rooster—who seemed to cheer himself on, punch out his breast feathers and make waves, whenever on a podium or before others of his kind. Moreover, Rodriguez's fame preceded him: he was the Braveheart of chickendom, the Great Liberator of Roosterville.

Of course, what Marigold had failed to reason through were the stultifying varieties of public inertia and fear. People distrusted strangers, new models of behavior, words like 'ecology' and 'veganism'. New Mexico was, Sannazaro pointed out, a state populated by more poor people, hunters, meat-eaters, heavy drinkers, gamblers, wife and child abusers, outlaws and sagebrush rebels than nearly any other state in the union.

"All the more reason to be supremely optimistic," the Commander replied. "If we can change their hearts here, we can do it anywhere."

To Sannazaro, the Commander's intimation was clear. He was planning to go all the way with this.

But, as the coming few weeks would have it, Marigold took an unprecedented drubbing in the press, and the polls thrashed him. He was unmercifully castigated by his opponents: ridiculed by the Greenies for dividing the environmental coalition; hammered by the Republicans for alleged treasonable statements against the nation; fired upon by Democrats for fundamentalism of a new and higher order than was ever before witnessed; sued by a dozen minorities for what they took to be the last word in racist grammar; and enjoined from even speaking in many communities, and over countless radio stations, that feared for their children, their wives and daughters, sisters and brothers. The police and fire departments were ordered to protect the Commander because it was clear that his pro-choice stand was a proving ground for assassination attempts or fires, his position celebrating the Swiss model of euthanasia even more so, his solid support of prostitution as a noble profession such a wildcard, and his stern condemnation of large Catholic families so dangerous that even the authorities who protected him soon felt the need to be protected themselves. Moreover, the Commander's Lieutenant Rooster frequently took blood-letting jabs at any cockers he and his Commander might meet along the campaign trail.

All this turbulence sent a provocative signal throughout Santa Fe's bureaucracy, for no one had quite expected the backlash. What the Commander had succeeded in doing was raising a mirror to the hypocrisy of liberalism in New Mexico. In the end, what it got him, and Rajibai as well, were more troubles. Twice his Tesuque hacienda was fired upon. A fire bomb blew up in the mailbox. The boy was no longer welcome at the public school and was beaten up on more than a few occasions.

When the election tallies came in, Mr Marigold had succeeded in capturing fewer than 900 votes. And most of these were for Marigold not as Governor but as City Manure Spreader.

Tired of bullets whizzing by in the night, Sannazaro was the one who suggested they leave the country for good. New Mexico was no longer friendly to them.

"But where can we possibly go that's any better?" the Commander entreated. "We failed here, we will surely fail no matter where we venture. I think I'm quite depressed."

"That all depends on what you want to do," the wise Italian rejoined. "Stay out of politics, keep your ideas to the sand, enjoy a good cocktail without feeling compelled to dictate the terms of the party."

"Those are words I will take to bed with me," the Commander lamented, feeling worse than ever.

Across the path, adjacent to the bridge, beyond the well, Mr Marigold slipped into his nightgown and dunce cap, kissed Rodriguez and Rajibai on their respective cheeks, and with a wax candle burning feebly headed to his dusty chamber and sinking bed. Surrounded by the myriad literary swarms that had been his legacy since childhood, he collapsed onto the mattress, still damp from the night Anastasia had graced it, his face clustering three Russian down pillows, and rolled into the dark waters of his own disappearance.

CHAPTER 151
The Commander's Mid-life Crisis

IT BEGAN WITH the conventional symptoms of a flu, the Commander's body wracked with acute aches in every joint, of which there seemed to be hundreds of thousands. No knight in tarnished armor was more in need of lubricating oil, Fleetwood's Fisherman's Friend and a general overhaul. Then he thought he'd had a stroke. Couldn't remember a thing.

With spring in the air, Sannazaro's garden next door was an engine of color and medicinals, and the good Senator brought over a basket of potions: Menzies' rattlesnake orchid to recover memory, edible flowers of sulfur paintbrush to restore the blush of youth, telegraph weed for the temper, yellow eriogonum to revive taste. All had been deciphered and decocted according to some medieval Italian prescription whose formula derived from vegetable respiration, the northeast wind, a retrograde eddy in the sea, an affirmation by Pliny and the Abyssinian plain.

The Commander had his own medicine cabinet, equally compelling, though thanks to Anastasia's rough ways much of it had been mingled on the floor, strange ingredients wrongly bottled with other ones, capsules wed, fluids intercoursed, powders fused. Nonetheless, feeling as he did, the defeated Master of Cremations did not hesitate to sample every possible remedy available to his despondency, except all gel caps and those with any other animal derivatives. With no maid to look after him now, it was up to the Victor of the Desert, as Rajibai was sometimes referred to in recognition of his heroic efforts to disarm India's nuclear capability, to look after his father who, it must be admitted for purposes of a clear posterity, was not an easy patient. Sickness outraged him and he took the slightest ill-health as a personal insult, which one might suppose it always is. He was resolutely stubborn about staying in bed and, with his restive jawbones directly joined to the idea-center of his brain, tended to bite down too hard on thermometers, with occasional mercury poisoning being the result. The slightest idea prompted an inelegant lurch from the resting position into an angle more easily oriented to action, instigating an undoubted collapse backwards and a sigh of agonizing proportions.

Rajibai had never seen so sickly and spindly a figure of a man, and told Sannazaro so, though he could see that for himself. The huge expenditure of energy to run his campaign, and the bitter disappointment of defeat, left its toll. He lay in bed reading the best of Edward Earle Purinton—*The Philosophy of Fasting.* Marigold ranked his "Declaration of Faith" as one of the Great Works of Humanity down through the ages, and returned to it constantly in times of trouble.

But on this day, even Purinton's remarkable belief system, Blitzguss, Priessnitz Compress and system of tepid showers were of little assistance.

Though the Commander bathed heavily in Homburg Salts and tried some Jeyes' Fluid, in his dizziness he inadvertently took Hooper's Female Pills instead of Kirby's Compressed Tablets; he drank Laville's Gout Mixture when Lamplough's Pyretic Saline would have sufficed; he tried Powell's Embrocation over Potts' Corn Plasters, and consumed far too much of St Raphael's Livelong Potato Fritters when a little Cod Corn Cure, Mustard Leaves and Digestive Cocoa Mineralis would have surely been preferable. Who was to know?

Ginevra had been traveling during the Commander's political campaign, but now had returned and made herself ubiquitous by his side. His lean, rugged indifference to the excess all around him only excited her; the changeable color of his eyes—one day gray, the next silver—added to the desire that had been evolving in her. Now that he had broken out of his hermit's shell and examined the world, his whole character had gone from being a worm to a meteorite shower and back to a worm. He was in pain, and Ginevra took to the calling of being needed, not merely by him but by his boy too.

In short, she was having unexpected family feelings for the Commander, and they had increased by the hour, though to one as worldly wise and experienced as Ginevra de Martin such sentiments were no more logical or describable than an uncommon hayfever. Both Rajibai and Sannazaro detected something more, but Marigold remained oblivious to her blandishments and was most wretchedly focused on the fact of his bedridden existence, or the various colors of phlegm—the warm palette of Tintoretto, the green slime of Rubens, at certain hours the dangerously inflamed walnut-black of Francis Bacon—exiting his considerably rough-housed nostrils. For an entire week he'd stumbled round betwixt and between, from room to room, no purpose in mind, waddling in a ridiculous tattered nightgown, the figure of an old dromedary, from bed to bathroom, back again. Ginevra showed up with ministrations of hot cider, minestrone, tofu salad sandwiches and any number of other preparations, which he ceremoniously waved off with an annoyed, self-deprecating gesture. His stubborn tally of abnegations said it all. The ascetic in him wished to die—*sallekhana* in Jainism, explained Rajibai; to renounce all that more than half a century had accumulated by way of wit, wisdom and weariness.

"But what about all your new-found responsibilities?" Ginevra inquired, addling his brain with repeated commentaries whose every degree of clarity and rationality served only to send him spiraling further towards the opposite pole of unreason and stubbornness. "You have a son now who needs you."

"He is a billionaire whilst still a lad. I believe that means he'll do fine."

"That's just plain stupid!" she scolded him. "Do you think a father's duties are no more than the number of zeroes at the end of his bankroll?"

The Commander knew, of course, that he was talking nonsense. But he enjoyed pulling her cork, biting her onion, chewing her bell pepper, muttering nonsensical non sequiturs nonstop.

"What of all the charities you've begun, and the Oasis of which Sannazaro has told me everything? Would you simply abandon all of your inspirations before they've even learned to stand, on account of a minor stomach upset or back pain, the makings of an everyday flu?"

"It is no flu, dear neighbor mine."

"You could call me Ginevra, Murillo."

"Ginevra. You're quite right. I shall call you by the familiar form. Surely that is correct. But what is incorrect is your labeling my ailment a flu, for I have insider information which has solidly convinced me it goes much deeper than that."

"So go see a doctor. When did you last have a physical?"

"I have never had a physical."

"There, you see." She opted for a different tactic. "You might truly be dying, after all. And what a loss for all those chickens that ever feared a well. Of course, the only way to know for sure whether it's cancer of the scrotum or rectal fission is to visit a qualified professional."

Marigold insisted his scrotum was fine but that he undoubtedly suffered from the rarest form of rat encephalitis as a result of the many occasions on which the odor, or physical manifestation of a rat, or rat feces had managed to find its way into his soufflé or toothpaste. Yet, in spite of his own diagnosis, he was not particularly concerned by the cohabitation of species—indeed, did all he could to encourage it, so that between the squirrels and rats and fleas and cockroaches and stink bugs and spiders and who can say what others there was both a sizable population of non-human lodgers circumambulating the rooming house and considerable residua attendant upon such fraternization. It was a friendly home, and no threat of rare disease was going to dampen Marigold's enthusiasm for convivialities late into the day, not even now.

The stench of urine in his household, though, was overwhelming. It took Ginevra hours of mopping and scrubbing with ammonia to make even the slightest impact on its universality. Thomas Malthus was alive and vindicated in the Commander's hacienda, for the numbers of rats were multiplying at an exponential rate and, unlike Ebert's solution at the Oasis, there was no way to dissuade these room-and-boarders from their contract nonviolently. They constituted a significant labor force whose union leaders would hear of no relocation or new job-training program. Nor did certificates interest them. They were there for the long haul, had said so publicly, and had no reason to quit their Ritz. Especially in light of the Commander's decree pasted on the refrigerator: three quotes from George Bernard Shaw, Leonardo da Vinci and Dr Mayo, founder of Mayo Clinic, all professing to a deep fondness for rodents. Marigold could never go back on his own word. He had vowed, as candidate for Governor, to provide rat hospices throughout the state; to turn every home into an animal sanctuary, and every animal into a bacteria sanctuary, and every bacteria into a nigoda heaven, whatever nigodas were. (The rats were perplexed by these nigodas and scurried for days searching out any information that could be gleaned from the Commander's considerable library, but preferred eating the pages to reading them.) The King of the Rats at the Marigold Hacienda—Out-of-Kilter was his name on account of the heavy-set, chocolate chip-engorged stomach that always gave him a left-leaning stagger—finally figured it out, having devoured a Prakrit lexicon as far as N: Nigodas were atoms, he'dread. This brought a rousing applause, at 3.30 in the morning, from all 200 or 300 rats in the household. The Commander lunged from his bed in panic.

"All right, that's it!" he screamed, chasing them from room to room. Never had there been a greater chorus of rat hysterics. They laughed at the top of their little lungs from under the spider gate-leg tables they had already trashed; laughed from inside Regency recessed drawers and cabinet stands; they chewed with all their excess laughter at the giltwood jardinière and Queen Anne bureau. They peed ferociously in a William and Mary satinwood seaweed marquetry chest and shat voluminously in the rosewood bookshelves. A racing horde of them saw the looming Lord of the Manor in the ebonized and parcel gilt mirrored wall panel abutting the Commander's bathroom, and shrieked at the awful sight, for he appeared in a wrathful state, no doubting it.

Had there not been more pressing issues with which to contend, namely Marigold's depression and the fear it instilled in his son, only presently becoming accustomed to his new home but having few friends there as yet, there surely would have erupted a rat war in the Marigold household, at least if Ginevra had anything to do with it. She was meticulous; her Camp of the Spirits was a spotless, livable, immaculate conception of Santa Fe leisure style and architecture, devoted to the ammonia memory of Fritz Haber. Whereas her neighbor's domicile was a crumbling hovel, albeit historical and charming, and in her opinion truly uninhabitable. She lobbied to get Rajibai out of there before he, too, caught scrotum cancer or rat encephalitis.

It so happened that a doctor made a house call, at the behest of Ginevra. He examined the recalcitrant patient, and determined that he was experiencing a mild form of Chronic Fatigue Syndrome; gram-negative bacteria, probably the result of rat urine contamination, which explained the low-grade running fever; and slight malnutrition, attributable to his nature and, without doubt, said the doctor, to a psychological mid-life crisis. Perhaps a psychiatrist could help lift him out of the worst of it.

"But you'll have to do the rest," the doctor admonished the Commander, who scarcely acknowledged his presence, except to scold him for taking his blood pressure and other samples.

"A medieval quack," he carped. "Next he'll be applying suction cups and sucking blood."

Several days later, with his fluids testing in order, the Commander was persuaded to get dressed and visit the most highly regarded psychotherapist in Santa Fe. Marigold was horrified by the idea—people of his stature didn't go to shrinks—but was so astonished by the person's professional name—Dr Quicker Wickerpecker—that he figured an hour of his time was worth the levity.

But what's in a name? Wickerpecker was far more than might have been surmised. His office was a territorial-style single-story building sequestered behind the Georgia O'Keeffe Museum. It rested upon a former fragment of lava flow and, in subsequent eons, a grassy knoll, nowadays the site of flea markets and forest lawn through which to muse upon the fleeting hours unobserved. Wickerpecker wore designer jeans, argyle socks (his boots off in a corner) and a dark magenta shirt. He smoked Algerian cigarettes. Not until his forties, as was evidenced from the framed accolades on his wall, had he graduated Summa Cum Laude from Princeton. His grandfather had studied with Freud.

"The afternoon is yours," Wickerpecker began. "I've kept my calendar free. Your friends Ginevra and Iacobo—is it?—said you wanted to talk."

"What's the Wickerpecker?" Marigold continued. "Not your everyday family name?"

"A kind of woodpecker, of course. French, originally. To peck repeatedly. But our clan hailed from the weirdest region in Germany. Bat Canyon. Poison Rock. Names had a different sound, a different skew. I thought of changing it. You can imagine the school-grade barbs and harassments. I tried alternatives at times—Gregory Peck, Warrior Bob, Wicked Joe, even Clark Gable. In the end, nothing could match the very name I was born with, however impossibly silly it sounds in English. The girls in college all found it worthy of assorted dares, pursuing its etymology and physical innuendoes with cheerleader zeal. I actually married one of them. So what do you want to talk about? Politics?"

"That's not funny."

"I voted for you, if that counts for anything."

"You're kidding?"

"Yes. I heard you speak for a few minutes on an NPR interview and read some of the news pieces.

Compared with your opponents, whose only concerns were new four-lane highways, school vouchers, the death penalty and securing space launches in the New Mexico desert, your elaborate scheme to bulldoze the south side of Santa Fe and engineer miles of dragonfly habitat sounded quite refreshing. Now that you've lost, I suspect we'll soon be seeing a host of repressive inanities and public deceptions—no more sex education or the study of evolution; demons in the war chest thought of as a kindness, slavery as freedom, a toxin construed as a blessing. A storm, blue sky."

"Well I appreciate that. I truly do. But honestly, I'm here for due diligence reasons. I've been in bed with some fatigue syndrome or other, but in fact I've been depressed—or I guess that's what you'd call it—for some time."

"Yes. I can see that."

The Commander could not fathom how a degree from Princeton gave anyone the authority instantly to judge a stranger. "How can you see that?"

"Because I've never seen you in my life and thus have probably a better shot at telling you what you look like than anybody else."

"So what do I look like?"

"Saint John the Baptist with a bad cold."

Actually, Wickerpecker had never seen anyone quite like the Commander. So wizened and elegant a bearing; such remarkable continence, a moderation so weathered, encinctured, immune as to connote the absolute in self-sufficiency. Yet, there was also a mournful outward giving whose spirit could be deemed generous with a look; soulful yearning without a friend, or great love affair suggesting holy closure. He seemed healthy in a monkish, belabored way, foggy skinned, luminous eyed, brackish haired and jeweline of thought.

"It's more than just losing a silly election, isn't it?" Wickerpecker suggested.

"I don't know that it's possible to summarize it in less than an hour."

"I've got plenty of time—this week, next week. No hurry."

"No. I am in a very great hurry."

"To do what?"

"The silly or the sober answer?"

"In the end, we all discover they're one and the same, I imagine."

That impressed the Commander. "This morning," he continued, "after the hail last night, and all that rain and lightning, I looked out from my inner sanctum, the drapes still stained with buffalo feces and squirrel urine, and saw this enormous bumblebee cruising a flower bed, warming its wings, and I thought, I would give everything up, sacrifice the rest of my own life, to be able to spend one day and one night inside the head of that creature. Wouldn't you?"

"No, probably not. I'm allergic to pollen this time of year, I don't take honey in my tea, and, well, aerodynamically speaking, I'd rather be an albatross than a bumblebee. Besides, they don't live very long—two years at best, if I recall my high school zoology. Anyway, I like being a person. Don't you?"

"That is a very leading question," replied Marigold. "On account of the fact we're both people."

"Some people are depressed because the sun rises, others because it sets. But I've long known about a third category of individuals—and there's probably 30 million of them in America—who are unhappy simply because they're human. I suspect with buffalo shit and squirrel urine in my bedroom I'd be ranked among them."

"I can't honestly say. I thought I was content, until recently."

"You were running for Governor. That implies something. A desire to help people, no? Or were you more concerned with saving bumblebees and dragonflies?"

"Actually, if you read my position paper which they published in all the local newspapers, they accused me of preferring roosters to people."

"Yes. I did catch that, but, you see, I agree with you about cockfighting.

I think the previous Governor's position on animal rights is pathetic. We'll see what the new one does. But I'd like to think, and your presence only amplifies my impression, that you have a number of concerns; you are a member of the community; you put yourself out there in a way that would be unthinkable for most of us. Nobody runs for Governor, voluntarily copes with all that criticism and prying into one's personal life, unless they truly feel something—an idealism, a willingness to socialize with gusto. You have convictions. Ethical principles. A set of priorities. A reason to go on. You've got to be immersed in humanity, which is a sign of true mental health. Am I wrong?"

"I have some very close friends, though this is a recent phenomenon. You have to understand, I grew up in a state of complete aloneness."

"Was it lonely?"

"No. I'm not sure. I lived with my father, until he died, and then with a housekeeper from Mongolia whose influence was more time consuming than long-lasting."

"A new insight into physics."

"My mother passed away as I was seeing first light. Nature schooled me in nearly everything. I grew up without friends, you see. There were 18 of us at the Tesuque Public School in those days. But I rarely attended. Never graduated from anyplace. Never received a report card. I was the perfect underachiever. A perpetual immobility machine. And at the age of 50 was content with my books and dreams."

"That's pretty unusual. Who financed a lifestyle of daydreams?"

"My father left his affairs in a manageable way. There was property, and valuable art, loads of antiques—most of it in various states of decrepitude, I'm afraid... My fault, in spite of there having always been sufficient cash accumulated over several centuries."

"Lucky you."

"But I never went anywhere. A misanthrope preferring all forms of complexity to the slightest simple matter. In fact, simplicity harms my inner nature. I need a chaos every day, a room of anarchy and upheaval, caverns scattered with dark crystals, a laceway of incomprehensible fissures, directions and confusion. Give me a few easy breaths and I faint, a clear pathway and I trip up. I cannot abide those who favor simple things, simple concepts, simple anything. I need intellectual stimulation, to the point of total incomprehensibility. Short of that, I am easily bored. Until 18 months ago I was still residing in solitary, out beneath the cottonwoods in Tesuque. Happy as a squirrel."

"Why squirrel?"

"What do you mean?"

"You said squirrel."

"It's just an expression."

"Right, but you could have said bear, or eagle, or clam. Squirrel seems, well, simple."

"Oh, I see. You figure you have a window on some Oedipus complex or obsession with big breasts."

"No. I was just curious. And I shouldn't imagine that squirrels replaced your father, or have very big tits."

"Well, actually I happen to love squirrels, and have recently started managing several thousand of them on a ranch, in addition to a few who live indoors with me. Believe me when I say there is nothing simple about squirrels. Remember Rocky and Bullwinkle?"

"Pretty unsanitary, as you yourself complained. They're rodents, are they not? Carriers of the black plague, and the Hanta virus that wiped out the Anasazi?"

"Actually, the rat feces are the more unsanitary part. Archeologists allege that the peoples around Kayenta, Antelope Canyon, the other cliff dwellers, could not build slabs sizable enough to contain the rats from their granaries."

"But where do the rat feces fit into your equation?" Wickerpecker asked, shifting positions.

"I've got uncountable numbers of them inhabiting my home. Dr Dracula who took some of my blood samples thinks my condition might have been aggravated by eating rat turds in some of my food."

Wickerpecker paused, rephrasing what he had intended to say and shifting in his chair yet again, obviously uncomfortable with the drift of conversation. "That doesn't strike you as slightly eccentric, not minding rat turds in your food?"

"Oh, of course it does. Naturally I would prefer a good oatmeal in the morning without having to wonder whether those are really raisins or not."

Pause. "And 18 months ago? What changed this picture-perfect postcard?"

"I inherited what now amounts to over five billion dollars and have been trying to find ways to spend it that will help the world. It's more difficult than you think."

"Oh, I do see your problem. Another poor billionaire who has perceived through to the cold calculus of flawed human beings and human communities, of a world that is violent, often horrible, of dragons and dictators and cruel injustices of every variety. And there's not a damn thing you can do about it. Is there? You can't even beat a conservative sonofabitch incumbent in a trivial local election. Whereas all you really want is a world where one can sit back, read books and dream of being a bumblebee drifting from flower to flower. God, I'm glad you lost as Governor. New Mexico would have destroyed a very nice person. I just hope your money doesn't."

Marigold was stymied. He'd reached a plateau where no other chatter counted for anything. He and Wickerpecker stared at one another silently for 20, maybe 30 seconds. A long time.

Marigold perceived Wickerpecker as a kind of pleasant, unsmoked mirror, or calming reference work to which one returned in the aftermath, like the *Encyclopedia of the History of Art*, a mental spark plug, a cup of tea or tonic that facilitated, at best, the occasional inner dialogue.

"Actually, you've only hit upon the obvious part," the Commander said, brightening suddenly.

"We have to start somewhere."

"I think the greater truth is more facile. I'm just tired. Very, very tired."

"Excellent. A breakthrough. Now you have it all. The rest is self-evident."

"Yes?"

"Stop. Slow down. Take a vacation. Go to Italy. Have a torrid affair. Buy Verona. You can probably afford it. To hell with Sisyphus. You don't have to prove anything to anybody."

"True. But now I have a son."

"A blessing, and no disguises. You get what you raise. Take him with you."

"It's the raising part that terrifies me."

"How old is he?"

Marigold had to stop and calculate. "I believe eleven. Possibly twelve."

"That's interesting."

"What?"

"Most fathers would not have to guess."

"The circumstances under which we met, the conditions of our affiliation, the emotions that spring to mind—I cannot describe everything, except to say that it happened quickly, six months ago; his sister had been murdered in a Bombay slum—I should say Mumbai, the new Hindu fundamentalist name for the city—where they walked the streets begging for food. There he was, this orphan, sitting alone in a hospital corridor. And there I was. Two orphans. We were, as they say, destined for one another."

"Is he happy?"

"Under the circumstances, I think so. Why wouldn't he be? Of course, losing one's sister ..."

"No, I don't mean that. I'm suggesting that if you intend to raise him like you were raised, I might have some concerns. The absence of friends, the solitude. Not all children find a life of books under the cottonwoods necessarily gratifying. Not that there's anything wrong with it, obviously. I'm just throwing that out."

"Ahh. Not a chance. He has his Uncle Sannazaro, his Aunt Ginevra. Rajibai has no difficulty making friends. In fact, his complete absence of inhibitions has been an inspiration to one and all."

"Maybe a mother would complete the circle. Any prospects?"

"No."

"As a rule, or it just hasn't happened?"

"The latter, certainly. You really believe marriage would solve my situation?"

"We haven't arrived at any situation, Mr Marigold. I'm still trying to figure out why you're here. You seem quite aware. You have the benefit, which not all people do, of a powerful introspective facility, and you appear to have used it well. You have divined the basic unfathomables with respect to life and those existential imponderables which we all must confront late at night, whether in consideration of the fact that everyone we know and love will die eventually; that all of our connections are ultimately doomed to absolute, infernal, terrifying nothingness; that our possessions are trivial in the end; and that the universe is collapsing, as Woody Allen once reminded us, and therefore, by inference, why bother doing anything, least of all attempting to save the world, as they say?"

"Aren't we an uplifting voice in the wilderness," Marigold commented, more amused than ever by this grimace wrapped in a diploma parading as a health spa, all in one unflinching representative of the psychological profession.

"I'm simply pointing out that we all know, more or less, that to live is difficult. Courage does not come on a platter, or by rote. Storming the fortress of evil and inequity takes energy. Then again, these are small impediments compared with your benefits/cost setting. That is to say, most of us don't inherit five billion dollars as part of the deal. Let me ask you something."

"Please."

"Your friends, Iacobo and Ginevra. Do you have long heart-to-hearts with them?"

"I suppose I do."

"What have they suggested to you?"

"Pretty much what you recommended earlier. Calm down. Don't try to accomplish everything. Stop throwing myself into battle. Leave it alone, in other words. Relax."

"And you weren't paying them 400 bucks an hour."

"Is that what I'm paying you? And is that the answer? To simply relax?"

"If I might be so bold."

"By all means."

"Relax. And, it seems to me, you probably need to get laid."

The Commander tried to divine the psychiatrist's inner meaning for, in truth, he was not familiar with the expression just applied. Laid?

"Let's be honest, Mr Marigold. You are the richest man in New Mexico, probably one of the wealthiest in America and the world, for that matter. You can damn near buy anything you want. You're smart. You've had a unique upbringing, undimmed by the normal influences which skew lives and lock them in concrete. You walk out of here a free man. My advice to you? Fall in love. Disappear. Don't question your smelling the flowers. Life is precious. I don't need to tell you that. We have to live. You're obviously a very compassionate human being. Which means, you have nothing to worry about. Absolutely nothing. Goodness and virtue always prevail. There is no choice. The coward's way out is simply unacceptable. Worse. It's a bore. You've proven that. Now, I would think, it's time to stop proving anything. Be yourself. Have a family. Fall in love. What more can I say?"

The Commander listened well, appreciative. An hour flew by. He wrote a check for 800 dollars. He could not let a good tip get away. It was, in fact, one of the only pleasures afforded him by the ridiculous sums of wealth now in his name. And he walked out the door quite pleased with all that had transpired.

Later that evening, over Darjeeling tea at Ginevra's, Sannazaro mentioned how much better the Commander was looking.

"The sheer fact you've gotten yourself up, that is the cure in itself," Ginevra added.

"But what did the doctor actually say?" Rajibai asked. And both Ginevra and the Señor listened with curiosity.

"That I should get laid," replied the Commander. "I'm still not sure what he meant. Some kind of solid repose, I imagine. He also suggested I fall in love."

CHAPTER 152
Alvaro's Sex Life and the Mystery of the Egg Salad Sandwich

ALVARO HAD RELINQUISHED his honorific "Father" long before the quiet matrimonial occasion, as it had been presently conceived. In fact, this pretense of virginity, of a blazing *lumen christi*, all that painstaking miscellany of holiness had been wisely dispensed with just minutes after he first ravaged the weeping willow that was Raquel two years earlier and prior to his brief odyssey across Brazil. The lusting had been sustained down in his studio where her naked likeness leaned against the walls on so many untreated canvases, luscious unframed hues, unheralded portraiture, a smoldering secret between the two of them that promised of either eternal damnation or laughter, exile or matrimony. Alvaro was versed in all the contradictory ordinances of the Early Fathers of the Church, who had themselves been steeped in Aristotle's notion of semen as pure, unsullied substance capable of igniting life in whatever it chose. As a young neophyte he had certainly memorized the most graphic passages from St Thomas Aquinas on the nature of carnal desire, of original, even unoriginal sin, of profuse erections in the night, as well as those from St Clement of Alexandria on the matter of menstruation and infertility—all the alleged pitfalls associated with the woman's private parts.

But more than all this, Alvaro, being of the French race, remembered his country's national treasure, Victor Hugo's Marius, and Marius's Ursula, swathed in the spring breezes that caressed her limbs, lifted her skirts to the extremes of her garter, smothering him with desires as desperate and forbidding as those remedied by the "fauns of Theocritus" upon the altar of Isis.

To Alvaro, who kept his pleasures in cipher, entombed in Ginevra's basement, young Raquel was the ultimate sex scandal: not a wrinkle on the gleaming Hispanic visage, only the one upon which she sat, and squirmed, whenever she was in the presence of the painting monk. He worshipped her simple beauty, came to view it in the same way a Spanish Nobel Laureate once reveled in the presence of a burro. Her every gesture threw off an odor of resplendent ease. She could not fart or secrete. She was not human. His Heaven was remade in her fast-witted eyes, creamy smile, rambunctious arms and svelte musculature. Her tightly knit bottom, smooth yielding belly, silky black hair, all 20 years younger than any single part of his anatomy, had the collective value in his mind of a great work of art, of 24 carats. She belonged to her own Paris, descending a stairwell left unscathed by the Cubists. A pure treasure, an island, and for some reason as yet inconceivable to him, she was in love with Alvaro.

Sometimes he imagined it was really her love of being naked before a Church Father, a heightened thrill ride through exposure of herself to Christ in some surreal, vicarious manner. He would slowly remove her outer garments, then toy with her panties. Seeking her forgiveness, he gave equal time to each nipple.

She would murmur, "Desnuda, desnuda, el milagro ..."

These desperate antics continued without any recognition from the world above. Ginevra knew nothing about their frequent trysts; neither did any of the other inhabitants of the Camp of the Spirits who, in any case, had evacuated for various sectors of the unknown universe. Raquel would do her work, careful to avoid the tracking countenance of her amore, who came up from the studio throughout the day to take a glass of Cabernet, or a smoke, or to prepare the meals for Negrescu and the others. Not the slightest show of an affiliation. But he always had his side glances upon the steamy sylphide, whose manner with a vacuum cleaner, the pole she pressed between her legs whilst moving from carpet to carpet, left him dazzled; whose way with rags and "409" on a countertop, Mop & Glow on the ceramic tiles, her manner of applying Whiz, Chlorox, Windex, even Snuggle, was ultra ultra ultra, inciting riot in his blood. Even her method of placing dishes in the dishwasher, or of taking plants to be watered out onto the deck, where she'd perforce lift her skirt, or check a fake silver snap on her affecting jeans, drove him to delirium.

But now their multiple rendezvous—hot, worrisome, cloaked in unresolve and mad desire—had blossomed into a pact born of her unexpected pregnancy. While Alvaro fretted at first, there was no question, in the end, but that she should have the baby. Both of them were good Catholics.

Actually, nobody was entirely surprised.

"I always suspected," confessed Sannazaro to Ginevra. "There's been a rakish air about him ever since his return from South America. It's clear he sampled the goods of Brazil. I suppose there's something to that."

She threw him a scolding look, but secretly enjoyed the Italian's oblique manner when it came to the other sex. Sannazaro seemed to look upon these matters with a calm indifference, beyond the pale of any such corporeality. His devastating affairs of the heart in New York had long absolved him from carnal afflictions, he said, and now afforded him the verifiable height from which to look down upon the ways of men and women, to sigh regularly and care not. The thought of an involvement, and what it took to stoke the flames, he protested, was simply beyond the borders of his rather frail self-confidence.

In fact, Sannazaro did—as Ginevra suspected—have his weaknesses, and they had been uniquely pressured by the women of the waterfall. That was easy, though. Like dreaming of a unicorn.

Alvaro and Raquel's wedding plans, on the other hand, genuinely and visibly excited Sannazaro, who took an active hand in the flower arrangements.

Ginevra had invited very few people. This was to be a private ceremony. Marigold and Rajibai, of course; Hidalgo and his wife, back from their global gallivantings; Rajibai's teacher, Mrs Williams, from the Tesuque School; the odd friend from Chupadero—Hayberry Sanchez, a descendent of an early land grant family who owned several O'Keeffes; a fossil collector from Río En Medio; Father Coca from the sanctuary at Chimayo; a wealthy antiques dealer, Mary Hedges, who lived across from the Green Triangle on NM 591; a young scholar-in-residence at Bishop's Lodge who was writing her dissertation on Willa Cather; a Canadian woman named Susan from Rancho Encantado who was one of Ginevra's closest friends and, in every respect, according to Sannazaro, "magnificent"; Khalsa, a Sikh tightrope walker from Santa Fe whom Alvaro had long admired; and Leopold, a local sheriff who was probably Alvaro's closest confidant. They would sometimes sit in Leopold's patrol car out beyond the compound's adobe wall and talk about the crime scene in Santa Fe. Alvaro loved the gossip almost as much as he loved watching football, basketball, pay-per-view boxing and CNN.

Alvaro had a strong and scented opinion about every news item. A glutton for punishment, he transmuted the sins of the world into a glorious sarcasm that spared no public figure, outbreak of war, Congressional vote, or disaster. For a year he had been a slave to the O.J. Simpson trial.

Another year (during which time he also wrote his first and only book, a diary of imbroglios that revealed fascinating glimpses into his early friendships with Salvador Dali and Le Corbusier) he was devoted to Bill and Monica.

Leopold's insider knowledge of the crime scene around town and his good-humored approach to the sordidness of human nature set well with Alvaro's own dark ambivalences. Conversely Alvaro, with his bright canvases and European toasts, his flamboyant laughter and storytelling, provided relief to the sheriff whose world was otherwise easily engulfed by dreary details of low-rider pathology, drug overdoses, suicides, cow mutilations, homeless mutts, emaciated cats and wife beatings.

It was Leopold who first mused aloud whether Alvaro had been screwing the maid.

"Why do you ask that?" the shaken Frenchman replied.

"Because I think she's pregnant, and she's clearly looking to you to take charge," replied the sheriff.

Such an instinctive assertion on the part of Santa Fe's premier law man left Alvaro gravely ill for two days. He had no idea whether Raquel was pregnant or not. When he finally mustered the courage to ask her outright, her candor sealed his destiny with sweetness of breath and the despair of knowing he must leave the Church for good.

Nonetheless, Carlos de Montivan, a priest in good standing at San Sebastian de Pacheco, and old acquaintance of the religious Father, agreed to marry the couple outside of the normal Church rubrics.

"Do you accept that the world is overpopulated?" asked Carlos, when Alvaro and Raquel first went to him with their situation. She was six months pregnant by then. "Because things are different now than at the time of Jesus Christ."

"Certainly."

"Do you agree to raise the child a Catholic?"

"Naturally."

"Will you have other children?"

"Maybe," said Alvaro, trying not even to think of the word condom, for Carlos could stare right through him, had a cardsharp's instincts about such matters and, like a Grand Inquisitor, was on to even the slightest vibration of birth-control phrases in the brain.

"If God intends it," added the bulging nymphet for whom life was a dream, now that her married life was assured, and her chicken and rooster back in her possession.

"That's a very good answer," said Carlos, who winked nervously at her artist apostate.

The day in question had been selected weeks in advance, the service to be held at the Oasis.

On the morning of the wedding, however, while the ladies primped and preened, and guests began arriving, a contingent of army tanks rolled off the main highway and on to the property. Three hundred soldiers wearing gas masks and heavy gloves raced into formation.

"I'm looking for Mr Marigold," shouted the military roughneck in charge.

"That's me," said the Commander. "What is this? More Los Alamos nonsense?"

Mr E.C. Clayton, EC for short, head of some important-sounding agency in Washington, took him aside and launched without formality into a what-is-what and how-so and wherefore. "Let me be brief, sir. In 1966, a Soviet chemist living in the Urals was working at his lab, took a lunch break, boiled a couple of eggs for an egg salad sandwich and found that the water had turned quite unexpectedly to brown pudding, according to the rudiments of Boyle's Law. The fellow studied the substance, noting that the water had shown strange impurities, traces of squirrel urine, tannin, rust and radioactivity, as well as real freaky hydrogen bonds and weird polymers."

"What are polymers?"

"No idea. I'm not a chemist. Anyway, the Soviet scientist named it polywater. Others called it anomalous pudding, or squirrel scuzz. Most other investigators denied its existence, said it was a fraud, a bogus experiment. But additional US-based scientists offered support to the claim. The American and Soviet leadership were nervous. You see, if this stuff was shown to be real, and polywater escaped the laboratory, it could destroy all life on Earth."

Marigold was astonished by the prospect. "All from an egg salad sandwich in Russia? But how?"

"Because it might automatically infect all other water, causing a chain reaction by which all the oceans, every river, lake and source of drinking water, even the clouds and the H2O in our own bodies could turn to a substance with the consistency of jello, speaking generically."

"Good God!" exclaimed the Commander. "Not that I have anything against jello. I quite relish jello, actually. Banana or strawberry, preferably.

They make vegan jello, do they not? But what does this have to do with me and the wedding?"

"Two days ago, one of your staff brought the brown pudding home with her. Now, she's been confined to a hospital. Straitjacket, round-the-clock security. Prudence the Dim—do you know her?"

"Skinny intern, University of Eastern New Mexico. Walks around with eucalyptus breath, mops the world. Says she's a long-lost descendant of Rachel Carson."

"That's the one."

"Is she OK? Best tea tree applicator we've ever seen."

"Don't know yet. You got squirrels?"

"'Bout 4,000."

EC turned to the sergeant-in-charge: "Vamos."

"But wait a minute..." Marigold was confused, grave. "What are you planning to do with our squirrels?"

"Check their urine. Move 'um out, if need be. Bury the whole kit'n kaboodle."

"But there's a wedding taking place in about half an hour!"

"We'll try to stay out of your way."

"This is preposterous!"

But there was nothing he could do to deter the march of progress. Presidential orders, national security, the post-Cold War, the Pope's travel itinerary, the spelling of jello in the District of Columbia and rodents in Arkansas—all figured into it. The world had simply become too complicated, its sides pressing in upon the pages, for a mere marigold.

CHAPTER 153

How the Invasion of Polywater Caused a Wedding Fiasco

GINEVRA, DECKED out in her stunning Issey Miyake bridesmaid's attire, finished blow-drying Negrescu's freshly shampooed fur, and Sannazaro, dapper to the most delicate degree, put his maestro's touch to the flower arrangements around the ranch house. The weather was holding and it was going to be a splendid affair.

Or would have been.

Half a dozen bridesmaids, dressed in lavender, came out onto the lawn just as 20 soldiers went wheeling by.

The Commander made light of the military invasion. No point panicking or calling off a sacred matrimony. So Father Carlos de Montivan earnestly attempted a ceremony, whilst the Commander gunned off to warn Ebert and the others. As a recent survey had shown, bulldozers and army tanks had the heaviest impact upon biodiversity. Squirrels didn't stand a chance.

Marigold had a special whistle, and within minutes Ebert was there on his shoulder. Throughout the forests, meantime, hundreds of his fellow squirrels luxuriated in down comforters and devoured banana walnut granola, vegan energy bars, Dong Quai root and candies of shou wu chih, excreting delightful fluids.

"Here's what's happening," he impressed upon his little friend, conveying every urgency.

The military scientists were kneeling beside a creek, taking readings.

According to the current mumbo jumbo, they found an alarming entropy of vaporization. A form of exquisite, if lethal, vomit favoring what, in the physicist's parlance, was referred to as "Trouton over Hildebrand". In other words, asymmetrical atoms and unstable molecules, all tainted with so-called Raman spectra and condensed matter. None of it was meant to be understood.

"*Shhhh!* " the priest exhaled, reading from the *Bible*. Alvaro and Raquel held hands before him, the guests seated behind. "... And God forbade that you should lust wantonly."

"What's the matter?" one scientist asked the other.

"At a distillation of 5000 degrees Celsius, it's creeping along at 12 centimeters an hour."

"You may place the ring on her finger," said the priest.

Many of the women present shed Picasso tears, which hit the floor and set off a veritable spark-source mass, as chemists call them, aerosolizing the molecular substrate of the watershed that undercut the barn and picnic area.

"Please, ladies, stop *crying!* " EC pleaded.

But chemistry hiccups to its own protocols. "Stage three," declared a panicky soldier into his headset. "I smell ionic honey."

"Polydimethylsiloxane," said another.

"You may now kiss the bride," Carlos rejoiced. "*No kissing!*" screamed EC.

But the jello had begun spreading, from tear to tear, kiss to kiss, throughout the Oasis. Sannazaro made the logical but unfortunate choice of trying to hose it off, for the gardening spigot was right there at hand. Now the anomalous water was getting everywhere.

"The acequia!" screamed the Commander.

"The river," warned another.

Amid the harried commotions, Alvaro carried his bride down the stairs, away from the foolishness, and into the studio basement of the ranch. He locked the door and they threw themselves at each other, ravenous. "Desnuda, desnuda," she groaned.

Upstairs, army specialists evacuated the guests who tended to trample each other, and worked their tanks into a pontoon formation to try to head off the flow of earth-hydrogenizing puddy. Using the Derjaguar method, as it's known, a host of exchangeable cations, H-bonded water structure, silicated surface, old-time radiation, a dollop of pressure-lowering hair gel, a proton magnet and a wall of absorbent diapers, the soldiers managed to stave off inundation.

Lucky for New Mexico, the Oasis soil type supported the antidotes applied. The new evolution of frogs and crickets also helped. A soil type known as Franciscan, coarse, much rained upon, allowed for sufficient reverse osmosis, and militated against undue manganese turbidity. The purple needlegrass, forbs, barley and oat would die out, but not the hardwoods. It was a miracle, and the experts would require many days, weeks and months to sort out just what happened. Microprobe analysis would yield a most improbable interpretation: the squirrels were metabolizing their unprecedented diet in a manner that could only be described as "catastrophic" in the annals of world chemistry. Had the army's efforts been unsuccessful, and the squirrel efflua prevailed, the aqueous portions of the planet would have turned to a kind of unpleasant vomit.

Mr Marigold was greatly embarrassed by all this. After all, in his largesse he had been the one to suggest the specific ingredients of the daily culinary preparations for the squirrels, including the date bars, and diced avocado and pecan salads. The ecologist in him shuddered. His worldly bulk, purged upon a daily regimen, however meager, had not so properly applied where science and civil health demanded board simple and sure. Food, a proper pan of yokes and flockmeal, whose fluxion was the sense and matter of all beings, had gone astray by fodder-crazed and unversed victual; chewing gave no choice, nor herb a livelihood. Neither sustenance nor aliment an inkling of what far freak of nature had aroused the demon in the stomach. Nonetheless, Marigold remained ready to promote a utopian diet that should satisfy the sweet tooth of every sentient being. Asparagus spears for antelopes, tempeh burgers for the lion. How was he to know that squirrel urine, in combination with chocolate chips and various other salubritious oddities, might induce this polywater flop? He felt responsible, too, for Ginevra's gloom, for she had planned so meticulously for a nice day. He was especially concerned about Ebert, who, frankly speaking, would not cotton easily to a change of eating habit, no matter that they were orders of the President. This was going to be rough on him and his chocoholic cronies.

The day had also been hard on Sannazaro, who saw all his early spring flower arrangements flattened during the fiasco.

"I've come to an important decision," he told the Commander that night, driving back to Tesuque. "I'm going home, to Italy. I've had enough of this crazy country, where the infantry crashes weddings and the President can refuse a squirrel a granola bar."

"My thoughts exactly," sighed the Commander. "Since we've been back nothing good has come of it. I'm ready for permanent exile."

CHAPTER 154
The Last Herbs of Positano

IT WAS JANUARY, by all indications. A stunning misarrangement of frost crystals on every window, the sun languid, fieldfares hovering in the warm trenches of manure along the outliers and stubble of cut hay, titlarks diabolically hunting down pupae, slugs freely in the mezeron, bear's-foot ready to bloom, fieldmice tight in their retreats and red-dead nettle changing color. In town, the homeless were selling puppies, reclining under eaves in revealed sunlight along the Plaza.

With more time in coming days to contemplate his new determination, Marigold reviewed all of his scruples and antipathies, deeply seated nauseas which had arisen from the very start of his public persona. It is one thing to recline in a safe villa, musing on the woes of the day, decrying the system with philosophy born of the noblest sadnesses. But quite another matter to set out expressly for the conversion of profiteers in the agora, or senators piled glibly in the polis, to an ethic. The Commander was tired, simply, of the multiplication tables; of how human nature, when increased by the Malthusian numbers of inhabitants in any given space, seemed to drag down the normal arithmetics, mire the high-end, aggrandize the dregs. Like the inability to distinguish the loss of species from so many existing ones, the erosion of values had become imperceptible to most. Just as indifference to the standing inventory of nuclear weapons could be related to their lack of use. Even the decimation of 100,000 acres a day of rainforest was difficult for the human eye (though not all other animals) to delineate or make sense of.

Marigold, quite simply, was sinking, like a confined, feather-plucking parrot frantically speaking in whole paragraphs to attract the notice necessary to save her, where she languished in a fetid cage. But to no avail. He was a man, granted. But one who no longer felt bonded to his species; whose ability to function in the normal ways of a day were grossly impaired by the yawning chasm of ecological melancholy that ate into his tea time, bedtime, lunch hour, morning constitutional, early-morning shower, late-night Schnapps. In fact, no moment was spared the ruination and anxiety resulting from this condition. Victor Hugo had felt it in exile, one imagines. It was a deep and desperate syndrome, a plaint welling beneath the vocal cords, attaching severest importance to the destruction of the world, when nobody else seemed to acknowledge it. Where the community celebrated progress, or debated economic strategies, this one conscience ran amuck with a fever to save earthworms, vascular plants, bats, wasps, rats, primates and all mammals in general. He had become one of those old women seen daily near the Spanish Steps, or Baths of Caracalla, feeding cats, their only companions.

Marigold's ecological despair transcended psychoanalysis; made a mockery of cajolery; swept past all anodynes. Nothing could help him. But helplessness had become a colossal, inconsequential cliché in an age where, essentially, everyone was helpless. Whether one thought of the dynamic in terms of dehumanization (à la Ortega y Gasset) or one more in keeping with the Commander's existential sweet-tooth theory (read: J.P. Sartre—every tree limb evincing a window on destruction; every newborn child, a person who will die; each new highway, a mortuary). Harold Bloom had brilliantly devised a different way of understanding the alienation when he described Shakespeare's characters as individuals who changed upon hearing themselves speak, whereas Cervantes' puppets evolved only after subsuming the words and deeds of others. In Marigold's case, a third epiphany was at work: exile as the guide price of mental freedom.

"What bothers you most?" Ginevra asked, as she considered whether she should join the trio. She was inclined towards it.

"List I shall the ways?" He intimated his deepest frustrations, pinpointing the peevish congestion, the breakdown of the legal guarantees, the rise of fascistic multinationals like Cooties, and the resulting industrial metabolism of the cancer cell, first intoned in George Marsh and Rachel Carson many decades before. He described what he perceived as a generalized greed and callousness infecting the American way. One could detect it everywhere. For example, the country's average of energy efficiency was no more than 2 percent. That was a subtle indicator of a lifestyle that had ignored all else. With its high-decibel standards of living, electromagnetic buzzes, crowds and pollution along every horizon and more than 250 trillion pounds of waste produced each year in the US—less than 5 percent of it recycled—America had utterly lost its balance. Americans had become mere predators rendering their tripe in sweet address and honeyed disclaimers. Where was the leadership? The willpower? What happened to love? The hostilities cascaded in direct proportion to the disappearance of every natural service, whether clean air, clean water or fertile soil. At the expense of animals, plants, family and humility. Mothers shooting white-tailed deer for Christmas. Children killing their teachers and their parents even during non-holiday periods. There could be no way to make light of any of it. The proportions were too catastrophic to lend much further credence to that venerable aphorism, "Don't take it all so seriously."

These were not merely the pontifications of a spoiled eccentric or sour green grapes of a collapsed political campaign. This was a tea leaf stripped bare of its medicinal; true sadness at the foothill of the heart.

A history of psychosis embedding its critics, survivors, newlyweds and newborns into a fog of forgetfulness and complaisance. For who could fight the ocean? Alter the tides? Or make the sun stand still? This was World War Three and scarcely anyone even realized there was fighting going on all around. Victims in the billions. What was the hollow cry against such backdrop? As if, feckless from a paddy wagon, unheard, a game of checkers in an insane asylum sometime after midnight. Marigold could not stomach the fact he was human, that was the catch. Nor was he all that crazy about taking an overdose, or jumping off El Capitan. Which left him in a precarious and melodramatic air. Nowhere to turn. "What about Rajibai's desire to visit Disneyland?" asked Ginevra.

"May I interject?" ventured Uncle.

"Please, Señor."

"Rajibai, as we all have had the pleasure of discovering, is something of a genius at the dare. Give him a crazy idea and he will fashion an entire camp out. Like his father, I know him to be a gadabout at *tours de force*, a landloper willing to run a risk. With his larkish, perpetually up-beat temper, he requires, in my estimation, intelligent stimulation, not distractions for the masses. Neither the shopping mall nor cinema house can ever fulfill the quest that is inherent to the star in that boy's eyes. Wouldn't you agree, Murillo?"

"Absolutely."

"But listen, you two, he wants to go to Disneyland!" Ginevra reiterated, stressing the most basic appeal she could think of. "Gentlemen, would you deny him the world of Snow White? *Fantasia*? Castles in the air?"

At that very moment, who should enter the conversation but Rajibai himself, holding a beaten copy of *The Last Days of Pompeii* that Sannazaro had given him.

"I read it door to door," he announced. "Now, if it's all right with you, I should very much relish an expedition to that same mountain. I am ready if you are."

"That's the spirit, lad!" his father declared in ready conjunction. The galaxies were aligned. The portents in place. In the event, all was decided.

"Presto! Andiamo!"

Sannazaro was certain that the kid would find more happening at his Great Uncle Giorgio's cafe in Positano—a fabulous arrabiata, and ongoing games of chess—than in Anaheim, though Ginevra wasn't so sure. But the Squire had a more important motive than entertaining the little monster of adventure. He hoped to buy back his family's estate.

How well the Commander remembered Sannazaro's dismal tale of the breakup of his childhood paradise; how all his siblings had lost interest in perpetuating Arcadia while local real-estate lords divided up the spoils of a disintegrating family history.

"Ahh," the Señor rhapsodized, "when I think of the surroundings— Sorrento, Amalfi, Pompeii, Capri, Ercolano ... you can have Naples! But we must walk to truly imbibe the flavor."

"You, Sannazaro? The man with not an ounce of crusade left, walk?"

"It is the only way, trust me."

Defying a well-deserved inertia, Sannazaro mapped out the feverish travel plans that would see them all—for Ginevra had agreed to come along—climbing toward the Colli di San Pietro, touring Tiberius's Villa Jovis, picnicking on the cliffs of Anacapri, sampling the local fettuccine alla Sant'Angelo, risotto al tartufo, and of course the local pastiera, with its candied fruits and ricottas and orange essences all served up upon the finest ceramic plates from Villa Guariglia in Raito, with a lustrous bottle of limoncello to wash it down.

"Rajibai will love Monte Solaro and the huge marine grottos of Azzurra, and the canoe ride across the Lapis Sea to Costiera Amalfitana." He carried forth with exalted recollections of Ravello, the Galli Islands, the greensward of Monte Sant'Angelo a Tre Pizzi, the splendid polychrome majolica of the church of S. Maria Assunta, where his mother took him for haircuts as a child, up solitary, wistful back streets that remained cozily crunched in his memory, along with the free air of vine-ripened tomatoes and scent of fir trees and baked cheese, great art in the warm shadows of Roman prehistory and the al fresco Renaissance, all preciously perched for lovers above the Mediterranean.

It took little time to make the arrangements. With neither conviction nor ceremony, no ascribing of permanency to their exile, the Commander, Sannazaro, Rajibai and Ginevra departed American shores.

But not all was lost on the domestic front. Raquel and Alvaro would have twins, and would live happily ever after, at least some of the time. A driver picked up Marigold and his party in Rome, and whisked them away by limo down the A2 to Naples, the A3 to Salerno and then on to Costiera Amalfitana and Positano.

For Ginevra the sinuous Italian coast and its islands were her natural birthright, too, and touring them in the company of such loved ones gave her the same sense of pride now bursting from Sannazaro.

"The Amalfi Republic once vied with Venice for the title of most important trading center in the world," he remarked. With that paternal radiance which homecomings can elicit, he then explained how Emperor Tiberius had moved his household to Capri. "A good sense of real estate," he went on. "He loved our local wheat."

As they neared the village, however, it at once became apparent to the Commander that something was wrong. Sannazaro's fountain of youth, his encyclopedic regard for his upbringing, showed signs of distress. Though he had been in a steady stream of consciousness since Naples, infusing the ears of his accomplices with zealous talk of all the famous artists, and glorious traditions, which had called Positano home—luminaries like Pirandello and Picasso, Nureyev and Igor Stravinsky, Claudette Colbert and the choreographer Massine on his island, "Li Galli" (Isle of the Sirens); of the hundreds of young girls weaving silk for 576-strand European cotton pillow-lacing, a sea-fashion of cobwebs; of ancient parchments and Byzantine icons, relic-busts of Positano's patron Saint Vito, and rare stones ... the Governor-General was presently staring out at a veritable mob of spring tourists. Traffic converged from every direction and the roads were jammed. Horns and tempers flared. Tour buses unable to negotiate steep narrows ensured there be no movement behind or in front of them. Diesel smoke belched from tail pipes, veiling the roadsides. Prices in the millions of lira—sums which dishonored the simple Italian—bore down upon the Señor from shop windows to all sides. He thought he smelled sewage.

"It was never entirely quiet," Sannazaro mumbled by way of apology. "But this? What has happened here? We never picked up any of Rome's bad habits, all the unsightly trappings of a big city. I am mortified."

"It's Europe," the moderating voice of Ginevra added.

"No. This is too dreadful." He recognized few of the new additions: pizza parlors, flashy hotels, new fashion boutiques.

"Oh but it's charming," exclaimed the others. Ginevra, especially, had a more sanguine orientation, pleasantly engaged by the bustle, and the sleek apparel and elegant jewelry in the windows. She rather took to the crowds, who were enjoying themselves and had every right to. Having been back repeatedly to Europe over the years, the changes were not as shocking to her eyes. But then, she'd never harbored the same sense of historic loss that had so changed Sannazaro's life.

They at length arrived at the driveway of their leased villa overlooking the sea, near the Chiesa Nuova. The church bells sounded at sunset and Sannazaro pointed out the bas relief in the tower with its picture of a whale. The villa, one of probably 200 for rent in the immediate area, cost them 3,000 dollars a week, plus the 300 dollar deposit—a bargain by today's standards, thought Ginevra. It was considered off-season.

"In my day, to rent this place would have cost, maximum, 150 dollars for the week," Sannazaro pouted.

"That's simply a sign of your age," Ginevra warned him. He took the dig.

After they'd freshened up, the plan was to pay a surprise visit to Sannazaro's Uncle Giorgio.

"Shouldn't you call him first?" opined Ginevra. "I mean, how many years has it been since you've seen him? It might be dangerously unsettling for him."

"Twenty, at least."

"What if he's dead?" Rajibai declared unhesitatingly.

"Nonsense," replied Sannazaro. "When you meet him you'll understand what I mean."

They strolled down to Uncle Giorgio's cafe. "He used to prepare the finest soufflé Caruso in town," Sannazaro warned. "His sfogliatelle, or babà, as we called it, was amazing. As light as the wind, the sweetness of a young girl weeping on your shoulder, pastries that melted against the tongue."

But when they reached the restaurant, Sannazaro knew at once that, as elsewhere in town, nothing was the same. Gone were the walls of wine bottles and old antiquities cramming the dark corners, the photos from the early part of the century populated by half of Sannazaro's cousins—one-sixteenth of the town, then.

Sannazaro sat in a slump, reflecting sadly on the inevitable. His friends were not surprised. He had already told them how his uncle used to handwrite the different menu each day, how food for him was a culinary pact with God, a mouth-teetering art of subtlety culled from the sea and the hills.

But now, instead of the true grapes and sheep cheese, the products of sowing and turning the soil and, at early autumn, culling of the received bounty, there were "cheeseburgers", "New York steak alla Naples" and "tortillas capricciosa". No more brilliant crostate di marmellate e frutta, or Uncle Giorgio's equally captivating torta di pere Mastroantuono. Gone the heavenly odors of his ravioli mamma Rosa, and fettuccine "notte amalfitana". In their place were "pesce con Los Angeles" and "spaghetti Vecchia Baltimore".

As for Giorgio, the present manager thought he had retired ten years before. The restaurant had changed hands three or four times. He had no idea where the visitors might track him down. But a diner overhearing the discussions threw in that Giorgio had gotten colon cancer and was walled up alone in a nursing home in Sorrento. Still another reckoned he might be out with his last surviving grandchildren in their Montepertuso apartment, or with a hearing-impaired niece in Nocelle. Someone else suggested trying the priest in Laurito: *Fu colpito a morte.* A dispute over a bill, she went on.

In the morning, while Sannazaro stayed in the villa, making phone calls in search of any surviving relatives, Ginevra, Marigold and Rajibai hired a guide and spent an exhausting few hours circulating about the familiar locations and hearing the routine mouthful: cruddy invasions of the Saracens, the feast of Our Lady of Grace on July 2nd, boisterous Benedictines, magical laurel plants that unseated dictators or bore sextuplets (depending on the requirement), and the deep Grotta dello Smeraldo with its tradition of inducing hallucinations in visitors. Atop S. Angelo a Tre Pizzi they stared across to the smoldering Vesuvius, and to the three jeweline isles, Gallo Lungo, Rotonda and Castelluccio.

"Is an eruption predicted any time soon?" asked the boy.

"Heavens no," said Luigi, their guide. "Not since 1944." He crossed himself, though, never certain.

They visited the Fornillo and La Sponda sections of town, and then went back to check on Sannazaro.

He had made some progress and suggested they all pay a visit to his ancestral farm, the "paradise cloister of Campania", as he thought of it. Cassa Arcadia, the origin of *De Partu Virginis*, the *Piscatory Eclogues* and, of course, *Arcadia* itself, published in 1504 in Venice. Sannazaro's ancestor had divided his time between the two locales, Venice and the mountains of Montepertuso.

By the time they'd arrived, both Ginevra and the Commander felt for their companion. Indeed, the Commander more or less grieved, for Sannazaro's loss of Paradise could not be more palpably felt than by Marigold himself, who had personally vested so much faith in an enduring vision. His poor, relentlessly despondent Squire had risen in his eyes to a champion of sorrows, a commander in his own right of ruined armies, devastated dreams and personal misfortune. Marigold's heart tasted of the Italian's bitterness. As Chaucer had written, "this king gan wepe"; and in the words of the immortal Philip Sidney, "... then throwing himself sometime upon the floor, and sometimes upon the bed, then up again, till walking was wearisome and rest loathsome; and so, neither suffering food nor sleep to help his afflicted nature, all that day and night he did nothing but weep ..."[21] The fields had been covered with condominiums already showing severe signs of wear. The old terracing had been replaced by "Villas To Let". Tourists thronged to all sides and Cassa Arcadia was now a posh golf course shorn of vegetation, mired in sandpits and the whir of electric carts. A clubhouse of absolute sterility. Clay tennis courts. Enormous parking lots. Garbage trucks making the rounds, grinding and grating. Loud radio. Bumper-to-bumper. The burning heat, no shade trees to absorb it. Distant smokestacks. Fish-processing plants. Policemen searching the remains of a burnt-out utility vehicle. Foul play. A heated outdoor pool could be seen within the complex, and overweight visitors sleeping in the sun or working on their laptops. The far-off sea sounds of water skiing; a helicopter. Video games.

Uncle Giorgio had indeed been shot—but not over a bill. Rather, some complicated sewage scheme, of which he was a part, that went bad. Not a single other relative remained.

As they continued driving every possible dirt road around the perimeters, Sannazaro gaped upon one perversion after another. Nothing was the same. No trace of 500 years of biological or cultural history. Not a single plant spoke of the native past, save for the marginalized flowers cowering anonymously against the odd barbed wire in the highlands.

"Wait!" The pitiful gardener of Paradise brightened. "Stop the car." Iacopo got out of the limo and crawled on all fours along one such fenceline.

"What's he doing?" asked Rajibai.

Sannazaro had found some precious herbs, *Chamaecrista* and *Platycodon*, which rang true. He clung to their touch, hovering over these last remnants of a tradition, his nose to the flower, beyond the range of power mowers and insecticides. A final plot of wildflowers, perhaps ten-by-thirty meters entire, in which the whole of remaining Italian history, art, and nature— along with Sannazaro's memories—would have to be content.

"Why's Uncle crying?" the boy asked again. "They're just some old weeds." But he got no response.

"Jesus," said the driver. He was listening to the radio, RAI 2. "What?" asked the Commander.

"An alert at Pompeii. The mountain is acting up."

CHAPTER 155
The Graveyard and the Gladiator

SIXTY THOUSAND TOURISTS, and seismic activity up and down the Amalfi Coast which argued for evacuation. But the mayors would hear nothing of it, in spite of their mountain having the most closely watched records of any in the world: multiple eruptions from AD63 to 79; others in 202, 472, 512, 685, 1036, and so on. On December 16, 1631, at least 18,000 residents who had failed to heed the warnings perished. Then, beginning in 1766, there was huge activity, which continued for 250 years. In1906, Vesuvius lost 607 vertical feet from its summit. In 1926, and again in 1944, there were incidents.

Nobody really believed, in this modern age, that the experts would let the mountain erupt. Only the driver, now dropping the foursome at Pompeii's main gate, 90 minutes in traffic from their Positano villa, seemed to burrow in to his superstitions, and expressed his wish that his party at least not dawdle.

To Marigold's way of thinking, this preserved civilization with the telltale mountain looming above was as close as the human eye could come to seeing the future, with all its advantages and disadvantages, presentiments and intimations. He was as attuned to omens as the next fellow, and Pompeii was absolute fodder for speculation. Fatalistically enamored of all those secrets of which the past is written, the history of mankind with its tendency to catch everyone by surprise, turns in the road after which there was no retracing, absurdities with no compunction, he realized that this excursion had somehow been ordained; that his life had come to nothing, despite the recent spate of sallies; that even the destiny of his adopted son had its own genetic shadows against which the Commander's aging peculiarities were no match in terms of persuasion. What would work for Rajibai was as yet unexamined, unexplainable. His life would be his own, the Commander would be gone. That was how it all played out from one generation to the next. Maybe, for the first time, he was truly contemplating his mortality. There could be no better place to do so than on that ashen sea of bones, first brought to life by order of the Bourbon Kings.

The limo driver waited nearby. Armed with the foremost maps from the popular reprints of the *Topographicum Pompeianum*, Ginevra took the lead in traipsing across the oval-shaped ruins, up Strada dell Abbondanza, down Stabiana, across di Nola to Strade di Mercurio, then back again all the way to delle Scuole. Every exoskeletal arm, caked in its stucco and seeming to reach out, betrayed yet other faces, paralyzed, worm-eaten. All the vanities on display, a Broadway show, of sorts, but no inkling of joy, only the immortal dreams, sunk beneath the crowding of beetles and maggots. Every profile bespoke an agony. Each humanity revealed a horror in its place. The Commander could not fail to glean that which had taunted Philemon and Baucis with lost love. Of course, the flipside of this awesome tragedy was the entertainment it effected across the ages. Tourists streaming through in throngs. Curiosity-seekers perpetually snooping around, the sun on their faces. For all that, in the end Pompeii most certainly acted on the heart, a crash course in humility.

"God does not temper the lava to the fawn," the Commander improvised. "But weep not for the silent. They had their day, if not their dawn." And so on.

Eventually, passing an amphitheater, the Palaestra Grande, the Stabian Baths, they reached the Capitolium before continuing to the Temples of Venus and Isis. At length they drew near to the shrine of the imperial family in the Macellum, the Casa del Cinghiale, and then the Caserma del Gladiatori adjoining the two theaters, Scoperto and Coperto.

In all, Ginevra explained to the boy, about 2,000 people died in these homes and public office buildings during the eruption on August 24th, AD79. Those who fled, survived. But many sought refuge in their wine cellars, and that was a mistake. Then again, who could have known? A record of advertisements, doodles, epigraphy, dipinti, diddles, tablets with accounting records, amorous artwork, political campaign slogans and every imaginable sort of graffiti carpeted the ruins. How many tourists and students of every discipline had subsequently pored over the remains, seeking some meaning to human existence amid the plethora of fascinating details from daily life? Architectural styles, building materials, a million household goods, millstones, loaves of bread, frescoes commending every sexual position, thousands of bottles of wine unopened, the Latin language ... Just another hot steamy summer's day over 2,000 years ago.

Though no actual manuscript within Pompeii survived the disaster, there is little doubt that Pliny the Younger's two letters recounting the tragedy to the historian Tacitus were accurate in their portrayal of Pompeii, Herculaneum and Stabiae, the three towns that were buried, said Ginevra. From the guidebook she read to her three companions the well-known story of how Pliny's father had commanded a fleet which went to Herculaneum in search of survivors on the very afternoon following the eruption. How he and most of his men died that night of the fumes creeping into their bivouacs.

Herculaneum suffered a worse fate than Pompeii because the cinder was wet, not dry, and hardened quickly. The city was submerged in a gray cement-like tufa 20 feet deep, on average, and three times deeper in some places.

But of all these stories, what most impressed Rajibai was the amazing tale of Spartacus and his assailant, the praetor Claudius Pulcher.

"You mean he climbed into the volcano to escape?"

"It would appear so," Ginevra hazarded, uncertain herself of what was meant by the "unguarded fissures" atop the rim of the 3,000-foot rock wall of Monte Somma, down which the famed gladiator lowered himself on ropes fashioned from vine branches.

Overhearing Ginevra, a local tour guide came forth and told the boy that the electric railway took visitors to within 450 feet of the mouth of the crater and he could see for himself which way Spartacus went. Though not on this day, because the railway was closed due to earthquakes. Mount Aetna was also acting up; in fact, the whole country seemed to have loose screws that week. Nothing new.

Seeing his son's disappointment, the Commander resolved that they would drive as high on the mountain as possible, and then go by foot, an idea that met with absolutely no purchase in either Ginevra or Sannazaro, but ignited a rousing concordance in the boy.

At that very moment another temblor shook the ground, and for a few seconds all hands were clasped to whatever object of seeming solidity was nearby. A bronze penis, in Ginevra's case.

"Five point three," said the driver. "I think it's time to leave."

"No," the Commander rallied.

"No way," his son seconded.

"I think you're an irresponsible father, then," Ginevra applied.

"All yogis recommend danger as a way of clearing the mind," the Commander exhorted. "Of seeing the light."

"Don't inflict that on innocent children," she railed, her eyes as penetrating as J.P. Morgan's.

It was the driver who settled the dispute. They would pay a visit to the Osservatorio Vesuviano and talk to the experts. That would certainly deter any rash decisions about trekking on the mountain, where smoke was visibly rising.

Ginevra and Sannazaro, though unhappy to be a party to this madness, were not about to let the Commander and his very childish child go off alone, especially in view of the fact Marigold had detoured through town and bought out the first camping store he could find, provisioning the limo with two rucksacks, a climbing rope, a hammer and pitons and carabiners, some nylon webbing, a pair of binoculars, a flare, a compass (which he had no idea how to use), matches, two headlights and emergency mylar blankets, spare batteries, some chocolate, oranges and bottles of Evian water. At the last minute he thought to buy two pair of extra-heavy-duty hiking boots, sized 11 and 5. What was he thinking to do?

The Commander would not say, but having traipsed through the Himalayas similarly outfitted, neither he nor his son was in the least daunted by the technology.

"You may need these, as well," added the sales clerk, stretching the bonanza to its limits.

Marigold examined the odd contraptions.

"They are called jumars," said the clerk, "for ascending a rope." And he showed them how it was done.

The driver took his charges as far he could, then turned the vehicle around and informed them they could go no further. The Osservatorio had already been evacuated of its inhabitants.

"How much am I paying you?" asked Marigold, annoyed by this show of cowardice before his son.

"Not enough," replied the driver.

"I'll double it."

"Sorry."

"Triple!" Rajibai shouted, sporting with the numbers. "Quadruple!" Marigold went on.

Now the boy was stumped. "Five times?"

But the driver would have none of it: "Look, you've had your view, now let's get the hell out of here before we're either arrested or incinerated."

"Please, Murillo," Ginevra pleaded. "You're acting incredibly stupid. This is utterly irresponsible. I beg you not to be a fool."

"He can't help himself," Sannazaro chimed in. "But he is a fool, starstruck by the glittering bauble of the world. That's his strange, magnificent, underestimated affliction. A fuel that better had been precious than profligate. A man who is not his own man because of his terrible sense of impending propelling endlessly tempting adventure, which is, in fact, somebody else's sense of impending propelling and endlessly tempting.

What was I saying? Right—you see, the problem is, nobody has yet figured out the true identity of the real person behind these strange compulsions to constantly move out, up and over; to risk one's life in the cause of ... Well, come to think of it, I'm not sure which cause. It's as if the whole thing were being written down for some silent edification, a triumphant frieze or nameless statuary, all this for that? Or a factory for marionettes, perhaps. At Arctic Christmas time. Taking no account of the fact marionettes have their rights too. But who can say what's really going on? Awkward situation, really. And we're all caught up in the frantic puzzle."

"What? What are you blurting on about?" Ginevra had no patience, and was frankly terrified of their perch.

"I'll tell you what," the Commander began. "You see those tents—" He pointed to a campsite a few miles down the slope. The road passed nearby. "We'll meet you all back there in two hours. Check your watches. I have 3.20. Say 5.30? We just want to get closer to the caldera and feel the mountain under our feet shake a little bit. No other way to really speak with Mother Nature. This is a once-in-a-lifetime situation. I do not want Rajibai missing out on it. We're so close."

"You're a stubborn man," levied Ginevra. "Worse than Jacques."

"Jacques?" Marigold drew a blank.

"He was my husband."

Sannazaro eyed the Commander. "I once mentioned the fact. You just forgot."

"Yes. Jacques, or Jack, whichever you prefer, is a geographer. He teaches at Oxford. We're still very good friends. We just can't live together. He'd probably join you two imbeciles if he were here. He loves danger. I never could understand that side of him. Of men, I mean."

"Not all men," Sannazaro decreed.

The driver was in no mood for banter and finally managed to usher his two remaining clients back into the car. The sleek air-conditioned Mercedes with its dark tinted windows sped away back down the gravel mountain in a trail of dust.

CHAPTER 156
Mr Marigold's Paradise Beneath Mount Vesuvius

WHEN SANNAZARO AND Ginevra reached the tent encampment, they found on the grassy slope two emergency vehicles bearing UNESCO imprimaturs, engines running, whilst bristletail silverfish swarmed to all sides toward the dying azure sea and a small contingent of scientists engaged in what appeared to be delicate calibrations. Fluid dynamics. Soil sampling. Thermal imaging. Satellite uplinks. Snails uncharacteristically raced downhill, tarantulas fumbled towards some other refuge, wood ticks fled their nests, bees dive-bombed haphazardly, stink bugs flopped through the shifting dirt, chameleons changed colors in obvious uncertainty, neighboring lizards—anguid, bluntnosed leopard—moved out onto their little perches of chrysoberyl and bloodstone, peering quizzically in the same tremulous uphill direction, their throats bobbing.

"You're monitoring the mountain?" Ginevra asked.

One of the team members, a young Englishman, nodded, then politely advised her that they shouldn't be in the area. "The mountain is closed. Didn't somebody inform you?"

No, the driver intervened. What's more—he spoke in rapid Italian— he had just let off two clients, a father and son, who were hiking several miles above. The scientist was incredulous and scolded him, but then, interrupted by an even more pressing revelation, hassled by other priorities, merely waved his arms and gesticulated with an hysterical impatience that they should move back. Then, in English, he reiterated: "Madam, it is very dangerous here."

"But a man and his son—" Ginevra started.

"You see that hole?" the scientist said. "It opened up yesterday. Smell the rotten eggs? That crack of sulphides and phosphates, running towards the crater? Also new as of today. It's expanding. We're seeing crystal formation. Oxides of silica being spit out ... I'm sorry. What I'm telling you is ..." But he was called away mid-sentence to the site of activity.

"Expanding? Where? What will happen? What about our friends?" Someone in a silver firefighter's suit and large oxygen tank was being lowered by a winch on a wire into the very hole in the ground, while two others were sampling gasses from the rim of the running crack which spanned several hundred yards of upper slope.

Ginevra and Sannazaro watched and listened, not about to go anywhere.

"EAD? Come on, people, do your DECO calculations." ..."Transmitter?" ..."Good."... "Nitrox computer, ppO2-sensors?"... "Good." And mumbling throughout ... "Depth plus ten meters times 100 percent minus the percentage of the oxygen times 79 percent minus ten meters ..." Or something like that.

An echoing voice rang up from shallow subterranean depths: "We're getting cyanide steam."

"Temperature reading?"

"Celsius 55."

Far above, the Commander and Rajibai had also just descended into a hole, one they'd come upon not 20 minutes after the limo drove off. It was concealed by a shelf of quietly lichened erratics beneath clustering hovels of white bur sage and yarrow. Marigold had hammered two pitons into the hard igneous cracks and lowered the boy into the ever widening darkness.

"It's hot down here," Rajibai shouted back. His hands had touched malachite that was near smoking.

"I'm coming," the Commander grumbled, scraping and scrambling down the dangling doubled rope into the rush of blackness, where carbonate of copper met the glint of abysmal pyrite.

Soon, father and son stood perched together on a tentative ledge in the middle of a cavern of amber and jet, their headlights illuminating the sprawling cavalcade of down-pouring raindrops floating through the spiral of eerie ultraviolet, then disappearing into stellar depths.

"Hmmm?" the Commander puzzled, emboldened by circumstances which should otherwise have terrified him. A hundred drooling mineral species surrounded them. Before him, a rare mercury, its crystal flaring, hundreds of shimmering transparencies. Hexagonal prisms shone fires in the runes of darkening stone. Halites and galenas everywhere about, in octahedrons and cubes, spreading the light of the duo's headlights along every inch of cavern wall.

Suddenly, both of them heard a sizzling noise, then smelled an intensely burning odor.

"Hey?" the boy muttered, noting that the drops were eating into his clothes.

"Acid!" cried the Commander. With that he pulled the ropes through the carabiners above, fumbled to hammer two more pitons into appropriately sized cracks, passed the ropes through, tossed them out over their ledge, and descended once again into an allowable fissure, though crumbling to all sides. No thought whatsoever for dinner, or where they were heading, or why. And no quarrel from Rajibai, who took it all in with his own attention-excess-eagerness disorder. The deeper they submerged, the higher his voice quavered. If he was terrified he subverted it with deep-source enthusiasm. It was a game of chicken, each goading the other. They were perfect for one another. The young and the old philosopher, driven by an equally insatiable and insane curiosity; both adding to the relationship, and the expedition, with their mutually contributory stupidities.

The cavern was hundreds of feet deep. Perhaps thousands—no way to tell. In fact, the light bore evidence of reaching the center of the Earth. Perhaps even going out the other side. Smooth shining surfaces refracted yellow and red; other rock faces showed a lower index, appearing limpid to the eye. But the whole inner world was gem-like in its totality, as if given by some artisan. Bluish velvet, chrome yellow, jade-like Vesuvianite in pulverized floes, a dust rising up from the beyond below.

Now there was a rumble, then a slamming jolt. "Hold on!"

Both clung, their heads pressed into their chests, their hands grasping the 11mm Perlon rope on which they hung suspended over the vortex. Sulfurous whiffs inundated the chimney system into which they'd swung. A pattering of rocks, chalky and orange, pummeled the darkness. Within seconds, only dust remained.

Then another temblor, and another.

"Had enough?" the Commander inquired.

"No," Rajibai injected. Something goaded him on, a density of experience he longed to inhabit. He loved the sensation of hot fiery shadow on his brow.

Both headlights pointed towards a plateau within the shelf of rock. Ten thousand carats of pink and cobalt nuance, blue ground, isomorphous vanadium. Carbonates came unglued in their hands, chromiums and irons, too. Moss agates weeping sweat. By now the two travelers were probably three full rope lengths—or nearly 500 feet—down into the burning Styx. Reaching a sizable cleft, they squeezed through an apparent archway, manmade.

"...gold!" exclaimed the Commander.

Now all led by turns through a series of crushed doorways and expanding rock galleries. A scattering of bones—toad, viper, fox; the rinds and pits of some long-ago mystery.

"Someone lived here once," the Commander inferred. "But how?" The heat was oppressive, but on that trail, as it presented itself, a tolerable wind sucked upwards, carrying with it the fumes of toxic chemistries and eternal damnation down below and all around them. Fires smoldered, embers glowed, cauldrons bubbled. A steamy mire double-stitching the subterranean labyrinth through which the two adventurers progressed, in the direction of an ascending pathway.

Passing beneath an archway carved with the unmistakable signs of a Latin floral arrangement painted in parched hues, they soon egressed into a remarkable clearing of scoria, the size of a football field. Both were silenced, staring all around.

"Don't utter a word," Marigold whispered, spooked out of all contrivances. His eyes, in preternatural confusion, scanned no Ausonian sky, bore no Hesperus, saw no serried clouds. Only the underside of a massive cliff, suspended in the underground, a cave within a cave, earth within Earth. Oppressive, beleaguered, only the barest of molecules to breathe in.

Immediately in front, a vineyard, vast in its proportions: a veritable forest of petrified arbor. Desiccated down to the scorched remains, like a gallery of some heated metaphysic, outlining the human ghosts that once made of it an afternoon's eclogue. The dozens of rows stretched far off towards a villa that rose beneath the down-pressing shoulder of interior mountain wall. Sheds and baches, farming outliers of every size, pergolas, and a feast of strewn items left behind in the haste of the obvious. Then the villa itself. They moved towards it, passing along the way several caches of jewelry, Roman coinage, flasks and ancient bottles filled with the fermented results of what had once been a prosperous business.

They reached the mansion, elegantly proportioned, generous by the standards of any age, and entered. It comprised dozens of elaborate rooms, all perfectly preserved and dating, Marigold surmised, to the time of the eruption of the mountain in AD79. Marigold and Rajibai wandered like astronauts from room to room, gawking at the perfectly preserved ruins. Twenty-foot-high ceilings. Mirrored walls.

"... What is it? ..."

Marigold raced to an adjoining room to find his son staring at a collapsed canopy bed stained gold, covered in chalk, and an old couple in their nightgowns, clinging to one another. Their eyes were tightly shut, the flesh on their bones mummified. Even their coloring remained, though add a tinge of lead, a dash of copper, a pinch of salt to truly catch that light of doom which materialized in the flames spurting intermittently from the thousands of crannies below.

In an adjoining room, seven children of various ages, all hiding under their covers, were frozen forever. Their sleep seemed undisturbed. The childhood way had buffered them. Dreaming forever.

A girl, no older than Rajibai. The most perfect sculpture he'd ever seen.

"Don't touch her, Son!"

But it was too late. He could not help himself. His finger was compelled to open her eyes, and there he beheld a flawless blue sea that led forwards to the very summation of girls and all that they fancy, pray for and divine. Her hair was caked platinum, laced with gold dust; her eyelashes seared, the follicles erased, like a well-brushed spine of the most precious quarto; her face as white as southeast Alaska's Mount Fairweather in harshest winter. She stared back at her admirer through 80 generations of perfect vacuum.

Upstairs, the parents stared with undoubted panic, their faces a hideous congestion of incredulity and terror, so different from the serenity of their children in the chambers below.

Rajibai heard well-tempered chimes. The winds were picking up above.

Marigold opened the windows, ochre-colored leaded glass with multiple inclusions. He looked up at the inside wall of Mount Vesuvius and reasoned that a mighty chunk of the mountain had slid off into the direction of this estate, only to become jammed on the mountain slope, thereby providing a true bridge over which the rest of the eruption passed: an adamantine buttress that then sank into the Earth, allowing for eternal cover for this one family and their estate, lost eternally beneath the inferno, and far from the probing busywork of posterity's armada of archeologists.

In their sunken tomb, this aristocratic family, with their servants and a dozen members spanning a century, were all sequestered: their skin, the color of their eyes, their exotic risottos, pennes and cornstalks, their wine, their precious pets—a strange Egyptian-looking poodle curled up asleep, a bright orange bobcat staring into the netherworld undaunted by time, and an enormous blue-footed wood stork.

"They must have slowly suffocated, then dried up," Marigold reasoned.

Rajibai went back downstairs to peer into the face of the child. As he did so, forlorn ululations rose in his breast which, feeling no more piercing cry, or more strident prayer in the dark, and across time, recited the one lullaby he knew by heart: ..."Little girl's boats, the silver moon, sailing through the sky, sailing o'er the sea, asleep as the clouds go by. Sail, little girl, baby sail, far across the sea, only don't forget to sail back again to me."

Marigold wiped acid tears from his cheeks. "Where did you learn that?"

"From my sister," said he.

Solemnly, they went out into the pergola beside the villa and there discovered an entire ceiling of magnificent frescoes—a Paradise of luscious depictions: nymphs and satyrs at play in lily ponds, lions, saints, deer, parrots, sheep, horses, monkeys, leopards, hares, tortoises all communing in the original Eden.

Suddenly the painted landscapes were changing before them, as a rush of air was somehow forced downwards with its oxidizing effects. Rumbles shook the entire estate. A fluid began its percolation off the painted walls. Cyan transmogrified to black; red velvet to ochre; gold to gray. An accelerated chemistry of decomposition.

"We've got to remove ourselves," the Commander underscored, incommoded now with utter urgency, grabbing his son. "The time is upon us, like it or not."

They raced from the ancient manse. There were glorious striations of sunlight striking the ribboned band of rock wall above, coming from inside the center of the caldera.

"We'll have to climb," the Commander implored, "that way, this way, anyway you can ...", galvanizing all his wits in one robust out-of-body seizure of verbiage and bubble-talk. The Yoga of confusion, Tao of panic, Zen of wits' end.

The gasses of unknown origins were swirling around the estate. As they fled the scene, Rajibai filled his pockets randomly with precious trinkets. A hairband of solid gold. Coinage. A pen case. A scarab.

Far down the mountain, a mile out on the exterior ramps of sulfurous steep, another group of cave explorers was also retreating, hoisted back up via electric pulleys in their million-dollar re-breather suits. They had found a skeleton bearing an eighteenth-century signet—a farmer who had fallen in his own vineyard, probably broke his leg, and was not discovered in time before the next lava flow.

Sannazaro and Ginevra were frantic now, for the mountain was clearly fragmenting. All were told to evacuate or perish. The summit was belching iron-dark smoke, translucent topaz, meteorites, porphyritic diabase, and the ground was continually shifting ... An inch, two inches, three inches each minute.

To his exquisite credit, the limo driver was not about to forsake a father and son, however frightened he might be, and took it upon himself to drive back up to the point where Marigold and Rajibai had departed, just two hours before. With helicopters circling overhead, and the scientists gathering up their gear, pulling their tents, and heading out, Mount Vesuvius was the scene of an eerie causation, all of its historical antecedents fixed in the minds of those frail human minions now fleeing her shoulders and surroundings.

Down at the earth-strewn ruins, a high-decibel siren of the air-raids generation evoked undisciplined terror among tens of thousands of tourists who now spared no selfish gene, antipathy or cuss word to escape, taking mass flight by whatever means. The roads were flooded with refugees; police vans had cordoned off certain routes; officers were firing their weapons to force the redirection of the exodus into unidirectional flows. Officials at Pompeii were supposed to be prepared for this kind of event. It had happened countless times before.

The limo driver reached the spot, but the Commander and his son were nowhere to be seen. He honked his horn in repeated spurts, but to no avail. With ash beginning to rain down, there was no point, he figured, in adding a third body to the tomb of imbeciles. He ignited the gas and retreated down the steep dirt road, the vehicle spraying the air with a dust storm of uprisen charcoal all the way into town, where he met Sannazaro and Ginevra in a well-stationed hotel lobby they had hastily agreed upon.

During this time, up in the guts of Vesuvius, the two adventurers struggled to find a way out. Marooned beneath a sheer face, they had no other option but to go back down into the maw and search for another route out.

Despite their predicament, Rajibai's curiosity was undiminished. The mountain's vroom, he pointed out, was more like a series of fantastic farts, giant trombone-sized heaves from unfathomably deep Italian sources. The air, too, reeked of sulfuric flatulence and counter-spells.

"... iyouhhh!" exhaled the boy, clutching either nostril.

"*Cover your eyes and mouth!*" screamed his father, who was smashing in the last of their pitons in order to fix the rope and facilitate a rappel back to a more suitable ledge from which they might make their escape.

With one more geophysical outburst of flatus came a spectacular silence, augmented by a gentle snowfall of white ash falling back into the giant pit in the earth. The winds had ceased; calm was temporarily regained.

"It can't last. We have to move more quickly."

They lowered themselves over the lip of the rock ridge, descending the sheer dihedrals, until they attained an elevated platform leading to another series of cracks and tunnels. All was shiny with the strange metallica of daylight and ash. Beneath them, a mere ten feet, lava which had risen, tantalized by the waiting caldera, gave in to gravity, out of steam, reversing its flow and retreating like a sluggish river into a sullen depth, leaving the estate with its perfect little girl, a princess who had stabbed the boy's heart and made him want to linger in antiquity. There she was, untouched. Forever in hiding.

Miles away, researchers with binoculars were watching, waiting, while the Italian Emergency Management Agency staff were commandeering the evacuation procedure, arms gesticulating, all the way up to Naples. Millions of people were stumbling over each other to get away.

"It's going to blow!" guessed one expert, peering across the walls of the Vesuvian landscape.

The silence lingered palpably above the coast of Italy, one bay, one village after another. Hypnotized by this sudden tranquillity, those taken to premonitions of *Sturm und Drang* sensed the eruption to be but minutes away. But what the experts with their high-powered sensing devices, satellite tracking, telescopes and binoculars witnessed instead were two skinny guys, man and boy, clambering over the rim of Mount Vesuvius, slightly dazed, judging by their uneven gait down through the deep detritus and shifting talus slopes, but otherwise making a surprisingly carefree beeline towards Pompeii. A cloud of ash trailed every footstep.

"What do you feel like for dinner?" Marigold shouted across the slope to his wunderkin, who glissaded with unhurried ease.

But the thunder coming from the mountain's bowels made all such mundane verbosities inaudible.

That night, however, Marigold discovered that Rajibai had lifted precious artifacts from the tomb of the villa. He was not pleased.

"We must go back, Son," he applied sometime after midnight. "It will not do to scavenge a sacred site like that. There's not a moment to waste."

Having met up with the others at the hotel, a rushed bite, and then more preparations, by three o'clock that morning, their headlights recharged, their reticent driver sworn to secrecy (they did not want to alarm anybody), the Commander and Rajibai were headed back up the mountain of ash. Once at the spot, they retraced their terrifying steps to the boulderfield, found the cavern entrance, undid the chaos of ropes, made the necessary adjustments to their harnesses and rappelled down into an eerie glow. They discovered the cavern to be lit up as a result of fresh lava blocking the entranceway to the crucial tunnels that had seen their free passage only nine hours earlier. That left no other choice: they would turn over the precious souvenirs to the museum in Pompeii.

On the other hand, Marigold got to thinking, if they were to do that, even worse damage might be incurred, encouraging archeologists to interpret secret data embedded in the relics and to mount their own expedition in search of the villa. That could only result in a new excavation and total trespass.

The Commander had experienced a similar guilt complex on a beach in Ecuador many decades before, when his own father had chastised him for picking up shells. "Never take from Nature," Pecos had challenged him.

"That settles it," Marigold presently concluded.

As they stood leaning out over the last rocky perch within the cavern, they ceremoniously tossed the dozen or so heirlooms and keepsakes into the lava.

"It's better this way. You will see. Never doubt that the gods are always watching!"

CHAPTER 157
A Venetian Misanthrope

A PARTY OF FOUR IS guaranteed to make monumental mischief in a place like Italy, when all constraints of Nature are removed. So it was that the Commander, his boy, their uncle and his madam made like petrels across the night, storming village after village with the *joie de vivre* of Alexander the Great, or Samson Carrasco, the most famous bachelor in the history of Western Europe. At length, they arrived at the Venice train station hours after dark—not that this had been the plan. But the Commander had insisted upon an impromptu stop along the way in Verona in order to visit the Cassa Romeo and Juliet and there fondle the hallowed bronze breast smoothed down to a gleaming palimpsest from so much devotional ardor and, in addition, divine some ordination amid the heartswells of graffiti on the right-facing wall, as was customary.

Neither Pollock nor Willem de Kooning could have splashed a more fashionable chaos than that monolith with its million chalky hues and ten million stabs at posterity: Jane, I love you; Ruggiero worships Deidamia, ad infinitum. To Marigold, this honeycomb of love notes and haiku, petrified crayon, necrotic pen and ink, febrile adorations and muted sonorities bespoke high purpose worthy of contemplation. A code in the cipher of *amore*. Hidden blueprints to any number of paradises awaiting us on Earth. He was wise enough to know there wasn't just one such Eden. The trick was in finding the right one. Sannazaro had reconciled himself to this harsh truth, as well, in the aftermath of his sorrowful visit to his home which no longer existed.

Both men stared at the wall, tracing its amorous alliterations with delicate fingers, searching for a directive, some elusive meaning to it all that transcended the ages. Every lover had his moment, a vast spasm of singular importance, whose vision of purest radiance in the guise of someone else to love came besieged by the ineffable. Graffiti that longed to be granite, names etched into an eternity made flamboyant by popularity and one million similar aspirants. The result was a wall of permanent inexpressibles, silent passions, all that desire unable to inhabit the thing it wanted most. These remnants of eternal want were like so many ghosts of a world that never was, a diaspora of desires.

Or, thought of entirely differently, said Ginevra, taking a wholly optimistic stance, a charming record of love nests that should empower any believer in the senses and ensure a long prosperity to all those who would place the heart before the head.

Still, the Commander was troubled by the many futile ejaculations whose only faint memory was a restive name, a transient couplet, barely distinguishable amid the desperate daze of so many other signatures all crowding towards the center to avoid that fringe where the wall ended and the Great Void of Being began. Where one had to accept that one was born into this world alone and died alone.

"Have you never considered the dangerous consequences of such nonsense?" Ginevra openly chastised Marigold, upon hearing the dribble of his existential hangover. "Especially given your new duties, and your hopes to raise a normal child. My God, at this rate you'll turn him into a monk with no interest in life, happy times or positive things."

"If that was the impression I imparted, I apologize," the Commander volunteered. "Surely you realize that I mean only to instill a love of reason and passion in the boy. Let him understand the power of distant horizons and the sheer joy of the song thrush and the Leonardo."

"Then lighten up. No more talk of Great Voids and permanent inexpressibles."

This, Ginevra began to sense, was not the man who had interested her. Never before had she encountered so weird a mixture of morbidity and hyperactivity. Perhaps he was a classic manic-depressive, without any Lithium? She did not know about the clinical baseline, no way to judge. But it was clear that his long-winded elocutions on subjects of grave unsuitability to a child contradicted his own childish abundance and zest for every hotspur, gauntlet and madcap. He might seem the hunched, retiring recluse, despising intimacy, misanthropic to the extreme, but there was that other side of him: the man of valor and enterprise, adventurousness and boldness. He had, after all, rescued the boy; defied a whole state, a nation; nimbly confronted opposition with the spirit of a harebrain and soldier of fortune rolled into one pluck.

A stuntman at heart, he brooked all weather, heeded few cautions. She liked his temerity, but could not understand the dark side. What to do but carry on? Perhaps his riddle would clarify itself. If not, nothing lost. He'd certainly been generous with everyone. Millions of dollars, just like that.

Sannazaro suggested they continue on into Venice. "There are no such voids or harsh realities there, where poets and artists have been expressing themselves quite nicely for 1,000 years."

In Venice the weather had turned to wind and cold rain. Waves were churning the surface of the Grand Canal. Sannazaro hired a private vaporetto which delivered the four weary voyagers to their pensione near the Accademia. Though it was after 10 p.m., everywhere they could see Venetians in a quandary. Dozens of earthquakes throughout Italy had left hairline cracks in tarmac, marble, cement and stone. That, in combination with unprecedented storm surges in the northern Adriatic, had injected volumes of seawater from the outer lagoon into the city proper. The water had risen six feet higher than normal for winter, and each cranny-distended chink and corner of the city's damaged infrastructure was vulnerable to the sinister flood. Residents who dared to enter public spaces did so in rubber waders and gumboots.

Sannazaro had studied art in Venice for a year during his time in university. He'd also sung in a choir at the Basilica of San Giorgio Maggiore. "Twelve months in a lagoon," he reminisced. "One of the best times in my life." His fascination with the painters and architects of Venetian history was what had brought him there in the first place, particularly the Doges' Palace, built over successive centuries, and completed under the guidance of Giovanni and Bartolomeo Buon during the fourteenth and early fifteenth centuries, he explained.

The clincher was all in the details, he insisted, tying, somehow hazily, the length of the palace (499 feet), the rose-colored upper story, the Asiatic filigree in the parapets and pointed arcades to some sophomoric theory concerning a mesh of glancing eyes and buoyant egos in a city known for the most beautiful women in the world.

"You've lost me," Marigold politely interposed. "Look at the capitals," Sannazaro rallied. "And there—such wide corridors, such slowly ascending banisters of marble and onyx. What do they say? To me, they are hewn of a desire to temper immensity with an open invitation to the everyday."

"Damn it, stop! Your academics are a blabber. Let the boy enjoy. The lady dally. And myself, I want to gaze, unraveled, no spelling bee. Not another detail or my brain will hemorrhage."

"Not to mention that we've heard mention the same theory, and every last detail, in 35 languages just since lunchtime," Ginevra pointed out.

Poor Sannazaro, proud of his heritage and assorted facts, had underestimated his companions, who wanted only to enjoy themselves.

But their pleasure was short-ended, for even their boatman was another of those tour-guide fonts who insisted on dazzling his charges with a steady stream of trivia: "Ahh, signora and signori, those same columns, edifices, architectural impulses are vanishing in a pelagic purgatory." (Actually, what he really said was, "Venice is sinking. Just as well. I'm retiring to Rome where my Uncle Eddie has a taxi concession.") But the point was too obvious. A hundred museums, more than 3,000 pieces of public art and 10,000 private villas were disappearing beneath a high tide that had come to stay. Most of the great Venetian Gothic structures by Andrea Palladio were threatened with seawater. Sannazaro had studied the great master in some depth, and was particularly dismayed by the man's prediction.

Even St Mark's basilica, the essence of Venice with its interplay of light and shadows, blatant beauty and retreating modesty, was now a foot underwater. Pigeons were finding it difficult to congregate in their normal manner. Everywhere, water was turning alleys into moats, lapping galleries and cafés. Pedestrian traffic had been re-routed in dozens of areas, though local residents pretended to ignore the confusion of annoyances and backstreet disasters, not wanting to acknowledge the looming chaos, or dispel the magic which translated into whole lives, and not a few tourist dollars. Venice, if anything, was also the idea of Venice.

While the rich were jacking up their mansions with improbable Japanese and Danish technologies, the poor were orchestrating sandbags with the help of frustrated carabinieris. The Benedictine Abbey at San Giorgio Maggiore, the Scuola Grande di San Rocco, San Zaccaria, the Guggenheim Museum, every significant location in the city was in danger of becoming a bog. Early next morning this air of doom wafted even into their pensione, for it was all the chambermaids spoke of. One after another they rattled off ever more dire prognostications.

Desperate to show his friends the city before it sank, Sannazaro led his troop to all the familiar outposts of greatest grandeur—Tintoretto's "Paradise" at the Ducal Palace; a ceiling filled with Tiepolos, another with the works of Veronese. Walls done over in the name of Carpaccio; portraits and landscapes from the astonishing studio of the Bellini brothers; the workshop of Tiziano, painters from Ferrara and, of course, the one and only Giorgione. All of these masterpieces had little time left, according to local gossip. And what was the Italian Government doing about it, asked the Señor?

Studying the situation, apparently. One gaggle of retired army officers suggested tenting most of the city, as if for termites, inflating it with air and pumping the water out through reverse osmotic pressure.

A Moroccan firm vaguely modeled its recommendations after Aldo Rossi's spectacular Il Teatro del Mondo near the Customs House. The concept was this: the best of the city would be removed, reassembled and fortified with tubular steel shells, a floating, living museum 1,000 stories high, three miles wide, much like Frank Lloyd Wright's hotel in Tokyo built in the 1920s, impervious to typhoon, flood or earthquake. The city would simply embark on a global journey, leaving the site of Venice behind, commemorating the great stage play that is life. The first city to become a ship.

Others relying on perfilograph data had suggested a massive anaerobic digestion program whereby algal blooms might be encouraged, red tides, bioaccumulations, garbage, all the fecal matter of the Ticino Commune, allowed to create a polywater-like land-form. This was seen as a way to halt the incoming floods with a buttress that would slowly turn from brown pudding to marsh, then solid earth.

Cynics disagreed, suggesting that there would be an outbreak of cholera and all of Italy would succumb. Sceptics complained, atheists battled Catholics, ecologists fought with art students, politicians fashioned glamorous and strident platforms over the quagmire with promises of a New Venice, a New Century. Chefs, maestros, gallery owners, mask-makers, venders, gondola *tassisti*—all carped among themselves. "Se la Regina Isabella non avesse aiutato Cristoforo Colombo ... chi avrebbe scoperto il Nuovo Mondo!" shouted one college student at the government official who was deemed to represent the remarkable inertia of those in power. "Forse voialtri giovani ..." he tried to reply, but was cut off by the angry mob.

Meanwhile, the scientists at Laboratorio Venezia scurried to and fro. In the early 1990s, a forecast system known as Operational Storm Surge—Segnalazioni Maree—was developed to monitor water levels, meteorological changes and atmospheric pressures throughout the Mediterranean. The Gulf of Venice and the Venetian Lagoon were tracked via satellite, wind fields were taken, sea swells, tidal flux, every possible datum inputted in mathematical grids that might provide some substantive picture of the rising water. But no one knew, exactly, how to save an entire city, especially in view of the Global Warming scenario.

The Falklands, Seychelles, Zanzibar and every KOA campsite on the Gulf Coast of America faced the same problem. Except that Venice had a trillion dollars in historical properties and art. It was, by some estimates, the most precious city in the world.

Sannazaro had his own solution: "Everything will simply have to be carried away by hand," he summarized. He was seated with his friends in the Café Serenissimo, where he had spent long hours of blissful oblivion as a student. "Italians have a long history of brilliant engineers. Remember Leonardo da Vinci who came up with the submarine in 1502. In those days Venice was at war with all her neighbors and the great artist/inventor, visiting from Rome, devised it for the occasion."

"What happened?"

"True to Italian form, nobody was willing to make a decision. Everybody argued. In the end, the Doge rejected it. A lack of vision."

"You're suggesting we all go live in submarines?" asked the head camaneri, opening a fine Chinzano.

"Nothing like that. A group effort, though, to be sure. Public altruism. Enough of this dissent. Let every man carry a wooden beam, a building block, a painting in its frame; every child a tile, a book, a public document; every woman a mirror, a load of antique linens, an icon. Padua is only 30 miles away, and high enough to serve as a dry hospice. After all, the trains, the vaporetti, Alitalia are still functioning."

"And what of the buildings themselves? Look around. This café. That marble bathroom. Those stairs. This bar top, which is 400 years old. The apartments upstairs—700 years old. It was next door that Goethe wrote his essay on glaciology; Ruskin copped a cigaretto right there, and Canaletto painted his remarkable scene of the Thames from that balcony. Ungaretti wrote his greatest poetry in the courtyard, and Woody Allen had a drink here during his honeymoon. Every building throughout the city has its own unique history."

"Forget Venice," came a somber voice from a strange figure in a burgundy turban at the rear of the café. His gray hair fell like silken tassels into his dark, bunched-up overcoat. "For that matter, forget the whole of Italy and of Europe. We are all history."

"Ignore him," said the bartender. "He is a lonely old Arab fisherman from Morano and times have not been friendly to him. No sponges or squid for many months. And every night for the last year he has come in here, ordered drinks for two, and sat there all alone. You see, he's waiting for his wife, who died 14 months ago."

"But that's so sad," said Ginevra.

"The world is coming to an end," the old man continued, speaking out in old Italian to all those who cared to listen, while Sannazaro managed a nearly simultaneous translation caked with his own layers of elaboration.

"The millennium came and went, good sir, not to mention this week's earthquakes, and we're all still here," Marigold volunteered, trying to cheer the fellow up, taking a seat at his table. "What are you drinking?"

"Moron! Imbecile! You understand nothing! Venetians are blind, fretting over their petty palaces, women flocking to rescue a jewel case, a canopy bed, a set of masks. Men their Lamborghinis. People have gone mad in favor of their meaningless possessions. When soon the whole world will disappear. Not even the gondolas will survive."

"Water levels are rising a few feet. True enough. That is a taxing problem. But the death of someone we love—now that I would describe as a true tragedy. Though we've all been there. My condolences, sir."

"Yes, my wife died a year ago. And you do me honor by your homage. But pity not this one lonely Arab, for soon I shall be reunited."

"Of course you will."

"We all will," the bereaved man carried on with poignant enunciation.

The bartender served them house liquors from Castelfranco. Rajibai ate potato chips.

"You're depressed. I understand. Have you no relatives?"

"Relatives? Sir, you fail to catch my meaning."

"Then speak clearly, friend. Just a few days ago I found redemption beneath Mount Vesuvius. So there is little about the so-called Apocalypse that can possibly hold any news for me. I have seen the truth of devastation—skeletons charred in the last anxious moment of their life on Earth—and know that therein lies a kind of honeyed salvation. Lovers entwined eternally. It is not so bad."

"That may well be, but Vesuvius is for amateurs. I'm speaking of a collision with Mars. The red planet. It's getting closer and closer to Earth. Whatever our species has dreamed or hoped will be banished in an instant. Nothing will remain."

"Really? On what authority?" inquired Sannazaro, intrigued by this novel species of dyslogia. "I've heard of water on the brain, and canals on Mars that were once filled with water, but did not know that those canals could affect these canals."

The Arab was not amused. "You ask by what authority? Why, by the most famous astronomer in the world," said he.

"And who is that?"

"Sheikh Abdul Hamidi," declared the old man.

"Where might one find his observatory?" asked the Commander. "In the mountains of Soqotra," replied the Arab.

"In what far-removed exile of hinterlands would one find such mountains?" asked the Squire, quite certain, if not fearful, that the Commander's little atlas, the one inside his brain that never slept, was already scheming on the edge of his chair.

"What does it matter," replied the old man in a deadening voice which signaled such a true resignation that the Commander could not help but register a certain uneasiness himself. There was something about the man's command of doomsday, his confidence in its finality, that drove shivers throughout the foursome. "Soon, even those ancient mountains— so venerable and blue, 5,000 feet of solid rock wall, the scourge of the Wadibootans—will be erased from memory; dust in a fiery pit of floating astral chaos."

"Soqotra ... Isn't that part of Saudi Arabia?" hazarded the Commander.

"No longer. Now it is Yemeni," replied the misanthrope.

"You have been to see this Hamidi?"

"He is my brother," replied the old man.

CHAPTER 158

The Strange World of the Wadibootans

SO CHILLING WAS THE old man's mocking style and calamitous caveats that all who heard his warnings could not help but tremble. There was no other task of worthy presentiment than that Abdul Hamidi should be forthright consulted.

Thus did the valorous Commander, Baron of the Four Seas, Professor of all Oddities, round up his waterlogged compatriots and announce an expedition far to the perilous south in search of this solitary astronomer on his grave of a mountain. If, as the old Arab seaman had alleged, the world was coming to a sorrowful close, Mr Marigold wanted to know the date and time so as to put right a ballroom full of loose ends.

Their introduction to Yemen was most peculiar. En route from the airport to the storybook capital Sana'a, the taxi driver, nestled beneath his heavy-fitting turban and layers of caftan, asked them 100 odd questions: their preference in napkins, Belgian linen or white damask?; their position on camel races, water desalinization, their views on good government, marriage vows, children's cribs and the prettiest coins. Only later did they learn that this man was the Crown Prince of Yemen, posing for two hours as a taxi driver; he had miraculously escaped his confining palace in order to find out for himself what life was really like out on the street, and what the people wanted.

To all of his entreaties Rajibai told him a thing or two straight from the fantastic heart of child gossip and calculation; and if a logical sequence of events may ever be predicted, and if the Crown Prince were truly listening, then surely Yemen's turbulent history, the map of her political relief, was about to change radically.

Rajibai, after all, was not merely a dzeren (Central Asian gazelle) of acrobatics and perdurable carefree ways. Or some too-easily impressed international parvenu. He numbered among his finer traits a rating badge of honor, a highly evolved auditory meatus and nuclear membrane, a parbuckle of instincts for catching new whiffs of possibilities. And he accomplished these vast antics with the grace and precision of a jai alai basket. So that what he had to say to the taxi driver-cum-Crown Prince was as penetrating as a cymbal, or pan pipe, or triangle. A new primary substance and tissue: new schools, roads, reserves and rainbows.

A priming charge that would provide for universal sensuality and literacy. Pure propositions culled from that obscure high-point of mathematics known as Reynolds Number; that, in addition to what future generations would come to regard as 'Marigold's Quotient', and guaranteed to get by any obstruction. He described a new world that dispensed with religion, division, pretension and exclusion. Expressed a keen satisfaction—right off his old man's block—with all forms of alcohol and wildlife, ginger snaps and brown sugar. He concluded his proposals for the new capital of Yemen with recommendations straight out of the Emerald City. By the time the astonished taxi driver dropped them off at their hotel, he had much to contemplate and no need for further polling among his people. The human condition had more than acquitted itself in that one little boy.

Unlike their altogether reasonable Prince, the Yemen authorities were, it seemed, counter-intuitive at every step. They firmly discouraged the Commander and his party from venturing to the remote island on account of the southwesterly monsoons which pummeled the jagged coastline with gigantic breakers day and night, week after week.

"Nobody goes, nobody can go, especially this time of year," the qat-chewing officer in charge on Al Zubairy Street insisted, emphasizing the lack of safe harborage, or any facilities for a famed billionaire.

"Why not go and enjoy our world heritage city, as well as other stupendous portions and tidbits of fair Yemen?" he admonished.

"We need to go to Soqotra," Marigold insisted. "Much hinges on this journey."

"Better you should visit the Suq al-Milh," the officer replied. "No poison spiders or sandstorms. And there you will find the finest raisins in all of Arabia."

"I'm allergic to raisins," admitted the Commander.

"That is a problem. Then certainly you must visit our 27 absolutely priceless mosques, each one a heaven, beginning with al-Mutwakil and al-Jami'al-Kabir. And after that, al-Aqil," he went on.

Now he sampled dates.

"I will certainly visit your mosques, dear sir, but only if you then promise to get us to Soqotra on the first available airplane."

"You must banish Soqotra from your mind. It is no place for a boy, and especially not for a woman."

"But women and children live on Soqotra! What are you talking about?

Why so disparaging?"

"Why not think it over in one of Sana'a's many saunas?" the man suggested with a wink intended for the gentlemen present, though it seemed to catch fire, repeating itself like a congenital stutter. He rubbed his eye and straightened his jacket. "And when you are hot and exhausted, you might then help yourself to a bundle of our finest Al-Rawdhi grapes, famed for aiding the digestion."

"My digestion's fine."

"Food is not to be trusted on those islands," he insisted. "But why are you so down on Soqotra?" asked Señor Sannazaro. "Yes, why?" reiterated the Commander.

The fellow brought up the fact that nearly everyone on the island had malaria or tuberculosis, or both; that the children sniffed gasoline, which messed up their brains, and one out of two died due to the extreme harshness of life out there; that if anything happened to any of them, only one doctor could be found on the whole island, and he had no medical supplies and little common sense. Dysentery was rampant. Jaundice and scabies, too. Just to give a newcomer the creeps, locals—60,000 farmers and fishermen—would steal his underwear. The dirt roads had been washed out five centuries before, never repaired. The walking trails were in even worse condition. Tarantulas got into your inner ear and nested there, feeding your brains to their young as they hatched. The only sure method for avoiding them was never to lie down, never to sleep. There was no electricity. All heating was occasioned by steam, which explained why most residents had terrible burns all over their bodies. Nobody read anything on Soqotra: the illiteracy rate was 99 percent.

"Add to our problems, we are slipping away from Africa at nearly one inch each year. A disaster!"

"Then why," asked the Commander, "is it called the Island of Bliss?"

"Ahhh ..." lamented the Customs official, almost nostalgically. ...And with that it became obvious to both the Commander and Sannazaro that this silly official had been giving them the round-about for a purpose: he wanted to keep Soqotra all to himself. Finally, he fessed up: "Because of its supreme beauty! All Yemeni people are addicted to beauty. Just look at Sana'a—the Venice of Arabia, is it not?"

He went on to admit that he had been instructed by higher-ups to discourage travelers from going to Soqotra because it had become Government policy to protect this precious place, said to be the best-preserved semi-arid tropical island in all the world. This heartfelt confession put all of them on the same map, for Mr Marigold let it be known that he had searched the world of late for such pockets of bliss and would not take 'no' for an answer, especially in view of the official being the one to confirm the aesthetic, cultural, intellectual and biological prominence of the island.

The Commander went on to cite confidently the Arabian bustard's migratory route this time of year, thus suggesting that flight patterns were possible around the island, and made reference to critical details from the famed first-century Greek explorer's treatise *Periplus of the Erythraean Sea*, in which were mentioned the island's plentiful food types, not least of which were the wild pomegranate and cow peas.

"Therefore I can anticipate little cause for worry, good sir," he concluded.

But seeing how these profound trivia exerted so little purchase on the Customs official, the Commander laid ten 100-dollar bills in his hand as part of the customary handshake. The officer examined his hand in the light, then added with a hearty grin, "Of course, sometimes there is a freak break in the weather."

The party chartered a military aircraft which carried them some 250 miles southeast to Mukallah. From there, after refueling, they soared out beyond the three other pearls of the Soqotra archipelago—Darsa, Samha and Abd al-Kuri. Rajibai gasped at the great flocks of cormorants that flew beneath their aircraft as it swung over the rugged-looking island, passing above the village of Qalansiya.

The pilot noticed something on his instrument panel. He pointed to a broad band of smudge that stretched for 100 miles.

"A typhoon?" Marigold asked.

The pilot didn't answer, but Marigold could see how he was beginning to sweat, his forehead giving vent to hot droplets of panic. The pilot had his orders, and knew there would be a substantial tip, and so was intent upon safely dropping off his passengers. Yet, something about that smudge terrified him. He'd never seen it before, only heard about it.

Now the reverse thrusters revved downward on their approach. There were high-flying sunbirds and grackles. Whitecaps were strewn across the sea like confetti. The mountains in the northwest were cloaked in a lugubrious fog, limestone walls plunging sheer into the rough waters. Down on the beaches the sandy spits had been transformed into dustbowls. Buntings, vultures, other sea creatures could be seen standing their ground against the tawny gales. After repeated efforts against strong headwinds, the aircraft managed to land on a sand dune two miles away from the town of Wadiboo, along the shores of the 1,300-square-mile island. The landing was raw and fast. All around them was a fury of wave action, the entire Gulf of Aden in terrible turmoil. Lonely was their perch, beleaguered their sensation. Not a soul between Africa and Asia.

"Does anybody here know what the hell we're doing," asked Ginevra, "when we could be shopping in Milan?"

None of the males deigned to answer.

The party of four toppled out, their baggage tossed after them from the aircraft's hull, along with a warning from the co-pilot, who shouted with a kind of desperation, "Quickly!"

The propellers never stopped turning, and soon the plane was gone again, the roar of its engines fading to the east. A squint of the aircraft remained, then that too vanished.

Marigold was equipped with two GSM telephones, and felt reasonably assured of being picked up once they had found their way to the top of the Haghir massif, with its renowned Mesozoic relic formations and species, met with the Venetian seaman's brother Hamidi, and acquitted themselves of the important information he might have for them. He hoped to glean whatever news of the Apocalypse was awaiting them, and return to Europe within a matter of days. Anyway, who could pass down such an opportunity, he explained to the dismal Ginevra who, with Sannazaro, was not so sanguine, standing nakedly in the brutal hot hamsin, trying to protect her Isabella Rossellini-like face from the stinging sand.

The Customs official had arranged, through a Yemeni travel service, to have the foursome met and taken care of. However, no one had arrived to greet them. There was no taxi. Only a deepening inferno of wind and flying gravel. No hotel representative. Not even a sip of cold water to be had. They stood in the barren spillway. A desert dune. No building for 20 horizons—or none that they could see—sunlight burning in their veins, dust demolishing their brains, sandworms collecting under their skin, carnivorous spiders eager to begin.

Ginevra suggested they all head towards the alleged town on foot, since no other choice presented itself.

"But which way?"

Battened down, their cheeks seeking cover between the upper portions of their partly zippered anoraks, they trudged across the barren plain with its decomposed cherts and horizontal razor-edged fissures. The landscape was as if from some other portion of the solar system that had been exposed to the primordial air for 135 million years while most of the world remained submerged beneath nurturing seas. This would have accounted for the strange shrubs and short-winged insects, the exotic birds and primitive lichen which everywhere confronted and confounded them. Green turtles and freshwater crabs shuffled unconcerned across the low tides.

Passing by scores of free-grazing camels, sheep and goats, they encountered a shepherd boy, probably Rajibai's age, with a kingfisher sound asleep on his head. Other birds slept in the trees, or atop the bushes: Forbe-Watson's swifts, rufous sparrows, hawks and eagles. This phenomenon of closed eyes in the middle of the day was especially peculiar given the fact most birds always keep one eye open in case of emergencies.

There was no way to understand the shepherd's eager stream of vocables, a language known to have its roots in the ancient Mahra quarters of southern Yemen, a nomadic tongue that predated Arabic and was scarcely understood by anyone at all. Even the Soqotri locals had problems with it, though certain Eteocretan, Portuguese and pan-African words could be made out by visitors from afar. "Iman? Souvlaki?"

But just as the travelers attempted to transcend conventional linguistic barriers by offering the lad a 100-dollar bill for his troubles, the shepherd pointed to the northeast, howled pitifully and started running. So shrill were his bellows that the birds heard the summons through their deep sleep, opened one or other eye (depending on the species), looked up anxiously and took flight in a gigantic wave of panic—a sudden exodus countered by a similar stampede among the camels. They, in turn, caused riot in the goats who terrified the sheep which made skittish and boisterous the buffalo whose mad flight scattered lizards, crushed snakes, pinioned tortoises and obscured the horizon, until the entire desert was like an agitated mirage beneath hysterical hooves.

Within seconds, the Commander's party understood that the cause was nothing Mr Marigold or Rajibai had said.

"Something's wrong," said Ginevra, feeling the humid avalanche of wind which presaged the front guard of ten billion frantic insect wings.

"*Locusts!*" Sannazaro shrieked. The locusts had arrived from Sudan and Eritrea, devastated Bani Fayid and Hawiya, covering 30 square miles before approaching the archipelago. These insects (scientists said half a billion, but Marigold counted well over one trillion) consumed in a day enough food to supply half a million people for a year. But although the foursome's initial fright was justified, it was soon clear that these red and pink marauders had nothing against the animals. They dominated the croton bush which covered the hillsides, clinging to every succulent vine, stem, trunk and leaf. In an instant whole forests of endemic *Soqotri adenium* and stinky *Dendrosicyos* squash vanished beneath the hordes, which could not decide whether to eat or to mate. Strands of frankincense and the famed Soqotrine aloe were gulped down by the long locust pincers. Grasses, gums and resins melted in their mouths; further afield, thatched rooftops also disappeared. No crop was spared. Millet, pea, potato, date, corn, almond, orange were consumed within hours. Wells were littered with millions of locust corpses, many half-eaten by other locusts in the feeding frenzy. A few sittingduck others were eaten as well: a kitten, a hen, a sparrow.

The foursome lay covering themselves in the ruins of an old fortress on the edge of town, hemmed in by stone mortars and a tent which they fashioned collectively from their wind parkas. Even so, there was locust ooze everywhere, in their mouths, their eyes, down their backs and their pants. Such a dark blizzard was the swarm that for nearly three hours no sunlight or dust could penetrate their mass.

In the aftermath, as they climbed out of their ancient confine, Marigold examined a living locust left behind while its havoc-wreaking extended family continued on in a pink, crepuscular swarm five miles by 30 miles thick towards some unknown and hapless destination across the Indian Ocean.

"Taken individually, he's quite the charmer, I would say," the Commander alleged, situating his eyes as close as possible to those of the aggressor. "Head to head, the locust is an admirable being. But place him beside his other comrades, and—just like a man—he loses every sense of decorum, bursts forth with a furious attitude, part papilla, part whelk, an inflammation of pustules and blackheads, and before you can say 'No', the mob rules. Napoleon usurps Paris, army tanks take Moscow, a conspiracy kills Kennedy, Nigerians are slaughtered, Hitler elected, and so on."

There seemed no fitter logic to explain the fact the individual insect appeared courteous, a slow-turning, intelligent, even affectionate bug— lonely, exposed, unsure of itself. Not one cantankerous cartilage in its elongated two-inch inverteframe. Collectively, however, he was no bargain. His billions of cousins constituted a sinful excess. The analogies with humankind were too delicious. Who knows what orgy-consciousness these bugs enjoyed; what dreams compelled their piercing bloodstreams. Sir Martin Conway had first analyzed their charters of havoc.

The Commander placed the insect down amid a sea of locust parts, many still writhing in one death agony or another. And meditated upon all the ethical ambiguities thereof, a Heraclitus in Yemen, wondering whether one invertebrate, amid a billion others, was nonetheless a valuable thing, a life unto itself worth rhapsodizing. His conclusion was inescapably affirmative. But there was no time for further contemplation.

The foursome must continue into the legendary village of Wadiboo. Residing a mere 1,400 camel paces from the nearest sea cliff, Wadiboo was, by worldly standards, quaint to the point of resembling a dried-out olive pit. The adventurers were easily enchanted by the enclave's silences; the town petite enough to be overpowered by the blue shadows of inaccessible granite, besieged by various hornets, poisonous woods, parlous declivities, each manoir with its unleavened screens worthy of an archeological expedition. A kingdom, in short, of dusty visages, of contented locals pointing in the opposite direction of yonder at every opportunity, of placid demeanors, innkeepers, offhanded philosophers, rueful recollections, ancient domestic charms, piles of speaking stones, peerless flotsam, vegetable-thick wadis, attractive misfortunes and lodgings to every side of description. No afternoon missed a beat. Every morning the same, century after century. Upon each courtyard, *F. socotras sigusmund*, a tarantula whose bravura, say the pundits, is distantly related to that of *Brontisaurus ethiopi*. On every outskirt, profuse white sharks; atop every slab of sandstone, sunning itself, a magnificent monitor lizard and, according to Arabic tradition, crocodiles 40 feet long.

But where were said crocodiles? Rajibai eagerly inquired, having never seen one. "Atop the sandstone with the lizards? Or out in the water?" But nobody had information. Nor was there a reliable source at hand to comment on the rumor that some rare variant of giant squid, immune to all pressure gradients and motion constraints, also frequented the shorelines, searching for breast of hyena.

But with all this going on, rarely in 255 years did the locals catch sight of a foreigner, and never in recorded memory did four such odd-looking holidaymakers show up on the occasion of the worst agricultural disaster in Soqotra's history. Did these mussy-mouthed vagrants cause it? In which case tradition demanded they be sacrificed to the island dragons known to lurk in the mountain fogs. Or, by a more heroic show, did they cause the locusts to give up the island? If so, this was grounds for making them each an honorary Sultan or Sultana. Such was the difficult question feverishly debated that night, around campfires across the whole of Wadiboo. The caliph himself placed a scimitar on his nose and danced dervishly for hours, attempting to divine the answer. If the scimitar even once fell to the ground, the decision would be made.

Now Wadibootans are renowned for their cooperative nature. A decision is a decision. Research by various United Nations scientists has shown them to be in favor of all those golden rubrics now classified according to the general parasol of 'sustainability'. Ecologists have long revered Soqotran society for its self-governance. For instance, those campfires were all fueled by dead wood. Those camels, which had returned to the safety of town and the companionship of shepherd lads, were prevented, as a rule, from free browsing. Fodder was revered, as were fruit trees. Seedlings were well protected from stock animals, dewdrops collected in the concavities of leaves, a system of wells long cultivated.

Arabian wildlife laws prevented the hunting of birds. In short, man and nature, beauteous each, withstood the kinks and idiosyncrasies of the other so that both might benefit from the relationship, and this contract had endured, as well as could be determined, for 10,000 years. At Wadi Ayhaft, on the rugged north coast, it was common for the beetle to confer with the lizard, the lizard the songbird, the songbird the feral cat, the feral cat the wild dog, the wild dog the billy goat, the billy goat a fair maiden, that very maiden her handsome consort, the consort the Sultan, and the Sultan the Almighty One who, in turn, was not above discussing life with the beetle if the soil needed turning in time of famine, or with the songbird if the dawns and twilights were bereft of music, or with the feral cat if the island for any reason lacked the soothing effect of a purr once in a while.

Somewhere in the middle of all this marvelous chatter and cohabitation of man and beast sat the unlikely tourists, three of them miserable, one of them characteristically bright-eyed. Rajibai, of course, had befriended a dozen natives his own age, or thereabouts, each whispering about some facet of the dragons in a language fervid with animal magnetism which children universally can understand. They were obviously testing either his gullibility or his courage.

"We must visit these dragons!" the boy demanded of his overburdened father.

"Even I must admit to hesitation where dragons are concerned, Son," replied he, shifting uncomfortably on the desert floor, insect blood and other exudations of the great locust aftermath itching his private parts, hardening his joints.

That night, Pluto and Uranus passed over them while the Wadibootans debated. Sannazaro, in his Armani shoelaces, complained of an anxious visceratonic gut and dreamt of cold Dos Equis. Ginevra fell fast asleep, sitting shoulder to shoulder with the Commander beside the fire, sparks cascading, whilst Rajibai danced with all the young girls. Nearby, the caliph came to the final climax of his whirligigs; a breathless pause entranced the hundreds of high-standing onlookers as they waited to see if that razor-sharp scimitar should be separated from the sweating, imperial schnozzola. A leap, a twist, a somersault, a gasp—yet, the scimitar remained glued to his nose! By midnight, the whole town was frolicking, for it had been decided: the foreigners were heroes. They had saved Wadiboo from being devoured.

At dawn, all were awakened by the royal clanging of gongs and call of the faithful from a high minaret, the only one on the island. Males were separated from females, although Ginevra was not required to distance herself whatsoever from her three male traveling companions. They all stood before the mosque.

The local caliph now commended the travelers in an ancient reverential tongue, utterly untranslatable. Little gifts of cormorant guano were passed around, commentaries from the *Koran* read aloud, and great excited cheers of adoration, along with gold coins and chocolate kisses, tossed into the air. Rajibai, too, was thrown around like a football, while Marigold and Sannazaro were carried aloft on the rampaging shoulders of ten dozen particularly wild Bedouins. This fanfare went on into the late morning.

By early afternoon, it was business as usual. Villagers had much to do. Millions of dead locusts needed to be swept into the fire pits, orchards replanted, cisterns de-loused. By this time, too, the Commander and his cohorts had become anxious to learn of the whereabouts of Abdul Hamidi. But upon the very mention of his name, a suddenly serious hush pervaded all who heard it, and frowns rose up in a unanimous negation that didn't bode well at first blush.

CHAPTER 159
The Enchanted Dragon

IT SO HAPPENED THAT there was a second band of islanders, most feared by the Wadibootans, who inhabited the highlands of Soqotra. They were called the Peekabouties. While the Wadibootans, descendants of the crocodile, were said to be sound of mind, of calm and conservative disposition, and religious comportment, the Peekabouties—whose ancestors were the ostrich—were taken to sneaking up on people and terrifying them. Though nobody was ever harmed in the land of Peekabou, there were certainly many who nearly died of heart attacks from fear. Angioplasties were common, stents were rampant, blood pressure and sugar soaring. There were natural anti-clotting agents spread generously about the island, but the Peekabouties tended to devour them. Because they lived in the terribly high mountains, it was believed that Peekabouties had a higher consciousness than others, but to what end they applied these greater wits remained a mystery. Even their geographical coordinates were unknown, because all maps were printed in disappearing ink for their said quadrants.

Whereas Wadibootans could claim responsibility for inventing the best in flyfishing footgear, the Peekabouties gave rise only to universal apprehension, hide and seek. While Wadibootans were confident, even brash on solid ground, they would not step foot, if they could help it, on a vertical stretch. In reality, as their race suggested, the Wadibootans were stuck, more or less, in a ditch, while the Peekabouties had free rein of the hills and let nothing attempt to curb their temperament, except by unspeakable peril to oneself. This fear and loathing on the part of the ditch people, and its accompanying false show of superior courage, was called by psychiatrists the 'Cowardly Lion Syndrome', and was reminiscent of a famed conversation between Goethe and Eckerman on the blatant mental differences between mountain people and flatlanders.

Adding to these primal barriers of mind separating Wadibootans from Peekabouties was the sheer inaccessibility of the Haghir escarpment. Nobody had ventured there in over 5,000 years, other than the Wadibootan children, who had always maintained good public relations with Peekaboutie youngsters. They seemed to be on the same wavelength and would think nothing of venturing into Peekaboutie territory (though never after dark) if only on a dare or to scare the wadibijeebies out of one another. And, as is the wont of children, there was considerable name-calling—no opprobrium intended—for their body types were quite different (for example, Wadibootans had gravel eyes, Peekabouties favored yellow), and much fun could be made at the other's expense.

It was of some academic interest to understand the untoward way in which a Wadibootan child, having grown up feeling comfortable, at least by daylight, in Peekaboutie territory, should as an adult grow out of that capacity to withstand the unknown; should become a veritable enemy of the mountain people, if not a racist. What age marked this sad reversion to a segregated world? What were the deep ethnographic inhibitions and superstitions that overtook a whole people? How was it that generation after generation of children never ceased to enjoy their curious and amenable neighbors whilst their adults carried on in the most fervent and public shows of antipathy? Clearly a serious division rent Wadibootan society, or, more likely, its genetics. The children were the wise ones, their adult peers diminished in sagacity and mother wit.

This sorrowful gap between old and young was instructive, lending a universal lantern to the state of affairs governing all such bifurcations. Marigold himself had detected the signs in other spheres, but never experienced such direct confirmation in a culture at large. The abyss between ages argued for a complete rethinking of public policy, the Commander determined. The adults had no clue, making government by the young an absolute necessity. His Children's Party, postulated in New Delhi, was clearly on the right track. Those who still believed in Santa Claus should rule Utopia.

Recent data from Iceland lent further confirmation to Marigold's hypothesis regarding the profound differences between the child's brain and that of his parents. In the case of Iceland, the entire population of adults—nearly 150,000 individuals—had been sampled; the specific gene for Alzheimer's identified. At what age was the onset? Over 50.

That meant that the child's universe had ample room to formulate exquisite fantasies and make them come true. There was time enough. Without dreams of Oz, airy castles, misty lakes, white-clad maidens and green serpents, lacking hope for mountains beyond the visible, and lotus-dwellers within the soul, the body predictably grew old and flimsy, prey to every degenerative disease. It was not a new idea, but never had Marigold seen it so palpably proven as on Soqotra.

He remembered quite poignantly the general disinterest exhibited by his 'mature' peers in matters pertaining to enchanted dolls, royal monkeys, hocus pocus and Palmer Cox brownies. How could people over twelve years of age be so blind? That did seem a fairly telling dividing line, thought he. By twelve, the shopping mall had conquered the child; video arcades and electric trains taken priority over the powerful bagpipe lungs of Wee Gillis or Thomas the Tank Engine. By thirteen "The Princess and the Pea" or "How Sir Turquine bare Sir Ector clean out of his Saddle" could no longer compete with Nintendo. Fifteen was truly a watershed year of nullification and abnegation. Of wiping the slate of one's past in order to become a bona fide bore. That was the year, and April the very month, when Victorian water-babies, Jumblies and carved lions were tossed out. By sixteen, snowboarding had replaced "The Fish with the Deep Sea Smile". By seventeen, Ian Fleming had usurped "Tiny Tadpole" and "Robin Hood and the Tanner". At eighteen, all halfpenny marvels had been burned, while bungy jumping was the vogue.

College years made the schism even worse: *The Education of Henry Adams* could not be read, evidently, in tandem with *The Jumping Lions of Borneo*, or Rosetta Baskerville's *The King of the Snakes*. But why was that? Did not Peter Rabbit have at least as much to say about the Western psyche as tattoos and other fashion statements? The ultimate irony was that many Nobel Laureates turned back to *Jabberwocky* and *The Wasp in a Wig*. That Einstein himself adored *The Three Sillies* and Madame Curie *Little Red Riding Hood*. Even President Truman was a fan of *The Last of the Huggermuggers*. While John Maynard Keynes studied the illustrations of Cruikshank, particularly those for the various *Testimonies to the Value of Fairytales* and, of course, the illustrations for *Oliver Twist*. But these were rare instances of the getting of wisdom. They were all tall men, high visibility.

By and large, in adults the child is lost. In adults, Marigold now understood, the wind is not the wind, and every earthly sign that in a gentler time gave some chance to dreams is but a forgone desolation. No hope of fancies, all dragons slain. That very grown-up, ripe with nothing, once a sterling child, is now alone in a land of pain, his memory clouded, his name erased, no fondness or nostalgia. Banished are the good things, replaced by scorn, competing in a skyscraper of others suited up, conniving, no jest, just seriousness; all borne upon a stream of jealousy, cruelty and self-regard. A benign Rajibai among

Argentine ants, Ethiopic hornets, ship rats out for a meal of fantail.

Whereas once upon a time, all were free, and some may still be.

Yet for most, the majority and many, such curiosity as carried the sandman and his crew, a tall sail, a wind so blue, had died, and the wonder with it. Night is black, no stars remain. And nothing any longer be true.

So that when the Commander asked for a guide to lead his party into the mountains in search of Abdul Hamidi, his request was met with horror among the adults and widespread chagrin amongst the children.

After several minutes, when nobody stepped forward to volunteer, and this in spite of the recent celebrity of the foursome, it was all the more peculiar that the caliph, or imam as locals referred to him, should recommend two five-year-old boys for the task.

"Their romps into the outer realm are stuff of fables," hazarded the imam.

"But surely there must be some mistake," replied Ginevra. "Those are very high mountains, and rugged too. That's no place for children."

Marigold knew instinctively that five-year-olds were probably the only ones who could ever guide such a fantastic journey.

"They know the way, they really do!" Rajibai interjected, having danced half the night with all the children of Wadiboo. He'd heard about the lunatical djins and hamadryads of Jebel Hamidi, the highest, most feared of rocky crags, and could think of nothing more enthralling than an expedition into those very precincts with the leading brats of Wadiboo.

"I know you're right, Son," availed Marigold.

Seeing how there was no apparent circumstance under which the imam, or any of the other adult Wadibootans would hear of such a journey themselves—in fact, they all cupped their ears tightly when the Commander proceeded to inquire, "What's the problem?"—it was presently resolved that the boys Miraj and Alibooboo would escort them to what was described as "The Edge of the World".

Notwithstanding the availability of the five-year-olds, the curmudgeonly imam implored his esteemed champions to forget this madcap notion, pointing out that Abdul Hamidi was a dangerous sorcerer, according to the children who had spied upon his fortress. He surrounded himself with dragons which did his bidding, and lived inside a huge dome of impenetrable metals which opened to the sky to admit the coming and going of evil spirits in the form of snowstorms—snow which fell nowhere else on Soqotra but in that dome—and lights of every pile-up and perfidy. Sickening radiations glowed across the barren soil; winds pummeled the crenellations of his castle; eerie monsters abounded. Abdul Hamidi conversed, in short, with the Devil, by way of elaborate instrumentation that sent and received sparks and hail and sleet to the outer reaches of the lost portions of Hell.

"But you have never met him yourself," said Rajibai. "So how do you know anything with certainty?"

"Your son speaks his own mind," said the Imam admiringly. Ordinarily he would have belted the little cretin.

"Yes, a custom among Marigolds," admitted the Commander, eliciting raised glances from both the Señor and Governess, as Sannazaro now referred to Ginevra in public; both of them realized that they'd never before heard the Commander use his family name in the plural form.

Nothing the elders could do or say would cause the Commander to alter his mental precinct. In fact, the imam's dire warnings simply encouraged him the more, as he recalled how the official in Sana'a had similarly tried hard to scare them from coming to the island in the first place. Neither a dozen virgins, 200 camels, twelve years' worth of locust pâté, nor 14 years of scorpion satay could persuade them to stay. In the end it was decided: Miraj and Alibooboo would lead them until four o'clock the following afternoon, when the sun would be at 17.5 degrees, which should suffice to point the general way. Then the boys must return to Wadiboo with all due haste, making sure to reach their village before dark, at which time the foursome would be on their own. The imam explained this very carefully to the two brats who seemed to understand perfectly well. Of course, they did not.

And by four o'clock the next afternoon, no one could quite obtain a proper reading of the sun's position in the sky on account of the dust storms at 20,000 feet that obscured the very mantle of all incoming light. Nor did either brat have the stomach to descend all the way back betwixt ghost and goblin, dragon and who-knows-what. Instead, not wanting to miss out on the adventure of a lifetime, they insisted on remaining in the more assured company of Rajibai, the Commander and the others. So it was decided. Darkness crept upon the six trekkers who, by that time had attained an altitude of probably 2,000 feet, as measured by the refraction of light on the spherical droplets of their sweat as calibrated by the arc of resplendent full moonlight rising above the last of the dust wall on the Venus side of night.

"Ask them how far to the sorcerer's abode?" the Commander requested of his son.

Rajibai fell easily into his children's Esperanto of elocutions and gyrations, and succeeded in gaining the necessary information.

"Miraj says it could be there, or it could be over there. Then again, maybe it doesn't even exist. Alibooboo is more certain that it's over that ridge. But because it's dark, it might be some other ridge entirely. One ridge leads to another, the another to yet another, and they insist that since, mathematically speaking, another plus another equals another, what's the point, after all, in splitting hairs?"

"They make their point," Sannazaro sighed, confounded by the least fact, overwhelmed by the last detail, exhausted by the tyranny of his own legs and Achilles tendons, frantic to lie down—which they presently set about organizing, along with a campfire and hastily concocted meal of Yemenite pasta à la rancid peanut.

"I could have stayed in Rome," the ever cosmopolitan Ginevra speculated, "although I will volunteer that the fire is nice and warm, the place seems free of ants, and just *look* at all those stars, will you!"

"Speaking of the fire, both Miraj and Alibooboo are in agreement upon the dire necessity of our keeping the fire good and strong, and of making sudden movements and noises all night long."

"Or what?" asked the Commander.

"Or we shall be fair game for the Peekabouties, they warn."

Rajibai proceeded to explain everything he had learnt about the local inhabitants of the cordillera in which they were bivouacked. It was not long after that fine dissertation that everybody began to see what appeared to be darting eyes in the darkness.

"Look there!" Miraj exclaimed.

"And *there!*" cited Alibooboo, in his own language. "Shhh!"

Howls issuing from the blank of night merged with the gusting winds that threatened to extinguish the party's tentative fire, forcing them to spend considerable energy gathering dry mountain oleander to keep the flames alive. Marigold, having learned an ancient method of keeping African wild dogs and panthers at bay, asked Ginevra to look away while he proceeded, with the help of the boys and Sannazaro, to pee in large concentric circles around their fire. This way, alleged the Commander, citing the bylaws of evolutionary biology and all the learned lessons of the Rift Valley, the periphery of their camping grounds would signal undeniable markings, sufficient to thwart the expansionary pranks and territorial imperatives of even the most aggressive Peekabouties.

His urinalysis faltered, however: upon conclusion of group micturition came an anticipatory patter of giggling, distinctly audible through the whining winds and creaking trees. Pee meant nothing to the adversaries. Boundary lines were mere ephemera in the night. Odors of no consequence. Clearly, these Peekabouties were formidable opponents. The temptation, some primeval urging for reunion, was too overwhelming, and before Marigold could stop them all three boys had wandered out into pitch blackness, guided by nothing rational. Before long there was ample evidence of a struggle: grunts, peals of—of what?—and every variety of physical mischief silhouetted in the jarring face of the moon, not 34 paces away.

"Rajibai!" Marigold shouted repeatedly. "Son, come back!"

But of course the boy was not persuaded. The Commander had no choice but to venture out after him. Sannazaro wisely refused to join him, and Ginevra had no intention of leaving their pee circle. "Please be careful," she cautioned.

Within minutes Mr Marigold encountered a windswept grove of enormously tall Chinese silk floss trees covered in 20-inch spikes. At the base of the trees Arabian ticks congregated in tremendous piles, and each little monster trundled upon its wee-tiny back a gargantuan balloon filled with pink blood. One by one the ticks leapt onto Marigold's face and promptly began screwing themselves into his cheekbone, which caused an odious sensation.

Now which way does one unscrew a tick, so that the little jaws and head muscles and bulging eyes do not remain? Marigold pondered. If left unbothered, surely it would munch its way through the bone marrow and cause irreparable annoyance? Finally he chose a counterclockwise method, which seemed to work, and he moved on.

He passed by the eye of a poison oak forest that was swarming with noxious ampules, and continued all the way into a five-acre cluster of enormous glacial erratics—boulders left over from the last Snow Cone Age 14,000 years ago. Each of the rocks, covered in jabbering fungus, was the size of a hand-squash court. The fungus was contiguous for miles, making it a clear cousin of Marigold's fungus friend in New Zealand's Fiordland. Marigold passed along greetings from the Antipodes, triggering a chorus of surprise that would not let the Commander get a word in edgewise. In fact, there was absolutely no known antidote against its incessantly rude gossip, though what, precisely, the fungus was mealy mouthing about, nobody could rightly say, as it spoke in most peculiar tongue. It didn't matter: the enthusiasm was contagious.

Soon the Commander found himself confronted by the oddest tree yet: a hissing cinnabar specimen whose knotted limbs were clearly ancient. By star glow, the enormous earthling resembled the Crab Nebula.

"Hiss!" went the fearsome tree, ambulating and rippling in the midnight gale.

"I'm looking for my son, and his two companions," said the Commander, softened to the oddity of talking trees by his communion with the fungus.

"They were somewhere out here just moments ago."

"Hiss!" the entire tree reiterated, this time with motives best described as sinister.

"I'm terribly sorry if I awakened you from sleep or frightened you. But, you see, he's my only son and a very good boy and not at all accustomed to these dangerous woods. All right, I get the point. Goodbye, then."

As the Commander began to walk off in another direction, the tree began to speak, first with a menacing "*Grrrh!*", but then a more calming and sympathetic, "They've gone thataway."

Just as soon as it had opened its knot, a mouth formed—or, more precisely, a cavity filled with enormous fangs dripping blood and a tail equipped with multiple razor-sharp spurs. Arms could now be deciphered—for this was no tree at all—with talons clothed in more talons, razor upon razor, and it reared up with a mighteous roar, burgundy and slimy in the silver light of night, three feet thick at the throat, 40 feet long if an inch, one of the most terrible, if enchanted, of dragons, and menacing, too, if one were less than courteous in her presence.

CHAPTER 160
A Hermit Astronomer Among the Peekabouties

I THOUGHT YOU WERE a tree. But seeing you are not, I must say you seem like a pleasant enough dragon," admonished Marigold, ignoring the brio all about, the feigning of fire and squirting blood. "Perhaps you'd be so kind as to reveal their whereabouts in greater detail?"

"On one condition," replied the dragon.

"Yes, speak up?"

"That you be my friend."

What a strange request, the Commander thought. To think that the Wadibootans had feared this lonely, aging monster, when all she wanted was companionship in the wild.

"Friends for life," Marigold assured the tall-standing beast.

With a hefty swing of her enormous head, the dragon turned towards the summit of the mountain. Looking up, the Commander noticed a meteorite shower, or something similar to it.

"But why are all those meteorites falling into what appears to be a place of singular interest to them?"

"That, sir, is Sheikh Abdul Hamidi's throne room."

"And if I were to venture there this very night?"

"It all depends," the dragon contemplated aloud. "Are you with the Wadibootans, or do you stand by the Peekabouties?"

"I am from the outside," the Commander said, without considering the potential for politics. "But I am given to a general dislike of all finks, fiends, perpetrators and underminers. I embrace sunny dispositions, and those who exemplify virtue."

"The outside?" puzzled the dragon.

"Yes, from New Mexico, where the dragons are far less intelligent or seemly than yourself, Madam." He felt proper in designating her gender, given the sonorous tone of her voice which could only be that of the female variety.

"You are a charmer," replied she. "If you care to hop on to my back I shall be honored to escort you to the throne room myself."

"I have two friends back at the fire. May they come, as well?" asked the Commander.

"If they are your friends, certainly. There is plenty of room, as you can see."

So the Commander ventured back to the fire pit, gathered up their supplies and explained about all he had encountered, concluding with the dragon. Sannazaro was not exactly thrilled by the prospect, but Mr Marigold used all of his special skills at persuasion and at last induced them to try a seat on the dragon and see if it was comfortable. But convincing Ginevra was another matter entirely. She was not accustomed to the Commander effectualizing reality out of stardust, or having phantasms materialize. Her doubts were heavy and charged with ratiocination.

"You can't expect me to sleep amid thorns, turn the other cheek beside scorpions, abide by buckets of locust blood and a Caliph's superstitions, feed upon desert mush, gravel in my hair, not a single bar of soap for 800 miles, and then assault me with the preposterous proposition of riding a dragon!"

"Ginevra dear," he proceeded, "this is the nature of adventure." And he continued by flattering her, in turn, with rhymes culled from the master of careless text, such as *The Tale of the King who Lost Kingdom and Wife and Wealth*, only to have them restored by Allah himself. In an idiom suited to every hidden happiness, he praised her valor, kindled a lamp of suasion that made her out to be heroine of the year, all of Arabia, and—in short—turned her adroit scepticism into flagrant eagerness, and outright terror towards singular curiosity. Captain Sir Richard Burton, translating *The Book of the Thousand Nights and a Night*, could not in twelve volumes have effected a greater transformation of character.

"Why, it's most comfortable!" said Sannazaro and Ginevra in nervous tandem, once they were properly fitted on the slimy, leathery surface of the *Dragonata sentimenta arabia*, which was her formal name. Actually, she was an Arabian subspecies of *bixie*, the Chinese Imperial Lord of the Netherworlds, part lion, part dragon, part phoenix, with a new set of scales suited to high-desert retirement thrown in. Her face was the size and texture of a Welsh coal mine; her skin the color of the rain forest, 40,000 shades of green and auburn, with spectacular stripes and dilettantish dots and fractal geometric patterns; and the thin filament of medical slime which covered it contained remarkable reflective properties such that the abundant firmament overhead was almost to a precise quasar mirrored on her back, thus promoting in her riders the sensation—once they were up and moving—of slithering through the Milky Way on a carpet of sinuous jungle.

As they entered a fog-saturated bog, Sentimenta cautioned her guests to close their eyes, which all three agreed to at once. "But why?" asked Marigold.

"We are crossing a Peekaboutie graveyard," the dragon answered.

And only seconds later each rider felt something brushing up against his or her skin.

"Ignore the white bony claws of the dead Peekabouties. They are merely seeking contact with the living. Not to worry," Sentimenta called.

"Worried not," replied the benumbed Commander.

They attained higher ground, and Sentimenta cautioned them to close their noses. "But why?" asked Sannazaro.

Just as suddenly the threesome smelled the grotesque odor of something new to their experience.

"Tallow works," replied the dragon.

"For whom?" asked Ginevra.

"Enemies," said the dragon.

"Who are the enemies?" Sannazaro nervously inquired.

"Adults bent upon acting like adults, and unbelievers of every species," advised Sentimenta.

"But believers or unbelievers, as the case may be, in what?" insisted the Commander.

"That is the question, isn't it!" concluded their magic carpet. "Forsaking folly, renouncing foolishness, betraying all that is silly, sentimental and sweet—those are the terms for disqualification."

"But belief in what?" the Commander again pressed. "All innocences," replied she.

"She sounds to my ears like a card-carrying Marigold," Sannazaro concluded.

Eventually they cleared the last hurdle, a stream with a garrulous penchant, mice-eating insects scuttling atop eddies, and weeping willows along the banks in such need of consoling that they were wont to wrap their limbs around any would-be journeyer with such force of intimacy as to squeeze every last ounce of oxygen from the lungs, inducing a perverse and unintended result. The whole landscape was dolorous and in need of companionship.

It was 3.30 in the morning, and they were now less than a mile away from the sorcerer's observatory. "We must proceed respectfully and quietly," the dragon advised. "He can hear us, and see us—every move, every thought, even a heart palpitation."

"Who can?" Marigold questioned.

"Why, Abdul Hamidi, of course. Whose brother you conversed with in Venice, was it not?"

"But how did you figure that out?" Sannazaro spilled.

"Because he told us so," said Sentimenta. "He saw you with one of his telescopes and could read your lips."

"But, if you knew that much, why did you bother to scare me with your hisses and grrrrhs when first we met earlier this evening?" asked Marigold.

"Simply to ascertain whether there was a child beneath that armor of adulthood," replied Sentimenta. "Since you were neither a Wadibootan nor Peekaboutie, I had no sure way of knowing much about you. If your tone had proved more haughty, or if you were too big a man to bother stooping to lower echelons of rhyme and unreason, or if you had shown yourself to be above speaking as children do with a tree, then I was certainly not about to divulge the speaking dragon inside of me. Fair is fair. Make sense?"

The threesome nodded. Before long they arrived before the main entrance to the hornet-engulfed 960-foot-high granite doors to the fortress. They could make out huge cosmic slurps from inside, and a kaleidoscope of lights as a star shower the consistency of fresh powder snow floated in massive arrays down into the dome. Then they discerned the giggles of four children: the two brats, the zany hysterical shivers of Rajibai, whose laughter was its own trademark, and a deep-throated convulsive chuckling which Sentimenta said belonged to Hamidi himself. A wise chortle of undulating profundities.

"Does that sound not remind you of something?" wondered Sannazaro.

Both he and Marigold formulated the same thought at the same moment: Crowquill! "But how did the brats and my son arrive here so quickly?"

"With the help of the Peekabouties," replied the dragon, who did not bother to explain but knocked three times on the amazing doors with her equally splendiferous tail, swinging it in gigantic loops that would, of course, prove fatal to any accidental interloper.

For 1,000 miles around, the moon illuminated the world: the eastern coast of Eritrea, the Gulf of Aden immediately to the north, the Indian Ocean further east, even the hallowed summit of Kilimanjaro, far to the southwest, though strangely lacking any snow on its summit. Down below, somewhere in the tangle of intersecting slopes and plains, forests and sloughs, the Wadibootans slept in their little mangers and huts, happy as could be, and safe, for their time, from the Peekabouties who now, in throngs, came to the granite doors to see who was there.

They were little people, as Marigold had envisioned, no more than 30 inches tall, on average, and naked through and through. Children, all of them, who had been waiting for the dragon to arrive.

"What kept you? Hurry up, then," they chided the great and lonely beast. "The sheikh has just commenced his latest and most urgent of observations."

With that the children all raced up the agate and amethyst spiral staircase to the domed observatory, the Commander, the Squire and Ginevra rushing to keep up. As for the poor dragon, the stairs were most inconvenient. She could not fly, due to the cramped interiors of the spiral tower; she could not slither efficiently, either. So she had no other choice but to climb the stairs, one at a time, clumsily and hard-breathing.

"My 14,678 arteries," she complained to the sheikh upon reaching the summit, "are hardening. I need a good bypass."

"One of these nights," replied Hamidi. "When I have time to find my surgical gloves."

Presently, the sheikh looked at Ginevra, took her hand in his own wrinkled way and, bowing with a steady demur and hunched humility, kissed it like a Frenchman. Then he examined the Commander and Sannazaro with his all-knowing almond eyes and bade each of them a formal welcome.

"But please, hurry. What took you so long?" he mumbled, annoyed, forgiving, on the intellectual edge of terrible anticipation. Something mighty was in the air, all could feel it; even the falling light was tinged with the tentative choreographies of snow crystals which could not decide whether they were six, seven or 700 facets, whether to reflect, refract, absorb or emit. Some were mirrors of themselves, queens of the albedo factor; others preferred to melt rather than endure the long-drawn waiting period. They simply couldn't bear the uncertainty. Still others simply sat frozen and still, glistening with perfect composure. The same could be said of many of the Peekabouties, who lounged about in a variety of anxious positions, squeaking amongst themselves, giggling, commenting, wondering, hoping, jesting. A vast assemblage of hugely excited little creatures.

"Oh well, no doubt Sentimenta's loneliness is what kept you. She's the last dragon in the world, be advised. Addicted to the mint bush which has transformed her fire into sweet-smelling breath. And aren't we all luckier for it. But that, no doubt, has had something to do with her deplorable plight. A friend to all, yet perpetually besmirched in the newspaper columns. The first fright of saints and utterly misled mythographers. Did she or her kind ever do anything to deserve such a reputation? Of course not. Then came all those hateful European scientists searching for specimens century after century; and American Presidents out on safari, not to mention the wrath of the Wadibootans who, up until just 62 years ago, used to mount expeditions to burn them out. They won't talk about it now; I think some guilt has crept in. But the result has been the decimation of dragons. Now there's just her. But who among you can look upon that pulchritude and not weep for her equipoise, her undying art, her every ounce of flesh which mirrors the best of the creation! Ahh, there is nothing like a dragon. And to have one in the neighborhood—why, it is bliss, I tell you!"

He gazed upon his elegant visitor, her 75,000 cubic feet of loving flesh and scales, stumbling along in the observatory, trying to fit in, wanting only to be loved and to love in return.

"Loneliness is surely the greatest cause of extinction. Now Sentimenta's getting on in age and nobody knows for sure the life expectancy of a dragon. Quite sad. But I don't mean to upset you. Just find a seat over there. And watch your heads. The astronomical mirror alone weighs 70,000 tons. Once the computer within the apparatus locks onto a starburst, I have no way of controlling the instrument's movements."

"Father!" shouted Rajibai, who sat on the other side of the circular pit of galaxies beside Miraj and Alibooboo. "Isn't it wonderful!"

Indeed, it was, for they were all exposed to the heart of the universe atop the sorcerer's tower on the summit of the deadliest crag in all of Soqotra. One hour before sunrise, floating on the rings of Saturn. And just now the planet Mercury was coming into full view as it never had before.

CHAPTER 161
How The Question of the End of the World Remains Unanswered

SEATED AROUND THE quartzite pit of galaxies, eagerly awaiting Sheikh Abdul Hamidi's astronomical observations and calculations, were not only countless Peekabouties, the two brats, Rajibai and his family, and an exhausted Sentimenta, but also two noteworthy plants, diplomats from Wadi Aloft.

This wadi was hidden in a deep and terrifying backside of Jebel Hamidi, a place that no sane Soqotran—not even the Peekabouties—had managed, or even tried, to set paw within. No hard feelings, either (despite the Peekabouties otherwise priding themselves on having spooked every square inch of the island). In this rare instance, one would be hard-pressed to discover a single pent-up longing to have visited that sordid vertical encampment with its dark, damp chasms, hanging gardens of noxious vine, plummeting cataracts of tannic acid, melons of mildew that burst upon even a nearby whisper, nodules chockful of pepper spray whose release was timed to the slighted trespass. Even the rock conformed to no other surface on the known Earth: slippery beyond all ice, razor sharp, surfaces of counter-inclining orientation that have no regard for direction, stability, a compass or a headache. This rock was bitterly antisocial, and was instituted for no other purpose than defiance, so that no climber, not even an ant, was spared lacerations. To add insult to oppression, the air was layered in primitive prions that lacked, among them, even a hint of oxygen; they were caked in cauliflower phlegm, which is a known derivative of cyanide. Not one atom of Wadi Aloft supported even a rudimentary safeguard, tranquillity or ease. It was so obnoxious and dacryocystitic a maelstrom that even the stinging gnats, pinching fleas, envenoming pincer bugs, cheese-paring spores and stabbing trilobites—a confederacy of vexing *primitifs* whose only purpose in life was to cause misery—all kept their distance.

The one futile attempt in biological history to alter this depressing state of affairs was initiated by a lone *Passer motitensis insularis*, that lovely endemic sparrow, peach-colored and overly brave. Legend has it he once stoked up his front courage feathers and entered Wadi Aloft with a walnut-sized mind to altering the evolution of the island and rendering the gorge habitable for birds and worms, prunes and daffodils. He'd noted down in his diary prior to setting forth (manuscript no. 8372 in the Royal Academy of Mecca) a host of high aspirations and logical deductions, citing learned references from co-evolutionary incidents involving Darwinian finches, sparrows, prunes, worms and daffodils (as well as plums and ploima) elsewhere in the world—the Galapagos, New Guinea, even Newfoundland. Bolstered by the confidence of such sententious precedent, this little Columbus made straight for the worst of the sickening steeps, hoping to negotiate a treaty with all seed-bearing poisons in the gorge in the same way Rockefeller wiped out his competition in Cleveland years before, consolidating wildcatters into one Standard Oil and secretly dealing with the railroads. Similarly, this one sparrow had tenaciously laid the groundwork for colonization and neighborly interactions, wheeling and dealing with all the venomous chiefs and noxious thugs. The result of this expedition—the emergence of two hardy plants at the zenith of biological abstinence—was strange beyond weird: lovely, tragic, preposterous and silly.

Hence, no Peekabouties envied the plants their homeland; in fact, upon seeing "w" and "e" arrive at the august congregation of stargazers looking not a little fatigued, they felt pity for them. But there was also an undeniable aura of awe surrounding these two latecomers, clear acknowledgment that they were the ultimate survivors. One could scarcely imagine the life they led down there in that ghastly cavern-bottoming world just 20 miles over the escarpment. The "w" and "e" plants resembled nothing at all. Yemeni twins whose tails, arms, legs, noses, eyes, musculature, bottoms and brows were inexplicably linked according to a never-before-tested vascular arrangement dependent for its biological success on nothing more than a treaty. No ordinary document, but a consensus of chloroplasts and amino acids—concord among every cell, passed down from generation to generation.

The "w" and "e" plants (usually written down as a royal "we" because they so often spoke in tandem; the lower-case was a function of etiquette, so that neither took offense at the other, or let a capitalization go to their heads, which was important, as will shortly be clarified) were the arbiters of all decisions of any importance in the world. This fact, however, was appreciated only by the residents of the Haghir Massif, particularly atop Jebel Hamidi.

Within living memory this congress of "w" and "e" stood firmly in favor of the physiological consolidation. Both were wont to cite their favorite precedents arguing for continued intimacy. "w" was fond of the Kellogg-Briand pact, while "e" typically singled out the Treaty of Versailles, intrigued by the mirror imagery. Both carried on endlessly with respect to Woodrow Wilson's notion of "the rule of law sustained by the organized opinion of plantkind", and took this to apply to their own unimpeachable title deeds, mastery of territory, collective self-defense and absolute veto power. Both "w" and "e" had been instrumental in informing the Soqotran Constitution on matters of water uptake, erosion, use of pesticides and fungicides, the inviolability of sacred land, and the juridical authority vested in stomas, permeable cell walls and, most of all, flowers in bloom. Diplomats to the extreme, both families—"w" and "e"—had studied their articles, clauses and exemptions, forces major, doctrines, extraordinary powers, allied protocols and, above all else, the principle of *pacta sunt servanda*. Asserting their right to independence, the "we" had obtained unprecedented advantages for plants everywhere. They had effected legislation defining "minor" so that no plant under the age of six months could be forcibly made to perform photosynthesis, or be unmercifully pollinated [read: tickled] by bees or wasps. Conversely, retirement from standing arrangements, manicured decorum and all evapotranspiration was calculated, according to the genus and species, as well as the basic characteristics (ornamental, perennial, and so forth) at an average of two years. Sun-sensitive stalks were granted exceptions.

Groundcover obtained full right of self-rule, while the tallest hardwoods were necessarily enjoined from independent authority, or the over-reaching negotiation tactics of plant unions and labour organizers, given the risks to the understory and surrounding community of any renegade behavior, or strikes.

"we" had carefully studied the workings of the joint committee charged with delineating the flower frontiers between Yemen and the Aden Protectorate. They were familiar with the sorry machinations that led to the uprooting of the Tulip King in 1948, and the emigration of nearly 50,000 bulbs to Israel a year later. It was also of utmost use to "we" to have examined in some detail the cultural ecology defining Yemen's diverse landscape: the Ashraf nomadic flowers—plants descending directly from the gardens of Muhammad; the southern Arabian Qabail, or trading plants, whose seeds were accessible and easily carried off by bees; and those mixed bloom-types, largely coming from Africa, and very exotic. By understanding these subtle facets of Yemenite botany, "we" had managed to control the frankincense trade, and could number among their constituencies nearly every oasis in the entire country. No fertilized valley would ever cross "we". Even the exquisite coffee beans in Manakha saluted "we" as their sovereign lord.

In fact, "we" was a subspecies of sage brush, changing colors from season to season—caramel in fall, ivory in winter, mauve in spring and orange throughout the summer. They could be said to be more akin to a perennial creeper one day, a succulent the next; an endosymbiant, a moss, a fungus, an algae, a slime during alternate months; they might tower like a sequoia, or cower like a pansy; devour like a venus flytrap, or cuddle your finger after midnight like the pale grayish leaf of the lamb's ear. For this reason, and despite the fact their actual locus was confined to the most treacherous piece of real estate in the country, they were universally loved by all plants and had thus secured unique geopolitical leverage over the soil, water and sunlight across Yemen. Because evolution is accelerated in harsh places, "we" could easily claim to be the most advanced plant in the world. And it was.

Inasmuch as form strictly follows function in the plant kingdom, the varieties that "we" would adopt depended entirely on the answer to the question posed previously, or the question itself. For both members of the"we" family lived their entire lives asking questions (in the case of "w") or answering questions (in the case of "e"), and usually the former, since there were so few answers to be had in their terrible fissure. Given these linguistic and conceptual ties, "we" exhibited unique growth rates and incarnations which fostered a remarkable range of concomitant behavior.

"we" was supremely adept at dishing out threats, dispatching seed casings drenched in perfume (when it was politically expedient to do so) and seducing members of other plant classes through the sheer exuberance of unabashed display. Not infrequently, insects and animals fell victim to their ploys. All for the good of the land, "we" could justly argue.

"What? Where? Whither? Which? Who? When? Why?" These were just some of the more important queries addressed by "w", who was instinctively attuned to the likes of Socrates and that same James Thurber who once openly cogitated on the matter of "what they are running from and where and why".

As for "e"—she usually deferred, out of politeness, to the first part of the "w" question, softening the abruptness or severity of the conjecture with lazily given answers like: "whatever, wherever, whichever, whomever, whenever". She lived, in truth, in ever ever land—a matter of some concern to "w", who frequently observed that "e" was simply incapable or unwilling to deal with practical matters of state, and there were certainly many gripes, grievances and distress calls in Wadi Aloft demanding their attention. "e" was a student of E. B. White, doomed to share a desk with the far more Thurberian "w". If, however, she met with difficulties, or was herself taken aback, or challenged, or made anxious, she would always ask, "Why Ever?" (in caps), which was a sure sign that something was dreadfully wrong and shouldn't have been posed in the first place.

It was all very confusing. Frankly, none of the Peekabouties could figure the "we" plant out. Was it one plant, or two? Were they related? Were they friends, lovers, mother and daughter, father and son, brother and sister or distant relatives? Did they eat together, compete, fornicate? All these questions tittilated the greater Peekaboutie society, and the tabloids were constantly supposing this and that. So reticent were "we" to give out any information about themselves (never once granting interviews) that all theories can only be described as suspect, any extrapolations dashed before they even got their start, all research positively smashed at the go-ahead. In fact, when the United Nations team of explorers came to Soqotra, it was the direct order of the Secretary General that no one even think about attempting a foray to Wadi Aloft. The US State Department had put out warnings for over a century to avoid coming within 500 miles of that dastardly gully. Most adventurers had never heard of it. Those who had wished they hadn't. At Princeton's Institute for Conflict Resolution, "we" was always held up as the goal of all human relations, but one least likely to achieve results. The Old Gauls, during the beginnings of the Dark Ages, had heard about Yemen and Soqotra, and somehow gotten wind of "we". Their simple minds misinterpreted the "we" for "oui", which provided an excuse for a man to take advantage of a woman, the subsequent birth of Charlemagne, and a revolution in European history that otherwise would not have been. Indeed, if not for "we", the French would still be saying "no" and Paris would never have been built.

All this by way of meager prelude to appreciate the stature these two little chameleons of the plant kingdom enjoyed whenever they made some excursion into neighboring climes around the Haghir Massif. Everyone bowed down before them. Marigold, catching the signs, instructed his son to do the same.

Hamidi looked out over the assemblage, noting the convergence of heavens above. His was a precise science, a timing of peculiarities that obeyed no other formulas than those of the cosmos. The moment had arrived. The astronomer announced the proceedings, with the formal kettledrumming of an ancient darabukka.

Hamidi had been tracking Mercury, an observation usually obtained from a C-141 military aircraft above 41,000 feet. That was because Mercury's resident sodium-rich plagioclases, the various rocky minerals strewn across its surface, reflected so much of the sun's radioactive energy that was not visible in Earth's vaporous troposphere. Ground-based observations were, as a rule, waterlogged. But in the case of Hamidi's observatory this was not at issue this time of year, on account of a combination of factors. Soqotra's etesian winds, locust swarms and infernal dryness tended to dispel most water vapor. The island's absence of air pollution clinched it.

"Everyone will please adjust their sunglasses," began Hamidi. "The last time anybody looked at Mercury directly, it burned their eyes out, and the whole observatory and mountain, as well."

All the Peekabouties—and there were dozens of them—put their own little Raybans into proper position. The dragon took great pains to fit her sunglasses, and even more so to ensure that "w" and "e" were properly protected. It is no small matter affixing sunglasses to flowers, for plants are very private when it comes to their eyes and it is rare that they will even divulge their whereabouts. Trees are less particular, and have no scruples about revealing their knots. But flowers have to be careful. Think of the consequences: if bees knew that flowers were watching them, they might become self-conscious and fail to pollinate the world. And if a groom saw a rose staring up at her, would he dare pluck it for his bride? That would spell the end of bouquets. As for rabbits, a single glance by a carrot or parsnip, and the shy forager would surely retreat to its hole for weeks and there most likely starve.

"But why are you tracking Mercury?" asked the Commander.

With his reflective fighter-pilot headgear, shoulder-length white locks and golden beard, the hunched astronomer, cloaked in azure magician's robe and felt knee boots, struck an annoyed countenance: "The world is coming to an end, and you ask for details?"

"But when will it come?" inquired "w" with some alarm. "Whenever," replied "e" calmly.

"The end of the world?" moaned Sentimenta.

"Ladies, gentlemen, all my dear Peekabouties, please, calm yourselves.

It won't happen for eleven, or 1,100 years. That is why this present observation must be perfectly timed," declared the sheikh. "In order for us to know which one it is, eleven or 1,100."

The dragon had a nervous twitch in her tail, a 75-foot swathe that was quite dangerous to anyone seated nearby, and this news only aggravated her condition.

"Sentimenta, dear, please watch your twitch!" insisted the sheikh, as he mechanically oriented the gigantic mirror into place. "To answer your question as quickly as I can, sir," he went on, addressing the Commander, "since we have only a few minutes left before the event, let me just explain that Mercury, the moon and Mars have been the subject of great debate during the past twelve months because of a gigantic gamma-ray explosion nine billion light years ago."

"What is that?" asked "w".

"Try to imagine the heat and light and radiation from 10,000 of our suns, over several billion years, all exploding in a millisecond. The light from that unbelievable outburst exposed our solar system in a way it has never been revealed before. I happened to be looking at Mercury at the time. A colleague at the Royal Greenwich Observatory was watching Mars simultaneously. A third compatriot at the Copenhagen planetarium had his eyes glued to the dark side of the moon."

"Well, what did you see?" the Commander plied impatiently.

"At first I thought it was a cosmic mirage, like the one discovered recently in the Abell 370 cluster—an illusion involving light that actually bends courteously downwards towards the observer. This is how mountains themselves, which are in fact hidden behind horizons, can somewhat be viewed on a solid plain, given a sufficient cantilever of cold air rising above hot air molecules. It's all about measuring red shifts in the arcs of light, and so on and so forth. My colleague in England deduced that Mars was moving out of its orbit, as astonishing as that sounds. But that is precisely what I discovered about Mercury, as well. Then my old friend in Denmark said the same thing about the moon, pending verification of a meteorite shower that collided with Greenlandia. He's leaving next week, in fact, to search for the meteorites and determine their chemistry, origins and anything else that might shed light on this most ominous escalation of anomalies. In fact the lunar data is the most crucial, given the moon's known behavior. The slightest deviation, as measured against those of Mars and Mercury, will complete the triangle of doom. What is most perplexing is that the speeds at which Mercury, Mars and the moon each appeared to be leaving their customary orbits—all three in the unfortunate direction of Earth, I might add—differed by a fraction of an arc, which translated into the discrepancy between eleven and 1,100 years."

"I'm totally confrazzled. A baked Alaska would have a better grasp than I do at this moment," the dragon cried. "Me too," "w" and "e" groaned in unison.

The brats threw in their own persnickety fidgets, for they had not come this far through Peekaboutie territory only to suffer an unintelligible lecture in the middle of the night. They had made the arduous climb on the promise of a wonderful entertainment. All the Peekabouties complained and murmured among themselves. But the Commander was feeling a hot sweat building on his temples, and Sannazaro was no less troubled by the news. Eleven hundred years—OK, I can live with that. But eleven years—no sir. Not good, he thought. Not after having survived the end-of-the-world madness just months before atop that Irish pyramid. And certainly not after all the great hopes stirred in their veins following those ordeals in the Tibetan paradise. To see it end in a flash? A collision with the moon? Absurd. Especially given the twilight of his retirement years ready to be indulged—10,000 cappuccinos, at the very least. As for Rajibai, anything so utterly catastrophic was worthy of excitement, though Ginevra strongly disapproved.

"But there's more," Hamidi continued. "With the afterglow of the mighty explosion I happened to catch a glimpse of faint blue froth at the edge of the universe: soft little clouds, 60 billion trillion miles long, that were formed just a few hundred thousand years after the birth pangs of the Creation, more than 15 billion light years ago. They lit up like fireworks for that remarkable millisecond and told me much about our destiny."

"What?" asked "w". "And *don't* tell me whatever!" he growled at "e", seated next to him. "This is too serious for your habitual complacency!"

"You don't know what I was going to say," whimpered little "e".

"The point is, 'w' is perfectly correct to be concerned. I know I am," exclaimed Hamidi.

This sent tremendous shivers through the assembled Peekabouties, whose naked little bodies seemed to shrivel up and cower down.

"You see," the sheikh continued, "those clouds long ago, towards the beginning, were here one moment, gone the next. This disappearing act went on for weeks. First, all the twinkles in the stars at night were gone, and then a moment later the twinkles resumed. There is some subterranean galaxy, of massive proportions, that is screwing with the twinkle in our universe."

"That's terrible!" the entire assembly gasped, appalled by the notion of such manipulations beyond their ken. It was downright unsporting. Everybody knew that the twinkle of stars was the smile of God; the hope for the future; the reason for being; the irony that gave every artistic instinct its calling and celebrity; the *je ne sais quoi* propelling all love affairs. No twinkle, no nothing. Lose the twinkle, all other lights might as well go out.

"Is the twinkle really that important?" Marigold inquired, just to make certain.

A stunned silence met his query. Hamidi began, "Good sir, you jest? Have you no memory of twinkling wings or twittering eyelashes? Is not the soul itself a flame of intermittent pulses, joy, mirth, sparkles, hill-orchards at dawn, heaven at all other times? Have you not yearned to visit Twinkledum, wherein such super-eminences as Mimas, Enceladus, Dulcinea and Proserpine dost gently to sleep, sweetly to oblivion, all in the eye's refrain? Know thee not the scintillation whose lamp didst wonder-fix the years, poise the vibrations, steady all authority, gather the waters, massage the astral motions? Whether speaking of Odysseus or Wordsworth, Chaucer or Herschel, Einstein or Shelley, there is no other substratum of worthy data than that the universe twinkles, faintly, brightly, a giant mirror of refraction from whose stardust all plant and animal breath derives."

"I'm afraid of the dark," the Commander stated.

"Then you understand."

"I suppose I do."

"Then know this: it gets worse," said Hamidi. "Not only Mars and the moon, but the sun itself is moving. In fact, if Mercury shows its true reflective splendor in approximately two minutes, the red shifts will prove whether or not half the universe is heading in our direction at a frightful speed of about 427 and a half miles per second."

Said Marigold, "But your dear bereaved brother was certain that Mars was the offending planet."

"He's not up on the latest data. Two months ago, yes, Mars was the more likely candidate of our destruction. But now it is a wait-and-see game. It could be Mercury; it could be the sun. Personally, I fear the moon. But what is more radically at stake is the time-frame. Now please, you will excuse me. Work to do."

A paralyzing hush rose up from all the ranks seated there as Hamidi situated himself comfortably beneath the pendulous mirrored contraption which he had built using designs from the multiple mirror telescope at Mount Hopkins in Arizona, from the Kapteyn Laboratorium in Groningen, from Cerro Tololo in Chile, and from the 305-meter radio dish at Arecibo.

"*Now!*" he whispered aloud.

The whole titanium mechanism of arms and levers creaked as the awesome mirrors crept into position along a translucent grid over the dome. Starlight in the form of snow crystals began falling into a cold, powdery depth, while Leonid showers rained down atop the mountain, all sluiced into the one treadmill of revolving mirrors and optical ping-pong. It was a curious system indeed that managed somehow to filter all the light in the known universe into the 162-square footage of two ricocheting mirrors.

Presently, the snow was a blizzard of light, all colors, millions of hues, as Mercury came into focus.

"*There!*"—and an astonished awe pervaded the crowd. "Sentimenta, watch your tail!" Hamidi cautioned. "And all you Peekabouties, sequester and decommutate your sensitive parts at once! Nipples and groins especially."

For the next minute it was like watching a continuous thermonuclear explosion, but up close. On one part of the planet the temperature was nearly 1,400 degrees Fahrenheit. At the other end, polar. In between, said Hamidi, Mercury seemed to harbor the distinct possibility, somewhere, of a small region with a perfectly acceptable temperature for the support of life forms, even that close to the sun. But it was not the search for life on Mercury which absorbed the old astronomer's gaze. Rather, the Fresnel light reflections on all the aluminum silicates, sodiums and calciums, the variable 12.6cm wavelengths, the scores of altimetry data, rms slopes and radar backscatters. Somehow, all this arcana gave him to understand whatever it was he needed to know.

Everyone present was now bathed in the calibrated radar lights, resampled in glows which seemed orange one moment, blue the next. With his hydrogen masers and antennas, he swung his slate around and began taking the data by hand with a no. 2 pencil, mumbling aloud to his Peekaboutie assistant, Bernie, who responded with a rigorous panic-stricken sobriety born of many slavish years' tutorializing with the great astronomer. Bernie was the envy of all the other Peekabouties, who could not imagine his courage in staring directly into the guts of a galactic situation and not hiding his face with all eleven fingers, as they currently did.

Target parameter? Uncertain, boss. Radius planet? Fully flattened. Magnetic moment? Eighty-eight zillion point one. Mass density? Dunno. Equatorial radius? Point 47320000. Pole right ascension? Got me. Longitude of perihelion? What's that? Parameter epoch? Yikes! Sidereal rotation period? Forget it, man! Mean solar day? Give me a minute, boss. *We don't have a minute, Bernie!* All 30 inches of poor Bernie ran on stumbly little legs from mirror to mirror, stanchion to stanchion, triangulation to computation, out of breath, trying to cope.

"The pressure!" he exclaimed between high-altitude wheezes, frantic telemetries, sneezes and raw visuals. Hamidi was a demanding taskmaster, and these high stakes real-time computations had destroyed Peekabouties bigger than Bernie. After four minutes, Mercury disappeared, the dome closed, the mirrors retracted and the snowstorm of starlights dissipated.

"What does it all mean?" the Commander pressed frantically, exhausted from so many incalculables and such apprehension.

Hamidi completed his final set of hand-scrawled computations, feeding little Bernie with the final constraint and patchwork of assumptions and hypotheses. He turned to Marigold and replied, "Normally, Mercury moves around the sun in 88 days. Three minutes ago it gave off an orbital rate of 235 days. Two minutes ago that rate had already changed to 500 days. What does that tell you?"

"I have no idea."

"It's moving away from the sun," Rajibai volunteered.

"Correct, lad. Smart boy. And it's coming this way. Four minutes ago Mercury was 92.6 million miles from our star. Now it's 91.3 million miles. The planet's axial spin is also changing. Part of it is going to melt, the other part will freeze. I don't know what will happen to poor Mercury—could end up like a pancake or a sausage, even a pineapple if it's not careful—but its new trajectories are in tune, precisely, with both the data from Mars and from the moon."

"So, are we talking eleven years or 1,100?" Ginevra puzzled, as yet unaffected by the consequences amid the anesthetizing snow cover of scientific mumbo-jumbo.

"Can't say," Bernie figured, "considering that one day on Mercury equals 176 Earth days. All the data is heavily confusing."

But Hamidi took a deep breath of clarity and began, "If you consider the ambiguous conclusions of Johann Hieronymus Schroeter, who first noticed and drew Mercury, or those later observations by Schiaparellit, Lowell and Antoniadi, one thing is very clear about the planet: its dense iron core, transparent magnetism and bare vestige of an atmosphere—one-trillionth that of Earth—makes a mockery of all predictions, throws off all conclusions, thwarts all gravity-based speculations, even alters the nature of discourse and perception so that no astronomer would dare propound anything in the guise of a certainty. Imagine trying to formulate an answer—any answer—on a planet with no atmosphere?

Why, it would be the equivalent of praying after you were dead. Humility is the first Law of Astrogeophysics. Fogged Lenses the second. And Dim Witted the third. All three apply in this case."

"But that's terrible, if what you and your colleagues suspect is true.

How shall we know whether we are all going to die?"

"And when?" exclaimed "w". "I had two birthday parties planned, one for me and one for 'e.'"

"What do we do?" asked Marigold.

"And what about me?" cried the dragon. "Should we mention this to our fellow Wadibootans?" inquired Miraj and Alibooboo.

"Do I need to look for a new job?" wondered Bernie.

"Whatever," yawned "e". Then, discerning the Mercury-rich sunrise across the coast of Africa, she recited her favorite lines from Kipling, who had once written, "His uninhabited island ... by the beaches of Soqotra and the pink Arabian Sea. But it's hot—too hot from Suez, for the likes of you and me."

Nobody knew what "e"—or Kipling for that matter—had in mind, but Hamidi had some excellent advice for the Commander: "I am too old, but you and your team seem reasonably fit. I deem it imperative you leave this very hour, go see Professor Dr Hingabajeegit Dingstboomst, tell him I sent you."

"Then what?"

"Implore him to bring you along on his expedition to Greenlandia, next week. Maybe—with your added incentive—he can discover the answer. Now hurry, there's no time to waste!"

"The answer to what?" asked the addled Commander.

"The movement of the moon. The origins of a certain meteorite. If his data confirms my data, then—verily—we are doomed, I'm sorry to say."

He then proceeded to aim his telescope at Denmark to show them the way to the Tycho Brahe Planetarium in Copenhagen, where Dingstboomst had his laboratory.

"We will do so straight away," replied Marigold.

"We'll talk about it," said Sannazaro.

"We'll think about it," added Ginevra.

"We are already gone there," the excited Rajibai exclaimed. Then he thanked the brats—"You have all been absolutely divine ..."—and said goodbye to everybody in a manner most suitable. ("May King Shah Zaman of Shahrazad, clad in those famous cramoisy chemisettes, favor you with moonbeams, eagle-wood and ambergris; may the clouds themselves bow down before your loveliness, and may Kaza was Kadar, the good fortune of all things, provide for you a shade tree in your later years, and lemonade instead of dog-teeth.") Even Marigold was enthralled by the boy's sudden powers of senselessness.

Rajibai then jumped on the back of Sentimenta. He signalled the Commander, his faithful Squire and doubting Ginevra to join him. All the Peekabouties were waving farewell.

"You've been most kind, Sheikh," Marigold conveyed. "Hold on tight," cautioned the dragon.

But within seconds she had collided head-on with a lopsided tree, and all her passengers were thrown from their seats. Their grazes and scrapes left blood on many of its branches, reinforcing the appropriateness of the tree's local name: the Dragon's Blood Tree. This wasn't the first time such an accident had happened.

"Take off your sunglasses!" shouted Hamidi from up in his observatory.

The great beast had forgotten to do so, and couldn't see a thing. With some embarrassment she cast them aside, helped her guests back on to her twelve-foot shoulders that were caparisoned in leathery scales and lethal spurs, and started down the northern side of Jebel Hamidi.

By noon they had reached a small settlement of oysters and sea otters, giant crickets and the ubiquitous and odious-smelling squash, a genetic precursor of a tropical meat flower in Borneo. A village of somnambulants who moved across the landscape of their dreams with the quality of gossamer. At the jetting fountain in the local square, sultans and wazirs conversed with boyish rogues, kings and Kasi-Askars with birds, about such matters of pressing urgency as the latest news of Nimrod, or the birth of three children to a 90-year-old woman near the golden spring. Wise minds and loose gutters unanimously appealed, on this day, to the Emir Zayn al-Asnam for a repeal of the gumdrops tariff, and this was all the talk; while elsewhere across town were implanted new and exalted decrees providing for every pleasure. Up the hill, in a palace of 40 incenses, a well-tuned poet, without the slightest shame of passion, was singing thus: "Shahwah daram ... I am craving love ..." A village, in other words, impossible ever to walk away from.

"Ordinarily I would simply fly you across to Aden," said Sentimenta. "But for a few thousand years the inhabitants outside Soqotra have not taken well to dragons, to put it politely. All the others were killed. So if you don't mind, I think I'll stay put."

The Commander expressed his great thanks and assured Sentimenta that she was, by and away, the most wonderful dragon they had ever encountered.

"You're not just pulling my tail?" she replied.

"Absolutely not." And in true unison the foursome showered her with affection, gave her heaps of little presents, fondled her prickly beard and oily wattles, kissed her gravelly talons, shed clouded tears of enduring truth, and all confessed to their deepest secrets, so that each would know, particularly Sentimenta, that they were a family now and should always be on the same path of vibrations through life.

Marigold then plucked mysteriously from his rucksack a radio telephone, a gift conveyed by Hamidi, and called the Customs official in Sana'a to see about securing a military aircraft to evacuate them. The official was taking a sauna and wasn't expected back for a day or so.

It would take some time, said the official. Was he speaking about hours, days or months? Nobody knew, and the telephonic connection did not make for clarification. Hence, with some time on their hands, Sannazaro prepared a good old zirbajah, or marinated stew with soured sheep's milk, oatmeal and pounded pears, all over an open fire in a shaded grove, and Marigold snoozed.

"I have an idea!" exclaimed Rajibai, who dragged Ginevra off in search of the local Il Haboul, that legendary meaninglessness, said by a bazaar-cook and fruitseller to inhabit the hill of widowed blueberries beyond the lake of rice milk. There, sayeth they, the old cobbler of Cairo had retired but was at least keeping himself active by making shoes for all the ants in the region.

And so on and so forth their marvelous day unrolled, devolved, escalated by degree, and evaporated gently like a rolling, quiet vegetable broth at dusk.

CHAPTER 162

Professor Dr Hingabajeegit Dingstboomst Prepares his Expedition to Greenlandia

AFTER SOQOTRA'S TRILLING wildsong, blazon cornet, crepuscular fire, Sentimenta, sea-green dragon blood divine, permanent grandeur in the woods of savagely free dustlight— all that and more—the steely clean halls of Danish Customs made Marigold and his weary companions feel as if they were checking into a sanitarium. The contrasts were instructive.

Once outside, they found themselves besieged by a well-intentioned driver by the name of Hans in his fabulous stretch limousine. His sole purpose that afternoon was the zealous imparting of Copenhagen's historic quarters: the tender pleasantries of Amalienborg Palace, the Queen's residence, the darker record of the Citadel, every tulip at Tivoli, the sconces of Rosenborg Castle and oddly hewn pews of St Ansgar Church. Rajibai clung to the bronze boobs of the Little Mermaid, before wandering off from Prinsessegade into Christiania on the pretext of buying an ice cream. In fact, it was the wafting suggestion of hashish that perked his sneaky little nose. He had his own American Express card in pocket, an impressive wad of kroners for frolic, and nothing the driver could say would dissuade the boy from entering the celebrated social experiment.

"Don't do anything foolish," Hans warned, echoing the words of Ginevra.

As for Marigold, he was not about to impede the boy's wonderlust. By now the elevenor twelve-year-old Rajibai (there was no birth certificate, his life spared tutelage, dancing lessons, precision, authority) knew quite a thing or two about the world. Mr Marigold never intended to exert the kind of parental control over the lad Ginevra argued for. But Rajibai was not her responsibility and all she could do was quietly proffer opinions. She knew by now that the Commander was the most stubborn man alive, German chocolate cake compounded by irresponsibility at every level—a fact that had begun to grow quite wearisome to her.

Hamidi had targeted laser signals via an ancient Soqotra Code to inform the famous professor at the Geologisk Museum on Øster Voldgade of Marigold's arrival. Ginevra declined to accompany the tempest-fostering toreadors, craving instead a long hot bath, a massage, facial and pedicure. Then she planned to stroll over to the Georg Jensen Museet. She would meet up with the Commander, Sannazaro and (she hoped) Rajibai for dinner at their sumptuous suites overlooking Orsteds Parken.

"You boys go figure out the trajectory of the solar system while I'm admiring the new me in the reflections of the world's finest silver," she declared. "If we're all going to die, I do not plan to waste one moment of my final days."

Meanwhile, Rajibai had entered Pusher Street, sampled all the hashish between slabs of pita bread, then stumbled off towards the Bathhouse. There, amid the promiscuous steams and fairytale conviviality, he slumped down beside a vision who only cemented his dizziness.

"Hi," he mumbled.

"Hello," eleven-year-old Natasha replied, her purple- and orange-streaked tresses floating above a quirky grin of (Rajibai thought) inconceivable guile and loneliness. A garnet pierced her tongue, aquamarines her nostrils, peridots her ears. Her incipient breasts with their sequined nipples cried out to be discussed. Her crotch greatly impressed him with its low voltage of platinum hairs seeding a pearly ampula, the shape of an anacardium nut. He stroked it—a moment of tactile inquiry inciting flying machines and drinking fountains. Only wolves on the tundra, lions in Zanzibar, are so abrupt with their entrées and introductions. Her eyes went slack, like rice pools in Bihar during the summer months.

They explored one another without preludes, commentaries or qualms for uncountable minutes, grappling in the rainforest of the senses which perfectly uninhibited freedom achieves at that tremulous age of darkness and dawn, lodged somewhere between playing doctor and guzzling lemonade, and only in little heavens of instantaneous innocence like Christiania.

They slipped back into their clothes—his jodhpurs, her farmer Johns— and dreamily meandered to the playground before Loppedbygningen. Rajibai was feeling the hashish. He burped, then helped Natasha onto a swing, Fragonard style, and thrust her towards the planets he now understood so well. They rolled in the bunched grass near the swan-bolstered Voldgraven Lake, where once the Danish military attempted to mow down the entire project, then went deeper into the maze of the free town, crossing the Dyssebroen, entering the Pagoda, kissing madly at the Floating House, making a show of their erogenous obeisances again somewhere beneath the waterlogged mangrove of weeping willows adjoining the Blue Caramel, where her family of tinkers resided.

Neither the mundane nor sublime mattered. Who you are? Which is your country? What's next? Nothing at all could weigh in between their mucilaginous heart throbs and convulsing fingertips. Destiny had been crossed. Certitudes established. They were the relaxed backpaddling of eternal sea otters, magenta butterflies home from migration. Matchsticks sighing like incendiaries: "I like your skin. Are you a Negro?"

"Your lips are so blue."

"Would you say it?"

"Which?"

"The word. Say it again. I simply adore the sound of it", and so on. Youth.

Within an hour both had proclaimed their frantic, all-encompassing, eternal love for one another.

"I will have all your children," she proclaimed forthrightly. "We shall of necessity remove the Queen to the garage and take up a life in the main palace," she went on. "Then we will make it a law that all people have to have sex eight hours per day, and give away all their money, and ride bicycles."

"Definitely," he replied.

Meanwhile, the Commander and Squire had arrived at the formidable Geology Museum, where they were seated in an outer office beside a case of specimens from Zealand, Baffin Island and Greenlandia. Chondrites, lodranites, ureilites of every density and porosity.

Eventually, the hugely famous Dingstboomst emerged from his dusty duties and heartily embraced the two newcomers. His wild hair, Victorian lorgnette, reddish complexion and muscular build sat well on the 63-year-old maverick, who was known to fellow Danes for his discovery of the cosmic origins of ... well, everything. Sheep turds, meteorites, even Denmark.

"Call me Dingst," he volunteered.

Formalities and all due explanations dispensed with, he walked them back to his laboratory, from where he and colleagues had first captured live video of the unprecedented explosion the previous year. He darkened the room and turned on the VCR.

"Here you see the event, about 100 miles into the uppermost stratosphere, crossing 93 degrees at the horizon," he proceeded. "There was what we call airglowing all over southwest Greenlandia. The air seemed to burn during meteoric entry. In the immediate aftermath, the lower atmosphere radiated halos and rainbows. Our friend Hamidi—how is he doing up there all alone, anyway?"

"Worried," Marigold replied.

"I understand," Dingst blurted. He nervously lit a cigarette, then continued. "I assume the Sheikh explained to you that he'd seen the scattering of light through his mirrors, even managing to capture some of the star particulates, granules of hydrogen-rich, 12-billion-year-old detritus. At least two dozen rocks of massive size hit the icecap somewhere in the vicinity of Greenlandia's Southern Cape. The idea is to fly into Kangerlussuaq. From there, a helicopter leased by the Museum will take me to base camp, using GPS to find the meteorites."

"How many are going on your expedition, and for how long?" the Commander inquired.

"I work more effectively alone," said Dingst. "Maybe for the summer."

"You'll need help," Marigold insisted. "No he won't," Sannazaro explained.

Marigold continued: "If it is your belief, as you were kind enough to intimate over the telephone, that it is not Mars, not even Mercury but the moon which threatens Earth, and not in 1,100 but eleven years, then I need to know. The sheikh himself is uncertain and bade me prevail upon your better senses. You must not keep Armageddon a secret. Let me finance your foray and benefit all of mankind with the resulting data, for better or worse."

They discussed these heady hazards and propositions at length. The Commander explained the turbulence around the waters of Venice, the neural agitation of the locusts and 100 other not coincidental perturbations across the planet.

"Silly man," Dingst replied. "You were focused on the rising water levels at the Adriatic, normal insect migrations across North Africa. The truth is far more arresting, but there's no point my speculating until I can determine whether the explosion comprised materials from the front side or back side of the moon. From what can be determined by the video, the meteorites were traveling approximately 70,000 miles per hour when they hit Earth's atmosphere and blew up. A few Inuit reported a flash as brilliant as the sun. In all, the airglow lasted less than ten seconds, but it was enough time for us here to obtain a satellite fix on the impact—or impacts. We're speaking of an area more than 60 miles across, here or there the size of greater Chicago, including Lincoln Park Zoo, but in a truly bad quarter of Greenlandia. Sinking fiords, uncrossable glaciers, sinister slushbowls."

Dingst explained these phenomena, peculiar to southern Greenlandia: vast tracts of collapsing earth, whole geological edifices of mushy subsidence where one footstep could result in six cubic miles of ice collapsing beneath the level of surrounding sea. Deadly quagmires of quicksnow. Meteorites that could split your head open. Polar bears that stalked you for weeks, then struck you down from the rear with a single swipe of the paw. Winds that mummified your entire surface area; cold akin to the surface of Mars; distances which conspired to enslave the senses to total disorientation. And added complications as a result of Global Warming that nobody could predict. The whole continent in turmoil.

"But what caused this coming calamity?" Marigold inquired. "We think it was the Chinese," Dingst offered.

"What? How's that?" Sannazaro asked.

"Bad pork."

"I have mortal ears. Do deign to explicate."

"One point three billion Chinese leaned to the left, all during the same 24-hour period."

Marigold looked puzzled and glanced at Sannazaro, who scratched his head as well. "You've lost us."

"One point three billion greasy dinners; heavy bacterial pork. It induces a lot of gas. The pork went bad during the full moon. You get that many Chinese venting fanatical flatulence, all leaning to the left, which Chinese people do if you've ever noticed, and the Earth's axis can't help but be affected. Even the tides are still registering the change, as you saw in Venice."

"Either he's totally mad," exclaimed Sannazaro, "or the most brilliant scientist in the annals of flatulology and astronomy—two disciplines rarely invoked together, I'd imagine."

The Commander stepped up to the challenge: "Professor, we're going with you. This is too big for one man."

"Greenlandia is cold."

"We've overwintered in the Antarctic. Greenlandia is a shopping mall by comparison."

"No. We were there but a few days and did absolutely no shopping. What's more, our brief stint nearly resulted in the complete meltdown of the South Pole," Sannazaro clarified.

They continued discussing all the particulars of Dingst's uncommon theories of Martian and lunar motion, orbital farts and asteroids. As the scientist expatiated on matters of gravitational potential, he stubbed out his cigarette and instead took up a piece of chalk at the blackboard beside a gallery of naked titanium puppets whose presence was as yet unexplained. "TE equals M times G divided by SMA squared minus AO," and so on, "whereas TE is the trace element coefficient of meteorite rubble, M the mass of those chunks which struck the atmosphere over Greenlandia, G the universal gravitational constant, SMA the semi-major axis of Mars and moon combined, and AO the axis of orbit of the Earth at the moment of contact, right out of Homer, et cetera et cetera." He powered his description of the crisis with a typhoon of other unintelligible equations and ferocious constants—irreligious periapses, turgid transfer orbits and puffy perihelions, millibars, occultation points, eerie electromagnetic waves, a concatenation of abstruse radio signals and hydrostatic disequilibria—until both the Commander and Squire were quite seasick. Neither was accustomed to such mathematical monstrosity.

Marigold begged Dingst to get to the point.

"Gentlemen, by calculating Mars's two-year orbit, and comparing it to the movement of other planets and moons in our immediate vicinity, it is clear that the entire Universe is on the move again. Where it's headed, nobody knows. Ludwig Wittgenstein once declared, *Es gibt eine und nur eine vollstandige Analyse des Satzes*. There is one and only one complete analysis of the proposition. Well, Hamidi and I have been back and forth on this issue for months. There is not just one but two distinctive analyses. In my estimation, the sheikh's calculations are off by 1,089 years. Moreover, it is not Mars that will strike us, as I told you on the phone, but the moon. Which somewhat commends Wittgenstein in his grave when he writes, *Wovon man nicht sprechen kann, daruber muss man schweigen*."

"Meaning?"

"Whereof one cannot speak, thereof one must be silent."

The Commander and Governor eyed each other with weary forlorn. If what they were hearing was true, then all of their great odysseys were of an even richer peel, promoted a more poignant sonority, given the coming flurry of dust that would reduce all heroics, loveliness and memory to an equal playing field. Who could truly be prepared for the end?

"How can you be sure?" Marigold said solemnly.

"Until I examine the debris at Nunatak Base, I am certain of nothing. But I have this hunch, and my hunches are seldom in error. I would advise you to get your estates in order."

"You mean to say," Sannazaro said, "the moon is actually going to collide with the Earth? Why, that's terrible."

"What is Nunatak Base?" the Commander asked.

Dingst explained how he had named the base camp to which he was headed after the mysterious and unexplored valley of granite spires rising out of the glaciers surrounding the impact point of the meteorites.

"Now, watch this," continued Dingst, his nimble science hands hovering in the ghostly twilight of the room as he placed some vials with dust in them between two sides of an enormous atomic laser, handed sunglasses to his visitors, turned off the lights and ignited the cathode ray beam.

The dust glowed in the dark and all the puppets started moving about the laboratory like moths to sunlight.

"My goodness!" the Commander said. "How is that possible?"

"Electrostatic pulses amplified by the lunar effect."

"But, are they coming alive?" Sannazaro wondered.

"They have been conditioned to communicate, in meter, song and common English while monitoring every atmospheric and biochemical disturbance, anomaly or change in their surroundings. The lunar dust has excited them. A scientist named Tully was their architect."

Each puppet clumsily walked on its own two feet towards the vials of dust, reaching out for them as their brains rattled off data displayed on their robotic counters. A few toppled to the floor, while still others reached out for contact with the humans in the room, doing an ingratiating little waltz that could not have been more well intended and polite. Still two others tried feebly to fondle one another.

"I have been studying them all to see which one will prove the most reliable," Dingst said. "Only one of them will join me in Greenlandia, and I think they instinctively know they are being tested. Their intelligence is certainly evolving—a hope factored into their working algorithms, but something hard to predict."

One of the puppets knelt down and tried to untie Sannazaro's shoes (suggesting an alternative color of socks as he did so), while another tall-standing creature kissed Marigold on the cheek—or licked him, to be more precise.

"Nice boy," the Commander said, patting him on the head, and rather blushing.

"That's Gerard," said Dingst proudly. "He is certainly the leading contender."

"But his lips and his hands do not feel like metal," Marigold observed.

"That's because he alone has been outfitted by the Danish military with a new skin-like material grown from human cells. They want to know whether epidermis affects intelligence. They have high hopes for Gerard, and so far he seems to be fulfilling every expectation—though the skin has had an unexpected effect, which is Gerard's need for affection."

"Certainly that says more about his heart than his skin," the Commander observed.

"So it would seem—except that he has no heart."

"But surely he has a heart?" said Sannazaro. "Just look at those mooning eyes and tender fingers."

"And who would not be moved by such an aria," added the Commander, acknowledging the melodious humming that issued from Gerard's roboticized lips. "*The Moonlight Sonata*, if I'm not mistaken."

"All very true," replied Dingst, "but the outstanding issue before us now is your dim-witted entreaty."

"We know exactly what we're doing," the Commander applied, using all his available suasion.

"No, we don't know anything," Sannazaro stated precisely.

"I have nothing else to live for, if what you intimate is true," Marigold went on. "And what's more, I can help you."

"And how is that?"

The Commander reached for his wallet and removed a credit card.

"Unlimited account," he said. And then spilled the details.

"You make a persuasive case, gentlemen," the scientist concluded, after hearing the magic words—a million-dollar donation to his own research.

"But you must promise me not to despair if things deteriorate. This is possibly the most physically challenging region on the planet. Your mind will feel the rigors, and every limb. People lose their bearings, their plot, their compass needle. Imagine sleeping with vomit in your mouth, red ants in your eyes, hungry leeches up your nose, hemorrhaging hemorrhoids, and maggots mass-producing in your stomach. It can be thoroughly disorienting. Do you think you can handle that?"

Marigold and Sannazaro looked at one another.

Marigold emitted a frantic chuckle as if to underscore his confidence. "We've seen it all," he explained.

"No we haven't!" Sannazaro adamantly added. "We've seen no such thing. Nothing like it and—" he made an exemplary sign of some cross "—I hope to God I never do."

This precipitated an argumentative exchange.

Finally, the Squire laid bare the embarrassing truth: "Professor, if there is an optical ailment responsible for absolute delusion, the Commander here is certainly afflicted. A regular champion of *ignis fatuus*. His orbicularis is downright mugwupian; where some have a wedge, a cup, a square and a rotation, he is all atmospheric haze and silly distortion. Sometimes I think it is deliberate, his way of erecting a buffer. One can hardly blame him, with lunar collisions, close shaves, slaughterhouses and creeping polywaters over every ridge. History would show that those who appear ridiculous are spared unkindness. Fools are always in demand, that is true. But think of the foreigner who makes out like a bandit the moment he so much as attempts a phrase in a new language. It somehow ingratiates him to a nation, especially the women. No reason why it should. But I am convinced—and I say this candidly—that my friend here actually enjoys making an idiot of himself to gain some strangely familiar sympathy. It is a psychological syndrome with no known cure or cigar calming. I am no man of science, but can assure you he is legally blind, though he denies it. Whereas I am a bona fide 20-80 in both eyes—no pretense, no chimera, no belief system to impede clear-headedness. With that in mind—"

But the Commander cut him off: "We're going to Greenlandia!"

"No, we're not."

"We are."

"Be my guest."

"Gentlemen, gentlemen, please!"

The old couple, their hackneyed spleens enlarged, pissed vinegar and shrank back to size.

Finally, Mr Marigold resolved all squabbles by simply writing out the check he had promised. Sannazaro was at pains to prevent the inevitable. Now he must miss out on the adventure of a lifetime, or tag along and hope the world didn't end. Feebly he inquired, "You say nobody has ever been to this part of Greenlandia?"

"That is correct," replied Dingst.

"So it could be worse than anybody has ever imagined?"

"Yes."

"Iacobo, just stop it, I insist," Marigold implored. "I have braved the very worst, and so have you."

Dingst walked them into the Museum warehouse, where the equipment had been assembled on wooden pallets. A forklift would lift the several tons of gear into the military helicopter.

"Now all we will need is a jet," said the scientist, looking meaningfully at the Commander.

"Money is not an issue," the Commander opined wearily. "Oh, and one last thing. My son Rajibai will be joining us."

The scientist liked the idea of all that money, grew accustomed to new-found riches within seconds, and thus could offer no good argument for rejecting the boy.

But what none of them expected—an event beyond the pale or commentary of any fortune—was the fact of a completely new element in the mix of forces dictating the foursome's destiny.

Ginevra had just received the most tragic missive; news at once terrible and fascinating.

CHAPTER 163
The Sun Spots in Van Gogh's Eyes

"MRS MARTIN?" the concierge inquired.

"Yes?..."

She'd been heading toward the elevators, looking forward to a blue-bubble bath, floating things bobbing about her long-starved imaginings after the riot of Yemen: ruinous heat, skin-torturing sunlight, alien forces; the husk of militant mountain, the locust pandemonium, the dragon of oily register, garlic fangs, purple emblazoning eyes. All of these rude and dusty exploits of her recent days—the communion of freaks who went peekaboo or groveled in ravines off the map—had left her wanting only the lulling of a quiet aria. No contests or danger. A simple life, centered in luxury.

The brightly upholstered guard in auburn suit and lavender tie turned over a large Danish-clean envelope that had been forwarded via rather elaborate means: Alvaro. Hidalgo. The tracking of Marigold's cell phone. Within was a less august-looking wrapping whose origins were English, legal. A royal seal of cobalt wax.

She scanned the letter from a law firm in Belgravia, and as she did so slumped low down with her back pressed against the corner of the elevator as it made its way to the twelfth floor. Jacques, her ex-husband, the professor of weird botany at King's College, had perished of lung cancer. He was in his early 60s. (She knew the actual age but could not say it to herself, exorcising precision.) Affixed to the letter from Jacques' solicitor was an executed, notarized copy of his quick will, signed six days before, according to the legalese.

Now, Ginevra stood benumbed before her door on the plush corridor. A chambermaid in black and white aprons, with her tray of late-afternoon orchids and chocolate biscotti, making her rounds to let down beds, assisted her into the room.

Ginevra and Jacques had been married 22, mostly good, years. Their divorce had been the occasion of no acrimony or even agitation, but a mutual pact, the product of frustrations that were too quirky and private to warrant discussion. And of sadness, too. Their son, Claude, had died at age 20 in the war in Mozambique where he'd gone with the International Red Cross. Claude had kept his parents together, two roamers bound by duty. Though their friendship was real and everlasting, neither of them had the desire to divulge certain windows of their respective souls—tacit last stands in life which even the best of partners will never know. They simply could not bring themselves to say whatever it was that nagged at the relationship, preferring the dignified closure to any chaffing heart-to-heart.

After Claude's death, Ginevra had wisely chosen to leave Europe, for New Mexico's open expanse did her soul good.

Sitting in her hotel room, reading Jacques' will, Ginevra discovered that, aside from leaving his library of flowery volumes to Oxford and 40,000 dollars to his younger brother Marc, a carpenter in Aix-en-Provence, the rest—all his personal belongings and transferable pensions—came to her. No point even starting the count. She had her own security, and whatever there was of Jacques' could only hurt her to contemplate out loud.

But there was more. Jacques also wrote by his own undeniable left hand a peculiar request which, he declared, only Ginevra could fulfill, and he conveyed with untrembling pen his every assurance and faith that she would not let him down.

This, she thought, is where the healthiest twists in life jerk around, so that a twist is no tortuosity but a bad joke. As she read more slowly, she recognized all the typical subtexts of outrageous, impossible Jacques. The bastard: he had no sense of practicality! A pre-eminent scholar of the rainforest, foremost in the study of narrow-waisted bees and wasps, *Hymenopterans*, the most critical order on the planet (he always insisted)—he had devoted 20 handwritten volumes to their jouvence blues, slender golds and iridescent oranges; enamored of their picnics, burrows, antennae, larvae, honey, beeswax combs and regional ballets— but he had, in preparing for death, evidently turned his back on the humid tropics in favor of an ice cube. He expressly wished to be buried naked, atop a mountain, over a glacier, in an arctic climate. Maybe out on some iceberg 200 miles east of Newfoundland's east coast, or, if it were possible, further afield. He knew this would cause some logistical difficulty but left what he considered to be enough money for Ginevra to work it out. He apologized for the hassle of gratifying his wish. Some weirdly narcissistic hope to remain unsullied in death, she supposed.

"Thank you, Jacques," she said dumbfoundedly.

She became aware of Marigold and Sannazaro noisily arriving in their adjoining suites. Subsequently, the excessive histrionics of a talk-show on the television. Shortly, there was a knock at her door. The Commander was concerned: had Ginevra seen Rajibai? She hadn't, but momentarily upstaged the Commander's concern for the boy with her own astonishing news.

Marigold took the dispatch badly, for he was an emotional gusher if given half the chance. Her plight touched each of his nerves. "I am so sorry, dear," he said, gathering no composure, only a depth of commiseration which she greatly appreciated. "What can I do?"

"There's nothing to be done. This is how it works. You know that." And she filled the Commander in on the startling details of Jacques' final wish.

"But wait!" Marigold suddenly avowed. "There is something we can do. Hello! It is timing like no other. It must be ordained, a wedlock of afterglows."

She looked at him with her usual scepticism.

"We must take Jacques to Nunatak Base!" he announced.

There was no point in Ginevra questioning the Commander's wild enthusiasm, nor the uncanny coincidence of it all, now that the Commander was financing the foray to the lost continent. It was clear, somehow, that this bizarre volition, cast in the shadow of a dead man, was entirely possible.

To her mind, Greenlandia sounded somehow appropriate for Jacques. No other piece of named Earth offered so implacable and cold a final resting place.

Without remonstration or to-do, Jacques would be placed in a large equipment crate, on ice, along with tons of other gear. Dingst's helicopter would be replaced by a larger aircraft from the Danish military to accommodate the greatly increased size of the expedition.

"It'll be fine," the Commander ruminated out loud, though he was absolutely unclear as to what it all boded.

A sudden curious panic enshrouded him just then. "Oh my God!" he burst, the query having been suppressed long enough to form a little volcano of worry. "Where's Rajibai?"

Nobody knew, but Sannazaro was the one to calm the Commander, reminding him that if the little squirt could survive the waterfall, he could manage Copenhagen after dark. Still, Marigold felt little comfort in that.

"The city is different," he insisted.

Rajibai returned dreamily sometime after midnight, while Ginevra sat up going through the letter from the barrister which described Jacques' final weeks and months. He'd been to a lecithin clinic in Mexico, but the fact could not be altered: he had few red blood cells. A picture showed Jacques sitting with sunglasses in his little Oxford greenhouse beside the south-facing portion of his cottage, his face gaunt, stoic and unflexing. He had outlived the prognosis by 27 days. Massive radiation therapy slowed down the metastasis, while he pored over learned papers by Roessel and Enderlein, drank bucketsful of Mucokehl, Wobe-Mugos, Notakehl and Quentakehl. His body was pumped with echinacea. But in the rapid end, despite these anti-tumor enzyme mixtures, he lost his immune system, went swimming one afternoon in the old green cement-encased puddle at University Club, got out, toweled down, swayed giddily, thinking the whole cancer business a dirty trick that would go away that very afternoon, only to burst out in an indignity of painful weeping blisters. By the time paramedics got to him, he was not breathing. His last words, according to Ronny Burns, the legal representative who happened to be there: "Oh shit."

"He did not suffer, I suspect," Burns went on in his letter.

Ginevra knew he was lying. Whatever they tell you, the dying suffer.

Silence amid a density of cloying memento moris, lying awake, for days.

While the Commander and Uncle made hasty preparations with Dingst, Rajibai continued his wondrous flirtation with Natasha. There was no tomorrow for the two children in love. They inhabited their own eternal island. Nothing mattered.

"This is how it should be," the boy mooned.

She idled before a storefront, admiring a display of black orchids. She'd never seen orchids in black. Rajibai promised that he would spend the rest of his life with her. He had no idea what he was saying. She didn't care, was hardly listening. It was the moment that mattered.

Later that week, notwithstanding Ginevra's own fears and weariness, the heavy concept behind the Commander's 'plan', she found herself drifting over a vast expanse of ice.

There they were, in a specially outfitted jet. The Commander, wondering to himself whether he had done the right thing by persuading Ginevra to bring her dead husband along, and Sannazaro, bemused by his own apparent masochism. He'd long stopped trying to figure it out. The rattling plant. The crazy man beside him. The little sprite. And poor Ginevra herself. Sannazaro could only empathize, for he saw written across her face a sad, inward compliance with forces beyond her ken; a caving-in of personality to the irresistible flow of Marigold's overbearing, impossible self. People either took to him or fled. And those who took were soon regretting it. No man could speak with him for long without being sucked in, or spat out, for the Commander could not have a normal effect on people. His extremes exceeded all decorum and normalcy, and because he had this childlike heroism, no rules, no guidelines, no contrary forces of nature: in truth, he was simply very, very dangerous. The proof lay way down under their incoming aircraft, on yet another far-flung maze of terrible terrain.

Ginevra too was looking down at the first fringes, far, far below, of a continental shelf—ghastly, really (was Greenlandia properly a continent? she wondered)—striations of ice, crocheted crevasse, rearing monolith and crazy sullen color across unimaginable desolation.

Sannazaro was wearing earplugs so he wouldn't have to listen to the twining groan of the Royal Danish Air Force Gulfstream G3 aircraft. He gazed down upon a foggy bottom, a sort of channel. The pilot informed them all that that was known as the Scoresby Sund, ice two miles thick, a land mass the size of two Europes or one West Africa (and the Caucasus thrown in for good measure) or 33 American states (including the big ones) or 1.7 Australias. From 40,000 feet, Dingst, the pilots and the foursome could see nearly forever. Illimitable ice. Most political contracts, and probably the Greenlandia Treaty (or whatever they called it), as well, forbade the introduction of non-native species to that wasteland, excluding people, obviously. Burial did not come up in the treaty, Dingst advised, citing the obvious fact that 53,000 people called Greenlandia—or its ice-free fringes—home. And anyway, Jacques had conceived of his final resting place with some calculation, benefited by his copious command of the biological details. He figured his body would never decay. When all the wars had been fought and the rest of the world transfigured for better or (probably) worse, there he'd be, lovely and human, however petrified his manliness.

They touched down at Kangerlussuaq. An International Airport, of sorts. Thirty-six miles to the north of the Polar Circle, which Rajibai had tried to see from the air, but could not make out. This was a mere refueling stop, where Rajibai played amid logs and larger-than-life plastic Inuit animals between the first summery wildflowers and military tarmac. Ginevra purchased mournful cheese sandwiches and watched that the boy did not venture onto any landing strip. Marigold and Sannazaro, however, were engaged in serious listening out in the hangar, where Dingst had been met by the assemblage of interested experts: members of the National Center for Remote Sensing, the Greenlandia Electromagnetic Coordinator, and somebody from the Niels Bohr Institute for Astrometrics and Geophysics.

"We've recovered a piece of it, Professor," the manager of the hangar reported, and handed him a thick plastic bag. Dingst slumped a little as he took its weight—12 solid pounds of meteorite. "A tourist from Kuala Lumpur kayaking at Kangikitsoq found it."

"Contaminated?"

"Yes, but we still have reason to believe it was traveling at 40 ksecs."

Marigold looked to Dingst, who evidenced some emotion. "What does that mean?"

"Forty kilometers a second, which is considerably faster than any known speed of a meteorite within our solar system."

"So?"

"So it could be older than 4.5 billion years."

"Does that argue for the eleven- or 1,100-year theory?" asked the Commander.

"We will see," replied Dingst.

The hovering experts estimated the impact site according to data fed by some previously jettisoned aperture radar about which Dingst and colleagues spoke in terms of fancy resolution, multi-frequencies, L-band and C-band, cross-track three-dimensional interferometric images yielded up despite deep snow and water. Sputters of nonsense.

"It broke up," explained the resident tracker, whose whole life had oriented towards these moments, "over portions of Frederikshåb Isblink. Other parts of the fireball careened into Lindenow and Tasermiut fiords. Residents at Nanortalik reported seeing an explosion on the face of Uiluit Qaaqa itself. Its size can be estimated by the northwest labyrinth of ceilings, four million tons of frozen brant and slate, cut down in an instant—a harpoon the length of Chicago. But the major chunks evidently hit further to the northeast. We've identified a glacier to land on. Nobody has ever been within 400 miles of there—not counting, probably, Bjarni Herjolfsson."

"Who's Barni?" asked Marigold.

"Bjarni," Dingst corrected. "The European who first caught a glimpse of America, allegedly after 985, excepting, of course, the possibility that St Brendan long preceded him. He had settled in Greenlandia, led astray like so many other feckless dreamers by the allure of the color green. He, and others like him, had come thinking they would find luscious pastures, not knowing that 83 percent of the watery land mass sits under permanent ice. Today, all that remains of his presence are the stones of an Augustinian monastery, erected 400 years after him, and some local mummies. Fascinating, really." He briefly expatiated upon the Saqqaq and Dorset peoples, moody ancestors of today's Inussuk, as well as the phenomenon of glaciers moving the distance of a football field every day, compressed by gravity into billions of undiscovered black diamonds lounging in the wrinkled thickets of sea beneath fast-traveling icebergs, each the size of Christiania, 95 Safeways, or Vancouver's China Town.

Turf too strange and forbidding.

The tracker went on to tell of six minutes of enormous glow across the southern half of Greenlandia, followed by hurricane-force gusts, as the energy equivalent of 100 trillion pounds, truncated down to the size of the Ritz Montreal, and with a density greater than Mozart's brain, a light more penetrating than Van Gogh's eyes, roared into Earth's atmosphere and exploded fitfully across 900 miles.

"Normally," began Dingst, "the thousands of meteoroids that strike Earth each day are invisible to the naked eye, weighing less than a hundredth of an ounce. On any cloud-free night you can make out about three every hour. Once in a while, something like a 60-ton monster comes down, as one did in Hoba, Namibia. Or bigger still, Tunguska in Siberia, taking out 30 miles of forest, the explosion heard at drinkeries in Antwerp—not that they would have guessed what in the hell was going on. The one near Winslow, with its 1,200-foot-deep crater, was traveling no faster than a Mercedes on the Autobahn when it collided with Arizona. Chicxulub was bigger, but the Yucatan today is none the less for it. This one, however, is different, in my estimation. Not huge, by any means. But a harbinger of billions of light years in motion just behind it."

His eyes, like those of Marigold, who gazed breathlessly upon him, were radiant with the thought of it. Most men might have spoken to themselves in desperation, shoring up the futile finalities of their lives—which is what Sannazaro now endeavored to do. He was tired of hearing himself think, or ask, Why? Still, he had his sense of duty, greatly amplified by his new mission in life to protect, harbor, conceal and temper the mad Commander by his side, and to nurture that lovely innocent, his son—to be a father in his own right, perhaps. Who could not fail to have observed the long suppressed feelings in Rajibai, bursting uncensored upon the Feminine, whose singular icon—his sister chopped down— bade him explore by way of revolt, embrace, memory, commemoration: the last sensualities. And what pubescent curiosity could ever stay idle after the girls atop that Himalayan cliff? Marigold and the boy were not dissimilar, in the sense that the Commander was enjoying something of a second wind, in his fifties. Seeing life through the eyes of a boy. With eyes that sparkled when they looked upon Ginevra, who sparkled back. For at this time in her life Ginevra had a great need for intimacy, and Marigold's companionship, despite the strangeness of it, was definitely welcome.

Sannazaro, too, continued to remain transfixed by Marigold's magnetism, though perhaps it was nothing more than an excuse to be oneself. That's how the Italian now thought of it, with a secret smile, all consuming and filled with confidence.

The onward flight took them above a quadrant of exotic placenames, the sheer number of which suggested significant habitation. Nothing could have been more unlikely. Ghostly nomenclature, cartographical comforts suggesting a community only of wind and ice. Eight-hundred-mile stretches and not a single human. Yet, there below them was a population arrayed like so many fabulist toponyms—peaks, points, abutments, glaciers, moraines, dates of discovery, national interests, dense declivities, magnetic contours, gradients, ice readings, biological zones, and history, all swathed in the intense colors of satellite reconnaissance data and real-life corroboration.

In addition to the Commander, Sannazaro, Ginevra and Rajibai, two scientists—Ingrid, a paleobiologist, and Tully, a physicist, materials engineer, and creator of Gerard—as well as Johannes, a colossus from western Denmark, able to lift and fix anything, had come along. The latter three were, in addition, consummate mountaineers. Dingst had wanted a tight, alpine-style reconnaissance. Now he wondered how the addition of four strangers and a corpse could possibly help it succeed. As he looked down at the shimmering Greenlandian plateau, he began to doubt the whole enterprise.

"Get your gloves and hoods on," shouted the rear pilot as they circled high above the enormous migmatised metasediments, a cirque of rock pyramids fanning out across a glacier that disappeared over the horizon.

"Belts tied tightly, please. Heads down. You'll feel the parachute dragging in the rear. A roar. Not to worry."

"That's our base camp," Dingst calmly proclaimed as the aircraft broke below the layer of shivering cirrus. Crystal formations glazing the arc of low windows further distorted the optics of 2,000-mile-long rivers of ice, sunlight haloed in circumpolar arcs the color of elephant seal urine. "Nunataks," he called them, pointing to the granitic upthrusts.

Mr Marigold gripped the sides of his seat as the jet blew open its chute, skidded 15,000 feet across crevasses and glistening monadnocks, and spun 180 degrees before finally coming to a halt.

CHAPTER 164
The Music in Beethoven's Ears

TO ALL SIDES were ferocious avalanche chutes, summits rearing into a hazy greyling afternoon. The high whine of the turbines remained. It took an hour to offload the gear through the rear hatches by means of an electrified plank and sophisticated winches. With binoculars Dingst could easily make out black fissures in the ice, enormous chunks of charred basalt, steaming granite, burnt trails across the floe flush with incineration. Abase one of the nunataks, a large rock fall had cut clean through the bergschrund, peppering the glacier for miles, turning névé to ember, black ice to cinder, green ice to gravel.

Dingst and his three technical colleagues determined the precise location for their camp. No place was safe. The hit of the meteorite had dislodged every ledge, shelf, overhang. The entire amphitheater of peaks spoke to teetering mayhem. They spent nearly an hour discussing pros and cons—where the largest avalanches were likely to run out, where the snow was soft, the crevasses lurking, rock fall the most likely. Finally, they reached consensus and each man, woman and child was allotted appropriate tasks.

"It's like that," Dingst told Marigold. "All the money in the world can't do it differently. We have to move these things by hand, roped together, one step at a time. But hurry!"

"I know well of what you speak," the veteran Commander replied, referring to his previous Happy Home and proceeding forthwith to violate the First Maxim. He stepped forward ten paces, his arms outstretched to greet the spectacular view, mumbling on about those great iceberg painters Frederick Church and William Bradford, turned to relay his exuberance and add an afterthought regarding the technique of Claude, when the air was kicked out of his chest and he vanished beneath the glacier in one microsecond of a swoosh.

There was much screaming and torment, as nobody had yet roped up. Fortunately, the Commander had hit an ice block four feet down which prevented him from plummeting another mile—not that he should have bothered much over it. After all, he later recited, his epic journey beneath Vesuvius had more or less prepared him for anything. But at present, only his upper torso remained visible, as he gesticulated wildly, a midget in the snow. Johannes, or Hans, as Dingst called him, was able to extricate him quickly with the adze side of the ax and Marigold suffered only bruises to his dignity.

"Here are the rules," Dingst began, once the flurry of near-death had been concluded. "Never step foot onto the ice alone. Never unrope. You keep water with you at all times in a canteen clipped to a carabiner affixed to your belt. Dehydration, sunburn, exhaustion, dizziness, disorientation, panic, agoraphobia, these are very real risks. And you always wear this—" he held up a whistle "—around your neck. If a polar bear should show up, only the whistle will save you. The polar bear stalks silently. He is a precision hunter. The bone, fat and sinew of his victims are crunched between granite-hard incisors. He slurps the rest. Or if you should be so unlucky as to find yourself out in a blizzard, again the whistle is your lifeline. Crevasses—"

But here Mr Marigold stopped him, claiming some expertise with regard to gaps in the Earth in polar climes. (A total figment of his imagination, referring to no skills whatsoever, insisted Sannazaro.) Nonetheless, the Commander's saga greatly impressed Dingst, who had in fact heard about the breakup of the Ice Shelf, and something about two hopelessly inept madmen rescued by the Indian vessel: "That was you?"

Ginevra stared out at the unreal miasmas around her. There were eerie afternoon shadows suggesting early sunset, and the onset of impenetrable cold, where the manacled spires lay swathed in incoming mists, frozen auroras and a sudden gale that foretold of darkness.

"Loewe's Phenomenon," Johannes mumbled. "Hold to the center," decreed Tully.

The katabatic had come in five seconds flat, from calm air to 80 miles an hour, thick with ice crystals whose density weighed down the surface area of the still incomplete tent city of connecting titanium domes. The causeways were yet to be erected; only the mainstays were in place. Their little wagon train was hammered by the storm.

Marigold, Rajibai and the others were squatting against the inside of a triangular dome, their legs pressing hard against the metal supports. For the Commander and Sannazaro, it was all unsettling déjà vu.

"Previously, the world was the world. Now, it is only Greenlandia," declared the Commander. "Are you all right, Son?"

"Will we blow away?"

"No worry, boy," said Johannes, who seemed capable of holding it all down by himself. "This is normal out here."

Outside, colder still, amid the flotsam of snow hurling in the gale, in his wickerwork crate sealed with 100 pounds of pulverized Cocoa Crispies among other cases of computer printout paper, circuit boards, spare parts, insulator materials, cans of tomato rice soup, lay Jacques. Dingst did not think it wise to mention the corpse to his colleagues, yet.

They might not cotton to the idea of an alien introduction. Ginevra, always acutely aware of her former husband's peculiar presence among them, had already become anxious about their eventual response to the idea. After all, from the looks of the configuration, Johannes was going to be the one to haul the body out somewhere.

As quickly, like a spook, the storm vanished, leaving the team's three scientists to recondite chit-chat over green tea, compliments of Johannes, who drummed up the makings, a teapot, a stove, fuel. Sannazaro and the Commander listened in to the superheated conversations, immune to the particulars—the notion of the Pasture point, 2.3 billion years ago; the end of terrestrial anaerobes; isotope curves, Late Proterozoic sulfates, banded iron formations and metaquarzite micro-fossils, all the stuff of Ingrid's coy discipline. Among the non-scientists, more mundane matters were pressing. Ginevra's nipples, said she, were frostbitten. Rajibai giggled over that. "It's not funny, Son," scolded the Commander, whose own physical discomfort was evident in nostrils that were undergoing color changes, the current phase resembling a Chardin multiplied by tobacco smoke.

In the morning, the Commander awoke to find an industry all around him. He stared thoughtfully through the window of the huge 900-square-foot tent, feeling dreadful. The first monumental signs of arthritis, like some prophecy or particularly chilling sermon coming in touch with his basal metabolism. The temperature was -15 degrees Celsius. Everyone was several layers removed from one another, between the mittens and wind shells, parkas, sweaters, shirts, long underwear, four pair of socks, two pair of underpants, down pants and Asolo AFS 100-style plastic boots.

"We picked a warm day to arrive," admitted Dingst.

"We're all going to die," Sannazaro replied stoically.

"That's just his way of getting used to a place," explained Marigold, who felt something other than cold bringing tears to his face. He was rejoicing inside, even as his cheeks smarted against the hurry of atmospheres, and every joint cried out. Their new bivouac was free and buoyantly brisk and God-perfect to the barometric point of euphoria.

"How the world was intended," he explained to Rajibai, who was helping Johannes address cracks in the dome surface with silica epoxy.

Chatter, strange brews, intimacies and masses of nerves, amid a thin red soup thickened with scallions and taken by all in tobymugs—photo-realistic heads of the various Kings and Queens of Denmark. Rajibai was at once preoccupied with a plethora of intricate mechanisms and private spaces. Marigold, too, was intrigued by one's ability to carve a niche from a mere sleeve in the fabric of the inner dome and secure for oneself a few moments alone amid a continental ice shelf. It was uncanny, he thought, how humans could make themselves at home in any environment. Such illusions, at least, meant everything in the frenzied greater scheme of things. Ginevra, too, was every bit the homemaker, at once arrested by the possibilities of fashioning certain amenities not obvious to their circumstances. These promptings were evolutionary in nature, Marigold figured, contemplating with anthropological distance and ease the strange setting-in syndrome of humans confined in the rude awakening of such a harsh outpost.

The lodgings had been completed. In the center, the kitchen and medical area. A kit consisting of respirator, splints, blood plasma, sutures, needles, every kind of pill, tinctures of opium and a host of esoteric medicines that the Russians had developed up on the Mir Space Station. In addition, a dietary program had been worked out that neatly combated depression, Arctic hysteria, bone demineralization, scurvy, boredom and the subtle forms of malnutrition—a diet replete with antioxidants, all the mainstream vitamins, amino acid cysteine, selenium and zinc, polyunsaturates, freeze-dried fibers, fruits, even dried avocado.

In their personal drawers were electronic helmets, boots and gloves: chips were fitted therein to trigger the robotic computer system that would flush heat throughout their life-saving apparel if core temperatures started falling. Optic sensors would line their little domestic microcosm, feeding data continuously into the petite think-tank mounted within the main dome of habitation. It was, after all, the twenty-first century.

"Gerard is the latest in biological-assay technology, suitable to desert and polar environments, invented for exploring Titan," Tully explained. The mechanical puppet had kind eyes, a shiny exoskeleton, and somehow maintained a stable interior environment, calculating caloric intake, recycling efficiency, rations, human vital signs, the condition of the soil in the greenhouse, as well as everything happening outside— from the state of pet lichens they intended to cultivate, to the advance of air masses across the continent.

All eventually ventured outside, standing huddled beneath the riddled escarpment, Ingrid with her zero compass, Tully his azimuth. The nunataks cast their everlasting shadows over the heavily crevassed plateau: a new alphabet for the foursome. Every breath, a venture. To freely persist, warm-blooded, amid such distances and gaping substance, pummeled in the face of extreme latitude, was to size up the whole Earth in a visceral connection that read, at once, of exile and allure beneath the ice-ringed troposphere.

Gerard joined the team in what was to be their first exploration up the glacier towards the base of the nearest nunatak. The robot, or puppet as Dingst thought of him, came equipped with a low-pressure Krypton-Argon lamp, powered by a KIVA microwave generator at 20 watts, with light attachments and parabolic mylar dishes. His normal tune was that of a summer popsicle truck in Queens. His filtered sleeves contained an array of sparkling lights that irradiated ice crystals or the renegade flora colonizing a square millimeter of some polar bear's feces, blown hither abreast innumerable squalls. Gerard was a computation robot, with his own little storehouse of test tubes, a chlorophyll counter, vacuum manifolds, rotary evaporators, silver wire, gas chromotography measures, Tesla coils, reaction vessels, a centrifuge and a host of other portable testing facilities. He emitted his own brand of flatulence, greasy and always accompanied by a twang. He could scoop, sniff, film and assess the many worlds around him on the atomic, molecular and cellular levels; could resolve an image down to minus 15 angstroms and determine innumerable genetic sequences in the same three seconds that he recognized a constellation by the ever-so-faint star pattern cast on the ice. His acoustic scanning capabilities enabled him to gauge a rock's internal structure, grain, fluidity, rate of chemoautotrophy and pore density, yielding an image from pyrite or a lodestone similar to that of an ultrasound of a pregnant cow. The puppet, said Tully, would receive transmissions from a polar orbiting satellite that gave him the means to print out lovely pictures of a hurricane over the Gold Coast of Africa, or barometric pressures within 15 yards of their base camp. He'd shown them that night.

Best of all, this robot exceeded at musical improvisation. Every piece of information that Gerard stored had a digital scale value, so that all of his information, in the end, became song. In short, Gerard was a singing puppet, trained in the fine art of allegory and cadenzas.

Sannazaro remonstrated vigorously. He'd brought four back issues of *New Zealand House & Garden*, and the English *Country Life*, and had no other intention than reading them, comfortably ensconced, a calm Merlot by his side. As for Ginevra, she too had no particular compulsion to join the icemen, knowing that Jacques' final wishes were in as good hands as possible. She chose instead to remain behind in the kitchen, where her sanity might find succor, becalmed and sautéeing amid a theater of irrational gymnastics, preparing dinner for the returning explorers, her senses filled with the warm scent of freshly baked chocolate chip cookies miraculously concocted from spare expedition dollops and dough—for Rajibai and his father, who vied for the most persistent sweet tooth, would doubtless be greatly fatigued upon their return. She had never seen anything like Nunatak Base. Who had? She could not deny the excitement of it all, an infusion into her world that would sustain her in later times, though she did not know that now.

There was, she thought, uncommon reason in the substance of these unknowns. Jacques had had more than vanity in mind, of that she was sure. But how had he known about the beauty? Why would he have forsaken the coziness of an English country garden, or heat of a Brazilian tropic, for this? Had the cancer so double-crossed him as to obliterate all his views regarding botany? Chlorophyll? The cloying life force which is the Earth's stock-in-trade? Had he, during his final months, seen some other light of alien purity? If so, what was he saying to her about long-term plans? There was a message, and not a very easy one.

As the expedition trailed off into gusting snows, an ever-so-faint melody could be detected back at base: some far-off pipes and chimes, sewn by a robot, of a vacant world transformed to blue and canticled airs.

CHAPTER 165
The Puppet and a Corpse

THE GIGANTIC FRAGMENT of meteorite had struck the cloud-swathed uppermost reaches of a nunatak, where it presently lay sunk in a molten cavity emanating crucial data. Reaching it was the goal of the reconnaissance. They would attain the summit and leave Gerard there. That way, the puppet could actually touch the wayfarer, get emotional with it, listen to its heartbeat, shoot the bull and record whatever biological news the chunk of rock had to report each day and night, relaying the interstellar gossip back to the computers at base camp miles below on the glacier, and all via Danish military satellite. These complex scientific high-wire gymnastics should duly accomplish the crucial task of ascertaining the horizon eleven years out: safety, or catastrophe.

With this extraordinary rendezvous in mind, Gerard, outfitted in snowshoes, came deliriously to life, flopping merrily along the magnetic glacier of translucent air, roped to the others as they made their first foray there. Rajibai protruded in the middle, directly behind the puppet, a rascal of all the antics known to childhood curiosity—and what a strange parade they made, sluggishly advancing across the meteorite-strewn white powder of planar fields. Gerard maintained his silly grin, galvanized by hard drives, as close to being happy as machines evidently can be, attuned now to the extraterrestrial chunk of matter high above, near the very summit of the nunatak. Busy with calculations, he purred and rumbled movements from Johann Hermann Schein's *Hesperion* 19 or 20 (a favorite of his repertoire).

"He's on to the meteorite," explained Dingst who was wearing his red Lederhosen and tasseled Peruvian mountain cap, the very Inca of Santa Clauses. Compared with the Commander, however, he exuded an altogether confident air of expertise. It was Marigold's lack of balance. His knock-kneed pigeon-toed squint-eyed spasm of fumbles from one deranged foot to the other was as painful to behold as it was to execute.

"Blast it!" retched the Commander, as repeatedly he fell flat on to his face. "Not fair! Stop laughing, all of you!" The snowshoes were not well suited to his particular canter. His gait was that of a spoiled French poodle.

Tully took the readings off Gerard: Fox microstructures, photo-degradations and electric discharges. Marigold rested. Rajibai gulped down lemonade.

Eventually, all reached the base of the nunatak.

Johannes examined the sky. "The weather could turn," he reckoned. "Forecast is good through tomorrow night," foretold Ingrid, unsure. "If so, then early in the morning we return, climb that crack system—"

Tully had already assessed the 900-odd-foot wall before them "—and haul Gerard to the ledge, then rappel back down. We'll leave him here tonight."

The team took its notes, marked its quadrants and departed, leaving the puppet strangely alone beneath the curvilinear dome of aquamarine heaven in the growing strands of late afternoon.

They arrived back at base that evening as exhausted as Ginevra had been expecting, each with algid hands and bitterly stinging body. An Arctic malaise that slipped tortuously down through each undergarment.

Rajibai had made out well, considering. The lad could not be daunted, but the Commander was in trouble, with scratching pangs at his throat which, they say, signal the onslaught of pertussis, grippe, rheum, catarrh and bug. That distant, adamantine pain that smarts the eyelids, cracks teeth, gives a hoarse, persistent ache in the alveoli. Cold that makes the hands feel stuck to frozen steel. Acute throbs in each toe, stretching to the groin. Blows more bitter still across the face. Frozen spheres that have settled in for good, even within the first few seconds.

"Don't feel surprised by it all," explained Ingrid, attuned to the Commander's symptoms. "To outsiders, this is no different from landing on Mars." She checked his pulse. "You'll be fine. Get some sleep. Take some hot chocolate."

This was of little comfort to the billionaire, or to Sannazaro who could not help but feel responsible for his foolish friend, and felt no better himself.

Tully's rhapsody on the freezing point, that temperature gradient which had purified the land, did little to ameliorate the uniform gripe growing among the non-scientific foursome, too accustomed by now to the comforts of fine lodgings. For all his meritorious ecologizing, the Commander had, by imperceptible degrees, become addicted to room service.

Marigold lay beside Rajibai on two foam pads atop the neoprene surface of the dome. No dreams for him, though his son's brain-of-embers was full of Ingrid's provocative boobs. In the morning, Dingst took a deep breath and called everybody together.

"I have something to tell you all," he began.

Ingrid was between mouthfuls of a slimy oatmeal. Tully was busy at his laptop, monitoring the first data back from the puppet.

"So here's the deal. Ginevra's husband—"

"Ex—but we were tied like a bowline-on-bight," Ginevra inveighed. "—He passed away a few weeks ago," Dingst eulogized. "His name—"

"Jacques," Ginevra intoned, addending her late husband's fascination with burial atop ice. And describing how Greenlandia had loomed, timing-wise, with the perfect characteristics of a deep freeze for an endearing gentleman.

Ingrid was alarmed and could not make light of the situation. "Where? In a crevasse?"

"No. There—" She pointed to the high peak at the far end of the glacier, the very nunatak beneath which Gerard awaited their return.

"I don't suppose anyone has checked on the corpse?" Ingrid asked, heating up to the concerns over biological contamination. "Should we not get an epidermal sample from his left forearm and armpit, as well as a few hairs from the eyebrow, a baseline for bacteria and follicle mites?

We mustn't spoil the meteorite."

The debate subsided quickly. The conversants knew there were ethics to be considered, but none of them had sufficient multidisciplinary perspective to cast a final judgement on the wisdom of anything. Scientists at least knew when they didn't know. Especially in the light of the one far greater priority which had brought them here: an end-of-the-world analysis of a piece of steaming rock now calculated to have landed on no lower ledge but on the very irregular zenith of the nunatak. In its mineral depths lay the resolution to all their fate. The speed of its collision with Earth; the chemistry of its origins—lunar, Martian, Mercurial or extra-galactic? And the message from the universe: removed or closing in fast?

Beside such colossal scientific judgement calls, Jacques was a smidgen of dust, a nobody like the rest of us, Ginevra thought as she lay half awake in her bed. She took private pleasure in knowing that her late husband was about to be positioned in the Earth's premier viewing gallery, from where he'd be able to watch over everything, oblivious to the perturbations of a violent universe.

In the morning, Dingst and his team exhumed Jacques from the crate and readied him for his final journey.

At 9 a.m. the entire team set off. Ginevra had never traveled this way before and required a good deal of steadying by Johannes. Ingrid took the lead, then Tully and Rajibai.

Dingst stayed to the rear, behind the three stragglers.

"There!" the Commander glistened in half rhymes of breath and incoherence. "Where the land is bare, and the ridge blows, and a portal opens to the otherworld, it is myself, my flesh, all my outgoing and incoming. I sing the song of this great Other; I bow to thee, I hail the sea of sensation. I—I—"

"Hello? Commander?" Dingst's voice rang out, carrying miles across the Epidaurus of glacier. "Might we focus our attention for one moment?"

"Huh?"

"Could you turn, please."

All did so.

"That's a mirage," Dingst explained. "The hyperboreal rimefrost effecting an inversion of the molecular Siberian. It's all in the x-y-squared Popsicle pattern. Not real."

"And I tell you I see something there. A sherbet on the move. Like a giant ostrich, and—see that—if I'm 50 and a day, over there, unmistakably etched against the stellar dawn, Sitting Bull himself. Or is it a platypus smoking a cigar? How queer. I'm certain of it. Along the far edge. Where mites are prancing on a bowling green and Queen Victoria is having her tonsils removed!"

Rajibai also witnessed something, though what it was could be deciphered only by its fringes: the ghost of Mowgli, a steam giant, a desert village, two shoes, Mother Goose and a bell-nosed northeast wind. Embarrassed jitters fluttered across the land, a steeplechase—poetry whipping science, dizziness enflaming unreason. In substance, only Levanter and glare abroad hard-packed snow and flowing ice. The party was surrounded by the cirque of impossibles. Concision of breath, fog pouring in, concept without foundation. Swirls of huge peril in the air.

In fact, they all were feeling peculiar, required a respite, plopped down in the snow, breathed each to him and herself. Johannes helped the Commander to some hot rum from a flask. Three miles further on, they approached something: a bundle of skin, remains of a life, blood tracks and a tooth, matted hair from nowhere, until—further still—a mummified bearded seal that had dragged herself all these fathoms from the sea. And strange butterflies waltzing in the air above it. Real butterflies, this time: Norwegian Fritillaries and Russian Satyr Commas. In the eviscerated black ice the seal's haggard head was large. The skin and hair had been eroded by the brazen elements, though enough of her fire-red mane was intact to interpret the creature, *Erignatus barbatus*.

They all stood staring at the petrified eye socket.

"It was a young one," said Ingrid, explaining how the seal had probably become lost amid some maze of pack ice and polynyas, had dragged herself inland for hundreds of miles before giving up, centuries, even millennia ago. A symbol, Marigold announced ominously, for their own times.

"It's unbelievable," Ingrid went on, as much to marvel at the Commander's eyesight—for he had detected it miles away—as for the sheer impossibility of butterfly biology on an inland glacier. She tried to catch one, but Marigold seized hold her arm and forbade it.

"No," he insisted.

"What's this?" she objected.

Rajibai, gliding on the airs of lambent inexhaustibility, aglow with all their effort, explained: "He doesn't approve of catching things. And since he's footing the bill ..."

She stood back when Dingst, by a look, confirmed what the boy had said. Tully fixed aluminum ladders across the narrow chasm that separated them from the actual rock wall. The summit roared 85 stories above them all, ferocious, weird, twisting upon itself, one isotope after another, a Ptolemy of design cleanly thrusting its many overhangs into their collective face. A monster of sheen and instability leaning under the weight of frozen firmament. An infinite wall, sheer, Yves Klein aquatints in blue.

Mr Marigold carefully moved on all fours along the ladder, peering down into the gaping chasm below. The ladder creaked, its instability heightened by the complaints whimpered by the itinerant above. Beneath him lay a green darkness never before viewed by human eyes. Hundreds, maybe thousands of feet deep, it yawned with a direct opening into the world of the dinosaurs.

The team, following one another, all reached the base of rock walls, and then pulled the ladders. Johannes went first, Tully belaying him with two 165-foot 11mm Perlon ropes. He inserted metallic chalks into an angling series of parallel cracks, affixing carabiners through which the ropes passed. Standard climbing technique. Ginevra could not look down. She was silently and continuously in prayer. It was her first time on high. Even for the three veterans of Tibet, this sheer riser was intimidating and no remembrance of immortal fluids in their blood was sufficient to ease the edge.

"I for one am not about to test our luck," Sannazaro smoldered aloud so that his two immediate companions could hear. But by that time they were quite high and all complaints were irrelevant.

"If you're going to bitch, you shouldn't have come," Marigold ridiculed him.

Eventually, they reached a ledge of suitable fourth dimensions for the placement of a winch. The sky remained complacent. But by Ingrid's satellite reconnaissances, they had all of five hours to summit, and rappel back down, before angry weather broke upon them. Even now an eruption of purple cumulonimbus could be seen churning up trouble to the north, a howler gaining confidence.

The party was equipped with jumars of the kind the Commander and Rajibai had used beneath Mount Vesuvius, and presently ascended the fixed ropes one at a time towards the ledge. It was there that Johannes waited for the others to join in, before he singly hauled up the dangling puppet and corpse.

Unbeknown to the entire company, the corpse was eliciting vibes from the robot, who had never traveled with a dead man before and thought it highly peculiar.

CHAPTER 166
Nunatak

"FIRST LIFE," Ingrid acknowledged with some fanfare, gently touching a mass of minute *Micrognathozoa* as a dry cold blustery zephyr pulled the moistureless salts off the back glaciers across the afternoon squint of 1,000 square miles of near-sterile ice, stinging the cheeks with uplifted bits of handsomely honed crystal.

Johannes belayed the others up to the small rock promontory. Sannazaro, already well adapted to his own vertigo, liked what he saw, and commented that it was akin to looking out over the summary of one's life. Such clarity was worth the price of the ticket, agreed the Commander. Some felt dizzy; others closed their eyes. Rajibai raised up his arms in socially responsible salute to self-destruction, and Johannes immediately attempted to prevent him.

"It's all right," Marigold assured the heavy-set climber. He knew well the temptation, waterfall or no waterfall, but also trusted his son's infallible good sense.

Dingst took a reading in the absence of a graspable reference point of mass or gravity of direction. The jaundiced granite monoliths formed a scattered dominion around the whiteout of glacial expanse. Far off, towards the center of the desert-like plateau, they could make out a minute smudge of black: Base.

Before them lay the partially embedded meteorite, which had slammed directly into the 285-foot-wide summit of verglass and metaphoric crest. To all sides, the sheer precipices fell away into sickening distance.

"Sit right there, boy," Johannes instructed Rajibai.

His family, breathing hard in the upper atmosphere, joined him against the rock face.

Gerard got his bearings and became silent. His arms, shielded with plexiglass gloves, went out to sample microbes and nutrients, preparatory to the geological inquest. Rotifers and tardiglades showed up at once in the clusters of névé. Mites and fungi were everywhere aboard the alien stone.

"*Ceratodon arcticus,*" declared Ingrid. "Waterbodies."

The robot Gerard proceeded to analyze the carbon flux and evident photosynthesis. He picked up a 44-pound chunk and placed it in the oxygen-free cabinet. At once, pre-solar system data emerged. The isotopes of nitrogen were not enriched, said Dingst, further confirming his elaborate anxieties.

"Outside the solar system," he clarified, "the argon/xenon ratios are different."

"Are we dead meat?" Rajibai bespoke.

"Yes and no," Dingst replied vaguely, his thoughts already reabsorbed in his theories. This rock sample, he went on, was no achondrite, so this ruled out the moon as a source.

Even the Commander and his crew were surprised by this, though it was among the scientists that the relief was most palpable. If not the moon, perhaps life eternal, after all? And it wasn't, said Dingst, a carbonaceous chondrite, either, thus excluding Mars. There was not even a jot of iron content, brown fusion crust, no magnetism nor metallic platinum insides. But this boded of other, even more cataclysmic events— a looming collision with some other galaxy, perhaps.

"The truth of the matter is, I don't know," Dingst concluded, his manner—huddled beneath his fur-lined parka—bespeaking more the grave doubts than any jubilation. "This could have originated at the edge of the known universe. It is a complete mystery."

Johannes hauled up the crate holding Jacques.

"Everybody, please, a moment of prayer," Sannazaro insisted.

All stood resolute and quiet. Then Johannes pried open the wooden casket. A burp entered the air, trailed by something terrible to inhale.

"Oh dear," Ginevra cried.

The epicanthic fold had visibly swollen around varicose eyes. For a second time Jacques' warped mouth broke silence with a belching from the afterlife. It leered open, and all beholding it gasped to see the tongue flop out.

"Gross!" Rajibai voiced miserably, noticing the froth bubbling over like swamp gas producing its ellipsis of methane. Ginevra stuck the tongue back in, and proved herself adept at other gruesome doctorings as well.

Abstruse untried capacities that flower upon their necessity.

"He must have been a good-looking fellow," Ingrid said appreciatively.

"Thank you." Ginevra's voice punctured a colossal hollow of air that lay trapped like a whisper against all eternity.

"Excuse me." Mr Marigold wandered to a far lip of the summit. His urine was off-yellow on account of all the space pills he and his party had swallowed. It vanished into the bitter indraft, coalescing indiscriminately with a continent.

Suddenly Ingrid cried out, "*Glossopteris!*"

There was little commotion since nobody else knew what in hell the word meant.

"Incredible!" she said, spraying this finding with a cascade of other revelations, her tone caught out between despair and enlightenment. "*Drupaceous.* Permian—coal-bearing gymnosperms. *Dicroidium, Struth-ioptera camachoi,* extinct sea shells—" and so on, her gab alive with fossil woods, conifers and endoliths. But something was wrong, as yet undefinable, her outbursts providing no clue. There was Jacques, laid out as nude as a lungfish. A center of attention, to be sure. And Ingrid, explaining now that the nunatak turned out to be a Cenozoic remnant, a lost asteroid come to rest on Earth. She sat down, wobbly. The weather was changing.

"I can't begin to tell you what this all means," she harped, her head visibly spinning on a top, somewhere between the altitude and the realization of a biological pillar cut off from logic: an antediluvian way-station that never got re-admixed into the stream of evolution, remaining, instead, in pure standoffish isolation.

"This defies everything I know about science," she said, her voice stifled by a rush of emotion. "It predates everything we know."

"But of course it does," the Commander explained with an easy flourish.

"Time to go," Johannes joined in, breaking the euphoria instantly. "Madam," he said to Ginevra, "you might like to say goodbye."

"Leave us," asked she.

All stepped aside, as much as the summit allowed. She leaned over to kiss Jacques. "You take care of yourself," the others heard her say, though most of her words were lost to a mistral.

"Maybe we shouldn't even be up here?" Ingrid suddenly burst out, panic rising in her voice. Then, "*Don't touch that!*" she cried, forcing Rajibai to leap away from the three-inch-tall lichen he had discovered at his feet.

Already Gerard was singing his torch song, a maiden probe across the deep seas of metallic cerebellum; calculations winding up through every parallel processor a billion gigabytes faster than the speed of human neurons. Between the miniature ecosystem atop the nunatak, the meteorite and now Jacques, the puppet looked forward to no rest. But Ingrid was now convinced that the meteorite had to be evacuated, and Jacques as well.

"You're suggesting a hybridizing of the DNA from a corpse and a meteorite, in this temperature?" Dingst asked.

"There's freeze/thaw up here, obviously," Ingrid said. "Look at this— pebbles. I'd wager on a dozen cycles before winter's done. God damn it, this is a bad idea. We're courting a mutation."

"What are you saying?" Ginevra broke in. "That your research is more important than my husband?"

Ingrid was silent.

"I'm cold, I'm terrified, I don't know how we're going to get down, and I've come halfway round the world to honor my husband, and since you don't have a gun I guess there's nothing you can do to stop me from upholding my vows. So screw you!" Ginevra continued politely.

Rajibai found this exchange hysterically funny and burst out appropriately. The Commander tried to comfort the ladies with equal turns. Sannazaro put his arm around Ginevra, but it was Tully who found the way out of intractable ethics.

"Gerard'll get up a baseline on his bacteria, as well as any chemical peculiarities. Fact is, we're all here. There's bound to be some kind of exchange between elements, no matter what. At least we have the computing power to track it."

Ingrid conceded this overwhelming point. They'd all been standing atop the nunatak for 20 minutes. In that time biological precursors of genetic change had probably been expelled, in breath and sweat and the sheer weight of footprints compacting the hair-thin soil. Even audio pollution constituted a change, as well as the electromagnetic pulses from human cellular metabolism. There had to be emotional and spiritual components, as well. And neutrinos passing through living tissue into summital ice, carrying biological trace materials. An exchange of unseen substances that eclipsed the relevance of any philosophy. And who could tell what Gerard injected into the mix. It was probably true that no dinosaurs had ever inhabited the nunatak, but ancient plant forms certainly had. Ingrid had little doubt that underfoot there was entire tundra of a new magnitude: landscapes within landscapes, a polar oasis teeming with microbes, even insects new to the *Bible*.

Dingst and Ingrid were on the same page. But neither counted on this dilemma. Ingrid reminded them, "I did not expect such a profusion of life. There is no way this ecosystem won't be damaged by a human corpse."

"Jacques is his name," Ginevra added, furious.

"It's been decided," Dingst declared. "I am the leader of this expedition, and you, dear—" he pointed at his younger colleague "—came along at the last minute. Seniority has its season, and this is it, here, now. Anyway, your compatriots have disturbed other lost worlds and lonely spires without catastrophic consequences. Do you forget the giant worms in sulfur vents of the deep sea, or Lake Yellowstone, or those microbes in the boiling muds of Iceland? And what about the scorched caldera of the Saharan volcano Emi Koussi down which biologists nosed around?"

"The weather!" Johannes reminded him. Mottled storm clouds were dumping snow not 35 miles to the east.

"Madam Ingrid," the Commander uttered, straining under the weight of his own fear and exhaustion, "nobody here would argue against your concerns, but we have bigger fish to fry, I think you'll agree? The world may end, in which case this discussion hardly matters. What more properly concerns me at this moment is that my dear friend Ginevra should keep her promise; that a human life be commemorated; that ritual be restored and mystery preserved. That's what we are: human beings one and all. Let the heavens collapse, worlds collide, but not at the expense of our humanity. Not while we still have a choice in the matter. Ceremony, honor, dignity. Never forget them."

"Well stated," Sannazaro chimed in.

"Let us make peace with the inevitable. Jacques is staying. The meteorite is staying. Gerard is staying. The rest of us are going," said Dingst. "That's it. Goodbye, then."

Tully tweaked Gerard's delicate calibrations, then joined Dingst and a deflated Ingrid on the fixed ropes, rappeling back down to the lower ledges. Johannes now helped Rajibai and Sannazaro, both of whom had become silent and morose. It was the barometric pressure, which had dropped significantly. Or the hallucinogenic fringe that arises under such circumstances of intense concentration upon minerals amid thousands of miles of snow and ice. Mountaineers frequently speak of it, in the aftermath. Or possibly it was the sheer fatigue of so much, so many, adventures piled up like indiscriminate affronts to man's inner calm—that state to which all rational beings aspire. Poets since the time of Aristotle have stepped up to the plate of undistracted contemplation, only to find themselves in the center of Yankee Stadium during a playoff.

Johannes stayed to the rappel point while Marigold assisted Ginevra with her husband. They laid him out atop the cracked and gravelly remains of a slab eaten through by gastrulated growths. The sand was ice free, embryonic, warm, and looked to be the place that could best receive him. Flaking underskin; desperate clusters of final blood; hairy, matted arms. He lay still and sterling atop crustaceous lichen; waxy, gentle feet atop moss hummock; long silver-white hair, patchy as a result of the chemotherapy, but uncut in years, strands of brilliant crimson still present against the scalp, draping the *Tortula, Bryum algens* and *Grimmia arctici*, the dark, heavy clumps of moss, a gossamer setting of inclines and final rest. And there, his fingers mutely feeling; his veins still shimmering marlin blue, positioned like an offering atop these filamentous substances unknown to nomenclature. As mysterious as Jacques, now, himself.

He lay on the granitic earth colored yellow and orange from the *Xanthoria* that had long ago colonized its surface. Ginevra plucked a few of the remarkable berries, and put the fruit in his mouth. The Commander ate one as well, unseen by the others.

"Here's to you, my dear," she said, or something to that effect, and then both added their weight to the ropes, belayed by the giant Dane who saw them all safely through the snow flurries down to the glacier.

By the time they'd reached their base camp, Marigold was clearly a ruined man. Rajibai was worried about him, and Ingrid too. She had calmed down, accepted things, and now transferred her concerns to the incoming data from Gerard. Ingrid was the closest thing amongst the expedition members to a doctor. She applied two nasal squirts of ephinephrin to the Commander, whose pulse had dropped to below 49. He was lingering confused, half a phrase lost, half an urging to rise, a yogi with no direction, professing fear of neither God, giants nor pestilential fevers.

"He needs to sleep," Ingrid explained to Rajibai. And she gave him two sedatives.

Within minutes the Commander was totally gone, and quickly followed by the Squire himself. Both would sleep through the following afternoon.

Sometime during his deep snooze, Marigold's dreams picked up the transmissions from the summit of the nunatak, via Gerard, to a satellite 400 miles above and back to base. His inner ear detected streams of zeros and ones which added up to a persuasive argument: evolution might require a million years. But it can also occur by some calamity, skipping countless generations in favor of opportunism. That's the kind of biological entrepreneurship that terraforming involves. You splice a million years with a few concerted punctuation marks, like the addition of some incredible chemical or biological agent that serves as a catalyst, a diving board, for a host of other microbes to follow. Jacques, and a meteorite, were those punctuation marks, and Gerard was feeling the heat. Something was happening. At 3.20 in the afternoon, the Commander lurched upwards.

"Huh???" Not minutes later, Ginevra also rose from her deep sleep. Her mouth felt odd, but when she went to clean her teeth to freshen up, she was appalled by what she saw. Her tongue was purple.

"Murillo! Ingrid!" she shouted. "Look at this!"

The Commander hurried over—and Ginevra screamed. "You've got it too!"

Both of their tongues were purple. Ingrid ran a culture, only to conclude that both of them had consumed some strange fruit.

"Like blueberries," Marigold explained.

"Seven million square miles of ice and you found a ripe blueberry?

Why didn't you tell me!"

"Why would I bother telling you?"

"You found rare and precious fruit atop an Arctic desert, the most inhospitable point on Earth, and you ate it?"

Ingrid pursued this astonishing oxymoron of biological anomalies, but missed the fact of Marigold's dreams, and Ginevra's as well.

By nightfall, each member of Dingst's expedition found himself and herself engaged in those diddly-squat distractions which make the hysteric polar night bearable. Rajibai watched a DVD movie—*The Wizard of Oz*— on Tully's laptop, while Ginevra made borscht with a heavy infusion of ascorbic acid to counter what Dingst had described as "pibloktoq": polar confusion known to cause outright dementia among Eskimos. Sannazaro played chess with the Commander. Ingrid examined the emerging database. Dingst studied the rain of incoming analysis as well.

Johannes, sinking beneath the moonless fog like a hulking pallbearer in Gogol, enjoyed the movie with the boy as the night suffused their camp in the palpable fire of the aurora borealis. Avalanches roared somewhere beyond. The glaciers moved. The sky was molten dark. Summery cold, infecting everything. Life reduced to groping and fumbling.

"It's good for spore migration," Ingrid said, noting the Commander's agitation. The gusts were growing more persistent.

"I could do without them," he replied.

Leonids were interrupting the computers. Power surged from silence to phosphor fuzz. Not a sound on the whole planet save for the morose musical performances that accompanied the machines, and the domed interior full of amateurish putterings-about, the occasional crash, out on the glaciers, of a sérac, and the imponderably sustained tempest.

Slack air, nothing to do. Absolutely nothing. The quintessence of twiddling thumbs and dozing off.

Then, late that night: "Jesus, he's moved!" Tully exclaimed. Everyone gathered around, sleepy-eyed, and Tully turned up the video relay.

"The wind?" asked Ginevra.

"Don't think so," Tully nervously replied, pulling more data, inching closer to the monitor. They were all crouched low and together.

It was 11.30 p.m. The polar wind was steady, grinding up molecules.

The temperature read minus 75. Yet, atop Jacques's nunatak, the readings showed an improbable 53—*above* zero! Then Tully said something that, to the Commander, smacked of artistic sense: "He is claiming authorship."

Some warming, Ingrid reckoned, was an expected effect of the human trespass, in line with her earlier warnings. But not a 128-degree temperature discrepancy! "If the reading is true," she said, hazarding any number of guesses, "the world as we know it is about to change forever."

An alien aboard the meteorite? The implications were startling.

But Dingst had his own theory, and it was even more alarming: this was a chemical, more infectious than polywater, suggestive of the Last Hurrah at the End of Time, a cosmological swan song.

"I need to go back up, to be certain," he said.

Marigold, not to be outflanked by a gentleman of similar age, insisted on joining him. Rajibai was already standing. And Sannazaro chimed in not a minute later. Johannes, and Ingrid, who was quite clear about the risks to the entire party, were there, and Tully, whose way with the puppet was crucial. All were intent on making one last inquiry to the summit. They would depart as soon as the weather permitted.

CHAPTER 167
A Sweet Pea in the Snowstorm

PINIONED IN THE FULLEST Greenlandian ambivalency, the whole history of philosophy and metaphysics freezing up in his nostrils like a ring of ammonia or dried orange rind, currency no longer relevant to this age, Marigold sat quietly in his low-light quarters, staring blankly out upon the Breughel-dark storm. Earthly whorls of apprehension masked their frail camp.

Dingst, Tully and Ingrid remained in their places throughout the night, monitoring the quickly metamorphosing summit. Satellite data relayed from inside the puppet's obscenely overstuffed brain revealed an exuberant, as yet undefinable host of changes: chytric fungus colonizations atop Jacques, strange plants sprouting out of rocks, the formation of a small pinkish-colored cataract spiraling down one of the precipices, a needling cabaret on the move, even a micrometeorology keeping the summit cloaked in forensic steam, a singular cumulus within the greater storm that would not abate or move on.

The implications were shattering. Ingrid's conceit of an alien algebraically squared was not so far-fetched, after all. Marigold struggled with the notion: three strange consumptions occurring simultaneously, stretching the system of symbiosis to a new meaning, a commons wherein every creature partook with the same gusto, resulting in a screwball love fest. He presided over this freak show of biochemistry, grabbing an equation from here, a bit of tent gossip there, at length arriving at a wholly original summary of life on Earth; a belief in some new power of spontaneous eruption that transcended evolution, relying for its effect on transpermias, granite crystals, mud and fog. Throw in a dollop or two of Jain atoms (nigodas), a large cliff with water streaming off it, a few words of Danish, Tibetan, Eskimo, Italian and English— enough in their collective utterance to formulate an Esperanto of the last 40 million years of Hominid development—and a half-dozen alloys (all contained within Gerard's make-up), and presto! Andiamo! A new life force.

If, as Marigold now firmly advanced, comets, meteorites, asteroids, galactic dust and cosmic background radiation had been showering the earth willy-nilly for eons, there should be no reason to doubt the occasional alchemistry, unlikely bed partners meeting in isolated quarters and moments, like that transpiring presently atop the nunatak. With enough subsequent weathering over time, one could reasonably deduce the emergence of other offspring elsewhere in the region, and eventually across the whole continent, as the inevitable outcome of chemical permutations guided by wind velocity and the travel itineraries of feeding birds.

Speaking of birds. A second event transformed the lives of those at base that morning: the arrival of a large, unknown avian, blown thither, seeking refuge. It was no skua, no petrel, no auk. Five to six times the size of a wandering albatross, it had the olive-green beak of a super-puffin and the bulky body of an emu, the tail feathers (frozen and looking worse for wear) of an Andean condor and the bulbous glint of a blind barn owl. It was colored more flamboyantly and an even greater show-off than the peacock. Her neck twisted sensuously like a trumpeter swan, and from this gorgeous mass—300 pounds if an ounce—issued the most delicate greetings and inquiries: sounds as refined and sonorous as that great troubadour Martim Codax, her every gesture the mating dance of a New Guinea bowerbird, her long-journeying sighs those of the Lacadive loggerhead or the Cameroon cuckoo.

Rajibai promptly ingratiated himself with this whimsical princess of nature, giving her hot saki and pumpkin pie, blow-drying her feathers and reviving her spirits. She, in turn, allowed her newfound savior to plump down on her back, as he had become accustomed to doing upon the dragon. Like Sentimenta, Sweet Pea, as the boy called her, could fly, even with the added weight of a little human. Bundled up, wearing ski goggles, the boy and his bird soared through the snowstorm, immune to all cares, happy to have found each other.

"Be careful, lad!" the Commander shouted as his son disappeared far away. But he wasn't overly concerned. Sweet Pea had arrived with the timing of grace, an adroit deliverance from all that was morbid and adult. She and the boy were made for one another. Why the world did not listen to its children, or all the avians, thought Marigold, was the question that would surely haunt the ages. Only the child's viewpoint was sufficiently distracted to center in upon that which mattered, those pranks, playthings, games and gallops to redress the adult disasters and imbroglios of history.

"But, Marigold, this is crazy!" cried Dingst. "What if he falls or gets eaten? How do we know the bird is not carrying him away to its nest?"

"What if, what if ! The boy can look after himself," the proud father unfalteringly replied, referring time and again to the first principles of biophilia.

Not long after, the Commander spotted them out among the nunataks, returning from afar, floating across the glacier on a wing span exceeding 15 feet. Sweet Pea was larger, even, than New Zealand's Haast's eagle.

Throughout the day all spoiled the fantastic avian, who sampled each human import, whether cooked lentils or walnut granola in microwaved soy milk and romaine lettuce bunches, especially the hard crunchy spines. Rajibai tossed her the frisbee, and later Sweet Pea took an active role in the team's last-minute preparations, chewing unnoticed on the blue diamond-patterned Perlon ropes, on gloves and sunglasses. She rejected the computer, however. No Internet interested her.

A decided softening of reason with respect to the bird pervaded the collective. No attempt was made to strip awe down to mere calculation. Sweet Pea had transformed the three scientists, who were shortly behaving like children. This phenomenon would not be lost on any of them: they deduced a carrier gene outside the body; an aerosolized microbe of influence, the derivative of a musk gland hormonally catalyzed in the presence of all retrograde suggestion. It was a complex theory, born in the ultimate clean room. Greenlandia was a laboratory, its present voyagers a cell culture. Growth was occurring along countless avenues of thought and phylogeny. Gerard kept track, but nobody could keep track of Gerard.

The night had witnessed winds atop the nunatak of 187 kpm, yet the summital temperature now registered a balmy 88 degrees. Ingrid suspected the workings of *Buellia*, a form of lichen first discovered in an Antarctic dry valley in 1976. These pertinacious life forms had managed to hide inside the rocks, or been plastered on the surfaces, like biological renegades, spurning the cold by the heat of their own metabolic frenzies, and keeping the entire summit as snug and inviting as any Polynesian sea resort. Everything Jacques had imagined was now collapsing. His body was decaying; had provided a jumbo hothouse for breeding organisms, a filter for the aggressive exchange of gasses and fluids. On the computer monitor Ingrid noted a bubbling froth of new endosymbiants that had laid claim to Jacques' gut and were taking over with the assembly-line efficiency of a cancer cell, 1.8 trillion in 14 hours—a wellspring of devolutionary forces to which Jacques had provided perplexing purpose. Infinitesimal swarms of microbiota were stirred by the windfall, like ants fornicating.

Jacques had bloomed into something rich and strange. No doubt about it. A real bobby-dazzler. He was up there, alone with his own private jungle of vegetal multipliers. This was not the scenario he had counted on. He'd hoped for pure untouchability—preservation amid the ice—but his corpse was shifting positions markedly now. The carrier for dramatic change. He was the confrontation of biology with imagination; free will exerting its impact after death. He had set himself out to be willingly crystallized, bonded into the minerals of a continent. Instead, his fibers, and those of a new biological renaissance, were meshing. All burials accomplish grandiose geological designs—the adding of one's body by miniscule increment to the global burden of coal or mountain, however slowly. This internment differed not by degree but by implication. Rebel invaders had arrived on the tail of a far-flung rock, traveling at high speeds from a distant galaxy, alleged Dingst. That suggested an incoming tidal wave of other crystal apostates, or an entire field of truant black matter heading this way. The robust example of Jacques, his afterlife transformed, was but a quiet precursor of cataclysmic events to come, he insisted. The first creepy steps into a new world.

But, in the end, all this talk and hubbub about one man, one nunatak, one set of new species, was of trivial importance. They were all going to die. It was only a question of time.

Rajibai thought little of these discussions, emboldened by his own fancies, unwilling to cede confidence to an unknown that was as far removed from his visible universe as death itself. Of course, it could happen any time. Which signaled no particular reason to get all worked up over Dingst's or Hamidi's theories. If, on a certain night, at the eleventh hour, the whole Earth were to vanish, so be it. Who would know or care? Did he remember falling asleep a year ago?

As for Marigold he only wanted to believe that if the world did vanish, it wouldn't hurt. Wouldn't hurt his son, or his two dearest friends, Iacobo and Ginevra. That was all.

"I'd hate to have to see it coming, though," he speculated aloud. "What do you think, Professor? Will it light up the night sky for weeks before impact, or strike us dead without a second's notice? How fast would it have to be traveling to accomplish the latter?"

Dingst already knew the answer, which any school-grade grasp of galactic light shows should have already clarified. "Light travels, as everybody knows, at a confirmed speed. 186,000 miles per second, give or take, is not very fast when you add up the sums of the Universe. We'll see it coming, possibly for years. But, happily, we won't actually perceive it, or single it out from any other galaxy. When it crosses into our solar system, the tides, the weather, air pressure, magnetism, blood flow, metabolism— everything will start to change."

The weather socked them in, confining them to their increasingly cramped quarters. Many days passed while the team continued to monitor vital signs and robotic lyricism from above. Greenlandia's storm system dumped vast sheets of slush. The mists froze like sculptured mid-air layer cake. No descriptive faculty in the cold could quite articulate the rapidity with which good manners and evenness simply slid away. Showers were more trouble than they were worth. Food became a bother. The prolonged stay indoors, with brief and painful dashes out along the jogging chain, had left the party with a queasy dread, the air heavy with an obsessive future. None of them was prepared for the mental effects or their physical deterioration. Apocalypse skulked the burdened group like a disease.

Marigold noticed peculiar things for the first time about the human body; how cramped, uniform, slovenly, uninteresting and unavoidable it was. He talked with his Squire about their past, now convinced that the end of their days was near.

"Your patience will not go unrewarded," the Commander applied. "Even if all that we take for granted should turn to cinder in one mighty flame, there is a divine order, I'm certain, and you will be remembered."

"That's lovely of you to say so," replied Sannazaro. "But not necessary. I am no longer frightened. In fact, I rather relish this dense obscurity to which we have sunk. It is a holy elevation, if you ask me. Thick enough a fog to escape notice. If I were to die tomorrow, which seems more than possible, I should not fret, for I have been fortunate to have such friends."

Marigold got up with some effort and hugged his Squire, something he had rarely done. The expression caught on and soon there was a general feel-good orgy of hugs and congratulations, commiserations and kisses. Dementia was setting in. Such demonstrations of affection left little doubt of their peril, thought Ginevra, who took in the scientific revelations, the horror-filled outbursts and that ghastly video from the summit as a sign of their collective disappearance. She was reading the early ravings of Michel Foucault on archeology and cognition—a feast of ideological caveats that set perfectly well with their situation. She could not blame Jacques, because his body's trigger effect—as Ingrid was calling it—was trivial compared with the assertion by Dingst of a pending cosmic disaster: an entire universe on the move. Hamidi had gotten only the part about Mercury right, Dingst illuminated. The moon, Mars—they too were moving. But then so were the other planets, and neighboring galaxies. And all were heading somewhere to the right, Saturn in the lead, Venus—spinning in an opposite direction—a close runner-up, which meant that Earth was also in terrible flux and in a dreadful mess. Jupiter, so much larger than the others, was also closing in fast.

"But aren't we all simply traveling together?" asked Rajibai, envisioning a great and wondrous train ride of stars and planets.

"Yes, lad," Dingst rejoined. "There is some comfort in that, to be sure. But the rate of flow is variable, depending on gravity. Orbits are all mixed up, after billions of years. Some are going to collide with others. It's bound to happen."

"Will we all die?" he asked forthrightly.

"The mathematical probabilities are certainly increased," replied the famed Dane, trying to allow for some hope. It was an extreme form of generosity given the umbrella of doomsday he had already formulated. But then, Danish men of letters were renowned for their exquisite oxymorons, from the sixteenth-century Palladius to the modern Klaus Rifbjerg. Dingst was particularly fond of Jens Peter Jacobsen, who hailed from the remote Faroes Islands. His novel, *Niels Lyhne*, had been called the Bible of Atheism in its seamless admixture of brute nature, romantic dreaming and compliance with forces greater than oneself. Jacobsen was dead before his thirty-eighth year, a pedigreed victim of a weakened immune system and chronic tuberculosis. Earlier, Schoenberg had written his haunting "Gurre-Lieder" in response to the writer's earliest poetry. Although no Dane quite captured the fatal sense of life like Søren Kierkegaard, the champion of heroic self-sacrifice.

The boy clung to the bird, staring into her dark retinal pools where every nuance of life on Earth was mirrored, a museum of living still stores, all those vantages she had crossed, retained in the multi-myriad glints of her hovercraft. Sweet Pea had navigated untold cosmographies. In her flight patterns, all the centuries of winged ideality, the primal memories that gave birds their distinctive edge. Rajibai could only gaze on, losing his arms in her bodily nest of layered down, lowing, mooing, gurgling with a desire to communicate.

Ginevra, in her dreams, recognized old familiar faces. Someone had bound her arms and legs, depositing trinkets of platinum, figs and pennies in her hands, honey and garlands in her hair, wrapping her corpse beside that of Jacques in a glue of linens, salts and oil to ensure that her afterlife would elude the captive web of degenerative worms and maggots.

But demons with hideous breath and glaring eyes surrounded her pure-air mountaintop habitation, drawing both Ginevra and her late husband into a panic attack, the muscles quivering in an attempt to escape. This image haunted her. What had begun as a group process, rational and whole, had started to shift.

It would snow for 19 days.

During that period, everyone moved slowly, hunched over, equivocal and turbid, an opaque surface of daily toils. Did one pee, drink, eat, sleep, say even a word to anyone else during those three weeks? The occupants had settled uncomfortably and cold into private thoughts and foregone conclusions. Collectively they had gained 70 pounds. Sluggish and irritable. Senses dulled. Time breaded like dough, flattened and pounded and made into something that perhaps it was, or perhaps was not. The improvised indoors, the impoundedness of being.

Then, suddenly, exploding into their dull recognition, the long storm began to fractionate. The very rhythms of the Creation were detectable. A faint curfuffled light egressed in hair-thin increments, negating the nihilism of the blizzard with needle-clear expressions. A messenger of successive tones hewing from the horizon to meet the flamboyant northern lights.

"It's time," Rajibai thought he heard Sweet Pea mutter.

Ginevra lurched from her sleeping bag.

Sannazaro threw an arm round to the left, accidentally smacking Marigold in the head. The Commander lunged for his dagger, smarting, shrieking.

"It's OK, it's OK ..." Tully pleaded, holding him back.

Sweat profuse. Fears, tingling restraints, slaphappy, itchy trigger fingers, cabin sickness in so many guises.

After so much infernal darkness, the sky broke clear and bountiful, accompanied by a new symphonic outburst from Gerard. Something extraordinary, or horrifying, was happening up there. Did Gerard sense the end, or see the approaching starfield before anybody else?

Gerard! Of course, thought Dingst. If anyone, the robot should have the answer.

CHAPTER 168
The Final Ascent

THE SCIENTISTS WERE all industry, tightening crampon screws, consolidating packs, Johannes checking ropes for any frayed areas or puncture holes. The language of chalks, friends', Chouinard biners,

55mm ice axes, snow seal, one-inch webbing, helmets, flashlight batteries. Just to stretch required a leap of faith. Static electricity was detonated off each touch. The thought of proceeding out-of-doors an absolute insistence. The weeks of stale confinement were at an end. All were anxious to make their peace.

In spite of the renewed vigor, Ginevra was queasy with these goings-on, reluctant to concede her little quadrant of acquired safety within the dome for another bout in the seismic outdoors. She was terrified of heights, and her previous foray had left her dismally aware of her susceptibilities. She'd had countless nightmares of falling, of space all around her, of rocks puncturing her lungs, cheeks, eyes, bashing out her brains. Horrible impacts. Mostly, her fears centered on Jacques and what he might have become. She'd deliberately avoided glancing even once at the video relay monitor all these weeks. The demons of anticipation lay buried near her surface. A monster lay beside her, reminiscence of a horticulture that was their well-tempered greenhouse of a marriage. Rotted insides that threatened, by all these scientific premonitions, the whole planet. It was too incredible, she reckoned. Better to renounce any connection; spurn all knowledge of the man, and the events leading to the present; to eschew every promise.

The party carried on with nervous chit-chat as they made ready. This was the worst part: nobody saying anything that mattered. They shared a tacit foreknowledge that there were hard times ahead. Marigold and Sannazaro both sported ragged beards by this time: the Commander's a rueful patchwork, Sannazaro's more trim, white against the wizened skin. Marigold noticed that his right hand trembled, a palsy of premonition. He knew it for what it was—in grand terms, an ontological fever. He had made out his personal master plan, poised to embrace death, if need be; to yield up in himself the full force of a mature culmination that accepted its fate in Greenlandia and held it in highest esteem. As art historian Frank Elgar once said of Rodin, his "art was too individual to be transmitted"; the idiom could not last. Marigold felt that way about himself at this great bridge in the flow of time. Contrary to whatever tonics Anna and her people had conveyed to him, he imagined that somehow or other he would die atop the nunatak; that nobody would ever understand what he had attempted, been all about. He too had dreamt of the moment, catapulted by the reams of enthusiastic data emerging on the computers in the dome. These uplinks, downlinks, end-of-the-world sciences, all so dense with ambiguity and complication—a dead man conversing with a puppet signaling a satellite dispatching telegrams to a doomed ensemble of curiosity-seekers off the map of the world. It had a rueful ring of finality to it which argued for no other encomium or gravestone. Perhaps an El Greco never painted.

It seemed to him, as it had so many times in previous months, that everything he had done—every gesture, each conceptual and spendthrift amalgamation, all the fanfare and legalities and airplane rides and bushwhacks—had been ordained, bringing him precisely to these coordinates so that it could be over. Done with. He even looked forward to the relief of a conclusion. Fifty, the year for philosophers and kings. Resolution. Let it be finished. High time. Nobody to answer to. No more compunctions or burning impulses. The end. Quietly. Anonymously. Peacefully.

But for the sake of his son, in whose eyes was the brightness of stars, the hope of a new century, Marigold's fatalism would admit to no nuance of sorrow or regret. Rajibai would survive him. Where it would take him, amid six billion *Homo sapiens* all clawing after the trapdoor and ventilator shaft, was anybody's guess.

Continuous mischief, that was the boy's inheritance. Good, decent hijinks for a better world. The bright lights of bedeviled lunacy whereupon the least conceivable prospect fructified the most fallow of absurdities. His treasure chest of hand-me-downs was larded with the Commander's last dying breath, and there were many of them. Countless gasps, innumerable shudders. There he stood, a knight in full glacial apparel, ready to tramp off in the bog of bad presentiments. Yet, who else could view the worst ideas in so favorable a manner? His foreign affairs were not reconcilable with any known government body; his purchase on the patience of those with real power was so negligible as to be better characterized as a nuisance. Nobody who listened to him for more than a minute was likely to be convinced of anything, save for Rajibai, who instinctively followed his every footstep, and Sannazaro, who knew better, of course, yet could not help himself. These three musketeers made for the most pitiable assemblage of carefree gullibility in the annals of inanity. And, to their credit, they were the only ones who did not know it.

For himself, Marigold never even questioned his modus operandi, or the impact he had on others. He was capable of change, but only upon inner reflection and discourse. He could not, however, respond intelligently to others. This meant that he was not ready to follow through with an argument, make sense in the conventional or unconventional worlds. If there was logic to his tirades and escapades, you had to be a child to understand it. But most children would never have the stamina or working vocabulary to get close to him. His difficulty with others of his own species was, in short, the problem of consciousness, as phenomenologists have for centuries contemplated it. A crisis of faith in humanity's capacity to save itself. Here was a man who had read through the great literatures of the world, in multiple languages; had delved into science, art, history, metaphysics; burrowing for nuggets, nesting for decades in the pile of his contusions, paraphernalia, anecdotes, translations and marginalia. Yet, he could not sit still for five minutes, add two plus two without recourse to other recondite emendations. His brain lived in a skillet, overheated, oversaturated, towards no end but the act of digestion itself. In trying to be virtuous, he was a menace. And still, all this was to his eternal credit. One could not help liking him. There had been no other Marigold of his delusional caliber for over a century.

The Commander looked adoringly at his son, patted him on the head, and consoled himself: "This will be fun, child," he said stoically.

Ginevra gazed out across the ice, churning inside but finally resolved to the love that had brought her here, all the more certain of her scheme and gratified to have been entrusted with so profound a realization. What she had not shared with anyone was her half-cocked vision of remaining beside Jacques, an ideal of welling syllogism, given the coming calamity to which she had been privy. In an odd way, she and Marigold had arrived at the same place at the same time for similar reasons.

The temperature was a mellow 15 degrees when they set out. A venticular cloud encased the northern horizon, delineating the frozen Bremen blue above from the vibrant orange eddies of the day below. In their down suits and outer wind gear, crampons tightly secured to double boots and roped together, they were lunar commandos, fumbling from weeks of inactivity. Behind the traveling team hopped the great bird.

Johannes patiently belayed the non-climbers with a double 9mm line, sinking his ax into every third foot, testing for crevasses. He knew by all of his training and instinct that a landscape of searing cavities loomed beneath. They stood upon a bridge, miles wide, miles long, that would eventually cave in.

"The glacier is totally different," Ingrid remarked almost at once, breathing heavily in the sledge-drawing dawn. Nineteen days of snow had covered the séracs and craquilures along the center of the vast glacier up which their doddering cortege tramped. In a canyon land of exposed black ice, impervious to their 12-point crampons, they entered a blinding, blistering, wind-bullied warp where time was measured in pain. They stumbled towards the hard obscure pinnacle in that distant gray-gold sky. Out there no idea lasted for long, frozen against the inner brain the moment it attempted to express itself.

They paused, breathing unsteadily. Pulse rates, on average, 160. "Let's keep moving," said Dingst, in a voice that revealed volumes of his fear and troubles.

They reached the 100-foot wide bergschrund at the base of the nunatak. It was 3.35 in the afternoon. One more hour of light. Everyone checked their headlamps, knowing they would shortly need to rely on them. Johannes launched into action at once, descending into an abyss, climbing out the other side and connecting with the granite wall. Tully belayed him, then fixed a line with a single foot of slack, so that the non-climbers could jumar across.

Marigold was exhausted and slumped against a corner of brilliant red flowering plants the likes of which, Ingrid alleged, had never been seen. The word 'protein' surfaced in somebody's mind. She had repeated it over the din of the gale starting up, unexpected weather, all over again.

Johannes was steadily ascending the darkening crag, his broken fingernails clawing after the slightest purchase amid the untouchable gardens that had descended the wet steeps, sprouting a barrage of lilies and viscous gonidia.

"Just hammer it!" a voice shouted, the declaration followed by the repeated action of a metal hexagon forced into a crack. A veil of obscurity blinded the team as they seemed to move higher and higher. A lapse of memory. Eyes to the wall. Fingers frantic after holds; bodies squirming towards any hospice, a ledge, no matter how pitiful its size. These labors seemed to go on for an eternity.

Until a bright light could be seen emanating from just 20 feet or so from the summit. Something was happening to Johannes, who was there, on top, in the lead. From down below they could all hear it—

groans, then shrieking.

"Oh no," Sannazaro cried instinctively.

The fear was instantly contagious, as if they'd heard an avalanche. Each member of the team hurtled inward, conjuring final prayers, flashbacks, seeing halos, epiphanies, lost tracks, calls. The Commander instinctively drew his son to his chest and managed to alert the Squire. "Don't let go!" he called as a large billowy cloud hurtled down at them, a gigantic cumulus moving with weight, deliberate speed and direction, its shape a palpating muscle. It was a man.

"No ..." Ginevra's voice trailed off. She sat on a corner of the ledge where the others stood, save for Johannes who was gone, his body creaming into the wall, slicing through the rope, bouncing dumbly into the void.

"What the hell is it?" Dingst screamed. "A *creature!*" Ingrid hollered.

Ginevra, obsessed with attaining the very Jacques, began clambering upwards again, Dingst following closely and calling, "My meteorite!"

"*Go, go, go!*" Tully shouted, more for himself than anybody else, as he too lunged upwards to rescue his puppet from the unknown transmogrification. With Ginevra's dazed and foaming hand in tow, he led them—Marigold, Rajibai, Sannazaro and Ginevra—through the dark world of the nunatak's biological revolution.

And as they neared the very tippy top of the obscure mountain, there was a substance drooling down the rock which no one could fail to recognize for what it was: feisty gray matter, or the equivalent, the color of cactus milk or whale sperm. Very gross, very intelligent and not unsucculent.

And there was the summit itself, Gerard aflame with his own metallic absorptions, chugging out compulsive figures, spinning analyses, rocking to and fro, disappearing beneath the fibrous super-strings engulfing them all.

Tully, starting down, was feebly groping under mucousy downrush. "... No choice ... goodbye! ..." he cried, before vanishing below. Marigold heard a faint thud as his body crashed somewhere in the lower mists, 500, 1,000 feet below on the glacier. And then a second thus, which was the body of Ingrid, who had succumbed to circumstances that were not entirely susceptible to description.

"The ropes!" yelled Sannazaro.

"No time!" the Commander cried out. All was concentrated, seconds condensed. Language itself a victim of the economy enforced upon them in this sudden horror of death and survival. Before these moments, there had prevailed the exquisite surreality of a mountain in Greenlandia.

Nobody, not even the ever-serene Commander nor his unflinching little boy, could have predicted actual pain, and terror, and a creature that was not accountable to the norms of biology on Earth.

But there were even weirder goings-on. Ginevra, clambering to the top, lay down beside her ex-husband. Marigold called out to her, but she did not respond, was as if in a trance, covered in the membranous plant material.

Dingst was also on the summit, staring at the living proof of some theory or other which he had concocted. But it did not fit the momentous juncture—nothing could—and the Danish scientist's mouth hung open, surprised by data he could not speak of.

Then suddenly Dingst exclaimed, "Everything is fine!" And at that instant there was an eruption of flesh, coming out of Jacques in a grinding pulse.

The Commander grabbed hold of Ginevra, dragging her away from the monster that had emerged from her deceased husband, as Sannazaro frantically tied off the ropes on one end, then tossed tangled hanks overboard, down the front wall up which they'd ascended. Now all five were attached to jumars and began the rapid descent, Sannazaro, for a change, in the lead.

There was a scream. It was Dingst, plunging away. Something had gone wrong. His jumar had snapped. No reason why, and no time to inquire. He was dead.

Rajibai and Ginevra were newcomers to the technology. Rajibai was a quick learner—the Commander showing him how—but Ginevra, still in a trance, had no clue. Her hands had to be forcibly clasped around the handle of the jumar, her legs pressed, manually, into a suitable position. Marigold hung off the ropes by her side, trying to help her. But it was difficult. He'd had a little practice—at Bandelier, long before—but that was not enough. Not for a situation like this. In the darkness, hands slime begotten, surrounded by spastic vegetal matter.

And then, suddenly, the main rappel rope tore apart, a poof of Perlon powder in the air.

"*Falling!*" whimpered the foursome as they plunged off the over-hanging wall.

The freezing breeze, the godspeed, out over the glacier in all directions. A near miss. A cornice. A dihedral. Glancing off a ledge. A smashed ankle. An arm.

Whence, from afar, sweeping all four of the plummeting humans from mid-air, a bird. Alert to the danger, flying in a hair's breadth from the cliff. Expert maneuvering. Twenty, perhaps 30, magical feet of tough, leathery, muscle-bound wingspan. Sweet Pea.

She had seen the goings-on, one must assume, and been intrigued, or alerted, or fearful, for her friends. No one will ever know. But with an instinct for falling bodies, she knew, miraculously, what to do, and arrived at the precise coordinates as four bodies, crashing at terminal velocity, smashed into her topside, heavily buffered in feathers. But, for all her strength, this combined weight constituted a heavy load. She could not sustain it and began, herself, to fall. But it was a controlled fall across the icy blue of Greenlandia, a glide straight down which ended in a skid, not a crash.

The puppet, meanwhile, in his final machinations, metal never before colonized, was crawling along the rim, through a molten slush of life, alien sparks, rock-borne galleries of fizzle, sizzle and writhing flesh, all concentrated atop Jacques' high-altitude throne room of New Science. Submerged in the gauze and feeble starts of a newborn, Gerard lay down beside the creature that was Jacques. Warm and cozy atop the jeweline morass. Sinking into the sweet and grasping globules of the rock and slime. In some future eon, a Darwin-type would describe it. Maybe colorful finches or a new species of butterfly would emerge.

Sweet Pea managed to land, a half mile from the domes. Her four passengers were safe, though needed some help across the ice. Rajibai was the one among them to prod and galvanize the others. He had no choice: if they stayed out in this condition, fatigue coupled with intensive cold, they would die. It was the boy's moment, and he acted upon it, saving the other three.

But it was Sannazaro who remembered the satellite phone, and figured out how to use it.

"Call out the cavalry!" ignited the fully devastated Squire. "We have to destroy it."

He had managed to dial the direct number of the Danish Air Force team that had worked out the preparations with poor doomed Dingst.

It was the middle of the night at Kangerlussuaq, and later still in Copenhagen. In the electricity of his hysterical elocutions, Sannazaro conveyed the broad strokes, and the more subtle details.

Marigold, revived by his life-saving half-mile trudge across the ice from where Sweet Pea had landed, grabbed the phone from his Squire.

"It is something magnificent," he decreed. "You mustn't hurt it!" Sannazaro forced the phone away from him. "He's mad! You must, I repeat. You gotta detonate this whole goddamned ecosystem—don't miss a square inch—or we're all gonners. How do you say that in Danish?" And he continued shrieking in this manner till the phone went dead. The batteries were gone.

For hours they waited on guard, arguing. The Commander was furious. Sannazaro would not apologize. He knew he was right. The danger of gravity-fed slimes coming off the nunatak from miles above was ever-present. But, for all that, relief pervaded their mood. Yes, their fine colleagues had perished and the world might be coming to an end ... But it wasn't. For Marigold believed sincerely that he had seen the light in the professor's eyes. "No question," he reported to his peers, "he meant to tell us it will be all right."

"How could you tell?" Sannazaro demanded, while Ginevra snored by his side, curled up under woolen emergency blankets.

"It was obvious," Marigold replied cryptically. As Danish jets streaked the skies the following dawn, the pilots looked down upon a glacier turned the color of puke. The glob was spreading, was no more than a half-mile from the base, when a flotilla of helicopters, followed an hour later by paratroopers, descended to rescue the foursome.

Sweet Pea!" Rajibai cried out.

But there was no point. Unhappy with the choppers, the mysterious bird set off to southward with a melancholic cry and one last look at the boy, leaving 15 feet of feather—a single plume—behind.

Soon after these agitations at base camp, the Tesuque quartet, wide awake now, passed what appeared to be the very horizon, if that is possible. They rode in military choppers this time, more comfortable than Sweet Pea, or Sentimenta. And from this safe vantage at 4,000 feet, traveling at 110 miles per hour towards Copenhagen, they witnessed a series of cataclysmic explosions—neutron bombs, perhaps—which appeared to vaporize the nunatak, and whatever it was about Jacques.

CHAPTER 169
The View from the Watch Tower

THE MIGHTY ROCK WALLS OF the nunatak had been thoroughly incinerated, 20 miles of glacier reduced to dust. A dark smoky plume drifting towards Newfoundland was all that remained of the indefinable imbroglio. Knowing that NASA and Defense Mapping Agency satellites would have picked up the explosions, authorities in Copenhagen had already formulated their carefully constructed press release: two Danish military planes on routine exercise over Greenlandia had collided.

Within minutes of returning to the Danish capital and checking into the Ritz Carleton, Ginevra booked herself a ticket back to New Mexico, and left the following afternoon. She was exhausted and verging on a nervous breakdown. Events which had begun with such purity of intent had succeeded only in turning her late husband into red algae and charcoal. She yearned to remember what had transpired, her last fixed image of the two of them together, as they had been so many years before, in a Paris hotel room or at Club Med in the Bahamas. They had lain side by side atop the unreal world. She'd touched a half-kiss to his enflamed cheeks and passed out. More precisely, that instant of lips-to-Jacques had been enough for the transfer of atoms. The goo that enlivened him had entered her veins, incapacitated her autonomic nervous system, infiltrated her glands, bubbled into her mind, just enough of it to slow down her heart and leave her transfixed. Incapable of interacting with this world.

The details accompanying her deliverance from the summit of the nunatak were hazy in her mind, and news of the deaths of Dingst, Ingrid and Tully was shattering. But seeing the vaporization of her husband had for her been, in some strange way, a rare reprieve from further complications, she thought. She knew how Jacques' dream of immortality had gotten quite out of hand, but she was unable to grapple further with the myriad spiritual dimensions of his disintegration and simply looked forward to sleeping for a year.

As for any love interest in Murillo Marigold, she had disinherited the idea with the strongest convictions. However one described his peculiar handicap, loving they neighbor, she concluded, was not all it was cracked up to be. Contagious stupidity could not make for a stable relationship. While his temper was mild, his incessant enthusiasms were exhausting. Nobody could stand up to one *idée fixe* after another. In the case of Marigold, these grand masquerades had become a philosophy, an attitude of unstoppable force that was loathsome to the pampered debutante in her. She did not want to die in the service of some altruism. Granted, hauling Jacques to the point of inaccessibility had been her desperate doing. But it was not her fault that this gesture of loyalty had unleashed a biological backlash, or whatever it was. Now, all she wanted was to forget, and soak.

Sannazaro, having endured similar questions at Los Alamos, knew very well about keeping to himself in the closed room of the emergency ward at Copenhagen General Hospital, where the military authorities presided over their recovery. Rajibai, whose condition (attributed to shock) of lapsing into giddiness just before bedtime had worsened, proved adept at spewing hairballs of nonsense. As for the Commander, who had been the one to try and spare the nunatak, he skimmed over a delicate drug-free dramaturgy. There was no point escalating the intrigue by mentioning Jacques. If he did, the Danish officials would never cease harassing them with questions. In truth, Marigold no longer feared the finale, and now thought of it as a strange game of scientific Chicken played out between the professor and the sheikh against a backdrop of the distant stars. Dingst's last words hung in the ruptured air of personal disaster, but suggested no general Armageddon. The Universe wasn't going anywhere. This Earth was good for another four billion years. And that hybridized creature atop the nunatak was nothing more than some algal bloom with the nagging powers of proliferation one sees from time to time in paint thinner or along the shores of Longboat Key.

But events occurring simultaneously across Europe intimated some other version of this, and did not take long to come to Marigold's attention as he slowly recuperated from his Danish bed, reading the city's English newspapers.

In the fair city of Budapest there exists a fine construction of mossy rubble. The ruins, long dozing betwixt the red walls of castle pieces and crenellations, have been re-engineered into a veritable cornerstone of Central European metaphysics. Hewn from quartz and onyx remnants of the continent's past, of whole centuries forgotten—wars, famines and marauding infidels—larger-than-life lions of feldspar seem to weep at its architectural junctures. Their tears form a confluence streaming all the way down the forested hill and rocky abutment towards that languorous portion of the Danube best known for its suspension bridges and the Hungarian Academy of Romantic Love.

This obscure building was collectively known as the Watch Tower by all those lovely virgins who used to bathe beneath the stone rudiments in a natural hot spring which issued from a cave in the mixed carstwood forest and served their ritual oblations. The ladies took secret delight in the knowledge that a certain hermit, otherwise famed for his pursuit of high thoughts, spied upon them from a turret with some sort of scientific instrument. In later times, Hungary's Department of Royals used the 80-foot tower as a secret gathering site during moments of historic gravity. By 1960, however, after 1,200 days of Soviet neglect, this pyramid of crumbling dimensions had been abandoned, become home only to migrating pigeons. With the advent of Hungary's freedom, the Women's League for Precious Places laid claim to the task, fired up some weary diplomats, achieved a UNESCO stamp of approval for World Heritage, and turned the Watch Tower into a site of iconographic charm and recognition. Less prominent than the Citadella, perhaps, or the vertical dome at Pannonhalma Abbey, or even the spires of Parliament, the Watch Tower nonetheless presided with its own unique capacity for inspiring curiosity. From as far away as Szechenyi lanchid, the odd little cupola of oozing flints was visible. Travelers were drawn to the Gellerthegy district in hopes of finding that one sequestered promenade that might lead them to the mysterious alcove atop the tower.

The only way up, however, was by a daunting vertical apparatus, always in motion, catapulted by the forces of the cascade nearby. Amid the wild jungle of Mongolian limes, variegated Kentucky-coffee trees and Japanese cherries, one's timing had to be just right or else the consequences could be dire—instant beheading. Ministries all over Budapest later adopted this style of lift, presumably to keep employees on their toes.

Three days after the foursome's escape from Greenlandia, a massive gathering of scientists converged on the Watch Tower to sort out the latest crisis affecting the stability of the European Union and all of mankind, for that matter: a detectable presence of dioxins in Yorkshire pudding.

As if that weren't sufficient cause for general despair, foul-tasting pig toes, mostly pulverized, were appearing in one Hungarian cream cheese after another. The young and dashing Hungarian Prime Minister, a soccer buff who in '89 had bravely bid the Soviets get lost, presently welcomed the delegates with a rousing and metaphorical speech about soccer's place in human history, and warned them: "Get those toes out of our cheese!"

But there were other untoward biological anomalies, as well. The number of Mad Cow (CJD) victims had gone from under 100 individuals to the entire spectrum of all those afflicted with dementia and Alzheimer's. Until autopsies were mandated, no one would know for certain. Nonetheless, the outbreak seemed somehow to have imbibed the virulence of BHD (bunny hemorrhagic disease). But how? Policy dragoons debated diethylstilbestrol hormone implants in sheep, subtherapeutic bacteria-resistant cortisone in piglets, and the washing up of nearly 50 million hen carcasses on a beach near Normandy five days earlier. A rash of polluted meats pervaded Europe and, in the opinion of many, North America as well. Indeed, pathologists were likening the cannibalistic kuru disease of the New Guinea Fore Highlanders to similar forms of transmissible brain-wasting ailments in cats, mink, deer, elk and cows. Even chickens, turkeys, pigs and goats were alleged to be susceptible, as were sheep in whom the scrapies disease had first been detected in the very country that first tried to suppress all data pertaining to BSE: England. With the transmission occurring in placentas, in blood, and between all mammals, a growing contingent of scientists had predicted that by 2015 all non-vegan humans would start going extinct. A Nobel Prize was given to one researcher who identified some of the amino-acid culprits. If that weren't enough, there had been a disastrous collapse of blue tuna, and newly detected yeast strains infected with North Atlantic fungus. To Marigold's way of thinking, all these strange occurrences had to be connected to Jacques. Even officials in Copenhagen were fearful of an international quarantine of their entire country, consistent with the earlier World Trade Organization protests on the streets of Seattle. International news briefs had implicated Denmark in the "strange accident over Greenlandia". Milk and blue vein Havarti were sure to be boycotted.

After a week's confinement at the hospital, Marigold, Rajibai and Sannazaro left Denmark and flew directly to Budapest. They arrived amid a countrywide groundswell of vocal public opposition to the new Ghent Directives on transgenic bristle and digestive tracts. With colorful placards condemning germline engineering, the manipulation of embryos, even somatic gene therapy, the angry crowds warned of human robot clones, and harassed the visiting delegates, who guzzled their cheap champagnes and devoured tidbits from their lunch trays—Marmite with treacle.

Sensing that he had been the key accomplice to all the apocalyptic mirages in question, Marigold had come to Budapest to strategize—an observer for once, not a crusader. He needed to listen and learn. There was no question but that the European continent was biologically deteriorating at an escalated pace, and he half hoped to be able to do something about it. Just what that was, he couldn't tell you. (Sannazaro, by contrast, had transcended these utterly confusing multidisciplinary alarm bells. He'd come along to the Danube in the pursuit, purely, of the best Tokay in the world, and the famed Roman hot baths. He had his priorities right.) Every major international scientific organization was represented at this freak show of big brains: the International Union for the Conservation of Preservatives; the Federation of Hopping Neutrinos; the Commonwealth of Independent States of Matter; the Association of Stem Cells. Collectively, these national associations of science and their highly paid representatives constituted a hotbed of denials, a bastion of hidden agendas. What the Commander witnessed were the many marvels of indifference and the mattresses of the male ego. Confirmation of everything Anna Christov had said about science. Nothing had changed in nearly a century.

Each delegate represented a pet peeve and priority; some agitated for superconductivity in Khirgizia. The Angolan envoys wanted Internet access; the Poles were looking for cheap desalinization technologies; the Columbians were there to discuss the eternal problem of the square root. Zimbabweans sought legal sanction for taking 'excess' elephants; Japanese wanted higher quotas on gray whales and basking sharks. Those nations with no basking sharks were quite happy to see them disappear, as long as the shark killers granted reciprocal rights allowing non-shark nations to cultivate their evergreen *Prunus africana* and quince monitor lizards.

Vanishing species were bartered as chattels, used as pawns in trading deals that took no notice or care of all the other threats to the planet.

Amid the parliament of self-serving rhetorics, conference tables were piled high with standard published papers and endangered caviars served by bored barmaids. There was no elbow room for small kindnesses; nothing to say about dreams or social causes. The view from up there was, in short, no less obscured than from elsewhere in the human world.

Amid all the scientific mumbo jumbo, no individual had once referred to the rights of animals, or seemed to care one Quaker oat for the fate of the world.

"Screw 'em," Sannazaro said. "Let's get the hell out of here."

"What should we do?" Marigold lamented over dark ale and lentil soup at the Aquincum Café, the oldest drinking spot in Europe rumors had it, dating to the period of third-century Pannonia, when Romans themselves stopped by to get slushed. On the television above the bar a live production of Haydn's "The Creation" was being performed by the Zenekedvelok Egylete—the Music Lovers' Society. Everything that happened—every flippant aside, odd nuance, number of ice cubes in his drink, the first violinist playing Haydn—the Commander took as a personal sign, a communiqué coming directly at him for a purpose. Not so Sannazaro, who dismissed everything as extraneous to what was really going on, or mattered. This was his salvation, and Marigold's martyrdom.

The two were fundamentally different, yet the boy bridged their gulf. Later, turning and tossing, the Commander could not sleep, so he got up, dressed, then strolled out across the soundless street and entered a grassy shimmering green drenched in late-night dews. There, on a bench, a man slept soundly, his terrier even more so. Never had Mr Marigold seen such contented slumber. No grocery cart, not even a rucksack to mark the spot. The ragamuffin of adult embers was attired in weary jeans and moth-eaten sweater, mauves, charcoals, no borrowed robes, but his own threads, and slept curled up, his unshaved face against his mottled hands. The comfort at the end of time. A biorhythm as blissful as those atop the waterfall. Right in the middle of Budapest. The dog slept on her own little rag of a pillow. No other possessions between them. Perfect.

Marigold stood there gazing on this remarkable scene. It was three in the morning. Crickets and frogs were parading and serenading. It was this moment, somehow, that translated into a master plan of typically Marigoldian bravura.

He meditated on the monkish, Zen-like absolute that was the man and his dog. No accoutrements. Not a trapping or ounce of excess. A Jain monk in homeless drag. Bingo! he concluded. The thing that would set the world right was the disappearance of all human assets! It was for him a profound stroke. A freeze frame of common-sense lullaby. Stop the mints, halt the flow of money, reverse 10,000, 20,000 years of accumulation. That was the answer! What did renunciation have to do with meteorite showers over Greenlandia, or biology run amuck in Western Europe? Everything. Was there some succor for the human species—for all species—in the advent of such pauperdom, and could one as rich as Marigold objectively speculate on such financial theories, given his recent ideological dependency upon his own riches? Some might correctly argue that a man that rich had necessarily lost touch with most of humanity. But they would be wrong, for Marigold's method—evolving in the wake of the late-night encounter, a man on a bench with his dog—suddenly grew up, not in his mind but in his heart, and would encompass all living beings.

He promptly returned to his hotel room and commenced a vast new formulation. He contemplated the early Engels; the transcripts of the first Bretton Woods gatherings; the confessional letters of Machiavelli to his mistress; and those of Alfred Wallace—lonely, stricken with malaria on the wild shores of Java— to the finch-smitten Darwin, relying upon the memory of the massive bibliophile that was Marigold, however scanty the details, to clothe his new humanism. He recalled Carl Jung's theory that a human being needs nothing to live—a prospect greatly amplified by Rousseau who argued that a man requires only sunlight and water for his sustenance. In its more consolidated hypothesis, John Ruskin's little book, *Unto This Last*—a strident call for an end to market forces, an embrace of universal depreciation, and the author's binding salute to the purity of poverty—had transformed one unlikely reader: Mohandas Gandhi. Marigold also recalled Sorenson's version of the *Life of Saint Francis*. No better paean, the source for Nikos Kazantzakis's own biographical rendition of the saint with no clothes. If all humankind adopted St Francis as their role model; moved through this world with the methodical gait of the Digambara monk, all but possessionless, consuming only those walnuts half-eaten by the squirrels, lounging in the spirit of Todaville, unencumbered by all aspiration, acquitted of goals, the world would quickly shape up, he believed. Poverty, Antonian asceticism, was the answer. Simplicity.

These philosophies all called for an economic revivification, in a sense; a reallocation of assets such that bankruptcy was aspired to; material wealth recast in the guise of village life, such as could be gleaned among the Bhutanese, or Karen tribe of Myanmar. Or the fifteenth-century Chinese renouncing their Navy; the Japanese, under Shogun Ieyasu, their guns. The deconstruction of the Broadway overpass in San Francisco, and the virtual decommissioning of the New Zealand Air Force. These small poetic gestures accumulated a significance of mendicancy in Marigold's mind; suggested the tonic of halting destruction by simply stopping.

An end, in other words, to all economic progress so that an alternative banner could be raised.

And what was that? Sannazaro asked wryly, after Marigold had seen fit to knock on the door of his adjoining suite, and rouse him from his slumber just so he could share his latest enthusiasm.

"Why, the realization that poverty is an asset; that a world of paupers would resemble the rainforests of the Amazon or Indonesia—a huge ecological sink that recycled itself and prevented destruction."

"That's crazy," said the Italian. "Yes, poverty all too clearly replicates itself. But we've had this discussion, and I would submit that you have, on previous occasions, fought to liberate victims from their slums. Or did I miss something?"

"You did miss one thing," the Commander importuned. "Liberate, yes, but not at the expense of the whole natural world."

"I fail to see your solution, old man."

"Then you are not looking artfully at the topic. Let crops be sown, mass unemployment transformed into simple tasks each day, as first outlined in Lycurgus's constitution for Sparta. After all, the relief paid out by welfare exceeded the income enjoyed by the wealthy yeoman of 500 years ago."

"Your point?" Sannazaro pressed, no less cynical.

"My point?" The Commander turned it around and around in his head. "My point is, simply, that there is more dignity in pennilessness than in all the fortunes of the world. I would rather be a beggar child in downtown Jakarta than a billionaire."

"Hmmm. You've yet to prove it. And even if you did, what would it actually prove?"

"You'll see."

But Marigold knew that those who studied poverty—scholars like the Rev. John McFarlane of Edinburgh who wrote *Inquiries Concerning the Poor* in 1782, or Amos Warner in the late nineteenth century—were not concerned with other species, but with blaming the poor themselves. Warner believed that at least 25 percent of all poor people deserved to be poor on account of their sloth. In the first half of the twentieth century, B. Seebohm Rowntree broke open the myth of mere indigence, conducted three surveys in York and determined that poverty was a function of too many dependants. Overpopulation, not laziness.

That for Marigold was the answer: a man and his dog should be the icon for the new century. Let one-child families define the shape and size of the human contingent. Let all excess destroy itself. Generations that had exceeded their family carrying capacity would (harsh though it sounded) die out. Draconian genetics, disease vectors, would accomplish that saving grace, he fathomed. Survival of the fittest. Let the fit be poor, the fittest the most poor. And as populations in country after country withered and expired, non-human populations would rebound. It was a certainty. Until, ultimately, would come a balance. The signs of renewal would show up initially in all those regions of greatest fallout, the wounded supersized Alzheimered tail piped and diaper sludged shadow towns of concrete, bad dream ecosystems, whether Sea of Gdansk, Shanghai or LA.

The collective weight of all these monastic novelties flooded Marigold's late-night fevers of computational urgency long after his Squire had returned to bed. His goal was no different from before. Only now he had added the muster of meteorite showers and the crisis of Jacques to his profound nonsense. Was he right, was he wrong? The new Malthus, or the old? It did not matter. Here was a billionaire with a plan for a radical social contract, and that was a dangerous thing. Would anybody listen, would anyone care?

However he got to his *éclaircissement*, the vision by which all pains, ills, incongruities, inequities and human falterings might be eradicated was overwhelming. He rushed out into the hallway, banged on his Squire's adjoining suite again, shouted, "Iacobo! I've hatched the solution!", then proceeded to lay out what was, indeed, an uncanny notion.

CHAPTER 170

A Summit in La Mancha

"TO BE UNILATERALLY relieved of their fortunes," the Commander contemplated aloud, the air of Spain in his lungs, as he sojourned past one princely, broad-stroked Velázquez after another in the company of his son and Squire. All around them, the Prado was hemorrhaging hikers, tote bags, Instamatics, as tour buses from Kiev and Hamburg disgorged their summery flocks.

The Commander was thinking back to everything Sam Turbovsky had said at Catherine Champion's house all those months ago in Santa Fe. He'd hit it right on the nose. Universal poverty, or (more precisely) pure, well-intended, benign and noble simplicity, was the answer to the world's environmental woes. Equal opportunity starting from scratch. A complete ruination of fiscal fashions and social discrepancies. A return to the Jeremiah Johnsons and medieval Jesuits of wilderness reclusion.

"Look at that little boy!" yelped Rajibai, impressed by the painter's barrage of velvety apparels. "Might I have such a suit, Father?" he implored.

His father, however, saw only the squandering of riches; the decadent history of empire, all belied by the superb green landscapes.

"But that is my point, Son." Marigold would never say "No" to the child, but let his vote remain in silence, a dangling modifier for further study—not that Rajibai entirely understood.

Feeling the first pangs of an ulcer, the Commander had hit the ground zero of futile excess; was wearied to breaking point by so much useless ardor. All around him, ineluctable desuetudes, debilitations. Carnage proliferating at the same speed as the reproducing flies atop it. There was every evidence of these disasters in the paintings before him, and in the canvases of life that had weighed on his mind since childhood. We are a species of spurious dimensions, no reason at all for being on Earth, he reasoned to himself. There was no purpose to humanity. Goodness, virtue—these were scarcely sufficient recompense for our inflictions. No destiny guided our way. No lamp lit our path. No God watched out for us. Why should He?

Whereas his son had never taken even one aspirin (though considerable quantities of more illicit drugs and alcohol since joining the Commander's unbridled retinue). For the father, a sustained pessimism punctuated by an occasional burst of life that harbored the seeds of self-destruction in every hope. Whilst his boy was just sitting down to enjoy the concert that was life, unconcerned, without dialectic. Or, as the busy writer Scott once alluded to, even a world turned upside down provided those with a mind to butter and break their bread the rudiments and community of kindred spirits with which to do so.

Still immersed in the immeasurable, unrivaled Prado, the Squire sat on a stone bench, quietly considering his own disturbing, invisible thoughts. He knew that he was somewhere in between his two companions, old and wise enough to reconcile both extremes of the human heart, though lacking sufficient patience to make the effort—the consequences of which translated in a peculiar, if life-affirming, symmetry between the three of them. But he was no dummy, either. He knew that being poor was no fun; that money could be used towards good, rather than ill. Surely he and the Commander had already proven that. But he failed to grasp the brilliance of the Commander's larger philosophy, a scheme which—if it were to work—might take the human race back to the time before radio, to a life in caves. Electronic mail superseded by signals in the smoke.

"It will make for a very smoky planet," the Squire commented. "CO_2 levels will skyrocket."

They hurried past the galleries, and through the streets of Madrid, out of town, their driver dispatching them towards La Mancha where the Commander had leased a castle and called a gathering of the world's more than 400 billionaires. The locale could not have had a more implicit recommendation or rationale, for this was Cervantes country.

Anyone familiar with that portion of south-central Spain between the capital and Andalucia knows it is here a steamy steppe of lurking bogs, there a desiccated vineyard, with scarcely a hint of any heraldic glory. The unsuspecting traveler, searching in vain for cooler airs, eyes glued upon the scorched upper atmospheres, catches sight, now and then, of a purple Iberian heron migrating elsewhere, and realizes only too latethat his feet are sinking in the treacherous quicksands of Ojos de Guadiana. Struggling to extricate himself, the hapless enthusiast is soon entangled to the point of madness or medical emergency in the wicked brambles of Ruidera, or endlessly condemned to wading tit-deep through those mosquito-multiplying lagoons which lead by inexorable turns for hundreds of legua, or Spanish leagues, to that notorious canyon of bandits—Desfiladero de Despenaperros—where is inscribed upon a high, leaning slab, *Lasciate ogni speranza voi ch'entrate* (All hope abandon, ye who enter here, from Dante). Little wonder most Castizo Spaniards think of this vast series of backwaters and barrens as a living Hell, despite the occasional farmer's daughter, charming innkeeper and happy-go-lucky brewer.

But the sunken flatlands are littered with menacing cul-de-sacs, back roads of melancholy fields and deserted horizons through the Campo de Calatrava, signs everywhere indicating *Este carretera no funciona* and warning of *averia*, and monastic ruins adrift in petrified sheep turd and various barbs. All this mire butts up against the inaccessible Sierra de Alandia, hills soured with the obnoxious tailings of mercury, coal and zinc.

In spite of the region's shortcomings, the great Cervantes had, hundreds of years prior to Marigold's own arrival, managed to find desirable lodgings for his wizened knight throughout this spooky La Mancha, at villages like Puerto Lapice with its Venta del Quixote; at Consuegra, noted for ten windmills and its famed saffron-larded paella; at El Toboso, where one lovely Dulcinea resides now for eternity; or at the Alpera Caves of La Vieja, known for their handprints and miraculous mirages.

Of course, all is not lost in La Mancha. Wine is still fermented in tinajas, gigantic Roman-storied jars, fashioned of earth, some—like those in the Valley of Stones, Valdepenas— holding more than 4,000 gallons. In fact, the great variety of jovens, crianzas and reservas makes the Avenida del Vino one of Spain's most attractive tourist haunts, the Napa/Sonoma of Europe. Perhaps it was on this account that the lonely, tortured Cervantes went searching one day, after years in prison, for a fine field of Cencibel grape and some excellent Manchego cheese, wandering with a flock of Merino sheep whose milk—properly treated by a liquor from the golden *Cynara cardunculus* thistle and rendered into a Torta de La Serena— made for the most excellent of cheese cakes, according to some; and that Marigold in homage to the ever-elusive artist had chosen a medieval castle in the very same vicinity of Campo de Criptana to host this unusual gathering.

The Commander's impulses were guided by a decisive ambition calculated to accomplish everything needed in the world, as he now perceived it. A vaporous pie in the sky of devilish and fantastically wrought details. Eco-political revolution; an ethical renaissance sweeping the entire human community; economic subterfuge on a global scale that sought to eliminate the culprit at the perpetual root of all woes: money.

So how did he propose to separate this money from its duly appointed owners? Sannazaro mildly inquired.

By implementing the worst scare in all eternity, the Commander vowed. Taking the most erudite, global message, and transforming it into a rallying cry that any sensible person could get behind. Giving the super-rich to consider that they alone possessed the means to save themselves and their loved ones, where the scientific community and those governments in the know had failed to do so. In short, he explained, to get out while there was still time.

Sannazaro scratched his head, feeling more than ever a slight pressure building behind his eyes, a foreboding of what it might be like to live somewhere other than on Earth. "Could you possibly clarify what it is you're actually saying? I don't like the smell of this."

"To build a lavish space station and the rockets to get them there; to colonize the moon in luxury!" Marigold announced. "Not since Eugene Cernan and Harrison Schmitt walked the moon in December of 1972 have humans trod there—a tragedy, considering what could be gained by evacuating the Earth of all people. Nixon was sensitive to criticisms that the money was better spent on more meat in school lunches. He abolished Apollo after that, no longer focused on the gains that could be reaped, like cranberry juice in the form of a pill."

"I still don't follow how you expect these rich cats to agree on anything, even if they do recognize the peril of which you speak," the Squire countered. "They are competitors, cutthroats, gangsters. What force of cohesion could accommodate their chaos or meld their antipathy into teamwork?"

Marigold carefully considered this. His Governor was no dunderhead. But, as he'd said, these billionaires were as much interested in wealth preservation as self-preservation, and that could only work in favor of their relocating from a doomed planet.

In essence, he intended to found a whole new biological civilization within the next eleven years, before it was too late—or that's what he'd tell them. Four hundred and twelve billionaires, multiplied, on average, by 51: the realistic average number of extended family members, cousins, secretaries, business confidants, lawyers and close friends each of the billionaires should be permitted to bring along, for a total of less than 21,000 people. It was doable, as long as the shuttles commenced their outgoing activities within seven years, he calculated.

Why should they believe him? Because he had the proof.

"What might that be?" Sannazaro finally pressed.

"Dingst's video," Marigold reminded him. They had seen it at the lab in Copenhagen, a composite of Hamidi's findings and a video of the screaming meteorite above Greenlandia. "What's more," he went on, "we have images from Gerard, and the confessions of the Danish Academy. It all fits together. I lend the indisputable glue—that and my money as an example."

"And if they confer with the National Academy of Sciences, NASA, JPL, or wherever else they're likely to go for confirmation?"

"Let them. Government denials are the essence of any conspiracy theory. In this case, it will be clear to our filthy-rich compatriots that the governments of the world do not want to induce a decade of global pandemonium. Especially if there is the slightest chance that Dingst was mistaken, which for purposes of this ruse we may assume he was, given his final reassurances that life would go on."

"So … We're going to send them all to the moon?" Sannazaro's voice tailed off. "What does it accomplish?"

"Moron, think! They will spend all of their trillions on this comic effort—collectively, we are probably looking at 30 trillion in assets, by my reckoning—which will more or less deplete the entire human population of 90 percent of its portfolios and long-term spending sprees. No more mutual funds, corporations, stockholders, board members, futures markets, speculations. The end of capitalization stocks, convertible securities, investment-grade and high-yielding bonds. *Fini* to equity asset classes, *nada* to all those yield-to-maturity manias. No more real estate, multinationals or investments. Goodbye to fees, distributions, concentrations, asset-allocation targets, goals and risk parameters. No longer the discrepancy between North and South, or the rampant disparities between the developed and developing peoples of the world. Imagine, Iacobo! Equity, egalitarianism, liberty. Like a man and his dog asleep on a park bench. No worries."

"Lunacy in the pit of their stomachs. Hunger in their eyes. You speak of tomfoolery! Your head shines like a vacant stare!"

"I want to go to the moon, as well!" cried Rajibai.

"You may consider this my last attempt at human redemption," exclaimed the Commander to his Squire as they checked in to their 40,000-square-foot castle, leased for the week from an astonished agency representative in Albacete who was more accustomed to dealing with agricultural colleges for a fortnight here, a weekend there. "And I assure you, once the gathering is in place, they will either buy into my argument, or not. Either way, we should have an outcome within an hour or so."

"I pray this be so," replied Sannazaro. "For honestly, I am in no mood for cold showers and humble meals, scorpions in my bed and the braying of mules all night outside the window. Moreover, I am sure you've noticed, the castle has no air conditioning. And the electricity is erratic."

"I noticed."

Marigold's concept was a simple one, if considered in the context of the last 60 or so Nobel Prizes for Economics. This was, more or less, how he described it to his companions once they were nicely settled beneath down comforters, their three Emperor-sized canopy beds forming, roughly, a little asterisk in the center of a 4,000-square-foot room. The walls were of a greasy reja, or grillwork, rounded out by a splash of second-rate designer Old Masters, from the 17th and 18th centuries. Obscure personages of a gentrified Spain.

"Consider," said he, "the world's poverty. Of what does it consist? Lack of money, certainly. But there is more to it than too few coins in one's pocket. Poverty such as you, dearest child, most certainly experienced is a pattern which proves itself 100 times a day. Success within poverty perpetuates poverty. Now what do I mean by that—"

"Indeed," Sannazaro interjected. "What do you mean by that?"

"The British laborer who works a full-time job now earns more than 20,000 pounds a year. With that, he can scarcely escape debt or fulfill his dreams. Yet, he works like a squirrel perpetually facing winter. And I don't mean our spoiled squirrels at the Oasis. He drives in a leased car (polluting no less) whose payments are killing him, or takes a large and noisy train, plastered amid other dreary commuters, five days of every week, through *Bleak House* surroundings that have the look and truth of bombed-out remains. Filth and concrete, steel and all that is inorganic about the world are his companions. Such scenery must weigh upon the human heart, I assure you. Prepare it for a life of dimmed hopes. He grows old, having grabbed two weeks here, a medical leave there, while his children go off to the pub for entertainment, with bullet-for-brains tattoos on their nicked arms and cheap earrings to make fools of themselves, then disappear altogether once they have found the means to jettison their crazy bones from the house of their ancestors, names forgotten. Go on to some accountant's life, salesman's life, insurance agent's life. Go on to high-cholesterol, marrow-sucking years with no particular point, just each day, staying out of trouble. Any concern for their neighbor? Community? The last grove of trees or the birds dependent on them? The odd outside chance of altruism, a little flame of courage, a spurt of high profile and patriotism. But beyond the rare largesse—the little gesture at the market, Sunday supper with the minorities on the block—"

"Why spoil the lad so early on with such cynicism?" Sannazaro wondered. But the Commander had his own ideas about the last of the necessities, as he thought of them; knew well how little time there really was to effect a damn thing, and was not worried as Sannazaro was of offending the innocence in his boy. After all, they were different now, each one of them. The waterfall, the Jains, Crowquill and 100 other events and personages had certainly cast them onto some alternative plateau, or island of conscience, thought the Commander. They had a responsibility, if they had anything at all, and making it clear what the boy was here to do meant everything now. The purpose in living. No more flexing of useless muscles in an unattended circus, no expression without an ear to hear it, passion without audience, love without receiver. Happiness alone in giving to others.

Sannazaro understood these things because he heavily comprehended his friend, had watched him go from nowhere to everywhere, and seen in a very short time a traumatized boy become a precocious young man, all on account of the Commander's remarkable way with him. So he listened.

"And this is considered success, by the Western model," Marigold continued, neither shrill nor dim, but clear; still referring to the poor English slattern, downtrodden like some historic model of oppression in the Commander's mind. "His whole of life, and that of his spouse, has been sacrificed on behalf of a certain security. Even the dreariest technical tomes in continental logic concern themes less stringent. Yet he does not see it. Every travel brochure to Majorca or the Canaries only excites his false sense of accomplishment that much more. If he makes it to 70, his semi-detached flat nearly paid off, his golf clubs, his deer antlers, the memory of some mistress 20 years before still ripe in his mind, and can claim no experience of prostate, colon, lung or pancreatic cancer, or a quintuple bypass, he considers himself the luckiest sonofabitch alive.

And why? Because he *is* alive, which may be enough. He can sup on his canned crabmeats, play darts with his mates, gamble on the races and read about the latest lottery winner. Defame the Royals, memorize the *Bible*, join a gun club, sample neighborhood garage sales, watch cable soft porn, lease an RV, drive to the Grand Canyon or Cornwall."

"But that's just one narrow vision," Sannazaro chided him.

"It's several billion narrow visions, I would wager," Marigold countered. "Meanwhile, his soul is nearly dead, and has been perishing for most of his life."

"But how can one actually know anything at all about the soul, Father?"

Rajibai threw out. "It's not visible, is it?"

"Son, I look at you and see a soul that is burning and alive, eager to explore each day anew, unmindful of trouble or want. Whereas—"

"Perhaps," Sannazaro said, "that's because his old man's a bloody billionaire!"

"Ahh, but take the slum dweller in Forlorn, for example. Since we all know what that's like—you, Son, far more than either Uncle or me." And he went on to formulate his philosophy of the poor—an undigested gruel of canned ideas and paperback assumptions, which is not to denigrate the Commander but simply to point out, if pointing is ever necessary, that Sannazaro was correct in saying "*Le style est l'homme même.*" There was no changing the Commander's habit of creating a world to suit his ideas. That went for the poor, as well, whom he idealized as surely as Poussin. Only the Commander could think of a garbage dump as a science exam; the chemical spill as a massive form of shock therapy; the end of the world as a sanitarium. These odd associations escalated in his mind like popping corn at the first mention of the billionaires' club— men and women whose colossally silly pleasures were surely draining the world of its vitality, he insisted, whilst ensuring that the majority of all other people had little food, water, sanitation, health care, education or money. Any money at all. While dark-skinned peoples despoiled in vast numbers, puny increments of ecological, plant and animal woes from Indonesia to New Jersey, an accumulating dark tunnel of jumbled squatting rights, toothpick-sized deforestation, tulip-weighted defoliation, other more serious white-appropriation loomed even larger: the bigger fellows, the ones driving the world trading organizations, manufacturing the hundreds of thousands of chemicals, fueling the consumption, setting the trends with advertising. These were the heaviest offenders. Diet aids, obesity, military budgets.

He had delicately calculated the rate of destruction occasioned by the rich, by contrast with the poor, using as his baseline the negative impact of wealth accumulation upon the health of biological communities and individuals. Charting such consequences was absolutely key, of course, to any meaningful computation of fiscal fanaticism, he explained: "We know that every medium household of four in the United States, for example, consumes x-number of pounds of meat, dairy and other animal by-products, while purchasing y-number of other environmentally unfriendly products. Their average income, 20,000 dollars per year. For every dollar, then, there is a known percentage of overall consumption directed against Mother Nature. The most harmful purchases comprise an automobile and a fuel-inefficient house, water use, land consumption, sprays, pesticides and building materials. The other deadly sector of consumption includes food, clothing, travel, paper and cleaning products, utensils, and medical (read: animal) testing. To all of these we can assign the full 20,000 dollar annual income stream. Now, hear this—I have oft repeated, every dollar equals, symbolically, one dead animal, though it's actually much worse."

"How did you come to that appraisal?" Sannazaro puzzled, not doubting, just wanting to understand, having forgotten the data.

But the Commander lost him in his vague stretch of formulas, equations, allocations and equivalencies. He argued that the cost per pound of chicken, multiplied by a family of four, divided by the dollars and cents invested in a lunch or dinner, was a fairly accurate portrayal of life in the twenty-first century, reflecting upon more than just chicken sandwiches, or T-bone steaks, but quantifiable with respect to every chemical, piece of wood, unrecycled sheet of paper, the trees lost to a new suburb, and the multiple generations of birds whose time would never come, because of a wealthy land speculator today. Indeed, the Commander had taken the early Club of Rome techniques, and those of the State Department's *Global 2000 Report*, and adjusted for medium income streams times the nine billion chickens killed every year in the US (nearly 55 billion per year worldwide) times all the other species (turkeys, cows, horses, sheep, pigs, et cetera), broken out into individual lives, country by country. The numbers were overwhelming and the only way to get a handle on them, he insisted, was by looking at the overall economy. He'd done it before.

"A 60-trillion-dollar global economy," he went on, "translates to 60 trillion dead animals. And that's just the first generation. Now think in terms of a century, each animal modeled in its life span somewhere between the butterfly (one year) and the Caspian sturgeon (300 years). If there are still 50 million species at large ..." and he went on to figure for himself certain coefficients, trying to stay on top of all the multiplication tables ... "well, I believe a single dollar actually translates into 150 parts of individuals, which is like one whole individual across a certain range of species, and that would mean 7,500 trillion animals each year, or 75,000 trillion animals per century. Divided by six billion present human citizens of the planet, that translates into roughly 12,500 dead creatures for every person, every year, or 34 per day. My blood boils for the victims of certain traditions—the rams slaughtered in Damascus during Id al-Adha, for example, or the bulls at Pamplona. But it is everywhere. Every child, every parent, somehow manages by his and her indifference and consumerist laziness to slaughter 34 such rams every 24 hours. And I am including only the known species. For every identified bug, there may be 10,000 unidentified. That puts us up into the quadrillions. If I were a Jain, I would also include the commensural bacteria living aboard those animals, but then the numbers of downed critters would be beyond anybody's powers to grasp. Or certainly mine. We're talking the number of dust motes in the whole world, or grains of sand, or atoms in the full universe." Reinvigorated computations.

Sannazaro could not keep up. "Get back to the point."

"The point, Señor? Lose the majority of wealth, and the whole battery of disastrous occupation crumbles. Undermine the battlements of the rich, tear away the covers of the invaders, plunder the vaults, rape the repositories, radically turn away all dollars and cents, impound the mints, break up the banks, terminate all trusts, gut the garrisons, and the rest might ever find a way to work it out. All the glaring discrepancies might be eradicated if only the super-rich would ... leave!"

"Hmmm..." Sannazaro applied, picking a sesame seed from his teeth.

"And can you think of a better place for them to go than the moon?" the Commander concluded with a naughty smile that he shared with his son.

"Mercury," replied his faithful Squire.

CHAPTER 171
A Praying Mantis in the Wondershed

THE THREE NUTCASES slept in the castle's coro, a finely filigreed room, darkened by the ages, segregated in soot of the Churrigueresque style, that once heard the belting harmonies of a local choir. The Republican Army had contributed many countertenors during the early 1930s, on each Sunday, the one day exempted from target practice. Much of the castle was bombarded during Franco's Civil War, and only restored at great cost by an hidalgo of high social ambition. His 400-year-old inherited coat-of-arms—the Brightly Sprayed Cuckold—became, by means of a suitable donation to the regional Documentation League, the Leaping Barbary Ape, to coincide with the launching of Sputnik and a political partnership with the Communists in the region. This embattled alliance accounted for the strange satellite-transmission facility housed in a dilapidated bach in one corner of the eleven-hectare estate. The parts for the receiving station did not amount to much: a radio transmitter that no longer worked, some odd bells and whistles now mobbed by cobwebs of various sizes, dust of several generations, old farm tools with no place else to reside and, most precious, a photograph of Kruschev bowling with Franco at an alley in Moscow, signed by both men and framed in shattered glass. Rajibai, of course, had no idea who these two old farts might be, as he occupied himself the following morning in the shed, turning over every mysterious pile, rummaging through painted tin picnic boxes and turd-infested shelves.

Outside, a herd of frisky Murciana bucks and gopher-eared does were foraging. On a distant ridge, there were nine windmills, their cylindrical stone towers painted white beneath the dark conical summits.

Across the lawns, inside the main manor, the Commander and his Squire sat waiting in the mahogany and red sandstone vestibule, ready to receive. Sometime after 11 a.m., a stream of security personnel swarmed down to sweep for any bombs, each reporting into his cellphone. Soon thereafter assorted limousines and unmarked helicopters began delivering the invited billionaires to their eccentric meeting point. How Marigold had managed to persuade those in control of 80 percent of all human wealth to show up in one ghastly castle stems from that side of the man little appreciated by most of the world: namely, his ability to enrich the truth, as they say, when necessary. In this case, his dramatic description of the impending catastrophe in eleven years.

Such chicanery was summed up in the way Marigold had handled himself at a certain press conference at the conclusion of the Budapest conference days previously. Newsmen had flocked to his sensational exposure of the Danish cover-up. NASA could not deny a mysterious explosion over Greenlandia, just as the Commander had alleged (there were too many amateur astronomers across Scandinavia to back him up), forcing the Danish Foreign Secretary to admit that two military jets had not collided as previously reported. The videos. The other data. The accumulation of incriminating evidence added up in the many minds of those present.

Presently, after all the news flashes across Europe, the Commander received his distinguished guests in the castle's reception room. Marigold personally spoke with the Sultan of Hay-Wain, who had made his gobs trading in museums, which he bought entire and sold without the slightest show of emotion. He then moved on to greet the Royal Court at Redmond, whose half-dozen billionaires controlled a large number of the world's digital technologies, and various moghuls from the U.A.E. to La Défènce. He'd needed to make more than 400 phone calls from his lodgings in Budapest to get them here. There was Victor Hamaz, whose family had refinanced Egypt in exchange for private ownership of the pyramids and the Nile; the 19-year-old Canadian pop phenomenon, Juicy Girl, who had acquired all the mining rights on the moon as a lark, only to learn of their significance in the present context; King Mayood Malcontenta, who owned most of the salt marshes in Iraq and Saudi Arabia, from which the resident mosquitoes had provided a miracle cure for malaria and yellow fever; Sir Galworthy Grim, the first man to break the 100 billion mark for having acquired all electronic rights to the *Bible*, and the copyright on apples—all apples; Douglas Surefire, the principal owner of the Amazon; Gajijahoohoo, proprietor of over 1,000 islands in Indonesia, and so on.

Some had traded in human organs, or weapons of mass destruction, like red mercury. Many had earned or inherited their fortunes off the misery of others—slave-trading in Thailand, sweatshops in Korea, porn, chemicals, fossil fuels, slaughterhouses, soap and shampoos, shoes, shipping, lumber, metals, real estate, re-insurance. A few had cleaner pedigrees—broadcasting, publishing, vaccines, virtual reality, computers. But only the Commander could claim absolute immunity to all sin, for who could fault the inherited proceeds of an innocent night of gambling more than 150 years before?

For each of these elaborate pomposities, personalities driven by bulwarks and bastions of family bullion, the Commander had the same message, which he now repeated to the assembled multitude. They were configured uneasily in the main chapel of the castle, name tags before each privatized pew, a rampart of security guards heavily bolstering the red earth and white plaster exterior.

"Welcome, all of you, to La Mancha. Collectively, you control the vast majority of all wealth in the twenty-first century. But to what end? In eleven years, the planet we inhabit will be reduced to burnt cinder. The greatest living astrogeophysicists have confirmed this, though—as can be expected—no government agencies will subscribe to the theory. We all, in combination, have enough money to finance our salvation and that of those we love ..."

And he went on to describe his plan for getting the 21,000 privileged ones out into space in time.

Whatever doubts—a hoax?—lingered, there was no mistaking the momentum of fear generated by the Commander's words. He pressed his advantage. "In earlier times," he said, "progress was often masked by scorn and ridicule. Oil, the automobile, electricity, the atom, the fuel cell, even the personal computer. Let us not similarly mask the end of progress with denial. There is still time, for those of us with the foresight, the spine, the spunk. Pitch in, do your part, embrace change. There is no technical reason why the standards to which you are all accustomed cannot be relocated to the moon. Granted, there will be no Paris or Milan for your wives to shop in; no gaming tables at Monte Carlo or yacht cruises in the Aegean. But together we will create equivalents on the spectacular lunar surface. And remember, with one-sixth the gravity, everyone of you will enjoy a whole new personal mobility."

He went on to describe in astonishing detail the metaphysics of life on the moon, using such rousing expressions as "astral catharsis", "planetary perspicuity", "the homelife of the sand king", "hegemonies untaxed, uncensored, unburdened by mass hysteria, global warming, or the market fluctuations, anxieties and jealousy of billions of other people". He enumerated the physiological advantages of lunar life for *Homo sapiens* (none of which bore even a grain of scientific accuracy), and outlined "a day in the life of the moon" that was certain to calm all fears of loneliness, heartbreak, nausea and diminished sexual appetite.

"Indeed," he concluded, "NASA specialists have frequently alluded to the fact lunar orgasms should prove far more satisfying and prolonged, for reasons combining low gravity with higher concentrations of oxygen in the bloodstream." (Again a Marigold, as it were.) "Where can we build the rockets so that the public will not catch wind of our enterprise?" inquired the richest man in Hong Kong—a real-estate tycoon, who'd recently purchased Mount Victoria for eight billion dollars and was only too mindful of that obvious scenario—the hoi polloi finding out, storming the elite command center, slaughtering the rich, undermining the whole effort for everyone.

"That is not a problem," replied a cigar-slurping boulder of a man from Amarillo, the most irritating of all the cattle barons in Texas. He knew security issues, and controlled his own paramilitary force to combat rustlers. And who could forget the secret Japanese launching site in the movie *Contact*.

For an entire day the champions of high finance worked out the elusive details. Each volunteered his net worth, most of them skimping on the edges, holding out hope the entire plan would prove unnecessary within a few years. But even so, their network as a group exceeded 45 trillion, if one took in their bonds, properties, stocks and other holdings. With that much money, the moon could well be re-engineered to resemble Rodeo Drive: dead craters transformed into Gulf Drive in Naples, Florida; inland seas fashioned with their own resorts. There would be no need of skyscrapers. The town would be built according to Santa Fe's master plan: adobe dwellings; homes an average 40,000 square feet; all energy manufactured with solar-powered fuel cells. Water would be sucked from deep in the moon's surface, where it existed between layers of magma. Nanotechnology would easily serve every need, from thermostats to control ambient indoor temperatures to surgical technology. Five hundred of the greatest opera singers, storytellers, aboriginal elders, bakers and gardeners would be brought along, as well as other professionals in natural sciences and healing arts. Plumbers and electricians, too. And of course, the Vienna Philharmonic. And all situated under a massive mesh to catch meteorites a mile high.

Marigold had carefully constructed his fantasy to appeal to the worst instincts in man, knowing that history would prove him right. There was no greater incentive than survival. He was certain that, confronted with disaster, and the corresponding hope of saving themselves and their families, the lunar scenario could only galvanize a desperate consensus. Moreover, each family would be entitled to one million acres, according to his plan. The rest of the moon would be held in common for mineral exploitation and old-fashioned exploration.

And the space station itself ? A gargantuan floating garden, a Zen monastery replete with spas, juice bars, squash courts, a media center and dry-cleaner, 1,000 other customary stalls, tavernas, art galleries, gourmet grocery stores, designer boutiques, antique shops, et cetera, all drifting in space like some cosmic Calder, overlooking the past, peering into the future (second and third cousins could work behind the counters.) It was all possible, reiterated Marigold. The rudiments had been prefigured for Mars in the guise of terraforming. The moon would be a snap, by comparison. Less than 700,000 miles away—two years' worth of Frequent Flier miles for some.

During these momentous discussions, Rajibai remained thrashing about in the wondershed with a family of curious goats, sifting through several centuries of antique castoffs and all the fascinating spare parts that had been lodged in a cellar. Brushing aside the spiders which hung in a gallery of protective looms, pulling off the accumulation of broken-down stone wall, hewing through bricks, charging past ceramic shards, dispatching old pieces of pipe, odd sections of timber, on all fours he broke into a treasure chest neatly hidden behind a stonemason's hurried attempt at concealment, and, using a pair of pliers to twist off the rusted King's lock, discovered to his profound disappointment nothing inside but a dried-up praying mantis, its peculiar body more than likely dead for centuries. Around its minute neck was fitted a name tag and handwritten instructions, though they were impossible to read, the arcane cursive having run together from centuries of damp. In addition, there was a large chunk of glittering lagoon-green crystal, its facets sparkling against a dried out inkhorn and pen; a lamp still glowing with a dim lead-yellow light (odd? he wondered), its limp wick a pale remnant of a fuse; and a partially moth-digested rug from the Levant or thereabouts, in whose delicately worn entrails was hidden a shiny copper salad bowl or barber's lather dish. Rajibai stared into it and saw instead an old man wearing a soldier's helmet in which was reflected a salad bowl reflecting a second soldier's helmet reflecting the goofy guileless dementia of a boy who looked identical to, and was in fact, Rajibai himself.

He threw down the basin for rightful fear of losing his Marigolded mind betwixt several advancing armies of salad bowls, barbers and soldiers.

A goat promptly snatched the bowl—or whatever it was—between its bicuspids, and sauntered off towards the castle.

Suddenly, the praying mantis began creaking, each of its severe appendages cavorting into motion, hovering around a first breath and a long-suppressed sneeze, whereupon it spat up a gob of tender slime, before shaking out its head, getting back some color to its tawny armament and sluggishly reviving itself by means of alchemical resolve. The eight-inch creature began speaking thus: "Good sir, what day is it?"

Rajibai gazed upon the braying animalcule and recited, "Saturday, of course."

The bug shrugged, leaping with one great reach 95 times his height in order to arrive upon Rajibai's shoulder, and yawned enormously. His head slowly jerked from angle to angle, spying upon the known world.

"How odd a sensation," he half-opined philosophically.

"Is something wrong?" asked the boy.

"There was a castle, a moat, a lovely maiden and my horse."

"The castle is there," explained the boy, and he took the mantis outside to see for himself.

"Ahhh! But what beasts of burden are those?" inquired the insect.

"Those are called Rolls Royces," said Rajibai.

Now the little creature sought cover: he had spied two parked helicopters, their rotors slowly turning. Rajibai tried to allay his fears, explaining that these were machines, not insect-eating birds.

"They must be Roman, then," whispered the unnerved stick figure. "They were the ones who introduced toilets and aqueducts to these parts, though long before my time. Now where were we?" The mantis scratched his head with his long stick of a paw and tried to remember. "Something left undone? A place to which we were headed?"

"Who is we?"

"I don't know." He scratched some more, perplexed as someone emerging after many hours of general anesthetic—which wasn't at all far from the truth.

"The crystal. Where is the crystal?" rallied the mantis.

The boy returned to the cellar, took up the crystal to the light and there beheld a melange of meaningless milestones and awkward nuances, half-explications and failed reincarnations, clarities darkling bright, personages obscured and unlikely creatures many. He held it so that the insect could see for himself, though at first glance could not quite make out the optical plane of sight. Then he caught the wave: "Don Fernando! Gines! Lady Oriana! You, Lion! And lo! Could that be my dear Don Diego de Miranda!" He went on this way until he slumped back, tears streaking his little face, despairing of so many obviously poignant memoirs.

"Oh Purgatory," the insect wailed.

"But what's wrong?" cried Rajibai, full of empathy.

"If they are visible in the crystal, then they are surely dead. Something terrible has happened!"

CHAPTER 172

The Tears of Angelica, the Wonderful Shoulder Blades of Ercilla

INSIDE THE CASTLE, an even stranger hubbub recommended the old adage that only under fire do cold hearts warm their portions in company with one another. So much greed had never in the history of our kind agreed. Who would buy the O-rings, the toilet articles, manufacture the hydrogen rocket fuel, or do the catering. Every detail needed working through. Multiplied by 21,000 calculating heirs, conniving cousins and ardent associates, every contribution, however hard-pressed, squeezed like an unripe lime, was significant.

There would be no taxes on the moon, no guns, no loud music. A one-child policy was codified as part of the Magna Lunarchia, signifying from the start a firm constitutional understanding by which the billionaires would sort out their inevitable gripes. Mr Marigold pointed out to his distinguished colleagues that they could not afford blood and guts, rubbish or fumes in a clean-room environment. That meant absolutely no fertilizers, fossil fuels or animal by-products. In short, an environmentally stable micro-environment—but one that would not suffer from the CELS syndrome. He was referring to NASA's "closed ecological life support systems" which had been enacted in Arizona at the Biosphere 2 project. Fewer than 100 representative species from all over the globe had been carefully selected and a small covey of scientists sealed themselves in for two years across a few acres. But the whole project collapsed because, as the Commander summarized its shortcomings, there was not a single "wild fruit". The moon, on the other hand, would offer more space, and the billionaires could pump trillions of dollars into seeing that tens of thousands of species took up residency in their new shared habitat. Life would be different, but life would be possible.

Moreover, no financial competition between them would be allowed until the 21,000 were well settled. Nor a word of this meeting in any document or transmission. Not so much as a whisper anywhere on Earth, but rather, a vast conspiracy of silence. All agreed, while their hundreds of billions began to flow into the useless Rube Goldberg of chimeras, to be housed in a rocket silo 800 feet beneath the Texas desert. Posterity should credit the Illustrious Mr Marigold (though not forget either Dingst or Hamidi) for ringleading the mischievous caprice.

Outside, Rajibai was touring the exterior of the castle with the creature riding shotgun. "But the moat is gone," remarked the *Mantis religiosa*, extending his strong spines, femur and coxae towards some unawakened past that was no more. Then a goat, the lather basin having somehow been affixed to its head by a cord, strolled by.

"The mitred Dapple!" shrieked the mantis, his little prothorax straining.

Rajibai rolled on the ground with laughter, nearly doing in the guest upon his shoulder, and rescued the goat from its predicament. Suddenly, the mantis hollered again: "By Christ, it is none other than my next door neighbor, my long-lost Señor Panza." For he had seen a long-suffering working man loitering near the entrance to the castle.

"But that is Sannazaro, having a slow old-man's pee against the wall," expostulated Rajibai, slapping his sides in tears for the sheer enjoyment of hearing the hysterical insect going on in such robust fashion.

They continued this way until the bug was certain he had seen Teresa and Sanchica and the shepherd Curimabro. Then, at the height of his fondest observations, he saw a girl coming down the lonely road on her bicycle, a long skirt maintaining her modesty, two dogs following her at a healthy clip.

"Goodness me, could it be, might it be—*yes*!" And he carried on with one rhapsody after another to sing the praises of his peerless virgin Queen, whom he hailed as Dulcinea, someone Rajibai had never heard of.

"But that mechanical contraption? What is it?"

"A bicycle," Rajibai instructed.

The insect attempted its pronunciation, and then, as the girl approached, recorded his praise for posterity: "Among a dozen Amarillises and Dianas, you are the fairest. And you two old dogs, Barcino and Butron, surely you recognize your old master?"

But the girl, who was no beauty, and the two mutts passed Rajibai at some distance with barely a glance in his direction. One of the dogs did race over to sniff, as an afterthought, then looked up at the insect, snarled viciously and ran off to rejoin its Mistress of the Ten Speed. The poor mantis fell off Rajibai's shoulder, dropped to its laminated limbs in a near devotional attitude of distress, and wailed: "But how could they fail to recognize me?"

"Your coloring rather disguises you," the boy advised.

With that the insect tried to examine himself, but could not. His head would not articulate to sufficient degree. "My armor—where is my armor?" he complained.

"But you are wearing it, good sir," Rajibai replied. "As fierce as any insect the world over, I am sure."

"Show me no dishonor by such analogies, lad, for I am in a most uncertain and emotional state. Wobbly, even. And know this: once I was the most feared of all, never to be conquered!"

But his absurd croon was interrupted by the emergence of a procession from inside the castle. Seeing hundreds of oddly dressed commoners coming forth, and led by one who appeared as none other than that scoundrel, Avellaneda of Tordesillas, the insect launched into an incantation composed by the famed Diego Perez de Vargas, surnamed Machuca for his having squashed a multitude of his Moorish enemies with nothing more than a limb from an oak tree: "... Near to the headlands of Lapice, adjoining a landfill of scum, with lance from Malta, a sword forged in the hot fires of Argamasilla, that fears not even Charon's ferry-boat and once outmaneuvered the great Amadis of Gaul, prepare for every thunderbolt of war!" And all this from the barely audible peep of a praying mantis.

"Why are you laughing?" the insect demanded.

"Because you are the most hilarious bug of all time," replied Rajibai.

"Why do you call me such things?"

"Bug? Because you are a bug. Look at yourself!"

"I can't. My eyes are not working properly, and a dizziness affects my every limb. My muscles have ceased to function. It is true, I consumed much wine the other night, but what previously seemed full of life and steady of hand now knows only a weightlessness I can scarce describe. I look down and see only a stick. As one who has lost touch with the forest for the trees. Am I dreaming or am I not? Do I live or do I die? I will not commit to a certainty, for there is none, not in this state. And so to hell, all you demons vying for my soul. I shall sleep it off and none shall gain entry in my head."

Amused even more, Rajibai thought it wise to hold up a mirror for the little strung-out fellow to see himself by.

The bug examined himself, carefully, with a mounting fascination ... and—an invisible thud—fainted straight away to the ground. Unfortunately, a herd of goats was just then ambling near, and one of them, answering to the call of goat nature, laid claim to the very spot in the grass with a direct hit, awaking the insect with a dolorous stream. It leapt into the air, only to knock itself out again by colliding head-on with the underside of Rajibai's jawbone.

The insect's long narrow legs dangled pathetically as the boy carried him gently back to the very spot where he had first found him in the shed, and did what he could to revive him. Slowly, the insect awoke.

"Where am I? What time is it? It is cold, yes, but my head is burning. And who are you?"

"Why, it is early afternoon, and cold indeed, though I have no idea what month it is. By the way, you hit your head. My name is Rajibai. I gather you're having a bad day."

The creature rubbed his eyes. Just a few hours ago, unless I be deceived, it was late spring. I was in my bed, surrounded by my dear friend Sancho whom I had led astray for so many years, as well as by the insufferable Carrasco who has chased every skirt in La Mancha. My long-annoying housekeeper, the local priest and my dear homely niece Antonia were there too. I was dying. For all my valor and Cid Hamete's flattering praise, nothing could unburden the melancholy that ate at my insides. And why was I depressed to the point of expiring? I cannot say, except to suggest that the early seventeenth century, we all know, has nothing to recommend it. My every play was a disaster, next to Lopa's. I had become a patchwork of twitching, self-conscious superfluosity, repeating words, bereft of new ideas, incapable of lending the necessary sobriety to my slapstick. Where the rest of Spain was awash in heaps and bastions of buffoonery, I was still taking seriously all that my characters did and felt. From Prague to the marshes of Leiden they laughed at me, missing entirely my intent."

The mantis now touched himself, awaking to the realization that he was, after all, a bug and nothing more. Rajibai could feel his panic. Witnessed within seconds the emotional arc that ranged across the whole feeble gallery of fits and starts: light-headed expressions in the eyes as large as any sea-change; a throbbing heart; a trembling all over, from top-gallant pincer to angling claw; and then the summation of woes, candidly conveyed in carefully considered meter and pause: "Were my noble calculations so heinous that the Lord should deem it appropriate to bring back this humble scribe and storyteller in so humiliating a form? The Chinaman, according to that legendary Marco Polo, would call it reincarnation, I believe. Taking one's chances in death, as in life. Which means that I have been punished for daring to incite the truth. Let all the world be forewarned: artists, poets, troubadors—sing of love, wax upon adventures, speak your heart and prepare to become a bug. Oh hideous fate!"

"You're saying you were a person?"

"Are you deaf! I was the greatest knight errant, and kisser, in the history of Europe."

"What did you do to earn the errant part?" the sagacious youth asked.

The insect replied with a long-winded testimonial to his times, and to himself, leaving no slave unliberated and no maiden unappreciated. He began by detailing his glorious service under the dwarf Captain Diego de Urbina and the gay Neapolitan Marquis of Santa Cruz. The killing of 500 Turks at Lepanto, which left him without a left hand and a sad case of hemorrhoids; the battles at Morea and Goletta; honors from Don Juan of Austria (a voucher for one year's free usage of the baths at Baden-Baden) and Don Carlos of Arragon, the viceroy of Sicily, who offered him his cousin. Even the Duke de Sesa recommended him to the King of Spain, which enabled him (along with his brother Rodrigo) to embark for home on the *El Sol* in hopes of some financial compensation. Anything would help. His wife was an addicted gambler.

Alas, just prior to taking possession of these duly won honors, he was abducted at sea and taken to the port of Algiers where, for five unbelievable years, he lived in and out of dungeons, a slave to the sadist Dali-Mami and then that bastard Dey Hassan Aga, who delighted in the use of burning candles to the skin. Later, after a successful ransom, he was present at the contest between French and Portuguese off Terceira. But all these adventures paled before the great love affair with Donna Catalina de Palacios Salasar y Vosmediano of the village of Esquivias.

Said the insect, "We were married on December 14, 1584, and I found myself the possessor of twelve acres of doubtful vineyard and several mite-eaten sacks of flour. Eventually I went to work for the Navy in Seville, though I had harbored dreams of going to America. I was particularly keen to visit New Spain, with its many Noble Savages. Unhappy me. At Tobosa, famed for the most beautiful women in all of Europe, I was arrested for soliciting tithings on behalf of the priory of San Juan. Some claimed that I had blocked their streams. What one has to do with the other is absolutely beyond me, and I said so at my convoluted trial, the consequence of which landed me in the Casa de Medrano. Surely it is still there?"

"I don't know," said the boy.

"And the Buscapie?"

"What is that?"

The insect sighed.

"I want to know what happened when you died. How did you end up a bug?" Rajibai pressed.

But the creature could not get a fix on the moment, or the strange hallucinations that overcame him: the caves of consolidated light, the tunnel of flares, a stairway to some island, and the poetry of the Sardinian, lo Frasso, who had composed his "Seven Homilies on the Good and Bad Fortunes of Love" and was there, hovering among the dust motes of the cellar, reciting them even now ... "The Tears of Angelica", "The Wonderful Shoulder Blades of Ercilla", "The Enormous, Hairy Nostrils of Thy Neighbor's Wife, Galatea", and so on.

"All I know is, one moment I was a man, and now—now *this*!" He buried his head in the Levantian blanket.

"What can I do?" appealed Rajibai.

"Go,"the insect sobbed. "I have been cursed. There is nothing anybody can do."

"But, if given another chance, who or what would you have preferred to be reborn as?" the boy asked. A logical question for a Jain.

But the insect was too choked up to answer, awash in ragged, inconsolable tears.

From outside Sannazaro showed up. "Master Rajibai, are you in there?"

The boy presented Uncle to the strange praying mantis.

"He talks! Go on then, say something."

The insect began speaking as he had been, lamenting his sad fate, but Sannazaro could hear nothing, though admitted that the amazing creature's pin-sized mouth seemed to be moving. He looked at Rajibai.

"That's all right, Son," he said. "Whatever you heard, it's got to be more interesting than the monologues of 400 billionaires planning their escape."

Rajibai was perplexed. He knew what he'd heard, but had no answer as to why only he, and not Uncle Sannazaro, was privy to the amazing creature's story.

"Why don't you take him outside and let him go free in the woods, where he belongs," Sannazaro urged him.

The eloquent mantis, hearing this, panicked again. "You mustn't listen to him! Please. There's owls and hawks and weasels out there for whom I'm just paté, an *hors d'oeuvre*, without the slightest concept of survival in this pitiable condition."

"Don't worry," Rajibai whispered, "we're sticking together from now on. But you need the fresh air. And then we're going to fulfill your dream of going to America."

"Really! Ohhhh! Ohhhh!"

The insect's excitement, amidst cries of incredulity and praise for the boy's common decency, was abruptly interrupted. As Rajibai took him outside, all the billionaires were heading for their vehicles, saluting one another, exchanging business cards, limos pulling out, French Squirrels— a type of a helicopter—revving up. And, in the skies overhead, something was coming, no chopper.

"Father!" Rajibai called as he greeted the Commander near the entrance to the castle. Sannazaro was following closely behind, watching the curious mantis sitting on the boy's shoulder and hovering close to the warm pineal gland in his neck. "Surely this castle is enchanted. A helmet is a barber's basin, an insect a knight errant. You have to meet somebody—" And he started to show him his new marvelous friend when the approaching thunder of an unseen fireball broke the sound barrier and there was a terrible explosion somewhere high above. It threw the insect off the boy's shoulder and down onto the ground where he groped amid the high treacherous grass, weed, and Scotch broom.

"Bug!" Rajibai called out. But he could not find him.

"*Look!*" cried the Sultan of Hay-Wain. "It's a—"

But not one among them could properly identify the falling object. Until it struck land with a thirsty thud.

"*Amigo!* " cried the Commander.

The nine-pound pollo, as plump as could be, had come from who-knows-where or by-what-chicanery. The Hopi shaman clowning around with his own rocket fuels, perhaps? Falling at such and such a speed, with an energy equivalent of such and such, its total mass amounted to that of a small meteorite. Enough to vaporize any insect. A fact that was now painfully clear. Aside from ruffled feathers, Amigo was in good spirits, but had landed, tragically, atop the bug whose flattened remains defied all attempts at revival. His eight inches of life had been ruinously pulverized. Nothing was left. One more road kill, of sorts.

Rajibai sat down and wept. It was over. Future generations would scarce believe that such a mantis as this had ever walked the Earth.

"Oh my little bug with no name!" cried he.

The billionaires all gathered round the fallen chicken, enthralled. No doubt about it: Mr Marigold's worst-case scenario was coming to pass, though none could quite put all the pieces and feathers together.

A scudding cloud. The hint of thunder as the heavens themselves sang their praises, unheard by mortals: "Such passion, such romance, such inventive imagination! A life cranked up magnificently between a bumbling brain and clod of soil. You lived your dreams, took endless swigs of that they call reality. Don't think that just because you presently seem a puddle, bug parts and Galician remains, we can't see you! Rest assured: each day up here in Micomicona they recite your full refrains. Angels of Fortune, Trinitarian nuns, monks on leave, the other errants. And down there at the Plaza de las Cortes, young girls prostrate themselves before your bust, shedding all the proper tears of the world. Even outside La Mancha, everywhere they echo your sentiments ... Oh, flower of our brigade, in Elegie and Earth have you been laid. To this final resting place of yours, all faithful squires, goatherds, mantises, maidens and lords arrive by gentle ass and horse to bid fond greetings well ...". Then added, "No Chicken Little, that one," and "Bad timing is everything it's cracked up to be". Such choir practice carrying on for years, up there.

But not all was rejoicing, for it was obvious to the Commander and his Squire that Rajibai was deeply upset about his late bug. How to console a child under these circumstances? A Jain, for whom it was no surprise at all that the precious and long-suffering insect had endured numerous incarnations. All Rajibai knew was that life was eternal, or was supposed to be. Moreover, he had found new playmates since his exile from India. The Danish Natasha, briefly; his girlfriends above the waterfall. But none who could be said to be a steady amour—which was just as well, as far as the Commander was concerned. But it underscored his present commiserations. He held his son. "There will be other insects," he said.

A flotilla of freshly polished vehicles and an armada of choppers were departing the harsh environs of La Mancha, carrying men and women whose eyes were locked onto the new frontier of space.

Said he to the boy, "You're going to grow up in a world where there is no poverty, because there will be no rich people. Nothing by which to measure worthlessness. No warehouse crammed with riches to ridicule the lonely material good. Lacking comparisons, no ill will or bad feelings. No pollution. No crime. No greed. No cruelty. Few people after a generation or two. All these hand-me-downs of the rich will be reserved for the moon. And with no more income flow, no more destruction. The animals, the plants—all of us—have won!"

Sannazaro, of course, had a slightly different take on the scenario. "What about our own money?" he said suddenly. "I'll be damned if I'm parting with it!"

"Who said you had to?" Marigold applied, grinning. "What, you think I'm that stupid?"

The Señor looked at the Commander. "But what happens when, after a year or so on the moon, they see that Earth has not been demolished as predicted? Won't they return?"

"By then they'll be broke, their bones demineralized, brains addled, hormones demolished, DNA deprived. They'll all have shrunk down to puny people, puny hands, no money. Pathetic jokes that once were human beings. There'll be not enough money in all the world—nor the motivation—to mount a rescue mission. What? For *the traitors*, people will say. Best of all, they'll be sterile. We'll have nothing to fear. And of course, one final irony: who could ever forget that the moon is receding slowly, inexorably, from the Earth. They will be lost in space."

To Mr Marigold's way of thinking, the course of tides had been ultrafavorable. Nothing had gone wrong, everything right. For one nearly killed 25 times in as many months, his optimism was profound, if harebrained. In his mind, of course, he had systematically courted destiny, and won. Despite every perversity, pernicious power, unruly force of humankind; beyond all the vagaries of dark imbalance, he had fought bravely, not merely with his brood pouch of ideas, but his bronze-winged duck. His foes had submitted. Philosophers and kings been brought to their knees. Scraps on the far fringes of Himalaya and South Pole, dangerous dunks in the Indian Sea, time travel and legendary leaps to boot. Neither locust swarm, Greenlandia's ice cap, demented Neanderthal nor thunderous sea could keep him from his mercies and ministrations, whether of rat, dragon, or little boy.

All these qualities Sannazaro admired, no doubt. Had caved in from sheer boredom in any other company, it must be admitted. The world, it seemed, was finally righted by their efforts. Though none of this was a foregone conclusion.

And strangest of all, outside a castle wild, in the velvet fields of La Mancha, a reincarnation had been revealed in the open palms of an innocent lad. Though no eyes had been capable of viewing it. Or not quite yet, as Rajibai carefully gathered up the leaking glues of his friend's fleeting remains, carried them with religious pomp into the castle's extensive library room, and placed them within a fancily carved box beside some rare books in Spanish, devoted to the picaresque. Even then the tidbits of limb, antennae, little heart still warm, veins rushing with latent prose, were beginning to twitch, a life force—both literary and beyond compare.

Part Five

Rites Of Passage

CHAPTER 173
Mr Marigold Makes an Official Visit to an Insane Asylum
Beneath the Streets of Los Angeles

THE WORD EVENTUALLY leaked out: it had to. "NEW MEXICO BILLIONAIRE GOES ON PHILANTHROPIC RAMPAGE. COERCES 400 OTHERS TO DO SAME."

Call it a garish goof with the contagion of moveable type. A driver had overheard a Japanese saki baron discussing the "new minerals" with a captain of the French plutonium industry. His wife had a brother whose dry-cleaner knew the baron's broker's hairdresser who regularly lunched with a very senior level comptroller whose lady friend was an editor at the *Yonkers Tribune*, and so on. Big news with unpredictable implications. The Dow Jones plunged 9.8 percent in one day, though many argued the bull would not die so easily. Yet, 52 percent of the American public saw 225 billion dollars vanish from their portfolios overnight—a payout equivalency of five Hurricane Andrews. Most governments refused to comment until they had "studied" the situation.

The Eritrean Treasury Secretary, however, declared at a United Nations session that such unprecedented humility would clear out the markets, replacing the robber barons, brokerage houses and day traders with a whole new generation of responsible entrepreneurs, unburdened by the trusts, monopolies and high-polluting regimes of the past. Even the International Finance Corporation, that arm of the World Bank dealing with private investments, vowed to draft a new set of principles that would pressure banks and other financial institutions into an embrace of ecological guidelines.

"Tarantula wasp economics," argued one Argentine naturalist. "Spiritual rebirth," claimed the Right Reverends from every parish in every diocese. Third World NGOs called it the "best news" since the *Bible*, declaring an end to Western consumerist domination. Representatives for the La Mancha Summit who were handling the vast and secretive organization of the Lunar Project issued a formal statement from Switzerland, putting a cap on the more flagrant rumors. Nothing about meteorites, Greenlandia, the moon or the end of the world. Instead, a smokescreen of "natural capitalism" with bright-sounding bromides: resource depreciation, biodiversity accountability, transgenerational Marxism, Agenda 21 and ecological economics.

Strictly speaking, the billionaires were concerned about the quality of life for their grandchildren. That required no leap of the imagination. How had they suddenly gotten religion? By listening to a flower. Genus *Tagetes*, to be precise. That was no lie, either.

Now there happened to be a little-known organization lost in Andorra's capital, La Vella, which was devoted to North/South issues and responsible for continuing the lucrative Plotinus Prize. Originally devoted to the dissemination of the *Enneads*, as well as the master's love letters, as translated by Porphyry; funded by the six parishes of Andorra and overseen by the Département des Pyrénées-Orientales, the organization had transferred to private hands following the demise of Communism, soliciting donations from wealthy Catalan churchgoers towards the goal of planetary harmony and a *bona fide* noosphere, as predicated upon Plotinus' theory of the Nous: a transcendental science. The Prize constituted the interest on well over US10 million dollars, which enabled its committee to dole out a substantial monetary award each summer. The time was upon them, and Mr Marigold emerged quite overnight as their champion. He was offered the PP, as it was known, for 2001, a high-profile commendation that carried with it honorary citizenship in Andorra, one set of mountain goat earmuffs (any color of his choice), a dinner for three at his favorite Andorran restaurant, followed next day by a Grand Tour of the country, said itinerary to include visits to a high-altitude home for wayward girls, tobacco and marmot farms, limestone quarries, several abandoned villages, Roman railway bridges and a Benedictine cliff monastery renowned for its innovative avalanche fences.

All this was a mere prelude to the ceremony itself, during which he would be given a one-million-dollar check should he wish to embrace his new 175-square-mile homeland with its peculiar patchwork of desolate valleys, 7,300-foot peaks, five passes impassable in winter, and 4,000 lonely shepherds of doubtful stability who fretted perpetually over the miserable state of the world.

After all due consideration, fearing yet more publicity, scandal, noise, Marigold gratefully declined the honor. After all, wasn't he already in the celebrated process of disbursing his own funds to good causes? Furthermore, stated he, no one could tempt him with citizenship, no matter how desirable the nation, for he now preferred the life of a nomad, inconsolably wandering from mountain meadow to lake district. No country to call his own. No home state. All had become obsolete in his mind; his image of himself twisted away like a mollymawk in an Antarctic gale, forever curving out beyond. Never situated, always on the loose, catching thermals, soaring where no petrel or albatross had ever ventured. A wild Tibetan ass. A grasshopper in the Central African Republic. Ticks in Connecticut; horseflies in the Brooks Range. He saw himself in all of them. Splendidly, forever anonymous. No cares. A breeze to content himself with. Nothing more. Where the hell was Andorra, anyway? No hard feelings: he at least agreed to sit on their nominating committee in search of an alternative winner, unaware that this simple gesture of accommodation would alter the remaining course of his life. And more.

For who can say, by any given cause, what effects lie in store for us? An unseen melanoma on the chest, gazing at you for the first time in the morning mirror, as it prepares to kill you day by day. A yacht flipped by a whale; accidental drowning in the Atlantic. Camus' unfortunate head-on with a tree. And so forth. Given all that, who knows how to embrace freedom? Marigold or Sannazaro? Surely Rajibai? And if we should take seriously for even a moment this shooting gallery of untoward hostilities and heavy consequences, what then our stuttered, interceded lives? Each moment a contemplation, every act inhibited by paralysis, no method or undertaking safe from the ruinous omens or proliferating alternatives competing with it? The da Vinci dilemma. In that case, we must stop, stand still, neither blink nor breathe. Collect ourselves for another day. Reconcile. But then, we remove ourselves from good fortune whilst stubbornly remaining beneath the avalanche.

Stasis versus mobility. No doubt, the trees and flowers fared well, in a state of nature. But then again, Mr Marigold reasoned, how few people, if given the outright opportunity, actually left to their own devices, would ever choose that happy state of our original forbears? Was man rotten to the core, as can be divined, for example, from the historical record of every decade, whether the enflamed whorls surrounding Stalin, or the Hundred Years' War? Had there ever been a tranquil period in man's upbringing, some truthful force of noble savagery? When professors weren't lynched in Prague, nor children disemboweled by soldiers for the sport of it. Surely the Todas were living proof—in the long debate spanning such worldly philosophers as Raymond Dart, Iraneus Eibesfeldt and Ashley Montagu. In the one camp, vivid portrayals of bloodshed between Cape York and Northwest Greenlanders, or Copper and Netsilik Eskimos; ambushes employing poisoned arrows and sickle-shaped knives.

Whereas other anthropological camps argued nearly the opposite: Tahitian society, the Mbuti, !Kung and Tasaday—portraits of passivity that convinced at least some students of human culture that peace and Paradise were possible. Had not a Marigold seen, felt, known it? But what then? If in fact he had partaken of all that was kind and gentle and antithetical to the 405 Freeway in Los Angeles, why had he left South India? Wandered away from the waterfall? Abandoned Crowquill's perfect lighthouse? Was leaving somehow inherent to our genes? He himself had cited his nomadic character. Moving out, packing up, constantly at sea, a high-plains drifter. Was there actually a physiological component forcing constant relocation, rebuking the good, ignoring the virtuous, yawning before perfection?

Even from adolescence these queries had never ceased to harass the Commander, for he never found an acceptable answer. No sourcebook provided even a thimble or parrot's breath of a clue. In the whole addled narrative of philosophy, the memoirs of religion, ethics and science, all the eclectic annals of art, not one example of a contented person. The Todas migrated every year. Crowquill roamed the world. Jain monks carried forth barefoot over rough backwoods, hot tarmac, rude stubble, constantly on the lookout, perpetually on guard. Only Anna had bridged the gap, it seemed. And Namgyal as well.

What then for a bombastic trio, feckless wanderers second-guessing planetary ecology when thousands of scientists had failed to do so? Had Marigold never listened to Hidalgo, he could have remained a poor hermit—well, not exactly poor, but certainly not famously rich. He had closed the final text—every word—of Aquinas. And Chaucer, too. Was nearing the end of the Great Books, which he'd first tackled in his youth and had never let up. His daily walks. Nightly candle vigils. Gin Rummy. Ten points for knocking. Learning to maneuver on a baby Steinway. Lunch, green tea a dozen times a day. The flowers. So much to do, even in the small space of his hacienda. Why go far away? He was no gypsy, not by birth. Or training. Or inclination. Why bother? Why become what was so much easier to dream? Why why, even?

This fixation on saving the world. Rubbish. Didact. Missionary madness. Boredom thrust upon others. Pedant, attitudinarian, predicant. Toady. Lickspittle. Had he already forgotten Bhopal? The rooster rings of southern New Mexico?

And this back-to-Nature idiocy. Had he lost all sense of himself ? His pride, dignity, reason? Was it not enough to open the window, enjoy the west breeze, commend the day, without stuffing it down one's throat or throwing one's face into it? These were schoolgirl gymnastics suited to a summer's afternoon, not a life.

What was true Nature? Those nameless ciliated creatures who spent all day feverishly paddling around the seas? If that was the wilderness, so what? Not even a pretty picture, at that. After all, weren't these creatures fair game at all times for larger predators? *Who needs that?* he mused. Or those in between— starfish, sea urchins, lizards—who seemed ideally situated to exploit the best of both worlds. Yet, once a lizard always a lizard. Even the wild flings of a lammergeier or nocturnal soirées of the wolf could grow old quickly. And how to reconcile the grisly truth that all were prey to hunters, illness, those who stayed home, others who went out? No, going back to Nature was no solution for a complex idiot.

But who was immune to the rigors and tribulations of this world? A pigeon, short lived? An albatross? Perhaps. The Jain monk, constantly aware of travail all around him, enduring by those many principles of vicarious substitution inherent to his empathy the whole life of a truly spiritual person? His grace conflicted, his joy embittered, even his revelations standing alone. A dreadful predicament. Did that empathy breed calm in the face of torment? Help victims? Or simply reflect pain at the highest batting average? And what of the philosopher, ceaselessly picking over the bones of conceptual contention, resurrecting the grammar of ideals, a slave to logic, forever stillborn as a person? Or the mind of the historian, roaming amongst those endless details no longer capable of exerting purchase in the now, and at the price of never knowing anyone or anything for sure. The archeologist, condemned to the ruins of our ancestors and their richly diverse follies, and realizing at some late day that we too will have been subsumed, are vanishing even now, and probably with lesser trace. Even that blithe spirit of the arts— thinkers, players and composers, musicians and lyricists, set designers and fanciers. Poetasters and those who work for effect with their hands. So many passions abiding in the ephemeral, rooted to the instant of delight or insight, forever feeding a hunger for more by turns ecstatic or despairing, so that the entire panoply of human life might be sampled in an evening of otherworldly romance, astonishing technique, whimsy, the voice of angels, reconciliation, but—again—at the expense of craving daylight, true love affairs, imbroglios, comic missteps, real causes and aftermaths. What would ultimately satisfy a thirsting soul?

"I'm tired of thinking," he resolved, his face dark in a stupor of rejected introspection. He was stymied. Could not head right or left. Felt claustrophobic sitting still, but feared to be anywhere else. A condition that led to catatonia, which was somewhere north of Andalusia ... and this eventually brought him, and his companions, back to Madrid where, having shaken his head out, he agreed to be part of the Plotinus Prize Committee, mostly on account of Rajibai, the little tuning-fork at the culmination of all their collective fopperies. The boy, who embodied pure freedom. That was the answer. Glowing, reckless, imperturbable, undaunted. What to the Commander read of deep thicket and undoing, a square one of false consciousness and oblivion, to Rajibai was the brightest of beginnings.

Marigold accepted this fact as a gift. The child was working his miracle upon both father and uncle, as he had upon Ginevra, who now soaked in a hot bath back in her beloved Tesuque.

That afternoon, news arrived that one Alex Smart, of Los Angeles, California, had been nominated, in place of the Commander. Though Marigold himself was to have superseded this new nominee, his humility in the event prompted a phone call from the committee requesting that, as a member, he agree to visit Smart, verify his genius, obtain his release from the inexplicable custody in which he'd long been placed, then escort him back to La Vella for the ceremony.

"What kind of custody?"

"We believe him to be an orphan."

The Commander was at once attuned. "Is he a child, then?"

"We can't tell. Obviously underage."

"But what has this kid accomplished that's so worthy?" the Commander inquired.

"It would appear he has discovered the missing kink," whispered the committee chairperson, "and all through strenuous self-analysis."

"I don't follow you."

"We're not entirely sure about it, either." The chairperson's voice was steeped in ambivalence. A real local dork, country-bumpkin-sounding. The Commander, as usual, invited his trusty Squire and son along with him, and the three of them headed off straight away. The flight to Los Angeles was uneventful, except that the last 30 minutes of it was over the city proper, reminding Marigold yet again of the malignancy that was humankind.

"Don't you sometimes get the feeling we're just drifting, with no reason for being?" Sannazaro mused. "Like marionettes in somebody else's melodrama." He'd had the same sensation before. Somebody was manipulating his strings, calling the shots, driving him into battle.

"Take comfort in knowing how much worse off we'd be if it were our own melodrama," the Commander aired.

It was early evening during that invigorating transition between one nondescript season and another; the streets harried and gargantuan, a sense everywhere of painful break-up, pointless construction; a landscape drenched in varicolored soots, dense with tawdry multitudes, the air noisy and thick with a too definable violence. The trio hailed a taxi and headed out towards the Pink Leviathan. This plaza of consumption was the most famed shopping mall in the greater megacity, from Santa Barbara to Encinada: the pride of city planners, nationally recognized for its 274 leather shoe and torn-jeans boutiques under one sky dome, and for collectively selling more cosmetics each year than the total value of all US Government annual expenditures directed at preventing crime in schools and curtailing unwanted teenage pregnancies. Marigold also had heard that this area of Los Angeles was famed for having more psychiatrists per square mile (2,400) than anywhere else in the world.

They entered the mall, at once bewildered by its sheer size and throb. Fifty movie theaters. One hundred decal, poster and baggy-pants shops. Ear piercing. Videos. A serial killer, famed for having taken out nine lawyers one morning, freed on technicalities (no lawyer would defend her), was there signing her memoirs. A large queue. Pizza. Ice cream. Skateboards. Girls everywhere looking up to her.

"Paradise!" exclaimed Rajibai.

"Certainly a welcome change after La Mancha," Sannazaro added.

"You're both deranged!" Marigold chaffed.

The Commander was loath to ask directions, to speak with anyone, touch anything. America—this America—gave him the creeps. They descended to the parking lot, were met at a kiosk, then driven through a dark tunnel. The facility that housed Mr Smart was underground, a decommissioned nuclear bunker converted to an insane asylum.

"Yes?" the head nurse declared matter-of-factly. "A new admission?" She directed her glare upon Rajibai, who recoiled.

"We're here to see Alex Smart," the Commander ventured. "Alex sees no one," she said, and nervously lit a cigarette. "Didn't you receive the fax from the Plotinus Committee?"

"Nobody gets out of here alive," she barked.

There was an awkward pause, then a buzzer signaled the opening of the metallic security doors adjoining the nurses' station. "Just kidding," the woman said. "This way, gentlemen."

She escorted them past the flotsam of inmates—contorted remnants of the LA experience—to her private office, where she withdrew Alex Smart's considerable file. Sannazaro noticed the calendar on her wall: the best truck stops in America. This month, Squat & Gobble in Winnemucca.

"How much do you really understand about Alex?" she began. "Only that many consider him to be a bona fide genius."

"The word means nothing down here. Alex is stable, that's the most that can be said for him."

"What is this place?" asked Sannazaro. "A hospital?"

"We like to think we're the finest insane asylum in the country."

Sannazaro was greatly unsettled by everything around them. The woman's manner of speaking, the deplorable Dark Ages conditions. She detected his unease, and pointed with her finger.

"I see a bleeding heart liberal! Let me just stop you before your sympathies verge towards a scene. Our institution dates back to that honored tradition when doctors called a spade a spade. No political correctness here. We are quite comfortable with the word 'insane', however much it may make you cringe. We are not here to apologize for the freaks of Nature, nor pamper them. That might sound callous but it is, in truth, an essential technique. The cases that land here are desperate. We help them, if we can. It's that simple. In the years I've worked at this facility, I have only seen two people leave, both in caskets. Up there, at street level, I suppose social graces and ethical responsibilities have their place. But folks, you're in the depths, now. Mind you, it's not their fault—nobody says it is. Although we do have a trainer from India on staff who believes firmly in the theory of karma. According to him, everyone here, whatever their circumstances, deserves to be here."

"A trainer?"

"Sure. Our therapies can get quite physical. Take Alex, for example. We've tried everything from dunking, to electric shock, to typical NASA-style deprivation. We've taken core samples from his teeth, examined the pollen in his snot, measured the veins around his legs."

She recognized Marigold's confusion, outrage.

"His condition is inoperable."

"But I don't understand," perplexed the Commander. "What condition? What's wrong with him? I've got to get him out of here and back to Andorra. The award ceremony is in three days."

"That would be quite a miracle. Alex has never even seen the shopping mall up above, which is for the best. The trauma could kill him. You see, he's been with us for over 25 years."

She then proceeded to tell the Commander, Rajibai and Sannazaro the sorrowful tale of Alex Smart, as best she knew it.

CHAPTER 174
The Odyssey of Alex Smart

"EVERYTHING WE KNOW about Alex's past comes from my predecessor's personal interviews with Sammie Smart, his late uncle, the last surviving relative of Alex, the man who had him committed."

She pulled forth the untranscribed scrawl of conversations, whose tenor soon revealed a guilt-ridden man, the obtuseness of a strange repulsion wracked by family schism and tragedy.

"What happened to your predecessor?"

"The details are too gruesome, and they are protected under work product privilege. I'm sorry."

"What about Sammie Smart?"

"A casualty of the Berlin Wall."

"In what sense?"

"It fell on him."

"But that's very funny!" The Commander laughed so much, he required a hankie. It was one of the few times in recent months that Sannazaro had seen him give vent to his comic side.

"And his nephew?" Sannazaro added.

"Alex. Little Alex. Here's what we know. His father, Boris, was a scientist who'd gone out to Africa as a young professor on sabbatical leave to study hair mites."

"Hair mites?"

"Yes. A primatologist who was evidently onto something very big, according to his colleagues. Supposedly to do with the DNA of follicles in various monkey species. Who knows what's real. He moved around a lot. Eventually the world lost track of him. He stopped communicating. His university mounted a rescue mission, but no clues as to his whereabouts ever surfaced. His only brother, Sammie, a condom manufacturer from New Jersey, went searching for him; their parents had both died years before.

"Sammie's tale was incredible, to say the least. If I didn't know Alex, I'd say it was apocryphal. But I do know Alex. Apparently, Sammie arrived at the last known campsite of his brother, some remote jungle outpost midway up an unmapped river between two contested tribal regions. Villagers remembered Boris, and indicated that he'd hired two natives to take him farther on, where nobody ever went. All unexplored territory. So Sammie hired his own locals and went off after him. He described sleepless nights penned into a canvas tent, his fists perpetually gripping a rifle and a lantern, surrounded by horrible predators: nocturnal nematodes that entered the nose, man-eating fungi, giant Cape buffalo that were blind and raged in all directions, venomous rabbits, poison-spitting sloths, piranhas the size of sharks, a new species of flying cobra, plants sadistically equipped with deadly stingers, trees swarming with ferocious ticks, army ants scouring the swamps, and vampires of every variety, including human ones. More on that later.

"Mind you, Sammie might have exaggerated some of these things. Imagine the night-time paranoia of an overweight slimebag from New Jersey. This was no Johnny Weismuller. But to hear him describe that purgatory was to glean an insight into every worst-case biological scenario, a true nightmare landscape. From a nurse's perspective, quite intriguing, I must say. He couldn't have invented such things. His native guides abandoned him, refusing to continue."

"But no place could be that bad," Marigold said, impatient to hear the end of the story so that they could walk down the corridor, connect with Alex and get him out of there.

"Perhaps only Alex's genes know for sure."

"But what do you mean?"

She went on: "After many months in the jungle Sammie crossed over into the lowlands of Bongo Bongo."

"Never heard of it."

"It's the least known African nation. State Department says it doesn't exist. In fact, the denials stacked up. But Sammie made a convincing argument, and Alex—well, you'll see for yourself—seems to be living proof of a physiological heritage previously unknown, at least on the streets of Los Angeles, and that's saying a hell of a lot. For weeks Sammie grappled with the dense brush, crawling in the mud. He lost half of his blood to biting insects, suffered several snake attacks, even managed to lose three of his toes to the rare toe-sucking jungle fungus. One night, camped on the edge of a gassy swamp, he had a mild stroke while protecting himself from poison darting frogs. All of his commentary loses something after that. His memory began to fail him. And it was at that time Sammie heard the unmistakable sounds of the Bongo Bongo echoing across the dark interior."

"What sound was that?" Rajibai asked, riveted to Nurse Pullman's tale.

"Bongo drums," she replied.

"That's novel," said Sannazaro.

The nurse continued: "So Sammie sought refuge with the tribe, for it had been weeks since he'd seen a human face. He knew the risks—they might be the feared jungle draculas he'd heard about months before. And guess what—they were!"

"*No way!*"

"*Yes!*"

"They sucked his blood?" Rajibai exclaimed.

"No, but they wanted to. Something intervened."

"What?"

"You have to understand the Bongo Bongo. You see, they had, by cruel and mysterious necessity, surrounded themselves by mile upon mile of methane-spewing quicksand. One little strike of the match and the entire jungle would have exploded. Hence, they had no fire."

"That's amazing!" declared Rajibai. "We know of another tribe without—"

"Let her finish, Son," the Commander inveighed.

"The tribe, which had taken the name of the country, the Bongo Bongo, lived in elaborate tree houses more than 100 feet above the swamps. For a very good reason, it must be added."

"Which was?"

"The Creature. Sammie says the tribal people both worshipped and despised her. She was their God and their curse. For thousands of years the Bongo Bongo had remained confined to their swamplands, never going beyond its unrelenting borders. Staying high up in the air to avoid contact with all the poisons everywhere about. They drank blood, probably, and gathered their rainwater up high."

Marigold shared a familiar look with his son and with Sannazaro.

Nurse Pullman certainly understood their scepticism. "I know. But hear the end of it. So Sammie is captured the moment he shows his face. And they're now all industry, sharpening their blood-sucking fangs, and all the women and children are dancing and singing in their trees. They've never tasted blood from anyone in New Jersey before."

"Yum," said Sannazaro with a darkening frown. He sensed a too-familiar unreality about all this, compounded by a fear of the Commander's own fascination, which seemed to be increasing by the second. History had shown a terrible propensity for repeating itself in Marigold's company, and Sannazaro wanted no part of those vampires, or venomous rabbits. The very idea of it violated his basic trust in Nature.

"Then what?" Rajibai pressed. "This is the best!"

"Then Sammie's recounting of the story gets truly convoluted. He was frightened for his life, as you can imagine. That plus the stroke—who knows. But apparently the Creature showed her face on the edge of the forest. One assumes that the vampires were going to sacrifice Sammie to her. And who should be keeping company with the Creature but—"

"Boris?" Marigold divined.

"No. Little Alex," said the nurse.

"But how? And what about Boris?"

"Impossible to know. What can be assumed is that Boris had died, but not before mating with one of the vampires."

"Absurd," Marigold declared.

"Impossible," said Sannazaro.

"Well, we believe Alex was the offspring. How else to explain his keeping company with the beast—a beast who might well have been their revered Queen? We just don't know. Sammie insisted that the Bongo Bongo recognized his similarity to the little white freak, and that alone saved him, temporarily. The tribe placed Sammie in his own hut in the highest part of the forest canopy. They had every reason to believe he wouldn't be going anywhere, and were probably going to use him the way Masai milk their cattle of their blood for years. A cash cow. A blood Sammie.

"But they never realized their food bonanza. The following night, despite anemia, hallucinations brought on by one fever or another, his right arm having seized up, his memory fast fading and his legs dangerously swollen, his abdominal wall infected with river flukes, cramps, spasms and other precocious parasites, Sammie enacted his escape, finding little Alex and taking him with him, shimmying down the tree by the sickly light of the moon, swimming through the poison swamp, his flesh turning permanently the color of zinc, and getting out of there. When we finally met him, there were worms living in every orifice, millions of skin mites inhabiting his limbs, a never-before-seen bacterium in his lungs, and the smallest snakes in the world—each a micron in size—populating his eyeballs. The poor man was dying of overpopulation, of dozens of disgusting microscopic species that had multiplied by the millions and were infesting his every cubic inch of tissue, lymph, blood and muscle fiber."

"OK. Charming. That's the boy's uncle. But who, or what, was Alex's mom?"

"We don't know. We can only imagine. Whoever she was, she was not around when Sammie kidnapped her child."

"How did they escape?" Marigold wondered, elaborating the whole scene in his mind—the pale white Alex by moonlight, the poison swamp, getting down the tree.

"They were lucky. Sammie said the only reason they got away was because the whole tribe was out feeding."

"Feeding?"

"Surely you've seen how vampires feed?"

"And Sammie and Alex made it all the way back to America?"

"Eventually. Yes."

"But why here, beneath a shopping mall in Los Angeles?" the Commander asked, struggling to understand.

"Even then, Sammie was no match for Alex. He couldn't control the child. And he himself was a walking time bomb: all those microbial species were about to erupt. Maybe you'd better see for yourself. Are you ready to meet Alex? It happened in Berlin. Not a pretty picture."

She led them down the corridor in the company of two large security officers, their guns drawn.

"Is that really necessary?" Marigold chastened her.

"We never know. We're not dealing with a normal person here," she explained. "Alex is not his real name."

"What, then?"

"We can't begin to pronounce it. It's more like the squawk of a bird."

"But he speaks English?"

"If he wants to."

CHAPTER 175
A New Species

NURSE PULLMAN KNOCKED on Alex's door. "Alex? You have visitors. Alex? May we come in?"

There was no response.

"Alex, they're scientists. And they've come to tell you some very good news."

"What kind of scientists?" a pale voice issued from inside.

She whispered to Marigold: "You're in luck. He chooses to speak."

"I asked who are they?" he repeated.

"We're here on behalf of the Plotinus Committee, young man," Marigold announced in a full voice. "You've been selected for the prize based on your recent contribution to the field of genetics."

Up and down the corridor other inmates were listening, their eyes and fingers straining behind the bars. These were the true victims of Southern California. Sensitive outcasts of the American way, the juggling of chainsaws on rollerblades.

"You can come in," the voice braved. He'd been reading Thomas Mann, a former fellow Los Angelino.

The guards opened the vault-thick door to Alex's containment area. Marigold and company entered. The room was a cold pastel, the color of undercooked tongue, and took a minute or so for the eyes to adjust. Eventually, they could discern the medley of sophisticated gadgets strewn across the inmate's boudoir. Interferon measuring devices; potassium counters; a plasma spectrometer tied to a Nintendo machine hooked into an electron microscope. On a large worktable were several computers, their screens lavender and electric with ongoing activity. Wires, test tubes, vials, samples of blood and other biological materials were arrayed in neat and purposeful configurations. Scores of videos and CDs. A small and esoteric library. In the very center, a dinner table for one, plates stained with the aftermath of a feeding— cockroach and cricket parts, and the tail and rectal sections of a rat. But Alex was to be found nowhere.

Nurse Pullman nodded upwards at the ceiling. Then: "Now come down and be polite to your visitors."

There was Alex, clinging to a jungle gym and hanging upside down on the ceiling. Beneath him, a sand box. His face was bearded with a brown fuzz; his eyes were bright and sharp, golden colored; his hair was long and waxy. His arms appeared cloaked in tissue. Was it a jacket? Or some skin deformity. Alex alighted on the rattan-covered octagonal floor, extended his hand and shook Marigold's. The Commander instantly withdrew from his clammy clutches. His long bony fingers, unusually dagger-like dentition, unnaturally broad shoulders, and huge flaps of skin congealing between his forearms and ribcage suggested nothing other than a kind of human bat, standing hunched at just over three feet tall. His baggy jogging clothes concealed the rest of his tragic anatomy.

"*Gross!* " exclaimed Rajibai.

Marigold grabbed the boy. "I'm very sorry. He speaks his mind." But Alex smiled with genuine understanding. "That's all right. I'd probably say the same thing if I were him."

"You're a bat!" the boy continued.

"It's true, you do strike an odd resemblance to one," Marigold stated as gently as possible, more in the manner of one scientist to another.

"My father preferred life in the frontier," replied Alex. "He will be remembered for the boldest of all experiments."

"Which was?"

"I don't know. Look at me. Judge for yourself."

The nurse felt compelled to speak up, lest there be some received nuance of implication—her job performance; and came forward to snip any wrong impressions in the bud. "When he was first brought to us he was a wild child, an anatomical freak of Nature. I say that with all due respects. Had his uncle delivered him to us via conventional means, the boy would have been impounded at the border, placed in quarantine with other animals. They would never have seen the child in him. Instead, Alex was smuggled here in a crate. How he survived is a miracle. Holes for breathing, I suppose."

"Twenty holes which my dear uncle hammered into the box with a pick ax. I was allergic to the wool blanket. He forgot about water. Three days. At least it was dark."

"Just so you get the full picture: when he arrived here he'd already been turned down by other hospitals and vets. Each institution sent Alex somewhere else, thinking him a deformed bat. That's what he resembled. Nobody would touch him. The US Fish and Wildlife Agency heard about him from one of the vets and put out an all-points bulletin. There was a fear of rabies. But by then fate had brought Alex to us, where no government agent dared come near. Alex was at death's door. Sugar water revived him, and lots of mice. We had no idea what else to do. We could have put him to the use of fundraising—donated him to the LA Zoo, or UCLA. But we didn't. We kept Alex a secret, for his own protection. He spoke a language that was indecipherable, more akin to the calls of, well, yes—a bat, or bird. He squeaked. Show him your high squeak, Alex."

"Blah blah blah!" he aped, frustrated by more than two decades of captivity, and helpless, save for the Internet, to effect his escape. "What she really means is that I grew up among a very different language group, a tribe that remains undiscovered. Biodiversity seen nowhere else on the planet. In particular, a certain mammalian species about which science has no precedent. Having not been back in many years, I have had only my own blood and genes to work with. This portrait of a captive species I have tried to communicate to the outside world."

"Magnificent! Indeed you have, my boy. Which is why we're here!"

Alex's words and gestures had already struck Marigold to his old marrow. Rajibai, too, sensed the pitiful dilemma that had just spilled open before them in such elephantman English. Refined, struggling, breathtaking. All their adventures, the Commander realized, had come down to this pivotal moment: the saving of a life in limbo. Not just any life, but what appeared to be the sole emissary of an entirely new mammalian organism. Everything he wanted emerged presently in the clearest light—his opposition to the city; to all those billions of people who madly scavenged; to that whole edifice of civilization that masqueraded as Necessity, Progress, Development when, in truth, it was a ghastly disease unleashed upon the world. And Alex Smart, whoever, whatever he was, seemed caught at the very nexus of that paradox. Marigold was also caught, as had been Rajibai. Their links welled up in a fever of kin altruism which the Commander now embraced, rising to the occasion with but one intention. To fly with his wildest idealisms in the face of all that was callous, brutal, indifferent. To brook no other option, break clear of every last inhibition, go for the gold. He had to liberate Alex Smart, in every respect. With his own lunar scheme well under way, and 40 other projects—not least of them, the Oasis—puttering forward, life seemed suddenly quite bright for the trio. Now this grandest of all opportunities. If he could be the one to reform the silence between species with an individual who spanned both worlds so fluently, as Alex obviously did, the effect might transform human consciousness forever more. And there was no risk in doing so: Alex was a willing emissary who had already captured the attention of the world via the Internet. They just didn't know what he looked like, who he was, or of what it all boded.

Nobody could allege this Alex was simply a bat who had learned to mimic human sounds—the accusation leveled by some scientists who had all but undermined any hope for real human dialogue and parity with other animals, whether primates, any of the marine mammals or psittacines. Once the poor fellow's incarceration had been exposed— already a priority on Marigold's list—scientists worldwide would be induced to re-think the whole laboratory setting, as deep ethological luminaries like Marc Bekoff and Jane Goodall had been demanding for many years. Cast out the metal cages, concrete bunkers, jail cells; abolish the Gulags that had confined to endless hell every generation of non-human; forbid the hideous regimens of debilitating tests, torture and captivity. Marigold recalled the scientist at a university somewhere in Chile who had recently named others in his field who, in his words, had "sadistically tortured and killed scores of capuchin monkeys, for the sheer joy of seeing them suffer". *Rattling the cages* had become a catchphrase for the growing movement of outrage. Even oysters had sophisticated consciousness.

Get back out into the field, go naked, dispense with all tools, preconceptions, preparations; observe *as* Nature, confronting in shock and surprise, without pretense, pretext, regularity or anything proper; no name, definition, compass reading, routine, margins of error, calculations, tables, pre-ordained contrivances, measurements, manipulations, or ulterior plan. Be without priority, assignment, conditionals or expense account. Have no title, territory, clue, hope of promotion, bright future, publication, recompense, responsibility, bearing or register; release expectations; deconstruct all affiliations from one's mind; vigorously renounce all ties to the human world; be wild.

This was his maxim, and the treatise fast shaping his mind around a New Science of Engagement. Without pure food, pure intentions, pure behavior, there could be no innocence. Without innocence, no valid research. Embrace in nudity, on all fours, that was the answer.

This ancient legacy—whether Aurignacean, Taoist or Jain—took as its starting point the absolute reunion of all naturalisms, and presently swelled in the Commander's brain. He stared into the cul-de-sac of ruination that had claimed yet another victim from the wilds. At the antipodes of cruelty, beneath the megacity of millions of bipedal, carnivorous desperados, all their former instincts gone awry, this cage with its prisoner named Alex Smart, in English, no bat-equivalent, was the emblem for all of Mother Earth's biological suffering, come home to roost in a Marigold.

Release all the other millions of tragic figures like Alex Smart at the tens of thousands of universities, institutes, government agencies and corporations, where they were drummed into misery and then slaughtered for the satisfaction of stockholders and the arrogant frauds parading under the rubrics of science, the Food and Drug Administration, market domination, legal liability and consumer product safety.

Release them all, free their habitat, hire armed posses to protect them. (He made a mental note to send a million dollars to the Yemao-niu Dui, the Wild Yak Brigade in Tibet's western Qinghai province, to help the guerrilla anti-poaching force of 32 men and women stop Chinese hunters from killing the antelope, and intercede in the international trade in shahtoosh fur. The money would not only honor the Tibetan antelope, but the two martyrs, Suonandajie and Zhabaduojie, who in the early 1990s gave their lives to save the animals.) His adamant sense of right, splayed to its far fringes, now marshaled one universal doctrine of liberation. A concept that can eat at the nerves, bearing down with endlessly more acute consideration as the layers and impediments peel away, more and more victims and refugees emerging in the limelight of the human crisis of cruelty. Cambodia's Tuol Sleng. Genocide in Rwanda. One hundred people killed in wars every hour throughout the world in the twentieth century, excluding an even more chilling number of victims of political tyranny. From East Bengal to Timor and Mozambique. Fascists like Idi Amin and Macias Nguema, inheritors of Nietzsche's Nazist "Be Hard!" Four thousand gorillas and 3,000 chimps exterminated in the African rainforests; 93 million pigs and six million horses slaughtered every year in the United States. Nearly 800 million chickens expiring even before reaching the slaughterhouse. A rising tide of endless pain in all its miserable guises: with Pol Pot, people forget Hitler. With the butchers of Chechnya, people forget Pol Pot. That was the *raison d'être* of Alex Smart, Marigold duly reasoned, sparks mingling with tears, electricity streaking his face: to bring to perdurable consciousness the reality of suffering, billions of animal and plant prisoners, and help them take a life of their own, each one an individual, with a soul. Rajibai was fluent in that arena. Now the entire ensemble held a candle for the world's woes.

And so had Marigold become. This night, then—the result of all his madly questing force and feeling against an outer world engulfed in the brute denial of everything the Commander stood and prayed for.

His séance out of immediate time merged with the continuing conversation, coming back loud and clear.

Nurse Pullman was speaking. The Commander had missed something.

"What?" he asked.

"I said, we've been through this countless times with him. He harbors a grudge. But he has no idea how cruel the real world out there can be. Alex, you can appreciate that we've all made the best of a difficult situation. Have we ever denied you the diet of your choice? Or a dark room? Haven't our benefactors gone out of their way to ensure that your considerable intellect is nurtured with all the learning toys of your choice? Did we ever exploit you, profit by you, harm you when it wasn't deserved?"

This last point sent shivers to all.

"You don't get it," Rajibai interjected angrily. "He just wants to go home."

"Bless you, lad," declared Alex. "Now what was that prize you mentioned?"

CHAPTER 176
A Tuna Fish in the Heart of Africa

BY 9.30 P.M. ALEX SMART BADE fond adieu to the pit, and to his human captors of over two decades. At least the nurse had tempered her sadism, mostly from fear of actually touching the monster. Never a moment's tenderness in 25 years, during which time she'd seen the half-bird, half-man, as she thought of him, evolve, missing entirely the distinction between an avian and *Chiroptera*. But he was not entirely a bat, either, though he possessed most of the bat's better qualities. Instead, he was something new and extraordinary. Perhaps, over the years, Nurse Pullman sensed greatness in him. But because she herself had so little confidence, or love or greatness, so little interest in others, or in the world of discovery, it never occurred to her that Alex, and Alex's kind, needed help.

Presently, in his release by darkness, it was obvious that the 43-pound hybrid needed to be stowed away rather than risk any exposure to thousands of late-night sojourners sampling the shopping plaza. Hence, under protective cover of Rajibai's Toda shawl, Alex was carried out of the Pink Leviathan, a delicate swaddling folded up neatly in his own wings within the Commander's arms. Two walnut-sized black orbs gazed out in panic from beneath the embroidery, and witnessed for their first time a cineplex, a bowling alley, the lights of the times, a live rock concert in the mall, and passers-by of every size, shape and color.

"You all right?" Rajibai whispered, feeling a profound bond with the little fellow, hearing his heart beating furiously, as they passed a tattoo and body piercing parlor.

But Alex could not reply. He was hyperventilating, his little ears sinking before the onslaught of heavy-metal frequencies and alien confusions. Partly stifled tears.

They got him into the dark limo around the corner from Melrose Street and pushed off towards the airport where Marigold had summoned a private jet.

But it was obvious to both the Commander and Sannazaro that Andorra was no place for Alex. The very process of taking him there might do him in, what with Customs formalities and a whole new host of strangers bearing down at every awkward juncture. Moreover, those judges of the Plotinus Prize could have no idea what Alex was. After all, they had assumed by their nomination that he was a human person. The committee members had emanated a conservatism, paid-for lackeys touting policy and publicity. They had gone after the Commander more for his own riches than anything else. But Alex was most assuredly no poster child, no charismatic diplomat with blond hair who could represent the largest monetary prize for science in the world.

Notwithstanding his physical aberrations, the three-foot, partially winged creature had, indeed, discovered something miraculous which would have warranted a Nobel, let alone Plotinus Prize: genetic markers suggesting an alternative bloodline contemporaneous with the advent of the human species; the first scientific self-portrait in history involving not merely such superficial observations as a double chin at the age of 35, as in the well-known case of a Rembrandt, but the divergent trail of Cytochrome C, leukocytes, hemoglobin, caudal tails, wings and fur-bearing pouches. And this collective thrust of a whole new science could be had at a glance in the form of oneself. The greatest autobiography in history. From his insane cloister, Alex had backtracked to his own personal beginnings, the ultimate in genealogical rummagings; shown courageously that there was a new mammalian genus hiding somewhere in the heart of Africa. A little furry Nosferatu unknown to science and with its own indecipherable appeal; a biological Rosetta Stone that declared, in Alex's own emails alerting attention to himself, "the Power of Pollination". Those Internet transmissions from his Los Angeles dungeon were like the radio beacon of a plane gone down, a mummy awaking atop Cotopaxi, a signal from deep within the Earth of a whole new foment. Something was coming, and his name was Alex.

But for all that, Alex himself was condemned. The offspring of a heretofore-untried experiment. No analysis or point of fact could quite capture an appropriate characterization of the results. Yes, it was true that everything about Alex Smart, or whatever his real name was in *Chiroptera*, suggested a new departure for humanity, some alternative future that was more kind, perceptive and gentle. But how could such a future be realized? And what might the Plotinus Committee do with the revelations? Breed its own in-house freaks? Sell off the genetic property rights the way the Russians and Indians had tried to do in Arunachal Pradesh? Anna and her tribe might now be caged in a New Delhi research lab had Marigold and team not shown up. Irrational enthusiasm for genetic high tech was closing in. History was repeating itself within the space of a year, and poor Alex now faced a similar plight to those miraculous people of the waterfall.

The more the Commander pondered the strange story of Alex's Uncle Sammie Smart, the clearer their mandate burgeoned in his febrile mind: they had to get Alex back to where he came from, even if it necessitated transport, which it surely would, through the tenebrous night of African doom.

He had no fear about such a journey; he had already discovered that adult logic nearly always failed to grasp the elegance of those things that really mattered. He was immune from harm. Knew that only the child's imagination—locked away within the grown-up, a Puddleby-on-Marsh of gray matter waiting to be rekindled—had a chance. Desperate to return somewhere, to be a single memory for all eternity. Thought of differently, without the courage to turn our backs on every worn habit, on all those assumptions of middle years, we are without hope. Mediocre. Lost. To nurture the possibility of a restoration might require every separation, cancellation, turnabout. It could bode of absolute instability, ire, impoverishment. Those in our direct emotional orbit might feel the brunt of betrayal, assault, outrage. The repercussions could be devastating in the short term. But for the rest of our lives there is the certainty of profound accomplishment. A relocation of such magnitude meant, ultimately, freedom. That was its definition. Break-up of family ways; the forced separation of comforts. No placations. Direct action in the line of fire.

As they headed towards the airport, Marigold ruminated on the way certain encounters could shake us from our lassitude, act like a whetstone of ridiculous fate upon which we might have the good sense to sharpen our wits, confirm our convictions and wake up to tomorrow. Otherwise, we should one day die with our head thrown through a car window, or surrounded by breathing machines and life supports, forgotten, unheralded, only to be buried beneath concrete and astro-turf. No one deserves that. All people possessed the possibility of Taoist shamanism, the Commander sincerely believed. Though he no longer had the time nor patience to focus on *all* people. Alex was quite enough.

"I think we should get you back to Africa," the Commander finally volunteered.

Alex looked up at him and tears were glistening in his eyes. "I would be more grateful than you can imagine," he replied.

Rajibai's own cheeks showed a similar streaking. In a rapture of complexity, all the journeys he had taken in the company of his new father and uncle seemed consolidated into a single thought. "We shall go this very moment," he declared. "Nothing else matters, eh Father? And will we see a zebra, eh Uncle?"

Sannazaro nodded, contemplating the strangeness of the night. Somehow he knew they'd confronted a turning point in Alex Smart. How attenuated and obscure that trail which led to him. Every adventure had been a deliberate piece of the riddle, or maybe not? If destiny—which Marigold was a firm believer in—was non-existent, then all this ardor and great fortune, these near-misses and astonishing discoveries had been proverbial chance, the purposeless meanderings of light beams in a dust bowl. But then, if that's all they were, why Marigold, why Rajibai, why Alex, in particular, as opposed to three others? These inner cogitations spanned no more than the diameter of a few million brain cells, but when he was finished— traffic speeding by, ugly lights of the city—he knew beyond all shadows that there was a reason, a purpose, a true path; that those Hong Kong chickens had died in order that he and the Commander should learn of the moa, and then of Crowquill; be marooned in Antarctica, and liberated in India; that the monkey should have bitten his hand that he might, in turn, pave the way for little Rajibai's own deliverance, and so on, all the way up to the top of the waterfall, and then to the summit of a nunatak, and now to darkest Africa. A thousand and one days and nights of liberation theology: bizarre connections that might mean many things to many people but were, to the Squire, Fate—Fate at her best.

He recalled lines from his own childhood of Carlo Collodi's *Le Avventure de Pinocchio*, which he abstractedly, inexplicably, began to recite: "*Io sono abbastanza filosofo e mi consolo pensando che, quando si nasce Tonni, c'è più dignità a orir sott'acqua che sott'olio!...*", rhapsodizing the formative realm of the one great Italian who had managed—none had done before, and none since—to provide an urgent, genuine rationale for the imagination. Here was a set of strange and crazy circumstances demanding the full vent of a creative freedom in order to resolve that terrible rash of dilemmas—to fight or not to fight; to be engaged, to be unengaged—that are endemic to most lives splashed across the visual and mental senses. It didn't matter whether the rash erupted during the most impressionable, formative or retiring years, either. The demands were the same: Stand up to meaning, give in to art, reject dogma, embrace your dreams. The point of the tuna fish, as Sannazaro reckoned, was that we were all caught in the net of chance, on the one hand, but fully in control of our own signature, on the other. Collodi gave posterity a platform by which we might each engender our own interpretations, make sense of our reveries, lavish peculiar metaphors on a case-by-case basis.

"But what does it mean?" asked Rajibai.

"Yes, do tell?" Alex seconded. "They did not teach me Italian in the asylum."

"Well, let's see—" and the Señor commenced to translate in a rough, Sannazaroan fashion, appropriate to the occasion, the enlarged version: "Because I am more or less of an obsessively soulful frame of mind, condemned to being a puppet at the hands of my benefactor—" he threw that part in, and others up ahead "—and attuned enough to know that when you're a tuna fish, well, you're a tuna fish and not a little boy, or a piece of chocolate, or even a modest mixed salad; and consequently since you've got to live out your life, however many years allotted, then for heaven's sake, do so in peace and joy, make yourself immune to all the silly tribulations. And be sure to stay in your own neighborhood, if possible, where you belong, with a loved one, someone you trust for all time."

"That is splendid advice," Alex relayed. "All that from a single line. How marvelous Italian must be!"

"Oh, but there's more to do," Sannazaro added, for he wasn't done translating. Other appropriate injunctions entered into the stream of his remembrance: "Be sure to find that secret garden that is yours, waiting for you, forever, where your chances of reincarnation in a place that you cherish are assured. All this, in the case of a tuna fish—and forgive me Carlo," he continued, veering far away from the great poet of simplicity, "happens to be way down deep under the ocean, tranquil, silent, far removed from all that oxygen which people breathe, and not in a festering can of wicked oil, or in the mouth of some idiot, or both. As far as I'm concerned, let mine be Tesuque, or Africa, where I personally have never been, but am not afraid, for it is said by somebody or other we were all there once. With such dear friends as these, I am grateful, Lord. I have nothing to fear."

At length he made the sign of the cross, intuitively aware of the crossroads he had just communicated, the change-of-life plans that might very well prove dramatic. "It's all right with me," he echoed.

"Words sweet and purely spoken," Marigold commended, well aware that the author of *Pinocchio* had uttered only one in ten of them. His Squire, like every good Italian, stretched the elastic truth of Collodi to take in every latitude and philosophy for every occasion.

"Sweet is good," Sannazaro said without the slightest hesitation. His literary memory had given him legislative powers and he was now fully at the helm.

"Driver, to Africa!" the Commander hailed, as they entered the stream of traffic on the 405. Then he placed a call to the head of the Plotinus Committee. It was breakfast time in Andorra.

"Good day to you, sir. Marigold here. I'm sorry to report that Alex Smart is totally unsuited for the Plotinus Prize ... That's right. He's a bat. You'll need to look elsewhere for a new candidate."

And he suggested several alternatives, beginning with Francis Bacon.

CHAPTER 177
War in the Chasm of Communions

A FEW DAYS LATER, the Marigold Jetstar landed at Abijan, in the Ivory Coast. Swarms of vinegar-flies, *Drosophila melanogaster*, in every colorful marketplace; rainforests cut down beside the continuous surge of lorries; whole communities out carving up the wood, smoking meat, slapping laundry at river's edge. Nearby, a sea swirling with visible brown streaks of hepatitis, meningitis, cholera. Inland, a maze of weary cattle being led past jeering hooligans to slaughter.

Upon seeing this all too familiar horror Marigold, true to form, stepped in, found the nearest bank and obtained with no small effort 80,000 dollars' equivalent in local currency—enough to purchase every last buffalo and cow and free them into the nearest outback, paying two dozen shepherd lads handsomely to coordinate the drama. In addition, thanks to the prudent oversight of Senator Sannazaro, a videographer from State Television was hired, rushed up to the location, and recompensed generously to memorialize the transaction and make it official. This way, in the aftermath, superstition might check the impulse of locals to seize the opportunity of the quartet's absence.

From there by arranged helicopter the foursome were taken to a disputed border area, recently the site of an expedition in search of a living Brontosaurus which ended with the discovery, instead, of 17 new species of carnivorous fleas, and the striking revelation that one of these was a flea as large as a man. Given its unique gymnastic capabilities, it would have no difficulty jumping from San Francisco to the Bahamas in one leap. And, probably, it already had.

Covered in these dreadful, if impressive *Orchestoidea* (mostly young ones not yet the size of people), the group was ferried in dug-outs upriver to the hushed Neutral Zone, a region so dense with poisonous brambles and warring raccoons that the guides cautioned against so much as a whisper, lest they give their location away. From there, they were further escorted down smaller tributaries wherein the incredibly skinny Measles People lived, feeding on mosquito larvae, and addicted to war with their neighboring Polka Dot People. Many wonderful tales were told about this longstanding enmity. It made little sense: the Measles People insisted that their skin pattern showed without doubt that they were smarter, more virtuous and genetically fit than the Polka Dot People, conferring their right to oppress and savage their inferior neighbors at will. But the Polka Dots argued just the opposite. For 25,000 years these two groups had been burning each other's fields, raping their children, eating their chimpanzees, killing the grandparents.

No killing, no dispute, explained the quartet's escorts; no dispute, nothing else to do in the jungle. Furthermore, the great African biologist, Darlose had speculated a century before that children, chimpanzees and grandparents of the Measles and Polka Dot regions were firmer and more agile as a result of all the adverse pressures on their existence. Oddly, commented Marigold, to outsiders' eyes, there was little if any difference between these particular measles and polka dots.

"The whole thing is politically incorrect," he waged. "It's not even as if there's any visible difference between these particular measles and polka dots. It's no different from what the rest of the world has been doing since time immemorial, and I am, frankly, surprised. I expected something more from Africa."

"Well, then, just wait until nightfall," urged one of the guides, an Oxford-educated chemical engineer who, upon discovering the height of his cholesterol, had made the wise decision to return to his West African village and row boats for the rest of his days.

"What happens then?" asked Sannazaro, not the least incommoded by each new horror. He had, Marigold noticed, taken his philosophy of Pinocchio to heart; nothing seemed to perturb him any more.

"You will see," the guide cryptically alluded.

And so they did. By night the foursome had made their way through a dozen other similar war zones, each with far-reaching disturbances to the general air and psyche: escalated political imbroglios, internecine debacles, the remains of massacres littering the land. They followed a herd of wise elephants who knew exactly where to go to avoid the poaching areas. It was during this silent séance, on the move with the Pachyderms, that Alex—Nature's freshest child—began to reveal some of his special skills. For example, he could hear elephant whispering, echo-locating the bounced pulses of language at 15,000 hertz, navigating with incredible ease.

They were eventually abandoned by their guides upon the far edges of The Veldt For No Man, a vast, hostile barren land of disrepute. Not two hours later, a black sandstorm swept across the interminable dunes, 900-foot walls of acidic silica. Alex, however, was able to lead his worried companions on their bellies a foot or so beneath the blackout. He did so by tracking a conglomeration of wide-winged migratory 24-carat bugs with his special sensors. These glowing pointillist life forms were no larger than one six-hundredth of a millimeter, and festered in dense arrays across the desert floor, their microscopic cilia giving them the resiliency and speed of bumper cars. Imagine interstices in a Seurat, caesuras in a Pollock, such was the all-inclusive scope of these unknown West African microslugs which moved out in mile-long love fests across the sinking aquifers as they had done every week for 500 million years, arriving ultimately at their secret oasis.

Fifty hours later, recovering amid a flamingo-thick mud flat of carotene and salt thrush, the party was met by a band of lanky, wandering Kuchis, covered from head to toe in blue silken veils, along with their five gas-emitting garlic in the air dromedaries.

"Gentlemen," said Marigold, "we are looking for Bongo Bongo Land and are in sore need of a ride. I can reward you greatly for any assistance."

The Romanies understood nothing but, seeing little Alex, fell to their knees, crying out the name "Allah" three times. Then they advised the Commander by the most serious of imprecations that they'd be only too happy to oblige and that the dromedaries were at their disposal. But while the Bedouins had every intention of assisting the strangers, the camels were not so eager to comply. The moment the foursome had mounted them, they charged off, impervious to counter-instructions, in the direction of Gnat's Escarpment, that dreaded cordillera known throughout Africa for its unrelenting chasms filled since the dawn of the dew point with armored divisions of lethal gnats, no-see-ums and spotted hyena flies. By the time the Blue Nomads were able to round up their rogue dromedaries, the foursome had long since been troubled, tried and tossed like rag dolls before the very entrance of the worst of the canyons.

There was a yawning silence. Not so much as one half-mile of breeze.

"Something's not right," Rajibai whispered to his ruffled Monseigneur.

"I, too, sense trouble," the Commander replied, wiping off the dust after his exhausting gallop across the desert sands. He had done so backwards, his peerage in reverse, blue blood turning pale.

In the canyon's ten million crannies, swarms of little howlers were awaking to the long-awaited scent and electromagnetism of four juicy warm-blooded meals. Only Alex, of course, was able to detect the vast megaphonic twitch of carnivorous frequencies gaining on the inert, 125-degree air of the sandy bottom lands.

"Don't move!" Alex whispered.

"What is it?" said Marigold the Trepidatious.

At that instant, antennae all the way to the horizon were growing erect; jaws were cranking up into hateful position, razor-sharp teeth rubbing rudely back and forth with knife-like anticipation; talons of gnat growing feverish; translucent wings beginning to rev. The foursome, in short, was about to be eaten alive.

"Unlike the locusts of Soqotra, I sense real hostility here," said Marigold. "What to do? And what is it with our karma and insects?"

Already Sannazaro was frantically searching for shelter amid the petroglyph-stained cliff walls. But it was Alex whose special skills would save them.

"Follow me," he squeaked precociously.

Along a stream they thrashed, racing to reach a cave which Alex knew to be there, by powers yet to be fully revealed.

"What was that?" Rajibai cried out.

"What? What did you hear?" his father countered. "I'm not sure—"

Suddenly ten sets of baby jaws snapped from beneath the surface of the water, and Rajibai began laughing in a rush of boisterous guffaws and tears.

"What is it?" Marigold again implored.

But to no use. The boy, who was deeply allergic to any sort of tickling, was out of control. Sannazaro began laughing, as well, a mad kind of underwater hysterics. Then Marigold himself fell swoon to the canyon chuckles.

"Are you all crazy? We have to move, quickly now!" Alex squeaked, hearing by their frequencies the army of bugs that were hurling themselves from the upper canyon towards the four meals, dead center, like rush hour on a descending 65-lane freeway. "They're coming. For God's sakes, *hurry!*" He urged his three tickle-stricken companions onwards towards a great bat-infested cave.

As they made their way through the creek bed, baby crocodiles leapt up from the water like flying fish, and continued nipping at the invaders. They were in the larval stage, no larger than thimbles, so that their teeth exerted only the most benign of teases upon their skin. But the Commander was barely mollified.

"The parents must be somewhere!" he cried.

"It's worse than that," said Alex. "Our giggles are the triggers, primed by evolution. The bugs and the crocs are in cahoots. Crocs tickle, bugs fly in for the kill. Again, I urge you, all of us, make haste!"

With that they ran into the ferocious entrance of the cave, which rose above the creek and required all their effort to get inside. Just as they did so, the first ranks of the swarm smashed past the final rim rock like dive bombers of the ages in deadly *Star Wars* formation. Thousands careened into the sandstone abutments, killing themselves instantly, blood and guts staining the walls. Other millions of stingers hurled in about-faces, searching angrily for their prey. Their collective buzz was louder than a chainsaw, sharper than a guillotine. To think that Mother Nature had allowed, indeed divined, a necessary niche for such mean-spiritedness was most disturbing to the Commander.

"I can't see a thing," cried Rajibai, as they all proceeded away from the fray of inconceivable sorrows into the penetralia of the yawning cavern.

"What's that?" warned Sannazaro, hearing some nauseating signal from the very depths of the abyss before them.

"Shhh!" squeaked Alex.

He oriented his very pointed ears in the direction of the stellar darkness to the rear.

"*Duck!* " he cried, just as a whole new swarm of winged creatures not entirely dissimilar from Alex came rushing out to greet the vast army of killer flies—*Epydra riparia larvae grotesquae, Tabanus punctifer cannibilis, Culex pipiens massacrex*—that were just now entering the cave in search of the foursome.

"Don't utter a word!" Alex whispered. "Heads down!" cried Marigold.

In the diagonaling shafts of purgatory the war of two primeval enemies commenced. A million bats confronted ten million bugs, while three humans and a batman lodged in crannies beneath and out of the way. For nearly an hour the two warring families—bats and insects— fought on, a blood bath of multicolored oozes flushing the grotto. The foursome was covered in it. Rajibai, insect-loving Jain that he was, recoiled in abhorrence. Eventually, the stinging creatures retreated, as did the bats. But the blood-soaked battleground was left with many wounded microchiropterans, and this caused great pain in Alex, as well. His flower-like nose was receiving the cries of those in need and emitting pained prayers in return as he set about helping the myriad injured. A bat had become a florence nightingale.

The floor of the cave was a tragedy of mangled mammals. Of the nearly 1,000 known species of bats in the world, at least a dozen were represented among the hemorrhaging bodies there. To Alex, who could hear what his human companions could not, there was no greater disaster. A traumatic first reunion with those of his own ancestry that would leave its mark on him forever. Before him lay a gorgeous little *Antrozous pallidus*, her throat bleeding heavily from 50 no-see-um puncture wounds; two dying free-taileds—a couple, it would seem—who had been converged upon by easily 300 horseflies; a mouse-eared who whispered something to Alex, a message to carry forward, though none of the Marigold trio could understand it; a pretty young baobab-loving transilluminator, out of breath, her nostrils bleeding, her beatific black eyes fading; a big brown extending her wings but unable to fly, chanting an African love psalm of profound resignation; several downed Ruwenzori long-haireds, little tendrils in the mesh, a whole family wiped out; and a magnificent spotted bat, proud, quiet, unmoving, accepting her fate with dignity beside hundreds of less experienced *Rhinolphus hildebrandti*, yellow *Lavia frons* and long-eared *Lonchorina auritas*, each of whom she tried to console with doleful sonnets by their Queen, a great poetess. All were reaching out in agony, sending their final ultrasonic SOSs into the farthest reaches of their domicile, never to be heard from again.

"You can't save everybody," Rajibai said, his eyes welling up with the flow of commiseration. "That is the nature of the world."

Alex Smart had not grasped that fact, not beneath the Pink Leviathan, where his only sound frequencies had been those of AM and FM Los Angeles, of power lines and overhead aircraft and 15 million telephone communications every minute. But the cave was now exerting a symphonic commentary on events within this war zone, and Alex was pulled in deeper by deeper as his companions trudged on behind him.

"I can't see," Sannazaro yelled out. "Just hold on to my tail," Alex said, leading the way.

For nearly an hour they continued, until the three humans could hear what Alex had heard from the beginning: millions of bats debating their gains and losses, certain individuals going out to bat for new policies of reconciliation, others mobilizing for an all-out assault on the insect world and justifying their calls for aggression on grounds of new priorities of pollination in the twenty-first century. It was mightily confusing, with little in the way of protocol or order. All were hanging upside down, which meant that the blood rushed to their little heads, and they spoke out of turn and tended to formulate impressive Utopias of their own without considering the impact of their high twines and grunts. For all that, thought Marigold, there was a refreshing wild-west absence of civic decorum; these were free thinkers, no quiet desperation or nine-to-fivers among them.

But bat society was obviously wrought of a very unique form of parliamentarian entropy. A town-hall meeting conducted without any concern for a conclusion. All that mattered in the end were how many tens of thousands of pounds of insect biomass had been consumed. It was, alas, a consumer-driven society. The measure of success was the depth of guano, or financial indices of nitrogen and phosphorus. Those few philosophically minded bats who strode toward an alternative barometer of achievement were deemed outcasts, and these were the first to be encountered by Alex and his companions on the very outskirts of the bat village deep within the cave.

"Who are *you*?" asked one of these furry frown bats.

"I am Alex," replied Alex in a tone of voice utterly untranslatable.

"But are you one of us or one of them?" inquired the brown's female companion, who hung beside him, tensed.

"I am both," replied Alex. "Son of the Mother of all Bats, the Queen of Bongo Bongo."

From the ceiling came a dreadful gasp, expelled at a frequency which quickly traveled along all the inner rock walls until it reached the central pillar of bat society, a 400-foot cliff of quartzite upon which more than ten million working bats hung in suspended animation, digesting their victory over the invading stingers.

"You? Can it be, at last?" murmured the furry contagion, their little heads weaving back and forth like a Nebraska wheat field by moonlight, their wings fluttering, their little hands fumbling in the ague of their excitement.

"I need the map, for we are lost," said Alex, anxious to find any foreknowledge of Bongo Bongo Land.

"This way," replied the inner core of leaders, who held sway over the millions of bats' governing body. Their lair was presidential, white guano encaking the multiples of high-level parterre stations, not less fine than the Managing Director's box at the Paris Opera.

Alex took the lead; the Commander, his son and then Sannazaro followed on all fours. Within a short time they were inside the last of the hidden chambers, able to see by the dim light multiplied and magnified like charged coupling devices in all the millions of sets of eyes which looked down upon them; a kind of Olympic torch, carried from those radical, introspective, philosopher bats on the outer corridors—their light coming directly from outside the cave by minute increments—to all those other working bats who feared exposure to UV-B and had by evolutionary necessity to remain in darkness.

"Imagine," whispered the Commander, as they crawled deeper and deeper into the cave. "Their eyeballs are illuminating their habitat, making clear the political hierarchy. I would imagine there to be a dozen PhD dissertations in neurophysiology and physics laid out before us."

They pushed on further, then Marigold called a sudden halt.

"There!" he gasped, seeing on the wall the unmistakable signs of a map. "Cave paintings executed how many tens of thousands of years ago?" Alex studied the intricate drawings of ochre, orange, burnt umber and lavender with care. "I think it is the way into Bongo Bongo Land," he said. "It appears to be about 200 miles to the southwest of here."

"Is it really a map?" Sannazaro asked, struck at last by the doubtfulness of such a stunning coincidence. "Maybe they're just traces of primeval guano formed by the leaching of minerals and erosion of moisture?" But, amazingly, Latin and Old English. Whatever the markings were, Marigold made a mental picture of their apparent instructions while directing hundreds of other burning questions at Alex. By now his resemblance to the bats' mythic ancestor had become too obvious, though Alex professed to utter uncertainty with respect to such matters, and diplomatically avoided committing himself to any impression for fear of stoking high-frequency ululations of hope or, conversely, eliciting anxiety, strengthening doubts, provoking ire or undermining confidence. Bats, he explained later, aside from keeping the world a heavenly place to live, were the most sensitive of all mammals, incapable of coping with disappointment or too much excitement. They easily took to fever; succumbed to depression, chilblains and coronary heart disease. Adult-onset diabetes was their scourge, but even so nothing could deter their sweet tooth, a fact eliciting great admiration amongst the existentialist trio.

"They need to be encouraged, not daunted; emboldened rather than undermined. Their hearts are all a ripple, though they try to conceal their delicate constitution with intimidating teeth. It is a big put-on. They are lambs of Lucretius, fur balls of Betsy Ross, soapy sentimental cuddlers from *Winnie the Pooh* who just happen to have a taste for insects."

"What about Dracula?" asked Rajibai.

"The insulting fabrication of a novelist, nothing more. Ask nearly any Transylvanian, let alone African: they've never heard of him."

When he, Marigold, Rajibai and Sannazaro eventually took their leave, ten million eyes wept. The quartet had remained with the elected officials no more than 35 minutes, but it was long enough to have solidified into a rumor-mill of emotional spasms.

"They're not good at saying goodbye," explained Alex, between bouts with his own hankie.

CHAPTER 178
How Alex Reached Bongo Bongo Land and What Adventures Awaited Him and the Marigolds Among the Heebie-Jeebies and Yoo-Hoos

BACK OUTSIDE THE GROTTO, all confirmed that the map they'd seen in the Cave of Communions—splashed in all the colorful painterly doodles that weathered guano is heir to—was probably on the mark. Its runes and rocky hieroglyphs seemed to point to the left, and down a wee bit, directing them away from the deadly chasm of biting insect hordes and beyond, across the dried-out ancient sea bottom and leading by miserable turns to Bongo Bongo Land.

They anxiously traversed a secret ravine whose arching walls of slate were smeared with petroglyphs painted long ago in ivory white The remarkable gallery depicted happy hippos copulating in the marshgrass. There were cavalier cranes tiptoeing about, century after century. And albino whales breaching to their heart's delight. They had all once lived in an inland sea, famed among the local green velvet ants who still carried the memories. In those times, a 1,200-mile sargasso provided a veritable nursery—the finest *hors d'oeuvres* and bedtime rhymes—for every young sand dollar, demur tunicate and brittle star. The ooze primeval, larded with high-protein goodies, stretched across most of the western sub-Sahara at a time when Africa could still boast of the juiciest cumulous clouds and most lubricated wetlands in the world.

But presently, the foursome found only an exasperating alkaline flat, desiccated shores of spiny exoskeleton stretching from one mirage to another. This deathtrap harbored only the echoes of waves, the ghosts of extinct genera, no real water. On further scrutiny, it seemed to Marigold that they were submerged, horizon to horizon, within an invisible conch shell. Sultry tar pits. Surface temperatures of 153 degrees, by the Commander's dizzy reckoning.

The sweat that commingled with their tear ducts was poisoned by acrid pestilences swirling, thickening, sucking in all of the continent's inert gases into this one basin. It languished in the throb of windless heat, 400 square miles that were stuck below sea level.

"We must move in measured paces," Alex suggested. He was swathed head to carnelian webbed foot in Banana Republic attire that succeeded only partially in keeping the sun out of his puffy face. He covered his enormous weepy eyes with fighter-pilot goggles. Marigold had acquired them at a welding shop adjoining the tarmac for private jets at LAX.

"What am I seeing?" the Caballero hastened, rubbing his eyes. "Methinks there is a caravan of giant sowbugs across the land!"

Upon closer scrutiny, that's exactly what it was: common pillbugs, *Armadillidium vulgare africanus*, members of the crustacean class, which thus situated them somewhere between antediluvian trilobites, lovesick lobsters and beetle-brained beetles, the common everyday kind that show up between bricks in Commonwealth gardens ... with one stupendous exception, acknowledged by all present. These were the older ones, 90 feet long, their shells as thick as Stegosaurs'.

"There must be thousands of them!" Rajibai delighted, racing across the hard stubble flats to see if it might be possible to ride on one, since they were all going in the direction of Bongo Bongo Land.

"I wouldn't do that!" Alex shouted out, but too late. The fast-stepping lad had leapt onto the first bug before him, only to see it close down into a tightly fortressed rolling ball. That translated into a 60-foot-high spheroid in topspin, at the zenith of which Rajibai clung to boiler-plate slabs of enameled skin with his bare fingers, his legs dangling over the abyss. Quite a feat of calisthenics, considering the moving hull he had to grip. Fortunately for him, all of the other 1,000 or so bugs took their cue and did the same, so that the desert seemed suddenly decorated with gray Ferris wheels. The infants stood only ten feet high, so it was upon their backs, one by one, that Rajibai was able to leap in descending order from the highest to the lowest, until he reached the sea floor, at which point the pillbugs spread out once again and recommenced their slow caravan towards the southwest.

"That alone was worth the whole price of admission to Africa," Rajibai rejoiced.

"Can you hear them?" Alex asked, his long ears minutely attuned to the chorus of sowbug sonorities.

"Not a word," remarked the *valet de pied*; "Nothing," said the Commanding boots; "Gripes and complaining," aired the boy. Alex could hear it all.

As they moved across the candescent landscape, a slow-coursing flock of curious ancient storks caught up with them, gabbing all day long. Alex could understand numerous words of their language and occasionally threw in his own opinions on some teleological matter or another.

Later on, the foursome encountered ladybugs thicker than caramel who had arrived from all over Africa to mate on the precipitous slopes of an extinct volcano. They also found scores of rainbow trout and golden salmon flashing through knee-deep brine, heading (Alex deduced) upstream from the ocean.

Eventually, after considerable travail, they reached a refreshingly wind-savaged timberline, where branches were bare or burnt out: aspen, birch, fruits and Russian olives uniformly petrified; seed-bearing cones no more than fossil memories. It was in this bewitching gulch of final stands and fateful glens that the muggy odor of salt enveloped the travelers in a labyrinthine mist. For two nights and three days they waited for the air to clear.

By nightfall of the third yellow moon, Alex took it upon himself to scout the immediate Beyond, sniffing the peripheries of their hastily assembled bivouac, his stout little body and cloak of cloven tissue hunched over the duff of charred guava seeds, running spiders and lapis-wings of bygone *Lepidoptera* that littered the ground underclaw. Rajibai joined him for company, but the Commander and Sannazaro would not quit their bedrolls, using their backs as buffers against the infernal hurricane that roared around them, dispersing the embers of their campfire for 1,200 miles. Moreover, Sannazaro's lower back had become a living hell, the discs drying up, his fissette joints swollen around the L4, legs tingling. Movement did not come without a price.

Alex looked afar.

"What?" Rajibai whispered.

"I'm not sure ..."

He stared towards a supra-darkness. The winds caught his little frame, his nostrils worked the air, his arms rose up, and Alex Smart for the first time since infancy raced alongside the currents, then leapt upwards toward the moon. The sky received him.

"Away!" he whistled, in a language Rajibai could not comprehend. Alex spiraled high into the luminous night. Rajibai watched him spin and curl, glide and free-fall with an enviable glee. Suddenly, others were arriving, night creatures hurtling towards him. "Alex!" the boy screamed.

But there was nothing to fear. Bats, attracted to his avant-garde accent and rusty pronunciations, had picked up his eccentric echo-locations.

"Hello! Hello!" exclaimed Alex in exulted tonalities.

"You're too big to fly. Get down, you idiot!" the first one protested. "Where do you come from speaking that way?" asked another in a sweet seductive screech. She flew directly beside him, skimming the tops of trees, grabbing the odd grasshopper or mosquito with her little fangs along the way.

"From Bongo Bongo Land," Alex replied. "By way of an annoying 25-year detour through Los Angeles."

"Yum," went the lovely Ruwenzori connoisseuse, who made mincemeat of all the arthropods she'd nabbed in a matter of rapacious mouthfuls. "And did they teach you to squeak like that at the Los Angeles district school?" she mocked.

"Let's just say it's been many years since I have spoken my native tongue," Alex confessed, flying cartwheels and Arabians.

"Well then, that explains the SssssUuu instead of a DddddOooo; the past-perfect WHEeeeeeNee where most of us prefer the more precise and evocative consonant. But don't worry. The bats of Bongo Bongo are so agitated over everything else that's going on, your silly enunciation should prove, if anything, a bit of light relief in a jungle of worries and pitfalls."

"What do you mean? What's happened?"

But she was already returning in a dive bomb towards the rigid limits of her own territory, which she had exceeded by several hundred yards. "And get out of the sky before you kill yourself!" she added instructively, and with a disappearing chuckle unique to bats.

"Wait! At least tell me which direction, won't you?" shrieked Alex, sweeping low towards some rocks.

She looked back, nodded her elegantly pointed head to the south, then flew off. But it was too late for Alex, whose query had distracted him from his flight plan. He smashed headlong into a weeping pistachio and fell to the darkling earth.

Rajibai was there within minutes. "I saw what happened. Wow! What did she say?"

"We're just 40-odd miles southwest of the border," Alex exclaimed, lifting himself up from a swarm of obnoxious mountain ants that had gotten onto his wings and were wedging their pincers between his delicate cartilage. "Get off!" he flailed, shaking the buggers out and sweeping up a few with his tongue.

He was not, in principle, opposed to ants. Rather liked them, actually. But these ones were very aggressive, without apology or rationale, and he did not cotton to them one iota. Annoyed by their persistence, he urged the party back to camp—nearly a mile away. There they mulled over the map and revisited by starlight the particulars of their hurried odyssey. The world was at stake, Alex waged.

The next day all headed downhill, into a fabulist forest of relic podocarps and thickening *Marantaceae*, of iron weed and taro root so high and thick as to be sunless. Any light that dared to penetrate these scabrous and tubercular woods was sucked up in a black hole of swampland where not an iota of chlorophyll managed to flourish. Rajibai was itching all over. His head was sinking, his throat parched, his palms sweaty.

"I think I've got the heebie-jeebies," he warned.

"You said the HJ word! You mustn't!" Alex cautioned, remembering a warning from long ago.

"Don't scare me. You're giving me the heebie-jeebies too," he complained even more loudly.

"Stop it at once!" Alex reiterated.

"Would you two just give it up? Now *I'm* getting the heebie-jeebies," inveighed Marigold.

"Three times. We're doomed!" cried Alex. And ...

"*OK. That's it!*" rang out the creepiest voice any of them had heard, as out from behind a grove of dead bramble thickets leapt the head honcho of the Heebie-Jeebies themselves, followed by ten dozen of his merciless brigands. Rajibai was the only one rational enough to note that they were dressed like eight-foot-tall bipedal turkey vultures, beards covered in swollen pimples, neck muscles bulging with all the gory meals they must have pirated on the run, talons as sharp as German butcher knives, cheeks bulbous and boil-enflamed, eyes bloodshot, temples maimed, toes more enormous than gargoyles, skin, tissue and bones eroded by super parvo or lingering leprosy or some other anomalous affliction, though without the customary weakening of tone, vim or vigor. They stood like deceased African Vikings, blunt, rude, callused living corpses that haunted forests, felled virtue, despoiled all virgins, drew to the brink the slightest wish, intercepted goodness, stole every holiday and, generally speaking, played vexatious pranks on all those who dared cross their paths of black urine, and/or recited their names three times.

"Of course, if one should somehow inconceivably manage to get them on your good side, there is nothing they wouldn't do to help you," Alex whispered to Rajibai, who was closest to his size. "Even give up their last stick of chewing gum."

"Who ... who are you?" demanded Mr Marigold, recovered enough to find words.

"I am Aristotle's lantern, Dr Pollieri's clubfoot, Schiller's rotten apple, Casper David Friedrich's monk with his back turned on the world in a blizzard," recited the leader of the HJs.

"Those aren't clothes you're wearing, are they?" asked the perspicacious Rajibai.

"Nope," replied all ten dozen at the same time. "They're Heebie-Jeebies," Alex trembled aloud. "I told you not to—"

"Quiet, cretin!" barked the grotesque-looking leader. "Now what do you want?"

Said Alex, "I must find the Queen of Bongo Bongo Land."

Mocking laughter erupted from the HJ ranks.

"What makes you think she wouldn't kill you the minute she even heard you dare to utter her name in vain, which in these troubled times and woods of turmoil constitutes nothing less than a capital crime?" asked the leader.

"Because she is kind and generous and good," replied Alex.

"Hummm ..." He and his colleagues had no choice but to mull that one over.

"Who told you so?" the leader eventually inquired.

"Nobody told me. I remember her that way."

"You've *met* the Queen? He's met the Queen!"

"*He's met the Queen!* " The Heebie-Jeebies' refrain rose up in flabbergasted self-doubt.

"Impossible!" rang one voice; "Ludicrous!" another; "What arrogance," a third. "She'll rip him bare limb by limb," said a fourth, whose verdict elicited a unanimous refrain: "From limb to bloody limb!"

"But wait," the leader pointed out in quieter tones. "He does, come to think of it, resemble the very Queen an odd bit, does he not?"

All took their leader's cue, addled by the mere suggestion, which led their simple minds to see what they had now fixed in thought. "By Heebie, by Jeebie, he does, doesn't he!"

All concurred. There was no doubting it by that point. Spitting image. Remarkable! Identical twins. Kissing cousins. Formally linked.

"That's on account of the fact she's my mother," replied Alex calmly, his tone belying the sweating terror that he and his friends were still experiencing, despite the Heebie-Jeebies' excitement. For the Heebie-Jeebies, much like porcupine fish, had a habit of inflating their muscles, bellies, necks and cheeks with foul-smelling airs which they exhaled all over the place when they meant to intimidate invaders. When doing so, a steam rose from the tops of their heads and spittle drooled down their pimply cheeks.

"His *mother!* " Their faces and other parts deflated before the sheer power of the idea. Arms and legs gesticulating out of the sack of their middle portions. Body tissues rolling off.

"But that's not possible," the leader declared at last, inhaling more intimidating air all over again. "The Queen's one son was kidnapped thousands of moons ago."

"Now I'm back. It's truly me. You see!"

And Alex revealed a scar on his third metatarsal.

All examined it with pathological interest. Still, protocol required more.

"If you are her son, what's the password?" demanded the leader.

Mr Marigold looked to Alex, who looked to Rajibai, who looked to Sannazaro, who looked to the sky. But Alex couldn't remember.

"There, you see! He doesn't know it! A liar and fabricator in our midst," shouted the mob, who now began quickly to work themselves up into a frenzy of destructive force. Their mandate was clear. They always followed their leader.

But just then Alex's unique acoustical sensitivities detected an odd whispering noise emanating from behind a large canopy of balsam.

"Yoo-hoo," went the voice.

"Excuse me one moment," Alex begged the leader, who had made himself once again ferocious. And without waiting for a reply, he ducked behind the trees and there met face to face with—who else but the Yoo-Hoos.

"Why, I remember you ..." went Alex. "You're Veg. And that's Tweety and Bartok."

"What a memory!" cried the sentimental old sergeant of the Yoo-Hoos, who reminded all those hiding with him of the magnificent identity of Alex Smart. The two respective reminiscences embraced with awkward hugs, given their vastly differing physiognomies.

A palpable sigh issued from the many Yoo-Hoo cavalry. Suddenly, they threw themselves into the defensive, spears raised, when Rajibai appeared behind the canopy and cried out with a start, causing many of the Yoo-Hoos, the Commander, Sannazaro and Rajibai himself to jump three feet in the air with an awful fright. The setting was not conducive to calm untheatrics.

"It's all right. He's with me," Alex assured the sergeant.

"Who are they!" the boy shrieked. They were the queerest-looking creatures he'd ever seen, after the Heebie-Jeebies. Like upright slugs, or chocolate croissants, with Oriental faces as hairy as muskrats' and the size of ping-pong tables.

"They are the Yoo-Hoos. Old friends. They always travel off to the side of the Heebie-Jeebies, daiquiris in hand, for just such occasions as these."

Tweety offered Rajibai a beaker. A genuine gesture of friendship. "What's the password? Hurry!" pressed Alex.

The sergeant whispered it into his ear, guano-à-guano, adding, "Of course, it changes every week. Has to, given what's going on."

"What's going on?"

"You don't know?" began Veg. "Humans have occupied all the beaches in Bongo Bongo, and the forests too. They're destroying everything. The last remaining Bongo Bongos are in hiding. Were you not surprised to hear such silence?"

"Why, you're absolutely right. When I was a child the tribal people— though their numbers and scope of activities was minimal—played drums day and night. Totally annoying, never understood it. That's why my mother and I, and all the other bats, retreated high up into the mountains where the bongo drumming was less audible and you could get a good night's sleep. Now, there's not even a single drumbeat."

"That's right. Everything is coming to a terrible termination and nobody knows how to stop the mayhem. The innocent drumbeat has been replaced by all these enormous hotels, rivers dammed up to make swimming pools, forests mowed over for golf courses, and beaches entirely cleared for badminton. By the way, what's skiing? There's talk of building ski slopes, whatever they are, through the upper jungle. They say it will require artificial snow machines. And they've captured all the birds and placed them in disgusting little cages, put chains on many of our finest unicorns, turned countless charcoal colobus monkeys into stew, and enslaved the pointillist zebras. They've trapped hundreds of mermaids and dolphins in their swimming pools, placed reins on their rostrums and drugged them so that all the fat greasy disgusting human tourists can ride on their backs. Worst of all, according to Heebie-Jeebie intelligence, the owners of the hotel chain have put out a reward for the Queen herself. They've gotten it into their heads that she might serve humans as the ultimate tourist attraction, so they've built an enormous cage in which to house her once they capture her. And have begun taking soldiers by helicopter into the highlands where they've systematically been burning one hectare after another of forest. It won't be long before the Queen Mother has nowhere to go. It's a state of war."

"How long as this been going on?" asked Alex.

Veg sighed. "Over a year. I'm telling you, Alex, you won't believe it.

The wetlands are almost gone. Stingrays are not welcome by moonlight. The Ridleys, greens and leatherback turtles are all confused and have stopped laying their eggs because the hatchlings can't figure out which lights are which. For 200 million years they've been going out to sea, attracted to the reflections of stars and the moon on the waves. Now they're hatching and heading in the opposite direction, directly into the three newly built discotheques. We've tried to help them, but they can't make out Yoo-Hoo language. It's a disaster. By our calculations, the Queen Mother has less than a month before her forests are gone. So naturally the Heebie-Jeebies are suspicious of any humans entering from the rear of the territory. Say, how did you manage that, anyway? You would have had to come across the Infinite Desert? The Howling Mountains? The Mirage Marshes? Not to mention Gnat's Escarpment!"

Alex described their taxing adventures, but the Heebie-Jeebies were losing patience and demanding the password, which Alex—with prompting from Veg—whispered to the leader. With that, and other tidbits of mounting proof, the Heebie-Jeebies decided that Alex and his compatriots were bona fide, bowed down before them, then proudly escorted them directly to the Queen Mother.

"You'll have to shimmy across miles of muck, disguise yourself with fire, breathe through crushed gravel and do as we do," said the leader. Alex explained everything to the trio. The Squire fortified himself with Tiger Balm smeared atop his buttocks and buckets of alcohol down his gullet. Marigold resolved without further ado to decimate the developers and have them tried for crimes against Nature before an international tribunal in The Hague, adopting all the new legal precedents that had been employed against the Serbian military. This plan ignited cheers from all the Heebie-Jeebies and Yoo-Hoos, none of whom had been to The Hague, but all imagined French fries there, which they craved, doused in mayonnaise. Adding additional juridical precedent, the Commander resolved to somehow induce the US Commerce Department to sue the French nation under the *Pelly Amendment to the Fishermen's Protective Act of 1967* allowing a President to enforce sanctions against another country that has violated the *Convention on International Trade in Endangered Species.* In this case, a blatant corporate policy akin to The Final Solution, targeting Alex's entire tribe, who were endemic to Queen Mother Mountain. Neither the Heebie-Jeebies nor Yoo-Hoos had heard of Pelly, or the convention, but all agreed to march on Washington if Marigold thought it would help.

CHAPTER 179
Lambs Hiding in the Pit Viper's Pants

AFTER FIVE DAYS' journey, Mr Marigold looked out upon the highlands of Bongo Bongo from a wide promontory and saw only cumulus clouds of smoke: rainforest burning for hundreds of square miles. Beside him were his faithful liveried Squire, his indefatigable son, and his most recent crusader in the person of Alex Smart, whose reunion with his mother, the Queen of Bongo Bongo, had taken on planetary dimensions. The enemy was there before them—a French hotel monopoly and its mercenaries—and if it could not be conquered, then every Jain principle of non-violence Rajibai had imparted to his old man, each pearly intuition passed along by Sannazaro, all that subantarctic mirth of Crowquill, and the lessons of Anna's exquisite world were wasted passions. Surely the collective wisdoms of these profound individuals and their beliefs were more powerful than these heinous misfits who saw profit in a carcass and passion in every wasteland? Was there not more pleasure to be taken from gentleness than crime? Veganism over prostate cancer and male impotency,the results of clogged arteries induced by meat-eating and the consumption of milk? Had not the twenty-first century learned its lesson? Were we incapable of transcending the conspiracy of comfort, the locket of futile familiarity, that mind-numbing nemesis of alarm clocks, school bells, telephones, the judge's hammer, the Internet, city sirens, sterile statutes and petty tyrants, every burden of alleged duty and patriotic gore, the sweltering idolatry of populist superstition, the shackles of male and female mythology, all those certitudes of science and doctrines of progress? Wall Street? Or were we forever condemned to the same atrocious treadmills and outrageous trespasses of history, without the capacity to remake ourselves, to reinvent the future? Had we lost our ability to be animals, children, gods and humans?

But it would be difficult, thought Rajibai, to tempt Alex and his kind off a diet of insects.

Seeing Veg, Tweety, Bartok and all the other Yoo-Hoos shedding tears as their forests went up in malevolent torchlight, Marigold spun 1,000 times round in his own solitary flame of untouchable frustration. His vigilante's clamoring for justice shredded his heart, scorched his bone marrow. The Heebie-Jeebies sensed the wrath swirling within him.

The leader, known to his immense army as Fireball was standing side by side with the much smaller Veg, and patted him on the back. "We have a plan," he exclaimed. "And you—" he was addressing the Commander "—happen to have arrived at the very moment of its brash execution."

Marigold had little confidence that his new allies, the Heebie-Jeebies and Yoo-Hoos, were any kind of match for the French. These were the same Frenchmen, after all, who'd murdered a Greenpeace anti-nuclear activist in New Zealand and irradiated islands in the South Pacific. The same French aptitude that thought nothing of sautéeing snails and pulverizing geese livers, force-feeding the birds down their throats, to satisfy dilettante palates. Moreover, it was clear from their disposition that the Yoo-Hoos were somehow genetically related to the dainty, delicate Peekabouties of Soqotra—which argued for a new theory of continental drift and the migration of Paleolithic peoples, but also undermined their credibility as warriors. As for Fireball and his battalions, it was true that their appearance was frightful; that they lived almost exclusively upon the physic mash of bellyache bushes mixed with crushed limestone, seasoned with ticks that had already died of tuberculosis. But they suffered from one overwhelming limitation, which, it must be confessed, none of them had noticed about themselves: they were physically incapable of harming any living thing. The Deputy Commander, Jackcreek, was terrified of the wind, spooked by beavers and pigeons, as bellicose as a butler. If they struck out at someone, their punches never landed. If they threw a stone, jettisoned a spear, laid a trap of any kind, their efforts were in vain. They could not kick even a ball or harass a fly. Nothing connected; no contact whatsoever was possible when initiated with ill-will. Their demeanors were less offensive than kittens, more contrite than the Brothers of Piety.

Now an even bigger surprise made itself known. Their freakish demeanor was but a clever ruse, a transparent edifice devised, one must assume, over millions of years as a kind of protective shield, much like Tibetan demonology behind whose ghastly veils presided polished Penstemons schooled in all the ways of restraint. Presently, as the Heebie-Jeebies marched out in guerrilla formation towards the uplands, the foursome was able to see through their silly disguise.

"Goodness me!" proclaimed Rajibai, seeing how their voices were now soft and mellifluous, their swollen pimples sweet little dimples, their eight-foot-tall turkey vulture aspects nothing more than the helplessness of baby does or ambling fawns. No more the street-shark grimaces and necrotic facial tissues, the menacing eyeballs or maggot-infested claws. For all their Lilliputian self-importance, the Heebie-Jeebies behaved more in accord with the legendary Lullaby Tribe of Zanzibar, reflected Marigold, than Heebie-Jeebies. All of which spelled very bad news indeed for the prospect of winning any battle. Even their diet was different. Poison nuts and chunks of gravel were in this environment replaced by a pabulum of plantain cooked in teardrops and seasoned with soft touches and packaged in pampers.

"They're goners," ventured Sannazaro.

"But do we dare tell them how really very gentle and loving they are? Won't that destroy their self-esteem, humiliate them to the point of wrecking Heebie-Jeebie civilization?" Marigold contemplated aloud, as Fireball and his top colonels stomped by, proudly thrusting their imagined talons forward.

"But I've got an idea," said Alex who, after all, was very smart. "See that cliff yonder, jutting above the highest of the coral trees? From there, we should gain a strategic position over the whole of the ridgeline. I'm no sapper, but the stratification suggests limestone, which means of course a network of caves therein. That must be the location of the openings to the underground network, where I was born, and where the Queen Mother and her attendants maintain the bat nursery. The plan, therefore, is this ..." And he went on to outline an ingenious initiative.

Several hours later, the multitudes of Heebie-Jeebies and Yoo-Hoos arrived at the very crest of angling cordillera that Alex had spied earlier. From their high point on the couloir it was possible to view the Amazonian-style devastation occurring to three sides below. Not since the felling (also by the French) of ten million baobabs for cotton planting in Mali during the early 1950s had West Africa seen such devastation. There were no fewer than 38 bulldozers plowing down primeval gardens; hundreds of African laborers working the cranes, unloading helicopters, setting fires, chopping and uprooting, ripping and detonating, hunting the yellow boar and orange Easter lizards, poisoning the under-stories of canopy, tossing grenades down gopher holes, and pursuing the shy hairy halloweens—a subspecies of mountain marmot with mask-like faces and singular pouches in which they stuffed all the marshmallows and matzoth balls, licorice root and fickle fennel they could find.

It was, in short, a terrible and murderous sight. If something weren't done soon, all of Bongo Bongo Land would be erased from living memory, and the remarkable forests of Queen Mother Mountain obliterated.

"If you wouldn't mind holding back all the troops for just a moment," Alex asked of Fireball and Veg. "I believe there is a way to stop this madness."

"Certainly," replied the two gallants.

Alex scrambled to the entrance of the largest of the caves and there spent much effort clearing his throat, twisting spit into his whiskers, rubbing banana leaf on his hands and exercising his wingtips.

"Do re me fa so la ti do ..." he practiced. When he felt confident about his arpeggios, he launched into higher frequencies of musical expenditure, squeaking louder and louder until that little ultrasonic engine in his throat had the throw-weight of a penetrating alarm bell—a strident whistle with carriage across the whole mountain range of Bongo Bongo.

Something from deep within the mountain started to stir. Whistles meeting whistles from every cranny of rock face, fissures in the earth, seams and alcoves in the ironwood, pores in the alpine wall, carried thither from the dungeon reaches of 10,000 subterranean chambers.

Suddenly, the army of bats came pouring forth into the smoke-engorged day, all squinting in pain but biting the bullet.

The swarming mammals were a familiar sight to the Marigolds after the Chasm of Communions. Millions upon millions of precious flying bats, all arriving along the ridge, where they alighted in formation and, mouths agape, gazed upon their mythic ally. A roar of remembrance went up, as they saluted their long-lost Prince Alex.

"It's wonderful to have you back, sir," said the Queen's lieutenant. "We knew you were coming. If you would permit me, sir, your mother is expecting you."

"Where is she?"

"I believe she's preparing your room in the deepest of the caves, fluffing up the pillows and toasting you some bat muffins and guano cheese the way you used to like it."

"That's my mom," he said with an embarrassed roll of his eyes. "The world is going up in flames and she's worried about the color of my bath towels."

"Rouge, sir, with lavender chevrons and azure rectangles, a bit like early Mondrian."

"Thank you, Lieutenant."

"What's the plan, sir?"

"It's very simple and, frankly, I'm surprised you've not yet thought of it yourself."

"We were waiting for your orders, sir."

Alex then described the play. It was, indeed, a simple maneuver, and one that came naturally to bats.

"About fangs!" the lieutenant squeaked at the 15,000 Herz necessary for him to be heard by the millions of soldiers awaiting their commands.

At that moment both Fireball and Veg arrived atop the ridge, out of breath.

The lieutenant bowed in greeting.

"What's the deal?" asked Fireball, eager to involve his thousands of Heebie-Jeebies, still believing them to be the fiercest warriors of all.

"Yoo-hoo," muttered Veg to the leader.

Fireball leaned over so that he could hear what Veg was urgently trying to tell him. "I'm afraid they can see us," whispered the chief of the Yoo-Hoos. "They know the truth."

Fireball looked all around and began to detect the bemused conspiracy that surrounded him and his troops. His confidence at once evaporated and it was as if he were suddenly an emperor without his trousers, or even his briefs. Now all the Heebie-Jeebies hid themselves with a horrified embarrassment.

"I'm sorry," Fireball apologized.

"No need, no need. You meant well," said the lieutenant.

"Of course you did," applied Alex. "There's nothing wrong with being gentle and hopelessly sentimental."

"And everybody truly appreciates your having escorted us through the most dangerous country of all time," Mr Marigold concluded. "Who else could have done it?"

"What should we do?" Fireball asked with appalling meekness.

"Wait in the caves," said Alex, "and protect all the baby bats who are too young to fly."

"What of the Queen Mother herself," added the lieutenant. "She's probably busy washing some fresh sheets for our beloved Crown Prince. Speaking of whom, if you'll permit me, sir, I must insist that you too wait in the cave. You must not risk your life. Nor those of your companions, to whom we owe a great debt."

"Agreed," said Alex wisely. He knew not to upset the lieutenant, or rearguard. Bats are easily discomfited; their highly evolved but delicate bat brains plunge into self-doubt at the slightest hint of uncertainty. Alex understood that the best policy was a mixture of conciliation, discretion and adulation. In any event, it was crucial that the lieutenant maintain his boldness if he and all his minions were to carry out their dangerous mission successfully.

And so got under way the preparations for the most important battle in the history of the world.

CHAPTER 180
The Battle for Queen Mother Mountain

THE DONNYBROOK POSITIONS were assumed; every station, combat zone, blitz bottom, cross hair, red flag, platoon of dragons, joust, tussle and scuffle-point well rehearsed. The vast battalion of bats practiced their butchery and uproar, stoked themselves into meditative frenzies of dissension, got about their circumvallations and balustrades with mottos cached from all the famed theaters of operations across African history and Texas Stadium. Trumpets and brays, hoots and barks. Squeaks high pitched enough to crack human teeth or induce a peccary to pee. They were ready to beat those Frenchmen into soufflé.

Meanwhile, Alex, Marigold, Rajibai, Sannazaro, the Heebie-Jeebies and Yoo-Hoos entered the Master Cave, forming a protective semicircle around the thousands of suspended baby-bat hammocks at fluttermouse school. It was there that the softest poetry in the world was taught—lines from the bat equivalents of Petrarch and Coleridge, which Alex attempted to translate. Los Angeles had perverted his linguistic touch. The rhymes lacked for that special high-toned hexameter:

"Oh glorious bat, these eyes are yours,
Reflect the heavens in whose blue night soars;
Of jocund din, commotion wild,
Uncharted freedom, Nature's child ..."

... and so on, lyrically, until poor Alex was back in nursery school himself.

"It just doesn't read in English," he said apologetically. "Try to imagine a squeak so kind-hearted and fine that all sound rhymes, all meanings, combine; every word is the tutelage of pure reciprocity, each smile incarnate in all loving smiles, circumstances so complicit with the divine that there is nothing in your universe that threatens. Paradise looms for all time. Flight, feeding, sleep, yawns, music, touch—everything you do in your hammock of webbed claw; every sound you hear, feel, believe, know to be true, *is* true, and forever. To be raised by the entire colony, hanging effortlessly beneath the gold stalagmites with their dripping calcareous ooze down cool stone. A fountain of eternal youth. Granted the freedom of ten million mothers' viviparous dreams. The immunity of all those fathers' pride. The safety of ten million siblings. The warm glowing dark of the cave. Food in plenty. That is the normal life of the infant bat, who sleeps as soundly as the Amazonian sloth, dances in the dark like the Japanese crane, preens and plays with all the vigor of the Yosemite cliff swallow. And, like quadrupeds, sucks vigorously the gold milk which is their passion. As streamlined in their flight as the effortless leaps at 70 kph of the pintapeds down under."

Meanwhile, outside, 18 million soldiers lined up in one phalanx after another atop the reeling ramparts. How to imagine this number of altruists, waging non-violence with the physiological means at their desperate disposal? Neither on horseback nor upon jackals; with no armor, firepower or GPS, only the hooks and claws of mammalian evolution, bolstered by the cause of a century, righteous self-defense and an instinctive command-and-control formation that took no prisoners, granted no ambiguity, was ethically resolved. There could be no more vivid and rich exposé of the Righteous Few, survival of the Fit, of that gene guaranteed to maximize poetic justice over short-lived extremes. Here, in this battalion of level-headed passivity, was a ferocious ethic determined to make good on the promise of loyalty to one's kind. It was a frightening truth that demarcated the species, made religious separate orders, kingdoms, families, phyla and taxa. In short, gave historical precedent to all those explanations at the heart of zoological sciences.

The lieutenant issued the directives, one by one: "All right now, bats. This is it. I'm not going to make a flowery speech, quoting Richard the Bathearted, or those infamous words from the Battle of Battysburg. You all know what's at stake here. So first, I want you all to hold hands and meditate on those you love ... That's it. Now give the bat standing next to you a big hug ... Very nice. Now gargle, snort and cough up as much sputum, hockers and saliva as you can. More! Even more! Let me hear that phlegm issuing with gusto. Now piss off your lice, get them swarming; polish your fangs and prepare to void your bowels."

It was a terrific speech, the lieutenant thought to himself. So he went on in that Baroque vein until he was certain that the army was feeling thoroughly invincible, pornographic with power.

Then, by sudden command that rang so rudely true, all 18 million of the Chiroptera began fanning their shiny varicolored wings so that a mighty squall could be felt, even far back in the cave where the others waited. And a shadow passed across the limestone bend in the wall, as the hordes volplaned out onto the warpath.

It didn't take long. Let the annals note that 18 million enraged West African bats are a formidable force. Multiply each bat by several thousand lice, and eleven ounces of picric ornithocopros, not to mention a few million bat-loving germs in each hocker, and the terms of their engagement might be surmised. A few hundred Frenchmen didn't stand a chance.

The thousands of pounds of expelled guano destroyed all their equipment. The army sank their fangs in the workers' cheeks, ejected annoying micro-organisms in their hair, drooled all over their faces and down their shirts, bit their lips, sucked their blood, jettisoned feces into their eyes. Moreover, even before the bats had arrived, billions of insects fled their own ground to escape the coming shadow, flying right into the encampment of the French forest-clearing team. Their biomass added kindling to the conflagrations spreading across the sylvan highlands. The lieutenant had known this would happen. Part of the plan. The workers fled, confused, panicking, many into the flames which had by now been fanned out of control and in all directions.

At that very instant, the lieutenant, flying high above the battlefield so that he and his colonels could obtain an overview of the action, uttered a death-defying order which triggered a massive release of deftly targeted urine to put out the fires. Every last bat contributed his and her storehouse.

Within an hour it was over. A vast, ureic steam rose up from the ash and galenobismutite of several hundred humans burnt beyond recognition, and from the thousands of smoldering hectares of hardwood. The sweet smell of fresh guano covered the countryside.

Quite simultaneous to the final hue and cry, the executives of the French multinational happened to be having their biannual board meeting in the free-roaming bottlenose dolphin pools 6,000 feet below, at the heart of the hotel lagoon, wading waist-deep, their drinks in hand. Scantily clad native sylphides of the Bongo Bongo tribe—interns training for careers in hotel management—strolled through the waters beside the busy fat-cats. Little Maui's dolphins scouted in wide elliptical loops, eyeing the distant whitecaps, forever searching for a way out into the ocean.

When suddenly Monsieur Louis, his majesty of all 28 other Paradise Magnifiques throughout the world, heard tell from an underling: "Sir, I bring you news from the mountains. Perhaps you should take a seat."

"Go on, spit it out," Monsieur Louis said.

"Rebel forces have attacked our people," said Bridger, the underling head foreman, in urgent blurs. He handed Lou a pair of high-powered binoculars.

"Call NATO. Call Putin. The NRA. No limits. Bring in the French Navy seals. Kill the bastards! Attach steel cables, rip them apart. No Geneva Convention, no mercy. Mutilation is our policy. Damn it!"

Meanwhile, the millions of surviving warriors had returned to the Mother of all Caves and held a silent vigil for those Chiroptera who had not been so fortunate. They had sacrificed themselves for the noblest of all causes: the saving of the forest and survival of the nursery. There was no pomp, and only modest ceremony, under the circumstances: 263,466 bats had perished. Who will ever know what great chefs, philosophers, first violinists, large format photographers, and brain surgeons were lost to the world among them. But eventually, after solemn remembrance, it was time to proceed into the lowest echelons of the cavern, convey the news of overall success on the battlefield to the Royal Court, and reunite the Queen with her son.

The little twinkling eyes of the baby bats gazed on from their suspended jungle gyms as the procession neared, and profound emotions flooded the perpetual twilight of the inner recess.

"Dear boy," Alex's mother cried. "You've come home at last."

Little Alex wept, enfolded in the Queen's adoring chiropterygia and wings. The Commander and his company were deeply moved. Nothing could be more touching. Just days before, Alex had been a prisoner of Los Angeles. Now he was a free—what? The Commander didn't rightly know how best to think of Alex Smart.

Later that night, over tea, the Queen described everything that happened so many years before. How Alex's father, a scientist working in remotest batland, had saved the nursery from the clutches of merciless army ants but not without extreme injury to himself. When surgeons with the Royal College of Bat

Medicine found him, he was comatose. Miraculously, he pulled through, on a diet of intravenous guano, lice pudding and bat-snot sodas. His strength largely recovered, he and the Queen began meeting every afternoon, talking with the help of a translator, a linguistically precocious parrot. The Queen was greatly impressed with Alex Senior's supreme act of inter-species heroism. After all, an entire generation of new clutches and creches owed their existence to this oddly stirring human.

After some time, the Queen and Alex Senior each sensed that something more than fascination was inspiring their afternoon trysts. Neither risked admission of feelings that were not of this Earth—or not in the beginning, anyway.

"We tried to deny them," the Queen Mother admitted. "After all, humans, to our eyes, were about as grotesque as any creature could be. Imagine legs so long and skinny, a head of patchwork hair so severe and bone belabored. A belly button, for god sakes! Not to mention spindly arms and upright spine which, frankly, makes most bats want to puke at the very sight of it. Yet, I found myself increasingly attracted to this ungainly giant. He stood over six feet, compared with my more seemly 37 inches. Yet, the mammal in each of us somehow recognized the other. One thing led to the next. The night was warm, but there was a cool wind from the south; I won't describe how it actually happened—the touch of his fingers on my wing; the fur here, the gleaming shaft there. I could get all steamy and anatomical but it would not be proper. The fact is, biologies coalesced and an experiment never before tried took place. They say species are distinct. But we proved a higher order of consanguinity. We learned one another's language. Shared ethical standards. He recited John Donne and Pablo Neruda, while I expatiated on Chestnut Consciousness and Bougainvillea Brains. He recited the *Old Testament*, the best of *Job*, *Jeremiah* and *Isaiah*; I contributed Chiropteran crossweb puzzles late into each night. Your father explained Back-to-Nature to 15 million of us—an odd concept, simple and redundant at best—while we, in turn, taught him to see the higher trialectic, which is the unity common to us all. I tried to teach him how to fly, but, alas, it resulted only in embarrassment and several broken bones."

She looked directly at her son and declared, "You, however, have what it takes, and that is due to the recessive genes and dominant chromosomes of every queen bat in your ancestral line, from whence you were gestated. All mammals issued from the same universal impulse to nurture another. You are living proof of the possibilities for true love, young Alex. You got the best of both of us."

Alex, whose romantic nature blossomed full and fair, tears streaking his faraway face, feared to ask: "Where is Papa?"

She paused, then, finally, pointed over the ridge: "Buried in that forest. The fires came close. Thank goodness not too close. His place is eternal. I will take you there tomorrow."

"What happened? How did he die?"

"I don't know," she admitted. "He could not breathe by the age of 45. He smoked inordinate quantities of mistletoe, consumed bundles of truffle. Perhaps there was some connection. Of course, what would we bats know? We never smoke, as it disturbs the population of bacteria living inside the abdominal regions of the lice without whom our entire society would suffer something intangible, indescribable. You can imagine the biological woes these Frenchmen have unleashed upon bat civilization. And I am told they detest lice. Can you imagine? That would be like detesting the air one breathes, the water one drinks."

"But it is probably true," said Alex. "Most humans are strange. And none more so than the Bongo Bongo themselves. Why on earth they fear us I shall never know."

He was quiet for a moment, thinking about his father, and what his parents' relationship must have been like. "Strangeness notwithstanding, you truly loved each other, didn't you?" he asked at last. He had to know.

"Yes. Very much. Your father called me Flora," she confided. "I suppose because of my insatiable appetite for night nectar."

Later, the Queen Mother inquired of Alex's friends, and Alex told her of the extraordinary circumstances of his meeting with the Commander, Sannazaro and Rajibai in a Los Angeles dungeon. Curtsies and royal discussions ensued for half the night, but were then followed by all the eternal matters at hand; questions of life and death, the nature of bat conscience, high frequency semiotics, Erasmus's folly, Darwin's facial expressions, Malinowski's Trobrianders, Planck's Constant, and the human legends of Bat Man. The Commander saw no reason to elucidate upon Alex's incarceration in an LA insane asylum. Queen Mother had suffered enough on his behalf and, as he would later learn, bats possessed a very different internal timepiece than humans, rendering them even more vulnerable to memory and loss.

Seeing how Mr Marigold remained troubled, Flora asked him the source of his agitation. The Queen Mother was called "Mum" by all the millions of her bantering choir, the worker bats, whose population, Marigold had already worked out, had not increased whatsoever over the years. Somehow bat society had managed a demographically stable ZPG. The Commander explained his quest for peace on Earth. He was not in the least reticent about impugning his own species, knowing that she would have no problem understanding.

"He is mad for serenity," threw in Sannazaro. "Let me tell you the ways—" and he started to roll off one fray after another into which he, in the intrepid company of his pronounced peer, had been hurled.

"But it seems that what you are really searching for is a complete elixir," the Queen Mother suggested.

"I suppose I am."

"But surely you accept that what has been is done. The past is accomplished. What will be depends upon certain, already met preconditions—though none are immutable. You can inject yourself. Your ideas. Even your personality, and it will work an effect. On the horizon line. Beneath the storm. At the edge of your uncertainty, where all takes flight upon bat wings, sailing heavenward on the deck of the human imagination, if you prefer. That is where the elixir is to be found. Go there. You will see."

"Gracious Queen Mum, are you speaking of an actual place?" Marigold replied honorifically.

"Indeed I am."

"But surely you have not failed to note that you and your kind possess much higher aerodynamics than I am accustomed to. And that goes for your thinking processes, as well."

"In other words," Sannazaro said, reformulating his Commander's eloquent muddle of a reply, "you've lost him, and that goes for both of us."

Taking her time, she began a more generous explanation, a medically-potent saliva coating every word and philosophical throw-weight.

CHAPTER 181
The Elixir at the Edge of the Ocean

"THINK OF IT LIKE this," she tried. "If it is the singular Idea that explains all others, the Word, the Moment, the Great Gasp, then you are not too far away. That Logos towards which your kind has dreamt for millennia is just out yonder. But it is not a geography for sissies," she warned. "This is a place where all beings wake up in solipsism, take lunch communally, dine romantically, sleep autistically. Where dreams merge with daylight and there is absolutely no way, or reason, to distinguish foolishness from the most profound, senselessness from sensible. Topography schools the heart, the heart the touch, the touch all of history. Taken in reverse, the way most mammalian minds work (unlike insects, who never looked back, ferociously, dutifully enamored of the future), a bat's sense of longing— located halfway between the nostrils and the fingertips—might well make a nation state, or formulate a plateau at sunset upon which the grandest schemes and greatest ideals are set forth. Live them. Become them. Fear nothing. Hope for everything. That is battology at its battiest." And she seemed to glance out towards the yawning southwest for confirmation.

She spoke in soft hybridized words that carried equal truck in bat and human eminence; a livewire *lingua franca* straddling two worlds as fiercely disconnected by the bias of history as any could be. Yet, in this woman who so strongly resembled her son were all the graces of the mammalian evolutionary line. Warm-blooded affection and its generous expression were evident in everything she touched, each gesture. Standing just over three feet tall, with a wing spread twice that, her gold eyes shimmered in a buoyancy that rose, widened, fell, dilated according to the linguistic pitch whose native tongue was pink, gentle and meandering.

"There really is such a place? And it really is good, and kind, and far away from all troubles?" Marigold asked.

"Oh yes. Unless you be carrying your dirty laundry with you, or thinking mean-spirited thoughts, expect little resistance or strife ... Assuming you can get there, of course."

"But how unfair that we might not, given the *idée fixe* now forming in my brain," reckoned the Commander.

Sannazaro noticed the howling subtext at once. How could anyone fail to divine the catch? It embodied all the dense acronyms of the world's fisheries and beehives.

Flora meantime waxed on: "A pristine stretch of inaccessibles, upon whose quaint shores Nature has seen fit to lavish every extravagance and blessing, greets the wayfarer. A commonwealth of pleasure, sequined ridges, warm breezes, not a misstep in 1,500 years; sheep sequestered in infinity; avuncular bushes, parental forests, flowers favoring the aesthetician, bumblebees waltzing to the air and nocturne of the very wind. Such latitudes scarcely exist in the normal imagination. You cannot just go there. Wishing it is not enough. The steady heart requires a courageous backbone. You cannot simply formulate the desire, or calculate the geographical positioning. I cannot convey the necessary techniques for reaching there, as much as I would like to. A mystery precludes easy instruction. You must present your modest sail to the gods and hope for the best."

"I'm ready," Marigold resolved. "It has been yesterday and tomorrow since we three have sought out this marvelous quadrant of no-worries. But I should add, were any data available, I might make informed preparations rather than landing merely with the shirts on our backs."

"I doubt there is any other way to land. Never mind, what sorts of data?"

"Well, for one, what's the population? Demographic mix? Economic outlook? Is there a social welfare net? What about consensus-building, the resolution of any conflicts? Is there a Green Party, by chance? Are there orderly assemblies, underground parking lots, canned and bottled food? Is the food labeled properly, lest some transgenic gobbledygook be included? Do they have a ballet or opera? What about medical bills, or the wheel—I presume it is known to the inhabitants? And anesthetics? A good dram, now and then, which presupposes a local pub with a dart board. Do they play darts?"

My God, thought Sannazaro. The man is getting more dog-eared all the time. If we do not arrive there soon, I don't dare speculate what form his demon will take.

The illegible laureate babbled on with annoying and irrelevant queries that had no possible bearing on the deeper meaning of the quadrant in question. His foot lackey was embarrassed by the Commander's irrelevant gusher of a reaction. Perhaps all the excitement had gone to his head. Or was he simply trying to be as cautious and practical as could be, for his son's sake? Certainly it wasn't on behalf of Sannazaro, who had no interest in darts whatsoever. As far as he was concerned, a baby-bat hammock would suffice as well as any, and that included the hotel complex down on the beach, which he showed no interest in visiting even for a cappuccino or shower. If indeed true Paradise was to be their lot, why question the number of floorboards or spigots in the place?

Queen Mum, who despite a bonny demeanor had to be breaking 90 years of age by the gray mantle of fur under her regal chin, and evident arthritis in her elbows, observed a Commander who had fought too many battles; a man who was, in her estimation, in need of a long rest.

For his part, Marigold manifested no inkling of his own purple prose or over-the-top temper. He never did. This funfair of circumbendibus locutions, loquacious principles and infinitesimal isms was the link to childishness that had saved him on most occasions.

The hidalgo of so many battlefields marveled at Flora's tranquillity in the face of such overwhelming threats from outside. Not just her way of life, but life itself, imperiled by the very species to whom she had once wedded. Alex was her Prince, the hybrid best of both parts, now returned home from Purgatory. She embraced him with emotions that swelled beyond either bat or human world, Marigold noted. She favored by all that motherly affection not only her own son, Alex, but all the other tens of thousands of bat babies, each thimbleful of mohair she quite knew by name. And more: she obviously included in this pantheism of love Rajibai, whose lively demeanor struck her with motherly interest. She wondered whether he might not even like to stay on in the nursery and school all the kindergartner bats in the ways of little boys. It might serve them well later on, she figured, when they sometimes had to make their way into the outer kingdom.

But Rajibai was already busy with sextant and compass, eagerly plotting their course towards the Great South, anxious to explore that island chain which had become the center of their gravity. No classroom for him, ever again, he demurred politely.

Seeing that they could not be stayed, she felt it best to warn the trio: "What you believe, or do not believe, all of your facts and figures, peculiar history and raging future are of little consequence to bats, other than to admit that you are indiscreet, abrupt and too abrasive for words—as a species, I mean. We can only hope and pray to betake our kind from your borders. But we would never fault a man, or celebrate him for his beliefs. They are justified only by modest silence. Their proof can be determined only by their realization in the living and practice of them. Better that a man's beliefs should be accorded false, and a bat's too, than that he should live with no beliefs at all," she explained. "You see, right or wrong, the will to believe is everything. That said, you will appreciate that this place you are seeking is on no map."

"But why not, if it is really as real as you make out?" Rajibai charged, suddenly deflated.

"Yes, and without a map, or some sort of instructions, how will we know how far to travel, or when we've even arrived? What if we're off by one half of one arc second, or a few notches or degrees—why, we might keep going forever, and never know to turn back or re-plot our graphs?" Marigold felt frustrated and stymied, knowing how important this final part of their expedition was to Rajibai. He did not want to disappoint the lad. But there was even more at work in his psyche, a foreboding that this expedition somehow intimated the final resolution of reunions. For everyone involved. He sensed destiny. Could sniff it. Sannazaro, tagging along reluctantly, sensed a notch above destiny, but was so inured to fantastic calamity that every insanity pleasantly escaped him.

But she resolutely pointed to the Great South, as if to decree that was all that was needed. "Out beyond the furthest limits of Bongo Bongo, there is an ocean. Somewhere in the middle of that liable sea, when the sinking sun is just so, and the restive light's refraction even more so, the angle of fugitive incidence that way, an albedo or two to the left, a stream of truant moon beams to the right. As long as your boat remains buoyant, your oarsman heroic, it will appear to you. There, somewhere out there, the gravity will take hold and away you'll go. But only *if*," she underscored, "you have faith that it really does exist."

It was a fair warning.

"But what is it, actually?" the Commander, bustling with excitement again, pressed on. "You mentioned shores?"

"The Archipelago, of course. Though none of my ancestors has been there for quite a while—no reason to—so I wouldn't want to comment on the accommodations, milk or sugar supply. Now keep in mind that non-believers aren't likely to find it, as the whole region remains invisible to them. It simulates an atmospheric deception, a simulacrum of mists resembling a caved-in cemetery or mile-high wall of flypaper. Sometimes it takes the form of an enormous army of Samurai braced to strike, or a vast labyrinth of bankruptcies or Pogroms. It may effect some other doom, like an ozone hole stretching to eternity, or a terrible storm, or all those worst instincts catalogued in Lucifer, made palpable in all who look upon him, or even vaguely in that direction."

"But it all sounds strangely like human nature itself: our worst violence, stench, fears and self-fulfilling prophecies articulated in a stretch of land and marine velvets, does it not?"

"There, you see!" She pointed with her talon. "You've got something. You really do. Doesn't he?" She looked to the Commander's comrades for cloying confirmation. They all smiled.

"But make no mistake," she went on, a flatterer with cause. "The veil is a deception, a miasma, though sometimes, if you get caught up in its whorls, real enough. There are storms out there, be not smug."

"Is it dangerous?" asked Rajibai.

"Not ultimately," she replied with half-a-clarity. "For beyond that chimera lies a world of substantialities, the scintillation of every asseveration, somewhere well concealed within the bedeviling woods long after the rain-soaked travails, past all privations and private woes. Which is the point of it all. Where things have simmered down and life is kind and willing to accommodate you. All us mammals got started there. At that precise junction of Empyrean clouds, circles and roses, centers and heavens, spheres and gravities. The clouds are unmistakable. You are near when they turn cloysome and purple, when cloudland clotters and cloudage grows black. If you have traveled wisely, in harmony with the trade winds and vapor, then you will have successfully floated somewhere intermediate between substance and rhetoric, fog and heaven. Look there, for you can well imagine it. You see there! A twinkling, and then—misshapen—it is gone for another, leaving a void between the Southern Cross and the mist in yourself. Think of smoke and dimness that has gotten an idea; a slur, an entire nation's busy affairs, an epithet from Zeus as related by your Homer; or girt, dividing, opening, vanishing, curtained, drowned, eclipsed, Upannishaded, and enveloped all at once. Understand?"

"What is the understanding, when compared to a bat speaking of girts and busy affairs, of scintillations and asseverations!" exclaimed Sannazaro dreamily. He didn't even know what asseverations were. But then, it didn't matter. Not at all. Whenever he came upon a word or notion that was over his head, he thought of it just like that very cloud upon whose lovely shape Flora waxed, and he was content to admire, to let a floating mist be itself, enjoyed for all of its internalizing and ephemerality, without imposing his own knowledge of the source and chemical composition upon it. A rainbow its golden promise, with no responsibility to photons or electromagnetism. A musical air its oxygen, no necessity for dating the composer's manuscript, nor the orchestral theory. To live one's life studying the clouds, he thought. How refreshing. How unconnected to man. How free of human meddling. To be a disciple of the clouds. Nothing else was necessary. No explanation. No guidance, apology, taxes, final papers or administrations. Nothing at all. To live and die as a cloud, in the image of cloudiness. Mystical and perfect, these caveats. That was the geography of which she spoke. The words themselves. A music to his ears.

"If you believe in lakes of light, love which moves the stars, lofty hosannas and precious fantasies," the Queen Mother continued, "you will find everything you're looking for. These cloudy renowns will be your guide. Proper names from ancient times. Traditions and seascapes that you will come to love as your very own. I imagine you've been there before and just didn't recognize it. This happens frequently. How many beaches have you strolled? How many grains of sand considered? Can a man, or bat, speak with them all? Nonsense. Yet there is a comfort in their patterns, arrays, densities. We seem to familiarize ourselves with the sea and the shore from infancy, no? And note, will you not, how we universally rest upon their warmth for pillow and for safe harbor. Walk barefoot along their silky smooth byways. You do not address a grain of sand by name, but know it nonetheless.

"Of course, if you feel compelled to remake any part of the grand itinerary to which I am alluding, be my guest, at least where humans are concerned. If it's the origins of wrath, of violence and greed, of discontent you're fixing to remedy, then that's the place to effect your handiwork. Reconstitute Eden starting right there in the sand, upon the shoreline. Tweak a little, rub off the odd smudge, salt a silhouette, nod towards favorable nuances, add a pinch of sweetness here. Change just one combination in those heavenly boondocks, and soon enough—50, 100 years of strong winds carrying fertile spores, half-digested seeds, the odd turd or lousewort, algal blooms or riboflexis, even a message-plugged bottle or two—and the whole world should get the idea sooner or later. Maybe even overnight. Because at that place, time, like genetic and linguistic drift, goes sideways, up and down, erratic, crinkled and around, no beginning, endless ends. It is this randomness which gives to death its tasty sting and makes the island so unpredictable, alchemical, elusive. Sow oats, spread seed, till a great idea. Punctuation marks are its stock and trade. You will discover certain anomalies, island errata, which purport to no faith for very long that isn't unexpectedly undermined by some new novelty or other. Every shattering a veritable beginning. So do not fear. But whatever you do, by what means, orientation or chaos you should manage to arrive, please talk some sense into those Frenchmen."

Marigold listened well.

"And there is one thing more you must keep in mind, by way of a caution: stay to the human trail. Only at your own personal risk, and that of your compatriots, do you dare meddle with anything else. You see, it's just fine as it is."

"I think we've got a clear picture," Sannazaro summarized, not wanting to invite further sermon. It was obvious that this was one of those 'tricks of destiny' in which you just played it by instinct and hoped heavenful for the best. That was good enough for him.

There was considerable squeaking of bat commentary in the background. Like a radio station with bad signal power. Buzzy clicks, free-tailed peeps and whines, late-night mealworms, burps, hiccups and national gasses. Marigold was astonished by the range of gray-headed fig-eating long-nosed bat communiqués. Countless little pharynxes telling of small island tales, blue beaches and great expectations.

Before long, millions of bats began succumbing to weariness. Some just slumped away, their snores almost audible. At least ten million of them had struggled to keep their eyes open in order to be polite about saying good night. They each threw a kiss and farewell at the voyagers, then dozed off. Marigold, Sannazaro and Rajibai, in turn, bid their adieux to Alex, who had found his permanent nesting ground. The outside air was redolent with a blue iguana moon, as they say in these parts. Alex and his mother would share a nightcap of neesberry and papaya smoothies, disgorged in unison. What's more, they had 25 years to catch up on.

In the morning, when all the bats were still sound asleep, sunning themselves in splendid darkness, Marigold, Rajibai and Sannazaro tiptoed out of their guano bags into the forest and soon found a path leading them down, down towards the sea through forests of lilac, rata, lemon and black walnut. The Commander had a plan already hatched.

In the nick of time, too, because a terrible troop of mercenaries from all over Africa was that very day heading towards Bongo Bongo, equipped with electromagnetic, ultrasound and infrared interceptors, bazookas and flame-throwers.

Eventually, the trio staggered forth from a river canyon, pulling themselves free of a chaos of deep bramble glens to arrive in the center of the hotel greens, where a game of badminton was in progress.

"Excuse me," the Commander interjected, after waiting on a long play. "Can you tell us who owns this, this—" He could not find the words, but eventually uttered some profanity that succeeded in bringing security guards to their doorstep, and the trio, in turn, to the offices of the owner. The tycoon, Louis XXIX (or Lou, as his inner circle of executives knew him), had styled himself after the former Emperor of France, had named his yacht *Bonaparte* and his pet crocodile Josephine.

"You are the owner of this monstrosity? The perpetrator of this crime against Batmanity?" the Commander began tactfully. "I have a mind to flog and impale your sorry ass!"

Lou snapped his fingers and half-dozen armed thugs surrounded the trio. "Is that so?" he replied.

"What would you estimate to be the value of the entire hotel complex, as well as the holdings you have stolen from Mother Nature up on the mountain?" Marigold went on.

"Eight hundred million. US dollars. With write-offs and long-term capitalization, twice that."

"A deal," proclaimed Marigold.

Sannazaro rubbed his eyes. Rajibai smiled. Familiar ground, this.

"What deal?" Lou asked.

"Global warming's round the corner. You'll never keep the snow on those proposed slopes. What's more, they're giving way, undermined by army ants. Not good for tourists. And red tides are coming, last detected out at sea, about 400 miles. There goes your scuba and snorkeling activities. In addition, whole covens of great whites are trying to outswim the coming tsunamis. Eruptions in the Philippines. A virus moving in on bottlenoses. Poisoned anchovies from Peru. Krakatoa acting up for the first time in 200 years. Not only that, there's seismic activity in these slopes. Remember Montserrat. Your forest clearance has aggravated the watersheds, over-lubricated the fault lines. I'm telling you. We've been there. And that's if the bats don't suck all your blood first. Twenty million of them. Big fangs. Lice in their talons. Boys and girls. The little white ones from France, the spoiled brats, their parents boycotting the Government's oil prices. That's who they go for. Getting worse every day. Put that in your tourist brochures. I don't think so."

Without pausing for breath, the Commander went on to detail the first blush of obvious engineering deficiencies in the hotel's construction— stuff he'd picked up from the Oasis: "Just look at those cripple walls, in need of bracing; and that breaker box, too close to the sauna; and where's your hypochlorite?"

"My what?"

"Not to mention that urea-formaldehyde foam insulation in your waferboard in all the suites; the radon beneath the asbestos-lined boilers; the lead and copper in your spigots—I can smell it—" He turned to his son: "Can you smell it? Causes brain damage in kids, just when they thought they were having a good time. Do I dare mention the wave of termites down from the Central Sahara—seen 'um coming this way. Point is, I'll take the whole mess, no questions asked. No reports needed. I'll take your surveyor's report and deed resolution as is. Full indemnification. You walk away. Bury yourself in oblivion. No worries. Lest the *Utrecht Jamboree for Human Whimsies*, the *Chiroptera Chapter of the United Nations*, the *International Congress of Mixed Bloods*, or the *League for the Empowerment of Oppressed Personalities* get wind of your little shenanigans. Slaughtering bats, enslaving virgins, abusing aboriginal children, blowing up mountains, driving countless species to extinction ... Lou, Lou, wake up! These tactics went out of fashion centuries ago."

As if by some rare deliverance, the faint distant sound of a Bongo drum could be heard for the first time in years. The sign of a rebellion brewing.

"And there you have it! The natives are getting restless. Are you with me, or should I claim not to know you when the cannibal hordes arrive?"

Then smoke signals appeared from high on the mountain.

"You see?"

"Who the hell are you? And where are you going to come up with that kind of money?" Lou asked pointedly.

"A single phone call. My name is Marigold. Sound familiar?" It did. No entrepreneur could ignore the ring of that name.

"The one from La Mancha? In all the papers recently?"

"The same."

And so it happened that the Commander persuaded Lou XXIX to part with his Paradise Magnifique. He coerced him into shipping all the luxurious thatched hotel rooms and banquet halls to poor rural communities across Africa where the structures might be used for roller boards or bowling night. And he sent a runner back upslope to halt the rearguard attack plans and present to Queen Mother a very solid proposal for regenerating the forests that involved nothing more complicated than a massive defecation-cum-pollination program—something bats were the very best at.

Throughout the lagoons, the many beach barricades were lifted, the dolphins led to freedom, the Virgins of Bongo Bongo liberated.

Eventually, after a dinner of sautéed banana pudding, roasted garlic plugs, impaled squash flower and withered tomato paste, the trio bid farewell to the mainland, having acquired as part of the deal Lou's own 156-foot yacht, which they equipped with the best remaining stores and tin cans from the Paradise.

"We're leaving an unknown shore for a nonexistent chain of islands," Sannazaro pointed out. "In a boat none of us knows how to steer. What makes you think that bat knew what she was talking about? She admitted it had been millions of years since any of them had gone there. What if the islands have moved? Or the sea's too fierce? Our navigation skills are nullified by dint of our collective stupidity, I dare say; and not one of us is good at infecting the others with courage. We are a sorry lot, made more sorry by our lack of a gameplan."

"Since we don't know exactly where the islands are, what difference does it make if they are somewhere else?" Marigold deftly assayed.

"Yes, but what if they've sunk, or been churned up in friable tidbits by some continental drift or other? Denuded by goats, guanified by giant sea lizards, abandoned by all but the hairy spiders and ringworms? We could get out there and sit for a year without aid of a lighthouse. Run out of sparkling water and truffles; perish at 1,000 points along the compass. I have an eerie foreboding. A mild headache that suggests more than a sea change. Why leave a swimming pool and king-sized beds?"

"My dear Governor. You are esquire, senator, squire and fool, but I have never doubted your instincts, you will give me that?"

The Señor nodded agreeably.

"Whenever you have asked why, I have answered with far more than why not. When you have questioned the wisdom of a thing, I have multiplied your query with other concerns. As a squad with utmost custodial duties, I would assert we have done service to the cause of reality, examining her hijinks and orifices from a multiplicity of proprieties and angles, some opaque, others as pellucid as a fine claret. Add to the team our central pillar of brash wisdom here, and I dare say this trio does honor to the cause of the world. Hence, I do not take your superstitions—a special gift of the Latin races we both share—lightly. I cannot guarantee this outcome. I testify to equally grave concerns. Were I the writer of our travails, I should simply skip this page and formulate a more even-tempered and predictable assignment. Alas, it is not so. We must abide by the unknowns, embrace them, wonder not at our blind corner which is the condition of man. To command the aftermath would lose in variety and sensation what it might gain in comfort. Naturally we would prefer more certainty. Imagine the energy savings, to be rid of these nerves: no more exercise of anxiety, an end to all those anticipatory pangs crisscrossing the humors. Yet, to lose no more sleep might well incur its own negations of another sort: narcosis, nullification of all that is fair, to sleep through life, dream atop its churned-up storms, never once taste the darkness, feel relief, pertinacity, triumph. Like a lotus-eater, to miss out on all that constitutes synthesis and resolution. Surely you see that we must march off into mystery if we are to enjoy this gift..."

And he went on by such hortatorical aplomb that the waning Señor allowed that a tidal wave might be preferable to a ruined ear. Indeed, his mind so wearied of his wooden-faced companion's sermonizing that an open sea now seemed a refreshment. Moreover, the boat—with its Blue-period Picasso, *Boy with Bongo*, over the smooth onyx dinner table—was engineered with something like 14 million dollars of nickel-plated technology, satellite and sideways sonar scanners to see them through any squalls, past any hidden underwater volcanoes, or sea mounts. Notwithstanding that none of them knew the first thing about operating the vessel, there was general concord that this was one ship that would never sink, or lose its way. She was as robust a vessel as was ever anchored at St Tropez.

The following morning, after rifling through the instruction manuals, loading supplies of fresh water, cantaloupes, jars of mushroom pâté, virgin olive oil and kelp patties, tomatoes, scallions and assorted other essentials, the trio made the heroic departure, beneath a flurry of excited gulls. Sannazaro noticed tears welling up in the Commander's eyes, but refused to take this as a sign. Instead, breathing deeply and consigning the rest of his days to the whims of an unknown ocean, he simply bid his farewell to the continent as they buzzed off over a tidal shoal and rocky narrows into the harbor, running 8,400-horsepower motors, turning ambiguous semicircles and rough-edged circumlocutions owing to miscalculated digital settings that placed them closer to Texas, or the moon. It was only with the guidance of a school of grateful, carousing dolphins that the dashing vessel, with its frazzled, yelping, self-absorbed and queasy Commander at the controls, was able to bumble more or less in a patternless fit and herringbone start towards the left flank of sunset.

Rajibai figured without to-do how to jettison the mainsail. It was a button that read, "Mainsail". The jib, too. With a whipping, nearly catastrophic turnabout, a plank ahead of his swift shadow, 300 pounds of murderous steel went slicing through the air of the upper deck.

The boy climbed upon the airy ladder, 55 feet to the raven's roost, and there instead of ahoy fell asleep in God's halo, curled up in a fishermen's fine-mesh larded with a topspin of Buller's Albatross feathers and honeyed moist light, gold-slashed at one moment, vermilion the next. Addulcently, the heaving sea surrounded his dreams, as if all were a toy fair, pastel and blue.

And all was fine, quiet and good, at last. With the wind at their back, ballast underfoot, a throwing weight of their craft zeroing in on the unknowns of a beckoning horizon before them.

CHAPTER 182
How Rajibai and Crew Brave the Hurrinado

LIVING ASTACITES—blue-blood crustaceans not seen for 100 million years—glomming on amid other relic *Cymba*— fossils come to life—aboard the fast sides, rusting plug and overworked rails; the fresh brash of the salt fray, dreamery holes of an earlier day, putting to sea in the archival bays—Hartlepool, Margate Pier—as the boatswain blows yonder his boy whistle, China bound, moored in open stretch. "Ahoys" from the upper deck, the boat's noisy mechanisms—knall-gas thunder, reciprocator, piston, smell of diesel—rudely greeting the broad expanse of ocean. Puff birds, *Chelidoptera*, trailing the sea readers in their slumbering palace, frightful bravura alone in the lonely construction, barreling through increasingly high waves.

For weeks they ascended amid bloated sea cucumber follies, solemn urchin trains and schools of petrels floating on their buns in the unnavigable doldrums of wherever they were. Lampblack nights, Quaker-blue mornings, verdigris afternoons. Floating shoals of crazy kelp, lobsters migrating from the West Indies, writhing pincer, rapier and doublet, jabbering in their native Arawak. Cetaceans uncharted in any seas, mooned, sojourned and breached in vast numbers, leaving trawls of exoskeleton-rich puke, hundreds of miles long, the remains of their gargantuan appetite for poor little whiting squid and reddish krill. Dreamers interrupted. Lunging fish of every nuance, from all the surrounding neighborhoods, soared in sphygmic rhythms through mauvecaps of raspberry glacé in pelagic yearning or confusion.

Never had human eyes witnessed such heaven-directed displays. Most astonishing of all, millions of *Hippocampus gianteus*—green, blue, gelatinous sea horses the size of Clydesdales—scooted towards the same horizon which now preoccupied the skipper Marigold and crew, though at far greater speeds, skimming the surface of the water like Neptune's chariot, rocking back and forth in erect dispositions. Many of the males were quite pregnant.

One day a rare school of super *Crossopterygii* swept nearby en masse, slithering up alongside the seaworthy *Bonaparte*. In addition were tens of thousands of their groupies and groupers: idolatrous fans, mooning fins.

"Where do you go?" spouted one of the colossal creatures with its elongated scales, rhombic shoulders, enameled face.

"You can speak?" Rajibai exclaimed, though he shouldn't have been surprised by anything in these waters, not even a talkative *Polypterus bichir*, as it was known locally.

"Certainly."

"How wonderful," replied the boy. "Well, actually, we're quite lost, I think."

"Not possible in this sea," supposed a second *Polypterus*, this one even longer than the first. Longer than the yacht entire.

"Really?" asked Rajibai. "Then where are we?"

"You're here," confirmed yet a third fish, longer than the first two combined.

Night after night the trio floated ponderously, deeper and deeper into an ocean that could not be located even on the vessel's own maps, which meant, of course, that they had entered the Realm referred to by Queen Mum.

Marigold knew that every previous anxiety had merely reaffirmed their present course. Keen to all the appropriate portents, he announced, "Each trial is a tribute, every foreboding a happy harbinger. This itinerary was fixed long before we were born."

"Nonsense. And don't go scaring junior," applied Sannazaro senatorially, and he pulled a sherry bottle from the captain's corner. He knew the Commander's fondness for the slippery melancholy of the great sixteenth-century Portuguese humanist De Goes, who for three years contemplated the death of the world from the monastery of Batalha. And others of his ilk—Proustians possessed of glib forlorn, like Hsieh Ling-yun, Yukio Mishima, or Boethius. Philosopher dissidents who spoke of their deaths with fond and steady anticipation, elevating their mortality, constructing their posterity. He wanted none of it. Sorrows. Werther.

"Look at that!" shouted the boy, who stared from the quarter deck at the phosphor glow far, far in the distance, a monolith of clouded moonsickness as thick as tuberculosis and Saturn-ring rearing along the horizon lines.

By morning, the walls of platinum haze surrounded them. Marigold noted their existing stores of fuel, 150 gallons—enough, if rationed, to power them through the deathly inert gas phase that intermezzoed the trio somewhere in the South Atlantic, and to see them another 1,846 miles, if necessary. But how far away from present positions was the Archipelago of which the Queen Mother spoke? They could always go by sail, except none of the three knew quite how to do so.

"We are more than lost," figured the Squire, his bruited reason appalled by their evident condemnation. "We are trapped in the biggest moat in the world. Now what?"

"Go back," cried a manta ray, as it wheeled circumpolar carousels through the upper hypolimnion just aft. The boy heard its warning. Then others chimed in. Punky little perch, squeamish squids, all hollering, "Be warned!"

Minerals, decomposed organic material, denitrifying hordes of bacteria, frightened bioluminescent diatoms and vast seething frictions of benthic anaerobes careened into the *Bonaparte* in their haste to head north. But it was no good. All were being swept southward. There was no longer any escaping the clockwise deepwater circulations below and in the air. A black marine hole.

"I can't stop it!" shouted the Commander, befuddled by wind drag, errors of calculation, unresponsive controls. His frantic button-pushing only brought them further towards the wall. "*Alis volat propriis!*" he shouted.

Yet the wall kept progressing at the same speed—about 15 miles per hour.

"Weird, don't you think?" he puzzled, an awe unnamable.

"Feels like a hurricane," Sannazaro concluded around noon, voicing what all had felt and feared openly to acknowledge. Opaque furor. A weather of storm ruffs on the collar of the azimuth.

They were somewhere in the South Equatorial Current, sucked along by strong atmospheric vortices, trade winds and tropical depressions. Curvilinear thunderclaps, purple and mean, issued from the hot bloat ten miles directly before them and to all sides, a fable of Coriolis accelerations. The air was moist and steaming; the sea swelling in terrible troughs that rolled by at elevations of 30 feet. The air pressure read 820 millibars; water temperature just over 29 degrees Celsius. A red frog—the Mark Twain species—fell from the purple skies and smacked onto the deck. Then another. Soon, the cornicles and quills of water raking over the millpond of their previous pancake days were replete with heaven-sent crossed-eyed newts and flichtered toads, each frog more stupefied than the next. They had fallen from the sky, been swooshed beyond every horizon in tornado darkness, some speaking Rhineland, others Calaveras Indian. A steady howl augured of real troubles.

"What does it mean?" asked Rajibai.

None could compose a firm idea. Sea frogs, they finally concluded, attracted to the scent of Mr Marigold's underarms, or their tea lights.

As they advanced, the currents became stronger, the distance between the enormous ceratoid sea swells shorter and shorter. Frogs, toads, salamanders multiplied on deck. Even the days were being jerked, so that not 24 but 16 hours seemed to constitute a single day/night. At other times, no fewer than 42 hours would do for the same consequences. What could it mean? Foams and lathers, yellow pigments off the Forel scale; blue and green spectrums absorbing a new kind of radiation from the disappearing sun. New surface tensions, too, on the chlorine-rich density of wave water. Every sea spider was frantic to get out; even the most sluffish of all pelagic species, the filefishes, were pressing their even-bordered anal fins with unusual frenzy, slobber dispersing over the tops of the waves.

"I know what I'm going to do," bemoaned the Italian, who proceeded to scavenge the captain's corner for enough silken drink to propel him into an unrecoverable happy time.

Marigold was unresigned. He had spotted a brave little *Angelichthys ciliaris* frothing at the mouth, a jumble of paradise vernacular and calming effects. "Fear not," the kind-hearted fish cried out. "Just follow me!"

A summoning metaphor, thought the Commander, sufficient to quell the dead reckoning of his two declining first mates. "We'll be fine," he avowed.

Suddenly, the troubled waters quaked with consuming ventrals and pectorals. Tooth carps and lungfish, spotted morays and gulpers, babbling blennies and goofy grenadiers, large mouths teeming with pointed barbels and soft rays darting in the darkening light, bleeding-heart bonitos and lantern-bright *Myctophidae*, poisonous plectognaths, blind swellfish, flying marlins and svelte swordfish, pre-adamite whales and naughty wrasses, blunt grinders, high-surf mackerels, free swimmers and spinous cichlids.

There was never a Renaissance of fishies more fair, and all now seemed to escort the *Bonaparte* towards its final destination.

"Batten down, boys," commanded Monsieur Marigold. "Lee ho! Starbird brash! Westward fling!"

Each did his part to bolt a door, lock a window, latch the silverware drawer, pin down the toilets and affix the pyxis, secure the goblets, bag the bric-a-brac, tie up the medicine chest and button up the ironing board. Unbeknownst to his currant-faced father, the gnomic Rajibai sneaked off to climb to the raven's roost to see if he might not gain an insight into what was happening out among the madcaps of fish escorts and mammalian flotillas.

From not far off Rajibai heard the roar at the very moment that elsewhere, down below on deck, an eerie silence greeted his companions. The waters were saying two things. Ominously, not a single fish remained, where just an hour before they had been surrounded by communing sea cows and giant kelp spiders, by tuna schools and mobs of phytoplankton. Gray spalding waters seethed now. One aqueous explosion after another rocked the air, grew by decibels each minute, until it was right upon them. Rajibai, up high, hid beneath the blanket of netting.

The waves tore into the windows, water smashed the galleys, and the *Bonaparte* lurched as if shot from a cannon.

"*Son!*" cried out the Commander.

"Have you seen him!" he screamed to Sannazaro, who clung for all his life to the side railings in the lower deck, drunk and oblivious, a nutty smile stashed in his lips.

Out of the eye of the storm they traversed into the second, deadly layer of five-mile-high hurricane darkness.

"Can you hear me, anyone, anywhere? I'm Marigold, this be the *Bonaparte ... Help!*" Marigold repeated into the useless mechanism that was the ship-to-shore, before being slammed into the waist-high swivel chair and thrown spastically against a wall, where wine glasses slid in shattered arrays beside the waterlogged Picasso.

"How do I use the computer? Quickly!" he screamed again, but Sannazaro was gone, washed underboard.

The futtock plates were ripped from the topmast rigging, and with them every iron rod and deadeye. The bands, shrouds, hoops and staves snapped and shot free, clouting a head, smashing into a human face standing in the way.

A dizzy, timeless ferocity, moving forty miles per ounce, 75 knots per inch, ten stories of water per hectare of Hell; a squall that, only seconds below the surface of the ocean, was merry-go-round of tall tales and whirligigs; of painter's light pinioned in the gray-green-maroons of seasonal massage. To be thrown, 250 carousels at a time, careening and sinking and being catapulted where no worries clouded the singular moment of pleasure, was the full brunt of hurricane to a given fish, who needn't breathe the air in our conventional manner, after all, or worry about sinking. But along the stricken deck it was another story, another way of thinking. There Marigold and his flopping Señor struggled to secure just two humble breathing spaces. Serene matinée idols below water, tragedians up on board.

"Do you see the boy?" Marigold screamed above the din. But Sannazaro could only hang on, spitting out water, not words.

Eight days this went on, havoc uncoordinated, black ocean drenching them in ruin. The sleep dream of horribles, witchcrafted into the consistency of celery, emblazoned in St Elmo's Fire, the corposant descending steadily the maintopgallant. The troughs had grown 500 feet, such that the *Bonaparte* vanished from sight, every 30 seconds, day and night. And the winds—200 miles per hour—became a silence—so continuous, unbroken, and hastening towards pain were they. Expiration easily stalked the lower bunks, almost a comfort after a time in its sheer familiarity.

The intermittent flooding was no longer a shock, but the rule of thumb that quenched all hope and made it their fatality to live. Vomit of tomato bisque rained upon the aisles. Salt water rinsed their veins, chelated their arteries. The many millions of dollars expended on her construction ensured that *Bonaparte* could not be sunk, only tortured. Twisters rang the edges of the hurricane.

But on the ninth morning it was Rajibai who, still conscious, departed his nest, climbed down the suddenly motionless ladder off the mainsail, and searched out his father and uncle.

There they were, their faces the color of gaunt mold, Belgian ash, lead-streaked Death's Door, smothered in watery rhymes, curled up under a steering column and demolished bed. Liters of fluid poured from their nostrils and mouth. Gobies fled from their eyes. A baby eel slithered out of the Commander's ear.

"Wake up!" Rajibai clawed. He gave them mouth-to-mouth, slapped their brains silly, revived them from a deadly stew. "There's land ahead!"

And sure there was, protruding from the gray mistral-like whey, whacked with beetling-cliff and burgundy sea. Homeric. Homeopathic.

"Huh? What time is it?" the Commander mumbled, coming to, going higher, lightly stepping in no shadow or footshoe. Without hint of breath, bearing or imperative. A lullaby of a man, his face as lovely as a little girl's, unmarked somehow by catastrophe, awarded a xiou-xiou, as Chinese sages describe that greatest of all gifts, an unmistakable trace of the everlasting, as in the savoring of a miracle, grace under pressure. No concept whatsoever of what had happened during the previous week or more. No memory, preamble or even questioning. Flat, glorious, watery aspect to it all, biolysis. Calm cessation.

As for the Señor, he presently crawled out from gold pilot-cloth. "Coraggio!" he stammered.

Now the inundated men gawked upon the glad vista thrown up in a mist of June fancy: a marble-veined seacoast. Like children at play in the scudding vision of solid ground that met their gaze, both burst with laughing peals of relief. Twelve nautical miles, no more. The clinging crew, the lonely boat, a storm that had abated, sky-hawks flying off, sharks fully gorged, and the glorious shroud of sun-lidded morning obfuscating the memory of their former wretchedness.

It was a full stretch of beachhead that appeared, a spot along an illimitable topaz stretch of coastline whose oracular mountains—Delphic, denuded—reared far back into another set of rain clouds, terrestrial sorts, deep and rooted, a firmness that applied to longevity, giving stock to the oceanic infinity out of which they lumbered. All the dreamy distant sights of creamy-white sand, of palm-galleried hopes and bathing girls that such waterlogged seamen had imagined era after era, now appeared in that sweet fetching glimpse of shared proprietary surmise, whose fashionable blur surpasseth dashed hope. Here all was gigantic desire, such that there was no other piece of land left on Earth. This was it.

The closer they came, so other points of apiculate rock and file and palm-laden beach broadened out, watery gaps between. There could be no doubt about it: an archipelago had welcomed the threesome home.

CHAPTER 183
Jovita

THE COMMANDER KNEW the moment he saw those satin, schiller shores, faraway fiords and rain-drenched Dosso Dossi tropics dissolving into mangrove that he had truly found that elemental substratum known by some as the Self. Of course, it wasn't like that—not Bingo! Not Lamb, nor Jade Temple nor Hiero's Golden Crown. There, where Mantegna mountains jagged and fine receded into the azure-liberated morning. No more dredging through the literal; no longer the Fact, or Reality. Shorn of overweening monstrous detail, Jean-Paul Sartre's Hole, regurgitated to trembling, undefined beginning, wild and succulent. Tyrannies of past tense were all finito! Ahead, a course of his own choosing. The slave only of open sunlight, wind through his portals, fresh water his tears. Whatever happened in that storm presently converged to wake him up, make every step, each glint of light, a radio beacon of new ways and deeds. Complete unto Marigold.

Sannazaro shared in this perplexing hopscotch of freshness, buffeted by the stardom and wind checkers of chance. It was a weather fine, as pure as Chamonix, North Wales or Half Dome in one chilled blend. One moment, lambent and fair. The next, a downpour of hail the size of kidney stones.

By these pungent stalemates and ambiguities of rapture they drifted closer to land. The Italian noticed serious abrasions of his forearms, and the odd fever blister cracking the Commander's lips. Both men, by contrast to the boy, had been drained of all color, a pallored corporeality in tandem. Yet, notwithstanding their apoplexies and jubilations, a peculiarly soft management of extremes comforted the trio, as if they'd been borne into the salvo of harbors. The closer they drew to the fine sandy reef, the more the eye of the starfish, the nose of the dolphin, the transverse coordinates of the coral cocoons began looking familiar. There was no escaping this interdependency of mind.

For Marigold there was no question they had arrived at point zero on the map of paradises. "It must be the same chain of islands Queen Mum described, wouldn't you think?"

"For now, I would argue for any prayer that it be so!" Sannazaro gasped, acknowledging the terror before them, a hazard of historical proportions lying in wait for all who dared, or blundered, any closer to land. The presentiment was devastating: a thunder of arriving waves smashing into a rock-strewn chaos of lethal fulminations and no trespassings. Manfred on the Jungfrau translated into a watery self-abnegation.

"We can, we must, we will," replied he. "I have not braved a hurricane so that, just moments from deliverance, our due prospects should be thwarted by a mere wave or two." And he kept on at the helm, though lacked any instrumentation or mechanical device for seeing them through. They were, verily, at the mercy of the tides or the slightest suggestion of the Fates.

With no unanimous decision to leap overboard yet, the threesome anchored themselves by one-inch webbing and bowline-on-bights to the ruined mast. "Hold your breath, son!" Marigold stated with dignity.

The *Bonaparte* lurched forward into the broil, where it pitched, canted, and was hammered into splinters. The beating went on for interminable moments: destruction that would not part with its toy, or choose a direction in which to spit out the final tidbits.

By and by, they saw themselves through the worst of the pitfalls, a dozen Scyllas and Charybdises whose anger was their beauty, seen from inside the church of tumult whose power was no more than a hiss to be forgotten: a shield to protect all who made it to the islands. And there was someone to greet the adventurers: a giant squid, tentacles 87 feet long, eyes blond, its body turning multiple colors, sunning itself beside the rapturously clear tide pools in which 10,000 crabs held court. Kelp shone brilliantly scarab-green, dozing in the explosive incoming, outgoing rollers that combed diagonally 100 miles of coast beneath monsoon alp and parting thunderbowls.

"We made it," the Commander downplayed as he untied the webbing and coughed up seawater from hours before.

"But it's not salty, not at all," Marigold beheld quizzically. "How is that possible?"

"The four rivers," yawned the squid, taking a slithering ten feet per water-bound stride in the direction of the *Bonaparte*, so vast was its body, so facile its scoops and plows. "And *who* might I have the pleasure of addressing?" wallowed he, with deep, beguiling antispasmodics, and the range of an underwater sousaphone. Flocks of raucous mollymawks circled the dialogue, whilst purple pelicans low to the ocean surface skimmed after the quicksilvered army of silver-flashing anchovies. Now a million and one butterflies the size of pomegranate petals hovered over the transparent waters, their wings trembling ten times a minute as they touched down to quench their thirst.

"That's my dad, and Uncle Sannazaro, and I'm Rajibai," volunteered the lad.

"What about those rivers?" Marigold went on, without the slightest fear of the monster.

"So very, very fresh," replied the squid, coming closer.

"What's that? I couldn't hear you. Why are you whispering?" asked Marigold.

"I don't like this. Something's wrong," groaned the Italian. "Don't go any nearer," warned a young bird. "It's a trick!"

"*Shhhh!*" scolded another.

Too late. With one mighty surge, the giant squid's tentacles grabbed the Commander, who'd leaned over to hear better, and yanked him off the deck, dragging him down beneath sea level.

Rajibai dived in after him, and Sannazaro too. All promptly vanished. Just furious bubbles rising to the surface and 1,000 birds I-told-you-soing above.

After several long minutes, all three humans reappeared, looking no worse than before.

"What happened?" Sannazaro lug-lugged, swimming back towards the ladder on the rear of the boat, helping the others up on deck, where gulls and curlews stood preening and gossiping with mentholated breaths. "Did we descend 20,000 leagues only to be sexually molested?" he implored, beyond patience. "Humiliating!" he stuttered.

"I think he liked us," commented the boy. "He kissed me on the cheeks."

Overhead, flocks of air creatures gabbed excitedly. Marine molestations were one of their favorite topics.

"It is a great day," Marigold muttered, crawling in no particular manner, neither south nor north, west nor east, dragging a supermarket worth of seaweed with him.

"Look there!" Rajibai now ignited, seeing they were drifting toward a half-sunken ship.

"Man the forestay, top the main, gaff the jib!" Marigold hollered, fortifying his nonsensical bravado, unaware that their sails had been shorn a week before.

As the *Bonaparte* approached, the remnants became clear. Not one, but countless mariner remains were scattered among the bashing rocks. Double halyards, port lids, stern galleries, shattered gangways and forecastles of the Renaissance. Sculptures, too: here a royal leopard or Genoan scutcheon, there an armillary sphere from the bowsprit of an East Indiaman. History had washed up on these treacherous sea stacks. Tudor Gothic inboards, as they're known, Chinese decorative gunwales, Stuart clench work, strakes of planking from the period of George the First, flamboyant bulkheads, a pale blue figurehead from a black, monolithic Viking ship far off course, left trapped inside an antediluvian cranny. They could see hundreds of brown recluses, adapted to sea action, dangling in the half-light. A Roman low-oared vessel, now populated by busily mating sea dwarfs, upended against a rock. Rigols of a Burgundian clinker. Carronades, hancing pieces and rails from a Phoenician exploratory. Female busts, one goddess after another, rammed upright into an overgrown wall of hanging tropic. A priapic male member, off some other ship, fitted delicately to their sides. Too resolute and finely choreographed to have been an accident.

All took solemn note of the sculptural edifices of the ages lodged in the twilight of so many shipwrecks. "What happened here?"

Of course the answer was no secret: had they reached the islands a few days earlier, during the storm, they too would have disintegrated upon the reef.

Even now, without rudder or steering column, they were at the mercy of the inbound breakers. The *Bonaparte* seized up along the crest of the perpetual wave action, threatening to topple, then stabilized for a few minutes before the next set rolled in. But the weather was fine and it was only a matter of minutes before they should reach the inside of the last portion of atoll.

"Hold on, boys!" the Commander warned, seeing that there was no way to avoid a direct hit upon the outer limestone caves.

Then it happened. They ground into the razor-sharp monadnocks, where pieces of single side-rudders on the starboard quarter floated beside keels, stems, sternposts and ribs—some outrigger or trireme from eras past. A deck beam and thwartship tiller jutted from a blow-hole directly in front of them. Then, suddenly, the hole exploded, a fricassee of spitchcock flashes, jewelry-heavened, from the spouthead of the seas, ejecta amid geyser. A treasure chest that had been sucked down and ruptured for all time inside the vortex. A vast emerald landed on their waterlogged deck. There a Phoenician bracelet, amethysts the size of pumpkins. A large ruby smacked the window. Diamonds in an airborne gallery disappearing in the sea all over again.

"Take a plank, like this," the skipper urged.

They leaned over from the diving platform on the back of the boat and grabbed hold of whatever wooden flotsam might be used as a paddle, then began rowing frantically towards shore, trying to avoid the peril, through the ever shallower portions of the inner bauble-larded bay. But the blowhole was too powerful, its swirling yards' worth of suction exerting extra-gravitational pull. Into the cavity their wind-jammed boat was pulled like a Solar System retinue finalizing its orbit, where all was suspended in a moment's build-up. And then it came, like the Pohutu Geyser herself, or the finest carbonated Pellegrino, sea-blasted with salt and brine.

The *Bonaparte* was detonated upwards 1,550 feet—slowly do boats rise through air, recollections, astonishments, winds to the east, risers west, thermals south, the history of the Aztecs, or Hapsburgs, or Italianate opera—and came crashing back down again, along with a Czar's portfolio of precious stones. Hardly useful here, their boat upside down, and moving no more, capsized in an eddy that guaranteed a century or more of anonymous stasis between boulders, currents and indefinable rigors of Nature. "Boy With Bongo" went floating off, a great Picasso made sport of by frolicking sea lions.

Now the waters were far calmer, as they passed by the rear end of an authentic Thai pirate vessel and a Lowlands barge, Belgian from its looks, rather off course. Even a rotted Nydam boat and the bare leavings of an Indian canoe; a sea-slimed caravel and gouged-out galleon; a paddle wheel and chunks of rusted iron from a Swedish dreadnought. There a tattered sail and after-mizzen, printed with the royal insignia of Cape Verde. A veritable regatta of disasters that foretold of bounty layering the rich veins of beachhead before them. They could see the sparkling doubloons, escudos, pieces of eight. And a scattered shimmering of sapphires and tiaras that poked out like children's sequins or abalone shells up and down the curving littoral.

A black cow watched from just inside the forest, and other pairs of eyes as well. There in the final breakers, three bobbing Brussels sprouts struggling toward shore.

"Smoke!" cried Marigold, as they dragged themselves belly and fingertips onto the cool pink and charcoal-washed sand. Sea gravy spun into white filaments that lathered the shoreline for miles. Sand hot to the heels, water fresh to nostril. Infant crinoids frolicking every which way.

"What is this place?" Rajibai inquired of the cow, who had strolled towards the margins of beach to greet the ridiculous newcomers.

"Jovita," replied her 1,100-pound Eminence, before attempting with little influence to hump the wretched Sannazaro who ran, tumbled—his trousers weighed down by gallons of water—and ran some more. "That's it. I'm outta here!" he screamed, breathless, from 100 yards down the beach.

"OK then, bye now," Rajibai shouted, with a straight face ... that then burst with the giddiness of a repressed century. He and Marigold wrestled one another to the ground, tossing hilarity upon hilarity, so relieved were they to have arrived, rolling over and over again. On the giving sand. Homeward thrust. Just screaming with delight to be alive, in this particular NoPlace.

The cow, in no less a playful mood, showed her attitude, and took up her chase after the sorely confused Italian whose panic could be heard for miles around.

CHAPTER 184

A Preponderance of Preposterous Poets

THE THREE INDOMITABLE SAILORS met up a mile down the seaside strand, beside a darkly pregnant creek that suspired in discrete shade, flowing from interiors as yet incalculable, mountains ripping the serenade of heaven with tropic-clad mayhem—foliage the wise botanist, Señor Squire, had ne'er encountered. So many melifluosities sweetened this teeming air.

The ground shook, throwing all three face forward. Then it was over.

"That's just dandy. We've landed on another fault," Sannazaro lamented, reflecting back to the seismic hell that was the waterfall in Tibet, and to Vesuvius, too.

The leveling ground shook again. They paused, counting the seconds, and then it was over. Thunder from a distant place, lightning strike, and the first crazy hint of a flying snowflake that splashed like a love drop against the boy's cheek. At the same neural instant came a hint of smoke, then, more distinctly, an elliptical haze trailing into the upper beyond.

"I say head for that smoke," Rajibai initiated, assuming it a sign of human settlement. The boy had become more than a man. In so few months he had acquired depth in 63 directions—tracker of gold bugs, high-seas anjin, connoisseur of sallies, Middle Eastern astronomer, premier ethologist, baffling polyglot and secret sensualist; his street smarts had blossomed and seemed to embrace the whole volcano of human experience. His hair had grown long and dark, his green eyes brighter by three F-stops (ever since the waterfall, Marigold had noticed), gold flecks having accumulated in the wild iris. Most comforting to the Commander, the boy had taken to his adoption with great dignity, and no longer referred to the tragedy of so many sleepless nights in the slums of Mumbai long ago.

In fact, for one whose life had become a whirlwind, it was remarkable how little, if ever, he looked back. This was a lad who consumed a feast of experience each day, ever on the move and untroubled.

His two elder statesmen nodded in the direction of the smoke.

They bushwhacked towards the spot, and found less than a mile away from their present position an open caldera, lava writhing hundreds of feet down in the ghastly cavity.

"Spare me further revelation. It is that village of the damned we always heard spoken of as children," whispered the waning Squire, soft in mind as the cuckoo's egg, wobbly as a noodle. "I swear this island is haunted, alive, vindictive, all three. Along with a fourth I don't dare speculate. First that randy squid, and now a cow in heat."

"What does that say about you?" Marigold asked, straight-faced.

All around the hard-shelled carapace of earth, where the caking forests had withered, hot pools spouted white liquid clay rich in all the known and unknown chemicals. Waltzing fairies of scalding mud. A suzerainty of thermal baths that heated up the surroundings. The geologic pandemonium attracted strange thermophilic cnidosporonts the size of tootsie rolls and color of fizelyite. A weird primordium, to be sure.

Above them, rearing miles, were the peaks, frosted tumult pouring out of strange auric summits, though no glaciers were evident. Nor was there obvious altitude to support higher snows.

"Look there. Do you see?" pressed the bewildered Sannazaro.

"So bright!" mulled Marigold. "Snowbows?"

"No. It's gold, I mean solid gold, got to be, though I don't understand it," he said, noticing how every summit resembled those capitals and religious cupolas hewn in precious filigree from Washington to Jerusalem. But these Jovitan citadels were neither informed nor hypothelated by the hand of man.

The astonished trio's speculations were cut short by a geyser erupting not 73 yards away, throwing its dense congeries of bacterial water 1,000 feet into the air. The three were hurled down, barely missing one of the boiling pools. The water trajectory formed a veil that drifted in the winds, perfuse with pure Victorian blue, diazo-brilliant orange, chromotrope and napthol yellow, the entire curtain floating in a lethal acidic haze, each droplet of water reflecting a pulp of pigments, so that the intense glare of the midday sun made soluble the potent mix, reflecting all who looked upon it.

"Don't stare into it!" Sannazaro, the most superstitious of the three, exclaimed, closing his eyes. He had Italian recipes for averting disaster, though few, so far, had succeeded at the task.

They got up a trio and ran, tumbling discordant between temblors. The whole island was alive.

Within an hour they were back on the beach. They could see the *Bonaparte* turning slow deranged circles out between the reefs, upside down but unsinkable, 2,000 feet from shore. And for the first time they noticed dozens of sharks patrolling the inner bay.

"Hey!" the boy whispered.

All looked to the same coordinate, where a man, trailed by three unleashed leopards, seemed to stalk warily from the fringes of the forest.

"What do we do?" Sannazaro asked: sharks in the water, leopards on the affront.

"They'd outrun us in seconds. We hold our ground as a team ... Bonjour!" Marigold called.

The far-off man in his tattered white linen pants and Panama hat gestured with his hand. He seemed to proffer no harm. Now the leopards sprang toward the threesome, and stopped only inches from them. The great cats sniffed out hands, crotches, bare toes, then made as if to play. Remarkable beasts, not quite leopards, nor tigers, nor lions. More like pumas, their fur the color of cerulean such as was baked into the lustrous porcelain vessels of the Korean Koryo period. Each with the horn of a unicorn and the regal tail of a long-winded orange howler monkey.

"Don't worry about them," sported the arriving man. "They're only two months old. Lovedoves."

"My goodness," the Commander started. "So the island is inhabited, after all?"

"Population about 150, I should imagine. Though it's always in flux, of course."

The man stood nearly the height of Marigold, and seemed not to have changed his trousers in as long a period as the Commander. His untrimmed beard shone silvery and rouge. His eyes stared blankly. Rajibai whispered something to his father.

"That's right," acknowledged the attuned man. "Blind as the heart for 15 years."

The Commander was reminded of their dear old friend Madame Vignette. "I hope you won't think me too brash for asking—"

"Certainly not. It's quite wonderful, actually. I was sitting beneath the tree, my favorite tree, the one at the center of the island. Archives from countless millennia have been carved into its unfazed bark. A giving tree. In fact, a coconut palm, largest, tastiest in the world as far as can be determined. There I was writing poetry, which is what I do, more or less, and one of those damned coconuts fell down and hit me square on the head. Cracked open my skull, and a bone sliver evidently severed the optic nerves. Not much in the way of surgical theaters out here. I recovered over time. But never my eyes. They see quite well, internally. There's just no way to reconnect them to the plug at the base of the skull, or wherever it is. Name's Saul Leibowitz."

Saul extended his hand, which the threesome collectively embraced, and immediately offered them a swig of his koa pipe. They all eagerly sampled.

"Coconut tobacco," mooned Saul, "with some underwater guava and misty papaya blend. A little methyl iodide from the kelp for added punch. Has the air of salt."

Then he led them toward the village of Jovita, followed by the three great spotted cats who gamboled infectiously along the way.

At length they reached a hamlet of some twenty ramshackle bowers cradled in the lap of jungly oblivion, yet blessed with the sea breezes. Other huts, outside the immediate pale of the community, were discernible in the surrounding hills. Half the village, at least, had been flattened, the debris of bamboo and thatch scattered everywhere. Yet nobody seemed the least concerned. Those few industrious types visible were seated beneath trees reciting poetry in languages unfamiliar, surrounded by a motley clutch of weird creatures—tricephalous snakes, their tongues promiscuously addressing one another, chattering boars, monkeys tippling their meerschaums, lambs their corncobs, and wild stallions demonstrating their prowess with dozens of mares. Many of the residents, young and old alike, of all colors and persuasions, were seated writing.

"What happened? What's going on?"

"Hurrinado. We lost two dozen villagers, countless others among the animals. These three pups' mother, I'm afraid. Of course, we're used to it. Not to be callous, but on a small island chain, with stragglers arriving and multiplying over thousands of years, you might think of it as population control. We've got all of Nature's most bizarre counter-measures. Even Malthus would blanch. Four electrical rivers, hazardously bumptious erogenies, daily sun strikes, Leonids attracted to the island's gravity, with resulting firestorms every night, quicksucks, geyser acids, 300-league hurrinadoes (no doubt of the sort that brought you to us), naughty bumblebees and falling stars that take it too far, to name a few."

The visitors in triplicate had some vague notion of what he was talking about, Sannazaro particularly.

"Where is everyone buried?"

"Blown thither, yon and further still, I imagine. The natural flux is so intense on Jovita that there's rarely a need to bury anyone."

Marigold chanced a different avenue of inquiry. "What are they writing?"

"Poetry," Saul replied matter of factly. "We have a preponderance of them on Jovita. In fact, everybody's a poet. That's how we cope. Virtuosos, each, of yeoman marinations. Hard to know for sure."

"Why's that?"

"I've never been able to read any of it."

"I understand, but surely they recite their work?"

"It's like talking to a coconut. Nobody understands anybody else."

"But that's preposterous."

Saul smiled: "That's what it has come down to out here. It doesn't matter—the true meaning, that is. Not when you're this happy. Everyone stopped trying to figure things out, or understand, centuries ago."

"But why?" pressed the boy.

"No understanding? Then what?"

"Understanding is not what it's cracked up to be," replied Saul.

"I'll underscore that," motioned the Squire.

"By quirky coincidence, no two people on Jovita have ever spoken anything like the same language, at least since I've been around—or not until this momentous occasion of your arrival. I must say it's quite shocking to understand another."

"But statistically, that's quite unusual, I should imagine," Marigold opined. "Considering the probability factor favoring English-speaking arrivals. The Commonwealth nations occupied 75 percent of the known world, at least politically, until 100 years ago. Shakespeare was *au courant* by 1650. Universal hegemonies were fashioned by Spanish, Portuguese and Dutch trading vessels. Together with the English, that's four languages, with considerable cross-breeding."

Saul interjected: "That's my point. There you go trying to understand, applying fancy theory, *OED* logic, precedent, rationality—all those things—to a situation which simply doesn't care about your one lonely brain. Out here, circumstances have somehow conspired to impose a linguistic isolation; to deliberately cut people off from the unnatural crutches of rumor, opinion and gossip, of incisive squabbles or vote-taking. It keeps the playing field quite level and congenial. Of course, on a different note, all the other plants and animals understand one another quite well. Tulip trees converse readily with lady bugs (infrasonicacoustics off the known spectrum), bats with tree shrews. We have migratory grazers from the Kalahari who know every fiddle pitch of platypus; a two-horned rhino desperately in love with a Newfoundland caribou who has her attention diverted by a silly skunk from Paraguay. We have Albanian newts chattering with Siberian ginger root and *Althaea officinalis*, the riparian marshmallow flower endemic to Jovita, gossiping all day long about the out-of-sort devilfish which swim upriver and make eyes at them. Ten-foot wide flowering rafflesia absorbing their grapevine, smelling atrocious, their spore brought here from somewhere high in Borneo—Kinabalu I think it said, though its speech is hard to determine: a cross between Sumatran Rhino, Slipper Orchid and Crested Lizard. It's a circus out in the language world."

"But without readers, or anybody to appreciate one's work, why bother writing poetry?"

"That is the question," marked the blind Wizard of the Three Cats. "I suspect it has something to do with the way we are as individuals, outside any group behavior or social gratification. There are all kinds of poetry: food and wise, errant and winnowed. Social salads. Porcupine and gauzy, threadbare and over-bloated. There is meter, brook, cataract and sea wall. Parnassian and parmeliaceous—belonging, that is, to the class of lichens who are most jejune and unconcerned with our own kind. There are hymned priests and flimsy woofs, gossip suckers, ploughmen of nectar, frenzy rollers, utterances in the sunlight and in the darkest hour. There are hiatuses of equal worth, whose poetic is all in the silence; common Roman poesies that are like an herb for Ptolemy or chest of tea. We all know there is cosmical and acronychal, heliacal and zodiacal verse; there are poetasters in the jungle, the valley and the church, learned and fantastic, skillful and devotional. Versing, cursing, searching, and all in common with that comprehensive soul to whom there is the very sheer love of mumbling to oneself, of imagining one's own ideas and fashioning the solitary *soirée musicale* without any need of confirmation from another. Which isn't to say the inhabitants aren't among the friendliest people you'll find anywhere. There is a feeling, shared by most if not all, that we are here for a special reason. That bond all by itself commands a common assent whose language is more like a tacit recognition—a group consensus requiring no discussion. Come, I'll introduce you to some."

"Neat!" exclaimed Rajibai, thrilled by so many abstruse notions, and by the sheer energy of Saul's own excitement. The words about whose meaning he had no clue infiltrated his innards like music. Which was the point of poetry in the first place, he reasoned.

They strolled past one elevated rattan hut after another, nodding their hellos and good-days to residents all busily engaged in their unintelligible, unreadable sonnets, haikus, attenuated prose, abbreviated epithets, massive tomes and epic hypercatalexes.

"Cauparome!" uttered the first poet, trailing off an iambic hexameter devoted to—who knows what?

"That's the Right Reverend Monsignor. He seems to speak some Roman galley-slave dialect."

"But that was a variation of the Latin phrase for sweet-smelling itinerant or peddler, no? *E italiano*?" Sannazaro called out.

The Monsignor, with his demonstrably deviated septum (the result of one of the island's more legendary storms) stared dumbly and with an undeviating smile.

"*Egli non e italiano*," Saul advised. "Nobody else on the island even comes close to a modern European language."

Another individual greeted them with an even stranger, part gymnastic verbal hieroglyphic: "Daeie dodne alle habbed!"

Then another, in a tongue more harp or chimes than reason. Some of it rhymed, some seemed seasonal.

"Mein liebes Fraulein, how are we today? Old High Anglo-Saxon: a former Baron. And there, the Most Honorable Marchioness: Cuneiform. Moderator of the General Assembly: a seventeenth-century Goudan, a prosody of sibilants the thickness of cheddar. Court Chairman: the odd idiolect of Lycaeus, in the fashion of Homer's Maeonian springs. Duchess of the Blood Royal: Kwakiutl."

They passed by speakers wielding sonorous Tungusic, attenuated Laughing Goose from somewhere in Mongolia, Out-of-Work Giraffe (a languorous-sounding Tanzanian dialect from the slopes of Kilimanjaro, explained Saul), Tremoloso Tocharian, Sunrise Faroese, Charitable Illyrian, Mountain Northern Song, Lost Rhaetic, Noon-Day Yap, a shrill Indo-Hittitian, cryptic Tupi-Guaranian and steel-yard Mon-Khmerian. It was a Babel of babbling brook proportions. There was no chance of exchanging even the most basic of information. Such a complete lockout suggested something monumentally awry, or unexpected, with regard to human linguistic origins, or origins in general.

"But how do differentiate Hittitian from Tupi-Guaranian?" asked the Commander, mightily confused. "And how did you figure out it was Kwakiutl, or attenuated Laughing Goose, to begin with?"

"Research," replied Saul. "Raised on *Rasselas*. I used to haunt the ziggurats of Mesopotamia and catacombs of Cappadocia, if that's any sort of explanation."

Later, they came around towards Saul's own Sunnybrook with white pickets and hanging bougainvillea, and saw that a coral tree had crashed during the last storm, severing his bachelor kitchen from a master bedroom with whirlpool ensuite. But Saul seemed indifferent to the chaos and all the nesting birds inside the northern portions of his living room; he invited his guests to seat themselves, and offered them what few trappings of civilized cuisine were available.

"Now, I suppose there is a reason you're here?" he began.

Chapter 185
Archives from the Tree of Life

THE COMMANDER'S HEAD was bombinating and gravitating with all this linguistic fiddle play and puddle plunges. They had arrived at what appeared to be the phylogenetic swamp at the beginning of human evolution, with one very strange twist: all of history had accumulated in the same living laboratory. What was he supposed to do now? Lie back and simply resonate? Spawn holy vibrations? Absorb the electricity in the air without so much as a whimper? He had no clue how to sit still, be at peace, shorten the half-life of his frissons or conduct himself with equipoise. These good graces of the satisfied life were beyond him, beneath him, to all sides. Whereas he was free-flying in the land of unease. Nothing quite fit. His imaginings remained truant and wanting. A restive forethought plagued even the hour of his fondue, like that beast, according to Spenser, who had no hope of any bliss. Nature may have heaped 10,000 happinesses in his lap, but only to the effect of nearly crushing his insides. The sum of all denominated pleasures could not negate the aggregate pains. No harborage, nor heartward compact was likely to settle him down—and this much Sannazaro now appreciated. Nowhere else to go, either. Unless, of course, Queen Mum had intended some yet-to-be-revealed expedition. Unlikely, thought the Squire. Her enlightened enjoiners would not resolve the Commander's dangling modifier. He was a wayfarer by birth, it was now clear; the lost clan of the dragonfly all in one soul.

Another earthquake rocked the whole village, throwing sparks from the red charcoal burner across the floor of the hut. Saul deftly put them out.

"How did you notice them?" raised Sannazaro. Even he, with sight intact, could not have found such embers amid the hodgepodge.

"That pinch of coconut tobacco you bibbled—well, I suppose I should have warned you: it induces heightened sensitivity."

"What sort of heightened?" Marigold asked.

"It varies from individual to individual."

At that very moment, Rajibai was waking to a cacophony of frequencies and canary calls emanating in a free-for-all in the surrounding jungles. He was beginning to tune in to everything, and it was giving him a slight headache. He shivered with acoustical receptivity.

"You hear that? They're all talking about the quake," Rajibai foraged. One group of Macedonian songbirds, he reported, was insisting it was a 5.9, while some worms from Azerbarrimus were making light of their exaggeration. Leaves discoursed with woodpeckers hailing originally from Ontario, whilst a small carouse of finger frogs from Upper Connecticut agonized over the constantly changing arnebia flowers, throwing them into an infernal temper on account of the plants changing color from day to day— violet on Monday, yellow on Tuesday, silver every other Wednesday, black during earthquake season.

"You see," Saul broke in. "The island is nothing but gossip. Now you can understand how a small community of 150 people have so little time, patience or inclination at the end of each day, or the beginning, for that matter, to speak amongst themselves, what with all this other clamor crowding the airwaves."

"So everybody can understand the animals and plants? Is that what you're saying?" wondered Marigold.

"After a time, yes, assuming they're open to the experience."

"Let me see ..." and the Commander put his ear to the air. "I'm waiting ..."

"Smoke some more pitch."

He did, taking several deep drags on the koa pipe, coughing up dinner from months before.

"Wait!" he ignited.

"What is it, Father?"

"I hear something ..." The Commander remained motionless. "There! Shhh! It's singing. Grapes. Vines. The strength of the Holy Spirit something something ... *Sed nos pisciculi* ..."

"Ahh! That's the tree you're hearing."

"Which tree?" Sannazaro wanted to know. He couldn't hear anything other than the popish madbrains, snipings and billows of his companions.

"The vintaging of St Hippolytus, a passage from Tertullian, a mosaic decoration—it's calling to you. We'll go soon," Saul assured his three new visitors.

"Now *you're* sounding as bad as them!" Sannazaro lamented.

"Calling? To me?" the Commander puzzled.

Saul prepared an avocado soufflé for his guests, served up with candied pear and unleavened eucalyptus bark toasted with orange peels. Over dinner he eagerly expatiated on his own background, grateful for human ears that would listen, and recited in his flat gaze of illumination a blank verse that summarized his days. The passing Fall, the heart of a girl in an old man's look—faces, dreams, whole lives that were, went, no recall. He described how, sometimes in the sweet cool afternoon, he could hear their quiet mooning from years before. It lived. So real. How he took her hand in his, ever so gently, stared into her dark eyes, peering through to that which forever inhabits the imagination. How he still dreamt of all those rain-washed midnights on a cozy side street in Paris, an uprising in his chest. A love affair that carried him onward forever.

"Who was she?" Marigold inquired.

"That's the really peculiar part," the poet went on. "I've only imagined her, ever since first hearing the account."

"What account?" the Commander hastened.

"Wait a minute," Sannazaro broke in. "You've rhapsodized some girl you've never met? I don't follow."

Marigold scolded his Squire with a frown. "My dear man, have you not even an itch of a soul, no sting of romance to remind you of that female ideal to which chivalry, philosophy and every nostalgia have always been oriented?"

"Sure, I have an itch, and a sting, bites and bruises on every limb, and a crack somewhere in my skull. And I prefer it that way. Better real flesh, and a compass to boot, than nothing."

"The queen of the night: there is no better compass reading than she, and I would gladly go to my grave just carrying her in my thoughts."

"To be perfectly frank, you look like you're there already," Sannazaro concluded.

"And you smell like a rotting badger," Marigold chastened. His nose was all crunched up.

"You two are best friends, I see," Saul rhymed in.

"Actually, they bitch more than any two adults in the history of the world," Rajibai divulged, in a tone that told Saul everything he needed to know.

"So what did you hear about her?" Marigold pressed on. "This damsel of the islands."

"Well, actually, there was a precocious female bat who spoke English in the days when I still had my sight."

"My, but that bat gets around!"

"You know her?" Saul exclaimed.

"Oh yes, but you must continue. What advice did she convey? Surely she's not the one you are in love with?"

"Heavens no. I like European girls, preferably over 36 and from northern France. Well seasoned, in other words, their beauty fully emergent. But you must understand, this poor bat had evidently been searching among all the islands in all the nearby seas for her one son, whom she missed something terribly."

"That problem has been solved," Marigold advised. "We found him and reunited him with his mother."

Saul was visibly moved. "That's marvelous!" he contemplated, going off on some inward journey, until the Commander's impatience broke the spell.

"So what did she say?"

"Ahh, right. 'Find her. Love her. Learn her secrets and thereby save the world.'"

"That all sounds perfectly sensible," Marigold reasoned.

"But that was it?" Sannazaro asked with a hopeless bickering air.

"Actually," Saul began, "the bat hinted at a cannibal's daughter. Not the sort of woman you'd expect to meet on a backstreet in Paris. Said to live alone. There were certain problems, things that didn't add up. I sensed all was rumor. The bats had heard it from the bees, who are known for their make-believe. More likely, a decent girl. An orphan. A lonely icon lost in the uplands. I imagined her, all right. Was desperate to find her. I don't know why, exactly; but that bat—the world's foremost pollinator—thought it quite important. In any case, it wasn't to happen. That coconut knocked out my noodles, cut short my expedition."

They slept that night in Saul's hut, on a dead manta ray who'd washed up in the storm yet gave off death warmth. Twelve feet in width, it was a small one by Jovitan standards, but young, which meant its skin was as soft as Egyptian cotton. Saul gave Rajibai a down pillow, 200 years old, an heirloom, the only surviving possession of his own shipwreck on Jovita, other than his trousers. The great cats—Vivendi, Activa and Contemplativa—curled up beside him, taken at once with the boy's charm.

Sometime after midnight, Sannazaro's hallucinations, born of the coconut pitch, reversed directions, making for the most obnoxious snores. But by morning all snores were forgiven. Jovita had the appearance and feel of no other island, or none that equally reliable testimony dare describe. Some things cannot, must not, be detailed. Fifteen hundred miles, give or take, south or southeast of the Gold Coast of Africa is as close an itinerary as should be permitted. But followers beware: even if you were to penetrate to the core of the approximate circumference, the absolute magnetic center would elude you entirely, in inverse proportion to the length squared of the radius from point of origin to moment of greatest confusion, minus the distance from your berth to the bathroom, given the perpetual seasickness that brings all heroics to its knees.

Moreover, no satellite imagery will ever find Jovita. No helicopter can land there. Only utter ruin to a ship and its crew is likely to jar forth the invisible gates. This truth is clear enough by dawn, when some force scatters the light as if to mock the explorer with heartbreaking clarity: explosions similar to lightning, but emanating in ionized atoms, electrical discharges, photon to photon. Direct transit to the island from the sun's coronal outgassing. The only receiving end on Earth. Yet the heat is moderated. All remains cool, tranquil, ensconced in enchanted puff clouds.

All these random and mutational sun strikes were not easily translated into any literature, or blueprint for electrical wiring. The effect upon the trio was disorienting, of course, but posed a potentially lethal challenge. Each strike amassed with no prior warning: no clouds to indicate the coming surge; no thunder to presage the devastation that cleaved trees in two, separated cliffs, burned hectares of unsuspecting wood in a microsecond. Every morning, every year. Any object was a suitable receiver.

There was no escaping it. Luck, only luck, dictated who lived, who died. This meant that every creature had a price on her head, lived with the inevitability of random mortality. It induced not prayer, but philosophy, explained Saul; and as one wearied of epistemology, metaphysics and logic, poetry and sex emerged as the only two expressions of the short-lived Jovitan soul.

Paradise had its limitations, though some, as in normal worlds, managed to escape death. It was all in the throw of the cosmic dice.

The "cannibal", for example, Saul said, was thought to be over 100 years old.

Moreover, there was no doubting the fantastic beauty of the sun strikes. Even the three terrified voyagers acknowledged this, as they stood on the beach watching the intrastellar kaleidoscope wreaking its savagery in ten minutes' worth of destruction across the entire cordillera of the Jovitan archipelago.

"When was the last time a sun strike hit the village?" asked Sannazaro, agitated to the point his lips would hardly move.

"About a week ago," replied Saul. "Roasted an anteater, the Baroness, who used to wander about reciting one of her ancestor's epyllions. Too erudite for me, though the rhyme scheme was clear enough. A remarkable lady, considering her diet was, well, ghastly, in my opinion. Grub larvae were her favorite, seasoned with tick urine. But never mind that. Here's the real catch, which I forgot to mention: it's not *our* sun that's causing all the havoc. No. It's a hidden star, only a few thousand years old. At the far edge of the universe. Said to look like a papaya. The dust shells surrounding it are actually 547,000 times brighter than all the light added together in our little solar system. Brighter, even, than Eta Carina. When the moon breathes at night, you can sometimes see it: gray-blues, lime greens, weighing 120 times the size of our sun.

"But where did you acquire your astronomy?"

"From a barn owl, Serpius, that lives in the attic of the Right Honorable Marchioness' hut. You met her yesterday. The one with the talking banana tree."

"Ahh, yes."

Later that day Saul finally got round to leading the weary foot soldiers to the Tree of Life. He knew his way about this part of the island instinctively. Didn't even need a cane. His three cats led him with exquisitely well-defined nudges and instructive purrs, gaining ground over any irregularity or subversion of land surface, avoiding all obstacles and hives.

Long before reaching the base of the mighty tree, the trio could feel its colossal presence rearing up in their nostrils, their brains, forming strange ideas. Their palms began to sweat, every hormone to react. They could hear its music.

Several local poets were gathered about the grandiloquent monster that reared 12,000 feet into the lemon-thick mists. Other theories as to its height abounded. Some reckoned it could be no less than 47 miles abiding. Poets had spent lifetimes formulating exquisitely rendered calculations, based upon length of shadow, density of murmurings, profligacy of dewdrop, spectral analysis of the 15 million hues and intimations of green, meteorological corollaries, the fall into time of a soft downy feather, or the plunge of a liberated nut casing, taking into account the variables of wind sheer, microclimate, humid season. The tree had harbored a poetic symmetry of pleasurable impressions and counter-impressions that was the essence of all mirror images. Though all poets universally agreed that it was born on the first day of spring.

The tree was so magnificent, its bark so articulated, the height, stature, canopy and coconuts which it fostered so utterly, inexpressibly sublime, as to render all speech triply useless. Hence, the gathered ensemble of versifiers was of little consequence, like the human race itself: an afterthought of testimonials. Saul showed the trio everything he knew about the tree, stroking the Braille and Rosettas of its elaborate bark, pictographic portions from 140,000 years of continuous Jovitan history. Even recent cave-finds from Namibia stopped short of such enduring evidence of humanity's evolution.

"Before my injury, when I could see, I used to wonder what was at the top. Something—a nest, or tunnel leading higher, into the highest atmospheres. I was never sure. Maybe you see something?"

They all strained their eyes.

"There is a dark nest, I believe," managed Rajibai, who had the sharpest vision of them all. "And you were right, some kind of channel, white on gold, or yellow against gray."

"Goya's colors," Sannazaro gasped, "leading higher and higher. But then again, I'm not certain of it."

"I can't tell," stated the Commander.

"One limb after another, an infinite tree," Sannazaro added.

"Well, there's an easy way to solve the riddle," Rajibai declared, proceeding to climb upwards, grabbing hold of the uneven finger ledges of bark.

"Son? Are you sure about this?"

"What's he doing?" Saul asked. "Ascending the tree? Splendid!"

"It might be better not to," appealed the Squire. "There are no upward Himalayan thermals to buffer your fall this time, Son."

"No worry, Uncle. Father, watch your head!"

Other poets stopped work on their masterpieces to gather round and observe as the boy continued into unimaginable eco-regions of height. They watched the scattering of his puny limbs making like an eagle, an ascending lark, a racing spider, a charging ant, vertically inspired, nothing to stop him. A remarkable show, fearless.

"Won't this be interesting. I am sure no human has ever attempted it," Saul declared. "You must inform me of his passage. And if he ever returns, whether he has aged."

CHAPTER 186
The Sermon of the Coconuts

THE BOY GREW FAINTER and fainter as he ascended into one misty layer of upper canopy after another. From Todea to Oleandra, through spheres of De re rustica and Hodaibaya. Marigold showed not the slightest misgiving about this new vertical sortie, though he couldn't actually remember anything about the terms of immunity afforded them since Tibet. Whether that special grace included falling out of trees. "He knows what he's doing," said he, in uncertain summary of Rajibai's inexhaustibility.

All the other poets gawked radiantly at the boy's seamless gymnastical endeavor, full of sacred fires and church oak benedictions, helping themselves to the sweet swigs of the smoldering coconut pitch served up generously from Saul's hardwood pipe. There would be propitiations, pregnancies, fine weather. The fine little scamperer was heading straight towards God's mouth, the Endendros, Chapel of Our Lady, realm of the tree nymphs and silk-cotton jinns.

Marigold walked around the tree, staring far up into the fetching cumuli, trying to follow the movement of his son and grasp the miracle that swayed Brobdingnagian above.

"Will you just look at those Atlantean proportions," he echoed reverentially. "Why, they defy the compass of comfortable perceptions. Let me see ..." He began multiplying, adding, dividing, though never once subtracted, and came up with a startling calculation: "If my numbers have not failed me, there are, gentlemen, approximately 400,000 cubic feet of sapwood, cambium, phloem, bark and leaf-mass before us. That would have to make this tree by far the largest living thing on Earth. Forty times the size of a blue whale. More substantial, even, than our fungus friend in the fiords of New Zealand. And that's merely the *visible* tree. If, as you noblemen and women have carefully divined, the ancient wood wanders into or beyond the stratosphere, then I would have to say there is as much living mass in this one being as in all the rest of Earth combined. Which would fairly argue for a central pillar, a ballast, a masthead, right here before us."

"That's a long fall if he slips," Saul warned, gazing into his own dark imaginings and memories.

But the Commander was not the least concerned. Nor was Rajibai himself, who was by now lost in a maze of his own, shimmying along the vertical coliseum of vascular networks, arboreal engines and wind stabilizers which held up the living skyscraper. For all its colossal size, the tree spent the vast majority of its time nurturing the most delicate of upper epidermises, palisade layers and chloroplasts. Rajibai put his ear to the sponge, heard the coursing veins, tens of millions of stomata singing the melody of photosynthesis. Cells as glib as a talk-show host. All the raw materials that went into its august introspection, internal debates, incessant groans and rhapsodies were a hybrid of the world's foremost trees, its one gigantic heart pounding with the steadiness of Ravel. Its wooden armada was equivalent to 1,000 Norway maples, or 700 giant sequoias, stacked one atop the other. The width of 8,000 river beech or 9,000 London plane trees. Its lateral and feeder roots spread across the entire island, based upon its standing size, translating into well over two million gallons of dissolved nutrients which it required every hour from the soil. In exchange, it exhaled 2.4 million cubic feet of the purest, sweetest oxygen, and these were all conservative estimates by a factor of ten hundred hundreds, thought Marigold, who related these amazed conjectures to Saul and Sannazaro. Numbers nullifying reason. The taproot must have extended into the thermal vents 20 miles below the surface, which meant this tree had a literal fire in its belly.

Even the leaves departed all the Commander's expectations. Looking at the faraway apex of the creature, it was indeed a *Cocos nucifera*, named by the Portuguese for "monkey with one thing on its mind and one thing only—sex". Its compound flower stalks, woody spathes, tens of thousands of athletic masculine flowers and hundreds of erotic female ones all tracked accordingly: graceful embryos, white kernels, liquid endosperm, three ovarial cavities in every flower. Each ellipsoidal fruit came encased in a fibrous husk— the meat of 100 industries elsewhere in the world, from shampoo to copra meal, and all this decipherable from the remains of scattered coconuts on the mossy floor.

But the coconut flowers were only part of the great Being, as Rajibai himself now realized. Somehow, uncannily, it had acquired along its infinite library of bark hundreds of other commensural vines, roseate bromeliads, sugary *Sphaeradenia* and lounging *Laetia*. There were anxious anthuriums and noisy bryophytes. And there, where the boy continued climbing higher and higher, symbionts and seeds that had all roosted in cubby holes so that there was, up and down its elegant mass, a riotous parade of Paul's scarlet hawthorn, glabrous chinaberry, sharp-leaved jacaranda and the most gentle of Jerusalem thorns.

On the lower reaches Sannazaro recognized a remarkable diversity that had fused into one. There was the rare Yulan magnolia as well as a most fragrant mazzard. Higher up, Yoshino cherries crowding a cranny embroidered with flowers of the Japanese pagoda tree. Rajibai dragged himself, squirmed, pulled up through golden-rain, tree of heaven and Crimean linden all chaotically arrayed amidst a constellation of fringe, crab and mulberries. The boy helped himself to a Chinese pistachio and smelled the redolent sweet gum all around him. Flowering *Eucalyptus regnans*.

Even the husk and sheath transgressed the fundamental laws of biology, as it combined what appeared to be an African variety of European white birch, a ribboned paperbark cherry, fine silky maple, rough and wild Korean mountain ash, even the thorny *Castor aralia*. All trees in one.

Crustaceous lichens, known as opegrapha, had left a subtle hieroglyphic up and down the length of the giant, Saul recalled, merely to point out that this one genus actually comprised all the appointed scribes of Nature busily translating 10,000 languages into a universal code of readable wood.

"In addition to a full complement of seeds, berries, fruits and edible leaves, it yields over 2,000 coconuts each year," explained Saul. "Six per day. One every four hours. Usually right on time, too. I learned the hard way. Uh-oh!"

The three men leapt to four sides as a coconut came crashing down. Fortunately, Rajibai was not with it.

"A good omen," Saul suggested.

"Why didn't the other poets scramble?" asked the Commander.

"They are more familiar with the flight patterns."

The poets. They sat on a mossy carpet busily writing in their diaries, using quills from the mountain peacock and white invisible ink from the coconut pulp. The great tree of life, *Etz Hayyim*, gave loft to every vowel and consonant. Any poet, no matter the language, could feel its urgings: tryw, trough, trey, triy, treuwe, trauwe, trau ...; all the special bugs, birds, deities, structures, vents, myths, movements, responses, causes and effects known to the etymology of apples, liberty and paradise; and the moss carpet—golden barbary—extending 35 miles in every direction. All part of the same tree.

"Do you think it's safe to sit back down?" Marigold asked.

"Why not," Saul said. "Surely you'll have four hours before the next clunker."

They helped themselves to the little spring at the base of the giant: a perpetual flow of cold pure coconut milk. On a little ledge above was a similar puddle of pure liquid chocolate that issued as a result of the very trigonometry of pressures encasing the cocoa beans lodged high up within the bulk of the tree.

A self-tapping system. From one hole, lemonade; from another, diet cranberry juice. Beers and other spirits of every variety. Together with the abundant diversity of fruits falling like leaves in autumn, the canopy— a crepuscular damp stretching out in the manner of so many Corots, Constables, Gainsboroughs, Lorrains, maybe even a few others—allowed for an eternal youth in the breezy shade of itself: a sylvan dark such that the sky was scarcely visible for 180 degrees. Or even more where the boy now clambered, 800 feet—or was it eight miles?—into the crown.

Rajibai's hand clung to the utopic tissue of rind which insinuated to his open mind a million microworlds: mites, leaf-cutting ants, peach-borer moths, walking sticks, leaf crickets, aphis-lions, golden eyes, termites and katydids. Each had an attitude, a prayer, a song. Each metamorphosed before his eyes as if time had rallied behind one momentary consolidation of insect civilization for the benefits of this child among the upper branches. In just one nook, two million tent caterpillars swarming around the mass of eggs from whence they'd just moments before hatched, emitting a weird song of science fiction, clearly evangelical in its address. A hundred thousand giant cecropia and polyphemus moths slowly fluttered in the haloed light, multiple layers of living wing fluttering through the upper canopies. Mayflies, speaking a distinctly Paleozoic dialect, tinged with Carboniferous sibilants, explored the mid-latitudes of the giant, whilst pale snowy tree crickets, *Oecanthus niveus*, sailed transparently through the lower ranges of the shadow world. The blues and golds and ochre blurs all breathed language; the wood vibrated stanzas from living prophets; in idyllic rhyme each butterfly whispered mating calls after the style of Lucan and Catullus. The overall effect was mesmerizing, Lamellas lining the luminous air. Five hundred million years of free-standing shade-green cornucopia. A comedy of metrical romance, lyric charms, metaphysical triumphs, ballads and reliques.

Among all the poetry of the world, no ideas were expressed so purely as in that tree. No sounds so seductive as far out on one limb after another. *Idylls of the King*, "Salut au Monde!", a *Carmina Burana*. Rajibai got all of it under his nails as he crept towards infinite riches above, in a trance sure enough.

A kinkajou, that small honey bear of the Procyonidae family, scooped out bright purple whip scorpions from hollows, taking off the heads first, then dining on the lethal tails. It offered one to the boy, who politely resisted. Jumping spiders shouted their glee at the newcomer as they swung from filament to strand and back again in search of mosquitoes.

All was savory, bellowing, cartilaginous speech, aria and bravado. Sneezing wasps, burping frogs, aerial intelligence cavorting through the ages with a patchwork crescendo of illustrated manuscripts rendered out of leaf, iterations of the here, prophecies of the now. Monteverdi's finesse, Purcell's profundity. Limbourg. De Berry. Hour after hour.

But what was it really like to be there, Marigold wondered. He stared into a cloud of unknowing. Should he dare follow after his son? He gave that inspired look to Sannazaro, who was more or less snoozing, immune to impulse, subordinated by the colossal weight everywhere. He felt the effect of the mass, an inertia bearing down upon him. The gardener in the man preferred sitting at peace upon the shaded moss carpet in the company of a blind sage. He no longer yearned to be heroic. He could easily ascribe to such poetry, his days passed in the quiet meditation of a good coffee, a few lines from Browning or Milton, reminiscences for all time.

Upon second reflection, neither did the Commander aspire any higher, for he knew not the first thing about tree climbing, in any event. Nor did he have the proper toes. Cliffs, high mountains were one thing. But surmounting this infinite tree was altogether a higher order of propositions.

He stared up at the boundless stretches above and around him and knew this tree to be his own soul. He did not have to ascend its heights to be part of it. His boy was no longer visible. He sat down and began to muse dreamily, without any notion of a direct object, no person to whom he was speaking, as if to incite the realization that true love abounds without purpose or reason. It just is. Like never before, he felt completely whole. The tree, without so much as a didactic inference, had overwhelmed him. A veritable sermon of coconuts that went straight to the heart.

"I am no parishioner," sighed Marigold. "But this is prayer divine."

CHAPTER 187
Mr Marigold's Final Utopia

MANY THINGS WERE happening to the Commander, though in truth he was no more than a tired man sitting under a tree, somewhere in the known or unknown world. All that he had tried to do, or hoped to do, came back to demand some fitting finale, a reconciliation of disparate suspensions and idealisms. Where there was a bark, now a ping; what once roared, now quivered. That which had impugned and indicted became sweet and sentimental, whereas the earlier quietude of his Tesuque retreat was presently a raging torrent of love, frustration and hope regained. What did they mean, these many contraries and resolutions?

With so much agitation flogging failing brainpower, it was enough for him to begin: "I cannot recall precisely how I once lived, what catapults and tension hurled me forward, the particulars of passion precariously sieved, nor those infernal caves down which I lowered. But a general impulse I picture well enough, whose deeply secretive ordeals admit no trespass, though the yearning memory would take this shady grove of dream's desire and plead all day and night to make it last. The sentiments accumulate into the way I would become. A matter of complicated verb tenses which I cannot explain. A swoon depiction that evades the present era. It fails to capture time between the self and its vague mirror. Or take hold of the pulse of life between its joys and tears. Each step, every instinct, throws with a bodily abandon that savors no confession. Arranges its inventions randomly, despite whatever lessons, and ultimately emerges in a paradise. This is the first day of any usefulness. All the messages of bright heaven drift in and out of me, to which I now surrender, as if no less than to a fair maiden."

"What *are* you talking about?" Sannazaro chided him. "It's not that I don't appreciate a good poetaster once in a while. I just don't have a bloody clue what you just said."

"I do," said Saul more confidently, his eyeless shadows ablaze with the Commander's light.

"Enlighten me, then."

They didn't have to. The coconut pitch was just then beginning to exert its unpredictable effects on the Squire as well. He started grinning, rolled over on the moss, looked up at the giant, with her 4.6-billion-year-old cholesterols, and knew at last what Marigold had just intended and intoned.

In the spirit of the moment, he too proceeded to recite some of the writings on the wall of his own soul, which happened to be none other than the famed Ballad of the Boisterous Bark Beetle, beginning with the Age of Darkness. Squeaking lapwings harmonizing up and down the *arbre familier* added a certain lyric-soprano tension to the Squire's recitativo, which dated from the time of Aristotle, who was himself familiar with the tone-poem of Abyssian lands, silvery sap and colored streams.

But what arborescent vision had actually ramified inside their softly suffused brains cannot be adequately described for present ages, or for those of posterity either. The fact will always remain that the twosome and their anything-but-blind guide were caught up in the odoriferous fruit-giving wisdom of the coconutty Tree of Life, otherwise known as the Giant. Everything henceforth was explained to them.

But, as most who make a compound study of zoosemiotics, the New Novel, *les mots et les choses* will no doubt attest to, every act of explanation is, in truth, an act of translation, which could not be entirely trusted to the likes of the Commander. He paraphrased all that he heard from the marvelous tree, adding a dollop and two toes of philosophy here, a semblance of unknown sociology there, until he had actually reconnoitered the metaphysical phraseology appropriate to describe this new vision of Utopia laid out directly before him, and which he proceeded therewith to convey to all who would listen, knowing that a single word might verily restore a kingdom, as a tender touch doth make a King.

It started with his lofty plans for gun control, a topic of absolutely no interest amongst the leaf-cutting ants and ivory weevils, let alone the other lounging poets, but one which Marigold extrapolated from the entire tree. Bridging metaphors and similes between species, attempting by way of new frequencies and bandwidths to explain himself to the growing confederacy of solipsists all around him, the Commander formulated a plan, however many deaf ears it fell upon, again based largely on the memorable Shogun Ieyasu, to have all guns throughout the world confiscated and melted down into a big bread oven. Gun owners and their descendants would be entitled to wholesale prices on all loaves of sourdough and Russian rye thereafter. Anyone caught with a gun would be made to swallow live ammo, then removed to some tropical country where their life would be spent planting trees.

"The other poets have fallen asleep," Sannazaro noticed.

"It is that time of day," Saul stated, trying to be polite about it.

"Never mind them," Marigold said. "Mount Everest is not Mount Everest to those who live directly on its lower slopes. Ask any Sherpa."

The Commander continued to elaborate his theological wish-list, as he had done so many times before, following on with his plans for tearing up several million square miles of the known world's road surface, where not a blade of grass could grow, and billions of animals and hundreds of thousands of people were killed each year. Marigold described his plans for using the chunks of tarmac to fill in the San Andreas fault. In the US alone, a region the size of Georgia had been denuded for freeways—land which might be rejuvenated. Losing all road surfaces, he calculated, would effectively undermine the continued use of automobiles, as Al Gore recommended, and thus eliminate all future tailpipe emissions. Moreover, by replacing concrete and asphalt with mixed crops, one could grow enough additional food to feed every hungry person on the planet.

"That's ingenious. But will it work?" Saul wondered, pitting the pragmatism of John Dewey, which was Sannazaro's preferred methodology, against the transcendentalist hazes of Immanuel Kant, whose every whiff and joint animated the Commander.

But Marigold wasn't one to belabor outcomes. Ideals were more important. And he had other striking plans for the hundreds of millions of scrapped vehicles: there were, he suggested, easily 500 extinct volcanoes around the world into whose calderas and deep caverns the junk might be amassed, causing no obvious deterrent to the natural world, much like the system of disposing nuclear wastes beneath Nevada. After all, a lightning blast turned a road surface into glass, and Nature was certainly not the less for it.

But with those very sentiments, noble as they appeared, came a mighty roar from several hundred miles away.

"What's that?" the duo implored.

"A volcano on one of the other nearby islands," Saul figured. "Happens from time to time."

"Are we in danger?" Sannazaro asked.

"Possibly. Nothing to do about it, though. Where will you go? How will you breathe there, versus here. Might as well carry on, Commander."

So notwithstanding a distant black streak in the sky and a rain of ash and sparks from hundreds of miles away, Marigold continued with the eloquent description of his plans to re-seed 52 percent of the planet, the NPP or Net Primary Production—all those chlorophyll-producing regions that had been usurped by human accommodation. The Commander then spoke of delousing all those fouled and frightened waters, starting with the Mississippi River, and his ingenious concept for hydrogen fuel-cell particulate-matter strainers. At that instant, they all heard another roar.

"A flood," Saul cautioned calmly. "That grinding sound happens to be the heaps of forest being uprooted along the banks. We've had a lot of rain of late in the highlands. Very sad, if you consider the loss of fish lives. Especially Jovitan fish, which sing Handel. It's true, I've heard them in the night."

"Should we flee?" Sannazaro begged to know.

"Not necessary," replied the blind poet. "It will, or will not, carry us away. No sense worrying about it. Please, continue. You have no idea how much I'm enjoying a conversation in my native tongue, more or less."

The Commander brushed impending disasters from his mind and launched into an inspired financial formulation that would solve the crisis of poverty throughout the world, based upon his plan to find the money to remedy those crippling diseases that Western pharmaceutical giants and governments had refused to bankroll, namely, schistosomiasis, AIDS, malaria and lymphatic filariasis.

"But my dear friend, have you forgotten that you've already plunged the planet into fiduciary bankruptcy, delegating every billionaire to the moon?" Sannazaro began.

"Did I?" Marigold scratched his head. He had forgotten all about that. "What a foolish idea. It is true that the rich corporations and taxpayers are doing nothing for the poor, whose own governments are without any resources. But surely the solution will not be found on the moon, but through the mechanism of pledging—no, not pledging, but adamantly pouring several tens of billions of dollars into immediate research. Vaccines can be and will be found. Rid these poor people of disease, and they will rid themselves of poverty," he chimed, citing the philosophy of a great Harvard economist named Jeffrey Sachs whom he had probably misunderstood on more than one occasion. In the next instant, he was misinterpreting the Federal Banking Chairman, as well as Dr Sen.

"And who will finance this heady research scheme?" retorted Saul, who was as sceptical about such things as Sannazaro, a true poet who had nothing to say on the matter. He'd been through it with Marigold too many times before, though had not expected so lucid a rampage under a coconut palm. Granted, the size of the palm seemed to impact by direct proportion on the scope of Marigold's latest Utopia.

"First we must encourage the 70-odd Unbearably Indebted Squatter Nations to take back the intellectual property rights that have been stolen by the rich. South Africa, which has nationalized foreign patents pertaining to AIDS research, has set the initial precedent. The poor must simply negate all claims for royalties by the rich. What nation would go to war with poor people who only wanted to heal their sick?"

"But are you able to borrow those billions of dollars?" Saul wondered, though he found everything else in the Commander's proposal rather plausible.

"He is, but it will forever put him out of business," Sannazaro reminded his friend. "Which would be the best thing that could happen at this point."

"By the time the lawyers start chasing me down, the cures will have been delivered to a billion people. Let them throw me in debtors' prison. Do I care? The soul defines its boundaries. Some see themselves behind bars, while others characterize the very same confinement as springtime. There will always be those who describe the zero as nothing, and others still who will look through the zero as if it were a marvelous looking glass. The value of my billions of dollars is its exponential leverage. That's obvious. Think of it as a new instrument for good will, monk bonds. What's more, there are yet additional mechanisms for generating still more billions."

"To hear him speak of mechanisms, one could be deceived into believing he has elbow grease, or some magic way with cogs and dowels," Sannazaro observed. "The truth is, if he puts on a watch, it breaks; he cleans out a chimney, the neighborhood burns down."

"That is patently unfair. It is true my learning came from books, mostly. But both Archimedes and Henry George—practical men, to be sure—were on my reading list. What's more, you will admit I've had my share of complicated frays lately. I have not ignored the subtleties of commerce, or social contradiction."

"So what's the mechanism?" Sannazaro yawned, looking up to see if he could spot the boy.

"Let one nation set the example by taking all multinationals to task under the alien tort law of 1789, intended originally to combat slave traders. How many US corporations doing business abroad might be guilty of at least one significant transgression, whether the case of a Bhopal, which we know well, or a copper mine in New Guinea, slave labor in Saipan or child abuse and the abrogation of women's rights along the US/Mexican border? Whether the manufacture of dangerous chemicals, or of golf balls that are too hard and have contributed to fractured skulls universally. There has been a conspiracy among the rich to destroy natural resources, habitat and tribal communities. Not to mention the sinister withholding of all information pertaining to golf balls, aluminum baseball bats and bowling-ball injuries. And why is that?

"But I love such sports," Saul replied. "And never noticed any dangers!"

But Marigold had already made up his mind: "A man doth not profit if his family perishes and his house is taken from him; if the air he breathes is fouled, the water mired, the soil blown thither. A man destroys only because he is able to get away with it. That is why."

He resolved to engineer new golf balls, and to finance the reform of the world's copper smelters.

Sannazaro had good reason to be sceptical: "How will you finance anything, my dear Captain Lunatic? You've probably already destroyed the world's leading financial institutions through your lunar ruse. Second, by my calculations, as a family we are several billion dollars, rupees, florins and francs in debt."

"That can't be true. Remember how well our tech stocks were doing?"

"Yes, you engaged, as they say, in profit-taking, but you gave most of those billions away to the children. Plus a bit more to save rats in Taiwan after the earthquake. "

"I did? I don't remember that?"

"What a lovely gesture," Saul added.

"Yes. And now he's broke," Sannazaro figured.

"We will see about that. I do not trust your calculations. When we have a moment, we will regroup with Hidalgo and see. In the meantime..." And then he went on to outline his concept for putting an end to all greed, violence, hatred, wars, ill-will and stupidity, as he had done for many months. A congress of cows and fanfare of repetitions that now sounded more like an engine's idle than a revolution. He imagined a carbon-emissions tax on all farts expelled by meat-eaters. And a sound method for funneling billions of borrowed dollars to every single up-and-coming President and Prime Minister of vegetarian vision in each country of the world. Again, by the time the banks came to collect from Marigold, those leaders would be in power, spawning a new generation of liberalism and empathy, not to mention debt forgiveness. If worse came to it, they'd simply print more and more money, since they'd be in control of the mints.

"It didn't work that way in Greece," Sannazaro reminded him. "And what about Weimar Germany? And Argentina? Inflation."

"Let inflation come. At least by that time hunger and worriment will have been eradicated."

With each far-reaching suggestion, the poets seemed to snore the louder for it, although the Commander was not in the least daunted by the reception. Eventually, even Sannazaro chose to bask in the midday shade, covered his eyes with the remains of his tattered shirt, and passed out. Saul, on the other hand, was all ears, clearly inspired by this grand vision for saving the world. It was, of course, only the first time that he had heard of it, and the Commander was adept at impressing people at first blush (it was only later that he bored them to tears), whereas Sannazaro had been assaulted by the barrage of self-important hokum on a daily basis since long ago and far away—how long, how far, he could no longer remember. In any case, it didn't matter. He had lapsed into the soundest, dreamiest sleep in many years.

Somewhere in the forested heavens above, Rajibai had reached an apex of sorts: the nest beyond all nests. Traces in the bark—however unlikely—of anadromous salmon. A Cenozoic lullaby of twigs and hollows wherein, once, the first mammal conceived and birthed an ideal. A lullaby of mammary glands and warm-blooded intimacies, of shared food stocks and reciprocal courtesies, of language and belly laughs, of hair and milk. The nest provided a vantage point over the romantic cirque of tropical-storm mountains rising above the furthest haunted reaches of the island.

He stared down through the lush vertical jungle. Hispid cyan glows. Cinnamon mists. A dozen blue kingfishers in deep discussion. Shocking mustard-crested hummingbirds hovering. Ten thousand doves taking flight. The absolute in stardust and fabled villages. No thought of putting junked automobiles inside volcanoes. No talk among the caterpillars of war or depression or the EPA. No mention among the 8,500 species of night beetle of advanced technologies for sewage control or soil aeration. And, frankly, the Giant herself was not eager to hear the Commander's endless statistics with regard to deforestation. It made her very nervous. Trees, after all, were masters of self-fulfilling prophecy. Once they got an idea into their heads, there was no telling where they might take it. Some trees were terribly gullible, hearing soft blandishments from lumbermen who had extolled the virtues of fast-growing timber, making all sorts of promises. In short, trees destined to be assassinated had acceded to their own doom, hearing what they wanted to hear—the promise of endless sunshine and sugars, amino acids and chlorophyll. Were shortsighted, in others words. Others were more savvy, setting up defenses against manhandling and fire.

Rajibai sat up there for a good hour or two or three, for there was no sense of time. "My goodness," he finally thought, alert to the lapse of hours. "I'd best be getting down." He was beginning to blossom.

But the moment he started his perilous descent, he dislodged an enormous coconut which went flying down the uncountable stories, crashing just above the Commander's head, spraying all three men with precious coconut juice. The three great cats who always accompanied Saul lapped up the white meat.

Such a near-miss definitely cut the wind in the Commander's sail. Stretching out his legs, he placed his head against the gnarled base of the mighty tree, where a soft carpet of moss was clumped inside and out, a cushion fashioned by evolutionary time for nothing more remarkable than taking a snooze, and promptly went to sleep.

Soon, Saul laid down to dream as well.

That night, when the three men awoke from their long and glorious stupors, all was peaceful beneath the Giant. Except that Rajibai was still nowhere to be found and no amount of shouting his name could bring him back.

"He must have decided to sleep in the nest at the top," said Saul.

"I don't know. I'm a little worried," issued the Commander. "He usually turns up, however far he's strayed."

CHAPTER 188
The Revelation of Amigo

NOT ONLY WAS THE BOY GONE, but a remarkable commotion greeted the waking Marigold, Saul and Sannazaro—a shrieking shambles of fast-moving talons, feathers, paws, thrusts, as the indefatigable chicken Amigo, having somehow miraculously arrived on Jovita, was fending off two of the overly curious cats—Vivendi and Activa—who tried every which way to play mincemeat with him, while the third, Contemplativa, watched on unmoved, insouciant, a poet in the making.

"Amigo, my long-lost friend! Hold on!" the roused Commander cried, sweeping up the family bird from the near clutches of Saul's cougar-sized kittens.

"As you once did," sighed Amigo. "Alas, your good-will notwithstanding, that damned well was unforgiving a second time. And why I should have failed to remember the paramount risks, when thirst could have been quenched a dozen other ways, I shall never live down."

"But what do you mean?"

"What do you mean what do I mean! I'm dead."

Saul had not counted on the news being broken in this perfunctory and unexpected manner. "You see ..." he began.

"Don't be silly. Of course you're not dead, you're in my arms, and those feline ruffians will never bother you again. My word on that. But, pray tell, how did you find your way to Jovita?"

"Yes, do tell," Sannazaro prodded, genuinely perplexed by so wide-roving an avian. He knew, of course, that chickens were notorious for tale-telling, though, in this case, there was no disputing the fact Amigo was a world traveler of renowned proportions, his uncanny method of propulsion the result of that Hopi shaman whose motives were never entirely clear. But there was more, and Sannazaro had always seen what Marigold was blind to recognize: Amigo was some kind of chivauchier, a courier of news with cosmic ambitions. There was nothing provincial or customary about this chicken; nothing either soupish or timorous; no chicken knots, thieves, stakes or eggs. No hazard was too great, for Amigo—vetch, weed, meat or pox. He spurned all terror, made sport of enemies. But none of the two-foot bird's spectacular courage explained his showing up at the least imaginable hour: in wells, upon icebergs, and now—the jungle! So far from home, across the seas.

Amigo began, "There I was drowning, but Raquel was indoors, as usual, with her lover, Alvaro. Oh, you did know they were married? Always in bed together, clucking more raucously than my solid upbringing permits expatiation. But on this occasion, their frivolities exceeded the bounds of all decorum. While they lay merrymaking, my Lord!, I was losing ground by the inch, second and claw to a waterlogged state of no return. And where were you, I might add? Well, that's an interesting point of discussion, because I longed for you to rescue me as you once did, and in my final death agonies I saw you and Sannazaro there sleeping beneath the Tree of Life, and I flew to you, on my very own, without the help of that crazy rocket scientist who has made my life miserable for years—what with Antarctica ..."

"And Spain."

"That's right, and a dozen other unplanned-for destinations. No sir, this time I got here on my very own."

"But, again I must ask you: by what improbable athletics, and to what end?"

"By dreaming of you at the terrible moment of my underwater demise."

There was an awkward silence, and Saul was not comfortable breaking the spell.

"You're telling us you truly drowned?" the Señor rejoined, casually enough, at first.

"Of course I did. And as tragedies go, more pleasant than most, I should think."

Then, and only then, did it begin to dawn upon the Commander: the distant cerebral nerve ending where man was born, before the 9.8 which ripped through his skull, mortified his senses, replaced the habits of a lifetime with a stark lunar authority. Yet, that was not all. These three seconds of fact-finding in the ruins of his mortality merely preceded a veritable volcano of horror. It struck his jawbone, clasped the air passages in his throat, detonated his tear ducts, sent shrapnel into his knees so that he wobbled, then collapsed. It invaded his lungs like some occupying force, scissored both nostrils, exploded the veins in his eyes, hammered every square inch of his body with punches. As if Rocky Marciano had stamped out every last ember of his soul on the punching floor. And as that memory struck, visible in the blanched face and terrorized eyes, the wave of realization pervaded Sannazaro's emaciated demeanor with an equal gasp. They looked upon one another, scrutinizing their respective suspicions from the throbbing basal metabolism of their traumatic deconstructivisms: the recall of their respective deaths by drowning. Any sign? Blood? Crooked joints? Bones jutting out? The slightest anatomical hiccup, exoskeletal glitch, dimmed cornea? Even a donkey's ears?

Now the Commander felt a semblance of weird tickling between his bare toes, glanced down at his feet and saw that maggots were swarming there in dizzying layers, by the thousands exhuming the flesh, writhing in his bloodstream, cavorting between the layers of muscle, bone, tendon and flesh. While roots of a chemoautotropic nature were emerging from his thighs, ants and lice burrowing into his crotch. Even his nose was becoming the habitat for some putrid genealogy of mites. And there was Saul, a skeleton now, floating vertically in an air of blood. Hideous! True! Revealed!

Both men screamed and screamed some more, wringing themselves out like washrags in a frantic *danse macabre*, hoping to shake the galling dream. Amigo, the wiser of the three, looked on his silly comrades with empathy.

Overhead, the moon was cutting a zigzag throughout the cobalt swathe of sky. That they had all awakened in the middle of the night should have provided some clue to their condition—that, or the fact the crickets were making music in reverse, and 10,000 other things that were backwards, and had been from the moment the last set of 300-foot waves slammed into the *Bonaparte* and left the Commander and Sannazaro underwater for hours.

Now it all came back to Marigold: the horrible week and a half of storm; the fact that Rajibai had managed to liberate himself up to the raven's roost, where his altitude was sufficient to protect him from the ferocity on deck. When the boy had revived his two elders, it was not to this life that they returned. But such a subtle transition had it been, out at sea, with the hurrinado abating, and other distractions to take their minds off the unnerving but frequently ignored truth that both Mr Marigold and Señor Sannazaro were dead. Drowned. Finished. And had been for several days now.

Saul had been so ever since his own shipwreck, he said. And all the poets, as well. In fact, Jovita was an island of the dead. An island of dreamers, strange as that may seem.

CHAPTER 189
Afterlife

"BUT I AM MIGHTILY confused," pleaded the Commander. "How can a chicken know such a thing, and a man not?"

That elicited a scornful rebuttal from Amigo. "First off, you have been terribly preoccupied, ever since the day we met."

"That's true," Sannazaro confirmed.

"And secondly, we chickens are far more sensitive to death than you humans. You may speak of the Holocaust, and a history of murders and wars; of Hiroshima and Nagasaki, the massacre of this tribe and that tribe. But we live with ten Holocausts every day. And don't tell me that does a disservice to what you humans call the Holocaust. Over 50 billion chickens have been slaughtered by you assholes, and that's just recently. I think we know a thing or two about death. Yet, you know that I remain your friend, in spite of everything. Most chickens have forgiven your kind."

"Oh dear bird ... How can I say what's in my heart? Everything you declare is more than accurate. And I apologize on behalf of everyone. But you alone know that I have fought for chicken rights."

"You needn't go on. No apologies required."

"But, but ...." Marigold was bumbling, terrified, crazed, appealing to reason. "What of the Tree of Life? Of all the thousands of butterflies; even your three pet cats, Saul? Is this all a dream too?"

Saul approached the subject with finesse. "Yes, and no. A question of transcendental epistemology, with its characteristic tractatuses."

"Say what?" Sannazaro groaned.

"It's as real as you make it. I know because once I was a starving poet in Paris, a taxi driver in Baghdad, an elevator operator in Stockholm, a postal clerk in Jerusalem, the broomkeeper at Royan-ji in Kyoto, a nuclear physicist in Odessa, a little boyin Vilnus. I've seen too many incarnations within my own life to doubt the ambiguities that assail us."

"That's no help whatsoever. You can't philosophically convince me I'm dead. No Continental Logic here. Look at these robust hands, darting eyes; feel those muscles. I hear Stravinsky. I see a Leonardo. I am equipped for everything. Hunger strikes, great plans swarm in my brain. There is simply nothing wrong with me. All right, we were shipwrecked. I was struck on the head, my lungs filled temporarily with water. It was a shocking near-death experience. But here I stand, my own Wittenberg, if you will. Alive and well. This whole scenario which you and my long-lost chicken friend have presented must be in error. Furthermore, if this archipelago be a place for the dead, how is it my child has arrived here unharmed?"

"It can happen."

"Are there others?"

"Yes, though few of them. It's sometimes very hard to distinguish living from dead. Conversations are possible between worlds, which further complicates delineations. And as for the Tree of Life, know that this is the land of rebirth, where new genes are strewn willy-nilly— sown—throughout the world. That's how it works and has worked since time began—if in fact it ever did. Those who end up here, rather than somewhere else, are prime candidates for sowing. Think of Jovita as the Land of Betsy Ross and this whole landscape as a place constantly amending. Gradations are many. Souls casually and carelessly arrayed, some animated, others buried up to their necks."

"Who is Betsy Ross?" asked Amigo. "A person or a chicken?"

"Will we remember where we were strewn from?" added the Commander.

"I don't know the answers to any of these things. Except to make one general comment which appears true: namely, that the longer you remain on Jovita, the more you will forget everything in your life preceding it. In that sense, it is the Island of Forgetfulness."

"But that's dreadful. I don't want to forget anything. I'm actually at the near beginning of all my intellectual accumulations!"

"Does all this mumbo jumbo matter?" countered Amigo. "As long as you keep those tigers away from me, and let me dine on some of those maggots, I would be more than happy to forget that damned well."

"It does matter," insisted Sannazaro. "We can't be dead. We would have noticed by this time. If for no other reason than the odor, shall we say."

"Not so," Saul interjected. "We die a little bit every day. And it smells good."

"That's different."

"How can you be sure?"

"Hmmm ..." Sannazaro paused, uncertain of his reality. "But if it's true, surely there must be some kind of Paradise gingko to help us remember?"

Tears began to flood the Commander's face, as he thought back to Madame Vignette, Ebert and Anastasia, Anna and Paramatman, Ginevra ... Ginevra!

"Wait a minute ... We all drank a special potion in Tibet not too many moons ago. We were promised immortality."

"Impossible," avowed Saul. "Never heard of it."

"It was urine, larded with all kinds of special plants. It assured us of an immunity to natural death."

"Someone convinced you to drink their urine?" Saul inquired.

"Surely drowning counts as a natural death," Sannazaro declared defiantly, remembering back to the rules of the game, as Anna had described them. Already the turncoat, hedging new bets.

The Commander was beginning to slump down. He understood. "Aging is a natural death," he now inveighed, the wiser for these sudden speculations. He recognized the hazards of compliance with what now demanded of him a noble, if incredulous, resignation. But drowning not. It was a catastrophe, like that which had overtaken Anna's lover. A hurrinado cutting off a man's breath was not given to the promised lifeline ordained atop the waterfall. No quarrel or angry contest was going to alter that fact. He scratched his head, shed a final tear. It was true.

But Sannazaro was ready to fight to live. The *coup de foudre* struck him as expressly impossible.

"I can't have died. I just began to live!" he remonstrated, suddenly fighting like the fish out of water, he too, had strangely become.

"We always say that," Saul reminded him.

But he could not, he would not, accept that this was happening.

"Who says so? I pick my judges, you can pick your own. I say, death in the sea, death on land, death in the air, even death by overeating and overdrinking and too much lovemaking—may I be so lucky—these too are all natural, are they not?"

"This question is the question, of course. Are synthetic chemicals natural? Was World War II natural? Is man himself—whom Nietzsche nicknamed the sick species, born too soon—natural? If Manhattan is not natural, what about a beaver dam, an 80-foot termitary in Tanzania, a honeycomb in Hungary, or dioxins, fission, americium?"

As their debate escalated, the implications became increasingly severe for the Commander, whose head was spinning out of control—and whose wouldn't?

"If we are truly dead," he said at last, "how can we be conversing thus? Is this Paradise or is it not? Is there a God with whom we must register, show our ID cards, discuss the future? What happens? Where do we go, and for how long? Do we need food, or is that merely the illusion from earlier times, a carryover for several months before the desire, the memory, fades? Is this it? I mean, where is everybody else? Can we let go of fear? Was this all pre-arranged? From the very first day of my life? Or from the moment I met this chicken?"

He had placed Amigo in Saul's arms when he and Sannazaro danced their exorcism of the maggots. Now he retook hold of the plump, contended bird.

Saul felt it was time for him to throw in his seven good cents. After all, ever since his own fatal wreck upon the outer reef, he'd had plenty of time to meditate on the condition of the Afterlife.

"You see, good friends, the confusion arises, as it arose for me, on account of there being no discernible break in continuity between life and death. One moment you were fighting the waves, were you not; the next, coming to on account of some remarkable agency. Try as you might, you will find no gap. But what did coming to actually mean? Trace your endeavors backwards in time, as I myself have done a thousandfold, over and over and over. You will likely discover that every one of your adventures was leading to the next, even though they might, at times, have seemed random, serendipitous, a matter of jolly or rotten luck, timing or coincidence. Yet, I would submit, all was purposeful in terms of the end. Maybe not in view of the next day. But if one is suddenly taken up by the task as you are now, then by accounting for all these past links and subtle connections, by embarking upon a life-circumference of due diligence, making amends—which is the essence of evolution—then you will see that you did, indeed, drown, and everything in your lives was preparing you for that moment. You—all of us—were blessed to have experienced death in these waters. Think of the countless alternatives."

"In my lover's arms," lamented Amigo.

"In bed with a good book and a glass of port," Sannazaro imagined. "In my sleep, dreaming the best of dreams. No fuzz, no mess, no pain," Marigold professed. "All three, gentlemen, here, now," said Saul, a leaven of comfort and confidence.

"Then it really is true? The bridge from life to death is painless, seamless, harmless?" Sannazaro wondered, enthralled with the possibilities.

"It is what you see," repeated Saul. "There is no pain. Not in retrospect. Only the massing of phenomena. Gape, bewilder, shout about like a frigate bird: there is no woeful countenance upon these shores."

CHAPTER 190
The Question of a God

THE COMMANDER HEARD the explanations, listened patiently, but refused in his way to grasp it. He struggled with that far-off sequence of events as best as he could reconstruct them.

"Rajibai performed mouth-to-mouth. He'd been spared up above. Whereas we were tied at the base. When the waves inundated the *Bonaparte*, we could not see to untie. I believe I was struck on the head. I can't remember. But how, upon my revival, could I be dead if my son was still alive and I saw him endeavoring to save us? I recall vividly the resuscitation, air returning to my pipes, nose and lungs relieved of water. I remember the refreshing explosion of clear air, pure light, cool wind, first sight. The roar of outer waves, the mauve of the reef, the embrace of that giant squid. And most of all, the heroic feats of my son. Surely there could be no normal exchange between us if, as you say, I was chopped liver—yet there was, and continues to be. I mean, for God's sake, what have we been doing for the last two days if not living, observing, wondering?"

"All qualities of the Afterlife," explained Saul.

"Damn it. I can't have died. I wasn't ready. You have no idea how much I've left to do."

Sannazaro nodded how true it was. But Saul merely grinned. "I refuse to accept it," Marigold concluded.

"That's good. That's a start."

"Don't."

"Don't what?"

"No therapies or clever ruses. I will not accept this verdict. And if it's true, I refuse to let it slow me down."

"Was it any differently in life?"

"Yes, it was." He felt himself slipping, entangled in the bitter ambiguities of what his lips unsparingly now confided. "In truth, I began my life at 50. Prior to that, I did not exist. I was dead, save for the occasional memory."

"Then you perfectly understand your situation this night, which happens to be day among the living. And day be night."

"So things really are in reverse?" Sannazaro mused, for it explained a number of odd perceptions.

"Why don't we just all agree it never happened ..." the Commander brainstormed in order to sidetrack a very sticky, unresolvable quagmire.

"It never happened," resounded Sannazaro.

" ... and get on with it."

"If that will make it easier," Saul avowed.

"No. Forget the *it*. There's no it. Never happened."

"You'd prefer denial?"

"There's nothing to deny, so it's not denial."

"You heard the man," voiced Sannazaro, fully in sync with the rejection process and happy to proceed along other avenues.

"No it!" all rejoiced.

"On the other hand," Marigold suddenly speculated, "perhaps I have over-reacted. Let's consider the options. Might there be any advantages to it, in terms of effecting change here on Earth? Like an invisible man able to sneak into hard places, effect the impossible? Hmmm."

"Oh yes," Saul enlightened them, with a remarkably broad smile. "You went on about utopias, sustainability, birds and bees. Why, the dead are the ultimate ecologists. Need I elaborate?"

But Sannazaro had his own priorities: "Let's first ensure that our deaths do not, in any way, preclude our First Principles."

"Meaning?"

"Dinner."

"If anything," replied Saul, "your appetites—all of them—will increase the further in time you drift away from that fond moment of transfiguration. As for changing things on Earth, you're both angels now, and your son will not, cannot, perceive you as dead. I would say there's much you can do."

"But if he doesn't recognize our death, why should anybody else?"

"There's no predicting who can see whom, or what one man hears over another. Anyway, what does it matter?"

"Has nobody ever been tempted to leave Jovita?"

"All the time, in one form or another," replied Saul ambiguously. "But why did Queen Mother send us here, if not to accomplish some great task?" Sannazaro asked, trying to grasp the miracle, as he now appreciated it.

"Because we asked," Marigold now recalled.

"She knew we would perish in the effort. She planned it," Sannazaro reckoned.

"Hard to say," said Saul. "But there is no doubting that you are men on a mission, and Jovita somehow is meant to be a part of it."

All of this struck Marigold with startling applicability. What began moments before as an end-of-the-world nihilism had now become its beginning. After all, hadn't the Queen Mum intimated the world's source of original genes, virtues, impulses, suggesting that the Commander might well find what he was looking for here, on Jovita, amid seas of malleable Nature? Might he not effect the revolution he had for many months contemplated? Going back to the very roots of human violence and greed to engender an all-new human nature? He need only influence all those quiddities of matter and microbes of flesh whose DNA carried the torchlight of evolution. That way, he might rework the curve of human behavior, though at a much accelerated pace of reform, as Alfred Wallace himself had speculated, in *Island Life*. The Queen had prophesied everything, in her way. So had Alex, whose research conducted from that Los Angeles morgue had shown the way to Bongo Bongo Land, which, in turn, would never have become a reality had it not been for the Summit of La Mancha and the various adventures in Greenlandia, Budapest and, of course, Yemen.

But this great chain of being went back further still, prompting the Commander to consider the very nature of predestination, which he aired aloud for his companions, particularly Amigo, who seemed the most difficult to convince. The chicken found it impossible to pronounce Chimborazo, for some reason. "Chickorzao", he kept insisting.

Marigold began with St John of Damascus, whose notion of salvation had God allowing for all beings to partake of Paradise, at least in the age prior to Sin. But Marigold did not believe in Sin, finding more in common with the ancient Pelagians who embraced the notion of Grace and Free Will as the two primary mechanisms by which the human animal might transcend all obstacles in the path to deliverance. St

Augustine added his own twist to this liberation theology by suggesting that, no matter what freedom man possessed, God worked in his own mysterious ways.

"So what are you saying?" asked Amigo. "Have we arrived or have we not? Is this Paradise? If so, please don't tell me they consume chicken soup here. Speaking of which, am I a chicken or the ghost of a chicken?"

"Is God on our side, in other words?" the Squire asked, trying to get at the heart of the matter.

"I don't necessarily believe in God," Saul added.

"But that's pointless," the reformed Catholic in Sannazaro chaffed. "Why deny something whose affirmation costs you nothing? It's like a free life-insurance policy."

"I know. I just don't think much of the concept."

"Sannazaro's absolutely right. That's terribly uneconomical," said the Commander, who had no qualms accepting God, or presuming God behaved—which was indeed a tricky mathematical theory—all causes contemplated. More times than not, it appeared, God had let his or her creatures down. Mice, rainforests, cows, chickens, turkeys, tigers, sheep and pigs, for starters. "But I certainly sympathize with your doubts. Frankly, I would have expected more from the moment of death if there *was* a God. Not this vague clamor of uncertainties that have left us standing here debating whether we're even dead. Do I believe this is personal, that there is some master plan that said, Get thee to Jovita! I will need some time to work on that. But my first instincts—assuming I have any left—tell me that there is a good reason we're here."

However, the more he thought about it, the more he could no longer remember. Had he been to London? Was Ireland a place, or a dream? The same with Fiordland, Hong Kong, Antarctica, the Long March across India. The leap off the waterfall. His tiring court hearing in Santa Fe, a card game 150 years before. Controversy, critics, great plans. Dragonflies. Everything was slipping away. A blessed blank. Not a certainty to be had. No worry. The light was going out. All those pages of travail were becoming foxed to the point of unreadability. And who cared any more? He was here. Whatever had previously transpired had obviously intended it to be this way. Innocence beyond experience.

The Commander continued in this amorphous sea, getting bent up in the computational precepts that attended the so-called gratuities of predestination which had absorbed monks like the freckle-faced ninth-century Gottschalk of Orbais, or that seventeenth-century son of a cobbler, Jacobus Arminius of the Dutch Reformed Church, whose mother specialized in heels, his father riding boots. Such icons of church history, and their massive, infamous arguments favoring God's authority, limiting human choice, upholding the rigid precision of divine law, were known to Marigold but fell on deaf chicken ears. Alas, Amigo wanted no such rubrics, parameters, rancid religion or spiritual noise. He calmly made talon tidbits of that great and lasting book, *Summa Theologica*, and argued strenuously against any and all talk of the Apocalypse. Such ideas scared him—you could see his little orange pores perking up—and he rightly pointed out how inappropriate such bleak visions were on so lovely an island. Amigo had class, *joie de vivre*, and wanted none of Marigold's stubborn idealism. Jovita, with its incredible varieties of pebble, earthenstone and groundcover to peck at, was more than enough.

Finally, Sannazaro broke up the two intelligentsia. "While you all debate the course of life and death, chicken mores and human perfectibility, time is escaping us, and a young man is somewhere up in the tree, or off in the geyser-imperiled woods. I suggest we find him, pronto."

Contemplativa, ever the partial observer, was the one who described how the boy had descended the Tree of Life only to find his human companions sound asleep. The boy seemed possessed of an unearthly energy and glow, and was attracted to a certain *je ne sais quoi* up in the mountains. The cat gestured uphill, prepared to lead the way, though neither of his two feline kin would budge from their coconut and chocolate licks.

"He's gone off in the direction of the cannibal and his daughter," Saul intuited, never such dead words so enlivening. "How I envy him."

CHAPTER 191
Lost Atop the Invisible Cliffs

THIS WAS NOT THE first time Rajibai had disappeared in the middle of the night. Marigold should not have given it a thought. But the word 'cannibal' was sobering, and the Commander rallied his forces, leaping up in the darkness to have a go at the wilderness and bring back his little wanderer. Somehow the knowledge that Rajibai was still in the bloom of youth gave him so much more concern. Had the hurrinado killed him, so be it. Little to fear at this stage. Now the tables were turned, and the Commander and his Squire both felt as never before a dreadful sense of responsibility to the living. Nothing could shake it. No other sentiment resembled it. New turf. If before they were concerned about cow lives, the psychological well-being of monkeys, orphans and the citizenry of Santa Fe, now the sensation was tantamount to all-out hysteria in the ravine of earthly possibilities.

Towards that conviction, they set off, with Saul, in the firm hope of preventing any untoward happenstance. Rajibai was prone to impulse, that much was known and accepted. But these terrains were unlike the tamer dragon-haunted strangelands of Yemen or girl-scented enclaves of Christiania. In fact, just minutes of off-trail bushwhacking landed all three men in a precarious swamp, where fevers had become palpable, like Roman pikes or fungus balls.

"We're sinking," Saul observed. "It's hotsuck—the saltwater marsh, tar and lava-heated quicksands that pervade these lowlands."

"How can you remain so calm?" Sannazaro upbraided him.

"Because we're already dead. From henceforth you must think of all physical travails, insults, foment and injury as amusements and attractions to be enjoyed. Decay, decrepitude and obliteration are banished from your world. All is renewal, experience, being."

"Spoken like a true poet, but I have no intention of spending all eternity beneath oozy hotsuck," said the Italian, who started squirming frantically to reach a nearby oleander branch in flower.

It so happened that a small female gorilla with ulterior motives helped them out. But upon their reaching the edge of the marsh she pinned poor Sannazaro to a pumpkin tree and tried to have her way with him by pale romantic moonlight. Extricating himself from her clutches, but minus his trousers, Sannazaro ran back through the jungle towards the beach, his outrage echoing for miles around, along with the angry cluckings of an equally terrified Amigo racing, wings extended, behind him.

"I think he may have reached his limit," Marigold sighed reflectively, parting the dense fronds of flaming forest as they, too, moved away from the overheated primate. She wailed bitterly, standing alone, abandoned.

"She lacks for a mate," Saul explained. "That is one of the terrible things about the Afterlife. The population of Jovita is so tiny, there simply aren't two of everybody, and a gorilla can expect little pleasure mating with a butterfly."

"Those are wise words, practical words," Marigold confirmed, poised to go forward or back, up or down, he couldn't decide which.

"I'll go look after your friend. You'd best find your son, don't you think? But why do you hesitate?"

"I'm not sure. I suppose this is all so new to me. I feel the past fading away. It's disconcerting not to remember what I had for dinner last night."

"Are you afraid?"

"Yes."

"Understand that nothing can happen now. You're free. Free and wild, with the immunity of sunbeams and star frost, lunar dust and rebel DNA."

"I only lived half my life."

"That's perfect. The other half lies before you. True, it is the reverse image, but think of it as reflection. Or relocation. That's how I dealt with it, and it was useful. I mourned, but not for very long. Death stares back at you in the mirror but can do nothing to impede your continued curiosity, experience, ideas, joys, revolutions. It's true, my friend. And we are proof. Moreover, you obviously did something right in your earlier career among the living."

"What makes you think so?" Marigold was cynical on that score.

"You made it to Jovita—very few in history have done so. The barriers are not accidental, in my opinion."

These were kind words, but had less than useful impact on the grieving Commander. He was grieving not for himself, or his Squire, but for his son. Could they ever renew a regular relationship, father and son? Would the Commander lose his memory of the affiliation? He had no compass reading or precedent by which to gauge the outcome of these strange happenings, and his nerves, which had already been severely thrashed in previous months, were suffering as a result.

Add to that Saul's sudden caveat, warnings issued with no greater urgency: "Before I go back, there is something I ought to confess."

"What is that?"

"I don't know how to put it."

"I don't like the sound of that."

"The truth is, your son may be the only living person on the island. I don't know about all the other species—certain flies and fiddle ferns might well be among the living, hard to tell in such cases—but I expect that Rajibai is the only fully alive human."

"So? You were quite explicit about the impartiality of risks."

"I didn't expect him to go gamboling off into the highlands. You see, up there it's very dangerous, unless you're already dead."

"He's not unfamiliar with highlands. As you understand by his deft manner upon the Giant. Limbs present no hindrance, heights no barricade. He has made a mockery of the Himalayas, outwitted Assam. Can fend for himself, is what I'm saying."

"No need to elaborate. But I would be remiss if I didn't point out certain unique hazards on Jovita, even to the dead. Satan himself is said to inhabit a hidden valley somewhere up there, his terrible minions venting steam and lava through cracks that eat the spirit raw, and cook every caliber of a person, warthog, hippopotamus or shrew. They madden and unbalance the sanguine, dispossess the true, infect all health, and without scruples topple even the most brave-hearted goodness."

"You didn't tell me about that!"

"I'm telling you now. What did you expect—Paradise without any conflict, tension, night?"

"Anything else I should be concerned about?"

"Well, it might be a good idea to look out for the invisible cliffs."

"How does one do that?"

"I don't know. If you come up with a method, please do tell when you return. But hurry. At dawn the probability factor for increased sun strikes is very high. Rajibai wouldn't stand a chance."

"All right. I'm going. You'll look after Sannazaro?"

"A cup of cappuccino should settle him down."

They hugged farewell and Saul oriented the Commander, then stumbled down towards the village of Jovita, deftly avoiding the swampmeal, badger heights, poison palisades and sandfly desert. By the time he reached his hut, at something like 4 a.m., Sannazaro was there noshing on leftover guava pie.

"I couldn't sleep. I don't think I'll ever sleep again," he announced.

"You will," Saul coddled mercifully. "Give it time, of which you have plenty."

In the morning, Saul welcomed the weary Italian refugee with a hot drink from his private stash. Sannazaro's inimitable sniffer zeroed in on the familiar aroma whist one eye was still landlocked.

"My God!" he exclaimed. "Now I know I have gone to heaven." And he sat up with innumerable groans—a leg ache and backache only the recently dead can fully attest to—and religiously took the cup and saucer into his hands, warmed by the foaming apotheosis.

"How is it?"

The Squire studied the lather, then indulged. There was a pause.

"You do this for me, every morning for the rest of my death, and I shall gladly be your amanuensis."

"Deal."

"Throw in a governorship along the way. I was promised one by the Commander, who never came through, for either of us."

"Nobody will mind, or even notice," Saul said. With a palm frond he thrice tapped Sannazaro on the shoulders and declared, "I pronominate thee newly enshrined, magnanimous and fine, our Governor of Jovita. How's that?"

Governor Sannazaro could only smile in complete, complicit bliss.

While this smarmy couplet was getting along down on the beach, a less cozy situation was unraveling in the treacherous highlands, where the Commander struggled like the last angry drunk between clumps of biting bramble and billowing tick-infested nests. He negotiated haunted hollows, morbid miasmas of 12 lifetimes, aggressive ectoplasms, savage phantasms, shadowy hobgoblins and fiendish mirages. Every ferocity stood in his way: Briareus, Pantagruel, pitiless titans—trees that stalked journeymen—and bogeymen mired in mud-caked materializations. All the while he called out the name of his son, but received only the haggard remains of his echo, mocking the very effort, dwarfing the intent amid vaster priorities of Nature.

Turning circles on himself, arriving upon a brink and knowing it to be the same invisible cliff, he sat down beside a river filled with mother-of-pearl at the very moment a sun strike detonated twelve hectares of misty forest directly before him. All the hair on his head was singed, his face tanned within half a second, the tender little hairs in his nostrils on fire. Exhausted, defeated, he put out his nose and exclaimed to a dangling twelve-foot-high daddylonglegs directly before him, "I'm finished!"

CHAPTER 192

A Wise Hornbill Leads the Commander into the Highlands

A LIGHTING WITH uncommon weight, a varicolored hornbill, the size of seven large 1933 *OED*s, crashed through three layers of leaden plumbago, spilling herbaceous calyxes every which way.

Marigold leapt, his nerves' labor on high alert—every leaf, vesicle and filament of his insider organization resigned to being taken unawares. To his relief, it was instantly apparent that the bird was no common threat. Indeed, it emanated a bioluminescent decorum that instantly put him at some rest. There was no easy way to describe the sensation—an intimacy and camaraderie more fluent than any human companionship, and established in the flicker of a tail feather.

"G'day," hollered he.

"Hello," voiced the Marigold.

The Commander knew something about birds, of course; gauged quickly the presentiment of a hornbill, described by the aboriginals of New Holland as Engang, meaning, evidently, "creature that defies a flat universe". These birds were also once famed among residents of the Côte de Coromandel for their especial tenderness towards all those deprived of feathers or flight. Deemed the Bird of Knowledge in Bengal, according to Boddam, curiously cuneiform in shape, toes equidistant all the way to their origin, gibbous, carinated, his bill convex and contrived for purposes of nurturing, the great bird appeared to take some pity on the hapless wayfarer. His plummet through the adjoining bush caused him some embarrassment. Landing upon the Commander's shoulder, he was at no small disadvantage in terms of hornbill protocol and etiquette, which are legendary.

Blanched and bumbling, he offered apologies, then requested that Marigold preen those hard-to-reach russet and cobalt feathers that had been so ruffled on his backside. In exchange, he promised to fulfill the Code of Abiding Reciprocity and Amorous Persuasion that informed all avian transactions in the world.

"You needn't go out of your way," Marigold improvised.

But the hornbill was insistent—fair is fair—leaning over to produce all manner of middle-of-the-day birdie snacks from his golden casque: a regurgitated ooze of scorpion legs, pesto of ant, bowel worm broth, all greatly enhanced by the freshly ground feces of sloth, which are make-or-break for most hornbill delicacies.

Marigold declined the food fest, claiming that this was his day of fasting, and so allowing the bird to save face. He preened the hornbill for some time, then described his terrible plight, whereupon the bird resolved to lead the Commander along a steep furrow through the under-thicket, skirting precipice and hotsuck. He'd seen the youngster sure-footedly canter hours before in that direction.

"By now, he will have reached the plateau," he explained. "By the way, do you have any pens?"

"Pens? Why pens?"

"For a bird, the presence of a pen, almost any pen, is a profoundly diverting pastime. A way to wile away the hours harmlessly, whilst partaking of a venerable tradition."

"And what might that be?" Marigold asked, all curiosity.

"Well," he began. "Consider the Age of Metaphor, which is our present time-frame of the last 165 million years, the whole period my family has been around. The pen is the Tree of Metaphors, is it not?

From its quill, or ballpoint, arises every ..." and he went on, leaving no category or philosophical subset of pens unturned—the fact it touches the central pillar of bird existence, every testimony, towering purpose, Cloud of Unknowing, Hope for Avianity—not to mention the fact inks themselves, some of them, are delicious, the feel of outer plastic sheaths against the tongue simply mesmerizing. Though there was no disputing their toxicity.

Suddenly there was another sun strike, far off in the mountains. Like lightning, it was accompanied by a blue thunder that cleaved the morning mists and the speed-of-scent vapors of licorice, a vellum glow spreading out over the surface of the jungle like a traveling flame.

"An aphrodisiac," offered the bird, whose ability to detect one part per ten million with his nose, two parts per ten billion with his eyes and one part per 100,000 with his talons was legendary. Unless, of course, he was distracted, which happened, in his own telling words, one fateful morning not too long ago.

"I was formerly ensconced in a little private jungle within a greenhouse adjoining the state room of a Georgian manor in Sussex, until one day a temp served me a lethal pâté of avocado and parsley. How well I remember. Mr Penguin, Furry Lambkin and I were all watching a particularly riveting prime-time special about exotic fruits on BBCWorld. Now, normally, I would have detected the adulterated food. But I was glued to that documentary and it slipped by me ..."

"I should very much like to continue such fascinating repartee, but I need to find my son," Marigold went on in haste. "If you could please just lead me in the right direction ..."

And so the Commander and his Laotian hornbill companion, Lord Nelson (or, the Lord, as he rather relished, grin in tow), headed towards the highest of the mountains on the island, easily ten miles away. The Lord rode on the Commander's shoulders, and in this manner cleared the darkest depths below and reached more airy ridges. The bird's grasp of detail was astonishing. He knew every knob, soil type and grub. Expostulated on all the gravies, larvae and dewdrops. Could separate out ten million shades from one another, and tell you the names of every ant that passed their route. They even got on to their respective curtains.

"You see, death, from what I can conclude, was only an instant. One moment I was caught up in the best of the BBC, the next my heart was seizing up, my esophagus lined with bumps as if allergic to wholewheat, my chest heaving, my brain dull. It was all over before I could count to three or pass judgment. And then, just as suddenly, here I was, in this marvelous place."

"Do you remember the last living image?"

"Why, come to think of it, yes. An island of glorious fruits very much like this one. How very curious! But what about you, was death any different?"

"Not very. I drowned, dreaming of reaching sunny dry land at the very moment I was inundated with a ton of seawater."

"Now that would make me nervous," shivered the bird. "But the point is clear: death is a momentary transition between worlds, which are all in our heads. Evidently, from this survey of two, it is important to fix in your mind where it is you wish to go for the next afterlife. Otherwise, you could end up anywhere, like England, where I was originally kept in a horrid pet store—may all pet store owners be reborn inside a cage within their own sordid perimeters!"

"If you could change the world, what new rules would you impose?" Marigold asked as he slipped across a muddied gully, lunging for a trunk to hold on to.

"Our revenge fantasies are endless, if you must know. First, I would totally reverse the cards, so that 80 percent of your kind, not mine, were on the verge of extinction. I would like to hear from your elected officials once they see how it feels. Then I should restore the world to its original temperate rainforest, which would mean nine-tenths of the terrestrial globe was swathed in luscious, impenetrable canopy. A platter of festive flowers and fruits and insects with it, naturally. Galloping frogs, burping orchids, lusty lemurs, frisky and benign bee-eaters, the rare fellow *Rhyticeros cassidix*—nothing like your own kind to stir up a good cry. If that weren't all, those absolutely unintelligible butterflies with the two feet of wingspan, largest in 200 years, and, of course, unnamable millions of others ... I could go on. But one thing's for certain, I would delegate your species to the caves, naked, without fire, feeding on slime molds."

"I get the picture," admitted Marigold. "That would certainly alter the hierarchy. If I have anything to say about it—which, given the recent course of tidal changes, is unlikely—I should be the first to endorse and finance your scenario."

Lord Nelson shared his thoughts with the Commander on a variety of intimate matters, some of strictly historical interest, others pertaining to the most vital and contemporary of issues. He was fond of quoting all the great poets on bird topics, beginning of course with Walter Scott, Barry Cornwall and Robert Roscoe. He was fluent in the sonnets of Mrs Hemans and Charles West Thompson; knew Charlotte Smith and the Earl of Surrey. Could cite lyric leaves from Cornelius Webbe's *Summer Extract*, and Richardson's lonesome "Ode To the Bullfinch", penned when he was at Queen's College, Oxford. Sacred melodies, a natural touch, hymns, allegros, crystal streams, gusting thermals, happy strains were his usual fare. *When the moon rains and the soul is upborne on wings wandering in haunted places*: that was his exalted style.

Lord Nelson combined power and privilege. He was terribly aware that birds everywhere were vanishing, but could nonetheless minister with such sentiments as: "When Joseph stated, 'I am your brother, Joseph, whom ye sold into Egypt'", or that destitute sentiment conveyed by Priam to Achilles, "'Judge of the excess of my misery, when I kiss the hand that slew my son.'" Most curious of all, he expatiated on the life of the great hornbill philosopher, Rrraaack, whose saga had been memorized by all hornbills wherever they are. For reasons unknown—perhaps he was simply too different—Rrraaack had been kicked out of the nest when still a mere fledgling, and if it had not been for the companionship of a white rhino, who fell in love with the little furball and carried him on his hump, would have been devoured in one night. Rrraaack thus developed a pantheistic orientation to the jungle, tempered by the realism of predation. His earliest writings addressed the problem of abandonment in bird society. The very plinth of his philosophy, explained Nelson, was the need for universal adoption. Every bird for himself was no longer an acceptable notion. No bird is an island was closer to the truth. This empathic response hailed all creatures as brothers, beginning with the rhino, however contrary to that other sense of outrage regarding humans indicated earlier by Nelson (a perspective, it should be added, that Nelson himself could never wholly embrace, as evidenced by his loving way with the Commander from the first instant of their acquaintance).

"Rrraaack was a Nature mystic," Nelson delineated, "and all subsequent hornbills are proud to share in that legacy. By his eightieth year in the jungle, Rrraaack had seen through to the core of all reflections; had analyzed the Great Goo and knew that what mattered most was not one more piece of regurgitated pomegranate, or additional 100 percent down fluff to make a nest super-luxurious, but the Essence of Grace. Fashions changed: one year tuft feathers standing unmatted were considered très chic; other years the gnarly look was in. I remember once when a ratty little hole in a flight feather was deemed very stylish. Vogues come and go. Even the boldest flight patterns soon became tiresome. Hornbill arias also passed through endless incarnations: one year C-minor ague was the rage, another year F-major tremulo. In short, there had to be more to the life of a hornbill than social standing and endless gratification. Hence, Rrraaack's famed Theory of Love, circa 1887, which took on such profound dimensions, its depth much remarked upon by all bird species. I bet you can't guess where he wrote down the main points?"

"I have no idea."

"In a nest atop the Giant, our very own Tree of Life."

"Rrraaack is here, on Jovita?"

"He was, for nearly half a century. Then he moved on."

"What do you mean?"

"There are numerous accounts. The bugs side with one theory, birds another. Monkeys have their own version. Even the air molecules have had something to say about it. From all the documentation available, Rrraaack was incinerated during the great volcanic eruption of 1933. He's somewhere out there, as we speak, in his third or fourth or fifth reincarnation."

"Did Rrraaack ever discuss the Afterlife?"

"Naturally. If anything, adoption and love are ever more critical after death, he reasoned, inasmuch as every one of us feels abandoned at that critical juncture, and usually is. Everything is written high in the Giant, above the upper canopy, in a mahogany crook guarded day and night by the spirits of a rhino and half-dozen hornbill elders."

"Could a living person make head or tail of what is written?"

"That's a tough one," Nelson replied, scratching his pompadour. "I've never thought about it. Logic suggests, why not?"

Knowing that his son had been there, this gave Marigold much to ponder. What had Rajibai learned? Had some new knowledge compelled him to make so risky a solitary journey into the highlands?

The twosome traveled throughout the day together, encountering all the ghosts that had anything to say, and quite a few did. They met up with a Brontosaurus who'd been wandering the Jovitan highlands for 64.6 million years ("Say, you wouldn't have a pen?" Nelson asked), and a megabat ("Pen?") who'd been searching on his hands and feet for Bongo Bongo Land for decades, but had been restricted to the island by his fear of flying over water. He had open sores on his palms, his frail little knees were banged to hell, and he'd developed a pitiful hunch from groveling for so long. This meeting offered what was a good opportunity to take a breather, as the rocks had formed a rampart of disorienting magnitude, an escarpment blocking any obvious entrance to the higher worlds. Further progress would require some serious route finding. So Marigold took the chance to psychoanalyze the bat and see if he might not be disabused of his phobia. Sure enough, it was no mental challenge that prevented the bat's liberation, but a deformed wing. Lord Nelson had a brainstorm, dropped four of his largest flight feathers and supervised the surgical transplant.

Marigold stood upon a high outcrop overlooking the entire island, held up the trembling bat, whose name was Melville, counted to ten— which was far too many numbers to count, given the suspenseful nature of the circumstances—and made the toss. The sleek black mammal soared, squeaking hysterically with his newfound freedom, flying off, albeit in a lopsided manner, toward the ocean with not a minute to spare.

"When his friends see those gorgeous flight feathers—you'd never find them on a bat in a million years— Melville's going to make a major splash," said Lord Nelson, and they continued towards their destination.

CHAPTER 193

How an Ornithocyrus Reunited Marigold and Rajibai

SOME TIME later—hours, days, who could say?—they were standing looking over the entire visible archipelago when they heard screams of "Help!" from upwind.

"Goodness me!" cried the bird.

"That's Rajibai!"

And they raced in his direction.

Within minutes, they attained a new vantage that allowed for a direct prospect out over a parallel ridgeline along the ultimate finale of cliff.

"Oh dear," the hornbill said.

"What?"

"It appears he's crossed the boundary."

"I hope you're not referring to that Chasm of Satan I've heard tell?"

"Can't say. Never been there. Never seen it. Probably just an ugly rumor propagated expressly to keep too many tourists from visiting Jovita. One person per 20,000 square miles is about all we birds can handle."

"But that's probably a size larger than all of Jovita."

"Is it?" The Lord gave a downright quizzical expression. "Well, I'm not noted for my trigonometries, but what I can tell you is that the Boundary refers to what locals call Never Never Land. Unless you're lucky enough, wise enough, loving enough to be a bird, one wrong move, one slip, and it's back to the ironing board."

"What would you suggest?" Marigold's addled brain bespoke, bridled on the one hand by some sense of mounting miasma, and on the other by a freedom the likes of which his pounding heart had never entertained.

Nelson scanned the possibilities before them. Ten thousand feet of sheer cliff separated the ridge from the tumultuous ocean below. Three hundred-foot breakers detonated every 20 seconds against the vertical beach front. Optical hallucinations were occasioned by a 25-carat sunset whose gauzy effects were those of a palette knife cutting paramount swathes of every golden hue into the equally rugged terrain, such that a proliferation of mini-canyons and crests tormented the wandering eye, leading by tortuous turns to a tropics of alpine prolixity and confusion, the seeming entranceway spanned by an ancient rope bridge.

"There!" he exclaimed in the full light of enantiomorphic faculties.

On the far side could be discerned a little hut, some evensong from George Inness or Frederick Church, in the storm of illuminated vegetable patch, defiant trees emanating from its fringes. But on the bridge itself was Rajibai, who had broken through a section of roped plaiting and was now dangling by his arms.

"Excuse me, Madam!" the boy was heard to call out again, against the prevailing cold easterlies.

"He should never have used the bridge. It's been out of commission for as long as I've been on the island," exclaimed Nelson.

"Look!" Marigold blurted.

A woman—was it?—quite naked, had suddenly appeared from below the hut, running deftly through the steep granite-slated tropics until she'd reached the far side of the frayed suspension bridge. Moving with indescribable delicacy, a wolf spider with the feet of a Kirov ballerina, an Anna minus military fatigues, she made her way towards the sagging center where Rajibai was trapped.

"You mentioned that your son had never died?" Lord Nelson asked.

"Not that I know of," Marigold replied.

"Well then, this could prove quite traumatic for all involved. Bridges are bad ways to go, I'm told. I know several mice and hamsters who have fallen to their deaths in this manner. But I shouldn't elaborate, should I?"

Marigold was already racing to the edge of cliff. "Rajibai!"

Now the woman saw the Commander and stopped in her rocky tracks, bewildered, just inches from reaching the boy's hand.

The minute the Commander started across the bridge, it began sway-ing and giving way. Marigold was mesmerized, conflicted, trembling. What to do? He remembered an odd journey just then: 45 years before, with his father, on a pilgrimage of sorts to Mark Twain's house, just west of the Connecticut River, down the street from the chateau-like Aetna Life Building, on Farmington Road, or Boulevard, or Street—he couldn't remember—in Hartford, Connecticut, as the whole history of the United States flooded Marigold Senior. All the adventures that had figured in Twain, and the sad state of Hartford today, with its burnt-out mills and attempts to revitalize a downtown. Why had he thought of Twain, and Huck Finn, and the wilds, and his youth and—well, nearly everything? It was an epiphany, a remembrance of a life lived, suddenly endangered. Not by fierce centipedes, or waterfalls, but by the vision of a mysterious woman.

"*Father, don't come closer, it'll break!*" Rajibai eviscerated, his guts spilling real panic now.

Below, the canyon disappeared into mists and rainbows. A hidden valley in the heart of Jovita, surrounded on all sides by impossible steeps, water pouring from every direction, a deep plateau of penumbras and penultimate optics as sacrosanct in its geological removal as a foreign funnel cloud or steaming caldera. Something was astir down there: a mighty spring from which four rivers seemed to head in four distinct angles. Sulfurous water spouting upwards from the island's thermal underpinnings, each bubble—and there were thousands of them—a floating prism of gaseous color, a crystal ball reflecting on all past and future lives, one might well have extrapolated from even a vertically removed and passing glance. Strange creatures mingled there, but they were so minute from two miles above as to resemble nothing more than mites cavorting in the hot pools like little Vargas Girls or floating pumpernickel seeds, depending on your eyesight.

Nelson joined ranks with the Commander atop the bridge. Now their attention was focused on the amazing young woman who'd grabbed hold of Rajibai— —and, at that same instant, the whole bridge collapsed! She swung back towards the hut side, clinging to the boy, smashing into the rock wall, but was undeterred. Holding tight to the kid, she managed to climb up the remains of the hemp ladder to safety. It was a gallant effort, much Tibetan in its topographical evocations.

"I'm OK!" Rajibai shouted from across the 1,000-foot abyss. "But now what?"

The woman, having seen Marigold at length, had already vanished up along the ridge toward the hut, leaving Rajibai alone on the exposed ledge.

"Is there any other way round?"

"It would take you weeks," Lord Nelson explained. "I've flown most of it." He pointed with his soft yellow talons towards a far mountain range. "The canyon extends that far. You'd have to traverse every ridge between here and eternity, cross over a highly suspect avalanche chute, then make your way all the way back along the other side. A good 200 miles of ridge-climbing. Alternatively, I could call in a favor."

"What is that?"

"Umm, a dinosaur dissident who owes me. I shared my walnut grove with him and he's never been the same. You have no idea how many denizens were searching for an alternative to coconuts. How many stone are you?"

"Well, let's see—14 into 150 ... I guess I weigh just under eleven stone. Or I did when I was alive. Do weights change after death?"

"That's strictly dependent upon your attitude. Septic, non-septic. Clean, unclean. I know some dead people who live on air and water in the Afterlife. And others who will settle for nothing less than pastrami on rye. It really depends."

The Lord made some mental calculations. "It's only 1,200 talons from here to there. If you two can handle it, I'm sure my friend can."

"I'll do it!" Marigold exclaimed.

Lord Nelson issued the secret distress call that is universally recognized by all birds, transcending translation, dialect, species, order, phylum, kingdom, genus, even class. Oddly, Mr Marigold heard nothing.

"That's because it is a psychic energy," explained the Lord. "An appeal that issues from the heart. The sort of thing Rrraaack taught us."

He must have known what he was talking about, because within minutes an ornithocyrus, several barn owls, hundreds of sparrows, macaws, trace maries, canaries, eagles and others showed up on the narrow ridge. There was not room for all of them.

"I need a few of you to fly my friend across the gap," Nelson announced.

"He weighs 10.7 stone. Who volunteers?"

Of course he already knew the game plan. They would all volunteer, but the sparrows and canaries were obviously in over their beaks. The Lord did not want to make any of them feel unwanted, so he suggested that the ornithocyrus (Sir Joseph Odyssey to his closest dinosaur and bird associates, his wingspan being 77 feet) provide the primary means of transport, as he'd been unemployed for several months, and that everyone else render a full escort with all their feathers proudly displayed.

It took a few minutes to situate the avian parade of kin or next-of-kin altruists. "Go ahead," Sir Joseph said gently, "don't be afraid. Hold on to these neck reins. It won't hurt me."

Nelson took Marigold aside momentarily and gave him enough details to make the Commander more than comfortable with the idea: "He is a veteran, you see, of every Ice Age and asteroid. Some say his veins are laced with iridium, his strength that of seven tyrannosaurs. So there's absolutely nothing to fear."

"No worries. I'm used to flying upon dragons," Marigold replied.

"Dragons? You're not serious?" Nelson was utterly captivated by the notion. He'd never seen one.

In this way, so full of conversation that he barely even registered lift-off, the Commander (with Lord Nelson still riding on his shoulder) dangled by both outstretched arms from the ornithocyrus's chains and was expertly flown across the great chasm overlooking the seed bank of Jovita, the place of renewal, where the four rivers originated and then flowed towards the Tree of Life 30 miles away—as the hornbill flies. Or that was one version of the vista below. Others claimed more nefarious goings-on, though nobody among the hundreds of dignified escorts really wanted to talk about it at all. Somebody suggested Hell, which cast a whole different perspective on the gaseous prisms and rising plumes of black soot, confirming Saul's own recapitulation of the ambiguous myth. But for now Marigold must put such counter-tenors out of his footlocker.

Upon attaining the far side, and before flying off to their own appointed nests, each of the birds stopped to drop a feather in tribute to the reunited father and son. Seeing how there was no shortage of yummy-looking fruit trees there on the wind sheer of ridge, the Lord decided to stay a while too, which sat very well by the Commander, who sensed that other psychic ministrations, silent frequencies and universal appeals from the heart might again be necessary before the day was done.

But what was really on his mind was that woman. Never had he seen a more lustrous, innocent and beguiling female of any species! Not even atop the waterfall. Her uniqueness seemed indescribable just then. No frame of reference in which to couch it. Or maybe Marigold himself was simply a different set of feelings now.

"What's this?" the Lord referred. "You're blushing. I hope not on account of me. Snack time. Want some scorpion legs?"

CHAPTER 194
A Vision

MARIGOLD HAD FOR one brief instant suffered an apparition of unobstructed, unselfconscious, naked lust as he watched the woman scramble back up the jungly cliff to her inglenook. Twenty, 30, 40 years old? She resembled the girls of the waterfall, but her aloneness struck a significantly different tuning fork in his veins. Along the Tibetan frontier, he had felt only anthropological curiosity, the intensity of a cathartic pathos.

Her hips, buttocks to drink from, nipples that were milk messengers from 100,000 years ago, a face that shone too glorious for translation, and a crotch whose rippled curvature—even at 1,000 paces—shredded his gut ... Suffice it to say, the animal in Marigold was detonated. Every verb by which one sinks, presses, plunges, rises, catapults and preys for reciprocity—dies, in other words, and dies again—assailed him now with the tickling aggravations of teenage love, made over in the mammoth accumulation of a hermit's long denial. Female mitochondria from Neanderthal times drifted in the air like gossamer seedlings. The sexual beast beneath the dusty armor arose in Marigold for that woman with no advance warning.

How odd that it should happen for the first time in my life only after I'm dead, he thought to himself.

His boy had escaped the bridge, was safe, crouched now by his side, clinging to a stand of teak that jutted from the wall, whipped by the South Atlantic gales. He had been not in the least surprised to see the dinosaur. Blue day. Racing fogs. No apparent way back. Back where? To the sea of storms? Transfixed, resolved that this was the final place, he sank his head into his father's chest and wept, for joy, for sadness, for fear.

"Where's Uncle?" Rajibai inquired.

"He stayed behind with Saul."

Marigold held him lightly, afraid, now, of contaminating him in any way; afraid of the unknown; unsure where, or whether, the flesh, blood and spirit boundaries of life and death were meaningful.

"You scared us. Why did you disappear in the middle of the night? What brought you to this place, Son?"

The boy wiped clear the liquid in his eyes. He stood gravely still, pondering the imponderable, as if gripped by some seizure of unearthly philosophy or rapture. Then he pointed, and the word issued from his quarantined lips: "Her!"

The Commander looked. There she was, jarringly still, her own *Moonrise Over Hernandez*, *Rest on the Flight to Egypt*, facing both of them from 30 paces. The Lord flew off Marigold's overburdened shoulder into the nearest ripe pear tree.

"Who are you?" the Commander inquired, his whole steadiness of being gone berserk. The matrix of all personal puzzles cried out from beneath the veneer of the worldly-wise ambassador, environmentalist, knight errant, billionaire. His Boy Scout camping skills had lost their nerve; whatever practical streak he'd had was locked out. If he had learned anything about the wilderness, the natural sciences, a wind tunnel in his heart now sucked it all away, leaving not one half cubic inch of bone marrow, street smarts or wherewithal. His hands trembled, his legs swayed.

A look from her, that particular look, was devastating. It meant everything, but spoke not a word. Was she dead; was she alive? And if so, which life? Questions that had never taxed him in the past. He moved closer, she moved the equivalent distance away. Her nudity bore holes in his loins. Something within him begged to consume her and be consumed.

"I am Murillo Marigold, and this is my son, Rajibai. You saved his life."

Her eyes were bright with wonder, her porcelain expression one of absolute perplexity.

"Do you speak English?" he pressed gently.

Deep reticence. Silence.

"I understand. But you have nothing to fear from us. We're new to the island. We mean only good tidings here. I just want to thank you." Marigold nudged his boy.

"Me too, thank you, Miss," Rajibai said.

It was Nelson who, unseen by the Commander, gave her the sign.

"You're most welcome, child," she said at last.

Marigold's heart was stammering. "You speak English! What's your name?"

She thought about a proper reply. The Commander noticed it did not come easily.

"My name is Rachel. Too many surnames. You want some sponge cake?"

It was some time much later—moments, hours, days, weeks? —that the Commander inadvertently let fly the three words he had never in his life uttered: "I love you."

A wave of shock ricocheted off every corner of her country seat, but the Commander felt no shame in realizing this admission. After all, hadn't he earned the right of candor? Could there be any possible advantage to delaying the inevitable? None, Lord Nelson indicated, who welcomed this rallying force of human chutzpah. It was the manly thing to say and feel, he suggested in hornbill vernacular.

Who Rachel was cannot be versified in any court of poetry. To limit the Female by trying to wrap one's arms around the Commander's fancy, or clasp her reality by placing his head in a vise, however light-touching its long-stemmed affections, would only steer far from the truth of hersurreal importance to the very center of the universe, and all its weights and measures. She was the sinecured cornerstone, plucked like the middle C-major of the first Harp that ever intoned the first Heaven. Her Eden was the very fact she was, is, will be. The grammar attendant on her ontology should well constitute the one and only Prolegomena to every future metaphysic. Marigold heard nothing but a one-time, all-encompassing murmur. He floated away in the free-fall of her presence, absorbed by timelessness and heritages beyond recall or investigation. Never before had he abandoned himself in such a manner. She entailed the grand finale which every other experience prior to that time had merely intimated in so many splendid shards.

Now they came together to make a whole in which he saw clearly his life spelled out, with its meaning firmly upheld, in her arms.

She came quietly to him, head adrift in taciturn clouds of deliberation, paused, then pulled him towards her. They collapsed onto the ground with free-for-all abandon. She tightened her legs around his emaciated body, and smothered him with her lips, frantically questing after every intimacy, knowledge, taste, and they made ecstatic love there on the perilous ridge.

And then the dream? premonition? hallucination? subsided. A blue flash, the scent once again of pervasive licorice. The Lord flew off, circled and returned to the tree limb.

Marigold held himself steady. Shook out his head. No woman stood before him. Rajibai was ten paces away, beneath the branch on which perched the Lord, both of them gazing upon the Commander with anticipatory wonder. He'd just been hit on the head by a sun strike and glowed as blue as a Matisse.

"You OK, Dad?"

"Never felt better. Why?"

"That's the spirit!" the Lord piped.

"But where's the Princess?" Marigold puzzled.

"What do you mean?" replied his son. "She went to her hut after saving my butt. You saw the whole thing. I think she's maybe a little shy, like Anna."

The Commander stared absentmindedly through the caesura, uncuffed his discontinuities, retied his spectral vision into a knot and tried to sort out what was happening. Have I already spoken to her? Does Rajibai know that I am dead, or does he not? Did anything happen?

Quiet your confusion, he told himself, his chest heaving. Let it breathe. Let it go.

"Let's remove to higher ground," he went on, staunchly holding on to his wits, however deteriorated. "This is no place to play pinochle."

His boy grinned.

The glints of jungle light penetrated his innermost sight, refracting truant thoughts, each surface a boomerang, cheval glass and sounding board. The lucubratory man, his rapt son, moved up among the hanging rocks and cloven rim towards the inhabitancy. No offscourings or grounds, no sign of human refuse whatsoever. A purity as resplendent as he imagined from that fugitive encounter. She was real, though. Staring at him through the peepholes of her estate, between boscage and stone trellis work. It was the volcanic mortar that held her humble abode to this earth, in spite of the routine storms which swept through. He would learn about them soon enough. Up high, the hurrinadoes made what happened further down look amateurish.

They moved closer now. The habitation had obviously withstood every inclement weather, a steadfast English-style country cottage with elements culled from all the Equatorial portions of the globe. Set back, slightly—30 feet was all—from the final drop-off down into the ocean miles away. Her latitude for free prancing was desperately limited, and now, with the bridge gone, her options were even more extraordinarily claustrophobic. A ridge line, 200 feet wide, stretching for hundreds of miles. She had clearly chosen this course for decisive reasons. Rajibai read tragedy into the configuration. But Marigold harbored another idea.

"We shouldn't approach further," he whispered. He sat down on a comfortable slab, and urged silent solicitude and patience. They waited, though for what Marigold was unsure. It didn't matter. They had all the time in the world.

CHAPTER 195
Rachel of Never Never Land

THEY PAUSED, REFLECTED, waited all through the latest weather-tormented and afternoon hours. A rainstorm was abating in the wake of rare and precious snowbows 100 miles to the north ... was it true north? Even the sun followed an unpredictable arc, the moon in tow. The North Star? Or was it Jupiter? The Lord gathered grugru grubs from a nearby coppice, took no offense at his human companions' rejection. Tried offerings of guava, papaya, and the yellow fruit of the long pepper, which went over much better. Started on, for Rajibai's benefit, about the later years of Rrraaack's glorious career, his *Tractatus Rhyticeros plicatus Philosophicus*. Remarking on the deep significance of the hornbill's gular pouch, pinion coverts and corrugated bill, given to metabolic cogitation and contemplative immunity to life's vicissitudes. Rajibai asked all the right questions, cutting to the chase. Did Rrraaack have children? Answer: He made it a point of moral necessity to adopt all the hornbills of the world. Rhinos, too. He had never a moment's hesitation when it came to embracing the Universal Principles of the High Mark of Virtue first intoned by Baron Munchausen's Scythians (the Baron was evidently a good friend to the hornbills): "Hrornbegh dna skoohtop" meaning, "All hornbills are of heavenly origin and all others should be treated with equal understanding and respect." Question: But not in reality? Answer: Philosophically speaking. Question: That's not the same thing. Answer: Smart ass! Beak-brain! Little Dick! Bigger Than Yours!

"Are you two primary adolescents going to bicker for the rest of the day?" Marigold inquired.

Suddenly, Rachel appeared again, laughing, having heard every word of the enlightened conversation. She'd squeezed into a loincloth— scarcely what one would call a retreat to modesty—and walked out into the closest likeness to a clearing anywhere for miles. She seemed to stand just inches above the scudding cloud that traveled at her bare toes, socking in the lower gorge, so that the four of them emerged in dramatic relief atop the known world. She stood surrounded in birds. A macaw—a true genius— on her right shoulder.

A thousand questions between them. One at a time.

The most pressing: "What are you doing here?" asked she.

"We came from the village. I was looking for my son, Rajibai, whom you've met. I am unspeakably grateful for your heroism."

"Hi!" The boy grinned from ear to snot-nickering nose.

"I'm Murillo Marigold. We were all three lost. From ridgetop to circumjacent ivy; inexpressible stone towers in our past, the sound of musketry, months and days of compassless disappointments, hundreds of Botany Bays, Dutch speakers, distant Krakatoas, Devil's Punch Bowls, parts of the moon, absence of refreshments, consequences too horrible to enumerate. I apologize if we've frightened you, or intruded. We mean no harm."

"I am Lord Nelson, I don't believe we've had the pleasure."

She smiled gracefully at the trio, more radiant than the Commander had imagined, her eyes revealing.

There was an ungainly silence, which Marigold finally surmounted: "But what a spectacular abode of rarified oxygen, the very nature of air affirming a new motion of particles, a suzerainty of platinum shadows, their aerial architecture embossed by ambrosial dews. Even the plants are everywhere aspiring. A place, in other words, where gods alight, casting their anchor momentarily before setting off again. Might I inquire how long this aeriality has been graced by your magnificent company?"

She seemed at ease with the outsiders. In truth, she knew that if the worldly hornbill were riding on a human shoulder, it was all right. Hornbills were known throughout the land for their intuitive powers, and as sticklers for integrity and wise intentions. "Since my childhood," she said. The macaw gazed upon them with circumspect curiosity.

"You've never gone away? Change of setting, different pace?"

"In time," she said cryptically.

"Better coffee somewhere else?"

That drew a rather omniscient grin but no other commentary.

He had other questions, but they could wait—clouds had a way of coming back, circling the Earth.

She appeared, up close, to be in her late twenties, the more remarkable considering the glowing skin, few freckles or blemishes, not the slightest hint of excess sunlight; clear azure eyes, flagrant dark cast of hair with flecks of sporangia and leafless kale entangled, a gleaming body seemingly untouched by the elements. None of it made sense, given her precarious patch of foothold along this furthest cul-de-sac in Never Never Land.

"Come!" She led them into her quarters, an immaculate dwelling rooted to solid rock, yellow lichens, hydrangeas blue, flowering moss merging every which way. Suspended *Cypraeidae* shells jingled in the trees, a spring bubbled up from a rock warren within, and an enormous flowering Chinese silk floss formed the center of the main room, around which she had fashioned a pool, spawning sea creatures living there from time to time. Petals floated on the surface. Chalky opaque windows of mica had been hewn and fitted precisely by her. There was a table of old oak, heavy and dark, cluttered with memories of various pasts: photographs of family—parents? siblings? lovers? —and some pastels framed in metals unknown to the Commander. A library—the librettos of the ta'ziyas, and Jamal-zada's famed *Yaki bud, yaki nabud*, or, *Some of it was, some of it was not*, published in Berlin in 1922 where, she contended in an uneventful aside, she'd been living at the time with Nikos Kazantzakis.

The information did not slip by Marigold, who announced his wonder only to be intercepted by other pressing mementos: a single thin gold fibula stamped and granulated; a sea-dragon finial; a cornelian and faience collar from Eritrea; a few Italian brooches; Egyptian jade scarabs; an onyx parure from Arabia; and a very large diamond. Only later would Marigold discover that this was no ordinary diamond but the 507.5 carats remaining of the Great Mogul, as it was known. The Venetian cutter Ortensio Borgis, stationed in India, had taken the original and whittled it down, hoping to shape a rose cut for the Mogul Emperor Aurangzeb. Somehow, the carats were purloined from Delhi at the time of the Emperor's death and hidden in a burlap sack aboard the *Brahman*, which shipwrecked on the outer reefs of Jovita in the year 1699, said Rachel.

"How do you figure all that?" asked Marigold.

"I was on the ship," said she.

All was beginning to make sense to the Commander. "You can remember?"

"Most of my past has escaped me. The price one pays for all that cosmic dust in our eyes. But some things a woman never forgets." Over coming weeks and months she talked more of her bygone escapades, hopes, tragedies. It was no secret, now, that Rachel had died repeatedly—a fact that settled quite easily with Rajibai. He'd grown up amid multiple lives. The essence of his faith. Indeed he now hoped that his own sister might be joining them soon, given the island's apparent magnetic allure when it came time for karma and reincarnation. Rachel had been washed up at least three times on Jovitan shores. One of her uncles was Ponce de Léon. She described her family connection to the English librarian, Sir Anthony Panizzi, and knew every Codex in the British Museum. Descending from an ancient King of Croatia, she alluded to a distant relation in Aeschylus, as well as to an ancient Hebrew prophet, the man known to modern exegesis as "Q".

"And what of a certain cannibal?" the Commander asked.

"My father? That was his idea of a good joke. A way to raise me without intrusions from below. He was protective, after everything he'd been through in his life. Nobody had ventured here either before or since—that is, until now. Of course, *we* ventured, and I thought we'd never reach the end. I remember him carrying me on his shoulders. I have no idea how he managed it. When we attained the ridge, he realized there was no end, not really. He chose this place, and disappeared just a few months later."

"What happened?"

"I have no idea. I assume he fell into the gorge, possibly the sea."

"How old were you?"

"Four. My father was never able to make it back. I cannot account for it. Death and its effects, however familiar, are never predictable."

"You mean to say you've grown up alone, surviving on your own, all those years? You were never curious about the village?"

She had been only once to the village of Jovita, and described how she and her father had arrived there in the midst of one of the worst hurrinadoes ever, winds exceeding 300 miles per hour. The village was not much to look at by that time. A blind man greeted them, she recalled. But as she spoke it became even more clear why her return was never necessary. Speechless reckoning. Contentment. The essence of human oneness with Nature. She had it all. The passage of eternity as registered in her smoky mirror atop the oak table, circa 1772, its wooden upper piece painted by Fragonard on commission from Madame du Barry (for her chateau at Louveciennes), which Rachel had collected at a flea market in Nice in the mid-nineteenth century. One of his women on a swing. It had weathered poorly on Jovita, but these modest trappings of her itinerary from one life to the next counted; gave her endless small joy.

Scarcely a day passed, she told them, when she wouldn't wrestle her way down the precipitous trail to the hidden cove two miles below. The path dropped steeply through ten microclimates, skirting the Everest-like face of deep, jungle-clad sandstone walls. Down on the beach, she would do what bathers since time immemorial have done. Her daydreams had merged with her nights. Sometimes she tempted the waves, swam out to the horizon. Twice, she believes, she drowned, and arrived promptly back at her Pierrefonds on the ridge. How she was able to do so, but her father not, she could not explain. The mechanisms were unclear to her. They certainly were to the Commander.

Moreover, no matter what it might appear, she said, the dead are never bored: a fact amplified during the coming months, when Marigold and Rachel were truly getting to know one another.

How the Commander broke out of his intellectual skein was in itself no small miracle. Even Rajibai acknowledged it.

"You're different, Dad," he said matter-of-factly one day.

"What do you mean?"

"I mean you're ... real."

"Then what have I been?"

"It's hard to explain."

"Try."

"I don't want to hurt your feelings."

He shrugged off the very possibility. "Go on, say what's on your mind."

"Well, you're the finest father in the world. But you have a few ticks."

"I'm listening."

"You avoid certain things."

"You couldn't be referring to volcanoes or waterfalls or hotsucks."

"No. You do pretty good for an old man where they're concerned."

"What, then?"

He was hesitant, but the Commander bridled him on. He felt it proper to unburden chests.

"OK. When was your heart ever captured?"

"The moment I laid eyes on you in that dreadful hospital ward."

The boy was at a brief loss. Then: "Father, I mean by girls."

"What you really mean is Rachel, isn't it?"

"Yeah."

"You like her as well."

Long airing memory that to a woman cottoned, tried, wanted, hoped, with no mother, no sister, and prayed aloud, "She's unbelievable," Rajibai stated, in tune psychically with his father's coming-of-age.

Then, "Believe, Son."

CHAPTER 196
Jungle Jane

THEY SHARED IT ALL, never questioning the deeper significance of two shadowless corpses in Heaven tempting fate, which both accepted gratefully.

Mr Marigold's very first time was not the stuff of legends. She was kind and gentle in every way, and it didn't help that Rajibai, with the Lord on his shoulder, happened upon the desperate couple *en flagrante*. The growing son knew much more about these matters than his father. One day the question of embryology declared itself. Rajibai, who had occupied himself in hundreds of conversations with the Lord, and many other creatures who eventually came around to investigate the newcomers, learning everything there was to be known about paradise, was the first to detect Rachel's pregnancy. He had a nose for the flood of hormones and pheromones and women's moods, and eyes to catch the slightest incremental change in the natural surroundings.

"It is my first," Rachel declared.

"In all those lifetimes?"

But as it turned out, those lifetimes were incomplete. During the sixteenth century, she had fallen in love with Michael Servetus, who was editing Ptolemy's *Geography*, and she had been shackled to an iron stake and burned beside her lover on the hill at Champel, thanks to the infamous sadist John Calvin, who testified to their intellectual heresies. During the seventeenth century Rachel had died three times, and always before the age of 12. All of history swirled through her bloodstream, and now additional nutrients as well. The Lord regurgitated fruit puddings for her, from rare endemic varieties that she could never obtain for herself, for they sprouted only at the precarious outer branches of one particularly inaccessible cliff palm. Marigold did most of the cooking over an open pit: Sally Lunn bread, old-world orchid stew, taro pâté. Their nights were spent tracing lineages to delight one another, prodding their respective memories, which waned and ebbed with each passing day. Rachel had kept diaries throughout the centuries, always lost in the effect, of course, but the process at least enabled her to remember a considerable amount of one past after another. The Commander was less fortunate. Apart from certain shared experiences during the previous year with his son, his earlier life was quickly dissipating from his head.

They smoked an upland coconut pitch whose impact was heavier at this altitude, drank dark palm wine that fermented in the seed, lay in a kapok hammock gazing upon the show of stars over the rough hibiscus sea.

"Do you suppose we always come back in human form?" she asked him.

"Why, do you remember something?"

"No. But I wouldn't mind being a bird."

"If I came back a chicken," Marigold postulated, "which seems a distinct possibility given my own crèche of acquaintances, I would certainly stir revolution. Cause a great pestilence from the dust in my feathers. Perhaps I did at one time, and was cut down. I don't remember. All the billions of beleaguered, suffering creatures have entered my heart. I am exploding with their pain and would gladly endure every last tear of it on their behalf if there were only enough lifetimes for me to do so."

"There are," she comforted him. "And you have every reason to look forward to your sacrifices."

They exchanged all they knew and dreamt and were. For Marigold, it was a release from himself that he had never thought possible—had never thought about at all. Rajibai was right. He had spent his life reading books. Had broken out only recently, going through billions of dollars, millions of Frequent Flyer miles, with no other blueprint than the creation of Utopia on Earth. But it had all been one elaborate artifice, the product of newspaper clippings, chance encounters, moral outrage, intellectual uprisings. He had no real plan, no consistent approach, little education. When all was voiced, tried and intended, he had nothing to show for his feverish 1,000 days since his court appearance in Santa Fe.

A few properties scattered to the winds. Some new friends, but equally dispersed. He had found a son, and a best friend, and that would count for everything. But now, strangely—too strange for any reasonable explanation—he was dead, allegedly, although he had no sure proof of it, and nothing could be more peculiar than that. If his emotions had been repressed, inhibited, inert for most of his adult life, now they were jejune, confused, weeping, wanting, naked day and night. Rachel stood unafraid before that flood.

With Rachel, the Commander would find the strength to give himself away totally—a prerequisite, he knew, for assuming the sweet sentient composure of other species, which had become his primary aim in this or any other life. Nevertheless, once he had stared into the clear pools of her eyes, stroking that unsullied flesh, touched her most delicate nuances, all these other campaigns took second fiddle. Even the lessons from the Tree of Life seemed of minor importance now. Gone were the hopes of sending all the billionaires to the moon, of worrying about Mercury colliding with Earth. How he could ever have wanted to be Governor of New Mexico escaped him. What a futile and absurd ambition, as odious as it was miniscule. All the clever advantages of fortune now appeared in a clear light of cloying disadvantage: connections to mortality and doomed aspirations; to a frail body that was susceptible to every ill-wind, bruise and bang. On Rachel's windswept ridge, a harbor in the timeless elements, he knew he had somehow risen above himself. Which only placed in stark relief all those desires which had preceded him and seemed now to be a vast confusion of monstrous and predatory proportions. He felt ashamed, in fact, by his earlier dispositions, his wasted affiliations, trivial expectations.

"And to think that I had been so long a victim of those whims, throwing myself from country to country, crisis to crisis, and for what? To save the last moa? Find redemption for the lost souls of the Cooties disaster? Satisfy the endless cravings of a squirrel?"

In confessing to these alter-egoistical expeditions, Marigold was more alive than he had ever been. He not only insisted but proved he was a new man.

"I thought I could shape a new human nature when my very own was as dumb and gullible as clay. How could I have been so blind? Saul sees it all. I see nothing. I've thrown myself into hand-to-hand combat without the slightest idea what I was doing. I thought I could save all the chickens of Hong Kong. Instead, I got most of them killed. I tried to buy the Presidency of Greece, to launch a vegetarian ticket, only to trigger an Interpol investigation. I could go on. Every effort has backfired."

"You saved a tribe in Tibet. Rajibai told me all about it. And the roosters. The cows. The bats. Rajibai himself. You're too hard on yourself. You have done what nobody thought to do," she plied. "I failed to change."

"The world?"

"Yes. The horrors."

"It's not possible. I was once present for the slaughter of 60,000 Huguenots in Paris. And my grandfather, in this century, survived Auschwitz in a cage made for chickens. Next to him, in another cage, was a man he knew as Tex, a British Army officer famed throughout the war for his miraculous escapes. They were both dragged before a Gestapo firing squad, yet managed miraculously to escape. Eventually, they were both liberated from the death camp. In the end, they died, having done nothing to change this world, however much they presaged other possibilities."

"He told you all this?"

"I read it in his diary," she said, and produced it from a drawer. "You can't imagine the crown of thorns, so don't tell me about horrors. Tell me about good things. Read to me from the annals of your magnificent efforts; don't renounce them. That is simply a cowardice."

"No saner words ever spoken. I apologize."

They hugged, and lay down together.

"I tried, but I have not managed to sleep for many years," Marigold said. "I always said I would sleep when I was dead. Clearly, that is not how it works."

This admission triggered in Rachel much open contemplation. Her eloquence had enjoyed centuries of seasoning, which gave her a little of Plutarch and Virginia Woolf, of Sappho and Isabella D'Este.

"You were right, and remain right, to try to save everything that could be saved, even if—in the end—it couldn't be; even if a second's amelioration of pain was the limit of your effectiveness. You were wise and good to cherish that which deserved your love. Don't think that death makes it all irrelevant. That is not true. You have perished only once, or once that you are aware of, and so are truly a newcomer to the universe. I speak from having ridden a little more of the rollercoaster ride. And can assure you that the worst sin of all is to waste a life. Such lives are very short-lived, as a rule; interregnums that must—they must—foster every boldness; campfires for fueling dreams. Just because the greater truth of our deaths allows for all the absolutes—freedom, immunity, joy—the search is always there. A longing, even if it cannot be articulated. We make love not just for the moment but in craving something beyond ourselves. My father, who had died countless times, always told me: Live as if there is no death to save you."

Marigold suddenly caved in, discounting in one stroke whatever he might have accomplished, or tried to do. Nothing, in his estimation, was worthy of the slightest remembrance, not beside this young beauty who had experienced at least a dozen lifetimes to his one—or at least as far as he knew. She had suffered terribly. In fact, her detailed description of how she and Michael Servetus were burned alive while the Calvinist elders of Geneva's council watched with righteous glee would not leave him. The pain had no translation. Even now, having merely heard about it, he could not shake it. But then, multiply that one unimaginable instance billions of times and he began to sense the outlines of the tragedy of the last several hundred years for other species.

Since the chances of accomplishing anything were nearly impossible, and because Marigold had tried nonetheless, he might have been a ruined man. All his money could not save even one human community from itself—a fact which Sannazaro had reminded him of every day. Yet, like himself, and in spite of the odds, Sannazaro had tried, had conjured his own castled airs, allowing himself to be dragged from one crazy war zone to another. The Italian had begun taking to a life of tourism. Insanity had never daunted him. As long as a good triple shot of some dram or heady caffeine could be downed by day's end in close company, he was game to try anything. In this way he served, without knowing anything of the chemistry, as the perfect reaffirmation goading the Commander beyond himself and his years. They were made for one another, however much they bitched back and forth.

Marigold loved that man, and he missed him. For ten months or so they had been apart. Sannazaro had remained down in the village of Jovita, beachcombing, gabbing all day long. The Commander, up in the highlands, sorely felt the absence of his Squire's foolish carping and inflated hallelujahs. There was no better companion, no wiser mentor, no more sprightly, chaffing, ruinous laughter; no more astute observer or poet's restraining order, Marigold thought. Rational to a fault, Sannazaro's complaints and fears were seldom ill-founded. He was a refreshing hydrant in the midst of steamy ghetto summers, and could always be counted on to distinguish between a nut and a bolt. Moreover, Sannazaro never tired, not really. Just kept going. Was truly a burro of divine domains.

There in Jovita, the Italian had spent his days drinking cappuccinos, taking long walks, rearing three leopards, engaged in leisure games of chess and the duties of Governor which consisted of nothing whatsoever. Never in his lifetime had he felt so free and childlike. A terrible burden had been lifted from him. Death had served him magnificently. He felt not one jot of fear or apprehension and, most strange of all, began to feel intense and original cravings all centered upon one woman—Ginevra.

But he too missed his old friend, and the boy. Amigo seemed to crave their companionship as well, as much as said so to the Italian. The two of them would awake each dawn (Amigo having taken on the noisy characteristics of his old friend Rodriguez, who always greeted the sunrise three or four times, commencing in the dark, when everyone else was asleep), resolved to go searching for them. But by evening the Italian was exhausted from the day's heavy lounging, helplessly condemned to the sedentary pleasures of the beach, though he would always vow all over again: 'Tomorrow!'

Tomorrow never came, or not with sufficient energy to induce so risky an expedition to the highlands, where Sannazaro knew there would be trouble and misery of every kind. Moreover, nobody would journey with him. Not even the leopards, who'd grown acutely lazy. His new friends among the Jovitans were likewise immovable, and Saul was too busy preparing cappuccinos for the whole village, or those who remained. There had been another earthquake, a serious one, which leveled a dozen huts, killing a third of the villagers. Some of the victims drifted back; some did not. Reincarnations were quite fickle, alleged Saul.

And what about Rajibai who, like Rachel, seemed to fear nothing? Hope for nothing? He simply lived with an ardor that defied analogy. No tragedy fazed him. His tears were plentiful and unabashed but never dissuaded him from going on to third base. He'd been bashed countless times in his young life, but it never mattered: he would always peer forth, curious, insatiable. What would become of him now? What were the rules about a dead father and a living son?

Marigold's mind raced back to the *New Testament* for any guidelines or Holy Ghosts. But the whole book was a muddle of pages stuck together like duff to pine resin in his brain. Shakespeare? Any guidance from Falstaff? A hundred other characters and situations? Or how about Milton, surely Milton? Again, nothing. Not so much as a line remained. He rifled through the vast library of his past—Kuo Hsi, Dom Francisco Quevedo, Erasmus Darwin, Allan Lerner, Wilhelm Busch, Sir Richard Fanshawe, Knight—only to discover that Jovita truly was an island of forgetting, where gophers and turnips were the same, the oxen lost their grazing patterns, wedding rings vanished, slights and overlooks prevailed, and even the omission of care or propriety was the forgetful quick of common day. His eyelids were now steeped on this perfect jungle. He was an abbey whose bricks had crumbled. A man become a clean slate, without anchor or reliance whatsoever on all that mumbo jumbo, arcane illusions and endless references which had once invariably saved him from going to the core, expressing the underpinning, voicing the deepest reality. His charismatic endeavors had always to rely on the sheer magnitude of the effort for their effect. But now he had to confront his situation shorn of any intellectual buttressing. He had to rely on his pure emotions, the essences of himself. A new world. How, he wondered, does one do it? Find that which matters? Let go of excess?

Atop that windy ridge beyond the known world, ten months of sublime wear and tear passed as if it were a day. Murillo, as his lover normally called him, was schooled on the nerve endings, good taste and mystery of Rachel, who had no last name. Then, one afternoon, she came to him and said, "Rachel Marigold. I like the sound of it. "

When the earthquake hit, Rachel was in labor, but having a hard time of it. The rain had not let up for days and nights, and Marigold had found it difficult to keep the hut heated—which was a hardship for all its occupants, including Lord Nelson.

The quake lasted for one minute—and it made all the difference. In the throes of a 7.3 Rachel produced a healthy, eight-pound girl, the offspring of two spirits very much in love.

"Rajibai, meet your sister," Rachel said, and she handed the suddenly diffident lad his swaddling kin, ruby cheeks, vermilion fuzz on her elegantly shaped little head. Eyes as darkling blue as the sea in a morning mist encircling the island of Jovita.

She looked at the Commander, who gazed back upon her, and upon these two children. "Marry me?" he said with sudden aplomb. No stranger words had ever been uttered by him.

She hugged him. Tearful.

And they named the newborn Jungle Jane.

CHAPTER 197
The Vale of Naked Fairies

THERE WERE NO bylaws or corollaries upon that ridge of biotopia; no science or methodology. To the discerning intellect, not even a pattern attending to the Afterlife. *Dictum de omni et nullo*, that most revered foundation of syllogistic logic which held, ultimately, that all parts reflect the whole, was not the only story, or even the most interesting one. By present standards, perceptions and company, it appeared that anomalies, strange attractions, a deepening diversity beyond any the biologically oriented Marigold had ever imagined were more expressly the natural order of things. The Commander rested quite comfortably on the supreme laurel of having died. A little known fact, rarely mentioned in the spiritual corpus: death can be wonderful.

Those mysterious gravesites, implements and ornaments bestrewn about the paleolithic strata all suggest to the appreciative eye great assurances of continuity. From Predmost in Moravia to Mount Kailasha in

Tibet. Karens, Chaldeans, Chorotegans, Bonpo and thousands of other tribal individuals performed rites for expediting the passage of the soul. For how many millennia were belongings burned alongside the corpse, or sent out in the canoe, or buried, lest the deceased require such things on that journey? The unifying presumption was that life transmigrated; that souls, spirits, even bodies reappeared in other forms. Rajibai had grown up in such a culture of belief.

Add to this anthropological maelstrom the revelations of zoologists like the famed tissue-culture experimenters Carrel and Ebeling who sustained the heart of a chick embryo for a quarter century, or the work of Bidder in the 1920s with respect to immortal fish—fish that were simply incapable of dying naturally. Even by the mid-twentieth century, scientists knew that every organ of an animal—all the cells and tissues, the heart and the nerves—could go on living indefinitely. Put them all together in a live being and the possibilities were endless.

Marigold had by this time discussed the drowning with his son, who fortunately showed no ill effects or psychological fallout from the realization. He had, in fact, managed to save his father and uncle, as the philosophical tenets would confirm, aiding their own transmigrations with mouth-to-mouth. What both Marigold and Rajibai found particularly curious was the nearly invisible hairline between life and death. Like a flawlessly restored painting, or Italian parterres so deftly laid down as to conceal the edges forever. Not even a blur to signal transition.

Death on Jovita was simply indistinguishable from life. Sometimes Marigold found himself going for weeks without once feeling tired, craving food or needing to pee. Rachel, on the other hand, snacked and nibbled all day long, took lengthy languorous naps, and sported two bountiful, elegant breasts which never lacked for a globulin-rich, coconut-tasting colostrum. In her body, the world's *historia naturalis*.

Their lives were animated by the little girl. Jane was the name of Rachel's most recent mother, a woman half her father's age who had disappeared during a political mission among Eskimos in the Northwest Territories.

"Some day," Rachel said, "my mother will come back. She can't possibly like the snow that much."

"But back where?"

"Wherever I am."

"Does it work that way?"

"Dreams have a way of materializing. We're both proof."

"How strange and foreboding, all these things," Marigold pondered. "Am I dead, am I alive? Am I on a journey, or am I still? What are these veils, concealing chimeras, compassless perceptions, these past and future tumults? Why is there no certainty, even now?" Then: "I'm sorry about your mom."

"I was three at the time. I remember a million flying geese, like a blizzard on a sunny day. And the ancient souls of musk oxen stampeding across the flowering tundra. My mother laughing. An expedition to collect wild strawberries. I'll never forget those things," she said, and she started to cry.

Marigold held her. "Rachel, your mother did not abandon you. Something incredible happened, over which she had absolutely no power."

"Yes, you're probably right."

"Where did they find you?"

"Asleep on the ice somewhere."

The "Jungle" part of the baby's name was contributed by Rajibai, who relished the alliterative and was well versed in the tales of Edgar Rice Burroughs, thanks to Lord Nelson's incessant conversational skills. Rajibai had become fluent in Hornbill, as well as a dozen other local dialects, including Pterodactyl. He had an ear, a growing seriousness that seemed to become more sober by the night. There was the ever-present rascal in him, fired up, ready to leap, a crusader amidst the Milky Way, but also an increasing introversion, as if he was happy to stare meditatively and pick up all the nuances around him, which only silence was better at fathoming.

Meanwhile, there were changes occurring in the Commander, as well. A much-softening heart, and a head of absolutely unredemptive, disheveled hair. Red hair, silver hair, tips blanching to beneath his pale shoulders. His eyes had begun to droop, or suspend themselves in pools of green, so doting were they on the baby. A baby surrounded by every shade of verdant light and inaccessible jungle. Marigold's prominent brow had settled; the look of an aristocrat less observable. He was no more formal these days, content to play on his knees in the dirt, to prate and babble for hours undistracted. The infant had conquered him. A crazy stitchwork of Sir Francis Drake and Jonathan Winters.

Play was infectious on the ridge. The Lord recited long passages from the 500-year-old *Volksbuch*, known as *Till Eulenspiegel ... the Rare and Comical Conceits of Master Owlglass*. Nobody could laugh like a hornbill—except for Sir Joseph Odyssey, on whose enormous wings both the Lord and Rajibai, even the Commander on occasion, took rides out over the abyss, both east and west. The strangest things induced his guffaws: a tickle in the updrafts, the sight of mountain crows hounding monkey-eating eagles, or whenever anyone touched a small region of wrinkled gray flesh just under his enormous beak. If Sir Joseph happened to start laughing whilst in flight, it could be very serious indeed—which is exactly what happened the morning that Marigold, Rajibai and Nelson opted to take a ride down into the Valley of Four Rivers to explore what they presumed and hoped to be Paradise proper.

On loping wings they were heading beneath the collapsed bridge when Sir Joseph saw a large snapping turtle that had slid off the top of the cliff and was dangling by his jaws from a tatter of hemp. His little paws were swimming pathetically in mid-air above the 10,000-foot drop-off, and he might have been there in that mess all night long, given the tenacious strength of his jaws, and his powerful will to live.

"Now that is a ridiculous sight!" Sir Joseph quipped, chuckling without reservation. Chuckles becoming mighty wind-sucking har-har-hars.

"Please don't laugh!" cried the Lord, who was familiar enough with the risks.

But it was too late. Sir Joseph had failed to take into account the volumetric pressure in his lungs as against the forced expiration rate as measured in kilovolts of static electric pressure on his posterior maximus. No Pterosaurian was malleable enough to do both: laugh and fly. He plunged, and the trio held on to the rough scales at the base of his neck, their legs flying out behind them.

"Don't let go don't let go don't let go!" went the Lord's panic attack. "Two hundred, 300, my God we're flying 400 miles per hour!"

"I got you, Son," the Commander hailed, his old bony hands like ratchets on the beast. Nothing could pry him loose.

But the speed was too great. Both the father and son passed out.

For all his massive ungainliness, Sir Joseph—taking his bloody time— managed to save the situation, admittedly a mere 100 vertical feet above a steaming cauldron below—far too close to all-out catastrophe to inspire any kind of regular confidence in his aeronautical livelihood. Yet, to their astonishment— Marigold and Rajibai regaining consciousness—in the dinosaur's delicate talon was the snapping turtle, which he had plucked from certain death on the way down, a gesture of exquisite timing and sensitivity that transcended any likeness in other animal communities.

"No problem," said Sir Joseph, touching down beside a stream along which ambled beasts of every description, none seen by humans on Earth before, and certainly not by the Commander or Rajibai.

"Lower Jurassic, that one," commented Sir Joseph on the gorgeous, mammoth-sized okapi crossing before them. "Very singular sweet tooth."

"Never mind that, you could have killed all of us!" the Lord scolded.

They soon dismissed their rapid descent as one more adventure and went about their morning, exploring the endless attractions of the Vale. Warm-water slips that snaked their descent through 100 fern forests; vines that resembled fine jewelry cloaking the lower trunks of an endless variety of softwoods; strange species of kitty cat, their faces made of crystal in which all reflections were broken down into their component parts and past lives, like paintings by Braque and Duchamp; the gaseous prismatic bubbles seen from high above over a year before, which now proved to be a type of naked fairy who traveled lighter than air, their purposes unknown to the visitors. Marmosets atop dolphins.

And much more.

CHAPTER 198
The Commander's Last Glimpse of Civilization and its Discontents

I sent my Soul through the Invisible,
Some letter of that After-life to spell:
And after many days my Soul return'd
And said, 'Behold, Myself am Heav'n and Hell'
—Rubaiyat of Omar Khayyam of Naishapur

A PENGUIN CROSS, part Jackass, a portion Macaroni, who stood three times the size of ordinary Emperors, bristling ultramarine in exposed aspect, with a face as striking and as golden as King Tut's, passed them by obliviously, musing, then turned, started to speak, thought the better of it, continued on his way, mumbling even more solemnly, turned again and pondered the practicality of it yet a second time.

"All right, come along, then," crrraaaked he, then proceeded to escort the present company to the complicated entrance of a fantastic castle. It was 20 times the size of Neuschwanstein, in Bavaria, and huge rookeries of *Spheniscidea* were seen lounging around the inflows from the four rivers. As their guide started off to join his other ranks, Rajibai threw at him a universally resonant question: "Where can somebody get a good breakfast around here?"

The penguin never shirked from a discussion of food: "What did you have in mind?"

"A waffle smothered in blueberry jam," he replied.

"Just over there!" The proud avian pointed towards a huge mechanical device that stood hundreds of feet tall, was cloaked in slime and perpetually vomited up more slime, which slid down funnels that led to pools that were feasted upon by the penguins and billions of bioluminescent tunnel worms. The drainage area was alive with teeming bog herbs. Groans and howls. Weary laments and musical beatitudes. There was no easy way to characterize the scene. Frightening. Feisty. Fully lived in the moment. "You don't want to go near there," Sir Joseph cautioned.

"What an amazing machine!" cried Marigold, ignoring him, moving closer.

"What is it?" wondered Rajibai.

"Here," replied the penguin, "select souls of all the ages past are ground up and regurgitated for the new penguins. The worms get the leftovers."

"But don't you find that slightly grotesque?" the boy remarked.

"Ahhh! We have here a child seeking answers," declared the penguin, prompting a heated debate among his vociferous kind. Was he a child or a man? A man, argued several hundred thousands of the birds. A child, insisted an equal number of others.

"Who built the castle?" interjected Marigold.

"Ahhh! We have here a man seeking knowledge," answered another tall-standing avian. Yet another debate broke out among the birds, with equally numbered battalions taking their favorite positions.

Marigold looked to his companions, the Lord and Sir Joseph. "Doesn't he understand that some things cannot be explained by simple question and answer?" Sir Joseph replied. "Dissent and vote-taking? Why, if that were the case, we'd all simply ask the right questions and end up knowing everything, which we certainly don't. I, for one, don't want to. The fact is, you'll save yourself much time and trouble by simply not asking. The end results will be the same."

The penguins were still deep in debate, 220,900 birds agreeing with Marigold, over a million unsure, when Rajibai recommended they all climb the highest turret for purposes of a view towards clarity.

"Nix that," said the Lord.

"Ditto," went Sir Joseph.

"Gentlemen, what's the problem?" asked Marigold. "This is Paradise."

"Don't be misled," wisely voiced the hornbill. "This is the bottom of Paradise, in case you forget, the place where all the hard work, the blood and guts that goes into making angels gets accomplished. I have a feeling it may not be the pretty part."

They traversed a huge hallway lined with the exhibited bones of 1,001 extinct creatures; little educational signs designated their individual tragedies, illuminated by darkly glowing candles. Every one of the displays emanated its particular pain. You could not pass by without feeling it. Though each pilgrim sensed and saw something different.

Sir Joseph was the first to collapse, his wings flapping desperately against the hard, glassy-smooth stone floorwell. Staring into the reflective surface he saw a vision: it was him! The bones of the mighty *Ornithocyrus*, though none of the others could see what Sir Joseph saw. (He had much larger eyes than the others combined.) The sleekest flyer in the annals of biology was here reduced to a mere mug-shot of its former glory, scavenged coracoid, sternal keel, zygomatic arch and pygostyle. And a petrified heart. Across the sweep of the planet, expeditions of vicious fossil hunters were digging up whole skeletons of his cousin dinosaurs, removing them from sacred burial sites to noisy museums.

"Help me!" he cried out.

Over there, grimly splayed upon the gallery wall, *Archaeopteryx lithographica*, the size of a stellar jay, 140 million years old, ancestor to the hornbill. Nearly two million bird species, less than half of one percent of them actually familiar to science, known to have gone extinct since that time—a rate rapidly increasing. On islands, the extinction rate was nearly 95 percent. Behind the grisly display cases there was the real McCoy: horrors beyond description. Real men, slitting the throats and plucking feathers from the live birds. Billions of chickens, reflected in a gallery of mirrors, their throats succumbing to round, flat guillotines. Mechanical devices eviscerating them.

The endless blood. A melancholy spreading like a wildfire in Lord Nelson's walnut-sized brain. He fell to the floor, snapping several primary feathers, gripped by a grand mal. "Oh dear!" he yammered, passing out.

Then it was Rajibai's turn, as he was suddenly confronted with all his old friends—Singh, Annand, Radha, Kiritbai, Budjo—slaving in the pits of Forlorn, molested and horribly abused all over again. No progress. Nothing gained by their week-long revolution. And there, the very corpse of his own sister, hacked to shreds amid communal violence, the callous indifference, pale frost, illnesses and woes of all the poor people throughout time. She stared at him, piecemeal, hideous effigies of her ruin displayed like trophies marked up for special notice by time. Along with the heads of caribou and moose and 15-racks, mounted on Bavarian oakboards. Weapons proudly displayed behind glass—the ten-thousandth centennial of man: Becketts, obsidian fore-shafts, Kimbers, Remingtons, Valmets, .700 heavy-barreled varmint specials, cuirasses, bamboo spears, throwing clubs, boomerangs, pellet bows, daos and cord slings. Even the odd vial of red mercury. A flood of sobbing poured from the veins in her brother's eyes.

The Commander who wasn't even a Commander: all the commanders of all the wars and ecological hells there on the wall. It was no secret that hundreds of millions of people over time had killed each other, just as they had prevailed upon all other animals. Commanders themselves had been much to blame, for taking charge of the ground troops, enthusiastically endorsing the mayhem, goading on the killings by their own example. But only one face stared back at him: a profile daubed in war paint and writhing in the sea, the pain unbearable—he felt every ounce of what he had been through (there was no escaping it now), in the nostrils, in the brain, the lungs, the arms, condemned forever. Karma catapulting its minions without delineation. The countering face was not that of Marigold, precisely, but the gaunt untouched-up countenance of all men, implicating, naming and revealing all men, and women too, in the sorry, senseless doom to which they had committed themselves since the dawn of human imagination. These were no fables.

He stepped away embittered, helped his son, held on to the Lord, until his seizure subsided, and then, together, they wrestled the 19,000-pound Sir Joseph up on to his talons so that he could move, albeit with oppressive difficulty out of the long colonnade, his gigantic feathers hunched over. His heart crushed. He kept slipping, as on plantain peels, upon his own tears.

At the end of the cloistered arcade, the miserables came upon a workshop of sorts, spilling out onto a marble ballroom floor surrounded in reflective surfaces. There, the image of man, not God's image, surely, but some other misshapen concatenation of freaks, dementia and despair from the beginning of known and unknown history, where hundreds of heavy-jawed ancestors of all orders and families and kingdoms exhumed, fitted, devised, composed, shaped and generally manufactured their own rebirths and, by implication, others'. It appeared as if this was the normal course of all biology, working and struggling towards some nauseous conclusion—little gain, complete ruin, pointless ruin starkly diffused across the ages. A Buddhistic inevitability: all life comprised of nothing more than suffering. The materials from which they worked consisted of a ghastly jumble of remains—dead corpses, cold meat, washed-up cadavers, half-eaten carcasses—delirious with foot-and-mouth bacteria. In such calamitous times, chivalry was no longer an option. Some of these bundles of rotting flesh were not corpses at all but stubborn sparks of life, and the builders would hammer them hard, breaking up the bones in all the heads, despite the agonized pleadings, until so many mushes and squirming aggregates were definitely dead and could then be reassembled according to some allegedly visionary plan.

Those half-corpses which clung to the past, still fighting their reincarnation, were fed into gigantic furnaces distinguished by volatile green outgasses, the workers continually shoveling the charred powder from the kilns into a looming orifice which evidently led to the very center of the Earth, surmised the Lord. Down there, all the evidence, identity and reason for being was expunged from the record of life, or any future tribunals of justice. It was as if those tenacious ashes had never lived at all. That was their reward. To be forgotten. The building blocks of more earth, without even a redemptive murmur. Unfair. Unrealized. Only too imaginable.

"They call that cosmic necessity," uttered Sir Joseph, revealing to the others a stalwart philosopher amid chaos and unredeemable disheartenment. This dinosaur of remarkable courage who seemed to have seen it all began, "Sixty-odd millions of years ago there was a senseless flash in the sky, a fireball as I recall, that struck the Earth. Most of my friends succumbed to it, but I can assure you, each and every one of them—at least the ones from my circle of immediate relations—remains a living memory. I see them all as if it were yesterday, lounging in a meadow, feasting on a plum tree in the sunshine. I remember my first true love, Herbivorous Sally, possessed of the most gentle of talons: she could point out a single star from among the millions, or kneel down fascinated to trace the path of an ant on its tiny way to a tiny grocery store, yet she weighed 19,000 stone, stood 33 feet high. How to describe her sinuous neck, fleshy thigh muscles and soft little tuft of yellow head-feathers, not to mention that naughty glint in her eyes which suggested she would never die. She wanted only to make little Sallies. I will always be looking for her. Because this is Jovita ..." He trailed off in tears. The Commander offered him a hankie.

"I know you're in mourning, but wouldn't it make sense, after 60 million years, to let her go?"

Lord Nelson shrugged, knowing full well how attached dinosaurs were to each other—a legendary point of fact in the animal kingdom. It was simply futile trying to get them over their bereavement.

"Wait a minute," Rajibai ignited. "How do you feel about dragons?"

"Brilliant!" Marigold cried. "Why hadn't I thought of that!"

"Dragons? I love dragons. Never met one, though," Sir Joseph exclaimed.

"Why do you ask?"

"A match made in Heaven," Rajibai declared, though he was not yet at the point of figuring out how one would travel from Jovita to Soqotra, or vice versa. But those were mere details. And, of course, if no sparks flew between Sir Joseph and Sentimenta, there was always Sweet Pea, though she might be harder to locate.

The group, in their exercise of some hasty departure, read before them a sign at the front of the workshop with a dozen arrows and distances: Utopia, that way; the Kingdom of God, over there, where sunbeams, moonlight fancies and a universal thirst for useless adventure converged in a stream of dust motes. And finally, Erewhon Flats, Tibet, Disneyland, even Tesuque—thataway. And looming beneath this cartography of wishful thinking, Hell, two steps back for every step forward. All measured in distances that made no sense. None at all: exhausting miles, minus the superficial inches, divided by all those profoundly revealing visions, and all multiplied, humiliated, distanced beyond compare by an array of dizzy stars and galaxies that taunted the explorer with logic, hope and science, whilst growing ever fainter; poetry, governance, in shambles.

"We have to get out of here," the Lord urged. "While there's still time."

CHAPTER 199
The Night of Falling Stars

AT THAT MOMENT, Marigold looked across the piazza of pain into the mirror, and saw himself asleep, stretched out atop the keys of a harpsichord in some secluded oasis high away from it all.

He closed his eyes and opened them again. To find himself crinkled against the far wall of the hut. Neither the Lord nor Sir Joseph was anywhere to be seen. Rachel was breastfeeding Jungle Jane. It was late afternoon. Rajibai had just awakened.

"You two slept all day. I think you're smoking too much of the coconut snuff," Rachel suggested. "It can make your brain do peculiar things."

Marigold and Rajibai shared a nervous glance.

"But I haven't touched the snuff in days," the Commander protested. Neither, it seemed, had Rajibai.

"What do you think it means?" the Commander asked Rachel, having enumerated all the details he could remember.

"I've been down there," she went on. "It was nothing like what you just described. Nothing at all. There were four rivers, butterflies in profusion, some beautiful grasslands, a rare species of wild buffalo, tens of millions of talkative parrots, but no penguins that I've ever noticed. Way too warm for them. And certainly no kitty cats with crystal faces, or naked fairies riding around inside gas bubbles. Waves in a castle moat? Workmen committing those unspeakable acts? You want to know what I think? I think you're exhausted. You had a frightful dream. I know just the remedy."

"How could you and I have perceived such vastly divergent pictures of the same place? What happened to you afterwards?"

"Nothing. I returned here. Years went by."

"But why did I have such a nightmare when I'm so happy? I've never had a nightmare, ever, in my entire life. It was dreadful."

"You needed to get it out of your system. That's how it works. Nightmares. Whole lifetimes, if it comes to that. No fancy theories. Just let it happen. Give in to it." She hugged him.

"I'm afraid," he said. "It was disgusting, poignant. It seemed altogether real, had a sort of logic to it, even boded of—I don't know what. Something. And worst of all, it was definitely personal."

They napped, cuddling in an aerie, his body shivering in surf upon crashing surf of premonitory fear.

Later that night the rains came. A tropical cyclone that dumped 10 feet of water, turning the few trails from the garden into deep mud. It stormed all the next day. But by evening the winds had been quelled, the rains evaporated, and the sun made one of its legendary eleventh-hour appearances across the enflamed archipelago. Mists floated off like ozone. From their nearly 11,000 feet of altitude they could see the curvature of the sea, as it lay spellbound and shimmering, churning with cod, beneath the green and aquamarine flashes of twilight.

They had supper. Sautéed coconut, white asparagus, a wild lettuce salad with avocado, mushrooms, scallions, a dressing made from pulverized licorice root and ginseng that bunched up in profusion at their very doorstep. Tangerines and plum pudding for dessert. A fine, aged palm wine.

Later, Rajibai sat out on the large limb of the Mongolian sequoia upon which he had constructed his own little tree house months before in order to give some privacy to his parents. He was happier out there, with the Lord as his companion, and some of the Lord's other friends— neighborhood rakehells; an Indian falcon; an African tree shrew; a very clever giant panda who had died in squalid captivity during the Cultural Revolution, crying every night for years while the locals gathered his bile; a hook-billed pigeon from Madagascar and her lover; a variegated tinamou of Guinea. Wonderful games.

They made love, Rachel and Murillo, to the emergence of Canis Minoris, the Persei and Coronae Borealis. The quiet happy sounds of Jungle Jane snug in her tattered flannel comforter—the one her grandfather had managed to hold on to, even through Auschwitz. The moon was faint. On the sea shone the millions of reminders of their happiness: Rasalgethi, Canopus, Betelgeuse, Arcturus, Pollux.

"Come on!" she murmured, supreme joy breaking out from every pore.

There was an open clearing, deep soft grass the consistency of cashmere, a soil of shelled facies, soft uplifting stalks of relict *Graminae* that first germinated 600 million years before, when 11,000 feet of Jovitan mountain wall were under water. Remains of the cliff were discernible, jutting out through the luscious, slippery pasture just 20 yards down the allée from the Giverny. It was to this precise and perilous spot that the lovers came—to an aerial vantage point where, if one had been there in the past, it would have been possible to observe Jovita rising, sinking and rising again from the ocean some 25 times throughout Earth's history.

And from here there was now the chance to view the entire island chain, cheeks to the warm midnight breeze. They were naked, the mud oozing between their toes. Both were giddy from considerable drink, and everything else.

"Hold on, tight."

Their fingers entwined, forever.

"I love you," Marigold whispered.

Stars in their eyes gloaming. "I love you," she groaned, face streaming upwards.

Then, suddenly, first Marigold's, then Rachel's enveloping bodies were sliding, unexpectedly, at first ambiguously, loam teasing the practitioners, then out of control, the grass giving way to mud, mud that became steep embankment, then a drop-off. Two bodies plunging, beholden to the gravity at the beginning of the all-embracing sea.

CHAPTER 200
A Tea Party For Siberian Cranes

IN THE MORNING RAJIBAI straddled across the enormous tree limbs towards his residence. He craved a toasted onion papadam, mango chutney and palak paneer and maintained a curious view as to how to prepare them. Jungle Jane was giggling at the play of mottled light upon the stone interior, her little legs upended, slowly twisting like a glossy beetle in the air of her crib. Her eyes shone inquisitively but neither her father, nor Rachel, was to be found.

Rajibai called out to them, searched everywhere, then decided they must have gone down for an early-morning swim in the sea, despite the nearly 22,000 feet of combined descent and ascent, the same as climbing Mont Blanc for a morning constitutional.

He started down the trail, only to slip royally on his butt. The mud was deep and impossible to negotiate. Like gumbotil, dark, leached, glacial once. It was then that he saw the telltale signs of a mishap: toe prints leading to the grassy nook, and a sudden cavalcade of clues—the mud churned up as if a dozer or disc had run riot—right off the edge, where the sandstone walls plunged directly into the microscopic thundering of sea breach two miles beneath. He brought himself with utmost care to the very edge, digging in to combat the slippery clays. Now there was little doubt.

Rajibai sat there stunned, shaking, his brain occluded and without thought. For long moments he remained there. It couldn't be. Not those two, not now, when true happiness had finally been won.

Jane was crying audibly. He had to go back.

He was paralyzed with trepidation. The incredulity of sudden manhood had been forced upon him in the loneliness at the edge of the world. He climbed back up on all fours, grasping to vines, the thicker base of large shrubs, whatever gave substance to his desperate retreat from the impossible lip of the abyss where much had been mired by mishap.

Once back into the lodgement, he stared into Jane's eyes, so innocent of the inexpressible tragedy; she wanted only to be breastfed, cuddled, loved unerringly. He must exchange memory, hope, for certainty. Courage, he knew, hinged upon that trade-off. So he took Jane in his arms, folded her up in her luxurious comforter and pink damask, and smothered her in little kisses. Then, sitting at the stone table anointed for that purpose, he prepared breakfast for the two of them. Holding back his tears.

Once Jane was properly situated, he went outside and called for the Lord.

Nelson had spent most of his time napping in a tree adjoining the house. Eject the odd query, muse aloud, mumble a haiku, toss out a riddle, grill a coconut cake or invent a stinky pinky, and Nelson was there.

"They're gone. I think they're dead," the boy broke out hysterically.

"Calm down. What are you saying?"

"They're gone, I can't find them anywhere ..." Rajibai unleashed a flood of panicked confusion between sobs and valiant decrees.

Nelson, who had been around for more than a century, had seen everything, and this was not a first. Long ago—he remembered the day well—Rachel's father similarly disappeared. "The cliff."

"There were tracks," Rajibai stammered. "Too much mud. They slipped."

"Is your father a good swimmer?"

"Sort of."

"Then what are you waiting for? Get down there and see what you can find!"

"You'll watch after Jane?"

"Regurgitation on call. That's me."

Rajibai raced away, reached the trail, then stopped dead on his toes. Why not jump? It was high, horribly high, but nothing like the waterfall. He could save, easily, two hours. He inched towards the edge, his mind spinning. Anna's words came back to him. A prayer Namgyal had imparted. He stood, fixed on the immunity to harm he thought he understood. A swarm of particulars. Was it immunity, or only the countering winds of the waterfall? Would he live forever, or would he not? And what about Marigold? Did he need to take that drug, whatever it was? Drink his own urine? Pound himself on some particular portion of the heart muscle? Too confusing. Ambiguities crowded his thinking. Then he recalled the nightmare, and the machine with its slave laborers hammering people's heads.

He stepped back from the edge. Down below, the waves were ferocious, smashing into the sea stacks, throwing up spume 200 feet. The whole mountain rumbled with each incoming tidal rogue, and the mountain wall fell away to a point where breakers from two opposing directions clashed. No one could survive such savage seas.

He would not leap. Not with Jane all alone up there, albeit with the protective acumen and instincts of the Lord. And so he started down the trail. Soon he was bounding where the sheer declivity gave way to a less inclining slope thick in fern forests, multi-storied undergrowth and hundreds of intersecting creeks that plunged to the ocean.

At some length he reached bottom, scouring the rocky coves for miles on either side of the fall line. He spent most of the afternoon calling out their names. The night, too. A moon had risen, its harmony gold caressing every inch of sea night beneath a Leonid shower. Amid the softened roar of ocean in the darkness, there was no sign. No hint. Marigold and Rachel had vanished from this world.

By morning he was a philosopher, reconciled to the silence of the aftermath. For more than a year his life had been one of supple joy, nothing stopping it; now it was rigid with shadowed lamentation. But he'd been there before. This was no more or less difficult. At least he wasn't confronted by a corpse, arms and legs chopped off. He started up.

It was early afternoon when he reached the ridge. The Lord was there ensconced within their regal chambers, reciting fairy tales to Jungle Jane, whose Buddha smile and chirping wonderment had stolen the hornbill's heart for all eternity. Never had he enjoyed so thoroughly nor in turn entranced a human speaker. Just to listen, to gaze upon such innocence.

She was the beauty of all beauties. And for one as gossipy and nonstop as Nelson, this was true paradise Judging by the boy's aura and disposition as he drew close inside the roost, he could see that Rajibai came with no shred of evidence, or of a conclusion. If Rachel and the Commander were gone, they were fully gone. Into the next round. If not, then they must be fully found. Nothing in between. So he decided not to ask. Instead: "Do you think she understands what I'm saying?"

"Well, she's nearly two months old, I don't know why not. Soon I expect she'll be studying proper Hornbill, Greek and Latin."

Months passed, Rajibai hoping beyond conviction that his father and Rachel would suddenly show up. He looked each day, devoted whole weeks to searching along every remote outcrop and hidden cove. He himself was frequently marooned in his quest, trapped in sea caves, holed up on crumbling ledges. He became a friend of massive storm, killer waves and disintegrating walls of mud. Hope eventually settled down to trust, and trust to a distant reconciliation some might call by its proper name: faith. Faith in their memory. Faith in the belief that wherever they were, they were together and in joy, or so he told one mournful macaw.

His loneliness was exacerbated by his fear of telling Sannazaro who, he knew, would be devastated. Nor was he entirely sure how to manage the descent with Jane. But equally, it was Jane, and all his other new friends, who tempered the trauma. The Lord did a superb job in keeping the boy busy and arranging his social calendar, so that he would not sulk, or invest the air of the domicile with any other sentiment than serenity.

"It's important. For the sake of Jane," he'd often remind the lad.

Lunch and dinner invites went out on a regular basis and not even the most humble stink bug was excluded. Card games up in a gum arabic tree. Occasional bouts of hang-gliding with Sir Joseph, though he'd thrown out his back during that dreadful descent to Purgatory, as Rajibai now came to understand the place, and was not keen to push his luck. The Lord tried, but was no chiropractor, and succeeded only in ruffling 100 cubic feet of primaries and secondaries.

"Dinosaurs are very particular about massage therapy," the Lord advised. "And let's be serious: it's my eight pounds against his how many tens of thousands? One ant to his tree. And how many light years before a moonbeam melts the glaciers on Kangchenjunga? What he needs is that dragon you all talked about to smooth out his kinks and get his humors excited again. But I don't dare tell him. It would just work him into a funk. Last thing we need."

But there was much more to the hornbill's prescriptions than whatever insights he might have suggested regarding Sir Joseph's loneliness and arthritic condition.

One day, many months later, the Lord threw a tea party for several hundred Siberian cranes passing through. They were the last of their kind and had flown 15,000 miles, stopping at a hot spring in Concordia, then on to the Nubra Valley of Ladakh, spending a few days near a caramels factory in Sri Lanka (the scent drove them wild), crossing the Indian Ocean and heading towards their favorite nesting grounds on the remote island 100 miles off Tristan da Cunha. The old one among them was looking very frail, and the Lord took him aside and suggested he remain on Jovita. They chatted for some time, drinking a mix of poetic teas. The crane, one of the bird world's true elders, was meantime eyeing Jungle Jane, who'd been hoisted up onto the premier nookbuttock in the gum arabic, where the stage-wise princess sat humming arias and generally delighting all who gazed upon her.

"One day she'll sing in the Paris Opera or stun audiences at the Vienna theater," said the elder. "That's where this little girl's fortunes await."

"She's not interested in fortunes," Rajibai interjected. "This is her home."

"Of course is it, I'm merely suggesting."

"Don't go putting any ideas into her head. This is her home. We're not going anywhere!"

The Lord had never seen Rajibai react so defensively. It was not at all in character. Later, he understood the problem: it had been one year since Rachel and Marigold disappeared, one year to the day.

That evening, while the cranes partied up the ridge (they'd be gone before sunrise), he looked at the boy and addressed him with the following sentiments: "You must be getting on to 14 ... Am I correct?"

Rajibai nodded, though he wasn't exactly sure.

"And Jungle Jane is well into her second year. Right?"

"Yeah."

"My dear boy, there is a whole world out there." The Lord spoke to him as his own son, and with an undying affection. He had no other.

"I know that," Rajibai replied angrily. "You have no idea all the many adventures."

"We've all had adventures. That's not the point. Don't count them. Don't think about them, or not too much. I know it's been a year since your parents disappeared."

"They're going to come back. Sooner or later."

"Of course they will. I'm merely saying that it isn't fair to Jane, nor to you, to spend the rest of your life waiting. Believe me, wherever you are, they will find you."

"But I love it here. There's no better place. And where am I going to go? What are you really saying?"

"Your manor seat on the windy ridge will always be here for you. As steadfast and faithful as Jovita herself. Why not give the child a taste of the other side? Beyond the boundaries of Never Never Land, even of the archipelago? No harm done."

"What other side?"

"You mean—you don't know?"

"Know what?"

That was the first time Lord Nelson fully appreciated the fact Rajibai had never died, nor had a clue what his own words were insinuating. Nelson had known, certainly, that Rajibai was a living person. The Commander had informed him on their very first outing together. But hornbills have a wonderful way of letting things slip, in much the manner that birds in general will discount 95 percent of a perfectly acceptable dinner plate or squander large sums of seeds with no semblance of shame. Profligates, Epicureans, they are the same with facts and ideas. A loosely held approach to the world that has always stood them in the best light. The tragedy of their forgiving nature. As the famed Lao Tzu (himself a hornbill in a later life) advised, "Cling to it tightly and you shall surely lose it."

Rajibai had similarly let go of the significance of death, though his father had spent hours revisiting the hurrinado and its aftermath with his son. Yet the Lord now recognized the signs of traumatic denial: Rajibai had never really come to terms with the fact his father and Rachel had died prior to their plunge off the cliff; that Jovita was, technically speaking, beyond the mundane world, though it, too, had certain unsolvable quirks (the fact that every now and then someone made it to Jovita without going through a death to get there—Rajibai being a case in point). He felt uncomfortable being the one to have to break the news or to try explaining the unexplainable. What good could it do? There was no telling how the boy might react to the *Law of Unpredictabilities*.

"Know what?" he asked again, alarmed.

"I'm going to bed," the Lord declared.

"No. I want to know what you meant by that. Please."

So the hornbill conceded, sat him down, took a deep breath and explained it all. Finally, "Our lives are part of the weather."

Remarkably, Rajibai's sure-fire kid was now the quieter. He mulled for a moment, and then his coloring returned.

"I know that Father and Uncle drowned," he said. "We discussed it. But it didn't really matter. They weren't really dead. Uncle is probably having a merry old time right now, down in the village."

"That's the spirit, lad!"

The Lord needn't have worried. In fact, his careful explanation made everything tolerable for the young man, brought happy tears to his night, where only darkness had struggled for a flashlight. Now, that night of falling stars conveyed a true, lasting, though somewhat confusing evanescence.

"Maybe I died, too?" he conjectured. "I mean, that hurrinado was terrible."

"Yes, but you were the one who saved your father and uncle."

"But maybe I was already dead. I drank quite a few gallons of seawater up there on that masthead."

"I suppose it's possible. Which should tell you one important thing: death is not the end. My point exactly. You need to see how your uncle is doing. Maybe even inquire of your other loved ones? Did you ever think of that? What if they're worried sick about you?"

That night Rajibai lay awake thinking back to Tesuque and wondering whether it wasn't possible that he, too, was dead, or whether his father might not just show up one day at the hacienda or Camp of the Spirits. They'd all continue to church at Chimayo, and romp with Anastasia, and Ginevra would cook a Corsican carrot stew. Sannazaro, dear Sannazaro, would pour a silky red wine near the fire which Alvaro had fashioned from deadwood under the bridge that the bear had peed on.

A thousand other memories, too. In the morning, it was decided. He packed up the precious one, erecting a little backpack she could ride in—the Lord helped chop the wood with his dexterous beak, executing precise notches that allowed the pieces to fit tongue-and-groove style—and put everything in proper place, so that in the event his father and Rachel should one day return it would all be there for them. Food in the freezer box, dried saleps, plenty of palm wine and coconut oil in painted amphorae along the porch, the bed neatly done up, the floor swept, the windows closed, cracks in the lintel sealed with cocoa paste.

"Take a year, or two if you must. Fear nothing. Catch a sea breeze. The coast of Africa is always easy to find when leaving here. No storms in that direction. And when you're ready to return, just show your ticket. Return visits are risk free. That's how it works. I'll be waiting for you," Lord Nelson attested stoically. He held back his own tears until the young man had hugged him thoroughly, struggled with his goodbyes, given thanks to all the assembled neighborhood chums—every tapeworm, muskrat, bull moose, canary and albatross, not to mention the old Siberian crane who had stayed on indefinitely, and who had first divined that Rajibai and Jungle Jane would be moving on some day soon.

Rajibai sustained last-minute changes of heart, repealed all woes, rectified all errors, but eventually dispelled any fear, straightened his shoulders, pinched ever so lightly Jungle Jane's thirsting cheeks, and walked away down the steep rise towards the rendezvous point. The little girl waved goodbye to each and every multitudinous creature, whom she knew by name—her playmates one and all. They waved goodbye to her, tears raining down like dewdrops on the gardens of Paradise.

Rajibai looked around and mumbled, "I wonder where ...?"

Not two minutes later a gargantuan shriek ruptured the jasmine-haunted air of the highlands as Sir Joseph alighted, his head-feathers ruffled, his complexion a tad flushed, the discombolutated behemoth utterly out of breath. He had arrived in the nick of time to transport his two favorite humans down to the outskirts of Jovita.

"Thank goodness, sorry I'm late. You don't think I would have missed ... Not for a moment. Just one of those mornings. Don't ask."

On their way over the dangerous midlands they spotted a ridiculous sight. There, invisible to all but the most penetrating eyes of the Cretaceous, was Sannazaro stuck in a hotsuck. He had been there for weeks. A double outrage, given the cloud of no-see-ums swarming around his exposed head. His arms flailed madly.

Rajibai screamed delightedly, panicked by the reunion and all the emotions flooding over him. He had missed the silly, noble, glorious Italian with all his heart.

"Thank God, my lad. I was on my way to find you," Sannazaro cried out in return. "Weeks in this blasted wilderness. Not a single cup of coffee to be had; picking bones with every ant hill, falling off 10,000 knolls, skinning my knees and going crazy but for the burning hope of discovering your whereabouts. Only to end up in this miserable pothole. I'd have been dead all over again. Mercy on me! Where's the Commander? And who are they?"

"One revelation at a time," the dinosaur whispered, eyeing the boy.

"Uncle, meet your niece proper," Rajibai explained. "Her name is Jungle Jane."

"Gorgeous, simply gorgeous," he stammered, his spine blurting out in chills. "And—and—so many questions, but never mind. Not now. I'm afraid of heights, and can't talk and hang on at the same time!" he gasped, clinging to the dinosaur's bony back as Sir Joseph rose up from the hotsuck with helicopter force and the ease of a U-2.

CHAPTER 201
The Hypotreble of Devil Fish and the Journey Home to New Mexico

Where is to-morrow? In the other world.
To thousands this is true, and the reverse
Is sure to none.
   —Henry Fielding, Esq., *The History of the Life of the Late Mr Jonathan Wild the Great*

SAUL LIEBOWITZ, other poets, the three cats and Amigo were on hand to greet the adventurers who dismounted from Sir Joseph.

"An historical occasion!" Saul bellowed. Relief and gratitude scarcely describe the wondrous feelings that flooded him.

The cats, rearing up on hind legs, carefully licked the little face of Jungle Jane with all the affection older brothers are meant to bestow.

Only Amigo held back outright jubilation. "Where's the Commander?" he fretfully inquired.

Rajibai explained what had happened, and reactions were mixed. The poets yawned, well aware that Marigold and his young bride would show up somewhere, sometime, in some form. Saul, his arm encircling the bereaved boy, tended to agree, and he spouted pearly wisdoms about death and rebirth which no longer had the power to evoke much of any serious thought, though the sympathies were certainly appreciated. Amigo was desperate, however. Caterwauling, plucking out his breast feathers, inconsolable.

"That man meant everything to me!" he cried miserably.

And Sannazaro. He was simply stumped by the sheer magnitude of the news. He retreated to his own hut, governed by some higher law of silent reflection. The news would take some time to set in. We will never know what he thought about, exactly.

Eventually, Uncle removed from his coziest of quarters to rejoin the periphery of perplexities. "She's so beautiful," he said, lifting Jungle Jane into his arms. "I see her father in every luminous ounce. And what a goddess Rachel must be." His use of the present tense was not lost on Rajibai. Then, referring to the poets, Sannazaro added, "They're right."

"Give it a year. They'll be back," Saul speculated.

"Absolutely not. The duration between temblors is diminishing, their size increasing, the steam from the geysers getting hotter and hotter. The volcanoes are smoking, the hurrinadoes becoming more frequent. The girl must survive. And that means *you* must survive, young man." Sannazaro was adamant about it, and—after his own recent bout in a hotsuck, the lower half of his body badly sautéed—he was prepared to go to any length to evacuate the children from the island. These two were the last. All the other kids had perished and gone elsewhere.

"I now more fully comprehend the implications of the drowning," Rajibai confessed, unsure of the effect his words might have on Uncle. "I mean, I don't necessarily understand how it all works, or what exactly is going on. But I do accept it. I'm only sorry that I didn't get to you both sooner that day during the storm."

"Son, you succeeded in your efforts, don't think that you didn't. Why, without you, who knows where I'd be by now."

"I guess my poor father is going through it a second time."

"Don't you dare speak of it as something to be sorry about. I can tell you this: I've never been happier in all my times. Moreover, although you didn't hear it from me, it has done wonders for my sex life."

"I've caught him straying on numerous occasions," Saul boasted on the blushing man's behalf. "Of course, they're all corpses—hornier in Heaven—so I'm not sure it deserves much special notice."

"Yeah, you should see some of them," Amigo laughed, feeling better now.

"Shut up, you two," Sannazaro snapped, which caused even greater merriment all around. "But don't get me wrong: I love it here, best place there is. And Saul, your cappuccino is second to one."

"Which one?"

"My own. The machine is crucial, and it's presently in Ginevra's kitchen. But the island is not for children, especially first timers."

Liebowitz, who had expired in many previous circumstances, reflected on how the newlydeads were always the big experts. But he knew that Sannazaro was right. Jovita had become too dangerous for children. It didn't use to be that way, back in the Pre-Cambrian.

"The problem's going to be getting out to the *Bonaparte*. The vessel is still there, but jammed between reefs and smack dab in the center of the feeding area for all the sharks, and I'm not referring to the basking sharks, who nibble only plants, but to the great crayon sharks, and gray-golds, with whom I'd prefer a long-standing literary correspondence to any one-on-one conversation," said the Italian.

"Perhaps there's another way," envisioned Saul.

They strolled down to the beach, past arrays of carved tiki whose messages went unread, and ancient turquoise lanterns glowing by means never yet discovered. Recent storms had twisted gravity so that trees grew sideways, rivers flowed vertically, cliffs lay upside down, mountains had bottoms but no tops, and huge sections of driftwood littered the whole wild sea front, a baobab of bedlams.

"You're thinking of building a raft?" asked Sannazaro.

"Why not," opined Saul.

"There might be a better way," Rajibai figured, noticing a large charcoal body sleeking in the near waves. It looked to be about 20 times the size of a shark. "See that?"

A Selachian. The largest Pleurotrematan any had ever seen. The cats were in a frenzy of interest but had an even greater disdain of getting their toenails wet.

"What is it?" all asked.

The boy could hear a heaven-high frequency he seemed to grasp in rudimentary form. The grammar, known as Hypotreble clef, was not entirely strange. Unafraid, Rajibai waded out to where the breakers smashed high around his waist. The creature, called by some a devil fish, its enormous pectoral fins and circular disc rolling effortlessly, came right up to him, careful to keep its electric organs to itself.

"Good day to you, Ma'am," the wading boy greeted the sea centurion.

From the beach it was clear the two were getting on famously, discussing all the particulars of their respective situations. After some time, Rajibai returned to the group that awaited his news.

"You remember the dead creature we slept on when first we arrived on the island?" Rajibai began.

"Of course, I still sleep on him. Smoothest pillow and bed sheets in all the seas."

"Well, it's her mate and she wants him back."

"But he's dead, has been for over a year. His spirit went back out to the sea, no doubt. What's left is a pillowcase, a rubber sock, a leather flagon, with not the slightest ounce of gumption or sensuality left in it."

"That's what I told her—well, sort of. Guess what she said? Put his remains back in the water and she'll carry them into some life-reviving thermal vent 30,000 feet down, just a couple of miles offshore, where diamonds are crushed into pure oxygen and silicate bacteria, and sulfur-rich muds are crystallized into some new form of DNA."

"That would explain a lot of things," Saul said, thinking aloud how certain rocks on the island got up and started walking; how trees assumed the faces of animals, animals the height of trees; how poets could become lifeless, and lifeless things poetic. "But I'm particularly curious about her language. Do you think she'd allow me to do up a lexicon of devil fish, or manta ray as they denominate it at certain marine laboratories in the West?"

"Why not. Just ask her. She's as dignified as a Member of Parliament. In fact, she promised to give us a ride out to the boat. Of course Sir Joseph could also ferry us, but he would have a much harder time extricating the *Bonaparte* from the reef or guiding us through the labyrinth to safe waters. She knows the precise route."

So the die was cast. With the aid of Sir Joseph, they managed to get the male manta back down to the beach and into the waves, where its mate then gently guided the enormous body far away and down many fathoms. "I'll be back to get you soon," she called.

And three days later she kept to her word. The male—a vastly elegant ray, known in some circles as a mobula—was fully restored, his brilliant coloring and lofty strength of character intact. What once was a pillow had become a prized life force.

"There are no final farewells on Jovita," Saul cried with touching resolve, his once bright gaze welling up with salty tears. "This is an island purely for hellos."

And thus the foursome—Rajibai, Jungle Jane, Sannazaro and Amigo—headed out through thundering surf on the back of the 20-foot-wide female manta ray, her anterior end free thinking, like a horn of plenty, while her even larger mate glided ahead, explaining the situation to all the understanding sharks, reaching the luxury yacht with its helicopter port and satellite dish, and shambled interiors, dislodging it, setting it upright, and towing it out to a point beyond the reefs where it could be properly oriented towards New Mexico, wherever that was.

Thus, by understated, quiet ceremony, the party was delivered onto the back of the boat. The love duo, who never stopped holding their whip-tails in each other's barbs, then dispatched massive high-decibel queries out into the open sea—a kind of "calling on all rays throughout the world" short-wave transmission. Within minutes they began receiving instructions from all quarters of the water planet. Tropically minded *Torpedinidae* pointed forever west, while dozens of cosmopolitan shark rays insisted north; carefully worded replies from several conservative *Pristis perrotteti* indicated a distance of 6,920 leagues, while one very astute thornback, in exile near Christmas Island, refined that figure. Those formally known as stingrays, or Trygons among their own kind, had never heard of New Mexico. But it was one worldly-wise spotted eagle ray, a resident of the waters beyond Matamoros, who summed it up simply: "Boca Chica. And from there, head northwest all the way up the Río Grande."

"We have a fix on the coordinates," replied the manta, supremely happy to be reunited with her loved one. "Whatever they tell you, never fear sentimentality," she cried out. "It is the salvation of the world." Having gotten that off her chest, she and her doubly-enormous mate hooked their barbs onto either side of the 120-foot sailing vessel, tugged Rajibai and party out beyond the lateral gravitations of the archipelago, gave one resolute push with their double-horned snouts, saluted the crew with electric tails flashing high in the air, an alternating current of neon novelties, and turned round towards home in the happy scooping grounds of Jovita Bay.

The boat's petrol had been waterlogged during the hurrinado over a year before, the deck and interior cabins and bridge smashed to bits, so there was no possibility of running the engines. But a full breeze gave plenty of loft to the working foresail and flying jib, and Sannazaro knew how to tie knots, set a course and keep to it. Amigo searched out available rat feces for lunch, while Rajibai scoured the cupboards for any leftovers. Jungle Jane needed formula, at the very least. And an arcane, complicated one at that. She was not a simple child, as geniuses go. As temperamental, in fact, as Jovita.

In all, they managed. It was November, the weather steady and clear, a cold front from the great south, a moderating high down from the temperate north. An albatross, aged five, joined the crew, having circumambulated the world six times, by her count, in search of the finest squid. She was a self-proclaimed dilettante and would soon venture back to South Georgia Island, to the very grassy perch where she was born, in search of a love interest, as she described him. "He's out there, I just know it," she crooned, "despite what Coleridge would have you believe." Some nights, when the moon was full, hundreds of unidentifiable fish flopped onto the deck, inhaled the free oxygen until they were good and drunk, then threw themselves overboard again. It seemed to be a favorite pastime of the region.

In due course, after several weeks of sailing, it was clear to Sannazaro that they had re-entered the known world. Out on the horizon, they saw an ocean-going vessel. Upon closer scrutiny, it appeared to be filled with huge metal containers, marked in Chinese.

Another month passed by, abetted by a well-stocked kitchen and fair breezes from the east. One day, they came upon the distant greenswards of Saint Kitts, in the Leewards, and not long after they found themselves drifting past the Keys off Louisiana. By and by, they reached Brownsville, Texas; they found Boca Chica (a sign on a floating oyster bar), guided the *Bonaparte* on to the outflow of the Río Grande, and took her on to the North America continent.

"I'm singing, I'm dancing, I'm fine I'm fine I'm fine," rang out Governor Sannazaro's veteran vocal chords as the old goat gesticulated a little jig, a modest fillip, as they sailed on. Past the oldest continuously farmed lands in the Americas, Papago Indian children running with their sheep along the sandy banks and waving to the crew whose purple sails were fully inflated now, as if the whole vessel was ready to lift off.

A few weeks later they arrived in shallow waters at the intersection of the Río Grande and Highway 4 near Nambé, and plowed into the Santa Fe River, taking advantage of its unheralded tributaries and connecting network of acequias. Within a few hours had managed to shipwreck in an enormous mound of bison dung not 19 yards from the entrance to the Camp of the Spirits.

Rajibai had written everything down—every nautical mile, twist and sea-turn, all the while gaining important wind-vane information from Amigo. *The Governor's Log*, as it came to be known in deference to Sea Captain Sannazaro, Governor-General of Jovita, was Rajibai's guarantee of someday navigating himself back to his little hanging house in the Mongolian sequoia, adjoining the aromatic gum arabic tree, and the family chateau situated most comfortably and fine in Mr Marigold's final Utopia, there along the impossibly sheer ridge. Looking out over an invigorating eternity. That's where he knew he belonged, and would always be headed, no matter what he did, or thought. No matter the troubles he was likely to encounter in this life, or the disappointments in the next. Nothing mattered but that tree house and legacy of legacies it enshrined: the companionship of a blind hermit named Saul with his three great leopards, of a lonely *Ornithocyrus*, a wise Siberian crane and the Lord himself, that witty chatterbox of a hornbill.

In the coming days, confusion and the general dramas of life swirled about the hacienda and Camp of the Spirits. The pouring forth of so many emotions. News from all leagues and legalities. Sannazaro professed his love of Ginevra, who was looking glamorous and wise after her long quiet recovery since Greenlandia. And as fate would have it, she felt exactly the same about Sannazaro, and always had. Now there was nothing to stand in the way of their complete matrimony.

"Don't you dare say a word about my being dead and all," Sannazaro whispered to his best man, Rajibai. Anastasia crashed the party, literally. Ebert and friends, down for a wild weekend from the Oasis, where they had permanently taken up habitation, stole most of the fine cheeses and chocolates from the wedding table, which they have since been stashing in 100 wintering holes.

Alvaro and Raquel thought it a sensible motion to betroth Jungle Jane to their own eccentric son, who was three years older, and whom they'd named Misha. Rajibai conditioned the arrangement on a mysterious poem, written by Saul, dedicated to the Commander, sealed in an envelope, not to be opened for 20 years, at which time Jane and Misha could read it, and decide what to do, where to go and how to spend their own lives in fulfillment, should they want to.

Sannazaro and Hidalgo managed to borrow two billion dollars— despite unbelievable debts, complications, legal entanglements and a roar of contestation surrounding the Marigold estate. Using the remaining properties as collateral for a ten-year loan, paying a floating interest rate of 115 basis points above Libor, a deal carved out over monte on the Isle of Jersey, they were able—according to the Commander's wishes—to finance the complete revitalization of Zambia, including the support and transport of 100,000 orphans to New Mexico, personally championed by the Squire, who was guided by the foundling he now fathered.

But in the wake of this vast migration, redneck rifle-fire riddled the Camp of the Spirits. Unemployment throughout the state soared into double digits. The welfare rolls collapsed. Typical.

There were many who considered the beleaguered gardener's actions to warrant a Nobel Peace Prize, even if it did throw the state of New Mexico into turmoil, evincing race riots and every shade of hemophobia. But because most of those orphans' parents had died, by and large of AIDS, there was little noise from the State Senate to contest the humanitarian effort, even though all the newspaper columnists said there would be another 100,000 tomorrow, and the next day. Sannazaro had in fact taken a broad interest in immigration, applying the Commander's principles of unburdening imperiled regions of high biodiversity by diverting human populations across borders and regions. Opening up that biologically depleted zone from north Texas to North Dakota to all of the Yucatan's millions of unemployed, for starters.

Rajibai and Jungle Jane moved into the Camp of the Spirits to live with Ginevra and Sannazaro. But there was no discussion of adoption. Rajibai forbade it, and Sannazaro knew precisely why.

The Hacienda was turned into a museum of animal rights and nonviolence—of which the centerpiece was the Commander's bedroom—that study in magnificent chaos with its ancient treasures, family history that nobody could remember any more, plaster faces of unknown likenesses, a disheveled storm advisory of books, their many splendored words of some befuddled consequence, though nobody could tell what it was, and a broken-down suit of armor on the wall recalling all his futile dreams, lost memories and abandoned ruminations.

But for all that, it was a happy place.

EPILOGUE
Marvelous and Nearly Forgotten, The Illustrious Sallies of Mr Marigold

ON A COLD, CLEAR winter's day, Rajibai, Sannazaro, Ginevra, Jungle Jane, Amigo, Anastasia, Ebert, Hidalgo and his wife Shirley, Alvaro, Raquel, and their sterling little Misha, along with a Hopi rocket scientist recently inducted into the National Academy, paid their final respects to Mr Marigold, and to Rachel, in a fabled seance conducted on the pinion-and juniper-covered mountainside above the Hacienda, a wilderness stretching undeterred all the way into southern Colorado. A simple piece of tattered blue cloth was hung upon a branch—the last remains of the handkerchief a little boy named Murillo once carried in his back pocket, and which had protected his eyes and mouth and nose during the avalanche off Chimborazo that killed his father. A cloth he had carried with him all of his subsequent days. Whether underwater or in a fog. On mountaintops or languishing in hotsucks.

Carved onto a smooth mani stone that came from atop a certain waterfall were two words: "Thank you." The stone was laid to rest inside a folded-up Toda shawl at the base of a great ponderosa on which the fragment of windblown handkerchief was loosely tied. Sannazaro tried to elaborate upon some of the marvelous and nearly forgotten sallies of his illustrious friend. But lightly spreading sobs stilled his speech.

As they were all finally leaving the site, having paid their solemn respects, Rajibai noticed a vague, barely legible passage carved into bark, no telling how many years or generations before:

> ... *Y al fin yo tierra he de ser...*
> And in the end, I shall be earth.[22]

Then he continued on his way.

THE END

Endnotes

1. Marian Meyer, *Mary Donoho, New First Lady of the Santa Fe Trail,* Santa Fe, New Mexico: Ancient City Press, 1991.
2. ibid., pp.37-39.
3. W.H.H. Allison, "Santa Fe as it Appeared During the Winter of the Years 1837 and 1838", Old Santa Fe 2, 1914, pp.176-77.
4. Meyer, op.cit., p.40
5. Daniel Tyler, *Sources for New Mexican History 1821-1848,* Santa Fe, New Mexico: Museum of New Mexico Press, 1984.
6. Many of the details of Tome, as well as the Spanish translations of verse come from Roberto De la Vega, *Three Centuries of Tome,* New Mexico, printed at Saint Clement Church, Los Lunas, New Mexico, 1976.
7. R.L. Duffus, *The Santa Fe Trail,* Albuquerque: University of New Mexico Press, 1972, p.156.
8. Walter Briggs, with Howard Bryan and Fray Angelico Chavez, "Venal or Virtuous? The Lady They Called La Thules", *New Mexico Magazine,* Spring 1971, pp.9-10. See also Janet Lecompte, "La Tules and the Americans", Harwood P. Hinton (ed), *Arizona and the West, A Quarterly Journal of History,* Vol. 20, No. 3, Autumn 1978, p.223.
9. Patrick J. Rohan and Melvin A. Reskin, *Nichols on Eminent Domain, Cumulative Supplement* (3rd ed.) Vol. 8, Matthew Bender & Co., October 1997. See also *New Mexico Real Estate Law Reporter* Vol. 4, No. 1, Austin,Texas: Butterworth Legal Publishers, 1990; and "Restrictive Covenants: An examination of New Mexico Case Law and Application", p.3.
10. 348 US 26, 75 S.Ct. 98, 99 L.Ed. 27 (1954).
11. "Condemnation Procedures and Techniques" in Rohan and Reskin, op.cit.
12. US104, n.36, 98 S. Ct. 2646mn.36, 57L.Ed.2d631, 657, n.36P.14E-11in Rohan and Reskin, op. cit., Chapters 14-14F.
13. Julius Sackman and Patrick Rohan, 1997 *Supplement* Vol.2A; 1997 *Supplement* Chapters 6-7, *Nichols on Eminent Domain,* Sackman and Van Brunt, 4, Chapters 12-13, 1997 *Supplement* Vol. 4.
14. Christine A. Klein,"Treaties of Conquest: Property Rights, Indian Treaties,and the Treaty of Guadalupe Hidalgo", *New Mexico Law Review,* Vol. 26, No. 2, 1996.
15. Norman Todd, "Statutory Notice in Zoning Actions: Nesbit v. City of Albuquerque", *New Mexico Law Review,* Vol. 10, No. 1, 1979-80.
16. Jean Jacques Rousseau, *An Inquiry into the Nature of the Social Contractor Principles of Political Right,* p.11, London: 1791.
17. William Shakespeare, "King Henry VI," Part II, Act III, Scene 1, *The Plays and Poems of William Shakespeare,* William Pickering, London, 1825, Vol. 6, p.167.
18. "From Sonnet By The Late Nawab of Oude, Asuf Ud Dowla", Vol.1, p.xlix, *Narrative of A Journey Through The Upper Provinces Of India, From Calcutta To Bombay,* 1824-1825, by Reginald Heber, D.D., Third Edition, John Murray, London, 1828.
19. For the botanical and much cultural data on the Todas, see Dr Tarun Chhabra, "A Journey to the Toda Afterworld", *India Magazine,* September 1993. See also Dr Tarun Chhabra, "Nilgiris – Flowering Paradise", *Sanctuary Asia Magazine,* Vol. XVII, No. 2, 1997.
20. All word and phrase translations adopted from Herbert Joseph Spinden (trans.), *Songs of the Tewa,* New York: The Exposition of Indian Tribal Arts, Inc., 1933, pp.119-121. See also Elsie Clews Parson, *Tewa Tales,* Tucson, Arizona: University of Arizona Press, 1994.
21. Sir Philip Sidney, *The Countess of Pembroke's Arcadia,* Book III, London: Sampson Low, Marston. Searle & Rivington, nd. p.347.
22. From *Penitente alabado,* quoted in Frank Waters, *People of the Valley,* Swallow Press, Athens, Ohio, 1941, p.88; and in Malcolm Ebright, *The Tierra Amarilla Grant: A History of Chicanery,* Santa Fe: The Center for Land Grant Studies, 1980.

About Michael Charles Tobias

The author has already weighed down the beleaguered reader with enough cargo so as to render senseless, obviating any want of, biographical detail, which — in the event — is as uninteresting as it is obsolete, adding nothing to the work in question.

About Zorba Press

Zorba Press is an independent publisher of books, ebooks, audio books, and films on DVDs. From the gorgeous gorges of Ithaca, New York, we publish the paperback books *The Zorba Anthology of Love Stories; The Ithaca Manual of Style;* the anthology of wise quotations called *Zenlightenment;* and a wild novel about love and eros (for adults) *Thoreau Bound: A Utopian Romance in the Isles of Greece.*

Currently, we offer about 50 titles of fiction and nonfiction. Some of our popular books include *The Terrestrial Gospel of Nikos Kazantzakis; 50 Benefits of Ebooks: A Thinking Person's Guide to the Digital Reading Revolution; Lark's Magic* (a comic novel for children); and *Sing In Me, Muse, and Through Me Tell the Story: Greek Culture Performed* by Maria Hnaraki. In addition, we publish many works by the incomparable Michael Tobias, including *Biotopia; Central Park; The Misadventures of Pinocchio; Professor Parrot and the Secret of the Blue Cupboard; The Strange Life & Disappearance of English Milligrams;* and *21st Century Solitude.*

Our most recent publications are *Kazantzakis: A Film By Michael Tobias* (video on DVD); *Sappho At The Edge Of Love: 100 Poems by Michael Pastore* (paperback and ebook and audiobook); the paperback edition of *My Life On The Ragged Paths Of Pan: Selected Poems and Translations of Thanasis Maskaleris;* and the first paperback and ebook editions of a modern classic — Michael Tobias's colossal comic novel, *The Adventures of Mr Marigold.*

At Zorba Press, we practice what we call "Sustainable Publishing": publishing with a deeper sense of awareness, compassion, and responsibility. Zorba's mission is to promote the innovative ideas and the daring books that nourish children and childhood, point the way to a culture of non-violence, create a sustainable future, and nurture – for every living being – a new world of love, kindness, courage, creativity, sincerity, and peace.